PENGUIN  CLA

D0877851

GARGANTUA AND PANTAGRUEL

FRANÇOIS RABELAIS, born in the 1480s, is very much a Renaissance man. As a Franciscan turned Benedictine he studied Law; he graduated as a doctor at Montpellier in 1530. Living irregularly, he published in 1532 the first of his comic 'Chronicles', *Pantagruel*; it revealed his genius as a storyteller and creator of comic characters and situations. By early 1535 he had published *Gargantua*, outrageously mocking old-fashioned education and rash imperialism. Against monastic ideals it opposes an Abbey where noblemen and ladies live in evangelical freedom and Renaissance splendour. In January 1535 Rabelais fled from his post as physician in Lyons. His profound and audacious *Third Book* was published in 1546. He was then a secular priest. He fled to Metz. His *Fourth Book*, published in January 1552 not long before he died, contains some of his deepest, boldest and funniest pages. It enjoyed the public support of the King and two Cardinals. (It outlived the *Index of Prohibited Books* on which it was eventually placed.) A *Fifth Book* appeared under his name in 1564. His genius was acknowledged in his own day: his world-wide influence remains enormous.

M. A. SCREECH is an Honorary Fellow of Wolfson College and an Emeritus Fellow of All Souls College, Oxford, a Fellow of the British Academy and of the Royal Society of Literature, a Fellow of University College London, and a corresponding member of the Institut de France. He long served on the committee of the Warburg Institute as the Fielden Professor of French Language and Literature in London, until his election to All Souls. He is a Renaissance scholar of international renown. He has edited and translated both the complete edition and a selection of Montaigne's *Essays* for Penguin Classics and, also, in a separate volume, the *Apology for Raymond Sebond*. His other books include *Erasmus: Ecstacy and the Praise of Folly* (Penguin, 1988), *Rabelais, Montaigne and Melancholy* (Penguin, 1991) and, most recently, *Laughter at the Foot of the Cross* (Allen Lane, 1998). All are acknowledged to be classic studies in their fields. He worked with Anne Screech on Erasmus' *Annotations on the New*

Testament. Michael Screech was promoted Chevalier dans l'Ordre du Mérite in 1982 and Chevalier dans la Légion d'Honneur in 1992. He was ordained in 1993 by the Bishop of Oxford.

FRANÇOIS RABELAIS

Gargantua and Pantagruel

Translated and edited
with an Introduction and Notes by
M. A. SCREECH

PENGUIN BOOKS

PENGUIN BOOKS

Published by the Penguin Group

Penguin Books Ltd, 80 Strand, London WC2R ORL, England

Penguin Group (USA) Inc., 375 Hudson Street, New York, New York 10014, USA

Penguin Group (Canada), 90 Eglinton Avenue East, Suite 700, Toronto, Ontario, Canada M4P 2Y3
(a division of Pearson Penguin Canada Inc.)

Penguin Ireland, 25 St Stephen's Green, Dublin 2, Ireland
(a division of Penguin Books Ltd)

Penguin Group (Australia), 250 Camberwell Road, Camberwell, Victoria 3124, Australia
(a division of Pearson Australia Group Pty Ltd)

Penguin Books India Pvt Ltd, 11 Community Centre, Panchsheel Park, New Delhi – 110 017, India

Penguin Group (NZ), 67 Apollo Drive, Mairangi Bay, Auckland 1310, New Zealand
(a division of Pearson New Zealand Ltd)

Penguin Books (South Africa) (Pty) Ltd, 24 Sturdee Avenue, Rosebank, Johannesburg 2196, South Africa

Penguin Books Ltd, Registered Offices: 80 Strand, London WC2R ORL, England

www.penguin.com

This translation first published in Penguin Classics 2006

1

Translation, Introduction and Notes copyright © M. A. Screech, 2006
All rights reserved

The moral right of the translator has been asserted

Set in 10.25/12.25 pt PostScript Adobe Sabon
Typeset by Rowland Phototypesetting Ltd, Bury St Edmunds, Suffolk
Printed in England by Clays Ltd, St Ives plc

ISBN-13: 978-0-140-44550-3
ISBN-10: 0-140-44550-1

Contents

Chronology

1483 Possible date for the birth of Rabelais at La Devinière near Chinon. (An alternative date of 1494 is not well supported.)

1500–1510 Some time during these years Rabelais studies law, perhaps at Bourges, Angers and/or Poitiers.

1510–26 Rabelais, previously a novice and lay-brother (possibly in the Franciscan convent at La Baumette), is ordained priest, either there or at the Franciscan abbey of Le Puy-Saint-Martin near Fontenay-le-Comte, where he remains until 1526.

1520 Rabelais, a Franciscan at Fontenay-le-Comte, writes his first (lost) letter to Guillaume Budé.

1521 Second letter of Rabelais to Budé.

1522 Amaury Bouchard publishes *Of the Female Sex, against André Tiraqueau*. Rabelais remains friends with both Bouchard and Tiraqueau.

1523–4 Rabelais, in trouble with his superiors for studying Greek, has already translated into Latin the first book of Herodotus and some works of Lucian. He is supported by his bishop, Geoffroy d'Estissac. Rabelais ceases to be a mendicant friar and becomes a monk (a Benedictine).

1524–6 Based at the Benedictine house at Saint-Pierre-de-Maillezais, Rabelais works for, and travels with, his bishop.

1525 Rabelais possibly in Lyons.

February: A disastrous defeat for the French at Pavia. François I is prisoner in Madrid.

1526 By the Peace of Madrid, François I is released from captivity and the royal sons are kept as hostages for his ransom. Milan is ceded to Charles V.

1526–30 Rabelais leaves Poitou. He studies the great Greek medical authorities (Hippocrates and Galen), probably in Paris. Two of his three children, François and Junie Rabelais, perhaps born during this period.

1528 Late summer sees the beginning of over five years of disastrous drought in large parts of France.

1529 The Peace of Cambrai: the royal sons are to be released against a ransom of 2 million crowns.

1530 Rabelais signs the matriculation rolls at Montpellier and quickly graduates as Bachelor of Medicine.

1530–32 Rabelais in Montpellier.

1531 Rabelais lectures at Montpellier on the *Aphorisms* of Hippocrates and Galen's *Ars Parva*.

May: The Paris Parlement consolidates its powers over the Sorbonne's right to censor books.

1532 Rabelais, in the University of Montpellier, acts in *The Farce of the Man Who Married a Dumb Wife*. Practises medicine in the Midi, including Narbonne; by June, he is established in Lyons.

Dedicates his edition of Manardi's *Epistolae Medicinales* to Tiraqueau, his edition of works of Galen and Hippocrates to Bishop Geoffroy d'Estissac and his edition of Lucius Cuspidius' *Testamentum* to Amaury Bouchard. First edition of *Pantagruel* (if not in 1531). Appointed physician to the Hôtel-Dieu in November, the great hospital in Lyons, Rabelais publishes his *Almanac for the year 1533*. Writes to Erasmus; the letter is sent with a Greek manuscript of *Josephus* sought by Erasmus. The *Pantagrueline Prognostication* for 1533.

1533 February: Permission is given to wear masks in the streets of Paris during the Shrovetide revels. 'Anti-Lutheran' demonstrations and sermons are orchestrated by the Sorbonne.

May: An attempt by the Sorbonne to censor *The Mirror of the Sinful Soul* of Marguerite de Navarre as well as *Pantagruel*. The Sorbonne theologians Béda, Picart and Leclerc are exiled twenty leagues from Paris. Critical posters (*placards*) are displayed in Paris. Reprisals.

July: The Sorbonne authorizes Nicolas Bouchart and Louis

Théobald to supplicate François I on behalf of Béda. They are unsuccessful.

October: The Sorbonne denies ever having intended to censor *The Mirror of the Sinful Soul*.

Rabelais publishes an augmented *Pantagruel* and the *Pantagrueline Prognostication* for 1534.

The plague, endemic in Europe, spreads. Rabelais is praised for his devotion to his patients.

1534 Rabelais leaves for Rome with Bishop Jean Du Bellay, possibly entrusting a manuscript of *Gargantua* to François Juste in Lyons. He leaves Rome in March.

April: Rabelais in Lyons with Jean Du Bellay (who goes on to Paris). Rabelais' movements unknown between April and July. *Gargantua*, if not already published, now in hand.

August: Rabelais resumes his post as physician in the Hôtel-Dieu. He dedicates his edition of Marliani's *Topographia Romae* to Jean Du Bellay.

October: The (first) *Affaire des Placards* (17–18 October). Posters (now known to be Zwinglian) attack the Mass as idolatry. Repression follows.

November–December: The publication of the *Almanac for the Year 1535* and the expanded *Pantagrueline Prognostication* for 1535, critical of the suppression of Evangelicals.

1535 The *Affaire du 13 janvier*: a rash repeat of the *Placards* of October 1534. Violent repercussions. Many flee. All printing is forbidden but later restored through the influence of Guillaume Budé and the Du Bellays. A great national act of expiation led by François I; the Du Bellays remain in favour. Heretics are burnt.

January: The probable date for the publication of *Gargantua*. Rabelais' son Théodule, born about this time (?). *Pantagruel* published without the permission of Rabelais by the printer Saincte-Lucie dit Le Prince in Lyons.

February: Guillaume Du Bellay publishes for François I a letter to the German states defending the French alliance with the Turks even while 'heresy' is suppressed at home. Béda's *amende honorable* before Notre-Dame-de-Paris; he is exiled once and for all to Mont-Saint-Michel.

Rabelais abandons his post in the Hôtel-Dieu, Lyons; he publishes his *Almanac for 1536*.

May: Jean Du Bellay is named cardinal, amidst accusations of Lutheranism.

June: François I invites Melanchthon to Paris.

Jean Du Bellay and Rabelais in Rome: they may have travelled there together, passing through Ferrara. The second edition of *Gargantua*, specifically dated 1535, may have been left en route in Lyons with François Juste.

1535–6 Rabelais arranges a papal absolution for his 'apostasy'.

1536 February: Rabelais is installed in Jean Du Bellay's Benedictine abbey at Saint-Maur-les-Fossés; it is secularized, and Rabelais with it. A papal brief authorizes him to practise medicine. He is now a secular priest, a 'father'.

August: Rabelais figures among the canons of Saint-Maur.

1537 During this year, *Pantagruel* and *Gargantua* republished in Lyons and Paris.

January: Béda dies in exile at Mont-Saint-Michel.

February: Rabelais at a celebratory banquet in Paris with Etienne Dolet, Budé, Marot, Danès, Macrin, Bourbon and others.

April: Rabelais graduates, in Montpellier, as a *licencié* (a step towards his full Doctorate of Medicine).

May: Rabelais becomes a Doctor of Medicine.

June–September: Rabelais possibly in Lyons.

August: Guillaume Du Bellay passes through Lyons on his way to govern the Piedmont. Rabelais joins him.

October: Rabelais lectures at Montpellier on the *Prognostics* of Hippocrates. The course lasts until April 1538.

November: Rabelais presides over a public dissection performed as a lesson in anatomy.

1538 Fresh severe measures decreed against heresy in France.

Summer: Rabelais in Montpellier, from where he joins Guillaume Du Bellay (now the Governor of the Piedmont) in Turin. Publishes his *Stratagemata*, praising the military prowess of Guillaume Du Bellay. No copy is known.

First edition of the anonymous *Panurge disciple de Pantagruel* (seven editions follow, variously named).

1538–40 Rabelais possibly in Lyons. He may have made a visit to Bordeaux. His son Théodule may have been born in this period, rather than 1535.

1540 Rabelais' children François and Junie relieved of the stigma of illegitimacy by the papal curia.

December: Rabelais back in France (via Chambéry). Publishes an *Almanac for 1541*.

1540–42 Rabelais in Piedmont with Guillaume Du Bellay.

1541 Rabelais returns to France in November (when Guillaume Du Bellay reports on Piedmont).

1542 Guillaume Postel violently attacks Rabelais in print. Rabelais will mock him in his *Fourth Book*.

April: Rabelais passes through Lyons en route for Turin with Guillaume Du Bellay. The revised *Pantagruel*, published by François Juste, dates from this period. Etienne Dolet brings out a pirate edition without the revisions made by Rabelais. During his various stays in Italy Rabelais reads Celio Calcagnini, the mythographer.

November: Guillaume Du Bellay, ill, includes Rabelais amongst the beneficiaries of his will. He leaves Turin for France in December. Rabelais is with him.

1543 January: Guillaume Du Bellay dies near Roanne. Rabelais is present and escorts the body home.

March: *Gargantua* and *Pantagruel* figure on the list of censorable books drawn up by the Sorbonne for the Paris Parlement. Rabelais is present (with Ronsard and others) at burial of Guillaume Du Bellay in the Cathedral of Le Mans.

1544 August: The Sorbonne's revised list of censorable books is sent to the printers: Rabelais figures in it.

1545 January: François Bribart, secretary of Jean Du Bellay, burnt at the stake.

April: The massacre of the Vaudois.

September: François I provides the royal *privilège* for the *Third Book of Pantagruel* (signed by Delauney).

1546 Before Easter: *The Third Book* printed by Christian Wechel (Paris). At least three other printings follow.

Rabelais discreetly slips away to Metz. He is appointed Physician to the City. He reads works of Luther.

August: Etienne Dolet is burnt in the Place Maubert. Jean Du Bellay exchanges his bishopric of Paris for that of Le Mans (which is better than Paris for his health).

December: The expanded catalogue of books censored since May 1544 is published; it includes the *Third Book of Pantagruel*.

1547 April: Henri II succeeds to the throne. Jean Du Bellay remains in favour.

June: After the coronation of Henri II at Rheims, Jean Du Bellay leaves for Rome.

Probably the last of the payments to Rabelais as physician in Metz. He travels from Metz to Rome, possibly leaving the 'partial' *Fourth Book* with Pierre de Tours in Lyons. Remains in Italy until 1549.

1548 During this year, there are at least two printings of the 'partial' *Fourth Book*.

June: Rabelais in Rome.

1549 February: The birth of Louis of Orleans, second son of Henry II.

March: The festivities held in Rome in honour of Henry II are described by Rabelais in his *Sciomachie*.

September: Jean Du Bellay leaves Rome. Violent attack on Rabelais in a work, *Theotimus*, by an important theologian of the Sorbonne, Gabriel Dupuyherbault, whom Rabelais will mock in his *Fourth Book*.

1550 August–October: Rabelais is at Saint-Maur with Jean Du Bellay (convalescent). He meets the Cardinal Odet de Châtillon, who assures him of the royal favour and of his own support.

August: The royal *privilège* for all of Rabelais' works granted in the presence of Odet de Châtillon. Calvin attacks Rabelais in his *Treatise on Scandals*.

1551 The Sorbonne publishes a list of censored books which includes editions of *Pantagruel*, *Gargantua* and the *Third Book*.

Rabelais enjoys two benefices: Meudon and Saint-Christophe-du-Jambet (Sarthe). He does not reside.

1552 January: The *Fourth Book* is printed by Fezandat in Paris;

it contains a *Preliminary Epistle* addressed to Cardinal Odet de Châtillon.

March: The Paris Parlement condemns the new *Fourth Book* at the request of the Sorbonne. It provisionally forbids the sale of the *Fourth Book* pending directions from the king.

April: The triumphant entry of Henry II into Metz. Fezandat reprints two pages of the *Fourth Book* to insert a eulogy of the French victories.

October: (Untrue) rumour that Rabelais is in prison.

1553 January: Rabelais resigns his benefices at Meudon and Saint-Christoph-du-Jambet.

Before 14 March: Rabelais dies in La Rue des Jardins in Paris. He is buried in the cemetery of St Paul's Church.

1555 October: Calvin attacks Rabelais in a sermon.

1562 The *Isle Sonante* is published.

1564 Publication of the *Fifth Book*.

The Council of Trent concludes and publishes the *Index Librorum Prohibitorum*, which places Rabelais at the head of the 'heretics of the first class'.

Introduction

BAWDY, AND INCOMPARABLE

Rabelais has made us laugh for centuries. His name evokes fun, merriment, jests and bawdiness at its best. Yet his laughter is not all on the surface and not always easy to grasp: it leads to a smiling, charitable and tolerant wisdom which accepts and surmounts misfortune. He came to call it pantagruelism. Like Democritus in antiquity, Rabelais deserves the name of Laughing Philosopher.

Dictionaries define his comedy as gross, bawdy and often scatological. It certainly can be, but the *Oxford (New English) Dictionary* is wider in its terms. There *Rabelaisian* means 'an exuberance of imagination and language, combined with extravagance and coarseness of humour and satire'. Admirers of Rabelais can go along with that, but such judgements fall far short of the praise heaped on him. His countrymen never underestimated him. Calvin certainly did not; he read him, though he disliked him and may have feared him. Calvin's successor Theodore Beza both admired him and enjoyed him: he was astonished at the philosophical depths of Rabelais even when he was jesting and wondered what he must be like when he was serious.

Chateaubriand classed Rabelais with Dante, Homer and Shakespeare as a genius who gave suck to all the others. Flaubert placed him beside Homer, Michelangelo and Goethe. Rabelais was read by Francis Bacon, Molière, Diderot, Balzac and dozens of other giants.

We expect to find a taste for him in Jonathan Swift, Laurence

Sterne and James Joyce; but he was enjoyed too by men such as Charles Kingsley, the author of *The Water Babies*. He found his way amongst the Lake Poets, especially in Southey's delightfully rambling miscellany *The Doctor, &c*, in which figure two Lakeland physicians, father and son. Southey's elder Dr Daniel picked up the odd volume of his English *Rabelais* in Kendal. (They were shelved with his *Pilgrim's Progress* and Plutarch's *Morals*.) 'The elder Dr Daniel could make nothing of this book,' Southey tells us, and the younger Dr Daniel, who was about ten years old when he began to read it, understood of it 'less than he could of the *Pilgrim's Progress*. But he made out something.' That younger Dr Daniel 'was by nature a Pantagruelist'. Southey comments that true Pantagruelists are rare. 'Greece produced three great tragic poets, and only one Aristophanes. The French have but one Rabelais.' He held that 'all the greatest poets had a spice of Pantagruelism in their composition', seeing it as 'essential to their greatness'. Homer was a Pantagruelist, especially in his lost mock-heroic poem *Margites*. 'Shakespeare was a Pantagruelist; so was Cervantes.' And Southey concludes: 'until the world has produced two other men in whom that humour has been wanting equal to these, I hold my point established'.[1]

From the start the clergy appreciated Rabelais. His patrons included liberal princes of the Church with Lutheran leanings. (For many Luther meant freedom, joy and laughter.) Centuries later, Trollope's Archdeacon Grantly kept his *Rabelais* locked away in his book-room (safe, he fondly thought, from the eyes of his wife).

Grantly enjoyed him for his witty mischief; others liked his merry pranks. So did succeeding generations from the earliest times, but they often enjoyed him for much more. French revolutionaries tended to think of him as one of theirs. Nineteenth-century free-thinkers were sure he was one of them. (Those who do not like him and dismiss him as sordid include Solzhenitsyn's Soviet Commissar in *The Cancer Ward*.) His laughing philo-

---

1. Robert Southey, *The Doctor, &c*, (in chapters VI P.1 and XVII P.1 in that work's idiosyncratic numbering). Homer's *Margites* is known only from allusions, fragments and quotations.

sophy appeals to the humanity of so many in so many lands.
Like Erasmus, Rabelais is a deeply Christian author who is read
and enjoyed by readers who do not share his faith and who
do not even always recognize it in his writings. His satire of
superstition and hypocrisy is priceless. His thought welcomes and embraces the wisdom of the ancient world and the
kinds of laughter which lead us to look afresh at the world
around us.

Yet when readers come to him for the first time they are often
puzzled. What are they to make of these astonishing books with
their extraordinary and fantastical narratives which often push
back the frontiers of decency, with their long lists of words and
names, their arresting prologues which make the books read
like plays and their ability to give to print the allusion of speech
at many levels of the social scale? The answer to that question
is that the works of Rabelais really are *sui generis*: there is
nothing else like them. When Guillaume Budé (the great scholar
whom Rabelais admired) needed to define the Greek word
planos (a kind of wandering trickster such as the Panurge of
Pantagruel), he simply gestured towards François Villon: 'His
name alone is as good as a definition.' For *Rabelaisian* too we
might do the same, and point towards Rabelais. He is his
own definition. But we can be helped for example by knowing
something of Shakespeare. Rabelais and Shakespeare have
much in common: they intertwine tears and laughter, comedy
and tragedy. Their ghosts walk and their witches cast spells;
their peasants are funny; topsy-turvy standards reign during
Twelfth Night and Carnival, when reprobates and rogues are
sources of fun not indignation, when London youths or Parisian
students play outrageous tricks on the pillars of the establish-
ment and their prudish ladies.

The lack of moral censure of the lecherous companions in
Pantagruel (in, that is, the first of our books by Rabelais)
worries some readers. They might meditate on Charles Lamb's
defence of Congreve and Wycherly, the seventeenth-century
playwrights, against the dulling influences of bourgeois drama:
'We dread infection from the scenic representation of disorder,
and fear a painted pustule. In our anxiety that our morality

should not take cold, we wrap it up in a great blanket surtout of precaution against the breeze and the sunshine.' Lamb is 'glad for a season to take an airing beyond strict conscience'. He loves, 'for a dream-while or so, to imagine a world with no meddling restrictions'. He then comes back to his cage and to restraint 'the fresher and more healthy for it'. He is 'the gayer, at least, for it'. Those fictional immoralities and freedoms 'are a world of themselves almost as much as fairy land'.[2] Southey's younger Dr Daniel took especial delight in the bottom-wiping chapter of *Gargantua* when he read it as a boy. C. S. Lewis, a sound guide in matters of the bawdy, maintains that it is the Christian theology underpinning Rabelais which best explains the pleasure taken in that chapter. Human beings, unlike other animals, are not at ease with their condition, which they find comic (or in the case, say, of dead bodies, eerie). Something seems to have gone wrong with us. We are the only animals who find our sexuality laughable. Dogs and horses do not. So too for all the natural functions of the body, many of which we consistently hide. Most other creatures do not. So too death (which is often comic in Rabelais). Human beings veil their physical functions, so comedy tugs the veil cheekily aside.

It might be expected that graver sages would dislike Rabelais, but it is not so. Even the sober Dean Inge of Saint Paul's found 'the ribaldry of Aristophanes and Rabelais comparatively harmless'. It was part of his world as a scholar whose intellectual sphere embraced the normative laughter of the ancient world. But Rabelais was no more content than Molière to limit his comedy to ribaldry and slapstick. Molière needed his philosophical *Misanthrope*, Rabelais, his *Third Book*; Molière, his daring *Dom Juan* with its challenging of misused rank and power, Rabelais, the riches of his *Fourth Book*.

To enjoy Rabelais and Shakespeare is to delight in words. Both of them kindle our delight in language. (The volumes which Rabelais himself certainly saw through the press contain nothing but words: he had no need of woodcuts or illustra-

2.   Charles Lamb: *The Essays of Elia*: essay 'Of the Artificial Comedy of the last Century'.

tions.) Both delight in speech in all its diversity. Both enjoy complex word-play; both use puns seriously and in fun. Rabelais is far more erudite, but Shakespeare ranges more widely. Unlike Shakespeare, however, Rabelais, the erstwhile friar and monk, is simply not concerned to create realistic female characters. Both are at home, though, with popular farces and their often harsh conventions: Rabelais expounds some of his deepest thoughts in chapters presented as farces. The objects of our laughter in a farce on the stage (as in a cartoon on television or in a chapter of Rabelais or a scene in Shakespeare) are getting their comic deserts, often in terms of what would be extreme cruelty if the laughter were drained away and the cruelty taken to be real). But when all is said and done, Rabelais, who changes his comic norms from book to book, must be left to speak for himself (with a measure of help, at times, from his editors).[3]

RABELAIS THE MAN:
WINE AND SCHOLARSHIP

Rabelais studied deeply and travelled far, yet he never cut himself off from his own *pays*. He was profoundly learned in an age which respected erudition, yet he never lost the common touch. He seems to have had a happy childhood in a well-off family in Touraine. The family home was La Devinière near Chinon. He rejoices in the local wine; delights in the local place-names; revels in the peasants, friends and patrons he knew in Touraine. As children we live our lives amidst giants who may seem powerful but erratic and silly. For Rabelais reminiscences of childhood evoke happy memories of them: his great war in *Gargantua* is fought over the castle, fields, streams and ford which lie around the family home. Throughout his books, fantasy intertwines with the real, the personal, the local, the private.

---

3.   In this edition each chapter of Rabelais is preceded by an Introduction
      designed to clear the way. That allows footnotes to be reduced to a
      minimum.

He remained in touch with popular culture (culture, that is, which, at all levels of society, expressed itself in French not Latin). Yet he could never be a 'popular' author appealing to the uneducated masses. He wrote with the art and erudition of a Renaissance scholar. He makes great demands on his readers. Already in his lifetime those demands were accepted: copies of his books quickly made their way into the libraries of kings, convents and cathedrals as well as into more modest book-rooms.

Rabelais is the high-priest of wine happily drunk in good company. Wine in his writings is not usually a symbol of something else, though it can be. For Rabelais (as for David, whose psalms Rabelais had chanted, day in day out, in his convent chapel) 'wine maketh glad the heart of man'. There is a Dionysiac savour about many of his best pages. It is as a famous physician that he linked good wine with the laughter he aroused to make the sufferings of his patients more bearable. He held with the ancients that wine can delight and inspire. As a physician he was sure that (in moderation) it does us good. It can be drunk with delight as a means of quite literally raising our spirits. In his *Fourth Book*, published not long before he died, he presents wine – symbolized by the figure of the Wingèd Bacchus at Amyclae – as a God-given means of lightening our bodies and lifting our minds up towards things spiritual.

By then his knock-about giant has changed into a Renaissance Socrates, open to divine promptings. By then readers have discovered that the mechanics of sex, crapulence and gluttony are amusing as part of a wider vision of what men and women are, or may become.

Some delicious country foods were highly perishable: most entrails especially had to be eaten soon after the slaughter. In mid-winter a great many animals had to be culled so as to leave enough fodder for the ones to be kept. So country folk enjoyed mid-winter feasts of tripe as the February cull met the wine of the last autumn's *vendange*. Rabelais delights in those cherished intervals of merriment brought round by the rolling year with its Twelfth Night indulgences and Shrovetide revels. Even the lofty Pantagruel of the *Fourth Book* takes grateful pleasure in rare stately banquets. He presides over a companionable feast celebrating a longed-for change in the weather. Only the idle belly-worshippers treat their whole lives as though there were nothing else in the world but Twelfth Night feasts and carnivalesque debaucheries. And they are trounced for it in the *Fourth Book*.

RABELAIS THE MAN: MEDICINE, LAW AND OTHER STUDIES

From the outset medical men liked Rabelais. The earliest extant allusion to *Pantagruel* in print is found in a lecture delivered before the medical faculty at Nantes on 7 August 1534. The lecturer, an Italian physician, contrasts the modest contents of a proper enema with the enormous compound prescribed by a rival, more worthy, he thinks, of the giants in those recent books of *Pantagruel* enjoying such a success.

That Rabelais was a physician everyone knows. That he was a student of the law is less known. Law was his first love. He counted amongst his earliest friends in Touraine André Tiraqueau, a great legal scholar. Legal men and women may still feel a certain complicity with Rabelais. He can think like a lawyer: his *Third Book* was constructed by a man who knew his Roman Law inside out (and its glossators too). He can still arouse laughter even in his most legal mode. But not always: few readers today can laugh their lonely way unaided through the chapters on Mr Justice Bridoye in the *Third Book*. Yet, with a little help and effort, smiles, laughter and sudden guffaws can again break through.

As a young man Rabelais joined the Observantines (the stricter branch of the Franciscans). He read theology. He was ordained a priest. He must have studied Bonaventura, the glory of his Order. At the same time he developed a solid acquaintance amongst distinguished Touraine 'humanists' (scholars who gave pride of place to the 'more humane' writings of Greece and Rome). For humanists everywhere elegant Latin stretched from before Cicero and Seneca right up to Jerome in the fourth century (and even, exceptionally, to Bernard of Clairvaux in the twelfth). As for the study of Greek, it included almost everything written in that fluent tongue: Plato of course; Aristotle too, but also Aristophanes and Lucian amongst the laughers, the medical authorities Hippocrates and Galen, Plutarch the moralist, the New Testament and all the Greek theologians (including many disliked by Rome). Several humanists aspired to learn Hebrew, often very successfully. (Rabelais knew at least something of that tongue.)

Rabelais was hounded by his Franciscan superiors who disapproved of his studying Greek. (Greek encouraged dangerous thoughts.) He shared that ordeal with his learned friend Pierre Amy. In his *Third Book* Rabelais recalls how Pierre Amy had consulted Homeric and Virgilian 'lots' (which involved opening pages of Homer and Virgil and seeking guidance from selected lines of verse). He was led to renounce his vows and flee. Rabelais, however, had behaved more prudently: great folk intervened for him and he was transferred quite legally to the Benedictines.

Already, as a Franciscan, Rabelais was corresponding with Guillaume Budé, the leading French student of Greek and a towering legal authority. He found a generous patron in his local bishop, Geoffroy d'Estissac, who supported him even when he had abandoned his new Order to become a physician. After living in Paris (irregularly for a professed monk), he quickly graduated in medicine at Montpellier.

He retained mixed memories of his short Benedictine phase. In many ways he remained a Franciscan rather than a monk. (Franciscans are mendicants not monks.) Nevertheless his Frère Jean, one of the greatest comic characters of all time, is a Benedictine, often simply called 'The Monk'.

The break Rabelais made with the religious life was final. His two surviving children, François and Junie, were eventually legitimated (1540) by the Vatican bureaucracy. They bore the surname of Rabelais. He also fathered a son called Théodule, 'Slave of God'. The child was dandled on the knees of cardinals. He died in infancy. Rabelais, working as a physician with few outward signs of his religious vocation, was in Church law an apostate, a traitor to his vows. That was ingeniously put right. His champion in such matters was his patron Jean Du Bellay, the Bishop of Paris, who, despite (or because of) his Lutheran sympathies, was made a cardinal in 1535. Rabelais wrote and submitted to the Vatican a *Supplication for his Apostasy*: thanks to Jean Du Bellay, who knew how to thread skilfully through the labyrinthine ways of the Vatican bureaucracy, he duly ended up a secular priest (1536), living in the world and permitted to practise his 'art' (his medicine), though, as a man in holy Orders, forbidden to shed blood whilst doing so.

From 1536 he was 'Dr' Rabelais or 'Father' Rabelais, widely known and respected for his knowledge of medicine and law.

RABELAIS AND HIS PATRONS

Rabelais had several patrons, clerical and lay. All were liberal thinkers. Some at least had Lutheran sympathies. Even before *Pantagruel* and *Gargantua* he was supported by powerful protectors. Geoffroy d'Estissac helped him from the early days. Then he was favoured by Jean Du Bellay and his brother, the statesman Guillaume Du Bellay, the Seigneur de Langey. Rabelais served them both in turn as their private physician. He accompanied each of them to Italy more than once. He was with Langey on 9 January 1543 when he died near Roanne on his way home from the Piedmont. Langey was his hero, praised as such in the *Third* and *Fourth Books*. Dr Rabelais was with Jean Du Bellay (now Bishop of Le Mans) when he completed his *Fourth Book* of 1552.

He stood at the height of his reputation in the 1540s and early 1550s. He was encouraged and protected by his kings (not always effectively: French kings were not in all things above the law). Both François I and Henri II gave him fulsome *privilèges* (legally enforceable rights as an author). Quite exceptionally they covered not only books published or ready to be so, but books yet to be written. Over his *Fourth Book* of 1552 Rabelais was positively courted by Cardinal Odet de Châtillon. That cardinal was a member of a powerful trio, nephews of the great statesman Anne de Montmorency, the Constable of France. Two were openly won over to the Reformation: François d'Andelot and Gaspar de Coligny, the Admiral of France. Some ten years after the death of Rabelais, the Cardinal Odet de Châtillon too dramatically showed his colours. He fled to England and became an Anglican. From there he issued – on what authority? – letters of marque, licences (such as Elizabeth I granted to Francis Drake) permitting corsairs legally to harry enemy shipping. Odet de Châtillon lies buried with honour in Canterbury Cathedral.

In 1546 Rabelais was graciously permitted to dedicate his *Third Book* to Marguerite d'Angoulême, the Queen of Navarre, the liberal, mystical, platonizing, evangelical sister of François I. (An author in her own right, she was a protector of evangelicals, even of some disapproved of by her royal brother.)

Earlier, on 30 December 1532, while physician in the Hôtel-Dieu, the great hospital in Lyons, Rabelais seized an opportunity to write to Erasmus. It was a matter of sending to him a manuscript of Josephus on behalf of Georges d'Armagnac, the princely Bishop of Rhodez. Rabelais was at pains to demonstrate his grasp of Greek, the key to so much wisdom and knowledge. In his carefully calligraphed letter he hails Erasmus not only as his spiritual father but as his mother too, a mother to whose nurture he owed more than he could ever repay. Rabelais had then published little: it was not as a fellow author that he wrote to Erasmus but as an admirer of a sage who had changed his life. Erasmus had already influenced him as a man and was soon to influence him just as deeply in his writings. As an author his debt to Erasmus was to become immense. Erasmus showed that worthwhile things could be achieved outside the cloister. He showed how Christianity could be further enriched by the writings of the ancients. He knew how to laugh and he held medicine in high esteem. Rabelais became the kind of humanist doctor who risked his life for his patients during the plague: the kind of physician whom Erasmus could admire.

LAUGHTER AND BOOKS

Rabelais drew upon the world around him for his smiles and laughter, but he also drew heavily upon all his learned disciplines, law and medicine included. Those who urged Henri II in the 1540s to persuade Rabelais to write a sequel to his *Pantagruel* and *Gargantua* were 'the learned men of the Kingdom'. William Hazlitt, the eighteenth- and early nineteenth-century critic and essayist, captures a vital aspect of Rabelais' art when he imagined him

> with an eye languid with an excess of mirth, his lip quivering with a new-born conceit, and wiping his beard after a well-seasoned jest, with his pen held carelessly in his hand, his wine-flagons and his books of law, of school divinity, and of physic before him, which were his jest-books, whence he drew endless stores of absurdity; laughing at the world and enjoying it by turns, and making the world laugh with him again for the last three hundred years, at his teeming wit and his own prolific follies. Even to those who have never read his works, the name of Rabelais is a cordial for the spirits, and the mention of it cannot consist with gravity or spleen!'[4]

It is a pleasing picture but a partial one. All his special fields required sound Latin, but Rabelais was also at home with the culture of those who knew nothing but French. One of the works he most often evokes is *Maître Pathelin*, a French farce laughing at lawyers which was performed at Court by Songecreux, a great comic actor. Rabelais was also at home in the world of student farces and the tumultuous world of the Latin Quarter. He knew what bawdy songs were sung in college, town and royal palace. He delighted in the pranks associated with Tyl Eulenspiegel or the François Villon of life or legend.

---

4. William Hazlitt, *Lectures on the English Comic Writers* (Oxford University Press, 1907), pp. 34–5.

In *Pantagruel* he can show that he had read More's *Utopia* but also enjoyed the talk and jests of simple folk in town and country.

Anyway, not all the tomes that he read in Greek and Latin were grave and solemn. A major influence on him was Lucian, the late Greek mocker whom Erasmus too had taken as a model. Works of that grinning Greek (the joy of many a subtle writer) were being translated into Latin by well-known scholars and so made widely accessible. Erasmus translated some. So did Thomas More. So did the wise and tolerant Melanchthon, the Lutheran Preceptor of Germany. And so did Rabelais, while still a Franciscan. (His translation has been lost.) Already called the French Democritus, Rabelais became the French Lucian. Lucian is strongly present in each of his works. Yet for some critics of his day (despite Erasmus, Melanchthon and the like), even to admire Lucian suggested more than a hint of atheism: had not Lucian mocked Christians in his dialogue *The Passing of Peregrinus?*

Rabelais also became acquainted with the laughter found in ancient Greek or Latin comedies and Latin satires. He accepted (with most who wrote about laughter, many of whom were medical men) that laughter is the 'property of Man'. Laughter is an activity that humans share with no other creature. It is 'proper' to them. It defines the human being. It divides mankind from all the rest of creation. When Rabelais calls someone an *agelast* (a sad sobersides, a non-smiler, a non-laugher) the judgement is harsh and dehumanizing. For both his kings Rabelais was worthy of the highest accolade as defined by the Roman poet Horace: he 'mixed the useful and the sweet'. He is 'sweet' (enjoyable) but also 'useful' (a sound moralist).[5] Rabelais is a moralist in the French sense, often more inclined to paint folly than to inveigh against it (though he can do that too). He is a moralist who shows up human follies with humour, and who commends virtue in ways that make us want to go on reading him.

Such an author cannot be ignored, for he often stirs up great

5.   Horace *The Art of Poetry*, l. 343.

controversies. Rabelais was troublesome from the start. Each
book of his at once provoked a storm for, besides his many
admirers, he had powerful enemies who would willingly have
burnt his books (and him as well). It required courage to take
on the Sorbonne (the main body of French theologians), the
Vatican and the many who opposed his ideas and those of his
patrons. None of his books quietly glided into prominence.
Pantagruel was no sooner published when would-be censors
impotently condemned it. When *Gargantua* was being written,
Paris was in turmoil over heresy, with religious riots firmly
suppressed. Rabelais had to flee from Lyons to Italy in January
1535. After the *Third Book* (1546) he fled to Metz, then a free
German city. Censors tried to suppress his *Fourth Book* of
1552. They failed, but rumour suggested (wrongly, it seems)
that he was in serious trouble. In 1562, the Council of Trent
put him on their *Index of Forbidden Books* as a 'heretic of the
first class'. But he went on being read. And discreetly published
too, openly abroad, or in France under false addresses. (Molière
assumes that his audience has read him.)

THE BOOKS IN TURN

Pantagruel

Each of the books has its own very distinct personality. Behind
each one lie other books besides Lucian. Behind the first book,
Pantagruel, there lies an anonymous little French chapbook,
*The Great and Inestimable Chronicles of the Great and Enor-
mous Giant Gargantua*. (Rabelais' own *Gargantua* came later.)
Rabelais draws on it for his own 'chronicle' of funny giants,
and also on Pulci's *Morgante Maggiore* and on the curious
tales told by Merlin Coccaïe (Folengo) in his *Macaronics* (verse
written in a fusion of Italian and Latin). Rabelais also found
his way into a work then available only in Hebrew, *The Pirkei
of Rabbi Eliezar*, many of whose laughs derive from Old Testament stories. It supplied him with some of his best Scriptural
fun, above all with the giant riding astride Noah's Ark and
guiding it with his feet.

Before Rabelais, *Penthagruel* (as he was sometimes spelt) was a sea imp who shovelled salt into the throats of drunkards to increase their thirst. 'Penthagruel,' men said, 'had them by the throat'. Rabelais, writing towards the end of a dreadful four-year-long drought, turned that imp into a Gallic giant. He is now as huge as the legendary Gargantua. Pantagruel's name now is cheekily derived from *Pan*, all, and *gruel*, thirst!

Pantagruel is a Renaissance book of Twelfth Night and Mardi Gras merriment, when men and women in Court, town and village laughed for a while at their dearest beliefs. (Drunkenness is fun for a Twelfth Night Toby Belch: it is not so in normal times for a Michael Cassio, nor, indeed, for a Falstaff.) *Pantagruel* finds some of its best laughter in the Bible. Pantagruel is at times a sort of Shrovetide Christ, a comic parallel to the Jesus of Scripture.

Pantagruel is also an amused parody of tales of chivalry. A book of legal laughter, too. (The very title-page of *Pantagruel* in its first edition is done up to look like a Latin law-book.) It also had its say on education. More boldly, it laughs at *Magistri Nostri* ('Our Masters' as the theology dons were proudly called). Such laughter greatly increases in the second edition. In several pages *Pantagruel* is strikingly evangelical in tone. Rabelais laughs at the rights and privileges claimed by the University of Paris. (French kings did not always like those entrenched freedoms.) He trod on a great many toes, but his enemies had to work within legal constraints. No record of any legally enforceable condemnation of *Pantagruel* survives from the time of its first success. But in 1533 the Sorbonne had taken measures against *The Mirror of the Sinful Soul*, a committed, evangelical poem by Marguerite de Navarre, the king's sister. With the help of his troops the king soon put a stop to that! The Reverend Dr Jean Leclerc, trying to excuse his conduct, made reference to a mix-up with 'obscene' books: *Pantagruel* and *The Forest of Cunts*. Rabelais tacked bitter laughs against such censoring hypocrites on to the end of *Pantagruel*. He made wry remarks about them in *Gargantua* too, referring back to *Pantagruel*. The only surviving copy of the first edition of *Pantagruel* bears clear signs of a censor's pen. *Pantagruel* contains jokes about Scripture which horrified some. (Tastes were changing towards a sustainedly solemn treatment of Holy Writ.) Rabelais had dared to laugh at institutions such as the Sorbonne which could do him harm. He soon felt it wise to cut out or tone down some of his boldest gibes. Later editions of *Pantagruel* (and of *Gargantua* too) suffer for that prudence; that is why it is the text of the first editions of them (with later variants) that are translated here.[6]

Gargantua

Gargantua (early 1535 or autumn 1534) forms a marked contrast with *Pantagruel*. *Pantagruel* pretended to be a popular chap-book: *Gargantua* is afraid of being taken for one. *Pantagruel* revels in allusions to tall tales of chivalry: *Gargantua* evokes Plato from its very first lines. *Gargantua* is presented in its Prologue as a book which resembles Socrates. Both are *sileni*, a term drawn from Silenus, the jester of the gods, the gross, ugly old devotee of Bacchus. *Sileni* are presented as little graven images with a god to be found hidden inside them when they are opened up, or as pharmacists' boxes decorated on the outside with grotesques or, say, an ugly old flute-player. But open them up and look within and you find something precious, something divine. So too for Socrates and for *Gargantua*. Socrates, called a *silenus* by Alcibiades, hid divinely prompted wisdom within his ugly exterior. *Gargantua* may well look ugly on the outside, printed as it was in old-fashioned gothic type, yet, inside, it treats of 'the highest hidden truths and the most awesome mysteries touching upon our religion as well as upon matters of State and family life'. By referring thus to the *Sileni* Rabelais is, from the outset, underlining his debt to Erasmus. With another echo of Erasmus, *Gargantua* is likened to *Pythagorean symbols*. Superficially such symbols appear to be

---

6.   Rabelais made more changes and additions to *Pantagruel* than to the other three books put together: that is why the footnotes are so much more copious for *Pantagruel* than for the others.

odd and ridiculous, yet – like *Gargantua* – they contain within them 'precepts for right living.'[7]

In *Pantagruel* the ideal education produced a bookish scholar with his head crammed full. In *Gargantua* we are shown how a young giant, reduced to laughable insanity by paternal ignorance, crapulous old crones and dirty, syphilitic dons from the Sorbonne, can be turned into a Christian knight, cultured and healthy, trained to excel in the arts of peace and war. *Gargantua* touches on politics, including mockery of the dreams of world conquest of the Emperor Charles V. (His capture and ransoming of François I at the defeat of Pavia in 1525 still haunted the French nobility.) *Gargantua* – partly as a reply to a rash little book which laid down the meanings of colours in heraldry – devotes space to topics dear to the aristocracy: heraldry, emblems (then growing into a cult), the true and rational meanings of colours, the education of princes, the avoiding of war whilst prudently preparing for it, and the fighting of battles. Plans are laid for an ideal lay abbey, housing the rich, young, elegant and well-born sons and daughters of the nobility. Protected from the wickedness of the world, they live their lives free from what Saint Paul calls 'the yoke of bondage'. (But ideal freedom allows for great conformity in Thélème, as it did for the Stoics.)

After his uproariously mad education the young Gargantua is purged of insanity by Dr Rabelais and brought up in tempered freedom. The education he is given may have been first conceived as a model for the sons of François I; released in 1530 from their restraint in Madrid as hostages of the Emperor Charles V. (They had been held as pledges for their father's ransom.) The king, fearing that their sense of princely

7.   Renaissance comparisons with *Sileni* (including those of Guillaume Budé and Francis Bacon) owe virtually everything to the adage 'The Sileni of Alcibiades'. (It is translated by Margaret Mann Phillips in *The 'Adages' of Erasmus* (Cambridge University Press, 1964), pp. 269ff.) For Pythagoras, see *Adages*, I, I, I, 'Pythagorean Symbols'. Throughout his works Rabelais remains loyal to an Erasmian concept of Pythagorism.

independence might have been compromised, was determined to have them educated in freedom. Rabelais shows (a little late perhaps, in print) how ideally it could be done.

The reformed Gargantua raises fewer laughs: he was far more laughable as a boy giant obsessed with his hobby-horses and his bum. Rabelais accepted the maxim 'Contraries juxtaposed to contraries shine forth more clearly'. The education of the giant is such a juxtaposition. The young giant delights in suave ways of wiping his bottom: the reformed giant goes modestly to the jakes with his tutor, cleansing body and soul together. From then on it is Frère Jean, 'the Monk', who arouses our laughter. He represents the triumph of the constructive deeds of even the coarse-mouthed over purely passive verbal piety. He is eventually revealed as acting out a parable: he comforts the afflicted and succours the needy. And he guards the Abbey vineyard. What matters is not verbiage but right actions. Merely verbal piety turns prayers into magic spells. As a Franciscan Rabelais had learnt from Saint Bonaventura that justification lies partly with grace and partly in our free-will. Much depends on what we do. God's grace must not be received in vain. That is a recurring theme for Rabelais.[8]

Gargantua appeared during a long period of social unrest. Already in 1532–3, riots in Paris had been provoked by the preachings of evangelical clerics supported by Marguerite de Navarre and other great persons. Was the mob egged on by placards posted up by *agents-provocateurs* disguised as masked revellers and acting for the Sorbonne? It would seem so. But worse was to come. On the night of 17–18 October 1534, densely argued placards were posted up in Paris. We now know that they had been printed in Neuchâtel for followers of Zwingli, the Zurich reformer. The Roman Mass was attacked in

---

8.   In *Pantagruel* (following the Latin Vulgate) men must be 'God's *helpers*'. By the time of the *Fourth Book*, following the original Greek, men must be God's *co-operators*. Much laughter is provoked again on this theme by the Frère Jean of the *Fourth Book*. The technical name for the doctrine of Rabelais is synergism ('working together'). It can be made consonant with Classical wisdom. Cf. Erasmus *Adages* III, IX, LV. 'God helps industriousness'.

them as idolatrous. Suppressed, they appeared again (13 January 1535) when the royal reaction stunned the kingdom. Men and women were burnt. Printing was forbidden. A public act of expiation led by François I suggested that the enemies of liberalism had won. Yet within weeks the king, urged on by the Du Bellays, kept Noël Béda, the fiery and illiberal Syndic of the Sorbonne, under restraint and invited Melanchthon to Paris to discuss reform with selected theologians. (Melanchthon was every moderate's favourite Lutheran. He was invited to England too by Henry VIII.) Unfortunately he was forbidden to leave German lands, but for a while the Du Bellays had triumphed. *Gargantua* is markedly favourable to the causes of the Du Bellays and to the eirenic teachings of Melanchthon. But before any invitation was sent to Melanchthon, Rabelais felt obliged (in January 1535) to abandon his post as physician in the Hôtel-Dieu in Lyons and to flee from France. Laughter in *Gargantua* is not aroused by a man living an uneventful and comfortable existence.

The Third Book of Pantagruel

Over ten years were to pass before Rabelais was persuaded to publish his *Third Book* (1546). It is dedicated to the enraptured 'spirit' (or 'mind') of Queen Marguerite de Navarre, who was a deeply religious woman, both mystical and evangelical. (Rabelais treats her as a contemplative whose mind, caught away to Heaven in rapture, has to be tempted back to earth in order to witness the joyous deeds of his new book.) The *Third Book* is his masterpiece of philosophical comedy.

In form and matter it is an elegant, learned, comic Renaissance work. It too has a book behind it: Lucian's *To One Who Said to Him 'You Are a Prometheus in Words'* in which Lucian defends his fusion of dialogue with comedy: before him, dialogue was the domain of philosophy not laughter. Rabelais quotes him and follows him. The *Third Book* begins as a comic, philosophical dialogue between Pantagruel and Panurge. For the first twelve chapters, nobody else is present. Both characters are fundamentally changed: Pantagruel is now a giant in wisdom, Panurge, an ageing fool, progressively driven deeper into melancholy madness by his yearning to take a wife and his terror of being cuckolded, beaten and robbed if he does so. The stage is set by Panurge's ingeniously perverse praise of debts and debtors. The rest of the book too is taken up with monologue, dialogue and sometimes with comic exchanges like those heard between actors on the trestles in farces such as *Pathelin*. It is a feast of rhetoric and dialectic, twin subjects of study in Renaissance schools and colleges.

The framework of the book owes much to legal doctrines about how to deal with 'perplex cases' – legal cases where the law reaches an impasse. The advice of Roman Law is to follow two intertwining courses: to consult acknowledged experts and harmonize their opinions; and then, when (in the technical legal phrase) 'there is no other way', to seek counsel from dice, divination and lots. Rabelais runs through the gamut of methods of divination and of Renaissance wisdom and knowledge, all of which, as he expounds them, are wreathed in smiles or shot through with the sudden glory of laughter. It is all the more amusing in that a decision to marry or not should not be a 'perplex case' (as Thomas More remarked elsewhere with a smile). Panurge ought to make up his own mind about marriage.

But there are such things in law as truly 'perplex cases': cases which defy a clear, rational decision, cases where the law itself is clear but its application is not. The *Third Book* reveals how to deal with them in accordance with Roman Law and Christian simplicity.

Rabelais is indebted throughout to both André Tiraqueau and Guillaume Budé, the summits of French judicial studies. The *Third* is the most difficult of the four books. For many it is also the most rewarding. Its comedy is complex and profound. Such a book cannot please everyone: Rabelais tells us that his public found its 'wine' – here, its more easily accessible comedy – little but good. They preferred it to be plentiful and good. He took the hint.

The Fourth Book of Pantagruel

After the *Third Book* Rabelais, despite his royal *privilège*, prudently slipped away to Metz, a free city, a Lutheran city. Life for him there was marked by a degree of poverty. He had made more enemies, kept powerful friends, and gained more. And in Metz he was already reading Lutheran books destined to enrich his art and thought.

The *Fourth Book* has a puzzling history. In 1548 a shorter *Fourth Book* appeared, clearly unfinished and misshapen. It has a well-written Prologue, which is not that of the 1552 *Fourth Book*. It ends up in the air, in the middle of a sentence. Most striking of all, it does not sport its royal *privilège*. To fill up his space the printer padded out the book with old woodcuts drawn from stock. Had he somehow got his hands on an incomplete manuscript of Rabelais' future book? Was it printed without the author's knowledge or consent? It might seem so. But it remains a puzzle.

The *Fourth Book* of 1552 is a very different matter. The Rabelais of the full *Fourth Book* has greatly profited from his reading, some of it gleaned in Italy and in German lands. In Italy, with the Seigneur de Langey, he had read the works of Celio Calcagnini, who was long judged the best mythographer of the Renaissance. Unfortunately he wrote in Latin, so his myths are now all but unknown. His *Works* were a mine for Rabelais (and many others). Under his direct influence Rabelais was inspired to invent and develop myths which stretch across the world and into the heavens. He now begins to talk of his books as 'pantagruelic mythologies'. But even when plunged into works of erudition, Rabelais never overlooked more popular writings. For his *Fourth Book* he borrowed from a little work which had appropriated some of his characters, and tells of a sea-voyage, of Chidlings and of a giant Bringuenarilles. Thanks to Rabelais it has earned its modest place in literary history.[9]

9.   The little book goes by various names including *Le Disciple de Pantagruel* and *Les Navigations de Panurge*, as well as *La Navigation du Compagnon à la Bouteille*.

Rabelais already showed in *Pantagruel* his admiration for Plutarch's *Moral Works*. Some twenty years later they come fully into their own in the *Fourth Book*. Several of the most profound pages Rabelais ever penned were written with his Plutarch open before him. Especially important is *The Obsolescence of Oracles*; important too are *The Oracles at Delphi*, with *On Isis and Osiris* and *On the 'Ei' at Delphi*.

Another very different work also contributed much. In Metz Rabelais read a strongly satirical work by Martin Luther, *Of the Papacy of Rome, Constructed by the Devil*. It mocks an idolatrous respect for the Vatican and for papal power, buttressed as it is by the Decretals, edicts issued on the sole authority of popes. Some of the Decretals were already known to be forged. (They had misled Thomas Aquinas.) Luther also tells how zealous, generous boobies are sneeringly called 'Good Christians' by the unbelievers who, for him, dominate the papal Curia.

Rabelais transmutes Luther's bleak satire into the pure gold of the moral laughter which dominates the episode of the *Papimanes*. Far away on their island, isolated in zealous and intolerant ignorance, they innocently, gullibly, cruelly – and maniacally – worship the very objects of Luther's mockery. They worship the wrong god and venerate the wrong scriptures.

Cardinal Odet de Châtillon and others had hoped to persuade Henri II to break with Rome in 1551-2 and to set up a national Church of France, not unlike the Church of England. He met Rabelais and, assuring him of his own support and of that of his king, persuaded him to write under his protection. Safe at last, Rabelais could write as he dared. And in the *Fourth Book* – a book protected by a Royal *privilège* and proudly prefaced by an Epistle to the Cardinal Odet de Châtillon in person – he dared a great deal.

Another book to influence him was Plato's *Cratylus*. Before he had studied the *Cratylus* Rabelais worked within the standard linguistic ideas of Aristotle: to speak is natural, but no language is natural. Except for onomatopoeias, words are sounds on to which meanings have been arbitrarily imposed.

For Plato in the *Cratylus* words are more complex. Onomato-poeias, for Plato as for Aristotle, convey their sense in their sound, but the 'true' meaning of some words is to be sought in their etymologies. (Etymology involved seeking out the *etymon*, the word's *true* meaning.) In the roots of at least some words lie half-veiled truths.

Platonic 'ideas' dwell as *paroles* ('words') in the heavenly Manor of Truth. At long intervals some of those words drip down like catarrh on to our snotty world. When they do so, they contain divine revelations. And they will providentially do so 'world without end' – until, that is, the 'end of the age'. Some authors would have made heavy weather of such profundities: Rabelais turns them into part of a laughing venture of discovery. We discover areas of mystical truth. We learn how mankind must cooperate with grace. And all this in a comic book, with Dionysiac laughter never far away.

Love links Heaven and earth but our fallen world is driven by Signor Belly, by fear of hunger. We are conducted to the Manor of Truth, and then to the Manor of Virtue, where our guide is a famous myth from Hesiod which tells how the upward path is laborious, rough and stony, yet Virtue, once reached, dwells in smooth and pleasant uplands. The elevating powers of wine are praised. The ways of an inspired Pantagruel and of a self-loving, squittering Panurge are contrasted. Pantagruel becomes a Renaissance Socrates, divinely guided in his wisdom. In the purest comic tradition Panurge remains unchanged, cheekily fixed in his filth and folly. He now remains for ever where Gargantua the boy giant once was: delighting in the products of his anus. And the book, like its predecessors, ends up in the air.

All four books by Rabelais sport with signs. Signs and ges-tures may be real (natural) or conventional. From *Pantagruel* onwards Rabelais laughs at those who confuse self-evident, natural signs (such as pangs of hunger, messing one's trousers, as well as cocking a snook and suggesting coitus with one's fingers or pinching one's nose whilst pointing at someone) with signs which have conventional meanings. Conventional signs have to be learnt. They are understood only by those who know the conventions. The last book that Rabelais sent to the printers before he died ends with signs: Frère Jean des Entommeures is ready to make *entommeures* (mincemeat) of his foes: his very name is a sign of his bravery. The long-delayed laughter of Pantagruel is a sign of his wisdom and humanity. That Panurge has messed himself again is a sign of his servile fear, and the faeces which he delights in are signs of perhaps diabolical error.

The Fifth Book

Rabelais died little over a year after his *Fourth Book* of 1552. But his name sold supposititious books, something he complained of during his lifetime. In 1549 some pages had been passed off as a *Fifth Book of Pantagruel*. (Rediscovered in 1900, it convinced *The Times* for a while.) New books continued to be published under his name after his death. One is the *Isle Sonante* (the *Ringing Isle*) of 1562. Most but not all of it is included, with some variants, in another, which purports to be the *Fifth and Last Book of Pantagruel* of 1564.

It is essentially the *Fifth and Last Book* of 1564, not the *Fifth Book* of 1549, which has for centuries been printed together with the other four in the works of Rabelais. (There is also an incomplete manuscript of it, not in the hand of Rabelais, which gives variant readings.) Some think this *Fifth Book* is based on papers left by Rabelais at his death. (No such papers have been found. Not one page. Not one line. But authors' manuscripts were not often treasured then as they are now.) Others think it has nothing to do with Rabelais, that none of it bears his hallmark, and much of it certainly does not. That is my judgement. At all events, the complete book cannot be by Rabelais as it stands. More than a hint of its arranger (and part author) is given at the end of the first edition. There we find a poem signed NATVRE QVITE.

NATVRE QVITE is an anagram of Jean Turquet. Jean de Mayerne, called Turquet, was a doctor from a solid Piedmontese family. (French was the language of many in the Piedmont, long the citadel of religious reformers.) One Turquet – of the same family – eventually came to England to escape religious persecution, and became a well-known London physician.

The *Fifth Book* is religiously aware, with 'reformed' tendencies. It displays a knowledge of medicine. It also moves into the domain of the transmutation of metals, and of curiously mystical themes more obscurantist than profound. But, by Rabelais or not, it has been printed with the authentic works of Rabelais from the sixteenth century onwards.

Other great authors drag along a train of doubtful works. It may not matter much, but it can. An authentic play by Shakespeare is not likely to be interpreted in the light of a doubtful one. In the case of Rabelais, however, it matters a great deal. Ever since 1564 readers of Rabelais have been presented with copies of his works which include a book, published a decade after his death, which claims to round off his writings. It brings the heroes back to Touraine. It tells of the end of the quest for the 'Word' of the Dive Bouteille, of that 'Sainted Bottle' dwelling in a mystical Never-never Land. Some read back into the four Books the often cryptic meanings they find in the *Fifth*. For them, Rabelais' last word is essentially *Trinck* (Drink!), the 'Word' of the Dive Bouteille. And here *Trinck* risks turning the real, soul-uplifting wine of the wingèd Bacchus of the *Fourth Book* into something other: a quest for something symbolized by wine – knowledge, say, or even enlightenment. The *Fifth Book* is included in this translation, but its various endings leave the reader with a very different savour from that of the end of the *Fourth Book*.

RABELAIS, SCRIPTURE AND
HUMANIST FUN

Rabelais was a learned scholar and readers expect to be impressed. In parallel, at a popular level, restaurants named *Gargantua* or the *Moutons de Panurge* lead readers of Rabelais to expect to find in him a delight in lashings of rich food and wine. They often do, though habitual gorging and swilling may be greeted in Rabelais with wry laughter, even at times with indignation. An occasional banquet, Shrovetide revels and

rustic stuffing of tripe in mid-winter are a delight and presented
as such: idly spending the livelong year on gluttony and crapulence is another matter, as the *Fourth Book* makes crystal clear
through its sometimes remarkably bitter comedy.

What does surprise many is the importance of Scripture in
the four Books, Scripture exploited for both serious and comic
ends. Yet Rabelais was an ordained priest. He lived much of
his adult life amongst churchmen. Erasmus brought both the
Bible and Greek thought alive for him. Clement of Alexandria
had taught generations that what the law was to the Jews
philosophy was to the Greeks: Old Testament religion and
Greek thought were both inspired tutors. Rabelais accepted
that, but his own Erasmian theology was in happy harmony
with Dionysiac elements. Erasmus had no sympathy for them;
nor did he appreciate 'monkish' jokes derived from Scripture
twisted out of context. Rabelais did.

In *Pantagruel* and *Gargantua* especially we find plenty of
what is traditionally called 'monkish' humour. Monks, men
living closely with other men, often cut off from women and
concerned year in, year out, with the daily round of liturgy,
psalms and Scripture, turned to liturgy and Holy Writ, for
comfort, certainly, but also for their jests, some of them remarkably coarse. 'Unto thee I lift up' is the incipit of two psalms: it
is also a 'monkish' term for the rampant penis. 'Charity,' we
are told, 'covers a multitude of sins' (I Peter 4:8). So does a
monastic frock. Christ on the Cross called out, 'I thirst.' So does
the tipsy cleric in *Gargantua*. For pages at a time *Pantagruel*
is, in the spirit of Shrovetide, a parody of Scripture with plenty
of Mardi Gras humour. Rabelais' wider comedy remained
anchored in his grasp of the gulf which separates words from
deeds, bums from minds, rhetorical nonsense or smooth-
speaking hypocrisy from positive action.

Moral comedy needs its triggers to be clear, well-defined or
intuitively grasped. Once that is so, literally anything can be
turned into subjects of laughter: no topic is too awesome. To
leave everything to prayer is lazy, and can be turned into a
subject of laughter. To blubber instead of working hard is
ignoble, and can be turned into a subject of laughter. To prefer

your bum to your mind is odd, and can be turned into a subject of laughter. To worship human beings or objects is idolatrous, and can be turned into a subject of laughter. To interpret words and other signs wrongly is misleading, and can be turned into a subject of laughter. As for cruelty, in a farce it almost always is the subject of laughter. Both birth and death are veiled with awe: stripped of their veils and skilfully trivialized, they too can be turned into subjects of laughter. Rabelais gives his readers clear pointers. One may be simple and intuitive; the next may be a saying from, say, Saint Paul entwined with words from Plato. Rabelais presents them firmly in ways which satisfy. And at least in the background there is always room for pantagruelism – for comradeship, for friendship, for wine drunk in good company and for Dionysiac fun. More than mere smiles lie within an adage such as 'He is no dithyrambic who drinks but water'. Wine both delights and inspires.

There is a progression in the use of Scripture by Rabelais. The prompting came from Erasmus. In *Pantagruel* Rabelais cites Holy Writ as he had learnt to do as a Franciscan, associating type and antitype. For example, at the beginning of *Pantagruel* an amused reference to the Cain and Abel of the Old Testament leads on to a quiet allusion to 'the blood of the righteous' of the New. (Most readers nowadays probably overlook the linkage.)[10] Throughout *Pantagruel* one finds similar links being made. Not normally however in the later books. There Rabelais is more likely to link Plato and the Gospel, as he does for the first time in the *Almanac for 1535*. The *Third Book* links Paul with Lucian, and Roman Law with Lucianesque laughter. The *Fourth Book* is the triumph of Renaissance syncretism (unifying and reconciling the ancient world with mystical truth as Rabelais saw it). Paul is to the fore, but close at hand are Aesop, Plato, Pythagoras and Plutarch.

The fun with Scripture is closely paralleled by fun at the expense of great philosophers. An earnest moral saying of Plato, cited cogently by Cicero, may be turned on its head, only to be cited solemnly later. Platonic 'ideas' or Pythagorean triangles

10. That links Genesis 1 with Matthew 23:35.

are objects of fun before they become matters of deeper import. As Rabelais read Plato, Socrates made folly (or madness) not ignorance the trigger of laughter. And madness comes in myriad guises. Solomon said so: 'The number of fools is infinite.' Avicenna, the much-admired and much-studied Muslim philosopher and physician, says virtually the same. So there are plenty of idiots to laugh at, some of them very grand indeed. The *Third Book* lists dozens of them when ringing the changes on fools and folly.[11]

READ RABELAIS THROUGH, OR DIP INTO HIM?

Not everybody finds it best to start with page one of *Pantagruel* and to read solidly on to the end of the *Fourth Book* (or the *Fifth*). When Rabelais was on the syllabus of virtually every university in the United Kingdom, some prescribed only 'Rabelais, *Gargantua*: from Chapter 23 to the end' (beginning with the peasant strife leading to Picrochole's war). That may still to be a good place to start. Others find the *Fourth Book* the best to begin with. Each book can be read by itself. Others like just dipping in. Many do, keeping him as a bed-side book. Yet in the end, and when the time is ripe, there is nothing quite like starting with page one of *Pantagruel* and reading on. We enter then into a wise world of kaleidoscopic laughter.

THE ORDER OF THE BOOKS

Pantagruel (1532?) appeared well before *Gargantua* (early 1535 or autumn 1534). In editions it is normally placed after it. That order confounds the development of the art of Rabelais from book to book. Here *Pantagruel* comes first. The other works too appear in order of publication. However, the established general title, *Gargantua and Pantagruel* has not been

11. See Chapter 46 of the *Third Book* and Chapter 48 with its list of fools.

switched to *Pantagruel and Gargantua*. To do so would be pedantic.

Rabelais kept *Gargantua and Pantagruel* apart from his overtly learned works, which are often in complex Renaissance Latin. He also wrote French works long classed as minor. Only his *Pantagrueline Prognostication* and his *Almanacs* are given here. The other works remain little frequented by the gentle reader. Photocopiers and scanners make them easily and legally available in English from W. F. Smith's translation of Rabelais (long out of copyright): his scholarly, nineteenth-century English serves them well, but they add little to pantagruelism and its wise kaleidoscopic laughter whilst adding much to the price of the book – and to its bulk (some eighty-seven pages in the Smith edition).[12]

THE FOOTNOTES

Editions of Rabelais can be crushing, with notes taking up more room than the text. Here the footnotes are devoted mainly to variant readings. The sources of Rabelais are given in the introductions to each chapter only when they add to the pleasure or understanding. One exception is made: Erasmus. He is frequently mentioned for his *Adages*. Few books have ever had a greater influence on their times. Now that they are available in English, published by the University of Toronto Press, they are more accessible.[13]

12. *Rabelais. The Five Books and Minor Writings Together with Letters and Documents illustrating His Life. A New Translation with Notes by W. F. Smith, Fellow of Saint John's College, Cambridge, and Member of the Rabelais Club* (2 vols., Alexander P. Watt, 1893).

13. The Toronto *Adages* are far too dear for most pockets but are in many libraries. (The translations given there may differ from those given here.) The *Adages* with the comments upon them remain one of the surest and richest ways of entering into aspects of the mind of Rabelais.

ACKNOWLEDGEMENTS

Specific debts and the editions translated are mentioned in the
Introductions to each Book of Rabelais.

When it appeared in 1991, I read Donald Frame's translation
of Rabelais but have not regularly done so since. It was better
to work separately. That great scholar stayed in my home twice
and we talked about Montaigne and Rabelais. He wrote to me
during the last years of his life, years marked by great suffering
stoically borne. His letters were a pleasure to receive, often
painful to read, but always evoking affection and admiration.
Had he lived he would have eliminated from his translation, as
posthumously published, the gaps, errors and misreadings of
his manuscript. He was a meticulous workman, a warm friend
and a great scholar.

Kazuo Watanabe's work in Tokyo was also a constant encouragement, as he was himself during his lifetime.

My own approach to Rabelais and his text is one that colleagues will recognize. Much will always be owed to those
who laid the foundations of Rabelaisian scholarship from
the eighteenth century onwards. And good work is still being
done.

A great debt is acknowledged to the incomplete *Edition
Critique* of Abel Lefranc and his team. Another to the individual
texts of Rabelais published by Droz of Geneva. W. F. Smith's
translation is a mine of ideas gratefully acknowledged. Guy
Demerson's edited translation of Rabelais into modern French
has been a joy to consult. Mireille Huchon's very full *Rabelais*
for la Pléïade is not easy to handle but is a true cornucopia.

I first read Rabelais as a soldier in the classic seventeenth-
century translation of Urquhart and Motteux. I have not,
however, sought its guidance here. It is at times a recasting of
Rabelais rather than a translation. Its rich English is bound to
its time, and for that very reason remains a joy to read for its
own self. Any echoes of it here (if there are any) are attributable
to long-rooted memory. The only phrase that I know I have
taken from it is Frère Jean's unforgettable refrain, 'Breviary

stuff'. Other translations I have simply avoided for practical reasons.

It was Paul Keegan who first proposed that I translate Montaigne and then Rabelais for Penguin. I owe him many thanks for two decades of pleasant and rewarding work.

My greatest debts are to the many who, over the years, have read Rabelais with me round a table. Truly a joint journey of discovery, leading to a deeper understanding of the Renaissance and to many a good laugh.

A Note on the Translation

My aim here for Rabelais (as for my Penguin Montaigne) is to turn him loyally into readable and enjoyable English. Here too I have not found that meaning is more loyally conveyed by clinging to French syntax and constructions. French and English often achieve similar effects by different means; they very often fall naturally into different word-orders. Rabelais deliberately employs many rare words, words which would have baffled most of his contemporaries. That is a conscious stylistic device. His vocabulary is vast, drawing upon dialects and loan-words as well as on French at its richest. Italian, Dutch, German and even English and Scottish words may jostle with Greek, Latin or Hebrew terms. To translate him always by common-or-garden English terms would be to traduce him. Some of his words should fox readers and others challenge them. Their very rarity is their appeal. Their general meanings (if we need to know them) are normally adumbrated by their contexts. Save for made-up comic words and nonce-words, I try to pour Rabelais' riches into the ample lexical mould of the *Oxford (New English) Dictionary*. It was a joy to do so. There is nothing cramping about that dictionary! Rabelais uses more different words than any other French author. In that, and not only in that, he is like Shakespeare, to whom the same applies in English. Rabelais enjoys punning and elaborately playing with words. Puns may be comic. They may also be deadly serious. Plays on words rarely pass easily from one tongue to another, yet they must be rendered. Occasionally they are best transposed into English equivalents. If so, a more literal version is tucked away somewhere in an introduction or note.

There is no desire to bowdlerize Rabelais, but it is not always best to translate his grosser words by their apparently direct English equivalents. A stronger or weaker word may serve better. Taboo words are far from identical in both languages. *Shit* in English is far more arresting than *merde* in French (one of the words picked up on a first trip to France). *Shit* is by no means always the best translation of *merde*. *Pooh* or some other word may often serve better. The same applies to words such as *cunt* and *con*: *conneries* ('cunteries') is a word accepted in elegant French parliamentary debates or in a polished broadcast. Conversely *cul* may sometimes be better rendered by arse than by bottom or bum. It is not a regular taboo word, though it can be.

When the 'rude' English word is the right one it is of course used. Rabelais is not addressed to the verbally bashful. Yet he is less bold than may be thought. In his own days he was much read aloud: when François I wanted to judge whether Rabelais was orthodox he did not ask the Bishop of Sens, the 'best reader in France', what he thought of him: he ordered him to read him his *Rabelais* so that he could judge for himself. There is no word he read, no theme, no bawdy, which could not be decently read aloud by a bishop to his king, in the presence of his attendant lords and ladies.

Contemporaries were, however, struck by the scatology. The symbol of the physician was the urine bottle and the clyster (or enema), but Rabelais was not just being a doctor. He also associated faeces with error and sometimes with the Devil: piddling is a source of simple laughter; faeces, of laughter more complex and often fully condemnatory.

In the *Fourth Book* Rabelais (perhaps with death in view) ties up his knots. He confronts the comedy of cruelty of which he was a master but which had come to trouble him. Before the end he also reminds readers that scatology is to be found in refined Latin poets and elegant Italian *conteurs*. (Rabelais cites them in the original tongues and leaves you to make what you can of them. Here they are all translated.) Emphasis on the bodiliness of human beings is part of the stock-in-trade of the satirist.

There is *laughing at* and *laughing with*. Rabelais is an adept at catching us out: first trapping us into laughing *at*, when we are about to be led to veneration and awe; or making us laugh *with*, when we are soon to be led to laughing *at*. It is a translator's task to bring that out. Laughter often lies in the names Rabelais gave to his characters. Some of the names are appropriate whilst others very much are not: so names too may trip us up.

Here the names are mainly kept in French. That reminds readers that these are French books anchored in French Renaissance culture.

All Souls College, Oxford

*

This edited translation of Rabelais is dedicated to those students who read Rabelais with me at home and abroad, and especially to those in the University of Birmingham, 1951–61; at University College London and the Warburg Institute, 1961–84; and at All Souls College and Wolfson College, Oxford, from 1984 onwards.

PANTAGRUEL

Introduction to *Pantagruel*

The text as translated here is that of the first edition, which dates from 1531 or 1532.

The present text includes selected variants from the definitive edition of 1542. The variants are shown in two main ways: 1) interpolations are shown in the text and are enclosed within square brackets; 2) eliminations and modifications are given in the notes. Thus, to read the text of the first edition, ignore the interpolations inside square brackets and the variants listed in the notes. To read the definitive text of 1542, read everything.

The first edition of *Pantagruel* (by Claude Nourry of Lyons) is undated, though was probably published in 1532. In *A New Rabelais Bibliography* (NRB)[1] it is numbered 1. Since the Edition Critique the definitive text is taken to be *Pantagruel, Roy des Dipsodes* published by François Juste of Lyons in 1542 (NRB 12).

The text used as the basis for the translation is that edited by V.-L. Saulnier.[2] The Edition Critique[3] is consulted, as is the Pléiade edition of Rabelais edited by Mireille Huchon[4]

---

1. *A New Rabelais Bibliography* (Geneva: Droz, 1987).
2. Rabelais, *Pantagruel*, trans. V.-L. Saulnier (Geneva: Droz, 1946, with later reprints).
3. Abel LeFranc *et al.* (eds.), *Œuvres de Rabelais* (Paris: Champion): *Gargantua*: 1913; *Pantagruel*: 1922; *Le Tiers Livre*: 1931; and continued for *Le Quart Livre* (up to Chapter 17) by Paul Delaunay, Antoinette Huon, Robert Marichal, Charles Perrat and V.-L. Saulnier (Geneva: Droz, and Lille: Librairie Giard, 1955).
4. Rabelais; *Œuvres complètes*, ed. Mireille Huchon with the collaboration of François Moreau (Paris: Editions de la Pléiade, Gallimard, 1994).

and the parallel text version of Guy Demerson,[5] which gives a modern French translation.

5.   Rabelais, *Œuvres complètes*, ed. and trans. Guy Demerson (Paris: Editions du Seuil, 1995).

PANTAGRUEL

The horrifying and dreadful

DEEDS AND PROWESSES

of the most famous

PANTAGRUEL

KING OF THE DIPSODES,

Son of the great Giant Gargantua.

Newly composed by Maître Alcofrybas Nasier

Contents

[Dixain by Maître Hughes Salel to the Author of this Book]

[This poem is not in the only extant copy of the first edition. Hughes Salel, a court poet and valet de chambre *to François I, is the first to apply to Rabelais the highest literary accolade: he 'mixes the useful and the sweet'. As this poem appeared in the edition of 1534 published by François Juste in Lyons, the literary public already had time to judge the merits of* Pantagruel. *Hughes Salel is also the first to call Rabelais the French Democritus.*

The last sentence, 'Long live all good Pantagruelists' was first added in two editions published by François Juste (1534 and 1537).]

> [If mixing moral profit with the sweet
> Enables the good author praise to find
> You will such praises garner, as is meet.
> That I do know. Its laughing face behind,
> Within this book the reader sees your mind
> Build moral profit on foundations new.
> Reborn Democritus in you I view
> Laughing at human beings' silly ways.
> So persevere: should plaudits e'er prove few
> Below: in Highest Regions find due praise.
>
> Long live all good Pantagruelists.]

The Prologue of the Author

[Pantagruel was preceded by a modest little book, The Great and Inestimable Chronicles of the Enormous Giant Gargantua. It is a chapbook, not from the pen of Rabelais. Alcofribas Nasier (an anagram of François Rabelais, the 'author' of Pantagruel) pretends in his patter that his book is of the same kidney. The other books which it is compared to are mainly medieval romances, or parodies of them (much enjoyed in modernized prose versions).

The allusion to Raimbert Raclet, a professor of Law at Dôle who is supposed not to understand such a basic text as the Institutes of Justinian, *is a reminder that* Pantagruel *has many in-jokes shared with Law students.*

The nonce-word 'predestigiators' renders prestinateurs, *an invented word combining* prédestination *and* prestidigitation. *It was not predestination as such that Rabelais likened to a kind of juggling but Calvin's interpretation of it.]*

Knights most shining and most chivalrous, noblemen and others who delight in all things noble and decorous, you have of late looked in, dipped in and taken in the *Great and Inestimable Chronicles of the Enormous Giant Gargantua*, and as men faithful and true you have [gallantly] believed them like the text of the Bible or the Holy Gospel, and have often spent time over them with honourable ladies and gentlewomen, relating long and lovely tales from them whenever you have run out of topics of conversation. For which you are indeed worthy of great praise [and of being for ever remembered].

If only each one of us would abandon his own tasks, [stop worrying about his vocation] and cast his own affairs into oblivion so as to devote himself entirely to them, without letting his mind be otherwise distracted or impeded until he had learnt them off by heart, so that, if ever the printer's art should chance to fail or all books be lost, every father could teach them clearly to his children [, and pass them on from hand to hand to his descendants and successors as a religious cabbala]; for there is more fruit in them than is perhaps ever realized by a bunch of loud-mouths (scabby syphilitics all of them!) who understand such bits of fun less than Raclet understands the *Institutes*.

I have known a fair number of great and powerful lords out hunting game or hawking [for ducks] who, if their quarry was not tracked down or if their falcons remained hovering as their prey flew off, were deeply disappointed, as you can well appreciate, yet they resorted (for comfort and to avoid being plunged into boredom) to rehearsing the inestimable deeds of the said Gargantua.

There are folk in this world – this is no silly nonsense – who, being plagued with the tooth-ache and having spent their all on the physicians [to no avail], have found no remedy more expedient than to place the aforesaid *Chronicles* between two very hot strips of fine linen and apply them to the seat of the pain, sprinkling a little powdered dung over them.

But what shall I say about the wretches who suffer from the gout and the pox? O how often have we seen them after they had been well basted and duly daubed with unguents, their faces burnished like the clasp of a pork-barrel and their teeth clattering like the manual of an organ (or a set of virginals when the keys are struck) while they are foaming at the gullet like a wild boar which hound and whippet have hunted for seven hours [and cornered in the nets]. Then what did they do? Their only consolation lay in listening to a page read from that book. And we have seen some of them who swear that they would give themselves to a hundred barrelfuls of [antique] devils if they hadn't experienced manifest relief from such readings while sweating it out in their limbos (neither more nor less relief than women in labour experience when one reads to them the *Life of Saint Margaret*).

Is that nothing! I shall stand you half a noggin of tripe if you can find me another book in any tongue, field or faculty which possesses such powers, properties or privileges. No, my lords, no. [It is has no equal and no paragon; it is beyond compare. That I maintain up to the stake, exclusively.]

As for those who would hold otherwise, take them to be cheats, [predestigitators, mountebanks] and seducers.

You can, it is true, find certain occult properties in a few other memorable books,[1] including [*Toss-pints, Orlando Furioso,*] *Robert le Diable, Fierebras, William the Fearless, Huon of Bordeaux, Mandeville* and *Matabrune*; yet they cannot be compared with the one book we are now talking of.

Experience has infallibly convinced everyone of the great profit and utility to be derived from those *Gargantuine Chronicles*. Why! the printers have already sold more of them in two months than bibles will be bought in nine years.

So I, your obedient slave, wishing to extend your pastimes further, offer you now another book of the same alloy, except that it is a trifle more balanced than the other one and more worthy of credence. For unless you deliberately intend to go astray, don't think that I'm talking as Jews do about the Law: I was not born under such a planet as ever to lie or to assert anything which was not true: *agentes et consentientes,* meaning 'gents with nothing on our conscience'.[2]

I am speaking like Saint John of the Apocalypse: 'We bear witness of that we have seen':[3] that is, of the horrifying deeds and exploits of Pantagruel, whose retainer I have been ever since I stopped being a page until this present time when he has given me leave to have a turn at visiting my old cow-byres to discover whether any of my folk are still alive.

And so, to bring this Prologue to a conclusion: I give myself – body and soul, tripe and innards – to a hundred thousand punnets of fair devils if I tell you one single word of a lie in the whole of this history: so too, may Saint Anthony's fire burn you, the falling sickness skew you, quinsy and wolf-ulcers snip you; may you suffer from bloody-stools; and:

---

1. '42: . . . in a few other *tall-standing* books . . .
2. The Latin legal adage really means 'Doers and Abettors' (are punished with the same punishments).
3. '42: . . . which was *untrue.* I am speaking like *a Pelican lawyer – I mean a Vatican lawyer – talking of martyred lovers: I mean, like a protonotary talking of love-affairs:* 'We bear witness of what we have seen' . . .
   The quotation is from the first words of the First Epistle of John, who is identified with the author of the Apocalypse (the Book of Revelation).

> May the clap caught from your Fair,
> Dense as any cow-hide's hair,
> With quick-silver for cement
> Penetrate your fundament,

and may you fall into the sulphurous fire of the Pit like Sodom and Gomorrah should you not firmly believe everything that I shall relate to you in this present *Chronicle.*

On the Origins and Lineage of the great Pantagruel

CHAPTER I

[The tale is set in the context of Scripture which (in the spirit of Twelfth Night, Shrovetide and Mardi Gras, is for a while not taken too seriously, even when, as here in Pantagruel, *the Old Testament is traditionally interlinked with the New: the genealogy parodies those of the Old Testament, for example, but has links with both genealogies in the New. So too the murder of Abel by his brother Cain alludes to Genesis 4, but (as antitype and type) is quietly linked to 'the blood of the righteous' of Matthew 23:35. Rabelais does not need to draw attention to such echoes of Scripture by citing book and chapter (verses had yet to be invented). They are the very stuff of his humour in this book: his readers are supposed to recognize them.*

The mock Old Testament setting is further emphasized by the quiet citing of Eve's judgement on the forbidden apple (Genesis 3:6): 'pleasant to the eyes and much to be desired by the taste'.

Noah, the first to plant the vine, was also the first ever to get drunk (with lightning speed).

'Almighty and everlasting Guts' renders Ventrem omnipotentem, *a carnavalesque distortion of* Patrem omnipotentem, *the Father Almighty of the Creeds.*

Saucy songs were sung in the highest society. Rabelais echoes one set to music by Jean Molinet, in which the ladies sing, 'Those big cocks which fill your fist . . . Where are they now? They are no more.'

The tale of the giant who rode astride Noah's ark is taken straight from the Pirkei de-Rabbi Eliezar, *where the giant is the 'Hapalit', the 'He-who-Survived' (survived, that is, the Flood). He is associated or identified with Og, the King of Basan of the Psalms.*

The last word of the chapter was originally 'Lucian': Rabelais' first allusion to that Greek satirist, some of whose works he had translated when still a Franciscan.]

It will be neither fruitless nor idle [, seeing we are at leisure,] to recall for you the primary source and origin of our good giant Pantagruel, for I note that all fine historiographers have done likewise in their chronicles, not only those of the Greeks, Arabs and Ethnics but also the authors of Holy Writ, as Monsignor Saint Luke particularly, and Saint Matthew.[4]

You should note therefore that, at the beginning of this world of ours – [I am talking of long ago: more than twice-score twice-score nights to count like the ancient Druids –] it befell, one particular year soon after Abel was slain by Cain his brother, that the earth, steeped in the blood of the righteous, was so prolific in all the fruits which are produced from her loins but above all in medlars, that from time immemorial it has been called the Year of the Fat Medlars, for it took but three to make a bushel.

[In that year Kalends were found in the Greek missals; March failed to fall within Lent, and mid-August fell within May.]

It was in the month of October it seems to me or else in the month of September – so as not to fall into error: [I want scrupulously to guard against that] – that there occurred the week so celebrated in the annals which is called the *Week of the Three Thursdays*. There were indeed three Thursdays when the moon wandered more than ten yards from her course because of the irregular bissextile days.[5]

Now note this carefully: everybody ate the aforesaid medlars with delight, since they were pleasant to the eyes and much to be desired by the taste. Now, even as Noah – that sainted man to whom we are all beholden and indebted since it was he who planted the vine from which comes to us that nectar-like,

---

4.   '42: . . . not only those of the *Arabs, Barbarians and Latins but also the Greek Gentiles who were everlasting topers.* You should note . . .

5.   '42: . . . bissextile days *when the sun lurched like* debitoribus *somewhat to the left, and the moon wandered more than ten yards from her course. Then was clearly seen a libration in what is called the aplanic firmament: the central star of the Pleiades quitted her companions and declined towards the equinoctial, whilst the star named Pica abandoned Virgo and retrogressed towards Libra; which are most disturbing events and matters so hard and difficult that the astrologers cannot get their teeth into them. (They would need very long teeth anyway to reach that far!)* Now note . . .

Even those without Latin knew *debitoribus* from the Lord's Prayer, where it means 'our debtors' or, 'them that trespass against us'. It gives a comic solemnity to the word debtors.

precious, heavenly, [joyful] and deifying liquor that we call *piot*
– was deceived when he drank of it since he was ignorant of its
great virtues and power: so likewise did the men and women
of that time partake with great pleasure of that lovely plump
fruit.

But many a mishap befell them, for their bodies developed
very strange bulges, though not all in the same places.[6]

In some it was their bellies that swelled up, and those bellies
grew as convex as fat barrels. Of them it is written, *Almighty
and Everlasting Guts*. [They were all fine folk and good jesters.]
From that stock were born Saint Paunch and Mardi Gras.

Others swelled up behind the shoulders, and were so hunchbacked that men called them *montiferi* (mountain-bearers, as
it were). You can still see a few of them about, of different
ranks and sexes.

From that race sprang Aesop: accounts of his fair words and
deeds are still extant.

Others swelled in length along that member which we call
Nature's plough-share, so that theirs became marvellously long,
big, plump, fat, verdant and cockscombed in the antique style,
so much so that they used them as girdles, wrapping them five
or six times round their middles. If it were just right with the
wind in their poops, on seeing them you might have taken them
for men with lances up at the ready for tilting at the quintain.
That race, so the women tell us, has now died out, for they
ceaselessly lament that

No more do we find those great big . . .

You know how the song goes on!

[Others swelled up so enormously in the substance of their
bollocks that three of them easily filled a fifty-gallon cask. From
them descend those Bollocks of Lorraine which never dwell in
their codpieces but drop down to the base of their breeches.]

Others grew long in their legs. If you had seen them you

6.   '42: . . . But many *diverse* mishaps befell them, for their bodies developed
      most horrible bulges . . .

would have said they were cranes [or flamingos] or else folk
walking on stilts. Little school-boys in their grammar classes
call them *Iambus*.[7]

[Still others grew so long in their noses that they looked like
the beaks of alembics: noses bespeckled and bespangled with
papules, all purple, pullulating and inflamed, and enamelled
with pustules embroidered with gules. You've seen such men:
namely Canon Panzoult, and Piedebois the physician of
Angers.[8] Few of that lineage liked barley-water: all were lovers
of the liquid of September.

Naso and Ovid descend from them as well as all those of
whom it is written, *The great multitude of* Nos.[9]]

Others swelled up so hugely in the ears that, from just one
of them, they cut out a doublet, a pair of breeches and a
long-skirted jacket, covering themselves with the other as with
a Spanish cape. They say that's still an inherited trait in the
Bourbonnais – hence the expression 'Bourbonnais ears'.

Others grew in length of body. From them came the giants
and, through them, Pantagruel;

The first of whom was Chalbroth,
Who begat Sarabroth,
Who begat Faribroth,
Who begat Hurtaly, who was a good eater of sops and
  ruled from the time of the Flood,
Who begat Nembroth,
Who begat Atlas, who with his shoulders kept the sky from
  falling,
Who begat Goliath,
Who begat Eyrx [who invented the game of thimblerig],

7.   Since i and j were the same letter, there is a play on *jambe* (leg) and
     iambic (a metre of verse).
8.   Canon Panzoult's name (which is also that of a village in Touraine) plays
     on *panes*, (paunch); *Piedebois* means Wooden-foot.
9.   The Latin poet Ovid's surname Naso means nose. A common jest treated
     ne (not) in the Latin Vulgate as though it meant nose, as *nez* does in
     French. The text reads 'ne reminiscaris', echoing Deuteronomy 8:14 and
     Tobit 3:3, but to convey some of the humour to readers of English the
     translation transposes the jest to Jeremiah 46:25.

Who begat Tityus,

Who begat Eryon,

Who begat Polyphemus,

Who begat Cacus,

Who begat Etion [who, as Bartachino attests, was the first to catch the pox through not having drunk his wine cool in summer],

Who begat Enceladus,

Who begat Ceus,

Who begat Typhoeus,

Who begat Aloeus,

Who begat Otus,

Who begat Aegeon,

Who begat Briareus, who had one hundred hands,

Who begat Porphirion,

Who begat Adamastor,

Who begat Antaeus,

Who begat Agathon,

Who begat Porus, against whom fought Alexander the Great,

Who begat Aranthus,

Who begat Gabbara [who first invented matching drink for drink],

Who begat Goliath of Secundilla,

Who begat Offot, who developed an awesomely fine nose from drinking straight from the wine-cask,

Who begat Artachaeus,

Who begat Oromedon,

Who begat Gemmagog, who invented long-toed Crakow shoes,

Who begat Sisyphus,

Who begat the Titans, from whom sprang Hercules,

Who begat Enay [who was most expert in the matter of digging flesh-worms out of hands],

Who begat Fierabras, who was defeated by Oliver, Peer of France and the comrade of Roland,

Who begat Morgan [, who was the first in the world ever to play dice wearing glasses],

Who begat Fracassus, whom Merlin Coccaïe wrote about
    and of whom was born Ferragus,

Who begat Gob-fly [, who was the first to invent the smok-
    ing of ox-tongues in the chimney: before him they were
    salted like hams],

Who begat Bolivorax,

Who begat Longis,

Who begat Gayoffe [, whose bollocks were of poplar and
    whose cock was of mountain-ash],

Who begat Munch-straw,

Who begat Brûlefer,

Who begat Crested-fly-catcher,

Who begat Galahad [, who was the inventor of flagons],

Who begat Mirelangaut,

Who begat Galafre,

Who begat Falourdin,

Who begat Roboastre,

Who begat Sortibrant of Coïmbra,

Who begat Brushant of Monmiré,

Who begat Bruyer, who was vanquished by Ogier the
    Dane, Peer of France,

Who begat Mabrun,

Who begat Swive-donkey,

Who begat Hacquelebac,

Who begat Garnet-cock,

Who begat Grandgousier,

Who begat Gargantua,

Who begat the noble Pantagruel, my master.

I realize of course that you inwardly raised a most reasonable
doubt during the reading of that passage and so ask how it is
possible that such a thing could be, seeing that at the time of
the Flood all mankind perished except Noah and the seven
persons who were in the Ark with him: amongst that number
the aforesaid Hurtaly is never placed. Without a doubt your
query is well put and most understandable: yet [unless my wits
are badly caulked] my reply will satisfy you.

I was not there at the time to tell you about it as I would

like to, so I will cite the authority of the Massoretes, those
interpreters of the Holy Hebrew Scriptures, who say that
Hurtaly was never actually inside Noah's Ark[10] – he could never
have got in: he was too big – but that he did sit astride it with
a leg on either side like little children on their hobby-horses [or
like that fat bull-horn-trumpeter of Berne who was killed at
Marignano while riding astride a great, plump, stone-hurling
cannon:[11] a fine beast indeed for a jolly amble]. In that way
Hurtaly saved the aforesaid Ark from foundering, for he propelled it with his legs, turning it with his foot whichever way
he would as one does with the rudder of a boat. Those inside
sent him up ample food through a funnel, as folk fully acknow-
ledging the good he was doing them. And sometimes they
parleyed together as Icaromenippus did with Jupiter according
to the account in Lucian.

[Did you understand all that? Then down a good swig without water! For if you believe it not, 'Neither do I,' said she.]

On the Nativity of the Most-Redoubtable Pantagruel

CHAPTER 2

[This is the first hint that Pantagruel, with its echoes of the Bible,
especially but not only the Old Testament and its long-lived patriarchs,
is also set in a comic version of More's Utopia, still known only to
those who could read Latin.

The great drought of Elijah is mentioned in James 5:17, referring
back to I (III) Kings 17:1 and 18 and to Ecclesiasticus 48.

Dives is the rich man whose fate is contrasted with that of the poor
man Lazarus in Luke 16.

For five years or more France had been suffering from a ruinous
drought. With Pantagruel's nativity the comedy draws upon the birth

10. '42: . . . the Massoretes are those fine, well-hung and beautiful Hebrew
    windbags who affirm that Hurtaly was in truth never actually inside
    Noah's Ark . . .
11. At the Battle of Marignano, 1515, one of the enemy's horn-trumpeters
    stormed the French canons but was then killed astride one of them.

of John the Baptist and of Jesus in St Matthew and the synoptic
Gospels generally.

'Sage-woman' is an old term for midwife and allows of easy
puns.

Whenever 'The Philosopher' is mentioned, it refers to Aristotle.
Here the allusion is to his Meteorologia, *in which the ideas of Empe-*
docles are treated as myth.]

Gargantua, at the age of four hundred and four score four and
forty, begat Pantagruel of his wife Badebec, the daughter to the
King of the Amaurotes in Utopia. She died giving birth to him
for he was so [wondrously] big and heavy that he could not see
the light of day without suffocating his mother.

But fully to understand the occasion and reason for the name
which was given him at baptism you should note that for the
whole of that year there had been a great drought throughout
all the land of Africa since it had gone without rain for thirty-six
months [three weeks, four days and thirteen hours, plus a trifle
more], with the heat of the sun so mind-blowing that the entire
land lay parched.

It had not been more scorched then than in the days of Elijah.
Not one tree in the land bore leaf or bloom; the plants were
not green, the rivers had withered and the wells had run dry;
the fish – abandoned, poor things, by their natural element –
roamed squealing horribly over the land; birds tumbled out of
the air for lack of dew; wolves, foxes, stags, boars, deer, hares,
rabbits, weasels, ferrets, badgers and other creatures were
found scattered dead across the fields with their mouths gaping
wide.

As for men, it was most deplorable: you would have seen
them lolling out their tongues like greyhounds after a six-hour
course; many leapt into wells; others, whom Homer calls
Alibantes, sought shade inside the bellies of cows. The whole
land rode idly at anchor.

A pitiful thing it was to watch how those human beings
strove to protect themselves from that horrifying thirst: it was
a difficult enough matter to save the holy water from running
out in the churches, but things were so arranged by order of

their Graces the Cardinals and the Holy Father that nobody
dared to have more than one go at it. When anyone entered a
church you would have seen thirsty men by the score trailing
behind whoever was offering it to anyone, their mouths open
like that of wicked Dives to catch a little drop of it so that none
of it should go to waste. Oh how blessèd was he whose cellar
was well stocked and cool that year!

The Philosopher, on moving the question of why the sea is
salt, relates that, when Phoebus handed over the reins of his
light-shedding chariot to Phaëton his son, he, unskilled in the
art and not knowing how to follow the ecliptic between the
two tropics of the sun's sphere, wandered from his path and
drew so close to the Earth that he desiccated all the subjacent
lands, scorching that large segment of the heavens which philosophers call the Milky Way and the foolosophers Saint James's
Road [whereas the most tufted poets say that it is where Juno
let her milk dribble down as she was giving suck to Hercules].
Whereupon the Earth grew so hot that she suffered a colossal
muck-sweat and exuded the entire sea, which is therefore salt:
all sweat is salt. You will find that to be true if you would taste
your own or – it's all the same to me – that of syphilitics when
they are made to sweat it out.

Virtually the same happened that year, for upon a certain
Friday when all were at their devotions and conducting a handsome procession with ample litanies and fine sermons beseeching Almighty God to vouchsafe to look down upon them in
their affliction with an eye of compassion, great drops of water
were then clearly and visibly exuded from the Earth, just as
when anyone copiously sweats. Those poor folk began to
rejoice as though it were a thing beneficial to them, for some
said that, since there was not a drop of moisture in the air from
which they could hope for rain, Earth was making up for the
deficiency.

Other – learned – persons maintained that it was rain from
the Antipodes (of which Seneca tells in the *Fourth Book* of his
Natural Questions when treating of the source of the Nile).

But all were deceived: for when that procession was over,
each one sought to scoop up the dew and drink beakerfuls of

it, but they found it was only brine, worse and more salty than sea-water.

And because Pantagruel was born that very day, his father imposed that name on him (for *panta* in Greek means the same as 'all' and *gruel* in Hagarene means the same as 'thirst'), wishing to signify that at the hour of his nativity all the world was athirst, and foreseeing in a spirit of prophecy that he would one day be Ruler of the Thirsty-ones.

That was revealed to him at that very same hour by another, more evident, sign. For when Pantagruel's mother Badebec was giving birth to him, with her sage-women in attendance to welcome him, there first sallied forth from her belly sixty-eight muleteers, each leading by the halter a mule laden with salt; after which came nine dromedaries laden with smoked bacon and ox-tongues, seven camels with eels, and then five-and-twenty wagons with leeks, garlic, chibols and onions. Which terrified the aforesaid sage-women; but some of them said: 'Good victuals there! [We shall drink a trifle remiss, not like Swiss.] It's a good sign: those are spurs to wine-bibbing'.

And as they went cackling on about such light-hearted topics, out comes Pantagruel, all over hair like a bear. In a spirit of prophecy one of the sage-women declared: 'Born hairy was he! Wondrous deeds will he do! If he goes on to live, then old shall he grow.'

Of Gargantua's grief at the death of his wife Badebec

CHAPTER 3

[A rhetorical and dialectical dilemma. The tone is comic but deals with a real problem: so many children died at birth and so many women died in childbirth.

Traditional scholastic debates pro et contra were mocked by Renaissance humanists as scholastic exercises, not serious attempts to reach the truth.

Rabelais replaces 'Jesus' by 'Lord God'. Elsewhere too the name of Jesus proved too hallowed for him to play with.]

Who was befuddled and perplexed when Pantagruel was born? Gargantua his father, for seeing on one side his wife dead and on the other his son Pantagruel born and so big and fair, he knew not what to say or do. The doubt which troubled his mind was namely this: ought he to weep out of grief for his wife or laugh out of joy for his son? He had good dialectical arguments for both sides. They choked him, for he could marshal them very well in syllogistic modes and figures but he could come to no conclusion. So he remained caught like [a mouse in pitch, or] a kite in the nets of a fowler:

'Should I weep?' he asked. 'Yes. Why? Because my good wife is dead, who was the best *this* and [the best] *that* in all the world. Never shall I see her more! Never shall I see her again! Her loss to me is immeasurable. O God of mine! What have I done that you should punish me so? Why didn't you send death to me rather than her? To live without her is for me but to languish. Alas, Badebec, my sweeting, my belovèd, my quim so little and lovely' – hers covered three acres and two square poles though – 'my tenderling, my codpiece, my slippers, my slip-on: never again shall I see you! [Alas, my poor Pantagruel: you have lost a good mother, your gentle nurse, your most belovèd lady!] Ha, false Death, how malevolent, how cruel you are, to take from me her who, as of right, deserves immortality.'

And so saying he bellowed like a cow.

Then all of a sudden he remembered Pantagruel, and began to laugh like a calf:

'O my little son,' he said. 'My little bollock, my imp, how pretty you are; how beholden I am to God for having given me so fine a son, one so happy, so laughing, so pretty. Ho, ho! Ho, ho! How joyful am I! Let us drink, ho! and banish all melancholy.

'Bring out the best! Rinse the glasses! Spread the cloth! Get rid of those dogs! Put bellows to that fire! Light that candle! Shut that door! [Cut up bread for the soup!] Send those poor beggars away [but give them what they want]! Hold my gown:

let me strip to my doublet to entertain those good women better!'

As he was saying that, he heard the litany and the dirges of the priests as they bore his wife to her grave. At which he gave over his happy talk and was caught away in ecstasy, saying:

'Jesus! Must I go on being sad? That irks me. [I'm no longer young: I'm getting on.] The weather is treacherous: I could catch a fever and feel awful. Nobleman's honour! 'Tis better to weep less and drink more. My wife is dead. Well then, by God [– allow me that oath! –], I shall never resurrect her by my tears. She's all right: in paradise at very least, if not better. She's praying God for us. She's most blessèd. She's no longer troubled by our woes and calamities. We've all got it coming: God guard those who are left! It behoves me to think about finding another.

Now this is what you'll do,' he said to those sage-women [– but where are such sages to be found, good folk? I can't see any! –] 'You go off to her funeral, and meanwhile I'll stay here cuddling my son since I feel very thirsty and could risk falling ill. But have a drink before you go.[12] It'll make you feel good. Believe me, on my honour.'

Doing as they were told, they went to the funeral and the graveside, whilst our wretched Gargantua stayed behind in his Hall. During that time he composed the following epitaph to be engraved for her:

IN CHILDBIRTH SHE DIED: GOOD BADEBEC IS DEAD.
NOBLE SHE WAS: NOUGHT IN HER WAS AMISS:
HER FACE LIKE A VIOL, AS EVERYONE SAID,
SPANISH IN BODY, WITH GUTS LIKE A SWISS.
PRAY TO GOD FOR HER: HE LOVES HER I WISS,
FORGIVING HER ALL HER TRESPASSES SMALL.
SHE LIVED IN THIS CORPSE, THEN VICELESS, AS 'TIS.
SHE DIED ON THE DAY DEATH CAME: THAT IS ALL.

12. '42: . . . But have a *good swig* before you go . . .

The Infancy of Pantagruel

CHAPTER 4

*[Infancy narratives are common in the tales of heroes and the tales of
chivalry still much appreciated. Rabelais draws on them for parodies
and mock-heroics.*

As later (in Gargantua*) he turns to Book 7 of Pliny's* Natural History
*for details of monstrous births. Pliny was taken very seriously on such
matters by many, including students of the Law, but not here by
Rabelais.]*

I learn from the historiographers and poets of old that many
have been born into this world in very wondrous ways, which
it would take too long to tell you about, but if you have the
leisure read Pliny, Book 7.

Yet you can never have heard of a manner more marvellous
than Pantagruel's: for it was hard to credit that he could grow
so much in stature and strength in so short a space. Hercules
was nothing with his killing of those two snakes in his cradle,
for they were very tiny, flimsy ones: but when Pantagruel was
still in his cradle he wrought the most terrible deeds.

I will skip over unsaid how, at each one of his feeds, he
golloped down the milk of four hundred and six cows, and
how all the pot-makers of Saumur in Anjou, of Villedieu in
Normandy and of Bramont in Lorraine were employed in
making a cauldron to boil up his broth, which was served in a
huge stone trough (still to be found even now close by the
palace at Bourges). However, his teeth had already grown so
big and strong that he bit a great chunk from it (as is still most
apparent).

On one particular day, towards morning, when they wanted
to get him to suck the teats of one of his cows – for, as the story
tells us, he had no other wet-nurses – he burst loose from the
reins which strapped one of his arms to the cradle, seized that
cow under the hocks and bit off and ate her udders and half
her belly including her liver and kidneys. He would have

gobbled her all up if only she hadn't bellowed as dreadfully as if wolves had got her by the legs. Everybody ran up as she bellowed and pulled the said cow away from the said Pantagruel's hands, but they couldn't stop him from holding on fast to the hock-end, which he ate as we might a sausage. When they tried to take the bone away he gulped it down at once, as a cormorant might do with a little fish.

Then he started to say 'Goo', goo', goo'', for he couldn't talk properly yet but wished them to know that he had found it *very good* and that all he wanted was more of the same.

Seeing which, his attendants tied him down with hawsers as thick as those they make at Tain for towing the salt up to Lyons, or as those of the *Grande Françoyse*, which lies in the docks of Le-Havre-de-Grâce in Normandy. But one day a great bear which was being trained by his father came up and licked his face (for his nurses had failed to wipe his chops properly), so he snapped those hawsers as easily as Samson snapped his amongst the Philistines, grabbed hold of My Lord Bear and ripped him apart like a pullet, making himself a good warm-meat cure-gorge before his dinner.

Whereupon Gargantua, fearing that Pantagruel might hurt himself, had ingenious flying buttresses made for his cradle as well as four huge iron chains to hold him in. (You now have one of those chains at La Rochelle, where they draw it up at night between the two great towers in the haven.) Another is at Lyons; another is at Angers, whilst the fourth was borne away by devils in order to hold down Lucifer, who was furiously breaking out into madness because of an extraordinarily in-furiating belly-ache brought on from having eaten for breakfast a fricassee of law-serjeant's soul.

So now you can readily believe what Nicholas of Lyra says about that passage of the Psalter in which it is written, 'Og, King of Basan': namely that when the said Og was still a babe he was so strong and lusty that he had to be bound to his cradle by chains.

And thus did Pantagruel stay quiet and peaceful, since he could not easily snap those chains, especially since he did not have space enough in his cradle to swing his arms about.

But see what happened on the day of a great festival when his father was throwing a fine feast for every one of the princes of his Court. I think that all the flunkies were so taken up with their festive duties that they neglected poor Pantagruel, who remained stuck there in his corner-ium. This is what he did.[13]

He tried to snap the chains of his cradle with his arms, but those chains were too strong and he could not manage it. He therefore battered the cradle so hard with his heels that he snapped off the end of it even though it was a beam some four foot square. Once he had thrust his legs outside he slithered down as best he could so that his feet touched the ground. Then, with one mighty heave he stood up, bearing his cradle bound to his spine like a tortoise clambering against a wall. To look at, he resembled a big five-hundred-ton carrack stood up on end!

At that point he so confidently entered the hall, where everyone was feasting, that he greatly terrified all who were there. As his hands were tied, he could not pick up anything to eat but, with a great struggle, he bent over and licked up a tongueful. Seeing which, his father rightly concluded that he had been left with nothing to eat and so, on the advice of the princes and lords there present, he commanded him to be rid of his chains; moreover Gargantua's physicians said that if he were kept in his cradle like that he would be subject to the stone all his life.

Once he had been freed from his chains, they sat him down; he ate his fill and shattered his cradle into four hundred thousand pieces with one blow from his fist [angrily] striking at the middle of it and vowing never again to be put back into it.

13. '42: . . . corner-ium. *What did he do, my Good People? What did he do?*
     Listen. He tried to snap . . .

The deeds of noble Pantagruel in his youth

CHAPTER 5

*[This chapter appealed to many liberal-minded university men, past
or present, in the time of Rabelais, especially the devotees of humanist
Law. The 'Pierre levée' – a raised menhir – still plays a large part in
student life at Poitiers; other universities too had their legends and
myths which are recalled here.*

*'Barbarian Toulouse' was renowned for its religious intolerance: in
1532 a liberal regent, Jean de Cahors, a professor of Law, was burnt
at the stake. Saint Liguaire is omitted later.*

*Some see in this chapter a comic transposition of Rabelais' own
travels in the course of his studies. He certainly knew at first hand
some of the places mentioned here, including Fontenay-le-Comte and
Maillezais. There are also allusions to friends of his, including the
abbé Ardillon and André Tiraqueau, the great legal scholar.*

*It was at Montpellier that Rabelais became a 'doctor' – as Bachelors
of Medicine were already called – and, in the course of time, a full
Doctor of Medicine.*

*The quotation about poets and painters refers to the famous judge-
ment of Horace in his* Ars poetica, *lines 9 and 10.*

Epistemon's name means 'wise' in Greek.]

And so Pantagruel grew from day to day and visibly profited
from it; out of natural affection his father was delighted and,
since he was still but a little fellow, had a crossbow made for
him to play at shooting birds.

It is now in the great tower of Bourges.[14]

He then sent him to the universities to study and spend the
days of his youth. And he came to Poitiers to study, where he
profited greatly. Noticing that the students there did have
a little free time but never knew how to use it, he felt compassion for them. So one day, from the great ridge named

---

14. '42: ... birds. *It is now called the Great Crossbow at Chantelle.* He then
     sent him ...

Passelourdin, he took a big boulder, about two dozen yards square and fourteen span thick, and set it comfortably upon four pillars in the midst of a field in order that the said students, when at a loss over what to do, could pass their time scrambling on to the aforesaid stone, there to feast with plenty of flagons, hams and pasties whilst carving their names on it with pen-knives.

It's called the *Pierre levée* nowadays.

In memory of which nobody is now matriculated in the said University of Poitiers unless he has drunk from the Caballine fountain of Croustelles, scaled the *Passelourdin* and clambered on to the *Pierre levée*.

Afterwards, from reading in the fine chronicles of his fore-bears, he learnt that Geoffrey de Lusignan, called Geoffrey Long-Tooth – the grandfather of the cousin-in-law of the older sister [of the aunt of the son-in-law of the uncle of the daughter-in-law] of his mother-in-law – was buried at Maillezais, therefore, as a gentleman should, he rusticated himself for a while to visit the place.

So he and some of his companions left Poitiers, passed through Ligugé, [calling on the noble abbé Ardillon,] then through Lusignan, Sansay, Celles, Saint Liguaire, Colonges and Fontenay-le-Comte, [where they greeted the learned Tiraqueau,] and from thence came to Maillezais, where Pantagruel visited the tomb of Geoffrey Long-Tooth, whose portrait rather disturbed him when he saw it: he is depicted there as a man in a frenzy, tugging his great malchus half out of its scabbard. Pantagruel asked the reason for it. The canons of the place said they knew no other reason save that *Pictoribus atque poetis*, and so on, that is, *To painters and poets* freedom is allowed to portray what they like, how they like. Pantagruel was not satisfied by that answer, and said, 'He is not depicted like that without a reason. I suspect some wrong was done to him as he died, for which he is asking his kinsfolk for vengeance. I will inquire into it more fully and do what is right.'

He therefore turned back, not going through Poitiers, since he intended to do a tour of the other universities of France; and so, passing through La Rochelle, he took to the sea and sailed

to Bordeaux, where he never found much sport except for a
Spanish card-game played by the lighter-men on the strand.

From there he then went on to Toulouse, where he learnt
how to dance very well and to play with the two-handed sword
as is the custom amongst students at that university. But he did
not stay there long once he saw how they burnt their regents
alive like red herrings. 'God forbid,' he said, 'that I should die
like that: I'm thirsty enough by nature without being hotted up
further.'

He then came to Montpellier, where he found joyful company
and some very good Mirevaux wines. He considered starting
to read Medicine there but considered that calling to be far
too tedious and melancholy; and the physicians there stank of
enemas like aged devils.

And so he wanted to read Law but, discovering that the
Legists there amounted to three scurvy-heads and one baldy,
he went away, halting en route to build the Pont du Gard [and
the amphitheatre at Nîmes] in less than three hours, yet it looks
more divine than human.[15]

Then he entered Avignon, where he was barely three days
before he fell in love, for [, it being a papal domain,] the women
there enjoy playing at squeeze-crupper.

On seeing which, his moral-tutor, called Epistemon, drew
him away and took him to Valence in Dauphiné, where he
found there was little in the way of sport and that the toughs
of the Town beat up the Gown. Which annoyed him.

One day, when all the folk were having a public dance, an
undergraduate tried to join in, but the local toughs wouldn't
let him. On seeing which, Pantagruel gave chase to them as far
as the banks of the Rhône and would have drowned them all,
but they hid away like moles a good half a league under that
river. Their bolt-hole is still there to be seen.

After which he left and [with a hop and three jumps] came

15. The description 'more divine than human' is applied in the first edition
    to the Pont du Garde, not to the Amphitheatre at Nîmes. In '42 the phrase
    is plural, so applying to both.

to Angers, where he got on well and would have stayed for a while had the plague not driven them away.

And so he came to Bourges, where he studied for a long time, doing well in the Faculty of Laws. And he would sometimes say that his law-books seemed to him like a beautiful golden robe, triumphant and wondrously precious, which had been hemmed with shit. 'For,' he said, 'no books in the world are as beautifully written, ornate and elegant as the texts of the *Pandects*, but their hems (that is to say the glosses of Accursius) are so squalid, shameful and putrid that they are nothing but ordure and filth.

Leaving Bourges, he came to Orleans, where he found plenty of roisterous students, who gave him a good welcome on his arrival; they soon taught him to play royal tennis so well that he became a past master at it, since it is a sport the students there excel in.

They sometimes took him off to the Islands, where they would play bowls with their balls. As for cudgelling his brains in study, he did none of that, fearing that it might weaken his sight, especially since one of the regents often stated in his lectures that nothing is worse for your sight than an eye-infection.

And one day, when one of the students he knew graduated in Law (even though he had scarcely more learning than he could lug, yet making up for it by being very good at dancing and tennis), Pantagruel composed the blazon and device of the Bachelors of that university, which reads:

> In his codpiece, a tennis ball;
> A racket in his hand withal;
> A tiny bit of Law: that's all;
> A jolly jig, whene'er he would:
> He's got his academic hood!

How Pantagruel met a man from Limoges who distorted the French tongue

CHAPTER 6

[Laughter at excessively latinate French was well established. Rabelais is partly indebted here to the Champfleury *of Geoffroy Tory. Then as now, some words in this chapter are opaque to anyone without Latin, though a few of even the most outrageously latinate words are to be found in the* New English Dictionary.

There are brief explanations at the end of the chapter.]

One day, [I'm not sure when,] Pantagruel was going for a stroll after supper with his companions through the gate which leads into Paris. There he met a dapper student coming along the road. After they had greeted each other, Pantagruel asked him,

'Where are you coming from at this hour, my friend?'

The student replied:

'From that alma, illustrissime and celebrated Academe vocate Luctece.'

'What does that mean?' Pantagruel asked one of his men.

'From Paris,' he replied.

'So you come from Paris? And how,' he asked, 'do you young gentlemen spend your time as students in the said Paris?'

The student replied:

'We transfrete the Sequana at times dilucidatory and crepusculine, deambulating via the urbic carfaxes and quadrivia; we despumate the latinate verbocination, and, like verisimilitudinous amorevolous, we captivate the omnijudicious, omniform and omnigenous feminine sex. On certain *dïes* we invite ourselves to the lupanars of Champgaillard, Matcon, Cul-de-sac, Bourbon and Huslieu.[16] There, in venereal ecstasy, we inculcate our veretra into the most absconce recesses of the pudenda of those more amicitial meretrices; then, in those meritful taberns, the Pomme-de-Pin, [the Castellum,] the Madeleine and the

16. The names of these five places of ill repute are omitted in '42.

Mule, we consume spatulas of sheep performaminated with the
herb called petrosil. And if we should chance *by forte fortune*
to have a pecuniary paucity or penury in our marsupiums,
exhausted of ferruginous metal, to pay our scot we demit our
codexes and oppignerate our vestments, expecting the tabellaries to come from our paternal lares and penates.'

To which Pantagruel replied,

'What diabolical language is this! You, by God, are a heretic!'

To which the student replied:

'Signior, no. For most libentiously, as soon as the minutest
matutinal section is elucidated, I demigrate towards one of
those so-well architectured monasterial fanes; there I asperge
myself with lustral aqueous fluid, mumble a slice of some missatical precative from our missaries, with a sub-murmuration
of precatories from my Horary, I lave and absterge my animated
part of its nocturnal inquinations. I revere the Olympicoles; I
latreutically venerate the supernal Astripotent; I have in delec-
tation and mutual amity my proximates; I observe the prescriptions of the Decalogue, and, according to the minuscule
capacity of my vim and vigour, I do not discede one laterality
of a tiny unguis from them. To be veriloquous, since Mammon
never super-ingurgitates one ob into my pecuniary receptacle,
I am somewhat rare and lentando in supererogationally
eleemosinating to egenes who from ostiary to ostiary are quesit-
itious of a small stipendium.'

'Oh. Pooh, pooh,' said Pantagruel. 'What does this idiot
mean! I think he is forging us some diabolical language and
casting a charm on us like a sorcerer.'

To which one of his men replied:

'My Lord, without any doubt, he is trying to ape the language
of the Parisians; yet all he can do is to flay Latin alive. He thinks
he is pindarizing; he believes he is a great orator in French
because he despises the common spoken usage.'

'Is that true?' asked Pantagruel.

The student replied:

'*Seigneur*, [*Sire*]. My genius is not innately apt – as this
flagitious nebulon opines – for excoriating the cuticle of our

Gallic vernacular. But, vice-versally, I am assiduous at striving, by oars and by sail, at locupleting it with latinate superfluity.'

'By God,' said Pantagruel, 'I'll teach you how to speak. But first tell me where you come from?'

To which the student said:

'The primeval origin of my atavics and avics was indigenous to the Lemovic regions, where requiesce the corpus of that hagiarch, Saint Martial.'

'I get you,' said Pantagruel: 'You come from Limoges. That's what it all boils down to. Yet you want to ape Parisian speech. Come here, then, and let me curry you down.'

He then seized him by the throat, saying,

'You flay Latin! By Saint John, I'll make you flay up the fox: I shall flay you alive.'

Whereupon that wretched denizen of Limoges began to say:

'Whoa, there, Maister! Aw! Zaint Marsault zuccour me! Ho, ho. In Gawd's name. Lemme be! Don'ee touch me!'

Pantagruel said, 'Now you're talking naturally.' And he let go of him, for that wretched man from Limoges was shitting all over his breeches (which were tailored in cod-tails, not stitched along the seam). At which Pantagruel said:

'By Saint Alipentinus! What a stench there below. Reek of the civet-cat! The devil take the turnip-muncher: how he stinks.'

And thereupon he released him; but for the rest of his life he was so remorseful and parched that he often said, 'Pantagruel has got me by the throat!' After a few years he died the death of Roland, brought about by the vengeance of God, so demonstrating to us what the Philosopher and Aulus Gellius said: that we ought in our speech to follow the common usage, and also what Caesar said: that we should avoid silly words as ships' captains avoid reefs at sea.[17]

[*Explanations of some of the latinate words and phrases:*
We transfrete the Sequana at times dilucidatory and crepusculine: We cross the Seine at dawn and twilight
we despumate the latinate verbocination: we skim off latinate wordiness

17. '42: ... what *Octavian Augustus* said: that we should avoid *stray* words ...

dies: days

lupanars: brothels

inculcate our veretra: insert our penises

amicitial meretrices: loving whores

meritful taberns: money-earning taverns

spatulas of sheep performinated with the herb called petrosil: shoulders of
    mutton dressed with the herb called parsley

marsupiums: purses

demit our codexes: sell our books

oppignerate our vestments: pawn our clothes

tabellaries: messengers

missatical precative from our missaries: Mass-prayers from our missals

Horary: Book of Hours

nocturnal inquinations: sins (or stains) of the night.

discede one laterality of a tiny unguis: depart one tiny nail's breadth.

ob: a penny

eleemosinating to egenes: giving alms to the needy

from ostiary to ostiary: from door to door

flagitious nebulon: injurious good-for-nothing

locupleting it with latinate superfluity: enriching with overflowing latinity

*The primeval origin of my atavics and avics was indigenous to the Lemovic
    regions*: the ancient origin of my ancestors and forebears was native to the
    regions of Limoges.]

How Pantagruel came to Paris [and of the fine books
in the Library of Saint Victor]

CHAPTER 7

*[Another chapter aimed at present and past university men and a
literate audience. Many of the titles in the library of Saint-Victor are
in Latin; some parody real books; some are wider satirical comments
on learned error or popular superstition or mawkishness. Some are
seriously critical. Rabelais takes on opponents of Reuchlin and Erasmus. The Sorbonne comes in for sustained and increasing mockery.
Many new titles were added in 1534 (and so figure in the definitive
text of 1542).*

*In the original these book-titles are given in one continuous sen-
tence; here they are set out as a list. Out of respect for French royal
susceptibility, Rabelais replaces the Pépin of the first edition with
Turelupinus. He expanded the list several times, mirroring new*

experiences in Rome and elsewhere. The reference to Gargantua's
stealing the bells of Notre-Dame is to the account in the anonymous
Grands et inestimables Croniques. *That tale, there simply told, will be*
soon retold by Rabelais in his next book, Gargantua.*]*

After completing his studies most satisfactorily at Orleans,
Pantagruel decided to visit the great University of Paris. Before
he went he was told of an enormously huge bell which had been
left lying on the ground at St Aignan's in Orleans for nigh on
three hundred years.[18] It was so heavy that no contrivance had
been able to lift it up off the ground, even though they had
applied every method advanced by Vitruvius (in *On Architec-*
ture), L.-B. Alberti (in *On Matters Architectural*), by Euclid,
Theon and Archimedes, as well as by Hero (in *On Contri-*
vances), since all proved useless.

So Pantagruel, acceding to the humble petitions of the citizens
and inhabitants of that city, determined to carry that bell to its
intended belfry. And indeed he came to the very place where it
lay and lifted it up with his little finger as easily as you might
lift a sparhawk's tinkle-bell. But before bearing it to its belfry
he determined to ring an aubade with it all over the town,
clanging it as he bore it in his hand through all the streets.

At which everyone was delighted, but there arose one very
great inconvenience: whilst he was carrying it thus and ringing
it through the streets, all the excellent Orleans wines turned
sour and were spoilt. Nobody noticed it till the following night
when each one of them, having drunk some of that wine which
had turned, was parched and could do nothing but cough up
gob as white as [Maltese] cotton, saying: 'We have caught the
pantagruel! Our throats are all salty!'

That done, he reached Paris with his companions. As he
made his entry everyone came out to stare at him: as you well
know, the people of Paris are daft by nature [, a semi-tone
above and below natural pitch]. They stared at him with amazement, not without greatly dreading that he might bear off their

18. '42: . . . in *Aurelians* for *the last two hundred and fourteen years*. It
was . . .

Palais to some far-removed lands, just as his father had once borne off the bells of Notre-Dame to tie round the neck of his mare.

And after he had stayed there some time, thoroughly studying in all the seven liberal arts, he said that Paris was nice to live in but not to die in, since the down-and-outs in the Cimetière de Saint-Innocent warmed their bums at a fire of dead men's bones.

And he found the library of Saint-Victor to be quite superb, above all for some of the books he came across there, [of which this is the catalogue, beginning with] *The Handcart of Salvation*;

The Codpiece of the Law;
The Slipper of the Decrees;
The Pomegranate of Vices;
The Testes of Theology;
The Preachers' fox-tail duster, Composed by Pépin;
The Elephantine Bollocks of the Douzepers;
The Bishops' Henbane;
Mammaltretus, *On Baboons and Monkeys, with a commentary by Des Orbeaux*;
A Decree of the University of Paris Touching the Soutientgorgeousness *of Ladies of Easy Virtue*;
The Apparition of Saint Geltrude to a Nun of Poissy during her Child-birth;
On the Art of Discreetly Farting in Company, by Magister-Noster Ortuinus;
The Mus-tardy Pot of Penitence;
Cloth-Overboots, or, The Boots of Patience;
The Ant-hill of the Arts;
[*On the use of Clear Soups, and On decently Tippling, by Silvester de Prierio, a Jacobite*;
The Cozened about Court;]
The Cuntainer of Lawyers;
The 'Packet' of Matrimony;
The Crucible of Cuntemplation;
Niggles of the Law;
Goades to wine;

Cheese as a Spur;
Scrubbing Dons Clean;
Tartaretus: On how to Defecate;
[*Roman Fanfares;*]
Bricot: *On Distinguishing between Sops;*
Fundamental Floggings;
The Worn Shoe of Humility;
The Tripe-odd of Good Ruminations;
The Cauldron of Great-Souledness;
Confessors' Cavils;
[*Flickings for Clerics;*
Three Books On How to Chew Bacon, by the Reverend
    Father Provincial of Drivell, Brother Lubin;
Pasquino, the Marble Doctor: *On Eating Roe-deer with*
    Prickly Artichokes in Papal-Lamb time, as Forbidden
    by the Church;
The Invention of the Holy Cross, for Six Characters Played
    by the Clerks of Finessing;]
The Eye-glasses of Romiseekers;
Major: *On the Stuffing of Black-puddings;*
The Bagpipes of Prelates;
Beda, *On The Excellence of Tripe;*
[*The Laments of Advocates over the Reform of Their*
    Sweeteners;
The Cat-Scrabblings of Attorneys;
Of Peas and Bacon, with a Commentary;
The Profit-rolls of Indulgence;
Magister Pelf Rake-it-in, Doctor of Canon and Civil Law:
    How to Botch Up the Idiocies of the Glosses of Accur-
    sius. A Most Enlightening Repetition;
Examples of Generalship by the Franc-Archier de
    Bagnolet;
Captain Train-Band: *On Matters Military, with Plans by*
    Etienne Funk-it;
On the Practice and Utility of Skinning Horses and Mares,
    by the Author Magister Noster de Quirkus;
On the Rusticities of Priestlings;
Magister Noster Rostock-Assley: *On the Serving of Mus-*

*tard after Dining; Fourteen Books, with Postils by
Magister Vaurillion;*
The Stag-night Fines of Procurators;
A Most Subtle Question: *Whether a Chimera Bombinating
in the Void Can Swallow up Second Intentions: as
Debated over Ten Weeks at the Council of Constance;*]
The Munch-them-down-to-the-very-stubble of Advocates;
[*The Daubings of Scotus;*
Cardinals' Bat-wings;
Eleven Decades on the Taking-off of Spurs, *by Magister
Albericus de Rosate;*
By the same author: *Three Books on the Mensuration of
Army Camps in the Hair;*
On the Entry of Antonio de Leiva into Lands Frazzled like
Brazil;
Marforio, a Bachelor lying in Rome: *On Skinning and
Smudging Cardinals' Mules;*
An Apologia by the Same, Against Such as Affirm that the
Mule on the Foot of the Pope Drinks Only When It
Will;
A Prognostication beginning *Silvius' Balls, established by
Magister-Noster Songe-Creux;*
Bishop Boudarinus: *Nine Enneads on Profits to be Milked
from Indulgences, with a Papal Privilege for Precisely
Three Years;*
The Mincings of Maidens;
The Tired Tails of Widows;
Monastic Whoopings;
The Mumblings of Celestine Padres;
The Toll Charged by the Mendicants;
The Chattering Teeth of the Beggarmen;
The Theologians' Cat-door;
Putting Things into the Mouths of Masters of Arts;
The Scullery-boys of Ockam, Simply Tonsured;
Magister Noster Fripesauce: *On Finely Sifting the Canoni-
cal Hours (in Forty Books);*
Anon: *The Arse-over-tipery of the Confraternities;*
The Gut-cavities of the Mendicants;

Spanish Pongs, Super-refined by Fray Inigo;
Wormwood for Wretches;
The Far-niente of Matters Italian by Magister Bruslefer;
Raymund Lull, *Fooling about with Elements;*
A Quimnall of Hypocrisy, by Magister Jacobus Hochstrat,
   Measurer of Heretics;
Hotbollockius: *On the Drinking-shops of Both the Aspir-*
   ant Magistri Nostri *and of the Graduated* Magistri Nos-
   tri, *in Eight Most Humourful Books;*
Bum-volleys of Papal Bullists, Copyists, Scribes, Abbrevia-
   tors, Referendaries and Dataries compiled by Regis;
A Perpetual Almanac for Suffers from the Gout and the
   Pox;
Ways of Sweeping Flues, by Johannes Eck;
Thread for Shopkeepers;
The Comforts of the Monastic Life;
The Heated-up Leftovers of Bigots;
The Fairy-tales of the Grey Friars;
The Beggardliness of the Pennywise;
Of the Snares of the Episcopal Chancellors,
Stuffings for Treasurers;
The Sophists' Badinagium;
Discussion of Messers and Vexers: Anti, Peri, Kata, Meta,
   Ana, Para, Moo and Amphi;
A Liming Dictionary for Rhymesters;
Alchemists' Bellows;
Jiggery-Pokery of beggars bagged by Fr Seratis;
The Shackles of the Religious Life;
The Viol of the Clangers;
The Elbow-rest of Old Age;
The Nosebag of Nobility;
Ape-chattering with a Rosary;
The Manacles of Devotion;
The Boiling-pot of the Four Weeks of Embertide;
The Mortar-boards of Town Life;
The Hermits' Fly-brush;
The Face-mask of Penance-doers;
The Backgammon of Belly-bumping Friars;

Dullardus: *On the Life and Honour of Young Gallants*;

Lupoldus: *Moralizing Exegeses of the Academic Hoods of Denizens of the Sorbonne*;

Travellers' Trifles;

The Remedies of Bishops in potationibus infidelium;

Fuss and Bother of the Doctors of Theology of Cologne against Reuchlin;

Pompom for Ladies;

Martingale Breeches with Back-flaps for Turd-droppers;

The Quick-turns of Tennis-Court Boys, by Friar Ballfoot;

The Thick-soled Boots of Noble-Heart;

The Mummery of Will o'-the-Wisp and Robin Good-fellows;

Gerson: *On the Deposability of a Pope by the Church*;

The Sledge of the Ennobled and of Graduates;

Johannes Richbrothius: *On the Terrifications of Excommunications* (lacks the Preface);

The Skill of Invoking Devils, Both Male and Female, by Magister Guingolfus;

The Hodge-podge of Friars Perpetually Praying;

The Morris-dance of Heretics;

The Crutches of Cajetanus;

Dribble-Snoutius: *On the Cherubic Doctor's Treatise On the Origin of Hypocritical Velvet-paws and Neck-Twisters; Seven Books*;

Sixty-nine Fat-stock Breviaries;

The Fat-gut, Midnight Gaude Maria *of the Five Orders of Mendicants*;

The Hide of the Turlupins, Extracted from the Wild Boot Infiltrated into the Summa Angelica;]

The Doter over Casuistries of Conscience;

[*The Gorbellies of Presidents*;

The Abbots' Ass-pizzles;

Sutor, *Against Some Person Who Called Him a Wretch: and that Wretches Are Not Condemned by the Church*;

The Close-stools of the Physicians;

The Astrologers' Chimney-sweep;

Fields of Enemas, by S. C.;]

The Apothecaries' Draw-farts;
The Surgeon's Kiss-me-arse;
[Justinian: *On the Suppression of Bigots*;
An Antidotary for the Soul;]
Merlin Coccaius: *On the Homeland of the Devils*.

Some of which are already in print, and the others are even
now in the presses of this noble city of Tübingen.

How Pantagruel received in Paris a letter from his father Gargantua, and what it contained

CHAPTER 8

*[A sudden change of tone: Genesis together with Aristotelian physics
(which is based on the twin concepts of generation and corruption)
meet the New Testament. Generation and corruption will cease at the
end of Time when 'Jesus Christ shall have delivered up his peaceful
Kingdom to God, even the Father' (I Corinthians 15:34).*

*The good human father, having produced a son who naturally
mirrors his body, so educates him as to mirror his soul as well, thus
reflecting his whole persona (his unique individuality as a particular
body plus a particular soul).*

*The letter ends evangelically, calling amongst many other things
upon Christ's summary of the Law ('Love God, and thy neighbour as
thyself') and on the Wisdom of Solomon 1:4, (associated with a
common Latin adage punning on science and conscience).*

*The synergistic nature of the theology is quietly emphasized (citing
of St Paul's injunction in II Corinthians 3:1: 'Receive not the grace of
God in vain'). Human beings must 'work together' with grace. True
faith is never divorced from good works. It must in scholastic terms
be 'informed by charity'.*

*The whole chapter savours of the renewed enthusiasm for Ancient
learning. From the earlier times theologians such as Tertullian called
God the 'Plasmator', the 'Moulder', the 'Fashioner': like a potter he
made Man of clay.*

Rabelais had performed at least one public dissection.]

Pantagruel studied very hard – as I am sure you well realize –
and likewise profited since he had a double-cuffed understanding and a memory as capacious as that of a dozen leathern
bottles and tubs of olive oil. And while he was staying there, he
received a letter from his father framed in the following terms:

Dearest son:
Amongst the gifts, graces and privileges with which
Almighty God our sovereign Plasmator endowed human
nature in the beginning, that one seems to me to be surpassing and unique by which it can, in this mortal state, acquire
a species of immortality, and in the course of this transitory
life pass on our name and our seed; which is achieved
through lineal descendants issuing from us in lawful wedlock. Thus there is to some extent restored to us what was
taken from us through the sin of our first parents, to whom
it was told that, since they had not been obedient to the
commandment of God the Creator, they would die, and
by death that so-magnificent clay in which Man had been
moulded would be reduced to nought. But by means of
such propagation of our seed, what was lost to the parents
remains in their children and what perished in the children
remains in the grandchildren, successively, until the hour
of the Last Judgement, when Jesus Christ shall have
delivered up his peaceful Kingdom to God the Father,[19]
free from all domination and stain of sin; then shall cease
all generation and corruption, and the elements will be
without their constant transformations, seeing that
yearned-for peace shall be consummated [and perfected]
and all things brought to their End and period.
  So now, not without just and equitable cause, I render
thanks to God my Protector for having given me strength

19. I Corinthians 15 is the chapter in which Saint Paul stresses the reality of
    the resurrection of the dead and immortality.
      For the use of the Classical term *period* by theologians, cf. an adage of
    Erasmus: I, VI, LXVII, 'He lives beyond his thread'; Theologians call
    'period' that fated boundary of life beyond which it is wrong for anyone
    to run.

to see my hoary old age blossom anew in your youthfulness: for when at the behest of Him who governs and directs all things my soul shall quit this human habitation, I shall not consider that I have totally died but to have transmigrated rather from one place to another, since in you and through you I shall remain in this world in my visible likeness, living, seeing and frequenting honourable persons and my friends as I used to do; that frequentation was not, I confess, without sin (for we all have sinned and ceaselessly beg God to wipe away our sins) but, with the help of God's grace, beyond reproach. Therefore, as the likeness of my body will dwell in you, should the ways of my soul not similarly shine forth from within you, nobody would consider you the ward and treasurer of the immortality of our name; and so the joy that I would experience as I saw all this would be small, noting that my lesser part, the body, would remain, whereas the soul, my better part, through which our name may continue as a blessing among men, would be debased and bastardized.

I do not say that out of any mistrust I may have of your virtue, which has already been tested before me, but the more strongly to encourage you to advance from good to better.

[I write this now not so that you should adopt such virtuous ways, but rather that you should take delight in so living and having so lived, giving you fresh courage to do the same in the future.]

You may well remember how I spared no effort to accomplish and perfect this enterprise: rather did I help you as though I had no other treasure in this world than to see you, once in my life, both fully perfected in virtue, honour and wisdom and also in all liberal and honourable knowledge, so to leave you when I die as a mirror reflecting the *persona* of me, your father, and if not actually as excellent as I could wish you to be, yet certainly such in your desire.

And even though Grandgousier, my late father of

grateful memory, devoted all his zeal towards having me progress towards every perfection and polite learning, and even though my toil and study did correspond very closely to his desire – indeed surpassed them – nevertheless, as you can well understand, those times were neither so opportune nor convenient for learning as they now are, and I never had an abundance of such tutors as you have. The times were still dark, redolent of the disaster and calamity of the Goths, who had brought all sound learning to destruction; but, by the goodness of God, light and dignity have been restored to literature during my lifetime: and I can see such an improvement that I would hardly be classed nowadays among the first form of little grammar-schoolboys, I who (not wrongly) was reputed the most learned of my century as a young man.

I do not say that out of vain bragging – even though I could well and laudably do so when writing to you, for which you have the authority of Cicero in his book *On Old Age* and the judgement of Plutarch in his book entitled *How One May Praise Oneself without Envy* – but to give you a passion for tending higher.

Now all disciplines have been brought back; languages have been restored: Greek – without which it is a disgrace that any man should call himself a scholar – Hebrew, Chaldaean, Latin; elegant and accurate books are now in use, printing having been invented in my lifetime through divine inspiration just as artillery, on the contrary, was invented through the prompting of the devil. The whole world is now full of erudite persons, full of very learned teachers and of the most ample libraries, such indeed that I hold that it was not as easy to study in the days of Plato, Cicero nor Papinian as it is now.

From henceforth no one should be found in any position or company who has not been well burnished in the workshop of Minerva. I see even today's brigands, hangmen, mercenaries and stable-lads better taught than the teachers and preachers of my day. [What shall I say?] Even the very

women and children have aspired to such praise and to the
heavenly manna of sound learning. Things are such that
I have had to learn to read Greek literature at my age! I
had never despised it as Cato did, but when I was young I
never had the means of mastering it. Now I readily delight
in reading the *Moral Writings* of Plutarch, the beautiful
Dialogues of Plato, the *Monuments* of Pausanias and the
Antiquities of Athenaeus, as I await the hour when it shall
please God my Maker to summon and command me to
quit this world.

That is why, my son, I urge you to employ your youth
in making good progress in study [and virtue]. You are in
Paris; Epistemon your tutor is with you; both can teach
you: one directly and orally, the other by laudable
examples.

I intend and will that you acquire a perfect command of
languages – first Greek (as Quintilian wishes), secondly
Latin, and then Hebrew for the Holy Scriptures, as well as
Chaldaean and Arabic likewise – and that, for your Greek,
you mould your style by imitating Plato, and for your
Latin, Cicero.

Let there be no history which you do not hold ready in
memory: to help you, you have the cosmographies of those
who have written on the subject.

When you were still very young – about five or six – I
gave you a foretaste of geometry, arithmetic and music
among the liberal arts. Follow that up with the other arts.
Know all the canons of astronomy, but leave judicial
astrology and the Art of Lullius alone as abuses and
vanities.

I want you to learn all of the beautiful texts of Civil Law
by heart and compare them to moral philosophy.

And as for the knowledge of natural phenomena, I want
you to apply yourself to it with curiosity: let there be no
sea, river or stream the fishes of which you do not know.
Know all the birds of the air, all the trees, bushes and
shrubs of the forests, all the herbs in the soil, all the metals

hidden deep in the womb of the Earth, the precious stones of all the Orient and the South: let none remain unknown to you.

Then frequent the books of the ancient medical writers, Greek, Arabic and Latin, without despising the Talmudists or the Cabbalists; and by frequent dissections acquire a perfect knowledge of that other world which is Man.

And for a few hours every day start to study the Sacred Writings: first the Gospels and Epistles of the Apostles in Greek, then the Old Testament in Hebrew.

In short, let me see you an abyss of erudition.

For from henceforth, now that you are growing up into manhood, it behoves you to issue forth from that calm and restful pursuit of knowledge and to learn chivalry and the handling of arms so as to defend my House and come to the help of our friends in all their troubles against the assaults of evil-doers.

And then I want you shortly to find out how much you have profited, which you can best do by defending theses in any field of knowledge, in public, with anyone, against anyone and by haunting learned men both in Paris and elsewhere.

But since, according to Solomon, 'Wisdom will not enter a soul which diviseth evil,' and since 'Science without conscience is but the ruination of the soul,' you should serve, love and fear God, fixing all your thoughts and hopes in Him, and, by faith informed with charity, live conjoined to Him in such a way as never to be cut off from Him by sin.

Beware of this world's deceits. Give not your mind unto vanity, for this is a transitory life, but the word of God endureth for ever. Be of service to your neighbours and love them as yourself. Venerate your teachers. Flee the company of those whom you do not wish to resemble; and the gifts of grace which God has bestowed upon you receive you not in vain. Then once you know that you have acquired all there is to learn over there, come back to me

so that I may see you and give you my blessing before I
die.

My son: the peace and grace of our Lord be with you.
Amen.

From Utopia,

this seventh day of the month of March.

Your father,

GARGANTUA.

Once that letter was received and read, Pantagruel took new
heart; he was so burning to improve himself even further that
if you had seen him improving himself by study you would
have said that his mind was so tireless and keen among his
books that it was like a flame among the heather.

How Pantagruel met Panurge, whom he
loved all his life

CHAPTER 9

*[Every language has to be invented, accepted by convention and learnt.
(Rabelais here, follows Aristotle.) Unknown languages may seem awesome or funny. In the* Quartier Latin *of Paris Latin held sway but one
also heard the many languages of the 'Nations' studying there. Most
readers find it tiresome to try to make out what the following languages
mean. At all events they are above all used for the comic effect of their
sounds on ears attuned to French.*

*Rabelais was not restricting himself to tongues he knew. The Scots
for example is garbled; no attempt was ever made to put it right, yet
there were plenty of Scots in Paris. (It can still be amusing to hear
this chapter read aloud by a good mimic. Since Rabelais added new
languages the joke must have gone down well. A few readers must
have played with the coded, invented tongues.) There are invented
languages in More's* Utopia, *and also in the* Farce of Maître Pathelin.

*What each of the languages approximately means is given in the
footnotes – reluctantly: they are best enjoyed for their sounds.*

Panurge's name is from the Greek for a wiley man, a trickster.]

Pantagruel was outside the city one day, strolling near the Abbaye de Saint-Antoine, discussing and philosophizing with his followers and some students, when he met a man handsomely built and elegant in all his bodily lineaments but piteously injured here and there and so bedraggled that he looked as if he had just escaped from a pack of dogs, or better still like an apple-picker from the orchards of Perche.

As soon as he descried him afar off, Pantagruel said to those around him:

'Do you see that man coming along the road from the Pont de Charenton? I swear he is poor only by chance, for I assure you from reading his face that Nature produced him from some rich and noble ancestry, but the trials which befall folk who are eager for knowledge have reduced him to such poverty and penury.'

As soon as the man came right up to them Pantagruel asked:

'My friend, I beg you to be good enough to stay here a while and answer what I ask. You will never regret it, for I have a very great desire to give you all the help I can in the wretched state I see you in; for you move me to great pity. So, my friend, tell me: who are you? Where are you coming from? Where are you going to? What are you in quest of? And what is your name?'

That companion answered in a Germanic tongue:

'Juncker, Gott geb euch glück unnd hail. Zuvor, lieber Juncker, ich las euch wissen das da ir mich von fragt, ist ein arm unnd erbarmglich ding, unnd wer vil darvon zu sagen, welches euch verdruslich zu hoeren, unnd mir zu erzelen wer, vievol die Poeten unnd Orators vorzeiten haben gesagt in irem Spürchen unnd Sentenzen, das die Gedechtnus des Ellends unnd Armuot vorlangs erlitten ist ain grosser Lust.'[20]

20. In German: 'My Lord: God grant you happiness and good luck. First you must know, my good Lord, that what you are questioning me about is a sad and unfortunate matter which it would be nasty for you to hear and for me to relate, even though former poets and orators have said that recalling past poverty and misery is a great pleasure.' There is an echo of a well-known part of Virgil said during a tempest: 'One day perhaps we shall be pleased to recall this' (*Aeneid*, 1, 203).

To which Pantagruel replied:

'My Friend, I can't understand that gibble-gabble. Speak a different language if you want people to understand you.'

Whereupon the companion replied:

'*Al barildim gotfano dech min brin alabo dordin falbroth ringuam albaras. Nin porth zadikim almucathin milko prin al elmim enthoth dal heben ensouim; kuthim al dum alkatim nim broth dechoth porth min michais im endoth, pruch dal maisoulum hol moth dansrilrim lupaldas im voldemoth. Nin hur diavosth mnarbotim dal gousch palfrapin duch im scoth pruch galeth dal Chinon min foulchrich al conin butathen doth dal prim.*'[21]

Pantagruel asked those around him, 'Did you get any of that?

Epistemon replied,

'It's the language of the Antipodes, I think. The devil himself couldn't sink his teeth into it!'

Pantagruel then said,

'The walls might understand you, my good fellow but none of us can understand one bit of it!'

To which the companion replied:

'*Signor mio, voi videte per exemplo che la cornamusa non suona mai, s'ela non a il ventre pieno; cosi io parimente non vi saprei contare le mie fortune, se prima il tribulato ventre non a la solita refectione, al quale è adviso che le mani et li denti abbui perso il loro ordine naturale et del tuto annichillati.*'[22]

Epistemon rejoined: 'One is as bad as the other!'

So Panurge then said:

['*Lard, ghest tholb be sua virtiuss be intelligence ass yi body schal biss be naturall relvtht, tholb suld of me pety have, for nature hass ulss egualy maide; bot fortune sum exaltit bess, an*

---

21.   Panurge, in a kind of Hispano-Moorish, is apparently asking Pantagruel for Chinon cakes and stew: otherwise he will bugger him, Scottish-style.

22.   In Italian: 'You can recognize, Signor mio, that the bagpipe, for example, never sounds except when its belly is full. I likewise could never tell you of my fate unless my troubled belly be given its habitual food, for which my hands and teeth have lost their natural role and are reduced to nothing.'

*oyis deprevit. Non ye less viois mou virtius deprevit and virtiuss
men discrivis, for, anen ye lad end, iss non gud.'*[23]

'Worse still' said Pantagruel.

Whereupon Panurge said:

*'Jona andie, guaussa goussyetan behar da erremedio,
beharde, versela ysser lan da. Anbates, otoyyes nausu, eyn
essassu gourr ay proposian ordine den. Non yssena bayta
fascheria egabe, genherassy badia sadassu nour assia. Aran
hondovan gualde eydassu nay dassuna. Estou oussyc eguinan
soury hin, er darstura eguy harm, Genicoa plasar vadu.'*[24]

'Genicoa?' Eudemon replied, 'Are you there?'

To which Carpalim added,

'By Sain Tringan, either I fail to understan' ye, or shoo cum
fra Scotlan.'

Panurge then answered him:

*'Prug frest strinst sorgdmand strochdt drhds pag brledand
Gravot Chavigny Pomardiere rusth pkallhdracg Deviniere près
Nays, Bcuille kalmuch monach drupp delmeupplistrincq dlrnd
dodelb up drent loch minc stzrinquald de vins ders cordelis hur
jocststzampenards.'*[25]

Whereupon Epistemon said:

'Are you speaking Christian, or the Pathelinese tongue? No:
the language of the Lanterns.'

To which Panurge said:]

*'Herre, ie en spreke anders gheen taele dan kersten taele; my
dunct nochtans, al en seg ie v niel een wordt, myuen noot v*

23. In Scottish, with some guesses at the meaning: 'My Lord, if you be as
    strong in intelligence as you are by nature supplied in the body, you
    should take pity on me, for Nature made us equal, but some Fortune has
    exalted and some depressed; nevertheless virtue is often despised and
    virtuous men depressed; for before the last End there is no one good.'

24. In a peasant form of Basque: 'Great Sir, for all ills a remedy is needed;
    the difficulty is to act aright. I have so besought you! See that we can
    have some order in what we say. That will be without resentment if you
    make my satisfaction come. After that ask from me what you will. It will
    do you no harm to meet the expenses of both, God-willing.' At least the
    word *Genicoa* (God willing) would have been recognized: it was the
    'typical' Basque word.

25. Lanternese seems a vaguely Scandinavian-sounding tongue; here one can
    recognize some French proper names.

claert ghenonch wat ie beglere; gheest my unyt bermherticheyt
yet waer un ie ghevoet mach zunch.[26]

Pantagruel's reaction was: 'Enough of that!'

But Panurge said:

'*Señor, de tanto hablar yo soy cansado. Por que supplico a*
Vostra Reverentia que mire a los preceptos evangeliquos, para
que ellos movant Vostra Reverentia a lo qu'es de conscientia,
y, sy ellos non bastarent para mover Vostra Reverentia a piedad,
supplico que mire a la piedad natural, la qual yo creo que le
movra, como es de razon, y con esto non digo mas.[27]

Pantagruel commented:

'Gosh, my friend, I have no doubt that you can speak several
languages well, but tell us what you want in one we can
understand!'

[The companion then said:

'*Myn Herre, endog jeg med inghen tunge talede, lygesom*
boeen, ocg uskvvlig creatner! myne kleebon, och myne legoms
magerbed uudviser allygue klalig buvad tyng meg meest behoff
girereb, som aer sandeligh mad och drycke: hwarfor forbarme
teg omsyder offvermeg, och bef ael at gyffuc meg nogeth, aff
huylket jeg kand styre myne groeendes maghe, lygeruss son
mand Cerbero en soppe forsetthr. Soa shal tue loeffve lenge och
lyksalight.[28]

26. In Dutch: Panurge says, more or less: 'Sir, I am speaking no tongue but a
    Christian tongue; but it seems to me that, without uttering one word, my
    rags are enough to show what I want. Be kind enough to supply me the
    food I need.'

27. In Spanish: 'Too much talking has tired me out. That is why I beseech
    your Reverence to think about the commandments of the Gospel so that
    you be brought to what your conscience requires of you, and if they are
    not enough to move your Reverence to pity, I beg you to think about
    natural pity, which I think will move you as you ought, and so I cease
    talking.'

        '42 reads 'Seignor' not 'Señor'.

28. In Danish: 'Sir, even if, like babies and beasts, I spoke no language, my
    clothes and the skinniness of my body should clearly show what I need,
    that is food and drink. Take pity on me then and have enough sent to me
    to overcome the barking of my stomach just as one places sops before
    Cerberus; thus you shall live long and contentedly.'

'I think,' said Eusthenes, 'that the Goths spoke like that, and thus would we speak through our bums if God so wished.']

Whereupon the companion said:

'*Adoni, scolom lecha. Im ischar harob hal habdeca, bemeherah thithen li kikar lehem, chancathub: Laah al Adonai chonen ral.*'[29]

'That,' replied Epistemon, 'I do understand! That's ancient Hebrew, pronounced as an orator should.'

Whereupon that companion said:

'*Despota ti nyn panagathe, doiti sy mi uc artodotis? Horas gar limo analiscomenon eme atlhios. Ce en to mctaxy eme uc eleis udamos, zetis de par emu ha u chre, ce homos philologi pamdes homologusi tote logus te ce rhemeta peritta hyrparchin, opote pragma afto pasi delon esti. Entha gar anancei monon logi isin, hina pragmata, (bon peri amphibetumen), me phosphoros epihenete.*'[30]

'Why!' cried Carpalim, Pantagruel's footman, 'Greek, that is! I could understand it! How come? Have you ever lived in Greece?'

The companion then said:

'*Agonou dont oussys vou denaguez algarou, nou den farou zamist vous mariston ulbrou, fousquez vou brol, tam bredaguez moupreton den goul houst, daguez daguez nou croupys fost bardounnoflist nou grou. Agou paston tol nalprissys hourtou los echatonous prou dhouquys brol panygou den bascrou noudous caguons goulfren goul oust troppassou.*'

'I fancy I do understand that,' said Pantagruel. 'It's the

---

29. The hesitant Hebrew means: 'Peace be with you, sir. If you wish to do some good to your servant, give him at once a hunk of bread, as it is written: "He that hath pity on the poor lendeth to the Lord."' (The quotation is from Proverbs 19:17.)

30. In Classical Greek, transcribed in the modern form of which Lascaris approved but not Erasmus: 'Excellent master, why do you not give me some bread? You see me pitiably perishing from hunger yet you show me no pity and ask me irrelevant questions. Yet all lovers of literature know that talk and words are superfluous when the facts are clear to everyone. Discussion is required only when the facts discussed are not evident.'

language of my homeland, Utopia. Or else it sounds very like it.'[31]

And as he was about to make a speech the companion interrupted him:

'*Jam toties vos per sacra perque deos deasque omnis obtestatus sum ut, si qua vos pietas permovet, egestatem meam solaremini, nec hilum proficio clamans et ejulans. Sinite, queso, sinite, viri impii quo me fata vocant abire, nec ultra vanis vestris interpellationibus obtundatis, memores veteris illius adagi quo venter famelicus auriculis carere dicitur.*'[32]

'Gosh, my friend,' said Pantagruel, 'can't you speak French?'

The companion replied:

'Yes I do. Very well, my Lord. French is, thank God, my native tongue, my mother tongue, for I was born and brought up in the Garden of France, [in Touraine, that is].'

'Well then,' said Pantagruel, 'tell us your name and where you come from; for, upon my word, I feel so great a friendship for you that, if you will condescend to do as I wish, you shall never budge from my side: you and I will form a new brace of friends, like Aeneas and Achates.'

'My Lord,' said the companion, 'my real and true baptismal name is Panurge. I am now on my way from Turkey, where I was taken captive during the disaster of Mytilene. I would love to tell you of my adventures, which are more wonderful than those of Ulysses; but since you kindly wish to retain me with you – and since I willingly accept that offer, vowing never to leave you even if you were to go to all the

31. The third artificial tongue. It has not been deciphered, assuming that it can be. Sir Thomas More invented an alphabet for the language of Utopia.

32. In Classical Latin: 'Several times I have already besought you by things holy and all the gods and goddesses to relieve my need if any pity can move you, but my wails and plaints have had no effect. Allow me, I beg you, allow me, you wicked men, to go whither the Fates call me, and weary me no longer with your vain greetings, mindful of that ancient adage which says a hungry belly had no ears.' The texts read as printed: *deos deasque omnis*.

Erasmus, *Adages*, VI, II, XII, 'A hungry man is not to be addressed', is conflated with II, VIII, LXXXIV, 'the belly has no ears'.

devils – we shall at some more convenient time find ample leisure for relating them.

'Just now I have a more pressing necessity: to feed! Everything is ready: sharp teeth, empty belly, dry throat [and screaming appetite]. If you will please set me to work, you will find it soothing to watch me tuck in.

'Do give the order, for God's sake!'

Pantagruel then commanded that Panurge be taken to his lodgings and brought plenty of food. And it was done: that evening he fed very well, went to roost early and slept round to dinnertime next day [, so that from bed to table he made but three-skips-and-a-jump].

How Pantagruel fairly judged an amazingly hard and obscure controversy so equitably that his judgement was termed more wonderful than that of Solomon's

CHAPTER 9 *bis*

[In the original edition this chapter is erroneously numbered 9 like the previous one.

Bumkis renders Baisecul *and Slurp-ffart* Humevene.

An adage of Erasmus (III, IV, LXXXIII: 'A deaf man went to law with a deaf man: the judge was deafer still') sums up the course of the following three-part farce. Erasmus extends the adage to the stupidly incoherent. Rabelais applies it to the incomprehensibly verbose. Here we have lawyers' jokes against legal proceedings partly conceived in the spirit of Maître Pathelin *and partly arising from a medieval legal belief that the Greeks, misunderstanding the 'natural' gestures of the Romans and taking them for signs of profundity, judged the Romans worthy of learning from them the principles of law. Cf. chapter 13.*

Not all the legal authorities laughed at here are dismissed with scorn – it is not in the spirit of Shrovetide fun to do so – though several are, since Rabelais supports humanist Law in the Gallic Mode. Guillaume Budé was its champion. Humanist Law depreciates much of the work of the great glossators whose copious glosses swamped the texts with

dense, cramped, workaday Latin. The Gallic Mode favoured the study
of the meanings of texts with the aid of the widest historical and
semantic erudition. Like Budé Rabelais believed that law should be
conceived as moral philosophy. Hence the condemnation of Cepola,
who was renowned for his 'stratagems' designed to get guilty clients
out of scrapes.

Pantagruel's published theses for disputation recall Pico della
Mirandola's, which were On Everything Knowable.

Rabelais later prudently cut out 'Not that he stopped the said Sor-
bonnical Theologians from tippling and refreshing themselves with
their customary quaffing'.

The pleasure taken by Demosthenes in being recognized is men-
tioned by Erasmus in Adages, I, X, XLIII: *'To be pointed at with a*
finger'.]

Pantagruel, bearing in mind his father's advice, decided one day
to make trial of his erudition. And so at all the crossroads
throughout town he posted up nine thousand seven hundred
and sixty [-four] theses on all subjects, touching upon the
greatest controversies which existed in all disciplines.

First of all he defended himself against the dons, the arts-men
and the rhetoricians in the rue du Fouarre, tumbling them down
on their bums. Then, over a period of six weeks, he defended
himself against the Theologians in the Sorbonne from four in
the morning until six at night, except for a two-hour break to
enable the Theologians to feed and restore themselves. Not that
he stopped the said Sorbonnical Theologians from tippling and
refreshing themselves with their customary quaffing. Most of
the Law Lords were present, as were the *Maîtres de Requeste*,
presidents, counsellors, accountants, principal secretaries, advocates and such-like, together with the city magistrates, the
Medics and the Canon Lawyers. Some took the bit between
their teeth, but despite their crowing *ergo* and their flawed
syllogisms, he tied them in knots and clearly showed them
that they were merely calves [dressed up in gowns]. Everybody
began to talk so much of knowledge so wonderful and to noise
it abroad that whenever he went through the streets there were
no goodwives, washerwomen, peddler-women, kitchen-maids

or women hawking pen-knives who did not exclaim, 'That's 'im.' He was delighted, as was Demosthenes, the prince of Greek orators, when a hunched-up old crone pointed him out and said, 'It's that one there.'

Now in that very season a lawsuit was pending between two gross lords. One of them, the plaintiff, was the Sieur de Bumkis. On the other side was the defendant, the Sieur de Slurp-ffart. The contention between them was so high and hard in law that it was all Double Dutch to the Court of Parlement.

And so by command of the king there were gathered together four of the most learned and obese members from each of the *Parlements* of France and from the *Grand Conseil* as well as all the principal regents of the universities not only of France but of England and Italy, such as Jason de Maino, Philip Decius, Petrus de Petronibus [and other rabbi-like dunces].

Despite being thus assembled for forty-six weeks they had found nothing they could sink their teeth into, nor could they grasp the case clearly enough to set it to rights in any manner whatsoever. At which they were so annoyed that they shat themselves for shame like villeins.

But one of them called Du Douhet – the most learned, the most experienced and the wisest of them all – said to them one day when their minds were all philo-garbidged:

'My Lords: we have already been here a long time, doing nothing but squander money. In this matter we can plumb no bottom, reach no shore: the more we study it, the less we understand it. That is very shameful and a burden on our consciences. We shall get out of this, I think, with nothing but dishonour since we are merely raving in our deliberations.

'But this is what occurred to me: you have all often heard tell of that great personality Maître Pantagruel, who, in great public debates held against all comers, has been acknowledged learned beyond the capacity of this present age. In my opinion we should summon him and discuss this matter with him. If he cannot get to the bottom of it all, then nobody can.'

All the Counsellors and Doctors-of-Law readily agreed to it. They at once sent to find Pantagruel and begged him to peg out their case, go into it thoroughly and report to them as he saw fit.[33]

And they handed over to him the bundles and documents, which were enough to load four, fat, well-furnished asses.

But Pantagruel said,

'My lords. The two noblemen concerned, are they still living?'

'Yes,' they replied.

'Then what the devil is all this bumpf for, all these transcriptions you are handing me? Would it not be better to hear them relate their differences *viva voce* than to read through all these monkey-puzzles, which are nothing but deceptions, devilish ruses *à la* Cepola and subversions of the Law?

'I am convinced that you and all the others through whose hands this case has passed have produced all the *pro-et-contra* machinations that you can. Where the controversy was patently easy to determine you have obscured it with the daft and unreasonable reasons and irrelevant opinions of Accursius, Baldus, Bartolus, Castro, Imola, Hippolytus, Panormitanus, Bertachinus, Alexander, Curtius and other old curs who have never understood the least law of the *Pandects*. They were mere fatted glebe-calves, ignorant of everything necessary for the understanding of the laws (that is quite certain for they knew no languages: no Greek – and no Latin save the Gothick and barbarous kind). And yet the laws originally came from the Greeks, for which you have the testimony of Ulpian *on the posterior law of 'On the Origin of Justice'* – and are full of Greek words and sayings.

'Next, the laws are drafted in the most elegant and polished language in all the Latin tongue, not excepting Sallust or Varro or Cicero or Pliny or Seneca or Livy or Quintilian. So how could those crazy old madmen understand the text of such laws, they who have never seen a book in good Latin, as is manifest from their style, which is that of a chimney-sweep, a kitchen-lad or a scullery-boy, not of a jurisconsult.

'Moreover, since the laws are rooted in the contexts of moral

33. '42: . . . begged him *to net up the case, sieve it through* and report to them . . .

and natural philosophy, how on earth can those fools understand them, having gone less into philosophy, by God, than my
mule!

'As for humane letters and a knowledge of Antiquity and the
ancient histories, they are as burdened with them as a toad is
with feathers, and use them as a crucified uses a fife![34] Yet the
laws are full of them: without them they cannot be understood.
One of these days I will put pen to paper and demonstrate that
more clearly!

'Now then; if you want me to deal with this lawsuit, first burn
all those documents for me, and secondly, summon the two
noblemen to appear in person before me. When I have heard
them out I will deliver my opinion without feint or fiction.'

At which some of them raised an objection since, as you
know, there are more fools than wise in any assembly with the
majority party always overcoming the better [as Livy wrote
when talking of the Carthaginians]. But Du Douhet manfully
maintained the contrary, contending that Pantagruel had
spoken wisely and that all those minutes, testimonies, rebuttals,
[counter-rebuttals,] formal discreditings, affidavits and other
such devilish trickeries were nothing but subversions of justice
and ways of prolonging the process, and that the devil would
take them all if they did not proceed otherwise, following evangelical and philosophical equity.

In short, all the papers were burnt and the two noblemen
were summoned to attend in person. Pantagruel then asked
them,

'Are you the two who have this great disagreement between
you?'

'Yes, my Lord,' they said.

'Which of you is the plaintiff?'

'I am,' said le Sieur de Bumkis.

'Well then, my friend, explain your affair point by point in
accordance with the truth, for if you utter one word of a lie, by
Gosh I'll have that head off your shoulders and show you that
in matters of justice and judgement one must tell nothing but

34. '42 omits: and use them as a crucified uses a fife.

the truth. So in stating your case take care to add nothing and
subtract nothing. Now speak.

*

*[There is no chapter-break here in the original edition. Later texts read:
How the Sieurs de Bumkis and de Slurp-ffart pleaded their cases before
Pantagruel without legal counsel. Chapter 11.*

*The ramblings of Bumkis and Slurp-ffart nearly make sense: one
recognizes for example a comic Beatitude: 'Blessed are the dullards,
for they have stumbled' (cf. Matthew 5); contemporaries would have
been intrigued by teasing, glancing allusions to the 'privileges of the
University' (first added in the Juste 1534 edition) and the 'Pragmatic
Sanction of Bourges' of 1438, which, for the French at least, subordinated papal authority to that of Councils, which were topical issues
in Rabelais' time, when the royal powers in France were being
extended over Church, university and papal domains.*

*Philip Decius was the legal authority who persuaded the French
king to call the Council of Pisa against the warrior Pope Julius II. The
allusion to a year '36 hints at 1436, when stormy sessions of the
Council of Basle sought to restrain papal powers. Such powers (a
project to limit which dominated the Council of Basle) were subject
to arbitrary French royal decrees in the* Pragmatic Sanction. *Further
attempts against papal power dominated the (allegedly heretical)
Council of Pisa of 1511, called on the advice of Philip Decius. The
matter was settled in the French interest by the Concordat of 1517,
which ceded great powers to the French monarchs, not least in the
nomination of bishops, archbishops and abbots. Such points are
touched on lightly, but would not have been lost on students of the
Law and the inhabitants of the* Quartier Latin *or on a reasonably
educated readership.]*

At which Bumkis began as follows:

'It is, my Lord, true, that a goodwife of my household was
taking her eggs to the market . . .'

'Don your bonnet, Bumkis,' said Pantagruel.

'As your Lordship pleases,' said le Sieur de Bumkis. 'But to get to the point: she passed between the two tropics, [some sixpence-farthing] towards the zenith, diametrically opposed to Troglodytes because the Rhiphaean Mountains had experienced that year a great dearth of booby-traps on account of a sedition [of the Yappers] stirred up between the Gibble-Gabblers and the Running-curs of Accursius brought on by the rebellion of the Swiss assembled, up to a number of three, six, nine, ten, to go to the New Year's mistletoes[35] on the first *die* of the year, when sops are given to cattle and the key to the coal-shed to the maidens in order to supply oats to the hounds.

'All night long, pledged hand on pot, they did nothing but dispatch papal Bulls by foot-post and lackeys by horseback,[36] so as to restrain the boats, since the sempsters wanted to make the pilfered off-cuts into a coverlet for the Ocean Sea, which was at that time great with child, according to the opinion of the trussers-up of hay.[37]

'However, the physicians stated that from her urine they could recognize no clear symptoms

> . . . in the tread of a bustard,
> Of eating mattocks jellied with mustard,

except that the Lords of the Court should issue an order in B-flat that the pox should no longer glean after the silk-worms and thus walk about during divine service,[38] since the beggars had made a good start at dancing a Brigadoon at the right pitch: "head in the middle, one foot in the fire", as our good Ragot used to say.

'Ah, my Lords: God governs all things as He pleases, and a carter, against fickle Fortune, smashed his whip [to nose-flicks]. It was on the retreat from Bicocca, when Maître Dolt of the Watercress graduated as Bachelor of Blunders for, as the

35. '42: . . . up to a *well-biased* number to go to the New Year's mistletoes . . .
36. '42: . . . dispatch *bulls by foot and bulls* by horseback . . .
37. '42: . . . great with *a potful of cabbage*, according . . .
38. '42 omits: and thus walk about during divine service . . .

canon lawyers say, "Blessed are the dullards, for they have stumbled."

'But, by Saint-Fiacre-de-Brie! what caused Lent to be so high, is quite simply that

> Pentecost
> Much does cost.
> May is born:
> A little rain abates a storm.

'Seeing that the serjeant never put the white of the target so high at the butts that the clerk might not [orbicularily] lick his fingers, ready and erect, being feathered with gander's plumes, and we clearly see that everyone feels guilty-nosed, unless one were to gaze ocularily in perspective towards the chimney-piece from which hangs the sign of *The Wine with the Forty Girdles*, which are needed by twenty panniers [of debt-relief for a quinquennium].

'Whoever would not – at the very least – loose his falcon [before cheese tartlets] rather than remove its hood, since memory is often lost once a man dons his breeches back to front.

> God keep him from blame,
> Thibault Mitaine.'

At which point Pantagruel said, 'Whoa there, my friend! Whoa! Speak with restraint and without choler. I am following your case. Do proceed'.

'Truly [, my Lord],' said the Seigneur de Bumkis, 'It is just as folk say: it is a good thing occasionally to observe people, for one observant man is worth two. Now, my Lord, the aforesaid goodwife, when saying her *Rejoice ye alls* and her *Hear us O Lords*, could not protect herself from a back-stroke feint [, arising, by Golly's virtue, from the privileges of the University,] except by angelically bathing, covering it with a seven-of-diamonds and launching a flying jab at it as close as possible to the place where they sell such old rags as are employed by the Flemish painters when they wish dexterously "to shoe the grasshoppers"; and I am deeply astonished that society does not lay eggs, since it is so beautiful to brood upon them.'

At this point le Sieur de Slurp-ffart desired to make an *ex parte* appeal and say something, but Pantagruel said to him:

'By Saint Anthony's guts! Does it behove you to speak without sanction! Here am I, sweating under the strain of following the process of your quarrel, and you come pestering me! Be quiet! In the devil's name, quiet, quiet! You shall speak your fill when the one here has finished. Do go on' (he said to Bumkis) 'and do not hurry.'

'Seeing therefore,' said Bumkis, that

> The Pragmatic Sanction
> Of it makes no mention,

and that the Pope gave everyone permission to break wind freely and at will, provided that the whites were not bespattered however much poverty there be in the world, and that one did not sign oneself with the left hand, that goodwife began to dish up the soups by the faith of the little well-bollocked fishes, which, at that junction, were needed to understand the cobbling of old boots.[39], However, Jean de Veau, her cousin-german, excited by a brand from the scuttle, advised her most definitely not to put herself to the hazard of doing her washing[40] without first steeping the paper in alum at the spin of a top (tick tock tack) for,

> If from a bridge you wisely fall:
> You never cross it after all;

seeing that the Gentlemen of the Accompts were not in accord over the summonings of the German flutes, from which had been constructed *The Spectacles of Princes*, newly printed in Antwerp.

---

39. '42: ... not sign oneself with *ruffians: the rainbow freshly ground at Milan so as to hatch out the skylarks, he consented that* the goodwife should dish up *the sciatics through the protestation of the little fishes*, which ...

40. '42: ... of *seconding the tumbled* washing ...

'And that, my Lords, constitutes a very poor endorsement, and, I believe on this matter the party opposite upon his faith, or upon the clerge of a Wordyman; for, desirous of obeying the king's good-pleasure, I armed myself from top to toe, with padding for the belly, so as to go and see how my grape-pickers had slashed their tall bonnets, the better to tinkle about with their virginals, since the weather was a little dangerous for merchants with the runs, on account of which several free-shooting bowmen had been rejected at the muster, notwith-standing – *Baudichon, my Love* – that the flues were quite tall enough in proportion to the distended synovial bursa and malanders of the horses.

'And that is why it was a bumper-year for snail-shells throughout the whole country of Artois, which was no mean advantage to my lords the hodmen of the *vendanges* when, with unbuttoned bellies, the snail-shells were consumed [without a sword being drawn].

'Would that everyone had so fine a voice: far better tennis would be played! And those sleights that folk employ when wearing high-soled clogs[41] would flow more readily down into the Seine, there to serve forever at the Pont des Meuniers, as was heretofore decreed by the King of Canarre: which decision is herein in the Archives.

'Wherefore, my Lord, I plead that your Lordship state and declare in this case that which is reasonable, awarding costs and damages.'

Whereupon Pantagruel said, 'Have you anything to add, my friend?'

Bumkis replied, 'No, my Lord, I have said it all, right down to the *world without end, Amen*; and upon my honour I have falsified nothing.'

'And now, my dear Sieur de Slurp-ffart, it is your turn to speak,' said Pantagruel. 'Be brief, but omit nothing relevant.'

*

41. '42: . . . employ when *expounding the etymology of* high-soled . . .

[A new chapter begins here: The Plea of le Sieur de Slurp-ffart before Pantagruel. Chapter 12.

Bumkis meets his match in obscurity. For the glancing allusions to the years '36 and '17 see the Introduction to the previous section.]

At which le Sieur de Slurp-ffart began as follows:

'My Lord, my Lords: if the wickedness of men could be as readily seen by our [categorical] judgement as flies are in milk, the world [, Four Beeves!] would not be so nibbled at by rats, and there would be many an ear on earth most cowardly gnawed at. For – despite the fact that everything alleged by the plaintiff is eiderdownedly most true to the letter and historical fact – nevertheless, my Lords, artfulness, trickery and piddling little cavillings are secreted within the pot of roses.

At the very moment when I am eating my soup [at par], thinking no evil, speaking no evil, must I put up with someone plaguing and rasping my brain by dancing me a jig and chanting,

> Eat your soup while wine you drink:
> Dead, you'll have no eyes to blink.

And by our Sainted Dame, how many fat captains have we seen on the open field of battle (during the distribution of knocks of holy bread to the Brotherhood) playing the lute, trumpeting their bums and performing little exhibition dances in fine slippers decorated with prawn-beard slashes, so as the more honourably to be seated at table. But now the world has entirely lost her way on account of the angle-irons on the bales of Leicestershire serge: one of them sinks into debauchery; the other five into four plus two. And unless the Court were to issue an order, this year it will be as hard to glean as ever it was, or else take three weeks.[42]

'If some poor wretch goes to the stews and gules up his conk with a cow-pat or buys winter boots, and if the serjeants passing by, or the men of the Watch, receiving the decoction of an

---

42. '42: . . . or else *make goblets*. If some . . .

enema or the faecal matter of a privy on their clatterings, must they therefore clip testoons or make a fricassee in wooden cash-erolles!

'At times we propose one thing but God does another, and once the sun has set, all beasts are in the dark. I do not want to be believed over this unless I prove it helter-skelterly by folk worthy of remembrance.[43]

'In the year six and thirty I bought a horse – a German curtal, high and curtailed – well fleeced and, as the goldsmiths vouchsafed, dyed with red antimony. The lawyer however slipped in some *etceteras*!

'I am not such a clerk as to seize the moon with my teeth, but at the pot of butter where they were affixing seals on the vulcanic impedimenta, it was rumoured that salted beef enabled you to discover wine at high midnight without a candle even if it were hidden away at the bottom of a coalman's sack, booted and protected though he was by the greaves and leg-armour necessary to make a good *rusterie* (that is, a head-of-mutton fricassee).

'Now, as the proverb says: "A fine thing it is, while enjoying your courting, to look at black cows in a burnt wood." I obliged My Lords the Clercs to consult on this matter. By way of conclusion they resolved in the ninth mode of the first figure of syllogisms that there is nothing like doing your reaping in the heat of summer within a cellar well provided with ink and paper, pen and whore-pen (as in Lyons on the Rhone) tiddly-pom.

'For as soon as armour starts stinking of garlic the rust attacks its liver; then you can merely peck back twist-neckedly, flirting with an after-dinner nap. And that is what makes salt so dear.

'Never believe, my Lords, that when the aforesaid goodwife caught the female red-tail in birdlime in order the better to enfeoff the serjeant-at-law – and when the puddingly viscera tergiversated into the purses of the usurers – there was nothing better to guard against cannibals than to trade a wad of onions,

43. '42: . . . by *daylight* folk. In the year . . .

bound by three hundred *Ave Marias*[44] and a *soupçon* of calf's mesentery of the best alloy possessed by the alchemists – and to well bedaub and calcinate one's slippers, *blah, blah, blah*, with a fine hay-rake sauce, and to hide oneself away in some little mole-hole, always saving, of course, the bacon.

'And if one of the dice never wants to show you anything but always a double ace, or a triad, six and three, beware the ace, and put the dame in the corner of the backgammon bed, hey nonny, nonny and live under sufferance and fish me plenty of frogs shod in fine boots.[45] That will be for the little moulted goslings playing at snuff-me-the-candle while awaiting the beating of the metal and the heating of the wax for the quaffers of English good ale.

'In very truth, the Four Beeves in question had rather short memories, yet, despite knowing the gamut, they had no fear of cormorant or Savoy drake, and the good folk on my lands held high hopes for them, saying, "Those boys will grow up good at Arabic mathematics, which will be as a legal rubric for us."

'Nor can we fail to catch the wolf, making as we do our hedges well above the windmills mentioned by the party opposite. But the devil was jealous and ordered the Germans to bring up the rear, who had a devil of a time slurping it down: *"Trink, trink. Dass is goot; forlorn by God! a poor fight vass it."*[46] And I am very strongly amazed how the astrologers bother so much about it with their astrolabes or *almugantarats*.

'There is no likelihood whatsoever in crying "Free-range hens on Petit-Pont in Paris," even if folk were as hoop-crested as a marshland hoopoe, unless they did indeed scarify the printers' pumpet-balls with the freshly ground ink, of upper-case or cursive letters: it is all the same to me, provided that the head-band in the binding breeds no bookworms.

---

44. '42: . . . three hundred *turnips* and . . .
45. '42: . . . triad *at the big end*, beware the ace . . . bed and *lecher away* hey, nonny, nonny, and *drink to excess and drown the frog-ibuses* in fine boots . . .
46. A play on the cry attributed to cowardly Swiss mercenaries, 'Alles ist verloren bei Gott', which allows of a Latino-German pun between *ver-loren* and *frelorum* (meaning 'of the hornets'). The jest is omitted in '42.

'And, even supposing that at the coupling of the running-dogs the pugs had sounded the kill well before the lawyer had handed over his report by the cabbalistic art, it does not follow (deferring to the better judgement of the Court) that six acres of broad-cloth meadow-lands should amount to three barrels of fine anchor without forking out one's share, considering that at the funeral of King Charles you could, in the open market, buy the fleece for six silver pence:[47] I mean, *by my oath, of wool.*

'I quite normally find in all good houses that,[48] whenever men lure birds by their song, making three turns on a broomstick round their chimney-pieces and insinuating their nomination, one merely tenses one's loins and (if it should be too hot) puffs at the bum: Then, skittle and ball!

> Immediately the letter read,
> They returned the cows to his own cow-shed.

And in '17 a similar judgement was handed down on Saint Martingale's Day touching Misrule in our hamlet of Loge-Fougereuse, to which may it please the Court to pay regard. In truth I do not assert that one may not in equity lawfully dispossess anyone who would drink holy water as one does with a weaver's shuttle from which are made suppositories to impale those who have no wish to give up, except on the terms "Play well: pay well."

'[*Ergo*: My Lords, what is the law for minors?] For the precedent of the Salic Law is that the first fire-raiser to dishorn the cow which snuffs it out in musical plain-song without sol-fa-mi-doh-ing the cobbler's points must, at the time of the plague, load his poor member by means of moss,[49] gathered when you are starving with the cold at midnight Mass, so as to inflict the strappado on those white wines of Anjou which trip you up, neck for neck like Breton wrestlers.

47. '42: ... buy the fleece for *tuppence-ace*: I mean ... (Echoes of *Pathelin*, 252.)
48. '42: ... find in all good *bagpipes* that ...
49. '42: ... time of *Good Nelly sublimate the penury of his* member ...

'Concluding as above, with expenses, costs and damages.'

After le Sieur de Slurp-ffart had concluded, Pantagruel said to le Sieur de Bumkis,

'My friend, do you wish to make a rejoinder?'

To which Bumkis replied,

'No, my Lord, for I have spoken nothing but the truth; and for God's sake let us put an end to this controversy, for we cannot be here except at considerable outlay.'

*

[Another new later chapter begins here: How Pantagruel pronounced judgement on the controversy between the two Lords. Chapter 13.

The lawsuit concludes with Pantagruel outsmarting the litigants at their own game. The crowd is moved to ecstasy by such superhuman wisdom, as they were at times in the New Testament.

The difficult legal texts cited by Pantagruel (as usual by their incipits) were indeed recognized as hard to understand and to apply.

Rabelais later corrected 'Exemptor' *to* 'Emptor'.*]*

Pantagruel then rose to his feet and brought together all the attendant Presidents, Counsellors and Doctors, saying,

'Well, Gentlemen, you have heard *viva voce* from the oracle the controversy in question. How seems it to you?'

To which they replied:

'We have indeed heard it, but – the devil! – we could not understand what the case is about. Therefore we unanimously beg and beseech you kindly to pronounce such judgement as you deem fit; then we will agree with it here and now and hereinafter, and ratify it with our full assent.'

'Well then, Gentlemen,' said Pantagruel, 'since such is your wish I will do so, yet I do not find the case as hard as you do. Much harder in my opinion are:

– your paragraph *Cato,*
– the law *Brother,*
– the law *Cock,*
– the law *Five feet,*

- the law *Wine,*
- the law *If the Master,*
- the law *Mother,*
- the law *The Good Wife,*
- the law *If a Man,*
- the law *Pomponius,*
- the law *Fundi,*
- the law *Exemptor,*
- the law *Lender,*
- the law *Vendor*

and lots of others.'

Once he had finished speaking he took a turn or two about the courtroom, deep in thought as you can well realize, for he was groaning with anguish and farting under the strain like an ass[50] when its straps are too tight, as he reflected that he had to be just to all men, without bias or respecting of persons.[51]

Then he resumed his sitting and began to pronounce his judgement as follows:

'Having seen, heard and weighed the quarrel between the Lords Bumkis and Slurp-ffart, the Court says to them:

'THAT, having considered that the sun bravely declines from its summer solstice in order to flirt with the little nonsenses checkmated by a pawn-slurp on account of the evil provocations of the night-crows, light-shunners which are lodgers under the trans-Roman clime of a crucifix on horseback bending a crossbow at its loins:[52]

'THE PLAINTIFF was legally justified in caulking the galleon that the goodwife was sufflating, one foot bare, one foot shod, reimbursing him, low and stiff, in all conscience with as many scrotums as there are hairs on eighteen cows, with as many again for the sempster.

'He is likewise pronounced innocent of the crime which it was believed he had incurred since he could not comfortably

50. '42: . . . was groaning like an ass . . . (words cut out).
51. An echo of Acts 10:34: 'God is no respecter of persons.'
52. '42: . . . considered that the *oppilation of the spleen-bat* bravely declines from . . . provocations of the light-shunners . . . clime of a *monkey* on horseback . . .

defecate, owing to the decision of a pair of gloves perfumed
by walnut-candles such as are used in his Mirabeau country,
slackening the bowline with the bronze bullets.[53]

'At which the stable-lads mixed his vegetables, constable-
fashion, interlarded the decoy with hawks' tinkle-bells made
out of Hungarian lace which his brother-in-law, as a souvenir,
bore in a limitrophous pannier embroidered in gules with three
chevrons exhausted by canvas-work at the angular hide from
which one shoots at the worm-shaped popinjay with the
feathered broom.

'NEVERTHELESS: Insofar as he accuses the defendant of
having been a cobbler, a cheese-eater and a smearer of tar on
mummies, which has not been found [clangingly] true as the
aforesaid defendant well deliberated:

'THE COURT CONDEMNS him to three glass-dishfuls of
junket, seasoned, jiggery-pokered and smoke-dried (as is the
local custom): which sum is to be paid to the said defendant by
mid-August in May. But the said defendant will be obliged to
furnish hay and oakum to stop up the holes in the guttural
booby-traps jiggled with slimy gobbets from well-sieved
roundels.

'And friends again as before.

'No order for costs.

'The Court rises.'

After the sentence was announced the two parties departed,
both happy with the decree, which was all but unbelievable
[for never since the Flood have two parties contending in an
adversarial case ever been equally satisfied with a definitive
judgement: nor will they be for thirteen Jubilees to come].

As for the counsellors and the other doctors of law there
present, they remained [swooning] in ecstasy for three hours in
a rapture of amazement before the superhuman wisdom of

53. '42: . . . innocent of the *privileged* crime of *turds* which it was believed
he had incurred since he could not comfortably *defecate* owing to the
decision of a pair of gloves perfumed *with a volley of farts,* walnut-candle
style, such as are used in his Mirabeau country . . .

    Mirabeau was famous for its windmills. Reading *fianter* (defecate) for
fianser (affiance), as in all other texts.

Pantagruel which they had seen manifested in his decision of so hard and thorny a judgement. And they would still have been there, had not vinegar and rose-water been supplied to summon their accustomed senses and powers of perception back to them.

For which may God everywhere be praised.

Panurge tells how he escaped from the hands of the Turks

CHAPTER 10

[Becomes Chapter 14.

The Turks were a real threat and widely feared. One of the ways to reduce fear is to laugh at those who cause it. There is also some Lucianesque laughter at stories of prisoners escaping from the Turks. On the other hand Turks were being better understood thanks to Frenchmen such as Guillaume Postel; François I was actively seeking help from the Turk against the Papal States and the Holy Roman Empire.

As expected the trickster Panurge in this farce flouts all the normal rules of decency let alone taboos and pious superstitions. We are also being prepared to see Pantagruel, in the same spirit, as a comic Solomon, and later – in the spirit of Mardi Gras – even as a comic Jesus.

Any hint of a hunchbacked Sorbonagre is a gibe directed at Noël Béda, the Sorbonne theologian.

The wisdom of Solomon in I Kings 3 was legendary. Lot's wife and Sodom and Gomorrah are known from Genesis 13 and 19.]

Pantagruel's judgement was at once known and heard of by everyone; a great many copies were printed, and it was entered in the Archives of the Palais de Justice, so that folk began to say,

'Solomon, who on a conjecture returned a child to its mother, never produced such a masterpiece of wisdom as this good Pantagruel has done. It is a blessing to have him in our land.'

Indeed they wanted to appoint him official Receiver of Petitions and President of the Court, but while thanking everyone most graciously, he absolutely refused:

'For,' he said, 'there is much too great a slavery in such appointments and those who exercise them can be saved only with great difficulty given the corruption of men [; and unless the seats voided by the fallen angels are filled by people of a different sort, I believe that Nicholas of Cusa will be disappointed in his conjectures and that we shall not reach the Last Judgement for another thirty-seven Jubilees. I warn you now, in plenty of time.] But if you have any hogsheads of good wine I will be pleased to accept some as a present.'

They most willingly did so, sending him the best wine in their city, of which he drank quite a lot, but the wretched Panurge drank like a hero, since he was as emaciated as a smoked herring and crept along like a skinny cat. But someone reproved him, [semi-breathless from downing a great goblet of good red wine,] saying,

'Whoa, there, comrade! You're slurping it down like a lunatic!'

'By Saint Thibault,' he said, 'you speak truly:[54] if I upped as much as I downed I would already be above the lunar sphere with Empedocles! But I don't know what the devil this means: the wine is very good and quite delicious, but the more I drink the thirstier I get! I believe that the shadow of my Lord Pantagruel breeds thirsts in men as the moon produces catarrhs.'

The bystanders began to laugh. When he saw it, Pantagruel said:

'What are you laughing about, Panurge?'

'My Lord,' Panurge said, 'I was telling them how wretched those poor devils of Turks are for never touching a drop of wine. If that were the only evil in the Alcoran of Mahomet I still would never submit to his religion!'

---

54. '42: . . . lunatic!' – 'I give myself to the devil!' he said, 'You will never find here one of those puny little wine-sippers of Paris who can't down more than a chaffinch and never fill their beaks unless you rap their tails as you do with sparrows. O Comrade of mine, if I upped . . .

'Yes. But tell me now,' said Pantagruel, 'how you escaped from their clutches.'

'By God, my Lord,' said Panurge, 'I shall utter no word of a lie. Those bloody Turks had put me on a skewer, all basted up like a rabbit, [for I was very skinny, and otherwise my flesh would have made very poor eating. And at this point they were] roasting me alive. As they did so I commended myself to God's grace and remembered that good saint, Saint Laurence; I ever hoped in God, that he would deliver me from such torment. Which most strangely came to pass. For, as I was commending myself heartily to God and crying, "Lord God, help me, Lord God, save me! Lord God, deliver me from this torment in which these treacherous dogs detain me in defence of their religion," the turnspit fell asleep – because of the divine will or that of some good Mercury who cunningly put to sleep Argus, who had one hundred eyes. Now noticing that he is no longer turning me as I roasted, I look at him and see that he has dozed off. So I get my teeth into a brand – by the end which was not burning – and toss it into the lap of my roaster, tossing another as best as I can under a camp-bed near the chimney where there was plenty of straw.[55]

'At once the fire took hold of the straw, spread from straw to bed, and from bed to ceiling (which was of fir-wood planking with pendant *culs-de-lampe*). The best of it was that the fire that I had tossed into the lap of my bloody turnspit burnt all his pubes, and it would have spread to his balls, but he did not pong enough himself not to smell it quicker than daylight. He leapt up like a giddy goat, yelling out of the window as well as he could "Dal baroth! Dal baroth!" – which is as much as to say, Fire! Fire!

'He rushed at me, to cast me right into the flames. He had already cut the cords which bound my hands and was cutting the ropes which bound my feet, but the master of the house (hearing the cry of *Fire!* and already smelling the smoke even out in the road where he was strolling about with some other pashas and muftis) ran as fast as he could to give help and to save his valuables.

55. '42: . . . where *lay the palliasse of my Lord the Roaster*. At once . . .

'No sooner arrived, he pulled out the skewer on which I was spitted and killed my roaster stone dead: he died, I think, of lack of attention or something like that, for the skewer was thrust into his right flank a little above the navel, piercing the third lobe of his liver and, running upwards through his diaphragm, it then went through the capsule of his heart and came out at the top of his shoulders between his spondyls and the left scapula.

'It is true that when he withdrew the skewer from my body I tumbled to the ground near the fire-dogs and hurt myself a bit in the fall: not much though, since the basting took the shock. Then when my pasha saw that he was in desperate straits, that his house was hopelessly on fire and all his valuables lost, he gave himself to the devil, nine times invoking Grill-goth, Astaroth [, Rapacious] and Rumbleguts. When I saw that, I experienced a good five-pennyworth of fright, fearing that those devils might appear there and carry that idiot off. Were they the kind who would take me as well? Here I am, half roasted: my rashers may be the cause of my downfall, for those particular devils have a soft spot for *jambon*. (The philosopher *Jamblicus* provides authority for that, as does Murmaltius in his treatise *On Hunchbacks and the Deformed: In Defence of the* Magistri Nostri.)[56] But I made the sign of the Cross and shouted in Greek, "Holy is God and immortal."[57] And not one devil came.

'Realizing that, my villain of a Pasha tried to kill himself by running my skewer through his heart. He did indeed push it up against his chest, but as it was not sharp enough it would not go in. He was thrusting as hard as he could but all to no avail.

'So I went up to him and said:

' "You're wasting your time, Signor Buggero. You'll never kill yourself like that. You'll certainly do yourself an injury and

56. There is a schoolboy play on words between *jambon* (ham) and *Iamblicus*, made possible by i and j being then the same letter.
57. A jest is at the expense of Noël Béda, the hunchbacked syndic of the Sorbonne who was falling into disgrace: *Hagios athanatos ho theos* (Holy is God and immortal) is a Greek phrase embedded in the liturgy for Good Friday.

languish your whole life long in the hands of the barber-
surgeons. But if you want me to, I will kill you frankly. You
will feel nothing, for believe you me, I've killed many a man
who felt much better for it afterwards."

'"Ha, my friend," he said, "I beg you to do so! Do it, and
I'll give you my purse. Here it is. Take it. There are six hundred
gold seraphs inside and a few diamonds and rubies which are
all quite perfect."'

'And where are they now?' said Epistemon.

'By Saint John,' said Panurge, 'a long way off if they are
still in circulation! [*But where are the snows of yesteryear?* That was the great preoccupation of Villon, our Parisian
poet.]'

'Finish the tale, I beg you,' said Pantagruel, 'so that we may
know how you dealt with your pasha.'

'On my faith as a decent fellow,' said Panurge, 'I tell no word
of a lie: I bind him with a pair of dirty Turkish trousers, which
I find lying there half burnt. With my ropes I truss him up so
well, country-fashion, hand and foot, that he cannot budge.
Then I thrust my skewer through his gullet and hang him up,
hooking the skewer on to two big clamps used for holding
halberds. Then I stoke up a roaring fire underneath him and
flambé my Lord as we do with smoked herrings in our chimneys. Then, grabbing his purse and a little javelin lying on the
clamps, I sped off at a fine canter. And God knows how I stank
like a shoulder of mutton.

'Once down in the road, I found that everyone had run up
with plenty of water to douse the fire. When they saw me
half-roasted like that, they took pity on me – naturally – and
chucked all their water over me, making me delightfully cool;
which did me much good. Then they gave me a little food, but
I scarcely ate any, since, as is their custom, they offered me
nothing to drink but water.

'They did me no further harm, except for one ugly little
hunch-breasted Turk who was furtively munching my bacon.
I gave him such a green thwack on the fingers with my javelin
that he never tried that on again! Then a young German

maiden[58] brought me a jar of emblic myrobalans pickled in the local style, only to stare at my fly-bitten johnnie as it had escaped from the fire, for now it dangled no lower than my knees.

['It is worth noting that I had suffered from sciatica for over seven years but that fire entirely cured it on the side which that turnspit of mine had allowed to sear when he dozed off.]

'Now while they were lingering over me, the fire won the day – ask me not how – spreading to over two thousand houses before one of the crowd noticed it and shouted, "By the guts of Mahoun! All the town is burning, and here we are hanging about!"

'So off they went, every man to his manor.

'As for me, I made my way to the town-gate.

'When I was on a nearby hummock, I turned round like Lot's wife and saw the whole town ablaze like Sodom and Gomorrah.[59]

'I was so happy at it that I nearly shat myself for joy. But God thoroughly punished me for that.'

'How!' asked Pantagruel.

'Well,' said Panurge, 'while I was thus contemplating the flames with great delight and joking with myself, saying: "Ha! Poor little fleas! Poor little mice! You're in for a rotten winter: the fire has got into your bed-straw," six hundred [or rather thirteen hundred and eleven] dogs came out of the town, big and small, all in one pack, fleeing from that conflagration. At their first sight of me they came right at me, following the flair of my rotten old half-roasted flesh. They would have gobbled me up there and then if my good guardian angel had not inspired me.'[60]

'And what did you do then, poor chap?' said Pantagruel.

58. In '42, it was a young *Corinthian* maiden who was concerned. Since Greek antiquity the women of Corinth were associated with sexual licence.
59. '42 omits: like Sodom and Gomorrah.
60. '42: . . . inspired me, *telling me of a most opportune cure for tooth-ache.*
    – *'Tooth-ache!' said Pantagruel, 'Why were you afraid of that? I thought*

'I suddenly thought of my rashers of bacon and tossed them into the midst of them. Those curs then bared their fangs and fought one against another over those rashers. And in that way they left me – and I leave them too, scrapping with each other.

'And thus do I escape, lively and joyful. [And long life to roasting!]'

How Panurge taught quite a new way to build the walls of Paris

CHAPTER 11

[Becomes Chapter 15.

A tale in the current tradition of jokes about pudenda and the women of Paris. In the only extant copy of the first edition of Pantagruel, *the page on which most of this tale was printed was so heavily censored that it became detached and lost, leaving signs of the censor's ink on the facing pages. To fill the gap editors follow the second edition. Rabelais made several excisions, all prudential, none 'obscene'.*

The chapter is best replaced in the tradition of the Querelle des Femmes, *a quarrel about the status of women which produced bawdy at one extreme and a platonizing idealization of women at the other.*

La Follie-Gobelin was a bawdy house in the present rue des Gobelins.

Erasmus supplies the remark of Agesilaus (Adages, III, V, VII, 'A wall of iron not turf'; and Apophthegms I, Agesilas 30).]

Pantagruel, seeking recreation from his studies one day, was strolling towards the Faubourg Saint-Marcel intending to have a look at *La Follie-Gobelin*. Panurge was with him, still carrying a bottle under his cloak and a piece of salted ham, for he never went without them. He called them his bodyguard: and no

---

your rheumatics were cured. – 'By Cod and his Easter,' answered Panurge, 'is there any tooth-ache worse than when dogs sink their teeth into your legs? But I suddenly . . .

other sword did he bear. When Pantagruel wanted to give him
a sword, he retorted that it would inflame his spleen.

'All very well,' said Epistemon; 'but how will you defend
yourself if anyone attacks you?'

'With a quick bit of shoe-work,' said Panurge, 'provided that
stabbing is outlawed!'

On the way back Panurge contemplated the walls of Paris
and said mockingly to Pantagruel:

'Lovely walls, aren't they! Solid enough to protect moulting
goslings! By my beard, they're quite rotten enough for such a
great city as this, since with a single fart a cow could blow
down more than six arm-spans of them.'

'My dear friend,' said Pantagruel, 'do you really not know
what Argesilaus replied when they asked him why the great city
of Sparta was not surrounded by walls? He said, pointing to the
inhabitants and citizens of that city, who were so experienced in
the art of war, so strong and well armed: "These folk are the
walls of our city," meaning that there are no walls like back-
bones, and that towns [and cities] can have no more sure and
solid rampart than the valour of their [citizens and] inhabitants.

Thus our city is so strong from the multitude of warriors
within her that they never bother to build other walls. Besides,
should anyone want to throw a wall right round it as at Strasbourg, [Orleans or Ferrara,] it would not be possible: the cost
[and outlay] would be excessive.'

'True enough,' said Panurge, 'but it is nice to have some
semblance of stone-work when your enemies invade you, if
only to shout down, "Who goes there?" As for the enormous
expenditure you deem necessary if anyone wanted to throw
walls round it, why! if the Magistrates will tip me with a goodly
jar of wine, I'll teach them a most novel method of building
them cheaply.'

'How then?' asked Pantagruel.

'If I tell you, don't repeat it,' Panurge replied.

'I have noticed that, in this town, the thingummybobs of
women are cheaper than stone. You should build walls of them,
arranging them with good architectural symmetry, putting the
biggest ones in the front ranks, then sloping them back upwards

like the spine of a donkey, making ranks of the medium ones
next and finally of the smallest. Then provide an interlarding
of some nice little diamond-pointings as in the great tower of
Bourges, and with as many cocks as were lopped off from
wretched Italians at the Entry of the queen into that town.[61]

What devil could ever bring down such walls! No metal could
withstand blows better. And if cannon balls came and rubbed
up against them, you would, by God, see some of that blessèd
fruit of the great-pox distilled fine as rain! Cor! In the devil's
name! Moreover lightning will never strike them. Why? Because
they are all holy or blessèd!

I can see only one drawback.'

'Ho, ho! Ha, ha, ha!' said Pantagruel. 'What is that?'

'Well, the flies find them wonderfully tasty: they would all
readily gather round and leave their droppings. The work
would be ruined and slighted. This is how you could remedy
that: you would have to flick away the flies with beautiful
fox-tails or good fat pricks from Provençal donkeys.

'But on that subject, as we go back to supper, I can tell you
a fine exemplary tale, [which Friar Lubinus includes in his book
On the Compotations of the Mendicant Friars].

'Once upon a time, when beasts could talk (less than three
days ago) a poor lion was strolling through the forest of Bièvre
saying his little prayers. He passed under a tree into which a
villein (a charcoal-burner) had climbed to lop off some wood.
When he saw the lion, he hurled his axe at him, giving him an
enormous wound in the thigh. So that limping lion ran here
and there through the forest to find some help until he came
upon a carpenter who kindly looked at his wound, cleaned it
out as best as he could and padded it with moss, telling him to

61. '42: ... and with *those* many *stiff tools which, throughout, dwell in
claustral codpieces. What devil could* ...
    The allusion in the first edition is to the State Entry into Paris of
Queen Eléonore of Austria, the second wife of François I, in 1520: many
prisoners, instead of being pardoned, were sent to the galleys. Some
of them may have been castrated. (See Montaiglon, *Anciennes Poésies
Françoises*, 21, n.55.) As often, Rabelais cuts out a joke which could
offend his monarch.

swish that wound well to stop the flies from settling their bums
on it.[62]

'Meanwhile he would go and gather some carpenter's-
self-heal.

'And so that lion, cured, was strolling through the forest at
the time when some ageless old woman was cutting twigs and
gathering sticks in that very forest. When she saw that lion she
fell backwards from fright in such a way that the wind blew
her skirts, petticoat and chemise up over her shoulders.

'When he saw that happen the lion felt pity and came running
up to find out whether she had done herself any harm. He
contemplated her country-thing and said, "You poor woman!
Who gave you that wound?"

'As he was saying that, he saw a fox and called him over:
"Brother Renard. Hey! Here! Over here! There's good reason."

'When Renard came up, the lion said:

'"My fellow and friend, someone has given this good woman
a nasty wound between her legs. There is a manifest dissolution
of continuity. See how big the wound is: from her bottom to
her navel it measures four, no, a good five-and-a-half spans.
It's a blow from an axe. I fear it may be an old wound, so to
keep the flies off, give it a good whisking inside and out. You
have a bush fine and long. Whisk away; whisk away I beg you,
while I go looking for moss to put in it. We ought to thus
succour and help one another. God commands us to.[63]

'"Whisk hard; that's right my friend, whisk hard; that wound
needs frequent whisking: otherwise the person cannot be made
comfortable. Whisk well, my good little comrade, whisk on.
God has given you a brush; yours is becomingly grand and
gross. Whisk away, and never tire. [A good Fly-whisker, ever
whisking flies with his tassel, himself will ne'er fly-whiskèd be.
Whisk away, well-hung! Whisk away my little dear!] I won't
keep you long."

'Then he went off in search of plenty of moss. When he was
some little way off he cried back to Renard:

62. '42: . . . from *befouling* it. Meanwhile . . .
63. '42 omits: God commands us to.

' "Comrade, keep on whisking. Whisk on, my good little comrade, and never tire. I'll get you appointed stipendiary Whisker to Queen Maria and Don Pedro of Castille.[64] Only go on whisking, go on whisking, and do nothing else."

'Poor Renard went on whisking; and he did it very well, this way and that way, inside and outside, but that naughty old woman stank like a hundred devils as she [constantly] broke wind and let off farts. Poor Renard was most ill at ease, for he knew not which way to turn to evade the perfume of the wind of that old woman. Now as he turned aside he saw that there was yet another hole behind, not as large as the one he was whisking but that the foul stinking wind came forth from there.

'At last the lion returned, bringing more than three bales of moss,[65] and began to thrust some of it into the wound with a stake he was carrying; he had already stuffed in two bales and a half[66] when he cried in amazement,

' "What the devil! This wound is a deep one! More than two wagon-loads of moss could get in there. Ah, well. Since God so wishes . . ."[67] And he went on stuffing it in.

'But the Renard warned him:

' "O Lion, my comrade and friend, do not, I beseech you, stuff all the moss in there: keep a bit of it back, for there is another little hole down below which stinks like a hundred devils. The stench is so awful it's poisoning me."

'So we had better protect those walls from flies and employ some stipendiary Fly-whiskers.'

Pantagruel then said,

'And how do you know that the private parts of women are going so cheap? In this town there are plenty of decent women, virgin and chaste.'

'But where-um find 'em?' asked Panurge. 'I'll tell you something: not my opinion but something truly sure and certain. I am not boasting when I say that I have stuffed four hundred

64. '42 omits: Queen Maria and.
65. '42: . . . bringing more *moss than eighteen bales would hold*, and began . . .
66. '42: . . . stuffed in *sixteen-and-a-half bales* when he cried . . .
67. '42 omits: Ah, well. Since God so wishes.

and seventeen of them since I have been in this town – women theologians, kissers of images – [68] and that's for only nine days!

'Why, this very morning I came across a man who had a beggar's wallet slung over his shoulder as in Aesop's *Fables*. He was carrying two little girls, two or three years old at most. One was in the front pouch, the other in the back one. He begged me for alms, but I told him I had far more bollocks than pence. Afterwards I asked him:

'"My good man, are those little maids still virgins?"

'"Brother of mine," he said, "I have been carrying them about like this for two years now: as for this one here in the front whom I can see all the time, yes, I think she is, though I would never swear to it, finger in pyre. As for the one I carry behind, I simply do not know."

'You are truly a fine companion,' said Pantagruel. 'I would like to dress you in my livery.'

And he did have him finely accoutred in the style then current, except that Panurge wanted the codpiece on his breeches to be three foot long, and square, not round.

And thus it was fashioned.

And it was fair to behold.

And often would he say that people had not yet learnt the advantages and utility to be found in wearing a huge codpiece. But, one day, Time would tell them, since all things have been discovered by Time.

'God save from harm,' he would say, 'that fellow whose long codpiece saved his life!

'God save from harm that man whose long codpiece was worth to him one day a hundred [and sixty thousand and nine] crowns.

'God save from harm that man who, with the help of his long codpiece, saved an entire town from dying of hunger.

'When I have a bit more time, I will, by God, put it all into a book called *On the Benefits of Long Codpieces*.'

And he did indeed write a big and beautiful book on the subject, with illustrations. As far as I know it has yet to be printed.

68. '42 omits: – women theologians, kissers of images –.

On the morals and characteristics of Panurge

CHAPTER 12

[Becomes Chapter 16.

The 'malady' named 'shortage of silver' in the first paragraph is both shortage of cash and uncured syphilis, which was treated by silver and quicksilver. In that context Rabelais cites a widely known song, 'Faulte d'argent, c'est douleur nonpareil' (Shortage of Silver – of cash, or of a treatment for syphilis – as pain 'tis nonpareil). It had been delightfully set to music by Josquin des Prez.

'But that apart, the nicest young lad in the world' is a quip best known from Clément Marot's ironical judgement on his thieving Basque valet.

Jests at the expense of the Sorbonne and theologians generally are later suppressed, all of them. But the University Quarter, the Quartier Latin *and its colleges, streets and alleyways remain the background to the story.*

Rabelais replaced 'Fontarabia' with 'Foutignan and Foutarabia' so as to introduce a standard play on the verb foutre *(to fuck).]*

Panurge was of medium height, neither too tall nor too short. His nose, rather aquiline, was shaped like the handle of a razor; he was then about thirty-five years old and as fit to be gilded as a leaden dagger! In his person he was quite an elegant man except that he was just a bit of a rake and naturally subject to a malady which was called in those days,

Shortage of silver: as pain 'tis nonpareil.

However he knew sixty-three ways of raising money for his needs, the most honourable and most routine of which took the style of stealing, done with stealth. He was [, if ever there was such a one in Paris,] a felon, [a cheat, a tippler,] a loafer, a scrounger,

[but that apart, the nicest young lad in the world.]

And he was always involved in some machination or other against the bum-bailiffs and the Watch.

On one occasion he got three or four fine rascals together and made them drink like Knights Templar late into the evening, afterwards bringing them just below Sainte-Geneviève or close to the Collège de Navarre; then, as the Watch were making their way up – he knew when by placing his sword on the pavement and putting his ear to it: if he heard the sword vibrate that was an infallible sign that the Watch were near at hand – he and his companions got hold of a dung-cart and gave it a mighty shove, sending it rushing downhill, thus knocking all those wretched officers of the Watch to the ground like porkers. Then he fled down the other side, for in less than two days he knew the streets, alleyways and passages of Paris as well as he knew his grace after dinner. On another occasion, he laid a trail of gunpowder in a fine square that the Watch had to pass through, and just as they were doing so he set a match to it, making a pastime of seeing how gracefully they fled away convinced that Saint-Anthony's wildfire had got them by the legs. As for the wretched Masters of Arts and the Theologians he tormented them more than all the others.[69]

Whenever he met any of them in the street, he never failed to play some prank on them, sometimes dropping a turd into their graduate's hoods, sometimes tying little fox-brushes or hares' ears on to their backs, or doing some other prank.

One day, when all the Theologians were assigned to assemble in the Sorbonne to examine the articles of the faith,[70] he prepared a Bourbonese marmalade out of a mess of garlic, Persian gum, assa-foetida, oil of castor and still-tepid turds; he steeped it all in puss from cankered ulcers and, very early in the morning, theologically smeared and anointed all the gratings of the Sorbonne with it.[71] The devil himself could not have endured

69. '42 omits: and the Theologians.
70. '42: ... When *they* [i.e. the Masters of Arts] were assigned to assemble in *the Rue du Fouarre*, he prepared ... (Arts lectures were held in the Rue du Fouarre.)
71. '42: ... very early in the morning, smeared and anointed *with it all the pavement* ... (word cut out).

it. And all those fine folk were soon puking in front of everyone else as though they had been flaying foxes; some ten or a dozen of them died of the plague, [fourteen caught leprosy; twenty-two developed the gout and more than twenty-seven caught the pox,] but Panurge cared not a jot. [And he normally carried a whip under his gown: with it he would unremittingly flog any scouts he met carrying wine to their masters – to hurry them along.]

Inside his cloak he had over twenty-six pouches and pokes, always kept full. In one he kept a small leaden thimble and a small knife, sharp as a furrier's needle: with them he cut purses; in another, some verjuice, which he flung into the eyes of the folk he came across; in another, burrs, with tiny wings attached made out of gosling or capon feathers, which he stuck on to the gowns and bonnets of solid citizens, and he occasionally fashioned them into lovely horns which they wore everywhere about town, and sometimes all their lives! Made into the form of a male member he also stuck them on to the hoods of women from behind.

In yet another poke he kept a pile of little cornets full of fleas and lice borrowed from the beggars in the Cimetière de Saint-Innocent, which, using quill-pens or writing-reeds, he threw on to the collars of the most sugary of the young ladies, especially in church for, during Mass, evensong and sermon, he never sat up in the choir-stalls but always down in the nave with the women.

In another he kept an ample supply of hooks and pins with which he often tacked men and women together during tightly crowded gatherings, above all if the women were wearing robes of Italian taffeta: when they wanted to leave they ripped all their dresses apart!

In yet another he kept a tinderbox furnished with a wick, tinder-matches, flint and all other requisites; in another, two or three burning-glasses: with which he would sometimes drive men mad in church – and women too, upsetting their composure, for he said there was but an antistrophe between *Woman mucking about in the fane* and *Woman fucking about in the main*;[72] finally, in another, he kept a store of needles and thread which he used for countless little devilish devices.

As he was leaving the Palais one day just when a Franciscan was about to say Mass for the magistrates in the Great Hall, he helped him to robe and don his vestments. During the robing, he stitched the Franciscan's alb to his cassock and shirt. As my Lords of the Court came in to take their seats to hear the Mass, Panurge withdrew. But when, after the Dismissal, that wretched friar wanted to divest himself of his alb, he brought his cassock and shirt up with it, since they were well stitched together, and bared himself up to his shoulders, revealing his dick to all and sundry; which without a doubt it was not a small one. The friar kept on tugging, revealing all the more until one of the members of the Court said: 'Does this fair friar really want us to make our offertory by kissing his bum? Let Saint-Anthony's wildfire kiss it!'

From thenceforth it was decreed that those wretched caloyers should no longer divest in public but in their sacristies, especially when women were present, for it could give rise to the sin of envy.

And everybody asked why friars had such tools which were so long. But our aforesaid Panurge excellently solved that problem, saying:

'The reason why asses have such big ears is simply because their dams fail to put babies' bonnets on their little heads, as Petrus de Alliaco states in his *Suppositions*.[73] Likewise, what causes the tools of those poor, handsome fathers[74] to be so big is that they never wear breeches with crotches, which allows their poor old member freedom to dangle freely; but the reason why they have them correspondingly plump is because such

72. The jest is here transposed: the original equivocation is between *femme folle à la messe* (a woman foolish at Mass) and *femme molle à la fesse* (woman soft in the arse).
73. Petrus de Alliaco is a fourteenth-century theologian, cited for fun.
74. '42: . . . poor *blessed* fathers . . .
   The original phrase, 'handsome fathers', renders literally the Greek title *caloyer* (adopted also in English), which applied to the Orthodox clergy. Rabelais later uses it of himself.

wagging about causes the bodily humours to run down into the aforesaid members since, as the lawyers put it: *Continual agitation and motion are the cause of attraction.*'

Item: he had another pocket full of plume-alum itching-powder, some of which he would toss down the backs of the women he deemed most haughty, making them strip off before everybody, while others jumped about like a cock on hot coals or drum-sticks on a tabor. Still others charged madly about the streets: Panurge ran after them and, like a courteous and gracious gentleman, threw his cloak over the backs of those who were taking their clothes off.

Item: in another pocket he kept a little medicine-bottle full of rancid oil. When he came across either woman or man wearing a fine new garment he smeared it over them, spoiling all the nicest parts under the pretext of stroking them with his fingers, saying, 'Now here is good cloth! Here is good satin and good taffeta! May God grant you, Madam, your noble heart's desire. New dress: new friend. May God preserve you in it.'

And so saying he would put his hand on their collars. The filthy mark would stay there for ever, [so outrageously engraved on soul, body and fame, that] the devil himself could never remove it.

Finally he would cry, 'Madam, mind you don't fall in. There's a [dirty] great hole right there in front of you!'

Another pocket he kept full of euphorbium, finely ground into a powder; he also kept in it a beautiful lace-work handkerchief which he had purloined from that pretty laundry-girl in the galleries of the Sainte Chapelle[75] while removing a louse from her bosom – he had put it there!

Then, when he was in the company of some good ladies, he would get them talking about fine linen and place his hand on their bosoms, saying, 'Is this Flanders-wool? Is it from Hainaut?'

And he would then pull out his handkerchief saying,

'Take this. Take this. Look at the work in it. It's from Fontarabie.'

75. '42: . . . laundry-girl *in the Palais de Justice* while removing a louse . . .

Then he would shake it about really hard under their noses, making them sneeze for four hours without a pause. Meanwhile he would break wind like a cart-horse. And the ladies would giggle and say,

'What! Farting, Panurge?'

'Not at all, Madam,' he would say; 'I'm tuning myself to the counterpoint of the music you are sounding through your nose.'

In another pocket he kept a dentist's pincers, a hooked prod, a pelican and certain other implements: there was no door or coffer which he could not pick open with them.

In another he kept little thimbles with which he most craftily thimblerigged, for his fingers were adroit, like Minerva's and Arachne's. Once he was a quack touting theriac.

And whenever he changed a gold crown or some other coin, the money-changer would have had to be far more fly than Maître Mouche[76] if Panurge failed to make five or six large silver coins manifestly, openly and visibly vanish without causing any lesion or laceration: the money-changer would have felt but the breeze of it.

*

[Later a new chapter begins here: How Panurge gained indulgences and married off old women; and of the legal actions he undertook in Paris. Chapter 17.

'The farthing which has never known father or mother', is an echo of the Farce of Maître Pathelin.

The fun at the expense of pardons – indulgences – is in the Lutheran and Erasmian tradition of satirizing them as abuses, but it is perhaps even more in the comic wake of Folengo. Panurge's use of Hebrew to justify his theft was topical; Hebrew had been established, against the wishes of the Sorbonne, as the third language to be studied with Greek and Latin in the Trilingual Academy recently founded by François I. Rabbi Khimi's grammar had just been published in Latin by Sebastian

76. Maître Mouche (Master Fly) was the nickname of an Italian who gave financial advice to Philippe le Bel. He was held to have devalued the coinage.

*Muenster. Panurge's Hebrew examples are taken principally from the
New Testament.]*

One day I found him somewhat downcast and taciturn, and
supposed that he had not got a penny, so I said to him:

'You're ill, Panurge, as I can tell from your physiognomy.
And I understand your malady: you have diarrhoea of the purse.
But don't worry: I still have sixpence farthing which have never
known father or mother and which will no more let you down
in your need than the pox.'

To which he replied:

'A shit for the money! One of these days I shall have only
too much of it, for I possess a philosopher's stone which can
attract money out of purses as the magnet attracts iron.

'But would you like to come and get some pardons?'

'Upon my word,' I replied to him, 'I don't go in much for
pardons in this world: and whether I shall do so in the next, I
do not know. All right. In God's name let us go in for a
pennyworth, neither more nor less.'

'Lend me a penny then,' he said, 'against interest.'

'None of that,' I said: 'I'll gladly give it to you.

And he said, '*Grate vobis, Dominos.*'[77]

So off we went, beginning with the church of Saint-Gervais.
I obtained my pardons from the first booth only – a little of
that sort of thing goes a long way with me! – and then I set
about saying my brief prayers and *Orisons of Saint Bridget*.
Panurge, however, bought pardons at all the booths and always
tendered silver coins to each of the pardoners. From there we
proceeded to Notre-Dame, to Saint-Jean's and Saint-Antoine's
as well as to other churches which had a stall selling pardons.
I didn't acquire any more myself, but Panurge kissed the relics
at all the stalls and at each one made a donation. To cut matters
short, when we got back he took me for a drink at the tavern
called *Le Château* and showed me ten or twelve of his pouches
full of money. At which I made a sign of the cross, saying,

77. *Grate vobis Dominos* (for *Grate vobis Domines*) is, in ungrammatical
    Latin, a play on words, taking the *Do* of *Dominos* taken to mean 'give'
    and the *nos* to mean *nous* ('us').

'Where did you get so much money from in so short a time?'

He replied that he had helped himself from the pardoners' collecting-bowls.

'For in tendering my first penny, I did it so subtly that it appeared to be a large silver coin. Then I helped myself with one hand to twelve shillings change, or at least to twelve brass pennies or twopenny pieces, and with the other, to three or four florins. And so in all the churches we went to.'

'Indeed,' I said, 'you are damning yourself like a serpent. You're a thief, and sacrilegious.'

'Well, yes,' he said. 'So it seems to you, but it does not seem so to me, for those pardoners gave it to me when they said, as they offered me their relics to kiss, "Thou shalt receive an hundredfold" – that is, for one coin I may take a hundred. – For "Thou shalt receive" was spoken after the manner of the Hebrews who use the future for the imperative, as in the Law *Thou shalt worship the Lord thy God, and him only shalt thou serve*, and *Thou shalt love thy neighbour;*[78] in other cases too. Therefore, whenever a pardoner said to me, "Thou shalt receive an hundredfold," he meant "Receive an hundredfold". It is expounded thus by Rabbi Khimi, Rabbi Ben Ezra and all the Massoretes. [See Bartolus *ad loc.*].

'Moreover Pope Sixtus awarded me a pension of fifteen hundred pounds, drawn on his own inheritance and the treasure of the Church, because I cured him of a cankerous tumour which was so tormenting him that he thought he was crippled for life. So I help myself with my own hands. Nothing like doing that with the aforesaid ecclesiastical treasury! Oh, my friend,' he went on, 'if only you knew how I buttered my parsnips during the crusade you would be amazed! It was worth more than six thousand florins to me.'

78. In '42 the scriptural texts are changed to: 'Thou shalt love the Lord' and 'Love the Lord'. Originally the references are to Deuteronomy 6:13: 'Thou shalt fear the Lord thy God, and him only shalt thou serve' conflated with Luke 4:8, and with 'love thy neighbour', part of Christ's summary of the Law. 'Thou shalt receive an hundredfold' is adapted from Matthew 19:29.

'Where the devil have they gone?' I asked. 'You haven't got a farthing left now.'

'Where they came from,' he said. 'They have simply changed masters. But I used some three thousand of them to marry off – not young maidens: they can find husbands easily enough – but huge sempiternal old crones with no teeth in their gullets, considering that those good women had made very good use of their time in their youth, raising their bums and playing at squeeze-crupper with all comers until nobody wanted them any more; and therefore, by God, I will have them swived again for one last time before they die. And so I would give one of them a hundred florins; another, six score, another three hundred, depending on how horrible, ghastly and abominable they were; for the more horrid and ghastly they were the more they had to be given, otherwise the devil himself would never have wanted to service them.

'Then I would straightway go off to some hulking great builder's mate and arrange the marriage myself; but I would show him the coins before showing the crones, saying, "This is for you, my friend, if you are ready for a good bit of slap-and-tickle."

'The poor wretches would then stiffen up like old he-mules.[79] I would make them ready by feasting and drinking of the best, with plenty of spices to get those old women in the mood and on heat.[80]

'To cut a long story short, they worked away like all good souls, though in the case of the most horribly ugly and decrepit women I would have a bag put over their faces.

'I did lose a lot over my lawsuits as well.'

'And what lawsuits can you have had?' I said. 'You have no house or lands.'

'My friend,' he said, 'under the instigation of the devil in Hell the young ladies of this town had invented the mode of high-cut collars or neckbands which so hid their bosoms that you could

79. In '42 'stiffen up' (*aressoient*) has been replaced by 'play the buffalo' (*bubajalloient*).
80. '42: . . . in *rut* and on heat . . .

no longer slip your hands underneath, since they had placed the slits at the back, while in front everything was fastened tight; at which their doleful and dispirited lovers were not very happy.

'One fine day – a Tuesday – I presented my petition about it to the Court, constituting myself a party in a suit against the said young ladies, pleading the great damage I would suffer from it and threatening that if the Court did not issue an order against them I would, for the same reason, stitch my codpiece on to the backside of my breeches. To sum it up, those young ladies formed a syndicate [, exposed their fundamentals] and established proxies to defend their cause; but I sued them so vigorously that, by decree of the Court, it was declared that those high neckbands be no longer worn unless slightly slotted at the front.

'But that set me back a lot.

'I also had a very filthy and dirty little lawsuit against Master Pooh-pooh[81] and his lot, restraining them from clandestinely reading the books of the *Scentences* at night and permitting it only in the fair light of day and in the sight of all the theologians within the lecture halls of the Sorbonne. For that I was condemned to pay costs because of some procedural flaw in the law-serjeant's report.[82]

'On another occasion I formulated a complaint in the Court against the mules of the presidents, counsellors and others, contending that, whenever they were left to champ their bits in the lower yard of the Palais, the counsellors' wives should make them ample bibs in order that they should never befoul the

---

81. Master Pooh-pooh renders *Maistre Fyfy*, the nickname of the close-stool man who collected the night-soil.
82. Prudential changes made in '42: . . . reading *The Cask of Night-soil and the Quart of* the Scentences, *but* only in the fair light of day and in the sight of *the other Sophists* within the lecture halls of the *Rue du Fouarre; for which* I was condemned . . .
    This is a play on the *Sentences* of Peter Lombard; also on *quart*, the liquid measure, and the *Quart*, the Fourth Book of the *Sentences*. Again Rabelais replaces theologians by arts men and their place of assembly, which is not in the Sorbonne.

pavement with their slobberings so that the mule-lads of the Palais should be enabled freely to play on the aforesaid pavement at donkey-dice or at *I-deny-Gosh*[83] without splitting their breeches at the knee.

'The verdict was fine, but it cost me a good deal.

'And now add up the expenses of the little feasts I put on, day after day, for all those pages of the Palais.'

'To what end?' I asked.

'My friend,' he replied, 'you have no fun in this world. I have more fun than the king! If you join in with me we shall have a deuce of a time.'

'No, no,' I said. 'By Saint Up-in-the-air-ius, one of these days you're going to be hanged.'

'And one of these days you're going to be buried. Which is the more honourable: the air or the ground? O, what a dull beast you are! And Jesus Christ: was he not hanged in the air?

'But apropos:[84] while those lads of the Palais are feasting, I look after their mules for them, and I always make a cut in a thong of the stirrups of one of those beasts on the mounting-side, so that it is just holding on by a thread. Whenever the stout puffed-up counsellor or others come out to hop on, they fall down flat like pigs in front of everybody, providing a good hundred francs-worth of laughter. And what makes me laugh even more is that once they are back in their lodgings, they thrash my Lord the Page like green rye! So I never complain of the cost of feasting them.'

In the end he had (as I said above) sixty-three ways of procuring money, but two hundred and fourteen ways of spending it – not counting the replenishment of his sub-nasal maw.

---

83. 'Donkey-dice' is a pun: *baudets*, donkeys, and *beaulx dez*, beautiful dice. '*I-deny-Gosh*' will be one of Gargantua's games (see *Gargantua*, Chapter 20).

84. '42 omits: And Jesus Christ: was he not hanged in the air? But apropos.

How a Great Scholar from England wished to argue against Pantagruel, and was vanquished by Panurge

CHAPTER 13

[Becomes Chapter 18.

Any Englishman was long called Thomas. The fusion of Thomas with the Greek thauma (wonder, marvel) makes the English Thomas here into a thaumaturge.

Pantagruel is 'greater than Solomon'. In that at least, though comic, he is like Jesus. The debate by signs and gestures develops that theme. The Queen of Sheba 'tried Solomon with hard questions'. It was widely assumed that, not having a shared language, they communicated by signs. Jesus takes up the theme of her visit to Solomon in order to condemn by an emphatic repetition of the word 'sign' those who perversely still seek signs which do not lead to himself, who is greater than Solomon. Interlocking texts of the Old and New Testament form an essential backcloth to the comedy, but the laughter itself is centred on a linguistic truism: there are 'natural' signs we all understand and conventional ones we all have to learn. Conventional signs include such as are treated by the Venerable Bede, whose treatise on conversing by signs had been printed for the first time in Venice in 1525. Thaumaste, a monomaniac, assumes that Panurge's natural signs convey deep conventional meanings, whereas they are coarse natural signs (as can be proved by any reader who makes them).

Texts cited include the reference to 'the Queen of Sheba, who came from the uttermost parts of the East and the Persian Sea to see the order of the house of Solomon the Wise and to hear his wisdom' (based upon II Chronicles 9:1–12 and I (IV) Kings 10:1–13). In Matthew 12:42 the Queen of Sheba is alluded to as the 'The Queen of the South who shall rise up in the judgement with this generation and shall condemn it, for she came from the uttermost parts of the earth to hear the wisdom of Solomon: and behold, a greater than Solomon is here'. This is a good example of Shrovetide fun at the expense of otherwise hallowed parts of Scripture. Plato and the other examples of seekers after wisdom are serious ones too, but treated here in the same laughing spirit.

In the first line the original reading 'a grandissimo scholar called Thaumaste' later becomes 'a learned man called Thaumaste'.

In James 1:17, 'every good gift and every perfect gift is from above, coming down from the Father of lights'. Here used lightly in fun, that text will be used in earnest in the Third Book.

The phrase towards the end of the chapter placed between asterisks was added in the Juste 1534 edition but is not retained after the Juste 1537 edition. It was too audaciously funny.]

Now in those very days a grandissimo scholar called Thaumaste, hearing of Pantagruel's reputation and of his fame for unmatched erudition, came out of the land of England with one sole intention: to see the said Pantagruel, to meet him and to test whether his erudition corresponded to its renown. And, indeed, when he arrived in Paris he at once proceeded to the lodgings of the said Pantagruel in the Residence of Saint Denis, where Pantagruel was strolling in the garden discussing philosophy in the manner of the Peripatetics. When Thaumaste came in he first started with awe at seeing him so big and tall; then, as is the fashion, he courteously made his salutation, saying to him,

'What Plato, the Prince of philosophers, states is quite true: if the figure of knowledge-and-wisdom were to assume a body visible to human eyes she would excite the whole world to wonder: for if the mere rumour of her spreads through the air and strikes the ears of her studious lovers whom we call philosophers, it allows them neither to sleep nor to rest at their ease, so much does it spur them on and inflame them to run to the place and see the person in whom learning is said to have builded her temple and promulgated her oracles.

'That was made manifest to us:

– by the Queen of Sheba, who came from the uttermost parts of the East and the Persian Sea to see the order of the house of Solomon the Wise and to hear his wisdom;

– by Anarchasis, who journeyed from Scythia as far as Athens to see Solon;

– by Pythagoras, who visited the prophets of Memphis;

– by Plato, who visited the Magi of Egypt and Archytas of Tarentum; and

– by Apollonius of Tyana, who journeyed as far as Mount
Caucasus, passed through the lands of the Scythians, the
Massagetes and the Indians, and traversed the vast river
Physon[85] as far as the Brahmans to see Hiarchas; and through
Babylon, Chaldaea and the lands of Media, Assyria, Parthia,
Syria, Phoenicia, Arabia, Palestine and Alexandria as far as
Ethiopìa, to see the Gymnosophists.

'We have a similar example in the case of Livy: several
scholars came to Rome from the remotest parts of France and
Spain to see him and hear him.

'I dare not include myself amongst the number and ranks of
folk so perfect, but I do wish to be called a scholar and a lover
not only of learning but of the learnèd. Indeed on hearing tell
of your boundless erudition, I left my kin, my home and my
country, and brought myself here, discounting the length of
the journey, the dreariness of the seas and the novelty of the
lands, merely to see you and discuss with you certain texts
of philosophy, magic, alchemy and the cabbala[86] over which
I am in doubt and unable to satisfy my mind: if you can
solve them for me I will forthwith become your slave – I and
all my posterity – for I have no other gift which I deem a
sufficient recompense. I will set them down in writing, and
tomorrow will bring them to the attention of all the learned
men of Paris so that we may hold a public disputation before
them.

'But this is how I conceive of our dispute: I have no wish to
debate *pro et contra* as do the silly sophists of this town and
elsewhere. Similarly I do not want to dispute in the manner of
the Academics by declamations, nor by numbers like
Pythagoras and as Pico della Mirandola wished to do in Rome:
I want to dispute by signs alone with no talking, for the matters
are so arduous that no words of Man would be adequate to
settle them to my satisfaction. So may it please your Magnificence to be present in the Great Hall of the Collège de Navarre
at seven o'clock in the morning.'

85. '42: . . . *and sailed upon the great* river Physon . . .
86. '42: . . . texts of philosophy, *geomancy* and the cabbala . . .

After those words were spoken Pantagruel honourably addressed him:

'My Lord, insofar as it lies in my power, I would not deny anyone to share in the gifts of grace which God has vouchsafed me, for every good thing comes from him above, and his will is that it be multiplied when one finds oneself amongst people worthy and able to receive that Heaven-sent manna of sound learning, amongst the numbers of whom, as I well perceive, you now occupy the foremost rank, so I assure you that you will find me ready at any time to comply with each one of your requests, according to my modest power, even though it is I who should be learning more from you rather than you from me; but as you have publicly announced, we will confer about your doubts together and seek that resolution of them which you and I must find.[87]

'I greatly approve of the manner of disputing which you propose, that is by signs not words; for, by so doing, you and I will understand each other and be free from the handclappings of those [silly] Sophists just when we reach the very nub of the matter in our disputation. And so I shall not fail to appear tomorrow at the place and time which you have fixed for me, but, I beseech you, let there be no [discord nor] uproar amongst us and may we seek truth alone, not the honour and plaudits of men.'

To which Thaumaste replied:

'May God, my Lord, keep you in his grace; while I thank you that your High Magnificence has vouchsafed to condescend to my petty lowliness. And so, God's speed till tomorrow.'

'God's speed,' said Pantagruel.

You Gentlemen who read these present writings must not imagine that there have ever been folk more caught away and enraptured in thought than were Thaumaste and Pantagruel throughout that night. Indeed the said Thaumaste told the concierge at the Hôtel de Cluny, where he had taken up

---

87. '42: . . . resolution of them, *even in the depths of that inexhaustible well in which Heraclitus said that Truth lies hidden.* I greatly approve . . . (Rabelais confuses Heraclitus with Democritus.)

lodgings, that never in his life had he ever felt so thirsty as he did that night. 'I am convinced,' he said, 'that Pantagruel has got me by the throat. Do please give orders for some drinks [and make arrangements for us to have fresh water for me to rinse my palate].'

Pantagruel, on the other hand, had run to the top of the musical scale and had spent all that evening wildly leafing through:

– the book of Bede, *On Numbers and Signs*;
– the book of Plotinus, *On Things Which Cannot be Told*;
– the book of Proclus, *On Magic*; and
– those of Artemidorus, *On the Meanings of Dreams*;
– of Anaxagoras, *On Signs*;
– of Ynarius, *On Things Which Cannot Be Uttered*;
– the books of Philistion, of Hipponax, *On Things Not to Be Spoken*, and a whole lot more.

So much so, that Panurge was moved to say to him,

'Leave aside all such thoughts, my Lord, and go to bed, for I sense that you are so agitated in your mind from such an excess of thinking that you risk soon succumbing to a chronic fever.

'But first have a good twenty-five or thirty drinks and then retire and sleep at your ease, for tomorrow morning I shall answer the English Sire and dispute with him; and if I do not bring him to the point of no reply then speak ill of me!'

To which Pantagruel said:

'Yes, but Panurge, my friend, he is in truth marvellously learned; how will you satisfy him?'

'Very well!' said Panurge. 'Say no more about it, I pray, and let me deal with it. Is there any man as learned as the devils are?'

'Indeed not,' said Pantagruel, 'except by the special grace of God.'

'And yet,' said Panurge, 'many a time have I disputed with devils and landed them all befuddled on their bottoms. So where this [bumptious] Englishman is concerned, rest assured that tomorrow, before all the world, I shall make him shit vinegar.'

And so Panurge spent the night tippling with the page-boys

and gambling the very cords of his flies at *Rods* and at *Come first, come second.*

And so when the time for the meeting arrived, he escorted Pantagruel his Master to the appointed place. Surely there was nobody in Paris, great or small, who was not to be found there thinking, 'This devil Pantagruel, who defeated all those Sorbonicoles, will get but a pourboire this time![88] That Englishman is a devil from Vauvert.[89] We shall see who wins now!

So, with all the world assembled, Thaumaste was awaiting them. And when Pantagruel and Panurge arrived in the hall the undergraduates, dons and delegates all began to clap their hands as is their stupid custom. But Pantagruel cried out in a loud voice like a double cannonade:

'Quiet! In the devil's name, quiet! By God, if you beggars go on bellowing at me, I will cut off the heads of every one of you.'

At which words they stopped like thunder-stricken ducks. Even if they had swallowed fifteen pounds' weight of feathers they would not have dared merely to cough. They were driven so thirsty by that voice alone that they lolled their tongues half-a-foot out of their mouths as though Pantagruel had salted their throats.

Then Panurge began to speak, saying to the Englishman:

'Sir, have you come here to dispute contentiously over the propositions by you advanced, or to learn, and to find out the truth about them?'

To which Thaumaste replied:

'Sir, nothing brings me here but a right desire to learn and to know about things which I have been uncertain of my whole life long; I have found neither book nor man able to satisfy me by resolving the doubts which I have set forth. As for disputing contentiously, I have no desire to do that: it is moreover a thing most vile: I leave that to those stupid scoundrels the Sophists, *Sorbillans, Sorbonagres, Sorbonigenes, Sorbonicoles,

---

88. Again the allusion to the Sorbonne disappears, being replaced by: ... all those *wily green-horned Sophists*, will get but ...

89. The château de Vauvert near the Latin Quarter was thought by some to be haunted by devils.

Sorboniseques, Niborcisans, Saniborsans*[90] [, who in their disputations seek not the truth but wrangling and controversy].'

'Well then,' said Panurge, 'I am but a petty disciple of Lord Pantagruel, my master: so if I can set your mind at ease and absolutely and completely satisfy you myself, it would not be worth troubling my said master any further. For which reason it would be better if he were to take the chair, judging what we say and going on to satisfy you if I seem to you not to have fulfilled your studious desire.'

'That, in truth, is very well put,' said Thaumaste. 'So let us begin.'

You should note that Panurge had already attached to his ample codpiece a fair tassel of red, white, green and blue ribbons, while inside it he had placed a beautiful orange.

*

[Becomes: How Panurge made an ape of the Englishman who argued by signs. Chapter 19.

After the first few words, a long interpolation was made at this point in '42. It is given here between asterisks. The original text resumes with 'Panurge, without uttering a word, raised his hands'. The long interpolation shifts the comedy to the theme of the revealed wisdom of the mythical Hermes Trismegistus (also known as Mercury), who was considered an impostor by Erasmus but deeply venerated by Marguerite de Navarre as an ancient source of revealed spiritual truth dating back to the times of Moses. Rabelais in other contexts may have taken Hermes Trismegistus seriously: Shrovetide laughter by no means necessarily implies condemnation.

The felicity of the leper is perhaps an allusion to Lazarus.]

Then with everyone present and looking on in absolute silence, *the Englishman, raised both his hands high in the air separately and, knotting the tips of the fingers of each hand together so as

90. The words 'Niborcisans' and 'Saniborsins' suggest that the theologians of the Sorbonne are without *bourses* (without scholarships and scrotums).

to form what the people of Chinon call a hen's bottom, he struck the nails of both hands together four times, opened his hands and slapped one palm against the other with a resounding smack. Once again bringing them together as before, he clapped his hands twice, then four times, with open palms. He next put them together, stretched and conjoined, as though devoutly praying to God.

Panurge at once raised his right hand in the air, and stuck its thumb up his right nostril, holding his four fingers stretched out and squeezed together in due order in a line parallel to the bridge of his nose; he shut his left eye tight, meanwhile squinting with his right under a deeply lowered lid and eyebrow. He then raised high his left hand, strongly squeezing together and stretching forth its four fingers and, elevating the thumb, held it in a line directly corresponding to the position of his right, about a forearm-and-a-half apart. That done, keeping the same shape, he lowered both hands towards the ground; finally he raised them midway up as though aiming straight at the Englishman's nose.

'And if Mercury . . .', said the Englishman.

At which Panurge interrupted him:

'You spoke: you're unmasked!'

The Englishman now made this sign: he raised his left hand high in the air wide open; he then closed the four fingers into a fist and placed his extended thumb on the bridge of his nose. Immediately afterwards he raised his right hand, wide open, and wide open lowered it, placing the thumb in the bend of the little finger of the left hand, slowly wagging its four fingers in the air.

Then he switched round, doing with the left what he had done with the right, and with the right what he had done with the left.

Panurge, not at all surprised, lifted his trismegistical codpiece up into the air with his left hand and with his right drew forth from it a white splinter of bone taken from the rib of an ox, and then two identically shaped pieces of wood, one of black ebony and the other of scarlet brazil-wood, arranging them most symmetrically between the fingers of that same hand and clacking them together with the sound the lepers of Brittany make with their clappers – more resonant, though, and more harmonious – meanwhile, retracting his tongue into his mouth, he joyfully produced a buzzing noise, keeping his eyes still fixed on the Englishman.

The theologians, physicians and surgeons who were present thought that he was inferring by that sign that the Englishman was a leper: the counsellors, jurists and canon lawyers believed that by so doing he intended to conclude that some kind of human felicity consists in the leprous state, as our Lord maintained long ago.

The Englishman did not panic at that; he raised high both his hands, so holding them that in each case their three main fingers were bent right over, tightly squeezing each thumb between the index and middle fingers, while the little fingers remained extended. He then showed his hands to Panurge, bringing them together in such a way that the right thumb touched the left and the little finger on the left touched the one on the right.]*

Panurge, without a word, raised his hands and made a sign like this: he brought together the nails of his left-hand index finger and thumb, so making a space in the middle like a ring; he then squeezed all the fingers of his right hand into a fist, except for the index finger which he thrust repeatedly in and out of the finger and thumb of his left hand. Then he stretched forth his index and middle fingers, keeping them as wide apart as possible and pointing them towards Thaumaste. He placed his left thumb in the corner of his own left eye, fully extending the rest of his hand in the shape of the wing of a bird or the fin of a fish. He then waggled it most delicately to and fro.

He then did the same, with his right hand in the corner of his right eye. And that was spaced over a good quarter of an hour.[91]

At which Thaumaste started to blanch and to tremble, making him the following sign: he struck the middle-finger of

91. '42 omits: And that was spaced over a good quarter of an hour. At which.

his right hand against the muscle at the base of his thumb; he then made his right index finger into a ring, as he had done with the one of his left, but he placed it below not above, as Panurge had done.

Panurge thereupon clapped his hands together and whistled through his palms. That done, he once more placed the index-finger of his right hand into the ring made with his left, repeatedly pulling it out and pushing it in; then while gazing intently at Thaumaste, he thrust forth his chin.

Whereupon the crowd, who had understood none of the signs, now did get the sense: 'What can you say to that!'

And indeed Thaumaste began to sweat great globules and appeared like a man who was caught away in deep contemplation. He then came to, and placed all the nails of his left hand against all those of the right, opening his fingers to make semi-circles, as it were, raising his hands aloft as far as he could while maintaining that sign.

At which Panurge at once placed the thumb of his right hand under his jaw-bone, and its little-finger into the ring made by his left, and in that position melodiously clacked his lower teeth against the upper.

Thaumaste struggled up painfully, but in so doing let off a baker's fart – for the bran came afterwards – [and copiously pissed vinegar,] making a hell of a stink. Those present began to hold their noses, for he was messing himself in anxiety. He then raised his right hand, closing it in such a way as to bring the tips of all the fingers together, and the left he placed flat against his breast.

Whereupon Panurge pulled on his long codpiece with the tassel attached and stretched it out for a good arm-and-a-half's length, holding it up in the air with his left hand, and with his right he took out his orange, tossing it seven times into the air; on the eighth he hid it in the palm of his right which he quietly held up high. He then began waggling his beautiful codpiece about, exposing it to Thaumaste.

After that Thaumaste started to puff out his cheeks like a man playing the bagpipes and blew as though he were inflating a pig's bladder. At which Panurge stuck one finger of his left hand against his bum and drew air into his mouth as you do when slurping soup or gulping down oysters in their shells.

That done, he opened his mouth a little and struck the flat of his right hand against it, producing a sound which was both loud and deep, coming it seemed from the surface of his diaphragm via his trachea.

He did that sixteen times. But Thaumaste was still hissing like a goose.

So Panurge put his right index-finger into his mouth, squeezing it tight with his bucal muscles and then withdrawing it; by so doing he produced a loud plop such as little boys make when they blow lovely turnip-pellets through an elder-wood pipe.

And that he did nine times.

At which Thaumaste cried out, 'Oh! My Lords! The Great Secret! [He's elbow deep in it!]'

And then he drew out a dagger which he had, holding it downwards by the point. Panurge thereupon took hold of his long codpiece and shook it against his thighs as hard as he could. He then linked both his hands together like a comb and placed them on his head, poking his tongue out as far as he could and rolling his eyes like a nanny-goat dying.

'Ha! I understand you! But ugh . . . ?' said Thaumaste, making the following sign: he placed the handle of his dagger against his breast, pressing the flat of his hand against its point and bending his fingers lightly inwards.

Thereupon Panurge inclined his head to the left and put his middle finger into his right ear while sticking his thumb up high. He then crossed both his arms over his bosom, coughed five times and at the fifth stamped his foot on the ground. He then raised his left arm, closing his fingers into a fist and holding the thumb against his forehead, striking his breast six times with his right hand.

[But Thaumaste, as one not satisfied, placed his left thumb against the tip of his nose while closing the rest of his said left hand. At which Panurge put his two index fingers either side of his mouth, pulling it as far back as he could and baring all his teeth; and with his two thumbs he pulled his eyelids very deeply

down, making a very ugly grimace, or so it seemed to the
audience.]

*

[Becomes: How Thaumaste tells of the abilities and learning of Panurge. Chapter 20.

*'And, behold a greater than Solomon is here' (Matthew 12:42; Luke
11:31) reinforces the links between Scripture and Shrovetide fun: the
Pantagruel of this book is again a kind of comic Christ. That is
reinforced by Matthew 10:34 and Luke 6:40: 'The disciple is not
above his Master', the disciple here being Panurge and the master
Pantagruel. The connections with the Old Testament are maintained
by the citing of Psalm 143 (142):6, 'like unto a thirsty land'. Rabelais
quotes Matthew not from the Latin Vulgate but from the Latin version
of Erasmus in which 'Solomon' replaces the traditional 'Salomon'.
The Sorbonne disapproved of all such changes, including 'Moses' for
'Moïse'.*

*In French festive contexts, at least since François Villon, it was
common to praise 'Noah who planted the vine' (from Genesis 9:20).*

*By implication the 'signs' of the Jewish cabbala, geomancy, magic,
astrology, alchemy, and of certain kinds of philosophy are all condemned – but in Shrovetide terms.]*

Thaumaste next rose to his feet and, doffing his bonnet, thanked
the said Panurge politely. Then, in a loud voice, he addressed
everyone present: 'My Lords, now is the time to quote the
Gospel saying, "And, behold a greater than Solomon is here."

'For here, in your presence, you have an incomparable treasure, namely my Lord Pantagruel, whose fame drew me from
the depths of England to confer with him about inexhaustible
doubts weighing on my mind concerning magic, alchemy, the
cabbala, geomancy as much as astrology and philosophy.[92]

'But at present I am moved to anger against Fame, who

92. '42: . . . about *insoluble problems* concerning . . .
        The list of subjects to be discussed restores those cut out in Chapter 13
    (later, Chapter 18).

seems to me to be envious of him since she does not report a thousandth part of what he effectively is. You have seen how one sole disciple of his has satisfied me, telling me more than I ever asked for, and has in addition both revealed and solved for me other incalculable doubts. In that way he has, I can assure you, broached for me the true well and abyss of the encyclopedia of erudition – of such a sort that I, indeed, never thought I could find any man who knew merely the first elements of it – namely when we disputed by signs without uttering one word, nay, half a word. Soon I shall write down what we have treated and resolved so that nobody should ever think that it was all but tomfoolery, and I shall have it printed so that each man may learn from it as I have done. You can judge what the Master might have said when the disciple achieved such a feat, for *The disciple is not above his Master.*

'In all things may God be praised; and I humbly thank you for the honour you did me with this formal debate. May God eternally reward you for it.'

Pantagruel made a similar act of gratitude to all who were present. On leaving, he took Thaumaste off to dine with him. And you may believe that they drank guts to the ground, like all good souls at Hallowe'en, until they were slurring,[93] 'Eh! Where d'you sprung from?'

Holy Dame! How they swigged from the leathern bottle [while flagons went the rounds and all trumpeted out,

'Swig!'

'Pass it on!'

'Wine, boy!'

'Plonk it in, for the devil's sake, plonk!']

No man failed to drink some twenty-five to thirty hogsheads. And know ye how? 'Like unto a thirsty land.' For it was hot; and they had grown thirsty.

Touching the explanation of the theses advanced by

93. The text was changed after the first edition. '42 reads: . . . drank *with unbuttoned bellies – in those days, you see, they used to fasten their bellies with buttons just as nowadays we fasten our neck-bands –* until they were slurring . . .

The reference to Hallowe'en (*le jour des morts*) is cut out.

Thaumaste and the meanings of the signs used by them in their disputation, I would like to expound them to you according to their joint accounts, but I have been told that Thaumaste has produced a large tome, printed in London, in which he reveals all, omitting nothing; so for the while I shall desist.

How Panurge was in love with a great dame in Paris, and of the trick he played on her

CHAPTER 14

[This later becomes: How Panurge was in love with a great dame in Paris. Chapter 21.

Panurge's rhetoric works on a fair and gullible lady of Paris in the heartless spirit of the farce and the conte, *in which pomposity gets its comic deserts.*

Panurge's original equivocation was a play on à Beaumont le Viconte *(at the place called Beaumont-le-Viconte) turned into* à beau con le vit monte *(up fair cunt the cock mounts). Here it has been transposed into a similar English play on words.*

In the first sentence 'German-style' became 'Romanesque-style'.]

Panurge began to grow in reputation throughout the city of Paris because of the disputation he had won against the Englishman, and from then on embellished his codpiece, decorating it on top with embroidery-slashings in the German style.

Fashionable folk praised him in public and a ballad was composed about him which the little boys sang as they dragged themselves mus-tardily to school.

He was welcome at all social gatherings of dames and damsels, with the result that he became vainglorious, so much so that he set out to get on top of one of the great dames of the town.

In fact, abandoning all the long preambles and protestations usually made by doleful and contemplative 'Lenten lovers' [– the kind who shun flesh –] he said to her one day:

'Madam, it would be of very great utility to the whole commonweal, delectable to you, of honour to your lineage and essential to me, that you should be covered by my stock. Believe me, for the experience will prove it to you!'

At those words the lady thrust him a good hundred leagues off, saying, 'You wretched idiot: what right have you to address such words to me? To whom do you think you are speaking? Be off, and never appear before me again: it would not take much for me to have your arms and legs lopped off!'

'Well,' he replied, 'it would be nothing to me to have my arms and legs lopped off, provided that you and I should first have had a fine bit of fun playing the manikin with your lower pedals; for,' he said, displaying his lengthy codpiece, 'here is my John Thomas who would love to strike up a jig for you which you would feel in the very marrow of your bones. He's a chivalrous fellow who knows [full] well how to linger over preliminaries and nice little inguino-scrotal protuberances round your rat-trap. There's nothing to do after him but sweep up the dust.'

To which the lady replied,

'Go away, you wretched man. Go away. If you say one word more to me I shall call folk in and have you thrashed on the spot.'

'Ah!' said Panurge, 'you are not as nasty as you say you are. No. Or else I have been deceived by your physiognomy: for the earth would sooner mount to the heavens, the high heavens sink into the abyss and the whole order of Nature be perverted rather than that there should be a drop of venom or malice in such beauty and elegance as are yours. They do indeed say that

> Scarcely one belle can you find,
> Who's not a rebel and unkind;

but that is said of common beauties.

'Your beauty, however, is so excellent, so unique, so divine, that I am convinced that Nature set it in you as a model of excellence to enable us to understand what she can achieve when she wishes to employ all her power and wit. There is nothing in you but honey and sugar and manna from Heaven.

'Tis to you that Paris should have awarded the golden apple,
not to Venus. No! Not to Juno nor Minerva. Never was there
such magnificence in Juno, such wisdom in Minerva, such
elegance in Venus as there are in you.

'Ye gods and goddesses above! How blessèd is the man to
whom grace shall be given to enfold you in his arms, to kiss
you and to rub his slice of bacon against you. That man, by
God, shall be me! I know it. I can see it clearly, for fully you
love me already. [I am predestined to that by the fairies.] So to
gain time let us get on with it!'[94]

And he sought to take her in his arms, but she pretended to
make for the window to call on her neighbours for help. So he
got out quick, saying to her as he fled,

'Wait for me here, my Lady. I shall go and fetch them myself;
you needn't bother.'

And he went on his way, not greatly disturbed by the rejection
he had experienced, and having no less of a good time.

The following morning, there he was in church at the hour
she went to Mass. As she came in he offered her holy water and
deeply bowed before her. After that he went and familiarly
knelt down beside her and said,

'Madam, you should know that I am so deeply in love with
you that I can neither piddle nor pooh. What you make of it all
I know not, but what if I come to some harm?'

'Go away,' she said. 'I really do not care. Let me get on with
my prayers to God.'

'But,' he said, 'can you make an equivocation out of *Bucking-
ham Fair*?'

'I've no idea!' she said.

'It's *Fucking 'em bare*,' he said. 'And now pray God to grant
me what your own noble heart desires. And would you kindly
give me your rosary please?'

'Take it,' she said, 'and stop bothering me.'

So saying, she attempted to draw forth her rosary (which was
of Socatrine aloe-wood interlarded with marker-beads of gold),

94. '42: . . . enfold *this woman* in his arms, to kiss *her* and to rub his slice of
bacon against *her*. That man . . . for already *she loves* me fully . . . let us
thrust in-and-out-and-legs-astride!' Panurge sought . . .

but Panurge whipped out one of his knives, slashed it loose and
made off with it to the rag-and-bone men, saying,

'Do you fancy my dagger?'

'No,' she said. 'No!'

'But while on the subject,' he said, 'it is yours to command,
body and earthly goods, bowels and innards.'

The lady meanwhile was by no means happy about her
rosary, it being one of the things which gave her her standing
in church, and she thought to herself,

'That [fine] spinner of words is some lunatic from lands afar.
I'll never get my beads back. What will my husband say! He'll
be cross with me: but I shall tell him that some thief cut them
off inside church. He will believe that easily enough once he
sees this end of the ribbon still on my belt.'

Panurge went to see her after dinner, carrying up his sleeve a
fat purse stuffed with [lawyers' counting-tallies and] tokens.
He began by asking,

'Who loves the other more: you me, or me you?'

To which she replied,

'As far as I am concerned, I certainly do not hate you, since
I love everyone, as God commands.'

'While on the subject,' he said, 'you are in love with me,
aren't you?'

'I have told you many times already,' she said, 'not to address
such words to me. If you say anything more, I will show you
that I am not one to whom you should talk of dishonour. Now
be off; and give me back my beads in case my husband asks me
about them.'

'What, Madam,' said he, 'your beads? Upon my oaf, I shall
not do that, but I would like to give you others instead. Would
you prefer them to be of enamelled gold in the form of great
spheres, or of lovers' knots, or simply of massy gold as in great
ingots? Or would you prefer them to be of ebony, or of large
hyathcinthine gems, [of huge cut garnets] with marker-beads
of fine turquoises; or of beautiful engraved topazes, of fine
sapphires or fine balas-rubies interspersed with marker-beads
of twenty-eight faceted diamonds?

'But no, no! They are all too small. I know of a beautiful

rosary composed of fine emeralds with marker-beads of amber-gris [cut in the round]; its clasp is decorated with a Persian pearl as big as an orange. It costs a mere twenty-five thousand ducats. I would like to make you a present of it, for I have got enough cash.'

As he said that, he made his counters chink as though they were sun-crowns.

'Would you like a length of violet-crimson velvet, scarlet-dyed, or a piece of satin, either brocaded or dyed crimson? Would you like silver chains, gold-work, earrings, bejewelled fillets for you hair? Say yes, that is all. Up to fifty thousand ducats means nothing to me.'

By the force of those words he made her mouth water, but she said to him,

'No. I do thank you, but I want nothing from you.'

'By God,' he said, 'I want something from you, though: something which will cost you nothing, and you will have lost nothing. Get hold of this,' he added, displaying his lengthy codpiece. 'Here is someone [, Master Jack Daw,] looking for a lodging.'

After that he attempted to embrace her, but she began to cry out – not too loud, though.

Then Panurge revealed his trickster's face and said to her,

'So you won't let me have a little go then! Squitters to you! You don't merit such a thing nor such an honour: by God I'll have you ridden by dogs.'

So saying, he fled away fast for fear of a whacking [, of which he was by nature fearful].

*

[*Becomes:* How Panurge played a prank on that Lady of Paris which was by no means to her advantage. Chapter 22.

The Lady of Paris gets her farcical come-uppance.

Rabelais later added a Virgilian or Ovidian savour to his farce by replacing 'bitch in heat' by 'orgose lycisca'. In Virgil, Eclogue, 3, 18 and in Ovid, Metamorphoses, 3, 122, lycisca (wolf-dog) is the name

of a bitch; orgose *is apparently formed on the basis of the Greek verb* orgaō *(to be on heat).*

Here in the original text one of 'those ghastly dogs' 'beshat' the lady of Paris as well as piddling all over her. That is cut out. Faecal terms are indeed quite misplaced here: urine is made laughable in ways in which faeces never are elsewhere in Rabelais. Faeces imply a very different condemnation, frequently with devilish overtones.

Rabelais also twice replaced culleter, *a verb which, though it means here I think something like 'cocking a leg', has within it more than a hint of the* cul *(the behind) which is thus eliminated.]*

You should note that the following day was the great festival of Corpus Christi, when all the women dress up in their magnificent finery and when the said lady had donned for the occasion a most beautiful robe of crimson satin and a tunic of very costly white velvet.

Now on the Vigil of that festival-day Panurge searched far and wide for a bitch on heat.

Using his belt as a lead, he brought one back to his room; all that day and all that night he fed her very well. In the morning he put her down, abstracting from her a substance well known to the ancient Greek geomancers, chopping it up into the smallest pieces he could, hiding them thoroughly and carrying them off. He then went to the church where the lady would have to go to follow the procession customary at that festival.

Panurge offered her the holy water as she came in, greeting her most courteously. A short while after she had said her private orisons, he went and sat beside her in the pew and handed her a rondeau composed as follows:

RONDEAU

> Beloved Lady, since this once my case
> I told you truly, I have lost the race.
> Must I be chased away for good and all
> Who did no harm to you and showed no gall,
> By libel, letter, nor by action base?

You could have said, 'Dear friend, may God's
   good grace
Go with you now: I shall await your pace,
And warmly cherish your becoming face,
   Just now: this once.'

To tell you of my love is no disgrace,
Nor how my heart with love is all ablaze.
My Lady, I am bound in Beauty's thrall.
Nothing I seek but you my Love to call,
And cuntrify you, doing it apace
   Just now: this once.

And as she opened the missive to see what it was, Panurge
promptly scattered the *materia medica* he had brought over
various parts of her garments, especially in the folds of her
sleeves and gown.

Then he said to her:

'Poor lovers are not always at their ease, my Lady. Where I
am concerned, I trust that the bad nights, travails and torments
brought on by my love for you will lead to an equivalent
reduction in the pains of Purgatory. At the very least pray that
God may give me patience in my suffering.'

Panurge had not finished his speech before all the dogs in
that church came over to the lady following the flair of the
materia medica he had sprinkled all over her. Every dog came,
big and small, plump and skinny, all cocking a leg, sniffing
about her and piddling all over her.

[It was the most horrible trick in all the world.]

Panurge chased them up a bit. He then took leave of the Lady
and withdrew to a side-chapel to watch the fun. For those
ghastly dogs beshat her and piddled all over her garments, until
there was one huge hound which was pissing all over her head
while others did it over her sleeves and her crupper and the
puppies did it over her shoes, so that the women there had a
job to rescue her.

Panurge laughed and laughed, and said to one of the great

men of the town, 'I think that lady must be on heat; or else some hound has freshly lined her.'

When Panurge saw that all those dogs were growling round her as they usually do with a bitch on heat, he went off in search of Pantagruel. And in all the streets where he came across any dogs he gave them a kick, saying, 'Not going with your mates to the nuptials then! Off you go. [For the devil's sake] off you go.'

Having reached Pantagruel's lodgings, he said to him, 'I pray you, my master, come and see all the dogs in town, clustered round a lady – the fairest dame in this town – all wanting to have their knobs playing loose in her socket!'[95]

To which Pantagruel readily agreed, and witnessed the comedy, which he found most novel and beautiful. But the best was during the procession when six hundred [thousand and fourteen] dogs were to be found about her, inflicting a thousand ordeals upon her. And, wherever she had passed, fresh dogs came and followed her tracks, pissing all along the road where her garments had touched. Everybody stopped before that spectacle, contemplating the expressions of those dogs which were springing up as high as her neck and ruining her fine accoutrements; she could find no remedy but to withdraw to her mansion. And all the dogs came following after [while she hid herself – and her chambermaids laughed].

Once she had got in and shut the door behind her, the dogs from half-a-league around came and piddled all over her portals, forming a stream with their divers urines which ducks could have swum in.

[And that is the stream which nowadays flows through Saint-Victor and in which Gobelin dyes his scarlet-cloth on account of the specific qualities of those various dog-piddles: Magister Noster d'Oribus once publicly preached about it. Why, God

95. As usual Rabelais made several small stylistic changes in this episode to tighten up his text and eliminate awkwardness. They are not listed. One made after the original edition is worth noting: the change from 'all the dogs in town' to 'all the dogs in the *pays*' to avoid a clash with the next phrase, 'the fairest in the town'.

help you! a mill could have turned in it, though not as well as
the mills of the Bazacle at Toulouse.]

How Pantagruel departed from Paris on hearing news that the Dipsodes were invading the land of the Amaurots. And why the leagues are so short in France. And the Exposition of a saying inscribed upon a ring

CHAPTER 15

[*This becomes* Chapter 23, *and the third sentence of the title is then
omitted. In the first sentence of the text, Enoch and Elijah are replaced
by the medieval heroes Ogier and Arthur.*

  *Rabelais thrice uses the same verb 'to ride' (in a sexual sense) but
later varied the second and third to 'swive' and 'play the ram'.*]

Soon afterwards the news reached Pantagruel that Gargantua,
his father, had been translated to Faërie by Morgan (as once
were Enoch and Elijah) and that the Dipsodes, after hearing
the rumour of his translation, had issued from their frontiers,
laid waste a large stretch of Utopia, and were investing the great
city of the Amaurots. Whereupon, without taking leave of
anyone whatsoever, since the matter required speed, he left
Paris and made his way to Rouen.

  Now Pantagruel, noticing *en route* that the leagues in France
are shorter by far than in other lands, asked Panurge the why
and the wherefore. Panurge told him a tale related by the monk
Marotus Du Lac in his *Romance of the Kings of Canarre* which
says that long, long ago, countries had never been broken up
into leagues, miles, [stadia] or parasangs until King Pharamond
so divided them, doing so in the following manner: he selected
one hundred handsome, determined and gallant young fellow-
me-lads in Paris and a hundred fair maidens from Picardy,
causing them to be well treated and thoroughly spoiled for a
week. He then summoned them and bestowed a maid on each
youth, with plenty of money for expenses, commanding them

to travel this way and that to various places and to set up a
stone at every spot where they rode their maidens, each stone
marking a league.

So those lads went merrily on their way, and, since they were
fresh to the job and had time to spare, they rode their maidens
at the bottom of every field: and that is why leagues are so short
in France. But after they had journeyed further and were already
as exhausted as poor devils, they had no oil left in their lamps
and so rode less often. They were then quite satisfied – the men
were I mean – with one poor, wan little go a day; and that is
why in Brittany, the *Landes* and Germany, as in similar, remoter
lands, the leagues are so long.

Others suggest other reasons, but that one seems best to me.
To which Pantagruel readily agreed.

Leaving for Rouen, they came to Honfleur, where Pantagruel
went aboard ship with Panurge, Epistemon, Eusthenes and
Carpalim; but while they were waiting there for a favourable
wind and caulking their boat, he received a letter from a lady
of Paris with whom he had kept company for a good while.
The address on it read:

> *To the One most beloved of Beauties and*
> *the least Loyal of valiant knights:*
> PNTGRL.

*

[A new chapter later starts here: A letter which a messenger brought
to Pantagruel from a lady in Paris, together with an explication of a
saying inscribed upon a golden ring. Chapter 24.

*Rabelais was at times involved in secret diplomacy. He probably
had a practical interest in invisible writing. Many of the methods
listed were well known since Classical antiquity: the milky sap of the
tithymalus plant (euphorbia, a kind of spurge) is mentioned for
example by Pliny. The later citing here of the 'milk from the spurge'
is a doublet. The secret method explained by Aulus Gellius is cited by
Cicero: it consists in so writing a message on a piece of papyrus that
it can be read only when wrapped round a staff of the right size.*

The supposed works by Messer Francesco di Nianto of Tuscany,
Zoroaster and Calphurnius Bassus are imaginary.

Some of the erudite references are taken from the Adages *and*
Apophthegms *of Erasmus.*

The tale, with the light-hearted, indirect use of Christ's words on
the Cross, 'Why hast thou forsaken me' (cited from Psalm 22:1), is
borrowed from a novella by Masuccio

The jest further centres on a pun between 'diamant' (diamond) and
'di amant' (say, lover).

The boasting of the heroes before the battle corresponds to the
traditional 'gabbing' of knights before battle in the chivalrous
romances.

The harbour of Achoria later becomes that of Utopia. Both terms
are from Thomas More.

Zopyrus was a spy for Darius; Sinon tricked the enemy into admit-
ting the Trojan Horse.]

Having read the inscription, he was most surprised, and asking
the messenger the name of the lady who had sent it, he unfolded
the letter, only to find nothing written inside, simply a golden
ring bearing a square-table diamond. He then called Panurge
over and showed it to him.

At which Panurge told him that that leaf of paper was indeed
written upon, but so cunningly that the writing was invisible.

To reveal it he held it against the fire, to see whether the
writing had been done in sal ammoniac steeped in water.

Then he soaked it in water, to see whether the letter was
written in the sap of the tithymalus.

Then he held it up to the candle, to see whether it was not
written in the juice of white onions.

He then rubbed a part of it with walnut oil, to see whether it
was not written in a lessive made from the ashes of a fig-tree.

He then rubbed a part with the milk of a mother suckling
her first-born daughter, to see whether it was not written in
toad's blood.

He then rubbed a corner of it with the ashes of a swallow's
nest, to see whether it was written in the secretions within the
bladder-wort.

He then rubbed another part with ear-wax, to see whether it was written in raven's gall.

He then soaked it in vinegar, to see whether it was written in milk from the spurge.

He then coated it with the axunge of bats, to see whether it was written in the kind of whale-sperm which we call ambergris.

He then slid it gently into a basin of clear water and drew it out quickly, to see whether it was written in plume-alum.

And realizing that he had found out nothing, he called over the messenger and said:

'My good fellow: did the lady who sent you here not give you a staff to bring?' (He was thinking of the secret method explained by Aulus Gellius.)

The messenger replied, 'No, Sir.'

At which Panurge wanted to shave off the man's hair to find out whether the lady had caused what she wished to say to be written in jet-black ink upon his shaven scalp; but when he saw how long the man's locks were, he gave up the idea, considering that no hair could have grown so long in so short a space.

After that he said to Pantagruel:

'Master, by God's might, I don't know what to do or say. To find out whether anything was written here I have employed a part of what is set out by Messer Francesco di Nianto of Tuscany, who wrote on ways of reading invisible writing, and what Zoroaster wrote in his work *On Hidden Writing*, and what Calphurnius Bassus wrote in *On Writings Unreadable*.

'But I can see nothing there. All we have here, I believe, is that ring. Nothing more. Let's look at it.'

On examining it they found LAMAH HAZABTHANI written round the inside in Hebrew. So they called Epistemon over and asked him what it meant. To which he replied that it was a Hebrew phrase, meaning *Why hast thou forsaken me?*

Panurge immediately rejoined:

'I can understand it now! See this diamond? It's a false diamond – a *diamant faux* – hence the explanation of what the lady means: "Say, lover false" – *Di amant faux* – *Why hast thou forsaken me?*'

Pantagruel immediately grasped what it meant, remembering how he had left Paris without bidding farewell to his lady-love. It saddened him, and he would willingly have gone back to Paris to make his peace with her, but Epistemon recalled to his mind Aeneas' departure from Dido, as well as the saying of Heraclides of Tarentum, that when your boat is riding at anchor and necessity presses you hard, you should slice through the painter rather than waste time untying it: he too must cast all such thoughts aside and come to the aid of his native city in her peril.

And indeed, one hour later, there arose the wind we call a Nor'-nor'-Wester, to which they offered all their canvas and set out on the high seas; in a few short days they passed by Porto Santo and Madeira and touched at the Canary Islands.

From there, having sailed past Capo Bianco, Senegal, Capo Verde, the Gambia, Sagres, Melli and the Cape of Good Hope, they called at the port of the kingdom of Melinda.

From there, filling their sails with a Tramontane wind, they got under way, sailing past Meden, Uti, Uden, Gelasim, and the Faërie Islands off the kingdom of Achoria, finally touching land at the harbour of Achoria, which is a trifle more than three leagues from the city of the Amaurots. Once they were ashore and a little refreshed, Pantagruel said:

'Lads, the city is not far from here. Before going any further it would be good to settle what we ought to do, so as not to be like the Athenians who never deliberated until after the deed was done! Are you not determined to live and die with me?'

'Yes, my Lord,' they all replied. 'You can rely on us as on the fingers of your own hand.'

'Still,' he said, 'there is only one detail which keeps me doubtful and undecided: I have no idea of the disposition or number of the enemy who are holding our city under siege. For I would act with greater assurance if I could learn that. So let us discuss together a means of finding that out.'

They all replied in unison:

'Allow us to go and look. You wait here. We shall bring you definite intelligence throughout the day.'

'I,' said Panurge, 'undertake to go right into their camp

through the midst of their guards and their look-outs, to feast [and use my weapon] at their expense, and, recognized by no one, to review their artillery and the tents of all their captains, and to parade like a prelate through their troops without being rumbled: the devil himself could never catch me out, for I am of the lineage of Zopyrus.'

'I,' said Epistemon, 'know all the stratagems and exploits of the valiant captains and heroes of bygone days, as well as all the feints and subterfuges of the art of war. I will go; and even if I were discovered and unmasked, I would extricate myself by making them believe anything about you I liked. For I am of the lineage of Sinon.

'I,' said Eusthenes, 'in spite of their sentinels and all their guards, will go across their trenches, and, even if they were as strong as the devil, I shall pass over their bellies, snapping off their arms and legs. For I am of the lineage of Hercules.'

'And as for me,' said Carpalim, 'if birds can get in, then so shall I, for I am so nimble of body that I shall have vaulted over their trenches and driven through their camp before they have noticed me. I dread no dart nor arrow, nor steed however swift, be it the Pegasus of Perseus or the steed of Pacolet, from any fear of not escaping safe and sound before them. I undertake to tread over the ears of corn and the grass in the meadows without their bending beneath me.

'For I am of the lineage of Camilla, the Amazon.'

How Panurge, Carpalim, Eusthenes and Epistemon, the companions of Pantagruel, most cleverly discomfited six hundred and sixty knights

CHAPTER 16

[This later becomes Chapter 25.
A romp with comic chivalry crossed with mariners' tales.]

As he was speaking they descried six hundred and sixty knights, well mounted on light horses, who came galloping along to see what vessel it was which had just drawn alongside in the harbour, charging at full tilt to take them if they could.

Pantagruel then said, 'Now, boys, withdraw aboard ship, for some of our foes are charging up at full speed but I shall slaughter them like cattle were they ten times as many. Meanwhile withdraw and enjoy the fun!'

Panurge then replied:

'No, my Lord, it is not reasonable for you to act thus. On the contrary, you go back aboard – both you and the others – for I alone shall discomfit them here. But there must be no delay. Jump to it.'

Others added:

'Well said! Withdraw, my Lord, and we shall lend Panurge here a hand and you will soon learn what we are capable of.'

Pantagruel then said:

'I am happy to do so, but if you should prove the weaker I will not fail you.'

Panurge hauled forthwith upon two of the ship's great cables, made them fast to a windlass on the deck, cast them ashore and formed them into two big loops, one inside the other.

Then he said to Epistemon:

'Go aboard, and when I shout, wind hard that windlass [upon the deck], drawing these two cables towards you.'

He then said to Eusthenes and Carpalim:

'You wait here, boys. Greet the enemy frankly; do what they say and pretend to surrender. But take care never to step inside the circle formed by those cables. Withdraw, but stay outside.'

He then promptly went down into the hold, grabbed a bale of straw and a barrel of gunpowder and scattered them about inside the circle formed by the cables. He then stood by, holding an incendiary-grenade.

All of a sudden a great force of knights arrived, the vanguard charging up close by the ship: the embankment gave way and the men and horses came tumbling down to the number of four and forty. Seeing which, the other knights thought that they had been resisted on reaching the shore, so they closed in.

But Panurge said to them:

'Gentlemen, I believe you have brought some harm on

yourselves. We are sorry, but it was none of our doing: it was because of the lubricity of the sea-water – sea-water is always a lubricant – and we entrust ourselves to your good pleasure.'

His two companions said the same, as did Epistemon on deck.

Panurge meanwhile drew back and, noting that those men were within the circle of ropes and that his two companions had drawn back to clear a space for all the knights, who, crowding forward to see the ship, were now all inside, suddenly yelled out to Epistemon, 'Heave! Heave!' Epistemon then started to haul in on the windlass, and the two cables entwined themselves amongst the horses, easily bringing them down with their riders. But those riders drew their swords and tried to cut themselves loose: Panurge proceeded to set fire to the train of powder and burnt them all up like souls in Hell.

Of horse and man, not one got free, save for one single knight on a Turkish steed, which bolted and bore him off.

But when Carpalim saw it he ran after him with such speed and agility that he caught up with him in less than a hundred paces and, vaulting on to the crupper, seized him from behind and carried him off to the ship. The discomfiture accomplished, Pantagruel was very jolly, highly praising the ingenuity of his companions; he made them rest and eat a good meal on the shore, pledging drink for drink with their guts to the ground. The prisoner was treated like one of the family, except that the poor devil was never certain that Pantagruel would not devour him, something which, with his capacious throat, he could have done as easily as you could do with a grain of stomach-powder, for in his mouth he amounted to no more than a grain of millet in the gullet of an ass.

*

[A *new chapter begins here in* '42: How Pantagruel and his companions grew tired of eating salt meats, and how Carpalim went off hunting for venison. Chapter 26.

Vinaigre *in Rabelais means vinegar and also* piqué *(wine which has turned sour and also used for macerating), as well as wine for current drinking.*

The name of the chief of the giants, Loup Garou, means Werewolf.

Two numbers are changed: 'three thousand four hundred' men at arms become 'eleven thousand and four', and 'four hundred and fifty thousand strumpets' become a mere 'hundred and fifty thousand'.

'Saint Quimlet' renders Saint Quenet, a Breton saint whose name suggests such a pun.]

While they were feasting, Carpalim said,

'By the guts of Saint Quimlet, shall we never eat venison? This salt meat makes me all of a thirst. I'm off to get a thigh from one of those horses we burnt: it'll be well enough roasted.'

Just as he stood up to do so, he caught sight of a handsome great roe-buck at the edge of the forest: it had in my opinion come out of the woods at the sight of Panurge's fire. He at once started to race after it with such a thrust that he seemed like the bolt of a crossbow, and, as he ran, in less than no time he [had caught with his hands four great bustards, seven bitterns, twenty-six grey partridges, thirty-two red ones, sixteen pheasants, nine woodcocks, nineteen herons and thirty-two woodpigeons, all in flight, and] killed with his feet some ten or twelve leverets and conies, all but grown out of puberty [, plus eighteen braces of water-rails, fifteen young wild-boars, two badgers and three huge foxes]. So, striking the roe-buck across its head with his short cutting-sword, he killed it and, as he bore it off, he gathered up his leverets [water-rails and young wild-boars] and called from as far as his voice could be heard, 'Panurge, my friend, *vinaigre! vinaigre!*'

At which Pantagruel thought that it was his heart that was troubling him and commanded that *vinaigre* be brought out for him, but Panurge clearly understood that there was a leveret on the hook. Indeed he pointed out to our noble Pantagruel that Carpalim had a fine roe-buck slung across his shoulders and that his belt was all hung about with leverets.

Epistemon quickly prepared two handsome wooden spits in the antique style.[96]

Eusthenes helped him with the skinning while Panurge took two saddles which had belonged to the knights and arranged them to serve as andirons.

And they made their prisoner their roaster.

They roasted the venison over the fire in which they had frazzled the knights. And then good cheer, with lots of *vinaigre!* And the devil take anyone who held back! It was a treat to watch them guzzling away.

Then Pantagruel said:

'Would to God that each one of you had a couple of pairs of hawks' tinklers dangling from your chins, while dangling from mine were the great bells of Rennes, Poitiers, Tours and Cambrai: what a dawn peal we would ring as we champed our chops!'

'Yes,' said Panurge, 'but it would be preferable to reflect a bit on the matter in hand and how we can get the better of our enemies.'

'Good advice,' said Pantagruel.

He therefore addressed the prisoner:

'Tell us the truth, my friend. And if you do not want to be flayed alive, lie about nothing whatsoever, for I am the one who devours little children. Tell me the disposition, number and strength of your army.'

To which the prisoner replied:

'Take it as true, my Lord, that the army includes three hundred giants all clad in armour made of blocks of sandstone and all wondrously big, though not as big as you are, except for one who is their chief and is called Loup Garou, who is entirely clad in Cyclopic anvils.

Then there are a hundred and sixty-three thousand foot-soldiers, men strong and bold, all clad in an armour of Goblins' pelts; three thousand four hundred men-at-arms; three thousand six hundred double canons and any number of

---

96. '42: ... Epistemon, *in the name of the Nine Muses*, quickly prepared *nine* handsome wooden spits ...

siege-weapons; four score and fourteen thousand pioneers, and four hundred and fifty thousand strumpets as beautiful as goddesses . . .'

– 'They're for me!' said Panurge –

'. . . some of whom are Amazons; others hail from Lyons, Paris, Tours, Anjou, Poitiers, Normandy and Germany: from all lands and all tongues.'

'Indeed,' said Pantagruel, 'but is their king there?'

'Yes, Sire,' replied the prisoner. 'He is there in person. His name is Anarch, King of the *Dipsodes* (which means the *Thirsty Ones*, for you have never seen such thirsty folk nor folk more given to drink). He has his tent guarded by the giants.'

'Enough!' said Pantagruel. 'Up, boys. Are you sure you want to have a go at them with me?'

Panurge replied:

'God confound any man who abandons you. I have already thought out how I will make them as dead as porkers, leaving not a hough for the devil. There is one thing which worries me a little, though.'

'And what is that?' asked Pantagruel.

'How I shall go about servicing all those strumpets after dinner,

so that never a one
Escapes a drumming once I have done.'

Pantagruel laughed, 'Ha, ha, ha!'

And Carpalim said,

'The divel of Biterno! By God, I'll stuff one of them.'

'And what about me?' said Eusthenes. 'I've not once had a good stiff on ever since we left Rouen; let the prick point at least to ten or eleven o'clock, especially since mine is as hard and strong as a hundred devils.'

'Truly,' said Panurge, 'you will get the plumpest and most buxom ones of all!'

'Hey!' said Epistemon. 'You'll all be having a ride and I shall be left leading the donkey! The devil take anyone who tries that one on me. We shall enjoy the rights of war: *He that is able to receive, let him receive.*[97]

['No, no,' said Panurge, 'but tie your moke to the hook and enjoy a ride like everyone else.']

And that good giant Pantagruel laughed at everything; he then said to them:

'But you are reckoning without mine host! I greatly fear I may see you in such a state before nightfall that you will have little desire for an erection and be ridden down with great blows from pike and lance.'

'No, no!' said Epistemon, 'I shall deliver them to you all ready to roast, boil, fricassee or fold into pasties. They are not such a multitude as Xerxes led, for he had thirty thousand fighting men (if you trust Herodotus and Trogus Pompeius), yet Themistocles defeated them with his few. For God's sake do not worry.'

'Pooh!' said Panurge, 'pooh! My codpiece alone will dust off all the men, whilst Saint Besomhole who resides in it will mop up all the women.'

'Up then, boys!' said Pantagruel. 'Let us begin our advance.'

How Pantagruel erected a trophy in memory of their prowess, and Panurge another in memory of the leverets. And how Pantagruel engendered little men from his loud farts and little women from his quiet ones. And how Panurge shattered a thick stave over a couple of glasses

CHAPTER 17

[*Becomes* chapter 27.

Erecting trophies was the practice of the victors of Antiquity and therefore much admired during the Renaissance. Here it merits

97. Matthew 19:12, cited in the Vulgate Latin, 'Qui potest capere capiat', which allows a play on words: 'let him grasp' (both intellectually and physically).

mock-heroics and also a parody. In the next book, Gargantua, *trophies
built in the gratitude of men's minds will be preferred to such as are
built of stone.]*

'Before we quit this spot,' said Pantagruel, 'I would like to erect
a fair trophy in memory of your recent prowess.'

So every man, with great merriment and little rustic songs,
set up a big pike-staff on which they hung a soldier's saddle, a
horse's head-armour, caparisons, stirrups and spurs, a hauberk,
a full set of steel armour, a battle-axe, a broad-sword, a gauntlet, a mace, gussets, greaves and a gorget, with all the array
required for a triumphal arch or trophy. Then, in eternal
memory, Pantagruel composed the following song of victory:

> 'Twas here that valiant fights were fought
> By four brave men, as good as gold,
> Through good sense not good armour wrought,
> As Fabius and both Scipios told.
> Six hundred sixty lice, now cold –
> All powerful rogues – were burnt like bark.
> Kings and dukes from now must hold
>   'Tis wit not might lights glory's spark.
>   Each mother's son
>   Knows victory – won
>   Not by man – lies
>   Where God's writs run,
>   Whose will be done
>   Sans compromise.
> Not to the stronger comes the prize.
> But to whose works from grace have sprung.
> For him do wealth and honour rise
> Who hopes in faith in Him alone.

While Pantagruel was composing the above poem, Panurge
hung the horns of the roe-buck on to a big stake together with
its pelt and its front right foot, then the ears of three leverets,
the spine of a rabbit, the chaps of a hare, [the wings of a brace
of bitterns, the feet of four wood-pigeons,] a cruet of *vinaigre*,

a horn in which they kept their salt, a wooden spit, a basting stick, a wretched cauldron full of holes, a pan for sauces, an earthenware salt-cellar and a Beauvais-ware goblet. And in imitation of the verses on Pantagruel's trophy he composed the following lines:

> Here on their bums, great battles fought,
> Four gallant fellows, good as gold,
> In praise of Bacchus fun have sought,
> Quaffing like carps the wine out-doled.
> Saddles of hare and thighs untold
> Of master leverets left their mark.
> Scorpion-fish, salt, *vinaigre* old,
> Strain all their guts lest bellies bark.
>> Seize wine, each son
>> And drink for fun
>> 'Neath blazing skies:
>> Let the best run
>> Out from the tun:
>> Quaffed as a prize.
> But leveret's flesh – 'tis no surprise –
> Sans *vinaigre* is ne'er well done.
> Its soul-worth in *vinaigre* lies:
> Gainsay it not, then all are one.

Then Pantagruel said,

'Come on, boys. We have mused here too long about food: rarely do great feasters feature in feats of arms! There is no shade, but of a standard! No aroma, but of steeds! No clink, but of armour!'

[At which Epistemon began to smile and said:

'There is no shade, but of a kitchen! No aroma, but of pasties! No clink but of goblets!']

To which Panurge replied:

'There is no shade, but of bed-curtains! No aroma, but of bosoms! No clink, but of bollocks!'

Then leaping to his feet with a jump, a fart and a whistle, he cried:

'Pantagruel! Live for ever!'

Seeing which, Pantagruel strove to do likewise, but at the loud fart which he let off [the earth quaked for nine leagues around, from which, and the polluted air,] were engendered fifty [-three] thousand tiny men, all dwarfish and deformed: and from a quiet one he engendered the same number of bent-over little women (such as you can see in many places) who grow only downwards like cows' tails or round the middle like Limousin turnips.

'Well now,' said Panurge, 'is your flatulence so fruitful! Here by God are some fine old male down-at-heels and some fine female farts. We must marry them together and they'll beget gadflies.'

Pantagruel did so, and called them pygmies. And he sent them off to live on a nearby island, where they have since greatly multiplied. But the cranes ceaselessly make war on them; against which they defend themselves courageously, for those wee bit men – dubbed *Curry-comb Handles* in Scotland – are frequently choleric, the physiological reason for which being that their hearts lie close to their shit.

At that same time Panurge took up a couple of glasses which were there, both of the same size, and filled them to the brim with water. He placed one on one stool and the other on another, setting them five feet apart. He then took the pole of a javelin about five-and-a-half-foot long and placed it on top of the glasses in such a manner that the two ends of the pole just touched their rims. He then grasped a thick stake and said to Pantagruel and the others:

'Gentlemen, think how easily we shall win victory over our foes. For, just as I shall break the pole placed over these glasses without breaking or shattering them and, what is more, without spilling one drop of water, so too shall we break the heads of those Dipsodes of ours, without any of us being injured and without any harm to our affairs. But,' he said to Eusthenes, 'to stop you from thinking that there is any enchantment, you take this stake and you strike the pole in the middle as hard as you can.'

Eusthenes did so, breaking it cleanly in two without spilling one drop of water from those glasses.

Then Panurge said, 'I know plenty of others! Now let us go confidently on our way . . .'

How Pantagruel most strangely won a victory over the Dipsodes and the giants

CHAPTER 18

[Becomes Chapter 28.

The mock-heroic tale continues, echoing the style of the chivalrous romances and their wonders, with echoes too of ancient heroic deeds retold in the style of Lucian's True History.

There are lessons in warfare and justified strategic deceptions within the context of a faith which holds that God does not merely help those who help themselves.

Editions after '37 omit: . . . I do not say to you like those black-beetle humbugs, Help yourself and God will help you, for, on the contrary, Help yourself and the devil will break your neck! What I say is.]

After all that was said, Pantagruel summoned their prisoner and sent him back, saying:

'Go off to your king in his camp; tell him news of what you have seen, and that he is to arrange a feast for me tomorrow towards midday! For as soon as my galleys arrive – tomorrow morning at the latest – I shall, by means of eighteen hundred thousand fighting-men and seven thousand giants, each one bigger than you see me to be, prove to him that he has acted insanely and irrationally in thus attacking my country.'

By which Pantagruel feigned that he had a navy at sea.

The prisoner, however, replied that he was his slave and would be happy never to return to his own people, preferring to fight at Pantagruel's side against them; and that he should, by God, permit him to do so.

To which Pantagruel would not give his consent, but ordered

him to leave promptly as he had said. He then gave him a box full of euphorbia-resin and grains of *daphne gnidium* [pickled in brandy and reduced to a syrup], commanding him to bear it to his king and to tell him that if he could swallow one ounce of it without a drink he could withstand him without fear.

The prisoner thereupon clasped his hands together and implored him to take pity on him in the hour of battle.

Pantagruel replied,

'Once you have reported [all] this to your king, I do not say to you like those black-beetle humbugs, Help yourself and God will help you, for on the contrary, Help yourself and the devil will break your neck! What I say is, Put all your hope in God and he will never forsake you. As for me, although I am powerful, as you can see, and have an infinite number of men under arms, my hope is not in my might nor in my exertions: all my trust is in God my Protector, who never forsakes them that have placed their hope and thoughts in him.'

When he had finished, the prisoner [begged Pantagruel to come to a reasonable agreement where his ransom was concerned. Pantagruel replied that his aim was not to pillage or ransom men but to enrich them and to reform them in total freedom.

'Go on your way,' said Pantagruel, 'in the peace of the living God, and never follow wicked companions lest evil befall you.'

He] departed and Pantagruel said to his men:

'I have given this prisoner to understand, lads, that we have a navy at sea and that we shall not make an attack before about midday tomorrow, with the intent that they, fearing a great arrival of men, may spend tonight putting things in order and raising defences; but meanwhile my intention is to attack them about the hour of the first watch.'

But now let us leave Pantagruel and his apostles and tell of Anarch the king and his army.

So when the prisoner arrived he betook himself to the king and told him how there had come a great giant called Pantagruel, who had discomfited and cruelly roasted every one of the six hundred and fifty-nine knights, he alone being spared to bring the news. Moreover that giant had charged him to say that the king should prepare to have him for dinner about midday on the morrow, since he had decided to invade him at that hour.

He then handed the king the box containing the confection. But the very moment that he swallowed one spoonful of it he suffered such an inflammation of the throat with an ulceration of his uvula that his tongue peeled off. As a remedy he could find no alleviation except by drinking without a break, for as soon as he withdrew the goblet from his lips his tongue burnt him. They therefore did nothing but sluice wine [down his throat] through a funnel.

Seeing which, his captains, pashas and the men of his guard themselves tasted the specific to test whether it really did provoke such thirst; but what happened to their king happened to them: they all began to swig wine by the flagonful, so much so that it was noised through the camp how the prisoner had returned, that the assault must come tomorrow, and that the king was already preparing for it by crooking the elbow, as were the captains and the guardsmen. So that every man jack in the army began to tope, tipple and swill as on Saint Martin's Eve.

In short they drank so much that they lay scattered over the camp in a swinish sleep.

And now let us return to our good giant Pantagruel and tell how he comported himself in this matter.

On leaving the site of the trophy, he took their ship's mast in his hand as though it were a pilgrim's staff and stowed in its crow's nest the two hundred and thirty-seven casks of white Angevine wine left over from Rouen, and strapped to his belt the salt-boat crammed with salt as easily as the lansquenets' women bear their little baskets. And thus did he set out on his way with his companions. And when they approached the enemy camp Panurge said to him,

'My Lord, would you like to do a good deed? Send us down that white Angevine wine from the crow's nest and let us drink it, German-fashion.'[98]

Pantagruel readily condescended to do so, and they drank so

98.   '42: . . . drink it, *Breton*-fashion . . .

thoroughly that not one single drop from those two hundred and thirty-seven casks was left, except for a bottle made of Touraine leather which Panurge filled for himself – he called it his vade mecum – and some wretched dregs to make *vinaigre*.

After they had taken a good tug at the bottle, Panurge gave Pantagruel some fiendish pills compounded of round pastilles of alkegengi resin, Spanish fly and other diuretic specifics.[99]

That done, Pantagruel said to Carpalim:

'Go to the city and, as you do so well, scramble up the wall like a rat and tell those inside that they are to make a sortie at that very hour and fall upon the enemy as violently as they can. That said, scramble down again, taking a flaming torch with you with which to set fire to all the tents and pavilions in their camp. Then you will raise a great shout with that mighty voice of yours, which is more frightening than that of Stentor when heard above all the din of the Trojans' battle, and then leave the said camp.[100]

'Agreed,' said Carpalim. 'But would it not be good for me to spike all their guns?'

'No, no,' said Pantagruel, 'but do set fire to all their powder.'

In obedience Carpalim departed at once and did as Pantagruel decreed. So all the fighting-men on guard in the city came out. And when he had set fire to all the tents and pavilions, he glided lightly over those inside without their noticing anything, so deeply did they sleep and snore. He reached the emplacements of their artillery and set their munitions ablaze. But – O! the pity of it![101] – the fire took so quickly that it nearly engulfed the wretched Carpalim. Were it not for his wonderful speed and celerity he would have been fricasseed [like a pig].

But he sped away so quickly that no bolt from a cross-bow flies more fast. And once he had cleared their trenches he gave such a terrifying yell that it seemed that all the devils were unleashed. That din did awaken the enemy, but can you guess

---

99. '42: . . . compounded of a *lithonrhriptic, a nephrocathartic, some canthandarized quince-jelly* and other diuretic specifics . . .

100. '42: omits: which is more frightening than that of Stentor when heard above all the din of the Trojans' battle.

101. '42: . . . But – *there was the danger*: the fire . . .

how? They were as heavy as that first bell of mattins which the men of Luçon call *Scratch-your-balls!*

In the meantime Pantagruel began to sow the salt he had in his tub, and because the enemy were sleeping with their jaws gaping wide, he so filled up their gullets that those poor wretches began barking like foxes, crying, 'Ha! Pantagruel! Pantagruel![102] You are stoking up our fires! Suddenly Pantagruel wanted to do a pee on account of the drugs which Panurge had given him; and so well and copiously did he piss over their camp that he drowned them all, producing a Flood of their own for ten miles around. And the tale tells us that if his father's mule had been there too and had staled as copiously there would have been a flood more enormous than that of Deucalion, for she never staled without producing a river greater than the Rhône [and the Danube].

When they saw it, those who had issued forth from the city said,

'They have all been cruelly slain: see the blood flowing!'

Yet they were mistaken, thinking that Pantagruel's urine was his enemies' blood, for they could see only by the glow of the burning pavilions plus just a little moonlight.

After the enemy had woken up and seen, on one flank, the fire in their camp and then that inundation and deluge of urine, they knew not what to think or say. Some said it was the End of the World and the Last Judgement, which must be consummated in fire; others, that sea-gods such as Neptune [, Proteus, Triton] and the rest were persecuting them and that it was in fact sea-water and salty.

O! Who now could sing how Pantagruel comported himself against three hundred giants! O, my Muse! my Calliope! my Thalia! Inspire me now! Restore ye now my spirits, for behold: here is the asses' bridge of Logic, here the stumbling-block, here the difficulty of finding words to tell of the horrifying battle which then was joined.

Would that I now had a jar of the very best wine as will ever be drunk by such as shall read this so very true history.

---

102. '42: omits the second 'Pantagruel!'.

How Pantagruel vanquished three hundred giants who were armed with blocks of sandstone, and Loup Garou their captain

CHAPTER 19

[Becomes Chapter 29.

The mock-heroic savour is marked from the outset by the reference to the conduct of Anchises, the father of Aeneas, at the sack of Troy (Virgil, Aeneid, I, 866 ff. and II, 975 ff.) while the style again recalls that of chivalrous romances, especially perhaps pseudo-Turpin.

'That even Hercules could not take on two foes' is one of the Adages of Erasmus (I, V, XXXIX).

A prayer before battle is a feature of the chivalrous tales. Rabelais unexpectedly uses it for dense evangelical propaganda. Pantagruel's title for Christ is 'Servateur' (Servator). The theology is most arresting. A note commenting on it is placed at the end of this chapter for any who may want to go into it further.]

The giants, noting that their camp was submerged, bore King Anarch out of their stronghold as well as they could on their shoulders, as Aeneas bore his father Anchises from blazing Troy.

When Panurge saw them he said to Pantagruel:

'Look. The giants have come out! Whack 'em [vigorously], my Lord, with your mast in our old style of swordsmanship, for now is the time to prove yourself a man of valour: we, on our side, will never fail you.

'I am sure to kill many of them for you. Why? Because David killed Goliath easily enough: and I, who could knock down as many as a dozen such as David, for he was only a little shit of a fellow then, shall I not down a good dozen?[103]

'And that great lecher Eusthenes, who is as strong as four

---

103. '42: omits: and I, who could knock down as many as a dozen such as David, for he was only a little shit of a fellow then, shall I not down a good dozen?
(The allusion is to I Samuel 17.)

bulls, will not spare himself. Be of good courage: run them through with cut and thrust.'

'Well, I have fifty francs' worth of courage,' said Pantagruel, 'but then, even Hercules dared not take on two at once.'

'That's talking dog-shit up my nose!' said Panurge. 'Are you comparing yourself to Hercules! You have [by God!] more strength in your teeth and more sense in your bum than Hercules had in all his body and soul. A man is as good as he reckons he is!'

While they were saying such words, behold, Loup Garou arrived with all his giants and, spotting Pantagruel alone, he was seized by temerity and overweening recklessness from the hope he had of killing our poor Pantagruel.[104]

Whereupon he said to his companion giants:

'You lowland lechers, if any of you undertakes to fight against those fellows over there, I shall, by Mahoun, have you cruelly put to death.

'My will is that you leave me to meet him in single combat.

'Meanwhile your pastime shall be to watch us.'

All the giants and their king withdrew a short distance to the place where the flagons were kept; Panurge and his companions went with them, he mimicking men who have caught the pox, for he twisted his gullet, crooked his fingers, and croaked in a husky voice, 'I renounce Gosh, comrades! We are not making war. Allow us to feed with you while our masters battle it out between them.'

To which the king and the giants readily consented, making them join in their feast, during which Panurge related legends [of Turpin,] exemplary stories of Saint Nicholas [and a Mother-Stork tale].

Loup Garou then confronted Pantagruel with a mace weighing nine thousand seven hundred hundredweight [plus two quarter-pounds] made entirely of steel from Chalybes; its end was studded with thirteen diamond points, the smallest of which was as big as the biggest bell in Notre-Dame-de-Paris – well, perhaps it fell short by a nail's breadth or (I have no

104. '42: . . . killing *the* poor *little chap*. Whereupon he . . .

wish to lie) by the thickness of the back of those knives called
ear-loppers, a little more or less. And it was enchanted, so that
it could never be broken but, on the contrary, immediately
broke everything it touched. And then, as he approached with
great ferocity, Pantagruel, casting his eyes towards Heaven,
commended himself to God with a right good heart, as he made
a vow as now follows:

'O Lord God, who have always been my Protector and Servator, you see the distress in which I now am. Nothing brings me
here save the natural zeal which you have vouchsafed to human
beings for the saving and defending of themselves, their wives,
children, country and family, provided that it touch not upon
your own proper concern which is the Faith; for in such a
concern your will is to have no coadjutor except the affirmation
of Catholicism and the ministry of your word, forbidding us all
arms and defences: for you are the Almighty who, in your own
proper concern where your own proper cause is drawn into
action, can defend yourself far more than we can estimate, you
who have a thousand thousands of hundreds of millions of
legions of angels, the least of whom could kill all human beings
and spin Heaven and Earth at his pleasure, as was made most
manifest in the army of Sennacherib.

'Wherefore if it pleases you to come to my aid in this hour,
since my total faith and hope are in you alone, I vow to you
that, throughout all the lands in Utopia or elsewhere where I
shall have power or authority, I will cause your holy Gospel to
be preached purely, simply and entirely, so that the abuses of a
load of bacon-pappers and false prophets who have poisoned
the whole world with their human doctrines and their depraved
novelties shall be banished from about me.'

And then there was heard a voice from Heaven saying, '*Hoc
fac, et vinces*,' that is, This do and thou shalt conquer.

That said, Pantagruel, seeing Loup Garou approach with
his chops agape, bravely advanced towards him and yelled as
loud as he could, 'Death, you scoundrel, death!' (seeking to
frighten him with that horrific cry in accordance with the art
of war of the Spartans). Then from the salt-boat which he bore
on his belt he threw eighteen barrels [and one Greek pound] of

salt at Loup Garou, stuffing his gullet, chaps, nose and eyes
with it.

Loup Garou, enraged, aimed a blow at him with his mace,
hoping to bash his brains out. But Pantagruel was adroit, ever
sure of foot and quick of eye. He stepped back on to his left
foot, yet not so quick as to stop the blow from landing on his
salt-boat, shattering it into [four thousand and eighty-] six
fragments and spilling the remaining salt on to the ground.

On seeing which, Pantagruel [vigorously] flexed his arms
and, following the art of the battle-axe, whacked him with the
thick end of his mast, making a cut-and-thrust blow above his
breast, hacking it out leftwards and then slashing him between
the neck and shoulders. Next he put his right foot forward and
gave him a downward blow upon his balls with the top end of
the mast; it shattered the crow's nest and spilt the three or four
kegfuls of wine which were left: Loup Garou thought that
Pantagruel had cut through his bladder and that the wine was
his own urine escaping.

Pantagruel, not satisfied, tried to redouble his efforts to dis-
engage, but Loup Garou, raising high his mace, stepped towards
him and attempted to thwack it down on him. Indeed he aimed
such a vigorous blow that if God had not come to the aid of
our good Pantagruel he would have cloven him in two from
the crown of his head to [the base of] his spleen. Owing to
Pantagruel's brisk speed the blow swept past to the right and
the mace drove three score [and thirteen] feet into the ground
straight through a large boulder from which he struck more
than a barrel of fire.[105]

Pantagruel, seeing Loup Garou delayed by tugging at the
mace which was stuck inside the boulder underground, ran
at him, intending to slash his head clean off, but his mast
unfortunately brushed against the shaft of Loup Garou's mace,
which (as we have already told) was enchanted. By which means
the mast broke off three fingers' breadth from his grip. Pantagruel was as stunned as a bell-founder and cried out, 'Ha!
Panurge! Where are you?' On hearing which, Panurge remarked

105. '42: ... struck more than *nine hundred and six barrels* of fire ...

to the king and the giants: 'By God, if someone doesn't separate them they'll do each other some harm.'

But the giants were as merry as though they were at a wedding. Then Carpalim wanted to get up and help his master, but one of the giants said to him:

'By Golfarin, the nephew of Mahoun, if you budge an inch I'll stuff you up the bottom of my breeches like a suppository! I am constipated in fact and can only *cagar* by grinding my teeth.'

Then Pantagruel, thus stripped of his weapon, grasped the stump of his mast again, raining blows on to the giant this way and that, but he did him no more harm than you would do if you were to tweak a blacksmith's anvil. Meanwhile Loup Garou went on tugging his mace out of the ground, and having done so, readied it to strike Pantagruel, who was suddenly all movement, dodging every one of his blows until, realizing that, this time, Loup Garou was really threatening him (saying, 'You wretch! I'm now about to chop you up into chunks like forcemeat for pies; never more will you cause poor folk to thirst!') gave him such a kick in the guts that he knocked him on to his back with his feet in the air and then dragged him further than an arrow flies, scraping his bum along the ground. Loup Garou, spurting blood from his gullet, kept crying 'Mahoun! Mahoun! Mahoun!'

At that cry all the giants rose to come to his aid. But Panurge said to them: 'Gentlemen: if you believe me, don't go there. Our Master is mad, lashing out right and left regardless. He'd give you a nasty time.' But the giants, noting that Pantagruel was without his stave, took no heed. As they approached, Pantagruel grabbed Loup Garou by both his feet, and, [as though it were a pike,] raised his body aloft, armed as it was with anvils, and battered the giants with it – their armour was of sandstone – and knocked them down like a mason making chippings, so that none could pause before him without being battered to the ground. And at the splintering of their stone armour there was produced a din so horrible that it reminded me of the time when the great Butter-tower of Saint-Etienne-de-Bourges melted in the sun.

While that was going on, Panurge, Carpalim and Eusthenes were slitting the throats of those who had been knocked to the ground. And you can count on this: not a single one escaped; Pantagruel, if you had seen him, was like a mower who with his scythe (*i.e.* Loup Garou) was slicing through the meadow-grass (*i.e.* the giants).

But in that fencing-match Loup Garou lost his head: that was when Pantagruel was felling one by the name of Moricault,[106] who, from top to toe, was clad in armour of fully dressed grey-freestone, a sliver of which sliced Epistemon's neck right off. Otherwise the giants were lightly armed, some in tufa and others in slate.

In the end, seeing that all of them were dead, Pantagruel lobbed the body of Loup Garou as far as he could into the town, where it landed in the main square on its belly like a frog; and as it fell it struck and killed one scorched tom-cat, one drenched tabby-cat and one goose bearing a bridle.

[A note on Pantagruel's prayer. Rabelais goes so far with Luther but not all the way. Rabelais is no pacifist: it is a prince's duty, under God, to protect his subjects, but it is not right to start wars nor to fight battles in order to spread the Christian faith or even to defend it. Faith is God's own domain. God does indeed want Christians to be his coadjutors *elsewhere, but he never needs help from men's armies and battles where the faith is concerned: the help he demands in that domain consists in the confessing of Catholic truth and the ministry of his word. (Rabelais later changed 'ministry of your word' to 'service of your word'. Ministère may have sounded too Calvinistic, and no love was lost between Rabelais and Calvin.) The prayer is an example of an older style of biblical theology soon to be replaced by a humanist reading of the Greek New Testament, often in conjunction with Plato and the Greeks, but its central doctrine remains valid throughout the works of Rabelais, though the vocabulary is later refined. In the Latin Vulgate text of II Corinthians 3:9 Saint Paul states that 'We are God's "adjutores"' (his helpers). The Greek*

106. Immediately after the first edition Rabelais changed the name of the giant Moricault to Rifflandouille (Maulchiddling), a name borrowed from the mystery-plays and which he will use much later in the *Fourth Book*.

*original makes human beings God's 'co-operators', a term which
Rabelais came to prefer. What one single angel of God can do unaided
by men was shown by the slaughter of the entire host of Sennacherib
(II Kings 19:35, Isaiah 37:36, II Maccabees 15:22, and I Maccabees
7:41). That angel and his power is traditionally associated with a text
from Matthew 26 and its gloss: Jesus told Peter: 'Put up your sword.
Thinkest thou that I cannot now pray to my Father, and he shall
presently give me more than twelve legions of angels?' Lefèvre
d'Etaples, the theologian intimate with Marguerite de Navarre, wrote
on Matthew 26 words which draw upon the same urgent commonplaces as Rabelais:*

*Christ rebukes Peter because He did not need human help. For had He
needed help He could have asked the Father, and He would have sustained
Him with more than twelve legions of angels (that is, one legion of angels
for each of the apostles, one of whom was a traitor), troops more powerful
than all mankind put together. For we read in Isaiah [37: 36] that one single
angel 'went forth and smote in the camp of the Assyrians an hundred and
fourscore and five thousand', so what could twelve legions of angels have
done?*

*That one angel was more powerful than the whole army of Sennach-
erib. It is on the eventual authority of Dionysius the Areopagite that
Rabelais expands those 'twelve legions' into 'a thousand thousands of
hundreds of millions of legions of angels'. Those 'twelve legions' show
God as mighty: Pantagruel shows God to be almighty in the traditional
way, by juxtaposing and multiplying the greatest available numbers.
Again faith is conceived as evangelicals conceived it, as trust: trust in
God and his promises. The word 'Catholic' was never restricted by
such as Rabelais to mean Roman Catholic: evangelicals and reformers
of all kinds naturally retain the word in the creeds. The doctrine that
it is necessary to suffer for the faith but not to fight for it is that of
Luther, though not of him alone.*

*As Melanchthon insisted, Natural Law retained for men the right
to fight to defend their families ('family' being interpreted very widely
to include one's country). Erasmus held that the only vow Christians should ever make to God is a vow to spread the true and
living faith. Pantagruel does indeed make the one and only vow*

conceded to mankind by Erasmus in his treatise The Method of Praying to God.

*The phrase 'hoc fac, et vinces' ('This do, and thou shalt conquer')
is adapted from the Vulgate text of Luke 10:24: 'hoc fac, et vives'
('This do, and thou shalt live').*

*Luther held that the phrase in its context is ironical and so means
the contrary of its literal meaning: for Pantagruel that is not so.*

*Rabelais is deeply influenced by Luther, but he does not follow him
in everything.]*

How Epistemon, who had his head sliced off, was cleverly healed by Panurge; also news about devils and the damned

CHAPTER 20

[Becomes (with noddle *and* cut *confused in a Spoonerism): . . . who
had his coddle nut off . . . Chapter 30.*

*Medieval tales recount several resurrections. Descents into Hell are
common in popular religious stories. The reversal of roles in this list
of denizens of the Underworld forms the essence of the fun. Names
were added at various times, but here they are not individually dated:
all additions follow the '42 text.*

*Rabelais quietly excised the allusions to ancient French heroes,
almost certainly to meet royal susceptibilities.*

*Jean Le Maire de Belges would have subordinated popes to church
councils.*

Caillette and Triboullet were real Court fools.]

Having fully accomplished this rout of the giants, Pantagruel
withdrew to where the flagons were kept and summoned
Panurge and the others, who appeared before him safe and
sound, except Eusthenes (whose face had been somewhat
clawed about by one of the giants as he was slitting his
throat) and Epistemon, who failed to appear. Pantagruel was
so grieved at this that he felt like killing himself, but Panurge
said to him: 'Indeed my Lord, just wait a little, and we will go

and seek him amongst the dead and discover the truth about it all.'

Then, as they were searching, they found him stone dead, with his head all bloody and cradled in his arms. At which Eusthenes exclaimed: 'Ah! foul Death, you have taken from us the most perfect of men!'

At those words Pantagruel arose, with great grief such as was never before seen in this world [and said to Panurge:

'That augury of yours made from the pole and two glasses was far too misleading.]

But Panurge said:

'Shed no tears, lads. He's still warm. I shall restore him for you as sound as he ever was.'

So saying, he took hold of the head and held it warm against his codpiece to stop air from getting in. Eusthenes and Carpalim carried the body to the spot where they had feasted, not in the hope that he could ever be healed but so that Pantagruel should see it. Nevertheless Panurge comforted them all, saying, 'If I do not heal him may I lose my own head' – which is a lunatic's wager! 'Stop those tears and come and help me.'

Whereupon he carefully cleaned first the neck and next the head in some good white wine, sprinkled some powdered aloes over them – he always carried some in one of his pokes – and smeared some ointment or other over them and adjusted them meticulously together, vein to vein, sinew to sinew, vertebra to vertebra (so as not to make him a 'wry-neck', for he had a mortal hatred of hypocrites). He then used a needle to put in two of three stitches to prevent the head from toppling off again and applied all round it a little of an unguent which he termed a resuscitative.[107]

And suddenly Epistemon began to breathe, then to open his eyes, then to yawn, and then to sneeze; and then he let off a loud, homely fart, at which Panurge said, 'Now he is certainly healed.' He then offered him a glass of some dreadfully rough white wine to drink with some sugared toast.

107. '42: . . . powdered *diashit* – he always . . . put in *fifteen* or *sixteen* stitches *round it* to prevent . . .

And so in that wise was Epistemon skilfully healed (except that his voice was hoarse for over three weeks, and he suffered from a dry cough, which nothing but ample drinking could cure).

And then he began to talk.

He said he had seen devils, chatted familiarly with Lucifer and had a jolly time in Hell and in the Elysian Fields. Before them all, he maintained that the devils made good companions.

Where the damned were concerned, he said he bitterly regretted that Panurge had summoned him back to life so soon, 'For,' he said, 'looking at them afforded me a singularly pleasurable pastime.'

'How was that?' asked Pantagruel.

'They're not treated as badly as you might expect,' said Epistemon: it's their situations which are altered in an outlandish fashion: for I saw:

Alexander the Great eking out a wretched living by
  patching up old breeches.
Xerxes was a mustard vendor;
[Romulus, a salt-merchant;
Numa made nails;
Tarquin was a tar quean;
Piso, a peasant;
Sylla, a river-man;
Cyrus, a cow-man;
Themistocles, a glass-peddler;
Epaminondas, a maker of looking-glasses;
Brutus and Cassius, land-surveyors;
Demosthenes, a vigneron;
Cicero, a fire-raiser;
Fabius, a stringer of rosary-beads;
Artaxerxes, a rope-maker;
Aeneas, a miller;
Achilles, a dyer;
Agamemnon, a licker-out of casseroles;
Ulysses, a scyther;
Nestor, a rag-and-bone man;]

Darius, a cleaner of latrines;
[Ancus Martius, a bit of a caulker;
Camillus, a maker of galoshes;
Marcellus, a shucker of beans:
Drusus, an almond-crusher;]
Scipio Africanus, a peddler of wine-lees in a wooden
    clog.
[Hasdrubal, a fooler-about with lanterns;
Hannibal, an egg-man;]
Priam traded in rags and tatters.
Lancelot of the Lake ran a knacker's-yard.

'All the Knights of the Round Table were poor drudges, straining at the oar to cross the Cocytus, Phlegethon, Styx, Acheron and Lethe whenever Sir Devils want to enjoy a boat-trip; they are rather like the boat-women of Lyons and [the gondoliers of] Venice, save that they get but a tap on the nose for every crossing and, towards night-fall, a hunk of stale bread.

'The Douzepers[108] of France are there, doing nothing at all as far as I could see, but they earn their keep by enduring thwacks, tweaks, bonks on the nose, and great blows from fists on their teeth.

[Trajan was a catcher of frogs;
Antoninus, a lackey;
Commodus, an ornamentalist in jet;
Pertinax, a sheller of walnuts;
Lucullus, a meat-griller;
Justinian, a seller of knick-knacks,
Hector, a stir-sauce;
Paris, a tattered beggar;
Achilles, a baler-up of hay;
Cambyses, a mule-driver;
Artaxerxes, a skimmer of scum from off cooking-pots;]

108. All reference to the Douzepers (the twelve legendary Peers of France) is
    omitted after the original edition, presumably as offensive to touchy royal
    ears.

'Nero was a fiddler; Fierabras was his footman; but he plagued him in a thousand ways, serving him up coarse bread and spoilt wine while he himself ate and drank the best there are.

Jason and Pompey were tarrers of ships;[109]
Valentin and Orson were attendants in the hot-baths of
    Hell, and scraped clean the face-masks of the women;
Giglan and Gawain were wretched swineherds;
Geoffroy Long-tooth was a match-seller;
Godefroy de Billon, an engraver on wood;
[Jason, a toller of bells;]
Don Pedro of Castille, a pardoner;
Morgan, a brewer of ale;
Huon de Bordeaux, a cooper;
Julius Caesar, a scullion;[110]
Antiochus, a chimney-sweep;
Romulus, a botcher-up of old boots;
Octavian, a paper-scraper;
Charlemagne was a stable-lad;[111]
Pope Julius, a peddler of small pies [, but he no longer
    wore his big, buggerly beard];
Jean de Paris dubbined boots;
Arthur of Britain cleaned grease off headgear;
Perceforest carried a hod: I am not sure whether he was a
    vignerons' hodman;[112]
[Pope Boniface VIII was a skimmer of kitchen-pots;]
Nicholas (Pope) Tiers, sold tiers of paper;[113]
Pope Alexander was a rat-catcher;
Pope Sixtus, a greaser of syphilitic sores.'

'What!' said Pantagruel.'Are there syphilitics in that other world?'

109. '42: . . . best there are. *Julius Caesar* and Pompey . . .
110. '42: . . . a cooper; *Pyrrhus*, a scullion . . .
111. '42: . . . *Nerva* was a stable lad . . . (This avoids mocking a royal French
    hero.)
112. '42 omits: I am not sure whether he was a vignerons' hodman.
113. A pun: *Pape Tiers* (the third pope), papetier (a paper-monger).

'Indeed there are,' said Epistemon. 'I never saw so many. Over a hundred million. For you should believe that those who don't catch the pox in this world will do so in the next.'

'Golly,' said Panurge, 'That lets me off then! I've been in it as deep as the hole of Gibraltar [filling up the bungs of Hercules]; and I've shaken down some of the ripest!'

'Ogier of Denmark furbished ladies' armour;
King Pépin was a tiler;[114]
Galien the Restorer, a mole-catcher;
'The Four Sons of Aymon, drawers of teeth;
[Pope Calixtus barbered women's naughty cracks;
Pope Urban was a sponger;]
Melusine, a kitchen-maid;
Matabrune, a washer-woman and bleacher;
Cleopatra, a peddleress of onions;
Helen, an agent for chambermaids;
Semiramis, a comber of lice out of the hair of vagrants;
Dido sold mushrooms;
Penthesilea was a seller of watercress;
[Lucretia, a hospital sister;
Hortensia, a spinster,
Livia, a rakeress of verdigris.]

'In such ways, those who had been great lords in this world earned a poor, wretched, nasty living there below. Philosophers, on the contrary, and those who had been indigent in this world had their turn at being fat lords in that world beyond.

'I saw Diogenes, in a large purple robe, a sceptre [in his right hand], parading magnificently about like a prelate and driving Alexander the Great to distraction for having failed properly to patch his breeches; he paid him for it with great thwacks from his stick.

['I saw Epictetus, fashionably dressed in the French style, giggling beneath a bower with a bevy of young ladies, drinking,

114. '42: ... King *Tigranes* was a tiler ... (Again the change avoids mocking a king of France.)

dancing and offering everyone a fine old time. Beside him lay a
heap of gold coins – *écus au Soleil* – and these lines appeared
above the trellis as his device:

> To dance, to prance around, to sport,
> Wine red and white to swig all day:
> Doing nothing since our time is short
> But count my *écus au Soleil*.

'When he saw me he courteously invited me to join him in a
drink, which I willingly did. And we swilled it theologically
down. Meanwhile up came Cyrus to beg in the name of Mercury for a penny to buy an onion or two for his supper. "Nay,"
said Epictetus, "nay! I never give pennies. Take this gold crown-
piece, you good-for-nothing, and try to be a decent fellow."
Cyrus was delighted to stumble across such booty, but the other
beggarly monarchs down there, Alexander, Darius and that lot,
stole it from him during the night.]

'I saw Pathelin, [the bursar of Rhadamanthus,] who was
haggling over some tiny pasties peddled by Pope Julius; he
asked him:

' "How much a dozen?"

' "Three halfpence," said the pope.

' "What! Three whacks, rather! Hand them over, you lowest
of the low, and go and get some more."

'The poor old pope went off snivelling, and when he appeared
before the Master Pieman he told him they had taken away his
pasties. The Pieman gave him such a hiding that his skin would
have been no use for making bagpipes.

'I saw Maître Jean Le Maire playing at being pope,
making all those wretched kings and popes from this world
kiss his feet; he was showing off, giving them his blessing and
saying:

' "Come and buy your pardons, you rogues, come and buy.
They're going cheap. I grant you absolution from all your
pins; and by my dispensation you need never be other than
worthless."

'And he summoned Caillette and Triboulet and said,

' "Monsignori my cardinals, dispatch them their Bulls: and whack 'em with a stake across the kidneys!"

'Which straightway was done.

'I saw Maître François Villon, who was asking Xerxes:

' "How much for a pennyworth of mustard?"

' "One penny," said Xerxes.

'To which Villon retorted:

' "Die of the quartan fever, you rogue! Five pennyworth of it is at most worth a farthing. You're overpricing your food-stuffs!"

'Then he piddled in his bucket, as mustard-hawkers do in Paris.

['I saw the Franc-archer de Bagnolet: he was an inquisitor into heretics. He came across Perceforest pissing against a wall on which was a painting of Saint Anthony's fire. He pronounced him a heretic and would have had him burnt alive had it not been for Morgante, who, as a welcoming gift plus other petty fees, gave him nine barrels of beer.]'

'Well now,' said Pantagruel, 'keep those fine yarns for another time; only do tell us what they do with usurers.'

'I saw them,' said Epistemon, 'all engaged in looking in the gutters for rusty pins and old nails just as you can see the penniless doing in our world. Yet a hundredweight of such ironmongery is not worth a hunk of bread. And there is not much demand for it. Hence those wretched lack-alls may go for three weeks or more without eating a slice of bread or even a crumb, toiling away day and night and waiting for the coming fair. Yet so accursed are they and dehumanized that they remember nothing about that toil and misery provided that they can earn a wretched penny by the end of each year.'

'Now,' said Pantagruel, 'let's have a spot of good cheer! Drink, I beg you, for the drinking is fine [all this month].'

So they brought forth loads of flagons and enjoyed good cheer out of the victuals in the camp; but that wretched King Anarch could not be merry. So Panurge said:

'What trade shall we apprentice this kingly Sire to, so that he may already be a master of his art when he passes over and goes to all the devils?'

'That is truly a very good idea of yours,' said Pantagruel. 'Do what you like with him. I give him to you.'

'I am most grateful,' said Panurge. 'That present is not to be refused; and coming from you I love it.'

How Pantagruel entered into the city of the Amaurots; and how Panurge married off King Anarch and made him a crier of green sauce

CHAPTER 21

[Becomes Chapter 30.

Rabelais was amused by the New Testament practice of counting only the adult males of a multitude, simply adding 'besides women and little children'. He uses the device several times.

The jest on 'perverse' exploits the heraldic term for heraldic blue, pers or perse, *and for heraldic green, ver.*

The fate of the enemy captains in Gargantua *will be more in conformity to humanist ideals: they are made to work the printing presses.]*

After that prodigious victory Pantagruel despatched Carpalim to the city of the Amaurots to declare and proclaim how King Anarch had been taken and all their foes vanquished.

Upon hearing such tidings all the townsfolk poured out before him in good order. With holy joy and [great] triumphal pomp they escorted him into their city, throughout which superb bonfires were lit and round tables set up in the streets superbly furnished with an abundance of food and drink. It was a revival of the Age of Saturn, so great was the good cheer.

But once the whole Senate was assembled, Pantagruel said:

'Gentlemen: one must strike while the iron is hot. Before relaxing any further I want us to go on and take by assault the entire kingdom of the Dipsodes. Therefore let all who would accompany me be ready tomorrow after drinks, for I shall then set off on the march. Not that I need more men to help me conquer it, for I virtually hold it already, but I can see that this city is so packed with inhabitants that they have no room to turn round in the streets. I shall therefore lead them into Dipsodia as colonists and give them the whole country which is (as many of you know who have already been there) more beautiful, salubrious, fertile and pleasant then any other in the world. Each one of you who would like to come should, as I said, be ready.'

That decree and proclamation spread throughout the city and the next morning, in the square in front of the Palais, there gathered a multitude to the number of eighteen hundred and fifty[-six] thousand [and eleven], besides women and little children. And thus they began to march straight for Dipsodia, in such good order that they were like unto the Children of Israel when they came out of Egypt to cross the Red Sea. But before following up that enterprise, I should tell you how Panurge treated his prisoner, King Anarch.

He recalled to mind what Epistemon had told about how the monarchs and rich folk of this world are treated in the Elysian Fields and how they earned their living by doing jobs dirty and vile. And so one day he decked him out in a pretty little linen doublet, laciniated like the pennant of an Albanian estradiot, with matelots' breeches but with no shoes, 'for,' he said, 'shoes were bad for his sight'.

He added a little *pers* bonnet with one big capon's plume – no, I'm wrong there: I believe there were two – and a lovely belt both *pers* and *ver*, saying that such a livery became him as he was so *per-ver-se*. And he paraded him thus arrayed before Pantagruel and said:

'Do you know who this fellow is?'

'Indeed I do not,' said Pantagruel.

'It is my Lord the thrice-baked king! I intend to make a decent fellow of him. These devilish kings over here are like calves: they know nothing and are good at nothing except maltreating their wretched subjects and bringing havoc to everyone through wars fought for their iniquitous and loathsome pleasure. I want to settle him in a trade, making him a crier of green-sauce.

'So begin your cry: "Anyone want green-sauce?"'

And the poor devil did so.

But Panurge said, 'Too low!' and he tweaked him by the ear, saying, 'Sing it higher: *Do re mi fa sol*. That's right, you devil. You have a good throat. You've never been so happy at not being king!'

And Pantagruel took pleasure in it all; for I venture to say that he was the nicest man there ever was between here and the end of my stick.[115] And thus did Anarch become a good crier of green-sauce. Two days later Panurge married him off to an old strumpet from Lantern-land. He himself threw a wedding-party for them with lovely heads of mutton, lovely rashers of bacon dressed with mustard, lovely spit-roasted pork with garlic (of which he sent five pannier-loads to Pantagruel, who found them all so tasty that he ate the lot) and to drink, some very lovely perry and some very lovely sorb-apple cider.

And to get them dancing he hired a blind fiddler, who gave them the tune on his hurdy-gurdy.

Once they had dined, Panurge took the couple to the palace and showed them off to Pantagruel; then, pointing to the bride, he said to him:

'There's no risk of her going pop with a fart!'

'And why not?' said Pantagruel.

'Because she's well nicked,' said Panurge.

'And what on earth does that saying mean?' said Pantagruel.

'Haven't you noticed,' said Panurge, 'that chestnuts roasting in the fire pop like mad if they're whole? To stop them from popping you give them a nick. Well, this [newly wed] bride has been well nicked down below. So she'll never go pop.'

Pantagruel set them up in a little lodge close to the lower road and gave them a stone mortar in which to pestle up their sauce. And in such wise they established their modest household, and he became as courteous a crier of green-sauce as ever was seen in all Utopia.

But I have since been told that his wife pounds him like plaster, and the poor chump is such a ninny that he never dares defend himself.

115. '42: . . . he was the nicest *little chap* there ever was . . .

How Pantagruel covered an entire army with his tongue; and what the author saw within his mouth

CHAPTER 22

[Becomes Chapter 32.

The story is inspired by Lucian's True History *as well as by travellers' accounts of new worlds.*

Giants in most stories, and not only in Rabelais, vary immensely in size from tale to tale. The Almyrodes are the 'Salty ones'.

In the peasant's speech 'Sire' is later replaced by 'Cyre', since 'Sire' was widely thought to derive from the Greek kurios, *not, as it does, from the Latin* senior. *Spelled* Cyre it *could carry flattering echoes of Cyrus the Great – 'Cyre' in French.]*

And so, as Pantagruel and his entire band marched into the land of the Dipsodes, all the people [were happy and immediately] surrendered to him; of their own free-will they brought him the keys to every town he went to – save for the Almyrodes, who wished to hold out against him and who made answer to his heralds that they would never surrender except after good assurances.

'What?' said Pantagruel, 'are they asking for better ones than hand on jug and glass in hand! Come on, then: go and sack them for me.'

And so, as men determined to take them by assault, they all fell in, in good order. But marching en route through open country they were surprised by a downpour of rain, at which they started to shiver and huddle up together. When Pantagruel saw it he told them through their captains that it really was nothing, and that he could tell from seeing well above the clouds that there would be only a little shower: they should anyway get back into their ranks as he wanted to cover them. So they fell in again in good and close order, and Pantagruel poked out his tongue – only half-way – covering his men as a hen does her chicks. Meanwhile I who am telling you these tales so-true was hiding under a leaf of burdock which was

certainly no less wide than the arch of the bridge at Mantrible;
but when I saw them so well protected I went over to them to
find shelter. But I could not do so: there were so many of them,
and, as the saying goes, 'at the end of the roll there is no more
cloth'. I therefore clambered up as well as I could and journeyed
for a good two leagues over his tongue until I entered his mouth.

But, ye gods and goddesses, what saw I there! If I lie, may
Jupiter daze me with his three-forked lightning. There I wandered about as one does in Sancta Sofia in Constantinople, and
I saw huge rock-formations like the mountains of Dent-mark –
they were, I think, his teeth – and wide meadows, great forests,
and cities strong and spacious, no less big than Lyons or
Poitiers.

The first person I met there was a stout fellow planting
cabbages. Quite taken aback, I asked him,

'What are you doing here, my friend?'

'Planting cabbages,' he said.

'Why?' I said, 'and wherefore?'

'Well Monsieur,' he said, '[we can't all have bollocks
weighing a ton:] we can't all be rich. I'm earning me living; I
take 'em to market in the city back yonder.'

'Jesus!' I said, 'so this is a new world!'

'Well,' he said, 'it's certainly not new. They do say, mind,
that there's some new-found earth outside, with a sun and a
moon, and full of all sorts of fine things; but this one here's
older.'

'Indeed!' I said, 'but tell me, my friend, what is the name of
the town where you take your cabbages to sell?'

'Aspharagos,' he said. 'They're Christians. Good folk. They'll
give you good cheer.'

In short, I decided to go there. On the way I met a fellow
who was setting nets to catch pigeons; so I asked him,

'My friend, where do these pigeons here come from?'

'They come from that other world, Cyre,' he said.

I assumed then that when Pantagruel yawned great flocks of
pigeons flew into his throat, taking it for a dove-cote.

After that I went into the town, which I found very beautiful,
well fortified and of a fine aspect; but at the entrance the

gate-keepers demanded my Bill of Good Health. I was astonished and asked them,

'Is there a threat of the plague, gentlemen?'

'Ah, my Lord,' they said, 'people near here are dying so fast
that the death-carts go about the streets.'

'Jesus!'[116] I said, 'where?'

They told me it was in Larynx and Pharynx (which are two
towns as big as Rouen or Nantes, rich and full of merchandise)
and that for some time now the plague was being caused by a
stinking, noxious exhalation rising up from the depths: in the
last week some twenty-two hundred [and sixty] thousand
persons [plus sixteen] had died from it.

I then reflected and calculated, and worked out that it was a
stinking breath which had come out of Pantagruel's stomach
after he had eaten (as we told you above) so much garlic sauce.

Leaving there, I passed between cliffs (which were Pantagruel's teeth) and climbed up one, where I found some of the
most beautiful places in the world: beautiful wide tennis-courts,
beautiful colonnades, beautiful meadows, plenty of vines and
countless summer-houses in the Italian style scattered over fields
full of delights. I stayed there a good four months, and have
never had better cheer.

Then I descended by the back teeth to reach the lips, but on
my way I was robbed by brigands in a great forest situated
towards the ears. Further down I came across a hamlet – I
forget its name – where I found even better cheer and earned a
little money to live on. And do you know how? By sleeping!
For they hire journey-men to sleep for them: they earn five or six
pence a day, though good snorers earn seven pence-halfpenny.

I told the senators how I had been robbed in that valley and
they said it was a fact that the Transdental folk were evil-livers
and born bandits. It was thus I learnt that, just as we have
Cisalpine and Transalpine lands, they have Cisdental and
Transdental ones; but it is far better in the Cisdental lands, and
the air is better too.

I then began to think how true is the saying, 'One half of the

116. '42: . . . 'True God!' I said . . .

world has no idea how the other half lives,' for nobody has ever written about those lands over yonder in which there are more than twenty-five inhabited kingdoms, not to mention deserts and a wide arm of sea. But I have compiled a thick book about them entitled *A History of the Gorgeous* – I have named them thus because they dwell in the *gorge* of Pantagruel my master.

In the end I wanted to get back and, passing through his beard, I leapt on to his shoulder, slid to the ground, tumbling down in front of him.

When he noticed me he asked me:

'Where have you come from, Alcofrybas?'

And I replied,

'From your gorge, my Lord.'

'And how long have you been in there?' he asked.

'Since you set out against the Almyrodes,' I said.

'That was more than six months ago!' he said. 'How did you manage? What did you eat? What did you drink?'

'My Lord,' I replied, 'the same as you. I exacted a toll on the most delicate morsels that passed through your lips.'

'Indeed,' he said, 'but where did you shit?'

'In your gorge, my Lord,' I said.

'Ha! ha!' he said. 'A noble comrade you are! With the help of God we have conquered the entire land of the Dipsodes: to you I grant the Châtelainie of Salmagundi.'

'Many thanks, my Lord,' I said. ['You treat me better than I deserve.']

How Pantagruel was taken ill, and the method by which he was cured

CHAPTER 23

[Becomes Chapter 33.

A comic explanation of the origin of hot springs – 'hot-piss' is a gonorrhoeal flux – with a dose of medical humour.]

Shortly afterwards our good giant Pantagruel was taken ill, seized with such stomach pains that he could neither eat not drink; and since a misfortune never comes alone he developed a hot-piss which tormented him more than you might think; but his doctors effectively treated him with a mass of [lenitive and] diuretic drugs, making him piss out his malady.

And his urine was so hot that, from that day to this, it has never yet grown cold: you can still take some of it in divers places in France as it chanced to flow: we call them spas, as at Cauterets, Limoux, Dax, Balaruc, Néris, Bourbon-Lancy and elsewhere; and some in Italy, at Monte Grotto, Abano, San Pietro di Padova, Santa Elena, Casa Nova, Santo Bartolemeo and in the county of Bologna at La Porretta and at hundreds of other places.

I am greatly astonished by a pile of lunatic philosophers and physicians who waste their time arguing about where the heat of the said waters comes from: whether it is from borax, sulphur, alum or saltpetre in the sources; for they are merely raving and would be better employed scratching their bums with a hundred-headed thistle than wasting their time like that, disputing over things whose origin they know nothing about. For the solution is easy and there is no need for further inquiries: the aforesaid baths are hot since they spring from a hot-piss of our good giant Pantagruel.

Now to tell you how he was cured of his principal malady, I will pass over how he took for a gentle laxative four hundred-weight of scammoniate from Colophon, six score and eighteen wagonloads of cassia and eleven thousand nine hundred pounds of rhubarb, apart from other ingredients.

Now you must understand that, on the advice of the physicians, it was decreed that what was giving him the stomach-ache should be removed. In fact there were made seventeen copper spheres (each bigger than the one atop Virgil's Needle in Rome) so fashioned that they could be opened in the middle and closed by a spring.

Into one there entered a man of his, bearing a lantern and a flaming torch. And thus did Pantagruel swallow it like a little pill.

Into five others there entered some brawny fellows, each with a pick-axe over his shoulder.[117]

Into three others there entered three peasants, each with a shovel over his shoulder.

Into seven others went seven hodmen, each with a pannier slung from his neck.

And all were swallowed thus, like pills.

Once down in the stomach they all released their springs and sallied forth from their quarters. First came the man who bore the lantern; and thus they searched for the corrupt humours over half a league.[118]

Finally they discovered a small mountain of ordure. The pioneers hacked away at it with their pick-axes to dislodge it, and the others shovelled it into their panniers and, once everything was cleared up, each man retired into his sphere.

At which Pantagruel forced himself to spew and easily brought them up: and they were no more trouble in his throat than a fart is in yours; and they all came joyfully out of those pills. I recalled the time when the Greeks came out of the Trojan horse – and by such a method was Pantagruel cured and restored to his original health.

One of those brass pills you now have in Orleans atop the bell-tower of the Church of the Holy Cross.

*

117. '42: . . . each with a *spade* over his shoulder . . .
118. '42: . . . and thus they *all tumbled* over more than half a league *down into a horrid stinking abyss, worse than Memphitis or the Camarine Marshes or the putrid lake of the Sorbona described by Strabo. And were it not for the fact that they had taken an antidotary for the heart, stomach and 'wine-pot' – their name for your noddle – they would have been suffocated and snuffed out by those ghastly vapours. Oh what a perfume, what a vaporative with which to manure the nose-veils of our Gallic ladies of easy virtue! Thereafter, groping and flairing their way, they drew near to the faecal matter and the corrupt humours. Finally they* discovered . . .

[Becomes: The Conclusion to this Present Book, with the Author's apology. Chapter 34.]

You have now heard, gentlemen, a beginning of the Horrific History of my Lord and master Pantagruel. Here I will bring this first book to an end, since my head is troubling me a bit and I sense that the stops of my brain are somewhat befuddled by juice of September.

You will have the rest of this History at the Frankfurt Fair soon upon us. You will find there [how Panurge was wed, and cuckolded in the first month of his marriage;] how Pantagruel discovered the philosopher's stone, [how to find it] and how to use it; how he crossed the Caspian mountains, sailed upon the Atlantic Ocean, defeated the Cannibals and took the Perlas Islands; how he married the daughter of the King of India called Prester John; how he fought against the devils and burnt down five of Hell's chambers, [sacked the Great Black Chamber and cast Proserpine into the fire,] broke four of Lucifer's teeth and a horn in his rump; how he visited the regions of the moon to learn whether the moon is in truth not whole since women have three of its quarters in their heads; and hundreds of other merry little matters, all true: they are beautiful evangelical texts in French.[119]

Good evening, Gentlemen. Pardon me.[120] And think no more of my shortcomings than you do of your own.

Finis.

*

[Pantagruel *originally ended here.*

The expanded ending dates from 1534 and is a reaction against abortive attempts to censor Pantagruel *and to draw up articles of accusation against it and its author. Those hypocritical censors pretend*

119. '42: ... beautiful *matters*. Good evening ...
120. 'Pardon me' is in Italian.

to live like the austere Curii of ancient Rome yet lead lives which are
bacchanalian orgies. Rabelais cites a line from the Satires of Juvenal
(2, 5, 3): 'Et Curios simulant, sed bacchanalia vivunt' (They feign to
be Curii, yet live bacchanalia). He was guided by an Adage of Erasmus
(I, VI, XLV, 'In the manner of the Bacchantes'), where the line is
cited.

The accusation that the censors *'disguised themselves as masked*
revellers' is a serious one: the Sorbonne is being accused of having
acted as agents provocateurs, *causing men secretly to put up posters*
in 1532 while disguised as revellers. The accusation is repeated in the
Almanac for 1535 *and in Chapter 17 of* Gargantua.

'Sarrabites' were monks living irregularly: here and elsewhere Rabe-
lais makes them bovine *ones: 'Sarrabovines'.*

The devil's name in Greek, Diabolos, *means 'Calumniator'.]*

[Now, if you say to me, 'Maître, it would seem you were not
very wise to write us such idle tales and amusing twaddle,' I
reply that you are scarcely wiser to waste time reading them.
However, if as a merry pastime you read them, as I, to pass
time, wrote them, you and I are more forgivable than a heap of
sarrabovines, bigot-tails, slimy-snails, hypocrites, black-beetles,
lecherous shavelings, booted monks and other such sects who
disguised themselves as masked revellers to deceive the world.
For whilst making common folk believe that they have no
employment save meditation and worship, save fasting and
macerating their sensuality (merely, in truth, sustaining and
nourishing the meagre frailty of their human condition), they
enjoy on the contrary good cheer: God knows how much!

They feign to be Curii, yet live bacchanalia.

You can read that from the great illuminated capitals of their
red snouts and from their guts like crakow slippers, except
when they fumigate themselves with sulphur.

As regards their study, it is entirely taken up by the reading of Pantagrueline books, not so much to pass time merrily
but wickedly, so as to harm someone, namely by articulating,

arse-ticulating, wry-arse-ticulating, bumculating, bollockulat-
ing, diaboliculating, that is, calumniating.[121]

By doing so they resemble those village scavengers who, when
cherries or morellos are in season, poke about in the stools of
children and spread them out with sticks, looking for stones to
sell to the druggists to make up into oil of mahaleb. Flee them;
abhor them and loathe them as much as I do, and, by my faith,
you will find yourself the better for it. And if you desire to be
good Pantagruelists (that is, to live in peace, joy and health,
always enjoying good cheer) never trust folk who peer through
a hole.][122]

FINIS.[123]

121. The French words leading on from 'articulating' (drawing up articles of
     accusation) are, in order, *monorticulant* (mumbling), *torticulant* (a verb
     based on a deformation of a standard word for hypocrite, *torticol* (wry-
     necked), here changed to 'wry-arsed'), *culletant* (scratching one's bum or
     arsing about), *couilletant* (bollocking about), *diabliculant* (acting like the
     devil), and *callumniant* ('calumniating' or telling lies).
122. The 'folk who peer through a hole' are presumably delators or the censors
     themselves.
123. The definitive end in '42 reads:
                    The end of the Chronicles of Pantagruel,
                    King of the Dipsodes, restored to the
                    original, together with his deeds and
                    bold exploits compiled by the late
                    Maître ALCOFRIBAS, ABSTRACTER
                    of the Quintessence.

PANTAGRUELINE
PROGNOSTICATION
FOR 1533

Introduction to *Pantagrueline Prognostication for 1533*

This is a genuine almanac, in that all its astronomical and astrological data do indeed apply to the year 1533, are factually correct and fully confirmed by such impressive scientific almanacs as Stoeffler's in the early sixteenth century. Rabelais is allaying fears (perhaps royal fears) aroused by the appalling state of the heavens in the period 1533–6. With his scientific data Rabelais combines evangelical teachings and amused satire.

There are echoes of Lucian and direct borrowing from a Latin satire. From 1542 onwards Rabelais detached his *Prognostication* from a specific year and adapted his text so that it applied to any year (*Pour l'an perpetuel*).

The *Pantagrueline Prognostication* remained artistically close to *Pantagruel*, even after the publication of *Gargantua*. For example, identical names and metiers are found here and in the expanded account given by Epistemon of his descent into the Underworld in *Pantagruel*, Chapter 20; some identical titles also appear in, or are added to, this little work and to the Library of Saint-Victor (*Pantagruel*, Chapter 7). So too 'sarabovines' and other terms of reproach appear both here and in the addition to the end of *Pantagruel*.

The variants are given in the notes except for the four short chapters at the end, which are easily isolated. To read it as it first appeared in a real temporal and astrological context simply read the text and ignore the footnotes. The final version was so heavily expanded that the variants are many and intrusive.

The editions cited in the notes are as follows:

'33: no place or date (Lyons, François Juste); exists in two states, with slight variations of the text made during printing;

'35: [Lyons], François Juste;

'37: Lyons, François Juste;

'38: no place (Lyons, Denis de Harsy, but sometimes attributed to Denis Janot);

'42: Lyons, François Juste;

'53: no place.

The texts and variants translated are those of my edition of the *Pantagrueline prognostication pour l'an 1533 avec Les Almanachs pour les ans 1533, 1535 et 1541* in the Textes Littéraires Français (Geneva: Droz, 1974).

Pantagrueline Prognostication,

certain, true and infallible, for the year
one thousand five hundred and thirty-three,

newly composed for the profit and counsel
of natural blockheads and sluggards by
Master Alcofribas, Ruler of the Feast
of the said Pantagruel.

Of the Golden Number, nothing is said: no matter
what calculation I make I cannot find any at all
this year. Let us pass Beyond. Anyone who
has found one, may dump it on me; anyone who
has not, then let him look for it.[1]

Turn this leaf.

---

1.   In '42 the title reads: *Pantagrueline Prognostication, /certain, true and infallible, for the year perpetual,/newly composed for the profit and counsel of natural blockheads and sluggards/ by Master Alcofribas, Ruler of the Feast of the said Pantagruel./ Of the Golden Number, nothing is said: / no matter what calculation I make I cannot find any at all this year. Let us pass Beyond.*

   For the Golden Number see the note at the end of the *Almanac for 1535*.

Contents

To the Kindly Reader: Greetings and Peace in Jesus Christ

Having considered the infinite deceptions perpetrated by means of a mass of Prognostications from Louvain – made in the shadow of a glass of *vin* – I have here calculated one for you which is the truest and surest that has ever been seen, as experience will prove to you. For – given that the Royal Prophet said to God (in Psalm 5), 'Thou shalt destroy all them that speak falsehoods' – it is undeniably no light sin to tell lies knowingly as they do and moreover to deceive poor folk curious to learn things new (such as the French of all periods, as Caesar noted in his *Commentaries* and Jehan de Gravot in his *Gallic Mythologies*).[2]

We can still see that all over France where, day in day out, the first words addressed to those just arrived are, 'What's the news?' – 'Do you know anything new?' – 'Who's saying what?' – 'What's being bruited abroad?' – They are so keen that they often get angry with those who come from foreign parts without a budgetful of news, calling them calves and idiots. And therefore, since they are as prompt to ask for news as they are ready to believe what they are told, ought we not to place paid, trustworthy men at the entrances to the Kingdom employed exclusively in examining the news brought in to find out whether or not it be true?

Yes, certainly. And that is what my good Master Pantagruel has done throughout his lands of Utopia and Dipsody. It has worked so well and his lands have so prospered that people cannot consume all of the wine! Unless reinforcements of drinkers and jolly good wits come to help them, they will be obliged to tip their wines over the soil.

So since I want to satisfy the curiosity of all good companions, I have leafed through all the archives of the heavens, calculated all the quadratures of the moon, broached everything which

---

2. Jehan de Gravot is a spoof, but Caesar's judgement (*Gallic Wars*, 4, 5) was well known.

has ever been thought by all the astrophiles, hypernephalists, anemophylakoi, uranopetes and ombrophores, and discussed it all with Empedocles (who commends himself to your kind attention).[3]

I have then edited it all in a few chapters right down to the *World-without-end-Amen*, assuring you that I say no more than what I think, and think no more than what *is*: and that, in all truth, is what you are now about to read.

Anything said over and above that will be sifted this way and that through my coarse riddle and perhaps may happen or perhaps may not.[4]

I do warn you of one thing, however: if you fail to believe it all, you are doing me a bad turn for which you will be punished here or hereafter![5]

So now, my little lads, wipe your noses, adjust your glasses, and weigh well these words.

On the Governor and Lord of this Year

CHAPTER I

No matter what you are told by those idiotic astrologers of Louvain, Nuremberg, Tübingen and Lyons, you must never believe that there will ever be any other Governor of the entire world this year but God the Creator, who rules and directs all things through his holy Word, by whom all things consist in

3. *Astrophiles*: lovers of the stars; *hypernephalists*: those who are raised above the clouds; *anemophylakoi* cloud-watchers (a word forged, perhaps by Rabelais, from the Greek *anemos* (wind) and *phulaks* (watcher)), *uranopetes*: droppers-down from heaven; *ombrophores*: bringers of rain.

4. Reminiscence of a famous saying of Tiresias the ancient prophet, widely known through an adage of Erasmus (III, III, XXXV, 'A sign good or bad'), where Erasmus cites a satire of Horace (2, 39) which Rabelais echoes here too.

5. From '42: . . . will be *most grievously* punished! *Little towsings sauced with bovine straps will not be spared on your shoulders, and you will slurp in air as much as you like as though air were oysters; for, confidently, some folk will be very hot unless the baker drops off.* So now . . .

their nature, peculiarities and condition, and without whose preservation and control all things would in a moment be reduced to nothing, just as from nothing they were brought into being. For as Monsignor Saint Paul, that Trumpeter of the Gospel, says (Romans 11) all being, all goodness, all life and movement come from Him, exist in Him and are perfected through Him.[6]

And so the Governor of this year and all others will be (according to our veridical formulation) Almighty God; and neither Saturn, nor Mars, nor Jupiter, nor any other planet, nor, most definitely, any angels, saints, men or devils will have any virtue, efficacy, power or influence whatsoever, unless God of His good pleasure grant it to them. As Avicenna puts it, secondary causes have absolutely no influence or activity without the influence of the First Cause.[7]

On this year's Eclipse[8]

CHAPTER 2

This year there will be an eclipse of the Moon on the fourth day of August.[9] Saturn will be retrograde; Venus, direct; Mercury, variable. And a mass of other planets will not proceed as they used to.[10] As a result, crabs this year will walk sideways, ropemakers work backwards, stools end up on benches, and pillows be found at the foot of the bed;[11] many men's bollocks will

6. Romans 11:36.
7. '35, '37, '38 only: . . . First Cause. *And in this he is speaking the truth, even though elsewhere he raged beyond measure* . . .
     From '42: that sentence is replaced by: *The little chap's telling the truth, isn't he!*
8. From '42: On this year's *eclipses.*
9. From '35: . . . This year there will be *so many eclipses of the Sun and* the Moon *that I feel (not wrongly) that our purses will suffer from inanition and our senses from perturbation.* Saturn will be retrograde . . .
10. From '35: . . . they used to, *at your behest.* As a result . . .
11. From '35 omit: and pillows be found at the foot of the bed. Replaced from '37 by: . . . *the spits on the andirons, and the bonnets on the head-gear* . . .

hang down for lack of a game-bag;[12] the belly will go in front and the bum be the first to sit down; nobody will find the bean in their Twelfth Night cake; not one ace will turn up in a flush; the dice will never do what you want, however much you may flatter them;[13] and the beasts will talk in sundry places. Quarêmeprenant[14] will win his lawsuit; one half of the world will dress up in disguises to fool the other:[15] never was there seen such disorder within Nature. And this year will produce more than twenty-seven irregular verbs unless Priscian holds them on a tight rein.

If God does not help us we shall have a lot to put up with! On the other hand, if He is for us, nothing can harm us. As was said (in Romans 8) by that celestial Astrologer who was caught up to the heavens: 'If God is for us, who can be against us?'[16]

On this year's maladies

CHAPTER 3

This year, the blind will see very little; the deaf will be very hard of hearing; the dumb will hardly speak; the rich will keep themselves somewhat better than the poor, and the healthy than the sick. Many sheep, oxen, pigs, geese, pullets and ducks will die, whilst among monkeys and dromedaries the mortality will be less cruel. Old age will prove incurable this year because of the years gone by. Sufferers from pleurisy will have great

12. From '35: . . . game-bag; *fleas, for the most part, will be black, and bacon will avoid peas in Lent;* the belly . . .

13. From '35: . . . flatter them, *and the lucky throw you ask for often not come*; and the beasts . . .

14. Quarêmeprenant (Mardi Gras or approaching Shrovetide) always loses his annual battle against Lent.

15. From '35: . . . to fool the other *and will run through the streets like men mad and out of their senses*: never was there seen.

16. From '35: . . . 'If God is for us, who can be against us?' *Upon my faith, Nobody. For God is too good and too powerful. So here, in return, bless His holy name.* (For a joke *Nemo* (Nobody) was treated as though it were a proper name, introducing many surprising jests into the Latin Vulgate.) See Romans 8:31 for the quotation from Saint Paul.

pains in their sides;[17] those who suffer from a runny belly will frequently go to the jakes; this year catarrhs will flow down from the brain to the lower limbs;[18] and there will all but universally reign an illness most horrible, redoubtable, malignant, perverse, frightening and nasty which will so confuse everybody that they will never know what wood to use for their arrows, and will often madly write treatises in which they argue about the philosopher's stone;[19] Averroës (in Book Seven of the *Colliget*) calls it *Shortage of cash*.

And on account of last year's comet and the retrogradation of Saturn, a big beggar will die in the hospice all snotty and covered with scabs.[20]

Of Fruits and good things growing in the Soil

CHAPTER 4

I find that, by the calculations of Albumasar in his book *On the Great Conjunction* and elsewhere, that this will be a fine and fertile year, producing plenty of good things for those who have the means. But hops in Picardy will be somewhat fearful of the frost; oats will be very good for horses but there will be scarcely more bacon than there are pigs to produce it; it will be a good year for snails, because Pisces is in the ascendant. Mercury is bullying the parsley a bit, notwithstanding which it will remain reasonably priced.[21] Never shall you see more corn,

17. This phrase was omitted (by mistake?) from one of the editions of 1533.
18. From '42: . . . to the lower limbs; *eye-infections will be strongly inimical to sight; ears will be – more than is usual – short and rare in Gascony* and there will all but universally reign . . .
19. From '35: . . . the philosopher's stone *and Midas' ears. I quake with fear at the thought of it, for there will be an epidemic*; Averroës . . .
20. From '35: . . . scabs. *At whose death there will be horrid sedition between cats and rats, hounds and hares, falcons and ducks, monks and eggs* . . .
21. From '42: . . . reasonably priced. *Rue and sad herbs will thrive more than usual, together with choke-pears*. Never shall you see . . .
    My translation here is free: Rabelais plays untranslatably on *souci* (marigold, or care); *ancholie*, (columbine or melancholy); *poires d'angoisse*, (bitter, wild 'choke-pears' or pears of anguish).

wine, fruit and vegetables – provided that the wishes of the poor be heard.

On the state of various people

CHAPTER 5

The greatest madness in the world is to think that there are stars and comets for kings, popes and great noblemen rather than for the poor and the needy, as though fresh ones had been created since the times of the Flood or of Romulus or Pharamond, when kings were newly invented. Neither Triboullet nor Cailhette,[22] albeit folk of deep learning and high renown, would ever say that. And in Noah's Ark Triboullet might perhaps have had the same ancestors as the kings of Castille, and Cailhette be of the blood of Priam. But that entire blunder proceeds only from a lack of true Catholic faith. Holding therefore for certain that the heavenly bodies care as little about kings as beggars or about the rich as vagabonds, I will leave it to those other foolish prognosticators to talk of the kings and the rich whilst I shall talk of the condition of folk of low estate.

First, of folk under Saturn: such as those who lack money, the jealous, the mad, the evil-thinkers, the suspicious, the mole-catchers, usurers, mortgagers of other men's incomes, cobblers and the melancholy.[23]

This year they will not get everything they would really like; they will devote themselves to the invention on the Holy Cross,[24] will certainly not cast their bacon to the dogs, yet they will often scratch themselves where they ne'er did itch.

Under Jupiter: such as bigots, black-beetles, indulgence-mongers, Vatican copy-clerks, drawers-up of papal bulls,

---

22. Triboullet and Cailhette were real court fools.
23. '35, '37: ... cobblers, *tanners, debt-collectors, patchers-up of old boots* and the melancholy ... From '38: ... tanners, *tillers, bell-founders,* debt-collectors ...
24. The Holy Crosses they hope to 'invent' (that is, find) are on the obverse of gold crown-pieces.

apostolic dataries, pettifoggers, monks, hermits, hypocrites, purring pussies, paper-scribblers, parchment-scrabblers, notaries and fat-cats.[25]

They will live according to their incomes. And so many churchmen will die that there will be no one to confer benefices upon with the result that several clerics will hold two, three, four or even more.[26]

Under Mars: such as hangmen, murderers, soldiers, brigands, serjeants, bum-bailiffs, men of the Watch, garrison-men, teeth-pullers, bollock-cutters, cheap-jack physicians publicly shamed in the streets, blasphemers, tinder-match makers, fire-raisers, chimney-sweeps, train-bands, coal-merchants, alchemists and pinch-pennies.[27]

This year they will strike some fine blows, but some will be most likely to receive a few surprise blows themselves. One of the aforesaid will become a 'bishop-on-a-gibbet' – blessing with his feet such as pass by!

Under the Sun: such as trussers-up of hay, porters,[28] beggars

---

25. From '35: . . . such as bigots, black-beetles, *well-shod monks, indulgence-mongers, drawers-up of papal briefs, scribes,* copy-clerks, drawers-up of papal bulls, apostolic dataries, pettifoggers, monks, hermits, hypocrites, purring pussies, *pious dissemblers, velvet-pawed hypocrites, wrynecks,* paper-scribblers, parchment-scrabblers, notaries and fat-cats, *show-offs, sharp-eyes, registrars, image-mongers, medallion-pedlars,* rosary-sellers, ['42: *vendors of benefices,*] *registrars of precedence*: they will live according to their incomes . . .

    The term for fat-cat, *raminagrobis*, comes to the fore in the *Third Book* where it is challengingly used for the name of the good evangelical theologian.

26. From '35: . . . or even more. *Black-beetlery will jettison a great deal of its antique reputation, since the world has become a naughty boy and is no longer daft, as Abenragel states.* Under Mars . . .

27. '35, '37, '38: . . . bollock-cutters, *barber-surgeons,* cheap-jack physicians, *Avicennists, renegade Jews,* blasphemers . . .

    From '42: . . . bollock-cutters, *barber-surgeons, butchers, coiners,* cheap-jack physicians, *almanac-touters, renegade Jews,* blasphemers, tinder-match makers . . .

28. '35, '37, '38, '53: . . . such as *tipplers, conk-shiners, trussed-back gutses, brewers,* trussers-up of hay . . .

    '42, '53 . . . porters, *scythers, roofers, bearers, trussers-up, shepherds, cowmen, cowherds, swineherds, fowlers, gardeners, barn-men, farmers,* beggars from hospices, penny-labourers . . .

from hospices, penny-labourers, rag-and-bone men, de-greasers of bonnets, pannier-stuffers, ragged fellows, teeth-chatterers, snatch-bacons, and in general all those men who wear shirts knotted behind their backs.

They will be healthy and happy, with no inflammation of the gums when at a wedding-feast.

Under Venus: such as whores, bawds, debauchees, procurers, lechers, chambermaids in hostelries, women in professions terminating in -aids, such as barmaids, laundry-maids and second-hand-clothes-maids.[29]

They will be well esteemed this year; but, when the Sun enters Cancer and other signs of the Zodiac they should watch out for the pox, cankers, hot-pisses, pimples on the groin, and so on. Nuns will find it very difficult to conceive without the ministrations of a male, and hardly any virgins will lactate.[30]

Under Mercury: such as diddlers, cheats, deceivers, quack-chemists, thieves, millers, hangers-about, Masters of Arts, decretists, poetasters, jugglers, thimbleriggers, spell-binders, fiddlers, wafer-mongers, poets, scoriators of the Latin language and scourges of the sea.[31]

They will often pretend to be happier than they are, occasionally laughing when they have no desire to do so, and will be very liable to go bankrupt if they find less money in their purses than they need.

Under the Moon: such as colporters, lunatics, madmen, scatter-brains, hare-brains, harum-scarums, swindlers, messenger-boys, valets, glass-blowers, Italian mercenaries.[32]

29. From '35: . . . such as whores, bawds, *lechers, buggers, show-offs, sufferers from the malady of Naples, the scabby-arsed, the* debauchees . . . terminating in -<u>aids</u>, *such as linen-maids,* ['42: *soliciting-maids,*] barmaids . . .
30. From '35: . . . and *very few* virgins will produce milk *in their breasts* . . .
31. from '35: . . . decretists, *pack-bearers, trinket-pedlars,* poetasters, jugglers, thimbleriggers, spell-binders, fiddlers, wafer-mongers, poets, scoriators of the Latin language, *makers of rebuses, stationers, carters, scallywags,* and scourges of the sea . . .
32. From '35: . . . such as colporters, *huntsmen, stalkers, hawk-trainers, falconers, despatch-riders, salt-sellers,* lunatics . . . messenger-boys, *lackeys,* valets, glass-blowers, Italian mercenaries, *rivermen, matelots, stable-riders, gleaners* . . .

They will have hardly any respite this year. Nevertheless not so many Switzers will go to Santiago compared with 1524.[33]

A great crowd of pilgrims to Mont-Saint-Michel will come down from the mountains of Savoy and the Auvergne, but Sagittarius threatens them with blisters on their heels.

On the Condition of certain Countries

CHAPTER 6

The noble Kingdom of France will so prosper and excel in all things pleasant and delightful that, this year, foreign students will readily be drawn back there – little feasts, little parties and hundreds of frolics will take place during which each will enjoy himself. Never were there seen wines more plentiful and delicious, nor so many turnips about Limoges; so many chestnuts in Périgord and Dauphiné; so many olives in Languedoc,[34] so many fish in the sea; so many stars in the heavens; so much salt in Brouage; with an abundance of grain, vegetables, fruit, garden crops, butter and dairy produce.

No plague; no war; no foe; pooh to poverty; pooh to melancholy. And those old double-ducats, rose-nobles, angel-crowns and long-fleeced *Agnus-Dei*[35] will be back in circulation, together with an abundance of Byzantine seraphs and suncrowns. All the same, towards the height of summer there will be good reason to fear an attack of black fleas and of mosquitoes from La Devinière – for indeed, *Nothing is in all parts happy*[36] – but they will have to be restrained by collations after vespers.

Italy, Romagna, Naples and Sicily will remain where they

33. 1524 was, astrologically, an exceptionally frightening year. Many Swiss mercenaries had been won over to the early Reformation, especially that of Zwingli in Zurich.

34. From '42: . . . Languedoc; *so much sand at Olonne*, so many fish . . .

35. From '35: . . . angel-crowns, *seraphs, royals,* and long-fleeced *Agnus-Dei* . . .

36. A Quotation from Horace, *Odes*, 2, 16, 27, which appears in the *Adages* of Erasmus, III, I, LXXXVII.

were last year. Towards the end of Lent they will dream deep
dreams, and will occasionally go mad at the noon of the day.

Germany, Switzerland, Saxony, Strasbourg, *etc.* will do well
unless things go wrong; indulgence-pedlars should fear them;
and not many anniversary Masses will be founded there this
year.

Spain, Castile, Portugal and Aragon will be subject to sudden
thirsts and both young and old will have a strong fear of dying;
and yet they will keep themselves warm, and if they have any
money often count it.[37]

Austria, Hungary and Turkey: in truth, my good fellows, I
have no idea how they will fare, and I care very little about it
in the light of the plucky entrance of the Sun into Capricorn. If
you know more about it, utter not a word, but wait for the
coming of the Halting One.

Finis

*

APPENDIX: THE AUGMENTED TEXT OF
1535 ONWARDS

[*To avoid excessively long footnotes devoted to the additions to the
end of the original* Pantagrueline Prognostication, *the long variant
made before the penultimate paragraph together with the four
additional chapters are given here.*]

37. From '35: for the long additions made at this point and at the end, see
the following Appendix.

England, Scotland and the Hanseatic League will be pretty bad Pantagruelists: wine, provided it were good and flavoursome, would be as healthy for them as beer, but whatever is served at table they have to wait for it till dessert. Saint Trinian of Scotland will do a few more miracles but will not see a jot more clearly because of all the candles brought to him unless Aries trips over the clover and is of its horn forlorn.

Muscovites, Indians, Persians and Troglodytes will often pass bloody stools since (because of the course of Sagittarius, which is the ascendant) they do not want to be diddled by the churchmen of Rome.

This year Bohemians, Jews and Egyptians will not be brought to the fulfilment of their desires. Venus is bitterly threatening them with scrofula, but they will yield to the will of the king of the Butterflies.

Slimy-snails, Sarabovines, Incubi and Cannibals will be severely troubled by gad-flies, and only few will play at make-a-manikin and clash their cymbals if gaiac is not in demand.

CHAPTERS ADDED IN 1535 AT THE END
OF THE ORIGINAL TEXT

Of the four seasons of the year. And firstly, of Spring

CHAPTER 7

All this year there will be but one moon and she will not be a new one; you lot are greatly saddened by that, you who do not believe at all in God and persecute both his sacred, holy Word and those who uphold it. But go to hang. Never will there be any other moon than the one which God created in the beginning of the world and which was established in the firmament by the action of the said holy Word to lighten and guide mankind by night. I do not want to imply by God that she does not display to the earth and to those who dwell thereon a waning or waxing of her brightness as she approaches or draws away from the Sun. For why? Well, because, etc.[38]

Apropos: you will find in this season half as many flowers again as in the other three. And that man will be reputed no fool who, throughout this year, provides himself with money rather than spiders. The wild men and their guides in the mountains of Savoy, Dauphiné and the Hyperboreans (which enjoy perpetual snow) will be frustrated in this season and have no snow whatsoever (according to the opinion of Avicenna that spring arrives when the snow deserts the mountains).

Trust this reporter.[39]

Of Summer

CHAPTER 8

I do not know what the weather will be or what wind will be blowing,[40] but this I do know: that it will be hot and dominated by winds from the sea. Should it turn out otherwise you must not curse God for it since he is wiser than we are and knows what we need far better than we do ourselves. I assure you of that upon my honour, despite what is said by Haly and his faction. It will be a fine thing to stay happy and – despite those who say that nothing is more inimical to thirst – to drink your wine cool. Moreover, *Opposites cure opposites*.[41]

38. From '42: . . . etc. *And no longer pray to God to guard her from the wolves, for they will not touch her this year. That I can promise you. Apropos* . . .
39. From '42: . . . reporter. *In my days they dated spring from when the Sun entered Aries. If they now date it differently, I give way and say not a word* . . .
40. From '42, omit: what the weather will be or.
41. A scholastic axiom which was applied in most domains, especially in medicine.

Of Autumn

CHAPTER 9

The *vendange* will take place during, before or after the autumn: it is all one to me provided that we have plenty of plonk. Thinkers will be in season, for a man may be thinking of farting when in fact he will be gaily messing himself.[42]

Hypocrites, black-beetles and pedlars of pardons, perpetual Masses and other such trinkets will come forth from their dens: let all who will watch out for them. Watch out too for the fish-bones when eating your *poisson*: and from *poison* may God ever guard you!

Of Winter

CHAPTER 10

According to my modest intellect those who sell their furs and skins in winter in order to buy wood will not be wise. The Ancients, as Avenzoar testifies, did no such thing. Do not grow melancholy if it rains: you will have that much less dust on the road. Keep yourselves warm. Beware of catarrhs. Drink of the best, whilst waiting for Satan to amend. And from henceforth do stop shitting your bed.[43]

---

42. From '42: . . . himself. *Men and women who have vowed to keep their fasts 'until the stars are in the heavens' can by my authority and dispensation have a good meal here and now. They are very late about it too, for those stars have been there for some sixteen thousand days plus I-know-not how many more. And very well fixed there, may I say. So no longer hope to catch larks when the heavens fall in, for that will not happen in your lifetime.* Hypocrites . . .
43. From '42: . . . bed. *Oh. Oh, ye birds. Make ye your nests so high? – Finis.* (Perhaps the refrain of a song, and doubtless suggestive of bird-droppings.)

PREFACES TO
ALMANACS FOR 1533
AND 1535

ALMANAC FOR 1533, CALCULATED ON THE MERIDIAN OF THE NOBLE CITY OF LYONS AND THE LATITUDE OF FRANCE. COMPOSED BY ME, FRANÇOIS RABELAIS, DOCTOR OF MEDICINE, PROFESSOR OF ASTROLOGY, ETC.

[*As physicians still do, Rabelais, a Bachelor of Medicine, calls himself Doctor. He was genuinely versed in the domains of astrology and astronomy. This almanac deals with the year 1533, during which the state of the heavens was deeply worrying. There were fourteen conjunctions between the Moon and Saturn, and twelve between the Moon and Mars. Rabelais puts the governance of the world into the reassuring context of God's almighty power.*

The theme of the hidden 'privy council' of God is developed further in the Third Book *by the good theologian Hippothadée. To hope to know God's privy counsel is absurd, except insofar as he vouchsafes to reveal it.*

The abbreviation 'etc.' appears twice in the text: both are attributable to Le Roy who is interested in the theology but not in the astrological data of a year long passed.

The biblical texts alluded to include (in order) Tobit 12:7 and 11; Psalms 20:12; Acts 1:7 and Proverbs 25:27.

Antoine Le Roy's transcription of the subtitle reads The disposition of this present year 1553. *That is a manifest lapsus for 1533 and is corrected. His transcription is our only source for this text and the following* Almanac for 1535.]

The disposition of this present year, 1533

Because I find the prognostic and judicial part of astrology to be condemned by all learned men, as much on account of the nullity of those who have treated it as for the annual disappointing of their promises, I shall for the present dispense with telling you what I have discovered from the calculations of Claudius Ptolemy and others, etc. I venture to say (having considered the frequent conjunctions of the Moon with Mars and Saturn, etc.) that during the said year, in the month of May, there cannot but occur a remarkable mutation in both realms and religions contrived by the accord of Mercury with Saturn, etc.

But those are secrets of the privy counsel of the Eternal King, who, by his free-will and good pleasure, governs all that is and all that is done; which secrets it is better not to speak of but to adore in silence, as it is said (in Tobit 12) 'It is good to keep close the secret of the King'; and by David the Prophet (in Psalm 54) following the Chaldaean reading, 'Silence waiteth for thee, O God, in Zion.' And the reason he states (in Psalm 17), 'For He made darkness his dwelling-place.'

And so, in all circumstances, it is incumbent on us to humble ourselves and beseech him (as we were taught by Jesus Christ our Lord) that there be done not what we wish or ask for but what pleases him and what he has established before ever the heavens were formed, provided that by all things and through all things his glorious name be hallowed.

Anything beyond that we confide to what is written in the eternal Ephemerides which it is not licit for any mortal man to treat or to know, as is affirmed (in Acts 1): 'It is not for you to know the times and seasons which the Father has set within his own authority.' And the punishment for such rashness is fixed (in Proverbs 25) by the wise Solomon: 'He who is a searcher of Majesty shall be overwhelmed by the glory,' etc.[1]

---

1.   There is a lapsus in the Le Roy's transcription, wrongly reading *the same* for *the glory*.

ALMANAC FOR 1535, CALCULATED FOR THE NOBLE CITY OF LYONS, AT A POLAR ELEVATION OF 45 DEGREES 15 MINUTES IN LATITUDE, AND 26 DEGREES IN LONGITUDE. BY MAÎTRE FRANÇOIS RABELAIS, DOCTOR OF MEDICINE AND PHYSICIAN TO THE GREAT HOSPITAL OF LYONS

[There is a Humanist leap between these two almanacs as there is between Pantagruel *and* Gargantua. *Rabelais moves into the world of Erasmian theology with its respect for Plato. He cites or alludes to Ecclesiastes 1:8; Philippians 1:23; Psalms 16:15; Matthew 6:34 and 6:10, and Colossians 2:2–3. The adage of Socrates is in Erasmus' collection (Adages, I, VI, LXIX), and the good teaching of Plato which is better stated in Matthew 6 is to be found in the* Gorgias, *484 C–487. It was Platonizing Christians who, following certain versions of the Psalms, talked of the body in Platonic terms as the* prison of the soul.*

*A standard scholastic proof of the truth of the doctrine of the immortality of the soul is found for example in Thomas Aquinas (*Summa Theologica, *IIᵃ IIᵃᵉ V, articles 3, 4 and 5). Using the same Scriptural texts as Rabelais, it was based upon the conviction that Nature does nothing in vain. It took as its point of departure the famous opening words of the* Metaphysics of Aristotle: *'All humans naturally desire to know'. That is doubtless still true for Rabelais, but, he suggests, if you really want to face the problems of the coming year, Scripture – and Plato – refer you to faith, that is, confidence in God, and to Christian morality. The Lord's prayer is the true guide. Rabelais had just edited the* Aphorisms of Hippocrates *in Greek and Latin; its opening words are 'Life is short: the Art is long.' (The 'Art' referred to, as often in Rabelais, is the art of medicine. His astrologico-astronomical data probably derive from the tables of Stoeffler, in which the conjunction of Saturn and Mars, which had*

occurred on 3 May 1534, was predicted to occur again in 1535 on
25 May. In fact it occurred some three days earlier.]

The disposition of this year, 1535

The philosophers of Antiquity who demonstrated the immortality of our souls had no greater argument to prove it and advance
it than the admonition of an affection within us which Aristotle
describes (in Book One of the *Metaphysics*) saying, 'All humans
naturally desire to know': meaning that Nature has produced
in Man an eagerness, appetite and yearning to know and to
learn not merely things present but particularly things to come
(because a knowledge of them is higher and more wonderful).
But since we can never attain to perfect knowledge of such
things in the course of this transitory life – for the understanding
is never satisfied with knowing, 'as the eye is not satisfied with
seeing, nor the ear filled with hearing' (Ecclesiastes 1) – and
since Nature does nothing without a cause, nor gives an appetite
or desire for anything which cannot be obtained at some time
or other (if not, that appetite would be either ineffectual or
depraved), it follows that there is another life after this one in
which that desire will be slaked.

I tell you that because I see you keen, attentive and desirous
to learn from me, here and now, the state and disposition of
this year 1535. And you would judge it a miraculous advantage
if the truth about it were foretold to you with certainty. But if
you want fully to satisfy that fervent desire it behoves you to
wish (as when Saint Paul, in Philippians 1, said: 'I yearn to
be loosed asunder and to be with Christ') that your souls be
released out of the darksome prison of your earthly bodies
and joined to Jesus the Christ. Then shall cease all human
passions, affections and imperfections; for in the enjoyment of
him we shall have the plenitude of the Good, all knowledge
and perfection: as (in Psalm 16) King David sang of old: 'I shall
be satisfied when thy glory shall appear.'

To foretell it in any other way would be lightness in me, as
it would be simple-mindedness in you to believe it. Since the

creation of Adam there has never yet been born anyone who has treated or transmitted anything in which we should acquiesce or remain with assurance. Certain scholars have indeed committed to writing some observations passed on from hand to hand. And that is what I have always asserted, not wanting any conclusions about the future to be drawn from my prognostications but to have it understood that those who had reduced Man's long experience of the heavenly bodies to an Art have decreed as I myself have written.

And what can that amount to? Less than nothing, certainly: for in the first of his *Aphorisms*, Hippocrates says 'Life is short: the Art is long': that the life of Man is too brief, the mind too weak and the understanding too distracted to grasp things so remote from us. It is what Socrates said in his common adage, 'Things above us are nothing to do with us.' It remains therefore that following the counsel of Plato in the *Gorgias* or – better still the teachings of the Gospel (Matthew 6) – we refrain from any curious inquiry into the governance and unchanging decree of Almighty God, who has created and ordered things according to His holy pleasure, praying and beseeching that His holy will ever be fully done on Earth as it is in Heaven.

To expound for you summarily what I have been able to extract about this year from Greek, Arabic and Latin authorities in the Art: we shall start to feel this year last year's unfortunate conjunction of Saturn and Mars which will occur again next year on the twenty-fifth of May; with the result that, this year, we shall have merely the machinations, plottings, foundations and seeds of calamities to follow. If things do prosper, that will exceed the promises of the heavenly bodies; and if we do have peace, that will not be from lack of inclination to undertake a war but from lack of occasion.

That is what they say.

What I say for my part is that if Christian kings, princes and commonwealths hold the holy word of God in reverence and govern themselves and their subjects accordingly, we shall never have seen in our time a year more healthy for bodies, more peaceful for minds, more fertile in good things; and we shall see the face of the heavens, the raiment of the Earth and the conduct of the people more joyful, gay, pleasing and favourable than for any time during the last fifty years.

The Sunday Letter will be C; the Golden Number, 16; the Roman Indiction, 8; the Solar Cycle, 4.[2]

2.   A convenient way to understand and calculate the Sunday letter and the Golden Number is to consult the tables in the *Book of Common Prayer*. The *Roman Indiction* is the place of each year in the fifteen-year cycle which constitutes the fiscal period. It was used *inter alia* for dating papal documents. The *Solar Cycle* is the period of twenty-eight years, at the end of which the Sunday Letters correspond to the letters of the alphabet, beginning with A.

GARGANTUA

Introduction to *Gargantua*

The text as translated is that of the first known edition, probably dating from early in 1535. The original text of *Gargantua*, like that of *Pantagruel*, has a directness, freshness and boldness which later editions do not quite have. The title-page is missing from the only known copy.

The present text includes variants from the second edition, which is dated 1535, and from the definitive text of 1542, which incorporates the earlier variants. The variants are shown in two main ways: 1) interpolations are shown in the text and are enclosed within square brackets; 2) eliminations and modifications are given in the notes. Thus, to read the text of the first edition, ignore the interpolations inside square brackets and the variants listed in the notes. To read the definitive text of 1542, read everything.

The editions cited in the notes are as follows:

the first edition (Lyons: François Juste, undated (1535?));
the second edition (Lyons: François Juste, 1535): given here as '35;
the definitive edition (Lyons, François Juste, 1542): given here as '42

Variants are dated by giving the first edition in which the original text appears.

The text used as the basis for the translation is that of my edition with Ruth Calder in the Textes Littéraires Français (Geneva: Droz, 1970, with later reprints).

Contents

To the Readers

[To be 'scandalized' (from the Greek skandalizô) *is to lose one's faith through adversity or persecution. It used to be translated as to be 'offended', but that sense is now all but lost. The full force of 'to scandalize' appears at the very end of* Gargantua – *in the last ten lines of verse and the following prose.]*

Dear readers: hereon cast your eyes;
All sterile passions lay aside.
No offence here to scandalize;
Nothing corrupting lurks inside.
Little perfection here may hide
Save laughter: little else you'll find.
No other theme comes to my mind
Seeing such gloom your joy doth ban.
My pen's to laughs not tears assigned.
Laughter's the property of Man.

LIVE JOYFULLY.[1]

---

1. The poem is given here after the text of '35. It is missing from the first edition as it stands.

The Prologue of the Author

[*This prologue is a homage to Erasmus. The adage (and long essay) entitled 'The Sileni of Alcibiades' (Adages, III, III, I) throws great light on to the works of many Renaissance thinkers. It was externally that Socrates was like Silenus: hidden within his ugly exterior was wisdom, divine and inspired. Rabelais applies the comparison to his new book. It is printed in Gothic, not humanist, type and written in French, not Latin, yet it contains great truths concerning religion, statecraft and domestic life. Nevertheless we are warned not to read into Rabelais detailed allegorical nonsense of the kind which did indeed lead some to find all the Christian sacraments in a pagan poet such as Ovid!*

To Scripture was attributed four senses, the literal, metaphorical, tropological and anagogical. Naturally the 'higher' ones were most open to abuse and fantasy. Amusing in this context, and perhaps followed by Rabelais, is letter number I. 28 in G. F. Stokes's translation of the Letters of Obscure Men. *Amongst the other Erasmian adages that Rabelais exploits are:*

I, I, II: 'Pythagorean Symbols' (Pythagoras' injunctions may seem laughable, 'yet if you draw out the allegory you will see that they are but precepts for proper living'. Rabelais, like Erasmus, kept up a respect for Pythagoras.)

I, X, LXXII: 'A lid worthy of its pot';

I, VIII, XV: 'By hands and by feet';

IV, III, LVIII: 'He who drinks water is no dithyrambic';

I, VII, LXXI: 'It smells of the oil-lamp'.

Not in Erasmus but in Charles de Bouelles one finds two other adages important for the understanding of this Prologue: namely, 'To break the bone' and 'To extract the marrow'. When reading Gargantua, we should act like wise dogs with a good flair.]

Most shining of drinkers, and you, most be-carbuncled of syphilitics – for my writings are addressed solely to you – Alcibiades, praising in a dialogue of Plato's called *The Banquet* his teacher Socrates (beyond dispute the prince of philosophers), says amongst other things that he resembled *Sileni*.

Formerly *Sileni* were little boxes such as we can now see in the booths of the apothecaries, decorated all over with frivolous merry figures such as harpies, satyrs, geese with bridles, hares with horns, ducks with saddles, flying goats, stags pulling carts and other such paintings arbitrarily devised to make everyone laugh. (Such was Silenus, the Master of good old Bacchus!) But inside were kept rare drugs such as balsam, ambergris, grains of paradise, musk, civet, powdered jewels and other costly ingredients.

Such, he said, was Socrates, since on seeing him from the outside and judging from his external appearance you wouldn't have rated him above an onion skin, so ugly was he in body and so ridiculous in bearing, with his turned-up nose, his bull-like glower and his face like a fool's; simple in manners, rustic in dress, poor in fortune, unlucky over women, unsuited to any office of state, ever laughing, ever matching drink for drink with all comers, ever joking, ever hiding his God-sent wisdom: but, upon opening that 'box', you would have found within a medicine celestial and beyond all price: superhuman understanding, miraculous virtue, indomitable courage, unparalleled moderation, assured contentment, perfect confidence and an unbelievable contempt for all those things for which human beings wake, run, toil, sail and battle.

Now, in your opinion, what is the drift of this prelude, this apprentice-piece? Well, you, my good disciples – as well as some other leisured chumps – when reading no further than the titles of certain books of our devising (such as *Gargantua*, *Pantagruel*, *On the Merits of Codpieces*, *On Pease-pudding and Bacon, with a Latin Commentary* and so on), too readily conclude that nothing is treated inside save jests, idiocies and amusing fictions, seeing that their exterior epigraphs (their titles, that is) are normally greeted, without further inquiry, by scoffing and derision.

It is not however proper to estimate so frivolously the works of human beings. For you yourself say that *the habit maketh not the Monk*, that a man may wear a monkish habit who is inwardly nothing like a monk, and that another may be clad in a Spanish cape whose courage has nothing which becomes a

Spaniard. That is why you must open this book and scrupulously weigh what is treated within. You will then realize that
the medicine it contains is of a very different value from that
which its box ever promised: in other words, that the topics
treated here are not as frivolous as the title above it proclaimed.

And even granted that you do find, in its literal meaning,
plenty of merry topics entirely congruous with its name, you
must not be stayed there as by the Sirens' song but expound
the higher meaning of what you had perhaps believed to have
been written out of merriness of mind.

Have you ever cracked open any bottles? Dawg! Recall to
mind your countenance then. But have you even seen a dog
encountering a marrow-bone? It is (as Plato says in Book 2 of
The Republic) the most philosophical beast in the world. If you
have ever seen one, you were able to notice with what dedication it observes it; with what solicitude it guards it; with what
fervour it takes hold of it; with what sagacity it cracks it; with
what passion it breaks it open, and with what care it sucks it.
What induces it to do so? What does it hope for from its
assiduity? What good is it aiming at? Nothing more than a bit
of marrow. But the truth is that that *bit* is more delicious than
the *ample* of all the rest, since marrow is a nutriment elaborated
to its natural perfection (as Galen says *On the Natural Faculties*,
Book 3, and *On the Use of Parts of the Body*, Book 11).

Following that example it behoves you to develop a sagacious
flair for sniffing and smelling out and appreciating such fair
and fatted books, to be swift in pursuit and bold in the attack,
and then, by careful reading and frequent meditation, to crack
open the bone and seek out the substantificial marrow – that is
to say, what I mean by such Pythagorean symbols – sure in the
hope that you will be made witty and wise by that reading; for
you will discover therein a very different savour and a more
hidden instruction which will reveal to you the highest hidden
truths and the most awesome mysteries touching upon our
religion as well as upon matters of state and family life.

Now do you really and truly believe that Homer, when
composing the *Iliad* and the *Odyssey*, had any thought of the
allegories which have been caulked on to him by Plutarch,

Heraclides of Pontus, Eustathius or Conutus and which Politian purloined from them? If you do so believe, then you come by neither foot nor hand close to my own opinion, which decrees that they had no more been dreamt of by Homer than the mysteries of the Gospel by Ovid in his *Metamorphoses* (as a certain Friar Loopy, a filcher of flitches, endeavours to prove, provided that he can chance upon folk as daft as he is: 'Lids,' as the saying goes, 'worthy of their pots').

Yet even if you do not believe that, what is to stop you doing so with these merry new Chronicles even though I was no more thinking of such things when I wrote them than you were, who were perhaps having a drink just as I was! For in the composing of this lordly book I neither wasted more time, nor spent any other time, than what had been set aside for my bodily sustenance, namely for eating and drinking. That, moreover, is the appropriate time for writing of these high topics and profound teachings, as Homer well knew – he, the paragon of all men of letters – and Ennius, the Father of Latin poetry, as is attested by Horace (even though some clod-hopper said that his verse whiffed more of wine than of midnight oil).

Some tramp said as much of my books: but shit on him!

Ah, the bouquet of wine: how much more smiling, whiling, beguiling it is, how much more paradisiacal and delightful than that of oil! I would glory in it if they said of me that I more on wine than water spent, as much as did Demosthenes when it was said of him that he more on oil than wine did spend. To me it is an honour to be called a jolly fellow, and a glory to be reputed a good companion. With such a name I am made welcome in all good companies of Pantagruelists. Demosthenes was reproved by some grouser because his *Orations* stank like the apron of some filthy, dirty oil-monger. Expound therefore all my words and deeds in the most perfect of senses; hold in reverence the cheese-shaped brain which feeds you this fine tripe and, insofar as in you lies, keep me ever merry.

So enjoy yourselves my loves happily reading what follows for your bodily comfort and the good of your loins. Listen now, you ass-pizzles. May ulcers give you gammy legs: and remember to drink a toast back to me! And I shall pledge you double quick.

On the Lineage and ancient origins of Gargantua

CHAPTER I

[Amid the jesting Rabelais (as shown by the addition made at this time to the end of Pantagruel) is smarting at threats of censors over the genealogies of Pantagruel. Again 'devil' is juxtaposed to 'calumniator'.

A few of the themes of Pantagruel are lightly touched on here. The reference to Maître Pathelin's famous injunction 'Let us get back to our muttons' reminds us that Rabelais greatly admired that farce. The scene is set in Rabelais' own pays of Chinon and Touraine, with some place-names known only to the locals.

Rabelais exploits another adage of Erasmus, I, II, XLIX, 'Twice and thrice, that which is beautiful'.]

To learn of the ancient lineage from which Gargantua descended to us I refer you to the *Great Pantagrueline Chronicle*. In it you will hear more fully of how the giants were born into our world and how Gargantua, the father of Pantagruel, sprang from them in a direct line, so you will not be put out if I do not go into it at present – despite its being such that the more it is rehearsed the more it would please your Lordships, for which you have the authority of [Plato in the *Philebus* and *Gorgias* and] Horace, who states that there are some matters, including these [no doubt] which are the more delightful the more they are retold. Would to God that every man could trace his own ancestry as certainly from Noah's Ark down to this our age! I think that many today are emperors, kings, dukes, princes and popes on this earth who are descended from pardon-mongers or hodmen in vineyards, just as there are on the contrary many beggars in workhouses (wretched and needy) who are descended by blood and lineage from great kings and emperors, given the remarkable transfer of kingdoms and empires:

– from the Assyrians to the Medes;
– the Medes to the Macedonians;

– The Macedonians to the Romans;
– the Romans to the Greeks;
– and the Greeks to the French.

And to enable you to understand me who am talking to you now, I think that I'm descended from some rich king or prince of former times, for never have I seen a man with a greater passion than I have for being rich and a king so as to live in great style, never working, [never ever worrying] and enriching my friends and all good and scholarly folk.

But what comforts me is the thought that I shall be greater far in the next world than I could ever wish to be now. You too should comfort your sorrows with such a thought (or a better one) and if possible drink some cool wine.

But getting back to our muttons: I tell you that by a sovereign gift of God the ancient genealogy of Gargantua has been preserved for us more fully than any other – I am not talking of God, for it does not fall to me to do so, and the devils, that is the [calumniators and] black-beetles, object to it too.

Gargantua's genealogy was uncovered by Jean Audeau in a meadow near the Arceau-Galeau below the farm called *L'Olive* in the direction of Narsay. The diggers were cleaning out ditches with their pick-axes when they struck a huge brass tomb. It was immeasurably long: they never found the end of it because it plunged too deep below the sluice-gates at Vienne. On opening it up at one particular place (which bore on top the sign of a goblet, around which was written in the Etruscan script, HERE ONE DRINKS) they found nine flagons arranged as nine-pins are in Gascony. The one in the middle was placed on top of a great, grand, gross, grey, pretty little mouldy booklet with an odour more pungent than that of roses (albeit far less pleasant).

The genealogy, written in chancery script, was found inside it, not on paper, not on parchment, not on wax, but on elm-tree bark; the letters were so faded with age that you could hardly make out three in a row. I (though unworthy) was called in; with copious help from spectacles and by practising that art of reading indistinct writing taught by Aristotle, I transcribed it, as you may see by dint of pantagruelizing (that is to say, by being willing to have a drink and by reading the horrific deeds of Pantagruel).

That booklet ended with a little treatise bearing the title *Antidoted Bubbles*. The beginning of it had been gnawed away by rats and cockroaches – or (so that I may not lie) perhaps by other destructive creatures.

What remains I have appended here out of veneration for Antiquity.

The *Antidoted Bubbles* discovered within a monument from Antiquity

CHAPTER 2

[An enigma in the spirit of the satirical poems called coq-à-l'âne; *such sense as there is is hidden amidst a jumble of nonsense. Odd bits of fairly evident anti-papalist satire leave the rest of the poem still unexplained – if explanation there be. Is there satire of the Sorbonne and of the Emperor Charles V? The enigma remains tantalizing: there is a clear scriptural reference to God, who names himself I AM THAT I AM at the burning bush (Exodus 3:14).*

In the only substantive change Rabelais made to this poem amis *(friends) became* facquins *(porters) – a term often used derogatively.*

The opening lines are shown eaten away.]

> # ¡ ± , ≥ arrived the Cimbrian conqueror,
> Δ • ¿ : > ing through air for fear of all that dew,
> =. + \ ≠ e arrives, the tubs can take no more
> / · " ÷ resh butter pouring down like stew.
> ≈ ‡ bespattered grandma in full view:
> She cried aloud: 'Herren. Fish him right out!
> His beard cow-patted is as if by glue;
> Or hold him a ladder, better 'tis than nowt.'

To lick his slipper some said was true bliss,
Better indeed than pardoners to pay;
But an affected rascal came amiss
Up from that dip where roaches swim and play,
And said, 'My Lords, for God's sake, your hands
   stay!
The eel is in that booth quite unrevealed.
There you shall find, if you would look that way,
Deep in his amice a great fault concealed.'

He was about that Chapter to intone
But found, within, the horns of a young cow.
'My mitre's depth,' he said, 'is cold as stone.
It chills my freezing brain, I know not how.'
With turnips' reek they warm his icy brow:
He'd stay at home quite happily and glad
If they should find new harnesses somehow
For all those folk whose brains have turned quite
   mad.

They bandied words of Patrick's Hole afar,
Gibraltar too and holes of many kinds:
Could they be cured and end up with a scar,
Without producing coughs and throaty winds
Which all found unbecoming in their minds,
Seeing at every breath how they did yawn?
If all were tight restrained by cord which binds
They could be hostages to trade or pawn.

By that decree the raven lost its hide
Through Hercules who out of Libya came.
'What!' Minos said, 'Have I been thrust aside,
Apart from me all summoned to the game?
And yet they want me willing all the same
Of frog and oysters to provide a ration!
They'll never get me (in the devil's name!)
On distaff-vending to shower my compassion.'

Q.B. comes limping, all to check and mate;
Conducted safe, through sparrow-priests goes by;
The Siever, cousin to the Cyclops great,
Killed them. All wipe their noses and all sigh.
Within those fields few new-born buggers lie
Who were not diddled near the tanners' mill.
Come running all! War trumpets sound on high.
As ne'er before, rewards will come at will.

The eagle, the sole bird that Jove doth own,
Decided soon to back the worser side;
But seeing each in anger 'gainst his own,
Feared they'd raze low the empire in its pride.
Better by far to rush the heavens wide
And steal their fire, where herrings soused are sold,
Than th' air serene, against which many side,
To enthral in massoretic legal mould.

All was agreed, sharp pointed, in the raw,
'Spite quarrelsome Até with the heron-thigh,
Who squatted when she Penthesilea saw
Peddling, old crone, her cress to passers-by.
'Old coalman's wife!' to sneer they all did vie,
'You never venture should upon this way;
You stole that Roman banner from on high
Forged from stretched parchment as some men do
    say.'

Were't not for Juno 'neath the heavenly arc
Snaring her birds, helped by her hornèd coot,
Their blows against her would have left their mark
And ruffled her – at every point to boot.
It was agreed that her maw for its loot
Two eggs should have from Proserpine's own lay;
And should the 'flu in her ever take root
Bind her they would on hillsides decked with may.

Seven months then passed – take off a score plus two;
He who destroyed Carthage in days of yore
Set himself down politely 'twixt them, too,
Seeking his heritage but nothing more,
(Or else fair shares as settled by the law
Of cobblers true who stitch for stitch assign)
Dollops of soup distributing for the maw
Of those friends who that legal deed did sign.

The time shall be, marked by a Turkish bow
And spindles five and three pots on their bum,
When to a king's back none courtesy will show:
Poxy, he has a hermit now become.
How pitiful! A hypocrite you've won!
For her shall you engulf your acres wide?
Cease. Imitate not this play which now is done;
Withdraw and with the Serpent's brother bide.

That year once past, then peacefully shall reign
I AM, with those beloved as His own.
Nor blast nor slight shall govern to men's bane,
Nor good will, unrewarded, stand alone,
But Joy, long promised once for times to come,
To folk in Heaven, will draw into her belfry.
Then the stud-farms, amazèd once, will gain
Their triumphs true in a right royal palfrey.

And it will last, that age of sleight-of-hand,
Until the day when Mars in chains is bound.
Then one will come outstripping all the band,
Beautiful, gracious, none fairer to be found;
Lift up your hearts. Stand ye the feast around,
My faithful folk. For he has passèd o'er,
Ne'er to return, whatever goods abound:
Time past shall be regretted as no more.

At last, he shall be lodged (of wax once made)
In the hinge of the Manikin who strikes the bell.
That title 'Cyre!' shall never more be said
To him who holds the cauldron as men tell.
Alas! Who could his sword arrest would quell
And clean away bad cauli-headed uses,
With packing-cord could truss up firm and well
And tie up tight the factory of abuses.

How Gargantua was carried for eleven months in his mother's womb

CHAPTER 3

[*The maximum duration of a pregnancy was much discussed. All knew what the usual length is, but what is the maximum? Matters of legitimacy and inheritance depended on it. Greek and Latin authors assume that a pregnancy lasts ten months (lunar months, no doubt). Many doctors followed Aristotle, Hippocrates, Varro and Hadrian, who talk of eleven months and more. In the Renaissance, books of Roman Law were so glossed by scholars that the ten months attributed to gestation in Roman Law were clearly and firmly expanded to eleven. On the greatest legal authority, a child born after an eleven-month pregnancy was legitimate. Rabelais' friend André Tiraqueau treats the crux in a conciliatory manner in an austere and learned legal study of 1535. Tiraqueau's compromise is eleven months, meaning ten months plus a few days. Rabelais knew the work, perhaps before it was printed. The way in which Rabelais refers to individual laws by abbreviated title, book, paragraph, etc. was long the normal one. His abbreviations have been expanded to make them pronounceable.*

Page A8 is missing from the only surviving copy of the original edition of Gargantua. *The corresponding page in the second edition ('35) probably retains the original text word for word and is adopted here.*]

In his day Grandgousier was a jolly good fellow who loved to drink neat as well as any man then in the world. And he enjoyed eating salty things. To that end he normally kept an ample store of Westphalian and Bayonne hams, plenty of smoked tongue, an abundance of eels in season, beef cured in salt and mustard, supplies of mullet-caviar, a provision of sausages – though never those from Bologna, for he redoubted the 'poisoned morsels' of Lombardy – but always from Bigorre, Longaulnay, La Brène and Rouergue.

In his maturity he wedded Gargamelle, the daughter of the King of the Parpaillons, a fine filly with a goodly mug, and they so often played the two-backed beast together, happily stroking their bacon, that she became big of a fine son whom she bore up to the eleventh month.

For women are able to carry that long – even longer – especially when it is a masterpiece and a personage destined to do great deeds in his time (as Homer says that the child with whom Neptune impregnated the nymph was delivered after one year had gone by, that is, during the twelfth month). For (as Aulus Gellius states in Book 3) such a long time became the majesty of Neptune, so that within it his child should be fashioned to perfection.

For a similar reason Jupiter caused the night when he lay with Alcmene to last for forty-eight hours, since he never could have forged in a shorter time Hercules, who rid the world of monsters and of tyrants.

My Lords the Pantagruelists of old have spoken in conformity with what I say, declaring not only feasible but legitimate a child born to a wife eleven months after her husband's death:

- Hippocrates: *On food*;
- Pliny: Book 7, chapter 5;
- Plautus, in *The Cistellaria*;
- Marcus Varro, in the satire called *The Testament*, citing the authority of Aristotle on the subject;
- Censorinus, in his book *On the Day of Birth*;
- Aristotle, chapters 3 and 4 of Book 7 of *On the Nature of Animals*;

– Aulus Gellius, Book 3, chapter 16;
[– Servius, on the *Eclogues*, explaining the line of Virgil;
To your Mother, Ten Months', etc.;]

and hundreds of other idiots, the number of whom has been increased by the legal scholars. In the *Pandects*, see *On One's Own and Legitimate; the Law, To the Intestate, § On Sons*; and in the *Authentica, the Laws, On Restitutions*, and *On Her Who Gives Birth in the Twelfth Month*.

More copiously they have scrabbled together their lard-stroking law *Gallus* (in the *Pandects: On Children and Post-humous Heirs*, and *Law Seven, Pandects, On Man's Estate*) as well as certain others which I do not at present care to cite. By means of those laws, widow-women, for two months after the deaths of their husbands, can frankly play at bonkbum, pricking on regardless.

As for you, my good comrades, if you do come across any worth untying the flies for, mount them and bring them to me. For if they start to swell in the third month, the fruit will be heir to the deceased. And once the pregnancy is known they can confidently push ahead: *Let her run before the wind*, since the belly is full. Indeed Julia, the daughter of the Emperor Octavian, never let herself have a go with her drummer-boys except when she was gravid, just as a ship never takes her pilot aboard until she has been caulked up and laden. And if anyone should reproach them for getting country-bumboated on top of their pregnancies, seeing that the dumb beasts never tolerate the mating male once their bellies are swollen, they will retort that those are beasts whereas they are women, fully cognizant of the happy little rigid rights of superfetation (as Populia once retorted, according to Macrobius in Book Two of the *Saturnalia*).

If the divel does not want them to get pregnant, then one must twist the vent-pegs off tight – and keep mum.

How Gargamelle, when carrying Gargantua, took to eating [a great profusion of] tripe

CHAPTER 4

[The scene is again set in the pays *where Rabelais was brought up, and local terms are used. 'La Saulaie' (also called 'La Saulsaie') is the Willow-grove.]*

When and how Gargamelle was delivered is as follows – and if you do not believe it, may your fundament run loose. Hers did one afternoon (the third day of February) as a result of eating too many *gaudebillaux*.

– *Gaudebillaux* are greasy tripe derived from *coiraux*.

– *Coiraux* are cattle fattened up in stalls and in *prés guimaux*.

– *Prés guimaux* are lush meadows which produce two crops of grass a year.

Now they slaughtered three hundred and sixty-seven thousand and fourteen of those fatted beeves for salting over Shrove Tuesday so that in spring-time they would have seasonal beef in abundance to enable them [to say a grace for saltings at the beginning of their repasts and] to raise a better thirst for wine.

There was a profusion of tripe, as you realize, tripe so appetizing that everyone was licking his fingers over it. But the four-devil-mystery-play of it all was that tripe cannot be kept for long: for it will go putrid, and that seemed a shame. So they decided to gobble it all up and waste none of it. To do that they sent invitations to the citizens of the villages of Cinais, Seuilly, La Roche-Clermault and Vaugaudry, not forgetting those of Coudray-Monspensier, the Gué de Vède and others near by, all good wine-bibbers, good company, and fine skittlers with their balls.

That good fellow Grandgousier took great delight in it all and ordered them to ladle it out by the bowlful. He did tell his wife, though, to eat as little of it as possible, seeing that her time was near and that all that tripery was not a very commend-able food. 'Whoever eats guts,' he said, 'must really want to chew shit.' Despite such expostulations she ate sixteen tuns, two gallons and two pints of it. Oh, what lovely faecal matter there must have been swilling about inside her! After lunch they all went off pell-mell to La Saulaie, and there they danced on the lush grass to the sound of the merry flute and the bagpipes sweet, so joyfully that it was a celestial pastime to watch them having such fun.

*

[In '42 this exchange of drunken quips is expanded and turned into a separate chapter: Words from the tipsy. Chapter 5.

The jests come from educated tongues and conform at times to that kind of monastic humour which Erasmus loathed but which Rabelais knew how to exploit. A few of the sayings echo scriptural texts: all from the Latin Vulgate: 'cometh forth as a bridegroom' (Psalm 19/ 18:5); 'gaspeth unto thee as a thirsty land' (Psalm 143/142:6); 'Respect not the person' (Matthew 22:16, omitting the negative!); 'I thirst' (one of the last words of Christ on the Cross, John 19:28); 'And he hath poured it out from this into that' (Psalm 75/74: 9, Vulgate only).

A Canon lawyer is present: 'In the arid can no soul abide' is a quotation from the Decretum *of Gratian, 32, q. 2, cap. 9.*

There is also a quotation from Horace: 'Whom did most fecund cups not fluent make?' (Epistles 1, 5, 5, 19).

Jérôme de Hangest was bishop of Le Mans: Jacques Cœur was, since the fifteenth century, the archetypical rich man. The pope's 'mule' is his mount and/or his slipper (a constant source of jesting).

There is at least one woman present, one German-speaking Lansquenet, and one Basque: 'Lagona edatera' is Basque for 'Drink comrade'.

The translation is free at times, transposing some jokes, but not all the jests are complex or allusive.]

Then, at the appropriate place, they got round to conversing over dessert:
   – 'Swig
   – Give!

– Turn it on.

– Add some water.

– Shove it along to me, my friend, without the water.

– Whip that glass gallantly inside you.

– Produce me some claret in a cup dripping tears.

– A truce to thirst.

– Ha, foul fever! Will you never go away?

– 'Strewth my dear woman, I haven't even got started yet.

– Is your nose all bunged up, my sweeting?

– Indeed it is!

– By the guts of Saint Quimlet, let's talk about drinking.

[– I drink only by my Book of Hours like the pope's mule.

– I drink only by my Breviary like a fine Friar Superior.

– What came first, thirst or drinking?

– Thirst: in the days of Man's innocence who would have drunk without thirst?

– Drinking: for privation supposes habituation. A cleric, I am! *Whom did most fecund cups not fluent make?*

– Innocents like us drink all too much without a thirst.

– But not a sinner like me: if not for a present thirst then for a future one, preventing it you see. I drink eternally. For me drinking's eternity: eternity's drinking.

– Let us sing; let us drink; let's intone a motet. Just for fun.

– Just for funnel? Where's mine!

– Hey! I'm drinking by proxy.

– Do you wet your whistle to dry it, or dry your whistle to wet it?

– I understand nothing about the theory but I get by with the practical.

– Get on with it then.

– I moisten. I humidify. I drink lest I die.

– Drink for ever and you'll never die.

– If I drink not, I dry out. And there I am, dead. My soul will scamper off to some frog-pond or other. *In the arid can no soul abide.*

– Butlers, Ye Makers of new entities, change me from non-drinker into drinker.

– An everlasting asperging of my dry and gristly innards.

– In vain drinks he who feels it not.

– This one's going straight to my veins. My pisser will get none of it.

– This morning I dressed the veal-calf's tripe. Now I shall enjoy washing it!

– I've crammed my stomach full of ballast;

– If the paper of my pledges was as absorbent as I am, all the writing would be smudged when the time came to honour them and the creditors could whistle for their wine!]

– That hand of yours is spoiling your nose.

– O! How many other drinks will get in before this one gets out?

– This wine-cup is so shallow you risk bursting your girth-strap.

– You could call this one a decoy for flagons.

– What's the difference between a flagon and a butt?

– Immense: You plug a flagon with your bung, and a butt with your vent-peg.

[– A lovely one, that!]

– Our fathers drank well and left not a drop in their potties.

– Oh! What a shitty-shanty. Let's all have a drink.

– Have you got anything for the river? This one's for washing the tripe.

[– I can soak up no more than a sponge.]

– I drink like a Templar.

– And I, as one who *cometh forth as a bridegroom*.

– And I, as one who *gaspeth as a thirsty land*.

– Another word for ham?

[– A summons; commanding you to drink.]

– A drayman's skid: by the skid wine slides down to the cellars: by the ham wine slides down to the stomach.

– Get on with it then: drink. Let's have a drink then. *Respect the person!* – There's been no overloading. Pour out for twice: *for two* sounds *too much!*

– If I upped-it as well as I downed-it I'd be high in the air by now.

[Thus did Jacques Cœur in riches wallow:
Trees flourish in good land that's fallow:
Bacchus with wine did conquer Inde:
And search-for-wisdom reach Melinde.

– *A tiny shower smothers a gale*: lengthy toping foils the thunder.]
– If my member pissed such piddle, would you mind sucking it?
– The next round's on me.
– Page! Hand it over. When my turn comes I'll insinuate my nomination for you.
– *Guillot, Guillot, drink a lot: There's still more wine left in the pot.*
[– I appeal against thirst as an abuse. Page, register my appeal in due form.
– There's some left-overs.
– Once I used to drink everything up: now I never leave a drop.
– Let's not hurry but gather it all up.
– Tripe worth a wager, and *godebillaux* worth doubling! Such tripe would flatter that dun horse with the black stripe. Let's give him a good currying for God's sake. Waste not: want not!
– Drink up, or I'll . . .
– No, no, no! Say, 'Kindly drink up, I pray.' To get sparrows to feed you tap their tails: to get me to drink you have to coax me.
– *Lagona edatera*. There's not a burrow in my body where this wine doesn't ferret out my thirst.
– This one will track it down. And this will banish it entirely.
– Let us trumpet this abroad to the sound of bottles and flagons:

WHOSOEVER HAS MISLAID HIS THIRST,
LET HIM SEEK IT NOT HEREIN.
PROLONGED ENEMAS OF THIRST
HAVE EVACUATED IT FROM THESE LODGINGS.

– Our great God rules the welkin, and we rule the firkin;

– I have God's word in my mouth: *I thirst*.

– The stone called *asbestos* is not more unquenchable than the thirst of my Paternity.

– *Appetite comes with eating*, as Hangest Du Mans used to say, *and thirst leaves with drinking*,]

– A remedy against thirst!

– Flat opposite to the one against dog-bites: keep *behind* a dog and it'll never bite you: drink *before* a thirst and it'll never get you!

[– *I catch you at it and wake you up*.

– *Eternal Butler, bottle up sleep*.

– Argus had a hundred eyes to see with: like Briarus a butler needs a hundred hands tirelessly to pour with.

– Drink up, boys. A fine thing to dry out!]

– Some white! Pour it. Pour all of it, you devil! Pour it in here up to the brim: my tongue's pealing.

– Trink up, mein Freund!

– Here's to you, fellow soldier! All in good fun. All in good fun.

– O, la la! That's a good guzzle.

– *O Lacrima Christi!*

– It's from La Devinière. We call it *pinot*.

– O noble white wine!

– Upon my soul, it's a wine smooth as taffeta.

– Ho, ho, ho. One-eared wine! Fine stuff from a fine fleece!

[– Courage, comrade.

– With such cards we shan't lose points down: I'm raising a good hand.

– *And He hath poured it out from this into that.*

– Now there's no magic about it, folks. You all saw it: with goblets I'm a past master. Ahem, ahem: a mast pastor.

– O, ye drinkers! O, ye that thirst!

– Page, my friend. Fill it up with a crown of wine at the brim.

– It's all cardinal-red.

– Nature abhors a vacuum.]

– Would you say that a fly had drunk it!

– Drink up, Breton-fashion!
– Polish off this nippitate.
– Swallow it down: it's an herbal cure.'

How Gargantua was born in a manner most strange
CHAPTER 5

[Becomes Chapter 6.

Rabelais, recalling the old notion that the Virgin both conceived and delivered her Babe, the Word of God, through the ear, combines a medical romp with a comic sermon, both Erasmian and Lutheran. For the Sorbonnistes faith is the argumentum non apparentium *(Hebrews 11:1), Latin which French-speakers may ignorantly take to mean an 'argument of no apparency'. For them faith is believing something unlikely! Why then believe in the Nativity of Jesus yet not the nativity of Gargantua? Erasmus had shown that faith is not credulity. Faith, in the Greek original of Hebrews 11:1, is trust, trust in 'the evidence of things unseen' (in God and his promises). Mary did not at first trust the angel Gabriel: 'How can these things be?' Told of the conception of Elizabeth with its echoes of Sarah's conception of Isaac, she was reminded that 'with God nothing is ever impossible', cited in this chapter from Luke 1:37, echoing Genesis 8. That is the punch-line of this chapter, which remains joyful from start to finish.*

The texts amusingly cited from Proverbs 14 and I Corinthians 13 to defend credulity mean very different things in context.

Rabelais made the prudential cuts shown in the notes.

The place-names 'Busse' and 'Bibarais' both sound bibulous.

Rabelais returns again to the strange births in Pliny, 3.11, which clearly fascinated him.]

While they were exchanging such tipplers' chit-chat, Gargamelle began to feel pangs down below, at which Gargantua stood up on the sward and graciously comforted her, thinking that it was baby-pains and telling her how she was put out to grass neath the willows and would soon be bringing forth new feet: it behoved her to show fresh courage at the new arrival of

her little one; and though the pains would be rather irksome
for her, they would be short, and the ensuing joy would soon
so take away the pain that even the memory of it would not
remain.

'I will prove it to you,' he said. 'God – that is, our Saviour –
says in the Gospel (John 16), "A woman when she is in travail
hath sorrow, but as soon as she is delivered of the child she
remembereth no more the anguish."'

'Ah,' she said, 'you have spoken well; and I would far rather
hear such words from the Gospel (and I feel much better for
it) than to hear *The Life of Saint Margaret* or some other
black-beetlery.[2]

'But I wish to God you'd cut it off.'

'Cut what off?' asked Gargantua.

'Ah!' she said. 'There's a man for you! You know what I
mean all right!'

'My member?' he said. 'By goat's blood! If that's what you
want . . . – Bring me a knife, somebody!'

'Ha!!' she said, 'God forbid. God forgive me. I never meant
it seriously. Don't do anything whatsoever because of what I
said. But unless God helps me I shall have a rough time today
– all on account of your member, to make you feel nice.'

'Take heart,' he said; 'take heart. Worry no more: the four
oxen in front can manage the wagon. I shall be off for another
quick swig. If anything goes wrong in the meanwhile I shall be
near. Whistle in your palm and I shall be with you.'

Shortly afterwards she started to [sigh], groan and cry out.
At once, from all directions, there came piles of midwives who,
groping about her bottom, came across some bits of membrane
in rather bad taste and thought it was the baby, but it was her
fundament which had loosened because of the mollification of
the *rectum intestinum* – which you call the arse-gut – resulting
from her eating that excess of tripe which we spoke about
above.

2. From '42: . . . not remains. – *'Sheep's courage,' he said. 'Finish with this
    one and we shall soon make another. – 'Ah,' she said, 'you men can talk
    at your ease. All right. For God's sake I shall struggle through to please
    you. But I wish to God . . .*

Whereupon a dirty old crone in the throng (who, with a reputation as a leech, had settled there some sixty years ago from Brisepaille near Saint-Genou) concocted a constrictive for her so horrific that all her sphincters were obstructed and contracted to such an extent that you could only with great effort have forced them apart with your teeth. A horrible thought. (The devil likewise, who was recording the claptrap of two gossips during a Saint Martin's Day Mass, had to use his fine teeth to stretch out the parchment.)

As a result of that mishap, the cotyledonary veins of the womb were released from above and the child sprang through them, entered the *vena cava* and clambering through the midriff (which is situated above the shoulders where the aforesaid *vena* divides into two) took the left path and emerged through her left ear.

The moment he was born, he did not whimper *mee, mee, mee* as other babies do: he yelled at the top of his voice, 'Come and drink, drink, drink!' – inviting one and all, it would seem, to have a drink, [so well that he was heard throughout all the lands of Busse and Biberais].

I doubt whether you assuredly believe that strange nativity. If you do not believe it, I really don't care, but a proper man, a man of good sense, always believes what he is told and what he finds written down.

Does not Solomon say (Proverbs 1), 'The simple believeth every word,' and Saint Paul (I Corinthians 13), 'Charity believeth all things.' So why should you not believe it? Because you say there is *no apparency*. And I tell you that, for that reason alone you ought to believe it in perfect faith, for the Sorbonnists say that 'faith is the evidence of things having no apparency'![3]

Is it against our religion or our faith? Is it against reason; against Holy Writ? I for my part can find nothing against it written in the Holy Bible.

'But if thus were the will of God, would you say that he could *not* have done so?' Ha! For grace's sake do not mingle-mangle

3.   In '42 all is cut out from 'Does not Solomon' to 'no apparency'.

your minds with such vain thoughts. For I tell you that *with God nothing is ever impossible* and that – if he so wished – women from now on would have their children through the ear-hole.

Was not:

– Bacchus born from Jupiter's thigh?

– Rocquetaillade born from his mother's heel?

[– Croquemouche from his nurse's slipper?]

Was not Minerva born through the ear from the brain of Jupiter?

[– Adonis from the bark of a myrtle-tree?

– Castor and Pollux from the shell of an egg laid and hatched out by Leda?]

But you would be even more amazed and thunder-struck if I were to expound to you here the whole chapter of Pliny in which he tells of strange and unnatural births. Yet I am not such a confident liar as he is. Read the third chapter of Book 7 of his *Natural History* and stop befuddling my mind.

How his name was imposed on Gargantua, and how he slurped down the wine

CHAPTER 6

[Becomes Chapter 7.

The first idea of giving a comic etymology to Gargantua's name derives from the non-Rabelaisian Grandes et inestimables Croniques, *where* Gargantua *is allegedly a Greek name meaning 'What a beautiful son you have!' Rabelais is thinking mainly of the imposing of the name of John on the future Baptist, a practice which he attributes to Hebrews generally.*

The 'Scotist doctors' are doctors of theology who follow Duns Scotus. Duns was so out of favour with humanists that they drew from his name our term dunce. *The savour is however more one of joy than of theological contentiousness.*

The take-off of a condemnation by the Sorbonne ('scandalous,

offensive to pious ears and redolent of heresy') uses one of their
authentic formulas. Cf. Erasmus, Adages, *II, V, XCVIII, 'Esernius*
with Pacidianus'.]

That good fellow Grandgousier was joking and drinking with
the others when he heard the horrific yell which his son had
given upon entering into the light of this world, when he roared
out 'Come drink, drink, drink.' At which Grandgousier exclaimed *'Que-grant-tu-as!'* ('How great hast thou!') (to which
supply: *a throat*).

On hearing which words, those who were there said that –
in imitation of the example of the ancient Hebrews – he really
must be called *Gar-gant-tu-a*, since that was the first word his
father uttered at his nativity.[4]

His father graciously consented and it greatly pleased his
mother. To keep him quiet they gave him a longish drink; then
they carried him to the font and, as is the custom among good
Christians, had him baptized.

For his daily feed there were allotted seventeen thousand nine
hundred [and thirteen] cows from Pontille and Bréhémond,
since it was impossible to find in all the land an adequate
wet-nurse for him, given the huge amounts required to feed him,
(even though certain Scotist doctors alleged that his mother
breast-fed him and that she could draw from her bosom on
each occasion fourteen hundred tuns of milk [plus six quarts].
Which is unlikely, and condemned by the Sorbonne as [mam-
malarily] scandalous, offensive to pious ears and redolent from
afar of heresy).

Under that regimen he spent one year and ten months, at
which time they decided on the advice of the physicians to
transport him about, so a beautiful bull-cart was ingeniously
constructed for him by Jean Denyau, in which they happily
bore him hither and thither; he was a joy to behold, for he
sported a fine dial and had all but eighteen chins. He hardly ever
cried, but was always messing himself, since he was wondrously
subject to phlegmatic mucous of the backside, partly because

4.   From '35 Rabelais changed 'nativity' to 'birth'.

of his natural complexion and partly from an accidental disposition brought on by an excessive slurping of the juice of September.

And not a drop did he slurp down without good cause, for if he should happen to be crotchety, fretful, irritable or grumpy, or if he threw himself about and cried and bawled, it was enough to bring him a drink to restore him to his natural state, and he immediately remained quiet and contented.

One of his governesses told me [swearing *boy 'er vaith*] that he had grown so used to doing so that at the mere sound of cask or flagon he would be caught away in ecstasy as though tasting the joys of paradise, and that they, out of consideration for his devout complexion, would keep him happy in the morning by tapping glasses with a knife, or flagons with their bungs, or jugs with their lids. At those sounds he would cheer up, bob and rock himself about while wagging his head, humming through his fingers and playing a baritone with his bum.

How Gargantua was dressed

CHAPTER 7

[Becomes Chapter 8.

Gargantua is sumptuously dressed as befits a royal giant.

In Plato's Symposium (or Banquet) *Aristophanes playfully suggests that the first human beings were created double then split into two. A man and a woman truly love when they find their 'better half'. The androgyne was found by some in Genesis 1:27. Rabelais adopts the androgyne as an emblematic device on a badge for Gargantua to wear in his cap, supplying it with an appropriate motto taken from Saint Paul's praise of love in I Corinthians 13:5, 'Charity seeketh not her own'. He cites it in Greek capitals:* Η ΑΓΑΠΗ ΟΥ ΖΗΤΕΙ ΤΑ ΕΑΥΤΗΣ. *He does not translate it. Without help, his Greekless readers would have been foxed!*

Emblems were in fashion, and some found their way on to men's hats as here.

Andrea Alciato's Emblemata *had appeared in Paris in 1534.*

At Saint-Louand there is a Benedictine Abbey which Frère Rabelais
would have known. The 'Caballists' there are no doubt the monks.
The Fuggers of Augsburg were a family of great bankers.]

When Gargantua had reached that age, his father commanded
that clothes be made for him in his livery, which was of white
and blue: the work was indeed done and they were made,
all cut and stitched in the style then current. From ancient
muniments in the audit office of Montsoreau I find that he was
dressed as follows:

For his shirt they took nine hundred ells of Châtellerault
cloth, together with two hundred for the diamond-shaped gussets set under the armpits. There were no puckerings, since
such gatherings-up of cloth for shirts was not invented until
seamstresses, having broken the tops of their needles, started
to work with their bottoms.

For his doublet were taken eight hundred and thirteen ells of
white satin, and for the points fifteen hundred plus nine-and-a-
half dog-skins. Men began at that time to lace their breeches to
their doublets and not their doublets to their breeches – it being
unnatural [as was amply declared by Occam commenting on
the *Exponibilia* of Magister Topbreeches].

Eleven hundred plus five-and-a-third ells of white estamin-
cloth were taken for his hose, which were slashed in columns,
fluted and channelled on the back so as not to overheat his
kidneys. They puffed out the slashes from within with as much
damask-cloth as was needed.

And note that he had very fine tibias, well proportioned to
the rest of his body. For his codpiece were taken sixteen and a
quarter ells of the same cloth. In shape it was like a flying-
buttress well and merrily attached to two beautiful golden
buckles and fixed on by two enamel hooklets; in each of them
was mounted a large emerald as big as an orange (for as
Orpheus states in his book *On Precious Stones* and Pliny in his
final Book, it has properties for erecting and invigorating the
organ of Nature.

The opening of the codpiece was about a pole in length; it
was slashed like the hose, with the blue damask-cloth puffing

out as before. But on seeing the beautiful embroidery on it, with its threads of gold, its delightful strap-work garnished with fine diamonds, fine rubies, fine turquoises, fine emeralds and Persian pearls, you would have likened it to a horn-of-plenty such as you can see on antiques and such as Rhea bestowed on Adrastea and Ida (the two nymphs who brought up Jupiter). It was ever vigorous, succulent, oozing, ever verdant, ever flourishing, ever fructifying, full of humours, full of flowers, full of fruits, full of all delights. As God is my witness it was good to see! But I will expound all this much more fully for you in a book I have written *On the Dignity of Codpieces*.

But I warn you: long and ample though it was, it was nevertheless well furnished and well victualled within, in no wise resembling those hypocritical codpieces worn by masses of weaklings, codpieces full of nothing but wind, to the great prejudice of the female sex.

For his shoes there were cut four hundred and six ells of velvet of crimson blue. They too were most daintily slashed with a herring-bone pattern [in parallel lines united in regular cylinders]. For their soles were used the hides of eleven hundred dun cows, cut in the shape of cod-fish tails.

For his cloak were taken eighteen hundred ells of blue velvet, dyed fast in the fibre, embroidered round the edges with sprigs of vine and in the middle with pint wine-pots worked in silver-thread with interlacing rings of gold, and a great many pearls, thus indicating that he would be in his time a good whipper-back of pint-pots.

His belt was of three hundred and a half ells of silken serge, half white [unless I am much mistaken] and half blue.

His sword did not come from Valencia nor his dagger from Saragossa, since his father loathed all those boozy, diabolically half-converted Hidalgos: he had a fine wooden sword and a dagger of boiled leather, painted and gilded enough to satisfy anyone.

His purse was the scrotum of an elephant given to him by Herr von Pracontal, the Libyan consul.

For his gown were cut two-thirds of an ell short of nine

thousand six hundred ells of blue velvet (as above) all embroidered in unravelled gold-thread forming diagonals which, when
you looked at them from a particular angle, radiated a colour
which has no name, such as you can see on the necks of doves,
which marvellously rejoiced the eyes of those who contemplated it.

For his bonnet were cut three hundred plus two-and-a-
quarter ells of white velvet. It was large and round and fitted
the whole of his head, since his father held that those Moorish
bonnets raised up like pie-crusts will cause some evil to fall one
day on to close-cropped pates. For its plume he wore a large
and beautiful blue feather taken from the wilds of Hyrcania; it
hung most attractively over his right ear.

For the medallion of his bonnet he wore, on a tablet of
gold weighing some sixty-eight marks, a figure of appropriate
enamel portraying a human body with two heads, each turned
to face the other, four arms, four feet and two bottoms, such
as Plato says in *The Symposium* was the nature of Mankind at
its mythical beginning.

Around it was inscribed in Greek script:

HE AGAPE OU ZETEI TA HEAUTES[5]

To wear round his neck he had a golden chain weighing
twenty-five thousand and sixty-three golden marks, fashioned
in the form of huge berries, between which were set huge green
jaspers cut and engraved with dragons entirely surrounded by
sparks and rays of light such as was worn of old by King
Necephos. It hung down as far as the hollow below the breast-
bone. From it he enjoyed all his life such benefit as is known to
the Greek physicians.

For his gloves sixteen goblin-skins were used, and for their
borders three hides of werewolves; they were made from those
materials following the prescriptions of the Caballists of Saint-
Louand.

For his rings (which his father wanted him to wear to bring

5.   Charity seeketh not her own.

back that ancient mark of nobility) he wore on the index-finger of his left hand a carbuncle as big as an ostrich-egg, most attractively set in gold as pure as that of Turkish sequins. On his middle finger he wore a ring composed of the four metals assembled in the most ingenious fashion that has ever been seen, such that the steel never rubbed away the gold, and the silver never encroached upon the copper. It was entirely the work of Captain Chappuys and Alcofribas, his good factor. On the middle finger of his right hand he wore a spiral-shaped ring, in which were set a perfect balas-ruby, a tapered diamond and an emerald from the land of the river Pison; it was of estimable value. Hans Carvel, the Great Lapidary of the King of Melinde, estimated its worth at sixty-nine million eight hundred and ninety-four thousand [and eighteen] *Agnus Dei* crowns.

That was also the estimate of the Fuggers of Augsburg.

Gargantua's colours and livery

CHAPTER 8

[Becomes Chapter 9.

There is an abyss between the natural and the conventional sign as great as between word and action. Rabelais enters the lists against a popular book of heraldry, The Blason of Colours, *which, he maintains, makes the meanings of colours arbitrary, whereas colours in fact have natural meanings internationally recognized across the centuries by natural law.*

Rabelais also distinguishes between august, courtly emblems and fustian rebuses. Rebuses are essentially a matter of puns, puns such as Rabelais himself exploits with delight in other contexts. Some of the puns have become unclear even for French readers because the pronunciation of French has changed so much. Puns do not often lend themselves to translation. The links are as easy in French as a sprig of rue, say, is for 'rueful' in English, or as banewort, for 'baneful'. I have transposed some when it helps to convey the flavour of Rabelais.

One of the sources of the knowledge of the 'sacred writings' of Egypt was Horapollo's On Hieroglyphics, *which was already published with a translation by a protégé of Marguerite d'Angoulême, the Queen of Navarre. The basic work on emblems by Andrea Alciato was translated into French and dedicated to the Admiral of France, Chabot, a highly placed evangelical. It was printed in 1536 but Rabelais knows of it beforehand and of its dedication to the Admiral de France. The admiral's official emblem was an anchor entwined by a dolphin. It is linked to an adage of Erasmus, 'Hasten Slowly', (II, I, I, 'Festina lente'). It is the object of a long and rich commentary by Erasmus.*

The Dream of Polifilo of Francesco Colonna is one of the great illustrated books of the Renaissance, particularly interesting to Rabelais for its portrayal of ancient hieroglyphs and sumptuous buildings.]

Gargantua's colours, as you have been able to read above, were white and blue. By them his father intended it to be understood that his son was a Heaven-sent joy for him, since for him white signified joy, pleasure, happiness and delight, while blue signified heavenly things.

I realize that you are laughing at the old tippler when you read these words: you judge that his interpretation of those colours is far too gross and absurd and say that white signifies faith and blue firmness.

But without getting agitated, angry, overheated or thirsty – for the weather is dangerous – answer me this, if you want to that is: for I will use no further constraint against you or anyone else whoever they may be; I shall simply tell you one word of the Bottle: who is pushing you? who is prodding you? who is telling you that white means faith, and blue means firmness?

Why, a wretched book, peddled by hawkers and hucksters, entitled *The Blason of Colours*. Who wrote it? Whoever it was, he was wise not to put his name to it. I simply do not know what should astonish me more, his presumption or his stupidity:

his presumption: in that he has dared, on his private authority, without reason, cause or verisimilitude, to prescribe what colours should mean; such is the practice of tyrants, who intend their will alone to take the place of reason, not of the learned and wise who satisfy their readers with evident reasons;

his stupidity: in that he thought that the world, without further demonstrations or valid arguments, would govern their devices by his fatuous impositions. Indeed, as the proverb puts it, *A besquittered bum in shit abounds*: he has found a few nincompoops left over from the days when hats were tall who have placed their trust in his writings and have, in accordance with them, fashioned their mottos and apophthegms, bedizened their mules, dressed their pages, quartered their breeches, embroidered their gloves, fringed their bed-curtains, painted their medallions, composed their songs and – what is worse – secretly spread their frauds and dirty little deceits amongst honest matrons.

In similar darkness are plunged those show-offs at court, [those transposers of puns,] who, when they want to signify 'hope' (*espoir*) on their devices portray a *sphere*; for 'pains' portray the *pens* (quills) of a bird; for 'bankrupt,' a ruptured *banc*; for 'melancholy,' some ancoly; for 'a crescent life',[6] a hornèd moon; a *non* and an armoured breast-plate for '*non durabit*', [and a *lit* (bed) without a *ciel* (canopy) for a *licentié* (a graduate),] which are rebuses so inept, so insipid, so yokelish and barbarous that, from this day forth, we ought to stick a fox's tail behind the collars of anyone who would still employ them in France and make masks of cow-pats for their faces.[7]

By the same reasoning (if reasoning is what I should call it and not lunacy!) I could paint a hamper to denote that *I am hampered*, or a mustard-pot to signify *My heart most tardily moves*; I could paint a chamber-pot for a *chamberlain*; the seat of my breeches for a *vessel of* paix *and* pets (*of peace and farts*); my codpiece for a *wand-bearer*, or a dog's-turd for my *sturdy rod, Wherein lies the love of my lady*.[8]

Very differently acted the sages of Egypt in Antiquity when they wrote in those letters they called hieroglyphics, which none

6. A crescent life: that is, a growing, thriving one.
7. *Non durabit* means in Latin 'it will not last', but sounds in French like a *non dur* (not hard or durable) *habit* (robe).
8. The above translation is very free. Rendered literally, with explanations inside brackets): I could paint a *pénier* (that is, a *panier*, basket) to denote 'to suffer *peines*' (pains) , or a *pot è moutarde* (a mustard-pot) to signify 'My heart *moult tarde*' (much languishes); I could paint a *pot à pisser* (a chamber-pot) for an 'official' (both a chamber pot and an ecclesiastical

understood who did not know – and all understood who did know – the qualities, properties and natures of the objects portrayed. Horus Apollo wrote two books in Greek about them and Polyphilus developed them further in his *Dream of Love*. In France you have a taste of it in the device of my Lord the Admiral which was originally sported by Octavian Augustus.

But I shall let my skiff sail no further amongst such distasteful gulfs and shallows. I am returning to dock in the port I set out from.

I very much hope to write more fully about all this one day, demonstrating, both by philosophical arguments and authorities acknowledged and approved since the most venerable antiquity, which colours there are in nature, how many there are and what may be signified by each of them, if the Prince wishes and commands it – he who with his command grants power and knowledge.[9]

What the colours white and blue do signify

CHAPTER 9

[Becomes Chapter 10.

Rabelais argues that colours have meanings which are natural, not arbitrarily imposed. He starts from Aristotle's Topics. *His argument is impressive and convincing (flawed only if one denies that all joy is contrary in species to all sadness). The true nature of white is shown*

---

official); the seat of my breeches for a 'vessel of farts' (with the old pun between *pets*, farts and *paix*, peace); my codpiece, for a '*greffe des arrêts*' (a written declaration of judicial sentences); *un tronc de céans* (a branch here within), 'Wherein lies the love of my lady.'

9. From '35: . . . each of them, if *God saves the mould of my bonnet, that is, as my grandma used to say, my wine-pot.*

In the first edition, despite the hyperbole, there is probably not an allusion to the king (often called 'Le Prince' by humanists as a Latinism). Le Prince was also the nickname of two Lyonese printers who printed *Pantagruel*, Claude Nourry, who died in 1533, and Pierre de Sainte-Lucie, with whom Rabelais appears to have quarrelled precisely over his edition of *Pantagruel*.

*by the Greek of Matthew 17:2 and the Latin version of it by Erasmus
which Rabelais cites: the Lord's raiment became at the Transfiguration
'as white as the light'. (The Vulgate here wrongly says 'as snow'.) In
medieval times Bartholus followed the Vulgate and so was mistaken.
Lorenzo Valla scornfully corrected him. Erasmus finds Valla 'too
wordy' on the subject. Rabelais does not. Medieval artists often make
the light gold: Renaissance artists, white. Some of the greatest legal
scholars wrangled over the meanings of colours, Baïf, for example.
Rabelais' erudition is impressive but not necessarily rare or original.
Natural Law is universal but allows of cultural or perverse exceptions.*

*The account of the old woman who clung to life, saying 'Light is
good', is attributed to Varro in the* Adages *of Vulpius. She appears
also in the* Praise of Folly *of Erasmus.]*

White then signifies happiness, gladness, joy: signifying it not
abusively but with a good title. You may discover that to be
true if, setting your emotions aside, you listen to what I shall
expound to you.

Aristotle maintains that if you postulate two notions to be
contrary in their species, such as good and evil, virtue and vice,
cold and hot, black and white, pleasure and pain, grief or
sadness, etc., and if you pair them together in such a manner
that the contrary of one species corresponds rationally to the
contrary of another, it follows that the other contrary must be
appropriate to the remaining one.

To give an example: virtue and vice are contraries within one
species. So are good and evil. When one of the contraries of the
first species corresponds with one of the second, as *virtue* with
good – for one knows that virtue is good – so the two remaining
contraries, *evil* and *vice*, must also correspond, since vice is
indeed evil.

Once you have grasped that rule of logic, take those two
contraries, joy and sadness, and then these two, black and
white, since they are contraries in nature. Now, if black signifies
grief, then white will rightly signify joy.

And that signification was not laid down by any human
imposition but accepted by that universal consent which
philosophers term the Law of Nations, the *jus gentium*, the

universal law, valid in all lands. You are well aware that all peoples, all nations and tongues (I except the ancient Syracusans and a few Argives whose minds were askew) whenever they want outwardly to show sadness, don black. All mourning is in black. Such universal agreement is not reached without Nature providing some argument or reason which every person can immediately grasp without further instruction from anybody: that is what we call a Natural Law. By white under the same guidance from Nature the entire world has understood joy, happiness, gladness, pleasure and delight. In times past the Thracians and Cretans used white stones to signify the more auspicious and happy days, and black the sad and inauspicious ones. Is the night not malign, sad and melancholy? Privation makes it black and gloomy. And does not the light rejoice the whole of nature?

Now light is white: whiter than anything else there is. To prove it I could refer you to the treatise of Lorenzo Valla *Against Bartholus*, but you will be satisfied by the testimony of the Gospels: in Matthew it is said of our Lord at the Transfiguration that *his raiment was made white as the light*. By that luminous whiteness Jesus enabled his three apostles to understand the idea and form of eternal bliss.

All humans rejoice in light, as is shown by that old woman without a tooth in her head who could still mumble, *Bona lux* ('Light is good').

Did not Toby reply, after he had lost his sight and was greeted by Raphael (Tobit 5), 'What manner of joy shall be to me who see not the light of Heaven'? And by being clad in such a colour the angels bore witness to the joy of the whole universe at the Resurrection of our Saviour (John 20) and at his Ascension (Acts 1). Saint John the Evangelist too (Revelation 4 and 7) saw the faithful in the hallowed New Jerusalem 'arrayed' in similar 'white garments'.

Read the ancient authorities, Greek as well as Latin:

– *you will find* that the town of Alba (the prototype of Rome) was founded and named because of the discovery of a white sow;

– *you will find* that whenever it was decreed that a victorious

captain could enter Rome in triumph he did so in a chariot
drawn by white horses; so too a captain who entered with an
ovation, for they could not by any sign or colour more definitely
express joy at their arrival than by whiteness;

– *you will find* that Pericles, the General of the Athenians,
wished those of his soldiers who drew the white beans by lot
to spend the day in joy, happiness and repose, while the other
group were to be out fighting.

I could expound hundreds of other texts and exempla for
you, but this is not the place to do so.

By understanding the above you can solve a conundrum
accounted insoluble by Alexander of Aphrodisias: why does
the lion, which terrifies all beasts by its mere cry and roar, fear
and revere a white cock? It is (as Proclus states in his book *On
Sacrifice and Magic*) because the presence of the power of
the sun (which is the instrument and source of all light, both
terrestrial and sidereal) is more befittingly symbolized in the
white cock – both for its colour and for its properties and
specificity – than in the lion. He adds that devils have often
been seen in the form of a lion, only suddenly to vanish in the
presence of a white cock.

That is why the *Gali* (the French, that is, who are called thus
since they are by nature as white as milk (called *gala* by the
Greeks) delight in wearing white plumes in their bonnets: for
they are naturally joyful, candid, gracious and well loved, and
have as their symbol and device the whitest of all flowers:
the lily. If you ask how Nature brings us to understand joy
and happiness by the colour white, I reply that it is by analogy
and correspondences: for just as – externally – white scatters and
disperses our vision, producing a manifest disintegration of
those bodily spirits which make sight possible (according to the
opinions of Aristotle in the *Problems* and of the specialists in
vision, and as you yourselves can tell from experience when
you cross mountains covered with snow and complain of not
being able to see properly, which Xenophon describes as hap-
pening to his companions and which Galen explains in detail
in Book 10 of his treatise *On the Use of Parts of the Body*), so
too – internally – the heart is disintegrated by exceeding joy

and suffers a manifest dispersal of its vital spirits; which dispersal can so increase that the heart would be left bereft of all means of support and life consequently extinguished [by that excess of joy as Galen states in Book 12 of *On the Method of Curing* and] as the said Galen demonstrates in Book 5 of *On Parts Affected* and Book 2 of *On the Causes of Symptoms*; and as happened in the past (witness Cicero in Book 1 of the *Tusculan Disputations*), Verrius, Aristotle, Livy after the battle of Cannae, Pliny, Book 7, Chapters 32 and 53, Aulus Gellius, in Book 3, Chapter 15, and others, to Diagoras of Rhodes, Chilo, Sophocles, Dionysius the Tyrant of Sicily, Philippides, Philemon, Polycrita, Philistion, Marcus Juventius and others, who died of joy; and as Avicenna (in the *Second Canon*, and in his book *On the Strengths of the Heart*) says of saffron, which so stimulates the heart that, taken in excessive doses, it robs it of life by superabundant dissolution and dilation. [See Alexander of Aphrodisias in Chapter 19 of the First Book of his *Problems*. The case rests.

Hey!] I have gone deeper into this than I planned when I started, so here I will strike my sails, reserving the rest for my book to be entirely taken up with this matter. I shall merely say in one word that blue signifies Heaven and all things celestial by the same symbolism by which white signifies joy and delight.

Gargantua's childhood

CHAPTER 10

[Becomes Chapter 11.

From erudite declamations to moral fun, dominated in part by proverbs and saws. We see the uproarious results of leaving young Gargantua to himself in the hands of lubricious peasant women chosen by his rustic father.

'To skin the renard' (or, 'the fox') is to puke during excessive drinking. The expression appears twice in the long addition, which dates from 1535.

Gargantua's father was King of the Butterflies.]

From three years of age to five Gargantua, by order of his
father, was brought up and grounded in all the appropriate
disciplines. Like little country boys he spent his time drinking,
eating and sleeping; eating, sleeping and drinking; sleeping,
drinking and eating.

He was forever wallowing in the mire, dirtying his nose,
scrabbling his face, treading down the backs of his shoes, gaping
at flies and chasing the butterflies (over whom his father held
sway); he would pee in his shoes, shit over his shirt-tails, [wipe
his nose on his sleeves,] dribble snot into his soup and go
galumphing about.

[He would drink out of his slippers, regularly scratch his
belly on wicker-work baskets, cut his teeth on his clogs, get his
broth all over his hands, drag his cup through his hair, hide
under a wet sack, drink with his mouth full, eat girdle-cake but
not bread, bite for a laugh and laugh while he bit, spew in his
bowl, let off fat farts, piddle against the sun, leap into the
river to avoid the rain, strike while the iron was cold, dream
day-dreams, act the goody-goody, skin the renard, clack his
teeth like a monkey saying its prayers, get back to his muttons,
turn the sows into the meadow, beat the dog to teach the lion,
put the cart before the horse, scratch himself where he ne'er did
itch, worm secrets out from under your nose, let things slip,
gobble the best bits first, shoe grasshoppers, tickle himself to
make himself laugh, be a glutton in the kitchen, offer sheaves
of straw to the gods, sing Magnificat at Mattins and think it
right, eat cabbage and squitter puree, recognize flies in milk,
pluck legs off flies, scrape paper clean but scruff up parchment,
take to this heels, swig straight from the leathern bottle, reckon
up his bill without Mine Host, beat about the bush but snare
no birds, believe clouds to be saucepans and pigs' bladders
lanterns, get two grists from the same sack, act the goat to get
fed some mash, mistake his fist for a mallet, catch cranes at the
first go, link by link his armour make, always look a gift horse
in the mouth, tell cock-and-bull stories, store a ripe apple
between two green ones, shovel the spoil back into the ditch,
save the moon from baying wolves, hope to pick up larks if
the heavens fell in, make virtue out of necessity, cut his sops

according to his loaf, make no difference twixt shaven and shorn, and skin the renard every day.]

His father's little dogs would eat out of his bowl, and he would eat with them; he would bite their ears and they would scratch his nose; he would puff at their bums and they would lick his chops.

And what d'ye think, laddies! May the drams make 'ee poorly! That naughty little lecher was forever groping his nurses, above, below; before, behind. And – gee up, little donkey – he was already beginning to put his codpiece through its paces. Every day his nurses would bedeck it with posies, fine ribbons, fair flowers and tufts of lace, and spend their time working it between their fingers like dough in the kneading-trough, and, as though they enjoyed the game, guffawing when it pricked up its ears.

One called it my little bung; another, my little prickle; another, my corral brand; another my stopper, my wimble, my ram-rod, my bradawl, [my drooping stalk, my rough-and-tumble, my poting-stick,] my pretty little red chidling and my little trollopy-bollocky.

'It's mine!' said one.

'It's mine,' said another.

'And what about me!' said a third. 'Am I to get nothing? 'Struth then, I'll cut it off!'

'Oh!' said another, 'You'll hurt him, m'Lady. Do you go round cutting off little boys' whatsits?'

[He'd be just *Master*, with no appendage!]

And to keep him amused like the local children they made him a lovely whirligig out of the sails of a Mirabeau windmill.

Gargantua's hobby-horses

CHAPTER 11

[*Becomes* Chapter 12.

The boy giant, like many children, is a chatterbox and interested in his natural functions. His mad education emphasizes these traits.

In parts of France, including Rabelais' own pays, *houses built into cliffs have entrances at the top as well as below at ground level.*

'To land someone with the Monk' is to leave him holding the baby. It originally meant to submit someone to torture.

Plays on the word pape *(pope) are routine in the time of Rabelais but rarely translatable:* papelard *means 'a bacon-sucker' and hence a Lenten hypocrite.* Parpaillons *(or* papillons*) are butterflies.*

There is another play between sense *(side, direction) and* cents *(hundreds). The words are left as they are.]*

Then, so that he would be good once astride his whole life long, they fashioned a lovely big wooden horse for him, and he got it to prance, jump, run round circles, kick up its heels and dance, walk, trot, step high, gallop, amble, pace like a pony and a gelding, and then to run like a camel or a wild ass.

And (just as monks change their dalmatics according to the feast-days) he would change the colour of its coat to bay, sorrel, dapple-grey, rat-skin, dun-yellow, roan, cow-hide, black-spotted, red-speckled, piebald or lily-white.

Gargantua himself made another hunting hobby-horse from a huge woodman's drag, another everyday hobby-horse from the beam of a wine-press and a mule (complete with a sumpter-cloth for his bedchamber) from a gigantic oak. He had ten or a dozen other hobby-horses forming a relay, and seven more for riding at post. And every one of them he put to bed close by him.

One day the Seigneur de Grudge-crumb came to visit his father in great state and pomp. That very same day there similarly came le Duc de Free-meals and le Comte de Wet-whistle. Gracious me, with so many people about, space was a bit short, particularly for stabling. So in order to find out whether there were any unused stabling elsewhere on the estate, the major-domo and the lodgings-steward of the Seigneur de Grudge-crumb addressed themselves to Gargantua, a little boy, furtively asking him where was the stabling for the big horses – believing that children will readily tell you anything.

So he led them up the grand staircase of the château, through the upper hall into a wide gallery by which they went into a great tower. As they were climbing up yet more stairs the lodging-steward said to the major-domo,

'This lad is having us on: stables are never at the top of the house!'

'You're wrong there,' said the major-domo, 'for I know houses in Lyons, La Baumette and Chinon – in other places too – where the stables are at the highest point of the building. There may be a way-out at the top. But to be more certain I shall ask him about it.'

He then asked Gargantua,

'Where are you taking us, my dear little chap?'

'To my big horses' stables,' he said. 'We shall soon be there. Let's just climb up those steps.'

Then he led them through another great hall into his bedroom and, opening the door, said,

'Here are the stables you were asking about. Here's my Spanish-horse, here's my gelding, my courser, my ambler.'

Then, pressing a great beam of wood on to them, he said,

'This is my Friesland-pony. I got him in Frankfurt; but he can be yours now. He's a lovely little colt and can put up with a lot. With half-a-dozen spaniels, a couple of greyhounds and a male falcon you will be kings of hare and partridge throughout the winter.'

'By Saint John,' they said, 'a lot of good that's done us! This time we've been landed with the Monk!'

['That I deny,' said Gargantua. 'He's not been here for three days.']

Guess what it was better for them to do: hide away in embarrassment or laugh at the entertainment.

As they were making their way down in confusion, Gargantua asked them,

'Would you like to have a poogumajig?'

'What is that, then?' they replied.

'Five turds,' he said, 'to make you a face-mask.'

'Even if we were set to roast today we'd never get burnt,' said the major-domo. 'We've been too well basted! Well, my dear little chap, you've put bales of straw over our horns all right! One of these days I shall see you made pope!'

'A *pape* I mean to be!' said Gargantua, 'then you'll be a *papillon* and my nice little popinjay a perfect *papelard*.'

The lodgings-steward said, 'Well, well, well.'

'Yes,' said Gargantua. 'But guess how many stitches there are in mummy's mantle.'

'Sixteen,' said the lodgings-steward.

'You're not speaking Gospel truth,' said Gargantua. 'There's a front to it in one sense and a back to it in the other sense: you got the cents all wrong!'

'When?' asked the steward.

'That time they made your nose into a spigot to draw off a vatful of pooh,' said Gargantua, 'and your gullet into a funnel to pour it off into another pan as the bottom was all smelly.'

'Golly,' said the major-domo, 'we have come across a tongue-wagger! Well, Monsieur Chatterbox, may God keep you out of harm's way, for you have a sharp tongue.'

They scuttled on down, dropping under the stairs the great beam which Gargantua had loaded them with. Whereupon Gargantua said,

'What devilishly rotten riders you are. Your bob-tail will let you down when you need her.

'But if you had to get from here to Cahuzac would you rather get astride a gosling or lead a sow on a leash?'

'I,' said the steward, 'would rather have a drink.'

And so saying they went into the lower hall; all their companions were there and when they told them this novella, they had them buzzing with laughter like a bevy of flies.

How Grandgousier recognized the miraculous intelligence of Gargantua from his invention of a bum-wiper

CHAPTER 12

[Becomes Chapter 13.

Before the general use of lavatory-paper the leaves of many plants were used to wipe bottoms; some still retain their popular names such

as arse-smart. Rabelais prepares us, through laughter at a caricature
of the effects of the old education, for the evangelical-humanist propa-
ganda of the following chapters. Left to himself and to the minis-
trations of peasant women, Gargantua becomes a bouncing boy who
concentrates on his bum, on faeces and on graffiti on the wall of his
jakes composed by an old woman. The addition at the end, with its
evocation of Duns Scotus (Jean d'Ecosse) places this foul education
firmly under that 'Gothick' past which humanists (unfairly) associated
with that 'dunce'.

One of the few changes to the text was made in '42. The phrase
'the most royal' is cut out. (Sensitivities about royal backsides had to
be humoured!)

'Breton wine' came not from Brittany but from the vineyards of a
Monsieur Breton in Rabelais' pays. It still did some ten years ago and
doubtless continues to do so.

Saint Buddocks, a West Country saint later gentrified as Saint
Budeaux, is used here to catch the savour of Gargantua's patois oath.
'Par la mer Dé' ('By the mercy of God', with a pun on merde *(shit)).*
'Doctor of the Sorbonne' becomes 'Doctor of Gay Science' in '42.]

Grandgousier, on his way back from defeating the Canarrians,
came to visit his son Gargantua towards the end of his fifth
year and was delighted at seeing such a son, as such a father
could well be. Putting his arms round his neck and kissing him,
he asked him all sorts of little-boy questions. He drank drink for
drink with him, and with his nurses too, whom he meticulously
asked, amongst other things, whether they had kept him white
and clean. Gargantua replied that he had so ordered things that
there was no boy in the whole realm cleaner than he was.

'How did you manage that?' said Grandgousier.

'After long and careful experimentation,' said Gargantua, 'I
have invented a way of wiping my bum which is the most royal,
the most lordly and the most excellent one ever seen.'

'Which way was that?' said Grandgousier.

'I shall tell you now,' said Gargantua. 'Once I wiped my bum
on a velvet muffler belonging to one of your young ladies. That
I found good, for the softness of the silk gave great pleasure to
my fundament. It was the same another time when I used a

lady's lace bonnet; yet another time I used a neckerchief; another, some crimson satin ear-muffs, but the gilt-work on a pile of shitty pearls stuck into them skinned all my bum: may Saint-Anthony's fire scorch the arse-gut of the jeweller which made them and of the young lady who wore them! The pain went away when I wiped my bottom on a page's bonnet full of Switzer-style plumes. Then, when I was pooing behind a bush, I came across a March cat and wiped my bum on that: but its claws ulcerated my perineum. The following morning I made it all better by wiping myself on mummy's gloves, all redolent of her bad-crack. Then I wiped my bum on sage, fennel, dill, marjoram and rose-petals; on leaves of the vegetable marrow, of cabbages, of the vine, of mallows, longwort (which gives you a raw bottom), lettuces, spinach – which all did me a pile of good – pot-mercury, arse-smart, stinging-nettles and groundsel: that gave me the Lombardy squitters, but I cured it by wiping myself on my codpiece.

'Then I wiped myself on linen sheets, on a blanket, the curtains, a cushion, a carpet, a baize table-cloth, a table-napkin, [a serviette,] a headscarf, a handkerchief and a shoulder-cloth. I found even more pleasure in all of them than mangy folk do when you scratch 'em.'

'Yes, I'm sure,' said Grandgousier. 'Which arse-wiper did you find the best?'

'I was just about to come to that,' said Gargantua. 'You'll soon know it all, down to the *World without end, Amen*. I wiped my bottom on hay, straw, oakum, flock, wool and paper, but

> Use paper on your dirty bum:
> On your bollocks splatter some.'

'Well I never did,' said Grandgousier. 'Have you caught at the rim, seeing you've begun to rime!'

And Gargantua said:

> 'Yes indeed, King of mine:
> I can rime all the time:
> E'en when snotty in frost or rime.

But just you hear what our jakes say to all who pooh there:

> Squitter,
> Shitter,
> Farter,
> Thundering,
> Dropper,
> Dunger,
> Larder,
> Scumbering,
> Squirting,
> Turding,
> Fouling,
> May erysipelas bite you, sir,
> If failing –
> Your ring
> Cleaning –
> You wipe it not without demur.

Shall I go on?'
  'Yes, please,' said Grandgousier.
  'Well then,' said Gargantua:

> Whilst duly dropping yesterday
> The tribute owing by my bum,
> An unexpected smell did come:
> An evil pong about me lay.
> If only someone brought my way
> That girling whom I long to come,
> Whilst poohing;
> I would my tool to her display
> And get it then – I would, by gum –
> Into that pee-hole 'neath her tum,
> Whilst her fair fingers cleaned away
> My poohing.

Now dare tell me that I know nothing about such things! By Saint Buddocks, I never made them up myself, but on hearing them recited by grandma over there I have stored them in the game-bag of my memory.'

'Can we get back to the subject,' said Grandgousier.

'Which? Poohing?' said Gargantua.

'No,' said Grandgousier, 'the wiping of bottoms.'

'But,' said Gargantua, 'are you prepared to pay me a vat of Breton wine if I render you speechless?'

'Yes, certainly,' said Grandgousier.

'There is no need,' said Gargantua, 'to wipe your bum unless there be ordure upon it. No ordure can be there unless you have pooh-ed. We must therefore pooh before wiping.'

'O my!' said Grandgousier. 'How clever you are, my little boykin! One of these days – soon – I'll have you made a Doctor of the Sorbonne. By God I will. You are wiser than your years. Now do, I pray, get on with your bottom-wiping topic. And, by my beard, instead of a vat of that good *vin breton* (which grows not in Brittany but in the fair vineyards of Véron) you shall have sixty tuns of it.'

'I wiped my bum after that,' said Gargantua, 'on a head-scarf, a pillow, a game-bag, a basket – but oh, what a nasty bottom-wiper – then on a hat. And note that some hats are soft, others have bristles, others velvety, others smooth as taffeta or soft as satin; the best of all is one made of bristles, for it is very good for the abstersion of faecal matter.

'Then I wiped my bum on a hen, a cock, a pullet, on calf-skin, on the pelt of a hare, on a pigeon, a cormorant, a lawyer's bundle, a woollen hood, a night-cap and a stuffed decoy-bird.

'But to conclude: I affirm and maintain that there is no bottom-wiper like a downy young goose, provided that you hold its head between your legs. Believe me on my honour, for you can feel in your bumhole a mirifical voluptuousness, as much from the softness of its down as from the temperate heat of the young goose which is readily communicated to the arse-gut and the rest of the intestines until it reaches the region of the heart and the brain. And do not believe that the blessedness of the heroes and demi-gods in the Elysian Fields lies in their nectar, asphodel or ambrosia, as these old women would

maintain: in my opinion it consists in the fact that they wipe
their bums on a young goose.'

[And such is the opinion of Master Duns Scotus.]

How Gargantua was introduced to Latin literature by a Theologian

CHAPTER 13

[Becomes Chapter 14.

*The name of the preceptor Tubal Holofernes is revealing: Thubal
(worldly, confusion and ignomiry in Hebrew) and Holofernes, taken
to be the archetypical persecutor of the Church. The name of his
successor, Jobelin Bridé, means a bridled fool.*

*From '42, throughout this and the following chapter, Rabelais sys-
tematically replaced 'theologian' by 'sophist', and similarly for all
similar words like 'theology' and 'theologically'. Those important
changes are not further pointed out in the notes; they are made every
time without exception.*

*The old-fashioned books used in this wretched system of education
are all real ones, long since mocked by many humanists including
Erasmus. Sleep in Confidence was the title of a book of sermons to be
used by priests.*

*The long opening account of the wisdom and skill at horsemanship
of Philip of Macedonia is taken from Plutarch's Life of Alexander. It
implicitly condemns Gargantua's limitation to hobby-horses and,
later, to his old mule, thus preparing the way through laughter for the
new princely education which is to follow.]*

That fine fellow Grandgousier, having heard those words, was
caught away in wonder as he considered the higher meanings
and the miraculous intelligence of his son Gargantua. And he
said to the nurse-maids:

'Philip, King of Macedonia, recognized the good sense of his
son from the dextrous way he handled a horse, for the horse
was so intractable and terrifying that no one dared to mount

it: it threw its riders, breaking the neck of one, the legs of another, the skull and the jawbone of others. As Alexander watched it closely in the hippodrome (which was the place where horses were exercised and put through their paces), he spotted that the horse's skittishness arose from fear of its own shadow. At which he leapt astride it and headed towards the sun so that the shadow was cast to the rear; and thus he made it docile and malleable to his will. By which deed his father, recognizing the divine intelligence within him, had him very excellently taught by Aristotle, who was then rated above all the philosophers of Greece. Yet I can inform you that, from this one conversation which I have now had with my son Gargantua before you all, I recognize that his intelligence does partake of something divine, since I see him so acute, so subtle, profound and serene: I have absolutely no doubt that, if he receives a good grounding, he will in time attain to the highest degree of wisdom. I therefore intend to entrust him to some learned man to have him educated according to his abilities. I will spare nothing!

'In fact they recommended to him a great Doctor of Theology called Magister Thubal Holofernes. He taught Gargantua his ABC so well that he could recite it by heart backwards. He spent five years and three months over that.

'Then he read with him the Donatus, the *Facetus*, the *Theodolet* and Alan de Lille's *Parables*. Over that he spent thirteen years, three months [and a fortnight]. Note however that during this time his tutor taught him to write in the Gothick script, and he copied out all his books by hand, since the art of printing was not yet in use. He normally lugged about a bulky writing-desk weighing more than seven thousand hundred-weight. Its pen-and-pencil-box was as big and bulky as the great pillars in Saint-Martin d'Ainay; its ink-horn, which could hold a ton, dangled from it by great chains of iron.

'His tutor then read with him *On Methods of Signifying*, with commentaries by Windbaghius, Plodmannius, Too-many-Likemmius, Galahad, John Thickeadius, Billonius, Quimius and a heap of others. He spent over eighteen years and eleven

months over it and he knew it so well that he recited it backwards in the exam and proved to his mother on his fingers that
On Methods of Signifying has nothing to do with learning.

'The tutor then read the *Computum* with him; he had spent a
good sixteen years and two months over it when his tutor died,

> In the year of grace fourteen hundred and twenty,
> Killed by the pox of which he had plenty.

'He was then allotted another old cougher called Magister
Jobelin Bridé, who read to him *Hugotio*, Eberard's *Lexicon of
Greek*, the *Doctrinale*, the *Quid est*, the *Supplementum*, the
Mammotreptus, the *How to Behave at Table*, Seneca *On the
Four Cardinal Virtues*, as well as *Passavantus, with a Commen-
tary* and *Sleep in Confidence* for the feast-days and other books
of similar grist, on reading which he became as wise as any loaf
we have ever half-baked.'

How Gargantua was placed under other pedagogues

CHAPTER 14

[Becomes Chapter 15.
*After all the laughter we are brought to realize that the young giant
has been driven mad by his tutors. We have been laughing at a mad
way to bring up children.*

*'Mataeologian' is a word vulgarized by Erasmus, combining mataios
(vain, useless) with theologian.*

*Again 'theologically' is replaced in '42 by 'sophistically'. The change
is not further indicated in the notes.*

*The young page Eudemon, whose name means 'Fortunate', is in
most ways an ideal Renaissance youth, clean, healthy, skilled at Latin
and at elegant speaking, but his rhetoric is more eloquent than truthful
in his praise of the young giant!]*

His father eventually noticed that, although Gargantua was
truly studying very hard and devoting his entire time to it, he

was deriving no good from it, and what was worse becoming a fool and a dolt, quite stupid and mad. Grandgousier complained about it to Don Philip Desmarais, the Viceroy of Papeligosso, and was told that it would be better for the boy to study nothing at all than to study such books under such tutors, since their scholarship was sheer stupidity and their wisdom triviality, debasing sound and noble minds and corrupting the very flower of youth.

'To prove it,' he said, 'select one of today's youths who has studied for a mere two years: should he not show better judgement and a better command of words and arguments than your son, as well as a better deportment and behaviour in society, then for ever account me a bacon-slicer from La Brenne.'

That greatly pleased Grandgousier, and he ordered it to be done.

During supper that evening Desmarais brought in a young page of his from Villegongis named Eudemon, so neatly combed, so trim, so well brushed and so proper in his bearing that he looked more like a little cherub than a human being.

Desmarais then said to Grandgousier,

'See this young lad? He is not yet sixteen. If you agree, let us see what a difference there is between the learning of those mad old-fashioned mataeologians of yours and the young folk of today.'

Grandgousier was pleased to try it, and commanded the young page to address them. At which Eudemon asked his master the Viceroy for leave to do so, and then, standing up straight, bonnet in hand, with an open countenance, ruddy lips, and steady eyes looking straight at Gargantua with youthful modesty, he began to praise and commend him: first, for his virtues and good behaviour; secondly, for his wisdom; thirdly, for his nobility; fourthly, for his physical beauty; then for the fifth, he gently exhorted him to honour his father in every respect since he had taken such care to have him educated. And finally he begged him to retain him as the least of his servants, for at that present time he supplicated Heaven for no other boon than grace to please him by doing him some acceptable service. All that was advanced with such appropriate gestures, so clear an enunciation, so eloquent a voice, such elegant language and in Latin so excellent that he resembled a Gracchus, a Cicero, an Aemilius of antiquity rather than a youth of our century.

But Gargantua's behaviour was merely to blubber like a cow and hide his face in his bonnet: it was no more possible to drag a word out of him than a fart from a dead donkey.

At which his father was so incensed that he would have slaughtered Magister Jobelin, but the said Desmarais stopped him with elegant remonstrations, in such a manner that his anger was moderated. Grandgousier then ordered that the tutor be paid his wages and encouraged to tipple theologically.

That done, let him go to all the devils.

'At least,' he said, 'he wouldn't cost his host much today if he should happen to die, drunk as an Englishman.'

Once Magister Jobelin had quitted the house, Grandgousier consulted the Viceroy about which tutor they should provide for Gargantua. It was decided amongst themselves that the duty should be entrusted to Ponocrates, the tutor of Eudemon, and that they should go off to Paris together in order to find out what the youth of France were studying nowadays.

How Gargantua was sent to Paris, and of the enormous mare which bore him, and how she overcame the gad-flies of Beauce

CHAPTER 15

[Becomes Chapter 16.

'Out of Africa ever comes something new' is one of the best-known sayings of Pliny. It forms an adage of Erasmus (III, VII, X).

It was Froissart during the wars who made the famous remark (which Grandgousier inverts): 'Were it not for Messieurs the Clerics we would all live like beasts.'

Here and elsewhere Rabelais changed 'Languedoc' into 'Languegoth' by a false etymology suggestive of depised Gothic roots.]

In that same season, Fayoles the Fourth, King of Numidia, sent Grandgousier a mare from the shores of Africa: she was the biggest and most enormous that had ever been seen, and the most marvellous – you know of course that *Out of Africa ever comes something new* – for she was as large as six elephants, had hoofs split into toes like the horse of Julius Caesar's, and her ears hung down as far as those of the goats of Languegoth. On her rump she bore a tiny horn. For the rest, her coat was the colour of burnt chestnuts with a trellis-work of dapple-grey; her tail especially was quite horrifying, for – give or take a little – it was as wide and as square as the tower of Saint-Mars near Langès and had tufts of hair plaited like ears of corn.

If that astounds you, be even more astounded by those Scythian rams whose tails weigh more than thirty pounds, or by those Syrian sheep which (if Thenaud is to be trusted) have tails of such length and weight that they need carts attached to their rumps to bear them along. Yours are never like that, you low-country bumpkins!

The mare was transported by sea in three carracks and one brigantine as far as Les Sables d'Olonne-en-Talmondais.

As soon as Grandgousier saw her, he said, 'She's just the thing to bear my son to Paris. Now then, by God, all will go well. In times to come he will be a great cleric. Were it not for Messieurs the Beasts we would all live like clerics.'

So the next morning – after a drink you understand – Gargantua, his attendants and his tutor Ponocrates set out on their way together with their young page Eudemon. And because the weather was mild and moderate Gargantua's father had a pair of tawny boots made for him. (Babin the cobbler calls them *brodequins*.)

And so they journeyed merrily along the highway, always enjoying good cheer until just above Orleans. There they found an awesome forest,[10] thirty-five leagues long and seventeen wide or thereabouts.

It was so appallingly and copiously productive of gad-flies

10.   From '35: . . . an *ample* forest . . .

and hornets that it formed a veritable highwayman's snare for wretched mares, asses and horses. But Gargantua's mare honourably avenged all the outrages ever perpetrated therein against beasts of her kind, playing them a trick which they least expected. For as soon as the party had ridden into the said forest and the hornets begun their assault, the mare unsheathed her tail and drove them away, so fencing about that she felled the whole forest like a reaper scything grass, cutting this way and that way, hither and thither, lengthways and breadthways, upways and downways, so that no tree or hornet since then remains there: the whole of that land was reduced to a bare plain.

Seeing which, Gargantua was delighted. He did not go on to boast, but to his men he said, 'Beautiful, that! (*Beau ce!*). And *Beauce* has been its name ever since.

[But for breakfast they had nothing but yawns, in memory of which the noblemen of La Beauce still breakfast on yawns: they find it very good for them and gob all the better.]

Eventually they came to Paris, where Gargantua rested for two or three days, having a good time with his companions and finding out which learned men were then in town and what wine they were drinking.

How Gargantua paid the Parisians for his welcome, and how he took the great bells from the church of Notre-Dame

CHAPTER 16

[*Becomes* Chapter 17.

Serious and comic etymologies of the name of Paris were current. Ris is a word for laughter in Renaissance French. So per ris or par ris could mean 'for a laugh' or 'by way of laughter'!

The Order of Saint Anthony is suilline *('of the pig'): Anthony is the patron of pig-rearing and his Order begged alms of pork. Its Commander mentioned as friend is Antoine du Saxe, of Bourg-en-Bresse. (He wrote a poem,* The Wish of the Ham-man.*)*

Then comes bold satire extending over four chapters. It had to be toned down (as shown in the footnotes).

Evangelical preaching encouraged by Marguerite de Navarre was a feature of 1532, 1533 and of both Lent and summer in 1534. Such preaching aroused the wrath of the Parisian mob. The Sorbonne seems to have secretly arranged for hostile placards to be posted up by men disguised as masked revellers. (Cf. chapter 17; the longer end to Pantagruel *and the* Almanac *for 1535.) The satire here of the events of 1532–4 became overshadowed by the twin* affaires des placards: *that of the night of 17–18 October 1534, when densely argued Zwinglian placards with little booklets attached preaching against the 'idolatry' of the Mass were stuck up by zealous Zwinglian reformers all over Paris, and the even graver* affaire des placards *of 13–14 January 1535, when the same placards were daringly exposed even in the royal apartments.*

A public procession of expiation was led by the king: the original text of Gargantua *simply had to be toned down in the second edition Rabelais published, since the very word* placard *soon became tainted and associated above all with the* affaires des placards *and the persecution which they sparked off.*

The stealing of the bells of Notre-Dame forms part of the tale in the pre-Rabelaisian Chronicles of Gargantua.]

A few days after they were rested, Gargantua visited the town and was greeted by all with great amazement, for by nature the people of Paris are so daft, silly and stupid that a juggler, a pardon-monger, a mule with its tinklers or a fiddler at the crossroads will draw bigger crowds than a good evangelical preacher. They followed him about so relentlessly that he was constrained to rest upon the towers of Notre-Dame. Once seated there and seeing so many people around him he spoke with clarity:

'I do believe these scoundrels expect me to pay for my own reception and supply my own welcome-gift. That's only right! I shall tip them with some wine! But they shall only have it *per ris.*'

Then, with a smile, he untied his flies, aired his *mentula* and then so brackishly peed over them that he drowned two

hundred and eighty thousand and eighteen of them, without
women and children.

A number of them escaped from that deluge of piss by fleet-
ness of foot, and when they reached the heights of the University
quarter, sweating, choking, spluttering and short of breath,
they began to curse and swear:
– God's wounds!
– Damme!
– Gollysblood! D'you see that!
– By Saint Squit!
– By the 'ead of Gord!
– God's passion confound you!
– *Da heada di Christo!*
– By the guts of Saint Quimlet!
– Virtue of Gosh!
– By Saint Fiacre de Brie!
– By Saint Trinian!
– I make a vow to Saint Thibaut!
– Easter of God!
– God's good-day!
– The devil take me!
– Nobleman's honour!
– By Saint Chidlings!
– By Saint Godegrin, martyred with cooked apples!
– By Saint Futin the apostle!
– By Saint Vital Parts!
By our Lady, woe is me:
We're all awash in pee, per ris.[11]
And that is why that town is now called *Paree.*

Before that it was called *Leukecia,* which, as Strabo says (in
Book 4) means nice and white – on account of the white thighs

11. Some of the above oaths are changed or attenuated in '35: Rabelais cut
out the favourite oath of François I, 'Nobleman's honour'; replaced 'God'
with 'Gosh', then 'By Saint Cock' with 'O Gawd, my Gawd' (in the patois
of Touraine); and the Italian '*Da heada di Christo!*' by a German oath,
'Ja martre schend'. From '42 almost all the oaths are cut out altogether,
the text finally reading: . . . they began to curse and swear, *some in anger,
some per ris: Abracadabra.* – By our Lady, woe is me: *Per ris* we're all
awash in pee. And that is why . . .

of the ladies in the aforesaid place. When its new name was imposed on it, all the bystanders swore oaths by the saints of their parishes, Parisians – being composed of bits and bobs and ha'p'orths of all sorts – are by their nature good jurants, good jurists and just a trifle bumptious: (that is why Joaninus de Barranco (in his book *On the Copiousness of Signs of Respect*) reckons that they are called *Parrhesians*, that is, 'fine talkers', in Greek).

Which done, Gargantua turned his gaze towards the great bells hanging from those towers and he tolled them most tunefully. It occurred to him whilst doing so that they would make good tinklers for his mule: he intended to send her back to his father fully laden with fresh herrings and with cheeses from Brie; he did indeed take them to his lodgings.

Meanwhile round came a Commander of the Suilline Order of Saint Anthony begging for pork; he, wishing to be heard from afar and to set the hams a-tremble in their larders, sought to bear some off furtively, but out of decency he left them alone, not as too hot to carry but as a trifle too heavy! (He was *not* the Commander from Bourg, who is far too good a friend of mine.)

The whole of Paris was moved to sedition. The people of Paris are (as you know) so prone to such things that the foreign Nations are amazed by the patience – or, more accurately, the apathy[12] – of the kings of France who, in view of the daily inconveniences which arise from them, do not do more to repress them by good justice. Would to God that I knew the stithy in which such plots and schisms are forged to see whether or not I could make some fine be-shitten placards there. Believe me, the place where that troubled, stupid throng assembled was the Sorbonne,[13] where once dwelt, but dwells no longer, the

---

12. From '35: omit, . . . or, more accurately, the apathy.

   The original word *stupidité* means apathy not stupidity but was too strong to use of the king, not least after the *affaires des placards*. The very word *placard* had to be removed. So from '35 the phrase 'to see whether I couldn't make some fine be-shitten placards there' below is replaced by 'to reveal them to the brotherhoods of my parish'.

13. '42: . . . assembled was *Nesle*, where . . . (Was the 'oracle' which was the Sorbonne eclipsed by the Trilingual Academy founded by François I?)

Lutetian Oracle. There a motion was proposed and carried deploring the incongruity of campanological transportation.

After much ergoteering *pro et con* it was concluded in the first indirect mode of the first figure of syllogisms that they would despatch the oldest and most sufficient member of the Faculty of Theology to remonstrate with Gargantua over the appalling inconvenience caused by the loss of those *clochas*, those bells. And despite an objection on the part of some members of the University who alleged that the charge was more suitable to an Orator than a Theologian, the man elected to deal with this matter was Magister Noster Janotus de Bragmardo.

How Janotus de Bragmardo was sent to recover the great bells from Gargantua

CHAPTER 17

[From '42 becomes Chapter 18.

In '42 all hint of theology is dropped: Janotus' theological hood was changed into an 'ancient-style' hood. Twice the word 'theologian' is replaced by 'sophist', and likewise 'made to drink theologically' is replaced by 'made to drink rustically'. The changes are not further recorded in the footnotes. That the theologian and the delegation from the Sorbonne are mistaken for masked revellers again repeats the suggestion that, disguised as such, men acting for the Sorbonne had been up to no good in 1533.

There are plays on words, including 'veadles', a portmanteau word – beadle + veau (calf, veal) – and 'Masters Inerts' for Masters of Arts.

As Rabelais retells the tale, the bells are delivered back in the presence of real people: the Provost of Paris was probably Jean de la Barre (who died in 1534), who was also bailiff of the University with wide disciplinary powers.]

Magister Noster Janotus, his hair cropped Caesar-style and sporting his theological hood, having settled his stomach with quince pies from the oven and holy water from the wine-cellar, processed towards the lodgings of Gargantua, prodding before him three veadles with red conks and dragging behind him five or six really filthy – *Waste not: want not!* – Masters Inerts.

When they made their entrance, Ponocrates felt terror within him at seeing them thus disguised and thought they were some witless masked revellers. He then inquired of one of those Masters Inerts what was the purpose of their mummers' farce. It was said in reply that they were asking that their bells be returned. As soon as he heard that, Ponocrates went straight to Gargantua with the news so that he could be ready with an answer and could instantly discuss with them what should be done. Gargantua, duly warned, took aside Ponocrates, his tutor, Philotime, his major-domo, Gymnaste, his equerry, and Eudemon; he had a quick discussion with them about what to do and what answer to return. It was unanimously agreed that the delegation should be taken off to the buttery and made to drink theologically, but (in order that the old cougher should not fall into vainglory through having the bells returned at his request) they should, while he was downing his drinks, summon the Provost of Paris and the Rector of the Faculty together with the Vicar of the Church, to whom they would hand over the bells before the theologian had propounded his commission. After which, in their presence, they would hear his beautiful address.

And so it was done.

And once the aforesaid dignitaries had arrived, the theologian was conducted into the packed Hall and began as follows, coughing:

The Harangue of Magister Janotus de Bragmardo delivered before Gargantua for the return of the bells

CHAPTER 18

[*Becomes* Chapter 19.

*This chapter is partly in dog-Latin as satirized by Rabelais, a human-
ist for whom good Latin mattered and who mocked the scholastic*

terminology he had mastered in youth. *The confused grammar of Janotus leads him to apply to the Virgin Mary words which apply to the Father. Janotus innocently applies to the Sorbonne words from Psalm 49 (48):21, 'A Man that is in honour and understandeth not is like unto the beasts that perish'.*

Throughout this whole episode there is perhaps a sustained pun between clocher, *to limp, and* cloche, *a then obsolescent word for a lame man, and also the French word for bells,* cloches, *for which the theologian uses a low Latin word,* clochas. *Noël Béda, the syndic of the Sorbonne, was certainly a hunchback and doubtless lame. Did he have lame colleagues too?*

The praise of physicians and medicine in Ecclesiasticus 38:4, 'And a wise man will not abhor them', is applied by Janotus to his promised pair of warm breeches.

In this chapter words which are in Latin in Rabelais are printed in italics, including clocha *and its derivatives. The word of address* Domine *(Sir, Lord, etc.) is kept in Latin. Throughout there is a savour of* Maître Pathelin *and of the* Letters of Obscure Men.

Londres-en-Cahors and Bordeaux-en-Brie are hamlets, having nothing to do with the great towns their names evoke, London and Bordeaux.

When David says in the Psalms 'Per diem' (By day!) he is amusingly taken to be using an attenuated oath, avoiding Per deum *(by God!).]*

'Huh! Hem! Ahem! *G'day*, m'Lord; *G'day. You too*, Gentlemen. Nothing but good would come from your giving us back our bells. We badly need 'em. Huh! Hem! Hasch!

'We have in the past turned down good money for them from the people of Londres-en-Cahors and those of Bordeaux-en-Brie, who wished to purchase them on account of the substantificial quality of the elementative complexion which is enthronicized in the terrestreity of their quiddity, in order to extrude the mists and whirlwinds from our vines (not, in truth, from ours but from those hereabouts). For lose we our tipple, then lose we our all: both rates and rationality.

'Now, if you do give us them back at my request I shall win six links of sausages and a pair of breeches (which will be very good for my legs, or else they will fail to keep their promise to me). [Mm! By God, *Domine!* Mn! Mn! Not everyone who wants a pair of breeches always gets one. I know that myself.]

'Bear in mind, *Domine*, that I have now spent eighteen days dreaming and polishing up this beautiful address: *Render unto Caesar the things that are Caesar's, and unto God, the things that are God's.* [*There lies the nub.*] By my faith, *Domine*, if you would dine with me (by God's Body!) in *our charity room* we will *make much good cheerubim! – Me, one pig has I killed; and also has I goodly wine.* But from good wine you can't make bad Latin.

'Now, with God as *ex parte*, please *give us back our clochas*. Here, on behalf of the Faculty I offer you these *Sermons of Utino*, with our *utinam* – our earnest wish – that you allow us our bells. *Do you want any pardons? By Day! You shall have 'em, and fork-out-um nothing-um.* O Lord, *Domine, Let us be clochi-donated.* Those bells are truly *municipal property*. Everybody uses them. They may become your mule but they also become our Faculty, *which is 'compared to senseless mules, and made like unto them'.* (*That's in Psalm number . . ., um, I forget which*, yet I did have it down somewhere on a scrap of paper, [*and it's an Achilles of an argument*].).

'Huh! Hem! Ahem! Hasch!

'Now then. I shall prove to you that you must hand them back.

'*Thus do I argue:*

'*Every clochable clocha by cloching in a belfry – cloching in the clochative – makes the clochas clochably to cloche.*

'There are *clochas* at Paris.

'*Ergo . . . QED, but I'm stuck!*

'Ha! ha! ha! There's talking for you! It was *in the third of the first*, or *in Darii*,[14] or somewhere!

'Gosh! I can remember when I was a very devil at arguing; now I can only ramble: from henceforth all I need is a good wine, a good bed, my back to the fire, my guts to the table, and a deep, deep bowl.

---

14. Janotus is tautological: *Darii* is 'the third of the first' (the third mode of the first figure of syllogisms).

'And so you, *Domine,* I pray *in the name of the Father, and
of the Son and of the Holy Ghost, Amen,* that you render back
our bells. And may God keep you free of evil, and Our Lady of
Health *who liveth and reigneth world without end. Amen.*

'Huh! hasch! gren-hem, hasch!

'*Verily; whereas; far be it that; most true it is; given that;
indeed, indeed; by Faith, god of Jove*: a town without bells is
like a blind man without a stick, an ass without a crupper and
a cow without cow-bells. Unless and until you have given them
back, never shall we cease yelling after you like a blind man
who has lost his stick, braying like an ass without a crupper
and bellowing like a cow without cow-bells.

'A certain scribbler of Latin dwelling near the Hôtel-Dieu
said on one occasion, citing as his authority a certain Taponus
– no, I am wrong there, it was Pontanus, a layman poet – that
he could wish that bells were made of feathers and clappers of foxes' tails because they engendered a chronic in the
innards of his brain: but, one, two, buckle my shoe, bing, bang,
bong, he was declared a heretic: heretics are like wax in our
hands!

'The case rests. *Farewell, and applaud. Calepinus' play is
done.*'[15]

How the Theologian bore away his cloth and how
he brought an action against the Sorbonnists

CHAPTER 19

[*Becomes* Chapter 20.

*In '42 the 'Sorbonnists' of the chapter-heading are replaced by 'other
Masters'. Similarly 'theologian' is still replaced by 'sophist' in both the
chapter-heading and the first line of text. All traces of theology and*

---

15. A legal term of conclusion followed by a deformation of the phrase which
    ends the comedies of Terence: 'Farewell, and applaud. Calliopus' play is
    done.' Janotus, a figure of farce unto the end, confuses the Classical
    Calliopus (taken by Erasmus to be an actor) with Calepinus, the compiler
    of a famous contemporary Latin dictionary.

the Sorbonne are removed. The changes are not listed in the footnotes.

Again the savour of Maître Pathelin *(which the actor-manager Songecreux had recently acted before the Court) lends piquancy to the satire. The laughter of Janotus was then called 'sympathetic': the laughter of others made him laugh just as the yawning of others can make us yawn.*

Janotus' remark 'Limp not before the lame' (in French, 'Ne clochez pas devant les boiteux') once more may link the lame, the cloches, *to* cloches *meaning bells.*

In '42 it is the 'Masters', not the 'Sorbonicoles', who 'vowed never to wash'; similarly 'the congregation of the Sorbonne' becomes 'the congregation held in the Church of the Mathurins'.

The later Rabelais is severely weakened in this episode by sensible, wise and doubtless necessary self-censorship.

Democritus was the laughing philosopher, Heraclitus, the weeping one.]

The Theologian had no sooner finished than Ponocrates and Eudemon burst out guffawing so profoundly that while laughing they all but gave up the ghost to God, neither more nor less than did Crassus on seeing a well-hung ass eat thistles, or as Philemon did by dint of laughing on seeing an ass eat the figs prepared for his own dinner.

Magister Janotus began to laugh with them, each outdoing the other until tears came to their eyes from the mind-shaking concussion of the matter of their brains by which the lachrimatory fluids were expressed and sent flowing around the optic nerves. [By which, in them, Democritus was shown heraclitizing and Heraclitus democritizing.]

Once the laughing had entirely died down, Gargantua consulted his friends over what should be done. Ponocrates was of the opinion that they should get that fine orator drinking again. And, seeing that he had provided more amusement and laughter than even Songecreux could have done, they themselves should give him the ten links of sausages mentioned in his laughable address together with a pair of breeches, three hundred big, good-quality logs for the fire, five and twenty hogsheads of wine, a bed with three layers of goose-feathers and a very profound and capacious bowl – things which he said his old age required.

All was done as they had decided, except that Gargantua, doubting that they could find in time a pair of breeches suitable for his legs, [doubting also what style would best become that Orator, a martingale, say, which is a drawbridge for the bum, making it easier to crap, or sailor-style, to make it easier to relieve oneself, or Switzer-style, to keep his paunch warm, or in cod-tails, to avoid overheating of the kidneys,][16] ordered seven lengths of black cloth together with three lengths of white cloth for the lining.

The logs were carried by penny-porters: the Masters of Arts carried the sausages and the bowl. Magister Janotus carried the cloth as he himself wished, which one of the said Masters of Arts, Maître Jousse Bandouille by name, protested to be neither proper nor becoming to his Theological status, and that he should hand the cloth to one of them.

'Ha! You jackass,' said Janotus, 'you jackass, you have failed to conclude in *mode and figure*. A fat lot of use you have made of the *Suppositions* and the *Minor Logics*.

'Now then: *To whom does the length of cloth refer?*'

Bandouille replied,

'*Indeterminately*; and *distributively*.'

'I did not ask you, you jackass, *in what mode* it refers,' said Janotus, 'but *to what end*. And that, you jackass, is *for my tibia*. And that is why *I, ego, me myself* shall carry it, *exactly as the subject carries the epithet*.'

And so he crept away with it, as Pathelin did with his cloth.

But best of all was when that old cougher vaingloriously claimed his cloth and his sausages during a full congregation of the Sorbonne. They were peremptorily denied him on the grounds that, according to information received, he had already had them from Gargantua.

He protested that they had been given him *gratis* out of Gargantua's generosity, by which they were in no wise absolved

16. The above addition was made in '35, except for 'which is a draw-bridge for the bum', added in '42.

from their promises. That notwithstanding, he received the reply that he would get not a scrap more and should please see reason.

'Reason!' said Janotus. 'We have no use for that here! You miserable traitors you! You good-for-nothings! This earth bears no folk more wicked than you are: that I do know! Limp not before the lame. I myself have practised wickedness together with you. God's spleen! I shall advise the king of the enormous abuses forged in this place by your hands and intrigues. And may I be a leper if he does not have you all burnt alive as buggers, traitors, heretics and deceivers, enemies of God and of virtue.'

At those words they drew up articles of accusation against him: he on his part issued summonses against them. In brief, the lawsuit was reserved to the Court: and it lies there still. At this point the Sorbonicoles vowed never to wash – and Magister Janotus with his adherents, never to wipe their noses – until such time as there was pronounced a definitive judgement. They remain, to this present time, filthy and snotty, since the court has yet to finish scrabbling through all the documents. The judgement is due to be given at the next Greek Kalends, that is to say, never: for those judges, you know, can do more than Nature can, going even against their own Articles. For the Articles of Paris intone that God alone can make things infinite, whilst Nature produces nothing immortal but sees an end, a limit, to everything she brings forth; for *All that rises, falls*,[17] and so on. But those pettifoggers render such cases as lie pendant before them both infinite and immortal. By so doing they both provoked and proved true that saying of Chilon the Spartan enshrined at Delphi: *Misery accompanies lawsuits*,[18] since plaintiffs are wretched, their lives reaching their ends before their petitions for their rights.

17. All that rises falls (*Omnia quae orta cadunt*) is an Epicurean maxim.
18. 'Misery accompanies lawsuits' figures amongst the three famous adages of Chilon, one of the Seven Sages of Greece. It was sculpted on the temple at Delphi and commented upon by Erasmus in his *Adages* (I, VI, XCVII).

The Study and Way of Life of Gargantua according to the teachings of the Sorbonagres, his preceptors

CHAPTER 20

[Becomes Chapter 21.

In '42, 'Way of Life' is dropped from the title and 'Sophists' again replaces 'Sorbonagres'.

The canting 'theologians' who drive a youth mad are then weakened into mere dons.

'Animal spirits' are the spirits of the anima, *the soul, within the human body. They govern our higher actions.*

The name of Professor Almain, a former logician at the Sorbonne, lends itself to a pun on main *(hand) and manual.*

The 'Comic' cited is Terence, probably not directly but from two adages of Erasmus, II, II, XVIII, 'His mind is on the scourge', and III, VII, XXX, 'His mind is on the leather', both of which cite Terence's line, 'His mind is on the wine-cups'.]

After the first days thus spent and the bells restored, the citizens of Paris, grateful for such generosity, offered to feed the mare and look after her for as long as Gargantua liked – which pleased him very much – and so they sent her away to the Forest of Bière. [She is no longer there, I think.]

Once that was done, Gargantua wished with all of his being to study at the discretion of Ponocrates. But Ponocrates told him to carry on for a while in his usual manner so as to establish how his old tutors, over such a long time, had made him so daft, stupid and ignorant. He therefore so arranged his time that he would normally wake up between eight and nine – daylight or not! – for so his theological tutors had bidden him,[19] citing what David said: 'It is vain for you to rise before the light.'[20]

He then would stir his stumps, toss about and wallow awhile

19. '42, ... his *old* tutors had bidden him ...
20. Cant: the theologians justify their sloth with a verse of Psalm 127 (126): 2 wrenched from its context.

in his bed, the better to arouse his animal spirits. He would then dress according to the season but preferably don a heavy, long gown of coarse frieze-cloth trimmed with fox-skin fur. He would then comb his hair manually like Almain: (that is, with four fingers and a thumb) since his tutors used to say that otherwise to comb, wash and clean himself was to waste time over the things of this world.

He would then shit, piss, hawk, fart, [break wind, yawn, gob, cough, snivel,] sneeze and dribble snot like an archdeacon, and then – to counteract the dew and the bad air – break his fast with lovely fried tripe, lovely grilled steaks, lovely ham, lovely goat-meat roasts and plenty of monastical bread-and-dripping. Ponocrates raised the objection that he really ought not to have a meal as soon as he got up without first taking a little exercise. Gargantua replied:

'What! I've taken enough good exercise already, haven't I? Before getting up I toss about in my bed six or seven times. Isn't that enough? Pope Alexander used to do precisely that by order of his Jewish physician and, despite all those who envied him, lived till he died. My original Masters accustomed me to it, saying *Breakfast makes for a good memory*: they were therefore the first to be drinking. I feel better for it and enjoy my dinner all the more. And Magister Tubal (who came top for his degree in Paris) used to tell me that the advantage lay not in running fast but in making an early start: so too the full health of us humans does not consist in drinking cup after cup after cup like ducks but rather in starting to drink early in the morning. Hence these lines:

> Getting up early is never fun
> Drinking early is better for one.'

So, having eaten a proper breakfast, Gargantua would go to church, and they would carry for him in a huge basket a fat breviary, snugly slippered in its sleeve, which (what with grease, clasps and parchment) weighed some eleven hundredweight [and six pounds]. There he would hear some twenty-six or thirty Masses.

Meanwhile his private chaplain would arrive, swaddled up like a hoopoe-bird and having already taken copiously for his breath plenty of medicinal syrup from the grape. With him Gargantua would mumble all his responses, shelling them so carefully that not one grain fell to the ground.

As he left church they would bring him, on an ox-drawn dray, a jumble of Saint-Claude rosaries, each bead of which was as big as your noddle; then, wandering through the cloisters, galleries and gardens, he would tell more beads than sixteen hermits.

Then he devoted a measly half-hour to his studies, his eyes resting on his book, but (as the Comic poet puts it) his mind was in the kitchen. Then, pissing a full chamber-pot, he would sit down to table. And – since he was naturally subject to the phlegm – he began his repast with a few dozen hams, smoked beef-tongues, salted mullet-caviar or chidlings, plus other such precursors of wine.

In the meantime four of his household, continuously, one after the other, cast shovelfuls of mustard into his mouth. Then – to comfort his kidneys – he drank an horrific draught of white wine.

After that, according to the season, he would eat any food he liked, ceasing only when his belly felt extended. But there were no rules to end his drinking, for he would say that the bounds and bourns of drinking were when the cork soles of the slippers of the person tippling had swollen up by a good six inches.

*

[In '42, a new chapter-break is inserted here: The Games of Gargantua. Chapter 22.

In the list of games those inserted in '42 are marked with a cross (+) either individually or after the square brackets. The others within square brackets were added in '35. Games such as these are seen as ways of wasting time. Brueghel has a picture devoted to the theme.

The third game was omitted here and inserted later in the list.

'Banquet' provides a pun with banc *and* to banquet *is made to mean to stretch out on a bench.]*

Then while heavily gnawing through a few scraps of a grace, he would wash his hands in an overspill of cool wine, pick his teeth with a pig's trotter, and chat merrily with his people. Then the baize was spread out and on it were deployed masses of cards and dice and game-boards. And then he would play at:

flush,
discard,
primero,
trumps,
heads-or-tails,
triumphs,
Picardy spades,
[poor little girl,
sneak,
first-to-get-ten,]+
spinets,
one-and-thirty,
[post and pair,
three hundred points wins,
wretches,]
la condemnata,
guess-the-card,
the malcontent,
[lansquenets' gamble,]+
the cuckold,
'let him speak that hath it',
one, two, buckle my shoe,
matrimony,
I've got it,
opinions,
'who doth one does t'other',
sequences,
mimic-the-card,

Spanish tarot,
the winner loses,
be diddled,
[tortures,]
snore,
click,
honours,
the *morra*,
chess,
the fox,
ludo,
cows,
whites,
chance,
triple-dice,
knuckle-bones,
nick-knack,
lurch,
little queen,
sbaraglino,
tric-trac,
tables all,
dice-and-domino tables,
'I deny gosh',
huff,
draughts,
pouting,
'Come first, come second',
toss-the-coin-near-the-knife,
keys,
shove-a-ha'penny,
odds or evens,
heads or tails,
[Normandy knucklebones,]+
dibs,
croquet,
[Hunt the slipper,
owl-bird's cry,

cuddle the hare,
snakes,
cast the jack to the fore,
hopping magpies,
horns, horn upon my head,
the cow and the fiddle,
screech-owls,
I tease but don't you laugh,
tickles,
tickly, tickly your ass's foot,
ca' the sheep,
Gee up little donkey,
I sit me down,
gold-dust, gold-dust on your beard,
wild apples,
pull out the spit,
shitty yew-twigs,
friend, lend me your sack,
toss me the ram's ball,
king of the castle,
best figs from Marseilles,
chase the fly round the rick,
stop thief,
flay the fox,+
sledges,
trip her up,
sell your oats,
all in a ring,
blow the coal,
hide and seek,
judge alive, judge dead,
pull the irons from the fire,
fake villein,
quail beads,
the hunchbacked Doctor,
at Saint Found-it,
pinch-me-tight,
head-stands,

rumble bum,
skip in the ring,
put piggy into its sty,
the world upside down,
building-tricks,]
short staves,
cast-the-disk,
chuck the ball,
snuff-the-candle,
nine-pins,
skittles,
[feather-sticks,
cast spikes towards Rome,
shitty-face,
angel-nard,]+
biassed skittles,
quoits,
bowl-on-a-green,
cast at the stump,
shuttlecock,
hide-and-seek,
pass-round-the-pot,
as-I-will,
tops and whips,
tiddlywinks,
short-straw,
rackets,
hide-away,
piquet,
pétanque,
[open up, some pages are blank,
ferret it out,]
cock-shy,
knock-down-in-a-ring,
marbles,
whirligigs,
humming-tops,
monk-tops,

tenebri,
dismay-me,
hard-ball,
to-and-fro,
arse-over-tip,
ride a cock-horse,
smudge the face of Saint Cosme,
[brown snails,
catch him with no green in May,
fair and fine speed Lent away,]+
hand-stands,
leap frog,
all-in-a-line,
top and tail and fart-in-the-throat,
'I'm a piggy-back knight, give me my lance',
see-saws,
catch as catch can, the thirteenth man,
[birch-trees,]+
swat that fly,
Dainty, dainty to the cow:
Madame's near the fire by now,
whisper it round,
nine hands in a pile,
nut case,
broken bridges,
bridled booby,
hopscotch,
battledore and shuttlecock,
blind man's bluff,
'Where do you come from, my good chap?'
play the spy,
toads,
lacrosse,
pounding-sticks,
billy-goat, jump the ball,
queens,
'what's my track?'
odds or evens?

[cherry-stones,
shake, shake, thy little dead hand,
punch up the conk,]+
'Lady, lady, I'll wash your hair',
sieve us all, to and fro,
here comes the farmer to sow his oats,
greedy-guts,
windmills,
eeny, meeny, mainy, mo,
head over heels,
give-him-a-bumping,
ploughman, ploughman, plough the field,
go it alone,
scrub him like mad,
'Carry me, carry me, like a dead beast',
up, up the ladder, hand upon hand,
piggy is dead,
salty bums,
fly away, pigeon,
pass the parcel, group to group,
jump, jump, over the bush,
cross tag,
hide and seek,
farthing, farthing, up your bum,
'Hidden in the buzzard's nest. Where? Where? Where?'
run the gauntlet,
cock-a-snook,
blowing raspberries,
pestle the mustard,
[mind your legs,
trip me over,
darts,
leap-frog,
crows,
off the ground,
here comes the chopper,
tweaking noses,]

peck his nose,
pinch his conk.

And so, playing hard and passing [and sifting] time, it was
right to have a little drink – eleven quarts apiece – and, immediately after, a *banquet* – that is, a stretch-out for a good
two-or-three-hours' nap, on a good *banc* or a lovely deep bed,
thinking no evil and speaking no evil.

Once awake, he would shake his ears a bit, during which
cool wine was brought in and there he would drink away better
than ever. Ponocrates protested that it was a bad way of life to
drink after sleeping. 'It is,' said Gargantua, 'a true life of the
Fathers! I naturally sleep salty: sleep has saved me all that ham!'

Then he would begin to study, just a little, with his rosary-
beads to the fore, and so as to despatch them more properly he
would mount an ancient mule which had served nine kings.
And so, doddering his head and mumbling with his lips, he
would go and watch a rabbit caught in a snare.

On his return he made his way to the kitchen to find out
what roast was on the spit. And, by my conscience, he had a
very good supper, readily inviting round a few tipplers amongst
his neighbours, and, each one downing drink for drink, they
told each other tales of things old and new. His intimates
included the seigneurs Du Fou, de Gourville, [de Grignault] and
de Marigny.

Then, after dinner, out would come his lovely wooden
Gospels – that is to say an abundance of gaming-boards – on
which to play:

flush,
one-two-three,
or (to cut things short) double or quits.

Or else he would be off to see the local girlies to have little
suppers amongst them, with collations and late-night snacks.
After which he would enjoy unbridled sleep until eight in the
morning.

How Gargantua was given his basic education by Ponocrates with such discipline that he never lost an hour of his time

CHAPTER 21

[Becomes Chapter 23.

Rabelais may well have in mind the concern of François I to find a princely way of educating his sons once they had served as hostages after the defeat of the French at Pavia.

The name of the 'learned physician . . . Seraphin Calobarsy' is an anagram of Phrançois Rabelais, *who thereby directly engages his authority in this chapter. In '42 he changed that name to 'Maître Théodore' since the name Seraphin Calobarsy had been pirated by an unknown compiler of shoddy almanacs.*

In Greek Theodore means 'gift of God'; Anagnostes, 'reader'; and Rhizotome, 'root-cutter'. Since Gargantua had been literally driven mad, he is first purged by Dr Rabelais with hellebore, the Classical remedy for insanity.

The medical adage in the first sentence is straight from the Aphorisms *of Hippocrates, which Rabelais edited in 1533 and republished in 1543.*

The education of the Renaissance prince is here set in Rabelais' home province of Touraine. In later editions he changes it to Paris. To do so he replaces 'the Loire at Montsoreau' by 'the Seine', omits completely the reference to the 'lake at Savigny' and turns 'Bessé' into 'Saint-Victor', and 'Narsay' into 'Montmartre'.

There were famous tennis-courts at Le Braque.

The rare word 'poppism' is taken straight from the Latin. It means a clucking sound made to encourage a horse.]

Once Ponocrates had taken cognizance of Gargantua's vicious manner of living, he determined to introduce him to letters by a different method, but he let things go on for the first few days considering that Nature will not endure sudden changes without a strong reaction.

To give his task a better start he begged a learned physician of those days called Seraphin Calobarsy to consider whether it was possible to set Gargantua back on to a better path; he, according to the canons of medicine, purged him with Anticyran hellebore, and by means of that medicament he also cleansed all squalor and corrupt tendencies from his mind. Ponocrates also made him forget by that method everything he had learnt under his old tutors, as Timotheus did for any of his pupils who had studied under other musicians.

To do things better, Ponocrates introduced him to the company of the learned men who were present, out of emulation with whom there grew in Gargantua a mind and desire to study differently and improve himself.

Ponocrates then set him such a course of study that he never wasted one hour in any day but devoted his entire time to letters and honourable learning.

Gargantua therefore woke up at about four a.m.

While he was being rubbed down, a passage of Holy Scripture was read out to him, loud and clear, with a delivery appropriate to the matter. A young page was appointed to do it: a native of Basché called Anagnostes. Following the theme and content of the lesson, Gargantua would often devote himself to revering, worshipping, supplicating and adoring God in his goodness, whose majesty and marvellous judgements were revealed by the reading.

He would then go to the privy to excrete his natural digestions. There his tutor would go over what had been read, elucidating the more obscure and difficult points for him.

On the way back they would consider the state of the heavens. Was it as they had noted the night before? Into which signs were the Sun and the Moon entering that day?

Once that was done, he was dressed, combed, brushed, perfumed and made elegant, during which time yesterday's lessons were gone over with him. He would recite them by heart and base on them some practical matters concerning our human condition; they might extend it to some two or three hours but normally stopped once he was fully dressed.

Then he would be read to, for three solid hours.

That done, they would go outdoors, still conferring together

on the subjects of those readings, and enjoy sports in Le Grand
Braque or in the meadows; there they played ball or royal-
tennis, [or three-men quoits,] nobly exercising their bodies as
they had previously exercised their minds.

Their games were all played freely, for they stopped whenever
they wanted to, normally when they were tired or all of a sweat.
At which point they were thoroughly sponged and rubbed
down; they would change their shirts and gently stroll over to
see whether dinner was ready.

While waiting, they would clearly and eloquently repeat some
maxims remembered from their lessons. Meanwhile Sir
Appetite would come, and they would opportunely sit down to
table.

At the beginning of the meal a pleasant tale of ancient deeds
of chivalry would be read until he had taken his wine. Then (if
thought fit) the reading would be resumed or else they would
enter upon enjoyable discussions, talking (during the first few
months) of the qualities, properties, efficacy and nature of all
the things that had been served up at table: bread, wine, water,
salt, flesh, fish, fruit, herbs and roots, as well as how to prepare
them. In doing so they quickly learnt all the relevant passages
in Pliny, Athenaeus, Dioscorides, [Julius Pollux,] Galen,
Porphyry, Oppian, Polybius, Heliodorus, Aristotle, Aelian and
others. When talking about such things, they would have the
books of those authors brought to the table for greater certainty. And he so fully and totally kept in his memory what was
said in them that at that time there was no physician who knew
half as much as he did.

Afterwards they would discuss the lessons read that morning,
finishing off their meal with some quince jelly, picking their
teeth with a sliver of mastic-wood, washing their hands and
eyes in clear fresh water and rendering thanks to God with
some beautiful canticles in praise of his bounty and loving
kindness.

That completed, the cards would be brought out – not for
play but to learn from them hundreds of little delights and
novelties all of which derived from arithmetic.

By such means he developed a passion for the science of

numbers, and every day after dinner and supper he would pass his time as pleasantly with it as he once had done with dice and playing-cards. Eventually he had mastered so much arithmetic (pure and applied) that Tunstal the Englishman, who had amply written on the subject, truly confessed that in comparison with him his own knowledge was but Double Dutch – and not only in that but also in other mathematical sciences such as geometry, astronomy and music; for while waiting for their meal to be concocted and digested they would make hundreds of amusing little geometrical shapes and figures or practise the laws of astronomy. After that they enjoyed singing music in four or five parts, or else on a set theme as it suited their voices.

As regards musical instruments, he learnt to play the lute, the spinet, the harp, both the traverse and the nine-holed flutes, the viola and the sackbut. Having spent one hour and completed his digestion, he would purge himself of his natural excreta and apply himself again to his principal studies for three hours or more, as much going over again that morning's readings as getting on with the book they had started or practising writing, forming and clearly making the letters of the ancient Roman script.

That done, they went outdoors, taking with them a young nobleman from Touraine called Gymnaste, the equerry, who showed him the art of chivalry. So, changing his clothing, Gargantua would mount a charger, a war-horse, a Spanish jennet [, a barbary horse] and then a light horse, which he would put through a hundred paces, making it jump, leap over a ditch, take a fence and perform tight caracoles to right and left.

There he did not 'break a lance', for it is the greatest lunacy in the world to say, 'I have broken ten lances in tilt-yard or battle!' – a carpenter could do as well! – but the glory is worthwhile when, with one single lance, you have broken ten of your enemies. So with his lance, sharp, fresh and strong, he would batter down a portal, pierce some armour, uproot a tree, spike a ring and spear an armed saddle, a hauberk or a steel gauntlet. All of which he did armed head to foot. As for riding in step to the trumpet and making little poppisms for his horse, none could do it better than he. (Why, that acrobat from Ferrara was but a chimp in comparison!)

He was singularly accomplished in leaping smartly from horse to horse without touching the ground – on what were called 'vaulting horses' – jumping into the saddle from either side, without a stirrup but lance in hand, and directing his horse at will without using the bridle. Such accomplishments are of service in the arts of war.

Another time he would practise with the battle-axe, which he would so supply brandish and crash down that he was by any standard an acknowledged knight-at-arms in the field or before any ordeal.

Then he flourished the pike, made thrusts with a two-handed sword, a bastard sword, a Spanish rapier, a dagger or a poniard, with armour, without armour, or with a buckler, cape or small targe.

He hunted the stag, the roebuck, the bear, the deer, the wild-boar, the hare, the partridge, the pheasant, the bustard. He played with the weighted ball, sending it high in the air with fist or foot. He wrestled, ran and leapt, not doing any hop-skip-and-jumps, one-footed springs or German leaps (for, as Gymnaste said, such feats are of no use in war) but leaping over a ditch at a single bound, sailing over a hedge and springing six paces up the side of a wall, thus breaking a window at the height of a lance.

He would swim in deep water, on belly, back or side, using his whole body or his feet alone, or else (keeping one hand in the air while holding a book aloft without letting it get wet) swim across the Loire at Montsoreau, dragging his cloak behind him with his teeth like Julius Caesar.

Then, by main force, he would haul himself up into a boat by one hand, immediately dive head-first back into the water, sound the depths and plunge deep through the rocky hollows and chasms of Lake Savigny. He would turn the boat about, guide it, manoeuvre it quickly then slowly downstream and upstream, keeping it steady in a flash-lock and steering it with one hand while fencing with a long oar; he would spread the sail, clamber up the mast by the shrouds, scramble over the yard-arms, set the compass, pull tight the bowlines and hold fast to the rudder.

Coming straight out of the water, he would dash up a steep mountain and as readily come down again, climb up into trees like a cat, leap from tree to tree like a squirrel and hack down great branches like a second Milo.

By means of two keen-pointed daggers and two reliable marlinspikes he would clamber up on to the roof of a house like a rat and then leap off it, so composing his limbs that he was in no wise hurt by the fall.

He would hurl the spear, the weight, the stone, the javelin, the stake, and the halbert, bend tight the bow and put his back into readying the great rack-bent cross-bows by the strength of his thighs; he would aim the harquebus, set up the cannon and shoot at the butts and the target-parrots upwards from below, downwards from above, straight ahead, from the side, and finally behind him like the Parthians.

They would tie him a rope, hanging down from some high tower: he would climb up hand over hand and then slide down so quick and sure that you could never have outdone him on a flat meadow. They would set up a great pole fixed between the two trees: he would hang down from it by his arms and move back and forth, hand over hand, touching nothing with his feet, so quickly that you could not have caught up with him by running full pelt.

To exercise his thorax and his lungs he would yell like the devil. On one occasion I heard him, from the gates of Bessé calling Eudemon at the fountain of Narsay. Stentor never had such voice at the battle for Troy.

And to tone up his muscles there were made for him two great leaden weights which he called *halteres*; each of them weighed some eight thousand seven hundred hundredweights. He lifted them off the ground, one in each hand, and raised them high above his head, holding them there without moving for three-quarters of an hour and more at a stretch, which shows inimitable strength. He would play martial-barriers against the strongest, and when the tussle came he would so sturdily stand his ground that (like Milo of old) he would expose himself to the strongest to see whether they could make him budge.[21]

He would also imitate Milo in holding a pomegranate, which he gave up to anyone who could take it from him.

Having thus spent his time, he would be rubbed down, cleaned up and given a change of clothing. Then he would leisurely walk back, passing through meadows or other verdant places where they would examine the trees and plants, comparing them with the books of Ancients who had written about them, such as Theophrastus, Dioscorides, Marinus, Pliny, Nicander, Macer and Galen, and carrying home great handfuls of specimens which were the responsibility of a young page called Rhizotome, as were the mattocks, diggers, hoes, spades, pruning-shears and other tools required for gardening and serious botanizing. Once they were back in their lodgings, while dinner was being prepared, they would go over some of the passages which had been read and then sit down to table.

It should be noted that, whilst his dinners were sober and frugal, since he ate no more than was necessary to stop his stomach from barking, his suppers were copious and generous, for he took as much as was needed to nourish and sustain him. That is the true diet, prescribed by the Art of good and reliable medicine, despite piles of silly physicians who advise the opposite, having been broken in in the workshop of the Arabs.[22]

During that meal they would go on as long as they wanted to with the same reading as at dinner; the rest of the time would be taken up with good conversation, entirely learned and useful.

Once grace was said, they would devote themselves to choral singing, to playing musical instruments or else to those lighter pastimes which use cards, dice or tumblers. And there they would remain, making good cheer and enjoying themselves, sometimes until bedtime; on other occasions they would drop in on gatherings of learned men or on folk who had visited foreign lands. Before retiring, once it was completely dark, they would go to the most open place in their lodgings to study the

21. From '35: . . . expose himself *to the most adventurous* to see whether . . .
22. '42: . . . in the workshop of the *Sophists* . . .

face of the sky, noting the comets (if there were any), the constellations and the locations, aspects, oppositions and conjunctions of the heavenly bodies. Then, in the manner of the Pythagoreans, he briefly recapitulated with his tutor every thing he had read, seen, learnt, done or heard throughout the livelong day.

Then they would pray to God the Creator, worshipping him and again confirming their trust in him, magnifying him for his immense goodness, rendering him thanks for all that is past and committing themselves to his divine goodness[23] for all that is to come.

That done, they would go to bed.

How Gargantua spent his time when it was rainy

CHAPTER 22

[Becomes Chapter 24.

'Apotherapy' is a term which goes back to Galen and means the restoration of an athlete after exercises; Rabelais uses it to mean indoor exercises to make up for those which cannot be done outdoors. 'Tali', as a Classical game newly rediscovered, was greatly esteemed by many humanists, not however as a means of divination. The short work of Leonicenus on the tali *appeared in his* Opuscula *(Paris, 1530). The game is played with four dice made from knucklebones. That Rabelais can claim friendship with Janus Lascaris is revealing. Lascaris, a refugee from Constantinople, taught Budé Greek and helped Erasmus with his* Adages. *He had contacts at the highest level in France and Italy. He died in 1534. The alleged experiment of separating wine from water with an ivy-wood goblet is recommended by Cato in* De re rustica, *3, 52, and Pliny,* Natural History, *115.]*

Should the air happen to be intemperate and full of rain, the whole period up to dinner would be spent as usual, except that a good bright fire was lit to correct the humidity of the air; but

23. From '35: ... His divine *clemency* ...

after dinner instead of their exercises they would stay indoors [and by way of apotherapy enjoy bundling up hay, chopping and sawing up wood, and threshing sheaves in the barn; then] studying the arts of painting and sculpture or reviving the ancient game of *tali* according to what Leonicus wrote about it and as our good friend Lascaris plays it: while they were playing they would recall passages in Ancient authors in which mention was made of their game or metaphors drawn from it.[24]

Or else they would go and see how metals are extruded or artillery-pieces cast; or else they would go and visit the jewellers, goldsmiths, gem-cutters or alchemists and minters of coins, or the weavers of fair tapestries, cloth-workers, velvet-makers, clock-makers, looking-glass-makers, printers, organ-builders, dyers and other similar craftsmen; they gave pourboires to everyone, noting the skills and weighing the originality of those trades.

They went to hear public lectures, formal legal proceedings, the interrogations, declamations and pleas of noble barristers, and the sermons of evangelical preachers.

He would make his way through rooms and halls prepared for fencing and try out every kind of weapon, proving to all that he knew as much or indeed more about fencing as they did.

Instead of botanizing they would visit the booths of chemists, herbalists and apothecaries, making a careful study of the fruit, leaves, [gums] grains and exotic unguents, and how they could be adulterated.

He would go to watch jugglers, thimble-riggers and mounte-banks, closely observing their gestures, ruses, sleight-of-hand and clever patter (especially those who came from Chauny in Picardy, for they are by nature great word-spinners and excel-lent fraudsters [of the green and gullible]).

Returning for supper they would eat more frugally than on other days, especially the more dessicative and leaner foods so as to enable the intemperate dampness of the air (communicated to the body by inescapable adjacency) to be corrected, and

24. From '42: . . . drawn from it. *Similarly* they would go . . .

so that they might not be troubled by having to forego their customary exercises.

And thus was Gargantua tutored, sticking to that course day after day, drawing such advantages as you know that an intelligent youth [of his age] can from practices thus persisted in: at first it did seem a bit hard, but sticking to it seemed pleasant, easy and delightful, resembling the pastime of a monarch rather than the curriculum of a schoolboy.

Nevertheless, to provide some relief from so stimulating a stretching of their minds, Ponocrates would choose one bright and serene day each month when they would leave town early in the morning, making for Gentilly, Boulogne or Montrouge or else for the bridge at Charenton, for Vanves or Saint-Cloud. There they would spend the whole day having the best fun they could possibly devise, joking, jesting, pledging drink for drink, playing, singing, dancing, larking about in a meadow, going after swallows' nests, hunting the quail and catching frogs or crayfish.

Yet whilst that day was spent without books or reading, it was not spent unprofitably, for in the beautiful meadows they would recite by heart some agreeable lines of Virgil's *Georgics*, of Hesiod or Politian's *Rustic Life*, compose a few pleasant Latin epigrams and then turn them into rondels and *ballades* in the French language.

As they were feasting, they would separate wine from water through an ivy-wood goblet as instructed by Pliny and by Cato in *On Matters Rustic*: they would drown the wine in a basin full of water and then draw it off through a funnel, sending it from one glass to another. They also devised several little 'automatic' – that is, self-moving – contrivances.

How a great dispute arose between the *fouace*-bakers of Lerné and Gargantua's countrymen, whence came mighty wars

CHAPTER 23

[Becomes Chapter 25.
A peasant quarrel: it will grow into dreams of world domination.
The extra insults are all added in 1535, except for the second, which dates from 1542.
'Fouaces', still a local delicacy, are baked flat-cakes made from the finest flour.]

Now at that time, (the beginning of autumn, the season of the vendanges) the local shepherds were guarding the vines and preventing the starlings from eating the grapes. At the same time the girdle-cake bakers of Lerné were just going over the great cross-roads leading ten or a dozen cart-loads of *fouaces* into the town. The said shepherds politely asked them to sell them some at the market-price, for note that it is a dish celestial to breakfast on fresh *fouaces* with grapes, especially the sauvignons, pineaux, muscadets or bicanes, and for those who are constipated, the *foyrards* which make them void turds as long as a stave: hence their nickname of '*vendange*-hopefuls', since, hoping but to fart, folk thoroughly shit themselves.

Those bakers were by no means disposed to accede to their request but, worse still, grossly insulted them, calling them superfluities, stubble-tooths, silly ginger-nuts, scoundrels, [shit-the-beds, good-for-nothings, sneaky smooth-files, do-nothings, tasty morsels, fat-guts, loud-mouths,] no-goods, clod-hoppers, rogues, scroungers, braggarts, pretty puffs, copy-cats, slackers, bad-'uns, twirps, boobies, scruff-'eads, smirkers, fat-'eads, teeth-clackers, cow-pat cowherds, shitty shepherds, and other such derogatory epithets, adding that it was not for the likes of them to aspire to eating such lovely *fouaces*: they should be content with gross chaff-loaves and cottage-bread.

At such an outrage, one of the shepherds named Frogier, a

decent fellow in his appearance and a worthy young man, quietly replied,

'Since when have you grown your horns and become so cheeky! Garn, you used to be pleased to sell them to us: now you won't. That's not a good-neighbourly deed. We never treat you like that when you come over here buying our best wheat to make your *fouaces* and your buns! We'd have throw in some grapes as well, but, by the Mudder of God, you'll be sorry for this. You'll need to trade with us one day: then we'll do the same to you. Remember that!'

Whereupon, Marquet, the Grand Verger of the Guild of *Fouace*-bakers, said to him,

'You'm quite a bantam-cock this morning. You ate too much millet lass night! Come over 'ere then! Come over 'ere! I'll give 'ee a bit of my *fouace*!'

Frogier, in all innocence, came over, pulling an elevenpenny-piece from his belt and believing that Marquet would take some of his *fouaces* out of his sack for him, but Marquet lashed him so hard across the legs with his whip that weals appeared. He then tried to run away, but Frogier cried murder and robbery as loud as he could, and threw at him a big cudgel which he carried under his arm: it caught his skull on the coronal suture, to the right-hand side of the superior maxillary division of the fifth cerebral nerve, with the result that Marquet tumbled off his mare, looking more dead than alive.

Meanwhile the peasant-farmers thereabouts who were knocking down walnuts came charging up with their long poles and thrashed those *fouace*-bakers as though threshing green rye. The other shepherds and shepherdesses, on hearing Frogier's yell, came up with their slings and catapults and chased after them, so densely showering them with stones that it seemed like hail. Finally they caught up with them and helped themselves to some four or five dozen *fouaces*. Yet they paid the going rate, adding a hundred walnuts and three basketfuls of ripe white grapes.

That done, the *fouace*-bakers, having helped Marquet back into his saddle – he had a nasty wound – abandoned the road to Parilly and made their way back to Lerné, uttering loud and violent threats against the cowherds, shepherds and peasant-farmers of Seuilly and Cinais.

Afterwards the shepherds and shepherdesses had a fine old time eating *fouaces* with fine old grapes, having fun together to the sound of the fine old rustic bagpipe and laughing at those fine old pompous *fouace*-men who had met such a rebuff for having crossed themselves with the wrong hand on getting up that morning.

And from fat 'dog-grapes' there was made such a dainty hot-compress for Frogier's legs that he soon got better.

How the inhabitants of Lerné, by order of Picrochole their king, made a surprise attack on Gargantua's shepherds

CHAPTER 24

[*Becomes* Chapter 26.

In '42, the name of the character here called Grippeminaud ('Grippenny') was changed to Trepelu ('Tattered'). In '42 he reappears in Chapter 46.

Picrochole is a choleric: his name means bitter bile. His complexion makes him impulsive and erratic. Toucquedillon means a boaster. Racqedenare is a Scrape-penny, and Engoulevant, a windbag.]

Back at Lerné, the *fouace*-bakers, at once, before eating or drinking, proceeded to their local Capitol and there, before their king, Picrochole, the Third of that Name, set forth their grievances, pointing to their broken panniers, their lacerated garments, their plundered *fouaces* and, above all, to the appallingly injured Marquet, alleging that all that had been done by the shepherds and tenant-farmers of Grandgousier near the great cross-roads beyond Seuilly.

Picrochole at once flew into an insane rage and, without further asking himself about the why or the wherefore, had Ban and Arrière-ban proclaimed throughout his kingdom: every

man, under pain of hanging, must forgather in the main square
before the Castle at the hour of noon.

The better to reinforce his enterprise, he had the drum beaten
through the town. He himself, while his dinner was being prepared, went to ready his artillery, to raise his standard and
oriflamme, and to load up a large quantity of supplies both for
armaments and bellies.

Over dinner he commissioned his officers: by his edict the
Seigneur de Grippeminaud was placed in the vanguard, which
comprised sixteen thousand men armed with harquebuses and
twenty-five thousand soldiers of fortune. The ordnance was
entrusted to Toucquedillon, the Grand Equerry; in which were
counted nine hundred and fourteen great bronze guns: cannons,
cannon-royals, basilisks, serpentines, culverins, bombards,
falcons, passe-volants, falconets and other field-pieces. The
rearguard was allotted to le Duc de Racqedenare. The king and
the princes of the realm took their places in the centre.

And thus summarily equipped, before they set out they
despatched three hundred light horse led by Captain Engoule-
vent to reconnoitre the land and find out whether any ambushes
had been laid in the country, but, having diligently searched,
they found all the land about them to be in peace and quiet,
without musters of any kind.

Upon hearing which, Picrochole ordered that each man
should march behind his banner, rapidly.

And so, without order or restraint, they started their campaign all jumbled up together, wasting and smashing everything
in their way, sparing neither poor nor rich nor any building,
sacred or profane. They made off with oxen, cows, bulls, calves,
heifers, ewes, sheep, goats and rams as well as with hens,
capons, pullets, goslings, ganders, geese, pigs, sows and piglets.
They bashed down the walnuts, stripped the vines, tore away
the vine-stocks and shook all the fruit from the trees. It was an
unparalleled havoc they were wreaking.

And they found no one whatever to resist them; all threw
themselves at their mercy and begged to be treated with greater
humanity, bearing in mind that they had long been good and

loving neighbours and had never committed any violence or outrage against them to be so suddenly mistreated; and that God would soon punish them. To such reproaches they made no reply except that they would 'learn 'em to eat *fouaces!*'

How a monk of Seuilly saved the close of his abbey from being sacked by the enemy

CHAPTER 25

[Becomes Chapter 27.

Enter Frère Jean (a Benedictine monk, as Rabelais had been for a while). In Gargantua *Frère Jean is normally called simply 'the Monk'. His surname, d'Entommeures ('Mincemeat'), suggests that he makes mincemeat of his enemies. He is one of the greatest comic figures of all time. He is also an acted parable preaching active virtue over merely verbal piety: see Chapter 38. After* Gargantua *he does not come into prominence again until the storm-at-sea in the* Fourth Book, *where he plays the same role and reference is made back to his defence of the abbey close.*

The plague kills evangelical preachers and medical men but not the devilish marauders. Why? Because the plague is not sent by God but by devils. (See Chapter 43.)

Until '42 the timorous monks were clearly chanting 'Impetum inimicorum ne timueritis' ('Fear not the assaults of the enemies'). Then their chants become all but incomprehensible: 'Ini, nim, pe, ne, ne, ne, ne, ne, ne, tum, ne, tum, ne, num, num, ini, i, mi, i, mi, co, o, ne, no, o, o, ne, no, ne, no, no, no, rum, ne, num, num'. Such repetitions even more evidently constitute battologia, *that 'vain repetition' condemned just before the teaching of the Lord's Prayer in Matthew 6. Rabelais was reinforced in his beliefs here by an adage of Erasmus (II, I, XCII, 'Battologia, Laconism').*

Before '42 Rabelais had discovered the Cratylus *of Plato, which influenced his attitude to language above all in the* Fourth Book *but also (as here) in some of his additions and changes elsewhere.*

'Da mihi potum' ('Give me a drink') is a monastic joke, sometimes

found written by the tired scribe at the end of a manuscript. It probably
echoes Matthew 10:42 (Vulgate).

  The war is fought over the countryside Rabelais knew as a boy
around his home at La Devinière.]

So they roamed thus about, thieving and pillaging until they
came to Seuilly, where they robbed the men and the women
and plundered whatever they could: nothing was too hot nor
too heavy. Now although the plague was in most of the houses,
they entered them everywhere and plundered everything inside,
yet not one of them ever suffered any ill effects; which is a
matter of great wonder, since the curates, vicars, preachers,
physicians and apothecaries who went to visit, bandage, treat,
exhort and admonish the sick all died of the infection whilst
those pillaging and murdering devils suffered no harm.

  How does that come about, Gentlemen?

  Think about it, I pray you.

  Having thus pillaged the town they proceeded to the abbey
with a terrifying uproar, but they found it bolted and barred;
the main body of the army therefore marched on further
towards the ford at Vède, save for six troops of foot soldiers
and two hundred lancers who stayed behind and breached the
walls of the abbey-close in order to despoil the entire vineyard.

  Those poor devils of monks knew not which of their saints
to invoke; but at all events they did toll the bell summoning *to
the Chapter such as vote in the Chapter.* There it was decreed
that they would take out a nice procession, reinforced by nice
sermons and litanies *against the snares of our enemies* as well
as by nice responses *for peace.*

  There was at that time in that abbey a cloistered monk called
Frère Jean des Entommeures, young, gallant, lively, lusty,
adroit, bold, daring, resolute, tall, slim, loud-mouthed, endowed with an ample nose, a galloper through of mattins, an
unbridler of masses [and a polisher-off of vigils]: in short, a
true monk if ever there was one since the [monking] world first
monked-about [with monkery; and for the rest a cleric up to
his teeth where breviary-stuff is concerned].

Upon hearing the din made by the enemy throughout the
close of their vineyard, he sallied forth to see what they were
up to. Realizing that they were harvesting the grapes on which
the entire year's drinking was based, he returned to the quire
of the church where the other monks were assembled, as dazed
as bell-founders. On seeing them chanting 'Im, im, im, pe, e, e,
e, e, e, tum, um, in, ni, i, mi, co, o, o, o, o, o, rum, um', he said,
'What a good little shitty-dog shanty! God Almighty! Why
don't you chant

Grape-baskets farewell: our vintage is o'er?

The devil take me if they are not inside our close, so thoroughly
lopping off fruit and branch that, by the Body of God, there
will be nothing but gleanings for four years to come. By the
guts of Saint James, what shall we poor devils be drinking in
the meantime? Lord God, *Give me a drink.*'

At which the claustral prior said:

'What is that hintoxicated fellow here going to do! Let him
be led off to the prison. Troubling Divine Service!'

'The Wine Service!' said the Monk. 'Let's see that it be not
troubled! You too, my Lord Prior, love to drink of the best. So
do all good men and true. *Never hath noble man loathed good
wine.* [That's a monastical apophthegm!] But those responses
you are chanting here are, by God, out of season. Why are our
services short during the harvesting of grain and grape yet so
long during Advent and winter? The late Frère Macé Pelosse of
blessèd memory (a true zealot for our Order or the devil take
me) told me – I remember it well – that the reason is so that we
may press and ferment our wine in that season and then quaff
it in winter. Harken to me, Gentlemen: He who loves wine, by
God's body let him follow me! For bluntly, may Saint Anthony's
fire burn me if any of those taste the wine who never succoured
the vine. Guts of God! It's church property! Ah! No, no! The
devil! Saint Thomas of England was willing enough to die for
it. If I died here wouldn't I be a saint too?

'But I'm not going to die: I'll make others do that!'

So saying, he cast off his great habit and grabbed the shaft

of the Cross; it was from the heart of a cornel-tree, as long as
a lance, rounded for the fist and scattered with a few fleurs-de-
lys all but effaced. He sallied forth in a handsome cassock, his
frock thrown over like a scarf, and with the shaft of his Cross
he lashed out so violently at the enemy who without order,
standard, trumpet or drum were harvesting the grapes in the
close (for those who bore banner or standard had left them
alongside the walls, while the drummers had knocked in one
side of their drums so as to fill them with grapes, and the
trumpeters were burdened by grape-laden vine-branches: all
had broken ranks) he fell so suddenly on them without crying
Cave, that he knocked them over like porkers, slashing this way
and that as one fenced of old.

In some cases he battered their brains out; in others, he
fractured their arms and legs; in others, he dislocated the
vertebrae of the neck; and in others, he ruptured the kidneys,
bashed in their noses, blacked their eyes, smashed their mandibles, knocked their teeth down their throats, stove in their
shoulder-blades, gangrened their legs, dislocated their thighs
and splintered their fore-arms.

If any one sought to hide amongst the thickest vines, he
bashed in his back-bone and walloped him like a dog.

If any one sought safety in flight, he shattered his head along
the lamdoidal suture.

If any one clambered into a tree and thought he was safe up
there he impaled him through the fundament.

If one of his old acquaintances cried, 'Ha! Frère Jean, my
friend, Frère Jean, I surrender!'

'You have to,' he would say; 'and surrender your soul to the
devils too!' And he would swiftly give him a few bonks.

If any person was so overcome with temerity as to wish to
face up to him, he showed him the strength of his muscles, for
he would skewer his chest through the heart and the middle
septum.

In other cases he would strike them below the rib-cage,
upsetting their tummies. And they would suddenly die.

In other cases he would run them so fiercely through the
navel that he made their innards pour out.

In others, he would pierce the arse-gut between their bollocks.

It was, believe me, the most dreadful spectacle man ever saw.

Some evoked Saint Barbara;

others, Saint George;

others, Saint Touch-me-not;

others, Our Lady of Cunault, of Lorette-en-Bretagne, of Good Tidings, of La Lenou and of Rivière.

Some made vows to Saint James;

others, to the Holy Shroud at Chambéry, but it got so well burnt three months later that they could never save one thread of it;

others to the one at Cadouin;

others, to Saint-Jean-d'Angély, to Saint Mesmes of Chinon, to Saint Martin of Candes, to Saint Clouaud of Cinais, to the relics at Javrezay and to thousands of other good little saints.

Some died without speaking: [others spoke without dying; some died speaking; others spoke dying.] Others loudly cried, 'Confession! Confession! *I confess! Have mercy upon us! Into thy hands I commend . . .*'

So great were the cries of the wounded that the Prior of the abbey came out with all his monks, who, when they perceived those poor wretches scattered mortally wounded amongst the vines, confessed a few of them. But while the priests were dallying over confessions, the little monklings ran up to where Frère Jean stood and asked how they could help. He told them to slit the throats of the ones lying on the ground. So, leaving their great capes on the nearest trellised vine, they began to slit the throats of the men he had already wounded, and finished them off. Do you know with what tools? Why, beautiful *gouvets* (which are those small short-bladed knives which little boys in our part of the world use to shuck walnuts).

Then, wielding the shaft of his Cross, he captured the breach made by the enemy. Some of the Monklings carried off the ensigns and standards to their cells to turn into garters. But when the men who had made their confession tried to get out through that breach, the Monk knocked them down, saying, 'Those who confess, repent and receive absolution go straight to paradise – as straight as a sickle or the track to La Faye!

And thus by his doughtiness were discomfited all those of that army who had entered into that close, to the number of thirteen thousand six hundred and twenty-two [, not counting the women and children, as is always understood]. Never did Maugis the hermit (of whom it is written in the *Four Sons of Aymon*), do such valiant deeds against the Saracens with his pilgrim's staff as were done that day against the foe by the Monk with the shaft of the Cross.

How Picrochole stormed La Roche-Clermault, and of the caution and reluctance of Grandgousier about going to war

CHAPTER 26

[Becomes Chapter 28.

The Monk's shaft of the Cross with its faded fleurs-de-lys is symbolic of the good old days when king and Church fought for the right.

As an admirer of Erasmus, Rabelais makes his giants first try the ways of moderation and appeasement.]

Now while the Monk, as we have related, skirmished with those who had broken into the close, Picrochole dashed precipitately with his men across the ford at Vêde and assailed La Roche-Clermault, where he met with no resistance whatsoever, and since night had already fallen he decided to billet both himself and his men on the town and to cool his excitable choler.

Come morning he took the bulwarks and the castle by storm, thoroughly strengthened the ramparts and provided the necessary munitions, intending to make the castle his redoubt if attacked from elsewhere since the place was strong both by art and by nature on account of its site and position.

Now let us leave them there and return to our good fellow Gargantua (who is in Paris, keenly engaged in the pursuit of good literature and athletic exercises) and to that good old

fellow Grandgousier, his father, who, after supper, is warming
his balls by a lovely, big, bright fire, waiting for his chestnuts
to roast, drawing on the hearth with a stick (burnt at one end
and used to poke the fire) while telling to his wife and family
fair tales of days gone by.

At that very hour one of the shepherds, called Pillot, who
had been guarding the vines made his way to him and told him
in full of the pillaging and excesses being wrought within his
lands and domains by Picrochole, the king of Lerné; how he
had pillaged and sacked the whole country and laid it waste,
except for the close at Seuilly which Frère Jean des Entommeures – greatly to his honour – had saved, and how the said
king was at present in La Roche-Clermault where he and his
men were diligently digging themselves in.

'O dear! O dear!' said Grandgousier, 'What is all this, good
people? Am I dreaming, or can what I am told be true? Picrochole, my old friend, bound to me by every bond of time, family
and fellowship, comes and attacks me! Who is driving him?
Who is goading him on? Who has given him such counsel? Oh,
oh, oh, oh, oh! My God and Saviour, help me, inspire me and
counsel me what to do! I declare, I swear before you – may
your favour be ever upon me! – that I have never offended
him, never harmed his people, never pillaged his lands. On the
contrary, I have supported him with men, money, goodwill and
advice whenever I knew it to be to his advantage.

'That he should thus come and affront me can therefore only
be through the Evil Spirit. God so Good, you know my heart,
for from you can nothing be hid. Should he have gone raving
mad and if you have sent him to me to rehabilitate his mind,
vouchsafe me the power and knowledge to restore him to the
yoke of your holy will by teaching him a good lesson.

'Oh! Oh! Oh! My good people, my friends and faithful vassals, must I burden you with aiding me? Alas! From now on
my old age sought nothing but rest, and all my life I have striven
for nothing but peace. But I see that I must now load armour
on to my weak, weary and wretched shoulders; must grasp
lance and mace with my shaky hands in order to succour and
protect my poor subjects. Reason so decrees: for by their labour

I am maintained and by their sweat I am fed, I, my children and my household.

'Yet I shall nevertheless never go to war before trying all the arts and ways of peace. Of that I am resolved.'

And so he convoked his Council and explained how matters stood. It was concluded that a man of wisdom be despatched to Picrochole to find out why he had thus suddenly abandoned his repose and invaded lands over which he had no right whatsoever; in addition that Gargantua and his men be summoned to save and defend their country in its hour of need. Grandgousier was entirely pleased and ordered it to be done.

Whereupon, within the hour, he despatched his manservant, the Basque, to summon Gargantua at all speed, having written him the following letter:

The purport of the letter which Grandgousier wrote to Gargantua

CHAPTER 27

[Becomes Chapter 29.

The letter, which starts off without any greeting, preaches the pacific virtues admired by Erasmus. That stratagems and ruses may be legitimately used in a just war was a moral tenet held by many, including Sir Thomas More in Utopia.

That free-will needs to be 'guided' by grace is an Augustinian doctrine emphasized by evangelicals and moderate reformers.

The adage on war in the first paragraph is taken from Cicero, Of Duties, *1, 22, § 76.)]*

'Your keenness for your studies would have required me not to recall you from your philosophical leisure for some long time yet, had not the arrogance of our friends and long-term allies now shattered the security of my old age. But since it is my fated destiny to be disturbed by those on whom I had most relied, I am obliged to summon you home to defend the persons and property enfeoffed to you by natural law. For, as arms are weak without, if counsel dwells not within, so too, vain is study and counsel futile if they are not virtuously practised at the opportune moment and put into effect.

'My intention is not to provoke but appease; not to attack but defend; not to make conquests but to protect my faithful subjects as well as my hereditary lands, which Picrochole has hostilely invaded without cause or occasion, daily furthering his mad enterprise with outrages unbearable to free-born persons.

'I have set myself the duty of moderating his tyrannous choler by offering him everything which I believed might satisfy him; several times I have sent friendly envoys to him to learn why he felt himself to be outraged, by what and by whom; but I have had no reply from him except wilful defiance and a claim to the right to do what he pleases in my domains. From which I learnt that God Eternal had abandoned him to the rudder of his own free-will and private judgement, which cannot be other than evil unless continually guided by divine grace, and that he has sent him here to me under such grievous auspices so that I may restrict him to his duties and bring him back to his senses.

'Therefore, my most dear Son, come quickly home – as soon as you can after reading this letter – to succour not so much me (which you should do anyway out of natural piety) as your own people whom by reason you should save and protect. The feat will be accomplished with the least possible shedding of blood, and if at all possible we shall, by using the most expedient devices and the wiles and ruses of war, save all those souls and send them back happily to their homes.

'Dearest son: may the peace of Christ our Redeemer be with you.

'Greet Ponocrates, Gymnaste and Eudemon for me.

'This twentieth day of September:

'Your father,

'Grandgousier.'

How Ulrich Gallet was despatched to Picrochole

CHAPTER 28

[Becomes Chapter 30.
  Appeasement is rightly tried, but we know that it will fail.]

Having dictated that letter and signed it, Grandgousier ordered Ulrich Gallet (his Master of Petitions, a man discreet and wise, whose virtue and good counsel he had already tried in diverse contentious affairs) to appear before Picrochole to warn him of what they had resolved.

This good man Gallet left that very hour, and having crossed the ford asked the miller how things were going for Picrochole. He received the reply that Picrochole's men had left him neither cock nor hen and that they had shut themselves up in La Roche-Clermault; he advised him strongly against proceeding any further for fear of their look-outs: their madness was beyond bounds.

Gallet readily believed it and lodged overnight with the miller.

Next morning he proceeded with his herald to the castle gate and requested the guards to arrange for him to speak to the king in his own interest. When the message was reported to the king he would in no wise consent to open the gates for him but betook himself to the ramparts and said to the ambassador, 'What news do you bring? What have you got to say?'

At which the ambassador spoke as follows:

The harangue delivered by Gallet before Picrochole

CHAPTER 29

[Becomes Chapter 31.
  Ciceronian rhetoric on subjects dear of humanists. Renaissance strategists and statesmen had to grapple with the possibility that their

enemies were deceived not only by ambition or greed but also by the
devil, that lying spirit who works through deceptive apparitions and
misleading illusions, against which the wise and prayerful Christian
must be ever on his guard.]

'No more rightful cause of grief can ever be engendered amongst
human beings than when, from the place from which they
justly expected graciousness and kindness, they receive pain
and injury. So not without cause (yet without right-reason)
several people, having met such an event, have found the indig-
nity of it harder to bear than life itself, and when they were
unable to put things right by force or ingenuity have cut themselves off from the light of life.

'It is no wonder then if my master, King Grandgousier, has
been overcome by great displeasure and is perturbed in his mind
by your insane and hostile incursion. The wonder would have
been if he had not been disturbed by the unparalleled atrocities
committed by you and your men against his lands and subjects,
in which not one example of inhumanity was omitted.

'That was grievous enough to him in itself because of the
heart-felt affection – which no man could exceed – with which
he has [always] cherished his subjects but more grievous still
by human judgement, in that those heinous wrongs were done
by your men and by you who, with your forefathers, had
conceived for him and all his ancestors, as far back into ancient
days as any can remember, a friendship held until now, by all
together, to be sacred and which you have so well guarded,
maintained and kept inviolate that not only he and his subjects
but the barbarous nations of Poitou, Brittany and Le Mans,
and those dwelling beyond the Isles of Canarre and Isabella,
have reckoned it as easy to bring down the heavens or to raise
the deeps above the clouds as to unshackle that alliance; and in
their own warlike projects they so greatly feared it that never
did they dare to exasperate, provoke or harm the one for fear
of the other.

'And there is more to it. That sacred amity has so filled our
heavens that few of those who dwell nowadays anywhere on
the mainland and the isles of the ocean have not ambitiously

aspired to join in it, through pacts with conditions drawn up by you yourself, valuing a confederation with you as much as their own lands and dominions. With the result that, in living memory, not one prince or league has been so presumptuous or overweening as to dare to move – I do not say against your lands but against those of your confederates.

'And if through rash counsel they have attempted to introduce some novelty, the name and terms of your alliance, once heard, led them quickly to abandon their enterprises.

'So what frenzy moves you now, having broken the whole alliance, trampled all amity underfoot, transgressed every law, hostilely to invade his lands without having been harmed, exasperated or provoked by him or his people? Where is faith? Where is law? Where is rationality? Where is humanity? Where is fear of God? Do you really think those atrocities are hidden from the immortal Spirits and from our sovereign God who is the just requiter of our enterprises? If you do so think, then you are deceiving yourself: for all things shall come to his judgement.

'Can fated destinies or astral influences be seeking to put an end to your peace and quiet? Thus all things have their ends and periods, and when they have reached their highest point they are sent tumbling down, for in that state they cannot long endure. Such is the end of those who cannot temper their fortune and prosperity by reason and moderation.

'But if you were so fated, and if your happiness and quietness must end, had it to be by disturbing my king by whom you were established in your power? If the house of Picrochole had to collapse, must it collapse on to the forecourts of him who had enhanced it?

'The matter so exceeds the bounds of reason and is so abhorrent to common sense that it can scarcely be grasped by human understanding and will remain unbelievable to foreigners until the deed, duly certified and attested, brings them to realize that nothing is holy or sacred to those who have broken free from God and reason in order to follow their own perverted passions.

'If some wrong had perhaps been done by us against your subjects and domains; if favour had perhaps been shown by us to such as wish you ill; if we had perhaps not aided you in your affairs; if your name or honour had perhaps been injured by us; or, to put it better, if the lying Spirit, striving to draw you towards evil, had perhaps, by deceiving apparitions or misleading illusions, put it into your mind that we had done anything unworthy of our ancient amity, you ought first to have enquired after the truth of it, and next rebuked us for it; then we would have so satisfied you that you would have had cause for contentment.

'But (O God Eternal!) what sort of enterprise is yours! Do you want to pillage and ravage my master's kingdom like a perfidious tyrant? Have you found him so craven and insensible that he would not – or so lacking in men, money, counsel and military skill that he could not – resist your iniquitous assaults?

'Be off at once. Spend all day tomorrow withdrawing to your lands without any riot or violence on the way. Pay one thousand golden bezants for the damage inflicted upon these lands, one half of which you shall hand over tomorrow, the other half on the coming Ides of May, leaving meanwhile as hostages le Duc Treadmill, le Duc Shortarse and le Duc de Little-trash, together with the Prince of Weals and Viscount Flea-pit.'

How Grandgousier, to purchase peace, made good the *fouaces*

CHAPTER 30

[Becomes Chapter 32.
*Appeasement is to be tried even when the concessions are extreme.
If appeasement fails, skilled battle is to be joined under God.
The insanely choleric Picrochole lives up to his name.
The tone and the ideas owe much to Lucian.]*

With those words that good man Gallet fell silent, but Picro-chole returned no answer to his address save, 'Come and get 'em! Come and get 'em! My lads have got fine balls and pestles! They'll pound you up a few *fouaces* all right!' So Gallet made his way back to Grandgousier, whom he found on his knees, bareheaded, bent over in a little corner of his closet, praying God to vouchsafe to mollify the choler of Picrochole and bring him to his senses without resorting to force. When he saw that his good man had come back, he asked:

'Ah, my friend, my friend; what news do you bring me?'

'Nothing but disorder,' said Gallet. 'That man is quite out of his mind and forsaken by God.'

'Indeed,' said Grandgousier, 'but my friend, what cause does he proffer for his excesses?'

'He expounded no cause to me whatsoever,' said Gallet, 'except that he said in his choler something about *fouaces*. I wonder whether anyone has done some outrage to his *fouace*-bakers?'

'Before deciding what to do,' said Grandgousier, 'I intend to get to the bottom of it.'

So he sent to find out about the matter and discovered that it was indeed true that a few *fouaces* had been forcibly taken from Picrochole's subjects; that Marquet had suffered a blow on the head from a cudgel; that all had nevertheless been properly paid for, and that the said Marquet had injured Forgier first by whipping him about the legs.

It seemed to Grandgousier's entire Council that he should defend himself by main force. Despite which, he said, 'Since it is but a matter of a few *fouaces*, I shall try to satisfy him, as I am extremely reluctant to go to war.'

And so he inquired how many *fouaces* had been taken and, on learning that it was four or five dozen, commanded that five cart-loads should be baked that very night, one load of which was to be made from the best butter, the best egg-yokes, the best saffron and the best spices and set apart for Marquet, to whom, for the hurt he had suffered, he would give seven hundred thousand [and three] Philippus-crowns to pay the barber-surgeons who had treated him; and, on top of that, he would further grant him the farm of La Pomardière, free for him and his heirs for ever.

To lead the convoy and see it all through, he despatched Gallet, who, on the way, near the Willow Grove, had a great many bunches of reeds and rushes cut and strung about the carts and each of the carters; he himself bore one in his hand to let it be understood that they were seeking nothing but peace and were coming to pay for it.

Once arrived before the gates, they requested to parley with Picrochole on behalf of Grandgousier.

Picrochole absolutely refused to let them in or to come out to parley with them, sending to state that he was otherwise engaged but that they should say what they had to say to Captain Braggart, who was up on the walls adjusting some cannon or other.

And so our good man said:

'Sire: to cut from you any handle for a quarrel[25] and to remove any excuse for not returning to our original alliance, we are making good to you now the *fouaces* over which this controversy arose.

'Five dozen our people took; they were amply paid for, but we so love peace that we send you five cart-loads of them, of which this one is for Marquet, who is raising most complaints. In addition, so as to satisfy him entirely, here are seven hundred thousand [and three] Philippus-crowns which I deliver to him; and for any damages he might claim I cede him the farm at La Pomardière, for him and his heirs to hold in fee-simple for ever. Look. Here are the deeds of conveyance. And for God's sake let us live in peace from now on, with you withdrawing happily to your own lands and giving up this fortress to which you have no right whatsoever as you yourself admit.

'Then let us be friends as before.'

Braggart related it all to Picrochole and increasingly poisoned his mind, saying to him: 'Those bumpkins are in a fine old fright. By God, Grandgousier is shitting himself, the poor old soak. His business is not going to war but emptying wine-pots! My opinion is that we keep both the *fouaces* and the money and hasten to dig ourselves in so as to pursue our good fortune. Did they really think they were dealing with a twit, feeding you

---

25. '42: ... to *draw you back from all this* quarrel ... (Rabelais' initial phrase is a Latinism which foxed some publishers.)

with those *fouaces*! But there it is: the good treatment and great intimacy that you have maintained with them up till now have made you contemptible to them: Flatter villein, he will batter: Batter villein, he will flatter.'

'Yeah!' said Picrochole. 'Yeah! Yeah! By Saint James, they're in for it now. Do as you said.'

'There is one thing I want to warn you of though,' said Braggart. 'We're pretty short of victuals and most meagrely furnished with belly fodder. If Grandgousier were to lay siege to us, I would here and now have all my teeth pulled out save three, doing the same to your men as to me: with three we would have more than enough to eat up our supplies.'

'We shall,' said Picrochole, 'have all too much to eat. Are we here to feed or to fight?'

'To fight, certainly,' said Braggart, 'but, Food short: no sport; and, Where hunger reigneth, power draineth.'

'All this yap!' said Picrochole. 'Seize what they've brought.'

Whereupon they did seize the money, *fouaces*, carts and oxen, and then sent the men back without a word, except that they had better not come so close again, and that they would teach 'em why tomorrow!

And thus, having achieved nothing, the men returned to Grandgousier and told him all, adding that there was no hope of bringing them to make peace save by war, quick and strong.

How some of Picrochole's governors put him in the ultimate danger by their impetuous counsel

CHAPTER 31

[Becomes Chapter 33.
A chapter with laughter directed at real events.

The effect of bad counsellors on stupid kings. Rabelais has read and digested Lucian's The Ship, *or the* Wishes *and Plutarch's* Life of Pyrrhus. *He directs the lessons they imply against the Emperor Charles V, whose device consisted of two columns with the motto 'Plus Ultra', ('Further Beyond'). (The Straits of Seville, or of Sybil, are the Straits*

*of Gibraltar: the twin columns of Hercules stretched only that far.
Charles V ruled over a much greater empire, 'Further Beyond').*

    *The Turkish admiral Barbarossa took Tunis on 22 August 1534;
from at least January 1535, Charles V began preparing a mighty navy
to reverse the Turkish successes. He invested Tunis for several weeks
from 20 of June 1535. The French were actively seeking an alliance
with Barbarossa and the Sublime Porte generally; there was no question of restricting French alliances to Christians only! Early in 1535
Guillaume Du Bellay wrote a general letter to the German princes
explaining why François I was suppressing seditious Christian extrem-
ists at home while Turkish emissaries were flitting in and out of Paris.
This part of* Gargantua *is best understood as referring to these events.
(The interpolation of Algiers, Bona and Corona in 1542 keeps up the
satire of Charles V: in 1541 the Emperor had undertaken a disastrous
campaign against those Moorish towns, and the French were pleased
at his reverses.)*

    *Dividing an army into two parts is a folly condemned by Rabelais
in a letter to his patron, Geoffroy d'Estissac, Bishop of Maillezais: the
Turk had divided his army and was defeated by the Sophy. Rabelais
adds, 'See here the ill counsel that it is to divide one's army before
victory.' (The Duke of Albany also drew off the flower of his camp
before the battle of Pavia when François I was defeated and taken
prisoner.)*

    *'Hasten slowly' is one of the best known of all emblems, represented
by the anchor and the dolphin used by the French admiral. It is the
subject of a very long and personal explanation in the* Adages *of
Erasmus (II, I, I), in which both Horappolo and Lascaris are mentioned.*

    *The name of the only wise counsellor, Echephron, means 'prudent'
or 'wise' in Greek.*

    'Spadassino' suggests an Italian; Squit's name renders merdaille, *a
name given to raw recruits.*

    *An error, 'Swedes' – for 'Swiss' – was corrected in '35. Such errors
suggest that Rabelais did not see his new book through the press.]*

Having plundered the *fouaces*, there appeared before Picrochole le Duc de Little-trash, le Comte Spadassino and Captain
Squit. They said to him:

'Sire: today we will make you the most sprightly and knightly prince there ever has been since the death of Alexander of Macedonia. Here is how:

['Please, please,' said Picrochole, 'do put on your hats.'

'We are most honoured, Cyre,' they said. 'We are merely doing our duty.][26] You will leave behind you here some captain or other with a small band of men to garrison the fort, which we believe to be sufficiently strong, partly by nature, partly because of the ramparts you yourself have devised.

'You will divide your army in two, as you well know how. One part will go and throw itself against this fellow Grandgousier and his men. He will be easily discomfited by them at the very first encounter. There you will put your hands on piles of money, [, for that villein has pots of it: we say *villein* because a noble prince never has a penny: saving is a villein's vice].

'Meanwhile the other part will make for Aunis, Saintonge, Angoulême and Gascony, as well as Périgord, Médoc and the Landes. Without resistance they will take towns, castles and fortresses. At Bayonne, Saint-Jean-de-Luz and Fontarabia you will commandeer all the boats and then coast along towards Galicia and Portugal, sacking all the maritime forts as far as Lisbon, where you will find all the shipping required by a conqueror. By Gosh! Spain will give in! They're nothing but yokels! You will pass through the Straits of Sybil: there, you will set up two pillars as magnificent as those of Hercules in perpetual memory of your name: and those straits shall be called the Picrocholine Sea.

'You've crossed the Picrocholine Sea and look! Barbarossa's becoming your slave.'

'I,' said Picrochole, 'shall have mercy upon him.'

'Indeed,' they said, 'provided he gets baptized!

'Then you will storm the kingdoms of Tunis and Hippo, [Algiers, Bona, Corona:] indeed all Barbary.

'Passing *ultra*, you will hold Majorca, Minorca, Sardinia,

26. When the addition was made in 1535, the phrase 'Here is how' was permanently struck out. For the flattery and the jest see *Pantagruel*, Chapter 10, at the break later numbered Chapter 11.

Corsica and the islands of the Gulf of Genoa and the Balearic Sea.

'Sailing leftwards along the coast, you will establish your dominion over Languedoc, Provence, Savoy, Genoa, Florence, Lucca. And then, God help you, Rome! Poor mister pope is already dying of fright.'

'By my faith,' said Picrochole, 'I shan't ever kiss his slipper.'

'Italy taken, look! Naples, Calabria, Apulia and Sicily are all ransacked. Malta too. I wish those funny old knights who used to be in Rhodes had resisted you, just to see the colour of their piss.'

'I would very much like to go to Loreto,' said Picrochole.

'No, no!' they said. 'Do that on the way back. From Malta we shall take Candia, Cyprus, Rhodes and the Cyclades; and then set upon the Morea. We've taken it! By Saint Trinian, God help Jerusalem, for in might the Sultan cannot be compared to you!'

'I,' said Picrochole, 'will therefore rebuild the temple of Solomon.'

'No,' they said, 'not yet. Wait a while. Never rush into your enterprises. Do you know what Octavian Augustus used to say? *Hasten slowly*. It behoves you first to hold Asia Minor, Caria, Lycia, Cilicia, Lydia, Phrygia, Mysia, Bithynia, Carrasia, Satalia, Samagria, Castamena, Luga and Sebasta as far as the Euphrates.'

'Shall we see,' said Picrochole, 'Babylon and Mount Sinai?'

'No need of that just now,' they said. 'Good Lord! haven't we done enough, slogging through the Caspian Mountains,[27] sailing over the Hircanian Sea and riding over the two Armenias and the three Arabias?'

'By my faith!' said Picrochole, 'We're in trouble! Oh! those poor wretches!'

'Eh?' they said.

'What'll we drink in those deserts? [For Julian Augustus and all his army died there of thirst; or so we are told.]'

---

27. From '35: omit: slogging through the Caspian Mountains.

'We,' said they, 'have already seen to all that.

'Upon the Syrian Sea you have nine thousand and fourteen large ships laden with the world's best wines. They have already arrived at Jaffa. There they found twenty-two hundred thousand camels and sixteen hundred elephants, which you had already captured during a hunt near Sidjilmassa when you rode into Libya, taking into the bargain the entire Mecca-bound caravan: that provided you with all the wine you needed, didn't it?'

'True,' he said, 'but it wasn't cool when we drank it.'

'Ha! [Cool!]' they said. 'By some little Cod's might! A valiant knight, a conqueror, a pretender to universal Empire cannot always have it easy. God be praised that you and your men have come safe and entire to the very banks of the Tigris.'

'But,' said he, 'what is being done by that part of our army which discomfited that soak of a peasant, Grandgousier?'

'They are not being idle,' they said. 'We shall link up with them soon. They have taken Brittany for you, together with Normandy, Flanders, Hainault, Brabant, Artois, Holland and Zeeland. They have crossed the Rhine over the guts of the Swedes and the Lansquenets.

'Part of them have quelled Luxembourg, Lorraine, Champagne and Savoy as far as Lyons, where they met up with your troops returning from their naval victories in the Mediterranean Sea and are now regrouped in Bohemia, having first sacked Swabia, Würtemberg, Bavaria, Austria, Moravia and Styria. Then together they fiercely attacked Lübeck, Norway, Sweden, Dacia, Gothia, Greenland and the Hanseatics as far as the Frozen Sea.

'That done, they conquered the Orkneys and subjugated Scotland, England and Ireland. From there they navigated through the shoals of the Baltic Sea, passed through the Sarmatians, vanquished and subdued Prussia, Poland, Lithuania, Russia, Walachia, Transylvania, Hungary, Bulgaria and Turkey, and are now in Constantinople.'

'Let's join up with them as quickly as possible,' said Picrochole, 'I want also to be the Emperor of Trebizond. We'll slaughter all those Turkish and Moslem dogs, won't we?'

'What the devil else!' they said. 'And you will bestow all their goods and lands on those who have done you honourable service.'

'Reason so requires,' he said. 'That is only just. On you I bestow Carmania, Syria and the whole of Palestine.'

'Oh, Cyre!' they said. 'That's most kind of you. Many thanks. May God make you ever to prosper.'

An old nobleman was there present, a man tried by many hazards and a true old campaigner. His name was Echephron. When he heard that discussion he said:

'I fear this whole enterprise of yours will be like that jug of milk in the farce, by which a cobbler had a mad dream of becoming rich: the jug was shattered and he had nothing for dinner. What is your aim in these fine conquests? What will be the end of such travels and travails?'

'We shall then rest at our ease,' said Picrochole.

Echephron replied, '[And what if you never come back, for the journey is long and perilous.] Would it not be better to take our rest here and now without exposing ourselves to such hazards? ["Nothing venture: gain nor horse nor mule," quoth Salomon. "Too much venture, lose both horse and mule," retorted Malcon.]'[28]

'Oh!' said Spadassino. 'By God, what a mad dreamer! Are we to hide in a chimney-corner, passing our lives and our time with the ladies, stringing pearls or spinning yarn like Sardanapalus!'

'Enough!' said Picrochole, 'Let us pass *ultra*! My only fear concerns those devilish legions of Grandgousier's. Supposing they attack our tail while we're here in Mesopotamia: what remedy is there?'

'An excellent one,' said Squit: 'a pretty little mobilization order sent by you to the Muscovites will instantly put fifty thousand elite fighters in the field. O! Make me but your Deputy and – I disavow, damme! the flesh . . ., the death . . ., the

28. The *Dialogues of Salomon and Marcolf* (or, Malcon) was a popular work consisting of an exchange of proverbs between Salomon, the wise King of Israel, and a man of popular wisdom.

blood . . . !²⁹ – Why! I'd kill a comb for a haberdasher! I snap,
I bay, I strike, I slay!'³⁰

'Up then and onwards!' said Picrochole. 'Hurry everything
along! Let him who loves me follow me.'³¹

How Gargantua quit the city of Paris to come to the help of his country; and how Gymnaste encountered his foes

CHAPTER 32

[Becomes Chapter 34.

From dreams of world conquest back to the pays *of Rabelais. All
the place-names would have been known to Rabelais from childhood.
'The devil take me' was an extremely common oath.]*

That self-same hour Gargantua (who, having read his father's
letter, had left Paris at once astride his great mare) had already
crossed over Nuns' Bridge with Ponocrates, Gymnaste and Eudemon, who had taken post-horses to follow him. The rest of
his train were coming at the normal pace, bringing all his books
and philosophical paraphernalia.

When he reached Parilly he was warned by the tenant-farmer
of Gouget that Picrochole had fenced himself round at La
Roche-Clermauld, despatched Captain Tri-ffart with a large
army to assail the forest of Vède and Vaugaudry and ransacked
the very hen-houses as far as the wine-press at Billard: the
excesses they were committing throughout the *pays* were outlandish and hardly credible. Gargantua was so alarmed that he
was unsure of what to say or do, but Ponocrates advised that
they should proceed towards le Sieur de La Vauguyon, who

29. From '35 omit: I disavow, damme! the flesh . . ., the death . . ., the
    blood . . . !
30. '35 reads: . . . I snap, *I knap*, I bay, I slay! . . .'42 reads: . . . I snap, *I knap*,
    I bay, I *disavow*! . . .
31. A deformation of a saying of Cyrus the Great: 'Let him who loves himself
    follow me.'

had always been their friend and ally: by him they would be better informed about all that was going on.

They did so at once and found him already fully determined to help them; his opinion was that he should send one of his men to reconnoitre the *pays* to learn how the enemy was situated so that they could act upon counsel based on how things actually stood at that time. Gymnaste offered to go, and it was decided that it would be better if he took along with him someone who knew the highways and byways and the local rivers.

So he left with Prelinguand, Vauguyon's equerry, and they fearlessly spied out the land on every side. Meanwhile Gargantua rested and had something to eat with his men, giving his mare a *picotin* of oats (that is, sixty-four hundredweight [and three bushels]).

Gymnaste and his companion rode on until they came upon the enemy scattered in disorder, pillaging and pilfering everything they could. When they espied him afar, they came dashing up in a mob to rob him.

Then he cried out to them:

'Gentlemen; a poor devil am I. Have mercy upon me, I pray. I still have one golden crown left: we shall drink it up [for it is potable gold]. And this horse here shall be sold to pay for my welcome. That done, retain me as one of yours, for no man knows how to catch, baste, roast, dress and indeed, by God, carve and season a chicken better than I do. And for my initiation gift I drink to all good fellows.'

He then unstopped his leathern bottle and took a decent swig without sticking his nose in. The poor wretches stared at him, gaping with jaws a good foot wide and hanging out their tongues like greyhounds waiting to drink after him. But at that moment up ran Captain Tri-ffart to see what was going on. Whereupon Gymnaste proffered him his bottle, saying:

'Here you are, Captain. Take a bold swig. I've tried it: it's wine from La Foye-Monjault.'

'Hey!' said Tri-ffart. 'This here bumpkin is taxing us with his mockery! Who are you, fellow?'

'A poor devil,' said Gymnaste.

'Ha,' said Tri-ffart. 'Since you are a poor devil you may

rightly pass through: "poor devils pass through without tax or toll". But it is not the custom for poor devils to be so well mounted. Wherefore Monsieur Devil, dismount so that I may have your steed. And if it doesn't take me, you, Monsieur Devil, will have to do so: I'd very much like such a devil to take me!'

How Gymnaste nimbly slew captain Tri-ffart and other of Picrochole's men

CHAPTER 33

[Becomes Chapter 35.
  Gymnaste shows skill and dexterity worthy of his name.
  'Agios ho Theos' *('Holy is God'* – Hagios ho Theos) *was retained in Greek by the Latin Church in the liturgy for Good Friday.*
  'Ab hoste maligno libera nos, Domine!' *('From the hostile fiend deliver us, O Lord') is again taken from the liturgy. The* 'hostis malignus' *(the 'hostile enemy') is the devil, the foul fiend.]*

On hearing such words, some of them began to be frightened and crossed themselves with all their hands, thinking that Gymnaste was a devil in disguise. One of them called Bonny Johannie [, a captain in the local trainband,] tugged his Book of Hours from his codpiece and bawled out, *'Agios ho Theos.* If you be of God, speak: if you be of t'Other: be off!'

But he went not off.

Several of the band heard that and deserted their comrades, all of which Gymnaste was noting and considering. He therefore made as if to dismount but, having swung down his horse's left flank, he twisted on his stirrup, his bastard sword by his side, and having nimbly slid underneath along the girth, sprang into the air, stood with both feet on the saddle, his bum facing the horse's head and said, 'My scrotum proceeds backwards!'

From that position, he then cut a caper on one foot, turning to the left and never failing to come back to his original stance without in any way varying it.

At which Tri-ffart said,

'I shall not attempt that just now: I have my reasons!'

'Ah well!' said Gymnaste, 'I did that wrong. I shall undo it.'

With great strength and agility he then repeated the caper, spinning to the right.

Having accomplished it, he placed his right thumb on the pommel of the saddle, raised the whole of his body into the air (with the entire weight bearing on the muscle and sinews of that thumb) and twirled three times round.

The fourth time he flipped over backwards and, without touching a thing, leapt between the ears of his steed; there he raised his body aloft, with all the weight bearing on his left thumb. In that position he spun round like a mill-wheel; then, slapping the flat of his right hand against the middle of the saddle, he gave himself such a twirl that he seated himself sideways on the crupper as the ladies do.

After which, with utter ease, he swung his right leg over the saddle and took up position on the crupper, ready to ride off.

'But,' he said, 'I had better put myself between the saddle-bows.' And so, pressing down with both thumbs on the crupper in front of him, he turned a backwards somersault and landed correctly between the two bows of the saddle. Then he somersaulted again into the air and came down, feet together, between the saddle-bows; then, with his arms stretched out like a cross, he spun round over a hundred times, shouting meanwhile, 'I am furious, ye devils, furious, furious. Hold me back, ye devils! Hold me! Hold me!'

While he was vaulting about like that, the yokels said to each other in great amazement: 'By Saint Buddocks, 'tis an hobgoblin or a devil done up in disguise, *From the hostile fiend, free us good Lord*!'

Then they fled in a rout, each glancing behind like a dog making off with a goose-wing.

Gymnaste, seeing his advantage, dismounted, unsheathed his sword and, with great swipes, fell upon the most substantial of those bumpkins and battered them into piles of injured, bruised and wounded. Not one of them offered any resistance (for they all thought he was a famished devil, partly on account of his miraculous vaultings and partly because of the words which

Tri-ffart had used when calling him a 'poor devil') save Tri-ffart alone, who treacherously attempted to split open his skull with his lansquenet's broad-sword, but Gymnaste's armour was so good that he felt no more than the weight of it and, quickly twisting round, hurled a flying blow at the aforesaid Tri-ffart, who was shielding only his upper parts, so that, with one blow, he cut through his stomach, colon and half of the liver, at which he fell to the ground, as he did so spewing up four tureens of sops with his soul all mixed up in them.

That done, Gymnaste withdraws, well aware that matters hazardous should never be pursued to the end and that knights should treat Good Fortune with reverence, never outraging nor provoking her.

And so, mounting his steed, he gives it the spur and makes straight for La Vauguyon, bringing Prelinguand with him.

How Gargantua slighted the castle near the ford at Vède: and how they crossed that ford

CHAPTER 34

[Becomes Chapter 36.

The war is still in the pays of Rabelais. There is an allusion to Aelian, On the Nature of Animals, 16, 25 a text that would have been appreciated by a chivalrous audience.

In the first edition, one of the speeches of Gargantua is wrongly attributed to Grandgousier. Corrected in '35, it is tacitly corrected here too.]

Once arrived, he gave an account of the state in which he had found the enemy and of the stratagem he had employed – he alone against their entire cohort – asserting that they were no more than peasants, pillagers and brigands, quite ignorant of the art of war, adding that they should set out in confidence, for it would be extremely easy to strike them down like cattle.

Whereat Gargantua, accompanied as we have already said, mounted his great mare and, coming across on the way a big, tall elder-tree (locally called Saint Martin's Tree because it grew from a staff which, long ago, Saint Martin had planted there), he said, 'Just what I wanted! That tree will double up for my staff and my lance.' And so he wrenched it easily from the ground, stripped off the branches and trimmed it to his liking. Meanwhile his mare, to relieve her belly, pissed so abundantly that she formed a flood seven leagues wide and all her stale sped down towards the ford at Vède, so increasing the flow that all that band of enemies – except for a few who had taken the path towards the hills on the left – were therein drowned most horribly.

On arriving at the forest of Vède, Gargantua was warned by Eudemon that remnants of the enemy were still inside the castle, so, to find out, he hollered as loud as he could, 'Are you there, or not? If you are, be off: if you're not, I have nothing to add.'

But a renegade gunner up on the parapet fired a shot from his cannon and struck him violently on the right temple: yet it did him no more harm than if he had hurled a plum at him.

'What *is* this!' said Gargantua. 'Chucking grape-seeds at us, are you!? The vendange will cost you dear.' (He did indeed think that the round-shot was a grape-seed.)

On hearing the noise, those who were delayed in the castle by their pillaging rushed up into the towers and fortifications, shooting over nine thousand and twenty-five rounds from their falconets and harquebuses, all aiming them so thick and fast at Gargantua's head that he exclaimed, 'Ponocrates, my friend, the flies here are blinding me: hand me a branch from one of those willows to brush them away' – thinking, you see, that the lead-shot and stone-shot from the guns were gad-flies.

Ponocrates informed him that the only flies about were the gun-shot fired from the castle. So Gargantua battered the towers and fortifications with his big tree, and with many a great blow razed them to the ground. By which means all inside were crushed and smashed into smithereens.

After leaving there, they came to the bridge by the mill-pond and found the ford covered with corpses forming such a mass that they clogged up the mill-race. (They were the men who had perished in the mare's urinal flood.)

There they wondered how to get across, given the hindrance of those corpses. But Gymnaste said,

'If those devils got across it, then so shall I, easily.'

'The devils did get across it,' said Eudemon, 'to bear away the souls of the damned.'

'Then by Saint Trinian he will do so,' said Ponocrates, 'as a logical consequence.'

'Indeed, indeed I will,' said Gymnaste, 'or stay stuck on the way.'

And giving his horse the spur, he confidently went across without his horse ever taking fright at the dead bodies (for, following the teachings of Aelian, he had trained it to fear neither weapons nor corpses, not by killing folk as Diomedes killed the Thracians, nor following what Ulysses did – as Homer tells us – by dragging the bodies of his foes before the hooves of his horses, but by putting a dummy corpse amongst its litter and making it habitually walk over it when he gave it its oats).

The other three followed him across without trouble, except for Eudemon, whose horse plunged its right hoof, fetlock-deep, into the paunch of a great, fat peasant lying drowned on his back, and could not pull it out again. And the horse remained there hobbled until Gargantua used the end of his staff to thrust the remainder of the peasant's guts deep into the water while the horse lifted its hoof. And, behold – a hippiatric miracle! – the aforesaid horse was cured of an exostosis on that hoof by a touch from the innards of that fat clod-hopper.

How Gargantua combed cannon-balls out of his hair

CHAPTER 35

[Becomes Chapter 37.

Philip of Bergamo's continuation of a Supplement *to his* Chronicles *gives rise to the smiling appeal to the 'Supplement to the Supplement of the Chronicles'. The antifeminist narrator of the first paragraph is Maître Alcofrybas, not Rabelais in person, but some did take Rabelais*

to be an antifeminist. For many at the time such antifeminist remarks
were part of standard comic cheek.

The Collège de Montaigu was the butt of much humanist satire.
The mockery of it is at the expense of Noel Béda. That Opportunity
has to be seized by the forelock since she is bald behind is a Classical
commonplace, mentioned by Erasmus (Adages, IV, IX, XXXIX, To
catch by the hair).]

Issuing forth from the banks of the Vède, they shortly came to
the château of Grandgousier, who was awaiting them with
great longing. On Gargantua's arrival they gave him a mighty
welcome: never were seen people more full of joy. For the
Supplement to the Supplement of the Chronicles states that
Gargamelle died then of joy. Personally I know nothing about
that, and care very little for her nor for any other woman
there be.

What is true is that Gargantua, while putting on fresh clothes
and tidying up his hair with his comb (which was seven rods
long,[32] and set with huge complete elephant-tusks) drew out
more than seven clusters of cannon-shot which had remained
in his hair from that demolition in the forest at Vède. Seeing
which his father Grandgousier mistook them for lice and said
to him:

'Well, my son, have you brought all the way here those
"sparrow-hawks of Montaigu"? I never intended you to take
up residence there.'

At which Ponocrates replied,

'Sire. You must not think that I placed him in that louse-
ridden college called Montaigu. Seeing the enormous cruelty
and wickedness that I found there, I would sooner have lodged
him with the beggars of Saint-Innocent's, since the galley-slaves
of the Moors and the Tartars, and murderers in their prison-
tower, indeed the very dogs in your house, are better treated
than the wretched inmates of that College. If I were King of
Paris, the devil take me if I wouldn't set fire to it inside and

32. From '35: . . . which was *a hundred rods long* . . .

burn both the Principal and the regents who tolerate such inhuman behaviour before their very eyes.'

Then, raising aloft one of the cannon-balls, he said,

'These are cannon-shot which, when he was passing through the forest at Vède, struck your son Gargantua through the treachery of your foes; but they have received such retribution that they all perished in the razing of the castle, as did the Philistines by the ingenuity of Samson and those who were crushed by the tower of Siloam (of whom it is written in Luke 13).

'My opinion is that we should hunt down the foe while luck is with us. For Opportunity wears all her hair in front: once she has gone by you can never call her back: behind, her head is bald, and she never returns.'

'Truly,' said Grandgousier, 'not just now, for I intend to feast you tonight. You are right welcome.'

Which said, supper was got ready, and as an extra there were roasted sixteen oxen, three heifers, thirty-two calves, sixty-three milk-fed kids, ninety-five sheep, three hundred suckling-pigs basted in good sweet wine, eleven score of partridges, seven hundred woodcock, four hundred capons from Loudon and Cornouaille-en-Bretagne, six thousand pullets and as many pigeons, six hundred guinea-fowl, fourteen hundred leverets, three hundred and three bustards, and one thousand seven hundred cockerels.

Venison they could not procure at short notice, but the Abbot of Turpenay sent eleven wild boars and the Seigneur de Grammond eighteen red deer; with that came two score of pheasants[33] from the Seigneur des Essars and a few dozen wood-pigeons, water-hens, gargenays, bitterns, curlews, plovers, [francolins,] grouse, woodcocks, [lapwings,] black-headed water-fowl, spoonbills, herons, lesser white herons, heron-shaws, fen-ducks, egrets, storks and bustards, [three orange-coloured flamingos (called phoenicopters), bustards, turkeys, with plenty of couscous,] together with an abundance of soups.

Nothing was lacking: they had plenty to eat.

33. From '35: . . . *seven* score of pheasants . . .

The dishes were prepared by Grandgousier's chefs: Lapsauce, Gallimaufrey and Straingravy.

Janot, Miguel and Bottoms-up made an excellent job of preparing the drinks.

How Gargantua ate six pilgrims in his lettuce

CHAPTER 36

[Becomes Chapter 38.

Evangelicals and reformers alike disliked pilgrimages, believing them to have been condemned by Saint Paul.

The first edition refers in error to 'five of the prisoners', instead of 'five of the pilgrims'. The error, corrected in '35, is tacitly corrected here too.

Solemn 'applications' of Psalms to real contemporary events were much appreciated at the French Court; but Renaissance taste delighted in laughing at matters which were elsewhere taken with the utmost seriousness. The Psalm cited is the 124th (123rd).]

Our tale requires that we narrate what befell six pilgrims returning from Saint Sebastian's near Nantes who, seeking shelter for the night and fearing enemies, hid in the garden upon the pea-stalks between the cabbages and lettuces. Now Gargantua felt rather empty and asked if it were possible to find any lettuces for a salad. On hearing that there were some of the biggest and loveliest in all the land – for they were as large as plum or walnut trees – he was pleased to go himself and bring back in his hands those he liked. With them he carried off the six pilgrims who were so terrified that they dared not speak nor cough.

As the lettuces were being first washed at the fountain the pilgrims whispered softly to each other, 'What's to be done? We're drowning here amongst these lettuce-leaves. Shall we say something? But if we do he will kill us as spies.'

And as they were pondering thus, Gargantua put them and the lettuces into a kitchen bowl as big as the wine-butt at

Châteaux, and was eating them with some salt, oil and vinegar to cool himself down for supper.

He had already ingurgitated five of the pilgrims.

The sixth was hiding under a piece of lettuce in the bowl, but his staff stuck out above it. On noticing it, Grandgousier said to Gargantua,

'That, I think, is a snail's horn. Don't eat it.'

'Why not?' said Gargantua. 'They're good all this month.'

And so, pulling on the staff, he brought the pilgrim out with it, swallowed him into his maw, drank an awe-inspiring swig of *pineau* and then waited for supper to be ready.

The pilgrims, thus devoured, avoided as well as they could the mill-stones of his teeth: they thought that they had been thrown into a deep dungeon within the prisons. When Gargantua took that huge swig they almost drowned in his mouth and the torrent of wine all but swept them down into the chasm of his stomach. However, leaning on their staves and stepping from stone to stone like pilgrims to Mont-Saint-Michel, they managed to reach safety along the line of his gums. But by mischance, one of them, prodding about with his staff to see whether they were secure, roughly struck the edge of a dental cavity and a nerve in the lower jaw, causing intense pain to Gargantua, who began to yell at the anguish he was enduring. So to ease the ache he called for his tooth-picks and, going outside towards a chestnut-tree beloved by rooks, he ejected Messieurs the Pilgrims; for he caught one by the legs, another by the shoulder, another by his pilgrim's wallet, another by his purse, another by his scarf. And as for the wretched fellow who had struck him with his staff, he was hooked by the cod-piece: which, however, proved a stroke of luck for him, since Gargantua lanced a cancerous tumour which had been torturing him ever since they had passed through Ancenis.

And thus those ejected pilgrims fled at a good trot through the young vines. And the pain was eased.

At that same moment, since everything was ready, Gargantua was called to supper by Eudemon and said , 'I shall go and piss away my misery.' He then pissed so copiously that his urine cut off the pilgrims' route and they were obliged to cross a great ditch. Following the line of the clump of trees called La Touche, every one of them, save Fournillier, tumbled into a trap set in the middle of the path to catch wolves. They escaped thanks to hard work by Fournillier, who tore through the ropes and cords. Once extricated, they lay down for the rest of that night in a hut near Le Coudray.

There they were much comforted in their afflictions by the good words of one of their company named Weary-legs, who proved to them that this trial of theirs had been foretold by David in a Psalm:

When men rose up against us, they had swallowed us up quick – i.e., when we were eaten in a salad taken with a grain of salt;

When they were so wrathfully displeased at us, Yea the waters had drowned us – i.e., when he took that long swig;

the stream had gone over our soul – i.e., when we crossed the great ditch:

Peradventure there had gone even over our soul an insupportable water – i.e. from his urine, by which he cut off our path;

But praised be the Lord: who hath not given us over for a prey unto their teeth.

Our soul is escaped even as a sparrow out of the snare of the fowler, when we fell into that trap, *the snare is broken* – i.e., by Fournillier – *and we are delivered. Our help standeth, etc.*

How the Monk was feasted by Gargantua; and of the fair words he spoke over supper

CHAPTER 37

[*Becomes* Chapter 39.

'*Deposita cappa*' *is a rubric meaning 'the celebrant having divested himself of his cope'. (Rabelais was at the time of* Gargantua *legally a Benedictine monk who had also 'tossed his frock to the nettles' and was living irregularly.*

A Picardy proverb said, 'Of all fish, the tench apart, take the back and leave the paunch.'

One 'monastic' joke has become quite obscure because of changes in the pronunciation of French since the Renaissance. The opening words of Isaiah 11 are, 'There shall come forth a shoot out of the stock of Jesse' – in the Latin Vulgate, 'Germinavit radix Jesse.' Since soif, *'thirst', was then pronounced* sé, *'Germinavit radix Jesse' could be distorted by speakers of French to sound, with a metathesis, like* Je r'nie ma vie: redis, j'ai sé, *that is,* I disavow my life: I repeat, I thirst. *Such jests were condemned by Erasmus but appreciated by Rabelais.*

Frère Jean's statement in appalling Latin, that 'magis magnos clericos non sunt magis magnos sapientes' *struck a chord with Montaigne, who cites it in his* Essays.

Since the use of corks, bottles open with a pop: before, they opened with a crack as seals were broken.]

When Gargantua was at table and the tidbits of the first course had been devoured, Grandgousier began to recount the source and occasion of the war waged between him and Picrochole. He had arrived at the point where he was telling how Frère Jean des Entommeures had triumphantly defended the close of the Abbey, praising the deed above the prowesses of Camillus, Scipio, Pompey, Caesar and Themistocles. At which Gargantua urged that he should be sent for at once, in order to confer with him over what was to be done. So, as they wished, their major-domo went off to fetch him and brought him joyfully back bearing the shaft of his cross and riding on Grandgousier's mule.

When he arrived he was greeted by dozens of hugs and embraces and How-do-you-do's:

'Hey there, Frère Jean, my friend!'

'Frère Jean, great cousin of mine!'

'Frère Jean, for the devil's sake!'

'Arms round necks, my friend!'

'Come to my arms!'

'Now then, old cock, Let me hug you till I skin you!'

And Frère Jean was delighted: never was man so courteous or gracious.

'Well now. Well now,' said Gargantua. 'Set a stool here at this end of the table, close by me.'

'Since it pleases you, it pleases me,' said the Monk. 'Now, page-boy! Water!! Pour it out, boy, pour it out: it'll cool down my liver. Give it to me to *gargle* with!'

'*Deposita cappa*,' said Gymnaste. 'Let's take off that cowl of yours.'

'Ho, ho. By God,' said the Monk. 'There's a paragraph in the statutes of our Order, good Sir, which wouldn't like that at all.'

'Oh, pooh!' said Gymnaste, 'pooh on your paragraph. That frock of yours is breaking both your shoulders: shrug it off.'

'My friend,' said the Monk, 'let me keep it: by God, I drink the better for it! It makes my whole body happy. If I were to quit it, these young gentlemen, the pages here, would turn it into garters, as happened to me once at Coulaines. Besides, I would have no more appetite. But if I sit down to table in this habit of mine, by God I shall drink to you and to your horse as well – and enjoy it! God keep this our company from ill. I've already had my supper but I shall certainly still eat no less now. I have a paved stomach, as hollow as the butt of Saint Benedict, ever gaping wide like a lawyer's pocket! *Of all the fish, the tench apart, take* . . . the wing of the partridge [– or the thigh of a nun: it's a merry way for a fellow to die, isn't it, bolt upright! Our prior has a weakness for the white of a capon.'

'In that, at least,' said Gymnaste,'he is not a bit like a fox, for foxes never eat the white of any of the capons, hens and chickens which they kill.'

'Why not?' said the Monk.

Gymnaste replied, 'Because foxes have no cooks to cook 'em: if they're not properly cooked the meat stays red not white. Redness in meats is a sign of their being underdone, except for lobster and crayfish, which cooking turns cardinal-red.'

'Corpus Bayard!' said the Monk; 'the hospitaller in our Abbey must have his head very underdone: his eyes are as red as an alder-wood bowl.]

'This leveret's thigh is good for the gout. Talking of wood: how is it that a damsel's thighs are always cool?'

'That problem,' said Gargantua, 'is not in Aristotle, Alexander of Aphrodisias nor Plutarch.'

'There are three considerations,' said the Monk, 'which keep
that place naturally cool:

– *primo*, because water runs right along it;

– *secundo*, because it lies in the shade, all dark and murky:
the sun never shines upon it; and

– thirdly, because it is continually fanned by wafts from the
wind-hole, the chemise and the codpiece too.

'Come on then, Page! On with the drinking: crack, crack,
crack. How good is the Lord who vouchsafes us this plonk.
Honest to God! if I had lived in the time of Jesus Christ I'd
have seen that those Jews never grabbed him in the Garden of
Mount Olivet. May the devil fail *me* if ever I failed to slit
the hamstrings of Monsignori the Apostles who ran away, so
cravenly deserting their good Master – after eating a good
Supper! – in his hour of need!

'I hate worse than poison a man who runs off when daggers
are to be drawn. Bah! If only I were King of France for four
score or a hundred years! By God, I'd have whipped the tails
off those curs who ran away at Pavia. A quartan fever take 'em!
Why didn't they die there rather than desert their good king in
his hour of need? To die bravely fighting is better and more
honourable – isn't it? – than to live by fleeing like villeins! We
shan't get many geese to eat this year. Ha! My friend, pass me
the pork. The Divil! We've run out of new wine! *Germinavit
radix Jesse.*

'This wine's not at all bad. What wine were you drinking in
Paris? Devil me, if I didn't at one time keep open house there
myself for over six months: anyone could come. Do you know
Frère Claude of Saint-Denis? What a good chap he is! What
bug's bitten him though? He's been doing nothing but study
since goodness knows when. Me, I never study. None of us ever
has in our abbey. Fear of the mumps! Our late abbot used to
say that a learned monk is a monstrosity. By God, my lord and
friend, *magis magnos clericos non sunt magis magnos sapientes*
(them biggest clerks ain't the most wisest). A lot of hares about
this year: never seen so many. Haven't been able to get my

hands on a hawk, male or female, anywhere in this world. The
Sieur de La Bellonnière did promise me a falcon but he wrote
to me recently to say it had grown short of breath. Partridges
will be nibbling at our very ears this year. No fun for me in
netting birds: makes me catch a cold. I'm never easy except
when chasing and dashing about. It's true that I lose a few
strands of my frock when leaping over hedges and bushes. Got
my hands on a nice little greyhound: I'll go to the devil if it ever
lets a hare escape. A lackey was taking it on a lead to the Sieur
de Maulevrier. I, well, relieved him of it. Did I do wrong?'

'No. Not at all, Frère Jean. Not at all,' said Gymnaste. 'On
behalf of all the devils: not at all!'

'And so,' said Frère Jean, 'here's to those devils, while they
last. Besides, what, by God's might, would that old hop-along
do with a greyhound? God's body! He's happier when presented with a couple of good beeves.'

'Swearing, Frère Jean!' said Ponocrates. 'How come?'

'Simply to enrich my language,' said Frère Jean. 'Flowers of
Ciceronian rhetoric!'

Why everyone avoids monks: and why some men
have noses which are bigger than others

CHAPTER 38

[Becomes Chapter 40.

Virgil is cited from the Georgics, *4, 168. Rabelais leaves it
untranslated.*

*That the wind named Caecias attracts the clouds is the subject of
an Erasmian adage, I, V, LXII, 'Attracting ills to oneself just as Caecias
attracts clouds'.*

*The comparison of monkish drones to monkeys is inspired by Plu-
tarch's attack against flatterers in* How One Can Discern the Flatterer
from the Friend. *(Rabelais restricts to monks attacks made by many
Reformers and evangelicals against priests and monks in general.)*

*The end of the chapter is deeply theological, citing Romans 8:26 to
declare monastic intercessions to be irrelevant: 'The Spirit himself*

maketh intercessions for us with groanings which cannot be uttered'.
On the other hand Frère Jean reduces with his jesting the awe attached
to the predestinationalist rigour of Romans 9:23, in which God is
likened to a divine Potter who makes out of clay such vessels as he
wishes, which have no grounds for complaint.

The final 'monastic' jest takes the incipit of Psalm 122 (113), 'Ad
te levavi' ('Unto Thee I lift up'), and applies it to the erect penis (which
many believed to be proportionate in size to a man's nose). But, coarse
though he is, the Monk is an acted parable: his virtues are the active
Christian virtues: 'He toils, he travails, he defends the oppressed; he
comforts the afflicted; he succours the needy.'

Puns between paix *(peace) and* pets *(farts) are rarely translatable*
but can be suggested.]

'By my faith as a Christian,' said Eudemon, 'I am amazed when
I reflect on the worthiness of this monk, for he cheers us all up.
How is it, then, that men banish monks from all good gatherings, calling them chattering trouble-feasts, just as the bees
banish the drones from about their hives? As Virgil said, "*Igna-*
vum fucos pecus a presipibus arcent"; "They drive the drones,
a slothful herd, far from their dwellings."'

To which Gargantua replied:

'There is nothing more true than that frock and cowl attract
people's odium, insults and curses exactly as the wind called
Caecias attracts the clouds. The decisive reason is that they eat
the shit of the world (the sins, that is) and as chew-shits they
are chucked back into their jakes (that is, their convents and
monasteries) isolated from polite company as privies are in
houses. But if you can grasp why a family's pet monkey is
always mocked and teased you will grasp why monks are
rejected by everybody, both young and old. The monkey does
not guard the house like a dog, does not draw the plough like
the ox, does not give us milk and wool like the sheep, and bears
no burden like the horse. All it does is to shit over everything
and spoil it. That is why everyone jeers at it and cudgels it. So
too a monk – I mean the lazy ones – never ploughs like the
peasant, never guards the land like the soldier, never cures
the sick like the physician, never expounds sound doctrine like

the good evangelical preacher and tutor, never transports goods and commodities vital to the kingdom like the merchant. That is why everyone rails against monks and loathes them.'

'True,' said Grandgousier, 'but they do pray God for us.'

'Not a bit,' said Gargantua. 'The truth is that they disturb the whole neighbourhood by clanging their bells . . .'

'True enough!' said the Monk. 'Well-rung Masses, mattins and vespers are already half-said!'

'. . . They mumble through a great store of legends and psalms which they have never understood; they count quantities of beads interlarded with long *Ave Marias*, without thought or understanding. That I call mockery of God, not orisons. But God help 'em if they pray for us and not for fear of losing their wheaten loaves and thick bread-and-dripping. All true Christians, of all estates, in all places, and at all times, pray to God, and "the Spirit prayeth and maketh intercession for them," and God grants them his grace. Now such is our good Frère Jean. That is why everyone wants his company. He's no bigot; he's not tattered-and-torn; he's decent, joyful and resolute. He toils, he travails, he defends the oppressed; he comforts the afflicted; he succours the needy. And he guards the close of the Abbey.'

'I do much more!' said the Monk. 'For while galloping through our mattins and anniversaries in the choir I make strings for cross-bows, polish up darts and arrows, and construct nets and traps for catching coneys. I'm never idle. But come on! Something to drink, now, something to drink! Bring out the dessert. Ah! chestnuts from the forest of Estrocs. With some good new wine you'll all be farting peace-makers.

'Nobody here has got going yet: me, I drink in every trough, like the proctor's horse.'

Gymnaste said to him, 'Frère Jean: do wipe that dew-drop off your nose.'

'Ha! ha!' said the Monk. 'Could I be in peril of drowning, seeing that I'm up to the nose in water? No, no. Why? Because!

> It can well get out but never get in:
> I'm protected by wine and a waterproof skin!

O my good friend: if a man had winter waders of such a hide
he could confidently fish for oysters: they would never let in
water.'

'Why is it,' said Gargantua, 'that Frère Jean has such a handsome nose?'

'Because,' replied Grandgousier, 'God so wished it; according
to his holy will he has fashioned us in a particular form and to
a particular end as a potter fashions his vessels.'

'Because,' said Ponocrates, 'he was one of the first to arrive
when noses were for sale. He chose one of the biggest and best.'

'Gee up, there!' said Frère Jean. 'According to true monastic
philosophy it's because my nurse had soft tits. When I sucked,
my nose sank in as in butter, and it expanded and rose like
dough in the bowl. But hey, nonny, nonny: from the shape of
his nose you can judge a man's *I lift up unto Thee*. I never
eat preserved fruit. Page! On with the tippling. And toasted
croutons!'

How the Monk sent Gargantua to sleep; and of his Book of Hours and his Breviary

CHAPTER 39

[Becomes Chapter 41.

*The 'Seven Psalms' are the penitential Psalms, placed together in
the liturgy, with indulgences for those who recite them. The second
(32) begins 'Beati quorum', 'Blessed are they'. Frère Jean and Gargantua cannot keep awake beyond that!*

*Two more examples of monastic humour: Frère Jean adapts to his
liturgical duties Christ's assertion that the Sabbath was made for Man,
not Man for the Sabbath (Mark 2:27); the 'Venite adoremus' – 'O come
let us adore Him' – of Psalm 95 (94):8 becomes 'Venite apotemus' –
'O come, let us a-pour Him' or, literally, 'O Come, let us drink.']*

Once supper was over they discussed current matters and it
was decided that they would set out on patrol around midnight in order to find out what watch and care the enemy were

observing. Until then they would rest a while so as to be fresher. But Gargantua could not drop off to sleep in any position. The Monk then said to him: 'I never sleep at my ease except at sermon or when saying my prayers. Let you and me, I beg you, begin the Seven Psalms to see whether you quickly drop off.'

The scheme delighted Gargantua and so, beginning with the first Psalm, they had just reached the *Beati quorum* when they both dropped right off. But the Monk was so used to the time of his mattins in the cloisters that he did not fail to wake up before midnight. Once awake he awoke all the others by full-throatily singing the song,

> O, Regnault! Awake, now, wake!
> Ho Regnault, awake!

When they were all stirring he said,

'Gentlemen: they say that mattins start with a cough and suppers with a drink. Let's do it the other way round, beginning our mattins with a drink and then, when supper arrives this evening, we can out-cough each other.'

Gargantua replied:

'Drinking so soon after sleeping is not a medically sound way to live. We must first scour our stomachs of superfluities and excrements.'

'A fine medication that is!' said the Monk. May a hundred devils jump on my body if there aren't more old drunkards than old physicians. [I've made a pact with my appetite: it always lies down when I do, and I pay due attention to it during the day; then when I get up so does it.] Throw up your purges as much as you like, but I am going after my *tiring*.'

'What *tiring* do you mean?' said Gargantua.

'My Breviary,' said the Monk. 'For, just as falconers make their birds tear at a *tiring* – a chicken-leg – before they are fed, so as to purge their heads of phlegm and whip up their appetites, so do I take my jolly little Breviary every morning and purge all my lungs: then there I am, ready to drink.'

'When reciting those fine Hours of yours,' said Gargantua, 'which Use do you follow?'

'The Use of Fécamp,' said the Monk: 'three lessons and three Psalms, or none at all if you prefer. Never shall I be a slave to my Hours: the Hours are made for man, not man for the Hours. That's why I treat mine like stirrups, shortening or lengthening them as I please:

> *Brevis oratio penetrat coelos:*
> *Longa potatio evacuat scyphos,*

> (A short orison to Heaven goes up:
> A long potation doth empty the cup.)

Now, where is that written?'

'Faith, I've no idea,' said Ponocrates. 'But you're really too good, my fine little bollock'!

'I'm like you in that,' said the Monk. 'But *O come, let us a-pour Him.*'

Then were prepared plenty of charcoal steaks and glorious slices of bread-and-dripping, and the Monk drank as he would. Some kept him company: others refrained. After which each man started to don his armour and accoutrements. They armed the Monk too, against his will, for he wanted no gear save his frock over his stomach and the shaft of his cross in his fist. However, he was armed from top to toe to please them and with stout broad-sword at his side was set on a royal-Neapolitan charger.

And with him rode Gargantua, Ponocrates, Gymnaste, Eudemon, and five-and-twenty of the most valiant men of Grandgousier's household, all duly armed, all lance in hand, all mounted like Saint Georges: each with a soldier seated on the crupper and bearing a harquebus.

How the Monk put heart into his comrades, and how he dangled from a tree

CHAPTER 40

[Becomes Chapter 42.

   *The Gregorian Decretals contain a rubric 'On the Frigid and the
Bewitched'; Cf. the* Third Book, *Chapter 14.*

   *Absalom with his long hair suffers a similar fate to the tonsured
Frère Jean's in II Samuel (II Kings) 18:9.]*

So off ride those noble champions on their adventures, fully
determined to discover when to pursue an engagement and,
come the day of the great and awesome battle, what they would
have to defend themselves from.

   And the Monk put heart into them, saying, 'Fear not, lads,
and doubt not. I shall surely guide you. God and Saint Benedict
be with us. If I had as much strength as courage, Gosh, I'd pluck
them for you like ducks. I dread nought but their ordnance. I
do know a prayer, though, which protects the body from all
firing-pieces; it was given me by the sub-sacristan of our Abbey.
It won't do me any good though: I don't believe in it. Nevertheless the shaft of my cross will do a devilish good job.

   'By God, if I catch any of you lot ducking, the devil take me
if I don't make him a monk in my stead. I'll truss him up in my
frock: it contains a remedy for cowardice.

   'Have you heard the one about the greyhound of the Sieur
de Meurles which was no good in the field? He tied a monkish
frock about its neck, and, by the body of God, not one hare or
fox got away from it. What's more, it covered all the bitches of
the land, yet before that it had been impotent (as in, *On the
Frigid and the Bewitched*).'

   The Monk, fierily uttering such words, passed under a
walnut-tree towards La Saulaie when he caught the visor of his
helmet on a stump jutting out from a big branch. Despite that,
he fiercely dug his spurs into his steed (which was sensitive to
jabs) causing it to give a great bound forward, while he, trying

to unhook his visor, let go of the bridle and hung on to the branch by his hands as his horse slipped out from under him. By such means was the Monk left dangling from the tree, yelling, 'Help!' and 'Murder!' and crying treason.

Eudemon was the first to espy him and, calling to Gargantua, said, 'Sire: come and see Absalom hanging!'

Gargantua came up, contemplated the countenance of the Monk and the manner of his hanging, and said to Eudemon, 'It's ill done comparing him to Absalom: Absalom hung by his hair, whereas this bald-pated monk has hanged himself by his ears.'

'Help me,' said the Monk, 'for the devil's sake. Is this the time for yapping! You're like those Decretaline preachers who hold that whoever finds his neighbour in mortal peril must, before helping him, under pain of a three-pronged excommunication, first admonish him to make his confession and put himself into a state of grace. If ever I find them fallen in the river and about to drown, instead of looking for them and lending them a hand I shall preach them a lovely long sermon *On Contempt for this world, and On Fleeing things temporal*; then once they're dead stiff I'll go and fish them out!'

'Don't budge, my dear one,' said Gymnaste; 'I am going for help, for you're such a nice little monkling:

> A monkling in his abbey,
> For two eggs you can have 'ee;
> But outside, for a cert, 'e
> Might just be worth say thirty.

I have seen over five hundred men hanged in my time but not one dangling with better grace. If I could do it as gracefully I'd hang that way all my life.'

'Preached enough yet?' said the Monk. 'Help me for God's sake, since you won't do so for t'Other's. By the habit which I wear, you'll repent of all this *tempore et loco prelibitis* (in due time and place).'

It was then that Gymnaste dismounted, climbed the tree, raised the Monk by the gussets with one hand and with the other freed the visor from the stump. He let the Monk fall to the ground and he followed after.

As soon as he was down, the Monk stripped off all his armour and tossed one piece after another all over the field; then, taking up again the shaft of his cross, he remounted his horse which Eudemon had arrested in flight.

And so on they went joyfully, taking the road to La Saulaie.

How a patrol of Picrochole's was encountered by Gargantua, and how the Monk slew Captain Dashon and was then kept prisoner amongst the enemy

CHAPTER 41

[Becomes Chapter 43.

Stoles are the scarves symbolic of Holy Orders: the enemy here use them as talismans. 'Gregorian water' is holy water, but Gregory's name is crossed here by Rabelais with that of Pierre Gringoire, a popular French author.

Again, the expression 'to land somebody with the monk' is used literally.

'To leave an enemy a bridge of silver' is cited by Erasmus from King Alfonso of Aragon (Apophthegms, 8).]

Picrochole, during the report of those who had escaped in the rout when Tri-ffart was de-triffarted, was seized by great wrath on hearing how the devils had attacked his men, and held an all-night council in which Rushin and Braggart declared that his power was such that he could defeat all the devils in Hell if they were to come against him: which he did not entirely believe, nor yet disbelieve. So, as a patrol to spy out the land, he despatched under the command of the Comte de Rushin, sixteen hundred knights, all mounted on light horses ready for skirmishes, all well sprinkled with holy water and each bearing for his ensign a stole worn as a scarf, prepared for all eventualities should they encounter any devils whom they would compel to vanish and melt away by the virtues of both their Gringorian water and their stoles.

They galloped to the lands near the Lazar-house of La Vauguyon but found no one to parley with, so they returned by the high road; there, near Le Coudray, in the 'pastoral tugury' – or hut – they found the five pilgrims, whom they led away, trussed up and bound as though they were spies, notwithstanding their loud pleas, protestations and adjurations.

Having ridden down toward Seuilly, they were heard by Gargantua, who said to his men: 'Companions, here comes a crunch. They are more than ten times greater in number than we are. Shall we charge at them?'

'What the devil else,' said the Monk. 'Do you reckon men by number not by gallantry and bravery?' Then he yelled out: 'Charge, you devils! Charge!'

Now when the enemy heard those words they were convinced they were real devils and began to gallop off at full tilt, save for Dashon, who lowered his lance and violently struck the Monk right in the middle of his chest; but, coming up against his horrific frock, the steel point buckled back as though you were to strike a little wax-candle against an anvil.

Whereupon the Monk whacked him with the shaft of his cross so hard on the posterior apophysis (between the neck and the shoulder-blades) that he stunned him, causing him to lose all his senses and all control of his movements so that he tumbled before his horse's hoofs. Then, seeing his stole, the Monk said to Gargantua: 'They're only priests, the mere rudiment of a monk! I, by Saint John, am an accomplished monk: I shall swat them like flies.'

Then he galloped flat out after them and caught up with the stragglers, thrashing them down like rye as he struck out right and left.

Gymnaste at once asked Gargantua whether they ought to pursue them.

To which Gargantua replied:

'Most certainly not; for according to the true art of war you should never drive your enemy into a desperate situation, since such straits redouble his strength and increase his courage,

which until then had been abject and weak: there is no better
remedy for bringing deliverance to confused and exhausted
men than their having no hope of escape. How many victories have been snatched by the vanquished from the grasp of
victors who were not content with the reasonable but tried to
massacre and utterly destroy all their foes, unwilling to spare
even one to bring the news. Always leave gates and routes open
to your enemies: indeed, make them a bridge of silver to escape
over.

'True,' said Gymnaste, 'but they've been landed with the
Monk.'

'Landed with the Monk!' said Gargantua. 'Upon my honour,
that will be to their harm. But to provide for all hazards, let us
not yet withdraw. Let us wait quietly here, for I think I well
understand the tactics of the enemy: they are guided by chance
not by counsel.'

So while they waited under the walnut-tree, the Monk continued his pursuit, charging at all those whom he encountered
and showing mercy to none until he came across a knight with
one of the wretched pilgrims slung across his crupper. Then, as
the Monk was about to weigh into that knight, the pilgrim
cried out,

'Ha! My Lord Prior! My friend! My Lord Prior, save me, I
beg you!'

All the foes, on hearing those words, looked behind them
and saw that it was the Monk who was alone causing the
commotion; so they loaded him with blows as one loads an ass
with sticks, yet so tough was his hide that he felt hardly anything,[34] especially when the blows fell on his frock.

Then they assigned him to two archers and, turning their
horses about, saw nobody before them. At which they surmised that Gargantua had fled with his band. They therefore
galloped towards the walnut-grove as fast as they could so as
to encounter them, leaving the Monk alone with two archers
on guard.

Gargantua heard the pounding and neighing of their horses

34. From '35: . . . his hide that *he felt nothing* . . .

and said to his men, 'Companions: I can hear the racket raised
by our enemies and I can already espy some of those who are
coming against us. Let us close here up tight and hold the road
in good order. By such means we shall prepare a reception for
them, to their ruin and our honour.'

How the Monk rid himself of his guards, and how
Picrochole's patrol were defeated

CHAPTER 42

[Becomes Chapter 44.
    Medical 'comedy of cruelty' at Rabelais' best.
    Rabelais drew the matter of his Virgilian simile from an adage
of Erasmus taken literally: II, VIII, LIV, 'Roused by a gad-fly'.
(Juno drove Io the cow into a frenzy by plaguing her with a
horsefly.)
    The sudden, empty terror known as 'panic terror' is also the subject
of an adage of Erasmus (III, VII, III, 'Panic events').]

The Monk, seeing them make off in disorder, conjectured that
they were on their way to attack Gargantua and his men, and
it made him wondrously depressed that he could not help them.
He then became aware of the comportment of the two archers
of his guard, who would have much preferred to chase after
their troops and seize some plunder: they kept looking along
the valley where the others were making their way down. He
moreover syllogized, saying: 'These folk here are very badly
trained in the ways of war, since they have never put me on my
word nor removed my sword.'

Immediately afterwards he drew forth that sword and struck
the archer who was holding him on his right, entirely severing
the sphagitid arteries in the neck – his jugular veins – together
with the uvula down to the two thyroid glands; then, withdrawing his sword, he prised the spinal marrow half-open between
the second and third vertebrae: at which the archer dropped
down dead.

Then the Monk, tugging his horse to the left, fell upon the other archer who, seeing his comrade dead and the Monk with an advantage over him, loudly bawled,

'Ah! My Lord Prior, I give in. My Lord Prior, my dear friend, my Lord Prior!'

And the Monk similarly bawled,

'My Lord Posterior, my friend! My Lord Posterior, you shall get it on your posteriors!'

'Ah!' cried the archer, 'My Lord Prior, my dearest Lord Prior, may God make you an abbot.'

'An habit! By the one I wear,' said the Monk, 'here I shall make you a cardinal. Ransoming men of Religion! From my own hand now you shall get a red hat.'

And the archer cried,

'My Lord Prior, my Lord Prior; my Lord the Abbot-to-be; my Lord Cardinal; my Lord of All: ah! ah! heh! heh! No!! My Lord Prior, my nice little Lord Prior! I give in!'

'And you I give to all the devils,' said the Monk.

Whereupon he sliced through his head at one blow, cutting his cranium above the petrous bone, removing both the bones of the sinciput as well as the sagittal suture, together with the greater part of the coronal bone; by so doing he sliced through both meninges and opened up deeply the two posterior ventricle-cavities of the brain: and so his cranium remained hanging down over his shoulders at the back from the membranes of the pericranium in the form of a doctoral bonnet, black above, red within.

And thus did he fall to the ground quite dead.

That done, the Monk gave his horse the spur and followed the route adopted by his enemies, who had encountered Gargantua and his comrades on the highway but were so reduced in number (by the huge slaughter wrought there by Gargantua with his great tree and by Gymnaste, Ponocrates, Eudemon and the others) that they were beginning to retreat in good earnest, all terrified, with their minds and their senses thrown into confusion, as though they had seen before their eyes the very species and form of Death.

And – as you may see a donkey, when it is stung about the

arse by a wasp or a Junonian gad-fly, dashing hither and thither, following nor path nor way, casting its load to the ground, yet no one knowing what is provoking it since no one sees anything goading it – thus fled those men, bereft of their senses, knowing not why they fled but solely pursued by a panic terror conceived in their minds.

When the Monk saw that they had no thought but to flee on foot, he dismounted and climbed on to a large rock overhanging the road and struck down the fugitives with his sword, making great sweeps with his arm, neither sparing nor considering himself. So many did he slay and cast to the ground that his sword snapped in twain. Whereupon he reflected that there had been killing and slaughter enough and that the remainder ought to escape to spread the news. And so he grabbed a battle-axe from one of the men lying there dead, rushed at once back to his rock and spent his time watching the enemy as they fled and stumbled about amongst the dead bodies; he simply made them drop their pikes, swords, lances and harquebuses. And as for those who were transporting the bound-up pilgrims, he made them walk and hand over their horses to the said pilgrims, keeping them by him at the edge of the forest, with Braggart who was retained as his prisoner.

How the Monk brought the pilgrims back; and the fair words which Grandgousier spoke to them

CHAPTER 43

[Becomes Chapter 45.

Strong criticism of pilgrimages in a jolly setting: the plague is not sent by God nor the Just and the Saints: it is ever the work of the devil. Attributions of powers over particular diseases to particular saints are often based upon similarities of their names and those of the maladies. This chapter answers the question about the plague raised at the beginning of Chapter 25.

Perhaps the harshest of the scriptural expressions hurled at a religious enemy in Rabelais' time was 'false prophet', which carried

with it the condemnation of Jesus himself (as in Matthew 7:15; 24:11)
and of all four Evangelists.

Saint Paul allegedly condemns pilgrimages when he urges Christian
men to look after 'the household of faith', taken to mean their families
(I Timothy 5:8, and Galatians 6:10).

It is the king himself, not a cleric of any kind, who decides to drive
off the 'black-beetles' – those hypocrites who are classed with the
'false prophets' who can deceive the very Elect (as in Matthew 24:24).
In so doing he is exercising the right of the Christian Magistrate to
suppress blasphemy.

It is also in Matthew (10:28) that we are told not to fear 'them who
kill the body' but them who are able 'to destroy both soul and
body'.

Plato's praise of the philosopher king was well known from an
adage of Erasmus (I, III, I, 'Either a fool or a king should be born.').]

That skirmish once over, Gargantua withdrew with his men
except for the Monk and, as dawn broke, called on Grandgousier, who was in bed praying God for their security and
victory. On seeing them safe and sound, Grandgousier
embraced them with true affection and asked for news of the
Monk. Gargantua replied that, without any doubt, the foe had
been landed with the Monk.

'They're in for a bad time then,' said Grandgousier.

And that had already been proven true. Hence the saying
(still current), *To land somebody with the Monk.*

He then commanded that an excellent breakfast be prepared
to refresh them. They called Gargantua when everything was
ready, but he was so upset when the Monk never appeared that
he would neither drink nor eat.

All of a sudden, the Monk appears and yells from
the backyard gate, 'Cool wine, Gymnaste, my friend, cool
wine!'

Gymnaste went out and saw that it was Frère Jean bringing
in five pilgrims and Braggart prisoner.

Gargantua then came out to meet him; they all gave the
Monk the warmest possible welcome and brought him before
Grandgousier, who questioned him about his whole adventure.

The Monk told him the lot: how the enemy had taken him, how he had rid himself of the archers, about the slaughter he had wrought on his way, and how he had rescued the pilgrims and brought in Captain Braggart. They then all began to feast happily together.

Meanwhile Grandgousier inquired of the pilgrims where they hailed from, where they were coming from and where they were going to. On behalf of them all Weary-legs spoke:

'Sire: I hail from Saint Genou in Berry; this one hails from Paluau; this one, from Onzay; this one, from Argy, and this one here, from Villebrenin. We've been to Saint Sebastian's near Nantes, and are making our way home by easy stages.'

'Indeed,' said Grandgousier, 'but what did you go to Saint-Sebastian's for?'

'We went there,' said Weary-legs, 'to make him our supplications against the plague.'

'Ah,' said Grandgousier, 'you reckon then, do you, poor fellows, that the plague comes from Saint Sebastian?'

'Yes, certainly,' replied Weary-legs. 'So our preachers tell us.'

'Oh!' said Grandgousier, 'Do those false prophets spread such abuses? Do they defame in that fashion the Just and the Saints of God, making them like devils who do nothing but evil amongst mankind – as Homer told that the plague was spread amongst the Grecian army by Apollo, and as poets feign a great mass of bogeys and maleficent godlings?

'Thus there was in Cinais a black-beetle preaching that Saint Anthony caused inflammation of the legs, that Saint Eutropius sent hydropsy; Saint Gilden, madness; Saint Genou, the gout: but I punished him so exemplarily – even though he did call me a heretic – that from that time to this no black-beetle has ever since dared enter my domains. And I am amazed that your king should allow them to preach within his kingdom such causes of stumbling, for they are more to be punished than those who spread the plague by magic or some other device: the plague kills but the body: such devilish preaching infects the souls of the poor and the simple.'[35]

35. '42: . . . such *impostors poison* the souls . . .

As he was uttering those words in came the Monk with a decided air. He asked,

'Where have you shabby lot come from?'

'From Saint-Genou,' they said.

'And how is the Abbé Tranchelion, that good tippler, getting on? And the monks: are they enjoying good cheer? God's Body, while you go traipsing about on pilgrimages, they're prodding your wives.'

'Hee, hee!' said Weary-legs: 'I'm not worried about mine. Nobody who saw her by day would break his neck to visit her by night.'

'You've played the wrong suit there,' said the Monk. 'She may be as ugly as Proserpine, but, by God, she'll enjoy a jiggedy-jog if there are monks about, for a sound workman makes use of any bit of stuff, indifferently. May I catch the pox if you don't find them all big-bellied when you get home, for the mere shadow of the bell-tower of an abbey is fecund.'

'If you trust Strabo,' said Gargantua, 'it's like the waters of the Nile in Egypt, which, according to Pliny, Book 7, Chapter 3, are good for cereals, textiles and bodies.'

Then Grandgousier said:

'Off you go, you poor wretches, in the name of God the Creator: may He ever be your guide. From now on do not be so open to such otiose and useless journeys. Look after your families, work each man in his vocation, school your children, and live as you are taught to do by that good Apostle Saint Paul. Do that and you will have with you the protection of God, the angels and the saints, and there is no plague nor illness that will harm you.'

Gargantua then took them to the hall for something to eat but the pilgrims did nothing but sigh, saying to Gargantua,

'O! blessed is the land which has such a man as its lord: we have been more edified and instructed by those words he has addressed to us than by all the sermons ever preached to us in our town.'

'It is,' said Gargantua, 'as Plato says in Book 5 of *The*

Republic: all states would be blessed if kings were to philosophize and philosophers to reign.'

He then had their shoulder-wallets filled with victuals and
their bottles with wine. To each man he gave a horse to ease
the rest of his journey together with a few carolus-crowns to
live on.

How Grandgousier humanely treated Braggart, his prisoner

CHAPTER 44

[Becomes Chapter 46.

*Real chivalry is contrasted by implication with the conquests and
wars of the Emperor Charles V. In the* City of God, *4, 4, 5, Augustine
calls imperial conquests sheer brigandage (*latrocinium*). Christian
princes should heed that judgement.*

*'Infinite riches are the sinews of war,' according to Cicero (*Philippics
5, 12, 32).]

Braggart was brought before Grandgousier and questioned
about Picrochole's enterprise and designs and the alleged purpose of this tumultuous and ruthless incursion. To which Braggart replied that Picrochole's purpose and destiny were to
conquer the whole land if he could, on account of the injustice
done to his *fouace*-bakers.

'That,' said Grandgousier, 'is to take on much too much:
Too much embrace: little retain. The time has passed for such
conquering of kingdoms to the harm of our Christian brothers
and neighbours. Such imitations of the ancient heroes – Hercules, Alexander, Hannibal, Scipio, Caesar and so on – is contrary to the teachings of our Gospel, by which we are each
commanded to guard, save, rule and manage his own realms
and lands, and never aggressively to invade those of others.
And what the Saracens and Barbarians once dubbed prowess
we now call brigandage and evil-doing. He would have done

better to confine himself to his own domains and to govern them royally than to come bounding hostilely into mine in order to pillage them, for by ruling his realm well he would have enriched it: by pillaging mine he will destroy it.

'In the name of God go on your way, and pursue enterprises which are good.

'Reveal to your king such of his errors as you shall recognize, and never give counsel out of regard for your own private interests, for when the common weal looses, the private weal does too.

'As for your ransom, I shall entirely forgo it; and my will is that your armour and your horse be returned to you.

'Thus should things be done amongst neighbours and old friends; this our difference is not properly speaking a war, just as Plato would not call it war but sedition when Greek took up arms against Greek. Whenever that does unfortunately happen, he commands total moderation. If war you call it, it is but a superficial one: it does not enter into the innermost chambers of our hearts, for not one of us has been outraged in his honour; it all amounts to redressing a wrong committed by our people, I mean yours and ours.

'And even if you had known of it, you should have let it flow by, for those quarrelling folk were more to be ridiculed than resented, not least when their grievances were being satisfied, as I myself offered to do. God will be the just appraiser of our controversy. Him I beg to take this life from me in death and to destroy my goods before my eyes rather than be offended by me or mine in anything whatsoever.'

Having uttered those words, he called for the Monk and asked him in front of them all:

'Frère Jean, my good friend. Did you take prisoner Captain Braggart here present?'

'Cyre,' said the Monk, 'indeed he's here present. He has reached the age of discretion. I'd rather you heard it from his own admission than from any word of mine.'

Whereupon Braggart said:

'My Lord: he did indeed take me prisoner and I frankly surrender myself to him.'

Grandgousier said to the Monk:

'Did you put him to ransom?'

'No,' said the Monk, 'I'm not interested in that.'

'How much do you want for capturing him?' asked Grandgousier.

'Nothing at all,' said the Monk. 'I don't bother about it.'

At which Grandgousier, in the presence of Braggart, commanded that sixty-two thousand angel-crowns be disbursed to
the Monk for his capture; it was done while they were preparing a collation for Braggart, who was asked by Grandgousier
whether he would rather remain with him or go back to his
king.

Braggart said he would do whichever he advised.

'In that case,' said Grandgousier, 'go back to your king. And
God be with you.'

He then bestowed on him a fine steel sword from Vienne
together with its scabbard of gold, decorated with handsome
gilt vine-leaves; a golden chain to wear around his neck – it
weighed seven [hundred and two thousand] marks and was
garnished with precious stones valued at a hundred and sixty
thousand ducats – and ten thousand crowns as a token of
esteem.

That said, Braggart mounted his horse. Gargantua assigned
to him thirty men-at-arms and six-score archers under the command of Gymnaste, who, to ensure his safety, were to accompany him as far as the gates of La Roche-Clermault if needs be.

Once he had gone, the Monk handed back to Grandgousier
the sixty-two thousand angel-crowns which he had received,
saying, 'Cyre: this is no time for making such gifts. Wait till
this war is over, for you can never tell what problems may turn
up, and war waged without a good supply of money has but
one puff of vigour. Riches are the sinews of battles.'

'Right then,' said Grandgousier. 'Once it is all over I shall
satisfy you with some honourable reward. So too everyone who
shall have served me well.'

How Grandgousier summoned his legions; and
how Braggart killed Hastyveal and was himself
killed by order of Picrochole

CHAPTER 45

[Becomes Chapter 47.
The battle returns with a vengeance to Rabelais' pays, and Picro-
chole's choleric madness leads him still closer to disaster.]

Now in those same days the people of Bessé, Marché-Vieux,
Bourg-Saint-Jacques, Le Traîneau, Parilly, Rivière, Les Roches-
Saint-Paul, Le Vau-Breton, Pontille, Bréhémont, Le Pont du
Clam, Cravant, Grandmont, Bourdes, Lavillaumer, [Huismes,]
Segré, Ussé, Saint-Louand, Chouzé, Panzoust, Couldreau,
Verron, Coulaines, Varennes, Bourgueil, L'Isle-Bouchard,
Croulay, Narsay, Candes-Monsoreau and other neighbouring
lands, sent embassies to Grandgousier to tell him that they were
informed of the wrongs being done to him by Picrochole and
to offer him, for the sake of their ancient alliance, everything
in their power: men, money and munitions too.

The tribute offered him by all their contributions amounted
to six score and fourteen millions in gold [plus two and a
half]; the forces, to fifteen thousand men-at-arms, thirty-two
thousand light horsemen, eighty-nine thousand harquebusiers,
a hundred and forty thousand soldiers of fortune, gunners
with eleven thousand two hundred cannons, double-cannons,
basilisks and spiroles, and forty-seven thousand pioneers. All
to be paid and victualled for six months [and four days] ahead.

Gargantua neither entirely refused nor entirely accepted the
offer but, warmly thanking the envoys, said that he would settle
this war by such a stratagem that it would not be necessary to
bother so many good men. He merely sent to tell his legions
(regularly maintained in his forts at La Devinière, Chavigny,
Gravot and Quinquenays) to come in good order. They
amounted in all to twelve hundred men-of-arms, thirty-six
thousand foot, thirteen thousand harquebusiers, the crews of

four hundred great artillery-pieces, and twenty-two thousand pioneers.[36] They were divided up into troops so well provided with paymasters, quartermasters, horse-smiths, armourers and other men needed for the battle-train, so well drilled in the art of war, so well armed, so sure of recognizing and following their ensigns, so prompt at hearing and obeying their captains, so swift at running, so strong in engaging the enemy, so wise in their daring, that they were more like clock-work or an harmonious organ than troops of soldiers or an army.

As soon as Braggart returned, he presented himself before Picrochole and recounted at length what he had seen and done. He ended by using powerful words to advise that a settlement be reached with Grandgousier, whom he had proved to be the most honourable man in the world, adding that it was neither profitable nor reasonable thus to molest neighbours from whom one had experienced nothing but good, and above all that they would never extricate themselves from their enterprise except at great cost and much misery to themselves, for the forces of Picrochole were not such that Grandgousier could not easily crush them.

No sooner were those words uttered than Hastyveal loudly yelled: 'Wretched indeed is the prince who is served by men such as that, men easily corrupted, as I know Braggart to be! His mind, I see, has so changed that, if only they had kept him as a retainer, he would willingly have joined our enemies, fought against us and betrayed us. But just as valour is praised and esteemed by all, friend and foe alike, so too perfidy is soon recognized and distrusted: and even supposing that enemies make use of it to their advantage, they ever hold perfidious traitors in abomination.'

On hearing those words Braggart, unable to bear it, drew his sword and ran Hastyveal through just above his left breast, and he died at once. Then, drawing his sword from the body, he frankly exclaimed, 'Thus perish all who loyal vassals blame!'

Picrochole suddenly went mad and, on seeing the bespattered

36. '42: . . . They amounted in all to *two thousand five* hundred men-of-arms, *sixty*-six thousand foot, *twenty-six* thousand harquebusiers, the crews of four hundred great artillery-pieces, and *six* thousand pioneers . . .

sword and scabbard, said, 'You, there! Were you given that blade so that you might maliciously slay my good friend Hastyveal in my very presence?'

He ordered his archers to hack him to pieces forthwith, which they did at once, so viciously that the hall was paved with blood. He then had Hastyveal's corpse buried with honour and Braggart's flung over the wall into the ditch.

News of these outrages became known to the entire army, so that many began to murmur against Picrochole – so much so that Grippeminaud said to him:

'My Lord, I cannot see what the outcome of this enterprise will be. I note that your men are unsteady. They judge that we are short of supplies and already much reduced in number by two or three sorties. In addition, great reinforcements are on their way to your enemy. If once we are besieged, I can see absolutely no outcome other than our total overthrow.'

'Crap!' said Picrochole, 'Crap! You're like eels of Melun: you squeal before you're skinned![37] Just let 'em all come!'

How Gargantua assailed Picrochole within La Roche-Clermault and defeated his army

CHAPTER 46

[Becomes Chapter 48.

Julius Caesar's verdict that the Gauls are valiant in the first assault and 'worse than women' afterwards is known from Livy, who is cited by Erasmus (Apophthegms, 6, Varia mixta, *100).

The name Sébaste means 'venerable' in Greek.

Le Duc Phrontistes appears only in this passage: his Greek name shows him to be a man of considered judgement.

The account of the fighting is quite realistic, moving away from pure fantasy into the kind of battle experienced by many contemporary readers. Rabelais edited and published (in 1539?) a book, now lost,

37. An error in the first edition ('Leave the eels of Melun') is corrected as above. ('The eels of Melun which squeal before they're skinned' were proverbial.)

with the title of Strategemata, *written in honour of his patron Guil-laume Du Bellay, the Seigneur de Langey.]*

Gargantua took supreme command of the army. His father remained in his fortress, putting heart into them with good counsel and promising great bounties to any man who performed deeds of valour. They then reached the ford at Vède, which they crossed at one go in boats and over lightly constructed bridges. Then, taking into account the site of the town (which was set on high ground giving it the advantage) he spent the night deliberating on what should be done.

But Gymnaste said to him, 'Such is the nature and temperament of the French that their value lies in the first assault. They are worse than devils then. If they delay, they are worse than women. My advice is that you should suddenly begin the assault as soon as the men have got their breath back and had something to eat.'

The advice was judged to be good.

Gargantua then deployed his entire army in the plain, positioning the support-troops to his flanks on the upward slope. The Monk took six ensigns of foot-soldiers with him and two hundred men-at-arms, struggled carefully across the marshes and reached a spot above Le Puy as far as the highway to Loudon.

Meanwhile, the assault went on.

Picrochole's men could not decide whether it was better to come out and confront them or to stay put and defend the town. He himself, however, dashed out like a madman with some small band of household troops, where he was welcomed by a great hail of cannon-balls from towards the hills, whereupon the Gargantuists withdrew to the valley so as to allow greater scope to their ordnance.

The men in the town put up the best defence they could, but their projectiles overshot the mark and hit nobody. A few men from their band who had escaped the artillery-fire made a fierce attack against our men, but to no avail for, caught between our ranks, they were being battered to the ground. On seeing which, they sought to withdraw, but the Monk had blocked their passage. They therefore fled without order or restraint. There were those who wanted to chase after them, but the Monk held them back, fearing that they might break ranks while pursuing those fugitives, and then the defenders of the town could swoop down upon them.

He waited a while, but no one came out to confront them, so he despatched le Duc Phrontistes to advise Gargantua to advance and take the hill on the left in order to cut off Picrochole's escape through that gate. Gargantua did so with due speed and despatched four legions from the company of Sébaste, yet they could not reach the summit before encountering Picrochole and a scattering of his men beard-to-beard. They attacked them, but were themselves greatly troubled by volleys of arrows and cannon-shot from the men on the walls.

Seeing which, Gargantua went to their aid with a considerable force; his artillery began to pound that section of the walls, so much so that all the forces in the town were summoned to it. When the Monk saw that his side of the town which he was investing was deserted by its soldiers and the guardians of the gate, he bravely made for the fort and succeeded in scaling it with some of his men. He believed that troops who suddenly appear inspire more fear and terror than those who are heavily engaged in the fighting. However, he made no noise until all his men (except for the two hundred soldiers he had left outside for any emergency) had taken the wall. Then he gave a horrifying yell and so did his men, slaughtering without resistance the guardians of the gate, which he opened to his own men-at-arms. Then they all ran most fearsomely together towards the East-gate, where all was in disarray; there, from the rear, they smashed all the enemy soldiers who, aware that they were hard pressed on every side and that the Gargantuists had taken the town, threw themselves on the mercy of the Monk. He made them hand over their swords and weapons, withdraw into the churches and sit tight while he seized all the shafts of the crosses and posted men at the church-doors to prevent anyone from escaping.

Then he opened that East-gate and sallied forth to assist Gargantua.

But Picrochole believed that help was coming for him from the town, and arrogantly took even greater risks than before, until Gargantua called out, 'Frère Jean, my friend! Frère Jean, you arrive in good time!' Only then did Picrochole and his men, realizing that all was hopeless, begin to run away in every direction. Gargantua pursued them as far as Vaugaudry, killing and slaughtering. Then he sounded the retreat.

How Picrochole was surprised by ill luck as he fled, and what Gargantua did after the battle

CHAPTER 47

[Becomes Chapter 49.
*Captain Tolmère's name shows he was bold (*tolmeros*).*
Picrochole lives on in mad disgrace, hoping to return to his throne.]

So Picrochole now fled in despair towards L'Ile-Bouchard. On the road to Rivière his horse stumbled and fell; at which he was so incensed that he drew his sword and killed it in a fit of choler. Then, finding nobody to provide another mount, he tried to steal a miller's donkey which was standing by, but the millers showered him with blows, relieved him of his clothing and tossed him a miserable smock to cover himself with.

Thus went that choleric wretch on his way. Having passed over the waters at Port-Huault, he related his misfortunes to an ancient sorceress who foretold that his kingdom would be restored to him when the Worricows come home.

What became of him afterwards nobody knows. Yet I have been told that he is at present a penny-labourer in Lyons, still as choleric as ever, always catechizing every stranger about the home-coming of the Worricows, in certain hope of being reinstated in his kingdom at their home-coming one day as that old woman's prophecy had foretold.

After their withdrawal, Gargantua first of all mustered his men and found that few of them had died in battle, apart from some foot-soldiers from the troop of Captain Tolmère;

Ponocrates too had taken a shot from an harquebus through his doublet. Gargantua then made his men refresh themselves, each in his unit, commanding the pay-masters to defray the cost of their meal and absolutely forbidding anyone to commit outrages in the town since it was his, and telling them to assemble after their meal in the square in front of the château, where they would receive six months' pay.

Which was done.

In that same square he then gathered before him all the remnant of Picrochole's men and addressed them as follows in the presence of all their princes and captains:

Gargantua's address to the vanquished

CHAPTER 48

[Becomes Chapter 50.

A lesson of clemency, with Charles V, the Rex Catholicus, *as its butt. The Emperor, whose title was the 'Catholic King', had nevertheless held the French King prisoner in Madrid after the Battle of Pavia (1525), exacted a huge ransom and held the royal sons hostage until it was at least partly paid. The speech is a mixture of history and fantasy. La Tremouille defeated the Bretons at Saint-Aubin-du-Cormier in 1488 but showed mercy; La Joyeuse was allowed to withdraw when Charles VIII demolished the fortress of Parthernay in 1487. Hispaniola, however, never dreamt of invading France, and Canarre is a fantasy.*

For Moses and Julius Caesar as examples of generous warriors who knew when to be severe, see Numbers 12:3 and Cicero, Pro Ligario, *38.]*

'As witnesses to the triumphs and victories they achieved, our fathers, forefathers and forebears, from time immemorial, have, by conviction and inclination, preferred trophies and monuments erected by their forgiveness in the hearts of the vanquished over any erected architecturally in the lands they had conquered: for they valued more highly the living memories of

human beings earned by their liberality than the mute inscriptions of arches, columns and pyramids exposed to the
depredations of the weather and the envy of every man.

'You can well remember the clemency which they showed to
the Bretons after the Battle of Saint-Aubin-du-Cormier and
the destruction of Parthenay. You have heard of the kindly
treatment of the natives of Hispaniola – and hearing of it,
have marvelled – for they had pillaged, laid waste and
ravaged the maritime frontiers of Les Sables-d'Olonne and Le
Talmondais.

'Our very heavens were full of praises and thanksgivings
offered by you and your fathers when Alpharbal, King of
Cararre, not satisfied with his good fortune, madly invaded the
lands of Aunis, acting the pirate amongst all the islands of
Armorica and the neighbouring regions. He was defeated and
taken in a regular sea-fight by my father, to whom God be
Protector and Guard.

'Why! Where other kings and emperors – indeed those who
style themselves *Catholic* – would have treated him wretchedly,
harshly imprisoned him and outrageously ransomed him, he
treated him with courtesy, kindly lodging him in his palace
and, with unbelievable affability, sending him home under a
safe-conduct, laden with gifts, laden with benevolence, laden
with every token of friendship. And what was the result? Back
in his domains, he summoned all the princes and estates of his
realm, told them of the humane treatment he received from us,
and prayed them to deliberate upon it to the end that, as the
world had found in us an exemplar of magnanimous grace, it
might find in them an exemplar of gracious magnanimity.

'It was unanimously decreed that they would offer us their
entire lands, domains and kingdom to treat as we wished.
Alpharbal in person quickly returned with [nine thousand and
thirty] eight great cargo-boats bearing not only the treasures of
his House and royal lineage but of virtually all the country: for,
as he was embarking to set sail with a West-nor'-easter, each
one in the crowd cast into the boats gold, silver, rings, jewels,
spices, drugs, sweet-smelling perfumes, parrots, pelicans,
monkeys, civets, genets and porcupines. There was no mother's

son from a good family who did not cast into the boats something rare that he possessed.

'Alpharbal once landed, he wished to kiss my father's feet:
the act was considered demeaning and not tolerated: he was
embraced as an ally. Alpharbal offered him his presents. They
were not accepted, as being excessive. He gave himself and his
posterity to be slaves and willing serfs: that was deemed unjust
and not accepted either.

'By the decree of his States-General he ceded his kingdom
and all his lands, offering the deeds of cession and conveyance,
signed, sealed and ratified by all concerned. The offer was
rejected outright and the documents tossed into the fire. The
result was that my father began to weep for pity and shed
copious tears as he considered the frank intentions and simplicity of the Canarrians, and by choice words and congruous
maxims played down the good deed he had done, saying that
treating them well had not cost him a button, and that if he
had shown them any courtesy he was honour-bound to do so.
But Alpharbal praised him all the more.

'What was the outcome? Although we, as a ransom pushed
to the extremity, could have tyrannically extorted twenty
payments of one hundred thousand crowns, holding his elder
sons hostage, they made themselves tributaries for ever, bound
to send us every year two million crowns-worth of pure, twenty-
four-carat gold.

'The first year that sum was paid to us.

'The following year they quite voluntarily paid twenty-three
hundred thousand crowns; the third, twenty-six hundred thousand; the fourth, three millions: and they continue to increase
it willingly by so much that we shall be constrained to forbid
them to bring us any more.

'Such is the nature of generosity: for Time, which diminishes
and erodes all things, increases and augments generous deeds,
since a good turn freely done to a man of reason grows and
grows from noble thoughts and memories.

'And so, not wishing to fall away in any manner from the
generous disposition inherited from my forebears, I forgive you;
I free you; I leave you frank and at liberty as before.

'On top of that, as you go through the gates you will each receive three months' pay to enable you to return to your homes and families; six hundred men-at-arms and eight thousand foot-soldiers, under the command of Alexander, my equerry, will conduct you home in safety so that you may not be ill-treated by the peasants.

'May God be with you.

'With all my heart I regret that Picrochole is not here, for I would have made him understand that this war was waged against my wishes, without any hope of increasing my lands or my reputation. But, seeing that he has now gone missing and that nobody knows how nor why he has disappeared, it is my will that his kingdom remain in its entirety with his son, who, being much too young (not yet fully five) shall have the older princes and scholars of his realm as regents and tutors.

'But because a kingdom thus left to itself could easily be ruined if one did not restrain the covetousness and selfishness of its stewards, I will and command that Ponocrates be set above the regents as superintendent with all necessary authority, assiduously watching over the boy until he judges him apt to rule and reign by himself.

'I bear in mind:

– that too slack and lax a readiness to pardon evil-doers is an occasion for them to do evil again even more lightly, from a pernicious confidence of being forgiven;

'I bear in mind:

– that Moses, *who was very meek, above all the men which were on the face of the earth*, bitterly punished the mutinous and seditious amongst the people of Israel;

'I bear in mind:

– that Julius Caesar, an emperor so gracious that Cicero said that his destiny was never more sovereign than that he could, nor his virtue ever better than that he would, save and pardon everyone, yet even he in certain cases rigorously punished the instigators of rebellion.

'Following such examples, my will is that you hand over to me before you leave: first, that egregious Marquet who, through his vacuous arrogance, was the source and prime cause of this war; second, his fellow *fouace*-bakers, who failed to put a stop at once to his crack-brained folly; and finally all the counsellors, captains, officers and intimates of Picrochole, who encouraged, advocated and advised him to break across frontiers and molest us.'

How the victorious Gargantuists were rewarded after the battle

CHAPTER 49

[Becomes Chapter 51.

'Nosocome', hospital, is a French neologism taken by Rabelais straight from the Greek.

For the great banquet of Ahasuerus, see Esther 2:18 ff.

There is a riot of transient characters with Classical names: Tolmère (tolmeros, bold), Ithybole (ithubolos, straight-hitting), Acamas (acamas, indefatigable), Chironacte (cheironactes or cheironax, one who is a master with his hands; doubtless a skilled engineer), Sébaste (sebastos, venerable), Sophrone (sophronikos, moderate).

The names are Greek but the place-names are all in Rabelais' pays.

The Royal printing press was established in the Louvre by François I. To work such presses required great physical effort: hence, to be made to work them forms a good, useful, Renaissance punishment.]

Once that address had been delivered by Gargantua, the seditious men he required were handed over, except for Spadassino, Squit and Little-trash who, six hours before the battle, had fled [one without stopping as far as the Col d'Agnello; another, as far as the Val de Vyre, and the third, without a glance behind or a pause for breath, as far as Logrono], and two *fouace*-bakers who had fallen in battle.

The only hurt which Gargantua did them was to require them to toil at the presses of his newly established printing-house.

He then had the dead buried with honour in the valley of the Noyrettes and in the fields at Brûlevieille. The injured, their wounds dressed, were treated in his great Nosocome.

After that he informed himself of the depredations suffered by the town, and by its inhabitants whom he compensated for all their losses against sworn affidavits. He further had a fort built there, stationing soldiers and look-outs in it so as the better to defend himself in the future against rash disturbances.

On departing he graciously thanked all the soldiers of his legions who had taken part in the defeat, sending them back to their barracks and garrisons for the winter, except some of the Decuman Legion, whose great deeds he had witnessed that day, and the Captains of each troop, with whom he set out towards Grandgousier. That good fellow was indescribably delighted when he saw them coming. He at once organized festivities: the most magnificent, the most lavish and the most delightful ever seen since the days of King Ahasuerus. As they all rose from the table, he distributed amongst them the valuable items of his sideboard: they weighed eighteen hundred thousand [and fourteen] golden besants, including large antique urns, huge pots, huge basins, huge cups, goblets, beakers, candlesticks, chalices, sauce-boats, vases, [dragée-dishes] and other such plate, all in solid gold, not to mention their jewels, enamel-work and embossings which – by any reckoning – exceeded the value of the metal itself.

In addition, he ordered that twelve hundred thousand crowns in cash be counted out from his exchequer for each one of them. On top of that he granted to each man in perpetuity (except for those who should die without heirs) whichever of his castles and adjacent lands they deemed most suitable. To Ponocrates he gave La Roche-Clermault; to Gymnaste, Le Couldray; to Eudemon, Montpensier; to Tolmère, Le Rivau; to Ithybole, Montsoreau; to Acamas, Candes; to Chironacte, Varennes; to Sébaste, Gravot; to Alexandre, Quinquenais; to Sophrone, Ligré; and so on for other of his strongholds.

How Gargantua caused the Abbey of Thélème to be built for the Monk

CHAPTER 50

[Becomes Chapter 52.

Thélème bears a name which means 'will', thelema, in New Testament Greek. It suggests free-will but also God's will since the word occurs in the Lord's Prayer: 'Thy will (thelema) be done'. The new abbey is said to be established for Frère Jean and according to his fancy. He refuses the preferment, untypically citing a saying attributed to Socrates: 'How can I rule others who can never rule myself?'

Apart from two jests which interrupt Gargantua's flow, the Monk in fact contributes nothing whatsoever to the plan of his new Religious Order.

Rabelais' serious pun mur, *wall, and* murmur, *murmurings (of discontent) is transposed here to 'railing' and 'railings' (of discontent).*

The play on 'bit-of-stuff' (a fancy woman, and cloth) freely transposes an easy pun: -t-elle, *'she', and* toile, *'cloth' (both pronounced the same in Renaissance French).*

When clerical celibacy is simply called chastity it risks undervaluing the chastity of marriage. Evangelicals, including Erasmus, and the reformers were fervent champions of matrimony, but none make it compulsory. Here Rabelais just stops short of doing so. In the context of Christian freedom and courtly evangelism, wealth and liberty replace poverty and obedience in this noble abbey. Marriage is not compulsory but clearly assumed as the way of living happily ever after.

The construction of the Abbey is described in the next chapter; in it six and its composites play a large part. Six (according to Renaissance mystical mathematics) is favourable to matrimony and harmony.]

Only the Monk was still to be provided for. Gargantua wanted to make him abbot of Seuilly, but he turned it down. He then wished to grant him the Abbey of Bourgueil or the Abbey of Saint-Florent, whichever he preferred (or both if they took his fancy).

But the Monk's reply was absolute: of monks he wanted

neither charge nor governance. 'For,' he said, 'how can I govern others who can never govern myself? But if you deem that I have done you any welcome service and may do so again in the future, allow me to found an abbey to my own devising.'

The request was pleasing to Gargantua, who offered him all his lands at Thélème, two leagues from the great forest of Port-Huault beside the Loire. He then begged Gargantua to establish his Order flat contrary to all others.

'First, then,' said Gargantua, 'since all other abbeys are fearsomely fenced in, no walls or railings are ever to be built around it.'

'That's right,' said the Monk. 'Railings at the back and railings at the front produce envy, railings and rival conspiracies.'

'To go on,' said Gargantua: 'seeing that in certain convents in our world the practice is to clean the places passed through by any women who come in – decent women, I mean, and modest – here it was decreed that, should any monk or nun happen to come in, they would scour clean all the places they might have passed through.

'And because in the religious Orders of our world everything is circumscribed, delimited and ruled by Hours, it was decreed that not one clock nor sundial should be there, but that all their activities should be arranged according to whatever was fit or opportune; for Gargantua used to say that the greatest waste of time that he knew was to watch the clock – what good ever came of it? – and that there was no greater lunacy in the world than to rule your life by the sound of a bell and not according to the dictates of good sense and intelligence.

'Item: because in those days no women were put into convents unless they were one-eyed, lame, hunch-backed, ugly, askew, mad, backward, deformed or defective, nor men unless they were runny-nosed, ill-born, daft and a burden on their family . . .'

– 'Apropos,' said the Monk, 'if a bit-of-stuff's neither good nor fair, what is to be done?'

'Make her into a nun,' said Gargantua.

'Yes,' said the Monk: 'or into shirts . . .' –

'. . . it was ordained that no women would be accepted here

unless they were beautiful, well formed and well endowed by Nature; and no men, unless handsome, well formed, and well endowed by Nature.

'Item: because men never went into convents of women except furtively and secretly, it was declared that here there would be no women except with men; no men, except with women.

'Item: because men and women, once professed after a year's probation, are obliged and forced to remain there for ever their whole life through, it was laid down that both the men and women professed here could leave openly and definitively as they saw fit.

'Item: because the Religious normally make three vows: namely of chastity, poverty and obedience, there the constitutions stated that all could marry, and everyone should be rich and live in freedom. As regards the legal age, women were to be admitted between ten and fifteen; men, between twelve and eighteen.'

How the Abbey of the Thelemites was built and endowed

CHAPTER 51

[Becomes Chapter 53.

Six and its multiples play their part in the construction. The Abbey is placed in Rabelais' pays, but the names of the towers are all Greek: Arctice, north; Calaër, fine air; Anatole, east; Mesembrine, southern; Hesperie, western, and Cryère, icy.

The chapels *mentioned are perhaps oratories, but the word had a wide range of meanings, not all religious. The description is not a blueprint: even lavatories are lacking.]*

For the building and furnishing of the Abbey Gargantua sent twenty-seven hundred thousand, eight hundred and thirty-one golden *Agnus-dei* in ready coin, and then, each year until all was completed, sixteen hundred and sixty-nine thousand Sun-crowns [and as many golden *Pleiades*] raised from tolls on the river Dive. For its basic endowment and maintenance he gave, in perpetuity, twenty-three hundred and sixty-nine thousand five hundred and fourteen rose-nobles from ground-rents, free of all liens and depreciations, payable every year at the portal of the Abbey. The deeds, duly executed, were handed over.

The building was hexagonal, in such a manner that there was built at each angle a solid round tower with an inside measurement of sixty paces in diameter. Each was exactly alike in size and construction; on the northern side flowed the river Loire, on one of whose banks was set one of the towers, named Arctice. Another, facing east, was called Calaër; the next one round was Anatole; the next again, Mesembrine; the next after that, Hesperie; and last of all, Cryère.

Between each tower there was a distance of three hundred and twelve paces. The whole was built in six storeys, counting the underground cellars as one. The vaulting of the ground storey was in the shape of basket-handles. The remainder had stuccoed ceilings with *culs-de-lampe* in Flemish plaster. The roof was clad in fine slate and had lead finials artistically interspersed with gilded figures of little manikins and beasts. Gargoyles projected from the walls between the casements, into pipes diagonally painted in gold and blue stripes right down to the ground, where they ended in great conduits all leading to the river below the edifice. The building was a hundred times more splendid than Bonivet, [Chambord or Chantilly,] for it contained nine hundred and thirty-two chambers, each including an anti-chamber, a dressing-room, a private closet, a chapel, and a vestibule leading into a large hall.

In the middle of the main structure, between each tower, stood an inner spiral staircase. The steps were [partly of porphyry, partly of Numidian stone, and partly] of serpentine marble, twenty-two-foot long and three fingers thick, arranged in flights of twelve between each landing.

On each of the landings were two handsome classical-style arcades which let in the light; through them one entered into a loggia, with lattice-work gratings as wide as the staircase itself which, mounting to the main roof, terminated in a slightly raised pavilion.

The stairs led on either side to a great hall and through rooms into the chambers. Stretching from the Arctice Tower to the Cryère Tower were the great and beautiful libraries for Greek, Latin, Hebrew, French, Italian and Spanish, arranged by language on different shelves.

In the middle was a miracle of a winding-staircase, entered from outside by an arcade six arm-spans wide. It was made so broad and symmetrical that six men-at-arms, lance on thigh, could ride abreast to the top of the entire building. From the Anatole Tower to the Mesembrine were beautiful great galleries, all with wall-paintings of ancient prowesses, histories and depictions of localities. On the side facing the river there was in the middle an ascent and gateway like the ones already described. Over that gateway was inscribed the following in large antique letters:

The Inscription set above the main Gate of Thélème

CHAPTER 52

[Becomes Chapter 54.

This 'Abbey of the Will' has no walls to keep people in but does have means of keeping out the enemies of the Gospel. It is an aristo-cratic fortress of evangelical truth which defends its noble inmates from a hostile world.

Aristocratic wealth is honoured, but not riches raised by venal lawyers and the like.]

> No hypocrite nor bigot come herein,
> Nor apes of goodness, shoddy and profane,
> Nor stupid Wry-necks, worse than Goths in sin,
> Nor Ostrogoths and all their frightful kin,
> Humbugs fine-shod or clad in hair-shirts vain,
> Tramps, fur-wrapped perverts, true religion's bane,
> Each puffed-up clown who to make quarrels chooses,
> Be off with you: here peddle no abuses.

Abuses and hates
Through my wicket gates
Would bring faithlessness;
And all your badness
My song's praise abates.
Abuses and hates!

Come not here-in, ye lawyers with tight fists,
Nor clerk, nor legist who poor plaintiffs cogs,
Scribes, Pharisees, new tortuous canonists,
Doddering judges fighting in the lists
'Gainst parish-folk to tie them up like dogs.
Your fees lie screened behind a gibbet's fogs;
Yell for them there! Here's no judicial maw
Nor anything to swell your venal Law.

Law with its gambles
Here knows no gambols
Where all live in joy.
Forensics deploy
Where for fat fees scrambles
Bad Law with its gambles.

Away vile Usury's filthy money-grubbers,
Foul beggars, pigs forever with vile snouts in,
Fat-cats and Scribes, judicial pettifoggers,
Bent, bluff-nosed rascals stuffing coins in coffers,
Unsatisfied though thousand crowns are crammed in,
All teeth on edge, save when there's gold to win
And pile up high, with lean and hawkish face:
May horrid death this day your life efface.

Efface brutish dial
Which we e'er revile!
Bray elsewhere you might:
Here never 'tis right.
Be off: you are vile.
Efface brutish dial!

Come not herein, ye foolish jealous curs,
Nor night nor day, by jaundiced envy led,
Nor you for whom sedition ever purrs,
Spirits of ill, whom Distrust ever stirs,
Latins or Greeks, more than the wolf to dread,
With syphilitic sores from heel to head.
Your filthy lupus elsewhere feed you might!
Your poxy scabs can Shame alone delight.

> Delight, honour, praise.
> Here-in we do raise:
> In shared common joy
> Good health we enjoy.
> Happily teach all our days
> Delight, honour, praise.

Come ye inside, and welcome now abide,
And doubly so of chivalry the flower.
Bring riches too: they are not things to hide
Revenues, wealth, shall have their use inside,
For Great and Small shall find them their Endower;
Thousands with me shall enter friendship's bower,
All merry friends, with joy beyond compare:
Wholly and ever true companions fair.

> Companions fair,
> Serene and sans care:
> Banished vulgarity:
> Welcomed civility
> Whose ways are so rare,
> Companions fair.

Come ye inside; who God's Good News declare
With subtle sense while enemies do chide.
Here find a tower and refuge from the snare
Of hostile Error whose wiles ever dare

With falsest style the Truth from all to hide.
Found faith profound, here ever to abide.
Then we'll confound with Truth, written and heard,
The vilest foes by our God's Holy Word.

By God's Holy Word!
Truth ever be heard
In this holy site.
With Truth gird the knight.
Dames' minds' depths be stirred
By God's Holy Word.

Enter herein you dames of good descent.
Come with frank minds and with us find true joy:
Beauteous Flowers, with faces Heaven-bent,
Upright and pure, on Wisdom all intent;
Here Honour abides true, without alloy.
The great lord who bestowed this to enjoy
By way of guerdon gave it you to hold,
Enabling all with his most ample gold.

Gold given for a gift
Earns our God's forgift.
For gold's wards may earn
Rewards in return:
Forgiveness comes swift:
For gold given for gift.

What the dwelling of the Thelemites was like

CHAPTER 53

[Becomes Chapter 55.

*Evangelism may well be on the defensive here in a hostile world,
but the youthful noblemen and ladies of Thélème live expansively in
elegant, disciplined luxury. Their Abbey recalls the splendours of the
Dream of Polifilo.]*

In the middle of the inner court stood a magnificent fountain of pure alabaster, topped by the Three Graces with horns-of-plenty pouring water from their breasts, mouths, ears, eyes, and other bodily apertures.

The inner parts of the building above that court were raised up on pillars of chalcedony and porphyry, with beautiful ancient-style arches, within which were beautiful galleries, long and spacious, decorated with wall-paintings as well as with the horns of stags, [unicorns and hippopotamuses, with elephant tusks] and other objects of note.

The ladies' apartments stretched from the Arctice Tower as far as the Mesembrine Gate. The men occupied the rest. Placed outside between the first two towers where the ladies could enjoy them were the tilt-yard, the hippodrome, the amphitheatre and the wonderful baths having basins at three levels, with all sorts of equipment and an abundance of distilled waters of myrrh.

Beside the river were the pleasure-gardens with a maze in the middle, all very beautiful. Between the two other towers were laid out courts for balloon and royal-tennis. Towards the Cryère Tower were orchards full of every kind of fruit trees arranged in quincunxes. Beyond stretched the Great Park, teeming with all sorts of game.

The firing-butts for harquebus, bow and cross-bow were sited between the third pair of towers. The kitchens were placed outside by the Hesperie Tower and were single-storeyed. Beyond them were the stables.

In front of them was the falcon-house under the control of expert keepers and trainers. It was replenished annually by the Cretans, Venetians and Sarmatians with all sorts of birds of surpassing excellence: eagles, [gerfalcons,] hawks, goshawks, female lanners, falcons, sparrow-hawks, merlins, and others, so well trained and tractable that they would leave the château, sport over the fields and catch everything they came across. The kennels were a little beyond, towards the Great Park.

All the halls, chambers and private rooms were hung with tapestries, varied according to the season of the year. All the paving was carpeted in green baize.

The beds were of embroidered cloths. In each of the anti-chambers stood a crystal looking-glass, framed in fine gold and surrounded by pearls; it was large enough to give a true reflection of the whole person.

Hard by the entrance leading to the ladies' chambers were the perfumers and hairdressers, through whose hands the men passed when they called on the ladies. They also furnished the ladies' apartments every morning with distilled [rose water,] orange-water and angel-water, as well as that precious thing, a perfuming-pot, exhaling many kinds of aromatic vapours.

How the monks and nuns of Thélème were dressed

CHAPTER 54

[Becomes Chapter 56.

This luxury Abbey has been reformed, but only by agreement over matters of dress. The 'sympathy' which existed between the noblemen and the ladies has wide implications. Renaissance sympathy is, as defined by the Oxford English Dictionary: *'A (real; or supposed) affinity between certain things' – here, people – 'by virtue of which they are similarly or correspondingly affected by the same influence, affect or influence one another (especially in some occult way) or attract or tend towards each other'. It embraces the harmony of the Thelemites over their elegant dressing and more widely their harmony and conformity in everything affecting their community.*

No time is wasted over elegant dressing any more than it was for Gargantua in Chapter 21. The dressing is done by others. There is one Greek-derived name, Nausiclète (nausikleitos): 'renowned for his ships.']

At the time of the original foundation, the ladies dressed according to their own fancy and judgement. Subsequently [by their free will] they were reformed in the following manner.

They wore scarlet or cochineal stockings extending exactly three-fingers above the knee; the selvedge was of a variety of rich embroidery and slashes. Their garters matched the colour of their bracelets and clung to the top and bottom of their knees. Their shoes, pumps and slippers were of crimson, red or violet velvet slashed with the shape of a cray-fish's beard.

Over their chemise each wore a beautiful kirtle of lovely watered silk. On top of it they wore a farthingale of various taffetas, white, red, tawny, grey and so on. Over that came a tunic either of silver taffeta embroidered with golden-thread arabesque needlework, or else (when it seemed preferable, depending on the weather) of satin, damask or velvets – orange-coloured, tawny, green, ashen-grey, blue, bright yellow, crimson-red or white – or else (depending on the Festivals) of cloth-of-gold or silver-weave, with gold-and-silver braid or embroidery.

According to the season, their gowns were of cloth-of-gold fringed with silver, of red satin covered with gold or silver braid, of various taffetas – white, blue, black or tawny – of silk-serge, watered silk, pure silk, velvet, silver-weave, silver-cloth, gold-tissue, or else of velvet or satin with gold fringes in a variety of motifs.

In summer, in lieu of the gowns they would on occasions wear loose robes decorated as above or else sleeveless Moorish jackets of violet velvet with gold fringes over silver braid or with girdles of gold, garnished at the seams with little Indic pearls. In winter they would wear gowns of the various coloured taffetas mentioned above with furs of lynx, black weasel, Calabrian martens, sables or other costly species.

Their prayer-beads, rings, chains and necklaces were of fine stones: carbuncles, rubies, balas-rubies, diamonds, sapphires, emeralds, turquoises, garnets, agates, beryls, pearls and unsurpassed unions.

Their coiffures were arranged according to the season: in the winter they chose the French style; in the spring, the Spanish; in the summer, the Italian, except on Sundays and Festival-days, when they adopted the French style as being more becoming and savouring more of feminine modesty.

The men were dressed in their own style: their hose of wool or of thick serge, scarlet or cochineal, black or white. Their breeches were of matching, or nearly matching, velvet, embroidered and slashed to their own designs. Their doublets were of cloth-of-gold, silver-weave, velvet, satin, damask, and taffeta in the same colours, slashed, embroidered and trimmed in the height of fashion. Their fly-cords were of like-coloured silk with tags of thick-enamelled gold. Their cloaks and jackets were of cloth-of-gold, gold-weave, silver-weave or velvet, with such embroidered borders as they wished. Their gowns were as costly as those of the ladies. Their belts were of silk in the colours of their doublets: each bore at his side a beautiful sword with a gilt handle; the scabbard was sheathed in velvet to match the breeches and hose; its tip was of gold and gilt-work. So too for the dagger. Their bonnet was of black velvet, furnished with plenteous jewels and gold buttons; above it rose a white feather, delicately divided by golden spangles, at the ends of which dangled pendants of fine rubies, emeralds and so on.

But there was such sympathy between the men and women that they dressed every day in matching clothing. So as not to fail in this, certain gentlemen were delegated to inform the men each morning of the style which the ladies intended to wear that day – for that entirely depended on the will of the ladies.

You should not think that either the gentlemen or the ladies wasted any time over those noble vestments and most rich apparel, for the Masters of the Wardrobe had everything ready each morning, whilst the Women of the Bedchamber were so expert, that their ladies were ready and dressed in next to no time.

And so that the apparel might be most conveniently supplied, a large building, half-a-league long, well lit and equipped, was erected by the edge of the wood at Thélème; there lived the goldsmiths, jewellers, embroiderers, tailors, drawers of gold thread, velvet-makers, tapestry-workers and artists. All plied their crafts there, entirely for the monks and nuns of the Abbey, being supplied with their materials and cloths by the hand of the Sieur Nausiclète, who, year by year, brought them the cargoes of seven ships sailing from the Perlas and Cannibal Islands bearing gold ingots, pure silks, pearls and precious stones.

If any of the union-pearls tended to age and lose their natural whiteness, the jewellers revived them by their art, passing them through some splendid cockerels just as one feeds castings to falcons to purge them.

On the Rule of the Thelemites: and how they lived.

CHAPTER 55

[Becomes Chapter 57.

The famous Rule of the Order of the Thelemites contains only one clause: 'Do what thou wilt'. Such a rule cannot apply to everyone: it is restricted to the well-born and well-bred who have a developed and trained synderesis. Synderesis is that guiding force of conscience which, though weakened at the Fall, was not obliterated by it and so can be cultivated. Rabelais calls it 'honour', but his definition of honour is word for word that of the more theological concept of synderesis. Honour is a term which all his noble readers would have understood: synderesis is not.

Pauline freedom (eleutheria) releases men and women from the 'yoke of bondage', the jugum servitutis (Galatians 5:1; 4:31): Christians are at liberty to do or not to do anything which is indifferent, that is, anything which, of itself, does not concern salvation.

The concept is central to Lutheran theology. So is the stoic Lutheran paradox met here in Thélème and in Luther: the Christian is free and subject to no one: the Christian is most obliging, the servant of all and subject to everyone. The Thelemites live in harmony because they are freely obliging and willingly subject to each other in all matters good or indifferent.

'We strive for the forbidden and yearn for what is denied' is cited from Ovid's Art of Love, 3, 4, 17. Rabelais is not alone in quoting that line of Ovid's beside Saint Paul. It memorably reinforces Pauline morality and theology.]

Their whole life was ordered not by laws, rules and regulations but according to their volition and free-will.

They got up when it seemed good to do so; they drank, ate, worked and slept when the desire came over them. No one woke them up; no one compelled them to drink, to eat nor to do anything else whatsoever.

Gargantua had laid that down.

There was but one clause in their Rule: *Do what thou wilt*, because people who are free, well bred, well taught and conversant with honourable company have by nature an instinct – a goad – which always pricks them towards virtuous acts and withdraws them from vice. They called it Honour. When such as they are oppressed and enslaved by base subordination and constraint, that noble disposition by which they were, with frankness, striving towards virtue, they deflect towards casting off and breaking down that *yoke of bondage* – for '*We all engage in things forbidden, and yearn for things denied.*'

By such freedom they all vied laudably with each other to do what they saw to be pleasing to any one of them. So if any one man or woman said, 'Let us drink,' they all did so; if, 'Let us have a game,' they all did so; if, 'Let us go into the fields for some sport,' they all went.

Whenever it was for hawking or hunting, the ladies, mounted on their beautiful familiar-horses and accompanied by their proud palfreys, each bore on her gloved hand a sparrow-hawk, a lannet or a merlin.

The men bore the other types of bird.

All had been educated so nobly that there was not a man or woman amongst them but could read and write, sing, play musical instruments and speak five or six languages in which they composed both prose and verse.

Never were there seen knights like these: so stout-hearted, so gallant, so full of dexterity on horse and foot, so vigorous, more active, or more talented in the handling of every sort of weapon. Never were there seen ladies like these: so neat, so dainty, less froward, more accomplished with their hands, with the needle, or at every activity which is womanly, honourable and free.

That is why, when the time arrived that any man in that Abbey should wish to leave (at the request of his parents or for some other reason), he took one of the ladies with him – the one who had accepted him as her suitor – and they wedded each other; and so well had they dwelt together in Thélème in loving-friendship that they continued all the more to do so in marriage, loving each other as much at the end of their lives as on the first day of their wedding.

I must not forget to write down an enigma uncovered during the digging of the foundations of the Abbey; it was inscribed upon a huge plaque of bronze. It read as follows:

An enigma uncovered amongst the foundations of the Abbey of the Thelemites

CHAPTER 56

[Becomes Chapter 58.

The enigma artistically balances the 'coq-à-l'âne' in Chapter 2, but is not written in the same baffling style. Except for the first two lines (with their Sursum corda*) and the last ten lines – here separated from the rest of the poem – the verse seems to have been lifted straight from the works the Court poet Mellin de Saint-Gelais, presumably with his consent. At one level the poem is an example of the (often easy to resolve) enigmatic verse enjoyed during the Renaissance: it describes a game of royal-tennis in Apocalyptic terms.*

The poem ends with the scriptural injunctions to 'persevere unto the end' despite persecution and not to be 'offended' ('scandalized') by the persecution of the Elect. Since 1532, real but limited persecution of evangelicals had become an urgent concern. After the second affaire des placards *of January 1535, when Marot, Rabelais and others had to drop what they were doing and flee for their lives, matters became far worse. And then, suddenly, François I changed his policy and, while keeping in prison Noël Béda, the Syndic of the Sorbonne, invited the moderate Melanchthon to Paris to debate reforms. So Bishop Jean Du Bellay, the liberal patron of Rabelais, had been vindicated.*

Gargantua takes up the theme of the persecution of the Elect who return to the Gospel: Frère Jean dismisses the suggestion that any evangelical message is implied by the verse: for him it is all about a tennis-match: no more. But the dense scriptural quotations cannot of course be ignored.

They are noted at the end of the chapter.]

Ye who seek happiness, ye mortals all,
Lift up your hearts and listen now withal.

If we may truly hold, with full intent,
That heavenly bodies in the firmament
Have influenced human minds, which have foretold
So many things the future then did hold,
Or if Almighty God may help us know
That which on us the future may bestow,
Or Destiny from far-off time may send,
News of all which is by free knowledge penned:
I tell you now, if only you will hear,
This coming winter – yes, the one that's near –
Then various kinds of men shall make an entry,
Tired of peace and bored of leisured plenty,
They'll openly proceed, in day's full light
Good folk of every quality to incite
To discord and to quarrelling. Indeed,
Listen and believe them, then they do succeed!
However things turn out, whate'er the cost,
They wish to see our family concord lost,
Friend against friend, each on a different side,
And men and women too by kindred tied.
Ah, moral horror! Even the brash son
Will bend his arm and make his father run.
Even the Great, from noblest forbears sprung,
Shall by their subjects have their withers rung.
The duty then of honoured preference
Will be o'erthrown! 'Twixt men no difference.
For they shall say that each man in his turn
Shall drive right high, and then to earth return.
Men form in bands and argue at this point:
Discord, and fights: the time so out of joint,
That even History, full of wondrous things,
Can find no parallel to such happenings.
Then we shall see how many a good man,
Answering the goad as only young men can,
Clinging a while to life but wrapped in gloom,

Will ever strive, only to die in bloom.
There is no man who, once he sets his hand
Unto this task, following his heart's command,
Who has not filled the air with raucous cries.
Running about and yelling to the skies.
Then shall all men have like authority.
Men of no faith, and men of Verity;
Men then accept the judgements, always crude,
Of ignorance and the so vain multitude.
The dud amongst them then the judge shall be:
And then a dire and dreadful flood you'll see!
Flood do I say, and say it with right reason,
For all this strife will not be out of season
Nor shall the world be freed of it at last
Until there pour forth waters, rising fast:
Waters abrupt, drenching the moderate
Who fighting hard, quit the court too late:
And rightly so, for then their heart and mind
Ne'er to this combat pardon had assigned
Nor spared the beasts – the innocent beasts –
     whose guts
Not sacrificed to gods with priestly cuts
But put to daily uses by mere Man
Who with their innards strives as hard he can.
May this be settled? I leave it all to you.
Think about it. Can discord struggle through?
Within discord may quiet reign in robe?
Can rest e'er touch the stuff of our round Globe.
Those most enthralled with it most happy are:
They try not lose nor spoil it from afar:
They strive and strive in many a different way
To make it slavish, and a prisoner stay:
Yet, to its maker, spoilt, return at last
Poor and undone it needs work on his last.
But – for the worst part of its accident –
The Sun, before it shines in Occident
Will let the darkness circle it around,

Deep as eclipse or veiled nights daily round;
So, at one blow, 'twill lose its liberty,
Favours from Heaven and the Sun's clarity.
But, at the least, abandoned shall it be
And, well before, its downfall shall we see,
Such that Mount Aetna like shock had not known
When by that son of Titan she was thrown,
Nor yet more sudden, though it does resemble
The motion which Inarime made tremble
When Typhoeus to such a range did fly
That mountains toppled to the sea from high.
And soon it shall to all appear so battered
That changed 'twill be for fresh ones, unbespattered;
That even they who held it in their sway
Will let newcomers with it have their way.
Then nears the time – time ever good and wise –
To put an end to that long exercise.
Nevertheless before away all go
There will be felt in clean air all aglow,
The violent heat of a great searing flame
Which ends the floods, and also ends men's game.

More is to come: then such as then travail
And whom, though heavy laden, pains avail,
Shall, by Our Lord's own will refreshed and blest,
Come unto Him and find eternal rest.
Then shall we all with certain knowledge see
The good and fruit brought forth from patience' tree:
To whom, before, most suffering did grieve
Shall be allotted most, shall most receive.
Such was the promise. How must we revere
Him who unto the End does persevere.

The reading of this muniment fully completed, Gargantua
sighed deeply and said to those about him: 'It is not only
nowadays that those are persecuted who are led back to belief
in the Gospel: but *blessed is he who is not scandalized* and who

ever aims at the target, the mark, which God has set before us through his dear Child, without being distracted or diverted by his carnal affections.'

The Monk said: 'What do you think to be intended by this enigma? What do you understand it to mean?'

'Why,' said Gargantua, 'the course and upholding of divine Truth.'

'By Saint Goderan,' said the Monk, 'I think it is the description of a tennis-match and that the "round globe" is the ball; the "guts" and the "innards" of the "innocent beasts" are the rackets; and the folk who are het up and wrangling are the players. The end means that, after such *travails*, they go off for a meal! And be of good cheer!'[38]

[Note on the last ten lines of the poem and the ensuing comments.

The poem of Mellin de Saint-Gelais concludes with the conflagration at the End of the world (II Peter 3:18). Then follows Rabelais' own evangelical Dixain in his new, densely scriptural style, mostly echoing texts concerned with persecution and perseverance unto the End. The main ones are: 'Come unto me all that travail and are heavy laden and I shall refresh you' (Matthew 11:28); '... and bear forth fruit in patience' (the parable of the Sower, where patience means suffering).

Gargantua's comments reinforce those scriptural teachings: 'Blessed is he who shall not be scandalized in me' (to be 'scandalized' – or 'offended' in the Authorized (King James) Version – is to lose one's faith through fear of

38. In '42 the end is considerably expanded, the Monk explaining the enigma as one of the very allegories he denies it to be: ... 'By Saint Goderan,' said the Monk, '*that is not how I expound it. The style is that of Merlin the Prophet. Give it allegories and meanings as grave as you like: for my part I do not think that any other meaning is contained in it save the description of a tennis-match couched in obscure terms. The "seducers of the people" are those who arrange the matches and who are normally friends; after the two "services" are over, the one who is in then leaves the court and the other comes in. They trust the "First" (the one who says whether the ball is above or below the cord). The "waters" are their sweating; the strings of the racquets are made of the "guts" of sheep and goats; the "round globe" is the tennis-ball (the esteuf). After the game, they are refreshed before a bright fire, change their shirts and enjoy a feast, but those who won enjoy it more. And be of good cheer!*

persecution) (Matthew 11:6; Luke 7:23). 'To sin' in the Greek of the New Testament is hamartanô, *to miss the target, to miss the mark. Good Christians who are not 'offended', that is, not 'scandalized', aim so as not to miss their target, who is the Son of God (here called 'Child' as in the infancy narratives of Matthew and Luke).*

That target 'is set before us'. The term used by Rabelais is préfix, *a word with a clear predestinationalist import. The final '42 version by Rabelais of the last ten lines of verse is more emphatically predestinationalist:*

> *More is to come: those great events once passed,*
> *God's own Elect, with joys refreshed at last*
> *With all good things and heavenly manna blest*
> *And honoured recompense with all that's best*
> *Enriched shall be. The others at the End*
> *Each stripped quite bare. Which to all doth portend*
> *That, travails ceased, at that point all await*
> *And firmly find their own predestined fate.*
> *Such is the Accord. O how must we revere*
> *Him who unto the End doth persevere.*

The key word 'refreshed' and the 'call to persevere' are linked with terms frequently in the mouths of the Reformers: the 'Elect', the 'Covenant' (accord) and the 'Last Judgement', but they are all at home with a cleric such as Rabelais who had developed a predilection for Saint Paul.

The expanded '42 version of Frère Jean's dismissive remarks is given in the footnote.]

ALMANAC FOR 1536

Introduction to *Almanac for 1536*

A manuscript copy of this part of an *Almanac for 1536* was discovered by Professor Pierre Aquilon, written by Brinctius Clinckart on the blank space after the *Erratula* of an edition of Macrobius' *Somnium Ciceronis* (*Dream of Scipio*, Cologne, 1526). The gaps represented here by [...] are, I think, gaps not in Rabelais, but left by Brinctius Clinckart, who intended to fill them in later.

The Latin phrases of the original are kept here, with the translation given in square brackets. The Latin titles of books are translated.

MAÎTRE FRANÇOYS RABBELAIS, DOCTOR OF MEDICINE AND PHYSICIAN IN THE GREAT HOSPITAL OF LYONS IN HIS ALMANAC FOR 1536

[Rabelais retains his title of 'Physician in the Great Hospital of Lyons'. He walked out of that post, without warning (30 February 1535), fearing persecution. Either he composed this Almanac *for 1536 before that date, or else he clung to his title even though he had abandoned his post.*

1536 was a leap year, and so a year worrying to many at all levels of society. In Latin the intercalated day of a leap year is called a bisectum, *a 'double sixth'. The leap year itself is called* bisextilis *(again with the meaning of double-sixth).*

The main target of Rabelais is Giovanni Michele Savonarola, who was well known for his works on hot springs. I have used his Practica Canonica *of Lyons, 1560. Having shown, just as Rabelais does, that leap years are a human invention, corresponding to nothing in the heavens, Savonarola adds that, following Aristotle's* Ethics, *Book 2, we should not dismiss popular opinions out of hand. He is alluding to the* Nicomachaean Ethics, *1, 8, 7, where Aristotle writes that it is probable that popular beliefs based on experience are at least partly correct.*

The authors towards the end are identified in the notes; one only of their editions is mentioned: in some cases there were many more.]

Judgement on the Leap Year

I will expound to you (said the aforesaid Maître Françoys) within the capacity of this booklet what a leap year is and, once it is all understood, you will know that it is nothing in Nature nor in the heavens but simply a name imposed by the pleasure of men. Whether it be or not, there will be no change in Nature and no variation whatsoever, and Savonarola the physician made a great error when he asserted that thermal springs and hot baths are dangerous in a leap year. Know therefore that a year cannot be exactly defined by a certain number of days and hours, as Hyppo[crates] says in the third book of his *Prognostics*, and Pliny, Book 18, Chapter 25. However, as in several other things which cannot accept a precise setting of limits by human industry, the Ancients aimed to be as close as possible and divided the year into days and hours: that is, they decreed how many days and hours passed in our sundials during all the time that the sun makes one full revolution along its eclyptical line: for that is what we call a year. Romulus, the first king of the Romans, simply put 360 days, which he divided into ten months, beginning with the month named *Mars* after his father. And since a great number of days were left over after that division, they would, after some time, intercalate a month which the Romans called *mercidinum* [?], *intercalarem* [inserted], *embolimum* [intercalary] and macedonium [Macedonian?], as Plutarch says and Macrobius.[1]

Numa, who succeeded him, seeing the great deviation in their almanacs and calendars caused by those remaining days, made the year to be 365 days and 6 hours; he added two months, January and February, and severally distributed the days between each month, ordaining that the six remaining hours should be gathered together every four years, and from them he would make one artificial day, which would be added to February *inter Terminalia et Regifugium qui est 6 kalendas martii* [between the Terminalia and the Regifugium which is

1.   See Plutarch, *Roman Questions*, 19.

the VI Kalends of March] that those tw
over one letter of the calendar.[2] And tha
bisectum, [the double-sixth], because we
Kalendas martii, and the year itself in whi
day is made we call bisextilis. That will
present, for I know that the skilled in the
year into 364 days, 5 hours, 44 minutes a
that Julius Caesar corrected the Roman cal
lation, and that several complain of the v
since been incurred.[3] If you want to know
Aug[ustine], Book 18, Against Faustus, G
On Method, and Book 3 of the Prognosti
Isagoge for Megan the Astronomer, Pliny, Bc
[. . .], Solinus, Book [. . .], Chapter [. . .],[4]
Censorinus, The Day of Birth,[6] Macrobius ir
[. . .], chapter [. . .], Alphonso [. . .],[7]
Avenzre, On the Reasons for the Tables, [...],[9]
recting the Calendar and others. On these mai
taries on the Compotus, and glosses on the san

1536, 2nd of May, I, Brictius Clinckart.

2. The VI Kalends of March is 24 February.
3. That Julius Caesar corrected the calendar was very
    the general reader. It is explained for example in
    Fasti of Ovid.
4. There was an edition of his De die natali published
5. The Venerable Bede. There is an edition of his De
    Aleandre (Venice, 1505).
6. Caius Julius Censorinus. His De situ orbis & de si
    published as early as 1473 in Venice. Other works
7. Alfonso X, King of Castille. There is an edition of
    tabule [Venice] 1483 and his Tabule astronomice e
    (Venice, 1492).
8. Abraham ben Me'ir Ibn Ezra, known as Abraham
    ing note).
9. Despite the gap I think this should in fact read Abr
    case the combined reference is to Abraham ben
    as Abraham Avenar. His De nativitatibus was
    1485 and edited by J. Dryander at Cologne, 153;
10. The Compotus (or Computum or Compost) of Ar
    reprinted. An early example in the British Librar
    mento, is dated [Paris ? 1500?].

THE THIRD BOOK
OF PANTAGRUEL

Introduction to *The Third Book of Pantagruel*

The *Third Book* is printed in humanist type, a change from *Pantagruel* and *Gargantua*, which both had 'Gothick' appearances.

The *Third Book* was first published in 1546 by Chrestien Wechel of Paris. The definitive text is that published by Michel Fezandat of Paris in 1552. The two texts, minor corrections apart, are all but identical. The first edition is translated here; the very few interpolations are placed within square brackets and changes of substance are given in the footnotes. Thus, to read the text of the first edition, ignore the interpolations inside square brackets and the variants listed in the notes. To read the definitive text of 1552, read everything.

The translation is based on my edition of the *Tiers Livre* for the Textes Littéraires Français (Geneva: Droz, 1974, with subsequent editions). I have also consulted the Pléiade edition of the works of Rabelais, edited by Mireille Huchon and the parallel text edition of Guy Demerson, which gives a modern French translation. (Publication details of both can be found in the Introduction to *Pantagruel*.)

The Third Book
of the
Heroic Deeds and Sayings
of the
noble Pantagruel,
composed
by Maître
Franç. Rabelais,
Doctor of Medicine
and
Caloyer of the Iles d'Hyères[1]
The aforesaid author begs the Kindly Readers
to reserve their laughter until the
seventy-eighth book[2]
AT PARIS
By Chrestian Wechel, in the rue Saint-Jacques,
at the Écu de Basle: and in the rue Saint-Jean-de-
Beauvais at the Cheval Volant.
M.D.XLVI
With the Privilège *of the King*
for six years

---

1. Unlike *Pantagruel* and *Gargantua*, the title-page here bears Rabelais' real
   name and his medical title. The word *Caloyer* also reminds his readers
   that he is a priest (strictly speaking, the word, meaning 'Good Old Man'
   or 'Venerable', is applied to Greek Orthodox monks). Rabelais being a
   secular priest, the word is used in jest. His connection with the Iles
   d'Hyères, real or imaginary, remains unexplained.
2. Seventy-eight may well have been a way of expressing an imprecise
   number, like the English 'a hundred and one'. It appears several times in
   this text. W. F. Smith in his translation refers to it as 'strangely affected'
   by Rabelais (*Rabelais. The Five Books and Minor Writings together with
   Letters and Documents Illustrating His Life* (2 vols., London: Alexander
   Watt, 1896) II, p. 320, note 1.

Contents

FRANÇOIS RABELAIS
to the Mind
of the
Queen of Navarre

*[In ecstasy or rapture the mind (*esprit) *is caught away from its body and soars upwards, even perhaps as Saint Paul's did to the Third Heaven. It is seeking its homeland in Heaven, longing for intercourse with other souls and yearning for union with God. Marguerite was a platonizing, mystical, evangelical Christian, attracted by the mystical philosophy of Hermes Trismegistus (taken by many to be a contemporary of Moses): it is not surprising to see her hailed thus as an ecstatic mystic whose body here on earth strives to conform itself to the highest flights of its enraptured mind. Marguerite de Navarre was a great patron of other evangelicals, striving to protect them even from agencies approved by her brother, François I. She was the author of the* Heptaméron, *a playwright and a poet of real achievement. She also had a lively sense off fun and humour. To have her as patron marks Rabelais off for particular approval, but also (in the eyes of some academics in the Sorbonne) as a particular danger to their concept of orthodoxy.]*

Abstracted Mind, enraptured, true ecstatic,
Who Heaven dost frequent whence thou derivest
(Leaving behind thine host and place domestic,
Harmonious body, which in concord striveth
To heed thine edicts: stranger, it arriveth
Bereft of senses, calm in Apathy)
Deignest thou not to make a lively sortie
From thine abode divine, perpetual,
This Third Book here with thine own eyes to see
Of the joyful deeds of good Pantagruel?

The King's privilège

[Few French authors have ever received as fulsome a royal privilège. *On the other hand Rabelais had petitioned for a* privilège *for ten years: he received one for six. A misprint of six for* dix *(ten) seems most unlikely in so vital a document. The royal* privilège *not only placed Rabelais under royal protection, it also displayed royal approval of him as an author of the highest rank. But even a royal* privilège *did not guarantee an author from sometimes effective legal actions from which it was wise to free abroad, as Rabelais in fact did.*

By calling the works of Rabelais 'no less useful than delightful', this privilège *is again citing the highest praise accorded to a work of literature by Horace in his* Ars Poetica: *the works of Rabelais are 'sweet' and morally 'useful'.]*

François by the grace of God King of France, to the Provost of Paris, the Bailiff of Rouen, the Seneschals of Lyons, Toulouse, Bordeaux, Dauphiné and Poitou, and to all other Our Justices and Officials, or to their deputies, and to each of them severally as is due: greetings and affection.

On the part of Our beloved and loyal Maître François Rabelais, Doctor of Medicine of Our University of Montpellier, it has been expounded to Us that the aforesaid suppliant, having heretofore delivered to be printed several books, especially two volumes of the Heroic Deeds and Sayings of Pantagruel, no less useful than delightful, the printers have corrupted and perverted the aforesaid books in several places, to the great displeasure and detriment of the said supplicant, at which he has abstained from rendering public the continuation and sequel of the said Heroic Deeds and Saws; being however daily urged by studious and learned people of Our Kingdom and begged to use and to print the said sequels: he has supplicated Us to vouchsafe him a *privilège* so that no person be allowed to print them nor put any on sale, save only such as he shall have printed expressly by printers to whom he shall have handed his own true copies: and that for a period of ten consecutive years, beginning from the day and date of the printing of the said books.

Wherefore, We, all things considered and desirous that good literature be encouraged in Our Kingdom for the use and erudition of Our subjects, have given to the said Suppliant *privilège*, leave, licence and permission to have printed and put on sale by such reputable printers as he shall decide his said books and sequential works of the Heroic Deeds of Pantagruel beginning with the Third Volume, together with power and authority to correct and revise the two volumes previously written by him, and to make and cause to be made a new printing and sale; establishing prohibition and interdicts from Us, on pain of defined and great punishments, confiscation of any books by them imprinted and an arbitrary fine, to all printers and others whom it shall concern: that they are not to print nor put on sale the above-mentioned books without the will and consent of the said suppliant within the period of six consecutive years, beginning on the day and date of the printing of the said books, on pain of the confiscation of the said printed books and on arbitrary fine.

To achieve which, to each of you severally as appropriate We have given and now give plenary powers, commission and authority; and order and command all Our Justices, Officials and Subjects to allow the said supplicant peacefully to use and enjoy Our present leave, *privilège* and commission, and in so doing you are to be obeyed, for it is Our pleasure so to have done. Given in Paris this nineteenth day of September, in the Year of Grace One thousand five hundred and forty-five, being of Our reign the XXXIst. Thus signed: on behalf of the Privy Council, Delaunay. And sealed with the simple seal of yellow wax.

The Prologue of the Third Book

[From the outset, Rabelais is deeply indebted to Lucian. By quotation, exposition and practice, Rabelais acknowledges above all his fundamental and enduring debt in the Third Book *to Lucian's treatise,* To One Who Said to Him, 'You are a Prometheus with Words'. *It is that treatise which guides and justifies his potentially 'monstrous' marriage of dialogue and comedy.*

In '52 the title is more explicit: Prologue of the Author Maître François Rabelais for the Third Book of the heroic deeds and sayings of good Pantagruel.

The first paragraph makes allusions to Ecclesiasticus 11:7 (for the light of the sun) and to the blind man who (in Mark 10:51, Luke 18:35, and Matthew 20:30) was restored to sight by Jesus of Nazareth, whose full deity Rabelais quietly underlines by giving him the title of 'Almighty'.

'Piot' means wine (originally in the jargon of the fraternity of Parisian beggars).

Many thought that the French were descended from the Phrygian Francus, son of Hector. The Persian 'otacusts' (eavesdroppers, spies) were already linked with the legend of Midas' long ears by Erasmus in his Adages *(I, III, LVII; cf. also I, II, II, 'The many ears and eyes of kings').*

Several other adages of Erasmus and their explanations are exploited in this Prologue, including:

I, IV, I, 'Not everyone may call in at Corinth', and IV, III, LXVIII, 'To corinthianize' (the women of Corinth being supposed to be of particularly easy virtue).

III, V, XXXVI, 'War is the father of all'.

IV, I, I, 'War is sweet to those who have not experienced it', in which we are reminded that Solomon *means* Peaceful *in Hebrew. (Solomon is thought to have likened divine Wisdom to an army set in battle array in The Song of Songs, 6:4.)*

I, VIII, XXXIV, 'To scratch one's head with a single finger' (taken to be an idle, effeminate gesture on the part of a man worried about his hair).

IV, III, LVIII, 'He is no dithyrambic who drinks water' (A vital saying for those who love and respect wine.)

I, IX, XXX, 'His treasures will be lumps of coal'.

The verbs employed for the trundling by Diogenes of his earthenware barrel are chosen as much for their sound as for their meaning and are translated with that in mind. In this Prologue Rabelais places his Third Book in the context of the energetic steps taken, under the direction of Cardinal Jean Du Bellay, his patron, to defend Paris from the threats of the Imperial armies.

An attenuated oath playing on lapathium acutum (the Latin name for the plant which in English is called patience-dock) is an indirect way of referring to Christ's passion. As patience in English no longer readily evokes the Passion of Christ, patience-dock is transposed here to 'passion-flower'. There are two references to the marriage at Cana, one through the term 'Ruler of the Feast'.]

[Good people,] most shining drinkers and you most be-carbuncled sufferers from the pox, have you ever seen Diogenes the Cynic philosopher? If you have, either you had never lost your sight or else I have truly quitted my intelligence and logical sense. A fine thing it is to see the sparkle of wine and golden crowns – I mean, of the sun! – I appeal to the man born blind, made so famous by the Holy Scriptures: he was given the option of choosing anything he liked by the command of him who is Almighty and whose word is in a flash put into effect. All he asked for was his sight.

Now you too are not young; which is a necessary quality for metaphysically philosophizing in vine (not in vain) and for attending from henceforth the council of Bacchus, there not to lop and dine but to opine about the matter, colour, bouquet, excellence, eminence, [peculiarities, powers, virtues,] effects and dignity of *piot*, our hallowed and beloved wine.

But if (as I am easily brought to believe) you have never seen Diogenes, you must at least have heard of him, for his name and renown have indeed remained memorable to the present day, being praised to the skies in every clime.

And (unless I deceive myself) you are all of Phrygian extraction, and even though you do not have as many golden coins

as Midas had, you do have something of his which the Persians
used to appreciate in their otacusts and which the Emperor
Antoninus also desired: that which gave its nickname to the
'serpentine' cannon of Rohan: *Big Ears*. But if you have never
heard of him I want to tell you here and now a tale so that we
can start on the wine (drink up, then!) and on the words (listen,
then!) informing you (so that you should not be tricked into
disbelief by your simplicity) that Diogenes was in his day a
philosopher in a thousand, excellent and full of fun. If he did
have a few blemishes, so do you and so do we. Nought is perfect
save God alone. Nevertheless, although Alexander the Great
had Aristotle as his private tutor, it is Diogenes the Sinopian
whom he held in such high regard that if he could not have
been Alexander he would have wanted to be Diogenes.

When Philip, King of Macedonia, undertook to besiege
Corinth and reduce it to rubble, the Corinthians, warned by
their spies that he was marching against them with a mighty
army and vast array, were all rightly alarmed, overlooking
nothing, all taking up their posts and doing their duty to resist
his hostile advance and defend their city. Some brought everything movable out of the fields and into the fortresses, with their
cattle, grain, wine, fruit, victuals and all necessary provisions.

Others repaired the walls, erected bastions, squared off out-
works, dug trenches, excavated countermines, reinforced
gabions, prepared emplacements, cleared clutter from the
casemates, refixed bars on to advanced parapets, built high
platforms for cannons, repaired the outer slopes of ditches,
plastered the courtines between the bastions, built advanced
pill-boxes, banked up earth parapets, keyed stones into barbi-
cans, lined the chutes for molten lead, renewed cables on
[Saracen-style] portcullises (or 'cataracts'), stationed sentinels
and sent out patrols.

Everyone was on the alert; everyone was carrying his hod.
Some were burnishing breastplates, cleaning corselets and
polishing the metal bands and head-armour of their horses, and
their own plated jackets, light armour, helmets, [beavers, iron
skull-caps, gisarmes,] headpieces, morions, coats of mail, [jaze-
rants, wrist-guards, tasses,] gussets, limb-armour, breast-plates,

joint-armour, hauberks, body-shields, bucklers, foot-armour, leg-plates, ankle-plates and spurs. Others were readying their bows, slings, crossbows, lead-shot, catapults, [fire-arrows,] fire-grenades, fire-pots, fire-wheels and fire-darts, ballistas, stone-hurling scorpions and other weapons for repelling and destroying siege-towers.

They sharpened spears, pikes, falchions, halberds, hooked spears, [sickles,] lances, zagayes, pitchforks, partisans, bladed maces, battle-axes, darts, javelins, light javelins, long stakes and leisters. They whetted swords, scimitars, broadblades, badlars, [scythes,] short-swords, rapiers, poniards, hangers, spiral-ferruled daggers, pricks, tucks, knives, blades, cutting-edges and dirks. Every man was exercising his prick: every man derusting his dagger. No woman was there, however old or matronly, who did not manage to furbish up her fanion, since you are aware that, of old, the ladies of Corinth would put up a good fight!

Diogenes, seeing all this fervent coming-and-going yet not being employed by the magistrates on anything whatsoever, spent a few days contemplating their behaviour without uttering a word. Then, moved by the martial spirit, he cast his cloke about him like a scarf, rolled his sleeves right up to his elbows, tucked in his robe like a peasant picking apples, entrusted to an ancient companion his shoulder-wallet, his books and his writing-tablets, went forth from the city in the direction of the Cranion (a hill and promontory hard by Corinth) on to the fair esplanade, and there trundled the earthenware barrel which served him as a shelter from inclement weather, and then, flexing his arms with great mental ardour, he turned it, churned it, upturned it; [spattered it,] battered it, bent it, bonked it, [dubbed it, scrubbed it, rubbed it, flattered it,] banged it, beat it; bumped it, topsy'd it, turvy'd it, dribbled it, tapped it, ting-ed it; stoppered it, unstoppered it, paced it, ambled it, shambled it, haggled it; tossed it, stopped it, [prodded it,] shot it; lifted it, laved it, louvered it; hampered it, aimed it, blamed it, blocked it; troubled it, huddled it, splattered it; fashioned it, fastened it; [walloped it, dolloped it, tickled it, tarred it, smutched it, touched it, hawked it, mawked it, hooked it, crooked it, twiddled it, twaddled it,] charmed it, armed it, alarmed it, saddled it, straddled it, caparisoned it, and – volleying it down from mount to vale – tumbled it along the Cranion, and then (as Sisyphus did with his stone) pushed it back up from vale to mount so that he all but holed it.

On seeing which, one of his friends asked him what had possessed him to make him so afflict his mind, body and barrel. Our philosopher replied that, not being employed by the State in any other task, he was storming about with his barrel so as not to be seen as the only one idle and dilatory amidst folk so ardent and busy.

It is the same for me: I am void of fear though not of care, caring that nobody thinks me in any way worthy of being put to work and seeing that everyone else throughout this most-noble Cisalpine and Transalpine Realm [of France] is urgently making preparations and toiling away, some defensively (fortifying the country), some offensively (repulsing the foe), everything so well ordered in so wondrous an accord and with such evident future benefit – since from henceforth France will have superb frontiers and the French will live assuredly in peace – that only a little holds me back from adopting the opinion of that good man Heraclitus that war is the Father of all that is good, and from believing that in Latin war is called *bellum* – 'fair' – not by antiphrasis (as has been conjectured by some pickers-over of old Latin scrap-iron), because in warfare, fair things are found not, but absolutely and straightforwardly because in warfare all species of the fair and good do appear whilst all species of the evil and ugly are spurned. To prove which, mark that the wise and pacific king Solomon found no better way of describing divine Wisdom than by likening her to an army set in battle array.

So since I was not assigned or allotted by our people to any rank on the offensive side – being reckoned too weak and infirm – nor employed on the other – defensive – side (were it but bearing hod, digging bog, [binding rod] or turning sod: it's all the same to me!) I accounted it more than a moderate disgrace to appear an idle spectator of so many valiant, able and chivalrous personages who, in a spectacle staged before the whole of Europe, were acting out their parts in that remarkable play and tragic drama whilst I never bestirred myself nor devoted to it that 'nothing' which is all that is left to me. For small honour accrues, I think, to those who merely look on, husband their forces, hide away their money, secrete their silver and scratch their heads with one finger like vulgar louts, yawn at the flies like a parson's veal-calves and at the song of the music-makers simply prick up their ears like asses in Arcady, tacitly signifying by their looks that they approve of the roles being played.

Having made that choice and election, I thought that I would be doing a task neither useless nor inopportune if I trundled my Diogenic barrel (which alone remains to me after my past shipwreck in the Narrows of Ill-encounter). But what shall I achieve, do you think, by traipsing about with my barrel? By that Virgin who tugged her skirts right up, I still have no idea![3]

Wait a bit while I take a swig from this bottle: it is my one true Helicon, my Caballine stream, my sole breath of Enthusiasm. While drinking from it I deliberate, ponder, resolve and conclude. After the peroration I laugh, write, compose and drink. Ennius wrote as he drank and drank as he wrote; Aeschylus (if you trust Plutarch in his *Symposiaca*) composed as he drank, drank as he composed; Homer never wrote fasting: Cato never wrote before drinking: so you cannot say I live without the example of men praised and highly esteemed. The wine is good and cool enough, say just above the threshold of the second degree. For which may God, the good God Sabaoth (of Armies, that is) be forever praised.

If you fellows also discreetly take one big swig or two little swigs at it I can see nothing wrong in that, provided that you thank God just one tiny bit for everything.

Since such is my lot or my destiny – for we cannot all enter Corinth and dwell there – I am determined to serve one and all. Far from me to be sluggish and idle. As for the pioneers, the sappers and the men strengthening the ramparts, I shall do what Neptune and Apollo did in Troy under Laomedon, and

3.   Perhaps an allusion to Mary the Egyptian.

what Renaud de Montauban did in the last days of his life: I will wait upon the masons, boil up for the masons and, once the meal is over, juggle up on my pipes a jig for the jongleurs.

[Thus by sounding his lyre in days of yore did Amphion found, build and extend the great and celebrated city of Thebes.]

For those fighting-men I am going to broach my barrel again. From the draught I shall draw off (which would have been very well known to you from my two earlier volumes if the falsifications of printers had not perverted and corrupted them) I shall pour out for those men a good *Third* and merry *Quart* of Pantagruelic Sentences from the cru of our epicene pastimes. You may rightly dub them Diogenic. And since I cannot be their comrade-in-arms, they shall have me as their loyal Ruler-of-the-Feast, refreshing them to the limits of my puny powers when they return from the fray, and (as I insist) the tireless eulogizer of their exploits and glorious feats of arms.

By God's own passion-flower I shall not fail in this, unless Mars fails to turn up in Lent: but the old fornicator will take care not to do that!

Yet I recall having read that Ptolemy, the son of Lagus, displayed to the Egyptians one day in an open amphitheatre, a Bactrian camel amongst the spoils and booty of his conquests – it was entirely black – and with it a parti-coloured slave, half black, half white, not divided at the diaphragm (like that woman consecrated to the Indic Venus who was discovered by the philosopher Apollonius of Tyana somewhere between the river Hydaspes and the Caucasus) but perpendicularly, things never seen before in Egypt. He hoped by the gift of such novelties to increase the people's love for him.

But what happened?

When the camel was produced everyone was horrified and affronted; at the sight of the parti-coloured man some scoffed while others loathed him as a ghastly monstrosity produced by some defect of Nature. In short the hope he had had of pleasing his Egyptians and so increasing their natural affection for him slipped through his fingers, and he learnt that they took more pleasure and delight in things which are beautiful, elegant and perfect than in things ridiculous and monstrous. He subsequently felt such contempt for both the slave and the camel that (from neglect and lack of ordinary care) they soon bartered life for death.

That example makes me waver between hope and fear, dreading that instead of anticipated pleasure I find what I abhor: that my treasure be nothing but coal-dust and that my knucklebones throw up not Venus but the Shaggy Dog; that instead of serving I offend; instead of pleasing I displease, and that my lot be that of Euclion's cockerel (made so famous amongst others by Plautus in his *Aulularia* and Ausonius in his *Gryphus*) which scratched up the treasure only to have its slizzard git!

Were that to happen to me, should I get mad? It happened before: it could happen again. But by Hercules it will not, for I recognize in all of them a specific form and an individual property which our elders called *pantagruelism*, by means of which they will never take in bad part anything they know to flow from a good, frank and loyal heart. I have seen them regularly accept good-will as payment and, when attributable to weak resources, be satisfied with it.

Having dispatched that matter, to my barrel I return. Companions, tackle the wine! Drink, my lads, by the jugful. But if it does not seem good to you, leave it alone. I'm not one of those importunate Switzers who, by force, violence and brutality, oblige their fellows to swill down their wine in a bottoms-up carouse. Any good drinker, any good sufferer from the gout coming thirsty to this my barrel need not drink from it if he doesn't want to. If any do want to, and if the wine be pleasing to the lordliness of their lordships, then let them drink frankly, freely and boldly, without payment and without stint. Such is my decree.

And there is no need to fear that the wine will run out as it did at that wedding at Cana in Galilee. As much as you draw off from the bung I shall funnel in through the lid. And thus will the barrel remain inexhaustible. It has a living spring, an everlasting stream: such was the liquor represented figuratively by the Brahmin sages which was held in the goblet of Tantalus; such was that mountain of salt in Iberia so celebrated by Cato;

such was the golden bough sacred to the goddess of the Underworld and so highly celebrated by Virgil. It is a real cornucopia
of joy and merriment. If it seems at times to be drained to the
lees, it will not have run dry: good hope lies there at the bottom
as in Pandora's bottle, not despair as in the cask of the Danaïds.

Now mark well what I have said and what sort of people I
invite. For (let nobody be misled) I am following the example
of Lucilius, who proclaimed that he wrote only for his own
townsmen of Tarento and Cosenza: my barrel I have broached
for you alone, [good folk,] my best-vintage drinkers and gouty
men of good alloy. Gigantic, fog-swallowing, munch-bribe
magistrates are already occu-pied-arsed enough, with bundles
enough on their hooks to serve as venison. Let them toil away
at it if they want to: there are no game-birds for them here. And
I beg you – by the venerated name of the four cheeks which
begot you and of the life-giving peg which then coupled them
together – never mention to me those doctorally bonneted legal
brains sieving through their amendments. And black-beetle
hypocrites even less, despite their all being outrageous drinkers
and scab-encrusted syphilitics, furnished with an unquenchable
thirst and an insatiable desire to masticate. Why? Because,
though they sometimes counterfeit mendicants, they are not on
the side of the Good but of Evil – indeed of that Evil which we
daily pray God to deliver us from. But you can never teach an
old monkey to pull a pretty face! Back, you curs! Out of my
way, out of my sunshine you fiendish monklings. Are you
coming here to arse about, drawing up arse-tickles against my
wine and pissing all over my barrel? Look! Here is the cudgel
which Diogenes ordered in his will to be laid beside him after
his death in order to beat off and belabour such corpse-burning
grubs and Cerberean mastiffs. Sheep-dogs, look to your flocks!
And you black-beetles. In the devil's name get out! Still there?
I renounce my share of Papimania if I can catch you! Grr, grrr,
grrrrrr. Get 'em, boy! Get 'em. May you never shit save when
lashed by stirrup-leather, [never piss save when on the strappado,] and never get it up except through a good cudgelling.

How Pantagruel shipped Utopians off to colonize Dipsody

CHAPTER I

[A lesson in colonization. It sets off the new Pantagruel as a princely statesman. A biblically based smile is again aroused by the New Testament practice of numbering crowds 'not counting women and children'.

'Ruling with a rod of iron' is biblical too (Revelation 2:27), but the references and tone overall are markedly Classical: Rabelais draws upon Cicero, Plutarch and Hesiod. Virgil is cited in French (Georgics, IV, 561) and Homer is directly alluded to (Iliad, I, 375 and IV, 236). There are continued debts to Erasmus, including to the Adages *(II, I, XCIV, 'On not remembering evils', and I, VII, LXXII, 'Things acquired badly perish badly'.]*

Once Pantagruel had entirely subdued the land of Dipsody he planted there a colony of Dipsodians numbering 9876543210 men (not counting the women and children), skilled workmen in all the trades and gentlemen professing all the liberal disciplines in order to reinvigorate, people and grace that country which was but a sparsely peopled and partly uninhabited land without them.

He moved them there not so much because of the over-population of Utopia, where men and women had indeed multiplied like locusts – without my going further into detail you are quite aware that the men of Utopia had genitals so prolific, and the women of Utopia wombs so ample, voracious, retentive and well-constructed of cells that at the end of every ninth month seven children at least, both male and female, were born of each marriage following the example of the people of Israel in Egypt, unless de Lyra was delirious; not so much, either, because of the fertility of the soil, the healthiness of the climate and the attractiveness of the land of Dipsody, but rather so as to keep that land dutiful and obedient by newly resettling there his old and faithful subjects who, from time immemorial, had never known, recognized or admitted any lord but him and who, as soon as they were born into this world, had with their mothers' milk been suckled on the sweetness and generosity of his rule, being forever infused with it and brought up on it, which gave a firm hope that they would rather abandon their bodily lives than that unique and primary duty which is owed by nature to monarchs by their subjects, no matter where they might be resettled or transplanted. And not only would they and the generations successively born to their blood live like that, but they would also maintain in the same feudal obedience the peoples freshly added to his empire.

That did indeed happen and he was in no wise frustrated in his plans. For although the Utopians had been loyal and faithful subjects before that colonization, the Dipsodians became even more so after having spent but a few days among them, on account of that curious zeal which comes naturally to all human beings at the beginning of any enterprise which they concur in; but they did have one complaint: they called on the heavens and the Intelligences which move the spheres to witness their regret at not having had the renown of Pantagruel brought sooner to their notice.

You will therefore, you drinkers, take note that the way to hold and uphold a newly conquered land is not (as has been to their shame and dishonour the erroneous opinion of certain tyrannical minds) by pillaging, crushing, press-ganging, impoverishing and provoking the people, ruling them with a rod of iron: in short, by gobbling them up and devouring them, like the wicked king whom Homer dubs *Demoboros*, that is, Devourer of his people.

I shall not quote to you the ancient histories on this matter; I will simply recall to your minds what your fathers saw, and you too if you are not too young. Like new-born babes they should be suckled, dandled and amused; like newly planted trees they should be supported, secured and protected against every wind, harm and injury; like convalescents saved from a long and serious illness they should be spoiled, spared and given strength, in order that they themselves should conceive the opinion that there is no king or prince in the world whom they would less want for a foe, more desire for a friend. Thus did Osiris, that great king of the Egyptians, conquer the entire earth, not so much by force of arms as by reducing drudgery, teaching folk how to lead good healthy lives, giving appropriate laws and by benevolence and graciousness. For which everyone (by a commandment of Jupiter given to a certain Pamyla) surnamed him the great King *Euergetes* (that is, Benefactor).

In fact Hesiod in his *Theogony* classes good daemons – call them angels [or Geniuses] if you so prefer – as intermediaries and mediators between the gods and men, superior to men but inferior to gods. And because the blessings and riches of Heaven reach us via their hands, and because they are always beneficent to us, continually preserving us from harm, he says that they perform the duties of kings, it being a uniquely royal action always to do good and never to do ill.

Thus did Alexander of Macedon become the emperor of the whole world; thus was Hercules possessed of all the mainland, delivering mankind from monsters, oppression, exactions and tyrannies, governing and treating them well, maintaining them in equity and justice, founding for them benign constitutions and laws appropriate to the site of each country, supplying what was lacking, turning to profit whatever was abundant, forgiving the past and casting all previous offences into eternal oblivion: such, after the tyrants were overthrown by the bravery and industry of Thrasybulus, was the 'amnesty' of the Athenians which was later expounded in Rome by Cicero and restored under the emperor Aurelian.

Those are the love-filters, spells and charms by which one peacefully retains what has been painfully conquered. And no conqueror can more happily reign – be he king, prince or philosopher – than by making justice follow hard upon valour. His valour was manifested in victory and conquest: his justice will be manifested when, with the love and good will of the people, he makes laws, publishes decrees, establishes religious ceremonies and treats each person aright; as the noble poet Virgil says of Octavian Augustus:

> Victorious, he founded laws, and meant
> The vanquished to obey them by consent.

That is why Homer in his *Iliad* calls good princes and kings *Kosmetoras laon*, that is to say, Ornaments of their Peoples.

Such was the intention of Numa Pompilius, the second king of the Romans, a just man, an urbane ruler and a philosopher, when he ordained that nothing that had died was to be sacrificed to the god Terminus on his festal day (which was called the *Terminalia*): he was showing them that the *termini* – the frontiers and the marches of kingdoms – should be guarded and governed in peace, friendship and courtesy, without staining one's hands with blood or pillage. Whoever does otherwise will not only lose what he has acquired but also suffer the stigma and opprobrium of being judged to have wrongly and evilly acquired it, as a consequence of its having perished in his hands. Thing evilly acquired evilly expires. Even though he might peacefully enjoy it throughout his own lifetime, if it perished under his heirs the dead man will suffer the same stigma and his reputation will be accursed as that of an evil conqueror, for you have a common proverbial saying, *Thing evilly acquired the third heir ne'er enjoys*.

And, you enfeoffed sufferers from the gout, note how, in that way, Pantagruel made one angel into two, which is the opposite to what happened to Charlemagne, who made two devils out of one when he planted the Saxons in Flanders and the Flemish in Saxony: for, not being able to keep in subjection the Saxons whom he had annexed to the Empire and restrain them from breaking out into rebellion at any moment every time he was diverted into Spain or some other far-off lands, he transported them to a country of his which was naturally loyal, namely Flanders, whilst the inhabitants of Hainault and Flanders, who were his natural subjects, he transported to Saxony, never doubting of their fealty even after they had migrated to foreign lands. But it transpired that the Saxons persisted in their rebelliousness and original obstinacy, and the Flemings, now dwelling in Saxony, became imbued with the manners and waywardness of the Saxons.

How Panurge was made the Châtelain of Salmagundi in Dipsody, eating his corn when 'twas but grass

CHAPTER 2

[In Gargantua *it was Alcofrybas (the 'author' of the tale) who was given Salmagundi. Here it is given to Panurge, who, greatly changed from the trickster of* Pantagruel *– he never appears in* Gargantua *of course – is now the spinner of words and arguments who can twist the most hallowed moral maxims so as to justify imprudence, profligacy and a contempt for thrift. He is so wrong-headed that he even admires the Sorbonne! 'To eat one's corn in the blade' (that is, 'when it is but grass') is the height of imprudence and folly. (Similarly for a landowner to cut down his tall trees was a sign of dire poverty.)*

A 'bishop – or, what amounts to the same thing, his beneficed income – for a year' is gobbled up by the annates *(the obligatory payment of his first year's income to his patrons).*

Cato the Censor, in his book On Agriculture, *teaches that a prudent householder should always produce and sell more than he buys.*

A celebrated maxim of Plato, cited by Cicero and so enjoying the support of the great Greek and of the great Roman, held that 'We are not born for ourselves alone, but of our birth our country demands a part and our friends demand a part.' Panurge can abuse even such a maxim, which Erasmus says is one of the most famous of all (Adages, IV, VI, LXXXI, 'No one is born for himself').

The Roman sumptuary laws cited with approval by Pantagruel derive from Macrobius (Saturnalia, III, 17) supplemented by the commentary of Erasmus on another adage (I, IX, XLIV, 'He did a Protervia').

The Thomas Aquinas of legend was said to have finished composing a hymn to Christ in his head just as he was also finishing a dish of lamprey. When, to allude to his hymn, he quoted aloud one of Christ's last words on the Cross, 'It is finished', the shocked bystanders thought he was referring to his lamprey.

Rabelais plays on the Latin etymology of dilapidate, *which is a compound of* lapis, *a stone.]*

In establishing the order of government in the whole of Dipsody Pantagruel assigned to Panurge the castellany of Salmagundi, worth an assured annual income of 6789106789 golden royals in cash, apart from an unsure income from cockchafers and snails which, year in year out, amounted to between 2435768 and 2435769 of those ducats stamped with a long-fleeced sheep. Occasionally, when it was a good year for snails and there was a run on cockchafers, the total reached 1234554321 seraphs. Not every year, though.

Now my Lord the new Châtelain managed things so well and so wisely that in less than a fortnight he had dilapidated both the assured and unsure income for the next three years. He did not, as you might say, literally dilapidate it by founding monasteries, erecting chapels, building colleges and hospitals nor, indeed by casting his bacon to the dogs, but spent it rather on hundreds of little banquets and jolly parties open to all-comers, particularly to good fellows, young girlies and big cuddly women, chopping down his timber, burning their trunks to sell the cinders, borrowing in advance, buying dear and selling cheap, and eating his corn when 'twas but grass.

When Pantagruel was informed of this he was, in himself, neither indignant, angry nor troubled. I have told you before and tell you again: he was the best little giant of a fellow who ever girded himself with a sword. He took everything in good part: every deed he interpreted favourably. He never tormented himself: he never took offence. He would moreover have quitted the God-made mansion of Reason if he had been otherwise saddened or depressed: for all the goods which the heavens cover and this earth contains in all its dimensions – height, depth, length or breadth – are not worth stirring our emotions or troubling our wits or our minds. He simply drew Panurge aside and gently pointed out to him that, if he chose to live that way without being otherwise thrifty, it would be impossible or, at the very least, hard to make him rich.

'Rich!' Panurge replied. 'Have you fixed your mind on that? Have you worried about making me rich in this world? Ye gude God and gude men all, think about living joyfully! Let there be no other care, no other concern within the sacrosanct mansion of your Heaven-given brain. Let its calm never be troubled by clouds of thought thickened by worry and care. As long as you are alive, joyful, merry and bright I shall be more than rich.

'All the world is crying, Thrift! Thrift! But some talk of thrift who have no idea what it is. Counsel should be taken from me. By me you would then be advised that what is imputed to me as a vice is done in imitation of the University and Parlement of Paris, places wherein dwell the true stream and living Idea of Pantheology (and of all justice too). He who doubts that and does not firmly believe it is a heretic. For they, in one single day, gobble up their bishop – or, what amounts to the same thing, his beneficed income – for a year, and sometimes for two: that is on the day he is inducted. No excuse, unless he would be instantly lapidated.

'I am also acting in accordance with the four cardinal virtues:

i: *Prudence:* by taking money in advance. Who knows who will be alive and kicking? Who knows whether this world will last for another three years! And even if it does, is there any man so daft as to promise himself to live three years more?

> No man is by the gods made sure
> That he shall see one morrow more.

ii: *Justice:*

– *Commutative*, by buying dear (I mean on credit) and selling cheap (for ready cash). What does Cato write on the subject in his book on husbandry? *The paterfamilias*, he says, *must be a constant vendor.* By which he means it is impossible for him not to be rich in the end, so long as there remain any goods in his barns.

– *Distributive*, by providing fodder for good (note *good*) and noble companions whom Fortune has tossed like Ulysses on to the Rock of Good Appetite with no provision of eatables; and for girlies who are good (note *good*) and young (note *young*), for, according to the judgement of Hippocrates, youth is intolerant of hunger especially when vivacious, jolly, bouncy and full of fun. Which girlies are willing and delighted to give pleasure to all fine fellows; so Platonic and Ciceronian are they

that they regard themselves as having been born into this world
not for themselves alone, but, of their very persons, they keep
a part for their country and a part for their friends.

iii: *Fortitude:* by chopping down trees like a second Milo;
felling those darkling forests (which serve as lairs for wolves,
wild-boars and foxes, and as dens for brigands and murderers,
mole-holes for assassins, workshops for counterfeiters and
hideaways for heretics) and flattening them into open moors
and beautiful wastelands, fiddling with my tall trees and preparing seats for Doomsday eve.

iv: *Temperance:* eating my corn when 'tis but grass; living
like a hermit on roots and salad-leaves, freeing myself from
sensual appetites and so putting money aside for the crippled
and them that suffer. And by so doing I economize on the
hoeing – which costs money – on the harvesters, who like a
tipple without water, and on the gleaners, who have to be given
fouaces, on threshers, who (as is authoritatively said by Virgil's
Thestylis) never leave a single bulb of garlic, onion or shallot
in your gardens; on the millers, who are normally thieves, and
on bakers, who are not much better.

'Are those negligible savings, apart from the depredations of
field-mice, the grain rotting in barns and the nibbling of weevils
and termites?

'From corn when 'tis yet but grass you can make a lovely
green sauce: it is easily concocted and readily digested; it
enlivens your brain, gladdens your animal spirits, delights your
sight, whets your appetite, flatters your taste-buds, steels your
heart, tickles your palate, clarifies your complexion, tones up
your muscles, tempers the blood, lightens the diaphragm, fresh-
ens up the liver, unbungs the spleen, comforts the kidneys,
settles the bladder, limbers up the spondyls, voids the ureters,
dilates the spermatic vessels, tightens up the genital sinews,
purges the bladder, swells the genitals, retracts the foreskin,
hardens the glans and erects the member; it improves the belly
and makes you break wind, fart, let off, defecate, urinate,
sneeze, hiccup, cough, gob, spew, yawn, dribble snot, breathe
deep, breathe in, breathe out, snore, sweat, and get your gimlet
up, together with hundreds of other extraordinary benefits.'

'I well understand you,' said Pantagruel; 'you conclude that those who are not very bright could never spend so much in so short a time. You are not the first to conceive that heresy. Nero maintained it and admired above all other human beings his uncle Gaius Caligula who, in a few days, with remarkable inventiveness, had managed to squander all the treasure and patrimony which Tiberius had bequeathed to him.

'So (instead of [keeping and] observing the Roman sumptuary laws regulating food and dress:

the lex Orchia,
the lex Fannia,
the lex Didia,
the lex Licinia,
the lex Cornelia,
the lex Lefridania,
the lex Antia,
and the laws of the Corinthians,

by which each person was rigorously forbidden to spend *per annum* more than his annual income) you have performed a *Protervia* – *Protervia* being for the Romans what the Pascal Lamb is for the Jews: everything edible had to be eaten and all the rest cast into the fire, keeping nothing back for the morrow.

'I can rightly say of you what Cato said of Albidius, who, after devouring by his extravagant expenditure everything he possessed, had nothing left but his house, so he set fire so as to be able to say, "It is finished," as was subsequently said by Saint Thomas Aquinas when he had consumed a whole lamprey. Not that it matters.'

How Panurge makes a eulogy of
debtors and borrowers

CHAPTER 3

[Panurge will never be out of debt.

Marsilio Ficino in a famous Commentary on Plato's Symposium *made the whole universe cohere in mutual love: Panurge twists that platonizing ideal of mutual loving dependency and applies it to his self-loving, one-way debts, never to be repaid.*

To claim to be a creator, sensu stricto, is to claim to be God.

Hesiod in his Works and Days *famously places virtue serenely on a plateau at the top of a mountain, only to be reached by toiling up a stony path. Once reached, Virtue is a source of constant delight. (Rabelais returns seriously to the theme in the* Fourth Book, *Chapter 57.)*

Especially perhaps for Renaissance Platonists, Man is a microcosm, a 'little world' corresponding to the great world which is the Macrocosm.

Erasmus is again present through the Adages: I, I, LXX, *'Man is a wolf to man', and I, I, IV, LXXIV, 'To fish in the air, to hunt in the sea' (that is, to give oneself useless trouble, or, to attempt the impossible).*

One of Aesop's most famous fables tells how the other members, selfishly conspiring against the stomach, are shown that they are wrong. Throughout these chapters Panurge is flouting the wisdom summarized by Erasmus in the adage I, VI, LXXXVIII, 'Live within your own harvest'. Cf. also the adages later exploited in Chapter 25.]

'But,' Pantagruel asked, 'when will you be out of debt?'

'At the Greek Kalends,' Panurge replied, 'when all the world is happy and when you can inherit from yourself!

'God forbid that I should ever be out of debt! For then I would find nobody to lend me a penny. Who leaven leaves not at the eve: no risen dough hath in the morn! Always owe somebody something, then he will be forever praying God to grant you a good, long and blessèd life. Fearing to lose what you owe him, he will always be saying good things about you in every sort of company; he will be constantly acquiring new lenders for you, so that you can borrow to pay him back, filling his ditch with other men's spoil.

'In days of yore in Gaul when, by decree of the Druids, the serfs, servants and attendants were burnt alive at the funerals and obsequies of their lords and masters, were they not greatly afraid that their lords and masters should die? For they had to die with them. Were they not incessantly beseeching their great god Mercury, with Dis, the Father of the ducat, long to preserve them in good health? Were they not concerned to treat and serve them well? For then they could at least live together until they died.

'Believe me, your creditors, all the more fervently, will pray God that you should live and fear lest you should die: more than the hand they love the hand-out, and more than their lives, their pennies. Witness those money-lenders of Landerousse who recently hanged themselves when they saw the price of corn and wine take a plunge as the good weather came back.'

Pantagruel making no reply, Panurge went on:

'True Gosh! When I think of it, you are trying to drive me into a corner by holding my debts and creditors against me. By Jove! For that one quality I considered myself to be venerable, revered and awesome, since despite the opinion of all the philosophers (who say nothing can be made from nothing), I, who possess nothing – no primeval matter – have been a Maker, a Creator.

'I have created. What? Why, all those lovely nice lenders. A lender – I maintain, up to the stake, exclusively – is a creature both lovely and nice. He who nothing lends is a creature unlovely and nasty, a creation of the great villainous divel in Hell.

'And make what? Why debts! – O thing most rare and with the patina of Antiquity! – Debts, I say, exceeding the number of syllables resulting from the combination of all the consonants with all the vowels, which was long ago cast and calculated by that noble man Xenocrates. If you estimate the perfection of debtors from the multitude of their lenders you will not go wrong in applied mathematics.

'Can you imagine how good I feel each morning when I see all those lenders around me, so humble, obsequious and prodigal with their bowings, or when I note that, should I bestow a more open countenance or a more cheerful welcome on one rather than the others, the scoundrel believes he will be paid off first and be the first in the queue, taking my smile for ready cash. I feel that I am still playing God in the passion-play at Saumur, accompanied by his angels and cherubims, that is by my guardian spirits, my disciples, supplicants, petitioners and perpetual bedesmen. And I took it for true (once I saw that everybody nowadays has such a fervent, strident longing to make debts and lenders new) that the mountain of the heroic virtues described by Hesiod – I got top marks for him in my degree – consisted of debts, to which all human beings are seen to aim and aspire but few can climb because of the ruggedness of the path.

'Not all who would can be debtors: not all who would can create lenders. And you want to boot me out of such downy felicity!

'Worse still: I give myself to bonnie Saint Bobelin if all my life I have not reckoned debts to be, as it were, a connection and colligation between Heaven and Earth (uniquely preserving the lineage of Man without which, I say, all human beings would soon perish) and perhaps to be that great World Soul which, according to the Academics, gives life to all things.

'That it really is so, evoke tranquilly in your mind the Idea and Form of a world – take if you like the thirtieth of the worlds imagined by Metrodorus [or the seventy-eighth imagined by Petron] – in which there were no debtors or lenders at all. A universe sans debts! Amongst the heavenly bodies there would be no regular course whatsoever: all would be in disarray. Jupiter, reckoning that he owed no debt to Saturn, would dispossess him of his sphere, and with his Homeric chain hold in suspension all the Intelligences, gods, heavens, daemons, geniuses, heroes, devils, earth, sea and all the elements; Saturn would ally himself to Mars and throw all that world into perturbation. Mercury would no longer bind himself to serve the others and would no longer be their *Camillus* (as he was dubbed in the Etruscan tongue), being in no wise indebted to them. No longer would Venus be venerated, for she would have lent nothing. The Moon would remain dark and bloody: why should the Sun share his light with her? He was under no obligation to her. The Sun would never shine on their Earth: the heavenly bodies would pour no good influences down upon it, since that Earth refrained from lending them food in the form of mists and vapours by which they are fed (as Heraclitus stated, the Stoics proved and Cicero affirmed).

'Between the elements there will be no mutual sharing of qualities, no alternation, no transmutation whatsoever: one will not think itself obliged to the other: it has lent it nothing. From earth no longer will water be made, nor water transmuted into air; from air fire will not be made, and fire will not warm the earth. Earth will bring forth nothing but monsters, Titans, [Aloidae,] giants. The rain will not rain, the light will shed no light, the wind will not blow, and there will be no summer, no autumn. Lucifer will tear off his bonds and, sallying forth from deepest Hell with the Furies, the Vengeances and the hornèd devils, will seek to turf the gods of both the greater and the lesser nations out from their nests in the heavens.

'That world which lends nothing will then be no better than a dog-fight, than a brawl more unruly than the ones for the Rector of Paris, than a devil-play more disorderly than in the mysteries at Doué. Amongst human beings none will save another; it will be no good a man shouting *Help! Fire! I'm drowning! Murder!* Nobody will come and help him. Why? Because he has lent nothing: and no one owes him anything. No one has anything to lose by his fire, his shipwreck, his fall or his death. He has lent nothing. And: he would lend nothing either thereafter.

'In short, Faith, Hope and Charity will be banished from this world (for men are born to help and succour others). In their stead will succeed Distrust, Contempt and Rancour with their cohort of every misery, malediction and mischief. You will justly think that it is there that Pandora has emptied her bottle.

"Unto men, men wolves shall be," werewolves and hobgoblins, (as were Lycaon, Bellerophon and Nebuchadnezzar), brigands, assassins, poisoners, evil-doers, evil-thinkers, evil-willers, each hating all the others, such as were Ishmael, Metabus and Timon of Athens (who for that reason was surnamed *Misanthropos*). As a result, easier will it be for Nature to nourish fish in the air and feed stags in the depths of the ocean than to maintain such a lewd rascal of a World which lends nothing. Faith, how well I hate them.

'And then if you picture to yourself that other World, that microcosm which is Man formed after the model of that nasty, depressive World which never lends, you will find in him a terrifying turmoil. The head would not lend its eyesight to guide the feet and hands; the feet would not deign to carry the head; the hands would cease to work for it; the heart, angry at having to bestir itself to lend pulsations to the limbs, will no longer lend them anything; the lungs will no longer lend them their breathing; the liver no longer supply blood to maintain it; the bladder will decline to be debtor to the kidneys and urine will be suppressed; the brain, contemplating so disnatured a process, will drive itself raving mad, bestowing no sentiment on the sinews nor motion on the muscles.

'In short, in that disordered world, owing nothing, lending nothing, borrowing nothing, you will see a machination more pernicious than that which Aesop figured in his fable. And beyond a doubt he will perish: not only perish but very quickly perish, even if Aesculapius himself were there. And his body will soon become putrefied whilst his soul, all indignation, will flee to all the devils – all after my money.'

Panurge's eulogy of lenders and debtors: continued

CHAPTER 4

[More comic effrontery from Panurge, whose ideal world is one in which he alone borrows and never repays. Ficino's Commentary on Plato's Symposium *remains a template of the ideas which he abuses.*

So do the standard medical notions of those who follow Plato, Aris-
totle and Avicenna (rather than always following Galen) of how food
is digested and eventually refined into the 'animal spirits' (the spirits
of the anima, *the soul).*

The 'rete mirabile' is a supposed plexus of blood-vessels in the
cranium at the end of the carotid artery. It refined the animal spirits.
Rabelais holds to its existence, although Vesalius proved that it does
not exist in Man.

In the name of mutual love and collaboration Panurge is in fact
exemplifying philautia, *selfish love of self.*

Black bile is melancholia.

Medical theories of sexuality come to the fore again in Chapter 31.
Hippocrates held that semen is produced as Panurge says here. Galen
denied it. It is Panurge's misuse of good Classical ideas which is
skewed as here, not the ideas themselves (as Chapter 31 emphasizes).

The 'marriage debt' is the duty of husband and wife each to be
attentive to the reasonable sexual demands of the other.]

'On the contrary: now evoke for yourself a different world, a
world in which each one lends, each one owes, where all are
debtors, all are lenders.

'O! amongst the regular motions of the heavens what harmony there will be! I believe I can hear it as well as Plato once
did.[4]

'What sympathy between the elements! O how Nature will
delight in the fruits she there brings forth: Ceres laden with
corn, Bacchus with wine, Flora with flowers, Pomona with
fruit: Juno, health-giving, delightful, and all serene in her air
serene!

'I lose myself in such contemplation. Between human beings,
from hand to hand there would trot peace, love, affection,
faithfulness, repose, banquets, feastings, joy, happiness, gold,

4. Plato never claims that he heard the music of the spheres, nor that it can
be heard. The contention is, rather, Pythagorean. Plato, *Republic*, 617
B–C does have the Siren in each Sphere uttering one note each which
together produce a single harmony. Aristotle does not believe either that
we can hear such music. (See *On the Heavens*, 290 B, 12.) Cf. below,
Chapter 17 of the Fifth Book.

silver, petty cash, necklaces, rings and merchandise. No lawsuits: no wars: no contentions: there, no one will be a usurer,
no one rapacious, no one tight-fisted, no one will ever turn you
down. True God! Will it not be the Age of Gold, the Reign of
Saturn, the Idea of those Olympic regions in which all other
virtues cease while Charity reigns, rules, directs and triumphs
alone? Everybody will be good, everyone beautiful, everyone
just.

'O happy world! O inhabitants of that happy world. O folk
thrice and four times blessèd! I think I am there already! I swear
to you by our Good Gosh that if in that world, [that blessèd
world, thus lending to all and refusing none,] they had a pope
abounding in cardinals and in fellowship with his Sacred College, then in the space of a few years you would see saints more
thick on the ground, working more miracles, with more vows,
lessons, banners and candles than all the saints of the nine
bishoprics of Brittany, excepting only Saint Ives.

'Consider, I beg you, how that noble fellow Pathelin wished
to render immortal the father of Guillaume Jousseaulme and
raise him by his sanctifying prayers even to the Third Heaven:
he said nothing except:

> . . . and his goods he would lend
> To those who wished for cash to spend.

How beautifully put!

'After such a model imagine this our microcosm, [i.e., this
little world which is Man,] with all his members borrowing,
lending, owing: that is to say, Man in his natural state. For
Nature created Man but to lend and to borrow. The harmony
of the heavens will not be grander than the harmony of his
polity.

'The intention of the Founder of this microcosm is to maintain therein its soul, whom he has placed within as its host, its
life. Now life consists in blood. Blood is the seat of the soul.
That is why one single task weighs down upon this microcosm:
continually to forge blood. And in that forging all its members
are in their proper roles, their hierarchy being such that each

borrows from the other, each lends to the other. The material – the substance – proper to be transmuted into blood is supplied by Nature: bread and wine. Within those two are comprehended every kind of food: hence the term *companage* in Gothick Provençal.

'It is to find, prepare and concoct them that the hands toil and that the feet walk and support the whole structure; the eyes oversee it; the appetite, within the orifice of the stomach, by means of a little black bile despatched by the spleen, warns it to load food into its oven: the tongue tastes it, the teeth chew it, the stomach receives it, digests it and turns it into chyle; the mesenteric arteries absorb from it what is good and proper (leaving aside the excrements which are voided through the expressly made conduits by an expulsive force) and convey it to the liver which at once transmutes it, turning it into blood.

'What joy do you think there to be amongst all those artisans once they have seen that golden stream which is their sole restorative! No greater is the joy of alchemists when, after long labours and vast trouble and expense, they see the metals transmuted in their furnaces. Whereupon each member readies itself and strives afresh to purify and refine that treasure. The kidneys strain out through the emulgent veins the fluid which you call urine and send it flowing down. There below it finds a specific vessel, the bladder, which voids it when appropriate. The spleen draws off the grounds and the lees which you call black bile. The gall-bag extracts from them the excess of yellow bile.

'The blood is then conveyed to another smithy to be further refined, that is, to the heart, which by means of its diastolic and systolic motions so well rarefies and calorifies it that it is brought to perfection by the right ventricle and dispatched to all the members through the veins. They – feet, hands, eyes, the lot – draw it to themselves and each in its own way finds nourishment in it: and so they which were lenders are turned into debtors. The heart, by means of the left ventricle, then renders it so refined that it is turned into what is called spiritous blood, which is then dispatched through the arteries to all the members in order to heat and ventilate the other kind of blood which is in the veins. The lungs ceaselessly keep it fresh with their lobes and bellows. Out of gratitude for this service the heart separates out the best of the blood and sends it back through the arterial vein. Lastly it is so refined within the *rete mirabile* that from it are eventually made the animal spirits thanks to which the soul imagines, discourses, judges, resolves, deliberates, ratiocinates and remembers.

'Golly! When I enter into the deep abyss of that lending, owing world, I am drowned, lost and lose my way! Believe you me: to lend is an act divine, and to owe is an heroic virtue.

'And that is still not all. This lending, owing, borrowing world is so benevolent that, as soon as its own alimentation is complete, it already thinks of lending to those who are yet unborn, and by that loan to multiply itself if it can and perpetuate itself in images like unto itself: that is, children. To which end each member pares off and cuts away a portion of its most precious nutriment and sends it down below. There Nature has prepared appropriate vessels and receptacles for it through which it descends to the genitals via long sinuous and flexile conduits; it receives its proper form and then finds private parts which, in both men and women, are appropriate to the conserving and perpetuating of the human race. All of which is achieved by loans and debts from one to another – hence the term, the marriage debt: for anyone who refuses it Nature establishes a punishment: an acrid torment amongst the members and madness amongst the senses; to the lender, as a reward, are assigned pleasure, joy and sensual delight.'

How Pantagruel loathes debtors and borrowers

CHAPTER 5

[Topics *is the title of a much-studied work by Aristotle, a compendium of which was given by Cicero. It formed a basis of education in an age which appreciated eloquence and skilled argument. But rhetoric and dialectic do not themselves lead to the truth. To overthrow the*

*perverse fluent ingenuity of Panurge one verse of Saint Paul suffices:
'Owe no man any thing, but to love one another' (Romans 13:8). The
words 'mutual love-and-affection' render that love which is* agape *(so
different from Panurge's self-love,* philautia*). Saint Paul is supported
by Plato (*Laws, *98) as cited by Plutarch in his treatise* On Avoiding
Usury. *Rabelais' big guns are out!*

*Apollonius of Tyana claimed to have encountered the Plague
personified: he found her horrifying.]*

'I understand you,' answered Pantagruel; 'you seem to me to
be good at your Topics and zealous for your cause; but preach
and patrocinate from now to Whitsuntide and you'll be amazed
to learn that you have failed in the end to persuade me. "Owe
no man anything," said the holy Apostle, "save mutual love-
and-affection." You are employing fine graphic terms and vivid
descriptions. I find them most enjoyable, but I can tell you this:
that if you picture for yourself a flagrant fraudster, a relentless
loan-taker, newly arriving in a town already warned of his way
of life, you will find that the townsfolk will be more agitated
and terrified by his arrival than if the Plague had arrived in
person, dressed as she was when the Philosopher of Tyana came
across her in Ephesus. And I am of the opinion that the Persians
were not in error when they judged lying to be the second vice,
the first being to run up debts, for debts and lies normally go
together.

'Yet I do not mean to infer that we must never owe, never
lend. None so rich but at times must owe: none so poor but at
times can lend. The time for it will be such as Plato states in his
Laws, where he rules that you should never allow neighbours
to draw water from your land before they had first trenched and
ditched their own meadows and found the soil called ceramite –
potter's earth, that is – without uncovering a source or even a
trickle of water; for that soil, by its substance, which is greasy,
tough, smooth and dense, retains humidity and does not easily
allow any [draining away or] evaporation. It is therefore a
great dishonour to be forever borrowing everywhere and from
everyone rather than working and earning. In my judgement

you should lend only when the person working has not been
able to derive any benefit from his labour, or when he has been
suddenly plunged into an unforeseen loss of his goods.

'So, change the subject, shall we? And from now on do not
be beholden to creditors.

'From your past debts I shall free you.'

'The least and the most I can do is to thank you,' said
Panurge; 'and if thanks are to be measured against the affection
of the benefactors, that will be endlessly, sempiternally: for
the love which you graciously bear me is beyond the dice of
judgement, it transcends all weight, number and measure; it is
infinite, sempiternal. Yet if you measure it against the calibre of
the gains and gratification of the recipients, it will be somewhat
slackly. You do many good things for me: much more than I
ought to receive from you; much more than I deserve; more
than my merits demand. That I must admit. But in this matter
nothing like as much as you may think. What grieves me, what
hurts me and gnaws at me is not that! But from henceforth,
now that I am free of debt, what shall I look like? Believe me.
I shall appear graceless during the first few months, seeing that
I am not used to it, not brought up to it. I am very much afraid
of it.

'Moreover, in all the land of Salmagundi, from this day forth
not one fart will be born which is not to be directed towards
my nose. For whenever they break wind, all the farters in the
world say, "That's for those who are out of debt!" My life will
soon come to an end: I can foresee that. I entrust my epitaph
to you. And I shall die, all peacefully pickled in farts. Should it
ever come to pass that the usual medicines fail to satisfy physicians seeking a restorative to enable good dames to break wind
when suffering from an extreme access of the gripes, powdered
mummy from my wretched be-farted body will be a ready
remedy for them. And taking the tiniest bit of it, they will fart
more than the physicians ever expected.

'That is why I would beseech you to leave me with a good
hundred or so debts, just as, when King Louis the Eleventh
had quashed all the lawsuits of Miles d'Illiers, the bishop of
Chartres, he was pressed to leave him just one to practise upon.

Why I'd rather pay them all off with my cockchafers and snails, without touching the capital though.'

'Let us drop the subject,' said Pantagruel. 'I have already told you once.'

Why newly married men were exempt from going to war

CHAPTER 6

[Rabelais seriously conflates two passages of the Mosaic Law: Deuteronomy 20:5–7 and 24:5. Rabelais uses the form 'Moses' not the traditional form 'Moïse'. It was condemned by some theologians of the Sorbonne.

Panurge on the other hand misuses and misapplies Scripture, twisting the sense of the Book of Life *in Revelation 13:8 and of the faithful men who are 'lively stones' to be 'built into a spiritual house', in I Peter 2:5.*

The story of Brother Screwum (in the French: Frère Enguainnant) *goes back to a tale of Poggio, but in his* Jests *ten virgins are concerned, not as here a hundred.*

'Courcaillet' and the 'Battle of Cornabons' remain unexplained, but may be a way of suggesting that Panurge will be a cuckold (with cornabon *loosely meaning 'good for horns').*

The final allusion to Galen is confused, Panurge mistaking Galen's On the Difficulty of Breathing *for his treatise* On the Use of Respiration. *There Galen in fact rejects the opinion attributed to him. A pure lapse or a learned joke?]*

'But,' asked Panurge, 'in which Law was it laid down and established that men who had planted a new vineyard, had built a new house or had newly wed, should be exempt from going to war for the first year?'

'In the Law of Moses,' replied Pantagruel.

'Why newly married men?' asked Panurge. 'I'm too old to worry about planters of vines – though I do agree that we should be concerned about the *vendangeurs* – while those fine

new builders of dead stones are not written in my Book of Life:
I build up only lively stones – men, that is.'

'As I judge it,' replied Pantagruel, 'it was to let them freely
enjoy love-making during that first year, working at establishing a family and producing heirs. If they were then killed in
battle during the second year, their names and family arms
would remain through their children; they would also know
for certain whether their wives were barren or fruitful – one
year seemed long enough for that, given the mature age at which
they married – so enabling them to arrange second marriages for
the wives after the death of their first husbands, bestowing the
fruitful on men who wished to multiply in children, and the
barren on those who did not wish to do so and would take
them for their virtues, knowledge and comeliness, purely for
solace at home and the running of their households.'

'The preachers at Varennes,' said Panurge, 'revile remarriages
as wanton and improper.'

'For them,' replied Pantagruel, 'they are like a strong dose of
quarten fever.'

'And so they are for Brother Screwum,' said Panurge, 'who,
when preaching against second marriages at Parillé, swore in
mid-sermon that he would give himself to the nimblest devil in
Hell if he would not rather deflower a hundred virgins than
cover one widow.'

'I find your reasons good and well-founded. But what if that
exemption were to have been granted them because they had
given their newly wedded darlings such a drumming during
that first year (as is right and proper) and so drained their
spermatic vessels that they themselves were left all floppy,
unmanned, feeble and flagging so that, come the day of battle,
they would rather go plunging down like ducks with the
baggage-train than go with the fighting-men and valiant
champions, there where Enyo harks on the fray and blows are
traded: they could never strike a worthwhile blow beneath the
banner of Mars since their mighty blows had already been well
aimed behind the bed-curtains of Venus, Mars' lady-love.

'That it is so, even now we can still see how, in all well-run
households, amongst the relics and vestiges of ancient times,

they send such newly wed husbands off (after Lord knows how many days) *to see their uncle*, in order to absent them from their wives, make them rest awhile and take on victuals the better to return to the fray, even though they often have neither aunt nor uncle; just as King Pétaud did not exactly dismiss us after the battle of Cornabons but sent Courcaillet and me back to our hearths. Courcaillet is still looking for his.

'When I was a little boy my grandad's godmother would sing to me:

> Saying a prayer and telling of beads
> Are meant for those who them do ken:
> A piper off to work in the meads
> Is twice the man trudging home again.

'What brings me to my opinion is this: that first year planters of vines could scarcely have eaten any grapes nor drunk any wine from their labours; nor could builders live in their newly constructed houses during the first year without the risk of dying of suffocation from a shortage of breath (as Galen learnedly notes in Book Two of *On Difficulties of Respiration*).

'If I asked you that, it was not without well-caused causation nor well-resonant reason. I hope you don't mind!'

How Panurge had a flea in his ear and gave up sporting his magnificent codpiece

CHAPTER 7

[As a mark of perpetual slavery, the Jewish master of a Jewish slave had to pierce the slave's ear if he refused his freedom after seven years' service (Deuteronomy 15:15ff.). In the time of Rabelais 'to have a flea in one's ear' meant to burn with lust. Panurge is the slave of his concupiscence.

Again the word-spinning of Panurge is answered by Pantagruel with a quotation from Saint Paul: this time Romans 15:5, one of the central texts favoured by liberal evangelicals and reformers: 'Let every man

be fully persuaded in his own mind'. Theologically and philosophi-
cally, that injunction is applied to 'things indifferent', that is, to every-
thing which, being neither good nor bad in itself, depends on one's
own mind. The mind itself, under grace, is the battle-ground of the
Evil Spirit versus the Good. For Christian liberals such monastic
institutions as celibacy, poverty and obedience were 'things indiffer-
ent', their value depending on how they were conceived and practised.
In the Renaissance as in Classical and Christian Antiquity the heart
was primarily the seat of thought not of the emotions.

There is a traditional, untranslatable pun on à propos *(with the*
same sense as in English) and âpre aux pots *(bitter to poes).*

A further pun plays on bureau, *brown 'bureau-cloth', and* bureau
in the sense of a desk in the Treasury (the Cour des Comptes*).*]

The next morning Panurge had his right ear pierced in the
Jewish style and hung from it a small golden ring inlaid with
silver-thread; in its culet was set a flea. Now (so that you shall
be in no doubt, for it is a fine thing always to be well informed)
that flea was black and the upkeep of it, duly accounted for,
amounted to hardly less per quarter than the nuptials of an
Hyrcanian tigress – say 600,000 Spanish pence. Once free of
debt he was annoyed by such an excessive outlay, thereafter
maintaining the flea in the manner of tyrants and lawyers: that
is, by the blood and sweat of those subjected to them. He
took four ells of coarse brown bureau-cloth and draped it over
himself like a long cloak with a single seam. He refrained from
wearing his trunk-hose and clipped a pair of spectacles on to
his bonnet. Thus arrayed, he appeared before Pantagruel, who
found his disguise very strange, especially since he could no
longer see the magnificent codpiece which was to Panurge a
sacred anchor, his last refuge from the shipwrecks of adversity.

Good-hearted Pantagruel could not fathom this mystery, so
he interrogated him, asking what he meant by such a proso-
popoea.

'I,' said Panurge, 'have got a flea in my ear: I want to get
married.'

'And good luck to you,' said Pantagruel; 'you have made me
most happy. But truly – though I would not swear to it on a

red-hot iron – it is not the style of lovers, is it, to wear their
hose dangling down, to let their shirt-tails hang over un-
breeched knees and to sport a long cloak of brown bureau-cloth
(which, amongst respectable and manly folk is an unusual
colour for ankle-length cloaks)? Although some followers of
peculiar sects and heresies once went thus accoutred (and
despite there being many who attributed that to charlatanism,
hypocrisy and a desire to impose upon simple folk) I nevertheless do not wish to condemn them nor to make an adverse
judgement on them.

'*Let every man be fully persuaded in his own mind,* especially
over things external, extraneous and indifferent, which are
neither good nor evil in themselves since they do not spring
from our hearts and thoughts which are the forge of all good
and all evil: good, if the emotions are good and governed by
the clean Spirit: evil, if the emotions are perverted out of equity
by the foul Spirit. I am however displeased by novelty and any
contempt for normal customs.'

'The colour,' said Panurge, 'is apropos – bitter to poes – it's
my *bureau*. From henceforth I mean to work on it and keep a
close eye on my affairs. You never saw a man as nasty as I shall
be, now I'm out of debt – unless God helps me.

'Look, here are my goggles. If you saw me from afar you
would rightly take me for Frère Jean Bourgeois: next year I
shall, I think, preach yet another crusade! Then God save our
bollocks.

'You see this brown bureau-cloth? Believe me: some occult
property resides in it, known only to a few! I just put it on this
morning, and I'm mad already, raging, and piping-hot to be
married and plough up my wife like a brown devil without fear
of a drubbing.

'O what a great head of my household I shall be! After my
death I shall be cremated on a pyre-of-honour, so as to have my
ashes as a memorial and exemplar of the perfect householder.
Crikey. My accountant had better not play about on my bureau,
stretching esses into efs – *sous* into *francs*! Otherwise blows
from my fist would trot all over his dial!

'Look at me, front and back: it's in the style of the toga, the ancient dress of the Roman in times of peace. I based the style of it on Trajan's column in Rome and on the triumphal arch of Septimius Severus too. I am weary of war, weary of soldiers' cloaks and tunics. My shoulders are all bowed down from wearing armour. May arms cease: may togas reign (at least for all the coming year if I get married, as you quoted to me yesterday from the Law of Moses). As for my breeches, my great aunt Laurence told me in days gone by that breeches were made for codpieces. That I do believe, using the same induction as that nice old twerp Galen in Book Nine of *On the Use of our Members*, where he says that the head was made for the eyes: for Nature could well have placed our heads in our laps or on our elbows, but, having ordained that eyes should discern things afar, she fixed them on to the head at the highest part of the body as on a pole, just as we find lighthouses and tall beacons erected high above our sea-ports so that their beams may be seen from afar.

'And since I would like to give myself a breather from the art of war – for a year at least – that is, to get married, I no longer wear a codpiece nor, consequently, my trunk-hose. For the codpiece is the primary item of a fighting man's armour. And I maintain up to the stake, (exclusively of course), that Turks are not properly clad in their armour, seeing that the wearing of codpieces is outlawed by their religion.'

How the codpiece is the primary item of armour amongst fighting-men

CHAPTER 8

[Rabelais has just mocked Galen on human sexuality. He is compared to Pathelin's aunt Laurence. Galen did indeed maintain that the head was made primarily for the eyes. Others maintained that it was made, more nobly, for the brain. Similarly Galen held and taught that the testicles form a 'principal member' so important that it would be preferable for a man to have no heart (the seat of thought as well as of emotions) than no testicles. The quarrel raged in the time of

Rabelais, for it centres on the production of semen: Galen – to the angry amusement of his opponents – held that semen was produced in and by the balls. Those who, like Rabelais, followed Hippocrates in this matter, believed that semen originated in all the principal members and, after descending the spinal column, was stored in (not produced by) the testicles. For Galen, the species is more important that the individual: for Hippocrates (and Rabelais who follows him) the perfecting of the individual man is more important that the good of the species. (That is less surely so for the individual woman. See below, Chapter 33.)

The discovery of the real nature of semen and its production lay a long way in the future. In the Renaissance the question was one of real actuality. Galen rejoiced that even idiots could produce semen and thus children: followers of Hippocrates did not, holding that semen should be sown responsibly and that the child, once born, be educated to resemble not merely his sire's body but his persona. *(See* Pantagruel, *Chapter 8, Gargantua's letter to his son.)*

For Man in his helpless state at birth Rabelais draws upon the preface to the Seventh Book of Pliny's Natural History *and, again, on* Erasmus *(Adages, IV, I, I, 'War is sweet to those who have not experienced it'). For Moses and his fig-leaf Panurge seeks to draw on the authority of Genesis 1.*

The priapic poem at the end appears in an anthology, Fleurs de la poésie françoyse, *of 1534.*

The works of Justinian and Chiabrena mentioned near the end are fictional. Chiabrena (in French, Shit-turds) sounds like a play on the Italian surname Chiabrera.]

'Do you wish to maintain,' said Pantagruel, 'that the codpiece is the primary item of fighting-armour? That is a very novel and paradoxical assertion, for we usually say that donning of armour begins with the spurs.'

'I do so maintain,' Panurge replied, 'nor am I wrong to do so. See how Nature, intending that the plants, trees, herbs and zoophytes created by her should endure and be perpetuated through all succeeding ages – the individuals dying but the species surviving – carefully clad in armour the seeds and buds in which such perpetuation lies; and so with remarkable cunning she furnished and covered them with pods, shucks, teguments, husks, calyxes, shells, spikes, egrets, skins or prickly spines, which form fine, sturdy, natural codpieces for them. Manifest examples are found in peas, beans, chick-peas, nuts, peaches, cotton, bitter-apples, corn, poppies, lemons, chestnuts: in all plants generally, in which we can clearly see that the seeds and buds are covered, protected and armour-clad more than any other part of them.

'Not so has Nature provided for the perpetuation of the human race: in the state of innocence, in the primeval Age of Gold, she created Man naked, tender, fragile, without offensive or defensive armour, as an animate being not a plant: an animate being, I say, born for peace not war, an animate being born for the mirific enjoyment of all fruit and vegetable life, an animate being born for peaceful dominion over all the beasts.

'When, with the succession of the Age of Iron – the Reign of Jupiter – there came an increase in wickedness between human beings, the earth began to bring forth nettles, thistles, thorns and other forms of revolt against Man on the part of vegetable life, and virtually all the animals, for their part, became fatally disposed to emancipate themselves from him and quietly conspired no longer to slave for him and no longer to obey him insofar as they could resist him, rather doing him harm according to their abilities and powers.

'Man therefore, desiring to maintain his original privileges and to prolong his original domination, and not being able easily to forego the servitude of many of the beasts, found it necessary to don some novel armour.'

'By Holy Goosequim!' exclaimed Pantagruel, 'since the last rains came you have developed into a great fill-up-it, Sir – I mean, philosopher!'

'Reflect,' said Panurge, 'how Nature inspired man to arm himself and which part of his body he first protected with armour. It was, by God's virtue, the balls.

> Sir Priapus, once he had done,
> Begged her no more, for he had won.

That is witnessed to by Moses, the Hebrew Captain and philosopher, who affirms that Man protected himself with a glorious and gallant codpiece, made – a most beautiful device! – from fig-leaves, which are in every way suited and naturally appropriate (by their strength, serrations, curl, sheen, size, colour, odour, quality and capacity) to the covering and protecting of balls (save only those horrifying balls of Lorraine which gallop unbridled down into the hose, loathing the mansion of proud codpieces and knowing nothing of good order: witness Viardière, that noble 'King' Valentin of Mardi Gras, whom I came across in Nancy one May-day when, in the name of elegance, he was scrubbing his balls spread out on a table in the manner of a Spanish cloak). So, unless you want to talk incorrectly, you should no longer say when you send a train-band soldier off to the wars, *Look after your wine-jar, Tévot!* – your noddle, that is – but, by all the devils in Hell, *Look after your milk-jug, Tévot!* – that is, your balls. Lose your head, and only an individual has perished: lose your balls, and there would perish the whole human race. That is what moved the gallant Claudius Galen (in Book One of *On Semen*) boldly to conclude that it would be better to have no heart than no testicles – by *better* meaning *less bad* – for in them consists, as in a sacred promptuary, that seed which conserves the human race. And for less than a hundred francs I would believe that such were the very stones by which Deucalion and Pyrrha renewed the human race which had been wiped out by the [poetic] Flood. That is what moved the courageous Justinian (in Book 4 of *On the Removal of Hypocrites*) to locate the *summum bonum* in breeches and codpieces.

'For that and other reasons the Seigneur de Merville, the better to follow his king to the wars, was trying on a new suit of armour one day (since he could no longer make good use of his old half-rusty one, the flesh of his guts having for some years by then distanced itself from his kidneys) when his wife reflected with a pensive mind that he was taking scant care of that billet-doux rod they shared in their marriage (seeing that he was protecting it with nothing but chain-mail) and decided that he should arm it most efficiently with a gabion, a great

jousting helmet lying useless in his closet. The following lines
about her are written in the Third Book of *The Maidens'*
Chiabrena:

> She saw her husband dear his armour don,
> Save for the codpiece: he on battle bent.
> 'I am afraid,' said she, 'It may get dent!
> 'That part I love the best put something on!'
> What! For such words should she be set upon?
> No, no, I say: she was concerned for it,
> Afraid of harm for that which she did long:
> That goodly part, her nicest tasty bit.

So stop being amazed at my novel accoutrements.'

How Panurge seeks advice from Pantagruel over whether he ought to marry

CHAPTER 9

*[A chapter in which the replies echo the last words of the question.
(Erasmus made the form popular and respectable in his colloquy
entitled 'Echo'.) Here it is a means of casting the decision back to
Panurge.*

*Two of the adages of Erasmus are relevant: I, IV, XXXII, 'To cast
every dice', and I, VII, XCIX (more or less) 'To scratch one another's
back'.*

*From Ecclesiastes 4:1 is cited 'Woe to him that is alone'. It was
often quoted by those arguing against enforced celibacy and in favour
of marriage.*

*It was Seneca who wrote (Epistle 94) that 'what you have done to
others will be done unto you'.*

*The Sage who said 'Where there is no wife he greatly mourneth who
is ill' is the author of Ecclesiasticus (36:27).]*

Since Pantagruel made no reply, Panurge went on and said with
a deep sigh:

'Sire, you have heard my resolve, which is to get married (unless all holes are alas locked, bolted and barred). For the love you have so long borne me, I implore you to give me your advice.'

'Once you have cast the dice, so decided and firmly resolved,' said Pantagruel, 'there should be no more talking: all that remains is to implement it.'

'Indeed,' said Panurge, 'but I wouldn't want to implement it without your good advice and counsel.'

'I do so advise you,' said Pantagruel; 'and that is my counsel.'

'But,' said Panurge, 'if you knew that it would be better for me to stay as I am, without embarking on some novelty, I would rather never marry.'

'Never marry then,' replied Pantagruel.

'Indeed,' said Panurge; 'but would you want me to live alone all my life without a conjugal mate! You know the Scripture, *Woe to him that is alone*. The single man never enjoys such comfort as those who marry.'

'Marry then,' said Pantagruel, 'for God's sake.'

'But,' said Panurge, 'suppose my wife made a cuckold of me! It's been a good year for cuckolds you know. That would be enough to make me fly off the hinges with torment. I'm quite fond of cuckolds; they seem nice fellows and I enjoy hanging round them, but I would rather die than be one. That is a jab to bear which I dare not.'

'Dare not get married then,' Pantagruel replied, 'for the judgement of Seneca is true without exception: "What you have done to others will be done unto you."'

'Did you say,' asked Panurge, 'without exception?'

'Without exception is what he says,' Pantagruel replied.

'Ho, ho!' said Panurge, 'by a tiny little devil, he means in this world or the next! Truly, though: since I can no more do without a woman than a blind man can do without a stick (for my bradawl must trot, otherwise I could never live), is it not better that I should keep company with one decent, honest wife than be changing about, day after day, in constant danger of a cudgelling or even worse of the pox? For no decent wife has ever interested me: no insult is implied to her Man.'

'Manage to take such a wife [then], for God's sake,' Pantagruel replied.

'But,' said Panurge, 'if God so willed and it came to pass that
I married some goodly woman who knocked me about, I would
be more than a tercelet of Job if I never flew into a towering
rage. For they tell me that those goody-goody wives are normally shrews, with plenty of vinegar kept in their homes. But I
would outdo her: I'd so knock her giblets about – her arms, I
mean, her legs, head, lungs, liver and spleen – and so rip up her
robes with blow after blow that the great Deil himself would
be waiting at the door for her damnèd soul. This year I could
well do without such ructions: happy I'd be to experience them
never!'

'Never get married then,' Pantagruel replied.

'True; but in the state I'm in,' said Panurge, 'out of debt and
unmarried (take note, I say, *unfortunately* out of debt, for if I
were heavily in debt my creditors would be all too anxious
about my coming paternity) but anyway, out of debt and
unmarried, I shall have nobody to care for me, nobody to show
me such love as conjugal love is said to be. Were I to fall ill I
would only be treated against the grain. The Sage says, "Where
there is no wife" (I mean a materfamilias within legitimate
wedlock) "he greatly mourneth who is ill." I have seen clear
proof of that in popes, legates, cardinals, bishops, abbots,
priors, priests and monks. Amongst such, indeed, me you never
shall find.'

'Find you a wife then, for God's sake,' Pantagruel replied.

'But,' said Panurge, 'if I were ill, incapable of fulfilling the
marriage debt, my wife might be impatient with my debility
and abandon herself to other men, not only never succouring
me in my need but mocking my misfortune, and worse still –
I've often seen it happen! – stealing from me. That would be
the last straw. With doublet undone, raving mad through the
fields I'd run.'

'Run not into marriage, then,' Pantagruel replied.

'Yes,' said Panurge, 'but in that case I would never have
legitimate sons and daughters through whom I might hope to

perpetuate my name and my coat-of-arms, bequeathing to them my wealth, both inherited and acquired (I shall acquire a lot of it one of these days, doubt it not, and be great at disencumbering my inheritances) and with whom, when I was depressed, I would enjoy myself, just as I see your kind and gentle father daily do with you, and as do all good folk privately in their habitations. Now if I were out of debt, not married, yet troubled by some misfortune . . . But instead of comforting me I think you're laughing at my plight!'

'Plight not thy troth then, for God's sake,' Pantagruel replied.

How Pantagruel admonishes Panurge that it is hard to give counsel about marriage; and of Homeric and Virgilian lots

CHAPTER 10

[The erudition displayed in this chapter and the quotations – including the additions of 1552 – derive from a treatise, On Nobility *by André Tiraqueau, the legal authority who had been a friend of Rabelais from his early days as a Franciscan at Fontenay-le-Comte. Rabelais must have read the treatise in manuscript, since the work was not printed until 1549. His reading of Cardano's* On Wisdom *would further have reinforced his respect for Homeric and Virgilian lots.*

The final example, that of Pierre Amy, a very learned Franciscan, a contemporary of Rabelais in the same convent, shows that such lots kept their validity in the time of Rabelais.

'Cowled Hobgoblins' (Farfadets) is a harsh name for the Franciscans.

Most of the original readers of the Third Book *could not have managed Greek script let alone Greek verse: the presence of the Greek verse, in Greek script, forms a strong claim by Rabelais to be taken as erudite. The translations which here follow the Greek and Latin verse do not directly render the original Greek and Latin but retranslate the looser versions which Rabelais provides in French.*

Brutus was not killed at Pharsalia: he committed suicide at Philippi:
Rabelais slipped up.

In '52 'self-contradictory repetitions' replaces the original technical
terms 'paronomasias' and 'epanalepses' in the first sentence.]

'Your advice,' said Panurge, 'resembles – under correction –
Ricochet's round. It is nothing but taunts, jests, paronomasias
and epanalepses, one lot undoing the other. I can't tell which
to hold on to.'

'In your propositions, too, there are so many ifs and buts,'
replied Pantagruel, 'that I can build nothing on them nor reach
any conclusion. Are you not sure of your will? The principal
point lies therein: all the rest is fortuitous and dependent on the
destined dispositions of Heaven.

'We see many couples so happily met that there seems to
shine forth in their marriage some Idea and Form of the joys of
Paradise. Others are so wretched that the devils who tempt the
hermits in the deserts of the Thebaid and Montserrat are not
more so. Once it is your will to enter upon it, you must embark
on it blindfold, bowing your head and kissing the ground,
commending yourself meanwhile to God.

'No other assurance can I give you.

'Yet if it seems good to you, this is what you shall do. Bring
me the works of Virgil; then opening them thrice with your
nail, we shall, having agreed which numbered lines to take,
reconnoitre the future lot of your marriage, just as many a man
has discovered his destiny through Homeric lots:

– witness Socrates, who, upon hearing recited in prison this
line said of Achilles by Homer, *Iliad*, 9,

Ἤματί κεν τριτάτῳ φθίην ἐρίβωλον ἱκοίμην

I shall arrive without a long delay
In fair and fertile Phthia the third day

foresaw that he would die three days later and said so to
Aeschines [as Plato wrote in the *Crito*, Cicero in the first book
of *On Divination*, and Diogenes Laertius also;

– witness Opilius Macrinus, to whom fell by lot the following judgement from *Iliad*, 8, when he yearned to know whether he would be the emperor of Rome:

> Ὦ γέρον ἦ μάλα δή σε νέοι τείρουσι μαχηταί
> Σὴ δὲ βίη λέλυται χαλεπὸν δέ σε γῆρας ὀπάζει·

Old Man, the soldiers from now on, no doubt,
Being young and strong shall surely tire thee out;
Old age is here: your vigour fully gone,
Age harsh and grievous thee hath fallen upon;

he was indeed already old and, having governed the Empire for a mere year and two months was overthrown by the young and powerful Heliogabalus and killed;]

– witness Brutus who, wishing to reconnoitre the outcome of the battle of Pharsalia in which he was killed, came across the following line said of Proclus in *Iliad*, 16:

> Ἀλλά με μοῖρ᾽ ὀλοὴ καὶ Λητοῦς ἔκτανεν υἱος

Through spiteful Fate's felonious breath,
By *Latona's* cruel *son* I met my death.

And *Apollo* was indeed the watchword for the day of that battle.

'Moreover in ancient times outstanding things and matters of great importance were known and revealed by Virgilian lots, even including the winning of the Roman *imperium*, as happened to Alexander Severus, who, in lots of this kind, came across the following line of Virgil, Book 6:

> Tu regere imperio populos, Romane, memento

Remember, son of Rome, the empire come thy way,
So rule the world that it does not decay.

And a few years after that he was really and truly made emperor of Rome.

'Then there was Hadrian, the Roman emperor, who, when worried, and anxious to learn what opinion Trajan had of him and what love he felt for him, sought advice from Virgilian lots and came across these lines in Book 6 of the *Aeneid*:

> *Quis procul ille autem, ramis insignis olivae*
> *Sacra ferens? Nosco crines incanaque menta*
> *Regis Romani*

> Who is't that, in his hand, so far from home
> Bears olive branches, with true majesty?
> From his grey hairs and sacred vestments see!
> I recognize the ancient King of Rome;

he was then adopted by Trajan and succeeded to the *imperium*.

['See also Claudius the Second, that highly praised emperor of Rome, to whom fell by lot the following line from Book 6 of the *Aeneid*:

> *Tertia dum Latio regnantem viderit aestas*

> Until by thee, ruling in Rome, hath been
> In public view thy third of summers seen: . . .

And indeed he ruled but for two years.

'To that same man, when inquiring about Quintilius his brother, there fell the following line from Book 6 of the *Aeneid*:

> *Ostendent terris hunc tantum fata*

> The Fates shall show these lands alone to thee.

And so it transpired, for he was killed seventeen days after he had been entrusted with running the Empire. (That same lot fell to the Emperor Gordian the Younger.)

'Claudius Albinus, anxious to learn of his good fortune, happened upon what is written in Book 6 of the *Aeneid*:

> *Hic rem Romanam magno turbante tumultu,*
> *Sistet eques, etc.*

> This soldier brave, when discord is Rome's fate,
> Will prove the pillar of the Imperial State:
> O'er Carthage and the Gauls if they rebel
> He will gain victories full fair to retell.]

'So too the venerated emperor Claudius, the predecessor of Aurelian, when worried about his posterity, came by lot upon this line [*Aeneid*, 1]:

> *His ego nec metas rerum nec tempora pono:*

> A long success, to them I now extend:
> Where neither bound nor time shall fix an end;

'And he did beget long strings of successors.

'Then there was Maître Pierre Amy, who, when he was reconnoitring to discover whether he should escape from the cowled Hobgoblins, came across this line [*Aeneid*, 3]:

> *Heu, fuge crudeles terras, fuge littus avarum*

> Leave now at once these lands so barbarous:
> Leave now at once these shores so avaricious.

And he escaped safe and sound from their hands.

'There are hundreds of other examples, too long to relate, whose outcomes fell out in conformity with the verdict of the lines encountered through such lots.

'Nevertheless, since I do not want you to be taken in, I have no wish to infer that such lots are infallible in every case.'

How Pantagruel shows that the use of dice
for lots is unlawful

CHAPTER II

[Beaux dés, ('fair dice') commonly led to a pun on baudet, *('donkey').
Making light use of dice in games of semi-serious prophecy was
rejected by Rabelais as evil. For him the devil is a force to be reckoned
with. The Book of the Pastimes of the Fortune of Dice must have led
to ructions amongst those who took it even semi-seriously, since it
claimed to reveal adulteries, secret* affaires *and so on. Rabelais' propaganda is hostile, advocating the total suppression of both the book
and its illustrations. Interestingly, if the numbers thrown by the dice
in this chapter were to be used in combination with that book they
would give the right result: Panurge's marriage would be a disaster!
Pantagruel is prepared to use dice in combination with Virgilian lots,
since, by such means, yes-or-no advice or even a limited number of
possible answers are not imposed by the cast of the dice by the thrower.
(How Roman Law allowed of the use of dice is treated later, from
Chapter 39 onwards, apropos of Mr Justice Bridoye.)*

*When consulting lots a wise man stays calm and awaits their replies
with indifference.*

Sixteen is considered a favourable number in tali *and* tesserae.

In royal tennis a fault costs fifteen points.]

'It would be quicker,' said Panurge, 'and more expedient to
throw three donkey-dice.'

'No,' replied Pantagruel. 'Such lots are misleading, unlawful
and a real scandal. Never trust in them. That cursed book
On Pastimes with Dice was long ago devised by the fiendish
Calumniator in Achaia near Bura, where, before the statue of
Hercules, he would lead many simple souls astray and tumble
them into his snares; he does so still in several places. You are
aware that Gargantua my father has outlawed it in all his
kingdoms, burnt it – woodcuts, illustrations and all – and
completely banned it, suppressed it and destroyed it as a most
dangerous pestilence.

'What I say of dice applies similarly to *tali*, which are an equally misleading form of divination. And do not cite against me that lucky cast of *tali* which Tiberius made into the fountain of Apona at the oracle of Geryon. *Tali* are hooks by which the Calumniator draws simple souls to everlasting perdition.

'To satisfy you, though, I would certainly agree that we should cast three dice on this table: then, from the total of the points thrown, we shall select the line of verse on the page you have opened. Have you any dice in your purse?'

'A game-bag full of them,' Panurge replied. 'Dice are the sprig of green which wards off the devil (as Merlin Coccai states in his second book of *The Land of the Devils*). The devil would indeed catch me napping if he surprised me without dice.'

The dice were brought out and cast.

They fell showing five, six and five.

'That makes sixteen,' said Panurge. 'Let's take the sixteenth line of verse on the page. I like that number and believe our encounters will prove lucky. If I don't screw my future wife that often on my wedding-night I shall go and bowl through all the devils like a ball through a set of skittles – ware devils who will! – or a cannon-shot through a battalion of infantrymen.'

'I'm sure you will!' replied Pantagruel. 'There was no need to make so horrific a vow: Your first go will be a fault – which counts as fifteen – and when you get up in the morning you will correct it, by such means scoring sixteen!'

'Is that how you understand it?' replied Panurge. 'Never has a fault been served by that valiant champion which stands sentry for me in my lower belly. Have you ever found me amongst the Confraternity of Faulty Deliverers? Never! Never! To the very end never! I do it without a fault like a Father, a blessèd Franciscan Father. I appeal to those I play with!'

When those words were said and done, the works of Virgil were brought in. Before opening them, Panurge said to Pantagruel:

'My heart is thumping about in my bosom like a mitten. [Just feel my pulse in this artery of my left arm! From its rate and intensity you would think that I was being battered defending a thesis at the Sorbonne!]

'Before we go any further, do you think we ought to invoke Hercules or the *Tenitae*, those goddesses who are said to preside over the lots' own chambers?'

'Neither the one nor the others,' replied Pantagruel. 'Just open it with your nail.'

How Pantagruel, with Virgilian lots, explores what marriage Panurge will have

CHAPTER 12

[The line cited from Virgil (Fourth Eclogue, 63) was known for its difficulty. In his interpretation Rabelais follows the commentator Servius in a standard note.

The legal erudition in the final paragraph may be found in the same work of Tiraqueau exploited in the previous chapter. It constitutes one of the principal guides to the structure and meaning of this Third Book. Once Roman Law had duly allowed a recourse to lots, that was the end of the matter: there was no appeal, Fortuna having no superior to whom an appeal can be made. Rabelais refers to the relevant Roman laws with the standard abbreviations of his time (in this case simply as L. ult. C. de leg. and L. Ait praetor, § ult. de minor. Such abbreviations, once absolutely standard, are expanded here to make them pronounceable.

There is echo of an adage of Erasmus: Adages, I, V, XXXIX, 'Not even Hercules against two'.]

Whereupon Panurge, on opening the book, fell upon these words in the sixteenth line of the verse:

Nec Deus hunc mensa Dea nec dignata cubili est

> Not worthy at the god's table to be fed,
> Nor have a place within the goddess' bed.

'That is not in your favour,' said Pantagruel. 'It means that your wife will be a slut and consequently you a cuckold. The goddess who will not be favourable to you is Minerva, that most redoubtable virgin, that puissant goddess who hurls thunderbolts, that enemy of cuckolds, paramours and adulterers, that enemy of lewd wives who break faith with their husbands and abandon themselves to other men.

'And the god is Jupiter, hurling thunder and lightning from the heavens. You will know that, according to the teachings of the Etruscans, the *manubiae* (as they used to call Vulcan's thunderbolts) pertain exclusively to that goddess – take for example her engulfing in fire the warships of Ajax, Son of Oileus – and to Jupiter whose brain-child she was. It is not licit for the other gods of Olympus to hurl thunderbolts: that is why they are less redoubtable to human beings. I have more to tell you, which you will take as being distilled from high mythology.

'When the Giants undertook their war against the gods, at first those gods laughed at such enemies and said that their pages could deal with such matters. But when they saw Mount Pelion already piled on to Mount Ossa by the labour of the Giants, and Mount Olympus already prised loose to be set on top of them both, they were all terrified. So Jupiter summoned a general meeting of his Chapter.

'There it was decided by all the gods that they would valiantly prepare their defences. And since they had seen many battles lost by the hindrances caused by women in the midst of armies, it was decreed that they would drive for a while out of Heaven and into Egypt and the confines of the Nile all those crappy sluts of goddesses disguised as weasels, stoats, bats, shrews and similar metamorphoses. Minerva alone was retained in order to hurl thunderbolts together with Jupiter, being the goddess of letters, war, counsel and execution, a goddess born clad in armour, a goddess redoubtable throughout Heaven, air, sea and land.'

'Guts upon guts!'[5] said Panurge. 'Am I to be a Vulcan such as our poet talks about! No! I'm not lame as Vulcan was, nor a coiner, nor a blacksmith. My wife will perhaps be as fair and comely as that Venus of his but not a slut as she was. Nor shall

5. '52: . . . 'Guts *of Gosh*,' said Panurge . . .

I be a cuckold. That ugly old hop-along was pronounced a cuckold by a sentence of all the gods and in view of them all.

'Therefore take it to mean the contrary. The prognostic signifies that my wife will be decent, modest and loyal, not armour-clad, surly or brainless, nor a brain-child like Pallas; nor will handsome Jupiter be my rival, dipping his bread in my sauce when we sup together at table. Just think of his deeds and the fine things he got up to! He was the most debauched, the most franciscanly – I mean the most frankly – lecherous male there ever has been, as rutting as a wild boar.

'Yes, and if Agathocles of Babylon is not lying, he was brought up more goatish than a goat by a sow on Dicte in Candia. Others say too that he was suckled by a nanny-goat called Amalthea. And then (by Acheron!) in one single day he rammed one-third of the entire world: beasts, humans, rivers and mountains – Europa, that is. On account of that ramification the Ammonians had him portrayed in the form of a ram rampant, a hornèd ram.

'But I know how to protect myself from that horn-bearer. Believe you me: he will not find in me some stupid Amphitrion, some complaisant Argus with his hundred goggles, some cowardly Acrisius, some dreamer like Lycus of Thebes, some lunatic like Agenor, someone phlegmatic like Asopus, some hairy-pawed Lycaon, some yokelish Corytus of Tuscany, some long-spined Atlas. Well might he metamorphose himself hundreds of times into a swan, bull, satyr, shower of gold, cuckoo (as he did when he deflowered Juno, his sister), into an eagle, ram, [pigeon, as he did when in love with that maiden Phthia who dwelt in Aegia,] fire, snake, even indeed a flea, into the atoms of Epicurus or, like a Magister Noster, into second intentions: I'll nab 'im with me 'ook.'

'And do you know what I shall do to him? Golly: what Saturn did to Coelus his father – Seneca foretold it of me and Lactantius has confirmed it – and what Rhea did to Atys: I will slice off his balls a hair's breadth from his bum. For which reason he will never be pope, "because he hath no testiculos".'

'Whoa there, my lad; whoa!' said Pantagruel. 'Just open the book for a second time.'

Then Panurge came across the line:

Membra quatit gelidusque coit formidine sanguis

Breaks his bones, shatters his limbs in a trice;
For fear thereof the blood doth turn to ice.

'That means she will maul you, back and belly.'

'On the contrary,' replied Panurge, 'the prognostication is all about me: it says that if my wife annoys me I will maul her like a tiger. My Saint Martin's staff will do the job. And in default of a stick, if I don't eat her alive – as Cambles, the king of the Lydians, ate his – the devil may eat me.'

'You,' said Pantagruel, 'are most stout of heart! Hercules wouldn't take you on in such an ecstasy! But that is what folk say: one johnnie counts as a double, and even Hercules dared not take on two.'

'I am a complaisant Johnnie, am I!'

'No, no, no,' replied Pantagruel: 'I was thinking of a score in tric-trac and backgammon.'

At the third go Panurge came across this line:

Foemineo praedae et spoliorum ardebat amore

She keenly burnt, as is the female's usage,
To go for loot and pillage all the baggage.

'That means,' said Pantagruel, 'that she will rob you. According to those three lots I can see you in a fine old mess: you will be cuckolded, beaten and robbed.'

'On the contrary,' replied Panurge, 'that line of verse means that she will love me with a perfect love. Our satirist was telling no lie when he said that a woman ablaze with the extremes of love sometimes finds pleasure in stealing from her beloved. And do you know what she steals? A glove, or the cord of his flies, to make him search for it. Some trifle. Nothing of importance.

'Similarly those little quarrels, those squabbles which surge up at times between lovers, reanimate and stimulate love, just as we sometimes find cutlers, for example, hammering their whetstones the better to hone up their tools.

'That is why I take those three lots to be in my favour.

'Otherwise: I appeal.'

'One can never appeal, said Pantagruel, against verdicts reached by lots and Fortune, as our ancient jurisconsults affirm and as Baldus states in the ultimate Law: *Codex: "Common matters concerning legates"*. The reason is that Fortuna recognizes no superior authority with whom an appeal against her or her lots can be lodged. And in such a case the minor cannot be fully restored to his former status, as Baldus clearly states, in the law: *"The Praetor says"; final paragraph; Pandects: "Concerning minors"*.'

How Pantagruel advises Panurge to foretell his good or bad fortune in marriage from dreams

CHAPTER 13

[Divination from dreams held a place of honour in the Classical and biblical sources and authorities consulted by Renaissance scholars. Rabelais, following many other erudite authors including Erasmus, believed that a man or woman's mind (or spirit) may leave its body in rapture or in dreams, or at least strive to do so. That belief was held by theologians, philosophers and scholars generally. Rabelais is well within the scholarly context of his time, but not all the books he refers to were extant, some being known only from being mentioned by other authors.

The interpretation of Homer's and Virgil's two gates, one of ivory, one of horn, derives eventually from Macrobius' Dream of Scipio. The gates were best known from the Aeneid, Book 6.

More than once Rabelais, as here, applies the Classical rule of the Golden Mean to feasting and fasting, which would have horrified many ecclesiastical traditionalists. There is an echo of an adage of Erasmus: III, VIII, XII. 'A hungry man is not to be disturbed'.

'Νοῦς' ('Nous') is the mind or spirit.]

'Now then, since we cannot agree together over how to expound Virgilian lots, let us try another means of divination.'

'Which?' asked Panurge.

'A good, ancient and valid one,' said Pantagruel: 'by dreams. For by dreaming – under the conditions described by Hippocrates in his book *On Dreams*, by Plato, Plotinus, Iamblicus, Synesius, Aristotle, Xenophon, Galen, Plutarch, Artemidorus Daldianus, Herophilus, [Quintus Calaber, Theocritus, Pliny, Athenaeus] and others – the soul often foresees what is to come.

'There is no need to prove that to you at greater length. You will grasp it from a common analogy: you know how nurses, after their babes have been properly changed, properly fed and given the breast, and lie soundly asleep, can freely go out and enjoy themselves, being granted leave, as it were, to do what they want for an hour since their presence about the cradle would seem unnecessary: in the same way each of our souls, while her body is asleep and concoction has been completed in all its stages, can go and enjoy herself, revisiting her homeland in Heaven, since nothing more is required of her before we awake.

'From there she is granted the signal favour of participating in her primal and divine origin and of contemplating that infinite [and Intellectual] Sphere [whose centre is in every place in the universe and whose circumference nowhere: God, that is, by the teachings of Hermes Trismegistus] in whom there is no becoming, no transience, no waning, all times being the present; there she discerns not only things past amongst the motions here below but also things to come; she bears them back to her body, and as she expounds them to friends via her body's organs and senses she is termed prophetic and vaticinatory.

'It is true that she cannot report them as purely as she saw them, being hampered by the imperfection and weakness of our bodily senses: similarly the Moon, on receiving her light from the Sun, does not impart it to us as bright, pure, vibrant and blazing as she received it. That is why, for divinations made during sleep, there is still the need of an interpreter (, an adroit, wise, rational and consummate *oneirocrites*, or *oneiropolos* as the Greeks call him).

'That is why Herodotus would say that nothing was revealed to us by dreams nor anything hidden: we are merely given some pointer, some indication of things to come, either for our own happiness and unhappiness or else for the happiness and unhappiness of others. The Holy Scriptures testify to it and lay history confirms it, revealing to us hundreds of events which happened in accordance with the dreams of the person dreaming or equally the dreams of others.

'The Atlantes and the people living on the isle of Thasos (one of the Cyclades) are deprived of that benefit: in their lands nobody has ever had dreams.

'So too were Cleon of Daulia and Thrasymedes, and in our days the learned Frenchman Villanovanus, none of whom ever had dreams.

'Tomorrow, then, at the time when the joyful, rosy-fingered dawn chases away the darkness of the night, devote yourself to dreaming deeply. In the meantime strip yourself of all human affections: of love, hate, hope or fear.

'For as, in days gone by, the great prophet Proteus never predicted future events when he was transformed and disguised as fire, water, tiger, dragon or with any other strange mask, but to make predictions had to be restored to his own natural form: so too, no man can receive divine inspiration and the art of prophecy unless that part in him which is most divine – that is his Νοῦς or *Mens* – be still, tranquil, peaceful, and neither preoccupied nor distracted by any exterior passions or affections.'

'I will do that,' said Panurge. 'Must I eat a lot or a little for supper this evening? I don't ask that without a cause: for if I go without a good substantial supper I get no proper sleep and have nothing at night but silly dreams, dreams as hollow then as my belly is.'

'No supper at all would be better for you,' replied Pantagruel, 'given your plumpness and your habits. Amphiareus, a prophet of Antiquity, required those who desired to receive his oracles through their dreams to eat nothing at all that day and to touch no wine for three days beforehand.

'We shall not follow so extreme and strict a regime. I do

indeed believe that a man stuffed with viands and awash with wine finds it hard to receive notice of matters spiritual: I am not however of the opinion of those who think that after long and stubborn fasts they can enter more deeply into a contemplation of matters celestial.

'You may recall that my father Gargantua (whom with respect I mention) often told us that the writings of such jejunating hermits were as insipid, jejune and vilely salivating as were their bodies when they wrote them, and that it is hard for a man's spirits to be good and serene when his body is in a state of inanition, seeing that the philosophers and physicians affirm that our animal spirits arise, are born and act through our arterial blood, purified and refined to perfection in the *rete mirabile* which lies beneath the ventricles of the brain. They cite us the example of a philosopher who, the better to mediate, reason and write, persuades himself that he is in solitude, far from the crowd, yet all about him dogs are barking, wolves howling, lions roaring, horses whinnying, elephants trumpeting, snakes hissing, asses braying, grasshoppers stridulating, turtle-doves uttering their lamentations: that is to say, he is more disturbed than he would be at the fairs of Fontenay or Niort because hunger is in his stomach: to remedy which, his stomach barks, his eyes are dazzled and his veins suck out some of the substance proper to the flesh-creating organs and draw down the wandering mind which is neglecting to look after its nurseling and natural host which is the body. It is as though a hawk on the fist, wishing to soar into the air and take to its wings, were to be at once hauled back lower by its leash.

'On this subject they cite the authority of Homer, the Father of all philosophy, who says that the Greeks stopped weeping out of grief for Patroclus, the great friend of Achilles, when, and only when, hunger showed itself and their bellies swore to supply no more tears. For in a body exinantiated by long fasts there remained nothing from which to produce tears to weep.

'In all cases the Mean is to be praised, and you will stick to it here. For supper you will not eat any haricot beans, hare or any other meat, nor octopus (polyp) nor cabbage nor any food which might obfuscate or confuse your animal spirits. For just as a looking-glass cannot reflect the likeness of objects exposed before it if its sheen is clouded by breath or darkened by age, so too the mind cannot receive ideas from divination by dreams if its body is muddied and disturbed by vapours and exhalations from the above-mentioned foods, on account of the indissoluble sympathy which exists between body and mind.

'You will eat good pears from Crustumenia and Bergamo, a short-start apple, a few plums from Touraine and some cherries from my orchard. In your case there is no reason why you should fear that your dreams will be rendered dubious, deceptive or suspect by such fruits, as the Peripatetics have indeed declared them to be in autumn-tide, when human beings eat much more fruit than in any other season, and as it is taught mystically by the ancient poets and seers that vain, deceptive dreams lie hidden beneath the leaves carpeting the ground, for it is in the autumn that leaves fall from the trees, since the fermentation which naturally abounds in fresh fruit and which readily evaporates by ebullition in the animal parts (as we can see happen with the must of wine) has already long since been exhaled and dispersed.

'And you will drink some clear water from my fountain.'

'The terms are a bit hard on me,' said Panurge, 'but I agree to them all the same, cost me what it may, while protesting that I intend to have my breakfast early tomorrow morning, right after my dream-session. In addition I commend myself to Homer's twin gates, to Morpheus, to Icelon, Phantasus and Phobetor. If they succour me in my need I shall set up a merry altar for them entirely composed of soft eiderdown.

['Were I in the temple of Ino betwixt Oetylus and Thalamae my perplexity would be resolved by her during my sleep through beautiful and happy dreams.]'

He then asked Pantagruel:

'Wouldn't it be a good thing if I stuck a few laurel branches under my pillow?'

'There is no need of that,' replied Pantagruel. 'It is superstitious; and what has been written on such matters by Serapion Ascalonites, Antiphon, Philochorus, Artemon and Fulgentius Planciades is full of abuses.

'I would say the same of a crocodile's left shoulder and (with due respect to Democritus) of a chameleon; similarly, of that stone of the Bactrians called *eumetrides*, and of horn-ammonite (which is the name given by the Ethiopians to a precious stone which, like the horns of Jupiter Ammon, is gold in colour and shaped like a ram's horn; they assert that the dreams of any who wear it are as true and infallible as holy oracles).

'Perhaps that is what Homer and Virgil meant by the two gates of dreams to which you have commended yourself.

– one gateway is of ivory; through it enter dreams which are confused, deceptive and uncertain, just as it is impossible to see through ivory however fine-drawn it may be: its density and opacity impede penetration by our visive spirits and so the reception of visible forms;

– the other gateway is of horn, through which enter dreams which are certain, true and infallible, just as all forms appear clearly and distinctly through horn on account of its translucency and transparency.'

'You mean to imply,' said Frère Jean, 'that the dreams of horn-bearing cuckolds such as Panurge will be – God helping, and his wife – are ever true and infallible.'

Panurge's dream and its interpretation

CHAPTER 14

[It is in Genesis 37:19 that Joseph's brothers say, 'Here comes our dreamer'.

Renaissance writers never seem to tire of jests about horns (cornes) and cuckoldry. The unfortunately named Petrus de Cornibus was a don at the Sorbonne.

It was a principle going back to Synesius that one should tell one's dreams to one's friends and then calmly abide by their interpretations, since such friends should be free from prejudice and emotion and above all from our own self-love, which leads us all too readily to twist divination in our favour.

The erudition is all supported by reputable sources.

The problem of Panurge is turning into what lawyers called a 'perplex case'. In such cases the laws are clear but their application to specific circumstances is not. Such legal perplexities can be made worse by the devil and his agents, and, as Saint Paul warns his followers (II Corinthians 11:14) 'the angel of Satan often transfigures himself into an angel of light'.

Panurge's perplexity is proving a diabolical one. Several adages of Erasmus are concerned with perplexity, including: III, X, XXX, 'Perplexed'; and III, VIII, XL, 'Perplexed and disturbed in mind'. Several other adages of Erasmus are relevant, including: I, III, LXXIV, 'To satisfy Momus'; I, I, LX, 'To annoy hornets'; I, I, LXIV, 'To disturb the Camarina', and I, III, XXXVI, 'ἐχθρῶν ἄδωρα δῶρα: enemies' gifts are no gifts', which Rabelais cites in Greek, as a common saying, without any concession to his readers.

'Fiat', (so be it) is good Latin: 'fiatur' is not. Fiat is the sign of approval written on papal Bulls.]

The next morning, about seven o'clock, Panurge presented himself before Pantagruel; in the chamber with him were Epistemon, Frère Jean des Entommeures, Ponocrates, Eudemon, Carpalim and others; to whom Pantagruel said as Panurge appeared, 'Here comes our dreamer!'

'Those words once cost most dear,' said Epistemon, 'and the sons of Jacob paid a high price for them.'

At which Panurge said,

'I'm at Guillot the Dreamer's, all bemused: I've had more than enough dreams but I can't make anything out of them, except that in my dream I had a wife who was young, elegant and utterly beautiful, who treated me with affection and caressed me as her own little darling. Never was man more carefree nor happier. She stroked me, tickled me, patted my hair, kissed me, put her arms round my neck and playfully placed two pretty little horns high up on my forehead. I fooled about and expostulated that she ought to have placed them below my eyes, so that I could more easily see where I should strike with them, and also so that Momus should find no imperfection in her (as he did in Nature's positioning of horns on bulls). But, despite my expostulations that dear little idiot thrust them further in. It didn't hurt me one bit, which is quite remarkable.

'Soon after that it seemed to me that I was somehow metamorphosed into a little tabor and she into a little owl. At that point my sleep was shattered and I awoke with a start, all troubled, perplexed and angry. There's a good plateful of dreams for you. Make a good meal of them and expound them as you understand them. Let's go have breakfast, Carpalim.'

'If I have any competence in the art of divining by dreams,' said Pantagruel, 'I do understand: your wife will not actually plant horns on your forehead where, as satyrs wear them, they can clearly be seen, but she will not be faithful nor loyal in her marriage, and will abandon herself to other men and make you a cuckold. Artemidorus clearly expounds the point the same way as I do.

'Moreover you will not be metamorphosed into a little tabor but she will beat you like a tabor at a marriage-feast; nor will she become a little owl but she will rob you, as is the nature of horn-owls.

'And so you can see that your dreams agree with the Virgilian lots: you will be cuckolded, you will be beaten and you will be robbed.'

Then Frère Jean gave a shout and said, 'He's stating the truth, by God. My good chap, you'll be cuckolded, I assure you. Tut, tut, tut: you'll be Magister Noster de Cornibus! God help you! Give us a couple of words of a sermon and I'll pass the plate all round the parish!'

'Quite the contrary,' said Panurge. 'My dream foretells that I shall have an abundance of good things in my marriage, a cornucopia. You say they will be satyrs' horns. Yea. Amen! Amen! I give you my *fiat* (or to be different from the pope, my *fiatur*). Thus shall I have my bradawl eternally at the ready and inexhaustible – something which all men desire but few are vouchsafed by the heavens – and therefore never shall I a cuckold be, since lack of the above is the *sine qua non*, the one and only cause, turning husbands into cuckolds.

'What makes vagrants beg? They have nothing at home to

stuff into their pouches. What drives the wolf from the woods? The need for a bit of meat. What turns wives into harlots? You get me! I appeal to the lawyers and to those gentlemen the presidents, counsellors, barristers, procurers and other glossators of that venerable legal rubric *On Wives frigid or bewitched.*

'You – do pardon me if I give any offence – seem evidently to err in interpreting horns as cuckoldom.

– Diana wears horns on her head in the form of a handsome crescent: does that make her a cuckold! She's never even been married! How the devil could she be a cuckold then? For goodness' sake speak properly or she might give you horns of the kind she gave to Actaeon.

– That good god Bacchus wears horns; so do Pan, Jupiter Ammon and many others. Are they all cuckolds then? Must Juno be a slut? – for that would follow by the figure of rhetoric called metalepsis, as calling a child a bastard or a foundling in the presence of its father and mother is a way of implying indirectly and implicitly that the father is a cuckold and the mother a slut.

'Let us put it better. The horns which my wife was giving me are horns of plenty, horns of an abundance of all good things. I can assure you of that. In the meanwhile I shall be as merry as a tabor at a marriage-feast, ever rumbling, ever rolling, ever beating and farting. Believe you me, that is a presage of my good fortune: my wife will be neat and pretty like a lovely little owl: Who believeth it not, then

> straight to gibbet from Hell!
> Noël, noël.'

'I note,' said Pantagruel, 'the last detail which you gave and compare it to the first. At the beginning you were steeped in delight by your dream: at the end you awoke with a start, troubled, perplexed and angry . . .'

'True,' said Panurge, 'for I hadn't eaten!'

'. . . I foresee that everything will be bleak. Take it to be true that any sleep which ends with a start, leaving the person troubled and angry, is either a symptom of ill or portends ill:

– a symptom of ill: namely of an illness which is obstinate, malignant, pestiferous and occult, lurking within the centre of the body; under the influence of sleep which (according to medical theory) always increases the powers of concoction, it would begin to manifest itself and move towards the surface; by that dire movement, repose would be dissipated and the primary sensitive organ warned to react to it and provide for it: it is as the proverbs say: *To stir up a hornets' nest*, or, *To trouble the waters of the Camarinus*, or *To wake a sleeping cat*;

– portends ill: that is to say when the soul, by her reaction to the content of somnial divination, leads us to understand that some ill is destined and prepared there, which will soon produce its effect. Examples:

– in the dreaming and terrifying awakening of Hecuba and the dream of Eurydice, the wife of Orpheus; from which, once it was over, they both awoke (says Ennius) horrified with a start; and indeed Hecuba saw Priam, her husband and her children slain and her homeland destroyed, while Eurydice soon died wretchedly;

– in Aeneas, who, while dreaming that he was talking with Hector, who was dead, suddenly awoke with a start: that very night Troy was indeed pillaged and burnt. On another occasion he dreamt that he caught sight of his Lares and Penates, awoke in terror and suffered next day a terrifying storm at sea.

[– In Turnus, who, incited to go to war by a spectral vision of a Fury in the underworld, awoke with a start, deeply troubled: then, after a long series of catastrophes, he was slain by that same Aeneas.]

'There are hundreds of other examples.

'While I am telling you about Aeneas, note that Fabius Pictor states that nothing was ever done or undertaken by Aeneas, and that nothing ever happened to him, which he had not known beforehand from divination by dreams.

'Those examples do not lack reason, for if sleep and repose

are a special gift and boon of the gods, as the philosophers maintain and the poet attests, saying:

> Then unto men the heavens sent gentle sleep,
> Their gift to weary humans, gracious, deep.

then such a gift cannot terminate in disturbance and anxiety without portending some huge misery. Otherwise repose would not be repose, boon be no boon but something coming not from friendly gods but from inimical devils: as the common saying has it, ἐχθρῶν ἄδῶρα δῶρα.[6]

'It is as if you were to see the paterfamilias, seated at a richly laden table with a good appetite, leap to his feet in alarm at the beginning of his meal. Any who did not know why would be astounded. What was up? Well, he had heard his menservants cry *Fire*; his maidservants cry *Stop thief*; his children cry *Murder*. At which he must needs abandon his meal and rush out to put things right and re-establish order.

'In truth I recall that the Cabbalists and the Massoretes (expositors of Holy Writ) when teaching by what distinctions one can judge the truth of any appearances by angels (for *the angel of Satan often transfigures himself into an angel of light*) say that the distinction is that, whenever the good angel of consolation appears to man, he frightens him at first but finally consoles him, whereas the evil angel of temptation delights him at first but finally leaves him perturbed, anxious and perplexed.'

---

6.   That is, 'Enemies' gifts are no gifts' (*echthrôn adôra dôra*). See the introduction to this chapter.

The Excuse of Panurge; and an exegesis of a monastical cabbala concerning salted beef

CHAPTER 15

[There is a sustained play on to hear *and* to understand *(both* entendre *in French.)*

Cabbalistic knowledge is semi-secret knowledge, handed down from person to person amongst initiates.

Erasmus supplies the adage, II, VIII, LXXXIV, 'The belly has no ears', and, above all, I, VI, XC, 'We do not see what is in the pouch behind us'. In his commentary Erasmus cites the fable of Aesop, which Rabelais resumes. It was one of the most authoritative condemnations ever of self-love, philautia, *the source of all errors.]*

'May God keep from ill,' said Panurge, 'him who sees well yet hears not. I can see you all right, but I can't hear you one little bit. I don't know what you mean. A famished belly hath no ears! By God, I'm roaring mad with hunger. I've just done a most enormous stint: it would take more than Signor Sly to trick me again into this dreaming business this twelvemonth. "Have no supper at all, for the devil's sake!" Crikey! Frère Jean, let's go and get some breakfast.

['Once I've well and truly breakfasted and have my stomach well and truly stuffed with fodder and grain from the stall, I can, at a pinch, if needs be, go without dinner. But without supper! Crikey! That's quite wrong. It's an offence to Nature.

'Nature has made the day for Man to do things, to toil, to work every one in his vocation. So that we can do it more fittingly she has furnished us with a candle: the bright and happy light of the Sun. At eventide Nature begins to withdraw from us and tacitly says to us: "You are good folk, my children. You have toiled enough. The night is coming: it is right to cease your labours and to restore your strength with good bread, good wine and good viands, to enjoy yourselves for a while, to lie down and rest so as to be fresh and eager for work on the morrow as before."

'Falconers do just that. Once they have fed their birds they do not make them fly on full stomachs. They allow them time to digest on their perches.

'That was perfectly understood by the good pope who first instituted fasting. He ordained that one should fast until the hour of Nones; the rest of the day was left free for feeding.

'In former times only few ever ate dinner: monks, say, or canons, for they've got nothing else to do. Every day is a feast day for them and they meticulously follow that monastic saying, From Mass to mess. Not even for their abbot would they delay settling down to table where, while stuffing themselves, they'll wait for the abbot as long as he likes: but not otherwise and under no other circumstances. Yet everyone would have supper, except for a few mad dreamers; which is why supper is called *coena*, that is, common to all.[7]

'You know that all right, Frère Jean. Come on, my friend, by all the devils, come on! My stomach, mad with hunger, is barking like a dog. Following the example of the Sybil with Cerberus, let us toss plenty of sops into its gullet to quieten it down.]

'You like a Prime-time sop of bread-and-dripping, Frère Jean: I prefer a soup of giblets associated with a slice of nine-lessons plougher.'

'I know what you mean!' Frère Jean replied. 'That metaphor has been served up from the cloister cooking-pot. The *plougher* is a bull formerly used, or still used, for ploughing; *nine lessons* means cooked to perfection. For in my days, whenever the monastic fathers got up for mattins, they, following a certain ancient practice – cabbalistic: not written but passed down from hand to hand – performed certain noteworthy preliminaries before going into church: they shat in the shitteries, pissed in the pisseries, spat in the spitteries, melodiously hacked in the hackeries and raved in the raveries, so as to bring nothing impure into divine service. Which done, they would devoutly proceed to the *Sainte Chapelle* (for that was their name for the monastery's kitchen in their enigmatic jargon) and there

7.   The fantastic etymology taken from Plutarch's *Table Talk*, 8, 6.

devoutly urge that the beef for the breakfast of Our Lord's
monastic brethren be put then and there on the spit.

'Often they lit the fire under the pot themselves.

'Now when there were nine lessons at mattins they quite
reasonably got up earlier than when mattins were selvaged with
but two or three, intensifying their hunger and thirst by their
yelping from their parchment antiphonaries. Now (following
the aforesaid cabbala) the earlier they got up in the morning, the sooner the beef was put on the fire; the longer it stayed
there, the longer it cooked; the longer it cooked, the more
tender it became: it was kinder on the teeth, gave more pleasure
to the palate and was lighter on the stomach, and provided
better nourishment for those excellent monks, such being their
Founders' sole aim and original intention, considering that
monks by no means eat to live: they live to eat. They only have
one life in this world. Come on, Panurge!'

'This time,' said Panurge, 'I can hear you, you bollock of
velvet, you bollock claustral and cabbalistic. I have a stake in
that cabbala. I will forego principal, usance and all interest. I
will be satisfied with the expenditures, seeing that you have so
eloquently expounded for us the culinary and monastic cabbala.

'Come on, Carpalim. Come on Frère Jean, me old money-
belt! And good day to you, my good lords all. I have dreamt
enough to deserve a drink. Come on.'

Panurge had not finished the last word when Epistemon cried
out in a loud voice, saying:

'To know, foresee, recognize and predict the woes of others
is, amongst human beings, common and ordinary: but O! how
rare it is one's own woes to predict, recognize, foresee and
know. And how wisely did Aesop illustrate that in his fables,
saying that every man is born into this world with a
beggar's-wallet over his shoulder; in the pouch hanging down
in front are kept the faults and defects of others forever exposed
to our gaze and knowledge: in the pouch hanging down behind
are kept our own faults and defects, where never are they
seen nor known save by those to whom the heavens show a
benevolent aspect.'

How Pantagruel counsels Panurge to consult the Sybil of Panzoust

CHAPTER 16

[Panzoust is a village in the pays of Rabelais, between Chinon and l'Ile-Bouchard.

The principal Mosaic text for condemning the consulting of witches is Deuteronomy 17:10–11. Thomas Aquinas cites it twice when distinguishing between licit and illicit means of divination.

An Old Testament savour is provided by the allusions to Tobias and the angel (Tobit 3:14) and to the 'shekel of the Sanctuary' (mentioned several times in Numbers 7).

Alexander's incredulity is taken from Lucian's A Professor of Public Speaking, *5.*

An adage of Erasmus is alluded to: I, III, XII, *'A woman of Thessaly'.*

Panurge's (twisted) list of philosophers who profitably consulted women is shown up as laughable when it ends with Magister Noster Ortwinus, who was mocked in the satirical Letters of Obscure Men *and by many humanists for his opposition to Reuchlin and the study of Hebrew.]*

A little later Pantagruel summoned Panurge and said to him:

'The love which I bear you, matured over long stretches of time, invites me to think of your good and your welfare. Now listen to my plan: I have been told that there is a most remarkable sybil at Panzoust near Le Croulay who foretells all things to come. Make your way to her, taking Epistemon along as a companion and hear what she has to tell you.'

'Perhaps she is a Canidia,' said Epistemon, 'a *sagana*, a witch and a sorceress. I am led to think so because that place is notorious for abounding in more witches than Thessaly ever was. I will not willingly go there. It is illicit, being prohibited by the law of Moses.'

'Well, we're not Jews,' said Pantagruel, 'nor is it an admitted and proven fact that she is a sorceress. Let us put off the sifting and sieving of such matters until after you get back. How can we tell whether she is not an eleventh Sybil, a second Cassandra. Even if she is not a sybil and unworthy of such a name, what risk do you run by consulting her about your perplexity, especially since she is reckoned to know more, and understand more, than is customary in that part of the world and amongst her sex. What harm is there in always learning something, knowing of something, even from a sot, a pot, a mug, a kitten or a mitten?

'Remember Alexander the Great: having won a victory over King Darius at Arbela, he, in the presence of his satraps, once denied a hearing to some fellow, only vainly to regret it thousands upon thousands of times. There he was, victorious in Persia, but so far from his ancestral kingdom of Macedonia that it deeply worried him that he could find no way of getting news from it, partly on account of the enormous distance between the two lands, partly because of the barrier of huge rivers, the hurdles of deserts and the obstacles of mountains. During such critical and anxious reflections – which were no small concern, for his lands might have been occupied, a new king installed and a new colony planted there before he could learn of it and counter it – there appeared before him a man from Sidonia, a merchant experienced and intelligent yet unprepossessing and fairly poor, who firmly declared that he had discovered ways and means by which, in less than five days, Alexander's own country could learn of his Indian victories and he could learn of the situation in Macedonia and Egypt. Alexander reckoned the claim to be so outrageous and unfeasible that he would not give the man a hearing nor grant him an audience. What would it have cost him to listen and to learn what that man had discovered? What harm or hurt would he have suffered from knowing what were the means and method which that man wanted to show him?

'It seems to me that it was not without cause that Nature fashioned us with open ears without imposing upon them any gate or closure as she has with our eyes, tongues and all other bodily apertures. I think that it was to enable us, night and day, continuously to hear and perpetually to learn from our sense of hearing, for it is of all our senses the most apt for learning. That man might have been an angel (that is to say, a messenger) from God, sent as was Raphael to Toby. Alexander despised him too quickly, and for very long afterwards he repented of having done so.'

'You put it well,' replied Epistemon, 'but you will never convince me that it is very profitable to seek counsel and advice from a woman, especially from such a woman in that part of the world.'

'I,' said Panurge, 'find that I have done very well by the counsel of women, especially old ones. Following their advice I have enjoyed one or two exceptional stools. Such women are, my friend, real pointer-hounds, real legal rubrics. And those who call them *sage-women* speak quite properly. My custom, my style, is to call them *presage-women*. Sage they indeed are, for they are skilled in knowledge, but I call them *presage* since they divinely predict and foretell all things with certainty. Sometimes I call them not *Maunettes* ('Unclean-women') but *Monetae* ('Admonishing-women') like the Juno of the Romans. For admonitions, salutary and profitable, come to us every day from them. Ask Pythagoras, Socrates, Empedocles and Magister Noster Ortwinus.

'In addition I extol to the high heavens the ancient custom of the Germans, who prized the counsel of old women as the shekel of the Sanctuary and revered it with all their hearts; to the extent that they had wisely accepted their counsels and replies the Germans prospered in fortune. Witness old Aurinia and that good-dame Velleda in the times of Vespasian. Believe you me, old age in women ever abounds in the qualities of the sable – I mean, the sybil.

'Come on. Come on. With the help and power of God, come on.

'Farewell, Frère Jean. Look after my codpiece.'

'All right,' said Epistemon. 'I will follow you, protesting that if she employs in her answers any lots or enchantments I shall leave you at her door and remain no longer in your company.'

How Panurge talks with the Sybil of Panzoust

CHAPTER 17

[In '52 the text begins: 'Their journey took three days. On the third they were shown . . .'

The Greek epithet applied to Heraclitus, skoteinos ('obscure'), led to punning condemnations of the obscurity of Duns Scotus.

Jupiter, Neptune and Mercury forged Orion by urinating into a chamber-pot.

Homer's 'old stoker woman' standing by the fire (Odyssey, XVIII, 27), to whom Ulysses is compared by Irus the beggar, is evoked by Rabelais in Greek, again with no concession whatsoever to his Greek-less reader. (He again had in mind an adage of Erasmus: I, VI, LXXXVI, 'Poorer than Irus', where Homer is mentioned.

Sibyls were associated with Virgil's Aeneid, 6, in which we also meet the Golden Bough (136ff., 406ff.). Rabelais' Sibyl becomes a burlesque figure partly based on that section of Aeneid, 6, as well as on 3, 443–53: 74–6, and, for the Hole of the Sibyl, 6, 9–11.]

Their journey took six days. On the seventh they were shown the house of the woman soothsayer set under a large, spreading chestnut-tree on the flank of a mountain. Without difficulty they entered the thatched hovel, which was badly built, badly furnished and all smoky.

'No matter,' said Epistemon. 'When Heraclitus, that great Scotist and opaque philosopher, entered into a similar dwelling he was in no wise put out, explaining to his followers and disciples that the gods could reside there just as easily as in palaces crammed with delights. Such I think was the hovel of [that most-famous Hecate when she entertained young Theseus; such too that of] Hireus (or, Oenopion), where Jupiter, Neptune and Mercury did not disdain to enter, eat and lodge, paying the bill by forging Orion in a chamber-pot.'

They found the old woman in the chimney-corner.

'She is a real Sibyl,' Epistemon exclaimed, 'a real naive portrait as drawn by Homer with τῇ καμινοῖ.'[8]

The old crone was in a bad way, badly dressed, badly fed, toothless, bleary-eyed, bent, snotty and droopy. She was preparing a potage of greens, yellow bacon-rind and an old meat-bone for its savour.

'Green and blue!' said Epistemon, 'we're wasting our time: we shall never get a reply out of her: we've not brought along the Golden Bough.'

'I've seen to that,' replied Panurge. 'I have here in my game-bag a golden ring in the company of some nice merry Carolus shillings.'

After saying those words Panurge made a deep bow and presented her with six smoked ox-tongues, a huge butter-jar full of fried meat-balls, a flagon full of drink, and a ram's-cod stuffed with newly minted Carolus-shillings; then finally he made a profound obeisance and placed upon her leech-finger a very handsome golden ring in which was splendidly set a toadstone from Beuxes.

Then in a few words he expounded the motive for his visit, courteously begging her to give him her advice and to foretell the future awaiting his projected marriage.

The old crone stayed silent for a while, thoughtful and sucking her teeth; then she sat down on an upturned barrel and took into her hands three ancient spindles, twisting and twiddling them between her fingers in a variety of ways. She tested their points and retained the sharpest one in her hand, tossing the other two under a mortar used for pestling millet. Then she took up her spools and spun them round nine times. At the ninth turn she gazed at them, no longer touching them and waited until they had completely stopped.

I next saw her tug off one of her *éclos* – we call them *sabots* – and place her apron over her head (as priests do with their amices when about to say Mass) tying it under her chin with an old pied and parti-coloured cloth. Thus bedizened she took a

8.   A reference to Homer's 'grimy old woman poking the fire' (*Odyssey*, 18, 27), to whom Irus the beggar compares Ulysses.

deep draught from the flagon, extracted three Carolus-shillings from the ram's cod and placed them in three walnut shells, which she deposited in the bottom of her feather jar.

Next she gave three turns round about the chimney-piece with her broom, cast into the fire a half-truss of heather, and then a dry laurel-branch, watching it burning in silence and noting that it made no crackle nor any other sound. At which she uttered a dreadful shriek and forced through her teeth a few outlandish words with strange terminations, such that Panurge said to Epistemon:

'By God's virtue, I'm all of a tremble! I believe I'm under a spell. [She's not talking Christian. Look: she seems to me to have grown four spans taller than she was when she covered her head with her apron. What's meant by that chomping of her chops? What's portended by that jectigation of her shoulders? Why is she humming through her lips like a monkey dismembering crayfish?] My ears are ringing. I think I can hear Proserpine kicking up a shindy; the devils will soon come bursting out just where we are! Nasty creatures! Let's get away quick. Serpent of God! I'm dying of fright. I do *not* like devils. They upset me and are nasty. Fly! Farewell, my Lady; many thanks for all your kindnesses.

'I shall never get married. No. I reject it now as I always have done.'

At which he started to scamper out of the room, but the old woman forestalled him, holding the spindle in her hand and going out into the backyard by her hovel where grew an ancient sycamore-tree. She shook it thrice; on eight of the leaves which tumbled down she briefly scribbled with her spindle a few short lines of verse. She then tossed them to the winds and said to Panurge, 'Go and seek them if you wish; find them if you can: the fated lot of your marriage is written on them.'

With those words she withdrew to her den; on the threshold of the door she drew her kirtle, petticoat and shift right up to her armpits and showed them her bum. Panurge observed it and said to Epistemon, 'By the blood of the wooden Ox: Behold! The Hole of the Sybil.'

She suddenly bolted the door behind her and was never seen

again. They chased after the leaves and gathered them up, but
not without difficulty, for the wind had scattered them all over
the bushes down in the valley. Then, after setting them in the
right order leaf by leaf, they found the following verdict in
verse:

> Shuck you she will,
> Your fame too;
> Swell up she will,
> Not with you;
> And suck she will
> Your good bit,
> But flay not will
> All of it.

How Pantagruel and Panurge diversely expound the Sibyl's verse

CHAPTER 18

*[Rabelais draws on an adage of Erasmus: I, X, LXXVI, 'Magistracy
reveals the man'.*

*'Palintokia' means either a second exacting of interest or a second
birth (tokos meaning both 'interest' and 'birth').*

*'Palingenesy' is a Stoic term for the restoration of the body after its
dissolution. Augustine uses it in the* City of God *(22, 28) to mean
rebirth.*

*'Glubere' and 'deglubere' in Latin (literally, 'to peel' or 'to skin')
are used with the sense of to perform fellation by Catullus (of Lesbia)
58, 5, and by Ausonius, Epigram 71, 5.*

*Women started on the task of skinning men at the Creation, then
widely taken to date from some five or six thousand years earlier.
'Artus Bumbler' renders the imaginary 'Artus Culletant'.]*

Having collected the leaves, Epistemon and Panurge returned
to the court of Pantagruel, happy in part, but in part put out:
happy, because they were back; put out, by the hardships of

the road which they found rough, stone-strewn and badly maintained.

They gave Pantagruel a full report of their journey and the circumstances of the Sibyl. Finally they presented him with the leaves of the sycamore-tree and showed him what was written in the short lines of verse.

Once he had read them through, Pantagruel said to Panurge with a sigh:

'A fine state you are in! The Sibyl's prophecy clearly expounds what has already been noted both by the Virgilian lots and your own dreams: you will be dishonoured by your wife; she will make you a cuckold, abandoning herself to another man, and by another man bearing a child; she will rob you of something important and she will batter you about, flaying and bruising some part of your body.'

'You understand the exposition of these latter prophecies,' said Panurge, 'as much as a sow understands spices. Be not offended by what I say, as I do feel a bit put out.

'Note my words: it is the contrary which is true. The old woman states that, just as a bean is not visible unless it is shucked, so too my qualities and perfections would never be widely known unless I were to be married. How many times have I heard you say that magistracy and office reveal the man (which means that we know for certain what a man's character is and what he is worth only after he is called upon to manage affairs). Before that, when a man lives in private, you never know for certain what he's like any more than you know a bean in a pod. So much for the first item. Otherwise, would you really maintain that the good reputation of an honourable man hangs on the backside of a whore!

'The second couplet says my wife will *swell up* – understand by that the greatest joy of marriage – but *not with me*. Golly, I believe that! She will swell up with some lovely little boy. I love all of him already: I'm quite dotty about him. He'll be my own little darling. From now on, no botheration in this world, however great and distracting, will enter my mind without my shrugging it off by simply looking at him and listening to him chattering away with his childish chatter.

'Blessèd be that old woman! Golly, I shall arrange a good income for her in my Salmagundian lands, not some running rent, as for some silly dons running courses, but a settled one like fine professors in their chairs.

'Otherwise would you really expect my wife to bear me in her flanks – conceive me, give birth to me – so that people should say, "Panurge is a second Bacchus: twice-born, born again," as was [Hippolytus, and as was] Proteus, first by Thetis and secondly by the mother of Apollonius the philosopher, and as were the two Palici hard by the river Simethos in Sicily – and say, "In Panurge is restored the ancient *palintokia*, (that *second-birth* of the Megarians) and the palingenesy of Democritus?"

'Wrong.

'Never mention it to me again.

'The third couplet says of my wife: *And suck she will Your good bit.*

'I am well disposed towards it: you realize that it refers to that one-ended baton dangling between my legs. I swear to you, I promise you, that I will keep it succulent and well supplied. She will not suck it off in vain: half-a-peck of juice at least shall be eternally therein. You expound this locus allegorically and interpret it as referring to thieving or theft. I approve of that exegesis and I like the allegory, but not with the sense you give to it. Doubtless the pure affection which you bear for me pulls you towards the opposite – refractory – side, since scholars say that love is a thing which is wondrously apprehensive and that without fear there is no good love.

'But I am sure that deep down inside you know that any theft in this passage means (as in so many other writers, Latin and Ancient) the sweet fruits of dalliance, which Venus wishes to be secretly and thievishly plucked. Why? Honestly, now! It is because that nice little thingummybob, done privily, between two doors, on the stairs, behind an arras, in hugger-mugger, or on a pile of loose faggots, is more pleasing to the Cyprian goddess – and I agree with that, without prejudice to a better judgement – than when performed Cynic fashion openly in sight of the sun, or between rich canopies, within gilded curtains, with plenty of time, in luxury, while crimson fans and tufts of Indic feathers waft away the flies, and the female meanwhile picks her teeth with a blade of straw pulled from the bottom of the palliasse.

'Otherwise can you really mean that she would rob me by sucking as one slurps oysters in their shells or as the women of Cilicia (according to Dioscorides) gather the grains of alkermes! Wrong! A woman who robs does not suck but pluck, she fills not her gob but her fob; steals, and conjures away by slight of hand.

'The fourth couplet says of my wife: *But flay not will, All of it.* How nicely put! You take that to mean assault and battery. Let's change the subject. Raise your minds, I beseech you, a little above earthly thoughts to a high contemplation of the wonders of Nature. Here you stand self-condemned for the mistakes you have committed by perversely expounding the prophetic utterances of that hallowed Sibyl.

'Supposing, but neither admitting nor conceding, that my wife, at the instigation of the fiend from Hell, desired to play me a dirty trick and undertook to do so, shaming me, cuckolding me up to the bum, robbing me and affronting me, she would never achieve her desire and undertaking. The reason which moves me to make that last point is extracted from the profundities of monastical pantheology.

'I was told it once by Frère Artus Bumbler – it was one Monday morning when we were both sharing a pint of andouillettes; it was raining, I remember; may God give him good-day! – women, at the beginning of the world or soon afterwards, seeing that the men sought to be their masters in all things, conspired together to flay them alive. And to that effect they vowed, confirmed and by the holy blood of Gosh, swore an oath amongst themselves. But O! The vain projects of Womankind! O! The frailty of the female sex! They began to flay Man – to *deglubere* him as Catullus puts it – with that member which they liked best, namely with the sinewy *vena cava*. That was more than six thousand years ago, and yet they have never got beyond flaying its helmet!

After a while Jewish men, out of vexation, began to trim it

and cut it off themselves by circumcision, since they preferred
to be dubbed cut-down and pruned-back Marranos rather than
men woman-beflayed, like other nations.

'My wife, in no wise derogating from that common project,
will flay me that bit (if it has not been done already). I freely
consent to that. But not flay all of me. I do assure you of that,
good my king.'

'You,' said Epistemon, 'say nothing about the fact that the
laurel branch (in our sight, with the Sibyl gazing at it and
shrieking in a frenzied frightening voice) burnt without a
crackle or any other sound. That, you know, is a baneful
augury and a most redoubtable sign, vouched for by Proper-
tius, Tibullus, that subtle philosopher Porphyry, Eustathius,
Homer's *Iliad* and others.'

'You really are adducing some ripe old asses,' replied
Panurge. 'They were as mad as poets, as raving as philosophers,
as full of the finest folly as is their philosophy.'

How Pantagruel praises the counsel of mutes

CHAPTER 19

*[We now see that Panurge is indeed deceived by the devil, who works
through self-love. Rabelais draws on Lucian's dialogue* Of the Syrian
Goddess *and, for Tiridates, on his* Dialogue of the Dance, *completed
by matter from Budé's learned treatise* On Money.

*Roman law plays an important part in this chapter: the account of
lip-reading by a certain Nello de Gabrielis is taken from a well-known
gloss of Bartolus, a medieval legal scholar who is not always honoured
by Rabelais, though this particular gloss is cited here with respect as
by Renaissance students of Law in general.*

*The tale of the Syrian boys who spontaneously spoke Phrygian is
taken from Herodotus (II, 2) an author whom Rabelais had worked
on and partly translated when still a Franciscan. The important
assertion that there is no natural language goes back to Aristotle's* On
Interpretation *and was taken up by Dante and Thomas Aquinas as
well as by many lawyers who were professionally interested in the*

origin of languages, the sense of words and their possible interpreta-
tions. (Under the influence of Plato those ideas will be deepened and
developed in the Fourth Book.)

The tale of the naughty nun appears – very chastely told– in two
works of Erasmus: Ecclesiastes *and* Fish-eating. *Erasmus claims to have*
heard it in a sermon delivered by a Dominican. ('Bottome' represents
'Fessue'; 'Stiffly-Redeem-it', Redimet.)]

Those words once said, Pantagruel for some time kept silent;
he seemed deep in thought. He then said to Panurge:

'You are seduced by the Evil Spirit; but listen: I read that
long ago the truest and surest oracles were not those delivered in
writing or uttered in words. Even people who were considered
discriminating and intelligent were many a time misled over
them, partly on account of the ambiguities, amphiboles and
obscurities in the words, partly because of the terseness of the
judgements. That is why Apollo, the god of divination, was
called *Loxias* ('oblique') in Greek. Oracles expounded by [ges-
tures and] signs were deemed truest and surest. Such was the
opinion of Heraclitus. And thus [did Jupiter vaticinate at Amon
and] Apollo prophesy amongst the Assyrians, which is why
they portrayed Apollo with a long beard, as a venerable old
person of settled wisdom, not naked, young and beardless as
portrayed by the Greeks.

'Let us employ that method and seek advice from someone
who is dumb, using signs not words.'

'I agree,' replied Panurge.

'But,' said Pantagruel, 'it should be one who is mute because
he was born deaf, for there is no purer mute than one who has
never been able to hear.'

'What do you mean!' replied Panurge. 'If it were true that no
one ever spoke who had never heard any speech I could bring
you logically to infer a proposition both paradoxical and
absurd. But let it drop. You do not credit, then, what Herodotus
wrote of those two boys who, by order of Psammeticus, the
king of the Egyptians, were confined to a hut, brought up in
perpetual silence and after a period of time uttered the word
becus (the Phrygian word for bread)?'

'Not in the least,' replied Pantagruel. 'It is misleading to claim that there is one natural language. Languages arise from arbitrary impositions and conventions amongst peoples: vocables (as the philologists put it) do not signify naturally but at pleasure. I do not tell you this idly: Bartolus (*On the First Law: "On the Obligations of Words"*) relates how there was in his day a certain Signor Nello de Gabrielis in Gubbio who had become deaf through an accident; he nevertheless understood anything that an Italian said, however quietly spoken, exclusively from his gestures and the movement of his lips.

'I have also read in a learned and elegant author how Tiridates, the king of Armenia in the time of Nero, visited Rome and was received with solemn honours and magnificent ceremonies aimed at binding him in a sempiternal friendship to the Roman Senate and People; there was nothing worthy of attention which was not then shown and displayed to him. At his departure the Emperor bestowed on him great and surpassing gifts and further gave him the option of choosing whatever best pleased him in Rome, with a sworn undertaking not to deny him anything he asked for. But he merely asked for one of the players in the farces whom he had seen in the theatre. He had never understood a word he said, yet he had understood what he had conveyed by signs and gesticulations, adding that within his dominions there were peoples of a variety of tongues, requiring several interpreters to reply to them and address them, yet that one actor would suffice for them all, for he was so outstanding at communicating by gesture that he seemed to talk with his fingers.

'You ought therefore to choose a mute who is deaf by nature so that his gestures and signs may be naturally prophetic, not feigned, falsified or affected.

'There remains for us to know whether you prefer to take such advice from a man or a woman.'

'I would willingly take it from a woman,' Panurge replied, 'were it not that I fear two things: one is that, no matter what they see, women always mentally conceive, consider and imagine it to refer to the penetration of the hallowed Ithyphallus. No matter what signs, gestures or gesticulations you make in their sight or in their presence, they relate them to the motions of the sieve. And so we would all be misled: the woman would think that all our signs were erotic.

'Remember what happened in Rome two hundred and sixty years after it was founded: a young Roman gentleman met on Mount Coelion a lady from Latium called Verona; she was born deaf and dumb but he, unaware of her deafness, asked her, while making Italianate gestures, what time it was by the clock on the Tarpeian Rock.[9] She, not knowing what he said, imagined it referred to what was ever in her thoughts and what a young man naturally requires of a woman. So, by signs (which are incomparably more seductive, efficacious and compelling in courtship than words), she drew him aside into her house and made signs to show that she liked the game. And so finally, without one word of mouth, they produced a beautiful sound of bouncing bottoms.

'The second is that the women would utter no reply whatever to our signs: they would simply fall flat on their backs, consenting practically to our unspoken requests. Or else, if they did make any reply to our propositions, it would be signs so fond and ridiculous that we ourselves would judge their thoughts to be erotic.

'You know how that nun, Sister Bottome in Croquignoles, was got with child by a begging brother called Stiffly-Redeem-it. When the bulge became evident she was summoned by the abbess to the chapter-house and taxed with incest. She made excuses, maintaining that it had not happened with her consent but by violence, through being raped by Frère Stiffly-Redeem-it.

'The abbess said, "You wicked little thing! It took place in the dormitory. Why did you not cry, 'Rape'? We would all have rushed in to help you."

'She replied that she dared not cry out in the dormitory: in the dormitory one kept perpetual silence.

'"But, you wicked little thing!" said the abbess, "why did you not make signs to the other nuns in the room?"

9.   '52; . . . Italaniate gestures, *which senators she had met on the way up.* She, not knowing . . .

' "I," said La Bottome, "did make signs as hard as I could:
with my bum; but nobody came to help me."

' "But, you wicked little thing," demanded the abbess, "why
did you not come straightaway to me, to tell me and formally
accuse him? If it had happened to me, that is what I would have
done to prove my innocence."

' "Because," said La Bottome, "fearing to remain in sin – in
a state of damnation – when overcome by sudden death, I made
my confession to him before he left the room. The penance he
gave me was not to reveal it and to tell it to nobody. To reveal
his absolution would have been a most enormous sin, most
odious before God and the angels. It might perhaps have been
the cause of fire from Heaven burning down the whole of our
abbey, and we might all have been cast down into the pit with
Datham and Abiram." '

'You will never get me to laugh at that,' said Pantagruel. 'I
know full well that the whole of the cloistered riff-raff are less
afraid of trespassing against the commandments of God than
against their provincial statutes.

'Take a man, then. Nazdecabre seems suitable to me: he has
been deaf and dumb from birth.'

How Nazdecabre replied to Panurge by signs

CHAPTER 20

[This chapter recalls the fun in Pantagruel at the expense of Thaumaste
with his signs and gestures. Nazdecabre's gesture when he touches
Panurge's navel describes an item in the games of Gargantua: 'Up, up
the ladder, hand upon hand'.

'Pistolandier' is a dagger, translated here by 'Pisstool'.

Davus is a common name for a slave in Plautus, Terence, Perseus
and others. Cf. Erasmus' Adage, I, III, XXXVI, 'I am Davus not
Oedipus'.

By citing the axiom 'Every truth is consonant with every other truth'
Pantagruel emphasizes that all those consulted agree over what is in

*store for Panurge if he marries, which they would not have done if
they had been false.]*

Nazdecabre was sent for and arrived the next day. On his
arrival Panurge offered him a fatted calf, half a pig, two barrels
of wine, a load of corn plus thirty francs in small coins. He
then brought him before Pantagruel, and there, in the presence
of the Gentlemen of the Chamber, made him the following sign:
he produced a very long yawn and while doing so formed the
shape of the Greek letter Tau with his right hand just before
his mouth, frequently repeating it. He then raised his eyes to
Heaven and rolled them about in his head like a nanny-goat
when she aborts, coughing as he did so and deeply sighing.
Having done that, he pointed to his lack of a codpiece, put his
hand under the hem of his shirt, grabbed hold of his pisstool
and flapped it melodiously against his thighs; he then leant
forward, bending his left knee and remained thus, holding both
his arms folded over his chest.

Nazdecabre watched him carefully, then raised his left hand
in the air and clenched all his fingers together in his fist, except
the index as well as his thumb, the two nails of which he
coupled gently together.

'I understand what he means by that sign,' said Pantagruel:
'it signifies marriage and also the number thirty according to
the doctrines of the Pythagoreans. You will be married.'

'Thank you very much,' said Panurge, turning towards
Nazdecabre, 'thank you my little Ruler-of-the-feast, my Master
of the galley-slaves, my Warder [, my Archer-of-the-Watch, my
Chief Sbirro].'

Then Nazdecabre raised his left hand higher up in the air,
extended all five fingers, stretching them as widely apart as he
could.

'Here,' said Pantagruel, 'by signifying the number five, he more
amply suggests that you will be married. And not merely
betrothed, engaged and married, but you will lie together and
live it up. For Pythagoras called Five the number for nuptials,
weddings and consummated marriages, because it is a compound

of Three (the first odd, superflue number) and Two (the first even number), representing male and female conjoined. In Rome they used indeed to light five wax torches on the wedding-night, and it was forbidden to light more even for the nuptials of the richest, or fewer, even for the nuptials of the most indigent. Moreover, in days gone by, pagans used to invoke five gods (or one god dispensing five boons) over those who were being married: Nuptial Jove, Juno, who presided over the marriage-feast, Venus the Beautiful, Pytho, the goddess of persuasion and fair converse, and Diana for succour in the labours of childbirth.'

'O what a delightful Nazdecabre!' cried Panurge. 'I would like to grant him a farm near Cinais and a windmill in Mirabeau.'

Whereupon the mute, turning to the left, gave a sneeze of such mind-departing violence that it shook his entire body.

'Wooden-Ox almighty!' said Pantagruel, 'what is he up to! That's not in your favour. It signifies that your marriage will be ill-favoured and wretched. That sneeze (according to the doctrine of Terpsion) is the daemon of Socrates, which, when turning to the right, signifies that one can confidently and assuredly do whatever, and go wherever, as projected; the beginning, continuance and outcome of it will be good and fortunate; turned to the left, it means the contrary.'

'You are always interpreting things for the worst,' said Panurge, 'forever perturbed like a second Davus. I simply do not believe it. And I know poor shabby old little-read Terpsion only for his failures.'

'Yet Cicero says something or other about him,' said Pantagruel, 'in the Second Book of *On divination*.'

Then Panurge turned towards Nazdecabre and made the following sign: he rolled his eyelids upwards, wrenched his chin from right to left and stuck his tongue halfway out of his mouth. That done, he opened his left hand flat, except for the middle finger, which he kept perpendicular to his palm, and placed it thus where his codpiece should be: the right he kept tightly clenched into a fist, (save for the thumb which he stuck up) and twisted it back below his right armpit, placing it firmly between the cheeks of his backside over the spot which the Arabs call *Al katim*.

Then he suddenly changed over, giving his right hand the form of the left and placing it where his codpiece should be, and giving the left the form of the right, placing it over *Al katim*.

Nine times he repeated that changing-over of hands. On the ninth he returned his eyelids to their natural position, doing the same for his chin and his tongue. Then he cast a cock-eyed glance at Nazdecabre, clacking his chops as idle monkeys do and as coneys do when nibbling at oats on the sheaf.

Whereupon Nazdecabre raised his right hand into the air, flat open, then placed its thumb just on the first articulation between the third juncture – between the middle-finger and the leech-finger – squeezing them quite firmly round the thumb, bending their remaining articulations back into a fist and extending the index and the little finger. His hand, thus composed, he placed on Panurge's navel, continually wiggling the said thumb and resting that hand on his little finger and index finger as on two legs. And thus he set his hand climbing in turn up over Panurge's belly, chest, breast and neck and finally up to the chin, sticking that wiggling thumb into Panurge's mouth. He rubbed Panurge's nose with it, then, mounting further still towards the eyes, made as if he intended to poke them out with his thumb.

At which Panurge grew angry and attempted to draw back and rid himself of the mute. But Nazdecabre, with that wiggling thumb, went on touching now his eyes, now his forehead, now the brim of his bonnet. In the end Panurge cried out, saying:

'By God, Master Idiot, you'll be thrashed if you do not let me be. Make me any more angry and my hand will slap a mask on your bloody face.'

'He's deaf, you silly bollock,' said Frère Jean. 'He can't hear a word you're saying. Make him a sign meaning a rain of blows on his conk!'

'What the devil does this know-it-all think he's doing?' said Panurge. 'He's all but given me an eye poached in black butter! By God – allow me to swear! – I'll treat you to a banquet of bonks on the nose interlarded with double flicks on the smeller.'

Then he went off, aiming at him a volley of farts.

The mute, seeing Panurge marching off, got in front of him, forced him to stop and made him the following sign: he lowered his right arm towards his knee as far as he could stretch it, squeezing all his fingers into a fist and thrusting the thumb between the middle and index fingers; with his left hand he then stroked the upper side of his right elbow and gradually, as he stroked, raised that hand into the air as far as the elbow and beyond, then suddenly brought it down to where it had been. Then he raised and lowered it at intervals and showed it to Panurge.

Panurge was angered by that and raised his fist to strike the mute, but out of respect for the presence of Pantagruel he held back.

Pantagruel then said:

'If the signs anger you, O how much more will the things they signify! Every truth is consonant with all other truths.

'The mute means and claims that you will be married, cuckolded, beaten and robbed.'

'I concede the marriage,' said Panurge, 'and deny the rest. I beseech you to do me the favour of believing that never had man such luck over women and horses as is predestined to me.'

How Panurge takes counsel from an aged French poet called Raminagrobis

CHAPTER 21

[It is Socrates, in Plato's Phaedo, 85 AB, who teaches that dying poets may be divinely inspired and therefore prophetic. This dying old sage, despite his comic pussy-cat name, is wise, as is the dying man in the Colloquy of Erasmus called Funus (the Funeral) in which the evangelical Christian wishes to be left to die in peace, untroubled by rapacious Franciscans, Dominicans and others, varied in their vestments but all after his money. The platonic explanation of the prophetic powers of the dying, which compares the departing soul to

a traveller exchanging signals with friends glimpsed from afar on the
quayside as their ship draws near to the harbour, is from a well-known
passage of Plutarch's On the Genius of Socrates. *The seriousness of*
the chapter for Rabelais is emphasized by the allusion to the death of
his late patron Guillaume Du Bellay, the Seigneur de Langey, the
statesman brother of his present patron Cardinal Jean Du Bellay.
Rabelais was present at Langey's death on the way back from Italy,
having served there in his household. For Rabelais he was, in the
strictest sense, a hero. (See in the Fourth Book, *Chapter 27.)*

The reference to La Grande Gorre, the second wife of Ramina-
grobis, producing the fair Bazoche, is obscure. It may well refer to a
Mardi Gras procession in which a grotesque figure representing La
Grande Gorre (the pox? an elegant woman?) gives birth to La Bazoche
(the whole company of lawyers' clerks in Paris), but its meaning in
context remains puzzling.

Two adages of Erasmus are exploited: I, IV, XXX, 'To move every
stone', and 'I, II, LV, 'Swan Song'.

The verse cited is by Guillaume Crétin, though Rabelais may not
have known that fact as the poem appeared anonymously in an
anthology.

The final words of Raminagrobis are markedly evangelical, echoing
well-known phrases of Scripture (from, for example, Deuteronomy
31:29; Matthew 6:8; Revelation, 17:14, etc.).

The name of Raminagrobis might suggest a fat-cat, a hypocrite, but
Rabelais is showing that names can be misleading.]

'I never ever expected to meet anyone as stubborn in his precon-
ceptions as I see that you are,' said Pantagruel. 'Yet I am sure
that we should leave no stone unturned to throw light on to
your problem. Listen to my suggestion.

'Swans, which are birds sacred to Apollo, never sing except
when death approaches – specifically on the Meander, which is
a Phrygian river (I add that because [Aelian and] Alexander
Myndius write of having seen many die elsewhere but none die
singing) – so that a swan's song is a sure presage of its approaching death, and it will never die before it has sung. Poets,
who are similarly under the protection of Apollo, normally turn
prophetic as death approaches, singing under the inspiration of

Apollo and foretelling things to come. I have often heard it said, moreover, that every aged man, when frail and near his end, may readily divine future events. I recall that Aristophanes in one of his comedies calls old men Sibyls: Ὁ δὲ γέρων σιβυλλιᾷ.[10]

'For when we are on a jetty and see the mariners and the passengers in their ships far off upon the high seas we can only gaze at them in silence and pray piously for their safe berthing; but when they draw close to harbour we can greet them by both word and gesture and congratulate them on having reached us ashore in a safe port; similarly, according to the doctrines of the Platonists, angels, heroes and good daemons, seeing humans draw close to death (as to a most safe and salutary port of rest and quietness, free from earthly cares and solicitudes,) welcome them, comfort them, speak with them and already begin to communicate to them the art of divination.

'I will not cite you the ancient examples as Isaac, Jacob, Patroclus with regard to Hector; Hector with regard to Achilles, [Polynestor with regard to both Agamemnon and Hecuba,] that man of Rhodes celebrated by Posidonius; Calanus of India with regard to Alexander the Great; Orodes with regard to Mezentius, and so on. I wish simply to recall to your mind that learned and gallant nobleman Guillaume Du Bellay, the late Seigneur de Langey, who died on Mount Tarara on the tenth of January in the year of his climacteric (1543 as we count it, Roman style).

'The three or four hours before he died he employed in vigorous words, calm and serene in mind, foretelling to us what we have since partly seen already and now partly await to happen, even though, at the time, those prophecies seemed to us strange and implausible because no present cause or sign was then apparent portending what he foretold.

'Here, near La Ville-au-Maire, we have a man who is both aged and a poet, Raminagrobis, who took La Grande Gorre as his second wife, producing the fair Bazoche. I have heard that

10. Rabelais gives this in Greek (from Aristophanes, *The Knights*, 1, 1, 61) and takes it to mean 'The old man plays the Sybil'. Yet again he supposes his readers can read Greek.

he is at his last gasp and on the point of death. Make your way to him and hear his swan song. Perhaps you will find out from him what you seek and your doubt be resolved through him by Apollo.'

'I want to,' said Panurge. 'Let us go there straight away, Epistemon, lest death should forestall us. Do you want to come, Frère Jean?'

'Yes I do, most willingly' replied Frère Jean, 'out of affection for you, my little bollock, for I love you with all my liver!'

They set out that hour and, arriving at the poetic abode, found the good old man in the throes of death, with a joyful demeanour, an open expression and a radiant look. Panurge greeted him and, simply as a gift, placed on his leech-finger a gold ring with an oriental sapphire set in it, large and beautiful. Then, in imitation of Socrates, he offered him a fair white cockerel, which, as soon as it was put down on the bed, raised its head, shook its feathers with great delight, and shrilly crowed. That done, Panurge courteously begged him to speak and expound his judgement on the problem of his projected marriage. The good old man ordered ink, pen and paper to be brought in. All was promptly provided. Whereupon he wrote as follows:

> Take a wife and take her not.
> Take her, there is good in view.
> Take her not and it is true
> You will find a measured lot.
> Gallop, and yet merely trot.
> Backwards go yet forwards too:
> Take her do: take her n . . .
> Fast, but eat a double lot;
> Undo what has been tied anew;
> Tie it again, retie it, do;
> Wish life and death to be her lot:
> Take her do: take her n . . .

He then put it in their hands and said to them:
'Go, my sons, under the protection of the great God in

Heaven and bother me no more with this nor any other matter
whatsoever. This day, the very last of May and of me, I have
chased from my home, with great labour and difficulty, a rabble
of wicked, filthy, pestilential creatures: black, parti-coloured,
dun, white, ash-grey and motley, who would not let me die at
my ease, and who, with their fraudulent goadings, harpyish
grasping, hornet-like solicitations fashioned in the forge of
some insatiable greed, call me away from the sweet thoughts
in which I found repose, contemplating, seeing, and already
touching and tasting that joy and felicity which God in his
goodness has prepared for his faithful elect in the life to come,
our immortal state.

'Decline from their ways: be not like unto them; trouble me
no more, and, I beseech you, leave me in silence.'

How Panurge pleads for the Order of the Friars Mendicant

CHAPTER 22

*[An amusing, challenging chapter, one which would have aroused the
ire of many censors. The chapter is markedly Erasmian and Lutheran
in its tone and implications. Panurge is now all superstition and
haunted by devils.*

*That the grasping larvae about the death-bed of Raminagrobis were
indeed variously garbed members of religious Orders seems clear from
what Erasmus wrote in his Colloquy Funus (The Funeral). Epistemon's
'innocent' and charitable interpretation of the larvae is perhaps analo-
gous to Frère Jean's interpretation of the enigma in the last words of
Gargantua.*

*Epistemon cites Tiresias from Erasmus, Adages, III, III, XXXV 'A
good sign, or a bad'.*

*There is an important echo of the colloquy of Erasmus entitled
'Fish-eating'.*

*Towards the end of the chapter Rabelais risked a mild enough jest
– which he was certainly not the first or last to make – by which he
first printed* asne *(ass) as a feigned lapsus for* âme *(soul). Since the*

play on asne *and* âme *is not possible in English, I have transposed* ass *to* mole *(with* mole *forming the lapsus for* soul*). Rabelais later eliminated the jest and printed* âme. *He maintains in the* Preliminary Epistle *to the* Fourth Book *that it was only a misprint, attributable to the error of a careless printer.]*

Once he was out of the bedchamber of Raminagrobis, Panurge, as one utterly terrified, said:

'By the might of God, I believe he's an heretic: or else may the devil take me. He's bad-mouthing those good mendicant Friars and the Dominicans, who constitute the two hemispheres of Christendom, through whose sententiously gyrating circunt-umbilico-vaginations – as though by two counterweights producing movements in the heavens – the [antonomastic asthenia of the] whole Roman Church, whenever she feels herself driven frantic by any gibbering of error or heresy, homocentrically flutters!

'By all the devils, what have all those poor devils of Capuchins and Minims done to him? Are they not woeful enough already, poor devils! Are they not smoky and smelly enough already from wretchedness and disaster, those poor sods drawn out of Ichthyophagia?

'Frère Jean, by your faith: is he in a state of salvation! He's damned, by God like a serpent, he's on his way to thirty thousand hod-loads of devils. Speaking ill of those good and valiant pillars of the Church! Is that what you call poetic inspiration? I can't stand it! He's villainously sinning by blaspheming against the religious orders. I'm greatly scandalized.'

'I don't care a jot,' said Frère Jean. 'They speak ill of all the world: if all the world speaks ill of them it in no ways bothers me! Let's see what he wrote.'

Panurge read attentively what the old man had written, then said to them:

'He was rambling, the poor old soak. I forgive him, though. I think he's approaching his end. Let's go and write his epitaph.

'After the answer he gave us I'm just about as wise as we bake 'em! Listen to it, Epistemon, old chap. Is he decisive in his answers, do you think! By God, he's a subtle sophist, born so, and full of *ergos*; I bet he's a half-converted Jew!

'Ox's guts! How careful he is not to choose the wrong words. Whatever he says is bound to be right; his replies are all disjunctive propositions: it is enough for one part of them to be true. It's worthy of Pathelin. By Santiago de Bressuire, is his race still thriving then?'

'The great prophet Tiresias,' replied Epistemon 'made similar avowals at the beginning of all his divinations, stating clearly to all who came to consult him: "What I say will either happen, or not happen at all." And such is the way of all wise prognosticators.'

'Juno poked both his eyes out though,' said Panurge.

'True,' replied Epistemon, 'but that was out of malice because he'd given a better judgement than she did over the doubt proposed by Jupiter.'

'But,' said Panurge, 'what the devil possessed Master Raminagrobis to make him – without any provocation, without any reason, without any cause – speak ill of these poor wretched and blessèd Fathers: Capuchins, Friars Minor and Minims? I'm deeply scandalized by it, I assure you, and cannot keep quiet about it. Grievously has he sinned. His mole has gone off to thirty thousand hamperfuls of devils.'

'I do not follow you,' replied Epistemon. 'It's you who greatly scandalize me, perversely applying to the Mendicant Friars what that good poet was saying about vermin, black, dun and so on. In my judgement he never intended so sophistical and fantastic an allegory. He was absolutely and literally alluding to fleas, bugs, flesh-worms, flies, mosquitoes and other such insects, some of which are black, others dun or ash-grey, others tanned or dusky, all of which are importunate, oppressive and bothersome, not only to the sick but also to the healthy and strong.

'Perhaps he had some ascarids, stomach-worms or *vermes* in his body. Perhaps he suffered (as is common and usual in Egypt in the confines of the Sea of Erythraea) from a puncturing of the flesh of his arms or legs by the smaller speckled guinea-worm which the Arabs call *meden*.

'You do evil to expound his words otherwise. You wrong that good poet by detraction, and the said Fathers by attributing such bad qualities to them. One should always interpret favourably whatever concerns one's neighbour.'

'Teach me to spot flies in milk!' said Panurge. 'He is, by God's might, an heretic. I mean a formed heretic, a scabby heretic, an heretic as burnable as a pretty little clock.[11] His mole is off to thirty thousand wagon-loads of devils. Know where? Golly, right under the close-stool of Proserpine, my friend, right inside that hellish basin where she discharges the faecal products of her clysters, to the left side of the Great Cauldron, six yards from the claws of Lucifer in the direction of Demogorgon.[12] Ugh. Nasty specimen!'

How Panurge argues for a return to Raminagrobis

CHAPTER 23

[Panurge talks of the devil as never before. The propaganda against the formalities of contrition would have sounded Lutheran. The reference to the wife of the Provost of Orleans is to a real event: the local Franciscan friars hid a novice under the high altar who pretended to be the dead woman's spirit. The trickery was discovered and became a public scandal. The feigned lapsus asne (ass) and âme (soul) is found in this chapter too, until it was 'corrected' by Rabelais. (Again it is transposed.)

Flagellation was often ritually accompanied by the singing of Psalm 50 (51). The threatened flagellation here would be kept up from the first words of that Psalm, 'Have mercy on me', to the last words, 'bullocks upon thine altar'.

The 'Doctor Subtilis' was Duns Scotus.

The reference to Aeneas and his descent to the underworld is to Aeneid, 6, 260 and context.

11. 'The heretic burnable as a pretty little clock' has not been satisfactorily explained.
12. In '52 Rabelais changed 'Demorgogon' (the father of the devils) to 'Demiourgon', which evokes the Classical demiurge.

Devils were said to fear the effects of sharp swords on the authority of Psellus, in his treatise On Daemons: *'Such cuts hurt them, though they cannot wound them.']*

'Let's go back,' said Panurge, continuing, 'to admonish him about his salvation. Let's go in the name – go in the might – of God. That will be a work of charity on our part. At least, if he loses his body and his life, let him not damn his mole. We will induce him to feel contrition for his sins and to beg pardon from the said most blessèd Fathers, both absent and present, and we will have it legally documented so that he mayn't be declared an heretic after his death and damned, something those cowled Hobgoblins did to the wife of the Provost of Orleans. He must atone for his outrage by establishing for all the good monastical Fathers in all the convents of this province plenty of collections, plenty of Masses, plenty of obits and anniversaries.

'And on the anniversary of his death they must all have their rations quintupled for all eternity; and may the huge flagon filled with the choicest wine trot from bench to bench along their tables, for the drones, lay brothers and begging brothers as much as for the priests and clerics, both novices and professed.

'Thus shall he obtain pardon from God.

'Ah! Ah! I am wronging myself, getting carried away by my own words. If ever I go back there may the devil take me! Might of God! His bed-chamber is already full of devils. I can hear them squabbling and having a devil of a quarrel amongst themselves over which will slurp up that Raminagrobitical soul and which will be the first to bring it to Lucifer's lips straight from the spit.

'Avaunt, foul fiends! I am not going to go. The devil take me if I do. Who knows: they might take tother for which, making off with poor old debtless Panurge in lieu of Raminagrobis! They often failed to get me when I sported yellow as a debtor. Avaunt, foul fiends! I am not going to go. I'm dying from a mad fit of funk. Fancy being amidst hungry devils, battling devils, functioning devils.

'Avaunt, foul fiends! I bet you that not one Dominican, Franciscan, Carmelite [, Capuchin] or Minim will go to his funeral – for the same misgivings! That's wise of them. Besides, he left them nothing in his will. If I go there, may the devil take me! If he's damned, he's self-condemned. Why did he bad-mouth those good monastical Fathers? Why did he hound them out of his bed-chamber just when he had greatest need of their aid, of their devout prayers and holy exhortations? Why did he never bequeath to those poor wretches, who have nothing in this world but their lives, some alms, a little fodder and something to line their guts with?

'Go there who will! If I go there, may the devil take me! He would do so if I did. Holy Crab! Avaunt, foul fiends.

'Frère Jean, do you want thirty thousand wagon-loads of devils to bear you off here and now? Then do these three things.

'*First: give me your purse:* for crosses work against enchantments, and there could happen to you what happened at the ford of Vède to Jean Dodin, the toll-collector of Le Couldray, when soldiers smashed up the plank-way. On the bank that prick-proud fellow came across Frère Adam Couscoil of the Observantine Friars at Mirebeau, and promised him a new frock if he would carry him across the river, slung over his shoulder like a dead goat. The Friar was a hefty rogue, you know. It was agreed.

'Frère Jean Couscoil pulled his skirts right up to his balls and, like a handsome little Saint Christopher, loaded Dodin, the said suppliant, on to his back. And so he merrily carried him (as Aeneas carried Father Anchises out of the conflagration of Troy), singing *Hail Mary, Star of the Sea.* When they had reached the deepest part of the ford above the mill-wheel, he asked him whether he had got any coins at all on him. Dodin replied that he had a game-bag full of them and that he was not to worry about his promise to provide him with a new habit. "What!" said Frère Couscoil. "You know there's a special section in our Rule which rigorously forbids us to carry any money on our persons. Cursed are you for making me sin in this matter! Why didn't you leave your purse with the miller? You shall be punished for it here and now, without fail. And if ever I get my hands on you in our chapter at Mirebeau you will be flagellated from *Have mercy upon me* down to *bullocks upon thine altar*."

'Then he dumps his load and pitches Dodin head first into the deep. After such an example, give me your purse, Frère Jean, my gentle friend, so that the devils may carry you off more comfortably: do not keep any crosses on you: the danger is obvious. If you have any coins with crosses on them the devils will drop you on to some rocks just as eagles drop tortoises to shatter their shells: witness the bald head of the poet Aeschylus; and you would do yourself some harm, my friend (and that would make me sad); or else they'll drop you into the sea like Icarus, I know not where, far away. And thereafter it will be called the Sea of Entommeures.

'*Secondly: be out of debt*, for devils love those who repay their debts. I know that from my own case: those riff-raff never stop making eyes at me and courting me now: something they never did when I was sporting debtor's yellow. I was owing money: and the soul of a man in debt is all emaciated and dried up. It is not fit meat for devils.

'*Thirdly: go back to Raminagrobis* with your frock and your fat-cat cowl. I'll pay for drink and tinder if thirty thousand boatloads of devils don't bear you away thus elegantly bedizened. And if you want to have someone go with you for your safety, don't come looking for me. No. I warn you. Avaunt foul fiends! I am not going there. If I do, the devil take me.'

'With this sharp brackmard in my grip, replied Frère Jean, 'I would worry less than you might perhaps suppose.'

'You have got hold of the right end of the stick,' said Panurge, 'and spout like a *Doctor Subtilis* in the 'eart of magic. When I was studying in the University of Toledo, Picatrix, the Reverend Father-in-the-Devil, the Rector of the Faculty of Diabolology, told us that devils naturally fear the glint of swords as well as the light of the sun. And indeed, when Hercules went to all the devils in Hell, he never terrified them as much with his lion's skin and his club as Aeneas later did clad in shining armour and furnished with his brackmard, duly de-rusted and brightly furbished with the aid and counsel of the Cumaean Sybil.

'That – perhaps – is why, Field-Marshal Jean-Jacques de Trivulzi, on his death-bed in Chartres, called for his naked sword and died with it in his hand, laying about him right and left all round his bed, and, like a valiant and chivalrous knight, put to flight with that sword-play all the devils lying in wait for him on his passing to death.

'When one asks the Massoretes and Cabbalists why devils can never get into the earthly Paradise, they give no reason apart from the fact that a Cherubim stands by the gate holding a flaming torch. For I admit that, according to the true diabolology of Toledo, devils cannot actually die from sword-cuts, but I maintain, following the aforesaid diabolology, that they can suffer a dissolution of continuity, as when you slash with your brackmard through a burning flame or a thick veil of smoke. And when they feel that dissolution they make a devil of a shriek since it is devilishly painful.

'When you see the shock of two armies, do you think, do you believe, gross bollock, that the great and horrifying din that you hear comes only from the voices of men, the ring of armour, the clatter of the bards of the war-horses, the thud of maces, the clash of pikes, the shattering of lances, the cries of the wounded, the sound of the tabor and trumpet, the whinnying of horses and the thunder of blunderbuss and cannon? That counts for something, I admit. But the most terrifying din and the principal uproar arises from the anguished howls of the devils, who, lying in wait in that confused garboil, receive chance blows from swords and suffer ruptures in the continuity of their substances, which are both aerial and invisible. It is as when the chef, Master Grubby, gives a rap over the knuckles to scullery-boys munching rashers from the spit. Then they howl and ululate like devils, as did Mars when he was wounded by Diomedes before Troy: Homer says that he yelled at a higher pitch and with more terrifying shrieks than ten thousand men put together.

'But what is all this! Here we are talking of furbished armour and shining swords: that doesn't apply to your brackmard. From disuse and lack of service it is, by my faith, rustier than the clasp of an old pork-barrel. Therefore do one of two things:

either truly and smartly de-rust it or, if you keep it as it is, all rusted up, take care not to return to Raminagrobis.

'For my part, I am not going to go. If I do, may the devil take me.'

How Panurge takes counsel from Epistemon

CHAPTER 24

[Like Gargantua after his foul education at the hands of Sorbonagres, Panurge needs to be treated with hellebore, the Classical cure for madness. (Cf. Erasmus, Adages, I, VIII, LI, 'To drink hellebore'.)

Epistemon criticizes the narrative style of Enguerrand de Monstrelet in the light of Lucian's How to Write History.

Rabelais edited and translated the Aphorisms *of Hippocrates. The first aphorism, dealing with 'the Art' (that is, the Art of Medicine) states that 'Art is long: life is short, and judgement is difficult'.*

Rabelais has read Plutarch's Why Oracles Have Ceased, *which comes into its own on his next Book. For Panurge's 'Ogygian Isles' he again turned to Plutarch, to his treatise* On the Face to Be Seen in the Moon.

He remembers an adage of Erasmus: I, V, XXIX, 'As mute as fishes'.

The wise Epistemon's hesitation about consulting oracles parallels the hesitations expressed in the poem cited in Chapter 21.

*A play on words (*souris, *mouse and* soubris, *smile) has been transposed to amusing/amousing.]*

Once they had left La Ville-au-Maire and were on the way back to Pantagruel, Panurge addressed himself to Epistemon:

'My old friend and companion,' he said, 'you can see my mental perplexity. You know so many good cures. Could you possibly help me?'

Epistemon took up the subject and firmly pointed out that the common talk was entirely devoted to mocking his strange attire: he advised him to take a dram of hellebore to purge his faulty humour, and to return to his normal clothes.

'I,' said Panurge, 'am disposed, Epistemon, my dear companion, to get married, but I'm afraid of being cuckolded and unlucky in my marriage. That's why I've sworn a vow to Saint Francis-the-Less (who is invoked with great devotion by the women of Plessis-les-Tours, since he was the original Founder of the Minims, those "Good Men" for whom they feel a natural desire) that I shall wear my spectacles in my cap and shall never wear trunk-hose until I find a clear resolution of my mental perplexity.'

'A truly lovely and laughable vow, I must say,' replied Epistemon. 'I am astonished that you don't come to yourself; don't summon your senses back from their wild wanderings to their natural tranquillity.

'As I listen to you I am reminded of the vow of the long-haired Argives, who, when they had lost the battle against the Spartans in the quarrel over Thyraea, swore never to let their hair grow long on their heads until they had regained their land and their honour. Also of the vow of that silly Spaniard Miguel d'Oris to sport only one part of the greave protecting his leg. I really do not know who is more worthy and deserving of wearing the green-and-yellow fool's cap with its hare's ears, that boastful champion or Enguerrand, who gives a long, intricate and boring account of him, forgetful of the *Art and Manner of writing Histories* given us by the philosopher from Samosata. For as you read his long narration, you think that it must be about the beginning of some fierce war or the occasion of some significant mutation of kingdoms; yet in the end you simply laugh at that boobyish champion, at the Englishman who challenged him and at Enguerrand their chronicler as he dribbles on worse than a mustard-pot.

'We mock them as we mock that Mountain in Horace which was hugely crying and lamenting like a woman in labour; at her cries and lamentation all the neighbours ran up, expecting to witness some wondrous and portentous childbirth, yet in the end all that was born of her was a trifling mouse.'

'No amousing trifle for me at this point,' said Panurge. 'The limper mocks the lame! I shall do as my vow requires. A long time has passed since you and I swore mutual faith and friendship by Jupiter Philios: now give me your advice. Should I marry or no?'

'The matter,' said Epistemon, 'is certainly fraught with risk: I feel quite inadequate to resolve it. And if ever what Hippocrates of Lango said of old was true of the Art of medicine, JUDGE-MENT IS DIFFICULT, in this matter it is true absolutely.

'I do have in mind certain arguments which could lead us to a resolving of your perplexity, but they fail to satisfy me by their clarity. Some Platonists state that whoever can see his Genius can know his destiny, but I cannot fully understand their doctrine and do not advise you to give it your adherence: a great deal of it is misleading. I have witnessed the experience of an East-Anglian nobleman, both learned and scholarly.

'That is point number one.

'And now for another.

'If the oracles – of [Jupiter in Amon], of Apollo in Lebadia, Delphi, Delos, Patara, Cyrrha, Tegyra, Praeneste, Lycia and Colophon [and in the fountain to be found amongst the Branchides of Castalia near Antioch in Syria]; or of Bacchus in Dodona; of Mercury in Pharae near Patras; of Apis in Egypt; of Serapis in Canopus; of Faunus in Maenalia and Albunaea near Tivoli; of Tyresias in Orchomene; of Mopsus in Cilicia; of Orpheus in Lesbos, and of Trophonius in Leucadia – still held sway, I would (though perhaps I wouldn't) counsel you to go and hear what their judgement on your undertaking might be.

'But as you know, they have all become as mute as fishes since the advent of our great Servator King, in whom all oracles and all prophecies found an end: as with the advent of the bright light of the sun there vanish all hobgoblins, lamias, lemurs, werewolves, bogies and spirits of darkness.

'Even if those oracles did still hold sway, I would not readily advise you to trust in their replies. Too many people have been deceived in them.

'I recall, moreover, that Agrippina rebuked the fair Lollia for asking the oracle of Apollo Clarius whether she would be married to the Emperor Claudius; for which Lollia was first banished and subsequently put ignominiously to death.'

'But let us do something better,' said Panurge. 'The Ogygian

Isles are not far from Saint Malo. Let us sail to them, having first spoken of it to our King. In one of those four isles (the one most facing the setting sun) they say – and I have read it in good and ancient authors – that many soothsayers, vaticinators and prophets dwell, and that Saturn lies bound there in beautiful chains of gold upon a golden rock, where he is fed on ambrosia and celestial nectar brought daily to him in abundance from the heavens by birds whose species I do not know (perhaps the very same crows which fed Saint Paul, the first anchorite in the wilderness): there he clearly prophesies to anyone who wants to learn of his lot, his destiny and what is to befall him. For the Fates spin nothing and Jupiter plans nothing, contemplates nothing which that good Father Saturn does not know while he lies sleeping.

'It would greatly abbreviate our labour if we were to hear him a while over this perplexity of mine.'

'That,' said Epistemon, 'is too evident an abuse and a fable too fabulous. I will not go.'

How Panurge took counsel from Herr Trippa

CHAPTER 25

[The caricature-figure of Herr Trippa is doubtless a laugh at the expense of Henry Cornelius Agrippa, the German author of a treatise On Occult Philosophy *and of a very widely read book* On the Vanity of All Sciences and of the Excellence of the Word of God. *The erudition in this chapter belongs to the common domain, much of it to be found in Cardano amongst others and (later) in Pictorius. For the definitive edition of the* Third Book *Rabelais also borrowed extra details from Celio Calcagnini, an author who was to revolutionize his art in the Fourth Book. The 'Mons Jovis' (Jove's mountain) is the small swelling at the base of the index-finger.*

Astrologers established a 'Celestial Mansion' as part of the art of divination. The seventh 'house' was that of marriage.

A comic song sung about Court begins 'When all the cuckolds congregate, My husband will lead them, carrying the banner'.

We have the joy of witnessing a maniacal expert in the occult arts being accused by Panurge of precisely the faults of philautia which are so manifest in himself and which he ought first to be condemning 'at home'. A vital part is played by a clutch of authoritative axioms against self-love, drawn from the same two or three pages of the Adages of Erasmus. They include, but are not limited to: the Socratic saying (I, VI, LXXXV), 'Things are done right or wrong at home' – where Rabelais came across polypragmôn, Plutarch's name for a prying busybody; (I, VI, LXXXVI), 'To go down into oneself'; the scriptural saying (I, VI, XCI), 'To cast the beam from another's eye'; and, not least, (I, VI, XCV), 'Know Thyself'.

Several other adages to be found on those pages of Erasmus are, have been or will be pressed into service.

From I, VI, LXXXVIII, 'Live within your own harvest' (wisdom which Panurge had so blatantly flouted in his praise of debts and debtors) Rabelais took the word ptôchalazôn, a braggart-beggar. He had already taken from them the adage 'We do not see what is in the pouch behind us'. Cf. Chapter 15.]

'All the same,' said Epistemon, continuing, 'if you trust me, this is what you will do before we return to our king. Here, near l'Ile-Bouchard, there dwells Herr Trippa. You know how he foretells the future by the arts of astrology, geomancy, chiromancy [, metopomancy] and others of the same kidney. Let us discuss your matter with him.'

'I know nothing about that,' Panurge replied, 'but this I do know, that while he was talking to the great king about matters celestial and transcendental, the menservants of the Court were swiving his wife at will, on the stairs and in the doorways, she being not unattractive. He, who could see all things empyreal and terrestrial without goggles, who was holding forth about all things past and present, and predicting all that is to come, failed in one thing: to see her jiggedy-jigging. And he never got news of it either.

'All right. Since you want to, let us go to him. One can never learn too much.'

They arrived next day at the house of Herr Trippa. Panurge gave him a wolf-skin robe, an ornately gilt short-sword in a velvet scabbard and fifty fine golden angelots. He then began to discuss with him privily about his affair.

As soon as Herr Trippa set eyes on him he looked him straight in the face and said: 'You have the physiognomy and the metoposcopy of a cuckold: I mean a disgraced and notorious cuckold.'

Then, studying Panurge's right palm at every point, he said: 'This broken line on your *Mons Jovis* is never found except in the palm of a cuckold.'

He then rapidly pricked at a certain number of points with a probe, linked them together by geomancy and said: 'No truth more true: it is quite certain that you will be cuckolded soon after your marriage.'

Which done, he asked Panurge for his natal horoscope. As soon as he gave it to him, Herr Trippa established Panurge's Celestial House in all its particulars and, musing over its disposition and the aspects in their triplicities, he heaved a mighty sigh and said: 'I had already frankly predicted that you will be a cuckold. In that you cannot fail. And here I find a new additional certainty: I confirm that you will be cuckolded, and moreover that you will also be battered and robbed by your wife. For I find the Seventh Mansion to be malign in all its aspects and subject to assaults by all the signs of the Zodiac bearing horns, such as Aries, Taurus, Capricorn and so on. In the Fourth Mansion I find Jupiter in decline as well as with Saturn in a tetragonal aspect with Mercury.

'My good fellow, you are in for a good peppering!'

'I'll visit you with a quartan ague first,' Panurge replied, '[you idiot,] you disgusting old fool! When all the cuckolds congregate, you'll be carrying the banner!

But whence comes this flesh-worm here twixt my two fingers?' So saying he pointed his first two fingers straight at Herr Trippa, spreading them wide to form two horns while bending his thumb and the other fingers into his palm.[13]

Then he said to Epistemon:

'Behold the original Ollus in Martial, who devoted all his

13. This gesture makes horns at a cuckold.

study to observing the maladies and misfortunes of others; meanwhile his wife was on a debauch. He, on the other hand, poorer than Irus ever was, remained as boastful, as overweening and as unbearable as seventeen devils: in a word, a *ptôchalazôn*, as the Ancients most properly termed such scurrilous rabble.

'Let's leave this loony idiot with his familiar spirits – he ought to be chained up – raving away to his heart's content. Convince me some day that evil-spirits would serve such a wretch! He is ignorant of the first line of philosophy, which is KNOW THYSELF, and while boasting that he can see a mote in the eye of another he fails to see a great beam poking out of both of his. He is just the kind of *polypragmon* whom Plutarch describes; he is a second Lamia, she whose eyes were sharper than a lynx's in the houses of others, in public and amongst the common folk, yet in her own house she was as blind as a mole: at home she saw nothing, since as soon as she came back into her own place she took out her eyes from her head – they were removable like spectacles – and hid them away in a wooden clog hanging behind the door of her cottage.'

[At those words Herr Trippa took a branch of tamarisk.

'Well taken!' said Epistemon. 'Nicander calls it divinatory.']

'Would you like,' said Herr Trippa, 'to know the truth more fully by Pyromancy, Aëromancy [made famous by Aristophanes in his *Clouds*], by Hydromancy or by Lecanomancy, which was so honoured amongst the Assyrians [and tried out by Ermolao Barbaro]? Within a basin [full of water] I'll show you your future wife having it off with a brace of yokels . . .'

'Next time you stick your nose up my bum,' said Panurge, 'remember to take off your glasses!'

'. . . or,' continued Herr Trippa, 'by Catoptromancy [, by means of which Didius Julianus, an Emperor of Rome, foresaw all that was to come]. You won't need your glasses! – [In a mirror] you'll see her being screwed as clearly as if I had showed you her in the fountain of the temple of Minerva near Patras. By Coscinomancy [once so religiously observed within the rituals of the Romans]? Let's have tongs and a sieve and you will witness some devilry! [By Alphitomancy, as was indicated by Theocritus in his book *Pharmaceutria*, and by Aleuromancy (mixing together some wheat and some flour)? By Astrogalomancy? I already have some knuckle-bones to throw with. By Tyromancy? I've just what we need: a bit of cheese from Bréhémont. By Gyromancy? I shall spin a few hoops and, I assure you, they will all fall to the left! By Sternomancy? I say! Your chest is in poor shape!] By Libanomancy? All you need is a little incense. By Gastromancy, long employed in Ferrara by Dame Jacoba Rhodogina the engastrimyth? By Cephaleomancy [which used to be employed by the Germans who would roast an ass's head over red-hot charcoal]? By Ceromancy? In this case, from wax melted in water you will see the shapes of your wife and the men giving her a good pounding. By Capnomancy? We shall sprinkle poppy-seeds and sesame-seeds together over some glowing embers. How delightful! By Axinomancy? All you need to provide is a chopper [and a piece of agate which we will place in the brazier. How well Homer exploits it apropos of the Suitors of Penelope]. By Onymancy? We shall need oil and a little wax. By Tephramancy? Ashes exposed to the weather will show you your wife in a fine old state. By Botanomancy? I have some sage-leaves here just for the purpose. By Sycomancy? O! An art divine, using leaves from a fig-tree. By Ichthyomancy [once honoured and practised by Tiresias and Polydamas]: still as reliable as it was long ago in the ditch called Dina within the wood sacred to Apollo in the land of the Lycians? By Choiromancy? We shall need quite a few pigs: you can have the bladders! [By Cleromancy? It's like our looking for the bean in the festal cake on the Eve of the Epiphany.] By Anthropomancy, which was used by the Emperor Heliogabalus of Rome? A bit messy, but since you're destined to be cuckolded you can put up with that. By Sibylline Stichomancy? By Onomatomancy? What did you say your name was? . . .'

'Chew-shit,' said Panurge;

'. . . or else by Alectryomancy? I will trace here a nice little circle, which, in your sight, as you watch me, I shall divide into four-and-twenty equal sections in each of which I will draw one letter of the alphabet. Upon each letter I will place one grain of corn. Then I will loose among it a virgin cockerel. You will see it, I promise you, eating the grains placed upon the

letters, C. U. C. K. O. L. D. S. H. A. L. T. B. E. just as fatefully
as when, under the Emperor Valens (who was perplexed over
the name of his successor), the prophetic and alectryomantic
cock ate the grains over the letters T.H.E.O.D. Would you
be willing to learn from the Art haruspicine? Extispicine? By
auguries from flights of birds and the songs of the oscines?
From the ducks' tripudiation solistime . . .'[14]

'By Turd-ispicine,' replied Panurge.

'. . . or else by Necromancy? For you, Sir, I'll quickly resurrect someone recently dead (as Apollonius of Tyana did for
Achilles and as the witch did in the presence of Saul), who will
tell us everything, doing no more and no less than that dead
man did who, when evoked by Erichto, foretold to Pompey the
entire course and outcome of the battle of Pharsalia.

'Or if you are afraid of the dead – as cuckolds naturally are
– we shall merely use Sciomancy.'

'Go to the devil you raving idiot,' Panurge replied, 'and get
yourself buggered by an Albanian: he'll give you a conical hat
all right! Why the devil don't you also advise me to place an
emerald or a hyena-gem firmly under my tongue, or to provide
myself with the tongue of a hoepoe-bird and the hearts of green
frogs, or to eat the heart and liver of some dragon or other so
that (like the Arabs of old in the lands of Mesopotamia) I can
hear my destinies in swan-song and bird-song.

'May thirty devils take this horn-bearing cuckold, this
Marrano, this devil's own sorcerer, this caster of spells for
Antichrist! Let's get back to our king. I'm certain he will not
be pleased with us if ever he learns that we ventured into the
haunt of this be-cassocked devil. I'm sorry I ever came. I would
gladly give a hundred golden nobles – and fourteen commoners
– if only the thing which used to break wind in the bottom
of my trunk-hose would at this very moment shine up his
moustaches with its squitterings! True God! He's made me

14. Some technical terms now little known: *haruspicine*: the *haruspex*
examined entrails; *extispicine*: the *extispex* did likewise; the *oscines* are
the birds from whose song or cry divinations were made; the 'tripudiation solistime' (*tripudium solistimum*) is a measured, solemn liturgical
dance.

stink of loathing and devilry, of spells and witchcraft. The devil take him! Say amen to that, and then we can go for a drink. I shan't enjoy myself for a couple of days: nay, not for four!'

How Panurge takes counsel from Frère Jean des Entommeures

CHAPTER 26

[It is normal to link this chapter with the contemporary cult of poetic blasons (poems copiously praising, say, a beautiful young bosom and then having it answered by another poem piling up terms for an ugly old withered one). There are plenty of occasions for unexpected smiles in this list, where the terms applied to Frère Jean's bollocks are mainly those of vigour and power. In Chapter 28 we will find Panurge treated to epithets of weakness, scabbiness and debility. These blasons are later disposed in two columns only. Three epithets are later cut out of Chapter 28 (on Panurge's bollocks) and attributed to Frère Jean's: 'aborted b., – chalotted b.,– censored b.'

There are three quotations from Scripture light-heartedly made by Frère Jean as 'Breviary Stuff': 'Go forth – we that live – and multiply', which conflates the commandment given to Adam in Genesis to go forth and multiply with words from Psalm 112:18 – 'we that live' – which makes that commandment universal. For the Day of Judgement, 'when He shall come to judge', cf. among other texts, Psalm 95 (96) 13.

Words made up from mataeo (such as 'mataeologian' elsewhere in Rabelais and 'mataeobefuddledized' here) imply uselessness, emptiness and so on.]

Panurge was disturbed by the words of Herr Trippa, and once they had passed the village of Huymes, he approached Frère Jean and said to him in a tremulous voice while scratching his left ear:

'Perk me up a while, you old fat-guts. I feel all mentally mataeobefuddledized by the talk of that devil-ridden maniac. Hearken unto me, my dear bollock,

kindly bollock,
patted b.,
felted b.,
sculptured b.,
arabesque b.,
[antiquarian b.,]
mangled b.,
tin-smithed b.,
sworn b.,
primed b.,
swaddled-up b.,
tattered b.,
brazil-wood b.,
latin b.,]
long-sword b.,
passionate b.,
stuffed b.,
pretty b.,
positive b.,
active b.,
oval b.,
monkish b.,
respectable b.,
audacious b.,
manual b.,
resolved b.,
twinned b.,
fecund b.,
currycombed b.,
common-to-all b.,
prompt b.,
pendant b.,
high-warp b.,
great-fun b.,
scabby b.,
patronymic b.,

famous b.,
leaded b.,
bosun's b.,
stucco'd b.,
steel-braced b.,
assured b.,
embroidered b.,
hammered b.,
burgher's b.,
railing b.,
disposed-of b.,
varnished b.,
boxwood b.,
winch-braced b.,
frenetic b.,
heaped-up b.,
bloated b.,
well-seasoned b.,
gerundive b.,
giant b.,
don's b.,
virile b.,
reserved b.,
ten-ton b.,
gluttonous b.,
sinewy b.,
stylish b.,
fitting b.,[15]
gentle b.,
becoming b.,
nimble b.,
fatted-calf b.,
exquisite b.,
great-bum b.,
Guelfish b.,
cuddly b.,

fatted b.,
milky b.,
veined b.,
grotesque b.,
trussed-hare b.,
madder-red b.,
pied b.,
interlarded b.,
grained b.,
tarred b.,
doctoral-hooded b.,
ebony b.,
[organized b.,
hook-braced b.,
raving b.,
well-measured b.,
polished b.,
lively b.,
genitive b.,
vital b.,
claustral b.,
subtle b.,
idle b.,
wanton b.,
absolved b.,
rounded b.,
Turkish b.,
sibillant b.,
urgent b.,
brisk b.,
lucky b.,
everyday b.,
requisite b.,
prick-hot b.,
Ursine b.,
wasp-stinging b.,

15. In '52 'fitting' (*duisant*) changed to 'shining' (*luisant*).

alidadic b.,
[well-selected b.,
forceful b.,
insuperable b.,
[redoubtable b.,
profitable b.
palpable b.,
subsidiary b.,
transpontine b.,
convulsive b.,
sigillative b.,
[donkeynizing b.,]
thundering b.,
ramming b.,
resonant b.,
snoring b.,
frolicker b.,
knuckle-rapping b.,
censored b.,]
tumble-bum b.,

amalgamic b.,
well-connected b.,
graceful b.,
relievable b.,
horrible b.,
memorable b.,
muscular b.,
tragical b.,
repercussive b.,
incarnative b.,
masculinizing b.,
satisfied b.,
glistening b.,
ardent b.,
diaspermatizing b.,
lecher b.,
wiggling b.,
[aborted b.,
toussled b.,

algebraic b.,
house-affected b.,]
hungry b.,
agreeable b.,
affable b.,
notable b.,
horse-armoured b.,
satirical b.,
digestive b.,
restorative b.,
stallionizing b.,
fulminating b.,
beating b.,
aromatizing b.,
sprucifying b.,
robber b.,
waggling b.,
chalotted b.,
riddled b.,

Frère Jean, my friend, you fire-gun bollock, you joggle-bum bollock, I feel great respect for you and was keeping you for the ultimate tidbit. I beseech you: give me your advice. Ought I to marry or no?'

Frère Jean good-humouredly replied:

'Get yourself married, for the devil's sake; get yourself married, and ring me a double carillon with your balls. As soon as you can, I say, and I mean it. The evening of this very day order the banns and the bedstead! Mighty God! What are you keeping yourself for? Don't you know that the end of the world's drawing nigh? We're nearer to it by two poles and one yard than we were yesterday. Antichrist has already been born, so they tell me. True, he is still only pawing at his nurse and his governesses, for he's but a toddler and has yet to display his riches. As long as a sack of corn costs less than three silver patacoons, and a cask of wine but six copper blanks, *Go forth – we that live – and multiply.* Scripture that is: Breviary stuff. In the Day of

Judgement, *when He shall come to judge*, do you really want them to find you with your balls full?'

'You, Frère Jean,' said Panurge, 'have a very transparent and tranquil mind, you metropolitan bollock, and you speak to the point. That's just what Leander of Abydos in Asia prayed for to Neptune and all the gods of the sea while swimming from Sestos to Europe across the Hellespont to call upon Hero, his lady-love:

> If by your grace I swim across this Sound,
> What matter if, returning, I am drowned!

He did not want to die with his bollocks full.

'And my counsel is that from henceforth, in all my lands of Salmagundi, whenever it is decided by the courts to hang a malefactor, he will be made to pound away like a pelican for a day or two beforehand, so well that there will not be left enough in his seminal tools to write a Greek letter Y. So precious a substance must not be stupidly lost. He might possibly engender a man-child. And then he would die without regret, leaving a man for a man.'

[How Frère Jean merrily advises Panurge]

CHAPTER 27

[There is no chapter-break here in the first edition, yet the following chapter was already numbered 28. The interpolation of this chapter-break in 1552 therefore entailed no renumbering of the chapters which follow.

'Privileges are lost by non-usage' was a legal maxim.

There was a French saying: 'Those girls are like bells: you can make them say anything you want.'

There had never been a Marchioness of Winchester. Perhaps there is a confused allusion to the many brothels in the London domains of the Bishop of Winchester, whose inmates were known as 'Winchester Geese'.

Solomon, a sexually experienced man if ever there was one, classed the 'mouth of the womb' amongst the three things which cannot be satisfied (Proverbs 30:15–16). Aristotle held a similar opinion (Problems, 260).

Erasmus has an adage: (I, I, VII), 'Dodonaean Brass' and also (II, X, XXV), 'A wall of brass'.

Priapus as 'god of the gardens' was a fertility god for the Ancients.]

'By Saint Rigomé!' said Frère Jean, 'I'm not counselling you, my dear friend Panurge, to do anything that I wouldn't do in your place. Only give care and attention to leaving no gaps and to keeping up with your thrusts. If you stop for a while you'll have had it, poor wretch, and there will happen to you what happens to wet-nurses. If they give up suckling children they lose their milk. If you don't exercise your *mentula*, she'll lose her milk too and serve only as a pisser, and your bollocks likewise will serve merely as game-bags.

'I warn you. I've seen it experienced by many a man: they wouldn't when they could, so couldn't when they would. As the law-clerks say: *All privileges are lost by non-usage*. And therefore, sonny, keep all those humble little troglodytes and codpiece-ites down there sempiternally ploughing:[16] see that they never live off their means, doing nothing, like gentlemen.'

'No fear of that, Frère Jean,' replied Panurge; 'left bollock of mine, I believe you. You go roundly to work, you do. Without reservations or verbiage you have clearly dissipated any fear that might have intimidated me. And may the heavens grant you to serve the ball always hard and low.

'All right then: upon your word I shall get myself married, and not play a fault. And I shall always have a few pretty chambermaids for you when you come to visit me: you will be the patron of their sorority. So much for the first part of the sermon.'

'Hark!' said Frère Jean. 'The oracle of the bells of Varennes: what are they telling?'

'I can hear them,' Panurge replied. 'By my thirst, their ring is

16. '52, omit: *and* codpiece-ites.

more fateful than that of the cauldrons of Jupiter in Dordona.
Hark

> Marry thee, marry thee,
>   Marry, marry.
> If thou dost marry thee,
>   Marry, marry.
> Great good shalt thou find therein, find therein:
>   Marry, marry.

I shall get married, I assure you. All the elements invite me to.
Let those words of mine be unto you as a wall of brass.

'As for the second point, it seems to me that you have some
doubts about – indeed suspect – my potential paternity, as
though the erect god of the gardens were not favourable
towards me. I beseech you to be so good as to believe that I
have him under strict orders, docile, benevolent, all in all attentive and obedient. It suffices to loosen its leash – its fly-strings, I
mean – show it its prey close by and say, *Fetch it, boy!* Then,
even if my wife were as much of a glutton for the pleasures of
Venus as ever were Messalina or the Marchioness of Winchester
in England, I beseech you to believe that I would still have
plenty to satisfy her with.

'I am not unaware of what Solomon says – and he spoke like
a knowledgeable scholar – nor of what Aristotle declared after
him: that women are by nature insatiable; but I do want people
to know that, by the same measure, my tool is indefatigable
too.

'Don't bring up as models at this point those celebrated
lechers Hercules, Proculus, Caesar and Mahomet (who boasts
in his Alcoran of having more power in his genitals than sixty
bo'suns: the lecher was lying).

'Don't bring up that Indian so celebrated by Theophrastes,
Pliny and Athenaeus, who, with the aid of a certain herbal
simple, brought it off seventy times or more in a single day. I
do not believe it. That number is hypothetical. Do not trust it,
I beseech you. But do believe the following [, and you will
believe only what is true], that my natural organ, – my blessèd

Ithyphallus, my Signor Thingummybobba d'Albinga – is number one in the world.

'Now listen, my Bollockling. Have you ever seen the habit of the monk of Castres? When it was left in any house openly or secretly, those who dwelt or lived there suddenly – because of its horrifying powers – all started to rut: man and beast, men and women, down to the very cats and rats. Well, I swear to you that I have before now discovered certain energies even more lawless in my codpiece.

'I shall not speak to you of house or hut, of sermon or market, but of the passion-play which they were putting on at Saint Maxent: as I was coming into the pit one day I saw – on account of the powers and occult properties of my codpiece – everyone, actors and audience both, suddenly fall into such awesome temptation that there was not one angel, one man, one male or female devil who did not want to fornicate! The prompter abandoned his copy; the fellow playing Saint Michael slid down like a *deus ex machina*, the male devils burst out of Hell and bore away all the poor little females. Even Lucifer raged and broke his bonds.

'In short, on witnessing such disorder I quit the place, following the example of Cato the Censor, who, on seeing that the festivities of the *Floralia* were thrown into disorder by his presence, ceased to be a spectator.'

How Frère Jean gave support to Panurge in his doubts over cuckoldom

CHAPTER 28

[Panurge's rhetoric fails to convince even himself. He becomes the ageing comic husband of the farces, destined to be cuckolded, bullied and robbed by his future wife.

The 'Motor Intelligences' are moral and spiritual beings who guide the heavenly bodies and may show their approval of spiritual men and women. Panurge would dislocate the whole universe if he were ever successfully to oppose them. He would be acting 'worse than the

Giants' (who attacked the gods by piling Mount Pelion on to Mount
Ossa). Cf. Erasmus, Adages, III, X, XCIII, 'The Arrogance of the
Giants', cited again in Chapter 51. The basic tale of the ring that saves
from cuckoldom appears in Poggio, Ariosto and the Cent nouvelles
nouvelles.

The epithets applied to Panurge's bollocks suggest flaccidity, weak-
ness and bad qualities generally. The text given is essentially that of
the first edition with the additions as usual in square brackets, but
some epithets were dropped: they figure in the notes.]

'I see what you mean,' said Frère Jean, but time overmasters all
things. There is no marble, no porphyry but has its old age and
decline. Even if you're not there yet, in a few years' time I shall
hear you confessing that some folk we know have balls dangling
down for lack of a game-pouch.

'Already I can see the hair greying on your head. Your beard,
with its shadings of grey and white and tan and black, looks to
me like a *mappamundi*! Look. Here is Asia; here are the Tigris
and the Euphrates. Here is Africa and the mountains of the
Moon. Here are the marshes of the Nile. Over there is Europe.
Can you see Thélème? This tuft here, which is completely white,
is the Hyperborean Mountains. 'Pon my thirst, my friend, when
the snows are on the mountains (I mean the head and the chin)
there is no great heat in the vales of the codpiece.'

'Chilblains, to you!' Panurge replied. 'You don't understand
your *Topics*. When the snow is on the mountains, then thunderbolts and lightnings, shooting-pains and hypertrophies, red
flushes and rumblings, tempests and all the devils are in the
valleys. Would you like to experience that? Then go into
Switzerland and contemplate Lake Wunderberlich, four leagues
from Berne over towards Sion. [You reproach me with my greying hair, failing to see that it is of the nature of the leek, for the
head to be white when the tail is green, stiff and full of vigour.]

'It is true that I can just about make out one sign in me
suggestive of old age – I mean a green old age. Don't tell anyone.
It'll remain a secret between the two of us. I do find good wine
more delightful to my taste than I used to: and more than I
once did, I fear encounters with poor wine. Note that that does

somehow suggest the westering sun and signify that noon-day is past.

'But what of it? I – still as pleasant a companion as ever, or more so – am not worried about that. Devil! No. What I fear is that, through some prolonged absence of Pantagruel, our king, of whom it is my duty to be the companion [even if he went to the devil], my wife should make me a cuckold.

'There you have the operative word; for everybody I have spoken to about it threatens me with it and asserts that it is predestined to me by the heavens.'

'Not every man who would be cuckolded is so,' replied Frère Jean. 'If you are a cuckold, *ergo* your wife will be beautiful; *ergo* she will treat you well; *ergo* you will have many friends: *ergo* you will be saved. Monastical topics, they are. You, you old sinner, will be better off for it: you'll never have had it so easy! You'll have lost nothing. You'll grow even richer. And if thus it were so predestined would you want to go against it? Say on, wilted bollock,

musty b.,	macerated b.,	mouldy b.,
cold-kneaded b.,	dangling b.,	chilly b.,
[appellant b.,]	fallen-down b.,	paltry b.,
faded b.,	pod-shelled b.,	exhausted b.,
[incongruous b.,	failing b.,	done-in b.,]
tired-out b.,	screwed-out b.,	prostrate b.,
beshitten b.,	crouching b.,	slumbering b.,
creamed-off b.,	squeezed-dry b.,	passed-by b.,
caitive b.,	restive b.,	putative b.,
minced b.,	worm-rinsed b.,	pinchbeck b.,
bowed b.,	cowed b.,	poor old b.,
ill-complexioned b.,	ill-tempered b.,	ill-graced b.,
corked b.,	flabby b.,	diaphanous b.,
drained b.,	dripped-dry b.,	[squashed b.,
shattered b.,]	scattered b.,	tattered b.,
mitred b.,	chapter-housed b.,	whipped-cream b.,
quibbled b.,	shrivelled b.,	pimpled b.,
dirty b.,	daubed b.,	voided b.,
furrowed b.,	chagrined b.,	haggard b.,

unhelved b.,
gloomy b.,
scabby b.,
frustrated b.,
engraved b.,
leprous b.,
[gangrened b.,
nobbled b.,
dull-brown b.,
podgy b.,
trepanned b.
emaciated b.,
puff-pastry b.,
extirpated b.,]
mildewed b.,
buffeted b.,
shredded b.,
gob-smacked b.,
chapped b.,
stinking b.,]
ale-stinking b.,
scrupulous b.,
defective b.,
downing b.,
ugly old b.,
macerated b.,
antedated b.,
gammy b.,
glower-back b.,
hauled-in b.,
desolate b.,
ponging b.,
skinny b.,
assassinated b.,
sluggish b.,
heavy-cake b.,
threadbare b.,
[feverish b.,]

glum b.,
poohy b.,
weary b.,
ablated b.,
gawky b.,
hernia'd b.,
wormy b.,]
ragged b.,
watered-down b.,
abject b.,
smoke-dried b.,
castrated b.,
marinated b.,
gutted b.,
pock-marked b.,
watered-down b.,
cupping-horned b.,
[picked-bare b.,
bitter b.,
barrel-reeking b.,
frigid b.,
[languorous b.,
decrepit b.,
frowning b.,
vainly hoping b.,
unworthy b.,
degraded b.,
rattled b.,
farty kick-back b.,
gravelled b.,
disconsolate b.,
solecizing b.,
grill-barred b.,
botched-up b.,
nonchalant b.,
zero b.,
crumpled b.,

wormy b.,
fagged out b.,
castrated b.,
sphacelated b.,
[mealie-skin b.,]
varicose b.,
pox-sore b.,
gewgawed b.,
too-cocky b.,
worm-riddled b.,]
sun-dried b.,
mule-prick b.,
[ulcerated b.,
bowel-bound b.,
cut-up b.,
adulterated b.,
cupping-glassed b.,
slashed-faced b.,
wheezing b.,
bottle-stinking b.,
fistulous b.,
crack-pot b.,]
diminutive b.,
ape-like b.,
blighted b.,
paralytic b.,
one-armed b.,
bat-back b.,
jaded b.,
disparate b.,
declining b.,
appellant b.,
[ulcerated b.,]
stripped b.,
as-nothing b.,
mawkish b.,
clientless b.,

you bollocked away [to the devil], Panurge, my friend.[17]

'Since thus it is predestined for you, would you make the planets run retrograde, dislocate all the celestial spheres, suggest to the Motor Intelligences that they should go wandering astray, blunt the spindles of the Fates, accuse their spinning-rings, slander their spools, discredit their dividers, condemn their threads and unwind their clews? Quartan fever to you, old bollock! You would be doing worse than the Giants. Come on now, Big-balls: what would you rather be, not cuckold but jealous, not knowing but cuckold?'

'I'd rather be neither one nor the other,' Panurge replied. 'But if ever I did find that I was a cuckold, I'd soon knock things into shape, or else the world would have run out of cudgels!

'Faith, Frère Jean, it would be better for me never to get married.

'Harken to what the bells are telling me now we are closer:

> Marry not; marry not,
> not, not, no, no;
> If thou dost marry –
> marry not, marry not –
> Thou shalt regret it,
> gret it, regret it;
> Cuckold shalt be.

'Might worthy of God! I'm beginning to get really annoyed. Do all you robed-wearing big-heads have no remedy at all? Has Nature left humans so bereft that a married man cannot go through this world of ours without falling into the dangerous deeps of cuckoldom!'

'I am quite willing to tell you of a device,' said Frère Jean,

<hr/>

17. The blason of Panurge's sorry bollocks was subject to some minor rearrangement and omissions in '52. Omitted are: 'aborted b.' (after 'drained b.'), 'censored b.' (after 'mitred b.'), 'farinated b.' (before 'marinated b.'), 'extirpated b.' (after 'ragged b.'), 'chalotted b.' (after 'scattered b.'), 'mortified b.' (after 'scrupulous b.'). Three of these were transferred to Frère Jean in Chapter 26. One epithet appears twice: wormy.

'by means of which your wife will never cuckold you without your knowledge and consent.'

'I beseech you to tell it to me,' said Panurge, 'my velvety Bollock.'

'Take,' said Frère Jean, 'the ring of Hans Carvel, that great lapidary of the king of Melinda.

'Hans Carvel was a learned, experienced and scholarly man, a good man, sensible, of good judgement, courteous, kind, a giver of alms, a philosopher full of fun moreover, and a good and merry companion if ever there was one, with a bit of a paunch, always wagging his head and somewhat ungainly. In his old age he took to wife the daughter of Concordat, the bailiff; she was young, beautiful, active, comely, welcoming and gracious (too much so towards her neighbours and servants).

'And so it befell that after a few weeks he grew as jealous as a tiger and began to suspect her of getting her bum drummer-boy'd somewhere else. To counter which he gave her her fill of many a fine tale of the havoc wrought by adultery. He frequently read to her from *The Legends of Good Wives*, preached to her about pudicity and compiled for her a treatise in praise of conjugal fidelity in which he inveighed good and strong against flirtatious wives, and gave her a lovely collar studded all over with Orient sapphires. Despite which he found her so froward and so welcoming to her neighbours that his jealousy grew and grew.

'During one of the many nights that he was lying beside her racked by such torments, he dreamt that he was addressing the devil and telling him of his misery. The devil comforted him and placed a ring on his big finger saying: "This ring I give you: as long as it remains on your finger your wife will never be carnally known by another man without your knowledge and consent."

'"Thank you kindly, Monsieur Devil," said Hans Carvel. "If ever anyone takes that ring off my finger I shall renounce Mahoun."

'The devil vanished, and Hans Carvel awoke full of joy, finding himself with his finger up his wife's thingummy.

'I was forgetting to tell how his wife, when she felt it, drew back her bum as if to say: "Yes! No! That's not what goes in there!" And it seemed to Hans Carvel that some man was trying to steal his ring. Is that not an infallible remedy? If you trust me you'll follow that example and ever wear your wife's ring on your finger.'

Their road and their conversation ended here.

How Pantagruel brought together a theologian, a physician, a legist and a philosopher over the perplexity of Panurge

CHAPTER 29

[In subsequent editions Rabelais changed his good theologian's name from Parathadée to Hippothadée. He is almost always called Hippothadée today, so his name is exceptionally changed here by anticipation to its later form. Para + Thadée might mean 'Another Thadeus', that is, another Saint Jude. Hippothadée could possibly be a very oblique allusion to Melanchthon, whose followers were called Philippists. At all events he is modest and pious, the ideal evangelical and Erasmian theologian.

Self-love deceives. That basic belief is underlined by serious word-play (in the spirit of Plato's Cratylus): in French, amour de soi (love of self) more than hints with its near-homophone at the effects of self-love – not least in the case of the self-loving Panurge – it déçoit, it deceives, the self-lover.

As Roman Law and its glossators recommend in perplex cases, we now leave individual consultations on what in legal terms is the hypothesis (namely, Should Panurge marry?) for expert opinions on the thesis (Should any man marry?). The various roles attributed to the theologians, physicians, lawyers and jurisconsults are standard: Baldassare Castiglione's Book of the Courtier (written in Italian for the French Court) takes the line which Panurge supports and which Pantagruel rejects.

The legal phrase 'the dice of judgement', used here in its usual, metaphorical sense, is soon to be developed in unexpected ways.]

On arriving at the palace they gave to Pantagruel an account of their journey and showed him the ditty of Raminagrobis. Pantagruel read it once, read it twice, then said: 'No reply so far has pleased me more. He means, in sum, that when venturing into wedlock each man must be the arbiter of his own thoughts and seek counsel from himself. That has always been my opinion and I told you as much when you first brought it up with me: but you quietly laughed, I remember, and I realized that your *amour de soi* – your philautia – *vous déçoit.*

'Let us proceed otherwise. Here's how. All that we have and are consists in three things: soul, body and possessions. Three kinds of people are severally devoted nowadays to the conservation of each of them: theologians for the soul; physicians for the body; jurisconsults for our possessions. My advice is that we have a theologian, a physician and a jurisconsult round to dinner on Sunday. Then, together, we can discuss your perplexity.'

'By Saint Picault,' Panurge replied. 'we shall achieve nothing worthwhile. I can tell that already. See how our world is out of joint: we entrust our souls to theologians, most of whom are heretics; our bodies to physicians, who all abhor medicines; and our possessions to lawyers, who never go to law with each other.'

'You are talking like *Il Cortegiano*,' said Pantagruel, 'but I deny the first assertion, noting that the main, indeed the sole and unique occupation, of good theologians is to extirpate heresies by word, deed and writing (far from being tainted by them), and to implant deeply within human hearts the true and living Catholic faith.

'The second I approve of, noting that physicians so order the prophylactic and health-conserving side in their own cases that they have no need of the therapeutic, which cures by medicines.

'The third I concede, noting that good lawyers are so preoccupied with pleading and making legal rejoinders on behalf of the affairs of others that they have neither time nor leisure to pay attention to their own.

'And so for our theologian next Sunday let us take our own

Père Hippothadée; for physician, Dr Rondibilis; and for legist, our friend Bridoye.

'I further advise that we should move into the tetrad – the perfect number of the Pythagoreans – and so make up the fourth by inviting our loyal subject Trouillogan the philosopher, especially seeing that an accomplished philosopher such as he is replies affirmatively to all doubts expounded to him.

'Carpalim. Arrange for us to have all four of them here to dinner next Sunday.'

'I believe,' said Epistemon, 'that you could never have chosen better ones throughout the kingdom. I don't simply mean as touching the accomplishments of each one in his vocation (which are far beyond the dice of judgement) but because, as a bonus, Rondibilis is now married and used not to be; Hippothadée is not married and never has been; Bridoye once was married and now isn't; Trouillogan is and was.

'I'll relieve Carpalim of a chore. If you agree I shall go and invite Bridoye myself; I have known him for years and want to speak to him in the interests of the career of an admirable and learned son of his who is studying law at Toulouse under the aegis of the most learned and virtuous Boissoné.'

'Act as you think best,' said Pantagruel. 'And let me know if I can do anything to advance the son of Seigneur Boissoné, and the honour of Boissoné too, for I love and revere him as one of the most capable men of his profession. I shall be most delighted to see to it.'

How Hippothadée the theologian gives advice to Panurge about the undertaking of a marriage

CHAPTER 30

[*Much turns on a sentence of Saint Paul:* 'It is better to wed than to burn' *(I Corinthians 7:9), taken to mean, as it generally was, to burn with lust, not to burn in Hell). By quoting Saint Paul as saying:* 'It is far better to wed than to burn', *the theologian pre-empts any attempt to make* 'better' *here mean* 'less bad'. *Hippothadée rejects those many*

denigrators of marriage who, since Saint Jerome, made Saint Paul's
judgement into a morose and coarse alternative to celibacy. It is further
interpreted in the light of Matthew 19:10–11, from which evangelicals
deduced that celibate chastity, being a special gift from God, cannot
be imposed on anyone ever. Hippothadée gives a markedly evangelical
turn to his questions and answers, drawing on the Lord's Prayer, the
teaching of Saint James (1:17) that God is 'the Giver of all good gifts'
and on the marriage service (with formulas still in use today). For his
Classical wisdom Rabelais draws above all on Plutarch's Marriage
Precepts, doubtless following Erasmus.

The allusion to a 'goose which my wife won't roast' is another echo
of Pathelin.

For the 'privy counsel of God' see Rabelais' Almanac for the Year
1533.

The 'valiant woman' (in Latin, the mulier fortis) described by Solo-
mon is to be found in Proverbs 31.]

Dinner was no sooner ready the following Sunday than the
guests appeared, except for Bridoye, the puisne judge of
Fonsbeton. When the dessert was brought in Panurge gave a
deep bow and said:

'Gentlemen: but one word: should I marry or not? If my
doubt is not resolved by you I shall take it to be insoluble
[like the *Insolubilia* of Petrus de Alliaco], for each of you,
respectively in his vocation, has been selected, chosen and
picked out like fine *petits pois* on the sorting-tray.'

Père Hippothadée, at the bidding of Pantagruel and to the
respectful acclaim of those present, answered with unbelievable
modesty:

'Beloved, you have asked me for counsel, but first of all you
must seek counsel from yourself. Do you feel in your body any
importunate prickings of the flesh?'

'Very strongly,' replied Panurge. 'May that not offend you,
Mon Père.'

'No, Beloved, it does not,' said Hippothadée. 'But in that
struggle do you have God's special gift and grace of contin-
ence?'

'No, by my faith,' replied Panurge.

'Then get married, Beloved, for it is far better to wed than to burn with the fire of lust.'

'That,' exclaimed Panurge, 'is what I call talking graciously, with no circumbilivaginating about the pot! I deeply thank you, Monsieur Notre Père.

'Without fail I shall get married, and that right soon. I invite you to the wedding. Cock's blood! We shall have a fine old feast. You shall wear my wedding-ribbons and, Beef's Body! we shall tuck into a goose which my wife will never roast. Moreover, if it would please you to favour me with so great an honour, I shall invite you in return to lead the maidens in their first dance.

'There remains one little ounce of doubt to dispose of – a little one, I mean, less than nothing. I shan't be cuckolded, shall I?'

'Indeed not, Beloved,' replied Hippothadée; 'if it please God, no.'

'Aah!!' cried Panurge. 'The might of God comes to our aid! Where are you despatching me to, good people? To conditionals, which in dialectics allow of all contradictions, all impossibilities: *If* my transalpine mule could fly, my transalpine mule would have wings. *If* God so wishes, I shall not be cuckolded: but then, *if* God so wishes, a cuckold I shall be! If it were a condition which I could obviate I would not be entirely without hope, but you are referring me to the privy counsel of God and to the Chamber of his minute pleasures. How do you Frenchmen find the way there, then?

'I think it would be better for you, Mon Père, not to come to my wedding. The din and hurly-burly of all the guests would disturb all your testament. You like repose, silence, solitude. I think you'd rather not come. And then you dance pretty badly and would feel awkward opening the ball. I'll have some rillettes sent up to your room; some wedding-ribbons too. And if you like, you can drink us a toast.'

'Beloved,' said Hippothadée, 'take what I say aright, I beseech you. When I say to you *please God*, am I treating you wrongly? Is it badly put? Is that a condition which is blasphemous or an obstacle to your faith? Is it not to honour our Lord, our Creator,

Protector, Servator? Is it not to recognize Him as the only Giver of all good gifts? Is it not to declare that we all depend on His loving kindness; that we are as nothing, are worth nothing, can do nothing, unless His holy grace is infused upon us? Is it not to apply a canonical proviso to everything we undertake, is it not to remit everything which we propose to what He may dispose by His holy will, in earth, as it is in Heaven? Is that not truly to hallow His holy name?

'Beloved, you will, please God, not be cuckolded. To know what is His pleasure in this matter there is no need to fall into despair as being something over which one must consult His privy counsel and journey into the chamber of His holiest pleasures: God is good and has granted us the boon of having revealed it, declared it and clearly explained it through Holy Scripture. There you will find that you will never be a cuckold – that is to say, that your wife will never prove shameless – if you take a woman who is the issue of decent people, one instructed in virtue and in all things honourable, never having haunted nor frequented any but moral company; one loving and fearing God: loving to please God by keeping His holy commandments; fearing to offend Him and forfeit His grace through lack of faith or by any transgression of His holy law, in which adultery is rigorously forbidden and the wife told to cleave to her husband alone, to cherish him, serve him and entirely to love him after God.

'To reinforce such teachings you for your part must support her in your conjugal love, continue to behave like a wise and decent man and set her a good example: you will live purely, chastely and virtuously within your habitation, just as you wish her, on her part, to live; for it is not the mirror which is highly decorated with gilt and precious jewels that is called good and perfect but the one which most truly reflects the objects set before it: so too that wife is not to be most esteemed who is rich, beautiful, elegant or born from a noble lineage, but she who strives, with God's help, to form herself in good grace and conform herself to the morals of her husband. Look at the Moon: she does not accept light from Mercury nor Jupiter nor Mars nor any other planet or star in the heavens: she accepts it only from her husband, the Sun, and never receives more than he bestows upon her by infusion while he is turned towards her. And in the same way you will be the model and exemplar of virtue and honour for your wife, and will ceaselessly beseech the grace of God for your protection.'

'Well, then,' said Panurge, twiddling the ends of his moustache, 'do you want me to marry the *valiant woman* described by Solomon? She's dead; no doubt about that. God forgive me, but as far as I know I've never set eyes on her.

'Many thanks all the same, Father. Eat this slice of marzipan: it'll aid your digestion. And drink a bumper of mulled claret: it's a tonic and good for the stomach.

'Let us get on.'

How Rondibilis, the physician, advises Panurge

CHAPTER 31

[Behind Rondibilis probably lies Dr Rondelet, a distinguished physician at Montpellier. Rondibilis advocates the teachings about semen of the Platonico-Hippocratic school which, on this matter, was opposed to Galen. Rabelais draws freely on the Laws of Marriage *of his friend Tiraqueau.*

For the tale of Cupid, see Lucian, Dialogues of the Gods, *19.*

At least one adage of Erasmus is relevant: II, III, XCVII, 'Venus is cold without Ceres and Bacchus'.

For Socrates, to be a philosopher means 'to practise dying'. (Plato: Phaedo, 67D–68B). Because a true philosopher strives to liberate his soul from his body in philosophical rapture, philosophy is truly a practising of death, death being conceived as the final separation on Earth of body and soul. For Erasmus and his followers that idea of Socrates is central to the whole of Christianity, conceived as the philosophy of Christ.]

Panurge, continuing to talk, went on to say:

'After he had dealt with Fray Cauldaureil, the first words uttered by the man who was castrating the brown-clad monks at Saussignac were "Now for the others!" I say the same: now for the others! Come on, Notre Maître Rondibilis: dispatch this for me! Should I marry or not?'

'By the amblings of my mule!' replied Rondibilis, 'I have no idea how I ought to answer that problem. You state that you feel within you the barbed prickings of the flesh. I find from our faculty of medicine – and we have taken it from the conclusions of the ancient Platonists – that carnal concupiscence can be restrained by five means: *By wine*.'

'I can believe that,' said Frère Jean. 'When I am really drunk, all I ask is to go to sleep.'

'I mean, by wine taken intemperately, since lack of temperance produces a lowering of the temperature of the blood, a slackening of the sinews, a dispersing of the generative semen, an hebetation of the senses and a subverting of locomotion, all of which are impediments to the act of generation. You do indeed find Bacchus, the god of drunkards, painted beardless, dressed in women's attire, as being entirely effeminate, a eunuch, a gelding.

'It is otherwise with wine taken temperately, as is pointed out by that ancient proverb which says that without the company of Ceres and Bacchus Venus is frigid. According to the account in Diodorus Siculus it was the opinion of the Ancients (and particularly of the Lampsacians, as Pausanias bears witness) that Signor Priapus was the son of Bacchus and Venus.

'*Secondly*: by certain drugs and simples which render a man feeble, spell-bound, and incapable of the generative act. Experiments have shown that to be true of *nymphea heraclia*, the Amerinian osier or willow, hempseed, honeysuckle, tamarisk, *agnus-castus*, mandrake, hemlock, the lesser orchis, the skin of an hippopotamus, etc., which, within the human body, by their elemental powers and specific qualities, freeze and deaden the fertile seed or alternatively disperse the spirits which must conduct it to the organs destined by Nature to that end, or else oppilate the passages and conduits through which it can be ejaculated: as, on the contrary we have other substances which increase a man's ardour, excite him and dispose him towards the act of Venus.'

'Thank God,' said Panurge, 'I have no need of those.

'And thank you too, Notre Maître. Do not feel upset by what I say about them: it is not from any ill-will towards you.

'*Thirdly*: by assiduous toil, for by that is produced such a relaxation of the body that the blood, which is spread throughout it for the alimentation of each member, has not the time, opportunity nor ability to produce that secretion which is semen, that residue from the third concoction, Nature reserving it expressly for herself as far more necessary for the conservation of his individual person than for the increase of the human race and species. That is why Diana – who is continuously engaged in her work of hunting – is called chaste. That is why the camps of the Ancients in which soldiers and athletes were engaged in their work were called *castra*, from *casta*, chaste. Hippocrates too, in *Of Air, Water and Places*, writes of some contemporary peoples in Syria who were as effete as eunuchs in the sports of Venus because they were always at work and out riding, just as philosophers tell us that sloth, on the contrary, is the mother of lust.

'When Ovid was asked what made Aegistus an adulterer, he just replied that it was because he was slothful and that if anyone were to banish sloth from this world the arts of Cupid would soon perish away: his bow, quiver and darts would become a useless burden to him, for he is far from being so fine an archer that he can – as the Parthians could – "strike cranes flying through the air or stags bounding through the forest" (meaning human beings toiling and moiling). Cupid requires them to be tranquil, sitting and lying down, and at leisure. And indeed when Theophrastus was once asked what sort of beast, what sort of thing, he took passing love-affairs to be, he replied that lechery was the occupation of folk not otherwise occupied. That is why, when the sculptor Canachus of Sicyon wished to convey that idleness, sloth and languidness governed debauchery, he carved his Venus sitting down, not standing up as his predecessors had done.

'*Fourthly*: by fervent study, for in that activity is produced such an unbelievable dispersal of the spirits that not enough are left to drive the seminal secretion to its intended organs and

so to swell up the *vena cava*, the duty of which is to ejaculate
it for the propagation of humankind.

'That such is the case, contemplate the form of a man concentrating on any subject of study: you will see all the arteries of
his brain as taut as the string of a cross-bow in order skilfully
to provide enough spirits to fill the ventricles of his common
sense – that is, of his imagination, apprehension, ratiocination
and judgement, memory and recall – and to flow expeditiously
from one to the other through the conduits at the extremities
of the *rete mirabile* (manifest in dissections) in which terminate
those arteries which originate in the left ventricle of the heart
and which, along their complex circuits, refine the vital spirits
into animal spirits: with the result that in such a studious
person you will see all his natural faculties suspended and all
his external senses cease: in short, you would conclude that he
no longer lives inside himself but is abstracted out of himself
by ecstasy, and you would say that Socrates did not abuse
the term when he said that philosophy was nothing else than
practising dying.

'That may perhaps explain why Democritus blinded himself,
preferring to lose his sight rather than decrease his contem-
plations which he felt to be interrupted by his restless eyes.
Thus Pallas, the goddess of Wisdom, the protectrix of studious
folk, is called Virgin; virgin too are the Muses; and the Graces
dwell externally in chastity.

'And I remember having read that when Cupid was once
asked by Venus his mother why he never shot at the Muses, he
replied that he found them so beautiful, so pure, so comely, so
chaste, and all so continuously occupied – one in contemplating
the heavenly bodies, one in calculating numbers, one in measuring geometrical figures, one in devising rhetoric, one in writing
poetry and another in composing music – that as he drew near
them he unbent his bow, pressed shut his quiver and doused
his torch, in fear and trembling lest he should harm them; then
he stripped the blindfold from his eyes so as to have a clearer
view of their faces and listen to their chants and their poetic
songs, finding in them the greatest pleasure in the world, so
much so that he often felt himself caught away by their beauties

and moral graces and lulled to sleep by their harmony: far be it from him to wish to shoot at them or distract them from their studies.

'Under the same heading I include what Hippocrates wrote in the book already mentioned when talking about the Scythians as well as in his treatise *On Generation*, where he says that all humans are incapable of generation once you have severed their parotid arteries (which are found beside the ears), for the reason which I have already expounded when I was talking of the dispersal of the spirits and their blood of which those arteries are the vessels; he also holds that the greater part of the generative substance derives from the brain and the spinal column.

'*Fifthly*: by the act of Venus.'

'I was waiting for you there,' said Panurge, 'and make that my own! Anybody who wants to do so may use the previous ones.'

'That,' said Frère Jean, 'is what Fray Scyllino, the prior of Saint-Victor-les-Marseille, calls macerating the flesh; and I opine (as did the hermit at Sainte-Radegonde above Chinon) that the hermits in the Thebaid could not more appropriately macerate their bodies, tame their lewd sensuality and subdue the rebellion of the flesh than by doing it some twenty-five or thirty times [a day].'

'Panurge, now, I see,' said Rondibilis, 'is well-proportioned in his limbs, well-tempered in his humours, well-complexioned in his spirits, of the proper age, at the appropriate moment and with a balanced determination to get married. If he were to meet a wife of similar temperament they would beget offspring worthy of some transpontine monarchy. And the sooner the better if he wants to see them provided for.'

'Monsieur Notre Maître,' said Panurge, 'and so I shall: never doubt it, and right soon. During your learned consultation this flea I have in my ear tickled me as never before. I will keep a place for you at the marriage-feast. We shall have a good time and a half, I promise you! You'll kindly bring your wife with you – and her neighbours: that goes without saying.

'And now for some honest sport.'

How Rondibilis declares cuckoldry to be one
of the adjuncts of matrimony

CHAPTER 32

*[S.P.Q.R. stands for Senatus populusque Romanus (The Roman
people and Senate). To Panurge it means si peu que rien (so little as
to be nothing). The jest is here transposed in the translation to an
English equivalent.*

*Rondelet's domain is the Natural. He draws on sound authorities,
including the Letter to Dionysus of Pseudo-Hippocrates, The Laws of
Marriage of Tiraqueau, and the Marriage Precepts of Plutarch.*

*In this chapter woman, as in Virgil, is 'fickle and variable' (tacitly
cited from Aeneid, IV, 569).*

*Woman's instability is explained with the help of Plato, but (as was
true of other medical authorities of the time) it exploits a passage
ripped out of context. Plato in the Timaeus, 91 A–D, made both male
and female human beings each subject to a different 'animal' which
drove them to sexual intercourse. Galen (in On Affected Parts and
elsewhere) cited – in total isolation from its context – only the 'animal'
which worked in woman: the womb, 'an animal avid for generation'.
(The parallel 'animal' of the male is simply not mentioned.) The animal
within a woman makes her whole life unstable and precarious. Many
insisted as here, on Plato's authority, that the womb was indeed an
animal in the strictest sense: it is capable of self-movement and can
distinguish between smells, qualities used in the diagnosis and treatment of hysteria. Others insisted that its movements were 'accidental'
(incidental and secondary). Here such contentions are severely
rejected.*

*The only change later made is to turn 'five hundred times' into 'five
hundred and five'.]*

'There remains,' continued Panurge, 'one little item to void.
You have, sometime or other, seen on the gonfalon of Rome,
S.P.Q.R., that is, *Such a Piddling Question Really*. I shan't be
cuckolded, shall I?'

'Haven of Grace!' cried Rondibilis, 'What are you asking of

me! Will you be cuckolded! My friend, I am married, you soon
will be; but inscribe this saying on your brain with a pen
of iron: every married man is in danger of being cuckolded.
Cuckoldom is naturally one of the adjuncts of matrimony. The
shadow no more naturally follows the body than cuckoldom
follows married men; and whenever you hear these words of a
man, *He is married*, you will not be thought an inexperienced
construer of natural consequences if you say, *He therefore is,
has been, will be, or may be cuckolded.*'

'Hypochondriums of all the devils!' Panurge exclaimed.
'What are you telling me!'

'My friend,' replied Rondibilis, 'one day when Hippocrates
was leaving Lango for Polystylo to visit Democritus the philosopher, he wrote a letter to his old friend Dionysius asking him
(since he did not want his wife to remain at home by herself)
to take her to her father's and mother's during his absence.
They were decent folk of sound reputation, but he nevertheless
should keep a careful eye on her and spy out where she went
with her mother and what sort of people called on her at her
parents' place: "Not," he wrote, "that I distrust her virtue and
modesty, which in the past have been known and proven to
me: but she is, after all, a woman."

'My friend, the nature of wives is figured for us by the Moon
in the following way amongst others: they efface themselves,
restrain themselves and hide themselves away in the sight and
presence of their husbands: when they are absent they seize
their opportunity, have a good time, roam and trot about, lay
aside their hypocrisy and manifest themselves, just as the Moon,
when in conjunction with the Sun, is never visible in Heaven or
earth, yet when in opposition – being farthest from the Sun –
she shines forth in all her fulness, revealing all, especially at
night.

'So, too, all women are . . . women.

'When I say woman I mean a sex so weak, so fickle, so
variable, so changeable, so imperfect, that Nature – speaking
with all due reverence and respect – seems to me, when she
made woman, to have strayed from that good sense with which
she had created and fashioned all things. I have pondered over

it five hundred times yet I can reach no solution except that
Nature had more regard for the social delight of man and the
perpetuating of the human species than for the perfection of
individual womanhood. Certainly Plato does not know into
which category to put women: rational animal or irrational
beast; for Nature has placed within their bodies, in a hidden
intestinal place, an animal (an organ not found in men) in
which from time to time certain humours are engendered –
saline, nitrous, boracic, caustic, gnawing, stabbing and painfully irritating – from the sharp pangs and painful throbbing of
which (since that organ is all sinews and quickened sensitivity)
their whole body is convulsed, all their senses ravished, all their
emotions heightened and all their thoughts confused, to such
an extent that if Nature had not dewed their foreheads with a
little modesty you would see them hunting the fly-cord as
though they were mad, more awesomely than the Proetides ever
did, or the Mimallonides or the bacchic Thyades on the day of
their bacchanalia, because that terrifying animal is colligate
with all the principal parts of the body, as is evident from
dissections.

'I call it an *animal* following the doctrines of the Academics
as much as the Peripatetics, for if having its own proper motion
is a clear indication that a body is animate (as Aristotle puts it)
and if every entity which can move of itself is termed an animal,
then Plato is right to call it an animal, recognizing in it as
he does its own proper motions (of suffocation, prolapsus,
corrugation and irritation) so violent indeed that all other sen-
sations and motions are withdrawn from the woman on
account of them, as though she was suffering from lipomythy,
[syncope,] epilepsy, apoplexy and a real likeness of death. In
addition we can discern in it a clear distinguishing between
smells: women can feel it recoiling from foul odours and being
drawn towards aromatic ones.

'I am aware that Claudius Galen strives to prove that its
movements are accidental, not proper to it and autonomous,
and that others of his faction strive to demonstrate that there
is no sensory discrimination between odours in it, only diverse
reactions proceeding from the diversity of the odorous sub-

stances, but if you studiously examine their words and arguments and weigh them on the Balance of Critolaus you will find that, in this matter and as in many others, they have spoken frivolously, out of an urge to correct their elders rather than from any seeking after truth.

'I will not go further into that disputation: I shall merely say to you that those virtuous women merit no small praise who have lived chastely and blamelessly and who have had the power to bring that raging animal to submit to reason. And I will end by adding that once that animal is satisfied – if ever it can be – by the nutriment that Nature has prepared for it in the male, then all its own peculiar movements have attained their object, all its appetites are slaked and all its frenzies calmed. But be not surprised if we men are in perpetual danger of being cuckolded, we who do not always have the wherewithal to pay up and satisfy it to its contentment.'

'By the power of Other than a Spratling!' said Panurge. 'Don't you know of any remedy whatsoever in your Art?'

'Indeed I do,' Rondibilis replied; 'a very good one which I myself use; it was written down over eighteen hundred years ago by a famous authority. Listen.'

'By God's might,' said Panurge, 'you're a fine man and I love you up to the blessèd brim. Eat a bit of this quince tart: quinces have the property of stopping up the orifices of the stomach on account of a certain jolly styptic quality in them; they also assist the first concoction. But what's this! I'm speaking Latin before the clergy! Wait, and I will offer you a drink from this goblet worthy of Nestor. Would you like another draught of white hypocras? Have no fear of the squinzy: there is no squinant, ginger or grains of paradise in it, only some choice screened cinnamon and some choice fine sugar with good white wine of the local cru of La Devinière, from the vineyard with the sorb-apple tree in it and above that walnut-tree beloved by the crows.'

How Rondibilis, the physician, prescribes
a remedy for cuckoldry

CHAPTER 33

[Dr Rondibilis is about to provide a remedy for Panurge, adapted 'from a famous authority'. That authority is Aesop, whose relevant fable is known from Plutarch in two of his Consolations, *one* To Apollonius *and the other* To his wife. *Rabelais substitutes 'Cuckoldry' for 'Sadness'.*

'Saint Typhany' is a popular perversion of the Epiphany. The jest is expunged in the final version and Saint Typhany replaced by the Epiphany, but the reference to the Fall in Genesis remains as a serious contribution to the debate from Hippothadée.]

'At the time,' said Rondibilis, 'that Jupiter drew up the roster for his Olympian household and the kalendar of all the gods and goddesses, once he had ascribed a day to each of them and a season for their festivals, and once he had assigned them sites for their oracles and pilgrimages, and provided for their sacrifices . . .'

'Did he not act as did Tinteville, the Bishop of Auxerre?' asked Panurge. 'That noble pontiff loved good wine as does every worthy man; he therefore had a particular thought and concern for that forebear of Bacchus, the shoots of the vine.

'Now it befell that, over several years, he saw those vine-shoots distressingly spoiled by ground-frosts, mizzles, hoar-frosts, black-ice, freeze-ups, hailstorms and other disasters which arrived on the feast-days of Saints George, Mark, Vitalis, Eutropius and Philip, and of Holy-Cross day, the Ascension and so on, which occur when the Sun passes under the sign of Taurus. He therefore conceived the opinion that the saints aforesaid were frosting saints and hailstoning saints, spoilers of the vine-shoot. And so he desired to have their feast-days translated to between Christmas and Saint Typhany (as he called the mother of the Three Kings) granting them licence to hail and to freeze as much as they liked then – with all honour and reverence – since at that time the frost would in no way be harmful to the vine-shoots but clearly beneficial. He would transfer in their stead the feasts of Saint Christopher, Saint John-the-headless, Saint Magdalene, Saint Anne, Saint Dominic, Saint Laurence and even mid-August, to May, when, far from there being any risk of frost, no trade in the world is more in demand than that of the sellers of cold drinks [, purveyors of junkets, makers of leafy bowers] and coolers of wine.'

'. . . Jupiter,' said Rondibilis, 'overlooked that poor old devil Cuckoldry, who was not then present: he was in Paris, pleading at the Palais de Justice in some beastly lawsuit on behalf of one of his tenants and vassals. I am not sure how many days afterwards, Cuckoldry heard of the shabby trick played on him and threw down his brief, having a new brief: not to be excluded from the rosters; so he appeared in person before the great Jupiter pleading his previous meritorious actions as well as the good and agreeable services that he had formerly rendered him, earnestly petitioning that he be not left without feast-day, sacrifice or worship.

'Jupiter made excuses, pointing out that all his livings had been already distributed and that his roster was closed. He was so importuned by Signor Cuckoldry, however, that he did eventually include him in the kalendar and put him on the list: worship, sacrifice and a feast-day were ordained for him on Earth. But since there was not a single void or vacant slot in all the kalendar, his festival was arranged to run concurrently with that of the goddess Jealousy, his sway to be over married men, specifically over such as had beautiful wives, and his sacrifice to be suspicion, lack of trust, cantankerousness, the setting of traps, fault-finding and spying by husbands on their wives, with a strict instruction to every married man to revere, honour and celebrate his festival with double fervour and to offer him the aforesaid sacrifices under pain and threat that Signior Cuckoldry would never help, succour nor favour such as did not honour him as stated; he would take no account of them, never enter into their abodes, never haunt their company no matter what supplications they made unto him, but leave them, rather, to rot alone with their wives without a single rival, avoiding

them for ever as heretical and sacrilegious, as is the custom of
other gods towards such as do not duly worship them (as of
Bacchus with wine-growers, Ceres with ploughmen, Pomona
with fruit-growers, Neptune with seamen, Vulcan with black-
smiths; and so on).

'To which was subjoined an opposite, infallible promise that
those husbands who (as they say) took the day off for his
festival, refrained from all business and let all their affairs go
in order to spy on their wives, lock them in and mistreat them
out of jealousy (as set out in the order of his sacrifices) would
find him ever favouring, loving and frequenting them, living
day and night in their dwellings so that they would never be
deprived of his presence.

'I have spoken.'

'Ha! ha! ha!' said Carpalim with a laugh; 'there's a remedy
even more simply natural than Hans Carvel's ring! The devil
take me if I don't believe in it! Such is the nature of women:
just as lightning never burns or breaks anything but hard, solid,
resistant substances and never strikes anything soft, hollow or
yielding (burning the steel blade without harming the velvet
scabbard, and destroying the bones in a body without touching
the flesh which covers them) similarly women bend the contentiousness, ingenuity and contrariness of their minds towards
nothing except what they know to be proscribed and forbidden
to them.'

'Certainly,' said Hippothadée, 'some of our doctors of
theology say that the first woman in the world (whom the
Hebrews call Eve) would hardly have been led into the temptation of eating the fruit of all knowledge if it had not been
forbidden her. That it is so, reflect on how the crafty Tempter,
in his very first words, reminded her of the prohibition against
it, as though to imply, "It is forbidden thee: thou needs must
eat it; thou wouldst not be a woman else."'

[How women normally desire forbidden things

CHAPTER 34

[There was originally no chapter-break.

The speech which begins in the second paragraph is originally attributed to Pantagruel but later given to Ponocrates.

The tale of the nuns and the papal bird is retold after the late-medieval author Johannes Herold in his Sermon 90 and perhaps also from a violently antifeminist poet of the time, Gracien Dupont de Drusac.

In '52 the abbey of Fonshervault becomes the abbey of Coigneaufond (Wedge-it-in-deep).

The play at the end again evokes the Farce de Maître Pathelin *through one of its best-known lines: 'Let us get back to our muttons'). Here Rabelais provides a similar farce, with physicians laughing at physicians, put on by students of medicine, all of whom are named and most of whom had become famous.*

We learn that Panurge is a man of law: he alludes specifically to a law from the Digest entitled Concerning the Examination of the Belly.

The Digest (also known as the Pandects) is the compilation of early Roman jurisprudence made by Tribonian for the Emperor Justinian. It was much cited in the Renaissance, though the integrity of Tribonian was often attacked by many legal scholars.]

'Whenever,' said Carpalim, 'I played the ponce in Orleans I had no rhetorical flourish more efficacious and no argument more persuasive with the ladies for luring them into my nets and drawing them into the game of love than showing them spiritedly, openly and with curses how much their husbands were jealous of them. I didn't invent it: it's been written down and we have rules for it; reasons, examples and daily experiences of it. Once they have got that conviction into their noddles they will infallibly cuckold their husbands, even by God (no swearing!) if they have to do what Semiramis did, or Pasiphaë, Egesta or those women of the Islands of Mendes in Egypt slated by Herodotus and Strabo, and other such bitches in heat.'

'Truly,' said Ponocrates, 'I have indeed heard tell that when Pope John XXII was calling one day at the abbey of Fonshervault, the Abbess and the discreet Mothers-in-council begged him to grant them an indult permitting them to confess each other, contending that women in convents had a few little intimate failings which are unbearably embarrassing to reveal to male confessors; they could tell them more freely and intimately to each other under seal of confession.

' "There is nothing," the Pope replied, "which I would not willingly grant you: but I do see one drawback. Namely that confession must be kept confidential; you women could hardly keep it secret."

' "Yes we could, very well," they said; "better than men."

'So that very day the Pope entrusted a box to their keeping (in which he had caused a tiny linnet to be put). He gently begged them to shut the box away in some safe and secret place, promising them – Pope's honour – that he would grant them the tenor of their request if they did keep it secret, nevertheless strictly forbidding them to open that box under any pretext whatsoever under pain of ecclesiastical censure and eternal excommunication.

'That interdict was no sooner uttered than their minds were seething with a burning desire to see what was inside and longing for the Pope to leave by the gate so that they could get to work on it. The Holy Father, having given them his blessing, withdrew to his quarters. He hadn't taken three steps outside the abbey when those good ladies ran and crowded round to open the forbidden box and see what was inside.

'The next morning the Pope paid them a visit with the intention – they thought – of speedily granting them their indult; but before addressing the subject he ordered them to bring him the box. It was brought to him, but that tiny bird was no longer inside. Whereupon he proved to them that it would be too hard a thing for them to keep confessions confidential seeing that the box, so earnestly entrusted to them, they had kept secret for so short a time.'

'Monsieur Notre Maître, you are most welcome. I have greatly enjoyed listening to you, and I praise God for it all. I haven't seen you since you acted in Montpellier, together with our old friends Antoine Saporta, Guy Bouguier, Balthazar Noyer, Tolet, Jean Quentin, François Robinet, Jean Perdrier and François Rabelais, in *The Moral Farce of the Man who Married a Dumb Wife*.'

'I was there!' said Epistemon. 'Her good husband wished she could talk. And talk she did, thanks to the Art of the physician and of the surgeon who severed a stricture under her tongue. Her speech once recovered, she talked and she talked, so much so that her husband went back to the physician for a remedy to make her shut up. The physician replied that his Art did indeed have appropriate remedies for enabling women to talk but none at all to make them shut up. The only remedy against a wife's interminable prattle lay in deafness for the husband.

'The poor fellow was made deaf by some magic spells or other. [His wife, realizing that he'd become deaf, that she was talking in vain and was never heard by him, went off her head.] The physician then asked for his honorarium, but the husband replied that he was deaf and couldn't catch what he said.

['The physician scattered some powder or other over the man's shoulder whose powers drove him mad. At which that mad husband and his raging wife joined forces and so beat up the physician and the surgeon that they left them half dead.]

'I have never laughed more than I did at that *pathelinage*.'

'Let us get back to our muttons,' said Panurge. 'Your words translated from Rigmarole into French mean that I should go ahead and get married and never worry about being cuckolded. You've followed the wrong suit there!

'Monsieur Notre Maître, I believe that you will be otherwise engaged in your practice on my wedding-day and so unable to put in an appearance. I will excuse you:

> *Stercus et urina Medici sunt prandia prima:*
> *Ex aliis paleas, ex istis collige grana.*

> (Excrement and urine are primary food for physicians:
> Glean straw from those, but grain from these.)'

RABELAIS

'You've got that wrong,' said Rondibilis; the second line should be:

Nobis sunt signa, vobis sunt prandia digna.

(Are symptoms for medics: for legists, the food you deserve.)'

'And if my wife were poorly . . .'

'I would want to examine her urine,' said Rondibilis, 'feel her pulse and then, before proceeding further, observe the condition of her lower belly and umbilical regions (as recommended by Hippocrates, *Aphorisms*, 2, 35).'

'No, no,' said Panurge, 'that is not relevant. It is for us legists to do that: we have the legal rubric, *Concerning the Examination of the Belly*. I'd be making up a barbary clyster for her. Don't neglect your more pressing appointments elsewhere. I'll send some potted pork round to your place and you shall still be our friend.'

Panurge then drew close and, without a word, slipped four rose-nobles into his hand.

Rondibilis gripped them firmly, then said with a start as though affronted:

'Hay! hay! hay! There was no need for that, Monsieur. Many thanks all the same. Nothing from bad folk do I ever accept: nothing from good folk do I ever reject. I am always yours to command.'

'For a fee,' said Panurge.

'Yes, of course,' said Rondibilis.'

How Trouillogan the philosopher treats the difficulty of marriage

CHAPTER 35

[Was originally Chapter 34. The '52 numbering is adopted from now on for convenience of reference.

A key chapter for the philosophy of the Third Book.

Gargantua, last heard of as translated to the Land of the Faeries (Pantagruel, Chapter 15) is present here, unexplained, as the wise and courteous king and (later) the ideal father.

The name of Trouillogan remains to be satisfactorily explained. He is a comic sceptic and leads to a chapter first dominated by farce and then by an authoritative harmonizing of expert opinion. Rabelais is following legal practice in matters perplex: 'after consulting the experts, harmonize their opinions'. The harmonizing is presented as the last word of wisdom by Pantagruel.

Erasmus is very present: in the adage I, II, XXVIII, 'To pass on the torch'; much more fundamentally in the authoritative moral adage (already misused by Panurge for his Praise of Debts in Chapter 2), IV, VI, LXXXI, 'No one is born for himself alone'; in the woman cited by Gargantua and the Spartan maidservant cited by Pantagruel (who are both drawn from the Apophthegms (III, Aristippus, 31 and II, Lacaenarum, 32). After the smiles Erasmus like Rabelais gives an entirely serious moral meaning to the anecdotes.

Wisdom is to be found in the Golden Mean, to which even Saint Paul is seen as pointing the way.]

Once those words were spoken Pantagruel said to Trouillogan the philosopher: 'Our liege-loyal friend: from hand to hand to you the torch is passed. It is now up to you to give your reply: Should Panurge marry or not?'

'Both,' replied Trouillogan.

'What did you say!' asked Panurge.

'What you heard,' said Trouillogan.

'What did I hear?' asked Panurge.

'What I said,' replied Trouillogan.

'[Ah-ah! So that's where we've got to!] No trumps,' said Panurge. 'I pass. [Now then:] Should I marry or no?'

'Neither,' replied Trouillogan.

'The devil take me if I'm not going raving mad!' said Panurge; 'and may he also take me if I know what you mean! Hang on. To hear you more clearly I'll put my glasses to my left ear.'

At that very moment Pantagruel glimpsed near the doorway of the hall Gargantua's little dog (which he called *Kyne*, for such was the name of the dog of Toby).[18] At which he said to everyone present, 'Our king cannot be far from here. Let us rise to our feet.'

Those words were hardly uttered before Gargantua came into the banqueting hall. Each man rose to make his bow.

Gargantua, having courteously greeted the whole assembly, said, 'Leave neither your places nor your discussions. Bring a chair for me at this end of the table. Allow me to drink to you all. You are all most welcome here. Now tell me: where had you got to?'

Pantagruel told him that, when dessert was brought in, Panurge had posed a problematical subject, namely, *Should he or should he not marry*. Père Hippothadée and Notre Maître Rondibilis had acquitted themselves of their replies, and, just as he came in the loyal Trouillogan was doing so. When Panurge asked him, 'Should I marry or no?' Trouillogan had first replied, 'Both together,' and then 'Neither.'

'Panurge is complaining about such inconsistent and contradictory replies, and swears that he can understand none of it.'

'I do understand it, I think,' said Gargantua. 'The reply is similar to that given by a philosopher of old when asked whether he had ever had a certain woman (whose name was mentioned); "I hold her dear," he said, "but she has no hold on me. She is mine: I am not hers."'

'A similar reply,' said Pantagruel 'was given by a parlour-maid of Sparta. Asked whether she had ever had anything to

---

18. Toby's dog is called 'Dog' in Greek (that is, Kyne from *kunos*). Toby and his dog represent both loyalty and, for evangelicals, a great exemplum to use against clandestine marriages.

do with men, she replied, "No! But men had occasionally had something to do with her".'

'That,' said Rondibilis, 'is how we reach the Neutral in medicine and the Mean in philosophy: by participating in both extremes; by abnegating both extremes; or, by compartition of time, being now in one extreme, now the other.'[19]

'The Holy Envoy seems to me to have put that more clearly,' said Hippothadée, 'when he says, "Let those that are married be as not married; those that have a wife be as though having her not."' 'I,' said Pantagruel, 'expound *having and not having a wife* this way: *to have a wife* is to have her as Nature created her, for the help, joy and companionship of man; *not to have a wife* is not to hang about her, not to sully for her that unique and supreme love which a man owes to God; not to shirk the duties which a man naturally owes to his homeland, the State and his friends; not to neglect his studies or his concerns in order to be ever indulging her. Taking *having and not having a wife* that way, I can see neither inconsistency nor contradiction in those terms.'[20]

19. As a platonizing physician, Rondibilis respects the Golden Mean, whereas Galenists were suspicious of it in medicine. He is using technical philosophical terms. The Mean may be reached either *per participationem* or *per abnegationem*, or by both in turn as appropriate. For the modest theologian, Saint Paul says the same thing more simply when, in I Corinthians 7:29, he advises his followers 'to have wives as though they had none'.

20. Pantagruel is diametrically opposed to Panurge. The good wife is the 'help meet' for man of Genesis 2:18. Woman was made for man (I Corinthians 11:9), but a man is not made for himself: a husband also has the duties to God, country, profession and friends summed up in the adage, 'No one is born for himself alone'.

The continuation of the replies of Trouillogan the Ephectic and Pyrrhonian philosopher

CHAPTER 36

[Was originally Chapter 35.

In the first sentence Rabelais again confuses Heraclitus and Democritus. The philosophical farce continues. Classical scepticism was still mainly known from Cicero's Academics, *but, according to Rabelais, it was becoming dominant. (Scepticism was widely seen at the time, though not later, as favouring evangelical teachings.) A maxim dear to lawyers said: 'Words bind men: ropes bind bulls' horns: a bull is caught by ropes: a man is bound by words.' Another maxim added that horses are caught by their manes or their fringes.*

Panurge is thrown back on to what he was told at the outset, and we are prepared for the paradox of Bridoye.]

'You pipe up harmoniously,' replied Panurge, 'but I believe I'm down in that dark well where Heraclitus said that Truth lies hid. I can't see or hear a thing. I feel all my feelings grow numb; I greatly fear that I may be under a spell. I shall speak in a different style.

'Liege-loyal friend, don't budge! Stuff nothing in your purse. Let's change the luck of the dice and talk without logical disjunctives. I can see that those ill-joined clauses confuse you.

'Now then: for God's sake: Ought I to marry?'

TROUILLOGAN: 'There is some likelihood.'
PANURGE: 'And if I definitely don't get married?'
TROU: 'I can see no impropriety whatsoever in that.'
[PAN: 'You can see none at all?'
TROU: 'None: or my eyesight deceives me.'
PAN: 'I can see more than five hundred!'
TROU: 'Enumerate them.'
PAN: 'I mean, improperly speaking, employing a definite number for an indefinite one, a precise one for an imprecise one, that is, many.'

TROU: 'I am listening.'

PAN: 'I can't do without a wife, in the name of all the devils.'

TROU: 'Avaunt: away with those nasty creatures!'

PAN: 'So be it, for God's sake: my local Salmagundians say that to lie in bed alone, without a wife, is a beastly way to live. And so said Dido in her lamentations.'

TROU: 'I am yours to command.']

PAN: 'By Gord's buddy, I'm all right then. Now: shall I get married?'

TROU: 'Possibly.'

PAN: 'Shall I find it all right?'

TROU: 'Depends on whom you meet.'

PAN: 'And if, as I hope, I am well met, will I be happy?'

TROU: 'Sufficiently.'

PAN: 'Let's go against the nap: and if I am ill met?'

TROU: 'No fault of mine.'

PAN: 'For pity's sake counsel me! What ought I to do?'

TROU: 'What you will.'

PAN: 'Fiddle-faddle!'

TROU: 'No invocations, I beg you.'

PAN: 'In God's name, so be it. I only want to do as you advise me to do. What *do* you advise me?'

TROU: 'Nothing.'

PAN: 'Shall I get married?'

TROU: 'I was never in on it.'

PAN: 'I shall never get married then?'

TROU: 'I can't help that.'

PAN: 'If I never marry I shall never be cuckolded?'

TROU: 'So I was thinking.'

PAN: 'Let's put it that I *am* married!'

[TROU: 'Put it where?'

PAN: 'I mean, take it that I'm married.']

TROU: 'My hands are full.'

PAN: 'Damme! Turds up my nose! Gosh! If only I dared to have a good quiet little swear, what a relief that would be! Good. Now then: patience! And so: if I am married I shall be cuckolded?'

TROU: 'So one would say.'

PAN: 'And if my wife is honourable and chaste I never shall be cuckolded.'

TROU: 'You appear to be speaking correctly.'

PAN: 'Listen to me.'

TROU: 'As long as you like.'

PAN: 'Will she be honest and chaste? That's all.'

TROU: 'I doubt it.'

PAN: 'You've never even seen her!'

TROU: 'As far as I know.'

PAN: 'So why are you having doubts over something you know nothing about?'

TROU: 'For a reason.'

PAN: 'And if you did know her?'

TROU: 'All the more so.'

PAN: 'Page, my dear little fellow; here, take my bonnet. I'm giving it to you, minus the glasses. Go down into the back yard and do a little half-hour's swearing for me. I'll do the same for you whenever you want me to. But who will make me a cuckold?'

TROU: 'Somebody.'

PAN: 'By the guts of the wooden Gosh! I'll give you a good scrubbing, Monsieur Somebody.'

TROU: 'So you say.'

PAN: 'May the devil – he with no white to his eyes – make off with me if I don't buckle up my wife in a Bergamo-belt whenever I go out of my seraglio.'

TROU: 'Mind your language.'

PAN: 'Shitty-shanty for my language! Let's reach a decision.'

TROU: 'I do not oppose it.'

PAN: 'Wait! Since I can't draw blood from that spot I'll bleed you from a different vein: are you or are you not married?'

TROU: 'Neither one nor the other, and both together.'

PAN: 'God come to our aid! By the death of Gosh, the effort is making me sweat; my digestion is upset, I can feel it. All my phrenes, metaphrenes and diaphragms are taut and fraught from infunnelizating your words and replies into the game-pouch of my understanding.'

TROU: 'No hindrance to me.'

PAN: 'Gee up, our Liege-loyal man! Are you married?'

TROU: 'So I am persuaded.'

PAN: 'And you have been married before?'

TROU: 'That is possible.'

PAN: 'Did it go well that first time?'

TROU: 'That is not impossible.'

PAN: 'And that second time, how do you find it?'

TROU: 'As bears my fated lot.'

PAN: 'But come on. Seriously now. Has it turned out well for you?'

TROU: 'That is likely.'

PAN: 'Come on, for God's sake! By the burden of Saint Christopher, I'd as soon undertake to get a fart out of a dead donkey as a decision out of you. I shall get you this time though. Our loyal liege-man! Tell truth and shame the devil: have you ever been cuckolded? I mean *you* – *you* here, not some other *you* down there on the tennis-court!'

TROU: 'No. Unless it were so predestined.'

PAN: 'By the flesh, I deny! [By the blood, I jib; by the body] I give up. He's getting away.'

At those words Gargantua arose and said:

'Our good God be praised in all things. As far as I can see the world has grown quite smart since I first knew it. So this is where we've got? Have all the most learned and wise philosophers of today joined the school – that is, the phrontistery – of the Pyrrhonists, Aporetics, Sceptics and Ephectics? Praise be to God in his goodness! From henceforth you can catch lions by the mane, [horses by the fringe,] oxen by the horn, buffaloes by the snout, wolves by the tail, goats by the beard, birds by the foot; but never such philosophers by their words.

'Farewell, my good friends.'

So saying, he withdrew from the company. Pantagruel and the others wanted to escort him, but he would not allow it.

Once Gargantua had gone out of the hall, Pantagruel said to the guests:

'Plato's friend Timaeus counted the guests at the beginning of their meeting: we on the contrary will count them at the end.

One, two, three. Where's the fourth? Our friend Bridoye, is it not?' Epistemon replied that he himself had gone to his house to invite him but he did not find him in. An usher from the Myrelinguian Parlement in Myrelingues had already cited and arraigned him to appear in person to justify before the senators a sentence which he had pronounced. For that reason he had already left the previous morning so as to present himself in person on the day assigned and not to be in default or fall into contumacy.

'I would like to hear more about that,' said Pantagruel. 'He has been a judge at Fonsbeton for more than forty years. During that period he has pronounced over four thousand definitive judgements. Two thousand three hundred and nine of those pronounced by him were subject to an appeal before the Sovereign Court of the Myrelinguian Parlement in Myrelingues by the parties condemned. All of those judgements were ratified, approved and confirmed by decisions of that court and the appeals overturned and quashed. That he, old as he is, should now be summoned to appear in person – he who, all that time, has lived so piously in his vocation – can only be attributable to something ill-starred. I wish to help him with all my might to get a fair hearing.

'I know that the malign forces of this world have grown so much worse that nowadays a good case has need of aid, and I intend to apply myself to it at once for fear of being taken by surprise.'

And so the cloths were removed. Pantagruel bestowed precious and worthwhile gifts on his guests – rings, jewels, vessels of gold or of silver – and, then, having heartily thanked them, withdrew to his rooms.

How Pantagruel persuades Panurge to
take advice from a fool

CHAPTER 37

[Was originally Chapter 36.

That Panurge is 'lolling' his head is proof that he is a fool of the wrong sort. (Compare Gargantua when badly educated, and contrast the prophetic 'jerking' of Triboullet's head in Chapter 45.)

Christian folly is about to come into its own. Prophesying is a gift of God (I Corinthians 12). It is a matter of grace, but people can make themselves apt to receive that gift. The Christian fool despises the things of this world but is considered wise by the Celestial Intelligences (the highest rank of angels to concern themselves with human beings). The true spiritual fool, by forgetting himself, may be inspired, caught away in prophetic rapture.

The tale of The Cook, the Smeller, and the Fool Who Judges *was one well-known to legal scholars and cited in law-books, including by Tiraqueau in* The Laws of Marriage *(naming the same authorities as Rabelais).*

Three of the adages of Erasmus are relevant: I, III, LXVIII, 'A mouse tasting pitch'; I, III, I, 'Either a fool or a king should be born', and II, IX, LXIV, 'More foolish than Coroebus'.]

As Pantagruel withdrew he saw from the gallery Panurge in the attitude of a mad dotard, lolling his head and doting. He said to him:

'To me you look like a mouse caught in pitch: the more it struggles to be free of it, the more bespattered it gets. You, likewise, striving to free yourself from the snares of perplexity are more caught up in them than before. I know of no remedy save one. Listen: I have often heard the popular saying, "The fool may well teach the wise." Since you have not been fully satisfied by the answers of the wise, seek counsel from a fool. It could well be that in doing so you will be more agreeably pleased and satisfied. So many princes, kings and states, you know, have been saved by the advice, counsel and auguries of fools, so many battles have been won, so many perplexities resolved. No need to recall the exempla: you will acquiesce in this reasoning: just as the one who keeps a close watch on his private and family affairs, who is alert and attentive to the management of his own household, whose mind never wanders, who never lets slip an occasion for acquiring goods or amassing wealth and who cleverly avoids the distresses of poverty, you dub worldly wise despite his being daft in the judgement of the Celestial Intelligences: so, to be wise in their sight – I mean wise and forewise by divine inspiration and capable of receiving the gift of prophecy – a man must forget himself, sally outside himself, void his senses of every earthly affection, purge his mind of all human anxiety and treat all his affairs as indifferent: which is popularly attributed to folly.

'That was why the great soothsayer Faunus (the son of Picus, the King of the Latins) came to be called *Fatuellus* (Buffoon) by the ignorant mob.

['And that is why we see, at the distribution of parts between the strolling players, the role of the fool or jester is always taken by the most skilled and accomplished actor in the troupe. And that is why the mathematical astrologers say that the same configuration of the heavens obtains at the birth of kings and of the feeble-minded, citing the example of Coroebus (a fool, according to Euphorion) and Aeneas, who both shared the same horoscope.]

'I shall not stray off course if I relate what Johannes Andrea wrote apropos of a canon in a certain papal rescript addressed to the mayor and citizens of La Rochelle (and later repeated by Panormitanus on the same canon, as well as by Barbatia on the *Pandects* and recently by Jason de Maino, Caillette's great-grandpapa.

'The case stood thus.

'In Paris, at the area of the Petit Châtelet where meats are roasted, a porter's boy, in front of the booth of a certain roasting-cook was eating his bread to the smell of the roast and found his bread thus flavoured to be hugely delicious. The cook allowed him to do so, but in the end, once all the bread was gobbled up, he grabbed the boy by the collar and tried to make him pay him for the smell of his roast. The porter's boy said he had in no way harmed his meats; he had taken nothing of his and owed him nothing. The smell in question was wafting away outside and so was lost in any case. It was unheard of that anyone in Paris could sell in the street the smell of a roast! The cook retorted that he was not obliged to feed porter's boys on the smell of roast meat, and swore oaths to the effect that if the lad refused to pay up he would confiscate his porter's hooks. The boy pulled out his stave and prepared to defend himself. Great was the altercation. From all parts of Paris the stupid mob came running up to watch the quarrel.

'There, most felicitously, stood the fool Seigny Johan, a citizen of Paris. The roasting-cook saw him and asked the porter's boy: "Would you trust this noble Seigny Johan over our disagreement?"

' "Gosh, yes," replied the porter's boy.

'And so, Seigny Johan, having heard their opposing cases, ordered the porter's boy to take a silver coin out of his purse, and the lad placed a phillipus in his hand. Seigny Johan took it and put it upon his left shoulder as if to discover whether it was of the right weight; he then tapped it against the palm of his left hand, as though to hear whether it was of good alloy; he then placed it close up against the ball of his right eye, as if to see whether it had been well minted. All of which was done amidst the deep silence of the gazing mob, with the roast-meat man confidently waiting and the porter's boy full of despair. Eventually the fool rang the coin several times on the stall. Then, with the majesty of a presiding judge and while holding his bauble in his hand as though it were a sceptre, he donned his fool's cap (which imitated fine fur but had ear-flaps of paper encircled by an organ-pipe ruff), gave two or three fine prefatory coughs and then loudly said:

' "The Court decides that the porter's boy who ate his bread to the smell of the roast has, in accordance with Civil Law, duly paid the roast-meat man with the ringing of his coin. The Court now commands that all go home, each to his each-one-ery. No order for costs. The Court rises."

'That judgement by the Parisian fool appeared so equitable,

so amazing to the scholars that they doubt, if the case had been judged by the local Parlement [, the Roman Rotta] or even the Areopagus, that it would have been more judiciously settled. So think about taking counsel from a fool.'

How Triboullet is blazoned by Pantagruel and by Panurge

CHAPTER 38

[*Was originally* Chapter 37.

A chapter for informed laughter. Triboullet was a real person, a fool at the Court of France. He lived under Louis XII and François I.

In the two blasons *Pantagruel attributes to Triboullet qualities which can be recognized as good and positive, whilst Panurge, as one would expect, gives him qualities which, on the whole, do not find favour in the eyes of Pantagruelists.*

Bonadies was an Arcadian god and Bonadea, the Great Mother, a goddess of fertility.]

'Upon my soul,' replied Panurge, 'I will do it. I feel that my guts have extended. They were all tight and constipated before. But just as we chose the very cream of wisdom for our advice, I would like this consultation to be presided over by one who is a fool to the sovereign degree.'

'Triboullet,' said Pantagruel, 'seems to me to be an appropriate fool. Panurge replied: 'A proper and complete fool.'

PANTAGRUEL	PANURGE
A fated fool,	A major-scale fool,
a natural fool,	a B-sharp and B-flat fool,
a heavenly fool,	a terrestrial fool,
a jovial fool,	a joyful and frivolous fool,
a mercurial fool,	a pretty, frolicsome fool,
a lunatic fool,	a be-tasselled fool,
an erratic fool,	a be-pimpled fool,
an eccentric fool,	a cap-and-bells fool,

an ethereal, Juno-like fool,
an arctic fool,
an heroic fool,
a genial fool,
a predestined fool,
an august fool,
a Caesarine fool,
an imperial fool,
a royal fool,
a patriarchal fool,
an original fool,]
a loyal fool
a ducal fool,
a standard-bearer fool,
a lordly fool,
a law-court fool,
a principal fool,
a praetorian fool,
a whole fool,
an elect fool,
a curial fool,
a Roman eagle-bearing fool,
a triumphant fool,
a vulgar fool,
a domestic fool,
an exemplary fool,
a rare and foreign fool,
an aulic fool,
a civil-law fool,
a people's fool,
a family fool,
a famous fool,
a favoured fool,
a Latin fool,
an ordinary fool,
a redoubtable fool,
a transcendental fool,
a sovereign fool,

a laughing, Venus-like fool,
a racked-off fool,
a first-pressing fool,
a first-*cuvée* fool,
a fermented fool,
a silly-original fool,
a papal fool,
a consistorial fool,
[a conclaval fool
a Bull-issuing fool,
a synodical fool,
an episcopal fool,
a doctoral fool,
a monastical fool,
a fiscal fool,
an *Extravagantes* fool,
a doctoral-bonneted fool,
a simply-tonsured fool,
a man-hole fool,
a Distinction-in-folly fool,
a table-mate fool,
a first-class BA fool,
a papal-train bearing fool,
a supererogatory fool,
a subsidiary fool,
an *a latere*, alterative fool,
a poor little fool,
a passing fool,
a newly fledged fool,
a free-falcon fool,
a nice fool,
a spotty fool,
a pillaging fool,
a new-sprouted-tail fool,
a wild-bird fool,
a doting fool,
a back-stay fool,
an inflated fool,

a special fool,
a metaphysical fool,
an ecstatic fool,
a categorical fool,
a logically assertable fool,
a decuman fool,
an official fool,
a perspective fool,
an algorismical fool,
an algebraical fool,
a cabalistical fool,
a talmudistical fool,
an amalgamated fool,
[a compendious fool
a papal-brief-holding fool,
an antonomastical fool,
an allegorical fool,
a tropological fool,
a pleonastic fool,
a capital fool,
a cerebral fool,
a cordial fool,
an inward fool,
an hepatic fool,
an hypochondriacal fool,
a flatulent fool,
a legitimate fool,
an azimuthal fool,
an almacantar fool,
a proportionate fool,
an architraval fool,
a pedestal fool,
a paragon of a fool,
a celebrated fool,
a jolly fool,
a solemn fool,
a yearly fool,
a festive fool,

a super-cockalorum fool,
a corollary fool,
a Levantine fool,
a sublime fool,
a crimson fool,
a well-dyed fool,
a burgess fool,
a feather-brush fool,
a cageable fool,
a modal fool,
a second-intentionary fool,
an almanac-making fool,
an heteroclite fool,
a Thomistical fool,
a papal-brief-writing fool,]
a papal-bullish fool,
a paper-mandatary fool,
a cowled fool,
a titulary fool,
a crouching fool,
a rebarbative fool,
a well-mentulated fool,
a weak-clawed fool,
a well-balled fool,
a scribbling fool,
a windbag of a fool,
a culinary fool,
a timber-tree fool,
a turnspit fool,
a scullery fool,
a catarrhal fool,
a spruce fool,
a twenty-four-carat fool
a bizarre fool,
a cross-wise fool,
a martingaled fool,
a baton-bearing fool,
a baubled fool,

a recreative fool,	a well-biased fool,
a village fool,	a high-tide-mark fool,
a pleasing fool,	a tripping-over fool,
a privileged fool,	a superannuated fool,
a rustic fool,	a boorish fool,
an ordinary fool,	a big-chested fool,
an all-hours fool,	a pompous fool,
a sonorous fool,	a splendidly arranged fool,
a resolute fool,	a foot-rooted fool,
an hieroglyphical fool,	a fustian-puzzle fool,
an authentic fool,	a boss's fool,
a valued fool,	a riding-hood fool,
a precious fool,	a wide-sleeved fool,
a fantastical fool,	a Damascene fool,
a lymphatic fool,	a Persian-style fool,
a panic fool,	a baritone fool,
an alambical fool,	a fly-blown fool
an un-boring fool,	a gun-shot-proof fool.

PANTAGRUEL: 'If it was reasonable in ancient Rome to call the Feast of Fools the *Quirinales*, in France we could rightly institute the *Triboulletinales*!'

PANURGE: 'If fools were all saddled with cruppers, his rump would be raw by now.'

PANTAGRUEL: 'If he were that god Fatuellus whom we spoke of – the husband of the Blessèd Fatua – his father would be *Bonadies* and his Great Mother, *Bonadea*.'

PANURGE: 'Despite his bandy legs, if all the fools did amble he'd be two lengths ahead already. Let's go to him without delay; we shall get a lovely answer from him. I'm counting on it.'

'I want to be present when Bridoye is heard,' said Pantagruel. 'I shall go off to Myrelingues, which is across the river Loire, meanwhile sending Carpalim to bring Triboullet here from Blois.'

Carpalim was then despatched.

Pantagruel, accompanied by members of his household,

including amongst others Panurge, Ponocrates, Frère Jean, Gymnaste and Rhizotome, set off on the road for Myrelingues.

How Pantagruel is present at the hearing of Bridoye, who decided lawsuits by the throw of the dice

CHAPTER 39

[Was originally Chapter 37.

In '52 the original 'Bicentumviral Court' becomes the 'Centumviral Court' (probably a double allusion to the Centumviral Court mentioned frequently by Cicero, and to the Parlement de Paris, *recently expanded beyond a hundred members).*

The comedy of the following chapters presupposes a certain knowledge of the Law. All the legal references are given by Rabelais in Latin and in the standard legal form of abbreviated incipits to laws, paragraphs, etc. They have become incomprehensible and even unpronounceable to most readers. (Here the references have been translated and sufficiently expanded to make them at least pronounceable.) Contemporary legal authors piled up dozens or even hundreds of such references per folio page. Bridoye's references are brocards, *that is, elementary principles, maxims and legal commonplaces, most of which appear as such in current booklets as the* Flores Legum *(Flowers of the Laws) or the* Brocardica Juris *(Legal Brocards). Others were available in the* Lexicon *of Alberico de Rosate. One or two, which touch upon matters sexual, notoriously aroused laughter amongst students in their lecture-halls. For Bridoye even his Gospel maxims are known through his brocards.*

Trinquamelle is all but an anagram of Tiraquellus, *the Latin name of Rabelais' legal friend.*

In the original there are no paragraphs or indentations. They have been supplied. For many the best way to enjoy these chapters is to treat the indented matter simply or mainly as part of the obsessive, monomaniac, legal muttering of Bridoye.]

At the stipulated time next day, Pantagruel arrived at Myrelingues. The President, Senators and Counsellors invited him to join them and to witness their hearing of the grounds and reasons which Bridoye would allege to explain why he had pronounced a particular judgement contrary to Toucheronde, the legal Assessor, which seemed not at all equitable to the Bicentumviral Court.

Pantagruel was delighted to join them.

He saw Bridoye seated in the well of the court, merely offering as his sole reasons or excuses that he had grown old and could no longer see as well as he used to, alluding to several of the afflictions and tribulations which old age brings with it,

as noted by Archidiaconus: Decreta: distinctio 86, canon, 'So Great').[21]

Because of which he had not been able to read the number of spots on his dice as clearly as he had done in the past and hence, just as Isaac when he was old and his eyes were dim mistook Jacob for Esau, he, when deciding the lawsuit in question must have mistaken a four for a five, particularly insisting that he was then using his small dice, and that by the provision of the Law natural imperfections cannot be arraigned as a crime,

(as clearly transpires in: Pandects: 'Of Things Military'; the Law, 'He Who Has but One'; Pandects: 'On the Regulations of the Law'; the Law, 'Almost'; Pandects: 'Of the Edicts of the Aediles', throughout; Pandects: 'Of Boundaries Displaced'; the Law, 'Saint Adrian'; resolved by Ludovicus Romanus on the Law, 'If it Be True That'; Pandects: 'Of the Dissolution of Marriages').[22]

Anyone who would act otherwise would not be laying an accusation against Man but against Nature,

21. Bridoye misuses a brocard which states that weakness in old age is compensated for by freedom from lusts, greater wisdom and maturity of judgement.
22. The brocards here really refer to physical disadvantages. The first, 'He Who Has but One', states that a man is liable to military service even if he has but one testicle.

(as is evident from the Law, 'The Greatest Defects', Codex,
§ 'Of Children Passed Over').[23]

'What dice, my friend, do you mean?' asked Trinquamelle,
the High President of the Court.

'Why, the dice of judgement, the *alea judiciorum*,

(of which mention is made by Legal Doctors on Decreta,
26, question ii, "Of Lots"; by the Law, "Nor the Purchase", Pandects: "On the Contracting of Purchases", and
Bartolus on the same);

the dice which you, my Lords, normally use in this your Sovereign Court, as do all other judges when deciding their cases
following what has been noted by Dominus Henricus Fer-
randatus,

and noted in the gloss on the final chapter, "Of Sorti-
leges", and the Law, "Since Both"; Pandects: "On the
Judgements";

where the doctors note that lots are very good, proper, useful
and necessary for the voiding of law suits and dissention. That
has been even more clearly stated

by Baldus, Bartholus and Alexander in the Codex, "Generalities Concerning Legates"; the Law, "If Two Persons"'.[24]

---

23. The gloss stated that there are 'accusers of Nature' who make a difference
between men and women!

24. Civil Law most certainly did allow eventual recourse to dice in *perplexities*
(where facts are certain but the application of the law to them is obscure.
Behind the smiles the ground is being prepared for an eventual volte-face.
26 q.ii Sors (translated here as Decreta, 26, question ii, chapter 'Of lots')
will be taken up seriously by Epistemon in Chapter 44. Previously, *C.
Communia de leg. l. si duo* (translated here as 'Codex, "Generalities
Concerning Legates"; the Law 'If Two Persons') was cited at the outset
by Pantagruel at the end of Chapter 12 to state authoritatively that no
appeal can be lodged against Fortuna.

'But what procedures do you follow, my friend?' asked Trin-quamelle.

'I shall answer that briefly,' said Bridoye,

following the teachings of the Law, "More Abundant", paragraph, "In Refutatories"; Codex: "On Summonses"; and what is stated by the Glossator, Law 1, Pandects: "That for fear": namely: "Moderns delight in brevity".

'I act just as you do, my Lords, in accordance with normal legal procedure, to which our laws command as always to defer:

as in the note of the Extravagantes; "Of Customs", the chapter, "From a letter", and, therein, Innocent IV.

'So having viewed, reviewed, read, reread, dug into and leafed through the complaints, summonses, depositions, commissions, informations, preliminary appearances, productions of documents, allegations, declarations of intent, rebuttals, requests, inquests, counter-rebuttals, replies to the counter-rebuttals; replies to the replies to the counter-rebuttals, written depositions, objections, [complaints,] exornatories, depositions, confrontations, direct encounters, libels, letters of attestation, appeals; letters – patent, productory, disqualificatory and anticipatory –, elicitings, missives, remissives, conclusions, claims to throw out the case, reconciliations, appeals to another jurisdiction, avowals, final notifications and other such sweet-meats and spices from defendant and plaintiff alike – as the good judge must do,

according to what has been noted by Speculator, "On the Ordinary's", paragraph 3, and by the title "On the Duty of Every Judge", final paragraph, and "On the Presentation of Rescripts", paragraph 1,

I place at one end of the table in my Chambers the bundles of the Defendant and throw the dice for him first, just as you do my Lords, and as is noted in the Law, "The Most Favourable"; Pandects: "On the Rules of Law"; and in the chapter, "When the legalities of the litigants are obscure, the defendant must be favoured above the plaintiff".

Which done, I place the bundles of the Plaintiff – just as you do, my Lords – at the other end of the table, face to face, for

"Opposites placed opposite shine forth more clearly", as is noted in Law 1, paragraph, "We see"; Pandects, "To Those who are Subject to Their Own Jurisdiction or to That of Others"; and in the Law, "Of Remunerations", 1, "Things Intermixed"; Pandects, "On Remunerations and Honorariums",

similarly, and without delay, I cast the dice.'

'But my friend,' asked Trinquamelle, 'how do you set about penetrating the legal obscurities alleged by the parties whose pleas are before you?'

'Just as you do, my Lords,' replied Bridoye. 'That is to say, when there is a goodly pile of bundles on either side. Then I use my small dice, as you do too, my Lords,

in accordance with the Law, "Always in Stipulations"; Pandects: "On the Rules of Law"; and the vital law which scans as verse,

Semper in obscuris quod minimum est sequimur

(Ever in matters obscure we follow whatever is smallest), which is canonized by the Codex, "In Matters Obscure", same title, Book VI.

'I possess other dice – big, beautiful and resonant ones – which I use, just as you do, my Lords, when the matter is more fluid, that is to say, when there are fewer bundles.'

'Once you have done that, my friend, how do you reach your judgement?' asked Trinquamelle.

'As you do too, my Lords,' replied Bridoye. 'I pronounce

judgement in favour of him on whom first falls the lot delivered by the hazard of the judicial, tribunian and praetorian dice. And thus do our laws recommend,

> Pandects: "Whoever is First in a Pledge"; the Law, "Stronger"; the Law, "Creditor"; Codex, "Of Consuls", Law 1, and "Of the Rules of Law", in Canon vi: *"Prior in Time: Stronger in Law"*.'

How Bridoye expounds the reasons why he first examined the cases which he decided by dice

CHAPTER 40

[Was originally Chapter 38.

Bridoye continues to show gentle and engaging madness, citing his legal brocards at length for the most obvious of matters whilst defending his using dice as a practice common amongst his fellow judges.]

'I see, yes ... But,' asked Trinquamelle, 'since you reach your judgements, my friend, by chance, by the casting of dice, why do you not avoid delay by appealing to chance the very day and hour that the opposing parties appear before you? What use to you are those writs and other procedural documents contained in those bundles?'

'As for you too, my Lords,' replied Bridoye, 'they serve me in three manners, exquisite, requisite and authentic.

'First, it is a matter of due process, the omission of which renders actions invalid,

> as is very well proven by Speculator, title, "On the Publication of Documents", and the title, "On the Presentation of a Rescript";

moreover you are only too aware that, in legal procedures, formalities often demolish materialities and substantialities, for, The form changed, the substance changes; Pandects: "For the Exhibiting"; the Law Julianus; note on the Law Falcidia; the Law, "If he who has forty"; and, Extravagantes, "Concerning Tenths"; the Canon, "For an Audience"; and "On the Celebration of Masses", the chapter, "In a certain case".

'Secondly, they serve me, as they serve you too my Lords, as an honourable and healthy exercise. The late Professor Othoman Vadere, a great physician (as in the Codex, "On the Officers and the Archiatrus", Book 12), has many times informed me that a lack of physical exercise is the sole cause of the poor health and shortness of life of judges like you, my Lords, and all officers of the Court;

as has been very well noted by Bartholus in Law 1, Codex, "Of the Judgements for That Which".

'And to you, my Lords, and consequently to us,

since, An Accessory conforms to the Nature of the Principal (as in "On the Rules of Law", Book VI, and the Law, "When the Principal"; and the Law, "Nothing by Trickery", Pandects, same title: "Of Guarantors", and Extravagantes, "On the Duties of Legates");

have been allowed certain honourable and recreational exercises,

as in Pandects: "On Games of Dice and Chance", the Law, "They usually"; and in the Authentica, "That all should obey", near the beginning, collation 7; and Pandects: "Of Words Prescribed"; the Law, "If Gratuitous"; and Law 1, Codex: "Of Displays", chapter 11.

'And such is the opinion of Saint Thomas, in *Secunda Secundae*, question 168, very appositely cited *by Doctor Albericus de Rosate, who was a great legal practitioner* and a renowned authority, as is attested by Barbatia in his *Counsels to Princes*; the reason for which is expounded *by the gloss, Preamble of the Pandects, "Not even of the third": Interpose at times joys betwixt thy cares.*

'Now, actually, one day in 1498, having as I did a financial problem in the Chambers of the General Secretaries of the Treasury, and securing an entry by a pecuniary arrangement with the usher, since you too, my Lords, know that *All things are obedient to money,*

so says Baldus in the Law, "Singularities"; Pandects: "If a Precise Demand"; and Salycetus in the Law, "Of Receipts"; Pandects: "On Financial Constitutions"; and the Cardinal, in the Clementines, 1, "Of Baptisms",

'I found them all healthily exercised in playing *Swat that Fly* – that *Muscus* – whether before or after a meal is quite indifferent, conceding – *nota bene* – that the game of *Muscus* is honourable, healthy ancient and legal, invented by a certain Muscus,

concerning whom see Codex, "Of Petitioning for an Inheritance", the Law, "If after a Removal"; and *Muscarii*[25] – *id est* such as play at "Swat that Muscus" – are in law excusable (Law 1, Codex: "Of the Excusing of Artifices", Book 10.

'Now on that occasion the part of the fly was played, as I recall, by Magister Tielman Picquet, who was laughing at the Gentlemen of the Chamber aforesaid who were all spoiling their bonnets by thwacking his shoulders with them. He nevertheless told them that they would not be found forgivable by

25. A joke for the initiate. The word *Muscarii* gave great difficulty to students of the Law, many of whom thought it required emendation. But it looks like *muscus* (fly, mouche); hence the game in which one man becomes the fly whom the others try to swat.

their wives when they got home from the *Palais* with battered bonnets;

> as in Canon 1, Extravagantes, "Of Presumption", and the gloss thereunto.

'Now then, I would dare say [like you too, my Lords,] that there is no exercise in the world of the *Palais de Justice* equal to, or more sweet-smelling than, the emptying of bundles, scrabbling over papers, annotating files, filling up brief-bags and examining cases

> according to Bartolus and Johannes de Prato in the Law, "On Errors of Conditions and Demonstrations", Pandects.

'Thirdly, just like you, my Lords, I consider that *Time ripens all things*; that Time brings all things to light, that *Time is the Father of Truth*

> as in the gloss on Law 1 of the Codex, "Of Servitudes"; Authentica, "Of Restitutions, and of the Woman who gives birth"; and Speculator, title, "Of Requests for Advice".

'That explains why, just like you, my Lords, I prorogue, stay and postpone my judgement in order that the suit, having been thoroughly ventilated, sifted through and disputed over, may come in due time to maturity, so that the decision thereafter reached by lots may be borne more kindly by the losing parties,

> as is noted by the gloss on Pandects, "Of Excusing the Tutelage", the Law, "Three Burdens":
> *Kindly is borne what is willingly borne.*

'If you were to judge it at the outset, when it is unripe and green, there would be a danger of the mischief which the physicians say occurs when one lances a boil before it is ripe or purges the human body of some nocive humour before it has been concocted, for, (as it is written in the Authentica: "This Constitution", Innocent IV, First constitution, and repeated in the gloss on the Canon "But"; Extravagantes: "Of Sworn Calumnies"): "What Medicines Do for Illnesses Justice Does for Difficulties".

'Nature moreover teaches us: to pick our fruits and eat them when they are ripe;

Institutes, section, "Of the Cause", paragraph, "The One to Whom", and in the Pandects: "On the Acquisitions of the Buyer, the Law Julianus";

to marry young girls when they are ripe;

(Pandects: "Of Gifts between Husband and Wife"; the Law, "When this Statute", paragraph, "If one Weds" [and question 27, chapter 1, as stated in the gloss: "Her virginity has blossomed and grown ripe in years for the marriage-bed"];)

and to do nothing save when fully ripe, (23, *question 2, ultimate paragraph*, and 33, *ultimate canon*).'

How Bridoye tells the story of an Appointer of lawsuits

CHAPTER 41

[Was originally Chapter 39.

'Appointers' arrange a settlement or bring opposing parties to reach an agreement out of court. (The name existed in English well before Rabelais.) The French equivalent, appointeur *allows of a pun on* à point *(ripe, as of fruit), which is exploited by Rabelais here.*

The reader is at last jokingly informed of what many in the Renaissance would have already realized: Bridoye's legal references are commonplaces taken from the Brocardia Juris *(and other accessible*

*legal works). Why, his very teacher was a lecturer called Professor
Brocardium Juris!*

*Concile de Latran with his red hat, and his wife Pragmatique Sanc-
tion are probably carnavalesque figures. The fifth Lateran Council
(1512–17) was convened by Julius II to invalidate the decrees of
the anti-papalist, French-supported Council of Pisa. The Pragmatic
Sanction of 1493 defended the liberties of the Gallican Church against
Rome. Rabelais was no supporter of such freedoms or of University
freedoms if they sheltered those bodies in France from the powers of
the French monarchs.]*

'While on the subject,' continued Bridoye, 'I remember that
when I was a law student at Poitiers under Professor Brocadium
Juris there was at Smarve a certain Perrin Dendin, a decent
fellow, a good ploughman, a good bass in the quire-stalls, a
trustworthy man and as old as the oldest amongst you, my
Lords, who claimed to have seen that grand old man Concile
de Latran with his red hat, together with his wife Pragmatique
Sanction in her grey-blue satin dress and her huge jet-black
prayer-beads.

'That good man settled more lawsuits than were adjudicated
in the whole of the *Palais de Justice* at Poitiers, the court-house
of Montmorillon, and the Hall of Parthenay-le-Vieux put
together, which caused him to be respected in all the neighbourhood. In Chauvigny, Nouaillé, Croutelle, Aigne, Ligugé, La
Motte, Lusignan, Vivonne, Mezeaux, Etable and their surrounding countrysides, all the quarrels, suits and controversies
were adjudicated by him as by the ultimate judge, although he
was not himself a judge but a good man.

See the Argument on the Law, "If of One Only", Pandects:
"Of Oaths", and "On the Obligations of Words", the
Law, "Continuously".)[26]

26. Bridoye misunderstands a brocard listed in the legal *Lexicon* of Albericus
     under both *Judex* (Judge) and *Vir Bonus* (A Good Man), which explains
     that in the context of the laws cited *Good Man* means *Judge*.

'Not a pig was slaughtered in the whole neighbourhood without his having a slice or two of roast pork and some black-puddings. He was almost daily a guest at banquets, feasts, weddings and christenings, at parties after the Churching of Women and in the tavern, in order, you understand, to arbitrate, for he never produced any arbitration without first obliging the opponents to drink together as a sign of their perfect agreement, reconciliation and new-found joy,

> as is noted by the Doctors-of-Law on Pandects: "Of the Perils and Concerns Touching the Object Sold", Law 1.

'He had a son called Tenot Dendin, a lumping great yokel and (so help me God) a decent fellow who desired to undertake similarly to reconcile litigious parties; for you know that,

> Similar to the father his son not seldom seems.
> And the daughter lightly delights in her mother's ways.

As state:

> the gloss, Question 6, Canon 1, "If Anyone", and the gloss on "Constancy", division 5, chapter 1, towards the end; and as is noted in the Codex by the Doctors-of-Law, "Of Those below the Age of Consent, and Substitutions of Others", the final law; and the Law, "Legitimate"; Pandects: "Of the Human Condition", gloss on the words "If he wish not"; Pandects: "Of the Edicts of Aediles"; the Law, "Who"; Pandects: on the Law Julia ref. *Lèse-majesté*:

I make an exception for the children begotten by a monk of a nun,

> as in the gloss on the Canon, "Shameless Persons", 27, question 1.

'Now amongst the titles he gave himself was Appointer-of-Lawsuits. In that business he was active and vigilant, for,

"To the Vigilant laws come in aid", according to the Law,
"Pupil", Pandects: "Things Fraudulently Believed", and
the same, the Law, "Not indeed", or in the Preamble to
the Institutes;

for, no sooner did he hear of a lawsuit or quarrel anywhere in
that country or have sense of it –

scent as in the Pandects: "If a Quadruped does damage",
the law "Ostler", gloss on the verb *olfecit* (flaired), that is,
"put its nose to her arse" –[27]

he would set about reconciling the parties.
'It is written, "He who labours not, let him manger not";[28]

and thus says the gloss on Pandects: "Of Damages
Caused"; 'the Law, "Although";

and, "From necessity the old woman trots *plus que le pas*,"[29]

as in the gloss on Pandects: "Of the Recognition of Children", the Law, "If a Man Acts for Some Woman"; the
Law, "If", Codex: "Of Conditions Inserted".

'But in that business he was so unfortunate that he failed to
settle any quarrel whatsoever, no matter how piddling it was.
Instead of settling them he further aggravated and embittered

27. A well-known cause of laughter. To explain the elegant Latin word
olfecit, used when a horse caused difficulties by 'flairing' (smelling) a mule,
a medieval glossator of the Law *Agaso* (Ostler) notoriously explained it
in basic Latin as 'put its nose to her arse'. Bridoye quotes the gloss with
comic automatism as soon as he hears himself using the verb *sentir* in
another sense.
28. An indirect quotation from II Thessalonians 3:10 listed in the *Flowers of
the Laws* and the *Brocards of the Law*, where it is cited, as in the *Third
Book*, in a Latin form slightly different from the Vulgate's. But the
deformation of *manducet* (let him eat) into *mangeducat* (let him manger
not) is Bridoye's own.
29. A legal brocard known for its mixture of French, *plus que le pas*, with
the Latin: necessity can make even an old woman run fast.

them. You know, my Lords, that *Speech is given to all: wisdom to few*,

> see the gloss on Pandects: "Of Transfers Made to Change a Judgement", law 2;

and the innkeepers of Smarve complained that, in a whole year under him, they never sold as much of the Wine of Appointment – as they called the good wine of Ligugé – as they did in half-an-hour under his father.

'So it came to pass that he moaned about it to his father, attributing the causes of his rebuffs to the waywardness of folk in his day and age, telling him frankly that if folk had previously been so wayward, litigious, unruly and irreconcilable, he – that father of his – would never have acquired such unshakable honour and title of Appointer of Lawsuits. By so doing, Tenot was acting contrary to the dictates of the Law, in which it is forbidden for children to utter reproaches against their fathers:

> according to the gloss (and also to Bartholus) on Law 3, paragraph, "If anyone"; Pandects: "Of Conditions for Causes"; and in the Authentica, "Of Nuptials", paragraph, "But what has been sanctioned", collation 4.

'"Dendin, my son," said Perrin, "you *must* act differently. You really *must*:

> When *must* in a law comes, never, never doubt
> Whatever it says is to be carried out.

as in the gloss, Codex: 'Of Appeals', the Law, 'Even they'. '"That's not where the hare's hidden. You never settle any differences, lad? And why? Because you take them at the beginning when they are still green and immature. I settle them all. And why? Because I take them towards the end of their growth, quite *à point* and digestible. *And so the gloss states:* 'Sweeter ripe fruit through many hazards grown'; see:

the law, 'He not about to die', Codex, 'On Contracts and
the Transmission of Obligations'.

' "Do you not know what that popular proverb says: *Happy
the physician called in when the illness wanes*? The illness had
spontaneously passed its crisis; even if a physician never arrived
on the scene it was drawing to its end. So too those litigants of
mine were spontaneously wilting before the last stage of their
lawsuit, for their purses were empty. They were spontaneously
ceasing to plead and prosecute. There was not a bean left in
their bag for pleading and prosecuting.

Where *in*- is lacking there lacks all -*come*.[30]

' "By then, all that was wanting was someone to act as best
man and mediator who would be the first to mention any
reconciliation, in order to spare each of the parties the baneful embarrassment of hearing folk say, 'He gave in first. He
was the first to talk of conciliation. He tired of it first. He
never had the stronger case: he felt where the shoe pinches all
right!'

' "And there, Dendin, is where I come in, as appropriate as
pork to peas. Therein lies my 'chance'. Therein, my income!
Therein, my 'good fortune'. Let me tell you Dendin, my pretty
lad, that by that method I could have established a peace –
or at least a truce – between the Great King and the Venetians;
the Emperor and the Switzers; the English and the Scots; the
Pope and Ferrara; and (need I go farther?) with God's help
between the Turk and the Sophy or the Tartars and the Muscovites.

' "Understand me properly: I would seize the moment when
both were tired of fighting, when both had emptied their war-
chests, exhausted the purses of their subjects, sold their estates,
mortgaged their lands and used up their food and munitions.
Then, by God or his Mother, they are forcefully forced to

30. A line of the ancient Roman poet Ennius, 'Deficiente pecu deficit omne
nia', remembered above all for its tmesis (its breaking of *pecunia* into
pecu and *nia*, as are the *in* and *come* of *income* in this translation).

recover their breath and moderate their crimes. That is taught in the *gloss to 37, distinction, "If when"*:

> I shall hate if I can: if not, unwillingly love." [31]

How lawsuits are born and how they grow to perfection

CHAPTER 42

[Was originally Chapter 40.

The legal joke continues.

No concessions to the solitary reader are made at the end, neither the Gascon tongue nor the German being translated in Rabelais' texts. It is not vital to understand them: read aloud by a good mimic those passages can still be made to sound funny. 'Hondrespondres' (Hundred-pounders) was a nickname of Swiss mercenaries.]

'That,' continued Bridoye, 'is why – just as you, my Lords – I spin out the time, waiting for the lawsuit to mature in all its limbs (that is, in its documents and bundles) and to be perfectly formed. See:

> Argument on the Law, "If Superior", Codex: "Of the Division of the Community", and "Of Consecration", division 1, canon "Solemnities" and the gloss thereupon.

'A lawsuit when it is born seems to me at first – as to you too, my Lords – shapeless and unformed. It is like a bear-cub which, when it is born, has no feet, paws, skin, hair nor head, being simply a crude shapeless lump of flesh: then the mother-bear licks its limbs into perfect shape:

> as is noted by the Doctors-of-Law, Pandects: "Of the Law Aquilia", Law 2, towards the end.

31. A line of Ovid (*Amores*, 3, 2, 35).

'And thus – as you too, my Lords – I see nascent lawsuits as shapeless and limbless. They have but a document or two: an ugly beast still! But once they have been well piled, set and bundled up, you can genuinely say that they have limbs and a shape: for, *Form gives a thing its being:*

'For which see:

the Law, "If He Who", Pandects: On the Law Falcidia, in the canon, "When Having Chosen"; Extravagantes: "Of the Rescripts"; Barbatia, Consilium 12, Book 2; and before that, Baldus in the ultimate Canon of the Extravagantes: "Of the Custom"; and the law Julianus, Pandects: "For the Exhibiting", and the Law Quaesitum, Pandects: "Of Legates", 3.

'The procedure is as is stated in the gloss on "Penance", question 1; canon, Paulus: *A weak beginning will be followed by better fortune.* Just like you too, my Lords, the serjeants-at-arms, the ushers, the sumners, the quibblers, the proctors, the commissaries, the barristers, the inquirers, the scriveners, the notaries, the scribes and the puisne judges (*on whom see Title 1, Book 3 of the Codex*) by sucking away very forcefully and continuously at the purses of the litigant engender limbs for their lawsuits: heads, feet, claws, beaks, teeth, hands, veins, arteries, sinews, muscles and humours. They constitute the bundles,

as in the gloss on "Consecration", Decreta, 4, Canon, "You have received: *The Clothes Reveal the Inner Man*".

'Now, *nota bene*, that in this sense the litigants are more blessèd than the ministers of Justice, for *It is more blessèd to give than to receive:*

See Pandects: Commentary on Law 3; and Extravagantes; "On the Celebration of Masses", Canon, "When to Martha", [and Question 24, Canon 1, "I hate", gloss: "Thundering Jove weighs the intentions of the giver."].[32]

---

32. Bridoye knows even his Bible from his legal texts and glosses. Here he is citing indirectly Acts 20:35.

'And it is in that way are lawsuits rendered perfect, elegant and well shaped, as says the Canon-law gloss:

Take, receive and hope are words which please a pope.

Something which has been stated more clearly by Albericus of Rosata, *s.v. Roma*:

Rome gnaws at hands: if she cannot, she loathes them;
She protects givers: non-givers, she spurns them and loathes them.

Why? Because, *An egg in the hand is worth two chicks tomorrow*,

as in the gloss on the Law, "When They"; Pandects: "On Transactions".

The opposite disadvantage is given

in the gloss on the Canon, "Of Alluviums", the concluding Law: "Work at a Loss and Mortal Needs Increase".

'The true etymology of *process* is that it must in its procedures solicit *prou sacs* (many bundles).
'We have several God-made legal axioms to that effect.

By litigation laws do grow:
By litigation is Justice acquired.

'The same is stated

in the gloss on "That"; Extravagantes: "Of Presumptions", and Codex: "Of Probations", the Law, "The Instruments"; the Law, "Not by Epistles"; the Law, "Not by Naked"; and,

When individual efforts fail, many efforts can prevail.

'True, but,' asked Trinquamelle, 'my friend, what is your procedure in a criminal action, when the guilty party has been caught in *flagrante delicto*?'

'Just as you do too, my Lords,' Bridoye replied. 'To start off the action, I order the plaintiff to enjoy a deep sleep. And I see that he has done so, making him appear before me bearing a judicially sound, documented proof of his having slept

[in accordance with the gloss on Question 32, Canon 7, "If Any Man Wish His": *Occasionally Good Homer nods*].

'That document begets another limb; and from that other limb is born another: *Link by link a coat-of-mail is made*. I eventually find that the action is duly formed by such informations and is rendered complete in all its limbs.

'Whereupon I return to my dice; but that interlude is not ordered without reason and impressive experience. For I remember that there was in the camp at Stockholm a Gascon called Gratianauld, a native of Saint-Sever; who, having gambled away all his money, was deeply disturbed since as you know, *money is a second blood*,

as Antonius de Butrio states in the canon, "Acceding", Extravagantes: 2, "As in Litigation not Contestable", and Baldus, on the Law, "If to Yours", Codex: "On Work by Freed Slaves", in the note; and the Law, "The Advocates", Codex: "Of Advocates of Divers Judgements" – *Wealth is the life of Man and the best guarantor in hardships*.

'As he staggered away from the gamesters he yelled out loud in front of all his comrades, in the Gascon patois:

'"By God'z head, you fellows, may barrel-fever bite 'ee! Now that I've lost my four-and-twenty pence I can bash and batter all the better. Would anyone like to have a go at me [in a bit of sport]?"

'Since nobody reacted, he went on to the camp at the Hondrespondres and repeated the same words, challenging them to come and have a fight. But the Hondrespondres said:

'"Der Guascongner thut schich usz mitt eim jedem ze schlagen, aber er ist geneigter zu staelen; darumb, lieben frauuven, hend serg zu inuerm hausraut." ("That Gascon would like to have a fight with each one of us, but he would rather steal. So, women dear, look out for the baggage.")

'Not one of their league offered to fight him. And so that Gascon went over to the camp of the French soldiers-of-fortune, repeating what he had said before and, with little Gascon jigs, gaily challenging them to a fight. But nobody took him up. Thereupon the Gascon lay down at the edge of the camp near the tents of that stout knight Christian de Crissé and dropped off to sleep.

'About then a soldier-of-fortune (who had also lost all his money the same way) came forth, sword in hand; simply because he too had been a loser, he was quite determined to take on that Gascon. [*Tears, for his money lost, wept he most true,*

as says the gloss on, "Penances", distinction no. 3, Canon, "There Are Many Who".]

'And indeed, having searched throughout the camp he came across him fast asleep. And he said to him:

'"Get up, me lad, for the devil's sake, get up. I've lost me money just as much as you have. Shall we have a proper fight, and bash our bacon about good and proper? Look, me sword's no longer than your rapier."

'The Gascon, feeling fuzzy, answered him in his dialect:

'"By Saint Arnaud'z head! Who be you to wake I up? May barrel-fever twist your guts! Ho! Saint Sebber, Patron Saint of Gascony, I was having a good snooze when this old sod comes pestering me!"

'The soldier-of-fortune challenged him to a fight on the spot; but the Gascon replied:

'"Hey, stop it, you poor little chap. Now that I've had a good rest, I could skin you alive."

'His money was gone and forgotten: gone too his desire to fight! In short instead of starting a fight and perhaps killing each other they went off together for a drink, each pawning his sword. Sleep had achieved that good result and calmed the fiery frenzy of those two stout champions. Appropriate here is,

> that golden saying of Johannes Andrea, in the ultimate Canon, "Of Sentencing, and the Matter Adjudicated" (Book 6): *The mind acquires wisdom by remaining seated and keeping calm.*[33]

How Pantagruel absolves Bridoye over judgements made by the lottery of dice

CHAPTER 43

[Pantagruel is now acknowledged to be an inspired sage, his wisdom being a gift from God, 'the Giver of all good gifts' (James 1:17; Romans 12:6–7; I Corinthians 12:4–11). The tables are turned: Bridoye is indeed mad, but with the good madness of the inspired Christian fool. (Cf. the criteria in Chapter 37, and I Corinthians 1:27.) As for his God-given madness, it is cognate to Pantagruel's God-given wisdom, both being gifts of grace.

There are several scriptural echoes, including one from Magnificat. The reference to the Provost of Montléry remains unexplained.]

Bridoye then fell silent. Trinquamelle ordered him to leave the court and said to Pantagruel once that was done:

'Reason demands, most august Prince – not simply because of the bonds by which, through your infinite bounties, you bind this our Parlement to you as well as all the marquisate of Myrelingues, but also because of the good sense, discerning judgement and wondrous learning which almighty God, the Giver of all good gifts, has placed in you – that we should present it to you to decide what to do in this affair (so novel, so strange and paradoxical) of Bridoye who, with you in attend-

---

33. A maxim from Aristotle's *Physics*: a well-known legal brocard, the last to be cited by Bridoye.

ance and in your sight and hearing, acknowledged that he reached his judgements through the lottery of dice. We beg you to be so kind as to announce the verdict which seems to you judicious and equitable.'

To which Pantagruel replied:

'My Lords, as well you know, my avocation does not lie in professionally deciding lawsuits; yet since it pleases you to grant me so great an honour, instead of fulfilling the duty of judge I shall assume the place of suppliant.

'I recognize in Bridoye several qualities which seem to me to merit clemency in the case which has arisen. Firstly: old age; secondly, simple-mindedness: to both of which you well know what readiness to pardon and forgive is shown by our laws and statutes. Thirdly, I recognize another factor which is similarly favourable to Bridoye and deducible from our laws: namely that this single fault of his should be treated as null and void, being engulfed in the immense ocean of those so many equitable judgements which he has reached in the past. For well over forty years, in fact, there has never been discovered in him any action worthy of blame: it is as though I were to cast a drop of sea-water into the River Loire: no one would notice it, nor, for that single drop, would anyone call it salty.

'And it seems to me that there is here something – I know not what – of God, who has so acted and disposed that, in verdicts reached by chance, all Bridoye's previous decisions have been judged sound by this your venerable and sovereign Court; of God who, as you know, often wishes his glory to appear in the dulling of the wise, the putting down of the mighty and the exalting of the simple and meek.

'But I will put all that aside, merely praying you (not in the name of those obligations which you claim to owe my family – which I do not recognize – but in the name of the sincere desire which you have long since found in us to uphold your estate and privileges in both Hither and Thither Loire) that on this occasion you vouchsafe to grant him pardon, under two conditions: firstly, that he indemnify, or promise to indemnify, the party wronged by the judgement in question (under that heading I shall myself see that all is done properly and satisfactorily);

secondly, that you nominate some young, learned, wise, experienced and virtuous counsellor as an auxiliary to his office, by whose advice he shall from now on carry out his judicial functions.

'And in the event that you should wish totally to depose him from his office, I would very strongly beg you to entrust him purely and simply to me. Within my kingdom I shall find plenty of places to employ him in and posts in which he can serve me.

'At which juncture I pray God in his goodness, our Creator, Servator, and Giver of all good gifts, perpetually to keep you in his holy grace.'

Having spoken those words, Pantagruel bowed to the whole court and left the courtroom. He found Panurge, Epistemon, Frère Jean and others waiting by the door. They all mounted and rode back towards Gargantua. On the road Pantagruel gave them, point by point, an account of Bridoye's trial.

Frère Jean said that when he had lived in the convent at Fontenay-le-Comte under the noble Abbot Ardillon he had known Perrin Dendin. Gymnaste said he had been in the tent of Christian, the stout Seigneur de Crissé, when the Gascon had reacted to the soldier-of-fortune. Panurge had some difficulty over believing in the success of judgements made by lots, particularly over so long a period.

Epistemon said to Pantagruel:

'There is a parallel story told about a Provost of Montléry. But what do you make of that successful use of dice continued over so many years? I wouldn't be surprised by one or two such judgements thus delivered by lots, particularly in matters intrinsically ambiguous, intricate, perplex and obscure.'

How Pantagruel tells a curious story of the perplexity of human judgements

CHAPTER 44

[Originally there was no chapter-break here.

The first words of the divinely wise Pantagruel smoothly take up the terms perplex *and* obscure *just said by the sage Epistemon. We now move into what are* perplex *cases in the strictest legal sense. In such cases recourse can be had to dice, but only when there is no other way (as the time-honoured legal phrase puts it). Cf. the conclusions in the* Institutions of Civil Law with Notes of Silvester Aldobrandinus *etc. (Venice 1568), p. 192 vo: 'Add that it is wrong in Law to allow judgements by Lots unless matters are* so perplex and obscure *that* there is no other way: see the Law 'If Two', the law, Common Matters Concerning Legates' (the law cited by Pantagruel at the end of Chapter 12).

Behind all the laughter Rabelais is advancing standard humanist Law. Thomas More implies that recourse to lots is typically Lutheran, but whilst not accepting that lots can apply to a decision whether or not to marry, he used exactly the same technical phrases as Rabelais here: it is legal; and just to use lots to avoid the perplexity but only if there were no other way.

The case which Pantagruel is about to relate was very widely cited by legal writers (for example by Tiraqueau in On Tempering Punishments).

In the original text of the Third Book, *the answer to Pantagruel is delivered by Pantagruel! In 1552 it is attributed to Epistemon. That correction is accepted here. The attack on Tribonian, the architect of the Pandects, puts Rabelais in good company, including that of Gillaume Budé and Montaigne.]*

'As was,' said Pantagruel, 'the problem argued out before Cnaeus Dolabella, the Proconsul for Asia. The case was as follows:

'A woman of Smyrna had a son by her first husband. His name was ABC. Sometime after the death of that husband she remarried and had a son EFG by her second husband. It transpired (and you are aware that it is uncommon for stepsons and stepmothers[34] to feel affection for the children of the original fathers and mothers, now dead) that the second husband and *his* son covertly and treacherously killed ABC in an ambush.

'The mother, apprised of the wickedness and treachery, had no intention that the deed should go unpunished and put them both to death, thus avenging the murder of her first son.

'She was arrested under the law and brought before Cnaeus Dolabella.

'She appeared before him and confessed to the facts, dissimulating nothing; she simply submitted that it was right and reasonable to have killed them.

['Such was the case.]

'He found the matter so equivocal that he had no idea which side to incline towards. The wife's crime was serious: she had killed her second husband and the son. But her reason for those murders seemed to him so innate, so well grounded in natural law (since the two of them together had treacherously ambushed that first son without being in any way wronged or injured by him, merely out of a covetous desire to take over the whole of the hereditament) that he sent it to the Areopagus in Athens for a decision so as to find out what their counsel and judgement would be.

'The Areopagites replied that, in order to answer certain questions not covered by the transcript of the indictment, the contending parties should be brought before them, in person, one hundred years from thence.

'That was tantamount to stating that so great were the perplexity and obscurity of the case that they did not know what to say nor how to judge. If anyone had decided the case by casting dice, he could not have gone wrong whatever happened: if it went against the woman, she did deserve to be punished seeing that she had taken retribution into her own hands instead

34. '52: . . . uncommon for *stepfathers, second husbands and* stepmothers to feel affection . . .

of leaving it to the Law: if for the woman, she had a plausible case from her appalling suffering.

'What astonishes me, though, in Bridoye is the continuance over so many years.'

'I cannot give an unqualified answer to your problem,' replied Epistemon, 'so much I must confess. But I would conjecturally refer Bridoye's good fortune in judgement to the propitious aspect of the heavens and the favour of the Motor Intelligences: they contemplate the simple-mindedness and pure emotions of Justice Bridoye, who (mistrustful of his own learning and abilities; aware of the antinomies and contradictions within laws, edicts, customs and decrees; conscious of the deceits of the Slanderer from Hell who often transfigures himself as an angel of light through his ministers, the perverted lawyers, counsellors, procurators and other such myrmidons who turn black into white, make it appear to both parties through misleading illusions that they have the Law on their side: for you know that there is no case so bad that it finds not its lawyer, without which there would never be any lawsuits in this world) humbly commends himself to God, the Just Judge, invokes the help of heavenly grace, confides in the Most-Holy Ghost over the hazard and perplexity of the decisive judgement, and by such lots reconnoitre his decree and good pleasure which we call verdicts; and then the Motor Intelligences might spin and turn the dice so that they fall in support of him who, furnished with a just grievance, was imploring that his rightful cause be upheld by Justice; since the Talmudists say that *there is no evil in lots, simply that amongst the anxieties and doubts of human beings it is by lots that is manifested the Divine Will.*[35]

35. Compare what is said here with Chapter 37 about the Celestial Intelligences and the selfless man, which prepared the reader for Bridoye's Folly to be inspired. Rabelais employs a second time a quotation from II Corinthians 11:15: 'for Satan himself is transformed into an angel of light' (Cf. above, Chapter 14). Rabelais goes on to apply the condemnation of Paul literally to the perverted *ministri justitiae* – the 'ministers of justice' – of his day (crooked lawyers and judges and so on, who are genuinely doing works of the devil). Devils work through *phantasmes*, 'misleading illusions', as was true of Picrochole in Chapter 29 of *Gargantua*.

'I would not wish to think or say – and I certainly do not believe – that the iniquity of the legal consultants in that Parlement of Myrelingues in Myrelingues is so lawless and their corruptibility so manifest that a lawsuit would not be worse decided by a throw of the dice, whatever happened, than it is passing through their hands full of blood and perverted passions; especially considering that their entire manual of current law was handed down to them by a certain Tribonian, a wicked, faithless and barbaric man, so malevolent, rapacious and iniquitous that he would peddle the laws, edicts, rescripts, enactments and ordinances to whichever party offered him the most; and who "cut them their slices" into those little bits and bobs of law which they currently use, whilst repressing and jettisoning all which made of the Law a totality, fearing that if the Law had remained whole and the books of the Ancient jurisconsults expounding the Twelve Tables and the Edicts of the Praetors had been there to read, the world would have clearly learnt of his wickedness.

'That is why it would often be better (that is to say, less evil would come of it) if the opposing parties walked over spiked booby-traps than relied for their law on their responses and expert opinions; indeed, Cato wished and advised that the law-courts in his time be paved with such spikes![36]

God the Father is called 'the just Judge' in II Timothy 4:8.

The term 'Talmudists' here is not used for the experts in Jewish Law but for the (Christian) Canon Lawyers. Rabelais is citing word for word the judgement of Augustine in his second Sermon on Psalm 30 (31):16 (15, Vulgate text): 'My lots are in thine hands'. The words of Augustine are quoted in the *Decreta* of Gratian, 26 *question 2 § Sors*, the very first law cited by Bridoye in his defence of the 'dice of justice' in Chapter 39. (Tiraqueau cites it too.)

36. Tribonian, the sixth-century jurisconsult who compiled the *Pandects* under the Emperor Justinian, is similarly attacked by Guillaume Budé in his *Annotations on the Pandects*, which in an earlier edition is one of the major influences on Rabelais in the *Third Book*. The law-courts and spikes are taken from Pliny, *Natural History*, 19, 1. The spikes are probably caltrops (iron balls with spikes so placed that one of them is always pointing upwards). Rabelais exploits the same chapter of Pliny apropos of pantagruelion-asbestos later in the *Third Book*.

How Panurge takes counsel from Triboullet

CHAPTER 45

[Was originally Chapter 42.

We now meet Triboullet, the real fool of the courts of Louis XII and François I. With him we leave the 'thesis' – should one marry? – and return to the 'hypothesis' – should Panurge marry?

The principal authority and source of the arguments and details in this chapter is Budé's Annotations on the Pandects, *commenting on a paragraph of the* Pandects *with the incipit 'if the slave amongst the Fanatics did not always jerk his head . . .'(In* Opera, *III (Basle, 1557), Gregg reprint, pp. 251–2). There is a crucial difference in Law between 'jectigation', the jerking of the head of the inspired person, and the lolling of the head shown by Panurge at the beginning of Chapter 37 of the* Third Book *(and, before that, by the young giant in* Gargantua *lumbering astride his decrepit old mule). Jectigation is caused by the inflowing of the spirit of prophecy, which produces a divine 'madness'. The lolling head is the sign of a very different kind of madness, bestial stupor, or the worse kind of heavy, melancholy madness.]*

Six days later Pantagruel returned home at the very time that Triboullet came by river from Blois, on whom, when he docked, Panurge bestowed a pig's bladder, blown up tight and loudly rattling from the peas inside it, plus a wooden sword highly gilt, together with a game-pouch made from a tortoise shell, a wickered demijohn of *vin breton* and a quarter-pound of *blant dureau* apples.

'What?' said Carpalim. 'Is he as daft as an apple-headed cabbage!' Triboullet girded on the sword and the game-pouch, took the pig's bladder in his hand, munched some of the apples and drank all the wine. Panurge gazed at him intently and said, 'I have yet to see a fool – and I have seen more than ten thousand francs worth of 'em – who didn't enjoy drinking and taking long swigs.'

Panurge then expounded his concerns to him in elegant, grandiloquent words. Before he could finish Triboullet gave him a big blow between the two shoulder-blades with his fist, thrust the bottle back into his hand, gave him a tweak on the nose with his pig's bladder, and, while very strongly jerking his head about, said nothing in reply save, 'By God, God! Raving fool! 'Ware monk! Horn of the Buzançais bagpipes!'

Having said which, he drew apart from the company, playing with his pig's-bladder and delighting in the euphonious sound of the peas. From thenceforth it was not possible to get another peep out of him; and when Panurge wanted to pose further questions Triboullet drew his sword and went to strike him.

'A fine pickle we're in. We truly are!' said Panurge. 'What a beautiful answer! He's a fool all right! No denying that. But bigger fool still the one that brought him to me. And I am the biggest fool who confided my thoughts to him!'

'That,' said Carpalim, 'is aimed right at my visor!'

'Without working ourselves up' said Pantagruel, 'let us consider his gestures and words. I note deep mysteries in them and am no longer as astounded as I used to be that the Turks venerate such fools as teachers and prophets. Did you notice how – even before he opened his mouth to speak – his head jerked and rocked about? By the teachings of ancient philosophers, the ceremonies of Magi and the reflections of jurisconsults, you can conclude that such a movement was produced by the advent and inspiration of the Spirit of prophecy who, rushing into a substance weak and small – you realize of course that a big brain cannot be contained in a little head – made it jerk about in the same fashion as the physicians account for the tremor which seizes upon the limbs of the human body: partly that is from the mass and violent shock of a weight sustained: partly from the feeble power of the organ which bears it.

'An obvious example is provided by those who, not having eaten, cannot hold a large beaker of wine without their hands trembling. That was prefigured for us of old by the Pythian prophetess who, before answering through the oracle, jerked the laurel about which she kept in her cave.

'So too Lampridius tells how the Emperor Heliogabalus, so as to be reputed a prophet, would, amongst the fanatical eunuchs during several festivals before his great idol, publicly jerk his head about. So too did Plautus declare in his *Asinaria* that Saurias would walk along, jerking his head as though raving mad and out of his mind, terrifying the people who encountered him; and again, when exposing elsewhere why Charmides would jerk his head about, he says that it was because he was in ecstasy. So too Catullus tells in *Berecynthia and Atys* of the spot where the Maenads, those bacchanalian women, those priestesses of Bacchus, dementedly prophesying and bearing laurel-branches, jerked their heads about, as did those castrated priests of Cybele, the Galli, when they celebrated their liturgies, from which, according to the ancient theologians, Cybele got her name, since *kubisthai* in Greek means to twist, turn and jerk the head about, and to act the wry-neck.[37]

'So too does Livy write that men and women during the bacchanalian festivals in Rome appeared to be prophesying on account of a certain counterfeit jerking and jectigation of their bodies, for the collective voice of the philosophers and the opinion of the common people held that prophesying was never granted by the heavens without there being frenzied motions in the trembling, jerking body, not only when it was receiving that gift but also when it displayed it and manifested it.

'Julianus, an outstanding jurisconsult, was, in fact, asked on one occasion if a slave was to be held sane who had frequented the company of fanatical and raging worshippers, had apparently prophesied without however such jerking of the head.

'He replied: "Held sane."

'And so to this present day we find teachers and school-masters giving the heads of their pupils a shake, pulling and vellicating their ears as one shakes a pot by the handles, the ear being the member dedicated to memory according to the teachings of the Egyptian sages, thus bringing their minds (which had perhaps wandered off into strange thoughts

37. Cf. Servius on Virgil, *Aeneid*, 3, 111; *kubisthai* is treated as a verbal noun.

and been terrified by ludicrous emotions) back to sound philosophical learning. Virgil claims that he was himself vellicated
by Apollo Cynthius.'[38]

How Pantagruel and Panurge diversely
interpret what Triboullet said

CHAPTER 46

[Was originally Chapter 43.

The portmanteau term 'morosopher' (combining moros, *a fool, with*
philosopher) *goes back to Lucian's* Alexander. *Erasmus spread it
widely in his* Praise of Folly.

*Those who bear religious titles such as Brother, Father or Sister do
not commit simple fornication or adultery: they commit incest.*

Fou (Fool) and Tou (All) are two nearby villages in Lorraine.

*Solomon says that 'the number of fools is infinite' in Ecclesiastes 1:
15. Avicenna says that 'the species of madness are infinite' (Canon:
Fen I, cap. 14, doc. xix. Tertii).*

*Two adages of Erasmus are relevant: IV, VIII, IV, 'Nothing can be
added or taken away' and, for the Emperor Domitian who enjoyed
catching flies, II, I, LXXXIV, 'Not even a fly'.*

For the Lesbia of Catullus and her sparrow see his Odes 2 *and 3.]*

'He says that you are a fool. And what sort of fool! A raging
fool who would bind and enthral yourself in marriage in your
declining days. He says to you, *'Ware monk.* On my honour
you'll be cuckolded by some monk or other. Yes, I risk my
honour upon it: I could not risk anything greater if I alone held
peaceful sway over Europe, Africa and Asia. See how greatly I
defer to Triboullet, our morosopher. The other replies and
oracles had quietly made it plain that you will be cuckolded,
but they never expressly stated who would make your wife an
adulteress and so you a cuckold. This noble Triboullet does tell

38.   In the Sixth Eclogue, verses 3–4: 'When I would sing of kings and battles
       Apollo Cynthius tugged my ear and warned me'. Cf. Erasmus, *Adages*, I,
       VII, XL, 'To tug the ear'.

us. And that cuckoldom of yours will be notorious and deeply
offensive. Must your marriage-bed be defiled by incest with a
monk?

'He also says that you will be the *horn of the Buzançais
bagpipes*, that is to say, you will be blown like a horn, horn-
piped and horny. And just as that fellow who intended to beg
King Louis the Twelfth to grant the farming of the Buzançais
salt-tax to one of his brothers but in fact asked for bagpipes,
you, likewise, thinking to wed a good decent wife, will in fact
wed a wife who is void of wisdom, blown up with arrogance
and as nastily droning as bagpipes are.

'Note moreover that it was with the pig's bladder that he
gave you a tweak on the nose and thumped you on the spine.
That foretells that you will be beaten by her, bonked on the
nose – and robbed, just as you robbed those little children in
Vaubreton of their pig's bladder.'

'On the contrary,' replied Panurge. 'Not that I want to
exclude myself unwisely from the Land of Folly. I admit that I
am one of its subjects: I belong there. All the world is a fool. In
Lorraine, by sound judgement, *Fou* (Fool) is near to *Tou* (All):
all is a fool!

'Solomon says that the number of fools is infinite. Nothing
can be subtracted from infinity: nothing added to it. Aristotle
proves that. And I would indeed be a raving fool if, fool that I
am, I did not reckon myself a fool. It is that which likewise
makes the number of maniacs and raving madmen infinite.
Avicenna states that the species of mania are infinite.

'But the rest of Triboullet's words and gestures make for me.
He says of my wife, 'Ware *moine*. By *moine* (monk) he meant
a *moineau* (sparrow) which she will delight in, just as Catullus'
Lesbia delighted in hers; it will flit about after flies, passing its
time as happily as did Domitian [the Fly-swatter].

'More. He implies that she will be a country-maid, as sweet
and lovely as bagpipes from Saulieu or Buzançais. That veracious Triboullet has well understood my nature and my inner
feelings; for I promise you that I'm more delighted by merry,
loose-haired little shepherd-girls whose bums smell of Our-
Lady's-bedstraw than by those ladies in our great courts with

their rich fineries and their cracks pungently smelling of navel-wort. I take more pleasure in rustic bagpipes than in the strumming of lutes, rebecs and aulic violins.

'Triboullet gave me a thump with his fist on me poor ole spine. By God's love, so be it: so much off the pains of purgatory! He meant no harm: he thought he was thumping some lackey or other. He is, I assure you, a *good* fool, an innocent. Whoever thinks ill of him is committing a sin. I forgive him with all my heart.

'He did tweak my nose: that means those little endearments between my wife and me as happens to all newly weds.'

How Pantagruel and Panurge decide on visiting the Dive Bouteille

CHAPTER 47

[Was originally Chapter 44.

The Divine Bottle, Dive Bouteille, *makes her first appearance.* Dive *(from the Latin* diva) *means divine or saint or saintly.*

There is word-play on debts *and* Lord Debity *(Deputy), the title of the English Governor of Calais.*

The 'trespasses' of the Lord's Prayer in English are 'debts' in Latin and French. Similarly 'them who trespass against us' are simply 'Debtors' (in Latin, 'Debitoribus'). The punning is at once obvious and obscure. There was a saying: 'He is all debitoribus', meaning he dares not face his creditors.

There is also play on the English word fellow *and the French words* fallo *or* fallot, *which mean a lantern or a fire-basket.*

Lanternois appears as a land in a little book which Rabelais did not write, The Disciple of Pantagruel, *1537, which went through several re-editions. Rabelais drew upon it for his Fourth Book.*

Amongst other meanings 'to lantern' may almost always suggest sexual intercourse.]

'And here is another point which you aren't taking into account, yet is the very nub of the matter: Triboullet returned that bottle into my hand. What does that signify? What does it mean?'

'It means perhaps,' said Pantagruel, 'that your wife will be a drunkard.'

'On the contrary,' said Panurge, 'for the bottle was empty. I swear to you on the backbone of Saint Fiacre-en-Brie that our morosopher – not the *loony* but the *only* Triboullet – is referring me back to the Bottle; so I freshly update my original vow: here in your presence I swear by Styx and by Acheron always to wear my glasses in my bonnet and never to wear a codpiece on my trunk-hose until I have, on this my enterprise, the Word of the [Dive] Bouteille.

'I am acquainted with a wise man, a friend of mine, who knows the way there, the land and the part of the country in which her temple and her oracle are to be found. He will guide us safely there. Let's go there together. I beg you not to let me down. I shall be an Achates to you, a Damis, a companion throughout all the voyage. I've long known you to be a lover of peregrinations, ever wanting to see and ever wanting to learn. We shall see wonderful sights, believe you me.'

'Willingly,' said Pantagruel, 'but before undertaking that long peregrination, full of hazards and evident dangers . . .'

'What dangers?' said Panurge, cutting him across. 'Dangers flee seven leagues from me wherever I am, just as the arrival of the king supersedes the magistrate, the arrival of the sun banishes the darkness, and the arrival of the relics of Saint-Martin at Candes causes maladies to flee.'

'That reminds me,' said Pantagruel, 'there are certain details we must quickly see to before we set out.

'First, let us send Triboullet back to Blois (which was done that very hour, Pantagruel giving him a coat of gold crêpe). Second, we must have the counsel and congee of the king my father. We must also find us a sybil to serve as guide and interpreter.'

Panurge replied that his friend Xenomanes would amply suffice, and that he was already thinking about travelling through the Lanternois in order to pick up there a certain learned and experienced female Lantern who would be for

them on their voyage what the Sybil was for Aeneas when he
descended into the Elysian Fields. Carpalim, who was escorting
Triboullet back, was passing by and, hearing what was said,
called out,

'Hey! Panurge! Lord Sans-Debts. Take my Lord Debity with
you from Calais, for he's *a good fellow*. And don't forget
debitoribus: they're Lanterns. [Then you'll have both *fellow*
and *fallo* – Companion and Lantern].'

'My forecast,' said Pantagruel, 'is that we shall engender no
melancholy on our way. I can see that clearly enough already.
My one regret is that I cannot speak good Lanternese.'

'I,' replied Panurge, 'shall speak it for all of you. I know it
like my mother-tongue. I use it as a vernacular:

> Briszmarg d'algotbric nubstzne zos
> Isquebfz prusq; albork crinqs zacbac.
> Misbe dilbarlkz morp nipp stancz bos.
> Strombtz Panrge walmap quost grufz bac.

'Now then, Epistemon. Guess what that means.'

'They're like the names of devils,' replied Epistemon, 'devils
errant, devils passant and devils rampant.'

'Words truly brayed, fair friend!' said Panurge. 'It is the
courtly form of Lanternese. I will compile a nice little lexicon
for you *en route*, but it won't last much longer than a new pair
of shoes: you'll have learnt it sooner than witness a sunrise.

'What I said, translated from Lanternese into our vernacular,
is a song like this:

> A lover was I: ever sadness
> Dogged all my steps and me befell.
> Married folk have every gladness.
> Panurge, now wed, knows all that well.'

'All that remains, then,' said Pantagruel, 'is to hear what my
royal father wills and obtain his congee.'

How Gargantua establishes that it is never licit for children to marry without the knowledge and consent of their fathers and mothers

CHAPTER 48

[Was originally Chapter 45.

By a curious error, still retained in '52, the second speech is attributed to Pantagruel not to Gargantua, to whom it clearly belongs. Most editors correct it, as is tacitly done here.

The chapter consists of diatribes against clandestine marriages, that is, against marriages entered into by young people without the prior permission of their parents and kinsfolk. Such marriages were legal in the eyes of the Church and for the civil authorities too wherever the law of the (unreformed) Church held sway. In this matter Church Law took absolute precedence, requiring simply the consent of the partners (expressed in an exchange of vows 'for the future' and then 'for the present', as still today in the English marriage service), followed (as still today) by consensual sexual intercourse. Normally a priest was present as witness, but his presence was not a sine qua non. *Rabelais is championing Roman Law against long-established Ecclesiastical Law. For the Church and its Law, it is the consent of the* partners *which validates the marriage service: in Roman Law it is the consent of the* parents, *who may punish as rapists and abettors of rape the men involved in marrying their daughter without their prior consent* whether the woman herself consented or not. *By sometimes changing his original term* 'myste' *(translated here by* 'mysteriarch'), *to* 'taulpetier' *(translated here by* 'mole' *but strictly more like* 'monk living like a mole in his convent'), *Rabelais increasingly aims his attacks specifically against the religious Orders. Clandestine marriages which involved the clergy were more likely to involve a monk or mendicant than a parish priest dependent on local patronage. (It was a Franciscan who married Romeo and Juliet.)*

The subject was very much in the air. All the variously reformed Churches took marriage in hand. There were forces trying to make the French government do so too, and override Church Law. The arguments and vocabulary of Rabelais are those shared, for example,

by the liberal French legal authority Coras and the Lutheran theo-
logian Martin Bucer. Rabelais was taking on the Roman Church in a
vital aspect of its role. To many traditionalists he would have seemed
simply Lutheran or Réformé, though many others shared his views,
not least amongst the nobility, whose daughters were most at risk.

The revenge taken by her brethren for the rape of Dinah in Genesis
is condemned by Jacob; it nevertheless became a prime example to be
cited with approval as by Rabelais. Erasmus is present in an adage: I,
X, XLV, 'diametrically opposed' for whatever is 'vehemently repug-
nant and incompatible.']

As Pantagruel came into the Great Hall of the château he found
his good father Gargantua coming out of his council-chamber
and gave him a brief account of their experiences, outlined their
project and begged him that they might execute it with his
approval and congee.

Our good Gargantua was holding in his hands two fat
bundles of petitions answered and memoranda to be answered.
He handed them to Ulrich Gallet, his long-established Receiver
of Requests [and Petitions]. He drew Pantagruel aside and said,
looking happier than usual:

'My dearest son, I praise God who keeps you in virtuous
desires. It greatly pleases me that you should see your voyage
through, but I could also wish that it similarly came to you too
to wish and desire to marry. It seems to me that you have now
reached the age when it is becoming to do so. Panurge has
tried hard to break down the difficulties which could be an
impediment to him. Tell me about yourself.'

'Father most gracious,' replied Pantagruel, 'I have yet to give
any thought to it. In all such matters I was showing deference
to your own good-favour and fatherly command. Rather than
to be seen married and alive without your good-pleasure, I
would, in your displeasure, pray God to be found stone dead
at your feet. I have never heard that there has ever been any
law, sacred, civil or barbarian, which allowed children to wed
without their fathers, mothers and closest kin consenting to it,
willing it and advocating it. All law-givers have removed such
a freedom from children and reserved it to their families.'

'My dearest son,' said Gargantua, 'I believe you; and I praise God that only good and praiseworthy matters come to your attention, and that nothing save liberal learning has entered into the dwelling-place of your mind through the windows of your senses; for during my time there has been found a land within our continent in which there are certain species of mole-like pastophors, hating wedlock like the pontiffs of Cybele in Phrygia (only they are not capons but cocks full of lechery and salaciousness), who have dictated to married folk laws governing marriage!

'I am not sure which I ought to abominate more: either the tyrannical arrogance of those dreaded Moles who do not remain behind the grills of their mystagogical temples but meddle in concerns diametrically opposed to their vocation, or else the superstitious passivity of the married who have sanctioned their barbaric laws and obeyed them, failing to see (yet it is clearer than the Morning Star) that those connubial edicts are entirely to the advantage of their mysteriarchs and of no good or profit whatsoever to married folk, which, in itself, is enough to render their edicts iniquitous [and devious].

'By a reciprocal temerity the married could establish laws for their mysteriarchs governing their rituals and sacrifices, seeing that they tithe the goods of the married and gnaw away at the earnings arising from their toil and the sweat of their brows in order to maintain themselves in abundance and keep themselves in comfort; and (in my judgement) such laws would be no more wrong nor more insolent than the laws the married receive of them. For (as you very well said) there used to be not one single law in the world which gave children the freedom to marry without the knowledge, permission and consent of their fathers.

'Now, thanks to the laws of which I have spoken, there is no pimp, blackguard or criminal, no vile, stinking, leprous bit of gallows-fodder, no bandit, no thief, no evildoer, who, in those lands, despite all her kinsfolk, may not seize and abduct from her father's house and her mother's arms any daughter he chooses, no matter how noble, beautiful, rich, modest and chaste, once that pimp has conspired with some mysteriarch who will eventually share in the spoils. Could a worse or more callous deed be done by Goth, Scythian or Massagete against an enemy fort, long besieged, taken at great cost and subdued by main force?

'Those heartbroken fathers and mothers see – abducted from their homes by some uncouth, unknown stranger, some putrid, syphilitic, cadaverous, sinister, penniless dog – their beautiful, delicate, rich and blossoming daughters, whom they have so fondly brought up in every virtuous activity and educated in all that is honest, hoping, when the time was opportune, to give them away in wedlock to the sons of their neighbours and long-established friends who had been brought up and educated with the same care, so as to attain to that joy of the married who see descendants born from them who are like them, not only inheriting the virtues of their fathers and mothers but also their goods and their property.

'Think what a sight it is for them!

– Do not believe that even the desolation of the Roman People and their Confederates was more enormous after hearing of the death of Germanicus Drusus.

– Do not believe that even the dismay of the Spartans was more heart-rending when they saw Helen of Greece furtively stolen by that adulterous Trojan.

– Do not believe that their grief and wailing were any less than those of Ceres when her daughter Proserpine was snatched from her; of Isis, at the loss of Osiris; of Venus, at the death of Adonis; of Hercules, at the loss of Hylas; of Hecuba at the abduction of Polyxenes.

'And yet the parents are so smitten by fear of the devil and by superstition that they dare not challenge it since the mysteriarch was there, plotting it all.[39]

'So they shut themselves away in their homes, robbed of the daughters they loved so much, the father cursing the hour and the day that he ever got married, the mother lamenting that she had not miscarried during so sad and wretched a pregnancy, both ending their days in tears and lamentations when it would

39. '52: . . . since the *Mole* was there . . .

have been right to end them happily in close union with their daughters.

'Some, beside themselves and as it were insane, have drowned themselves, hanged themselves, killed themselves from grief and sorrow, unable to bear such shame.

'Others have been of a more heroic mind and, following the example of the sons of Jacob avenging the rape of their sister Dinah, have discovered the lecher, in partnership with his mysteriarch[40] clandestinely seducing their daughters with words and suborning them, have at once hacked them to pieces, killing them like felons and scattering their corpses over the fields for the wolves and the crows.

'Confronted by a deed so virile and noble their companion mysteriarchal moles have trembled and made miserable lamentations, framing dreadful protests, most pressingly begging and imploring the secular arm and the civil power to act, wildly urging and advocating that such cases be visited with exemplary punishment. Yet there has never been found one paragraph, rubric or chapter anywhere in natural equity, the law of nations or Roman law, which threatens punishment or torture for any such deed. Reason resists it; Nature opposes it: for there is not one virtuous man in all the world whose mind is not more utterly distraught on hearing the news of the abduction, shaming and dishonouring of his daughter than of her death. Now any father discovering a murderer wickedly lying in wait to commit homicide against the person of his daughter can by reason, and must by nature, kill him on the spot: never will he be apprehended by Justice. No wonder, then, if he, coming across the lecher, abetted by his mystagogue,[41] suborning his daughter and ravishing her from his home, can and must – even if she be consenting – put both men to a dishonourable death and cast out their corpses to be ripped apart by wild beasts as being unworthy of sepulchre (as we term that sweet, desired and ultimate embrace of Earth, our great nursing mother).

'My dearest son, see that no such laws are ever introduced

40. '52: . . . in partnership with his *Mole*, clandestinely seducing . . .
41. '52: . . . abetted by his *Mole* suborning his daughter.

into this kingdom after my death. As long as I am alive with breath in my body, I shall keep all in excellent order, God being my helper.

'Now since you leave it to me to decide about your marriage, I am in favour of it and will make provision for it.

'Prepare for Panurge's voyage. Take with you Epistemon, Frère Jean and anyone else you choose. Make use of my wealth at your complete discretion: whatever you do can only delight me. From my arsenal at Thalassa fit out as many of my ships as you will, with such pilots, seamen and interpreters as you will, and when the wind is right, spread your sails in the name of God our Servator and under His protection. While you are away I shall be busy arranging a wife for you, and festivities for your marriage, which shall be glorious if ever there were any.'

How Pantagruel prepared to put to sea, and of the plant called *pantagruelion*

CHAPTER 49

[Was originally Chapter 46.

An artistically contrived display of rhetorical and dialectical virtuosity brings the Third Book *to a close. In Chapters 2 to 5 Panurge, as an expert in rhetoric and the* Topics, *gave us a display of perverted ingenuity: like a devilish lawyer he could make black seem white. Here again we have a display of great ingenuity, but one which properly reveals (under the veil of an easily pierced enigma), the vast and varied uses which a humble plant can be put to. The apparently miraculous plant* pantagruelion *is soon perceived to be hemp, or more correctly hemp-and-flax (taken since Pliny to be one and the same plant) together with asbestos, thought of as* linum asbestinum, *a plant of the same species. Rabelais is taking up a challenge. For Pliny, hemp-and-flax is a natural miracle with a thousand uses too many to relate.*

Pliny treats of smyrnium olusatrum *in his* Natural History *(19, 8, 48, §62).*

The immediate inspiration of Rabelais is the short enigmatic praise of hemp-and-flax in Calcagnini's posthumous Works, *where the plant is named Linelaeon. Calcagnini is to prove a major influence on Rabelais in the* Fourth Book *of 1552.*

Rabelais' botanical erudition is not original; it lay mostly in the common domain.

'Passer-over-Perilous-Ways' was the name which Jean Bouchet gave himself. Bouchet was a moralizing poet and a long-time friend of Rabelais. They exchanged poems, which Bouchet printed.

*The ships of Ajax numbered twelve (*Iliad, *2, 557).]*

A few days later Pantagruel, having taken congee of our good Gargantua, who was devoutly praying for his son's voyage, arrived at the harbour of Thalassa near Saint-Malo accompanied by Panurge, Epistemon, Frère Jean des Entommeures (the Abbot of Thélème) and others of his noble household – notably by Xenomanes the great traveller and Passer-over-Perilous-Ways, who had answered Panurge's summons since he held some minor property in feudal fee to the Châtellenie of Salmagundi.

Once arrived there, Pantagruel fitted out his ships, which numbered as many as Ajax once brought from Salamis to convey the Greeks to Troy. He took on board seamen, pilots, oarsmen, interpreters, craftsmen and fighting men, and loaded provisions, artillery, munitions, clothing, cash and other stores needed for a long and hazardous voyage.

I noticed that, amongst other things, he took on plenty of his plant *pantagruelion*, both the green, untreated kind and the dressed and preserved.

The plant called *pantagruelion* has a small root, somewhat hard and rounded, terminating in a bluntish point, white, of few filaments and penetrating less than a cubit below ground. From the root grows a single, round, ferulaceous stem, green outside, whitish within, hollow like the stalks of *smyrnium olusatrum*, beans and gentiane, woody, straight, friable, slightly grooved in the manner of shallowly striated columns, full of fibres in which consists the entire merit of the plant, particularly of the kind called *mesa* (that is to say, middle) and the kind called *mylasea*.

It normally grows to some five or six feet, although it sometimes exceeds the height of a lance, namely when it is found in a soft, greasy, light soil, damp but not cold (as in Les Sables-d'Olonne or the soil in Rosea, near Praeneste in Sabinia) provided it does not lack rain over the Festival of the Fishermen and at the summer solstice; according to Theophrastus it can even exceed the height of trees, as does the tree-mallow, despite its being a plant which dies back annually and not at all a tree with perennial roots, trunk, stem and branches; from its stem grow big, strong branches.

It has leaves thrice as long as wide, evergreen, somewhat rough to the touch like prickly-ox-tongue, rather hard, and crenate round the edges like a sickle or like betony, each ending in a point shaped like a Macedonian spear or the lancet which surgeons use. Their shape is not very different from the leaves of the ash or of agrimony and so close to that of the eupatorium that several botanists, having misnamed it 'garden eupatorium', have mistaken *pantagruelion* for wild eupatorium. The leaves grow equidistantly in rows round the stem, five or seven to a row. Nature has so favoured this plant that she has endowed it with leaves of those two uneven numbers, which are so holy and mysterious.

To delicate noses the leaves have a strong and unpleasant smell.

The seed [comes from near the head of the stem, just a little below. It] is as profuse as that of any plant there is; spherical, oblong or lozenge-shaped, bright black or somewhat tawny, fairly hard, enveloped in a fragile husk, relished by all songbirds such as linnets, goldfinches, larks, canaries, yellowhammers and so on, but in men it suppresses semen if eaten copiously and often [; and although the Greeks used to make the seeds into some kind of fried tidbit, tarts or fritters nibbled after supper as a delicacy and to enhance the taste of the wine, they are nevertheless difficult to concoct and hard on the stomach; they produce bad-quality blood and, because of their excessive heat, have an impact on the brain, filling the head with troublesome and painful vapours].

And just as there are two sexes in many plants, male and

female, as we can see in laurels, palms, oaks, holm-oaks, aspho-
dels, mandrakes, ferns, agarics, aristolochias, cypresses, tere-
binths, pennyroyals, peonies and so on, in this plant too there
is a male, which bears no flowers whatsoever but an abundance
of seeds, and a female, which proliferates in little whitish flow-
erets which serve no useful purpose and produce no worthwhile
seeds; and as in similar plants the female's leaves are broader
and not as tough as the male's, and the female does not grow
as high.

Pantagruelion is sowed at the first return of the swallow; it
is gathered in when the cicada begins to sound hoarse.

How this celebrated *pantagruelion* must be dressed and put to use

CHAPTER 50

[There was originally no chapter-break at this point.

*English versions of some of the Latin names have been slipped in
between dashes when it helps things along.*

*The men who earn their living by walking backwards are rope-
makers, who move backwards as they entwine the strands of rope fed
to them between their legs. Not all the explanations are clear. For
example,* Aristolochia *helps lying-in women with their lochial fluids.
Saffron comes from the crocus, which was named after the lover
Crocus in Ovid's* Metamorphoses, 4, 283.]

Pantagruelion is dressed over the autumn equinox in various
ways, depending upon people's ingenuity and local conditions.

The first directions which Pantagruel gave were: to strip the
stalk of its leaves and seeds; to macerate it in stagnant – not
running – water for five days if the weather is dry and the water
warm, or for some nine or twelve if the weather is cloudy and
the water cold; then to dry it in the sun, stripping off the outer
layer in the shade and separating the fibres (in which, as we
said, consist its excellence and its value) from the woody parts,
which are useless except for producing a bright blaze, or as

tinder, or, by children at play, for blowing up their pig's bladders.

Wine lovers secretly use them at times as straws for sucking and siphoning new wine through the bung-hole. Some Pantagruelists nowadays avoid the manual labour involved in separating the plants by using certain contunding machines (constructed in the shape made by ferocious Juno when she interlocked her fingers, heckle-shaped, to impede the birth of Hercules from Alcmene his mother)[42] by means of which they break and heckle out the woody part, setting it aside as useless but keeping the fibres.

That is the only way to prepare it which satisfies those who (against everyone else's opinion and in a manner deemed paradoxical by all philosophers) earn their living by walking backwards.

Those who desire more evidently to increase its value do what we are told to be the pastime of the three Fatal Sisters [, the nightly diversion of noble Circe] and the long-maintained pretext of Penelope to her fond suitors during the absence of her husband Ulysses. That is how *pantagruelion* realizes its incalculable properties, some of which I shall expound to you (for to tell you all is for me impossible) if I may first explain its name.

Plants are, I find, named for different reasons.

Some take their names from whoever first discovered, understood, demonstrated, cultivated, domesticated and acclimatized them: thus, herb-mercury, from Mercury; panace, from Panace, the daughter of Aesculapius; *artemisia vulgaris* – mugwort – from Artemis (Diana, that is); eupatorium, from King Eupator; *sedum telephium* – 'live-long' – from Telephus; *Euphorbia* – 'spurge' – from Euphorbus, the physician to King Juba; *clymenus*, from Clymenos; *alcibiadon*, from Alcibiades; gentian, from Gentius, King of Sclavonia.

And that privilege of imposing one's name on plants thus identified was formerly so highly prized that, just as there once

---

42. In Ovid (*Metamorphoses*, 9, 297 ff.) Juno kept her fingers interlocked in the form of a *pecten* (comb). In Latin to comb (*pecto*) also means to card and to heckle.

arose a quarrel between Neptune and Pallas over which of them should give its name to the land which they had discovered together – which was subsequently called Athens from Athene (Minerva, that is) – so too Lyncus, King of Scythia, strove treacherously to murder young Triptolemus (who had been despatched to men by Ceres in order to reveal wheat to them, which was then still unknown) so that, having killed him, he could impose his own name on it and to his eternal honour and glory be called the discoverer of that grain which is so useful and so necessary to the life of humankind; for which act of treachery he was metamorphosed by Ceres into a caracal or lynx. Likewise, there were once great and protracted wars waged between certain idle kings in Cappadocia: their sole dispute was over which of their names should be given to a certain plant – valerian – which on account of that conflict was called *polemonia*, meaning warlike.

Other plants have kept the names of the regions from which they were introduced elsewhere, as *malum medicum* for a citrus fruit from Media where it was first found; *malum punicum* for pomegranates brought from Punicia (that is, from Carthage); *ligusticum* (that is, lovage) brought from Liguria (the coast of Genoa); *rhabarbarum* – rhubarb – from the *barbarian* river *Rha* as Ammanianus testifies; and similarly santonica, fenugreek, castanea – chestnuts – *mala persica* – peaches – and *sabina herba* – juniper – and *stoechas* – French lavender – from my *Iles d'Hyères*, which the Ancients called the *Stoechades*; then *spica celtica* – spikenard – and so on.

Others take their names by antiphrasis and contradiction; hence absinthe, which is the opposite of *pinthe* – tipple – because it is *not* pleasant to drink; or *holosteon* (meaning 'all of bone') – by opposition, for there is no plant in nature which is more brittle and yielding.

Others are named from their virtues and effects, as *aristolochia*, which helps women with their lochial fluids in childbirth; lichen, which cures skin diseases of that name; mallow, which is emollient; callitriche, which *beautifies* the *hair*; alyssum, ephemerum, bechium, nasturtium (that is, Orleans cress), hyoscyame, henbane, and so on;

others from the remarkable features seen in them, as the heliotrope (that is, the marigold), which follows the sun, opening at sunrise, stretching upwards as the sun ascends, drooping when it sets and closing up when the sun hides itself; the *adiantum*, since, despite growing close to water, it never retains moisture, even if you plunge it into water for a very long time; *hieracia* – hawkweed – *eryngion* and so on;

others from the metamorphoses of men and women with similar names, as daphne (that is, the laurel) from Daphne; myrtle, from Myrsine; pitys – pine – from Pitys; cinara (that is, the artichoke); narcissus, saffron, smilax and so on;

others, from similarities: as *hippuris* (that is, horse-tail), because it does resemble a horse's tail; *alopecuros*, because it resembles a fox's tail; *psylion*, which does look like a flea; *delphinium*, like a dolphin; *bugloss*, like an ox's tongue; *iris*, which in its flowers is like a rainbow, *myosotis*, like the ear of a mouse; *coronopus*, like the foot of a crow; and so on.

And, by naming the other way round, the Fabii were called after *faba* (the bean); the Pisos, from the pea – *pisum*; the Lentuli, from lentils; the Ciceros from *cicer* (chick-pea). And from a more intimate resemblance still are named Venus' navelwort, Venus' hair, Venus' bath-tub, Jupiter's beard, Jupiter's eye, Mars' blood, Mercury's fingers [, the *hermodactyl*] and so on;

others, from their shapes, as the trefoil, which has three leaves; the pentaphyllon, which has five leaves; the serpolet, which snakes over the ground; *helxine, petasites* – sun-cap – *myrobalans* – plums – which the Arabs call *béen* since they resemble acorns and are oily.

Why this plant is called *pantagruelion*, and of its wonderful qualities

CHAPTER 51

[Was originally Chapter 47.

Pantagruel's plant pantagruelion provides the material for hang-men's ropes as well as for tablecloths, bed-linen, the 'bundles' (sacks) for lawyers and so on.

In this chapter Rabelais invites a comparison with Lucian's True History. *It ends (under the influence of Calcagnini probably) with the air of mythology. Pliny is a pessimist for whom one of the uses of hemp-and-flax is especially regrettable: the making of sails for sailing-ships. Not so for Rabelais. These chapters are full of smiles and optimism, foreseeing a time when another plant will be discovered which will take men to the Moon, shake the gods of Lucian in their heavens and find men seating at table with them and marrying their goddesses, the only two ways to immortality mentioned by Servius in his commentary on Virgil's* Fourth Eclogue, *explaining the line cited in Chapter 12.*

Rabelais cites for the second time an adage of Erasmus, III, X, XCIII, 'The Arrogance of the Giants'. Cf. the criticism of Panurge in Chapter 28.]

It is for all such reasons (except the fabulous, for God forbid that we should make any use of fable in this Oh-so-True His-tory!) our plant is called *pantagruelion*, for Pantagruel first discovered it. I do not mean the plant itself but one particular use for it, which is more loathed and feared by thieves and is more inimical and hostile to them than burdock and devil's-guts are to flax; the reed is to heather; [shave-grass to reapers; choke-weed to chick-peas; the straw-weed called *aegilops* to barley; hatchet-fitch to lentils; *antranium* to beans; tares to wheat; ivy to walls;] the common water-lily and the Heraclean variety to lecherous monks; birch and cane to undergraduates of the Collège de Navarre; cabbage to vine; garlic to the magnet; onion to eyesight; fern-seed to expectant mothers; willow-seed to wanton nuns; the shade of the yew to such as sleep under it; aconite – wolf's-bane – to leopards and wolves; the scent of fig-trees to mad bulls; hemlock to goslings; purslane to teeth, and oil to trees: for indeed many a thief have we seen end their lives hanging high from a short piece of *pantagruelion*, following the examples of Phyllis, the Queen of the Thracians, Bonosus, the Emperor of Rome, Amata, the wife of King Latinus, Iphis, Auctolia, Licambes, Arachne, [Phaeda, Leda,] Acheus the King of Lydia and so on, all of whom were angry for no other reason but that, without their being otherwise ill, it strangled the conduits through which good jests come out and good nibbles go in, more dreadfully than would a severe bout of angina or a deadly quinsy.

And we have heard others, at the very moment that Atropus was cutting the thread of their lives, grievously bewailing and lamenting that *Pantagruel had them by the throat*! Oh dear! It was not Pantagruel: he has never been a hangman: it was *pantagruelion* doing duty as a halter and serving as a neckerchief! They were speaking improperly; falling into a solecism, unless you excuse them on the grounds of synecdoche (that is, taking the discovery for the discoverer, as when one says Ceres for bread and Bacchus for wine). I swear to you now, by the jests contained in that bottle keeping cool in yonder tub, that our noble Pantagruel never took any persons by the throat save only such as are negligent about obviating an imminent thirst.

It is also called *pantagruelion* from similarity: for when Pantagruel was born into this world he was as tall as the plant in question, being easily measured since he was delivered during a period of thirst, just when that plant is harvested and the Dog star of Icarus bays at the Sun, turning folk into troglodytes, constrained to live in cellars and underground shelters.

It is also called *pantagruelion* because of its virtues and peculiar properties, for, just as Pantagruel has been the Idea and Exemplar of all joyous perfection – I suppose that not one of you drinkers has any doubt about that! – so too I recognize in *pantagruelion* so many virtues, so many powers, such perfection, and so many wonderful effects, that if only it had been acknowledged for its qualities at the time when (as the prophet[43] tell us) the trees chose a wooden monarch to reign and dominate over them, it would, without a doubt, have carried the majority of votes and ballots cast.

Shall I go on? If Oxylus, the son of Orius had spawned *pantagruelion* of his sister Hamadryas, he would have been more delighted with our plant than with all his eight children put together, children much celebrated by our mythologists whose names are kept in eternal remembrance: the eldest was a daughter, Vine; next came a son called Fig; another was Walnut; another Oak; another, Cornel-cherry; another, Sugarberry; another, Poplar, and the last one was called Elm, who was a great surgeon in his time.[44]

I will refrain from telling you how, when the sap of *pantagruelion* is drained off and dripped into the ear, it kills all species of noxious parasites which may have been engendered in it by putrefaction, as well as any other living thing which may have found its way in. Why, so great is its power that, if you put some of its sap into a pail of water you will see that water set at once like a junket; the water thus curdled is a good remedy for the gripe and convulsions in horses.

If you boil its roots in water it will relax tense sinews, contracted joints, podagric sclerosis and swellings caused by gout.

If you desire quickly to cure a scald or a burn, apply some *pantagruelion* to it, raw, just as it naturally grows in the earth, without any processing or compounding. And be sure to change the dressing as soon as you notice it drying out over the wound.

Without *pantagruelion* our kitchens would be shocking and our tables repellent even when laden with every kind of delicacy; our beds would be without charm, even though bedecked with gold, silver, amber, ivory and porphyry. Without it the miller could bring no corn to the mill and take home no flour.

43. The prophet is Jotham, who tells this fable in Judges 9:8 ff. The following myth of the Hamadryads, the tree-nymphs, is eventually from Athenaeus, *Banquet*, 3, 78.

44. The Ancients 'cured' bad behaviour in children and slaves by beating them with elm-rods.

RABELAIS

Without it, how would lawyers bring their bundles into court?

Without it, how could we carry plaster into the workshop?

Without it, how would we draw water from the well? Without it how could notaries-public, clerks, secretaries and scriveners manage?

Would not all legal deeds and rent-agreements perish? Would not the noble art of printing perish? What could printers make their tympans from!

How would bells be tolled!

With it the priests of Isis are vested, the pontiffs are robed, and all humans swaddled when first laid down.

All the wool-trees of Seres, all the cotton-trees of Tylos by the Persian Sea, all the cotton-bushes of Araby, all the cotton-vines of Malta could never clothe as many folk as this modest plant. It protects armies from rain and cold more efficiently than skin-tents ever did; it shelters theatres and amphitheatres from the heat; it nets off woods and coppices for the pleasure of the huntsman; it is let down into waters, both fresh and salt, for the profit of fishermen; with it are moulded and formed winter boots, summer boots, heavy boots, gaiters, ankle-boots, country-shoes, court-shoes, slippers and cobblers' down-at-heels. With it are bows bent, cross-bows readied and catapults fashioned. And, as if it were some sacred plant such as verbena (which is revered by the happy and unhappy souls of the dead) the corpses of dead human beings are never buried without it.

I will go further: by means of *pantagruelion* things invisible are visibly trapped, arrested, captured, and kept as it were in prison: once arrested and captured they briskly turn great heavy grind-stones, to the signal advantage of our human life, and I am indeed absolutely astonished that such a discovery was hidden for so many centuries from the thinkers of Antiquity, given the priceless benefits which derive from it and given the unbearable drudgery men had to endure in working their pounding-mills.

And by its means the billowing air itself is contained and huge merchantmen, spacious ships and great galleons with room for a thousand or ten thousand men, are propelled from their moorings and sail wherever their skippers desire. Thanks to such means nations whom Nature appeared to have kept apart, hidden away, inaccessible and unknown have come to us and we to them: something that the very birds could not do, however light their feathers, no matter what freedom Nature has given them to sail through the air. Taprobana has seen Lapland; Java, the Rhipean Mountains; Phebol shall see Thélème; Icelanders and Greenlanders shall drink the waters of the Euphrates; by such means the North Wind has seen the dwelling-place of the South, the East Wind has visited the West, so that the celestial Intelligences and the gods of both sea and land have all been terrified, seeing, by the use of that hallowed plant *pantagruelion*, the people of the Arctic come clearly into the angle of vision of the people of Antarctica when they cross the Atlantic, pass through both the Tropics, tack beneath the Torrid Zone, take readings of the entire Zodiac, disport themselves below the line of the Equinox and glimpse both the Poles at once, level with their horizons.

The gods of Olympus, similarly terrified, said:

'By exploiting the virtues of his plant, Pantagruel has put new and painful thoughts into our minds, worse than those stirred by those giant Aloïdae. He will shortly be married; by his wife he will have children. We cannot gainsay that destiny, for it has passed through the hands and spindles of the Fates, those sisters, daughters of Necessity. It could well be that another plant will be discovered by his children, one having similar powers, by means of which human beings will be enabled to visit the sources of the hail, the sluice-gates of the rains, the smithy of the thunderbolts; they will be able to invade the regions on the Moon, penetrate the territories of the Signs of the Zodiac and settle there, some in the golden Eagle; some in the Ram; others in the Crown; others in the Harp, and others in the silver Lion, sitting down at table with us and taking our goddesses to wife, the only ways by which humans can be deified.'

To avert which they finally referred for a remedy to a debate in Council.

Of a certain species of *pantagruelion* which cannot be consumed by fire

CHAPTER 52

[Originally there was no chapter-break here.

Pantagruelion asbestos can be used to preserve ashes during cremation.

In Pliny manna is a kind of vegetable juice which hardens into grains.

The history of Caesar and the people of Larignum is taken from Plutarch's Life of Julius Caesar.

That the entrance to Truth is hard and stone-strewn is perhaps an extension and an echo of Hesiod's fable about the path to Virtue in his Works and the Days, which will be developed in the Fourth Book, Chapter 57. For the ivy-wood funnel which separates water from wine see Pliny, Natural History, 16, 35, 63, and Gargantua, Chapter 22.

Sceptical Jews 'seek a sign' in I Corinthians 1:22.

The final lines in this very Classical peroration are an echo of Virgil's Second Georgic. Solid utility and even great new inventions and adventures have been derived, and will be derived in the future, not from verbosity such as Panurge's but from human ingenuity working on the qualities of a humble plant such as hemp-and-flax and, no doubt one day, of a newly discovered plant resembling it.]

What I have told you is already great and wonderful, but if you would venture to believe in some further transcendent quality in our hallowed *pantagruelion*, I would tell you of it.

Believe it or believe it not: it is all the same to me; it is enough for me to have told you the truth. And tell you the truth I shall. But to attain to Truth – for her entrance is very hard and stone-strewn – I ask you this: if I had put two measures of wine and one of water into this bottle and thoroughly mixed them, how could you separate them out? How could you so segregate them that you could return me the wine without the water and the water without the wine, in the same measures as I had put into it? Again: if those carters and bargees of yours who supply your households with a certain number of barrels, tuns and casks of wine from Graves, Orleans, Beaune and Mirevaux had pinched half of it, drunk it and then topped up the barrels with water (as the men of Limoges do by the clog-full when carting wines from Argenton and Saint-Gaultier), how would you get rid of all that water? How would you purify the wine?

Yes, I know! You are going to tell me about an ivy funnel. It's in print. It's true and confirmed by hundreds of experiments. You knew that already. But those who did not know about it and had never seen it would never deem it possible.

But to get on. Supposing we belonged to the time of Scylla, Marius, Caesar and other Roman Emperors or our Ancient Druids, when the corpses of their lords and kin were burnt, and supposing you desired to drink the ashes of your wives and children infused in some good white wine (as Artemisia did with the ashes of her husband Mausolus) or, alternatively, to preserve those ashes entire in some urn or reliquary, how could you keep the ashes apart, completely segregated from the burnt ashes of the funeral pyre? Tell me now! By my fig, you'd be embarrassed! But I will disembarrass you by telling you that if you take a length of that hallowed *pantagruelion* – enough to cover the corpse and wrap it up tight – binding it and stitching it with thread of the same material, you can throw it on to a pyre as big and as hot as you please: the fire will burn the body through the *pantagruelion* and reduce its flesh and bones to ashes; as for the *pantagruelion* itself, it will not only not be consumed in the fire, it will lose not one single atom of the ashes enclosed within it; and you will get with it not one single atom of the ashes of the pyre, whilst the *pantagruelion* itself will eventually emerge from the fire fairer, whiter, cleaner than when you cast it in. That is why it is called *asbestos*. You will find quantities of it going cheap in Carpasium and in the lands about Syene. O, what a great and marvellous thing it is! Fire, which devours all, wastes all, consumes all, uniquely cleans, purges and whitens that asbestine *pantagruelion* from Carpasium.[45]

45. Possibly a confusion between Carpasium, a town in Crete, and *carbasus*, a fine flaxen cloth.

If you remain distrustful and, like Jews and unbelievers, seek proof and a practical sign, take one fresh egg and tie some of this hallowed *pantagruelion* around it. Thus bound, place it within a brazier as big and as hot as you like. Leave it in as long as you like. Eventually you will take out your egg, cooked hard and burnt, yet without any deterioration, change or scorching of the hallowed *pantagruelion*. You will have performed that experiment for less than fifty thousand Bordeaux crowns reduced to the twelfth part of a farthing!

Do not compare that to the salamander. That is a fallacy. I quite agree that a small fire of straw invigorates the salamander and makes it happy; but I assure you that it is asphyxiated and consumed in a big furnace like any other animal. We have seen it from an experiment; Galen proved it and confirmed it long ago in *Book 3, Of Temperaments* [, and Dioscorides asserts it in *Book 2*].

Do not bring up here feather-alum nor that wooden tower in the Piraeus which Lucius Scylla could never get to catch fire because Archelaus, the governor of the town, had daubed it all over with alum. [Make no comparison here with that tree which Alexander Cornelius called *eon*, saying that it resembled the oak which harbours mistletoe. According to him, no more than oak-mistletoe can it be consumed by fire nor harmed by water, and from it was constructed and fitted out that most famous of ships, the *Argos*. Find somebody to believe that! Not me, though.]

Do not make a comparison, either, with that species of tree, however wonder-working it might be, which you can see in the mountains of Briançon and Ambrun: from its root it produces our good agaric; from its trunk it exudes a resin so excellent that Galen ventures to make it equal to terebinthina; it retains for us on its delicate leaves that fine 'honey from Heaven' we call *manna*, which cannot be consumed by fire despite being oily and sticky. In Greek and Latin you call it *larrix*; the Alpine dwellers call it *melze*; the Paduans and the Venetians call it *larege*, which gave its name to *Larignum*, that fortress in the Piedmont which eluded Julius Caesar on his way to Gaul.

For the use of his army on its passage, he had ordered all the inhabitants and citizens of the Alps and the Piedmont to bring stores and munitions to stage-posts stationed along the military road. Everyone obeyed except those within Larignum, who, relying on the natural strength of the site, refused to contribute. To punish them for their refusal that Emperor led his army straight to Larignum. Before the gate of the fortress stood a tower built of great beams of *larix*, bound alternately together like a stack of wood extending to such a height that from the holes in the projecting parapet they could easily rain down stones and iron billets to beat off those who approached them. When Caesar learned that those inside had no other defences but stones and iron billets which they could hardly do more than lob down at such approaches, he ordered his soldiers to toss a great many faggots round the tower and set fire to them. It was instantly done. As the fire took to the faggots, the flames were so great and reached so high that they engulfed the whole fortress. It was then supposed that the tower would soon catch fire and burn right down. Yet when the flames died away and the faggots were all burnt, that tower emerged whole and entirely undamaged. Reflecting on which, Caesar ordered that a circumvallation of trenches and dug-outs be constructed all round that tower, beyond the reach of the stones.

The Larignians did then agree to terms of surrender, and from their own accounts Caesar learnt of the astonishing nature of that wood which produces neither flame, fire nor charcoal.

For that one quality alone it would have been worthy to rank alongside the real *pantagruelion* – (all the more so since Pantagruel desired that every door of Thélème be made of it, as well as all the gates, windows, guttering, drip-ways and cladding, and since he similarly ordered all the poops, prows, galleys, decks, gangways and forecastles of his swift carracks, barques, galleys, galleons, brigantines, feluccas and other vessels in his arsenal at Thalassa to be clad with it) – were it not for the fact that when *larix* is engulfed in flames from other kinds of wood it eventually decomposes and disintegrates like stones in a lime-kiln, whereas *pantagruelion asbestos* is renewed and cleaned, not corrupted and degraded.

And so:

Indies, Sabia, Araby: take heed:
Myrrh, incense, ebony, cease ye to praise,
Accept our plant and bear away the seed,
Sow it at home, a gift for all your days
If in your fields ye luckily it raise,
Thanks give to Heaven, thanks by the million,
For France, wherein our happy plant doth breed:
Blessèd our realm for *pantagruelion*.[46]

The end of the Third Book
of the
Heroic deeds and sayings
of
the Good Giant Pantagruel.

46. Echoes of Virgil (*Second Georgic*, 109–22): 'Not all soils can bear every
    fruit . . .; see, tamed by tillage, the eastern houses of the Arab and the
    painted Gelonians: trees are divided by their homelands. India alone
    brings forth black ebony; to the Sabaeans alone belongs the incense
    branch . . . or nearer the seas the woody glades of India.' See an adage of
    Erasmus, IV, III, XX, 'Not every land produces everything', which gives
    place of honour to Virgil and the *Georgics*.

PROLOGUE TO
THE FOURTH BOOK OF
PANTAGRUEL (1548)

Introduction to the Prologue to *The Fourth Book of Pantagruel* (1548)

The 1548 *Fourth Book*, often called the *Partial Fourth Book*, is certainly based on the author's manuscripts, yet it appears under such strange circumstances that it seems unlikely that Rabelais authorized its publication. In 1546 he had obtained a most fulsome Royal *privilège* for both past and future works: there is no hint of it here, two years later. This partial *Fourth Book* ends in the middle of a sentence! The printer printed all that he had; he padded out the book with wood-cuts from his stock.

This Prologue to the *Fourth Book* is later abandoned, to be replaced by the superb Prologue of 1552. But the 1548 Prologue, too, is a fine piece of writing.

The Fourth Book of the Heroic deeds and Sayings of noble Pantagruel.

Composed by Maître François Rabelais Doctor of Medicine and Caloyer of the Iles Hyères.

LYONS
The Year five-hundred and forty-eight.

Prologue

[Rabelais cites the ancient Roman legal formulas Do – Dico – Addico *(I give – I say – I adjudicate) as though they were in the second person: 'You give – You say – You adjudicate'. This makes nonsense of those august formulaic utterances by which the Praetor, on auspicious days, solemnly authorized judgement to be done:* Do judicem *(I appoint the judge)* dico jus *(I state the case of the plaintiff) and* addico litem *(I hand over the cause to the magistrate to judge). In Ancient Rome those venerable formulas had to be scrupulously adhered to.*

Tales of battles between birds are found in several authors including Poggio and Fulgoso. There may be an element of legal fun in the story of the battle of the jays. Legists quarrelled over the sense of the word graculus *in a text of Ulpian (Leg. 15 D. locati).* Cujas *(Observationes, 25, xv) denied that the* graculi *of Ulpian can be jays, since* graculi *are gregarious and jays are not. Cujas cites Julius Caesar Scaliger (Exercitatio, 232) in support of his contention.*

There is a sustained play on pie *meaning magpie and* pie *meaning booze:* croquer pie *can mean either to hook a magpie or to gulp down one's booze. Commonly a* croc-pie *was a toss-pot. Croquer pie* or *croquer la pie* and similar phrases are kept here in French to allow of the sustained play on words.

Wine-flasks disguised as Breviaries did indeed exist.

An important part of this Prologue, that concerned with the art of medicine, will be taken up again in the Preliminary Epistle to the 1552 Fourth Book.]

Most shining topers, and you most-becarbuncled sufferers from the pox, I have perceived, received, harkened unto and believed the Ambassador dispatched towards my Fatherhood by your Lordships' lordships; and he seemed to me to be a very good and fluent orator. I can reduce the substance of his statement to three words of such great importance that, amongst the ancient Romans, the praetor replied with them to all petitions brought for judgement; with those three words he decided all controversies, all plaints, lawsuits and disputes. Any days on which the praetor did not pronounce those words were declared

inauspicious and legally improper, and any days on which he
did do so, legally proper and auspicious:

– *You give* –

– *You say* –

and

– *You adjudicate.*

Oh! good people, I cannot see you. May the precious might
of God be eternally your helper, and mine too. And so may we
never do anything before first praising his most holy name.

– You give me: what? A lovely capacious breviary. Golly, I
thank you for it. That is the very least I ought to do. I never
gave a thought to what sort of breviary it was, seeing as I did
its die-stamps, rosettes, clasps and binding, not overlooking
either the *crocs* – the hooks – and the *pies* – the magpies painted
upon it and scattered over it in a most beautiful pattern, by
which (as though they were hieroglyphic letters) you clearly
convey that there is no piece like a masterpiece and no courage
like that of *croqueurs de pies*. Now *croquer pie* means a certain
kind of merriness by way of a metaphor distilled from a prodigious event which occurred in Brittany a little before the
battle which was joined near Saint-Aubin-du-Cormier. Our
forebears have related it to us: it is right that our successors
should know of it. Wine was plentiful that year: they would
trade you a quart of good delicious wine against a fly-cord with
only one aglet!

From the Orient there came in flight on one side a host of
jays and on the other a host of magpies, all heading towards
the setting sun. So well did they fly side by side that towards
evening the jays withdrew to the left (the auspicious side, you
understand), and the magpies to the right, all very close to each
other. Through whichever lands they passed, there was not one
magpie which did not rally to the magpies, not one single jay
which did not join the camp of the jays. They journeyed, they
flew, so far that they passed over Angers, a town in France on
the marches of Brittany; they had so grown in number that, as
they flew, they shrouded the sun from the lands stretched out
below.

In Angers there dwelt at that time an aged uncle called

Frappin, the Seigneur de Saint-Georges. (He it was who composed and set to music those beautiful, merry *noëls* in the dialect of Poitou.) He delighted in a jay because of its chattering by which it invited everyone who came along to join in a drink. It never sang but of drink, and he called it his Old Goitre. That jay, moved by martial frenzy, shattered its cage and joined the passing jays. Now a neighbouring barber called Behuart had a tame magpie; she was most gallant. With her person she augmented the number of magpies and followed them into battle.

Now come things great and unexpected, true, though, veritably seen and verified. Note all this well. What happened? What was the end of it all, good folk?

Something amazing.

Near the cross of Malchara a battle so savage was joined that is horrifying merely to think of it. It ended with the magpies losing the battle: on the field were cruelly slain jays up to the number of 2589362109, not counting the women and children (that is, as you realize, not counting the female magpies and the little magpielets).[1]

The jays stood victorious, though not without the loss of many a fine soldier. Hence the distress was very great throughout all the land.

The Bretons are really quite human, you know, but if they had understood that prodigious event they would have quickly realized that misfortune would fall upon them, since the tail of the magpie has the form of their heraldic ermine, whilst the jay has some resemblance in its plumage to the arms of France.

Old Goitre got home three days later by the way, fagged out, fed up with fighting and nursing a black eye. Nevertheless, a few hours later it was in good spirits again, after its usual feed.

The fine people of Angers, townsfolk and the students, came running up in droves to gaze at Old one-eyed Goitre in such a state. Old Goitre invited them to have a drink as was its custom, croaking after each invitation, *Croquez pie!* (that, I assume,

---

1. Counting magpies as humans often are counted in the New Testament, without the women and children, a practice which amused Rabelais here and elsewhere.

was the watchword on the day of battle). All made it their duty
to do so.

The female magpie of Behuart never returned. She had been
crocked! Hence *croquer la pie* truly became a common saying,
meaning to match drink for drink, taking great gollops.

Frappin had his servants' hall and buttery decorated with
paintings to serve as a perpetual memorial, as you can see in
Angers on Saint-Laurence's Mound.

Now the decoration on that breviary of yours made me think
that it was somehow more than a breviary. And anyway, what
reason could you have for making me the present of one!
Thanks to you and to God I have breviaries ranging from the
oldest to the newest. In such uncertainty I opened the said
breviary and discovered that it was a breviary contrived with
marvellous ingenuity, with most appropriate die-stamps and
opportune inscriptions. So at Prime, Terce, Sext and Nones,
you want me to drink some white wine, do you, and likewise
some claret at Vespers and Compline? That is what you mean
by *croquer pie*. No wicked magpie ever hatched you! I shall
grant your request.

– You say: what? That I have in no wise perturbed you in
any of the books I have so far had printed. You will be even
less perturbed if I quote a relevant adage from an ancient
Pantagruelist.

> 'It is,' he said, 'no vulgar praise
> To have pleased princes in our days.'[2]

You go on to say that the wine of my *Third Book* was good
and to your taste. There was not much of it, that is true, and
you do not approve of what men commonly say, 'Little and
good'; you prefer what that good fellow Evispande Verron used
to say, 'Plenty and good'. Moreover you invite me to continue
my tale of Pantagruel, citing the utility and fruit gathered from
the reading of it amongst all good folk, and apologizing for not

2.   Cited from Horace (*Epistles*, 1, 17, 35) taking *principes* to mean princes
     not principal citizens.

having obeyed me when I begged you to reserve your laughter until my seventy-eighth book. With a very good heart I forgive you. I am not so fierce or as hard to please as you might think; but what I said to you was not bad for you, and I quote in return that judgement of Hector's published by Naevius: 'to be praised by the praiseworthy it is a beautiful thing'. Echoing that assertion, I say and maintain up to the stake (exclusively, you understand, judicially speaking) that you are fine, noble people, all descended from good fathers and good mothers; and I promise you (Foot-soldier's Honour!) that if ever I come across you in Mesopotamia I will so work on that little Comte George of Lower Egypt that he will make each of you a present of a beautiful crocodile from the Nile and a chimera from the Euphrates.

– You adjudicate: what? And to whom? Well: all the odd quarters of the moon to black-beetles, *cagots*, *matagots*, booted monks, bacon-pappers, monkish drones, pussy-paws, pardon-pedlars and catamites: the mere sound of such names is terrifying. I saw your ambassador's hair stand on end even as they were uttered. They are all Double-Dutch to me and I have no idea what sort of beasts you include under such names. After a diligent search in several countries I have found not one man who would accept them for himself or put up with being thus designated or labelled. I presume they were some monstrous species of barbarous beasts dating from the days when men's bonnets were tall (a species now naturally extinct, since all things sublunary have their end and period, and we cannot know how those words were defined: as you realize, once an object has perished its name quickly perishes too).

If by such terms you mean the calumniators of my writings you could more aptly name them devils, the Greek for calumny being *diabole*. See how loathsome before God and the angels is that vice known as calumny (that is when a good deed is called into question and good things are ill-spoken of) since the devils in Hell are named and called after it, even though several other vices might appear more excessive. Those men are not strictly speaking devils from hell: they are their servants and ministers. I call them black devils, white devils, tame devils, familiar

devils. Now if you let them they will do to all other books what
they have done to mine. But it is none of their invention – which
I say so that they may not in the future glory so much in the
surname of old Cato the Censor.

Have you ever thought what is meant by To gob in the basin?
Well, long ago, whenever those forerunners of such tame devils,
those architects of voluptuousness and underminers of decency
(like Philoxenus, Gnatho and others of the same kidney) were
in the inns and taverns where they regularly held their classes,
they would watch the guests being served with good dishes and
tasty tidbits, and would vilely gob into the tureens to put them
off the food set before them, nauseated by their filthy spittle and
snot: then all was left for those nasty snot-dribbling gobbers.

An almost similar tale, albeit not so abominable, is told of a
fresh-water physician[3] (the nephew of the late Amer's legal
adviser): he would pronounce the wing of a fat capon to be bad
for you and its rump dangerous (so that his patients should eat
none of those things, all being set aside for him to put into his
mouth) while its neck was very good provided all the skin was
removed.

That is how those new be-cassocked devils have behaved:
having noted that everybody enthusiastically desires to see and
to read what I wrote in my previous books, they have gobbed
in the basin: that is, every one of them has so handled my books
as to beshit them all over, decrying and calumniating them with
the intention that no one, apart from their Reverend Lazinesses,
should heed them, no one read them. With my own eyes (not
my own ears) I have seen them at it, going so far as to keep
my books religiously with their night things, as breviaries for
everyday use.

They have filched them from the sick, the sufferers from gout
and those unfortunate persons for whose amusement I had
written and composed them in their illnesses. If I could personally treat all those who are depressed and ill there would be no

3.   A fresh-water physician (on the model of a fresh-water sailor) is one of
     limited skill and experience. Rabelais has probably modelled his phrase
     on the 'fresh-water lawyer' of Pathelin.

need to publish and print such books. Hippocrates wrote a work specifically entitled *On the State of the Perfect Physician*. (Galen threw light on it with his learned commentaries.) In it he lays down that there must be nothing in the physician which could offend his patient. He goes so far as to single out his finger-nails. Everything about the physician – gestures, mien, dress, words, look, touch – must please and delight his patient. That, in my awkward old way, is what I strive and struggle to do for those whom I take into my care. So on their part do my colleagues, which no doubt is why we are dubbed long-armed, big-elbowed charlatans by the absurdly expounded and taste-lessly contrived opinion of a couple of dung-prodders.[4]

There is more to it than that. We have hectic arguments over a passage in the Sixth Book of the *Epidemics* of our venerated Hippocrates: not whether the gloomy, severe, rheubarbative,[5] displeasing and dissatisfied expression of a physician depresses the patient while his happy, serene, pleasing, laughing and open expression cheers him up – that is proven and certain – but whether such depressing or cheering-up results from the percep-tions of the patient as he contemplates those qualities, or rather from the pouring of the physician's spirits (serene or gloomy, happy or sad) from him into the patient, as in the opinion of the Platonists and the Averroists.

Seeing that I cannot be called in by everybody who is ill nor take all the sick into my care, what meanness is it that would deprive the sick and the ailing (since I cannot be there myself) of the pleasure and happy pastimes they find, with no offence to God or the king or to anyone else, when my merry books are read out to them?

Well then, since by your verdict and decree such evil-speakers and calumniators are lunatics who have been seized and taken over by the old quarters of the moon, I forgive them; so now we shall not all be able simply to laugh at them when we see those raging lunatics – some lazars, some buggers, some lazars and buggers – dashing through the fields, gnashing their teeth,

4.   It is not known who these two hostile quacks were.
5.   *Rebarbative* ('crabby', a rare word in English but not in French) is crossed with *rhubarb*.

bashing up benches, smashing the cobbles, knocking about paving-stones, hanging themselves, drowning themselves, throwing themselves about and galloping away with their bridle loose to all the devils on account of the energy, qualities and virtues of the lunary quarters which they then will have within their noddles: quarters crescent, quarters new, quarters gibbous, full and waning.

I shall, however, in the face of their wickedness and deceit, repeat the offer which Timon the Misanthropist made to his ungrateful Athenians. Timon, angered by the ingratitude of the people of Athens where he was concerned, came one day into the public council of the city requesting that he be given a hearing about an affair touching the common weal.

At his request, silence fell: they expected to hear matters of importance since he, who had for so many years avoided all company and lived on his own, had now come to the council. Whereupon he said, 'Outside my private garden, below the wall, there stands a spreading, fair and notable fig-tree; from it, Gentlemen of Athens, your men, women, youths and maidens are accustomed in their despair to slip away to hang and throttle themselves. I hereby advise you that I intend in a week's time to chop that tree down in order to improve my house. Therefore whosoever amongst you (or anywhere else in your city) needs to hang himself should promptly get on with it. Once that period has elapsed they will find no place more apt, no tree so convenient.'

Following his example, I announce to those devilish calumniators that they must all be hanged within the final phase of the present moon. I will supply the nooses. The place I assign for the hangings is half-way between Mid-day and Faverolles. Come the new moon they will not get away so cheaply and will be obliged to supply the nooses at their own expense; and, in addition, to select a tree for their own hanging (as did Signora Leontium who calumniated the most-learned and eloquent Theophrastus).[6]

6.   Taken from the *Adages* of Erasmus I, X, XXI, 'A tree to be chosen for one's hanging'. But Rabelais jumped to a wrong conclusion from his reading of Erasmus: Leontium the whore did not hang herself.

THE FOURTH BOOK
OF PANTAGRUEL
(1552)

Introduction to the *Fourth Book of Pantagruel* (1552)

The 1552 *Fourth Book* (referred to in the notes here as '52) greatly expands the *Fourth Book* of 1548 (referred to as '48). The notes indicate where the text of '48 varies from that of '52; however, the '48 Prologue is not indicated, as this appears in full earlier in this volume. Square brackets show a selection of the additions made in '52. The variants cease in Chapter 25 at the point where the '48 text breaks off.

The only complication with the '52 text lies in the cancels introduced into some copies. Cancels (reprinted pages) were made so as to celebrate the French Royal victories of May 1552 in German lands (see note 5).

The text translated is that of the *Quart Livre* in the Textes Littéraires Français, edited by Robert Marichal, first published by Droz of Geneva in 1947 and several times reprinted.

THE FOURTH BOOK OF
THE HEROIC DEEDS AND
SAYINGS OF OUR
GOOD GIANT PANTAGRUEL

Composed by Maître François Rabelais
Doctor of Medicine

AT PARIS
From the printing-house of Michel Fezandat, on Mount
Saint-Hilaire, in the Hôtel d'Albret.

With the *privilège* of the King

Contents

To the most-illustrious Prince and Most-Reverend Lord the Cardinal de Châtillon

[For the first time Rabelais prefaces his new book with a formal, signed letter of dedication addressed to a patron. That patron, Odet de Châtillon, had assured him of the support and encouragement of Henri II, his king. He adds his own encouragement to that of Cardinal Jean Du Bellay. Rabelais can at last dare say what he wants to say. Châtillon was a member of a powerful trio, the nephews of Anne de Montmorency. Two were already open Protestants. Well after Rabelais was dead, the third, Cardinal Odet de Châtillon, fled to Anglican England with his wife.

Rabelais, deeply influenced by the works of Celio Calcagnini, has turned his new book into 'mythologies'.

For the medical anecdotes here Rabelais retells what he wrote in the Prologue of the '48 Fourth Book.

For the Emperor Augustus and his daughter Julia see Erasmus (Apophthegms, IV, Octavius Caesar Augustus, 45).

Rabelais links rebarbative (crabby, unattractive) with rhubarb.

The Anagnost (Reader) who read Rabelais' works to Franqis I was Pierre Du Chastel, Bishop of Mâcon and later of Orleans.

For 'agelasts', non-laughers, see Erasmus, Adages, II, V, LXXII, 'Unlaughing stone'.

The 'Gallic Hercules' drew men to him by his eloquence.

Alexikakos, a title of Hercules applied by Rabelais to Cardinal Odet de Châtillon, means 'Averter of Evil'. The Cardinal's sympathies already lay with the Lutherans and Anglicans not with Geneva and the Eglise Réformée. Calvin was shocked by the likening of him to Moses.]

Most-illustrious Prince: you have already been duly informed how I have been daily solicited, begged and importuned by so many great personages for the sequel of my pantagruelic mythologies, on the grounds that many of the ailing, the sick, the weary or the afflicted have, when they were read to them, beguiled their benighted sufferings, passed their time merrily and found fresh joy and consolation. To whom I normally reply that, as I wrote them for fun, I sought neither glory nor praise of any kind: my concern and intention were simply to provide such little relief as I could to the absent sick-and-suffering as I willingly provide to those who are present with me, seeking help from my Art and my care. Occasionally I explain to them at some length how Hippocrates (describing in several places, and especially in the Sixth Book of the *Epidemics*, the formation of his doctor-disciple) as well as Soranus of Ephesus, Oribasius, Claudius Galen and others, included in their concerns a physician's gestures, deportment, look, touch, expression, grace and affability, as well as the cleanliness of his face, clothing, beard, hair and mouth, going so far as to single out the fingernails as though the physician were about to play the role of lover or suitor in some famous comedy or to go down into the tilt-yard to face a powerful opponent. Indeed, practising medicine is compared by Hippocrates to a combat and to a farce with three characters: the patient, the physician and the malady. Once, when reading that portrait of a physician, I was reminded of a remark of Julia to her father Octavian Augustus. On one occasion she presented herself before him in extravagant, immodest and provocative robes, which greatly displeased him though he uttered not a word. The following day she changed her wardrobe, dressing modestly in the style then customary amongst chaste Roman matrons. Thus attired, she appeared before him. He who, the day before, had never shown his displeasure by a single word when he had seen her in immodest robes, could not hide the pleasure which he took in seeing her thus changed; and he said to her, 'O, how much more becoming and worthy are such robes to the daughter of Augustus!' She had her excuse ready: 'Today,' she replied, 'I dressed for the eyes of my father: yesterday I dressed to please my husband.'

So too a physician, dressed up with the right mien and attire – especially if he were clad as used to be the custom in the rich and pleasant double-sleeved gown called the *philonium* (as Petrus Alexandrinus wrote in his commentary on the *Sixth Book* of the *Epidemics*) – could reply to those who found his role-playing odd: 'I have put on such accoutrements not to show off and be pompous but to please the patient on whom I am making a call, whom alone I seek entirely to please, avoiding all offence and irritation.'

There is more to it than that: we have hectic arguments over a passage in the *Sixth Book* of the *Epidemics* of our venerated Hippocrates: not whether the gloomy, severe, rhubarbative, Cato-like, displeasing, dissatisfied, glum and sullen expression of the physician depresses the patient whilst the happy, serene, pleasing, laughing, open expression cheers him up: that is proven and certain; but whether such depressing or cheering-up results from the perceptions of the patient as he contemplates those qualities in his doctor – assessing by means of them the outcome and final act of his illness: that is, by happy qualities a happy, desirable outcome: by gloomy qualities, an awful, gloomy one – or whether it results rather from the pouring of the doctor's spirits, serene or gloomy, aerial or terrestrial, joyous or melancholic, from that doctor into the person of his patient (as in the opinion of Plato and Averroës). Above all else the aforementioned authorities gave a specific warning to the physician about the vocabulary, topics, discussions and conversations which he should employ with the patients on whose behalf he has been called in: everything must aim at one target and tend towards one end, namely to cheer him up without offence to God and never to depress him in any manner whatsoever.

Thus a certain Doctor Callianax is strongly condemned by Herophilus since, when a patient questioned him and asked, 'Am I going to die?' he callously replied,

> A better man than you was overcome
> When Patroclus to death had to succumb.

Another patient wanted to know the state of his illness and questioned him in the vein of our noble Pathelin:

> ... my micturition, now,
> Tells it you not that I'm a dying man?

He idiotically answered: 'No: not, that is, if you were born of Latona, the mother of those handsome children Phoebus and Diana.'

Similarly Claudius Galen (in *Book Four* of his *Commentary* on *Book Six* of the *Epidemics*) strongly condemned his medical teacher Quintus, who, when a certain distinguished patient of his in Rome said to him, 'You've already had your dinner, Doctor: your breath smells to me of wine,' arrogantly retorted, 'And yours smells to me of fever: which has the more appetizing smell and bouquet, fever or wine?'

But the calumny of certain cannibals, misanthropists and agelasts had been so atrocious and unreasonable that it overcame my patience and I decided not to write another jot. For one of the least of the contumelies they used against me was that such books are all stuffed full of a variety of heresies, yet they could not produce a single example from any passage: merry jests, yes, in abundance, with no offence to God in them (that is the sole theme and subject of those books): heresies, no, not at all – unless by perversely inferring, against all rational and routine linguistic usage, things I would never have allowed to enter my mind even under threat of dying a thousand deaths, if so many were possible. It is as though one were to make bread mean a stone; fish, a serpent; egg, a scorpion.[1]

Once when I was complaining of this in your presence, I told you straight that if I did not consider myself a better Christian than they and their faction show themselves to be, and that if I were to recognize, in my life, writings, words or indeed my thoughts, one scintilla of any heresy, they would not be falling so detestably into the snares of the Calumniating Spirit – the Διάβολος'[2] – who through them as his ministers impute such a crime to me: I would, following the example of the phoenix, collect the tinder myself and light the pyre so as to burn myself on it.

Then it was you told me that our late King François of eternal memory had been warned of such calumnies, and that, after

1. Cf. Luke 11:11.
2. The Greek Διάβολος (Diabolos) means Devil or Calumniator.

carefully and attentively listening to a clear reading of my books from the eloquent voice of the most learned and faithful Anagnost in this Kingdom – of *my* books, I stress, since some false and infamous ones have wickedly been attributed to me – he never discovered one suspect passage in them and was horrified by some envious snake-gobbler who founded a mortal heresy on an N put for an M through the compositors' misprint and carelessness.[3]

The same was done by his son (our so good, virtuous and Heaven-blessed King Henri – may God long preserve him for us – with the result that he granted you a *privilège* for me and individual protection against such calumniators.

Those good tidings you later graciously repeated to me in Paris, and again when you came to visit my Lord the Cardinal Du Bellay, who, to recover after a long and distressing illness, had withdrawn to Saint-Maur, a place – or to put it better and more appropriately – a paradise of healthiness, pleasantness, quietness, convenience and delight, and of all the noble joys of husbandry and the rustic life.

That, my Lord, is why, at this present time, I give a good wind to my quill, free from all intimidation, hoping that through your kindly favour you will be unto me a second Gallic Hercules in knowledge, wisdom and eloquence, and like him an *Alexikakos* in power, might and authority: of whom I can truly say what was said by Solomon the wise of Moses, the great prophet and Captain of Israel (Ecclesiasticus 45): a man fearing and loving God, a man of happy memory, a man agreeable to all mankind, beloved of God and of men; God in His praise likened him unto the valiant, and magnified him in the fear of his enemies. On his behalf He wrought marvellous and awesome things; He glorified him in the sight of kings; through him He declared his will to the people, and through him shed His light. He consecrated him in faith and graciousness, and chose him out of all

3. This refers to the jest which puts *asne* (ass) for *âme* (soul). Can that really be attributed to the printers and not to Rabelais? And could even Sorbonagres have taken it seriously? The jest circulated independently of Rabelais, who may be suggesting that it was only through such silly humourless quibbles that his alleged 'heresy' could be found.

men living. Through him God wished His voice to be heard, and the life-giving light of learning to be announced to those who were in darkness.

Further still, I promise you that those whom I shall find commending me for these joyful writings of mine I will adjure to be grateful entirely to you, to be thankful to you alone and to pray our Lord to preserve and increase your greatness, attributing nothing to me save humble submission and willing obedience to your commands. For through your exhortations which so honour me you have bestowed upon me both courage and inspiration. Without you my heart had given way and the fountain of my animal spirits run dry.

May our Lord keep you in His holy grace.

From Paris, this 28th of January, 1552.

Your most humble and most obedient

servant, Franç. Rabelais, physician.

The Royal *privilège*

[This privilège *is every bit as fulsome as that given to Rabelais at the time of his* Third Book. *It repeats the highest praise of a literary work as defined by Horace: the works of Rabelais are again judged 'no less useful than delightful'. No work of Rabelais in 'Tuscan' (Italian) is now extant or even known.]*

Henry, by the grace of God King of France, to the Provost of Paris, the Bailiff of Rouen, the Seneschals of Lyons, Toulouse, Bordeaux, Dauphiné and Poitou, and to all other Our Justices and Officials, or to their Deputies, and to each of them severally as is due: greetings and affection.

On the part of Our beloved and loyal Maître François Rabelais, Doctor of Medicine, it has been expounded to Us that the aforesaid suppliant, having heretofore delivered to be printed various books in Greek, Latin, French and Tuscan, especially certain volumes of the Heroic Deeds and Sayings of Pantagruel, no less useful than delightful, the printers have corrupted and perverted the said books in several places. They have moreover printed several other – offensive – books under the name of the above suppliant to his great displeasure, prejudice and shame, books totally disowned by him as false and supposititious, which he desires to be suppressed under Our good pleasure and will; further, other books of his, acknowledged as his but depraved and distorted as said above, he desires to review, correct and newly reprint; similarly to bring to light and to sell the sequel of the Heroic Deeds and Sayings of Pantagruel; humbly begging Us to vouchsafe him Our requisite and appropriate Documents.

And because We freely incline towards the supplication and request of the aforesaid Maître François Rabelais, and being desirous of treating him favourably in this matter:

To him, for those causes and other good considerations moving Us thereunto, We have accorded and vouchsafed to him permission, and by Our certain knowledge, plenary powers and Royal authority do now accord and vouchsafe by this present document, that he may licitly have printed by such printers as he shall decide, and newly put and expose on sale, all and each of the said books and the sequel to *Pantagruel* by him undertaken and composed, both those books which have already been printed, which will be to this end reviewed and corrected, as well as those also which he intends newly to bring to light; and similarly suppress those which have been falsely attributed to him.

And so that he may have the means to support the costs necessary to the undertaking of such printing, We by this present document most-expressly have prohibited and forbidden, and do prohibit and forbid, all other booksellers and printers of this Our Kingdom and other Our Lands and Lordships to print, have printed, put on sale or expose for sale any of the above-mentioned books, both old and new, during a period and term of ten years, consecutive and successive, beginning on the day and date of the printing of the said books, without the will and consent of the said suppliant, on pain of the confiscation of the books which shall be found to have been printed to the prejudice of this Our present permission, and of an arbitrary fine.

And We wish and order that each one of you in whatever concerns him and shall pertain to him shall keep, guard and observe these Our present congee, licence, permission, prohibition and interdict. And if any persons were found to have contravened them, then proceed and cause to proceed against them with the above-stated and other penalties. And see that the said suppliant enjoy and use the contents of the above *privilège* during the said period, to begin and to be in all respects as is stated above; ending, and causing to end, all troubles and obstacles contrary thereto: for such is Our pleasure, notwithstanding any so ever ordinances, restrictions, orders or prohibition thereunto opposed. And because appeal may be made to these present Documents in several different places, We wish that on the simple examination of notarial copies made under the Royal Seal, faith be placed in them as in this present original.

Given at Saint-Germain-en-Laye, the Sixth day of August in the year of grace one thousand five hundred and fifty, and the fourth of Our reign. From the King:

the Cardinal De Châtillon in attendance.

Signed Du Thier.

Prologue of the Author
Maître François Rabelais
for the Fourth Book
of the heroic deeds and sayings
of Pantagruel

[Pantagruelism is further defined.

This, the longest of the Prologues, is a masterpiece of syncretism. Rabelais treats an episode in the Old Testament, another in the New and a fable of Aesop as 'pedagogues' leading to a fuller understanding of Christian faith – that is, of trust and hope in God. The objects of prayer should be governed by moderation. Many devoted Renaissance humanists thought the same. Erasmus in his Adages *(I, VI, XCVI, 'Nothing to excess') holds that every single thing should be governed by the Mean, except our love of God. Calvin says much the same: even in matters 'theological Man must remain within true moderation between extremes'. The key biblical references are to Luke 19:1–6 and to II (IV) Kings 6:1–7.*

*The fable of the woodcutter and the axe is related by Erasmus (*Adages*, IV, III, LVII, 'A river does not always bear axes'). Rabelais retells it in the style of Lucian. The name of the woodcutter, Couillatris, is here translated as Bollux.*

We are shown the reality and limits of free-will. Even when our choices (like Bollux's here) are not spotlessly pure, they are real and bring upon us their inevitable consequences. Christianity had long since taken over for God the Father the ancient title of Jupiter, God the Most-good and the Most-great (Optimus Maximus or D.O.M.). Rabelais strikingly and very unusually, applies it directly to God the Son. There is hardly any other term which would so completely emphasize the full divinity of Christ. He will do so again later where it appears among the most powerful of syncretistic elements in Chapter 28 apropos of the death of Pan.

Tiraqueau's treatise The Quick Seizeth the Dead *treats at length of the immediate cession of property on the death of the testator to the heirs and heirs presumptive.*

The followers of Ramus and Galland were forming factions for and against the authority of Aristotle and a new concept of dialectics. They should be turned into gargoyles (since pierre *means stone and both are called Pierre) and turned into an equilateral triangle, a Pythagorean form treated lightly here and perhaps in Chapter 34 – as in Lucian's Philosophies for Sale – but destined, like the Platonic Ideas, which are similarly lightly treated at first, to become associated with revealed truth in Chapter 55.]*

To the kindly readers:

Good people: may God save you and keep you. Where are you? I can't see you: wait while I tug on my glasses. Ha, ha! *Lent runs on, both fine and fair*: I can see you now. Well then: I'm told that you've had a good *vendange*: I would be by no means saddened by that! You've found an infallible remedy against all thirsts and distempers? That's worthily done. You, your wives, children, family and kinsfolk are all in the health you desire? Things are going well. That's good. I'm pleased. God, our good God, be eternally praised for it and (if such be his holy will) may you long be maintained in it. As for me, by his holy loving-kindness I'm still here and pay you my respects. I am, by means of a little *pantagruelism* (that is, as you know, a certain merriness of mind pickled in contempt for things fortuitous) well and sprightly and ready for a drink if you are. Do you ask me why, good folk? An incontrovertible reply: such is the will of the Most-good, Most-great God in whom I find rest, whom I obey and of whom I revere the sacrosanct word of Good Tidings – the Gospel – in which it is said (Luke 4) with dreadful sarcasm and biting derision to the physician neglectful of his own health: 'Physician, heal thyself!'

Claudius Galen kept himself in good health not out of respect for that saying (even though he did have some knowledge of Holy Writ and did know and frequent the saintly Christians of his time, as is clear from Book 2 of *On the Uses of the Parts of the Body*, and Book 2 of *On the Differences of Pulses*, Chapter 3, as well as, in the same work, Book 3, Chapter 2, and in *On the Affections of the Kidneys*, if it be by Galen), but out of fear of falling under this common and satirical mockery:

'Ιητρὸς ἄλλων αὐτὸς ἕλκεσι βρύων.

To doctor others he is well affected,
And yet he is by ulcers dire infected.[4]

He brashly boasts that he does not want to be reckoned a physician if he fails to live in completely good health – apart from a few, short-lived ephemeral fevers – from his twenty-eighth year until an advanced old age, even though he was not naturally one of the heartiest and his stomach manifestly weak. "For," he says (in Book 5 of *On Maintaining Good Health*), "a physician will hardly be trusted to take care of the health of others if he neglects his own."

Even more brashly did Asclepiades the physician boast of having made a pact with Fortune: he would not be thought of as a physician if ever he were ill from the time he began to practise his Art until his ultimate old age (which age he did reach, both vigorous in all his limbs and triumphant over Fortune). Finally, without any preceding illness, he exchanged life for death by accidentally tumbling down from the top of a decayed and badly mortised flight of stairs.

If, through some ill-stared event, the health of your Lordships has emancipated itself, then, wherever it may be – up or down, before or behind, right or left, within or without, far or near your domains – may you, with the help of our Blessèd Servator, quickly come across it. And once happily met, instantly reclaim it; let it be repossessed by you, seized and remancipated. The laws allow it; the king understands it; and I so counsel you, neither more nor less than do the Ancient law-givers who authorize a master to reclaim a runaway slave no matter where he might be found.

O ye gude men and Ye gude God! Is it not written and

4.   As in the *Third Book* Rabelais simply cites his Greek (*Metros allôn autos helkesi bruôn*) in Greek script, but this time he does provide a translation. For both the previous quotation from Luke 4:32 and this Greek quotation Rabelais is drawing upon an adage of Erasmus: IV, IV, XXXII, 'A physician for others'. In Luke Jesus claims that his enemies are using the saying against him.

practised in the ancient customary law of this our so noble, so
flourishing, so rich and triumphant kingdom of France that
The Dead Seizeth the Quick? Read what has recently been
expounded on this topic by the good, learned and wise André
Tiraqueau, so debonair and just, a Counsellor to King Henri the
Second of that name in his most-awesome Court of Parlement in
Paris). Our health is our life, as was so well proclaimed by
Ariphron of Sicyon. Without health, life is no life, life is not
liveable, ἄβίος βίος, βίος ἀβίωτος: without health, life is but
languishing, life is but a pale image of death.⁵

And so, when you are deprived of health (that is, dead), *Seize
ye the Quick*, seize hold of life (of health, that is).

My hope is in God that he will hearken to our prayers, seeing
the firm faith in which we make them, and that he will grant
us our wish because it lies within the Mean. By the sages of
Antiquity the Mean was called Golden, that is to say, precious,
praised by all, and everywhere delightful. Study the books
of the Holy Bible and you will find that the prayers of those
who asked with moderation have never been rejected. An
example: that tiny man Zachaeus (whose body and relics the
mullahs of Saint-Ayl near Orleans boast of possessing and
whom they call Saint Sylvanus). He simply wanted to see our
Blessèd Servator near Jerusalem. Nothing more. That lay within
the Mean, open to anyone. But he was too short to do so from
the midst of the multitude. He pranced and trotted about,
he pushed, he drew apart, he climbed up a sycamore. Our
Most-good God recognized the purity and moderation of his
desire, presented himself to his sight – Zachaeus being not only

5.   The Greek (*abios bios, bios abiôtos*) is paraphrased in the text but kept
in Greek script. The proverb is given in the comment of Erasmus on an
adage: II, VIII, XXX, 'A man of money'.
     A cancel was introduced in some copies to celebrate the victories of the
King of France in German lands in 1552; the text then read: . . . Is it not
written and practised in the ancient customary law of this our so noble,
so ancient, so beautiful, so rich kingdom of France that *The Dead seizeth
the Quick*? Read what has recently been expounded on this topic by
the good, learned and wise André Tiraqueau, so debonair and just, a
Counsellor to *the great, victorious and triumphant* King Henri the Second
of that name . . .

seen but also heard by him – visited his home and blessed his family.

A son of a prophet in Israel was chopping up wood near the river Jordan when (as it is written in 4 Kings 6) the head of his axe flew off and fell into the river. He prayed God to give it him back – something within the Mean – and with firm hope and confidence he did not cast the head after the helve (as the devilish little Censors chant with an offensive solecism) but (as you so rightly say) cast the helve after the head. At once there appeared two miracles:

– the iron axe-head rose from the depths of the water;
– it fitted itself on to the helve.

If he had wanted to be borne up into the heavens in a fiery chariot like Elijah, multiply his seed like Abraham, be as rich as Job, as strong as Samson or as fair as Absalom, would that have come to pass? You may well ask!

Apropos of wishes within the Mean where axes are concerned – let me know when it's time for a drink! – I'll tell you a tale written in his fables by Aesop the Frenchman (I mean Phrygian and Trojan, as Maximus Planudes affirms. From their stock, according to the most veracious chroniclers, the noble French are descended. Aelian writes that he was a Thracian, and Agathias, following Herodotus, that he was a Samian. It's all the same to me.)

There lived in his days a poor yokel, a native of the village of Gravot. His name was Bollux, a feller of timber and driver-in of wedges, earning a wretched living, jogging along in that lowly estate. And it befell that he lost his axe. Who was sorely troubled and saddened? He was: for his well-being and his very life depended upon that axe; through that axe he lived in honour and respect amidst all the wealthy woodmen: without his axe he would perish from hunger. Death, encountering him six days later without his axe, would have scythed and sickled him from this world. In such a predicament he began to yell and to implore, beseech and invoke Jupiter through many a fluent prayer (since, as you know, Necessity is the mother of Eloquence), lifting up his face to the heavens, with his knees to the ground, his head bare, his arms stretched out high and his fingers widely spread as, in a loud voice, he kept tirelessly chanting as a refrain to all his orisons: 'My axe, Jupiter, my axe, my axe! Nothing more, O Jupiter, but my axe, or pennies to buy me another. Woe is me: my poor old axe!'

Now Jupiter was holding a council about certain urgent affairs. The aged Cybele was then opining or, if you prefer, the young and radiant Phoebus. But so great was the clamour of Bollux that it was heard as a great din in the full council and consistory of the gods.

'Who the devil is it down there howling so horribly?' asked Jupiter. 'By the might of the Styx! were we not and are we not still sufficiently encumbered with decisions about controversial and weighty affairs? Have we not voided the dispute between Prester John, the king of the Persians, and Soliman the Sultan, the emperor of Constantinople? Have we not closed the gap between the Tartars and the Muscovites? Have we not answered the request of the Shereef, and done the same at the beseeching of Dragut Rays? The status of Parma has been dealt with and so has that of Magdeburg, Mirandola and Africa (as mortals name that place on the Mediterranean Sea that we call *Aphrodisium*). Tripoli, being badly guarded, has changed masters: its time had run out. Here are the Gascons, cursing and swearing and asking for their bells to be restored. Over in this corner are the Saxons, the Hanseatics and the Germans, folk once invincible but now *aberkeits* – ruined – and under the yoke of a little old cripple: they're crying out for vengeance, succour and the restitution of their original rights and ancient freedom.

'But what are we going to do about those fellows Ramus and Galland who, flanked by their flunkeys, henchmen and partisans, are sowing discord through the whole of the Parisian Academe? I am greatly perplexed by it. I have yet to determine which way to lean. Otherwise both seem good and well-bollocked fellows to me. One of them has golden Sun-crowns: I mean beautiful solid ones. The other would like to. One is quite learned. The other's no fool. One likes fine folk: fine folk like the other. One is a cunning and crafty fox: the other speaks evil and writes evil, howling like a cur against the Ancient philosophers and authors. Tell me how it seems to you, Priapus, you old ass's prick! Many a time I've found your counsel equitable and your advice pertinent: even your mentulate parts have mental capacities.'

'King Jupiter,' replied Priapus, baring his helmet, his head erect, red, radiant and firm, 'since you compare one of them to a howling cur and the other to a fully freighted fox, I am of the opinion that, without worrying or disturbing yourself any further, you should do with them what you did with a cur and a fox long ago.'

'Eh?' asked Jupiter. 'When? Who were they? When was it?'

'What a fine memory!' Priapus replied. 'That venerable father Bacchus you can see here with his ruddy face wanted to avenge himself against the inhabitants of Thebes. He therefore kept an enchanted fox: no matter what harm or damage it caused no beast in the world could catch it or hurt it. Now this noble Vulcan here had forged a dog of Monesian brass and by dint of breathing into it had made it animate and alive. He gave it to you. You gave it to Europa, your sweeting. She gave it to Minos; Minos, to Proclis; Proclis finally to Cephalus. That dog too was similarly enchanted: it could nab any creature it came across and let nothing escape it (like lawyers today).

'Now it happened that they came across each other! What could they do? The cur, by its fated destiny, must take the fox: the fox by its destiny must never be taken.

'The case was referred to your council. You professed never to go counter to Destiny. Their destinies were incompatible. The truth, the effecting and the accomplishment of two simultaneous incompatibilities was declared an impossibility within Nature. You sweated under the strain; it was from your sweat falling upon the Earth that round-headed cabbages were born. All this noble consistory of ours, in default of a categorical conclusion, developed a wonder-working thirst; and at that particular council more than seventy-eight barrels of nectar were drunk.

'At my suggestion you turned them both into stones. Immediately you were freed from all perplexity; immediately a truce with drinking was declared throughout Olympus. It was the

year of the flabby honing stones near Teumessa (between
Thebes and Chalcis).

'Following that example, I am of the opinion that you should
literally *petrify* that cur and that fox. It is not an unprecedented
metamorphosis. Both of them bear the name of *Pierre* – Stone
– and since a proverb from Limoges says that it takes three
stones to make the mouth of one oven, you will bring them
together with Maître Pierre Du Coignet whom you once petri-
fied for similar reasons. And those three dead *pierres* shall be
placed in the form of an equilateral triangle[6] upon the great
Temple of Paris or in the middle of its parvis, where (as in the
game of Fouquet's puff) they will serve to snuff out lighted
candles with their noses as well as torches, tapers, rush-lights
and flambeaux (since, when they were alive, they bollocked up
the fires of faction and dissention, of bollocking cliques and
divisions amongst idle students) as an everlasting reminder that
when such bollock-shaped, self-loving coteries came before
you, they were not so much condemned as contemned.

'I have spoken.'

'As far as I can tell, fair Signor Priapus, you're well disposed
towards them,' said Jupiter. '(You are not so well-disposed
towards all men!) For seeing that they yearn to eternalize their
name and reputation, the best thing that could happen to them
is to be changed into hard marble *pierres* after death rather
than to return to the earth and rot.

'You can see, behind us here towards the Tyrrhenian Sea and
the environs of the Apennines, what tragedies are provoked by
certain pastophors. Such madness will last out its time like the
ovens of Limoges. Eventually it will end, though not all that
soon. That will provide us with quite a pastime. But I can see
one drawback: we have only a small arsenal of thunderbolts
ever since you, my fellow gods, by my special permission,
showered them on to New Antioch for fun, just as those foppish

6. Rabelais enjoys playing with concepts he will later take seriously. Equi-
    lateral triangles are mentioned only in this Book. They will be mentioned
    again: in the fight against the physeter (Chapter 34) and then, most
    seriously, in the Manor of Truth (Chapter 55). He treats Platonic 'Ideas'
    in the same way.

champions who, following your example, swore to defend the fortress of Dindenarois against all comers squandered their munitions in shooting at ravelins. And so, having nothing to defend themselves with in their hour of need, they gallantly gave up the fort and surrendered to their enemies, who, mad with despair, were about to lift their siege, having no thought more pressing than how to retreat with the minimum of opprobrium.

'See to it all, Vulcan, my son. Wake up the slumbering Cyclopses – Asterope, Brontes, Arge, Polyphemus, Sterope and Pyracmon– set them to work and make them match drink for drink. Skimp not the wine for workers with fire! And let us dispatch that yeller down yonder. Go and see who it is, Mercury, and find out what he wants.'

Mercury goes and looks through the trap-door of the heavens (by which they listen to what is said on Earth here below and which actually resembles the booby-hatch of a ship: Icaromenippus said it looks like the mouth of a well).

Seeing Bollux there, who wants his lost axe, he reports back to the council.

'Truly now,' said Jupiter; 'a fine thing I must say! Have we no other item on the agenda but the returning of lost axes! We shall have to give it to him, though. That, you see, is inscribed in Destiny just as much as if it were worth the Duchy of Milan. It is in truth as highly prized and valued by him as his realm is to a monarch. All right! All right! Let that axe be returned. Let there be no more talk about it. Let's resolve that quarrel between the secular clergy and the moles of Landerousse. Where had we got to?'

Priapus remained bolt upright in the chimney-corner. On hearing Mercury's report he said with all courtesy and a jovial frankness:

'King Jupiter: during the period when, by your command and special grace, I stood as guardian in the gardens on Earth, I noted that the term *coignée* (axe) is equivocal, having several meanings. *Coignée* can signify a certain tool by the use of which timber is cloven and chopped down. It can also signify (or at least it used to signify) the female frequently and duly jiggedyjogged. And I noted that every good companion called his own girlie his *coignée*. For with such a tool (and so saying he displayed his nine-inch knocker) the men wedged themselves so tightly and boldly into the eyes of their sockets that the females remained free from a fear, epidemic amongst the feminine sex: to wit, that without such a buckling their sockets might tumble down to their heels from their bellies. And, since I have a lovely big *mentula* – I mean *mental* capacity: enough to fill a butter-pot – I remember that one day in May, during the festivities at the Tubilustra of that good fellow Vulcan, I once heard Josquin des Prés, Ockeghem, Obrecht, Agricola, Brumel, Camelin, Vigoris, De la Fage, Bruyer, Prioris, Seguin, De la Rue, Midy, Moulu, Mouton, Gascogne, Loyset, Compère, Penet, Fevin, Rosée, Richafort, Rousseau, Conseil, Costanzo Festa and Jacques Berchem melodiously singing this song on a beautiful lawn:

> Tubby Tibault wished soon to lie
> With his fond wife but newly wed;
> He did not want her to espy
> A mallet, large, placed near the bed.
> "O lover dear!" his sweeting said,
> "What means that mallet hidden nigh?"
> "To ram me right in by and by!"
> "No mallet," said she, "needs my tum.
> "When Fat John comes to me, O My!
> He batters only with his bum!"

Nine Olympiads and one intercalated year later – oh, I do have a good *mentula* (I mean *mental* capacity: I'm always being solecistic over the concordance and interconnection of those two words!) – I heard Adrian Willaert, Gombert, Jannequin, Arcadelt, Claudin, Certon, Manchicourt, Auxerre, Villiers, Sandrin, Sohier, Hesdin, Morales, Passereau, Maille, Maillart, Jacotin, Heurteur, Verdelot, Carpentras, Lhéritier, Cadéac, Doublet, Vermont, Bouteiller, Lupi, Pagnier, Millet, Du Moulin, Alaire, Marault, Morpain, Gendre and other merry music-makers all singing in a secluded garden under fair leafy boughs fenced about with a rampart of flagons, hams, pasties and divers well-coiffured Peggy-Partridges:

> The empty socket in a helve-less head
> Is useless quite, a rake without its pole;
> One in the other you must tightly bed.
> I'll play the helve, and bed it in that hole.

But we still need to know what sort of axe that bellowing Bollux is asking for.'

At which words the venerable gods and goddesses all broke out into laughter like a microcosm of flies. Vulcan, for the love of his lady, made three or four fine little jumps in a hop-along style on his gammy leg. 'Come on,' said Jupiter to Mercury; 'get down there at once and cast three axes at Bollux's feet: his own; another of solid gold and a third of solid silver, all of the same calibre.

'Give him the chance to choose.

'If he takes his own and is satisfied with it, give him the other two. If he takes either of the others, chop off his head with his own. And from now on, do the same with all such losers of axes.'

Having finished with those words, Jupiter contorted his head like a monkey swallowing pills and pulled such a horrible face that the whole of mighty Mount Olympus quaked.

Mercury, with his pointed cap, his cape, his anklets and his caduceus, jumped through the trapdoor of Heaven, clove the aerial void, alighted gently upon Earth, cast the three axes at Bollux's feet and said to him, 'You deserve a drink after all that bellowing! Your prayers have been answered by Jupiter. See which of these three axes is your own and take it away.'

Bollux lifted up the axe of gold. He stared at it and found it very heavy. He then said to Mercury, ' 'Pon my zole, that bain't moine. Don't want thickee.' He did the same to the silver one, saying, 'Not thackee. You can 'ave 'im.' Then he took up the woodcutter's axe: he looked at the base of the helve and recognized his mark; then, quivering with joy like a fox coming across stray hens, he said, smiling to the tip of his nose, 'Mudder

of God: this one's moine! If you'll leave 'im with me, I'll sacrifice a lovely big pot of milk to you, covered with a layer of
nice strewberries at the Ides' – that is, the fifteenth day – 'of
May.'

'My good fellow,' said Mercury, 'I leave it with you. Take it.
And because you have opted and wished for the Mean in the
matter of axes, at the behest of Jupiter I give you the two others.
From now on you have enough to be rich. Be a good man.'

Bollux courteously thanks Mercury, worships great Jupiter,
and clips his venerable axe on to his leathern belt, girding it
over his bum like Martin de Cambrai. The two other heavier
ones he carries over his shoulder. Then he processes prelate-like
through the locality, cutting a fine figure amongst his neighbours and fellow parishioners, repeating that little phrase of
Pathelin's: 'Done well, haven't I!'

Next day, wearing a white smock, he loads his two precious
axes on to his back and betakes himself to Chinon, a famous
town, a noble town, an ancient town, indeed, the best town
in the world according to the verdict and assertion of the
learned Masoretes. In Chinon he exchanges his silver axe for
lovely testoons and other silver coins, and his golden one
for lovely Annunciation-crowns, lovely long-fleeced *Agnus-Dei*,
lovely Dutch Ritters, lovely Royals and lovely Sun-crowns.
With them he buys a great many farms, a great many barns, a
great many holdings, a great many tenancies, a great many
fields and a great many domains, meadows, vines, woodlands,
arable lands, pasture-lands, ponds, mills, gardens, willow-
groves; bulls, cows, ewes, sheep, goats, sows, pigs, asses, horses;
hens, cocks, capons, pullets, geese, ganders, chicks, drakes and
various small farm-birds. And in no time he was the richest
man around – why, richer than lame old Maulévrier!

Now the substantial yeomen and the clod-hopping Jacks
noted Bollux's happy encounter and were struck with amazement; within their minds the pity and commiseration which
they had formerly felt for him were changed into envy of his
wealth, so great and unexpected. And so they began to dash
around to inquire, find out and discover in what place, on
which day, at what hour, how and under what circumstances

such great treasure had come to him. On learning that it came from the losing of his axe, they said, 'Aha! To become rich we only have to lose an axe, do we! The means is easy: the outlay, trivial. The revolution of the spheres, the disposition of the stars and the aspects of the planets are now such (are they?) that whosoever his axe shall lose immediately so rich shall be! Hmm! Hee, hee! Axe of mine, you shall be lost, if you don't mind.'

Whereupon they all lost their axes. Any man who kept one could go to the devil. For lack of axes no more trees were felled nor timber chopped in all the land.

That Aesopic fable goes on to say that certain little *bas-relief* Rack-rents amongst the local Spentry (who had sold Bollux this little meadow or that little mill so as to cut a figure at the revue of the train-bands), when once informed how such treasure had thus come to Bollux and by what singular means, sold their swords to buy axes in order to lose them like their peasants, and so acquire by that loss a mountain of gold and silver. (You could easily have taken them for Rushers-to-Rome, selling their goods and borrowing from others in order to buy piles of mandates-to-benefices from a new-made pope.) And then they yelled and prayed and lamented and invoked Jupiter: 'My axe, my axe, O Jupiter! My axe here: my axe there: O! O! O! My axe!'

The ambient air resounded with the cries and howls of those losers of axes.

Mercury was prompt in bringing axes to them; to each he offered his own lost one, another of silver and third one of gold. They all chose the one made of gold and went to pick it up. But, the very instant that they stooped and bent over to lift it from the ground, Mercury – in accordance with the edict of Jupiter – lopped off their heads. And the severed heads were equal and equivalent in number to the axes which were lost. Well: there it is. There you have what happens to those who innocently wish and opt for things within the Mean.

Learn from that example all you lowland nags who swear that you wouldn't write off your wishes even for an income of ten thousand francs. From now on do not talk with such impudence as I sometimes hear you do when you wish, 'Would to God I had, here and now, one hundred and seventy-eight millions in gold! Oh how I would strut about!' Chilblains to you! What more could a king, an emperor, a pope wish for? And you know from experience that, after you've made such outrageous wishes, all you get is foot-rot and the scab, and not one farthing in your purse, no more than those two beggarly wish-makers who followed the Use of Paris: one of them wished to have as much wealth in lovely Sun-crowns as had been expended, bought and sold in Paris since the first foundations were laid for its construction until this present hour, everything to be reckoned according to the rates, costs and prices of the dearest year occurring during that lapse of time. Had that fellow lost his appetite do you think! Had he eaten sour plums without peeling them? Were his teeth set on edge?

The other wished the shrine of Notre-Dame to be crammed full of sharp-pointed needles from the pavement to the apex of the vaulting, and to have all the Sun-crowns that could be stuffed into all the sacks that could be sewn by each and every needle until all were broken or blunted. There's wishing for you! And what do you think happened? That evening both of them had,

> Upon his heels a calloused skin;
> A painful tumour on his chin;
> A nasty cough his lungs within;
> Catarrh producing wheezings thin;
> A bum-sore to a boil akin,

and not the devil of a crust to pick his teeth with.

Wish for the Mean and it will come to you, all the more so if you then duly work away and toil.

'Yes, indeed,' you say, 'but God could have just as easily given me seventy-eight thousand crowns as the thirteenth part of a halfpenny. He's almighty. A million in gold is as little to him as a silver penny.'

Hey, hey, hey! And who taught you poor wretches to speak and discourse about the power and predestination of God? Be quiet: *st, st, st.* Humble yourselves before his sacred face and acknowledge your imperfections.[7]

The Genoese do not act thus each morning when (after having, discussed, schemed, and decided in their counting-houses and cabinets from whom and from what kind of folk they will be able to squeeze out money, and who shall be diddled, swindled, cheated and duped by their cunning) go out into the piazza and greet each other with *Health and wealth, Signor.* They're not satisfied with health: they want gold crowns as well, indeed the gains of the Guadagni!

From which it results that they often obtain neither.

Well now: in good health, cough a good cough; have three drinks; merrily shake your ears, and then, you shall hear tell wondrous things about our good and noble Pantagruel.

---

7.   Rabelais, like theologians everywhere who talk of the predestination of the Elect, sets a limit to the discussion by echoing Romans 9:20, 'Nay but, O man, who art thou that repliest against God.'

   The sounds '*st, st, st* ' commanding silence are taken from Terence and Cicero, as is stated in the *Briefve Déclaration* (*Brief Declaration*) appended to many copies of the *Fourth Book*. It is by no means certain that it is the work of Rabelais.

How Pantagruel put to sea to visit the oracle
of the Dive Bacbuc

CHAPTER I

[The 1548 Fourth Book does not include Eusthenes in the list of Pantagruel's followers. But it does include Ponocrates, who is omitted here in error.

In '48 the 'Dive Bouteille' (the Holy Bottle) is for the first time called 'Bacbuc', a Hebrew word taken to represent the sound of liquids being outpoured. In '48 Thalamege was called Thelamane.

The service marking the sailing is Protestant in tone and content. (The 1548 text adds the word 'common' before 'the prayer that is said'.) The Psalm which is sung is number 114, 'When Israel came out of Egypt', in the French metrical version of Clément Marot, adopted by the Eglise Réformée. That Psalm is indeed appropriate to navigation. It was also taken as a paean celebrating the freedom of the true Church from its 'Babylonian captivity' under Rome. There is no Mass, no priestly blessings as (for example) the future Invincible Armada will have. After the Cardinal de Châtillon had fled to England, he granted licences (letters of marque) to Protestant corsairs, whose religious observances were doubtless much like Pantagruel's.

The route to be followed by the ships is not clear and raises controversy. The heroes are going to sail westward and so presumably will find and follow the then topical Northwest Passage. In which case it might seem that 'larboard' and 'starboard' should here be reversed. But 'elevation' (in French and in English) once meant not only the elevation of a star but the latitude from which its reading was taken. Our heroes could be sailing with the latitude-line on one side on the way out, keeping it to the other side on the way back. But it was then thought that the Northwest Passage was part of a continuous strait running round the whole of the North Pole.]

In the month of June, on the day of the Vestalia – the very day that Brutus conquered Spain and subdued the Spaniards, and when greedy Crassus was overcome and defeated by the Parthians – Pantagruel received his congee from his good father

Gargantua who [, following the laudable practice amongst the saintly Christians of the early Church,] was earnestly praying for the success of the voyage of his son. Pantagruel then boarded his ship in the port of Thalasse, accompanied by Panurge, Frère Jean des Entommeures, Epistemon, Gymnaste, Eusthenes, Rhizotome, Carpalim and others of his long-serving courtiers and members of his household, together with Xenomanes, the great traveller and Navigator across Perilous Ways, all of whom had arrived a few days beforehand at the summons of Panurge. [Xenomanes had, for certain good reasons, left behind with Gargantua a copy of his great *Map of the Seas of the World* indicating the course they would maintain to visit the oracle of Bacbuc, the Dive Bouteille.]

The number of ships is such as I expounded in the *Third Book*, [under the escort of triremes, swift, slim row-barges, galleons and Liburnian ships-of-war in equal number,] all well equipped, well caulked, and well provisioned with an abundance of *pantagruelion*.

The muster of all the officers, interpreters, pilots, [captains,] sailors, ordinary seamen and ship's mates was held aboard the *Thalamege*. That was the name of Pantagruel's great flag-ship; as an ensign it had on its poop a large and capacious bottle, half of smoothly polished silver, half of gold with flesh-pink enamelling. From which it was easy to deduce that white and claret were the colours of the noble navigators,[8] and that they were sailing to have the word of the Dive Bouteille.

On the poop of the second ship was raised aloft an antiquarian lantern, industriously crafted from [alabaster and] translucent mica, denoting that they would sail via Lanternland.

For their devices:

– the third ship had a deep and beautiful goblet made of porcelain;

– the fourth, a golden bowl with two handles, as though it was an urn from Classical antiquity;

– the fifth, a magnificent vase of grained jasper;

8.   '48: . . . colours *and ensign* of the noble navigators, . . .

– the sixth, a monkish tankard made of an alloy of four metals;

– the seventh, a funnel of ebony richly embossed with gold, enhanced by gilt and silver incrustations;

– the eighth, a most precious, ivy-wood goblet, with beaten gold and damascene inlays;

– the ninth, a carafe of fine gold purified in the fire;

– the tenth, a cup of sweet-smelling *agalloch* (which you know as aloes-wood) interlaced with Cypriot gold decorated in the Persian style;

– the eleventh, a golden grape-hod with mosaic-work;

– the twelfth, a matt-gold barrel covered with a vignette formed of large Indian pearls[9] set out as in topiary-work.

And so there was nobody, however gloomy, worried, depressed or melancholic (not even Heraclitus the Sniveller had he been there) who did not burst out into fresh joy and good-humoured smiles on seeing that noble convoy of ships and their devices; nobody who did not say that those voyagers were all stout men and good drinkers; nobody who did not confidently anticipate that their voyage there and back would be achieved in joy and perfect health.

Everyone assembled therefore on the *Thalamege*, where Pantagruel gave them a short and devout exhortation entirely buttressed by reflections on the theme of navigation drawn from Holy Writ. When that was done, prayer to God was said loud and clear. It was heard and understood by all the citizens and burghers of Thalasse who had flocked to the harbour-breakwater to witness the embarkation.

After prayer, there was tunefully sung the Psalm of David [the Godly king] which begins, *When Israel came out of Egypt*. Once the Psalm was finished, trestle-tables were set up on the flush-deck and the food promptly brought in.

The inhabitants of Thalasse, who had also joined in singing that Psalm, had caused food and wine to be carried in from their houses. Everyone drank to them: they drank to everyone.

9.   '48: . . . of *little* Indian pearls . . .

That explained why not one of the ship's company ever got sea-sick during the journey or suffered from troubled heads or stomachs. They would never have avoided those ailments so conveniently by drinking salt-water for a few days beforehand (either pure or mixed with wine), by eating the pulp of quinces, lemon-rind or the juice of bitter-sweet pomegranates, by following some long-drawn-out diet, by covering their stomachs with paper, or by doing any of those things which stupid physicians prescribe for such as put to sea.

After drinking toast after toast, every man returned to his ship; in due time, they spread their sails to an east – 'Greek' – wind, in accordance with which their principal navigator, Jamet Brayer, had plotted their course and set the needles of all their compasses. For, seeing that the oracle of the Dive Bacbuc lies in Upper India, hard by Cathay, his advice and that of Xenomanes was not to follow the usual route of the Portuguese who, by crossing the Torrid Zone, rounding the Cape of Good Hope at the tip of Africa beyond the equatorial line and losing all sight and guidance of the Pole Star, make an enormous journey of it, but rather to stick as close as possible to the same parallel as India and sail westward round the pole so that, curving along beneath the North Star, they would keep it at the same elevation as it has at the port of Les Sables-d'Olonne (drawing no nearer for fear of entering the Sea of Ice and being trapped), following that regular curve along the same parallel so that when sailing eastwards they would keep it to starboard, having had it to larboard on their departure.

That proved incredibly advantageous to them, for without shipwreck, without danger, without the loss of a single man and in great serenity, [except for one day near the Isle of the Macraeons,] they made in less than four months the journey to Upper India which the Portuguese could hardly have completed in three years after a thousand hardships and dangers without number. And I am persuaded, saving better judgement, that such a route was accidentally fallen upon by those Indians who sailed to Germany and were honourably treated by the king of the Swabians when Quintus Metellus Celer was pro-consul in

Gaul, as described by Cornelius Nepos [and Pomponius Mela]
followed by Pliny.[10]

How Pantagruel purchased several objects in
the Isle of Medamothi

CHAPTER 2

*[After the first sentence, which is in the '48 text, all the rest is added
in '52 up to the beginning of Chapter 5.*

*Medamothi ('Nowhere' in Greek) is perhaps a fleeting glance
towards another 'Nowhere', More's Utopia. All is Classical: the king's
name, Philophanes, may mean 'fond of appearances' or 'manifes-
tations' or 'revelations'. (The Brief Declaration makes it mean 'fond
of seeing' or of 'being seen', which seems weak.) 'Philotheamon' does
mean 'fond of seeing'. The land of Engys is the land of Near-by.*

*Behind the comic notion of the heroes' buying portraits of the Ideas
of Plato and the atoms of Epicurus lies a hint of the importance that
the 'Ideas' are to play in this Fourth Book. The word Idea (normally
with a capital I) appears in both comic and serious contexts and is
always worth notice when it appears.*

*The dread tale of Procne and Tereus is told by Ovid, Metamor-
phoses, 6, 412ff.*

The 'tarand' of Antiquity was perhaps a kind of reindeer.

*There are echoes of an adage of Erasmus: I, IV, XVIII, 'By oars
and by sails'.]*

On that day and the two following no new land hove into sight
nor indeed anything new, since they had already ploughed those
seas before. On the fourth day they descried an island called
Medamothi, pleasing and fair to the eye because of its many
lighthouses and high marble towers by which it was beautified

10. The writings of Antiquity were scoured for knowledge which might be
of help to sixteenth-century navigators. The lost account of Cornelius
Nepos is known from Pliny, *Natural History*, 2, 67, and Pomponius
Mela, *Cosmographia*, 3, 5, 45; it considers these 'Indians' in the context
of a supposedly continuous Northern Sea circling the North Pole.

all round its circumference (which was no less great than that of Canada). On Pantagruel's asking who ruled over it, he heard that it was King Philomanes, then away for the marriage of his brother Philotheamon to the Infanta of the kingdom of Engys. He thereupon clambered down on to the harbour and, whilst the crews of the boats took on water, contemplated the great variety of pictures, tapestries, animals, fish, birds and other exotic foreign merchandise on sale in the street running along the harbour-breakwater and in the warehouses of the port, for it was the third day of the great local Festival with its fair which, every year, brought together all the richest and most famous merchants of Africa and Asia.

From their wares Frère Jean bought two of the rare and precious pictures, in one of which was realistically painted the sad face of an appellant, and the other was the portrait of a valet seeking an employer and showing all the desired qualities, gestures, bearing, mien, carriage, expression and emotions. It was conceived and executed by Charles Charmois, painter to the Great King.[11]

Frère Jean paid for them with the coin of monkey-tricks.

Panurge bought a large picture transposing in paint the theme long ago worked by Philomela with her needle to show and reveal to her sister Procne how her brother-in-law Tereus had raped her as a virgin and cut out her tongue so that she could never reveal such a crime. I swear to you by the handle of this fellow's phallus that it was a daring and wonderful painting. Do not imagine, I beg you, that it portrayed a man covering a young woman. That would be too stupid and gross. The painting was very different and easier to understand. You can see it in Thélème on the left-hand side as you go into the tall gallery.

Epistemon bought another picture on which the *Ideas* of Plato and the *atoms* of Epicurus were painted from life.

Rhizotome bought another on which Echo was drawn from nature. Pantagruel bought through Gymnaste the life and deeds

11. The Great King's name, in French *Mégiste*, is the Greek *Megistos* (Great) not the Latino-Greek *Megiste*, a name for a slave. Charles Charmois or Carmois was a painter in the royal service.

of Achilles told in seventy-eight richly worked tapestries, each measuring some sixteen feet long and some twelve feet wide, all of Phrygian silk embroidered with gold and silver thread. The series began with the wedding of Peleus and Thetis, continuing with the birth of Achilles, his youth as described by Statius Papinius, his deeds and feats-of-arms celebrated by Homer, his death and obsequies described by Ovid and Quintus Calaber, and ending with the apparition of his ghost and the sacrificing of Polyxena described by Euripides.

He also bought three handsome young unicorns, one male with a coat the colour of burnt chestnut and two females of dapple-grey, together with a tarand which was sold to him by a Scythian from the country of the Gelones.

The tarand is an animal as large as a young bull, bearing a head like a stag's but a trifle larger, with branched horns remarkably wide; it has forked hooves and long hair like a great bear's; its hide is slightly less hard than body-armour. The man from Gelonia said few were ever sighted anywhere in Scythia since it changes its colour according to the various places in which it lives and feeds. It adopts the colour of the grasses, trees, bushes, flowers, background, pastures, rocks and, in general, of anything it approaches. It shares that quality with the cuttle-fish (that is, the polyp), the thos and the lycaon of India, as well as with the chameleon, which is a sort of lizard so extraordinary that Democritus devoted one whole book to its figuration and anatomy as well as to its magic powers and properties. And yet I have witnessed it changing hue not so much at the approach of coloured objects as of itself, depending on the fears and emotions it experienced: as when I most certainly saw it turn green on green matting, yet after staying there for some time it successively turned yellow, blue, brown and violet just as you can see the crests of turkey-cocks change colour with their feelings.

What we found most remarkable in that tarand is not only that its face and hide take on the colour of neighbouring things, but so do all its hairs. When close to Panurge in his bureau-cloth toga its hair turned russet; close to Pantagruel in his scarlet mantle, its hair and its hide reddened; close to the navigator, dressed in the fashion of the Anubis in Egypt, its hide appeared entirely white. (Those last two colours are denied to the chameleon.) When the tarand reverts to its natural state, free from all fear and emotion, its hair is such as you find on donkeys in Meung.

How Pantagruel received a letter from Gargantua his father; and of a curious way of obtaining news very quickly from distant lands afar

CHAPTER 3

[Homing-pigeons were all but unknown. Rabelais seems to have learnt of them recently and wrote favourably of them in his Sciomachie *of 1549 (his account of a mock naval engagement arranged by Cardinal Jean Du Bellay to celebrate the birth of the short-lived Louis of Orleans, the son of Henri II). Whereas others judged miraculous, or almost miraculous, the speed with which vital news reached (say) Roman bankers, Rabelais opted for unmysterious and unmiraculous explanations based on the 'gozal', the homing-pigeon recently reintroduced into Europe from Egypt.*

Gargantua cites a saying attributed to Hesiod by Erasmus (Adages, I, II, XXXIX, 'The beginning is half of the whole').]

While Pantagruel was engaged in buying those animals, there was heard a ten-gun salute from basilisks and falconets in the harbour together with loud happy hurrahs from all the ships. Pantagruel looked towards the harbour and saw that it was one of his father Gargantua's swift cutters, named the *Chélidoine* after the Corinthian brass statue of a sea-swallow raised on the poop.

A sea-swallow is a fish as big as dace in the river Loire, all flesh and no scales, with cartilaginous wings (like those of bats), long and wide, by means of which I have often seen it glide some six feet above water further than an arrow flies. In Marseilles they call it the *lendole*. And indeed that vessel was as light as a sea-swallow, so that it seemed to skim over the sea rather than sail upon it.

On board was Malicorne, Gargantua's esquire-trenchant, despatched expressly by him to learn of the condition and circumstances of his good son Pantagruel and to bring him letters of credit. Pantagruel, after a brief embrace and a graciously doffed bonnet, asked – before opening the letter or addressing any other words to Malicorne – 'Have you brought with you the *gozal*, that messenger from the skies?' – 'Yes,' he replied, 'it is kept hooded inside this pannier.'

It was a pigeon taken from Gargantua's dovecot, just hatching its young at the very instant that the swift cutter was about to leave. If ill fortune had befallen Pantagruel, black rings would have been attached to its feet, but since all had turned out well for him and prosperously, once its hood was removed he attached a little band of white taffeta to its leg and, brooking no further delay, set it completely free. It at once took to the wing, slicing through the air at an incredible speed, since, as you know, there is no flight like that of a pigeon's when it has eggs or young, because of the stubborn concern to conserve and preserve its brood instilled into it by Nature; and so it was that in less than two hours it flew back over that long distance which the swift cutter had covered in three days and three nights working extremely hard and using oar and sail with a steady wind astern.

It was spotted entering the dovecot to the very nest of its young. Noble Gargantua then learnt that it bore the little white band and continued in joy and confidence because of the good start his son had made.

Such was the practice of noble Gargantua and Pantagruel whenever they wanted to have news quickly of something eagerly coveted and intensely desired, such as the outcome of a battle on land or sea, the storming or the defending of some fortress, the settling of some vital quarrel, the happy or unhappy delivery of a queen or some great lady, the death or cure of sick friends or allies, and so on. They would take the *gozal* and have it borne from hand to hand, from post to post, to the places from which they wanted news. The *gozal* bore a black or a white band depending on events and outcomes and, once it returned, freed them from anxiety, flying a greater distance in one hour than a succession of thirty post-riders could cover in a typical day. That really is to gain and save time! And you should accept as quite credible that you could find eggs or chicks in the dovecots of their estates during all the months and seasons of the year, and plenty of pigeons. That is something easy to arrange in a household by using rock-salt and the 'sacred boughs' of verbena. Having released the *gozal*, Pantagruel read his father's missive, the contents of which were as follows:

My Dearest Son:

The affection which a father naturally bears for his beloved son is in my case so greatly increased by respect and reverence for the gifts of grace personally bestowed on you through your election by God, that since you have set out no other thought has diverted me, leaving me this one and anxious fear: that your sailing might be accompanied by some mishap or trouble, since, as you know, good and pure love is ever annexed to apprehension. And since (according to the saying of Hesiod) *half of any undertaking is beginning it*, and since (according to the common saying) *Well-shaped loaves start off in the oven*, I (to void my mind of such anxiety have expressly despatched Malicorne in order that I may be assured of your circumstances during these first days of your voyage; for if they are prosperous and such as I hope, it will be easy for me to foresee, foretell and judge the rest.

I have acquired some amusing books which will be given to you by the present bearer. You will read them when you need some relaxation from your serious studies. The same bearer will give you all the news of this Court.

The peace of the Lord be with you. Greet Panurge, Frère Jean, Epistemon, Xenomanes, Gymnaste and the other good friends of mine in your household.

From your family home, this thirteenth of June;

Your loving father,
GARGANTUA.

How Pantagruel writes a letter to Gargantua
his father and sends him several things,
rare and beautiful

CHAPTER 4

[A perfect son replies to his good father. The exemplum *of Augustus Caesar and Furnius was well known from the treatise of Seneca* On Benefits, *1, 25, 1. Rabelais is further indebted to* On Benefits, *2, 2, 31ff. for the three parts of a beneficent action.*

The exemplum *of Furnius (but not the development of it here) is listed by Erasmus'* Apophthegms, VIII, *penultimate series of numbers, 42.*

Pantagruel's hyperbole leads him to compare himself to one of the 'unprofitable servants' of Luke 17:10, who, having done all that they were told to do, deserve no gratitude for simply obeying orders.]

After reading that letter, Pantagruel discussed several matters with Malicorne, the esquire, and was so long with him that Panurge broke across and said, 'When are you going to have a drink then? And when are we going to have a drink? And when is Monsieur the Esquire going to have a drink? Haven't you preached enough to deserve a drink?'

'Well said,' replied Pantagruel. 'Have them prepare a post-sermon bite for us in that nearby inn, at the sign of the *Satyr on Horseback*.'

Meanwhile he wrote a letter to Gargantua, as follows, to be despatched with the esquire:

Father most debonair:
From all unforeseen and surprising happenings in this transitory life our minds and spiritual faculties suffer disturbances more immense and uncontrollable (indeed frequently causing the soul to be dislodged from the body, even though such sudden news were pleasing and desired) than if they had been anticipated and foreseen beforehand: and therefore the unexpected arrival of your esquire,

Malicorne, greatly moved and thrilled me, for I never hoped to see any of your household nor to have any news of you before the end of our voyage; and I was ready to delight quietly in the remembrance of your august Majesty which is written, or rather chiselled and engraved, on the posterior ventricle of my brain and often vividly re-presented to me in your Majesty's true and natural form.

But since you have anticipated me with the benefit of your gracious letter and have, by the testimony of your esquire, enlivened my spirits with the news of your well-being and good health as well as that of all your Royal household, I now indeed must (as I spontaneously do) first praise our blessèd Servator: may He in his divine goodness keep you in a long enjoyment of perfect health: secondly, forever thank you for that ardent and long-established love which you bear towards me, your most-humble son and unprofitable servant.

Long ago a Roman called Furnius received from Caesar Augustus a grace and pardon for his father who had joined the faction of Mark-Anthony; and Furnius said to him, 'In doing me that favour today you have reduced me to such embarrassment that, whether I live or die, I must needs appear ungrateful on account of the total inadequacy of my gratitude.' Thus could I say today that your exceeding fatherly love for me has made me afraid that I must live and die an ingrate, unless, that is, I am relieved of such an incrimination by a judgement of the Stoics, who maintained there to be three parts in a beneficent action: the part of the giver; the part of the receiver; and, third, the part of the recompenser; and that the receiver very well recompenses the giver when he gratefully accepts the beneficence and retains it in perpetual memory; as, on the contrary, the receiver is the most ungrateful man in the world who would slight and forget the beneficence.

And so, bearing the weight of an infinity of obligations, all procreated by your immense benignity, and being powerless to make the smallest recompense, I shall at least save myself from calumny in that the memory of it will never be expunged from my mind, and my tongue shall never cease to confess and proclaim that to utter condign thanks to you surpasses my faculties and my powers.

I have confidence moreover in the mercy and help of Our Lord: the end of our peregrination will correspond to the beginning, and the whole will be done in joy and perfect health. I shall not fail to record in diaries and log-books the whole course of our voyage in order that, on our return, you may read a true account of it.

I have discovered here a tarand from Scythia, a beast which is strange and wonderful because it changes the colour of its hair and hide according to the different things it approaches. You will find it interesting: it is as easy as a lamb to handle and feed. I also send you three young unicorns which are more domesticated and tractable than little kittens. I have conferred with the esquire and told him how to treat them. They cannot eat anything off the ground, since the long horn on their foreheads gets in their way. They are obliged to seek their food from fruit-trees, from adapted mangers or else from your hand if you proffer them grasses, blades of corn, apples, pears, barley, white-wheat, in short all kinds of fruits and vegetables. It amazes me how our ancient authors call them ferocious, savage and dangerous, and state that they are never spotted alive. You might like, if it seems fit, to make proof of the contrary: you will find that – provided they are not spitefully provoked – there exists in them the greatest mildness in the world.

I similarly send you the life and deeds of Achilles in beautiful and ingenious tapestry-work, whilst assuring you that I shall bring you specimens of all the new animals, plants, birds and stones that we can find and procure during the whole of our voyage – God being my helper, whom I pray to keep you in His holy grace.

From Medamothi, this eighteenth day of June.

Panurge, Frère Jean, Epistemon, Xenomanes, Gymnaste,

Eusthenes, Rhizotome and Carpalim dutifully kiss your hand and return your greetings increased a hundredfold.

Your humble son and servant.
PANTAGRUEL.

While Pantagruel was writing the above letter, Malicorne was feasted, made welcome and firmly hugged by everyone. God knows how well it all went and how compliments were flying about from every side.

Once Pantagruel had finished his letter he feasted with the esquire, bestowing on him a heavy gold chain weighing as much as eight hundred crowns; at every seventh link of it there were set diamonds, rubies, emeralds, turquoises and pearls in succession.

He ordered five hundred Sun-crowns to be given to each of his seamen. To his father Gargantua he sent the tarand (covered with a caparison of satin with gold brocade) as well as the tapestries containing the life and deeds of Achilles and the three unicorns with caparisons of gilded frieze-cloth.

And then they sailed away from Medamothi, Malicorne to return to Gargantua, and Pantagruel to continue his voyage.

On the high seas Pantagruel had Epistemon read to them from the books the Esquire had brought. He found them amusing and enjoyable so I shall, if you really press me, most willingly make you transcripts of them.

How Pantagruel met a ship of voyagers returning from Land of the Lanterns

CHAPTER 5

[Chapter 2 of '48 is taken up here, but with '52 reading the 'fourth' (not 'fifth') day.

The Lanterns who dwell on this island are all female.

In Renaissance French lanterne *means 'lantern' but also 'nonsense' and the female sexual organs.* Lanterner *can similarly mean 'to talk*

*nonsense' or 'to lecher' in a variety of ways depending upon contexts,
and many puns turn about those overlapping senses.*

The merchant's red-coral stump is his penis.]

On the fifth day we were already beginning to work our way
gradually around the Pole while moving further away from the
Equator when we descried a merchantman in full sail off our
port bow. There was not a little joy both on our part and on
the merchants': on our part, from hearing news of the sea; on
their part, from hearing news of *Terra-firma*. Drawing alongside, we learnt that they were Frenchmen from Saintonge.
When talking and deliberating with them, Pantagruel gathered that they were on the way from Lanternland, at which he
felt a fresh access of joy as did all the rest of the company,
especially when, after inquiring of the condition of that country
and of the mores of the Lanternese people, we were advised
that a chapter-general of the Lanterns had been convoked for
the end of June, and that if we made harbour there in time
(as it was easy to do) we should see a fair, honourable and
happy company of Lanterns, and that great preparations were
being made as though they were going to thoroughly lantern
things up!

[We were also told that if we sailed via the great kingdom of
Gebarim we would be greeted and honoured by King Ohabe,
the ruler of that land, who, together with all of his subjects,
speaks the French of Touraine.][12]

While we were hearing that news, Panurge got into a wrangle
with a merchant from Taillebourg called Dindenault. The cause
was as follows. This Dindenault,[13] seeing Panurge without his
codpiece and with his glasses stuck in his bonnet, said to his
companion, 'Look: there's a freshly minted cuckold!'

---

12. The '52 text is much expanded here from 'chapter general of the Lanterns'
     to 'Touraine'. Many further changes are made to the text of 1548, a
     selection of which are listed in the notes below. In this addition of '52,
     the Gebarim (Cocks) whose king is called Ohabe (Friend) have Hebrew
     names but may allude to the French and their king, or to friends in
     Rabelais' own province of Touraine.

13. '48: . . . This *boastful* Dindenault . . .

Panurge was hearing things more distinctly than usual because of his glasses and overheard what was being said, so he demanded of the merchant, 'How the devil could I be cuckolded when I'm not even married – as you are, judging by your ugly conk?'

'Yes I am, indeed,' replied the merchant, 'and would not have it otherwise for all the goggles in Europe. Nor for all the spectacles in Africa.[14] Because I have one of the most beautiful, most comely, most honourable and most proper wives[15] in all the land of Saintonge; no offence to the others. As a present for her I'm bringing home from my voyage an eleven-inch red-coral stump. What's that got to do with you? Why are you meddling in such matters? Who are you? Where do you come from, you goggle-man of Antichrist! Answer me, if you belong to God!'

'What I want to know is this,' said Panurge: 'if by the consent and connivance of all the elements I had jiggedy-joggedy-tarty-fartied that O so beautiful, O so comely, O so honourable and O so proper wife of yours in such a manner that the erect god of the gardens Priapus (who dwells herein in freedom, quite exempt from any subjection to codpieces) were, through the malign influence of the stars, to remain eternally stuck inside her so that it could never come out but remain there for ever unless you yourself were to tug it out with your teeth, would you do it?[16] Would you leave it there for all eternity or would you tug it out with those splendid teeth of yours? Answer me, you ram-beguiler of Mahomet,[17] since you're of the devils' tribe.'

'I,' said the merchant, 'would give you a slash from my sword on your bespectacled ear and slaughter you like a ram!'

So saying, he went to unsheathe his sword, but it was stuck in its scabbard. (As you know all arms and armour quickly

14. '48: . . . Not for all the *codpieces of Asia and* Africa . . .
15. '48: . . . most *honourable* wives . . .
16. '48: . . . if, by the consent of all the elements, I had *swived that* wife of yours . . . to remain stuck inside her so that it could never come out but remain there *sempiternally* unless you yourself . . .
17. '48: . . . *O ye codpiece-monger* of Mahomet . . .

grow rusty at sea on account of the excessive and nitrous humidity.)

Panurge scuttled over to Pantagruel for help. Frère Jean put his hand to his newly whetted short-sword[18] and would have savagely killed the merchant were it not that the ship's master, as well as some other passengers, begged Pantagruel that no offence be committed aboard his vessel.

And so Panurge and the merchant shook hands and gladly drank a toast to each other as a token of perfect reconciliation.

How, once the wrangle was settled, Panurge haggles with Dindenault over one of his sheep

CHAPTER 6

['48: . . . How Panurge drowned the sheep and the merchant who was bringing them. Chapter 3.

In '48 Panurge confides his plot secretly to Pantagruel and Frère Jean, a notion incompatible with the developed Pantagruel of the 1552 Fourth Book, so he is replaced here from the outset by Epistemon.

Once more Rabelais turns part of his chapter into a farce, set out as for the trestles.]

Once the wrangle was peacefully settled, Panurge said secretly to Epistemon and Frère Jean, 'Draw away from here a little and merrily pass your time, enjoying what you shall see: a good bit of theatre, if the scenery-cords don't snap. He then turned towards the merchant and at once drank a full goblet of Lanternese wine to him. The merchant then pledged him merrily and courteously. That done, Panurge urgently begged him graciously to sell him one of his sheep.

The merchant replied:

'Alas, alas, friend of mine, and neighbour of ours, how well you know how to poke fun at poor wretches! A nice customer you are, truly! O what a bold buyer of sheep! Golly, you look

18. '48: . . . Jean put his hand *to his short-sword* and would have . . .

like a cutter of purses not a buyer of sheep. By Sain-N'colas, old chap! No fun carrying a full purse near you in the Triperies when the thaw sets in! Ho, ho! You'd take anyone in, you would, provided he didn't know you already! Just look at him, good folks. Cor! preening himself like an Historiographer Royal!'

'Patience,' murmured Panurge. 'But while on the subject do, of your especial grace, sell me one of your sheep. How much?'

'What can you mean, friend of mine and neighbour of ours?' the merchant replied. 'They're long-haired sheep as on the coins. From the likes of them Jason derived his Golden Fleece, and the House of Burgundy their Order of Chivalry. These are Oriental sheep, tall-timbered and highly fattened.'

'Maybe so,' said Panurge, 'but of your grace do sell me but one – I plead for no more – and I shall pay for it in Occidental coins, squat-timbered and low-fattened.'

['Neighbour of ours, friend of mine,' the merchant replied, 'listen a bit with your other ear!']

PAN: I am yours to command.
MERCH: You're on your way to Lanternland?
PAN: Indeed.
MERCH: To see the world?
PAN: Indeed.
MERCH: Right merrily?
PAN: Indeed.
MERCH: Your name, I believe, is Robin Muttonhead!
PAN: It pleases you to say so.
MERCH: Take no offence!
PAN: None taken.
MERCH: You are, I believe, the king's fool.
PAN: Indeed.
MERCH: Ha! ha! Let's shake on it: you're off to see the world; you're the king's fool; and you're called Robin Muttonhead! See that mutton over there? It's called Robin, just like you. Robin, Robin, Robin. *Baa, baa, baa, baa!* What a lovely voice!
PAN: Very lovely. And tuneful.

MERCH: Let there be a pact between me and you, our neighbour
and friend. You – Robin Muttonhead – will stand on this
pan of my scales and Robin, my own mutton, in the other.
And I wager one hundred Arcachon oysters that in weight,
worth and quality it'll tip you up sharp and high, just as
you'll be strung up and hanged one of these days!

'Patience,' said Panurge. 'But you would do much for me and
for your progeny if you were to agree to sell me that one, or
else some other one lodged lower down in your choir-stalls. I
beg you to do so, my Sire and Lord.']

'Friend of ours,' replied the merchant, 'neighbour of mine,
fine cloth of Rouen will be made from the fleece of those sheep:
compared with their fleece, skeins of Leicester wool are nothing
but wadding. Fine morocco leather will be made from their
hides and be passed off as Turkish morocco, Montélimart
morocco or – at the very worst – Spanish morocco. From their
guts will be made strings for fiddles and harps, strings that will
sell as dear as any from Munich [or Aquila]. What do you think
of that?'

'If it please you to sell me one,' said Panurge, 'I shall kiss the
bolt on your front door. Here's ready money. How much?'

While he said that, he was displaying his purse full of newly
minted Henricus-coins.

Wrangling between Panurge and
Dindenault: continued

CHAPTER 7

[This chapter-division was added in '52.

*It was once widely believed that the holy relic of Charrou in Vienne
(kept there in the Abbey) was a clipping of the foreskin of Christ. The
translation here reflects that fact.]*

'Friend of mine,' said the merchant, 'and neighbour of ours,
here is meat fit but for kings and princes. The flesh is so tender,

so flavourful and so toothsome that it is aromatic balm. I am
bringing them from a land wherein the pigs, God save us, feed
but on plums, and the sows [when they lie in (saving the honour
of all the company)] only on orange blossom.'

'Yet sell me one of them,' said Panurge, 'and I will royally
pay for it, foot-soldier's honour! How much?'

'Friend of ours,' said the merchant, 'and neighbour of mine;
these are sheep descended from the same race as the ram which
bore Phryxus and Helle over that sea called the Hellespont.'

['A plague on you,' said Panurge, 'you must be either a don
or an undergraduate!'

'Ita (meaning cabbage) and vere (meaning leeks)'[19] replied
the merchant. But brr, brrr, brrrr, brrrrr; ho! Robin! brr,
brrrrrrr. You can't understand that language! Incidentally,]
throughout the fields where those sheep have piddled, the corn
flourishes as though God himself had piddled there. No need
of further marl nor muck. More! From their urine the alchemists
make the best saltpetre in the world. With their droppings – do
excuse me – the physicians of our land cure seventy-eight kinds
of illnesses, the least of which is the malady of Saint Dropsy of
Saintes, from which God preserve and keep us! What do you
make of that, neighbour of ours and friend of mine? And they
cost me a goodly sum.'

['They can cost what you like,' replied Panurge. 'Sell me one
and I'll pay a good price.'

'Friend of ours,' said the merchant, 'and neighbour of mine,
just reflect for a while on the marvels of Nature which dwell
within these beasts which you behold: why even in a member
which you would judge to be of no use! Take those horns there
and pound them a while with an iron pestle (or poker: it's all
the same to me). Then sow them wherever you will in full sun,
watering them often. After a few months you will find asparagus
shoots springing up, the best in the world: and I would not

19. The joke on 'ita' and 'vere', added in 1552, turns on the fact that the
    Latin ita (thus) can be translated by ce in standard French and chou in
    the Picard dialect. But to Parisian ears chou means cabbage. There is
    presumably some such undergraduate pun on the Latin vere (indeed), but
    it remains unexplained.

deign to except even those from Ravenna. Try and tell me that the horns of Messieurs the Cuckolds like you have virtues and miracle-working properties like that!'

'Patience,' said Panurge.

'I don't know whether you are a scholar,' said the merchant, 'but I've known many a scholar – I mean important ones – who were cuckolds. Yes indeed. By the way, if you were a scholar you'd know that there lies within the lowest limbs of these divine beasts – in their feet, that is, – bones, namely heels (the *astragali*, if you prefer): with them alone, or else with bones from no other beasts save the asses of India and the gazelles of Libya, they used in ancient times to play the royal game of *tali*, at which the Emperor Octavian won 50,000 crowns in a single evening. Cuckolds like you haven't a hope of winning that much!'

'Patience,' said Panurge. 'But let's get on with it!'

'And,' said the merchant, 'when shall I ever have sufficiently praised for you (friend of ours, and neighbour of mine) their inward parts, their shoulders, their thighs, their legs, their ribs, their breasts, their livers, their spleens, their tripes, their guts, their bladders (with which we play ball), their spare-ribs (from which in Pigmy-land they make little bows for shooting cherry-stones at cranes); their heads (from which, with a little sulphur added, men make a wonder-working concoction for loosening the bowels of hounds suffering from constipation).']

'Oh pooh, pooh,' said the ship's master to the merchant. 'Too much patter. Sell him one if you want to, and if you don't, stop stringing him along.'

'I do want to,' said the merchant, 'out of my love for you. But he shall pay three Tournois pounds for each one he selects.'

'That's a lot of money,' said Panurge. 'In our part of the world I'd get five or even six for the same number of pence. Reflect whether it mayn't be too much. You're not the first man I know who, wanting to get rich too quick and to reach the top, has tumbled backwards into poverty – even indeed breaking his neck.'

['Catch a strong quartan fever!' said the merchant, 'you stupid clodpole. By the holy foreskin at Charroux, the least of these sheep is worth four times more than the best of those which the Coraxians of Tuditania (a part of Spain) used to sell for one golden talent apiece.

'And what do you think a golden talent was worth, you overpaid ninny?'

'Revered Sir, I can see and tell that you are getting hot under your armour!' said Panurge. 'All right, then: take it. There's your money.']

Having paid the merchant, Panurge selected from the entire flock a lovely big sheep and dragged it away bleating and belling while the other sheep all bleated together, watching where their companion would be taken.

Meanwhile the merchant said to his mutton-mongers, 'Our client knew how to choose all right! He knows what he's about, the old lecher. Really – I mean, really and truly – I was saving that one for the Seigneur de Cancale, knowing his character as I do. For by nature he is merry and bright when he has a comely and becoming shoulder of mutton in his fist, holding it like a left-handed racket and fencing at it (God knows!) with a sharp carving knife.'

How Panurge drowned the merchant and his sheep in the sea

CHAPTER 8

[This chapter heading and division was added in '52.

A well-known comic tale masterly retold. The conte *owes much to Folengo's Macaronics. Aristotle's opinion that sheep are the silliest and most stupid of creatures was widely known through an adage of Erasmus: III, I, XCV, 'The manners of sheep'.*

After all the laughter, the '52 addition at the very end, with its citing of 'Vengeance is mine said the Lord', is another indication that Rabelais is now confronting the moral implications of the comedy of cruelty of which he was master. The text cited is from Deuteronomy 32:35, quoted more than once in the New Testament, including Romans 12:19.]

Suddenly (I don't know how: it all happened at once and I had no time to take it in) Panurge, without further ado, cast his sheep, bleating and belling, into the sea. All the other sheep, likewise bleating and belling with similar tones, started to cast themselves headlong into the sea one after another, all pressing to find out which could be the first to jump in after their companion.

It was impossible to stop them: as you know, the nature of sheep is always to follow their leader wherever it goes. [Moreover, Aristotle says (in *On the Nature of Animals*, Book 9) that it is the most silly and stupid creature in all the world.]

The merchant, quite distraught at seeing his sheep dying – drowning before his very eyes – strove with all his might to stop them and to hold them back. But it was in vain: they were all crowding together, leaping into the sea one after the other and drowning.

Finally he grabbed a big strong ram on the deck of the ship, intending to hold it back and consequently to save all the remainder, but that ram was so powerful that (in the same manner as the ram of one-eyed Polyphemus bore Ulysses and his companions out of the cavern) it dragged the merchant into the sea with it and drowned him.

The other shepherds and mutton-mongers followed suit, some grabbing sheep by their horns, others by their legs, others by their fleece. And all were likewise borne into the sea, where they miserably perished.

Panurge remained by the galley holding an oar in his hand, not to help those mutton-mongers, but to stop them from clambering back on to the ship and so saving themselves from going under; he was eloquently preaching to them as though he were some little Frère Olivier Maillart or a second Jean Bourgeois, expounding to them, with rhetorical commonplaces, the miseries of this world and the blessings and felicities of the life to come, insisting that the dead were happier than the quick in this vale of tears, and promising to erect a fair cenotaph for each of them, an honourable tomb on the highest peak of Mount Cenis: wishing them, nevertheless (in the event that they were not averse to living still amongst men and found it inappropriate to drown) good luck and an encounter with some whale or other which, following the example of Jonah, would, on the third day, cast them safe and sound upon some Tapestry-land. Once the ship was emptied of merchant and sheep, Panurge said, 'Does not one single muttonish soul remain? [Where are the muttons of Thibault Aignelet, and those of Reginald Baa-lamb which sleep while all the others graze?]

'Of that I know nothing. It's an old ruse of war. What do you think, Frère Jean?'

'You did very well,' replied Frère Jean. 'I found nothing to criticize except that it seems to me that, just as on the day of battle or assault in war, soldiers are promised double pay for that day because if they win the battle there is plenty to pay them with, and if they lose it, shameful would be to ask for it (as those lansquenets from Gruyère did after the battle of Cérisole) you ought to have postponed payment. The money would have stayed in your purse.'

'Oh sing a shitty-shanty for my money!' said Panurge. 'God almighty, I've had more than fifty-thousand francs worth of amusement. Let's draw away now: the wind is favourable.

'Listen to this, Frère Jean: never did any man do good to me without being recompensed, or at very least thanked. I'm no ingrate. Never was. Never will be. But never did a man do me wrong without undergoing penance for it, in this world or the next. I'm not that daft!'

['You,' said Frère Jean, 'are damning yourself like an aged devil. It is written, *Vengeance is mine*, etc. Breviary stuff!']

How Pantagruel arrived in the Isle of Ennasin, and of the curious kinships in that land

CHAPTER 9

[In '48 this was Chapter 4.

Ennasin means 'lacking nostrils'. The noses like aces of clubs may be an echo of descriptions of the Eskimos.

Much of the humour in this chapter (such as it is, for it has not well

withstood the passage of time) depends upon French and Latin plays
on words and proverbial expressions, most lending themselves to quite
obvious sexual innuendos: explanations of French and Latin words
are added within brackets and the translation given some latitude
when helpful.

In the first line Rabelais gives the Sou'-wester its Classical name of
'Garbin'.]

Zephyr, helped a little by Garbin, was bearing us steadily along
and we spent a day without sighting land. On the third day
after dawn, at the hour when the flies come out, there appeared
a triangular land, strongly resembling Sicily in shape and situation. It was called the Isle of Kinships. The men and women
resemble denizens of Poitou with their red-stained faces, except
that they all, man, woman and child, have noses shaped like an
ace of clubs. For which reason the ancient name of the Isle was
Ennasin. And as the local Podestat freely told us, they were all,
as they boasted, of one kith and kin.

'You fellows from the other world consider it wonderful that,
from a single Roman family – that is, the Fabii – on one single
day – the thirteenth of February – through one single gate – the
Carmentalia subsequently surnamed the Calamitous [formerly
sited at the foot of the Capitol, between the Tarpeian Rock and
the Tiber] – against certain foes of the Romans – the Etruscan
Veientes – there once issued three hundred and six warriors, all
kinsmen [, together with five thousand fighting-men, all vassals
of theirs; every man of whom was slain near the river Cremera,
which flows out of lake Bagano]. From our land here there
could issue forth in their need three hundred thousand men, all
kinsfolk, all of the same family.'

Their kith-and-kinship is of a most curious fashioning, for
whilst they are all related to each other and closely knit, no one
there is the father, mother, brother, sister, uncle, aunt, cousin,
nephew, son-in-law, daughter-in-law, godfather or godmother
of anyone else – save, it is true, for one noseless old man who,
as I saw, called a little girl of three or four Father, whilst the
little maid called him Daughter.

The kith-and-kinship amongst them was such that one man

called a woman My Flatfish, and she called him My Porpoise. 'Those two,' said Frère Jean, 'must reek of the tides when they rub their haunches together.'

One called out with a smile to an elegant maiden, 'Good day, My *Estrille*' ('My Currycomb'). And she greeted him back, 'Good morrow my *Fauveau*' ('My Dun Stallion'). – 'O-ho!' exclaimed Panurge, 'o-oh! o-oh! Come and see a Currycomb, a scythe and a veal-calf: *estrille* + *faux* + *veau* amounts to *étrille-fauveau*, doesn't it? This vain stallion with its black stripe must often get a good currying!'[20]

Another greeted his sweeting by saying, 'God be with you, my Bench.' She replied, 'And also with you, my Lawsuit! – 'By Saintrinian,' said Gymnaste, 'that Lawsuit must frequently get laid on that Bench!'

[One called another girl *Mon Ver* ('My worm') and she called him her Coquin (her 'scamp'). – 'There,' said Eusthenes, 'is a good case of *ver-coquin*' (sheep's stagger-worm).]

Another greeted a maiden from a family allied to his with 'Good-day, my Axe-head.' And she replied, 'Good-day my Helve' ('my *Manche*'). – 'Gosh,' exclaimed Carpalim, 'that axe-head's well helved. And how well that *manche* fits its axe-head! But may it not mean that *mancia* (handful of cash) that Roman courtesans ask for? Or perhaps a Grey-Friar with his long sleeves (*manches*)?'

Pressing ahead, I saw another, a bumpkin who greeted a family friend and called her 'My Mattress'. She called him her Coverlet. And indeed he did look coverletly lumpish.

One called another maid 'My Crumb', and she called him 'My Crust'. One called another his Shovel and she called him her Poker. One called another girl his Pumps, and she called him her Slip-ons. [One called another his Bootie, and she called him her Socks.] Another called another his Mittens, and she called him her Gloves.

20. An '*estrille* + *faux* + *veau*' literally a currycomb, a scythe and a veal-calf. Rabelais is alluding to a common rebus found also in the poet Clément Marot. *Estrille fauveau* is used both for currying a horse and for stroking or flattering someone (with perhaps an allusion to the proverbial saying, 'Curry a horse and it may bite you back').

One called another his Crackling: she called him her Bacon.
And their relationship was as close as rind to rasher. In similar
relationships, one called his maiden his Omelette and she called
him her Egg. And they were as closely allied as an egg to an
omelette.

So too another called his girl My Twig. And she called him
her Faggot. (I could never work out what their relationship,
kith or blood-links were in comparison with our own common
usage, save that they said she played twig to his faggot.)

Another greeted his by saying, 'Greetings, My Shell.' She
replied, 'Same to you, my Oyster.' ('That,' said Carpalim, 'really
does amount to an oyster-in-its-shell!')

Another similarly greeted his girl, saying, 'Live well, my Pod;'
she replied, 'A long life to you, my Pea.' ('That,' said Gymnaste,
'is a pea in a pod.')

[Another ugly great tramp, perched high atop his wooden
clogs, upon meeting a plump, fat, stumpy young wench, said
to her, 'Good-day my Top, my Spinning-top, my Humming-
top.' And she aggressively replied, 'Look out for yourself, my
Whip.' ('Blood of Saint Grey,' said Xenomanes. 'Is that whip
up to servicing that top?')

A doctoral don, neatly brushed and combed, after having
chatted a while with an aristocratic young lady, took leave of
her, saying, 'I am deeply grateful, Good Face.' – 'But,' she said,
'deeper thanks to you, Bad Hand.' – ('It is not an insignificant
matter,' said Pantagruel, 'to put on a good face when dealt a
bad hand.')

An apprentice woodman said to a young maiden as he passed
by, 'Oh, oh, oh! How long it is since I last saw you, my Bag!'
– 'I am pleased,' she said, 'to see you, my Pipe.' ('Couple them
together,' said Panurge, 'and blow down their bums and you'll
have bagpipes.')]

Another called his girl his Sow. She called him her Hay. And
it occurred to me that that sow would love to sport in that hay.

I saw a little hunch-backed gallant fairly near to us who
greeted a family friend saying, 'God be with you, my Hole;'
and she greeted him back, saying, 'May God guard my Peg.'
(Frère Jean said, 'She, I think, is all hole, and he's likewise all

peg. Now to find out whether it's a round peg filling a round hole!')

Another greeted his lady with, 'God be with you, my Moulting.' She replied, 'Good-day to you, my Gosling.' ('I believe,' said Ponocrates, 'that that gosling is frequently moulting.')

A merry chap chatting with a pretty young thing said, 'Now remember that, Quiet Fart.' – And she replied, 'That I will, my Big Ditto.' – 'Would you really say they were relatives?' asked Pantagruel of the Podestat. 'I think they must be enemies, for he called her a fart. In our part of the world you can offer no greater insult to a woman than to address her thus.'

'Good folk from that other world,' replied the Podestat, 'you have few folk more closely related than that big fart and that little one. For in an instant they both slipped invisibly out of the same hole.'

'So the Gallant Nor'easter had lanterned his mother,' said Panurge. 'What mother do you mean?' asked the Potestat. 'Such relationships belong to your world. They have no fathers or mothers. That's a matter for outlandish folk, for clodhoppers.'

That good fellow Pantagruel saw it all and quietly took it all in but at those words he nearly lost control.

So, having carefully studied the site of the island and the customs of the Ennasian people, we went into a tavern for a little refreshment. They were celebrating a wedding there in the local fashion and having no end of a time. In our presence they merrily married together a Pear – a very buxom woman so it seemed to us, though those who squeezed her found her a bit soft – and a young Cheese with reddish down on his cheeks. I had previously heard rumours of such things, and several similar marriages have been celebrated elsewhere. They still say in my back-of-the-woods that Pear and Cheese match well together!

In another room I saw that they were marrying an old Boot to a supple young Buskin; Pantagruel was told that the young Buskin was taking the old Boot to wife because she was a good bargain, in a good state and so delightfully ample that she could even serve as an angler's waders.

In another – lower – room I saw a young Dancing-Shoe

marry an elderly Slipper. And we were told that it was not for
any beauty or elegance she had but out of covetousness and
greed for the gold coins with which she was stuffed.

How Pantagruel landed on the Island of Cheli over which ruled the saintly King Panigon

CHAPTER 10

[Was originally Chapter 5.

*This island is a kind of Land of Cockaigne. Panigon derives his
name from the Italian figure Panicone, a great eater. Cheli is Hebrew
for peace.]*

The Garbin was blowing on our poop when, leaving behind
those nasty Kinshippers each with a nose like an ace of clubs,
we reached the high seas. Towards sundown we touched at the
island of Cheli: a spacious, fertile, rich and well-populated
island over which reigned the saintly King Panigon, who,
accompanied by his sons and the princes of his Court, had
processed towards the harbour so as to welcome Pantagruel
and escort him to his castle. The Queen made her appearance
above the tower gate accompanied by her daughter and the
ladies of the Court. It was Panigon's wish that she and all her
suite should kiss Pantagruel and his men: such was the courteous custom of that country.

Which was done, except in the case of Frère Jean, who had
stood back and drawn apart with the officials of the King.

Panigon pressed Pantagruel to stay on for that day and the
next.

Pantagruel grounded his refusal on the calmness of the
weather and on the favourable wind, which is more often
desired by seafarers than acquired: it must be exploited whenever it comes, for it does not always come when you want it to.

After such an appeal Panigon gave us his congee, but not
before each man had downed some twenty-five to thirty drinks.

Pantagruel, on returning to the harbour and not seeing Frère

Jean, asked where he was and why he was not with the rest of the company. Panurge had no idea how to excuse Frère Jean and was just expressing a desire to return to the castle to summon him when up he came running, full of joy and gaily shouted, 'Long live the noble Panigon! By the death of a Wooden Ox, he keeps an excellent kitchen! I've just come from there. They ladle it out! I was hoping to pad out the belly of my frock to the profit of my monastical and liturgical Use.'

'So my friend,' said Pantagruel, 'still haunting kitchens then!'

'Body of Chick!' replied Frère Jean, 'I know the customs and ceremonials of kitchens better than all that squitty-shittying about with women: *Magny, magna, squitty-shitty*: bow twice, do it again; arms round their necks then touch their guts: I kiss the hands of *Vuestra Merced*, of *Vostra Majestà*; Be you welcome, tiddly-pom.[21]

'*Bren* – that's *shit* in Rouen – all that mucking and piddling about! I don't say, mind you, that in my rough old way I would never stir up the dregs if some lady permitted me to slip in my nomination: but all that squittery of bowing and scraping bores me more than a double-fasting devil – I meant a devilish double-fast – on the subject of which Saint Benedick never lied.

['You're talking about kissing young ladies. By the holy and worthy frock that I bear, from that I forebear, fearing that there might happen to me what happened to the Seigneur de Guyecharais.'

'What was that!' asked Pantagruel. 'I know him. One of my best friends.'

'He,' said Frère Jean, 'was invited to a splendid and sumptuous feast given by one of his kinsmen who lived near by. To it were also invited all the gentlemen of the neighbourhood and all the ladies, both *dames* and *demoiselles*. While waiting for him to arrive, those ladies took the assembled pages, making them up and decking them out as attractive and fashionable young ladies. When Guyecharais came in, those feminized pages came to greet him. With great courtesy and courtly bows he

---

21. '48: . . . I kiss the hand *of your Majesty, your Reverence*; be you welcome
    . . . Frère Jean later associates this flimflam with Spain and Italy.

kissed them all in turn. In the end the ladies (who were in the gallery, lying in wait for him) burst out laughing and signalled to their pages to take off their finery.

'On seeing which that good lord, out of embarrassment and irritation, would not condescend to kiss the real *dames* and *demoiselles*, asserting that, since they had disguised those pages for him, they themselves, by Gosh! must be their lackeys even more cleverly made up.]

'Mighty God! – pardon my swearing! – why don't we rather transport our human frailties to some fair and godly kitchen, there to contemplate the dance of the spits, the harmony of the racks, the aspect of the rashers, the temperament of the soups,[22] the preparations for dessert and the order of the wine-service? *Blessed are they that are undefiled in the way.*[23] That's Breviary stuff.'

[Why monks are readily found in kitchens

CHAPTER 11]

[There is no chapter-break here in '48.
The monk from Amiens has an appropriate name, Lardon (Rasher).
Rabelais is indebted to Erasmus for the anecdote about Antigonus.
See his Apophthegms, *IV, Antigonus King of Macedonia, 17.]*

'Spoken like a monk born!' said Epistemon. 'I mean a monking monk, not a monkèd monk. You do in fact remind me of what I heard and saw some twenty years ago in Florence. We formed a goodly fellowship of studious folk, lovers of travel and keen on visiting the learned men of Italy, the antiquities and the curiosities. We were duly admiring the site and beauty

22. '48 . . . Mighty God! why don't we rather transport our human frailties to some fair and godly kitchen, there to contemplate the dance *and harmony of the spits*, the temperament of the soups . . .

23. The quotation is from psalm 118 (119):1 ('Beati immaculati in via'), quoted to make a monastic joke of some kind, perhaps suggesting that the cooks should be immaculately clean.

of Florence, the structure of the Duomo, the splendour of the churches and the magnificent palaces, and were outdoing each other to see who could most properly extol them with condign praises, when a monk from Amiens called Bernard Lardon said to us, all irritated as though we had ganged-up against him,

'I don't know what the devil you find to praise so much here! I've gazed at it all as much as you have and am no more blind than you are. But what of it? There are fine houses, that's all. But (God and our good patron saint my lord Saint Bernard be with us!) I've yet to find one single roast-meatery in all this town. [And I have diligently looked, hunted about and – yes, I tell you – searched as though I were a spy keen to list and count how many roasting roasteries we could find on the right and on the left, and on which side.]

'Why, in Amiens, covering four times less ground than we did when looking at things here [– well, three times less –] I could show you more than fourteen roasteries [which are ancient and fragrant]. I don't know what pleasure you took over by the Belfry while gazing at those lions and *africans* (the name, I think, you gave to what the people here call tigers), as likewise at the porcupines and ostriches on the palace of Signor Filippo Strozzi.[24] By my faith, me boys, I would prefer one good, fat gosling on a spit. All that porphyry and marble is beautiful. I've nothing to say against them, but those flans of Amiens called *darioles*, are [to my taste] better.

'I'm prepared to believe that those ancient statues are well made, but by Saint Ferreol of Abbeville, the young wenches of our countryside are a thousand times more winsome!'

'You can always find monks in kitchens,' said Frère Jean, 'but never kings, popes or emperors. What does that signify? What does it mean?' 'Is it,' replied Rhizotome, 'some latent

24. Many minor changes are not noted, but one omission is interesting. '48 reads: . . . the name, I think, *or lybistide bears*, that you gave to what the people here call tigers . . .

The allusion is to Virgil, *Aeneid*, 5, 37, 'pelle Lybistidis ursae' ('the skin of the Libyan bear'). Rabelais seems to have taken *Lybistidis ursae* to mean Lybistide bears rather than (as it does) of a *Lybistis* (i.e., Libyan) bear. That error may explain why he cut the words out in '52.

power, some specific property, hidden within the cooking-pots
and the cooking-racks which attracts monks as the magnet
attracts iron, without attracting kings, popes or emperors? Or
is it some natural inductive power or proclivity inherent in
frocks and cowls which of itself induces and propels good
monks into kitchens even though they have never elected or
decided to go there?'[25]

'He means *Forms seeking matter*,' said Epistemon. 'Averroës
puts it that way.'[26]

'Yeah. Yeah!' said Frère Jean.

'What I am going to tell you,' said Pantagruel, 'is no answer
to the problem you propose, which is rather a thorny one:
you could hardly touch it without pricking your fingers. But I
remember having read that Antigonus, King of Macedonia,
went into his field-kitchen one day, and, finding the poet
Antagoras there with the pan actually in his hands, preparing
a fry-up of eels, asked him with a sneer, "Was Homer frying
conger-eels when he described the prowesses of Agamemnon?"

' "But, O King," replied Antagoras, "do you think that when
Agamemnon was performing those prowesses he ever thought
of asking whether anyone in his camp was frying up eels?"'

'To the king it seemed improper for a poet to be making a
fry-up in the field-kitchen: the poet retorted that it was far more
shocking to come across a king in a kitchen.'[27]

['I can huff you on that,' said Panurge, 'by citing you what
Breton Villandry replied one day to my lord the Duc de Guise.
They were discussing some battle or other of King François
against the Emperor Charles the Fifth; Breton had been resplen-

---

25. '48: . . . 'Is it *some natural inclination adherent to frocks which of itself*
     leads and propels those good Religious into the kitchen, even though they
     have never elected or decided to go there? . . .

26. Normally matter is thought of as seeking form, rather than form matter.
     Averroës was in the tradition of Aristotle, but I do not know where he
     wrote what is attributed to him.

27. '48: *The king found it bad that he should find poets in the field-kitchen:*
     the poet showed him that it was far more improper to come across kings
     there.

     This exemplum from Plutarch is listed by Erasmus. He adds that the
     king took it in good part as a joke among equals.

dently armoured, especially with greaves and shoes of steel; he was well mounted yet had never seen any of the fighting.

' "Upon my faith," said Breton, "I was there all right, and it is easy for me to prove that I was in fact in a place where you would never have dared to go."

'His lord the Duke took offence at those words as being too arrogantly and insolently uttered. He raised the tone. Breton easily quietened him down amongst general laughter:

' "I was," he said, "with the baggage-train: where your sense of honour would never have allowed you to hide as I was doing." ']

With such small-talk they came to their ships, and lingered no longer on that island of Cheli.

How Pantagruel passed Procuration; and of the strange way of life amongst the Chicanous

CHAPTER 12

[*On this island dwell 'Procureers' (pejoratively named 'Procurators', adepts at wrangling) and 'Chicanous' (litigious lawyers, adepts in chicanery, who serve their writs aggressively in the hope of earning damages for assault and battery). There is a sustained play on the expression* passer procuration, *to 'pass' procuration, that is to grant power of attorney. Here Procuration is an island which can be 'passed' (that is, visited en route).*

In '48 this is Chapter 6. It is entitled How we passed Procuration ... etc., *and begins:* Full and replete after the good treatment by King Panigon, we continued on our route. The next day we passed Procuration, which is a land all scrabbled up ...

Over half this chapter (beginning '"What was it?" asked Pantagruel') and all of Chapters 13, 14, 15 and the beginning of Chapter 16 were added in '52. There is about to begin a superb example of the comedy of cruelty: its laughter depends on the dehumanizing of the Chicanous.

Many cultures use painful practices to impress events on people's minds. Choirboys used not to beat the bounds but to be beaten at

them; a sharp pinch-and-a-punch marks the start of a new month.
Blows and buffets reminded men that the newly wed bride was indeed
a bride, to be treated from now on as a matron.

Basché is a real place and the Seigneur de Basché was a real man
who apparently had a quarrel with the Prior of Saint-Louand. Behind
the conte *and the laughter lie real events.]*

Continuing on our way, the next day we passed Procuration,
which is a land all pawed over and scrabbled up. I could make
nothing of it. There we saw Procureers and Chicanous – a hairy
tribe. They never invited us to eat or to drink: after a multiplicity
of learned bows they simply told us that they were ours to
command – for a fee.

One of our interpreters told Pantagruel how these people
earn their living in a very odd way. It is diametrically opposed
to that of the inhabitants of Rome. In Rome an infinite number
of people earn their living by poisoning, beating and killing: it
is by being beaten that the Chicanous earn theirs, in such a
manner that were they to go for long without a beating they
would die of starvation, they, their wives and their children.

'They,' said Panurge, 'are like those men who, as Galen
reports, cannot get their *vena cava* up above the belt of the
equator without a good whipping! On the contrary: if anyone
were to whip me like that he would, by Saint Thibault, unsaddle
me [by all the devils].'

'This is how they do it,' said the interpreter. 'Whenever a
[monk,] priest, usurer or lawyer has it in for some local nobleman, he despatches one of those Chicanous to him. Chicanous,
following his written instructions, will issue him with a summons, serve a writ on him, insolently affront him and outrageously abuse him so that the nobleman (unless he is suffering
from paralysis of the brain and is as dull as a tadpole) will be
constrained to batter him about the head with the flat of his
sword or thwack him on the back of his thighs, or (better
still) chuck him down from the battlements or windows of his
château.

'Once that is achieved, Chicanous is rich for the next four
months as though beatings were for him Nature's harvest, for

he will have such a good fee from his monk, usurer or lawyer,[28] together with damages so huge and excessive against the noble-man, that the said nobleman may lose everything he possesses, running the risk of wretchedly rotting away in prison as though he had struck the king.'

'Against such a misfortune,' said Panurge, 'I know a very good remedy. It was used by the Seigneur de Basché.'

['What was it?' asked Pantagruel.

'The Seigneur de Basché,' said Panurge, 'was a courageous man, virtuous, great-souled and chivalrous. On his return from a certain long war in which the Duke of Ferrara, with the aid of the French, valiantly defended himself against the fury of Pope Julius the Second, he was daily summoned, cited and chicaneered to serve as a pleasant pastime for the fat prior of Saint-Louand.

'Basché, being gracious and debonair, was breakfasting one day with his people when he sent for his baker (whose name was Loyre) and his wife as well as for as the curé of his parish (whose name was Oudart and who served as his wine-steward, as was then the custom in France). Then in the presence of the noblemen and others of his household he said:

' "You can see, my dears, into what exasperation I am daily provoked by those good-for-nothing Chicanous. I've made up my mind: unless you help me I shall leave the country and, damme, join the Sultan! From now on, whenever they come in, you Loyre and your wife must be ready to appear in my Great Hall clad in your fine wedding garments as though you were being married, exactly as when you were actually married. Take this: here are a hundred gold crowns which I give to you to maintain your robes in good condition. And you, Sir Oudart, do not fail to be there with them in your best surplice and stole and with holy water as though to marry them. And you, Trudon – that was the name of his drummer-boy – you must be there with your fife and tabor. When the declaration is pronounced and the bride duly kissed to the sound of the tabor, you will all give each other those little buffets with the fist which are

---

28.   '48: . . . good fee from his *priest* or lawyer, together . . .

reminders of wedlock. You will sup all the better for it. But when it comes to Chicanous, thrash him like green rye! Don't spare him. Beat him, I pray. Biff him. Bash him. Look: I give you here and now these brand-new jousting-gauntlets, covered with goatskin. Don't count your blows: rain them down on him from right and left. Whoever plasters him best I will declare to be the one who loves me most. Have no fear of being arraigned for it. I shall vouch for you all. Following the custom honoured at weddings, such blows shall be given in jest!"

'"Indeed yes," said Oudart; "but how shall we recognize Chicanous, for people arrive in your house every day from all over the place."

'"I have seen to that," replied Basché. "Whenever there arrives at our gates a fellow, on foot or ill-enough mounted, wearing a big, fat silver signet-ring on his thumb, that will be Chicanous. Once he has courteously ushered him in the gate-keeper will toll the bell. Be ready then and come into Hall in order to act out the tragic-comedy which I have outlined to you."

'Now, as God so willed, there arrived that very day an ancient, portly, red-faced Chicanous. As he rang the bell at the gate he was recognized by the gate-keeper by his thick, dirty stockings, his wretched mare, the linen-bag full of summonses attached to his belt, and notably by the big silver signet-ring on his left thumb. The gate-keeper was most courteous; he ushered him in most honourably and then merrily tolled the bell. At the sound of which Loyre and his wife donned their fine vestments and, with a straight face, appeared in Hall. Oudart put on his surplice and his stole. As he came out of his buttery he encountered Chicanous. He brought him back into the buttery for a lengthy drink while people on all sides were pulling on gauntlets; he then said to him: "You could not have come at a better time. Master is in the best of moods: soon we shall have plenty of good cheer. They'll be ladling it out. We're in the midst of a wedding. Here. Have a drink and be merry."

'Whilst Chicanous was downing his drinks, Basché, seeing his people in Hall all duly equipped, sent for Oudart.

'Oudart arrived, bearing the holy water.

'Chicanous followed after him. Coming into the Hall he did not forget to make several humble bows. He served his writ on Basché; Basché gave him the warmest of welcomes, bestowed on him a gold coin (an angelot) and prayed him to be present at the contract and the marriage. Which was done.

'Towards the end, buffets from fists began to fly about; but when it came to the turn of Chicanous they regaled him so thoroughly with great biffs from their gauntlets that he stood there all battered and bruised, with one eye poached in black butter, eight fractured ribs, his breast-plate stoven in, his shoulder-blades in four quarters and his lower jaw in three pieces.

'And all done with a laugh.

'God only knows how Oudart operated, hiding under the sleeve of his surplice a heavy steel gauntlet covered with ermine, for he was a mighty fellow.

'And thus did Chicanous return to l'Ile-Bouchart, striped like a tiger yet most pleased and satisfied with the Seigneur de Basché. And thanks to the care of the good local surgeons he lived . . . as long as you like. Never again was he spoken of. All memory of him died away with the sound of the bells which tolled as he was laid in the ground.'

How, following the example of François Villon, the Seigneur de Basché lauds his people

CHAPTER 13

[The macaronic verse is not translated by Rabelais: it is translated here.

Rabelais' tale of Villon is fanciful, but, insofar as the refusal to lend church vestments is concerned, quite realistic. There were known quarrels on the subject.

Rabelais treats us to more comedy of cruelty.]

'Once Chicanous had left the château and mounted his monocular steed (as he called his one-eyed mare), Basché, sitting beneath the arbour of his private garden, sent servants to find his wife, her ladies and all his household; he ordered up dessert wines accompanied by a number of pasties, hams, fruits and cheeses; then, light-heartedly drinking with his folk, he said to them:

' "When he was getting on, Maître François Villon retired to Saint-Maixent-en-Poitou under the patronage of a good man, the local abbot. There, to entertain the people, he took on the task of producing a Passion-play following the traditions and patois of Poitou. The parts were distributed, the players rehearsed and the theatre made ready; he then told the mayor and the magistrates that the mystery-play could be ready by the end of the Niort Fair; all that remained was to find the right costumes for the characters. The mayor and the magistrates made the arrangements. Villon, to dress up an elderly peasant who was playing God the Father, begged Frère Etienne Tappecoue, the sacristan of the local Franciscans, to lend him a cope and a stole. Tappecoue refused, maintaining that it was rigorously forbidden in their provincial statutes to give or lend anything to actors. Villon contended that the statute applies merely to farces, mummeries and licentious plays, and that he had seen it so interpreted in Brussels and elsewhere. Tappecoue nevertheless peremptorily told him that he could get them from somebody else if he liked but might hope for nothing from the sacristy: he would get nothing from there, and that was flat.

' "Villon reported that to the players with great disgust, adding that God would very soon inflict on Tappecoue exemplary punishment and retribution. On the following Saturday Villon was advised that Tappecoue, mounted on *Foal* – that was their name in the convent for a mare not yet leapt – had gone to Saint-Ligaire in quest of alms and would be on his way back by about two o'clock in the afternoon. Whereupon he paraded all his devils through the town and marketplace. Those devils of his were all bedizened with wolf-skins, veal-skins and goat-skins enhanced by sheep's-heads, cow's horns and great pot-hooks from the kitchen; they were girded about with stout leathern belts from which dangled great cow-bells and mule-jingles making a frightening din. Some held in their hands black staves studded with squibs; others carried long, lighted torches

on to which, at every cross-road, they flung handfuls of powdered resin from which issued terrifying fire and smoke. After
having thus paraded them to the delight of the townsfolk and
the terror of the little children, Villon eventually led them off
to feast in a country inn outside of gates on the road to Saint-
Ligaire. As they arrived at the inn, Villon caught sight of Tappecoue on his way back from his alms-raising and said to them in
macaronic verse:

> *Hic est de patria, natus de gente belistra*
> *Qui solet antiquo bribas portare bisacco.*

(Here comes a fellow, true born of the race of the Cadgers:
A man who bears old scraps in his battered old wallet.)

' "By the death of Gosh," the devils then said, "he refused to
lend a wretched cope to God the Father. Let's give him a fright!" '
' "Well said," answered Villon, "but let's hide until he comes
by. And prepare your squibs and fire-brands." '
'When Tappecoue did arrive at the spot, they all sprang into
the road in front of him, making a great hullabaloo, chucking
fireworks at him and his mule from every side, clashing their
cymbals and yelling like the devil:
' "*Hho, hho, hho, hho. Brrrourrrourrr, rrrourrrs, rrrourrrs.
Hou, hou, hou. Hho, hho, hho.* We make fine devils, don't we,
Frère Etienne!" '
'Foal was quite terrified; she proceeded to trot and fart and
bound and gallop, lashing out, bucking about and kicking out
with her heels while letting off a great volley of farts, so much
so that she threw Tappecoue, who nevertheless clung on to the
pommel of the saddle with all his might. Now his stirrups were
made of plaited cord, and one of his open-work sandals got so
tangled up in the off-side stirrup that he could not tug it free.
And thus was he dragged behind, skinning his bum, while the
terrified Foal doubled and redoubled her kicks as she took the
wrong track through hedge, bush and ditch so that she battered
in his entire skull: his brains fell out near the Hosanna Cross,
followed by his shattered arms, one here, one there, and likewise

his legs; then she made a long fleshy trail of his guts, with the
result that when Foal arrived at the convent all she bore of him
was his right foot entangled in its sandal. Villon, seeing that it
had turned out as he had intended, said to the devils, "You will
act well, Messieurs les Diables, you will act well, I assure you.
Oh, how well you will do it! I defy all the actor-devils of
Saumur, Doué, Montmorillon, Langeais, Saint-Espin, Angers
and indeed by God those of the Great Hall of Poitiers, should
they ever chance to be compared with you. Oh, how well you
will act!"

'"I can foresee," said Basché, "that from now on you too,
my good friends, will act well in this tragic farce, seeing that at
our first try-out and run-through Chicanous was so thoroughly
bashed, whacked and clobbered by you. I here and now double
all your wages. You, my dear," he said to his wife, "distribute
any presents you like. All my worldly goods are in your hands
and looked after by you. As for me: first, I drink to you all, my
good friends. Well, now, this wine is nice and cool. Second:
you, my Steward can take this silver basin. I give it to you. And
you, Esquires, take these two silver-gilt goblets. You pages: no
beatings for the next three months! My dear, give them those
beautiful white plumes of mine with the golden pendants. To
you, Sir Oudart, I give this silver flagon; and the other one I
give to the cooks. To the chamber-lads I give this silver basket;
to the stable-boys this silver-gilt sauce-boat; to the gate-keepers
I give these two plates; to the mule-boys, these ten spoons.
Trudon: you take all these silver spoons and this confit-dish.
And you lackeys, take this great salt-cellar.

'"Serve me well my friends and I shall never forget it. And,
God almighty! believe you me, I would rather endure in the
wars a hundred blows from maces on my helmet in the interests
of such a good king as ours than be served with one writ
by those dogs of Chicanous to provide a pastime for our fat
Prior."'

Chicanous drubbed in the house of Basché: continued

CHAPTER 14

[The comedy continues.

Yellow and green are the traditional colours worn by fools and jesters.]

'Four days later, another Chicanous, young, tall and skinny, came to serve a writ on Basché at the behest of the fat Prior. When he arrived he was at once recognized by the gate-keeper, and so the bell was tolled. At the sound of which all the folk in the castle were privy to the mystery. Loyre was kneading his dough; his wife was sifting the flour; Oudart was totting up his accounts; the gentlemen were playing tennis; the Seigneur de Basché was at cards, playing *Three-hundred-and-three* with his wife; the young ladies were playing with ivory knucklebones; the officers, at cards, were playing Imperial, whilst the pages were playing odds or evens with much flicking of fingers.

'Suddenly they all realized that Chicanous was abroad. Oudart again donned his vestments, and Loyre and his wife fetched out their fine accoutrements; Trudon blew his flute and beat his drum; everyone was laughing and getting ready, with gauntlets to the fore.

'Basché went down into his courtyard. Chicanous, when he met him, sank to his knees before him and begged him not to take it ill if he served him a writ on behalf of the fat Prior; he protested in an elegant speech that he was but an Officer of the Court, a Servant of Monkery, and a Sumner for the abbatial Mitre, ready to do as much for him – indeed for the least of his household – wherever it might please him to send or direct him.

' "Truly," said the Seigneur de Basché, "you will serve me no writ before you've had a drink of my good Quinquenais wine and joined in the wedding in which I am now engaged. (Sir Oudart: see that he has plenty to drink and cools himself down; then bring him into my Hall.) You are most welcome."

'Chicanous, once well fed and watered, entered the Hall with

Oudart; there all the actors in the farce were by now in position
and ready to go. On his arrival everyone began to smile and
Chicanous laughed out of politeness; Oudart muttered some
mysterious words over the Betrothed; they joined hands, the
bride was kissed, and all were asperged with holy water.

'Whilst the wine and spices were being brought in, buffets
from fists began to trot about. Chicanous rained a few on
Oudart. Oudart had his gauntlet hidden beneath his surplice;
he had pulled it on like a mitten. Then Chicanous was whacked
and Chicanous was thwacked, and from all sides blows from
young gauntlets were showered upon Chicanous. "A wedding!"
they all said, "a wedding! a wedding! And don't you forget it!"

'Chicanous was given such a good dressing-down that blood
spurted from his mouth, nose, ears and eyes. In addition he was
battered and shattered and hammered all over: head, neck,
back, chest and arms. Believe you me, even at Carnival times
in Avignon the young men never played more harmoniously at
Winner-grabs-all than was played there that day at the expense
of Chicanous.

'Finally he fell to the ground.

'They threw plenty of wine over his face, fastened a yellow
and green motley to the sleeve of his doublet and set him upon
his snotty old horse.

'After he was back in L'Ile-Bouchard, I don't know whether
he was well bandaged and nursed by his wife and the local
leeches, but he has never been heard of since.

'The next day – because no writ had been found in the bag
or pouch of that skinny Chicanous – a similar event occurred.

'On behalf of the fat Prior a fresh Chicanous was despatched
to serve a writ on the Seigneur de Basché. Two bailiffs came
along to protect him. The gate-keeper tolled his bell, making
all the household rejoice as they learned that Chicanous had
arrived.

'Basché was at table, dining with his wife and the noblemen.
He sent for Chicanous and made him sit by him and the bailiffs
to sit down next to the young ladies. And they dined very well
and merrily together.

'At dessert Chicanous rose from his seat at the table and, in the presence and hearing of the bailiffs, served the writ on Basché. Basché courteously asked him for a copy of his warrant. It was ready to hand. The writ was formally served and, once everyone had withdrawn for the farce, four sun-crowns were bestowed on Chicanous and the bailiffs. Trudon began to beat his drum. Basché prayed Chicanous to come to the marriage of one of his serving-men and to formalize the marriage-contract (with the fee duly and satisfactorily paid).

'Chicanous was courteous. He unstrapped his writing-case and, with the bailiffs standing by, promptly produced paper. Loyre comes into Hall through one door, his wife and brides-maids through another, all attired for a wedding. Oudart, sacerdotally vested, takes them by the hand, asks whether *They Will*, gives them his blessing without stinting the holy water. The marriage-contract is signed and sealed. From one side is brought in wine and spices; from another, an abundance of white and brown ribbons; and from yet another gauntlets are secretly produced.

How ancient marriage customs are renewed by Chicanous

CHAPTER 15

[Rabelais delights in 'Breton' wine, which is a Touraine wine perhaps named after a vigneron.

The so-called Christmas Saints, O and O are in fact the O-Antiphons of Advent (O Wisdom! O Adonai! O Stem of Jesse!, etc.).

The 'Philosopher of Samosata' is Lucian. Rabelais refers to one of his best satires, The Symposium of the Lapiths, *in which philosophers end up lambasting each other. Rabelais had relatives called Frappin through his maternal grandmother. Their name suggests* frapper, *to strike and leads to* frappard, *a tupping monk.]*

'Chicanous, after gulping down a large goblet of Breton wine, said to the Seigneur de Basché, "My Lord. What's going on here? Aren't we having a wedding? Oddsblood, all the good old customs are being lost! No more hares in their forms! No friends any more! Look how they've given up pledging in many a church those blessèd Saints of Christmas, O and O! The world's gone mad. It's drawing to its end. Come on: a wedding! a wedding! a wedding!"

'So saying he gave a buffet to Basché and his wife; then to the young ladies, and then to Oudart. Whereupon gauntlets so performed their exploits that Chicanous' skull was shattered in nine places, one of the bailliffs had his arm put out of joint while the other had his jaw dislocated in such a fashion that it hung half-way down his chin, exposing his uvula and causing a notable loss of his teeth (molars, masticators and canines).

'When the sound of the tambourine changed its note, gauntlets were hidden without their being in any way noticed. Amidst renewed rejoicing sweetmeats were again brought out in profusion. While all those good companions were all each drinking to each other and to Chicanous and his bailliffs, Oudart was cursing and inveighing against the wedding, alleging that one of the bailliffs had entirely desincornifistibulated his other shoulder, yet he was nevertheless happily drinking to him. The demandibled bailiff clasped his hands together and wordlessly begged forgiveness, being unable to talk.

'Loyre complained that the bailiff with the shattered arm had given him such a great thwack with his fist on one of his elbows that he had become all maulocrippled-lowerhazarded in his heel. "But," said Trudon, covering his left eye with his handkerchief and pointing at his drum, one side of which had been knocked in, "What harm have I done them? It was not enough for them to have gravely cowpatconked-windbagthrottled-thumptbumped-bangbong-shattered my poor old eye: they have knocked in my drum as well. Drums are regularly beaten at weddings: drummer-boys never: they are feasted! The devil can use mine for his head-gear."

'Chicanous, now short of one arm, said to him, "Brother, to patch up your drum I shall give you a lovely big old Letters-patent that I've got here in my pouch. And do, for God's sake, forgive us. By that beautiful Lady, Our Lady of Rivière, I meant no harm."

'One of the esquires, staggering about and limping, gave an excellent imitation of the good and noble Seigneur de La Rochposay. He addressed the bailiff whose jaw was hanging down like a visor, saying, "Are you a Frappin, a Tapper or a Tupper? Wasn't it enough for you to have shattersplattered-beggarbagged-pibrochdroned-cropperspondylitized all my upper limbs with great kicks from your heavy boots without giving us such gnawgrips-trifletricks-muddledkettledrummeries on our shins with the sharp points of your shoes? Call this a youthful game! By God I'm not game!"

'The bailiff, clasping his hands together, seemed to be begging forgiveness, mumbling with his tongue, *mon, mon, mon, vrelon, von, von*, like a monkey. The newly wedded bride laughed as she cried and cried as she laughed because Chicanous had not been satisfied with thumping her indiscriminately on her limbs but had severely ruffled her hair and, what is more, treacherously pubicfumbled-crimpywrinkled her private parts.

'"The devil," said Basché, "has had a part in this. Was it really necessary that this *Monsieur In-the-King's Name* (as Chicanous call themselves) should wallop me so on me poor old backbone. I wish him no harm, though. They are little nuptial caresses. But I can clearly see he cited me like an angel and then daubed me like a devil. He has a touch of the knocking friar about him. I drink to him with a very good heart. And to you too, Messieurs the Bailiffs!"

'"But," said his wife, "For what words or what quarrel did he treat me over and over again to great blows from his fists? The devil take him if I like it! But no: I don't like it. By Jove I will say this about him, though, he has the hardest knuckles I've ever felt on my shoulders."

'The Steward had his left arm in a sling, as though entirely swaggerbattered. "It was the devil," he said, "who got me to come to this wedding. By God's virtue I have my arms all gulletbaggy-bumpcontused! Call this a wedding! I call it shit-shedding! In fact it's the very banquet of the Lapiths described by the Philosopher from Samosata."

'Chicanous could no longer talk. The bailiffs apologized:

they had no evil intention when landing their blows; in God's name may they be forgiven. And so they departed.

'About a half-league away Chicanous felt rather poorly. The bailiffs arrived at L'Ile-Bouchard stating publicly that they had never seen a better man than the Seigneur de Basché nor a household more honourable than his, adding that never before had they been to such a wedding. But the fault was all on their side: they had started the punch-up. And they stayed alive for some few days more.

'From that time forth it was taken as an established fact that the silver of Basché was more pestilential, mortal and pernicious to Chicanous and Bailiffs than ever was, in days of yore, the gold of Toulouse, or the horse of Sejus to him who owned it.[29]

'Since then the said Seigneur has been left in peace, and "the Weddings of Basché" turned into a common saying.'

How Frère Jean assayed the temperament of the Chicanous

CHAPTER 16

[After the opening two paragraphs of this chapter the original text of '48 picks up again. Several small changes are passed over here since they are minor and distracting, though we may note that Lucius Neratius at first had only one valet and that Frère Jean produces ten crowns not twenty.

This Fourth Book of Pantagruel *is still confronting the problem of the comedy of cruelty. The previous chapters have been full of laughter, yet how is laughter at pain and death to be reconciled with morality? Pantagruel, no* agelast, *does not laugh here, nor anywhere else until the very last page of the book. Nor did Frère Jean simply*

---

29. Rabelais ends with an allusion to two adages of Erasmus which follow each other: I, X, XCVII, 'He has the horse of Sejus', and I, X, XCVIII, 'He has gold from Toulouse'. Both are linked and explained by Aulus Gellius, *Attic Nights*, 3, 9, 1–7: a Roman consul took Toulouse, but its plundered gold brought disaster to all who touched it, as did the famous horse of Sejus, all of whose owners met dreadful fates.

laugh at the end of Chapter 8, citing Scripture to make his point. Here Pantagruel starts off by alluding to Romans 3:18 or its source in Psalm 36. He does not cite it textually but turns a limited condemnation – 'There is no fear of God before their eyes' – into a general commandment.

'To land someone with the monk "by the feet"' usually means to trick him while asleep by tying a string to his toe.]

'That tale,' said Pantagruel, 'might seem funny were it not that we should ever have the fear of God before our eyes.'

'It would have been better,' said Epistemon, 'if the blows from those young gauntlets had rained on that fat prior. He was laying out cash for his own amusement, partly to annoy Basché and partly to see his Chicanous beaten up. Blows from fists would have aptly bedight his tonsured pate, considering the violent extortions we see today amongst those puisne judges under the elm. What wrong had those poor devils of Chicanous ever done?']

'While on this subject,' said Pantagruel, 'I am reminded of a nobleman of Ancient Rome called Lucius Neratius. He belonged to a family which was at that time rich and noble. He was of such an overbearing character that whenever he went out of his palace he caused the wallets of his menservants to be filled with gold and silver coins;[30] then, whenever he came across some mincing, spruced-up dandies in the street he would gaily punch them hard in the face without the slightest provocation. Immediately afterwards he would distribute his money amongst them to calm them down and stop them from bringing legal actions, thus satisfying and gratifying them in accordance with a law of the Twelve Tables. That is how he spent his income: by beating up people at the price of his money.'[31]

'By Saint Benedick's holy barrel,' said Frère Jean, 'I shall find out the truth of all that right away.'

Whereupon he clambered ashore, put his hand into his money-bag and drew out twenty Sun-crowns. Then, with a

30. '48: . . . caused the *purses* and wallets . . .
31. '48: . . . beating up people *with blows from his fists*, at the price of his money . . .

loud voice, in the presence and hearing of a great multitude of Chicanousian people, he asked,[32] 'Who wants to earn twenty gold crowns by getting a hell of a beating?' ['Me! Me! Me!' they all replied. You'll knock us silly with your blows, Sir; that's certain. But there's a handsome profit in it.'] And so they all charged up, crowding round and trying to be the first to be so profitably beaten.

From out of the whole crowd Frère Jean selected a Chicanous with a red nose who wore on the thumb of his left hand a big fat silver ring [in the bezel of which was mounted a very big toad-stone].

Once he had selected him I saw the crowd of them grumbling;[33] and I heard one [big,] young [, skinny] Chicanous (a good and clever scholar according to the common rumour, and a good man in the ecclesiastical courts) lamenting and protesting that old Red Snout was taking all their cases from them and that if there were but thirty thwacks from a cudgel going in all the land he always pocketed twenty-eight and a half of them. [Yet all those complaints and grumblings proceeded only from envy.] Frère Jean with his stave walloped Red-snout so very,[34] very hard over his back, belly, arms, legs, head and everything else that I thought he had been battered to death. Frère Jean then gave him his twenty crowns, and there was my rascal back on his feet, as happy as a king or two.

The other Chicanous said to Frère Jean, 'Sir Brother Devil, if you would care to beat up a few more of us for less money we are all yours, bundles, papers, pens and all.'

Red-snout yelled at them, loudly saying, 'Corpus Chrikey, you layabouts! Stealing my trade? Trying to lure away and entice my clients. I shall cite you before the Diocesan judge,

In a week from now,
tow-row-row!

32. '48: . . . put his hand in his *bag* and drew out *ten crowns*. Then, with a loud voice, *with a* great multitude of Chicanous people *hearing*, he asked . . . ('Ten' instead of 'twenty' throughout).
33. '48: . . . grumbling; *it was envy*; and I . . .
34. '48: . . . Frère Jean walloped *him* so very hard . . .

I shall scratch you like a devil from Vauvert.'

Then, turning a happy, laughing face towards Frère Jean, he said, 'My Lord, my Reverend Father in Devil, if you have found me to be good value, and if you judge the bashing smashing, I'll be satisfied with half the going rate. Spare me not, I pray you. I am, Monsieur le Diable, all yours – entirely: head, lungs, innards; the lot. I'm happy to tell you so.'

Frère Jean interrupted what he was saying and drew aside. The other Chicanous resorted to Panurge, Epistemon, Gymnaste and others, devoutly imploring them to beat them up for a tiny sum of money, otherwise they risked being in for a very long fast.[35] But none of them would listen.

Later on, when we were scouting for fresh water with the oarsmen from the galleys we came across two local old female Chicanous, pitifully weeping and lamenting together. Pantagruel had remained aboard his vessel and had already sounded the bell to rejoin ship. We, suspecting that these old women were relatives of the Chicanous who had been subjected to the beatings,[36] questioned them about the causes of such lamentations. They replied that they had a most equitable cause for weeping: that very hour two of the most decent men there ever had been in all the territories of the Chicanous had been landed with the monk 'by the neck'.

'My pages,' said Gymnaste, 'land their sleeping comrades with the monk by their feet. To land the monk "by the neck" must mean to strangle a man by hanging.'

'Yeah,' said Frère Jean, 'yeah. You're talking like Saint John of the Pocalypse.[37] When those women were asked about the reasons for those hangings they replied that the men had stolen

---

35. '48: . . . The other Chicanous said to Frère Jean, 'Monsieur le Diable, we are all yours. They said as much to Panurge and as much to Gymnaste and the others. But none of them would listen . . .

36. '48: . . . lamenting together. Pantagruel, suspecting that these old women were relatives of the Chicanous . . . (Words omitted, once again removing Pantagruel from the action of the farce.)

37. '48: . . . equitable cause, seeing that they had brought to the gibbet the two best men there were on the isle. You're talking like Saint John of the Pocalypse . . .

the irons of the Mass [and hidden them beneath the parish handle.'

'What a terrible allegory that is,' said Epistemon].[38]

How Pantagruel called at the islands of Tohu and Bohu and of the curious death of Bringuenarilles, the swallower of windmills

CHAPTER 17

[Bringuenarilles as a swallower of windmills is borrowed from a book which Rabelais did not write: Panurge, Disciple de Pantagruel (1538, plus other editions sometimes with other names).

Tohu bohu is the Hebrew term for chaos in Genesis 1:2.

Hypostases and enaioremata are sediments and solid matter in urine. (Rabelais was content with the simple term 'sediments' in '48.)

Rabelais knew his Plutarch well, but the reference to the 'Face which appears on the surface of the Moon' and its context are taken from an adage of Erasmus: I, V, LXIV, 'What if the sky were to fall?'

The reference to a certain 'Bacabery l'aisné' is intriguing, as the name of Rabelais appears in it as an anagram (Rabelais plus b c e y a n, not yet adequately explained.]

That same day Pantagruel called at the two islands of Tohu and Bohu, where we found we had no fish to fry since Bringue-narilles, the great giant, had swallowed up all the pots, pans, saucepans, frying-pans, cauldrons, gravy-pans and dripping-pans, there being a dearth of the windmills he normally fed upon. And so it befell one day, a little before sunrise when food is digesting, that Bringuenarilles had been taken gravely ill from a raw stomach brought on (as the physicians say) by the fact that the concocting powers of his stomach, which were by

38. This 'allegory' was already so obscure at the time of Rabelais that, in the *Brief Declaration* it is somewhat grudgingly explained: 'By a quite heavy metaphor, the villagers of Poitou call the "irons" of the Mass what we call the ornaments, and the "handle" of the parish what we call the bell-tower.'

nature appropriate to the ingestion of working windmills, had not been able perfectly to assimilate the frying-pans and the dripping-pans: he had coped very well though with the sauce-pans and the cauldrons.

The physicians explained that they deduced the above from the *hypostases* and *enaioremata* in the four barrelfuls of urine he had voided on two occasions that morning.

To treat him they used various remedies according to their Art: but the illness was stronger than their remedies so that the noble Bringuenarilles had passed away that morning in a manner so curious that you should no longer be astounded by the death of Aeschylus, to whom it had been predicted as his fate by the soothsayers that he would die on one specified day from the dropping upon him of some falling object. On that fated day he put a distance between himself and the town and all houses, trees, cliffs and other things which could fall and inflict an injury on him as they did so. So he remained in the middle of a spacious field, putting his trust in the clear open sky and feeling perfectly secure, unless the very heavens were actually to fall upon him (something he thought to be impossible).

And yet men say that the larks have a great dread of the collapse of the heavens, for if the heavens fell down they would all be trapped.

The Celts dwelling by the Rhine also dreaded it in days of yore. They are now the noble, valiant, chivalrous, warrior-like and victorious French.

Questioned by Alexander the Great about what they most feared in this world [– he was hoping that, out of respect for his great prowesses, victories, conquests and triumphs they would make an exception for him alone –] they replied[39] that they feared nothing save the collapse of the heavens [; they would nevertheless not refuse an alliance, confederation and friendship with so brave and great-souled a king (if you believe Strabo in Book 7 and Arrian in Book 1).

---

39. '48: . . . they would all be trapped. The *Gymnosophists of India*, questioned by Alexander the Great . . . replied . . .

Plutarch, too, in the book which he wrote *On that Face which appears on the surface of the Moon*, speaks of a man called Phenaces, who, greatly fearing that the moon might collapse on to the Earth, felt deep pity and commiseration for the peoples dwelling directly underneath her such as the Ethiops and the Taprobanians, lest so great a mass should fall upon them. He would also have been afraid for both the heavens and the Earth as well had they not been adequately supported and upheld by the pillars of Atlas, as the Ancients opined (as Aristotle bears witness in Book 5 of his *Metaphysics*)].

All the same, Aeschylus was killed when the shell of a tortoise was dropped from the claws of an eagle flying high in the air; it fell on his head and split his cranium.

– Add the poet Anacreon, who choked on a grape-seed and died;

– add Fabius, the Roman Praetor who died from a goat's hair in the bowl of milk he was drinking;

– add that embarrassed man who [held back his wind and] suddenly died from the suppression of a wretched fart in the presence of the Emperor Claudius;

– add that man who is buried in Rome along the Flaminian Way who laments in his epitaph that he died from a cat-bite on his little finger;

[– add Quintus Lecanius Bassus, who died suddenly from the prick of a needle on his left thumb, a prick so small it could hardly be seen;]

– add Quenelault, a physician from Normandy, who died suddenly at Montpellier from the slanting cut he made with a pen-knife when prising a flesh-worm from his hand;[40]

[– add Philomenes, for whom his servant-boy, having prepared some fresh figs as a first course for his dinner, put them down and went off to fetch the wine; meanwhile an amply balled donkey ambled in and immediately consumed them; Philomenes then arrived and closely noted the graciousness of that figo-phagic beast and said to the servant-boy when he came

40. '48: . . . a cat-bite on his little finger. *Guingnenauld, a Norman physician, a great swallower of green lentils and a most outstanding haunter of taverns who died from repaying his debts and* from the slanting cut . . .

back, 'Reason commands that, since you abandoned these figs to that devout donkey you should also produce for it some of that good wine you have brought in!' Having uttered those words he became so merry of mind that he burst out into such enormous and sustained guffawing that the strain on his spleen cut off his breath and he suddenly died.]

– add Spurius Saufeius, who died while slurping down a soft-boiled egg as he came out of his bath;

[– add that man who, Boccaccio says, suddenly died from picking his teeth with a twig of sage;

– add Philippot Placud,

> who, 'tis said,
> Fit and well and fully fed,
> Suddenly crumpled down quite dead,

without any previous illness: he was simply paying off an old debt;

– add Zeusis the artist, who suddenly died of laughing while looking at the grimacing portrait of an old woman whom he had painted;]

– add all the others which may be told to you by anyone including Verrius, Pliny, Valerius, Battista Fulgosa or Bacabery l'aisné.[41]

Our good fellow Bringuenarilles, while eating a pat of fresh butter by order of the physicians, died alas of suffocation close to the mouth of a hot oven.

There we were also told that the King of Cullan-en-Bohu had defeated the satraps of King Mechloth and sacked the fortresses of Belima. We subsequently sailed by the islands of Nargues and Zargues; and also of Teleniabin and Geneliabin, which were beautiful and fecund in materials for clysters. And also Enig and Evig, which produced such a backlash for the Landgrave of Hesse.[42]

41. '48 ... Battista Fulgosa, or *Rifle-Chidling*. Our good fellow Bringuenarilles ...
42. The sense of 'Mechloth' (though a Hebrew plural in resonance) is not certain: perhaps *mikloth* ('perfect'), as in 2 Chronicles 4:21, or it may

How Pantagruel escaped from a mighty storm at sea

CHAPTER 18

[In '48 this was Chapter 8.

*We now leave fantasy for laughter at the Council of Trent (Chésil)
and its supporters (presented as members of religious Orders). Panurge
becomes the model of fear and superstition, a role he will keep until
the end. 'Chésil' (Hebrew Kesil) means 'fool'.*

*Rabelais took his 'kataigides' (violent winds), 'thuellai' (stormy
gusts), 'lailapes' (whirlwinds) and 'presteres' (meteors) straight from
Aristotle's De Mundo, 4, 2, barely Gallicizing them.*

*In the penultimate paragraph, where there now appears 'zalas' (that
is, a form of 'alas' in the dialect of Saintonge) the text of 1548 read
'Jarus'. (Jarus was the Parisian dialect form of Jesus. (The changes are
vital but are not individually noted. Jarus is once struck out: after 'Be
be be: bous bous' and every other time that it appeared in 1548 it is
replaced in '52 by 'zalas'.*

*Panurge typically confounds the Virgin Mary with God, or at least
makes her equal to him. 'All is verlor' bi Gott', that is, 'Alles ist
verloren bei Gott' (' All is lost, by God') was the cry often attributed
to Swiss mercenaries.*

*'O! Thrice and four times blessed', cited more than once by Rabelais,
comes from the cry of distress of Aeneas in Aeneid, 1, 94.]*

The following day we crossed on our starboard bow nine car-
racks laden with monks, Jacobins, Jesuits, Capuchins, Hermits,
Augustinians, Bernardines, Celestines, Theatines, Egnatines,
Amadeans, Cordeliers, Carmelites, Minims and other holy

---

mean illnesses; *Belima* is Hebrew for 'nothing', as in Job 26:7; 'Nargues'
and 'Zargues' are made-up names meaning something like Pish and Tush.
'Teleniabin' and 'Geneliabin' are the Arabic names of substances used in
clysters. In 1547, in a treaty between the Emperor Charles V and the
Landgrave of Hesse, the words *ohne ewige Gefängnis* ('without perpetual
detention') were substituted for *ohne einige Gefängnis* ('without any
detention'), and the Landgrave was thrown in prison.

Religious[43] who were sailing to the Council of Chésil to sieve through the articles of the Faith against the new heretics.

On seeing them, Panurge entered into an exceeding joy, [as though assured of finding good fortune on that day and the following days in long succession] and having courteously greeted the blessèd Fathers and commended the salvation of his soul to their devotional prayers and minor intercessions, he caused there to be slung aboard their ships three score-and-eighteen hams, lots of caviar,[44] dozens of Saveloys, hundreds of dried salted mullet-roes and two thousand handsome angel-crowns, for the souls of the departed.

Pantagruel remained all thoughtful and melancholy. Frère Jean noticed it, and was asking him the origin of such an unaccustomed gloom when the pilot, having studied the way the pennant on the poop was jerking about and foreseeing a severe squall and a new-formed tempest, called out for everybody to be on the alert: officers, matelots, ship's boys and us passengers. He struck the sails: mizzen-sail, mizzen-topsail, lugsail, mainsail, lower-after-square-sail and spritsail; he had the men furl in the topsails, foretop and maintop and lower the great storm-mizzen, leaving aloft none of the yards save the ratlings and the shrouds.

All of a sudden the sea began to heave and roar up from the deep; the huge waves beat broadside against our vessels; a Nor'easter, accompanied by a frenetic hurricane, black squalls, terrifying whirlwinds and deadly gusting cyclones, came whistling through our yards. The heavens roared above us, thundering, lightning, raining and hailing; the air lost its translucency and grew opaque, dark and murky so that no light reached us save from thunder-flashes, lightning and breaks in the fiery clouds; all around us there flamed *kataigides*, *thuellai*, *lailapes* and *presteres* with their flashes and their streaks of forked and sheet lightning and other aerial discharges; all sight-

43. '48: ... The following day we crossed on our starboard bow a *carrack*, laden with monks, *Cordeliers, Jacobins, Carmelites, Augustinians, Celestines, Capuchins, Bernardines, Minims, Jesuits, Benedictines* and other holy Religious ...

44. '48: ... *sixteen dozen* hams and *two thousand* caviars ...

ings of the stars were confused and obscured; horrifying whirlwinds sucked up the mountainous waves as they flowed in. It
seemed to us, as you can well believe, like that Chaos of old
where fire, air, sea, land and all the elements were in jarring
confusion.

Panurge, having thoroughly fed the scatophagous fish with the
contents of his stomach, stayed crouching down on the deck,
thoroughly miserable, quite wretched and half-dead. He invoked
to his aid all the blessed saints, male and female, asseverating that
he would make his confession in due time and place.[45] He then
cried out in great terror, 'Chief Steward! Ho! My friend, my
father, my uncle! Serve up the salty bits! I can see that we shall
soon have all too much to drink! From now on my device shall
be, *Little food, lots of drink*. Would to God [and to the Blessèd,
worthy and sacred Virgin that now – I mean at this very minute –]
I was on *terra- firma*, thoroughly at my ease.

'O! *Thrice and four times blessèd* are those who plant cabbages. O Fatal Sisters, why did you not spin me the thread of a
planter of cabbages? O, how small is the number of those whom
Jupiter has so favoured as to be destined to plant out cabbages:
for they always have one foot on the ground and the other not
far above it. Let him who will debate of felicity and the sovereign good; but by my decree whoever plants cabbages is here
and now pronounced to be truly blessèd, with far more reason
than Pyrrho had, who when in such danger as we are now, and
seeing a pig near the shore which was eating some scattered
barley, pronounced it most blessèd in two respects: namely,
that it had barley in plenty and, moreover, was on the shore.

'Ha! For a God-given and lordly dwelling there is nothing
like good old cow-trodden earth! Servator God! That wave is
going to swamp us! O, my friends: give me a little vinegar. I'm
all of a sweat from the strain. Zalas! The halyards have parted;
our head-rope has shattered; our cable-rings have split asunder;
the yard by the crow's nest is plunging into the sea; our keel is
exposed to the heavens; our cables are nearly all broken. Zalas!

45. '48: . . . He invoked *both the twin sons of Leda as well as the eggshell
from which they were hatched*. He then cried out . . .

Zalas! Where are our topsails? All is *verlor' bi Gott.* Our topmast is in rack and ruin. Zalas! Whom will this wreck belong to? My friends! Lend me back here one of those spars from the foc's'le-rail. Lads! Your cordage has buckled! Zalas! Don't abandon the tiller; nor the guide-lines either! I can hear a pintle straining on the rudder. Has it given way? Let's save those trusses, for God's sake. Don't worry about the gun-stays. Be be be: bous bous. Please, please check from the needle of your compass, Master Astrophile, the direction this hurricane is coming from!

['By my faith I'm truly frightened. Bou, bou, bou, bou, bous. I'm finished. I am messing myself from a frenzy of fear. Bou, bou, bou, bou. *Otto to to to to ti. Otto to to to to ti.*[46] Bou, bou, bou; ou, ou, ou; bou, bou, bous, bous. I'm drowning; drowning. I'm dying. Good folks, I'm drowning.']

How Panurge and Frère Jean comported themselves during the storm

CHAPTER 19

[A superb example of a fable or parable (in '48) turned into a directly Evangelical lesson in '52. There is a sustained contrast between Panurge's use of passive pious formulas as magic charms and Frère Jean's cursing and swearing, which is allied to active virtue.

Throughout this chapter the 'Jarus' of '48 continues to become the 'zalas' of '52. The changes, whilst most important, are not individually noted in the variants: they apply every time.

There is no space at all between Candes et Monssoreau, two contiguous villages in Rabelais' pays. That fact gave rise to the local jingle cited in the text.]

Pantagruel, [having first implored the aid of our Servator God and offered public prayers in fervent devotion,] on the advice

---

46. *Otto to to to to ti* is a lamentation taken over from Greek tragedy, one of the features that introduce mock heroic elements into this storm.

of the pilot held the mast steady and firm. Frère Jean had stripped down to his doublet in order to help the seamen. So too, Epistemon, Ponocrates and the others. Panurge remained with his bum on the deck, yelling and wailing. Frère Jean noticed him as he went along the gallery and said to him, 'By God! Panurge the little bovine! Panurge the cry-baby! Panurge the blubberer! You'd be better off helping us over here than bellowing like a cow and squatting on your bollocks like a Barbary baboon.'

'Be, be, be, bous, bous,' Panurge replied, 'Frère Jean, my dear friend, my good Padre, I'm drowning: drowning, dear friend, drowning. I've had it, my spiritual Counsellor; had it, my friend. Your broad-sword can never save me from this! Zalas, zalas! We've shot above top doh, right off the scale. Bebe, bous, bous. zalas! And now we're way below bottom doh! I'm drowning, Ha! Father! Uncle! My All! Water's got into my shoes through the uppers. Bous, bous, bous, atishoo, ha, ha, ha, ah, ah, ah, ah, ah. I'm drowning. Zalas, ha, ha, ha, ha, ha, ha. Be, be, bous, bous, bobous, bobous, oh, oh, oh, oh, oh! Zalas, zalas! I'm doing hand-stands like a forked tree, feet up, head down. Would to God that I were, at this present time, in the carrack of the good and blessèd concilipetary Fathers we met this fore-noon (so devout, so portly, so merry, [so cuddly] and of such good grace). Zalas, zalas! Our ship is going to be swamped by that bloody wave – *mea culpa Deus*, I mean that holy wave of God. – Zalas, Frère Jean, my Padre, my beloved friend: let me make my confession! Here I am on bended knees. *I confess to thee, Father* . . . Give me your holy blessing.'

'In the name of thirty legions of devils come here and help us, you damn gallows-fodder!' said Frère Jean. 'Come on. Will he come, or . . . ?'

'Don't let's swear,' said Panurge, 'not just now, my Father and friend. Tomorrow as much as you like. Holos! holos. Zalas! Our ship is taking in water. I'm drowning. Zalas, zalas! Be, be, be, be, be, bous, bous, bous, bous. Now we really have struck the bottom. Zalas, zalas! I will bestow eighteen hundred thousand crowns a year on anyone who sets me ashore, all dirty and beshitten though I am, if ever man were so in my beshatten land – *I confess to thee* ... Zalas! [Just a word or two to make my will. Or at least a codicil.]'

'May a thousand devils vault into the body of this cuckold,' said Frère Jean. God almighty! Are you talking of wills at a moment like this[47] when we are in peril and must – now or never – exert ourselves! Hey, you devil: are you coming or not?

'Hie! Boatswain, me beauty! Hie, noble alguazil! Over here, Gymnaste, up here on the poop. [Good God: with this wave, we've had it! It's doused our navigation light! Everything's going to all the millions of devils.'

'Zalas, zalas!' said Panurge. 'Zalas. Bou, bou, bou, bous. Was it here that we were predestined to drown? Holos, good folk. I'm drowning; dying. *It is finished!* I'm done for.'

'Magna, gna, gna,' said Frère Jean. 'Ugh! How ugly he is, that snivelling shit.] Hey! cabin-boy! Look to the pump-house; by all the devils. Are you injured? God almighty, hang on to one of those bollards. Round there, in the devil's name. That's right, my lad.'

'Ah! Frère Jean,' said Panurge, 'let us not swear, my spiritual Father and friend. Thou sinnest. Zalas, zalas! Be, be, be, bous, bous, bous: I'm drowning, my friends, I'm dying. I forgive you all. Adieu. *Into Thy hands, O Lord* ...; bous, bous, bouououous. Saint Michel d'Aure! Saint Nicholas! Just this once, and never again. I hereby vow to you both and to Our Lord that if you come to my aid in this strife – I mean if you set me ashore out of this present danger – I'll build you a lovely big little chapel or two,

> 'Twixt Candes and Monssoreau (take heed!)
> Where never cow nor calf can feed.

Zalas, zalas! I've swallowed some eighteen bucketfuls or two of water! Bous, bous, bous, bous: how bitter and salty it is.'

'Virtues of the blood, flesh, belly and head!' said Frère Jean, 'if I ever hear you snivelling again, I shall wallop you like a fish-eating wolf. God almighty! Why don't we just chuck him

47. '48: ... Are you talking of *confession* at a moment like this ...

down to the bottom of the deep? Hey. Leading Oarsman! O, O, my noble fellow. Just so my friend, cling on tight up there. Here's real thunder and lightning for you. I believe all Hell's been let loose, or else Proserpine's in labour. And all the devils are jingling a morris-dance.'

[How the seamen let their ship run before the wind at the height of the storm]

CHAPTER 20

[There is no chapter-break here in '48.

'Cabirotade' is a goat-meat stew, considered a desiccative and a thirst-raiser.

The jest on the French name of Herodotus (Hérodote + Il radote is sport at the expense of etymologies as found in the Cratylus, *which are elsewhere taken very seriously in the* Fourth Book.

Again 'Jarus' is dropped or replaced by 'zalas'.

The addition to the first paragraph, 'I am nought', lends a Classical ring to the story. Nullus sum (I am nought) is an adage of Erasmus (I, III, XLIV), where we are told that it is an hyperbole found in Euripides and Plato and used when one is in danger of perishing.]

'Ah!' said Panurge. 'You, Frère Jean, are committing a sin, my former friend: [*former* I say, for I am nought: you are nought.] It grieves me to say so since I believe that swearing is very good for your spleen, just as a man splitting timber is greatly comforted if someone nearby grunts *ugh!* at every stroke he makes, and just as a player at ninepins is amazingly comforted, whenever he has failed to bowl straight, if some bright soul near by him twists his neck and half-turns his body towards the direction in which the bowl would have run if it had been properly thrown to hit the skittles. Nevertheless, you are still sinning, my dear old friend.[48]

---

48. '48: . . . It grieves me to say so since I believe that *it does you a great deal of good to swear that way.* But you are still sinning . . .

'[But supposing we were to eat some kind of *cabirotade* at this very moment, would we be safe from this storm? I've read somewhere that, at sea during a tempest, those men had nothing to fear and were ever safe who ministered to the *Cabiri* (gods so celebrated by Orpheus, Apollonius, Pherecydes, Strabo, Pausanias – and *Hérodote*.)'

'He radotes!' said Frère Jean. 'Poor old devil.] May a thousand million and hundreds of millions of devils seize hold of that diabolically hornèd cuckold! Hey! Come and help us here, tiger-boy! Is he ever going to come?[49]

'Here, to larboard. God's head stuffed with relics! What chattering monkeyish paternoster are you mumbling over there? That devil of a maritime fool has brought on this storm yet he's the only one not helping the crew. By God, if I get over there, I shall whip you like a foul-weather fiend![50]

'Cabin-boy! Here, my darling! Hold your thumb here, lad, while I tie a Greek knot. Oh, what a good cabin-boy you are. Would to God that you were now the abbot of Talemousse and the present abbot were the warden of Le Croullay.

'Ponocrates! You'll be doing yourself an injury, brother.

'Epistemon! Watch out for those bulwarks: I saw a thunderbolt strike them just now.'

'Heave!'

'Well said. Heave; heave; heave. Let the pinnace ride. Heave. Good God! What's that? Our prow's been knocked to smithereens. [Thunder away, devils! Fart, let off and dump your droppings.] A shit on that wave! Good God! it all but swept me away in its under-tow. All the devils in their millions are holding their provincial chapter-meeting, I think [, or bickering over the election of a new Rector].'

'Larboard!'

'Well said. Hey, cabin-boy: in the devil's name watch out for that pulley. Larboard! Larboard!'

49. '48: . . . Come and help us here, *you bugger, you sod of all the incubi, succubi and all the devils there are.* Is he ever going to come? . . .
50. '48: . . . the crew, *and he is still bothering us with his yelling.* By God, if I get over there I shall flog you like a *maritime* fiend! Cabin-boy! . . .

'Bebebebous, bous, bous,' said Panurge, '[bous, bous, bebe, be, bou, bous. I'm drowning.] I can see neither sky nor Earth. [Zalas, zalas! Of the four elements, all that's left to us here are fire and water. Bouboubous, bous, bous.] Would to God in his condign power that at this present hour I were in the abbey-close at Seuilly, or else at Innocent the pastry-cook's opposite the *Cave Peinte* in Chinon, stripped to my doublet if needs be and baking little fancy-cakes. My man! I wonder if would you mind just casting me ashore? [I've been told that you know a great many clever tricks.] If by your skill I find myself once and for all on *terra-firma*, I'll give you all the estate of Salmagundi as well as my great snail-farm. Zalas, zalas! I'm drowning.[51]

'Dear friends, since we can't make a good harbour, let us ride this one out somewhere in some roads or other. Drop all your anchors. Let us get out of this danger, I beg you. Good friend, please, please, swing the lead and drop the weight. Let us know the height of the Deep! Take soundings, my dear fellow and friend, for Our Lord's sake. Let's find out whether we could drink standing up without stooping down. I have my own idea about that!'

['See to the ties,' bawled the master-pilot, 'see to the ties! Hands to the jeer-lines. Bring those ties about! Cut down the topping-lifts! Look to those ties. See we don't gybe over! Ho, there! That clew-line. Pay out that clew-line. Ho there! Those ties. Bows to the sea. Unyoke the rudder. Run before the wind.'

'So we have come to that, have we?' said Pantagruel: 'Then may God our good Servator come to our aid!'

'Ho! Let her run before the wind,' bawled Jamet Brahier, the master-pilot. 'Let her run before the wind. Let each man think on his soul and turn to his devotions, without any hope of aid except for a miracle from Heaven.'

'Let's make some good and lovely vow,' said Panurge. 'Zalas, zalas, zalas! Bou, bou; bebebebous, bous, bous. Zalas, zalas. Let's have a whip-round and send off a pilgrim! Come on! Let everyone fork out some lovely nice pence! Come on.']

51. '48: . . . I'll give *you all that I have; just throw me there. Jarus. Jarus!* I'm drowning . . .

'Over here!' said Frère Jean, 'In the name of all the devils, over here, to starboard. [In the name of God, let her run before the wind. Unyoke that rudder, ho! Let her run before the wind! Run before the wind, ho! Let's have a drink: I mean of what's best for the taste and the stomach. Hey! Chief steward, up there! Can you hear me? Produce and display! All this is on its way to millions of devils too. Ho, page-boy! Bring me my thirst-raiser,' – his name for his breviary.] 'Hang on! A swig, my friend, a swig! God almighty, now this truly is hail and thunder! Hold on tight up there, I beg you. [When is the Feast of All-Saints? It's a beast of a Feast today: for All the Millions of Devils, I believe!']

'Zalas!' said Panurge; 'Frère Jean is damning himself on the cheap! O, what a good friend I'm losing in him. Zalas, zalas! Here comes worse than before! We are leaping from Scylla to Charybdis. Oh, oh! I'm drowning! *Unto Thee I confess* . . . Just one little word to make my will, Frère Jean, my Father; and you too Monsieur Abstractor, my friend, my Achates; and Xenomanes, my All. Zalas, I'm drowning!

'Two words for my will and testament. Hold on to companion way.'

The storm: continued. And a short discussion about wills drawn up at sea

CHAPTER 21

[*In '48 this is* Chapter 10, *with the title* The Storm: continued. And of the talk of Frère Jean and Panurge about wills drawn up at sea.

The talk of wills may be seen in the light of Tiraqueau's commentary, The Dead seizeth the Quick *mentioned in the* Prologue.

'*Jarus' is again avoided.*

'*The Broken-lancers' are the unseated cavalrymen fighting on foot mentioned in Caesar's* Gallic Wars, I, 39.

The '52 interpolations at the climax of the storm greatly increase both the tragic and the Evangelical elements. Panurge again puts the Blessed Virgin on a par with God, while Pantagruel quotes the apostles

*during the storm in Matthew 8:25 as well as 'Thy will be done' from
the Lord's Prayer. Frère Jean, too, prays in his grubby way, welcoming
his Breviary as his 'thirst-raiser' – his mouth gets dry when chanting
from it – and starting off with the first Psalm.*

*Towards the end of the chapter, an adaptation of a line of Horace,
'Horrida tempestas caelum contraxit' ('The horrid tempest contracts
the sky') is turned into a satire of Professor Tempête, the flogging
principal of the hated Collège de Montaigu in Paris.]*

'To draw up a will now' said Epistemon, 'when it behoves us
to exert ourselves and help the crew on pain of shipwreck,
seems to me to be an action as inappropriate and ill-timed as
that of those Broken-lancers and friends of Caesar's who, when
invading Gaul, wasted their time drawing up wills and codicils,
lamenting their fortune and weeping for their absent wives and
friends in Rome, whereas they ought, of necessity, to have been
rushing to arms and exerting themselves against Ariovistus their
foe.

'It is silliness like that of the carter who, when he got stuck
in a furrow, implored on his knees the help of Hercules without
even putting the goad to his oxen or lending a hand to raise up
the wheels. What use can it be to you to make a will? Either
we shall escape this danger or else we shall be drowned. Your
will, if we escape, is of no use to you. Wills are authorized and
validated only by the deaths of their testators. And if we do
drown, that will of yours goes down with us. Right? And who
will bring it to the executors?'

'Some fair wave,' said Panurge, 'will cast it up on to the shore
as it did to Ulysses; and some king's daughter, taking a pleasant
stroll in the cool of the evening will happen upon it, have it
carefully executed and erect a magnificent cenotaph to me hard
by the shore, as:
– Dido erected one to her husband Sichaeus;
– Aeneas, to Deiphobus on the Trojan shore near Rhaete;
– Andromache, to Hector in the city of Bathrotum;
– Aristotle, to Hermias and Eubulus;
[– the men of Athens, to the poet Euripides;]

– the men of Rome, to Drusus in Germany and to their emperor, Alexander Severus in Gaul;
[– Argentier, to Callaeschrus;
– Xenocrites, to Lysidice;
– Timares, to his son, Teleutagoras;
– Eupolis and Aristodice to their son, Theotimus;
– Onestes to Timocles;
– Callimachus, to Sopolis, the son of Diocleides;]
– Catulus, to his brother;
– Statius, to his father;
and Germain de Brie, to Hervé, the Breton seaman.'

'Are you raving mad?' said Frère Jean. 'Help us over here, in the name of five hundred thousand millions of wagon-loads of devils! Help us! May you get canker of the moustache with three lengths of sores (enough to make you a new pair of breeches and a new codpiece too).

'Has our ship struck a reef? God almighty, how shall we tow it off? What a devil of a sea is running! We shall never get out of this, or I'll give myself to all the devils.'

[Then was heard a devout call from Pantagruel, who cried, 'Lord save us. We perish. Yet may it not be according to our affections, but Thy holy will be done.']

'God,' said Panurge, 'and the Blessed Virgin be with us! O – o – o. O – o – o. I'm drowning. Bebebebous, bebebous, bous. *Into Thy hands, O Lord* ... True God, send me some dolphin to bear me safely ashore like some [nice] little Arion: I shall sound my harp well if it's not out of tune.'

'I give myself to all the devils' said Frère Jean, – 'God be with us,' muttered Panurge through his teeth – 'if I come down below I shall prove to you that those balls of yours are hanging from the arse of a horny, hornèd, dehorned, cuckolded calf. Mgna, mgna, mgna. Come over here and help us, you great blubbering calf, in the name of thirty million devils: and may they leap on your body! Are you going to come, you sea-calf? Ugh! How ugly he is, the great cry-baby.'

'Can't you say anything else?'

'Come to the fore then, my jolly old thirst-raiser. Let me pluck you against the grain: *Blessed is the man that hath not walked* – I know this off by heart! – Let's see the pericope for Monsignor of Saint Nicholas:

Horrida tempestas montem turbavit acutum.

(Horrid old Tempête troubled the Collège de Montaigu.)

'Tempête was a great flogger of undergraduates at Montaigu. If for flogging wretched little boys and innocent undergraduates pedagogues are damned, then, upon my honour, he's on Ixion's wheel, flogging the lop-tailed cur which makes it turn. If by flogging innocent boys pedagogues are saved, he must now be way above the . . .'[52]

The end of the storm

CHAPTER 22

[The last word of the previous chapter would have been cieux *(skies), but once the heroes have done all they can, God quietly works his miracle and so the next word – the first word of this chapter – is* terre! *(earth!, or land!) Even Frère Jean thanks God. Panurge does not: he goes back on his vows.*

Death is discussed in Classical terms.

The learned Epistemon employs two rare words from the Greek; he may be the only one to ever use them in French: celeusma *(a term Rabelais would have met in Lucian, Proverbs and in Thessalonians 4:15) and* obelischolichnia. Celeusma, *means shouts of encouragement such as might be given to oarsmen in a galley;* obeliscolychny *means*

52. This chapter ends differently in '48: . . . 'I give myself to all the devils' said Frère Jean, – 'God be with us,' muttered Panurge through his teeth – 'if *the close at Seuilly had not been thus lost, if I had done nothing but chant* Against the onslaughts of our enemies, Good Lord deliver us, *like those other devils of monks, without succouring the vine against the pillagers from Lerné.*'

strictly a light on a pole, and may do so here, or else by extension a
lighthouse. He also prefers to give Castor his Greek name, Mixarcha-
gevas.

It is Pantagruel who evokes Homer's Ucalegon, a Trojan who
avoided battle while the others were fighting.]

'Land! Land ahoy!' cried Pantagruel. 'A spurt of sheep's courage now, lads! We're not far from a haven. I can see the sky
begin to clear towards the polar star. Watch out for that
sea-wind.'

'Courage, lads,' said the master pilot; 'the surge has abated.
Up, now, to the yards of the maintop. Heave. Heave. Now for
the spankers of the after-mizzenmast.

['Cable to capstan! Heave away, heave away, heave away.
Hands to the jeer-lines. Heave, heave, heave. Yoke the rudder.
Steady the sheets. Ready the rigging. Ready the ties. Ready the
bow-lines. Set the starboard cables. Bring the helm to leeward.
Tighten the sheets to starboard, you son of a whore!'
– 'News of your mother, good fellow. How nice for you!'
said Frère Jean to the matelot. –

'Luff. Close to, face to the wind. Right the helm.'

'Right it is sir,' answered the sailors.

'Cut straight ahead. Bows to the harbour-roads. Clear space
to tack on the studding-sail. Ho.]

'Heave; heave.'

'Well said and well thought,' said Frère Jean. 'Up you go,
lads; up, up; hard to it. Good. Haul away. Haul.'

'To starboard.'

'Well put and right masterly. Happily the storm seems to
have passed its climax and to be coming to an end. [May God
be praised for it.] Our devils are beginning to scamper away!'

['Slacken the line.'

'Well and knowledgeably spoken. Slacken the line. Slacken
the line. Over here, for God's sake, noble Ponocrates, you
powerful old lecher. (He'll beget nothing but boy-children, the
lusty old codger.) Eusthenes, my brave fellow, spread the
foretop-sail.'

'Heave, heave.'

'That's well said. Heave, for God's sake; heave, heave.'
'I wouldn't deign to fear anything,

> For today's a holy-day, they tell.
> Noel, noel, noel!'

'That *celeusma* is not at all out of place,' said Epistemon, 'and it pleases me,

> For today's a holy-day, they tell.'

'Heave; heave. Right you are.']
'Oh!' cried Epistemon, 'I require you all to be full of good hope: I can see Castor over there to the right.'
'Be, be, bous, bous, bous,' said Panurge: 'I very much fear it may be [that bitch of a] Helen.'
'Truly,' said Epistemon, 'it is Mixarchagevas (if, that is, you prefer the denomination of the Argives). Ahoy! Ahoy! I can see land; I can see a port; I can see a great throng of people on the quayside. I can see flares on an obeliscolychny.'
['Ahoy, ahoy there,' said the pilot; 'round the cape. And avoid those sandbanks.'
'Rounded it is, sir,' the matelots replied.
'Away she goes,' said the pilot. 'And so do all the others in the convoy. Splice the main brace to help on the weather.'
'By Saint John,' said Panurge, 'that's talking, that is! O what a beautiful saying.'
'Mgna, mgna, mgna,' said Frère Jean; 'if you touch one drop may the devil touch me! Do you understand me, you ballsed-up devil? Here, good friend, is a tankard full of the finest and best! Bring out the drinking-pots, ho, Gymnaste! And that hunking great pasty. Is it *iambic* or *jambonic*? It's all one to me.]
'Mind we don't slew round.'
'Good heart,' cried Pantagruel, 'good heart, my lads. And let us be chivalrous: hard by our vessel you can see two bumboats [, three sloops, five ships, eight flyboats, four gondolas] and six frigates sent out to help us from the good people of that nearby island.

'But who is that Ucalegon weeping and blubbering down below? Was I not holding the mainmast in my hands more surely than a hundred cables?'

'It's that wretched devil of a Panurge,' Frère Jean replied. 'He's caught the calf-shivers. He trembles with fear whenever he's drunk!'

'If,' said Pantagruel, 'he felt fear during that horrifying hurricane and menacing storm, I do not value him one tiny hair less: provided that he had bestirred himself. For just as it is a sign of a coarse and cowardly heart to feel fear at every shock (as Agamemnon did: for which reason Achilles shamefully reproached him with having the keen sight of a dog and the faint heart of a deer), so, too, for a man not to be afraid when the situation is manifestly formidable is a sign of want or lack of intelligence. Now, if next to offending God there is anything to fear in this life, I will not say it is death – I do not want to get involved in the contention of Socrates and the Academics, that death is not bad in itself and so not in itself to be feared – I do say that either death by shipwreck is to be feared, or nothing is; for as Homer puts it, it is a grievous, ghastly and disnatured thing to perish at sea.[53] Aeneas, indeed, during the tempest which surprised his convoy of boats off Sicily, regretted that he had not died at the strong hand of Diomedes; he declared those to be *thrice and four times blessèd* who had died in the conflagration of Troy.[54]

'Here, not one man has died. For which may God our Servator be for ever praised. But this is all a bit of a mess. Right! We must repair the damage. And see we don't run aground.'

---

53. '48: . . . to perish at sea. *The reason given by the Pythagoreans is because the soul is of the substance of fire, so that when a man dies in the sea – an opposing element – it seems to them, though the contrary is true, that the soul is totally extinguished.* Aeneas, indeed . . .

   In '52 Rabelais rejects even a hint that souls may be quenched by sea-water, and returns to the subject in Chapter 26, where it is central to his adaptation of Plutarch.

54. A very Classical ending, with allusions to Homer (*Iliad*, 1, 225; *Odyssey* 5, 312) and Virgil (*Aeneid*, 1, 94), as well as to Cicero.

How Panurge acted the brave companion once
the storm was over

CHAPTER 23

[Rabelais turns a fable or parable into a comic sermon with a tragic dimension: men must 'cooperate' with God. The lesson is a more theologically precise version of the same lesson in Pantagruel's prayer before the battle in Pantagruel, *Chapter 19 and the parable of Frère Jean's fighting during the attack on Seuilly (*Gargantua, *Chapter 25ff.) though there it was 'helping' God that was mentioned or implied not, 'cooperating' or 'working together' with him. The basic authority is I Corinthians 3:9: 'We are workers together with the Lord'. In the Vulgate Latin we are God's 'helpers' (adjutores); Erasmus and others insisted that 'synergism' entails 'cooperators', or 'workers together' not 'helpers'. (God, being almighty, needs no help but by allowing human beings to cooperate with him he bestows on them the dignity of causality.) Such synergism forms the very stuff of the moral laughter in Rabelais.*

Panurge cites a saying well known as an Erasmian adage: I, II, XCI, 'The most delightful sailing follows the land, the most delightful walking follows the shore'.

Rabelais has taken over here and rewritten matter from the end of Chapter 21.

Frère Jean retains his role as a symbol of active virtue.]

'Ho, ho!' cried Panurge; 'everything's going well. The storm is over. I beg you, I pray you, do let me be the first to go below. I really would rather like to attend to a few things. Shall I help you again over there? Permit me to coil up that rope. Indeed: plenty of courage I have: of fear, very little. Give it to me, my friend. No, not a ha'porth of fear. It's true that that decuman billow which swamped us from prow to poop did rather desiccate my arteries.'

'Strike sails!'

'That's well said. What! Not doing anything, Frère Jean? Is this the time to be drinking? How do we know that the devil –

Saint Martin's foot-boy – isn't brewing up a fresh storm for us? Do you want me to help you again over there? Golly. I know it's too late now, but I'm sorry that I never followed the teachings of those good philosophers who say that it is a safe and delectable thing to stroll *near* the sea, and to sail *near* the land. It's like going on foot whilst leading your horse by the bridle. Ho, ho, ho! By God: everything is going well. Shall I help you again over there? Give it to me. I'll do it or the devil will be in it somewhere.'

Epistemon had all the palm of one hand flayed and bloody from having held fast to a hawser with all his might; upon hearing the words of Pantagruel, he said,

'Believe me, my Lord, I felt no less fear and terror than Panurge. But then what? I did not spare myself as I helped. I consider that if, in truth, dying is – as indeed it is – a matter of fatal and unavoidable necessity, dying at such-and-such a time and in such-and-such a manner is within the holy will of God. Wherefore we must ceaselessly implore him, entreat, invoke, petition and beseech him. But we must not make that our bounds and our limit: we, on our part, must duly exert ourselves and, as the Holy Envoy say, be *workers together* with him.[55]

'You know what Gaius Flaminius, the consul, said when he was cleverly pinned down by Hannibal near the lake in Perusia called Thrasymene: "Lads," he said to his soldiers, "you cannot hope to escape from here by making vows or imploring the gods: it is by our might and valour that we must escape, slicing our way through the enemy with the edge of our swords."

'So too in Sallust: "The help of the gods [said Marcus Portius

---

55. The first ('48) version of the storm was a fable with Classical gods, from which a Christian meaning is extracted as in a fable or parable. In '52 the Christian theology becomes precise. Contrast the above with the text of '48: ... dying at such-and-such a time and in such-and-such manner is *partly in the will of the gods, partly in our own will.* Wherefore ... we, on our part, must duly exert ourselves *and help them with the means and remedy. If I am not speaking in accordance with the decrees of the Mataeologians they will forgive me: I am speaking by book and authority.* You know what ...

Rabelais remains loyal to the partly/partly moral theology of Saint Bonaventura, which he studied as a Franciscan friar.

Cato] is not secured by idle vows or womanish weepings: it is by watching, toiling and exerting ourselves that all things reach [as we wish] a goodly port. If anyone is neglectful, unmanly and lazy in the face of danger and necessity it is in vain that he implores the gods, who are angered by him and outraged." '

['I,' said Frère Jean, 'will give myself to the devil . . .'

– 'And I,' said Panurge, 'will go halves with you!' –

'. . . if all the grapes hadn't been harvested and the abbey-close wrecked, if I had merely chanted *Against the fear of our enemies* (as those other monks were doing, the devils), without coming to the defence of our vines by thwacking those pillagers from Lerné with the shaft of the Cross.']

'*Sail on, O galley!*' said Panurge. 'Everything's going well. And Frère Jean over there is doing nothing. [His name is Frère Jean Do-nowt.] He's just watching me sweating and toiling away to help Matelot the First, this good fellow here.

'Hola, dear friend of ours! A couple of words, if it's not a bother. What's the thickness of the timbers of this vessel?'

'A good two fingers thick,' the pilot replied: 'Don't be frightened.'

'God almighty,' said Panurge; 'we're always two fingers'-breadth from death then! Is this one of the nine joys of marriage? Ha, my dear friend, you do well to measure danger by the yardstick of fear. Personally I feel no fear: I'm called William the Fearless: I have courage to spare. I mean not the courage of a lamb: I mean the courage of a wolf and the confidence of a cut-throat. There is nothing I fear – but dangers.'

How Panurge is declared by Frère Jean to have been needlessly afraid during the storm

CHAPTER 24

[*Panurge as often twists his sources, here cheekily applying Genesis 3 to himself, especially the curse laid upon the fallen Adam: 'In the sweat of thy face thou shalt eat thy bread'.*

The sayings of Anacharsis are commented upon by Erasmus
(Apophthegms, VII, Anacharsis Scytha, XIII and XV).

Chapelle *in French – as (just) in English – can mean an alembic as*
well as a place of worship.]

'Good morrow, gentlemen,' said Panurge. 'Good morrow to
each one of you. [Is every one of you faring well, thanks to God
and to you? Be most truly and timely welcome.] Let's clamber
ashore. [Ho there, ship's-boys: lower the ladder and bring that
pinnace alongside.]

'Shall I help you again over there?

'[I have a ravenous hunger for doing good and toiling away
like four oxen. This is truly a beautiful place; and the people
are good. Do you still need my help, lads? For God's sake,
spare not the sweat of my brow. Adam (that means, Man) is
born to plough and to toil as a bird is born to fly. Our Lord
wishes (do you hear it well?) that in the sweat of our face we
do eat our bread – not by doing nothing at all like Frère Jean,
that decrepit monk you can see tippling away over there and
dying of fear.]

'The fair weather has come. I now know the reply of that
noble philosopher Anacharsis to be true and well founded in
reason: asked which ship he believed to be safest: he replied,
The one in the harbour.'

['Better still,' said Pantagruel, 'was when he was asked which
were more numerous, the quick or the dead; he replied, *How
do you class those sailing the seas?*, quietly suggesting that those
who sail the seas are always so close to the risk of death that
they live as they die and die as they live. Thus did Portius Cato
say that he regretted three things only: ever having told a secret
to a woman; ever having idled a day away; ever having travelled
by sea to anywhere accessible by land.']

'By this worthy frock that I wear,' said Frère Jean [to Pan-
urge], 'you, my friendly old bollock, were frightened [during
that storm] without rhyme or reason: it is not your [fated]
destiny to perish by water; you will be high up in the air
(hanged, certainly, or else jolly well burnt like a Friar). [My
Lord: would you like a good mantle to ward off the rain? Drop

all those wolf-skin or badger-skin cloaks: have the hide off
Panurge and cover yourself with it. But for God's sake don't
approach the fire with it on or pass in front of a blacksmith's
forge: you would see it burnt to a cinder in a flash. Yet expose
yourself to the rain as much as you like, and to snow and to
hail. Dive deep down into water with it on, yet by God you will
never get wet. Make winter boots from it: they will never let in
the rain. Make bladders from it for boys who are learning to
swim: they will learn without danger.'

'His hide, then,' said Pantagruel, 'would be like the herb
called maidenhair fern, which never gets damp nor soggy: it
always stays dry even when kept as long as you like in deep
water: that is why it is called impermeable (*adiantos*).'

'Panurge, my friend,' said Frère Jean. 'Never fear water, I
pray you. Your life will be terminated by the contrary element.']

'Maybe,' replied Panurge, 'but the devil's chefs sometimes go
mad and err in their duties: they often put souls on to boil
which were meant to be roasted [, just as in our kitchens here
below the cooks often lard up their partridges, pigeons and
queests, presumably intending to roast them, only to end up
boiling them, the partridges with cabbage; the pigeons with
leeks, and the queests with turnips.

'Now listen, my fine friends: I contend before you all that
when I vowed a *chapel* to Monsieur Saint Nicholas *'Twixt
Candes and Monssoreau (take heed)* I meant a rose-water alembic, *Where never calf nor cow can feed*, because I shall toss it
down to the bottom of the river.'

'Behold the brave!' said Eusthenes: 'the brave, now a brave-
and-a-half. It proves what is asserted by the Lombardy proverb:
'The peril once off, the saint's worshippers scoff'].

How Pantagruel landed after the storm on the islands of the Macraeons

CHAPTER 25

[In '48 this was Chapter 11, the last of its chapters, which begins but does not come to a proper end. After 'It is true that' in the second paragraph, the '48 Fourth Book peremptorily breaks off with 'quia plus n'en dict' ('because, no more is said').

Macraeon and Macrobios mean long-liver, hence 'Macrobe'.

Macquerelle means a procuress. The Ile Maquerelle in Paris, apparently then known for its bawdy-houses, is now called the Ile des Cygnes.

Rabelais sometimes uses 'oysters in their shell' for women of easy virtue or for vaginas or cunnilingus.

During the storm God had regard for the 'simplicity and pure intentions' of Pantagruel and his men. Cf. the same qualities in Judge Bridoye (Third Book, Chapters 37 and 43). Behind the laughter serious thoughts are being prepared.]

We at once disembarked at the port of an island which was called the Isle of the Macraeons. The good folk there welcomed us honourably. An ancient Macrobe (such was the title of their chief provost) wanted to bear Pantagruel off to the Town Hall, there to rest at his ease and have something to eat, but Pantagruel refused to leave the jetty before every one of his men had come ashore. After reviewing them, he ordered each of them to change his clothes and the totality of the ship's victuals to be set out on the quayside so that all the crew could make merry. Which was done at once. And Lord knows how they drank and feasted. All the people of the isle also brought provisions in abundance: the Pantagruelists gave them even more.

It is true that their own provisions had been somewhat spoilt during the preceding storm.

Once the feast was over Pantagruel told every man to do his task and dutifully repair the damage. Which they all did with a good heart. The task of repair was made easy by the fact that the inhabitants of that island were all carpenters and craftsmen such as can be seen at the Arsenal in Venice; only the largest island was inhabited, and that in three ports and ten parishes: all the rest was given over to tall trees and was as thinly populated as the forest of the Ardennes.

At our insistence the old Macrobe showed us what was worth seeing or outstanding on the island: within those dark and deserted woodlands he revealed to us several ancient ruined temples and several obelisks, monuments and tombs bearing various inscriptions and epitaphs, some in hieroglyphics, some in the Ionic tongue, or in the Arabic, Hagarene, Slavonic or other tongues. Epistemon carefully copied them down. Meanwhile Panurge said to Frère Jean, 'This is the Isle of the Macraeons: *macraeon* in Greek means an *old* man, a man of many years.'

'What do you want me to do about it?' said Frère Jean. 'Undo it?' I certainly wasn't here when this land was christened.'

'While on the subject,' said Panurge, 'I think that the term *maquerelle* derives from *macraeon*, for *procuring* becomes only the *old* women: using their bums becomes the young ones. It makes you wonder whether this is the model and prototype of the *Ile Maquerelle* in Paris. Let's fish about for a few oysters in the shell.'

That ancient Macrobe asked Pantagruel in the Ionic tongue how and by what toil and labour they had managed to dock in their harbour on a day when there had been such a violent disturbance in the air and such a terrifying tempest out at sea.

Pantagruel replied that the Servator on high had regarded the simplicity and pure intentions of his people, who were not voyaging for gain nor dealing in merchandise. One single cause had brought them to put to sea: namely a scholarly desire to see, learn and visit the Oracle of Bacbuc and to have the word of La Bouteille concerning certain difficulties exposed by one of their company. It had not however been without sore affliction and evident peril of shipwreck.

Then Pantagruel asked him what he deemed to be the cause of that frightful storm, and whether the neighbouring seas were normally subject to tempests, as are the Raz-Saint-Matthieu,

Maumusson and (within the Mediterranean) the Gulf of Adalia, Montargentan, Piombino, Cape Melio in Laconia, the Straits of Gibraltar, the Straits of Messina and others.

How the good Macrobe tells Pantagruel about the Manor and the Departure of Heroes

CHAPTER 26

[Rabelais has meditated deeply on Plutarch's Obsolescence of Oracles. *Interpreting Plutarch and other Classical authors as veiled forerunners of Christianity is typical of the fifteenth-century Renaissance in Italy and of the first half of the sixteenth century for the Northern Renaissance. A reading of the* Obsolescence of Oracles *is interesting in itself and throws much light on to Rabelais' mind in this and the following chapters. (Even better would be to read all the treatises in Volume 5 of the Loeb bilingual edition of Plutarch's* Moralia, *each of which Rabelais draws upon). This chapter is particularly indebted to sections 419 E to 420 F of the* Obsolescence of Oracles.*

The 'unveiling' of half-hidden truths by Renaissance humanists is not to be confused with the absurd finding of the Christian sacraments in Ovid, which Rabelais mocked in the Prologue to Gargantua. *It is in a learned tradition which reaches back to Eusebius and his* Preparation of the Gospel *(third–fourth centuries AD). It is fully within the humanist syncretism prepared for in the Prologue to this Fourth Book. Origen and the Greek fathers encouraged it. So in their different ways did, amongst many others, Marsilio Ficino and Erasmus. Rabelais unveils the deeper meanings of Plutarch and in so doing brings precise changes to the text. Plutarch assumes that even exceptional human souls are eventually snuffed out like candle-flames, leaving nothing but stormy disturbances in the air. Rabelais does not: for him and his entire culture death is not extinction but the final separation on earth of body and soul. Plutarch's texts are adapted by Rabelais to such ends.*

'Hero' is used here as in Plutarch for someone who is above the normal human level in the scale of Being.

The mystical islands off Britain are, it seems, the Channel Islands.

For the last paragraph Rabelais turns to an adage of Erasmus, I, III, LXXX, 'When I am dead let the earth be mixed with fire', and probably to the following one, 'To mix sea and sky'.]

Whereupon that good Macrobe replied:

'Strangers and friends, you have here one of the Sporades: not those Sporades of yours in the Caspian Sea but the Oceanic Sporades; they were once rich, much visited, mercantile and densely populated, being subject to the Ruler of Britain: now, given the lapse of time and the world in decline, they are poor and abandoned, as you can tell.

'Within the darkling forest that you see yonder, which is over three-score and eighteen parasanges in length and breadth, there lies the habitation of Daemons and Heroes who have grown old; and (since the comet which had appeared to us over three full days before no longer shines) we believe that one of them has died, at whose death was aroused the dreadful storm which you experienced. For while they are alive, all good things flourish here and in the other isles near by: then at sea all is ever calm and serene. When one of them dies we regularly hear great and piteous lamentations throughout the forest, and witness plagues, disasters and tribulations on land, tumults and darkness in the air, storm and gales at sea.'

'In what you say,' said Pantagruel, 'there is every appearance of truth. For as the wax-torch or candle, all the time that it is burning with a living flame, shines on those who are near it and throws light on to its surroundings, gratifying each person and offering to each its light and its service, causing no harm or annoyance to anyone, yet the instant it is extinguished it infects the air with its smoke and vapours, troubling those who are near it and offending each one: thus it is with those noble and outstanding souls. During all the time that they inhabit their bodies, their dwelling-place is peaceful, fruitful, delectable, honourable: but come the hour of their Departure there commonly occur throughout the isles and mainland great commotions, darkness, lightning and storms of hail in the air; shocks, quakes and perturbations on land; gales and tempests at sea, with lamentations amongst peoples, mutations of religions, transfers of kingdoms and the overthrowing of common-wealths.'

'Not long ago,' said Epistemon, 'we saw that from experience during the demise of the learned and chivalrous knight Guillaume Du Bellay. While he was alive France was in such felicity that all the world envied her, all the world courted her, all the world feared her: immediately following his death France long suffered the world's contempt.'

'Thus,' said Pantagruel, 'when Anchises died at Trepani in Sicily, the storm caused great distress to Aeneas. And it perhaps explains why, once Herod (the tyrant and cruel king of Judaea) realized that he was close to a horrible, naturally terrifying death – he died of phthiriasis, consumed by worms and lice, as did before him Lucius Sylla, Pherecydes of Syria (the preceptor of Pythagoras), Alcman the Greek poet, and others still: and foreseeing that the Jews would be lighting joyful bonfires when he died, he caused all the nobles and magistrates from every city, town and fortress in Judaea to gather in his private palace under the colour of the fraudulent pretext that he wished to communicate to them matters of importance to the governance and safety of the Province. Once they had arrived and presented themselves in person, he had them locked up in his palace race-course. He then said to Salome his sister and to Alexander her husband:

' "I am convinced that the Jews will rejoice over my death, but if you grasp what I shall tell you and carry it out, my obsequies will be honoured ones: and there will be public displays of grief. The moment I am dead, order the archers of my guard – who have an express commission from me – to slaughter every one of the nobles and magistrates locked up in there. By your so doing, all the inhabitants of Judaea will start grieving and lamenting despite themselves: it will seem to foreigners that that is because of my death, as though some heroic soul had passed away."

'A certain irredeemable tyrant had similar pretensions: "When I die," he said, "let the earth and fire mix together", meaning, let the entire universe perish. Which that vile Nero changed, as Suetonius tells us, into "While I live !"

'That detestable saying (which Cicero mentions in his book

On the Ends of Good and Evil, and Seneca in Book Two of
On Clemency) is attributed to Tiberius by Dion Cassius and
Suidas.'

How Pantagruel reasons about the Departures of Heroic souls: and of the awe-inspiring prodigies which preceded the death of the late Seigneur de Langey

CHAPTER 27

*[For the second paragraph of this chapter Rabelais again turns to an
adage of Erasmus, I, V, LVI, 'Theta praefigere' ('To set up a theta');
however a capital alpha (A) was printed in error for the capital delta
(Δ) given by Erasmus. That misprint is corrected here.*

Another echo of the Adages *is of I, II, XXVI, 'The catastrophe of
a drama'. ('Catastrophe' in this sense is the third part of a drama 'in
which things suddenly change'.)*

Rabelais, developing what he wrote in Chapter 21 of the Third
Book, *gives us here the only account we have of the death of Guillaume
Du Bellay, the Seigneur de Langey, to whom he was a physician. As
we were told in the* Third Book, *Guillaume Du Bellay died at Mont
Tarare near Lyons on his way back from Italy. Named persons, lords
and physicians are mentioned as present at his death.*

*In scholastic philosophy a good or evil spirit may work something
against Nature; a true miracle, something against the* whole order *of
Nature, appertains to God alone.*

*When Rabelais was writing these pages he was, again as physician,
part of the household of Cardinal Jean Du Bellay, the brother of his
hero. We can assume that Rabelais read the* Fourth Book *privately to
him before it was published. The cardinal then heard how his brother's
death enabled Rabelais to unveil the true and deeper meaning of the
pages of Plutarch he is transposing. Beneath the veil of Plutarch lie
intimations of immortality.]*

'I wouldn't have missed suffering that storm at sea which so
greatly tormented and distressed us if it meant having to miss

what that good Macrobe had to say. I am moreover readily inclined to believe what he told us about the comet seen in the skies on certain days preceding the departure of such a soul. For some souls are so noble, rare and heroic that signs that they are to leave their lodgings and die are given to us by the heavens some days beforehand. And just as the wise physician, when he recognizes the signs portending that his patient is sinking towards death, warns the wife, children, kinsfolk and friends a few days beforehand of the imminent decease of their husband, father and neighbour so that, in the time he has left, they can warn him to set his household in order, counsel and bless his children, commend widowhood to his wife, make the necessary arrangements for the care of his under-age charges, and be not himself surprised by death before he has drawn up his will and made dispositions for his soul and his household: so too the kindly heavens, as though rejoicing at a new reception for such blessèd souls, seem to be lighting festive fires before their deaths with such comets and shooting stars, which the heavens intend to be reliable prognostics and genuine predictions for human beings that within a few days those venerated souls will leave their bodies and this Earth.

'In much the same way the judges of old in the Areopagus at Athens, when voting about the verdict to be reached over men imprisoned on criminal charges, wrote certain alphabetical signs depending on their conclusions: Θ (theta) signified the death sentence; T (tau) signified acquittal; and when the case was not yet liquid-clear, Δ (delta) signified *More amplification needed*. Those symbols were exposed to public view, thus freeing from anxiety and conjecture the kinsfolk, friends and others who wanted to know what would be the outcome and verdict on the malefactors detained in prison: similarly, by such comets (as though by notifications in the upper air) the heavens tacitly say: "Mortal Men: if there is anything at all you wish to know, learn, hear, understand or foresee from these blessèd souls touching the public good and your private concerns, present yourselves quickly before them and receive an answer from them. For the catastrophe of the drama approaches. Once that is passed, in vain will you regret them."

'They go further: in order to pronounce the Earth and its peoples unworthy of the presence, company and enjoyment of such worthy souls, they astonish and terrify them with marvels, portents, omens and other preceding signs formed against the whole order of Nature: as we saw several days before the departure of the illustrious, bountiful and heroic soul of that learned and chivalrous knight, the Seigneur de Langey, of whom you have spoken.'

'I well remember it,' said Epistemon, 'and even now my heart quakes and trembles within its tegument when I think about those marvels, so varied and terrifying, which we clearly saw five or six days before his departing; such that the Seigneurs d'Assier, Chemant, Mailly-le-Borgne, Saint-Ayl, Villeneuve-la-Guyart, as well as Maître Gabriel, the physician from Savillan, Rabelais, Cohuau, Massuau, Majorici, Bullou, Cercu (called Bourguemestre), François Proust, Ferron, Charles Girad, François Bourré and so many others – friends, intimates and servants of the dying man – stared at one another in silence, without a word passing their lips, all of them thinking and foreseeing in their minds that France would soon be bereft of so accomplished a knight, one so necessary to her glory and protection, and that the heavens were claiming him as owing to them as one naturally belonging to them.'

'By the tip of my cowl,' said Frère Jean, 'I'll turn scholar in my advancing years! Mind you: I have quite a fine intellect;

> I have a question that's quite hard:
> Like a king's unto his guard
> Or a queen's unto her ward:

these heroes and semi-gods you have spoken of, at death can they cease to be? Byre Leddy, I used to think in my Land-of-Thought that they were immortal like angels fair. May God forgive me for it. But this most-revered Macrobe says that they die a death that is final.'

'Not all of them,' said Pantagruel: 'the Stoics say that all are mortal save One, who alone is immortal, invisible and impassable. Pindar specifically states that there is no more thread (that is, *life*) spun by the unkindly Fates and Destinies from their flax and distaffs for the Hamadryads (who are goddesses) than for the trees of which they are guardians: namely for the oaks from which the Hamadryades sprang according to the opinion of Callimachus and also of Pausanias (in his section on Phocis); with both of whom Martianus Capella agrees. As for the semi-gods, pans, satyrs, wood-sprites, hobgoblins, sylvan goat-pans, nymphs, heroes and daemons, many, starting from the sum total of their various ages computed by Hesiod, have calculated that their lives last for 9720 years (that number being composed of unity passing to quadrinity, that entire quadrinity four times doubled; then five times multiplied by solid triangles. See Plutarch in his book *Why Oracles have ceased*.')

'That,' said Frère Jean, 'is certainly not Breviary-stuff. Of that I shall believe only what you want me to.'

'I believe,' said Pantagruel, 'that all intellective souls are exempt from the scissors of Atropos: all those of angels, daemons and humans are immortal. I will, however, relate to you a history on this subject, a very strange one but written and vouched for by several learned and knowledgeable historiographers.'

How Pantagruel relates a poignant History touching upon the death of Heroes

CHAPTER 28

[In the last chapter the extreme length of life of 9720 years is supplied by Plutarch (415 E–D), but the method of reaching it is not clear to many today as the language of mathematics has fundamentally changed. Pantagruel's statement of belief which closes that chapter is strictly orthodox, fully in accord with the recent insistence by the Church on the immortality of souls in the definitions and anathemas of the Bull Apostolici Regiminis *of Leo X (1513).*

Rabelais is now 'however' to retell not a tale but an histoire, *an historical event: the death of Pan vouched for by Plutarch's professor of grammar, Epitherses. If that god Pan really did die in the sense of*

his soul's having been snuffed out, then even the higher souls are
mortal and come eventually to an end. But with a second 'however'
Pantagruel will proceed to unveil the hidden truth. By inserting the
word 'god' into his text – 'the great god Pan is dead' – Pantagruel
opens the way for what is for Christians the only God truly to die,
Jesus, and his death is no snuffing out into nothingness. The dying
Lord who lies veiled behind Pan can be revealed by a deeper under-
standing of his name: behind Pan the Shepherd god (Πάν) lies the
great 'Shepherd of the sheep' of Hebrews 13:20; and there also lies
Pan in the sense of All (Πᾶν), for the crucified Lord is Pantagruel's
All, 'in whom we live and move and have our being', as he is for Paul
and for Luke (Acts 17:28). To his other veiled sources Pantagruel adds
Virgil in his Second Eclogue, *33 who is taken to mean that Pan (truly*
understood) 'Takes care of the sheep and their pastors too', of whom
Rabelais was one.

Once again Rabelais applies to Christ the title the Most-good, Most-
great God, the old title of Jupiter definitively adopted by Christians
for God the Father. That is arresting: it normally does not apply to
the Son. Cf. the introduction to the Prologue to this Fourth Book.*]*

'Epitherses, the father of Aemilian the rhetorician, was sailing
from Greece to Italy on a boat conveying a variety of merchandise and several passengers, when, the wind having dropped
one evening near the Echinades – which are islands between
the Morea and Tunis – their vessel was carried close to Paxos.
Having reached the coast (with some of the passengers asleep,
others awake, others drinking and dining) from the isle of Paxos
there was heard a voice of someone loudly crying, *Thamous.*
At which cry all were struck with terror. Thamous was their
pilot; he hailed from Egypt but was not known by name except
to a few of the passengers. That voice was heard a second time,
calling with a terrifying cry for Thamous. No one answered; all
remained silent and deeply perturbed, so the voice was heard a
third time, more terrifying than before. To which Thamous did
indeed reply: "Here I am. What do you require of me? What
do you want me to do?" Whereupon that voice was heard
more loudly still, telling him, commanding him, to state and
announce when he came to Palodes that Pan, the great god,

was dead. Epitherses said that all the seamen and passengers were struck with awe upon hearing those words and were deeply afraid. As they were discussing amongst themselves whether it would be better to suppress what they had been ordered to publish or to announce it, Thamous counselled that if they had a stiff wind astern they should sail straight by without saying a word, but if the sea were calm, to announce what they had heard.

'Now when they were off Palodes they chanced upon neither wind nor current, so Thamous mounted on to the prow and casting his gaze shorewards, cried as he had been commanded to: that the great Pan was dead. He had not finished the last word when there were heard great sighs, great lamentations and tumultuous cries from the land, not of one solitary person but of many together.

'News of this soon spread throughout Rome (since many people had been present). Tiberius Caesar, then the Emperor of Rome, sent for that Thamous and, once he had heard what he had to say, believed him. Upon inquiring from the many learned scholars then in his Court and throughout Rome who that Pan was, he discovered from their reports that he was the son of Mercury and Penelope. So had Herodotus written some time before, and Cicero too in the *Third Book* of *On the Nature of the Gods*.

'However, I would interpret Pan as alluding to that Great Servator of the faithful, who was shamefully put to death in Judaea through the envy and iniquity of the Pontiffs, doctors, priests and monks of the Mosaic Law. That interpretation does not seem to me to be incompatible, for in Greek he can rightly be called *Pan*, seeing that he is our *All*, all that we are, all that we live, all that we have, all that we hope, is in him, of him, by him. He is the Good Pan, that Great Shepherd who (as attested by the passionate shepherd Corydon) not only loves and cherishes His lambs but also his shepherds. At whose death were heard plaints, sighs, tumultuous cries and lamentations throughout the entire machine of the Universe: Heaven, earth, sea and Hell.

The date is compatible with my interpretation, for that

Most-good, Most-great Pan, our Only Servator, died near
Jerusalem during the reign in Rome of Tiberius Caesar.'

Pantagruel, on finishing with those words, remained silent in
deep contemplation. Soon afterwards we saw tears pour from
his eyes as big as ostrich eggs.

One word of a lie, then may God take me!'

How Pantagruel called in at the Island of Tapinois over which reigned Quarêmeprenant

CHAPTER 29

*[The previous mystic chapter ended with a smile. The companions
then sail away unusually happy. (It was a truism that diabolical inter-
ventions make you feel happy at first but leave you troubled: true,
Godly revelations trouble you at first but leave you exceptionally
happy.)*

*'Tapinois' means dissimulation, hypocrisy. 'Quarêmeprenant' is for
many the three days before Ash Wednesday but for Rabelais he is the
personification of Lent (Carême). He is a bleak, unnatural figure who
traditionally defeats fat and festive Mardi Gras. Mardi Gras is an
enemy to be overcome, whose excesses are encouraged by the dicipline
of Lenten observances of which Rabelais disapproves. Like Erasmus
Rabelais would replace (or perhaps limit) Lenten excesses by moderation. The followers of Mardi Gras were, and still ought to be, allies of
pantagruelism. Glum Lent is the enemy.*

*The name of the 'Ichthyophagi', the Fish-eaters, recalls a famous
colloquy of Erasmus with that name.*

*The theme develops into a variant of the Battle between Carnival
and Lent, widely known from the picture of Brueghel.*

Rabelais calls the North Wind 'Aguyon'.]

With the ships of the joyful convoy refitted, overhauled and
laden with fresh victuals, with the Macraeons more than contented and pleased about the money which Pantagruel had
spent amongst them; and with our folk more than usually
happy, the next day, in high spirits, our sails were set for a

delightful, gentle Aguyon. At high noon Xenomanes pointed out in the offing the island of Tapinois, over which there reigned Quarêmeprenant, of whom Pantagruel had already heard tell and whom he would have been pleased to meet in person had not Xenomanes discouraged him, partly because of the long detour and partly for the lean pastimes to be found, he said, everywhere in that isle and at the court of that lord.

'You'll find nothing for your pot,' he said, 'but a great swallower of dried peas, a great champer of snails, a great catcher of moles, a great trusser-up of hay, a semi-giant with a mangy beard and a double tonsure, of the Lanternland breed, a great lantern-lecher, the banner-bearer of the Ichthyophagi, a dictator of Mustardland, a beater of little boys, a burner of ashes, a father and enricher of physicians, one who abounds in pardons and indulgences (and church-visits to gain them) – a fine man, a good Catholic and of great devotion! He weeps three-quarters of the time and is never found at weddings.

'It is true that he is the most industrious maker of meat-skewers and larding-pricks to be found in forty kingdoms. About six years ago I carried off a gross of them and gave them to the butchers of Candes. (They esteemed them highly; and not without cause. When we get home I can show you two of them affixed to their main gate.) The fodder he feeds upon consists of salted hauberks, salted helmets and head-pieces and salted green sallets, for which he often suffers a heavy dose of the clap. His dress is merry, I must say, both in cut and colour, for he wears: grey and cold; nothing fore or aft; sleeves to match.'

'You would do me a pleasure,' said Pantagruel, 'if, just as you have portrayed me his vestments, his food, the way he behaves and his pastimes, you were to expound his form and flesh in all its parts.'

'Do it, I beg you, you cuddly Bollock,' said Frère Jean, 'for I have stumbled across him in my Breviary: he comes in after the Movable Feasts.'

'Willingly,' replied Xenomanes. 'We shall perhaps hear more fully about him when we pass through the Ile Farouche dominated by the chubby Chidlings who are his mortal enemies and against whom he wages a sempiternal war. Were it not for the succour of noble Mardi Gras, their good neighbour and protector, Quarêmeprenant, that great Lantern-lecher, would long since have exiled them from their dwellings.'

'Are they male or female?' asked Frère Jean; 'angel or mortal? Matron or maid?'

'They,' replied Xenomanes, 'are female in sex, of mortal condition; some are maids, others not.'

'I give myself to the devil if I'm not on their side,' said Frère Jean.

Warring against women! What sort of disorder in Nature is that! Let's go back and slaughter the great villein.'

'What!' said Panurge. 'In the name of all the devils, fight against Quarêmeprenant! I'm not that daft and daring too! What will the outcome be if we find ourselves squeezed between Chidlings and Quarêmeprenant, between the hammer and the anvil? Avaunt, ye fiends! Let's draw away. What I say is, Fare ye well, Quarêmeprenant. I commend the Chidlings to you. And don't overlook the Hog's Puddings.'

How Xenomanes describes
Quarêmeprenant anatomically

CHAPTER 30

[As for centuries past, medicine still worked through analogies. Those evoked for Quarêmeprenant in the next three chapters show him to be grotesque and unnatural.]

'Where his innards are concerned Quarêmeprenant has,' said Xenomanes, 'or in my time had:
  – a brain which, in size, colour, substance and potency is like the left testicle of a male tick;
  – the ventricles of it, like a surgeon's terebra;
  – the worm-shaped epiphysis, like a block-beetle;
  – the membranes, like a monk's cowl;
  – the infundibulum, like a mason's mortar-board;

- the trigone, like a wimple;
- the pineal gland, like a bagpipe;
- the *rete mirabilis*, like a horse's armoured frontlet;
- the mamillary tubercles, like a hobnailed boot;
- the eardrum, like a fencer's flourish;
- the petrosal bone, like the tip of a goose-wing;
- the neck, like a hand-lantern;
- the sinews, like a tap;
- the uvula, like a pea-shooter;
- the palate, like a mitten;
- the salivary gland, like a turnip;
- the tonsils, like a monocle;
- the isthmus of the throat, like a hod;
- the gullet, like a grape-picker's flasket;
- the stomach, like a pendant girdle;
- the pylorus, like a two-pronged fork;
- the windpipe, like a penknife;
- the throat, like a clew of oakum;
- the lungs, like an amice;
- the heart, like a chasuble;
- the mediastinum, like a stone jug;
- the pleura, like a surgeon's crow's-bill;
- the arteries, like a Béarnese top-coat;
- the diaphragm, like a Spanish cap;
- the liver, like a mortising axe;
- the veins, like an embroidery-frame;
- the spleen, like a quail-lure;
- the bowels, like a fishing-net;
- the gall, like a cooper's mallet;
- the viscera, like a gauntlet;
- the mesentery, like an abbatial mitre;
- the jejunum of the small intestine, like a forceps;
- the blind-gut of the large intestine, like belly-armour;
- the colon, like a mustard pot;
- the arse-gut, like a monastical sconce;
- the kidneys, like a plasterer's bowel;
- the loins, like a padlock;
- the ureters, like a chimney-hook;

- the renal veins, like two syringes;
- the spermatic cords, like a puff-pastry-cake;
- the prostate, like a barrel of feathers;
- the bladder, like a catapult;
- the neck of the bladder, like the tongue of a bell;
- the epigastrium, like an Albanian's conical hat;
- the peritoneum, like an arm-band;
- the muscles, like a bellows;
- the tendons, like a falconer's glove;
- the ligaments, like a money-bag;
- the bones, like cream buns;
- the marrow, like a beggar's wallet;
- the cartilages, like a tortoise from the moorlands of Languedoc;
- the lymphatic glands, like a bill-hook;
- the animal spirits, like a rain of heavy punches;
- the vital spirits, like tweakings of the nose;
- the boiling blood, Gnat-snapper;
- the semen like a hundred tin-tacks (and his wet-nurse told me that when he was married to Mid-lent he spawned nothing but a number of pardons stuffed with locative adverbs, plus two-day fasts);
- the memory which he had was like a game-bag;
- his common-sense, like a droning;
- his imagination, like a ring of bells;
- his thoughts, like a murmuration of starlings;
- his conscience, like a sedge of young herons leaving the nest;
- his deliberations, like a bag of barley;
- his repentance, like the yoked oxen hauling a double-cannon;
- his enterprises, like the ballast of a galleon;
- his understanding, like a tattered breviary;
- his intellect, like snails slithering out of a bed of strawberries;
- his will, like three walnuts in a bowl;
- his desires, like six bales of holy-hay;
- his judgement, like a shoe-horn;

– his discernment, like a mitten;
– his reason, like a cushion-stool.'

The Anatomy of Quarêmeprenant as touching his external parts

CHAPTER 31

[Historically anatomy was just being newly developed by Vesalius and others. Quarêmeprenant continues to be shown as grotesque and unnatural.]

'As for his external parts,' Xenomanes continued, 'Quarême-prenant was slightly better proportioned, save for seven ribs which he had over and above the usual norm. He also had:
– toes, like on a cross between a spinet and an organ;
– nails, like a gimlet;
– feet, like a guitar;
– heels, like a mace;
– soles, like an oil-lamp;
– legs, like a decoy;
– knees, like a stool;
– thighs, like a steel lever for bending a cross-bow;
– hips, like a brace-and-bit;
– a belly, with a pointed beak like crakow shoes, button-hooked back on to the chest in an antiquarian style;
– a navel, like a hurdy-gurdy;
– a groin, like a tartlet;
– a member, like a slipper;
– balls, like a double leathern bottle;
– the genitals, like a turnip;
– the muscles of the spermatic cord, like a racket;
– a perineum, like a whistle-pipe;
– an arsehole, like a crystalline looking-glass;
– the cheeks of his arse, like a harrow;
– the loins, like a butter-dish;
– a sacrum, like a cudgel;

– a back, like a siege-sized crossbow;
– spondyles, like a set of bagpipes;
– ribs, like a spinning-wheel;
– a sternum, like a baldachin;
– shoulder-blades, like a mortar;
– a chest, like a small hand-organ;
– nipples, like the mouthpiece of a hunting-horn;
– armpits, like a chessboard;
– shoulders, like a handcart;
– arms, like a great riding-hood;
– fingers, like common-room andirons;
– wrist-bones, like a pair of stilts;
– forearms, as though fore-armed with sickles;
– elbows, like rat-traps;
– hands, like a curry-comb;
– a neck, like a carousing-cup;
– a throat, like a filter for mulled wine;
– a larynx, like a barrel from which hang a pair of bronze
   goitres, handsome and harmonious, in the shape of an
   hour-glass;
– a beard, like a lantern;
– a chin, like a Saint-George's mushroom;
– ears, like a pair of mittens;
– a nose, like cothurns fastened with escutcheons;
– nostrils, like a babe's bonnet;
– eyebrows, like a dripping-pan; over the left one he has a
   mark in shape and size like a chamber-pot;)
– eyelids, like a fiddle;
– eyes, like a case for combs;
– optic nerves, like a tinder-box;
– a forehead, like a flat vault;
– temples, like a watering-can;
– cheeks, like a pair of clogs;
– jaws, like a goblet;
– teeth, like a long spear; of his milk-teeth you will find one
   at Coulanges-les-Royaux in Poitou, and two at La Brousse
   in Saintonge, above the cellar-door;
– a tongue, like a harp;

- a mouth, like a packhorse's sumpter-cloth;
- a face, incised (as though with a lancet) like a mule's pack-saddle;
- a head, like an alembic;
- a cranium, like a game-bag;
- cranial sutures, like that signet ring showing Saint Peter as Fisherman;
- skin, like a sieving-cloth;
- cranial hair, like a scrubbing-brush;
- downy hair: as already described.'

The physical features of Quarêmeprenant: continued

CHAPTER 32

[Laughter turns to satire. The formal list gives way to proverbial expressions (including some from the Adages *of Erasmus). Amongst these proverbial expressions for useless and preposterous activities are, from the* Adages, *III, VII, XXXIX, 'korubantian (to be mad)'; I, IV, LXXIV, 'To fish on the air; to hunt in the sea'; I, III, LXXV, 'To fix horns over the eyes'.*

The main debt is to the mythological fable of Physis *(Nature) and* Antiphysie *(Anti-Nature), which stresses the danger of Antiphysie's misleading analogies between the divine and the human. Pantagruel presents the fable as ancient, but it in fact comes directly from Celio Calcagnini, as does quite a lot of matter in this* Fourth Book.

At the very end of the Chapter the followers of Antiphysie are hypocrites of all sorts. In the midst of the usual creepy ones are found three powerful enemies who had each attacked Rabelais in print. They are treated as plurals, so becoming tribes not individuals. The 'maniacal little Pistols' refer to Guillaume Postel, an erratic genius who hated Rabelais and whose madness saved him from the stake; the 'Calvins' explain themselves (and serve as a reminder that many who admired Luther, as Rabelais did, might detest Calvin and his Eglise Réformée); *'Putrid-herb' is in Latin,* Putherbus, *a French Sorbonagre whose attacks on Rabelais in his book* Theotimus *were recent (1549) and extreme.]*

'It is,' said Xenomanes, 'a natural wonder to see the features of Quarêmeprenant, and to hear of them:

- if he gobbed: it was basketfuls of wild artichokes;
- if he wiped off his snot: it was salted eels;
- if he dropped tears: it was *carnard à l'orange*;
- if he shuddered: it was pasties of hare-meat;
- if he sweated: it was cod in fresh butter;
- if he belched: it was oysters-in-their-shells;
- if he sneezed: it was full barrels of mustard;
- if he coughed: it was vats of quince marmalade;
- if he sobbed: it was ha'p'orths of watercress;
- if he yawned: it was bowls of pea-soup;
- if he sighed: it was smoked ox-tongues;
- if he wheezed: it was hodfuls of green monkeys;
- if he snored: it was pans of mashed peas;
- if he frowned: it was larded pigs' trotters;
- if he spoke: it was coarse bureau-cloth from the Auvergne (far from being that crimson silk from which Parisatis wanted any words to be woven which were addressed to her son Cyrus, King of the Persians);
- if he puffed: it was money-boxes for Indulgences;
- if he blinked: it was waffles and wafers;
- if he scolded: it was March tom-cats;
- if he nodded with his head: it was carts with iron tires;
- if he pouted: it was rub-a-dub-dub on a drum;
- if he mumbled: it was morality plays for revelling law-clerks;
- if he stamped about: it was referred payments and five-year graces;
- if he drew backwards: it was salt-sea Worrycows;
- if he dribbled: it was bake-house ovens;
- if he grew hoarse: it was intricate morris-dances;
- if he farted: it was brown cowhide gaiters;
- if he quietly broke wind: it was booties of Cordova leather;
- if he tickled himself: it was fresh precepts;
- if he sang: it was peas in their pods;
- if he shat: it was Saint-George's mushrooms and morels;
- if he puffed: it was cabbage in olive oil, Languedoc-style;

- if he reflected: it was *The Snows of Yesteryear*;
- if he worried: it was about the shaven and shorn;
- if he gave something away: it was *a penny for the lying embroiderer*;
- if he dreamt: it was of flying phalluses scrambling up walls;
- if he went mad: it was lease-holders' rent-books.

'A curious case: he worked doing nothing: did nothing working; he corybanted as he slept: slept as he corybanted, keeping his eyes ever open like the hares in the fields of Champagne since he feared a night attack by his ancient foes the Chidlings. He laughed as he bit: bit as he laughed; ate nothing when fasting: fasting, ate nothing; he munched by suspicion and drank by imagination; he bathed on high steeples and dried himself off in rivers and ponds; he fished in the air and caught huge lobsters; he hunted in the depths of the sea, finding there ibises, bucks and chamois; he pecked out the eyes of all the crows which he trapped; he feared nought save his own shadow and the bleating of fat goats; on some days he pounded the pavements; he made complex puns on *ceints*, *saints* and *sins* apropos of the knotted-cords of the Cordeliers.[56]

'He used his fist as a mallet; he also wrote prognostications and almanacs on ill-scraped parchment using his heavy writing-case.'

'An elegant chap that!' said Frère Jean. 'That's the man for me. Just the one I'm looking for. I intend to send him a note of defiance.'

'There indeed is a strange and monstrous carcass of a man,' said Pantagruel, 'if man he should be called.

'But you have recalled to my mind the forms and figures of Amodunt and Discordance.'

'What forms did they have?' asked Frère Jean. 'God forgive me, but I've never heard of them.'

'I shall tell you,' replied Pantagruel, 'what I have read about them amongst the fables of Antiquity: as her first brood, Physis (that is, Nature), being herself most fruitful and fertile, gave

---

56. The puns are based on three homophonic phrases: *cordes des ceints* (the knotted cord girding the Cordeliers); *corps des saints* (the bodies of saints – relics); and *cordes des sins* (the ropes of church bells).

birth to Beauty and Harmony without carnal knowledge. Anti-physie, who has ever been the party hostile to Nature, at once envied such fair and honourable progeny and so, in rivalry, after copulating with Tellumon, gave birth to Amodunt and Discordance: they had heads which were spherical and entirely round like footballs, not gently compressed on either side as in the shape of human beings. Their ears were pricked up high like those of a donkey; their eyes, without eyebrows, were projected on bones resembling the bone of the heel and were as hard as a crab's; their feet were round like tennis-balls whilst their arms and hands were twisted back towards their shoul-ders: and they walked on their heads, constantly turning cartwheels, arse over tip with feet in the air. And just as mother-monkeys, you know, think their little ones to be the most beautiful things in the world, Antiphysie praised the form of her offspring and strove to prove that it was more beautiful and more becoming than the form of the offspring of Physis, saying that to have feet and heads that are spherical and to roll along with a circular motion constitute the appropriate shape and the perfect gait, both suggestive of some participation in the Divine by which the heavens and all things eternal are caused to revolve. To have one's feet in the air and the head down below was to imitate the Creator of the Universe, seeing that hair in Man is his roots as it were, and the arms his branches. Now trees are more properly bedded into the ground by their roots than they would be by their branches. By which exposition she claimed that her own offspring were more aptly and more closely likened to upright trees than were those of Physis, who resembled trees turned upside down.

'As for the arms and the hands, she proved that it was more rational to twist towards the shoulders, because that part of the body should not be defenceless, seeing that the foreparts are appropriately furnished with teeth which a person can employ not only for masticating but also – without use of the hands – as a defence against things harmful. And thus, by the witness and warrant of brute beasts, she drew all the foolish and the stupid to her judgement and was a wonder to all the brainless folk bereft of good judgement and common intelligence. Since which time she spawned the Aping-males, Bigot-tails and Bacon-pappers, the maniacal little Pistols, the demoniacal Calvins (the impostors of Geneva) as well as the raging Putrid-herbs and the Mendicant Greedy-gutses, the Black-beetles, the Sycophants, the Cannibals and other monsters deformed and distorted from contempt for Nature.

How Pantagruel descried a monstrous Physeter near the Ile Farouche

CHAPTER 33

[The name of this island (which means something like Wild Island) is inspired by the Disciple de Pantagruel.

A leap from mystic fable to apparent reality. A physeter ('blower' in Greek, a word adopted also in Latin) is the cachalot of Pliny, which was differentiated from the smaller, better-known whale. Rabelais could well have seen it illustrated, differentiated from a whale, on the Carta Marina *of Olaus Magnus (1539).*

The play on words over the name of Perseus is again in the spirit of Plato's Cratylus, *soon to be specifically mentioned (in Chapter 37). The original pun* Perseus *and* Percé jus *(pierced down) is kept as far as proved possible in English.*

The Pythagorean Y is the moral Y. *(One of the arms of the* moral Y *is much broader than the other, facing the traveller with a choice: the broad arm leads to vice; the strait, to virtue. That aspect of the Pythagorean Y is scarcely relevant here, but we may be being prepared for the renewed interest in Pythagorean doctrines in Chapter 37.*

The line 'celebrated flame-vomiting steeds of the Sun' is a quotation from the first-century Latin poet Corippus.

The fear and superstition of Panurge are again to the fore.

There is a confused memory of the drowning of George Duke of Clarence in a butt of Malmsey.]

About high noon we were approaching the Ile Farouche when Pantagruel descried from afar a huge monster of a physeter heading noisily straight for us, snorting and puffing itself up, rearing above the maintops of our boats and spouting ahead of it from its gullet water like a great river running down a mountain-side. Pantagruel pointed it out to the pilot and to Xenomanes.

On the advice of the pilot the bugles of the *Thalamege* sounded: *Keep a look out* and *Sail close to*. At the sound of which, following naval discipline, all ships, galleons, frigates and liburnian galleys took up position in the formation of the Greek Y (the Pythagorean letter), such as found in an acute angle, or as cranes adopt in flight. Positioned at its cone and vertex was the *Thalamege* in valiant fighting trim.

Frère Jean, gallant and most determined, climbed up to the foc's'le with the gunners. Panurge started to blubber and moan even more than before: 'Babillebabou,' he said, 'this is worse than ever! Let's run away. By the Death of an Ox, that's the Leviathan described by the noble prophet Moses in his life of that saintly man Job. He'll gulp us all down like pills, men, boats and all: within his great hellish maw we shall be no more to him than a musk-scented sweet-meat in an ass's gullet. There he is! Let's flee away! Let's reach the land. I believe he's the very marine monster which was destined long ago to devour Andromeda. We are lost, all of us. O that now, to kill him, there were here some valiant Perseus.'

'*Pursue us*: then pierced by me!' Pantagruel replied.

'God almighty! Set us free from the *causes* of fear!' said Panurge. 'When do you expect me to be frightened if not in evident danger?'

'If such is your fated destiny as Frère Jean expounded the other day,' said Pantagruel, 'you ought to go in fear of Pyroeis, Eous, Aethon and Phlegon (the celebrated flame-vomiting steeds of the Sun which breathe fire from their noses): there is no need for you to feel any fear whatsoever of physeters, which merely spout water through their gills and nostrils. You will never be in danger of death from any water of theirs. By that element you will be protected rather and preserved, not troubled nor attacked.'

'Try that on somebody else,' said Panurge. 'You've played a weak card there. Little-fish almighty! Have I not adequately explained to you the transmutation of elements and the ready symbolic harmony between the roasted and the boiled: the boiled and the roasted?[57]

'Aah! Look! There he is! I'm off to hide away down below. This time we're all done for. I can see harsh Atropos over our maintop, with scissors freshly honed to snip off the threads of our lives. Look out! Here he comes. O you horrible and abominable thing! Many have you drowned who never lived to boast of it! Gosh. If only he spouted good wine, white, red, delightful and delicious rather than water, stinking, salty and brackish, it would be a bit more tolerable; and could be a reason for putting up with the suffering, following the example of that English Lord who, once convicted of specific crimes, was allowed to choose his own death and opted to be drowned in a butt of Malmsey.

'Here it comes! Ah! Ah! Satan! Devil! Leviathan! You're so hideous and loathsome that I can't bear to look at you. Off with you to the Chancery: off to the Chicanous!'

How the monstrous Physeter was killed by Pantagruel

CHAPTER 34

[For a while Pantagruel becomes physically a giant again whose size and skills are emphasized. Tales of the killing of whales are current enough in seamen's tales as in literature. Rabelais' is a fine piece of writing and description. One might have expected the biblical leviathan to play a greater part than it does.

More sporting with equilateral triangles. The darts piercing the physeter form an equilateral triangle. Cf. the three Pierres (Peters) of the Prologue and finally, most seriously and with evident Christian and Platonic mysticism, the Manor of Truth in Chapter 55. Rabelais'

---

57. An allusion to Chapter 24: 'Maybe,' replied Panurge, 'but the devil's chefs sometimes go mad and err in their duties: they often put souls on to boil which were meant to be roasted.'

*description of great iron and bronze cannon-balls seeming 'to melt
like tiles in the sun' is strange: what kind of tiles did he mean?*

*There is a confusion between two Roman emperors, Commodus
and Domitian.]*

The physeter, venturing within the fighting angle formed by the
ships and galleons, spurted water by the barrelful on to the
leading vessels: it was like the cataracts on the Ethiopian Nile.
Darts, arrows, javelins, stakes, harpoons and spears flew at it
from all sides. Frère Jean never spared himself. Panurge was
dying of fear. The artillery made a very devil of a noise, thundering, lightning and doing its job of playing at pinch-me-tight!
But little was gained since great iron and bronze cannon-balls
seemed, viewed from a distance, to melt like tiles in the sun as
soon as they penetrated its skin.

So Pantagruel, after considering what was opportune and
necessary, flexed his arms and showed what he could do.

You tell us – and it is written – that Commodus, that scoundrel who was the Emperor of Rome, could aim from afar so
dexterously with his bow that he could shoot without grazing
them between the fingers of little boys holding up a hand.

You also tell us of an Indian archer (from the time when
Alexander the Great conquered India) who was so skilled that
he made his arrows fly through a ring from afar, doing so
despite those arrows being three cubits long, with iron heads
so big and heavy that he could cut through steel swords with
them as well as through thick shields, steel breastplates and
indeed anything at all that he hit, however hard, solid, resistant
and tough.

You also tell us marvels of the skill of the French of old who
were considered the best of all at archery: when they were out
hunting the black boar or the red deer they would rub the metal
tips of their arrows with hellebore, since the flesh of any animals
which were then shot was more tender, tasty, wholesome and
delicious; they did, however, cut round and remove the part
which had been struck.

You tell a similar tale of the Parthians, who shot behind them
with greater skill than other peoples do to the fore. You also

praise the Scythians for showing the same dexterity; an ambassador was sent from them to Darius, the King of the Persians, to whom without a word he offered a bird, a frog, a mouse and five arrows. He was asked what was implied by such gifts: had he been charged with saying anything? He answered, No. Darius would have remained surprised and puzzled were it not for Gobryes (one of the seven captains who had killed the Magi) who deciphered and explained it to him. 'By those gifts and presents,' he said, 'the Scythians are tacitly telling you that if the Persians cannot fly in the sky like birds, hide near the centre of the Earth like mice and conceal themselves in the depths of ponds and marshes like frogs, they will all be sent to perdition by the might and shafts of the Scythians.'[58]

Now our noble Pantagruel performed incomparably greater wonders in the art of hurling and shooting since, with his horrifying harpoons and darts (which can be rightly compared in length, thickness, weight and ironwork with the great beams which support the bridges at Nantes, Saumur and Bergerac, as well as the Pont au Change and the Pont aux Meuniers in Paris), he would open oysters in their shells from a thousand paces without striking their sides; snip through a candle-flame without dowsing it; shoot magpies through the eye; shave the soles off boots without damaging them; shear the fur from cowls without spoiling them, and turn the leaves of Frère Jean's breviary, one after another, without tearing them.

With darts such as those (of which there was a great store in his ship) he so pierced the forehead of the physeter as to go through both its jaws and its tongue so that it could no longer open its mouth, draw in water or spout it out. With his second blow he poked out its right eye; with the third, its left. Then, to the amusement of us all, the whale looked as if it bore three horns on its forehead, inclining forward to form an equilateral triangle, as it twisted and turned from side to side, reeling about and losing its way as a thing dazed, blinded and close to death.

Not content with this, Pantagruel hurled another dart against

58. The slaughter of these false Magi is related by Herodotus, 4, 131–2. As a young Franciscan Rabelais had translated the first book of Herodotus into Latin.

its tail; it too remained inclined backwards. Then he hurled three more, which stood perpendicularly in a line along its spine, spaced so as to divide its length from tip to tail into three exactly equal parts. Finally he launched fifty darts against its flanks on one side and fifty darts against the other, with the result that the body of the physeter resembled the keel of a three-master galleon, mortised and tenoned together by beams of the appropriate size, as if they were the ribs and channel-boards of the keel. It was a most pleasing sight to see. Then, as it died, it turned over on to its back as all dead fishes do, looking once it had turned over – as the ancient sage Nicander describes it – like a *scolopendra*: a serpent with a hundred feet.

How Pantagruel landed on the Ile Farouche, the ancient dwelling-place of the Chidlings

CHAPTER 35

[It might seem odd that the Chidlings should look like squirrels, but, whimsy apart, there is a stock illustration of a squirrel in one of the editions of the Disciple de Pantagruel *which would lead any reader to think that they did. In the* Fourth Book *they vary from looking like furry animals to looking like sausages.*

There is a sustained and serious play on reconcilier *(to reconcile) and* Concile *(Council). The Council of Trent is again called the* Concile de Chésil *(fools).*

It dismally fails in its duty to re-concile. *In 1548 hopes had been raised that some at least of the contending parties would, once invited to Trent, reach an understanding. Most were inflexible. Rabelais refuses to allow any* Catholic *(universal) quality to Trent. It is a* National *not a* Catholic *Council.*

An heroic element is introduced by an allusion to Dido and Aeneas from Aeneid, *1, 561ff.]*

Oarsmen from the *Lantern* trussed up the physeter and towed it ashore on to the nearby island called Ile Farouche so as to cut it up and recover the fat from its kidneys, which was said to be most useful, indeed necessary, for the curing of a certain malady called *Lack-of-the-Ready*.

Pantagruel did not pay much attention, for he had already seen several others very like it – indeed, even huger ones – in the Gallic Ocean. He did however agree to disembark at the Ile Farouche to dry some of his men who had been drenched by the ugly physeter and to allow others who had been bespattered by it to freshen themselves up in a little deserted haven towards the south situated by a pleasant grove of tall, handsome trees; from it flowed a delightful stream of fresh water, clear and sparkling. Field-kitchens were set up under beautiful awnings there being no lack of firewood. Each man changed into whatever clothes he wished; Frère Jean then tolled the bell. At which the trestle-tables were laid and promptly served.

While Pantagruel was merrily dining with his men, as the second course was being brought in he noticed certain cunning little Chidlings scrambling silently up a tall tree near to where the wine was kept cool. So he asked Xenomanes what sort of animals they were, believing that they were squirrels, weasels, martins or stoats. 'They are Chidlings,' replied Xenomanes. 'This is the Ile Farouche: I was telling you about it this morning. Between them and Quarêmeprenant, their ancient and venomous enemy, there has long since been a war unto death. I suspect that our cannonades against the physeter made them somewhat fearful, wondering whether that same enemy had come with his forces to take them by surprise or to lay waste this island of theirs, as he had striven to do several times before but to little effect in the face of the care and vigilance of the Chidlings who (as Dido told the companions of Aeneas when they wished to make harbour in Carthage without her knowledge or assent) were constrained to be eternally vigilant and on the watch because of the malignity of their enemy and the proximity of his lands.' – 'Indeed, my fair friend,' said Pantagruel; 'if you can see a way to put an end to those hostilities by some honourable means – and those foes to reconcile – then give me your advice. I would devote myself to it with a good heart and without stint, aiming to temper and season the controversies between both the parties.'

'It is not possible, for the present,' replied Xenomanes. 'Some four years ago, when I was travelling from this island to the island of Tapinois, I set myself the task of establishing a peace between them, or at least a long truce. And they would already have been good friends and neighbours by now if any in either party had rid themselves of their emotions over one single article. Quarêmeprenant would not include in the peace-treaty either the wild *Boudins* or the mountain-born Sausages, their ancient comrades and confederates. The Chidlings insisted that the Fortress of the Fish-barrel be at their discretion exactly as the Castle of the Salt-meat-barrel is governed and controlled; and that there should be driven from thence those stinking, villainous assassins and extortionists who now occupy it. No accord was possible, and the conditions seemed iniquitous to both the parties. So no accord was reached. They did, however, remain less severe and more gentle enemies than in the past. But since the proclamation of National *Concile de Chésil* by which they were provoked, harassed and cited, and in which Quarêmeprenant was proclaimed shitty, shabby and stinky if ever he made an alliance or any sort of agreement with them, they have grown dreadfully bitter, envenomed, incensed and intractable: there is no remedy to be found. More easily would it be to bring cat and rat, or hound and hare together, than them to *re-concile*.'

How an ambush was laid against Pantagruel by the Chidlings of the Ile Farouche

CHAPTER 36

[Chidlings often come linked in pairs: so they are 'double' (and so not to be trusted). They are excellent fighters, though: behind these meaty figures of fun – the very antithesis of Lent and Quarêmeprenant – may be glimpsed brave Swiss and German soldiery won over to the Reformation. As enemies of Quarêmeprenant they ought to be natural allies of the Pantagruelists.]

While Xenomanes was speaking, Frère Jean espied twenty-five to thirty lean young Chidlings withdrawing at great speed towards their city, citadel, castle and redoubt of Chimneys. He said to Pantagruel, 'I can foresee some assing about. Those worthy Chidlings could perhaps mistake you for Quarêmeprenant, even though you in no wise resemble him. Let us break off feasting here and be ready for our duty to resist them.'

'That would be not at all a bad thing to do,' said Xenomanes: 'Chidlings are Chidlings: always double and treacherous.'

At which Pantagruel rose from the table to spy out the land beyond the woodland grove; he quickly returned and informed us that he had definitely discovered to the left an ambush set up by the podgy Chidlings, whilst to the right, about half a league from where they were, one full battalion of different, powerful and gigantic Chidlings were in battle order, marching furiously towards them along a small hill to the sound of bagpipes and flutes, merry fifes and tabors, trumpets and bugles. Judging from the seventy-eight standards which he counted we estimated their numbers to be not less than forty-two thousand.

The good order which they kept, their proud step and their confident expressions led us to believe that they were not Meat-Ball rookies but veteran Chidlings, war-hardened female warriors. From their front ranks back towards their standard-bearers they were all fully armed, bearing pikes which seemed small to us at a distance but were certainly well pointed and sharpened; they were flanked on their wings by a large number of Sylvan Puddings, massive crusted Pies and mounted Sausages, all very well-built island folk, wild and fierce.

Pantagruel was deeply disturbed. Not without reason, though Epistemon argued that the practice and custom of these Chidling-lands might well be to greet and receive their foreign friends in such a fashion with a parade of arms; just as the noble kings of France are welcomed and saluted by all the loyal towns of the kingdom on their first formal Entries into them after their sacring, upon newly acceding to the throne.

'Perhaps,' he said, 'they are the regular Guards of the Queen of this land, who, being warned by the young Chidlings of the Watch whom you saw up that tree how your beautiful and majestic fleet had swept into their harbour, realized that some great and puissant prince was aboard and came to greet you in person.'

Pantagruel, remaining unconvinced, called his counsel in order to hear their summary advice on what should be done in this crisis, where hope was unsure and danger evident. He then pointed out how such practices of greeting under arms had often brought mortal danger under colour of a warm welcome and friendliness.

'It was thus,' he said, 'that, on one occasion, the Emperor Antoninus Caracalla massacred the Athenians and on another occasion, overcame the retinue of Artaban, the King of Persia, under the false pretence of wanting to marry his daughter. That did not go unpunished: he lost his life there soon afterwards.

'Thus did the sons of Jacob slaughter the Sichemists to wreak revenge for the rape of their sister Dinah. In that hypocritical fashion the soldiers within Constantinople were killed by Gallienus, the Roman Emperor; thus too, under pretence of friendship, Antoninus invited Artavasdes, the King of Armenia, and then had him bound, placed in heavy fetters and finally murdered.

'We find hundreds of similar cases in the ancient muniments. And to this day Charles, the Sixth King of France of that name, is rightly and greatly praised for his wisdom: for, when returning to his goodly town of Paris after his victory over the men of Flanders and of Ghent, he learnt at Le Bourget that the Parisians, to the number of twenty thousand fighting-men, had marched out of the Town in battle array, all armed with mallets (*maillots*, hence their name of *Maillotins*). Although they protested that they had, without deceit or ill-will, thus taken up arms to welcome him more honourably, he would not make his entry before they had gone back to their homes and disarmed.'

How Pantagruel sent for Colonels Poke-Banger and Spoilchidling, with a notable disquisition on the proper names of places and persons

CHAPTER 37

[The Captains are given meaningful names in a comic application of the theories of the Cratylus *and of the meaningful prophecies from proper names in the Homeric and Virgilian lots in Chapter 10 of the* Third Book. *Then serious examples follow, both ancient and modern.*

The general context is a renewed sympathy for Pythagorean symbolism encouraged in Rabelais by the works of Calcagnini and by many adages of Erasmus, as well as by the authoritative learned legal works of André Tiraqueau.

While Joshua fought, Moses, as instructed by God, kept his arms held aloft, so assuring God's intervention into the fighting (Exodus 17:8ff.).]

Their council resolved that they should remain on the *qui-vive* whatever happened.

Then Carpalim and Gymnaste (at the command of Pantagruel) were to summon the marines who were aboard *The Golden Carafe* (commander: Colonel Spoilchidling) and *The Golden Grape-hod* (commander: Colonel Poke-Banger the Younger).

'I will relieve Gymnaste of that chore,' said Panurge. 'Besides, you need him here.'

'By my cloth, you old Bollock,' said Frère Jean, 'you mean to steer clear of the fight and never come back. He's no great loss. All he'd do would be to blubber, moan and wail, disheartening our fine soldiers.'

'I,' said Panurge, 'shall certainly be back again soon, Frère Jean my spiritual Father, but do please arrange for those beastly Chidlings not to scramble on to our ships. While you're doing the fighting I shall be praying for you, following the example of that knightly captain Moses, the Leader of the people of Israel.'

'If those Chidlings should chance to assault us,' said
Epistemon to Pantagruel, 'the names of your two colonels,
Spoilchidling and Poke-Banger, augur assurance, good luck and
victory for us in the conflict.'

'You have grasped it well,' said Pantagruel, 'and it pleases
me that you should foresee and predict our victory from the
names of those two colonels. Such predicting from proper
names is no novelty: it was formerly made famous by the
Pythagoreans, who religiously observed it. Many great lords
and emperors of old have profitably used it:

– Octavian Augustus, the second Emperor of Rome, once
came across a peasant named Eutyche (that is, Fortunate) who
was leading an ass named Nicon (Greek for Victory); encouraged by the meanings of those names, both that of the driver
and that of his ass, he was convinced of a complete success,
happy issue and victory.

– Vespasian, also an Emperor of Rome, was alone one day,
praying in the temple of Serapis, when, at the sight and sudden
appearance of one of his servants called Basilides (that is *Royal*)
whom he had left far behind ill, he began to have certain hope
of ruling over Rome.

– And Regilianus was elected Emperor by his soldiers for no
other cause or reason than the regal meaning of his proper name.

See the *Cratylus* of the inspired Plato.'

('By my thirst,' said Rhizotome, 'I would like to read it: I
hear you frequently citing it.')

'See how the Pythagoreans concluded by reason of names
and numbers that Patroclus had to be killed by Hector; Hector,
by Achilles; Achilles, by Paris; Paris, by Philoctetes.

'I am amazed when I reflect on that wonderful discovery of
Pythagoras who, from the odd or even number of the syllables
in any proper name, could indicate on which side of the body
a person was lame, hunchbacked, one-eyed, gout-legged, para-
lysed, pleuritic or suffering from any other natural infirmity,
i.e., by assigning the even number to the left side; the uneven,
to the right.'

'Indeed,' said Epistemon. 'During a general procession at
Saintes, I saw that fact corroborated in the presence of that

good, virtuous, learned and fair presiding judge Briand Valée, the Seigneur Du Douhet: whenever a man or woman processed by who was lame, one-eyed or hunchbacked, their proper names were reported to him. At once, without seeing them, he declared that they were infirm, one-eyed, lame or hunchbacked on the right side if their names were of an odd number of syllables; on the left when the number was even. And it was true: we came across no exception.'

'From that discovery,' said Pantagruel, 'scholars have concluded:

– that the kneeling Achilles was wounded by the arrow of Paris in the right heel, for his name is of an uneven number of syllables; (and here we can note that the Ancients used to kneel on their right knee;)

– that Venus was wounded by Diomedes before Troy in her left hand; since her name in Greek has four syllables;

– that it was Vulcan's left leg which was lame by the same reasoning;

– that Philip, King of Macedonia, and Hannibal were both blind in their right eyes.

'We could also, by this reasoning of Pythagoras, determine cases of sciatica, hernia and those migraines which afflict one side of the body only.

'But to get back to proper names, just think how that mighty son of King Philip of whom we have already spoken – Alexander the Great – succeeded in one of his enterprises by interpreting one word. He was besieging the fortress town of Tyre; over several weeks he gave it the most mighty battering that he could, but quite in vain: his siege-machines and mines profited him nothing; everything he did was at once undone or repaired by the people of Tyre. He therefore took the decision to raise the siege (greatly depressed, since he saw his disengagement as a weighty blow to his reputation). Worried and distressed he fell asleep. During that slumber he dreamt that a satyr was inside his tent, leaping and prancing on its goat-legs. Alexander tried to catch it: the satyr always got away. Finally the king drove it into a corner and pounced on him. At that point he awoke; he told the philosophers and the sages of his Court about his dream and was informed that the gods were promising him victory and that Tyre would soon be taken: for if you divide the word *satyros* into two, *sa* and *Tyros*, that signifies *Thine* is *Tyre*. And indeed, at the very next assault which he made he took the town by force and, in a great victory, subdued that rebellious people.

'But consider how the meaning of a single name brought Pompey, on the contrary, to despair. Being vanquished by Caesar in the battle of Pharsalia, he had no means of safety but in flight. And so, fleeing by sea, he struck land on the island of Cyprus: near the town of Paphos he could make out a beautiful and luxurious palace near the shore. On asking the pilot its name, he heard that it was *Kakobasileia*, that is, *Bad King*. That name inspired him with such fear and loathing that he sank into despondency, sure that he would escape only to lose his life. The seamen and the others near him heard his cries, sighs and groans. And indeed, soon afterwards an unknown peasant called Achillas lopped off his head. Whilst on this subject, we could further cite what happened to Lucius Paulus Aemilius when, by the Roman Senate, he was elected *Imperator* (that is, the Commander-in-chief) of the forces which they were despatching against Perses, the King of Macedonia. That very day he returned home to prepare for this departure and, on kissing his daughter Tratia, noticed that she was somewhat sad.

'"What is it my dear Tratia?"he said, "Why are you so sad and upset?"

'"Father," she answered, "it's Persa: she is dead."

'Persa was her name for the little puppy she delighted in; and with that word, Paulus Aemilius became assured of victory over Perses.

'If time allowed us to go carefully through the sacred Hebrew scriptures we would find several remarkable passages clearly showing in what religious reverence proper names and their meanings were held.'

Towards the end of this discourse the two colonels arrived, accompanied by their soldiers, all fully armed and fully resolute. Pantagruel gave them a brief word of encouragement, telling them to prove themselves valiant in the field (if, that is, they were really forced to fight, for he could not yet believe that the Chidlings were as treacherous as that) but forbade them to start the engagement. And the watchword he gave them was *Mardi Gras*.

That Chidlings are not to be despised by human beings

CHAPTER 38

[*Mardi Gras is the watchword: the mock-heroic battle is soon to be joined fought out in the spirit of Shrovetide fun.*

The quotation about the serpent who tempted Eve is taken from Genesis 3:9. Henry Cornelius Agrippa had published a Disputable Opinion *suggesting that the serpent which tempted Eve in the Garden of Eden was in fact Adam's penis.*]

Here you are scoffing at me, you Drinkers, and do not believe in the truth of a word I am saying. I've no idea what I should do with you. Believe it if you will, and if you won't, go there and see it for yourself: I know all right what I saw: the place was the Ile Farouche. There: I tell you its name. Now recall the might of those Giants of old who undertook to pile lofty Mount Pelion upon Ossa, and then with Ossa to enwrap the tree-shaded Olympus so as to fight the gods and drive them from their nests in the heavens. That might was neither ordinary might nor within the Mean. Yet those Giants were Chidlings for only half their bodies – or, to tell the truth, Serpents.

The serpent which tempted Eve was of Chidling stock; nevertheless it is written that it was 'more wiley and subtle than any beast of the field'; so are the Chidlings. And it is still maintained in certain academic circles that the Tempter was a Chidling called Ithyphallus, into whom, long ago, was transformed good Messer Priapus, that great tempter of women in *gardens* (called *paradises* in Greek and *jardins* in French).

How can we be sure that the Switzers, a people now hardy and warlike, were not formerly Sausages? I shouldn't like to swear to it, finger in pyre. The Himantopodes, a famous people in Ethiopia, are (according to the description in Pliny) nothing but Sausages. If those arguments do not allay the scepticism within you, then, my Lords, go straight away – after a drink, I mean – and visit Lusignan, Parthenay, Vouvant, Mervent and Pouzaugues in Poitou. There you will find long-renowned witnesses, all truly wrought, who will swear to you on the arm of Saint Rigomé that Melusina, their original foundress, had the body of a female down to her prick-wallet and that all the rest below was either a serpentine Chidling or a chidlingesque Serpent. Yet she had a fine and gallant step, still imitated today by Breton dancers when performing their tuneful floral-dances.

What caused Erichthonius to be the first to invent coaches, litters and chariots? It was because Vulcan had begotten him with Chidlingesque legs, and the better to conceal them he preferred to go by litter than by horse, since already in his days Chidlings were not highly esteemed. Ora, the Scythian nymph, similarly had a body which was partly woman, partly Chidling, yet she appeared so fair to Jupiter that he lay with her and produced a handsome son called Colaxes.

So stop all that sneering now and believe that nothing is as true as the Gospel.

How Frère Jean allies himself with the kitchen-men to combat the Chidlings

CHAPTER 39

[In the Latin Vulgate Nebuzardan is, with Potiphar, a Captain of the Guard: in the Greek Septuagint he appears as a cook and so as a good mascot for the coming battle of kitchen-men and scullery-lads which will be fought with the tools of their trade and pots and pans. Mock-heroic elements are supplied by Genesis 39, II (IV) Kings 25 and by Erasmus in his Apophthegms, IV, Cicero, 19, after Plutarch.]

On seeing those zealous Chidlings marching forth so gaily, Frère Jean said to Pantagruel,

'As far as I can see, this will be a fine battle of straw! Oh, what great honour and magnificent praise will our victory bring! I could wish that you were aboard your ship and merely a spectator of this conflict, leaving the rest to me and my men.'

'What men?' asked Pantagruel.

'Breviary stuff,' replied Frère Jean. 'Why was Potiphar made the Master of the Horse of the whole kingdom of Egypt, he who was the master-chef in Pharaoh's kitchens, who purchased Joseph and whom Joseph could have cuckolded if he had wanted to? Why was Nebuzardan, the master-chef of King Nebuchadnezzar, chosen from amongst all the other captains to lay siege to Jerusalem and to raze it to the ground?'

'I'm listening,' said Pantagruel.

'By the game of Hole-my-lady,' said Frère Jean, 'I'd venture to swear that they had formerly fought against the Chidlings – or against folk as little esteemed as Chidlings are – since cooks are incomparably better fitted and suited to basting, lambasting, dominating and slicing them up than all the men-at-arms, Albanian hussars, mercenaries or foot-soldiers in the world.'

'You bring freshly back to my memory,' said Pantagruel, 'something found written in the witty and amusing sayings of Cicero. During the Civil Wars between Pompey and Caesar, Cicero was naturally more inclined to the side of Pompey (despite being greatly courted and favoured by Caesar). Hearing one day that the followers of Pompey had suffered considerable losses in a particular engagement, he decided to visit their camp. There he found little strength, less courage and plenty of disorder. Foreseeing then that everything would go ill and to perdition (as did happen later) he began to jeer and to mock them all in turns with bitter and biting jests in the style of which he was master. At which some of the Captains tried to brave it out as though they were resolute and determined, saying to him, "See the number of Eagles we still have." (The Eagle was then the Romans' standard in times of war.) "That," said Cicero, "would be all very well if you were waging war against magpies!"

'And so, since we have to fight the Chidlings, you imply that it will be a culinary battle and that you wish to fall back on cooks. Do as you please. I shall stay here and await the issue of these fanfaronades.'

Frère Jean made at once for the kitchen tents and said to the cooks most merrily and courteously:

'Today, my lads, I want to see you win honour and victory. Feats-of-arms shall be achieved by you such as have never yet been seen in living memory. Guts against guts! Do men take such little account of our valiant cooks? Let's go and fight those Chidling whores. I shall be your captain. Drink on it, my friends. There now: Courage!'

'Captain,' the cooks replied, 'you put it well: we are yours merrily to command! Under your leadership we are ready to live or die.'

'To live, yes,' said Frère Jean; 'to die, certainly not! Dying is for Chidlings. So now: fall in! Your watchword will be *Nebuzardan*.'

How Frère Jean set up the Sow; and of the doughty cooks enclosed therein

CHAPTER 40

[The Great Sow recalls the Trojan Horse. The 'Sow of La Réole' was a kind of testudo *armed with stone-throwing catapults and able to cover some hundred soldiers during the French attack on Bergerac in 1378 under Charles V (not VI), when the town was held by the English.*

This chapter is largely devoted to lists of names of cooks. Some of the names are transposed: strictly literal translations drain away the fun.

Jews and half-converted Marranos avoid pork.

The inventor of the Sauce Madame *is called Mondame in Franco-Scottish because of the difficulty Scots had with French genders (hence Mondame for Madame.]*

Thereupon, at the orders of Frère Jean, the master engineers set up the Great Sow stored in the ship *The Leathern Bottle*. It was a wonderful contrivance; its ordnance consisted of huge 'bollockers' ranged in tiers, around it which catapulted big-bellied stone-shot and great square-headed arrows with steel flanges for feathers, while within its innards over two hundred men could easily join in the combat while remaining under cover. It was modelled on the Sow of La Réole, thanks to which Bergerac was taken from the English during the reign in France of the young King Charles the Sixth.

Here follows the list of the names of the doughty and valiant cooks who entered that Sow as into the Trojan Horse:

Spiced-stew,
Jackanapes,
Rapscallion,
Sloven,
Lardy Pork,
Dirty,
Mandrake,
Waste-bread,
Weary Willy,
Ladle,
Cods-in-wine,
Breton Pancakes,
Master Slops,
Arse-gut,
Pestle,
Lick-wine, Clerk of the Market,
Buttered Beans,
Goat-stew,
Grilled Steak,
Fried Tripe,
Hot-pot,
Pig's Liver,
Scarface,
Gallimaufry.

As coats-of-arms, all those noble cooks bore *on a field gules, a larding-needle ver, charged with a chevron argent, bend sinister.*

Larding-bacon,
Rasher,
Sliced-bacon,
Chew-bacon,
Stretch-bacon,
Streaky-bacon,
Save-your-bacon,
Round-basting
Archbacon
Anti-bacon,
Frizzle-bacon,
Truss-bacon,
Scrape-bacon,
Mark-bacon,
Gay-bacon, a native of Rambouillet. Named by syncope,
    the full name of that Doctor of Culinary Arts being
    Gaybake-bacon. By syncope we similarly say *idolater*
    for *idololater*,
Crisp-bacon,
Self-basting bacon,
Sweet-bacon,
Crunch-bacon,
Catch-bacon,
Pack-bacon,
Spit-for-bacon,
Trim-bacon,
Fair-bacon,
Fresh-bacon,
Bitter-bacon,
Rolled-bacon,
Ogle-bacon,
Weigh-bacon,
Pipe-bacon,
Leech-bacon,
(Names unknown amongst Marranos and Jews.)
Big-balls,
Salad-man,
Cress-bed,

Scrape-turnip,
Pygghe,
Coney-skin,
Gleanings,
Pastry-cake,
Shave-bacon,
French-fritters,
Mustard-pot,
Sour-wine,
Porringer,
Bon-vivant,
Stupid,
Green-sauce,
Pot-nosed,
Pot-stand,
Stew-pot,
Shatter-pot,
Scour-pot,
Trembler,
Salt-gullet,
Snail-farm,
Vegetable-soups,
March-soup,
Grilled-meats,
Rennet-monger,
Macaroons,
Stir-fire,
Crumbs. He was taken from the kitchen to serve the noble
   Cardinal Le Veneur as *valet de chambre*,
Spoil-roast,
Dishclout,
Little Biggin,
Smallcock,
Faircock,
Newcock,
Feathercock,
Cock-of-the-Walk,
Oldcock,

Tancock,
Hasty veal,
Short-rib,
Gigot-man,
Sour-milker,
Mountain-goat,
Bladder-blower,
Ray-fish,
Gabardine,
Booby,
Eye-wash,
Fop,
Slash-dial,
Freckles,
Mondame, the inventor of the *Sauce Madame*, hence his
    name in Franco-Scottish;
Chatterteeth,
Big-lips,
Mirelinger,
Woodcock,
Rinse-pot,
Blubber-mouth,
Hardly clean,
Codfish,
Waffle-maker,
Saffron-eater,
Tousle-hair,
Antitus,
Turnip-basher,
Rape-eater,
Black-pudding-man,
Bowling-jack,
Robert. He was the inventor of *Sauce Robert*, which is so
    good for you and so necessary for roast rabbit, duck,
    fresh pork, poached eggs, salted cod fish and hundreds
    of other similar viands,
Cold-eel,
Red-skate,

Gurnet,
Belly-rumbler,
Crumb-cake,
Swagger-guts,
Squirrel,
Cess-pit,
Hash,
Merry-rogue,
Soused-herring,
Cheese-cake,
Big-beak,
Tuck-in,
Tasty-bullock,
Artichoke-spear,
Sieve-salt,
Frying-pan,
Layabout,
Great Gourd,
Turnip-dresser,
Shyte,
Big-nails,
Squittered,
Snotty,
Trout-slayer,
Topsy-turvy,
Worricow,
Cock-face,
Gazing-hoyden,
Veal-calf,
Elegantius.

Into that Sow now entered those noble cooks, gay, gallant, full of life and ready for the fight. The last to go in was Frère Jean (with his great scimitar), closing the doors behind him from the inside.

How Pantagruel broke Chidlings across his knee

CHAPTER 41

*[The tale adopts, in mock-heroic style, the tone of the medieval tales
of chivalry. All the various types of meaty sausages are enemies of
fishy, Lenten fare.*

*'To break chidlings over your knee' means to do things the hard
way, to go round the parish to find the church.*

Phoenicopters are flamingos, called flamants *in Languegoth (that is
in the Languedoc tongue which Rabelais again assimilates to a kind
of Gothic).*

In the Disciple de Pantagruel *which partly inspired Rabelais, these
Chidlings and their allies are slaughtered and sliced up. In Rabelais
their god appears and cures them with mustard, which goes well with
sausages and the like.*

*For these anti-Lenten Chidlings to dare to oppose the Pantagruelists
is a case of Ignorance opposing Wisdom. Rabelais exploits two adages
of Erasmus:* ΥΣ ΑΘΗΝΑΝ *(Hys Athenan), A Pig [teaching]
Minerva'. That adage (I, I, XL) is to be read together with the one
which follows it (I, I, XL, 'A pig undertakes to fight Minerva'). Both
were well known, meaning 'To teach your grandmother how to suck
eggs'.*

*The 'Bull of Berne' is the soldier who fought at Marignano in 1515
against troops led for the first time by François I. He is mentioned
towards the end of the first chapter of* Pantagruel, *in the variants.*

*'La Reine Pédauque', the Goose-footed Queen, is above all associ-
ated with Toulouse (as in the tale of Anatole France). Her toes were
webbed.]*

Those Chidlings drew so close that Pantagruel could see them
flexing their muscles and already lowering their lances. He at
once despatched Gymnaste to hear what they had to say and
on what grounds, without any formal challenge, they sought to
make war against their ancient friends who had done them no
wrong in word or deed. Gymnaste, facing their front ranks,

made a long, deep bow and shouted out as loudly as he could, 'Yours, are we, yours, all yours to command. We all hold to your ancient confederate Mardi Gras.'

Some have since told me that he said *Gradi Mars* not *Mardi Gras*.

Be that as it may, at that word a fat and podgy woodland brain-meat Saveloy ran ahead in front of their battalion and tried to seize him by the throat. 'By God,' said Gymnaste, 'you'll get in there only in slices.' And so he pulled out his two-handed sword yclept *Kiss-me-arse* and sliced that Saveloy in twain. Good God, how fat was he! It reminded me of that fat fellow the Bull of Berne, who was slain at Marignan at the defeat of the Switzers. He, believe you me, had no less than four fingers of fat on his guts.

That Saveloy loyally savaged, the Chidlings rushed upon Gymnaste and threw him viciously to the ground just as Pantagruel and his men came running up to help at the double.

Then pell-mell was that martial combat joined.

Poke-Banger poked Bangers: Spoilchidling spoilt Chidlings. Pantagruel broke Chidlings over his knees. Frère Jean was lying doggo within his Sow, seeing all and taking it all in, when, with a great hullabaloo, the Force-meat Pasties who were lying in ambush rushed out together against Pantagruel.

Then Frère Jean, witnessing the disarray and the uproar, opened the doors of the Sow and came out with his fine soldiers, some bearing iron spits, others holding andirons, fire-dogs, pans, scoops, grills, pokers, tongs, dripping-pans, brooms, casseroles, mortars and pestles, all in good order like a mob of arsonists, yelling together and most terrifyingly shouting: *Nebuzardan! Nebuzardan! Nebuzardan!*

With such shouts and commotion they charged the Force-meat Pasties and right through the Sausages. The Chidlings, suddenly aware of those fresh reinforcements, fled off at the gallop as if they had seen all the devils. Frère Jean, with his big-bellied stone-shot, swatted them as thick as flies; his men too never spared themselves. Pitiful was it to behold. That field was strewn all over with dead or wounded Chidlings. And the book says that if God had not intervened the whole race of Chidlings would have been exterminated by those culinary warriors.

But a marvel then befell.

You shall believe of it what you will.

From the direction of the polar star there came flying a great, gross and grey pig with wings long and ample like the sails of a windmill. Its plumage was crimson-red like that of a phoenicopter (called a *flamant* in Languegoth). Its eyes were red and inflamed with fire like a carbuncle; its ears, green like an emerald prasine-stone; its teeth, yellow like a topaz; its tail, long and black like Lucullian marble; its trotters, white, diaphanous and translucent like a diamond; and it had broadly webbed feet like those of geese, and, once upon a time, like *La Reine Pédauque* in Toulouse.

It wore a golden collar about its neck, on which was inscribed some Ionic letters from which I could read two words only, ΥΣ ΑΘΗΝΑΝ, 'A pig teaching Minerva'.

The weather was bright and clear, but it thundered to our left, so strongly that, as this monster appeared, we all stood there amazed. As soon as they saw it, the Chidlings threw down their weapons and arms and sank to their knees, wordlessly raising high their clasped hands as though they were worshipping it.

Frère Jean and his men still went on poking and skewering the Chidlings, but the retreat was sounded by the command of Pantagruel and all combat ceased.

The monster, having flown back and forth several times between the two armies, dropped seven and twenty pipes of mustard on to the ground; whereupon it disappeared, flying through the air and ceaselessly crying: *Mardi Gras, Mardi Gras, Mardi Gras.*

How Pantagruel parleyed with Niphleseth, the Queen of the Chidlings

CHAPTER 42

[The name of the fair Niphleseth, the Queen of the Sausages, derives from a Hebrew word for an 'object of shame' (a dildo).

'La Rue Paveé d'Andouilles' in Paris means 'The Paved street of the-Chidlings', but it can be taken in fun to mean 'The street paved with Chidlings'. In the Disciple de Pantagruel, *which Rabelais drew on here, the Chidlings do not become semi-human and so end up sliced and ready to eat.*

The sow is called a 'monster', a word which still retained its suggestion of a more or less miraculous 'sign', though here in a comic context.

'Sangréal', normally spelt Saint Graal, is the Holy Grail. In the spirit of the Cratylus *the spelling* sangréal *suggests Royal Blood. (In older French* réal *means royal, as in Montréal.) The sense Rabelais gives it is supplied by his letter to Antoine Hulot (see Rabelais, Œuvres complètes, ed. Mireille Huchon (Paris, Gallimard, 1994), p. 1018): 'also the good wines, especially one . . . which we are keeping here for your arrival as a* sang gréal *and as a second – or rather a fifth – essence.' Here this quintessential draught is not the best of wines: it is mustard. Mustard is the* sangréal *of the Chidlings: it is a wondrous restorative, a balm, an aromatic ointment which cures their wounds and brings them back to life.*

The Chidlings have their (Platonic) Idea of Mardi Gras just as the Papimanes will have their (Platonic but earthy) Idea of God: the Pope.

The inhabitants of the next island have their own sangréal too, one appropriate to them.]

The monster aforesaid no longer appearing and the two armies staying rooted in silence, Pantagruel asked to parley with Lady Niphleseth (for that was the name of the Queen of the Chidlings), who was in her chariot near her standard-bearers. That was readily granted.

The Queen alighted and greeted Pantagruel graciously and courteously received him. Pantagruel protested about the war.

She honourably apologized to him, alleging that her error
arose from a false report: her scouts had informed her that
Quarêmeprenant their inveterate foe had landed and was spending his time examining the physeter's urine. She begged him
kindly to pardon her offence, asserting that one was more likely
to find shit than gall in Chidlings, and proposed the following
terms:

– that she and all her successive Niphleseths would for ever
hold all their lands on that island from him in faithful homage;

– that they would obey his commands in all things
everywhere;

– that they would be female friends of all his friends, and
female enemies of all his enemies;

– that every year, in acknowledgement of such fealty, they
would despatch to him seventy-eight thousand Royal Chidlings to serve at the first course of his table for six months a
year.

Having done which, the very next day she conveyed that
number of Royal Chidlings to Gargantua in six great brigantines. They were in the charge of Niphleseth the Younger,
the Infanta of the island. Our noble Gargantua generously
despatched them as a present to the Great King in Paris, but
they nearly all perished from the change of air as well as from
lack of mustard (which is Nature's balm and restorative for
Chidlings). By the grace and favour of that Great King they
were piled up and buried in a place in Paris which to this very
day is called *La Rue Paveé d'Andouilles*, The road paved with
Chidlings.

At the entreaty of the ladies in the Royal Court, Niphleseth
the Younger was saved and honourably treated. She has since
married into a good and rich family and given birth to several
lovely children. For which God be praised.

Pantagruel graciously thanked the Queen, forgave her her
offence, refused her offer of fealty and bestowed on her a pretty
little penknife from Prague. He then carefully questioned her
about the monster which had previously appeared. She replied
that it was the *Idea of Mardi Gras,* their tutelary god in times

of war, the first Founder and the source of the Chidling race. That is why it looked like a Pig, for Chidlings are of porcine extraction.

Pantagruel inquired for what reason, and following what curative prescription, it had scattered such a quantity of mustard over the land. The queen replied that mustard was their *sangréal*, their celestial balm: by putting a little of it on the wounds of the stricken Chidlings the wounded recovered in next to no time and the dead were resuscitated. Pantagruel had no further conversation with the queen and withdrew aboard ship. So too did all those good comrades with their weapons and their Sow.

How Pantagruel landed on the Island of Ruach

CHAPTER 43

[Some learned banter: in Hebrew ruach *means both 'spirit' and 'wind';* anemos, *the Greek for wind, has given us the name of anemone (the flower); plovers were thought to live on a diet of air (or wind); the name Oedipus means 'Swollen leg' – hence 'oedipodic', applied to the gout.*

Professor Schyron was Rabelais' professor at Montpellier.

The inhabitants of Ruach have their own sangréal, *a restorative balm appropriate to their grossness: a choice wind.]*

Two days later we reached the Island of Ruach, and I swear to you by the Pleiades that I found the way of life of the people there stranger than I can say. They live on nothing but wind. Nothing do they eat, nothing do they drink, save wind. Their only habitations are weather-vanes.

They sow nothing in their gardens save three varieties of anemone. They carefully weed away any rue and other herbs which absorb or expel flatulence. To produce food, the common folk use fans made of feathers, paper or cloth according to their powers and resources, but the rich use windmills. When they hold a feast or a banquet, trestle-tables are set up under a windmill or two. There they feed, as happy as at a wedding. And during their meals they discuss the quality, excellence, rarity and health-giving properties of their winds just as you, good Drinkers, philosophize about your wines in your symposiums. One praises the Sirocco; another, the Libeccio; another, the Garbin; another, the Bise; another, the Zephyr; another, the Galerne; and so on for other winds. One favours smock-winds for lovers and gallants.

Where we prescribe draughts of thin broth for invalids, they prescribe draughts of thin air.

'O,' said one inflated little Ruachite, 'if only one could get a bladder-bag full of that good Languegoth wind called Cyerce. When travelling through our land, Schyron, the noble physician, told us one day that it is strong enough to topple laden wagons. O what great good it would do for my oedipodic leg! The biggest are not the best.'

'Maybe,' said Panurge, 'but how about a big barrel of that good Languegoth wine which is produced at Mireval, Canteperdrix and Frontignon!'

I saw a man of fine appearance, closely resembling a windbag, who was bitterly angry with one of his big, fat valets and with a little page-boy, giving them the devil of a beating with a slipper. Being ignorant of the cause of his anger I supposed it was his doctors' orders, it being wholesome for a master to whack and get cross and wholesome for valets to be whacked. But I heard that he was reproving his valets for having stolen half a leathern-bottleful of Garbin, a wind which he was saving up for late in the season.

In that island they never spit, piss nor leave droppings. To make up for which they copiously break wind, fizzle and fart. They suffer from maladies of every sort and every kind: every malady is indeed brought forth and produced by wind as is deduced by Hippocrates in his book *On Flatulence*. But the most infectious is the windy colic. To remedy it they employ huge cupping-glasses and so evacuate powerful ventosities. They all die of hydropic gaseous extension of the abdomen, the men, farting, the women gently breaking wind, so that their souls leave via their bums. A little later, when strolling through the island, we came across three fat windy-heads who were out watching certain plovers which abound there and which follow the same diet as they do.

I noticed that just as you topers carry flasks, bottles and flagons about with you, so too each one of them carries a pretty little bellows on his belt: if winds chance to fail them, they forge themselves fresh ones with those jolly little bellows by alternate attraction and expulsion (wind being in its essential definition, as you realize, neither more nor less than air flowing and undulating).

Just then we received an order in their king's name forbidding us, for three hours, to bring any man or woman of that country aboard our ships, since someone had stolen from him a bag full of the very wind that Aeolus, that good snorer, gave long ago to Ulysses to direct the course of his ship in a calm. And he religiously guarded it like another *sangréal*, curing several abnormal illnesses with it merely by releasing and delivering just enough for the patients to produce a virginal fart (the kind which nuns call a *son net*).[59]

How little rains abate great winds

CHAPTER 44

['Little rains abate great winds' was a current French saying.

Rabelais takes as his starting-point the windmill-eating giant of the Disciple de Pantagruel.

Hypenemian ('containing wind') was applied in Latin to wind-eggs (unproductive eggs laid with soft shells).

The medical specialists of Ruach are called Mezarims, *which possibly makes a Hebrew pun on north wind.*

'To skin the fox' means to vomit after excessive drinking.

Rabelais discreetly alludes to an adage of Erasmus: IV, IX, III,

---

59. A *son net* (a pun on *sonnet*) means a neat, clean, clear or brisk little sound.

'Vento vivere, *to live on wind*'. *He also cites from Horace (*Odes, II,
xvi, *27–8) an expression which had become proverbial:* 'Nothing is in
all things happy'.

To take one's 'ease like Fathers' *is to live well, like well-fed, idle
monks.]*

Pantagruel praised their polity and way of life and said to their
hypenemian Podestat, 'If you accept the opinion of Epicurus
when he said that the sovereign good consists in pleasure (I
mean, easy not toilsome pleasure) then I repute you most happy.
For you live on wind, which costs you very little or nothing;
you need but to puff.'

'True,' said the Podestat. 'Yet in this mortal life nothing is in
all things happy. Often, just when we are at table, feeding
ourselves on a God-sent wind as on manna from Heaven and
at our ease like Fathers, there appears some tiny shower which
abstracts it from us and abates it. And thus many a repast is
lost for want of victuals.'

'That,' said Panurge, 'is like Jenin de Quinquenais, who, by
piddling over the bum of Quelot, his wife, abated a stinking
breeze which was issuing from there as from some magisterial aeolian pot. I once wrote a pretty little ten-line poem
about it:

> Jenin, on tasting his new wine
> (Cloudy, fermenting on its lees),
> Said, 'Turnips, Quelot, would be fine:
> Boil some for us for supper, please:
> Of melancholy ne'er a tweeze!'
> Then off to bed, to swive and sleep.
> But Jenin's eyes ne'er closed would keep:
> Quelot broke wind at rapid rate.
> He pee'd upon her. A bit steep?
> But little showers great winds abate.

'There is more to come,' said the Podestat. 'We suffer from
an annual disaster; great and destructive: there is a giant called
Bringuenarilles, who dwells on the island of Tohu. Following

the orders of his physicians he resorts here every year in the spring for a purgation, swallowing like pills a great many of our windmills' bellows, of which he is very fond. That brings great suffering upon us, and so we have three or four Lents a year, without the special rogations and intercessions.'

'And have you no way of countering it?' asked Pantagruel.

'On the advice of our specialists, the Mezarims,' said the Podestat, 'at the season when he normally appears we concealed a great many cocks and hens inside the windmills. The first time that he swallowed them he all but died, for they went on cackling inside him and fidgeted about in his stomach, at which he fell into a lipothymic fit with heart pains and horrific and dangerous convulsions as though snakes had slipped into his stomach via his mouth.'

'That *as though* is most inappropriate and out of place,' said Frère Jean, 'for I heard tell some time ago that if a snake gets into your stomach it causes no discomfort whatsoever and will come out at once if you hang the patient up by his feet and place a bowl full of warm milk close to his mouth.'

'You,' said Pantagruel, 'have *heard tell*, and so had those who told it to you, but no such remedy has ever been seen or heard of. Hippocrates (in Book 5 of the *Epidemics*) writes of a case which occurred in his times: the patient died in a trice in spasms and convulsions.'

'Moreover,' said the Podestat, 'all the foxes round here ran after those hens into his mouth and he could have died at any moment were it not for the advice of some silly old spell-monger who, at the hour of his paroxysm, advised him *to skin the fox* as an antidote and a neutralizer. He has since received better advice: as a remedy he has a clyster administered to him composed of a concoction of grains of wheat and millet (which bring the hens all running up) and goose-livers (which bring the foxes all running up). He also takes pills through the mouth compounded of greyhounds and terriers.

'So much for our misfortune.'

'Fear no more, good folk,' said Pantagruel. 'That great giant Bringuenarilles who swallows up windmills is dead. He died, choking and suffocated, while eating a dish of butter beside the mouth of an oven: he was following the orders of his physicians.'

How Pantagruel landed on the island of the Papefigues

CHAPTER 45

[*The Papefigues care not a fig for the Pope.* Faire la figue *is to cock a snook (which the Papefigues, as sound Protestants, did to a picture of a pope). Behind the Papefigues lie the Vaudois of Provence, massacred in 1545, but regarded as loyal subjects by Rabelais' great patron, Guillaume Du Bellay, the Seigneur de Langey.*

The Briefve Déclaration *explains the name of Thachor the mule as 'a fig up the fundament: Hebrew'.*

The 'Gaillardets' are merry ones, or were so once, before they were oppressed and dubbed Papefigues *by their enemies.*

*The beginning of the tale of the peasant and the trainee devil. Rabelais calls the peasant a ploughman (*laboureur*). He seems to have been rather a peasant-farmer.*]

The following morning we encountered the island of the Papefigues, folk who once had been rich, free, and known as the Gaillardets, but now poor, unhappy and subject to the Papimanes. This is how it befell. On one annual festal day when the banners were out, the Burgomaster, syndics and the fat rabbis of those Gaillardets went to pass time watching the festival on the neighbouring island of Papimania. Now, on seeing the papal portrait (since it was a laudable custom to exhibit it to the people on high days marked by processions with banners) one of the Gaillardets cocked a fig at it, which in that land is a sign of manifest contempt and derision. To avenge it, a few days later the Papimanes all took up arms and without warning surprised, sacked and laid waste the entire island of the Gaillardets. Any male sporting a beard they put to the sword. The women and youths were spared on conditions similar to those which the Emperor Federigo Barbarossa imposed

long ago on the Milanese. It was during his absence that the
Milanese had rebelled against him and hounded the Empress
his wife from the city, mounted to shame her on an ancient
mule called Thacor, sitting astride and backwards (that is, with
her bottom turned towards the mule's head and her face
towards its crupper).

On his return Federigo, having subjugated the rebels and
locked them up, diligently traced and recovered Thacor, the
famous mule. Then, in the midst of the great market-place at
Milan, by his command, the hangman placed a fig in Thacor's
private parts, the captive citizens all being there to see it. Then,
to the sound of the trumpet, he cried in the name of the emperor
that whosoever amongst them wished to escape death should,
in public, extract that fig with his teeth and replace it, all
without using his hands. Whosoever refused would, on the
instant, be hanged and throttled. Some of them felt such shame
and horror at so abominable a penalty that they feared death
less than that and so were hanged. In others the fear of death
overpowered their sense of shame. When they displayed to the
hangman the fig which they had pulled out with their bare
teeth, they said, *Ecco lo fico* ('Behold the Fig').

The remnant of those wretched and desolate Gaillardets,
saved and protected from death by a similar public disgrace,
were turned into slaves and payers of tribute, and upon them
was imposed the name of *Papefigues*, because they had cocked
a fig at the papal portrait. From that time forth those wretched
folk have never prospered: every year since then they have
had hailstorms, tempests, plagues, famines and every sort of
disaster, as an everlasting punishment for the sin of their forebears and kinsmen.

On seeing the misery and the distress of the people, we would
have preferred to go on no further, but to find some holy water
and commend ourselves to God we went inside a little chapel
hard by the port: it was in ruins, desolate and lacking its roof
like Saint Peter's temple in Rome. Having gone into the chapel
and touched some holy water, we perceived a man inside the
water-bowl, dressed in stoles and entirely covered by the water
like a plunging drake, save for a bit of his nose to breathe

through. Around him stood three priests, all shaven and shorn, reciting from their book of exorcisms and conjuring away devils.

Pantagruel found it all very odd; upon asking what game they were playing he was advised that, for the last three years, a plague so dreadful had raged in their island that over half the land was depopulated and the fields without owners. Once the plague had passed, that man now hidden in the water-bowl had been ploughing a wide and fertile field and sowing it with white-wheat at a day and time when a young little devil (who had not yet learnt to hail and thunder except against parsley and cabbages, and who could neither read nor write) had obtained leave from Lucifer to come to play and amuse himself on this island of the Papefigues (the devils often coming for recreation, being well acquainted with the men and women there).

Once arrived, the devil approached that ploughman and asked what he was doing. The poor man replied that he was sowing the field with white-wheat to help him get through the following year. 'Well now,' said the devil, 'this field is not yours: it's mine. It belongs to me. For from the day and time that you showed that you cared not a fig for the Pope all this land was adjudicated, consigned and relinquished to us. But sowing wheat is not my *métier*: I shall therefore allow you to use the land, but on condition that we share the yield.'

'I agree to that,' said the ploughman.

'What I mean,' said the devil, 'is that we shall divide the yield into two parts. One will be the part which grows above the soil and the other the part covered by soil. The choice belongs to me since I am a devil descended from a noble and ancient family whilst you are a mere peasant. I choose the part which will be *under* the soil. You can have the part above. When will the harvest be?'

'Mid-July,' said the ploughman.

'Well then,' said the devil, 'I shall be there without fail. As for the rest, get on with your duty. Swink, villein! Swink. I'm off to tempt the high-born nuns of Pettesec with the merry sin of lust. The Bigot-tails and begging Brethren as well. I'm more than sure of their desires: battle once joined, then comes the attack!'

How that little young devil was outwitted by the ploughman from Papefigue-land

CHAPTER 46

[A comically young and ignorant devil is shown up by an astute peasant, but the devil still remains to be defeated. Meanwhile he dolefully admits the key role of Saint Paul in the lives of today's students. Saint Paul was particularly favoured by Evangelicals and Reformers.]

Come mid-July the devil turned up with a bevy of tiny little choir-devils. When he met the ploughman he said to him:

'Well then, villein, what have you been up to since I left? Now we must do our share-out.'

'That,' said the ploughman, 'is only right.'

Then the ploughman and his folk began cutting the wheat. The little devils likewise pulled up the stubble. The ploughman threshed his grain on the threshing-floor, winnowed it, bagged it up and took it off to sell at the market. The tiny devils did likewise and sat down in the market-place beside the ploughman to sell their stubble. The ploughman sold his wheat all right and with the money filled up an old boot which he wore tied to his belt.

The devils sold nothing; on the contrary: the peasants openly made fun of them in the market-place. Once the trading was over the devil said to the ploughman:

'Villein, you've cheated me this time. You won't do that next time!'

'Monsieur Devil,' said the ploughman, 'how could I have cheated you? You had the first choice. The truth is you thought you were cheating me over the choice, hoping that nothing would come up from the soil as my share whilst you would find below ground all the grain that I'd sown, and use it to tempt the wretched, the hypocrites or the greedy, and by temptation cause them to tumble into your snares. The grain you can see in the soil is dead and corrupted. From its corruption has sprung the new grain which you saw me sell.

'You chose the worst. That's why you are cursed in the Gospel.'

'Let's change the subject,' said the devil. 'What can you sow in our field next year?'

'To make a good yield for the prudent husbandman,' said the ploughman, 'one should sow turnips.'

'Well then,' said the devil, 'you're a decent villein. Sow plenty of turnips. I shall protect them from storms, and no hail shall fall upon them. But get this clear: for my share I retain whatever shall be *above* the soil: you can have what's underneath.

'Swink, villein, swink. I'm off to tempt heretics: their souls are very tasty when grilled over charcoal. Monsieur Lucifer has got the colic: they're tidbits while they're still warm!'

When the time came to gather the crop, the devil was there with a bevy of lackey-devils. Having come across the ploughman and his folk, the devil began to cut the turnip-tops and gather them in. After him came the ploughman, who dug deep, pulled out the great turnips and bagged them up.

And so, off they go together to market. The ploughman easily sold his turnips. The devil sold nothing. Worse: people publicly made fun of him.

'I can see, villein,' he said, 'that you have cheated me. I intend to finish once and for all with this field shared between us. These are my terms: we will claw one another, and whoever is the first to give in shall surrender his share of the field, which will go entirely to the victor. We'll adjourn for a week. Away you go, villein. I shall give you a devil of a clawing-over. I was on my way to tempt those pillaging Chiquanous, falsifiers of lawsuits, counterfeiting notaries and prevaricating lawyers, but I've learnt through an interpreter that they're mine already. Anyway, Lucifer is fed up with their souls: he usually sends them down to the devils washing-up in the kitchen, except when dredged with a seasoning. You have a saying,

No breakfast like a student's.
No dinner like a lawyer's.
No nibble like a grape-harvester's.
No supper like a merchant's.
No late-night collation like a chambermaid's.
And no meal in the world like a cowled Hobgoblin's.

It is true that, as an entrée, Monsieur Lucifer regales himself on cowled Hobgoblins. He used to breakfast on students but, through I know not what disaster, for some time now, they have (alas) annexed the Bible to their studies; for which reason we can't get even one of them to go to the devil. And I believe that if the black-beetles do not succour us by wrenching their *Saint Pauls* from their hands with menaces, assaults, beatings-up and burnings, we shall never again nibble another down yonder. Lucifer normally dines on lawyers who pervert justice and rob the poor – no lack of them! – but you get tired of always eating the same old fodder. He once said during a full chapter-meeting that he would love to eat the soul of just one single black-beetle who had forgotten to beg something for himself during his sermon; he promised double pay and a first-rate job to any devil who should bring him one back hot off the toasting-fork. Each of us set off in quest of one, but to no avail. All of them counsel high-born ladies to give to their convents.

'As for nibbles, he has kept off them ever since he suffered a bad colic arising from the ignominious mistreatment meted out in Northern Lands to his suppliers: the victuallers, carbon-grillers and pork butchers. He dines very well on usurers, apothecaries, forgers, debasers of the coinage and adulterators of merchandise. And from time to time, when he's in a good mood, he makes a late-night collation of chambermaids who drink some of their master's good wine and then top up the barrel with smelly water.

'Swink, Swain! Swink!

'I'm off to Trebizond to tempt students to leave their fathers and mothers, reject the established polity, exempt themselves from the edicts of their king and live in subterranean licence, despising everyone, jeering at everyone and, behind the fair and merry mask of poetic integrity, to all become noble, cowled Hobgoblins.'[60]

How the devil was deceived by an old woman of the land of the Papefigues

CHAPTER 47

[The triumph of a knowing peasant woman. Elsewhere the devil is a real person and a real source of evil for Rabelais, but devils as they appear in contes, *mystery-plays and farces are often stupid and can be outwitted by shrewd peasants.*

The Persian women shamed their men-folk who were fleeing the battle by baring their vaginas and inviting the cowards to hide away in them. It is related by Plutarch. It reappears, for example, in Tira-queau's Laws of Marriage. *It was also known from an apophthegm of Erasmus (VI, Varie mixta, 93).]*

On his way back home the ploughman was brooding and sad. When his wife saw him she thought he must have been done down in the market, but after she had heard the reason for his melancholy and seen his purse full of silver, she gently comforted him, assuring him that no harm at all would come to him from his scratch-up: all he had to do was to pose and repose on her: she had already thought how to produce a good outcome. 'If it comes to the worst I shall only get a scratching,' said the ploughman, 'for I shall give in at the first clawing and yield him the field.'

'No, no, no!' said the old woman. 'Pose and repose on me. Let me do it my way. You did say that he was a little-boy of a devil? I'll soon make him give in and yield us the field. If it had

60. 'Cowled Hobgoblins' are Rabelais' *Farfadetz*, his term for Franciscan friars. No convincing explanation has yet been found for this final paragraph, which seems to be attacking students in a town (Paris?) who, against their monarch's express wishes, are preparing to enter the hidden, lazy delights of the Franciscan Order.

been a grown-up devil we would have had something to think about.'

The day we landed on the island was the day they were due to meet. Early that morning the ploughman had made a very full confession and taken communion like a good Catholic, and then, on the advice of his *curé*, had plunged into the water-bowl to hide himself. In which state we had found him.

At the very instant we were told this tale, we received news that the old woman had diddled the devil and won the field.

And this is how: the devil came to the ploughman's door, rang the bell and yelled, 'Hey! Villein! Villein! Look: what lovely claws!' He then went into the house, sure of himself and fully resolved; but finding that the ploughman was not there, he noticed the ploughman's wife lying on the ground, sobbing and wailing.

'What's going on?' asked the devil. 'Where is he? What's he up to?'

'Ha!' said the old woman, 'where is he? He's a bad man, a hangman, a savage. He's given me such a wound. I'm done for. I'm dying from the harm he's done me.'

'Eh?' said the devil. 'What's wrong? I'll soon trounce him for you.'

'Oh,' said the old woman. 'He told me – that hangman, that bully, that clawer of devils! – that he had an appointment to claw it out with you this very day. So to try out his nails he just flicked me here between my legs with his little finger. He's totally done for me. I'm finished. I shall never get better. Have a look! And he's just gone to the blacksmith's to have his claws pointed up and sharpened. Monsieur le Diable: you've had it, my friend. Save yourself. Nothing can stop him. Get away, I beseech you.'

She then bared herself up to her chin (adopting the position of those Persian women who exhibited themselves to their sons as they fled from the battle) and showed him her what-d'you-call. The devil, upon seeing that monstrous solution of continuity in all its dimensions, exclaimed, 'Mahoun! Demiourgon! Megaera! Alecto! Persephone! He's not getting hold of me! I'm running away double quick! *Selah*! I quit the field.'

Having heard the *catastrophe* – the end – of the story, we withdrew to our ship and delayed there no longer.

Pantagruel put eighteen thousand golden royals into the box for the fabric fund out of consideration for the poverty of the people and the wretchedness of the place.

How Pantagruel landed on the Island
of the Papimanes

CHAPTER 48

[This and the following six chapters constitute the high point of Royalist-Gallican propaganda, especially enjoyed no doubt by Cardinal Odet de Châtillon and Cardinal Jean Du Bellay. The Papimanes make an idol of the Pope, who for them is a god who rivals the true God. (The Fourth Book *is concerned with the worship of false gods.) There were indeed papalist lawyers who did assert that the powers of the Pope were such that he was* quasi deus in terris, 'as though God on earth'. *Anti-papalists seized on that formula to 'prove' that papists are truly idolatrous.*

The false god of the Papimanes is supported by false Scriptures: the Decretals, many of the most pro-papalist of which were already known to be forgeries. False Decretals were seen as the buttress of papal power. As such they were rejected by reformers and many others. Decretals are known by the name of their collection, such as the Extravagantes. *Decrees are by contrast the concern of Councils.*

God declares 'I am that I am' (in Latin and French, 'I am he who is') in Exodus 3:14. *The insistence on the demonstrable masculinity of the popes is connected with the legend of Pope Joan. Many were convinced that, since the election of a woman as Pope Joan, all newly elected popes were required to sit upon a special seat so contrived as to allow their testicles to be felt from below.*

'Hypophète' is explained in the Brief Declaration *as one who tells of the past as distinct from a prophet who tells of the future.]*

Leaving behind the ravaged island of the Papefigues, we had most happily sailed for a day of calm weather when the blessèd isle of the Papimanes hove in sight. As soon as our anchors were dropped in the harbour and before we had made fast our cables, there came towards us a skiff with four persons each differently dressed.

One was a monk, frocked, filthy and finely booted.

Another, a falconer with a lure and a hawking-glove.

Another, a solicitor holding a great bundle of examinations, summonses, chicaneries and postponements.

The other was a vigneron from Orleans in handsome cloth gaiters, with a punnet and a sickle attached to his belt.

The instant they drew alongside, they called out, asking us in a loud voice:

'Have you seen Him, O travellers? Have you seen Him?'

'Whom?' asked Pantagruel.

'The One who is yonder!' they replied.

'Who is it?' asked Frère Jean. 'By the death of Beef, I'll give him a good walloping.' (He thought they were complaining about a thief, a murderer or a committer of sacrilege.)

'Why! Foreign travellers,' they said. 'Know ye not the Unique?'

'Sirs,' said Epistemon, 'we do not understand your terms. But do please explain to us whom you mean and then we shall tell you the truth without any dissembling.'

'We mean,' they said, 'He who is. Have you ever seen Him?'

'*He who is,*' Pantagruel replied, 'by the teachings of our theology, is God. With such words he revealed Himself to Moses. Certainly we have never seen him: he is not visible to fleshly eyes.'

'We're not talking about that high God who reigns in the heavens. We're talking of the god-on-earth. Have you ever seen Him?'

'Upon my honour,' said Carpalim, 'they mean the Pope!'

'Yes, gentlemen, yes,' replied Panurge. 'Yes indeed. Saw three of 'em. Never did me much good, though.'

'What's that?' they said. 'Our holy Decretals intone that there is never more than one alive.'

'I mean,' replied Panurge, 'one after the other, in succession. Apart from that, I have only seen one at a time.'

'O people, thrice and four times blessèd,' they said. 'Be ye welcome; most welcome.'

Whereupon they went down on their knees before us and wished to kiss our feet. We would not let them do so, objecting that they could not do more for the Pope if he were to come there in person.

'Yes. So we would!' they replied. 'That's already been agreed between us. We shall kiss his bum – without the fig leaf – and his bollocks, too. For he does have bollocks, the Holy Father. We find that in our beautiful Decretals. Otherwise he could never be pope. So there follows this necessary consequence in the subtleties of Decretaline philosophy: "He is a pope: therefore he has bollocks." When this world runs out of bollocks this world will run out of popes.'

Meanwhile Pantagruel inquired of one of the seamen in their skiff who these persons were. The reply came that they were the Four Estates of the isle. He added that we would be well received and well treated since we had seen the Pope!

Pantagruel explained it to Panurge, who said to him in confidence: 'There you are then. I swear to God that everything comes in handy if only you wait. Seeing the Pope has never done us any good up till now, by all the devils, I can see today that it will.'

We then disembarked, and there came out to meet us, as in a procession, the entire population of the country, men, women and little children. Our Four Estates cried to them in a loud voice: 'They have seen Him. They have seen Him. They have seen Him.' As that was proclaimed, all the people sank to their knees before us, clasped their hands together and raised them heavenwards crying, 'O Blessèd Ones! O Blessèd Ones!' And their cries lasted more than a quarter of an hour.

Then the schoolmaster came running up with his pedagogues and the boys from the junior and senior forms and set about caning them magisterially, as one used to cane little boys in our country-towns wherever a criminal was hanged: 'to impress it upon them'.

Pantagruel was angry at this and said to them, 'Messieurs, if you do not stop beating those children, I shall be off.'

The people were struck dumb when they heard his stentorian voice, and I noticed a little, long-fingered hunchback who asked the schoolmaster: 'By the might of the *Extravagantes*! Do people who see the Pope grow as tall as that one who is threatening us? O, how terribly keen I am to see Him and grow as tall that!'

So great were their acclamations that Homenaz came bustling up. (Homenaz was the name given to their bishop.) He was riding on a bridle-less mule with a green caparison; he was accompanied by his subjects (and what he called his 'objects' too). They were also carrying crosses, banners, gonfalons, canopies, torches and stocks for holy water. With all his might he too wanted to kiss our feet (as the good Christian Valfinier did to Pope Clement), saying that one of their hypophets, a glossator and de-greasator of their holy Decretals, had left a scripture saying that just as the Messiah so long awaited by the Jews eventually did appear, so too, one day, to their own isle would come the Pope. And while they were awaiting that happy day, should anyone land on their isle who, in Rome or elsewhere, had SEEN HIM they were to fête him and treat him with reverence.

We, however, courteously declined.

How Homenaz, the Bishop of the Papimanes, displayed to us the uranopetary Decretals

CHAPTER 49

[*In the* Brief Declaration *the word 'uranopetary' is explained as 'descended from the heavens'.*

Frère Jean alone is more or less at home with these Papimanes. The others are not. Bishop Homenaz has some superficial culture but no wisdom or understanding.

There are references to the Ten Commandments written by the hand of God (Exodus 32) and to a treatise of Plutarch, The 'Ei' *at Delphi.*]

Then Homenaz said to us,

'We are enjoined and required by our holy Decretals to visit churches rather than taverns. And so, without derogating from that beautiful principle, let us first go to church, and afterwards go and have a banquet.'

'Lead on, you worthy man,' said Frère Jean, 'and we will follow. You have spoken good words, like a Good Christian. It is a long time since we saw one. I find myself happy in my mind and believe that I shall feed all the better for it. Meeting worthy men is a pleasant thing.'

As we approached the doorway of the church, we noticed a thick gilded tome, studded all over with rare and precious stones: balay rubies, emeralds, diamonds and pearls, all more valuable than the jewels which Octavian consecrated to Jupiter Capitolinus, or at least as valuable. It was up in the air, hanging suspended by two massy golden chains from the zoological frieze over the door. We contemplated it with wonder. Pantagruel twisted and turned it at will, for he could easily reach it. He insisted that as he touched those chains he experienced a pruritis in his finger-nails and pins and needles in his arms, accompanied by a violent temptation in his mind to beat up an officer or two of the law, provided they were not tonsured.

Whereupon Homenaz said to us:

'Long ago the Law of Moses was given to the Jews, inscribed by the very fingers of God. At Delphi, on the façade of the temple of Apollo, this maxim was discovered divinely inscribed, *KNOW THYSELF*.

'Then after a certain lapse of time the word *EI* was found thus divinely inscribed and sent down from the heavens.

'The image of Cybele was sent down from the heavens to a field in Phrygia called Pesinunt; so too (if you trust Euripides) was the image of Diana in Taurus.

'The oriflamme was sent down from the heavens to the nobility and Most-Christian Kings of France for their fight against the Infidel. During the reign of Numa Pompilius, the second King of the Romans, *ancile* (the sharp-edged buckler) was seen coming down in Rome from the heavens.

'Long ago the statue of Minerva fell down from heaven into the Acropolis at Athens.

'And here, likewise, you can see the holy Decretals written

by the hand of an angel called Cherubim. You folk from beyond the sea won't believe that . . .'

'Hardly!' said Panurge.

'. . . and then it was miraculously sent down to us here from the Heaven of heavens, just as the river Nile is referred to as *coming down from Jupiter* by Homer, the Father of all Philosophy (always excepting the holy Decretals).

'And since you have seen the Pope – the Evangelist and sempiternal Protector of those Decretals – you will be permitted by us, if you so wish, to go in to see them and kiss them. But (as is divinely chanted to us by those holy Decretals over there) you will first have to fast for three days and regularly make your confessions, meticulously listing all your sins and so shucking them one after the other that not one bean of circumstance is dropped on to the ground. That takes time.'

'Worthy man,' replied Panurge, 'we have seen plenty of De-grease-alls – I mean, Decretals – on paper, vellum and glazed parchment, both manuscript and printed in moveable type. There is no need for you to bother to show us those. Your good intentions are quite enough. Thank you all the same.'

'Golly,' said Homenaz, 'you certainly haven't seen these which were written by an angel. Those in your lands are (as we find noted by one of our ancient decretaline scholiasts) but transumptions of ours. Moreover, I beg you to spare me no trouble: simply tell me whether you are prepared to fast for those three, lovely little God-given days, to confess and be contrite.'

'Cuntright!' said Panurge. 'We readily cuntsent to that. Only the fasting is not at all apropos: we have fasted so long, so very long, while at sea that spiders have spun cobwebs over our teeth. Just look at Frère Jean . . .' – on hearing which name Homenaz courteously gave him a friendly monastic accolade – '. . . for want of using and exercising his chops and mandibula, moss has grown all over his gullet.'

'He's telling the truth,' Frère Jean replied. 'I've fasted so much, so very much, that I've turned into a hunchback.'

'Let's go into church, then,' said Homenaz. 'And do forgive us if we don't *sing* you the lovely Mass of God: the noon-day hour is past, after which our holy Decretals forbid us to sing a

Mass – I mean a high and lawful one – but I shall read you a
low and dry one.'

'I,' said Panurge, 'would prefer a Mass wetted by some good
Angevine wine. Thrust ahead, then, low and stiff!'

'Gosh!' said Frère Jean, 'it grieves me that my stomach is
fasting still. For after I'd had an excellent breakfast and bloated
myself monkish-style, if he'd chanced to sing us a *Requiem*
I'd have contributed some bread and wine: *draughts for the
passed!*[61] Patience. Pull, push, and get on with it, but, I pray
you, shorten its skirts lest they drag in the mud – and for some
other reason too.'

How we were shown by Homenaz the
archetype of a pope

CHAPTER 50

*[It is a fool who proverbially covers himself with a wet sack (to protect
himself from the rain).*

*Again we meet misused Platonic Ideas: the Papimanes make their
'portrait' into the 'Idea' of the Pope! ('Portrait' is used with the sense
of 'Idea' and in combination with it: see below, Chapter 55.)*

*The whole 'papist' system is being turned to ridicule, contrasted
unfavourably with the 'heretics' of Lutheran Germany and Anglican
England.*

*Two adages of Erasmus are drawn upon: III, I, LXXXVIII, 'Give
me a basin' (to spew into); it represents the highest degree of disgust;
and I, VIII, LXXXVIII, 'Food for the gods', applied by Nero to the
poisoned mushrooms at his disposal.*

*Raminagrobis was the good dying poet of Chapters 21–3 of the
Third Book.]*

The Mass once over, Homenaz drew a great hotchpotch of keys
from out of a chest by the high altar. With them he opened

---

61. Wine and bread were symbolically brought to funerals. Frère Jean makes
    a pun: *trépassés*, the dead, and *traits passés*, draughts (of wine) gone by.

the thirty-two locks and the fourteen padlocks protecting an iron-framed, heavily barred grill set above the said altar; then, with great solemnity, he covered himself with a wet sack and, drawing back a crimson curtain, showed to us an image of a pope – pretty badly painted, in my opinion – touched it with the end of a longish pole and made us all kiss the end of it.

He then asked us,

'That image: what do you make of it?'

'It is,' said Pantagruel, 'the portrait of a pope. I can tell it from his tiara, amice, rochet, and slipper.'

'You put it well,' said Homenaz. 'It is the Idea of that good God-on-Earth, the arrival of whom we devoutly await and whom, one day, we hope to see in this our land. O blessèd, yearned-for, long-awaited day! And you, blessèd and most-blessèd, who have had the stars so favourable that you really have looked upon the living countenance of that good God-on-Earth, upon whose portrait we but simply look to earn plenary remission of all remembered sins, together with a third plus eighteen-fortieths of sins forgotten. And only during our great annual festivals can we ever see it.'

At that point Pantagruel said it was a work such as Daedalus made. And even though it was distorted and badly executed, it nevertheless possessed some hidden and occult energy where pardons are concerned.

'It is as when the vagrants at Seuilly,' said Frère Jean, 'were supping in their hospice during a feast-day: one was boasting of having collected six five-penny pieces; another, two ten-penny pieces; but a third could boast of three fine silver testoons. "Well yes," his companions retorted, "but you've got a God-leg, you have!" (as though some divine qualities were lurking in a leg gangrened and decomposing).'

'Whenever you tell such tales in the future,' said Pantagruel, 'remember to bring in a basin: I am close to vomiting. Using the name of God in matters so filthy and abominable! Appalling. Yes, appalling. If such vile language is current within that monkery of yours, then leave it there. Never bring it out of the cloister.'

'So too the physicians claim,' Epistemon added, 'that there

is some participation of the divine in certain maladies. Similarly Nero sang the praises of mushrooms, calling them (after a Greek saying) *the food of the gods* because he had used them to poison his predecessor Claudius, the Emperor of Rome.'

'It seems to me,' said Panurge, 'that this portrait is all wrong where our recent popes are concerned, for I have seen them not with an amice on their heads but a helmet topped by a Persian tiara: the whole of Christendom was enjoying peace and quiet while they alone waged the most brutal and cruel wars.'

'Then that,' said Homenaz, 'was against those rebels, heretics and hopeless Protestants who refuse to obey the Holiness of that good God-on-earth. That is not only permitted and legal, it is commended by the holy Decretals: emperors, kings, dukes, princes and republics must put them to the pyre the instant they transgress one iota of his commandments – and to the sword – and must despoil them of their goods, dispossess them of their kingdoms, proscribe them, anathematize them and damn their souls too in the depths of the hottest cauldron in Hell.'

'By all the devils,' said Panurge, 'they're not heretics here as Raminagrobis was nor as they are in Germany and England. Real hand-picked Christians you are.'

'Golly, yes,' said Homenaz. 'That's why we're all going to be saved.

'Let's have a drop of holy water: and then to dinner!'

Light conversation over dinner in praise of the Decretals

CHAPTER 51

[Christ's summary of the Law is short and clear: 'Thou shalt love the Lord thy God with all thy heart, and with all thy soul, and with all thy mind' and 'Thou shalt love thy neighbour as thyself'. The Papimanes infringe both commandments: they have a rival god, and their love of their neighbour is conditional. They replace the Scriptures by the Decretals and their papal-centred theology, which for Papimanes equals or supplants Saint Paul.

Specific collections of Decretals are named, each with a mocking epithet in imitation of those given to great theologians (Doctor Angelical, and so on): Sextum seraphical; Clementines cherubical and Extravangantes angelical.

When ordering new rounds of drink Homenaz repeats a Latin/ French pun: Clerice: éclaire ici: 'Clerk! (or Cleric!) Shine light here'. To keep some of the savour, that play on words is transposed throughout to 'Deacon! Be a beacon! Shine over here!' But Clerice! can mean both 'O male clerk!' and 'O female clerks!' The ambiguity may be at least once intentional but is not reproduced here.

There is again a deliberate ambiguity over 'farce', both a comic play and force-meat stuffing.]

Take note of this, you Drinkers: during Homenaz's dry Mass, three churchwardens went round the congregation each holding a large bason in his hand and crying aloud: 'Forget not the blessèd folk who have seen His face.'

When they left the chapel they brought Homenaz their basons, each full of papimaniacal coins. Homenaz informed us that it was to provide good cheer, and that one slice of this free-will offertory would be devoted to good drinking and the others to good eating, in accordance with a miracle-working gloss hidden away in a nook of their holy Decretals. That took place in a delightful inn somewhat resembling Guillot's place in Amiens. The fodder, believe me, was ample and the rounds of drinks copious. I observed two memorable features during that dinner: one was that no viands were served – capons, kids or indeed porkers (of which there are plenty in Papimania) or pigeons, rabbits, hares, turkeys or other flesh – in which there was not an abundance of magisterial *farce*. The other, that all the dinner and the dessert was served by the local marriageable maidens, beautiful little things (I assure you), buxom little things, blonde little things, sweet little things, all very graceful. They were clad in long, loose, snowy albs and were girdled twice about their middles; their heads were uncovered; their hair crowned with little headbands and ribbons of violet silk strewn with roses, carnations, marjoram, dill-flowers, lemon-balm and other scented blooms; every so often they proffered us wine to drink with studied, engaging curtsies. Everyone there found them delightful to look at: Frère Jean watched them out of the corner of his eye like a dog making off with a morsel of goose-wing.

As dinner was being cleared away there was melodiously chanted by them an epode in praise of the most-holy Decretals.

When the dessert was brought in, Homenaz, merry and mirthful, addressed a word to one of the master butlers, saying, 'Deacon! Be a Beacon!' At those words one of the maidens promptly presented him with a large chalice full of *Extravagant* wine. He took it into his hands and sighing profoundly, said to Pantagruel: 'To you, my Lord, and to all of you, my handsome friends, I drink this toast with all my heart. You are most welcome.'

Homenaz, his drink downed at a bound, handed the chalice back to the charming young lady and exclaimed with a heavy sigh, 'O Decretals divine! It is thanks to you that we know that good wine *is* good.'

'It's not the worst one in the hamper!' said Panurge.

'If they could turn bad wine into good,' said Pantagruel, 'that would be something!'

'O *Sextum* seraphical!' continued Homenaz. 'How vital you are to the salvation of us poor humans. O *Clementines* cherubical! How within you is rightly included and propounded the perfect institution of the true Christian man. O *Extravagantes* angelical! Without you, how those poor souls would perish who, in their vile bodies, journey here below through this vale of tears!

'Alas! When will that special gift of grace be vouchsafed to humankind that they may desist from all other studies and concerns in order to read you, hear you, know you, frequent, incorporate and transfuse you, placing you in the centre of the deepest ventricles of their brains, in the innermost marrow of their bones, in the labyrinthine mazes of their arteries. Then – not before and in no other way – shall this world be blessèd.'

At those words Epistemon got to his feet and said quite bluntly to Panurge, 'I'm in need of a privy: I must get away:

this farce-meat has unbunged my arse-gut. I really can't wait!'

'Then, O then,' continued Homenaz, 'there will be no more hail, frost, fog, nor storms. Then, O then, there will be an abundance of all good things in earth. Then, O then! there will be stubborn, infringible peace in all the world: no more wars, no more pillagings, exactions, plunderings and assassinations, except of heretics and cursèd rebels. Then, O then! there will be joy, gladness, happiness, bliss and delight amongst the entire human race. But O! what great doctrine, what inestimable erudition, what God-made precepts there are, mortised together by the divinely inspired chapters of those everlasting Decretals. O! by reading one demi-canon, one tiny paragraph, one single phrase of them, you feel ablaze within your heart the furnace of God's love and of charity towards your neighbour – provided he's not a heretic – an assured contempt of all things earthy and fortuitous; an elevation of your minds in rapture, yea, unto the Third Heaven; and a sure satisfying of all your desires.'

Miracles produced by the Decretals: continued

CHAPTER 52

[The last chapter ended with the Papimanes earnestly believing that their rival Scriptures, the Decretals, can bring them that very special privileged ecstasy by which Saint Paul was caught up to the Third Heaven (II Corinthians 12:2).

Gullible superstition is added to the defects of the Papimanes and their religion. In demanding for the Decretals the adoration of 'latria' the Bishop wants the Decretals to be worshipped as God; 'hyperdulia' is that highest veneration that many (though not, it seems, Rabelais) believed owed to the Virgin Mary.

Panormitanus was a famous commentator on the Clementines.

The 'decretalipotent' Scot was Professor Robert Ireland of Poitiers.

Parisian students used 'Clos Bruneau', still the name of a little passage in the Latin Quarter, as slang for the anus (Brown Close).

'Incagulating' is a nonce-word based on the Spanish cagar, *to shit.*

Herbault is famine and misery personified.

With the lines translated from the much-admired poet Catullus (23,
20) Rabelais makes a literary defence of scatological humour.
'To be in the yellow' is to be legally bankrupt.]

'Harmoniously piped,' said Panurge, 'but I believe as little of it
as I can, because when I was in Poitiers one day at the home of
their decretalipotent Scottish Doctor of Law, I happened to
read a chapter of the Decretals and, may the devil take me if,
as I read it, I didn't become so constipated that I never voided
more than one tiny turd for four – no, five – days. And do
you know what kind? Such as Catullus said were those of his
neighbour Furius:

> In one whole year of turds you void but ten;
> Rub them with fingers: crumble them again:
> No dirt upon those fingers will be seen;
> Those turds are hard as any stone or bean.'

'Gna! Gna!' said Homenaz. 'Perhaps you were, by Sinjin! in
a state of mortal sin, my friend.'
'That's wine from a different barrel,' said Panurge.
'One day,' said Frère Jean, 'I was at Seuillé when I wiped my
bum with a leaf from some wretched old *Clementines* which
Jean Guymard, our bursar, had chucked away in our cloister-
meadows: I give myself to all the devils if fistulas and haemor-
rhoids did not so horribly come upon me that the poor old hole
of my *Clos Bruneau* became all lacerated.'
'By Sinjin!' said Homenaz, 'that was divine retribution,
clearly avenging the sin which you committed by incagulating
those sacred volumes which you ought to kiss and to adore
with the adoration of latria, or at the very least of hyperdulia.
On such matters the Panormitanus never uttered a word of a
lie.'
'In Montpellier,' said Ponocrates, 'John Thomas had bought
from the monks of Saint-Olary a lovely Decretals (written on
Lamballe parchment, nice and wide) for its vellum to beat out
gold-leaf. The extraordinary thing was that not one single piece
thus beaten turned out well: all emerged tattered and torn.'

'Retribution,' said Homenaz, 'and vengeance divine!'

'At Le Mans,' said Eudemon, 'François Cornu, an apothecary, made cornets from a shabby old *Extravagantes*: I disavow
the devil if all the items wrapped up in them were not immediately poisoned, spoilt and putrefied: incense, cloves, cinnamon,
saffron, spices, cassia, rhubarb, tamarinds, indeed all his purga-
tives, sedatives and laxatives.'

'Vengeance!' cried Homenaz, 'and retribution divine! Fancy
putting sacred scriptures to such profane ends!'

'In Paris,' said Carpalim, 'Groignet the tailor cut up some
old *Clementines* to cut out patterns and measures. O! strange
event! All the materials cut to those patterns and made up from
those measurements were ruined and spoiled: robes, capes,
mantles, cassocks, skirts, overcoats, neck-bands, waistcoats,
tunics, riding-hoods and farthingales. Intending to cut out a
cape, Groignet would cut out the form of a codpiece; and
instead of a cassock, a hat crinkled like plum-stones; from the
design for an overcoat he would cut out an amice: from the
pattern of a doublet he would cut out the form of a canopy – a
canapé for frying chestnuts is what it looked like once his
apprentices had put in the stitches and cut the deep slashes!
Instead of a neck-band he would make up a buskin; from the
pattern of a farthingale he would cut out a riding-hood; believing that he was making up a mantle, he produced a Switzer's
drum. Things went so far that the wretched man was condemned by law to pay for the cloth of every one of his clients;
and now he's in the yellow.'

'Retribution!' said Homenaz, 'and vengeance divine.'

'At Cahusac,' said Gymnaste, 'an archery match was
arranged between the Seigneur d'Estissac and the Vicomte de
Lauzun. As they were to shoot at a target, Pérotou dismem-
bered a copy of the Decretals belonging to that good canon La
Carte and cut out the white bull's-eye from its leaves. I give
myself, sell myself and send myself dashing to all the devils if
ever one of the cross-bowmen in all that land (who are
renowned throughout Guyenne) could lodge one arrow in it.
All went wide. Nothing of that sacrosanct white was in any
way besmirched, ravaged or deflowered. Better still: the elder

Saint-Sernin, who was in charge of the bets, swore to us by his golden figgies – his great oath – that he had actually, clearly and incontrovertibly seen Carquelin's iron-tipped bolt homing straight for the bull's-eye in the very middle of the white and on the very point of hitting it and sinking into it when it turned a good six feet aside in the direction of the bakery.'

'Miracle!' cried Homenaz. 'Miracle! Miracle! Deacon! Beacon: Shine over here! I drink to you all. You seem true Christians to me.'

At those words the girls began to giggle amongst themselves. Frère Jean was whinnying from the tip of his nose as though ready to leap them like a stallion, or at least cover them like an ass (as Herbault does the poor).

'It seems to me,' said Pantagruel, 'that, inside those white targets, you would be safer from the risk of an arrow than ever was Diogenes long ago.'

'Eh?' asked Homenaz. 'What do you mean? Was he a Decretalist?'

'That,' said Epistemon, returning after having done his job, 'is very much to follow the wrong suit.'

'Diogenes,' said Pantagruel, 'seeking amusement one day, visited the archers who were shooting down at the butts. One of them was so maladroit, unskilled and incompetent that whenever his turn to shoot came round all the spectators drew apart for fear of being struck. Diogenes watched him shoot an arrow so askew that it landed some six yards off target. At his second shot the spectators pulled far back to left and right but Diogenes ran up and stood by the white target, insisting that that was the safest spot of all and that the archer was more likely to strike anywhere else but there, the white alone being safe from his arrow.'

'One of the pages of the Seigneur d'Estissac called Chamouillac discovered the charm,' said Gymnaste. 'On his advice Péroton changed the whites, using instead documents from the Pouillac lawsuit.

'Whereupon everyone on both sides shot very well.'

'At Landerousse,' said Rhizotome, 'at the wedding of Jean Delife, there was a splendid and sumptuous nuptial feast as was then the local custom. After supper several farces, comedies and amusing sketches were put on; then there were danced several morris-dances with jingle and drum. After which various sorts of masques and mummers were brought in. My fellow pupils and I (to honour the revels to the best of our abilities, for we had been given that morning fine white-and-violet favours) made masks with false beards for a merry masquerade, using plenty of snail-shells and Saint-Michèle cockle-shells, but lacking leaves of colocasia, burdock and the personate bugloss as well as paper, we made our masks out of leaves from an old discarded *Sextum*, cutting out little slits for our eyes, noses and mouths. Then, O wonder! Having taken off our false faces once our little capers and childish shows were over, we appeared more hideous and villainous than the boy-devils in the passion-play at Doué: so marred were our faces wherever the said leaves had touched them. One of us had caught smallpox; another, the plague; another, syphilis; another, measles; and yet another, huge boils. In short, the least disfigured was the one whose teeth had dropped out.'

'Miracle!' cried Homenaz. 'Miracle!'

'It's no laughing matter,' said Rhizotome. 'My two sisters, Catherine and Renée, had placed their wimples, cuffs and newly laundered ruffs, all starched up and white, between the pages of a beautiful *Sextum*, using it as a press (for it was bound with thick boards studded with nails). Well, by the mighty power of God . . .'

'Hang on!' said Homenaz; 'Which God do you mean?'

'There is only one,' replied Rhizotome.

'Well, yes,' said Homenaz, 'up in Heaven. We have another one on earth though, don't we?'

'Gee up little donkey!' said Rhizotome. 'Upon my soul I wasn't thinking about him. By the mighty power, then, of Paper-God-Pope-on-Earth,[62] their wimples, neck-bands, bibs,

---

62. 'Paper-God-Pope-on-Earth' renders *Dieu Pape terre*. In the list of great figures in the underworld visited by Epistemon (*Pantagruel*, Chapter 20) appears Nicholas Pape Tiers as a paper-merchant with *tiers* of paper. The papal-god of the Papimanes was a paper-generating one: Decretals, Indulgences, Bulls and so on.

kerchiefs and all the rest of their linen turned blacker than a coalman's sack.'

'Miracle!' cried Homenaz. 'Deacon! Beacon! Shine over here and record these beautiful histories.'

'How is it then,' asked Frère Jean, 'that folk say:

> Since men stuck *tales* on to decrees[63]
> And soldiers stuff bags as they please,
> Monks gave up sandals for riding-boots,
> Then evils everywhere send forth shoots?'

'I get you,' said Homenaz. 'Those are quirky little taunts from the new heretics.'

How gold is shrewdly abstracted from France by virtue of the Decretals

CHAPTER 53

[Royalist-Gallican indignation with a vengeance, expressing itself through laughter: papal superstition drains France of its wealth; the 'appalling chapters' of papalist law (cited as always by their opening words in Latin) all involve paying fees or fines or taxes, transferring riches from France to the Vatican.

For the cruel and maudlin Bishop of the Papimanes the Decretals absolutely replace Holy Writ, which could never justify what are for Rabelais now the evils of the papalist system as well as its corrupt monastic institutions and skewed theology.

Homenaz's gaffe ('Decretist' for 'Decretalist') is a real one: for Rabelais Gratian's Decrees are never in question. What is in question is papal absolutism and the (for Rabelais and his patrons) corrupt system which it brings about.

Rabelais is adapting to his laughter harsh Lutheran satire. Homenaz breaks Christ's summary of the Law: he worships the wrong God; he

63. In the 'heretical' verse *ales* (wings) are added on to the Decrees so turning them into *Decretals*. To get a similar effect in English the wings become 'tales' (with a hint of 'tails').

does not love his neighbour as himself. And he venerates the wrong
Scriptures.

In the Latinate phrase, 'vivat' means 'Long live!', while 'fifat' and
'bibat' are the same word as pronounced by German-speakers. The
Spanish pronunciation – 'bibat' – makes it sound like the Latin for
'Let him drink!']

'I would willingly have paid half a pint of gut-ready tripe,'
said Epistemon, 'if only we could have collated against that
archetype those appalling chapters,

> *Execrabilis,*
> *De multa,*
> *Si plures,*
> *De annatis* (in its entirety)
> *Nisi essent,*
> *Cum ad monasterium,*
> *Quod dilectio,*
> *Mandatum,*

and certain others as well by which over four hundred thousand
ducats are extorted from France towards Rome every year.'

'That's not a mere nothing, is it?' said Homenaz, 'yet it seems
little enough to me considering that France the Most-Christian
is the unique Wet-Nurse of the court of Rome. But just you find
me any books in the world – of philosophy, medicine, law,
mathematics, the humanities or indeed (by that God of mine)
Holy Writ – which could extract as much! No! Not a whit!
Not a whit!: in them, I assure you, you will never find such a
flow of gold-bearing energy. And yet the Decretals are neither
willingly learnt nor acknowledged by those devils of heretics.
So burn 'em, claw 'em, lop 'em, drown 'em, hang 'em, skewer
'em, bash 'em, rip 'em apart, gut 'em, carve 'em, fry 'em, roast
'em, chop 'em, crucify 'em, boil 'em, broil 'em, quarter 'em,
squash 'em, tear 'em limb from limb and grill 'em: wicked
heretics, decretalifugitives, decretalicides – worse than homi-
cides, worse than parricides – the devil's own decretali-
slaughterers.

'Now, good folk, if you wish to be called and reputed true Christians, then with clasped hands I beseech you never to believe anything, never to think, say, do or perform anything except what is contained in our sacred Decretals and their glosses: in that beautiful *Sextum*, those beautiful *Clementines*, those beautiful *Extravagantes*. O ye books made by God! Then you shall be in honour, glory, repute, riches, preferment and prelation in this world, revered by all, feared by all, advanced above all others, and above all others chosen and selected. For in no estate beneath the canopy of Heaven could you find folk more suited to doing everything and managing everything than such as have devoted themselves – by divine foreknowledge and eternal predestination – to the study of the holy Decretals.

'Would you choose a brave general, a good captain, a worthy chief and leader of an army in time of war, who knows how to foresee all troubles, avoid all dangers, bring his men to attack and to fight with enthusiasm, yet risking nothing, ever victorious, not losing his men, and knowing how to follow up his victory? Then choose me a Decretist – Oh! No, no! I mean a Decretalist!'

'Quite a bloomer,' said Epistemon.

'Would you, in time of peace, find a man apt and able to govern properly the State affairs of a republic, kingdom, empire or monarchy; to maintain the Church, the nobility, the senate and the commonalty in wealth, amity, concord, obedience, virtue and decency? Then take me a Decretalist. Would you find a man who, by his exemplary life, fair speech and saintly admonitions shall in no time conquer the Holy Land, shedding no blood and converting those wrong-believing Turks, Jews, Tartars, Moscovites, Mamelukes and Sara-bovines to the true faith? Then take me a Decretalist.

'What makes the people in many countries rebellious and unruly, the pages cheeky and naughty, the schoolboys stupid and asinine? Why! Their governors, squires and preceptors were not Decretalists. But, in all conscience, what is it that has established, supported and justified those beautiful religious Orders by which we can see Christendom everywhere graced, adorned and glittering as is the firmament with its stars?

'Why! The holy Decretals.

'What is it that has founded, buttressed, protected and now maintains, sustains and feeds those devout Religious in their convents, monasteries and abbeys, without whose diurnal, nocturnal and continual prayers our world were in danger of returning to its antique Chaos?

'Why! The sacred Decretals.

'What is it that, day after day makes the famous and renowned patrimony of Saint Peter increase in an abundance of all goods temporal, corporal and spiritual?

'Why! The sainted Decretals.

'What is it that makes the Holy and Apostolic See in Rome, from all times – and to this very day – so feared throughout the universal world that all kings, emperors, potentates and noble lords must willy-nilly be enfeoffed to it, crowned, buttressed and accredited by it, must come and prostrate themselves and kiss that wonder-working slipper which you have seen portrayed?

'Why! God's beautiful Decretals.

'I intend to make a great secret known to you: in their crests and devices the universities of your world normally have a book, sometimes open, sometimes shut. What book do you think it to be?'

'I really do not know,' said Pantagruel; 'I have never looked inside.'

'It is,' said Homenaz, 'the Decretals, without which the privileges of all our universities would perish. I caught you out there! Ha, ha, ha, ha, ha!' Here Homenaz began to break wind, fart, slobber and sweat; handing his gross, greasy square-cap with its four codpieces to one of the maidens. She (having lovingly kissed it as a token and pledge that she would be the first to be married) placed it most merrily on her shapely head.

'*Vivat!*' cried Epistemon: *vivat, fifat, pipat, bibat!* Oh, what an apocalyptical secret!'

'Deacon!' said Homenaz, 'Deacon! Beacon! Shine light over here with double lanterns. And girls: bring in the fruit.

'I was saying, then, that by devoting yourself to an exclusive study of the sacred Decretals you will be rich and honoured in this world. And I add that, as a consequence, you will be infallibly saved in the next, in that blessèd Kingdom of Heaven, the keys of which have been entrusted to our good Decretaliarchic God. O, good my God, whom I adore yet have never seen, open for us, by special grace – at least in the article of death – the most sacred treasure of Holy Church, our Mother, of which thou art the Protector, Guardian, Custodian, Administrator and Distributor. And ordain that those precious works of supererogation and those handsome Pardons fail us not in our hour of need, so that the devils may find nothing to bite upon within our wretched souls, and the horrifying jaws of Hell never devour us. If Purgatory we must suffer, sufferance show! Within thy power and volition it lies to deliver us from it when thou wilt.'

Here Homenaz began to shed thick, hot tears, beat his breast, cross his thumbs and kiss them.

How Homenaz gave Pantagruel some Good-Christian pears

CHAPTER 54

[For the echo of Virgil in the third paragraph compare the poem at the end of the Third Book. The anti-papalist convictions of Father Rabelais have just been revealed as being as absolute as those of the later Luther. During his time in Metz after the Third Book Rabelais had read a Latin version of Luther's harsh but effective satire Against the Popedome of Rome, Constructed by the Devil. From it he took the phrase Bon Christian ('Good Christians', a plural though it looks singular). For Luther the term 'Good Christians' is a sarcastic one, applied to simple, gullible, exploitable 'papist' folk by cynical men in the Vatican who themselves believe nothing and believe in nothing. Having read these chapters, one can understand why Cardinal de Châtillon eventually crossed the Channel to a royally reformed Church, for it is inconceivable that Rabelais would have written so boldly without the clear, prior, public support he enjoyed.

Poires de bon chrétien ('Good-Christian' pears) were, and are, excellent pears, but poire in French can also mean a booby.

With the word 'catastrophe', already taken from Erasmus, Rabelais again emphasizes the dramatic, farcical conception of these chapters.

Rabelais draws on another adage of Erasmus: (II, III, V, 'He calls a fig a fig, a hoe a hoe'. It is applied to simple folk who tell things as they are.

Here and throughout the Fourth Book *Pantagruel is portrayed as a model of princely pantagruelism, wise, charitable and tolerant.]*

Upon seeing this wretched catastrophe, Epistemon, Frère Jean and Panurge hid behind their napkins and began to cry *miaow, miaow, miaow*, meanwhile wiping their eyes and pretending to weep. The maidens, who had been properly trained, offered full chalices of *Clementine* wine all round, with an abundance of preserved fruits. And thus was jollity restored to the feast.

As dinner ended, Homenaz offered us a large number of lovely fat pears, saying:

'Take these, Beloved. They are very special pears: you will find them nowhere else. No land yields every crop: only India yields black ebony; good incense comes from Sabaea, and sigillate earth from the isle of Lesbos: and these beautiful pears are borne by this isle alone. If you would like to, plant some in a nursery-garden in your own land.'

'What do you call them?' asked Pantagruel. 'They look excellent to me and very juicy. If you were to simmer them, quartered, in a casserole with a little wine and sugar they would make a wholesome dish for both the sick and the thriving.'

'Just pears,' replied Homenaz. 'Since it so pleases God we are simple folk. We call figs figs, plums plums, and pears pears.'

'Truly,' said Pantagruel, 'once I am back home (and that, please God, will be soon), I shall splice and graft some of them in my garden by the river Loire in Touraine. And they shall be called *Good-Christian pears*, for I have never seen better Christians than these good Papimanes.'

'It would be just as good for me,' said Frère Jean, 'if he were to give us two or three cartloads of his maidens.'

'What for?' asked Homenaz.

'To phlebotomize them between their big toes with certain

well-honed pistons. By so doing we would graft some *Good-Christian* children on to them and their race would multiply in our lands (where folk aren't all that good).'

'Gosh,' Homenaz replied. 'We won't do that. You'll make them boy-mad. I can tell that from your nose, even though I've never seen you before. Alas, alack. A bit of a lad, you are. Do you really want to damn your soul? Our Decretals forbid it: I should like you to be well aware of that.'

'Patience,' said Frère Jean. 'But if thou wilt not give them, *Praesta quaesumus* (Lend them, we pray). Breviary stuff! I fear no man sporting a beard, were he a triple-hooded doctor de-crystalline (I mean, decretaline).'[64]

When the dinner was over we took our leave of Homenaz and all those good people, politely thanking them and promising that, in return for such kindness, we would, once in Rome, so deal with the Holy Father that he would speedily come to see them in person.

We then returned to our ship.

Pantagruel, out of generosity and in recognition of the sacred papal portrait, gave Homenaz nine pieces of cloth-of-gold, napped and friezed, to be hung before its iron-grilled window; he also filled their repair-and-fabric-fund box with Double-clog crowns,[65] and caused nine hundred and fourteen Annunciation-crowns to be distributed to each of the maidens who had waited on them at table during dinner, to be used at the right time as a dowry.

---

64. Frère Jean in the original speaks ignorant Latin for his Breviary stuff. Rabelais is playing on the fact that several prayers in the Breviary begin *Praeta quaesumus* ('Grant we beseech thee') but in his 'monkish' Latin Frère Jean takes *praesta* ('grant') to mean the same as the French *preste* ('lend'). What lies behind the pun on 'de-crystalline' and 'decretaline' is not clear.

65. Double-clog crowns are made-up coins, no doubt suited to clog-wearing peasants.

How on the high seas Pantagruel heard divers
Words as they thawed out

CHAPTER 55

[An ambitious chapter from Rabelais the mythologist. In a myth he reconciles the linguistic ideas of Aristotle and Plato (as did Ammonius Hermaeus in late Antiquity). Aristotle taught that onomatopoeias alone convey their meanings directly without that need to impose meanings on to sounds, which all other words require. But in the Cratylus *Plato and Socrates taught that the true meanings of many words may be found in their etymologies because of the wisdom of those who invented those words.*

Rabelais hints that etymologies are important. Here the French word discours *is thought of as being composed of the* di *of* divisans *(conversing) and of* cours *(short). Good* discours *is short talk. That etymology is transposed here, hinting that the English word* discourse *is formed from the* dis *of* discreet *and the* course *of* intercourse. *(Discourse is discreet verbal intercourse). He returns to similar hints in the last paragraph.*

Rabelais takes the platonizing doctrines of the philosopher Petron in Plutarch's Obsolescence of Oracles *(422B–F) and simplifies them to their (here serious) essentials: the Manor of Truth is, as it were, a celestial equilateral triangle in which dwell the Platonic Ideas ('the Words, Ideas, exemplars and portraits of all things past and future').*

For the 'equilateral triangle' cf. the three 'Pierres' in the Prologue and the stricken physeter in Chapter 34. It may be relevant that Plutarch states that the Pythagoreans called the equilateral triangle Minerva, that is, Athene, the goddess of Wisdom, and so a powerful symbol for the source of the Christian truths revealed in this episode (On Isis and Osiris, 381 F). Cf. the flying pig in Chapter 41.

The terms used for the Platonic 'Ideas' are quite usual – Words, Ideas, exemplars and portraits – but it is Rabelais who gives pride of place to Words (parolles). Around this 'Manor of Truth' lies the 'Age' (in Greek, the aeon*) which Christians alone interpolate between Time and Eternity. Some of those 'Words of Truth' drip down on to this world 'like catarrh' (a comparison taken over from the end of the*

Cratylus). *A scriptural example of such a dripping of divine Truth into this world is the account of Gideon's fleece (Judges 6: taken by many to foretell the fecundation of the Virgin Mary). The key lies in the last words of the Risen Lord at the very end of Matthew's Gospel: 'I am with you always, even until the consummation of the Age.'*

The original French is close to the Latin Vulgate: the allusion is less clear in traditional English.

Rabelais' term parolle *(Word) is given an initial capital in these chapters to distinguish it from the ordinary term* mot *(word) or the technical term* voix, *rendered by 'voice' but meaning simultaneously 'voice' and 'word'. Both 'voices' (Latin* voces*) and 'vocable' are technical terms. Erasmus is also present: first in two linked adages: I, IV, XV, 'By hand and by foot', and I, IV, XVIII, 'By oar and by sail'; then in IV, III, XXV, 'A cock – or a Gaul! – can do best on his own dunghill', and I, X, XL, 'A man who flees will fight again'.]*

When they were upon the open sea, feasting, singing and holding discreet intercourse in fair discourse, Pantagruel rose to his feet and stood scanning the horizon all round. He then said, 'My companions, can you hear anything? I seem to hear several persons talking in the air, yet I can see no one. Hark!'

At his command we were all attention, our ears lapping up the air like fine oysters-in-their-shells so as to hear any scattered word or sound. In order to let nothing escape us, some of us followed the example of the emperor Antoninus and cupped our palms behind our ears. We nevertheless affirmed that we could hear no voices whatsoever. Pantagruel was continuing to assert that he could hear in the air various voices of both men and women; then we too realized that either our ears were playing us up or we could likewise hear them too.

The more we strove to listen, the more clearly we could hear those voices, eventually making out whole words.

And it greatly frightened us.

Not without cause: we could see no one yet we heard a great variety of voices and sounds as of men, women, children and horses; so much so that Panurge exclaimed: 'Guts of Gosh! Is this a joke! We're done for! Let's fly from here. There's an ambush all round us. Frère Jean, my friend, are you there? Stick close to me, I beseech you. Have you got your short-sword? Make sure it's not stuck in its scabbard. You never do rub half the rust off it. We're lost! Hark! By God, that's cannon-shot that is. Let us flee. Not by feet and by hands, as Brutus put it during the battle of Pharsalia, but as I put it now: by oars and by sail. Let us fly. At sea I have no courage. I have more than enough in cellars and so on. Let's fly. Let's save ourselves. I don't say that out of any fear that I have: I fear nothing but dangers. That's what I always say; so did the *France-archer de Bagnolet*. Take no risks and get no biffs!

'Let us fly. Turn about! Pull round the helm, you son of a whore. Would to God that I were now in the hamlet of Quin-quinais, at the cost of never getting married. Fly! We're not up to them: they're ten against one, I tell you. They're on their own dunghills; we don't know this place. They'll kill us. Let us fly: there'll be no disgrace. Demosthenes says, "He who flies, will fight again." Let us at least fall back. Larboard! Starboard! Topsails! Studding-sails! We're all dead men. Let us fly, in the name of all the devils, fly!'

Pantagruel heard the racket Panurge was making and said, 'Who *is* that deserter down below? First let us see who these people are. They may be our friends. I still can't see anyone, even though I can see a hundred miles all round.

'Let us try to understand.

'I have read that a philosopher named Petron was of the opinion that there are several worlds so touching each other as to form an equilateral triangle at the core and centre of which lay, he said, the Manor of Truth, wherein dwell the Words, the Ideas, the exemplars and portraits of all things, past and future.

'And around them lies the Age.

'And during certain years, at long intervals, part of them drops down like catarrh on to human beings and as the dew fell upon Gideon's fleece, whilst part of them remains where they are, kept until the consummation of the Age.

'I also remember that Aristotle maintained that the Words of Homer are fluttering, flying, moving things and consequently animate.

'Moreover, Antiphanes said that the teachings of Plato were like those Words which (being uttered in a certain land in the depths of winter, and freezing and congealing from the coldness of the air) are not heard: so too what Plato taught to young boys was hardly understood by them as old men.[66]

'It is up to us to make a philosophical inquiry into whether this might perhaps be the very place where such Words unfreeze. And what a surprise if it were the head and the lyre of Orpheus: for, after the Thracian women had ripped Orpheus to pieces, they hurled his head and his lyre into the river Hebrus, which swept them down into the Black Sea as far as the isle of Lesbos, ever floating together upon the waters. And from that head there continually poured forth a mournful song seemingly lamenting the death of Orpheus, whilst, with that song, strokes from the winding winds made the chords accord.[67]

'Let us keep a lookout in case we see them hereabouts.'

How amongst the frozen Words Pantagruel came across words both of gullet and gules

CHAPTER 56

[A lighter chapter with more laughs than openly displayed erudition, one with Pathelin again in mind. There is a common legal source behind this chapter, the preceding one and the Third Book: the first title of Book 45 of the New Digest, headed On the Obligation of Words. It is from a gloss on that title that Rabelais cites the allusion to Exodus 20:18 (Vulgate Latin): 'All the people saw the voices'.

The Adages of Erasmus make further contributions: I, V, XLIX, 'To give words' – which means to deceive (as, says Erasmus, lovers

66. These thoughts on the words of Homer are taken from Plutarch (On the Oracles at Delphi, 398 A, and 404 F–405 A). Rabelais is also citing Plutarch's treatise How One Can Tell if One is Advancing in Virtue, 79 A, for the time needed to understand the words of Plato. Rabelais' authorities are reinforcing each other, for Calcagnini also treats of frozen words and cites Antiphanes in a fable (while mangling his name).

67. Virgil, Georgics, 4, 523.

do), and I, VII, XIX, 'To suffer from money-quinsy' (that is, Argen-
tangina pati*) as did Demosthenes who suffered from a sort of* bribed
aphasia *when paid not to speak.*

*Two Greek names are puzzling: in Antiquity the Arimaspians fought
the Griffons, not the Nephelibates, whose made-up Greek name means
'those who go through the clouds'.]*

The pilot replied:

'My Lord: there is nothing to be afraid of. We are here at the
approaches of the Frozen Sea over which there was a huge and
cruel combat between the Arismapians and the Nephelibates at
the onset of last winter. At that time, the Words and cries of
men and the women, the pounding of maces, the clank of the
armour of men and horses, the whinnying of steeds and all
the remaining din of battle froze in the air. And now that the
rigour of winter has passed and fine, calm, temperate weather
returned, they melt, and can be heard.'

'By God,' said Panurge, 'I believe it. But can we see one of
them? I remember that, at the foot of the mountain on which
Moses received the Jewish Law, the people actually *saw* the
voices.'

'Here: get hold of these,' said Pantagruel. 'Here are some
which have not yet thawed out.'

He then cast fistfuls of frozen Words on to the deck, where
they looked like sweets of many colours. We saw gullet words
– *gules* – and words *sinople*, words *azure*, words *or* and words
sable; after they had been warmed up a little in our hands they
melted like snow, and we actually heard them but did not
understand them, for they were in some barbarous tongue, save
for a rather tubby one which, after Frère Jean had warmed it
in his hands, made a sound such as chestnuts make when they
are tossed un-nicked on to the fire and go pop. It gave us quite
a start. 'In its time,' said Frère Jean, 'that was a shot from a
small cannon.'

Panurge asked Pantagruel to give him some more. 'Giving
Words is what lovers do,' said Pantagruel.

'Sell me some, then,' said Panurge.

'Selling Words is what lawyers do,' replied Pantagruel. 'I

would rather sell you silence more dearly (as Demosthenes did with his money-quinsy).'

He nevertheless tossed three or four fistfuls on to the deck. And I saw many sharp Words, and bloodthirsty Words too (which the pilot said come home to roost with the man that uttered them and cut his throat); there were dreadful Words, and others unpleasant to behold. When they had all melted together we heard: *Hing, hing, hing, hing: hisse; hickory, dickory, dock; brededing, brededac, frr, frrr, frrr, bou, bou, bou, bou, bou, bou, bou, bou. Ong, ong, ong, ong, ououou-ouong; Gog, magog* and who-knows-what other barbarous words; and the pilot said that they were vocables from battles joined and from horses neighing at the moment of the charge; and then we heard other ones, fat ones which made sounds when they melted, some of drum or fife; others of bugle and trumpet. Believe you me, they provided us with some excellent sport.

I had hoped to preserve a few gullet-words in oil, wrapping them up in very clean straw (as we do with snow and ice); but Pantagruel would not allow it, saying that it was madness to pickle something which is never lacking and always to hand as are gullet-words amongst all good and merry Pantagruelists.

Panurge annoyed Frère Jean somewhat and made him mad with anger by taking him literally at his word[68] when he was least expecting it. Frère Jean threatened to make him sorry (as Guillaume Jousseaulme was sorry he had sold his cloth to our noble Pathelin), and since Panurge had caught him out as you catch a man – by his words – he (if ever Panurge did get married) would catch him out like a calf, by his horns.

Panurge curled his lip as a sign of derision. Then he cried out, saying, 'Would to God that here – without proceeding any further – I could have the Word of the Dive Bouteille.'

---

68. For taking a man by his word; cf. Chapter 36 of the *Third Book*.

How Pantagruel landed at the manor of Messer Gaster, the first Master of Arts of this world

CHAPTER 57

[Rabelais invents a powerful myth in the wake of Calcagnini. First he gave us the 'Manor of Truth': now he gives us the 'Manor of Virtue'. Rabelais retells Hesiod's famous myth of the hard, stony path leading up to the serene plateau of Virtue (Works and Days, 289ff.).

Many Renaissance thinkers sought to discover the prime natural driving-force in this world. Love, Plato shows, links Heaven and Earth; but is not that driving-force. (Ficino, who is not mentioned, taught that it was.) For Rabelais Nature governs this world through the belly, through fear of hunger. In the Prologue to his Satires, Persius calls the Belly the world's 'Master of Arts and Dispenser of Genius'. All the earthly arts, crafts and accomplishments of men and beasts derive from him. Rabelais develops that theme.

The fifteenth-century Council of Basle led to the Pragmatic Sanctions of Charles VII. It deposed the Pope. It was for Gallicans a favourite Council.

Aesop provides a famous fable. Calcagnini, Plutarch and above all Erasmus often overlap and contribute much to this and the following chapters.[69]]

69. For the relevant adages of Erasmus, see (en passant) IV, I, LII, 'Reddidit Harpocratem' ('To impose silence'), but above all some of the very many which treat of hunger, want and poverty: I, V, XXII, 'Paupertas sapientiam sortita est' ('Poverty produces wisdom'); IV, II, XLVIII, 'Multa docet fames'('Hunger teaches much'); III, VIII, XII, 'Non interpellandus famelicus' ('A hungry man is not to be disturbed'); II, VIII, LXXXIV, 'Venter auribus caret' ('The belly has no ears'), which includes 'Contra famem etenim nulla contradictio est' ('There is no contradicting hunger'); II, VI, LV, 'Vulpi esurienti somnus obrepit' ('Sleep surprises the hungry wolf'); III, IV, LXX, 'Decempes umbra' ('Ten-foot shadow,' that is, time to eat, used again, more fully, in Chapter 69); III, X, IX, 'Molestus interpellator venter' ('The belly is a troublesome disturber'); I, IX, LXVII, 'Saguntina fames' ('Saguntine hunger'); II, VIII, LXXVIII, 'Gastres' ('Gastres, bellies'); III, VII, XLIV, 'Ventre pleno, melior consultatio' ('Better deliberation on a full stomach'). The list could be much prolonged: Erasmus is an important authority for Rabelais in matters of the

That same day Pantagruel landed on an island which was wonderful above all others both for its site and its Governor. At first it was steep, stony, precipitous and barren on all sides, ill-pleasing to the eye, very tough on the feet and hardly less inaccessible than that mountain in Dauphiné which is called *Inaccessible* because it is shaped like a toadstool and nobody in living memory has climbed it, except Doyac, King Charles the Eighth's Master of Ordnance, who got up to the top by means of ingenious contrivances. There he found an aged ram. It was anyone's guess what had transported it there: some suggested that an eagle or horned owl had carried it up as a kid and that it had then escaped into a thicket.

Overcoming the difficult approaches with great toil and not without sweat, we found the top to be so pleasant, fertile, wholesome and delightful that I thought it was the true earthly Garden and Paradise over whose situation our good theologians so much quarrel and strive.

Pantagruel assured us however – without prejudice to a sounder opinion – that it was the Manor of *Arete* (that is, Virtue), described by Hesiod. Its Governor was Messer Gaster, the first Master of the Arts of this world. If you think that fire is the Grand Master of the Arts as Cicero wrote, you are wrong and in error, for Cicero never believed it. If, as our ancient Druids used to believe, you think that Mercury is the first inventor of the arts, you are very mistaken. The judgement of the Satirist is true when he says that of all the arts Messer Gaster is the Master. (With him there peacefully dwelt Penia, that good Lady otherwise known as Want, the mother of the Nine Muses, from whom, in company with Porus, the Lord of Abundance, was born Love, that noble boy who mediates between Heaven and Earth, for which Plato vouches in *The Symposium*).

To Gaster, that chivalrous King, all of us were obliged to pay homage, swear obedience and do honour, for he is imperious, round, rigorous, hard, difficult and unbending. You cannot

---

proverbial truths he required for his myths. Even his short remarks on adage IV, VII, LV, 'Mistress Necessity', are deeply relevant to Rabelais.

get him to believe anything or to accept any contestation or persuasion.

He hears nothing whatsoever. Harpocras (the god of Silence whom the Greeks knew as Sigalion) was by the Egyptians called *astomé* (that is, mouthless): Gaster was likewise created without any ears, as was the statue of Jupiter in Candia. Gaster talks only by signs; but everybody everywhere obeys those signs more promptly than the edicts of praetors or the commands of kings. Over his summonses he admits no delay, no demurral. People say that at the lion's roar the beasts round about all shudder, as far that is as its voice carries. That's written down. It's true. I've seen it. But I assure you that, at the commandments of Messer Gaster, the whole welkin trembles and the Earth quakes. His commandment has been issued: obey it at once or die.

The pilot recounted to us how, one day, following the example (which Aesop describes) of the Limbs conspiring against the Belly, the entire kingdom of the Somata conspired together against Gaster and swore to withdraw their obedience from him. They soon felt the effects of it, repented and very humbly returned to his service: otherwise they would have all died of widespread hunger. In no matter what company he may be, there can be no argument about rank or precedence: Gaster always goes before, be the others kings, emperors or indeed the Pope. He proceeded first at the Council of Basle, despite people saying that that Council was seditious on account of the contentions and squabbles over the top places.

The whole world is taken up with serving him; the whole world toils for him. And in return this is the good he does for the world: he invents all the arts, all the tools, all the skills, all the instruments, all the crafts. He even teaches brute beasts arts denied them by Nature: ravens, jays, parrots and starlings he turns into poets; and magpies into poetesses, teaching them to talk, to sing and to utter human speech.

And all for their innards.

Eagles, gerfalcons, falcons, sakers, laniers, goshawks, sparhawks, merlins, hagards, passenger-hawks, unmoulted hawks – birds savage and wild – he so tames and domesticates that he can allow them the full freedom of the skies for as high as he chooses and as long as he likes, making them hover, proceed, fly and glide, paying him court and flirting with him from above the clouds, then making them suddenly swoop down again to earth.

And all for their innards.

Elephants, lions, rhinoceroses, bears, horses, and dogs he makes to dance, jig, jump, fight, swim, hide away, retrieve whatever he wants and carry whatever he wants.

And all for the innards.

Fishes from sea and lake, as well as whales and sea-monsters, he makes to surge up from the deep abyss; wolves he drives from the woods; bears, from amongst the rocks, foxes from their lairs, and snakes from the ground.

And all for their innards.

To be brief, he is so inordinate in his rage that he devours them all, beasts (and humans, as was seen amongst the Vascons when Quintus Metellus was laying siege to them during the Sertorian Wars, amongst the Saguntines besieged by Hannibal, the Jews, besieged by the Romans, and some six hundred other examples).

And all for their innards.

When his Regent, Penia, stalks abroad, wherever she goes all Parlements are prorogued, all edicts are mute; all ordinances, vain. To no law is she subject: from every law is she exempt. Everywhere everyone flees her, risking shipwreck at sea or electing to pass through fire, mountain or abyss rather than to be apprehended by her.

How in the Court of the Master-Inventor Pantagruel denounced the Engastrimyths and the Gastrolaters

CHAPTER 58

['Engastrimyths' were in the strict sense ventriloquists – men or women with a prophetic spirit talking from within their bellies.

The name of Jacoba Rhodigina's indwelling spirit, Cincinnatulus (in French Crêpelu) means 'Curly-head'. This anecdote, which seems so personal, is in fact not so. It is not an account of something Rabelais had witnessed in 1513. The words are lifted date and all – even the 'we' – from the Ancient Readings of Richerius Rhodiginus.

Rabelais could well have called these people 'Gastromarges' (Gastromargoi, Men mad about their bellies) following Aristotle, as cited by Erasmus in an adage which influenced him here (II, VIII, LXXVIII, 'Bellies'). But that term is too weak: the Fourth Book is concerned with idolatry. Monks are condemned not as men insanely devoted to the belly but as men who make the belly into a god. They are firmly condemned with echoes of the Ten Commandments and the Lord's Prayer and by a long and sobering quotation from Saint Paul. (Philippians 3:19).

The Belly, Messer Gaster, is a created driving-force within Nature. He must be acknowledged, but he is not God. Not even a god. He works within fallen Nature. The dread Belly-worshippers are monks, now all condemned as more than idle men concerned with vestments: they, like the Papimanes, worship a false god.

Rabelais confounds Hesiod with Homer over a quotation very frequently applied to monks by their critics and enemies.

He is still writing with his Plutarch open before him: his closing reference to the Cyclops is taken direct from the Obsolescence of Oracles, *435 AB. He also turns to the* Adages of Erasmus *for IV, I, XXXIX. 'Eurycles' (the name of a soothsaying ventriloquist in Antiquity). Rabelais starts off by calling Gaster 'maistre ingénieux'; at that time* ingénieux *meant both ingenious and engineer.]*

In the Court of that great Master, that ingenious engineer, Pantagruel noticed two kinds of retainers, both importunate and far too obsequious, whom he held in great abomination. Some were called Engastrimyths; the other, Gastrolaters.

The Engastrimyths (citing on this subject the testimony of Aristophanes in his comedy called *The Wasps*) claim to be descended from the ancient family of Eurycles. That is why they were called Euryclians in ancient times as Plato writes (and Plutarch too in *Why Oracles Have Ceased*). They are called Ventriloquists in the holy *Decretum* (26 question 3), and Hippocrates (in Book Five of the *Epidemics*) calls them in Greek 'ones talking from the belly' (Sophocles calls them

Sternomantes). They were fortune-tellers, casters of spells and deceivers of simple folk, appearing to speak, and to answer those who questioned them, not with their mouths but their bellies.

About the year of our Blessèd Servator 1513, there was just such a woman, Jacoba Rhodigina, an Italian of humble origins, from whose belly we, and an infinite number of others in Ferrara and elsewhere, often heard the voice of the foul Spirit (soft, certainly, weak and low, yet well articulated, clear and intelligible) after she was summoned and sent for out of curiosity by certain rich lords and princes of Cisalpine Gaul. To remove any suspicion of feint or hidden fraud they stripped her quite naked and stopped up her mouth and nose. Her wicked Spirit called himself *Curly-head* or *Cincinnatulus* and seemed to enjoy being thus addressed. When he was called by that name he at once replied to anything put to him. If questioned about matters past or present, he replied so pertinently that those listening were moved to wonder; when questioned about the future he always lied, never telling the truth once, and often seemed to be admitting his ignorance by letting off a fat fart in lieu of an answer or else by mumbling a few unintelligible words with barbaric inflections.

The Gastrolaters were in another place, huddled together in groups and bands, some merry, elegant and cuddly, others sad, grave, severe and sour: all lazy, doing nothing, never working, 'a useless load and burden on the world', as Hesiod put it. They were (as far as one could judge) terrified of offending and pinching their belly, and what is more so bizarrely masked, cloaked and disguised that it was a sight to see. You say – and it is written by several wise philosophers of Antiquity – that the intelligent workings of Nature are wondrously revealed in the joyous abandon she seems to show in the forming of sea-shells: we find such variety in them, so many shapes and colours, so many lines and forms inimitable by art. Well, I can assure you that in the vestment-shells of those Gastrolaters we noticed no less diversity and disguises. They all held Gaster to be their great God; they worshipped him as God; sacrificed to him as to their God Almighty. They had no other God before him;

they served him and loved him above all things; and as their God they hallowed him. You could say that the Holy Apostle was writing specifically of them in Philippians 3: 'For many walk, of whom I have told you often and now tell you even weeping tears: enemies of the Cross of Christ, whose end is destruction, whose god is their belly.'

Pantagruel compared him with the Cyclops Polyphemus, to whom Euripides attributes the following: 'I never sacrifice to the gods: only to me, and to the greatest of all the gods, this my belly.'

Of the absurd statue called Manduces; and how and what the Gastrolaters sacrificed to their Ventripotent God

CHAPTER 59

[Carnivalesque fun at the expense of a frightening idol and the sacrifices offered to it by its monkish worshippers.

Rabelais draws in detail upon the explanation by Erasmus of an adage, IV, VIII, XXXII, 'Manduces' (a term applied to the extremely hungry and thence to a carnival-type figure in Antiquity with clacking wooden teeth. The name of the equivalent figure at Lyons in the time of Rabelais was Maschecrotte or Mâchecroutte. It was both frightening to little children and comic. Rabelais would also have seen Graulli, the figure of a dragon with clashing jaws which was paraded through the city on Saint Clement's day.

Rabelais again lends a Classical Bacchic savour to his satire: 'dithyrambs' are wild Bacchanalian hymns addressed to Dionysius, 'kraipalokômics' are songs of crapulous Bacchanalian revelry, and 'epaenetic hymns' are songs of praise. All such hymns are addressed by the Gastrolaters to their belly-god.]

As we all contemplated in sheer amazement the grimaces and gestures of those lazy, great-gulletted Gastrolaters, we heard the impressive stroke of a bell at which they all drew up as for battle, each according to his charge, rank and seniority. Thus

they moved towards Messer Gaster, following the lead of a
portly, gross young Fat-guts who bore on top of a long golden
pole a badly carved wooden statue, coarsely painted, such as is
described by Plautus, Juvenal and Pompeius Festus. During the
carnival at Lyons folk call it *Mâchecroutte*; here they call it
Manduces. It was a monstrosity of an effigy, absurd, ghastly
and terrifying to little children, with eyes bigger than its belly,
with a head, bigger than the rest of its body put together, and
with capacious, wide and horrible upper and lower jaws both
lined with fangs, which were made to clack together by the
ingenious device of a small cord hidden within the gilded pole
(as is done at Metz with their Saint-Clement's dragon).

As those Gastrolaters drew nearer, I could see that they
were followed by a great number of fat serving-lads laden
with panniers, baskets, hampers, pots, sacks and saucepans.
Whereupon, led by Manduces, they chanted I-know-not-what
dithyrambs, kraipalokômics and epaenetic hymns as, opening
their baskets and their jars they offered up to their god:

White hippocras with soft dry toast,
white bread,
canon's baps,
six varieties of grilled meats,
couscous,
hazlet,
fricassees (nine kinds),
thick slices of monastical bread-and-dripping,
lyonese sops,
hot-pots,
savoury bread,
burgher-bread,
goat meat (roasted),
veal-tongues: roasted, cold, sprinkled with ginger and
     mustard,
pasties (small),
grey-bread soup (known as *greyhound*),
cabbages: (round-headed) stuffed with beef-marrow,
salmagundis,

amidst perpetual potations, with the good, taste-enticing white preceding, followed by the claret, chilled and red – as cold, I say, as ice – and each served in huge silver goblets.

Then they offered up:

chidlings dressed in fine mustard,
sausages (wet),
ox-tongues (smoked),
meats (salted),
chine-of-pork with peas,
veal (larded and stewed),
puddings (white),
saveloys,
sausages (dry),
hams,
boars' heads,
venison (salted, with turnips),
pig's-liver slices (grilled),
olives (pickled in brine).

All accompanied by perpetual potations.

Then they would shovel into Gaster's gullet:

legs of lamb in garlic sauce,
pasties in hot gravy,
pork cutlets with stewed onions,
capons, roasted, all basted with their own dripping,
capons, young,
goosanders,
goats,
fawns,
deer,
hares, leverets,
pheasant, pheasant-poults,
peacocks, peachicks,
storks, storklets,
woodcocks, jadcocks,
ortolans,

turkeys: cocks, hens and chicks,
woodpigeons: young ditto,
pork in beer-wort,
ducks in onion sauce *à la française*,
blackbirds,
corncrakes,
moor-hens,
sheldrakes,
egrets,
teals,
loons,
bitterns,
spoonbills,
curlews,
hazel-grouse,
coots with leeks,
robin red-breasts,
kids,
shoulders of mutton with capers,
beef-cutlets *à la royale*,
breasts of veal,
boiled hens with fattened capons in a rich cream-and-
    almond sauce,
pintails,
pullets,
rabbits, young coneys,
quails, quail-chicks,
pigeons, pigeon-chicks,
herons, hernshaws,
bustards, bustard-chicks,
beccaficos,
guinea-fowl,
plovers,
geese, goslings,
pigeons,
wild ducklings,
redwings,
flamingos,

swans,
shoveller-ducks,
snipe,
cranes,
red-shanks,
curlews,
whimbrels,
turtle-doves,
rabbits,
porcupines,
and
brook ouzels.

Reinforced throughout by wine.
Then followed huge:

venison pasties,
lark pasties,
loir pasties,
alpine-ibex pasties,
roe-deer pasties,
pigeon pasties,
chamois pasties,
capon pasties,
bacon pasties,
pigs' trotters in lard,
savoury pastry-fricassees,
broiled legs of capon,
cheeses,
peaches from Corbeil,
artichokes,
puff-pastry cakes,
white-beets,
rich cream cracknels,
fritters,
sixteen varieties of raised pies,
waffles,
pancakes,

quince pâté,
curds and whey,
eggs in whipped cream,
pickled myrobalans,
jellies,
hippocras: red and white,
fancy-cakes,
macaroons,
tarts (twenty varieties),
creams,
seventy-eight kinds of preserved fruits, both dry and in
    various liqueurs,
sweetmeats of one hundred different colours,
junkets,
wafers drenched in refined sugar.

For fear of the quinsy, wine was continuously served throughout.
    Additional item: toasted tidbits.

How the Gastrolaters sacrificed to their god during their interlarded fast-days

CHAPTER 60

[Once more there is the pun, with farce *meaning the play, force-meat
stuffing and by extension stuffing oneself.*

*Fasting as an unreformed Church discipline entailed abstaining from
flesh, not abstaining from gluttony. Fish, eggs and so much else
remained available as sacrifices to Gaster. Pantagruel's anger is a
pointer leading beyond the surface fun.*

*For the Erasmian climax of this chapter see the footnote at the end.
Gaster is a creature not a creator God.]*

When Pantagruel saw that riff-raff of sacrificers and the multiplicity of their sacrifices he was angry and would have stalked
off if Epistemon had not begged him to witness the issue of
such a farce.

'And what do these scoundrels sacrifice to their ventripotent god,' asked Pantagruel, 'during their interlarded fast-days?'

'That I shall tell you,' said the pilot.

'For their *entrées* they offer him:

caviar,
pickled mullet-caviar,
fresh butter,
pease-pudding,
spinach,
fresh herrings,
soused herrings,
sardines,
anchovies,
marinated tuna,
cabbage in olive-oil,
buttered beans,
hundreds of kinds of salads: of cress, hops, bishop's-
    bollocks, rampion, Judas-ears (a variety of fungus grow-
    ing out from ancient elder-trees), asparagus, woodbine
    and many others,
salted salmon,
salted eels,
oysters in the shell.

'Now drink is a must, or the devil will get you! Good arrange-ments having been made, nothing was lacking. And they then offer unto him:

lampreys in Hippocras sauce,
barbels,
friture of barbels,
grey mullet,
striped mullet,
rays,
cuttlefish,
sturgeons,
guernet,

whales,
mackerel,
shad,
plaice,
fried oysters,
periwinkles,
crayfish,
smelts,
red gurnets,
trout,
perch from the lakes,
cod,
octopus,
dabs,
carrelets,
meagers,
sea-bream,
gudgeons,
brill,
sprats,
carp,
pike,
Mediterranean palamides,
spotted dog-fish,
sea-urchins,
poules-de-mer,
sea-nettles,
crepidules,
sea-owls,
swordfish,
angel-fish squali,
lamprels,
snook,
carp small-fry,
salmon,
samlets,
dolphins,
porpoises,

turbot,
white skate,
soles,
limander soles,
mussels,
lobsters,
shrimps,
dace,
ablen,
tench,
grayling,
fresh hake,
sepia,
prickle-back,
tuna,
gudgeon,
miller's-thumbs,
cray-fish,
cockles,
spiny-lobsters,
sea-lampreys,
congers,
dorados,
bass,
shad,
morays,
charlings,
small dare-fish,
eels,
pickled-eels,
turtles,
serpens (that is, bush-eels),
sea-bream,
sea-ducks,
ruff,
royal-sturgeon,
loach,
crabs,

sea-snails,
frogs.

'Once those viands had been devoured, Death lurks but two
steps away if you weren't then drinking. That was excellently
provided for.
'They next sacrificed:

salted haddock,
dried haddock,
eggs – fried, buttered, poached, smothered, braised,
    roasted-in-the-ashes, smoked-up-the-chimney, scram-
    bled, whipped in verjuice, etc.,
salted cod,
thornbacks,
bergylts,
small marinated sea-pike.

'To assist their proper concoction and digestion, the wine
was redoubled. As the end drew nigh they offered up:

rice,
millet,
porridge,
almond butter,
whipped butter,
pistachio-butter,
pistachio-nuts,
salted ditto,
figs,
grapes,
caraway-seeds,
maize (powdered),
frumenty,
dates,
walnuts,
filberts,
buttered parsnips,

and
artichokes,

amidst perennial potations.

'Believe you me: if Gaster their god was not more sumptuously, richly and appropriately served in his sacrifices than the
idol of Heliogabalus – indeed, than the idol of Baal in Babylon
under King Belshazzar – that was no fault of theirs: yet Gaster
admitted that he was not God but a poor, paltry, wretched
created thing. And just as King Antigonus, the First of that
name, replied to a certain Hermodotus (who addressed him in
his verses as a god and Son of the Solar Deity) by saying to
him: "My Bearer of the Lasanon says no to that – *lasanon* being
an earthenware chamber-pot devoted to receiving the belly's
excreta – so too Gaster referred those apish hypocrites to the
seat of his privy, there to ponder, meditate and reflect upon
what godhead they found in his faeces." '[70]

How Gaster invented means of gathering
and conserving grain

CHAPTER 61

*[Throughout there is play between 'Master of Arts' (the university
degree) and Gaster, the 'Master' of the arts, sciences and skills of
mankind.*

'Apanages' allows of a play on panus, *(bread).]*

Once those devilish Gastrolaters had withdrawn, Pantagruel
attended to the study of Gaster, the noble Master of Arts.

You are aware that, by a basic institution of Nature, bread
and its apanages were adjudicated to Gaster as provender and

70. Rabelais' authorities continue to reinforce each other. The moral exem-
     plum of Antigonus the First has immense authority: it is twice in Plutarch
     (*On Isis and Osiris*, 360 D), and in *The Notable Sayings of Kings and
     Emperors*, 182 C, as well as in the *Apophthegms* of Erasmus (IV, Anti-
     gonus, 7).

nutriment; to which was attached this blessing from Heaven: that he would never lack means of getting and keeping his bread.

From the outset he invented the art of the blacksmith, and husbandry to cultivate the land and make it bring forth grain.

He invented weapons and the military arts to protect the grain, and the arts of medicine and astrology (with the necessary mathematics) to safeguard it over the centuries, so putting it beyond the reach of climatic disasters, thieving by brute beasts and stealing by brigands.

He invented watermills, windmills and hand-mills and hundreds of other ingenious devices for grinding the grain and turning it into flour; yeast to leaven the dough and salt to give it its savour – for he knew as a fact that nothing in this world would make human beings more subject to illness than unleavened and unsalted bread – fire to bake it; clocks and sundials to regulate the time of the baking of that which grain produces: bread.

When the harvest chanced to fail in one country, he invented the art of hauling grain from one country to another; with great ingenuity he crossed two kinds of animals (the ass and the mare) to give birth to a third kind, which we term mules: beasts tougher, less sensitive and more able to sustain hard toil than other animals. He invented carts and wagons to transport it more conveniently.

When seas or rivers obstructed the haulage he invented boats, galleys and sailing-ships – something which astonished the very Elements – so as to sail the seas, cross estuaries and navigate rivers in order to haul the grain and ship it from unknown, foreign lands afar.

And then some years it chanced that, having tilled the soil, Gaster lacked rain in due season, for want of which the grain remained dead and wasted in the soil; some years it rained too much and the grain was sodden; some other years the hail battered it down, the winds beat the grain from the ears, and the tempests flattened it. Before we came on the scene, Gaster had invented a method and art of calling down rain from the heavens merely by chopping up a particular herb, which he showed us, one frequently found in meadows yet known to but a few. (I reckoned that it was the same herb by which the pontiff of Jove, by placing a single sprig of it in the Agrian Spring on Mount Lycaeus in Arcady during a period of drought, once brought forth mists: from them heavy clouds were formed which broke up into rain, watering at will the entire region.) He invented an art and method of keeping rain suspended in the air and making it fall over the sea.

He invented an art and method of eliminating hail, suppressing the winds and turning away a storm, by the means employed by the Methanensians of Troezinia.

A further setback occurred: thieves and bandits pillaged the grain and so the bread in the fields: he invented the art of building towns, fortresses and castles to store it in and keep it safe.

Then it chanced that the countryside lacked bread, and he realized that once it was brought within the towns, fortresses and castles, it was more fiercely defended and guarded by their inhabitants than the golden apples of the Hesperides were ever guarded by the dragons. He therefore invented the art and method of reducing or slighting fortresses and castles by machines and contrivances such as battering-rams and catapults for slinging stones or arrows, the design of which he showed us, though it was badly understood by those architectural engineers who were disciples of Vitruvius (as was admitted to us by Messer Philibert de L'Orme the great architect of the Mighty King).

And when they could no longer be profitably used against the malicious cunning and the cunning malice of the builders of fortifications, he recently invented canons, serpentines, culverins, bombards and basilisks which, by means of an horrific compound of powder, can project cannon-balls of iron, bronze and lead weighing more than great anvils, at which Nature herself was aghast, confessing herself beaten by Art, despising as she does the practice of the Oxydracians, who, in the midst of the field, vanquished their enemies and caused them sudden death by exploiting thunder, lightning, hail, great flashes of light and storms: for one shot from a basilisk is more horrifying, more dreadful, more diabolical than a hundred thunderbolts: it maims, injures, shatters and kills more people; it leaves men more shocked and it razes more walls.

How Gaster invented the art by means of which one can remain untouched and unwounded by cannon-balls

CHAPTER 62

[Rabelais again draws very heavily on one of his principal authorities, Celio Calcagnini. He plays – how seriously? – with the fact that opposing poles of the magnet do not attract but repel.

'Nature abhors a vacuum' was a tenet of physics until the seventeenth century.

All the alleged facts, exempla, *arguments and mystical truths (from the herb called* aethiopis *which opens all the locks placed against it right to the end of the chapter have the learned Calcagnini behind them. The reader is left to question or accept them, but is brought to accept the higher, Pythagorean meaning of the elder-wood, guided by a detailed borrowing from Calcagnini and yet again by an adage of Erasmus: II, V, XLVI, 'Mercury – as a graven image – is not to be made from just any piece of wood'.]*

Now it befell that Gaster, having stored his grain in his fortresses, found himself assailed by enemies, his fortresses demolished by such thrice-dreaded, hellish devices, whilst his grain and his bread were seized and pillaged by great force such as that of the Titans. He therefore invented the art and method, not so much of protecting his ramparts, bastions, walls and defence-works against damage from such cannonades, but of causing the pieces of shot not to strike them at all but to hover short of them motionless, or else of so striking them as to harm neither the defences nor the defending citizens.

Against such mischief he had already made an excellent arrangement, and showed us a trial of it – a device subsequently employed by Fronton and currently figuring amongst the honourable pastimes and sports of the Thelemites.

The trial was as follows (and from now on be more ready to believe what Plutarch assures us that he tried out himself: if, when a tribe of nanny-goats are running away at full pelt, you push a twig of eryngo down the throat of the last straggler, they will all stop dead).

Within a bronze falconet Gaster placed on top of the gunpowder (which had been compounded with care, cleansed of sulphur and balanced by the right amount of refined camphor) a cartridge of iron of the appropriate calibre together with twenty-four pellets of iron-filings, some spherical, others tear-shaped. He trained his sights on one of his young pages as though intending to shoot him through the stomach; then, at some sixty paces, strictly midway between that page and the falconet, he suspended from a post a very large block of siderite (iron-stone, that is, otherwise called *Herculanea*, discovered long ago by a man called Magnes at Ida in Phrygia, as Nicander attests. We normally call it *aimant*, magnet-stone). He then touched off the powder through the vent in the falconet. The powder was consumed. And thus, to avoid a vacuum (which Nature so abhors that the entire structure of the Universe, the heavens, the earth, the sea and the land would sooner be returned to ancient Chaos than any vacuum be admitted anywhere in the world), the cartridge and the pellets were precipitously expelled through the mouth of the falconet to allow air to get through to the gun-chamber, which would otherwise have remained in the vacuum caused by the rapid consumption of the powder by the flame. The cartridge and the pellets thus violently fired seemed bound to strike that page-boy, but at the point where they approached the above-mentioned stone, they all lost their momentum and stayed hovering in the air, circling about the stone: not one of them – no matter how violently propelled – got through to the page, however violent the force.

Gaster also invented the art and method of making bullets return against the enemy, as furious and dangerous as when they had been fired and following the same trajectory.

He did not find that at all difficult:

– seeing that the herb called *aethiopis* opens all the locks placed against it; that the *echineis* (a puny fish) can stay the most powerful ships that sail the seas, countering gales and raging tempests; and that the flesh of that fish, preserved in salt, can draw gold out of the deepest wells that one can sound; and seeing that Democritus writes (and Theophrastus both believed it and proved it experimentally) that there is a certain herb at the mere touch of which an iron wedge, driven with great force deep into a great, hard block of wood, will suddenly pop out; it is used by woodpeckers (those *pics Mars* which you call *pivars*) whenever anyone has used an iron wedge to stop up the entrance-hole to their nests, which they are accustomed to build by hollowing out the trunks of mighty trees;

– and seeing that if stags and does that have suffered deep wounds from strikes by darts or arrows or bolts from the cross-bow come across the herb called dittany (which flourishes in Candia) and eat a little of it, the projectiles at once drop out and the beasts suffer no harm; (by its means Venus cured her dear son Aeneas when wounded in the right thigh with an arrow shot by Juturna, the sister of Turnus);

– seeing that thunderbolts are deflected by the mere scent emanating from laurels, fig-trees and sea-calves, and never strike them;

– seeing that at the simple sight of a ram, mad elephants are restored to their senses, mad bulls on the rampage are tamed if they come near to that wild fig-tree called *caprificus*, remaining fixed and unable to budge; and the viper's rage is calmed by the touch of a branch of the beech-tree;

– seeing also that Euphorion writes that on the island of Samos, before the temple of Juno was erected there, he saw beasts called *Neades* at whose sole cry the earth toppled down into chasms to the abyss;

– seeing, similarly, that the elder grows more sonorous and more suited to making a set of pipes in places when the voice of the cock is never heard; so wrote the ancient sages, according to the account in Theophrastus, as though the crow of the cock weakened, softened and troubled the woody matter of the elder-tree, just as, upon hearing such crowing, the lion, a beast of such might and constancy, becomes utterly dazed and bewildered.

I know that others have taken that opinion to apply to the wild elder growing in places so far from towns and villages that the crow of the cock could never be heard there. Doubtless its wood should indeed be chosen to make pipes and other musical instruments and be preferred to the domestic variety which grows close to rural slums and ruined cottages.

Others have taken it in a more elevated sense, not literally but allegorically, following the practice of the Pythagoreans, who interpret the saying that *A statue of Mercury should not be carved from just any wood* to mean that God should not be worshipped in an uncouth fashion but in an elect, religious manner. With that judgement they likewise tell us that wise and scholarly people should not devote themselves to trivial, vulgar music but to music which is celestial, angelic, marked by divinity, more recondite and borne from afar, namely from a region where no crowing cocks are heard. For when we wish to characterize a place which is isolated and little frequented, we say it is one where no cock-crow has ever been heard.

How Pantagruel dozed off when near the
isle of Chaneph, and the problems put
forward once he awoke

CHAPTER 63

[*The* Brief Declaration *explains 'Chaneph' as 'Hebrew, Hypocrisy'.*

In this world, signs, gestures and actions speak louder than words.

In sailors' language, men becalmed 'raise up good weather' by having a good convivial drink.

'Sympathy' may extend from humans to Nature (and vice versa). 'A hungry belly has no ears' is in yet another adage of Erasmus (II, VIII, LXXXI.'The Belly has no ears'). Here and in the next chapter there is also a reminiscence of another adage: II, VII, XLIV, 'Deliberation is better on a full belly').]

Next day we sailed on our way chatting together until we arrived off the isle of Chaneph, at which Pantagruel's vessel could not dock because the wind had dropped and the sea was calm. We could budge only thanks to our trailing-bonnets, tacking from larboard to starboard and adjusting the sheets of the spritsails. There we stayed, all pensive, sifting through vain thoughts, off-pitch, bored and addressing no word to each other. Pantagruel, holding a Greek *Heliodorus* in his hand, was dozing away in a hammock hard by the booby-hatch: such was his custom, for he more readily dropped off by writ than by rote.

Epistemon was checking the elevation of the pole-star with his astrolabe. Frère Jean, having betaken himself to the galley, was estimating what time it could be by the rising stars of the fricassees and the horoscopes of the roasting-spits.

Panurge, his tongue in a stem of *pantagruelion*, was gurgling and blowing bubbles.

Gymnaste was sharpening toothpicks of lentisk-wood.

Ponocrates was dreaming mad dreams, tickling himself to make himself laugh and scratching his head with one finger.

Carpalim was making a merry pretty little singing-windmill out of a hard walnut-shell, adding four sails from a sliver of elder-wood.

Eusthenes was strumming his fingers along a culverin as though it were a one-stringed fiddle.

Rhizotome was making a velvet-covered purse out of a piece of shell from a wild tortoise.

Xenomanes was mending an old lantern with some hawk-straps.

And our pilot was nose to nose with his sailors, worming out secrets, when Frère Jean came back from the galley-hatch and noticed that Pantagruel had reawakened. At which, with a loud voice, he broke the stubborn silence and in the best of spirits asked: 'How can a man becalmed raise up good weather?'

Panurge next followed suit and likewise asked: 'A remedy for boredom?'

Thirdly Epistemon laughingly asked, 'How to pass urine without the urge?'

Gymnaste rose to his feet and asked, 'A remedy against the eye being dazzled?'

Ponocrates, having rubbed his forehead a while and shaken his ears, asked, 'How to avoid sleeping like a dog?'

'Wait a minute,' said Pantagruel. 'By the edict of those subtle philosophers the Peripatetics we are instructed that all problems, all questions and all doubts propounded must be unambiguous, clear and intelligible. What do you understand by *to sleep like a dog*?'

'It means,' Ponocrates replied, 'to sleep as dogs do, fasting and in full sun.'

Rhizotome was squatting on the coursey. He raised his head and gave such a deep yawn that he caused his companions to do likewise from natural sympathy. He then asked: 'A remedy against gasping and yawning?'

Xenomanes, all languor from fixing his lantern, asked, 'A way to keep the bagpipe of your stomach in a balanced equilibrium so that it never sags one way more than the other?'

Carpalim, playing with his windmill, asked, 'How many antecedent motions are there in Nature before a person can be said to feel hungry?' Eusthenes, hearing their din, ran up on deck and cried out from near the capstan, 'Why is a fasting man in greater peril from the bite of a fasting snake than when both man and snake have fed? And why is the saliva of a fasting man poisonous to all snakes and poison-bearing creatures?' 'My friends,' Pantagruel replied, 'to all the doubts and queries you propound there is only one proper solution; and for all such symptoms and effects only one proper medicine. The answer will be delivered to you promptly, without long confused tangles and verbal discoursings: "a hungry belly has no ears". It hears nothing. It is by signs, gestures and actions that you shall be satisfied and have a solution which contents you, as once in Rome Tarquin the Proud, that last king of the Romans . . .'

– at which point Pantagruel touched the bell-rope, and Frère Jean dashed off to the galley –

'. . . replied by signs to his son, Sextus Tarquin who was in the city of the Gabini and had despatched a man expressly to inquire how he could thoroughly subdue the citizens and return them to perfect obedience. That king said nothing in reply, doubting the trustworthiness of the messenger. He simply led him into his private garden and, in his presence and in his sight, took his sword and sliced off the heads of the tallest poppies. Once the messenger had returned without an answer and told the son what he had seen his father do, it was easy to understand from such signs that he was advising him to cut off the heads of the most prominent citizens, the better to constrain the common folk to their duty and absolute obedience.'

How no answer was given by Pantagruel to the questions put forward

CHAPTER 64

[Further play on the unreconciling *Council of Trent* – the Concile de Chésil – *and to* re-concile.

It was on the authority of Aristotle's History of Animals, *8, 29, that a fasting man's saliva was held mortal to snakes.*

Since Rabelais has listed his snakes in alphabetical order so far as their initial letter is concerned, Latin or French names have been kept whenever necessary to retain that order. (Snake in the Renaissance embraced as here all animals which crept rather than walked, and even some others.)

Gluttony is one thing: merry feasting is another. The joy of a happy feast can have 'sympathetic' effects on the weather.]

Pantagruel then asked, 'What people dwell in this fair bitch of an island?'

'They,' said Xenomanes, 'are all Hypocriticals, Dropsicals, Bead-tellers, purring Counterfeits, Sanctimoniums, Black-beetles and Hermits: wretched folk, all of them, living on way-farers' alms, like the hermit at Lormont, between Blaye and Bordeaux.'

'I'm not going there: I can promise you that!' said Panurge. 'If I do may the devil blow puffs up my bum! Hermits! By all the devils: Sanctimoniums, purring Counterfeits, Black-beetles

and Hypocriticals! Avaunt! I can still remember those fat travellers of ours on their way to the *Concile de Chésil*: would that
Beelzebub and Astaroth had re-conciled them with Proserpine,
so great were the tempests and devilish deeds we suffered for
having seen them. Listen to me please, Corporal Xenomanes,
my little old fat-guts. These Hypocrites, Hermits and Pot-
scrapers here: are they celibate or married? Are there any of the
feminine sex? Could a man hypocritically pull out his hypocritical little shaft for them?'

'Well, truly!' said Pantagruel, 'there's a jolly fine question for
you!'

'Yes indeed,' replied Xenomanes. 'There you will find
fair and joyful Hypocritesses, purring Counterfeitesses and
Hermitesses: all women devoted to religious Orders. And there
are plenty of young Hypocrites, purring young Counterfeits
and young Hermits . . .'

– 'Avaunt!' cried Frère Jean, interrupting him. '*Young hermit:
old devil*. An authentic proverb. Note it down. –

'. . . otherwise, without such multiplying, this isle of Chaneph
would long since have been without inhabitants and quite
desolate.'

Pantagruel despatched Gymnaste in a skiff to take them his
alms: seventy-eight thousand of those beautiful little half-
crowns with a Lantern on them.

He then asked, 'What hour is it?'

'Nine o'clock and more,' replied Epistemon.

'That,' said Pantagruel, 'is the right time for dinner. For the
hallowed line approaches (made so famous by Aristophanes in
his comedy *The Ecclesiazousae*) when the shadow falls on the
tenth point of the sundial. Long ago in Persia a specific time to
take his food was prescribed for the king alone: belly and
appetite were everyone else's clock. In fact a certain hanger-on
in Plautus loathes and madly detests the inventors of timepieces
and sundials, since it is notorious that there is no clock more
accurate than the belly.[71]

71. In this paragraph Rabelais is following in detail the adage of Erasmus,
    III, IV, LXX, 'Decempes umbra' ('A ten-foot shadow'). It is concerned
    with the time to eat as shown by the shadow on a sundial.

'Diogenes, when asked at what time a man should eat, replied: "The rich when hungry: the poor man when he can."[72] The physicians more correctly say that canonical rule is:

> Up at five: break fast at nine;
> Sup at five: to bed at nine.

The sorcery of the famous King Petosiris was very different.'[73]

Those words were hardly spoken when the Officers of the Maw set up the trestles and sideboards, spread perfumed cloths over them and laid out plates, napkins and salt-cellars; they brought out tankards, pitchers, flagons, cups, goblets, basins and jugs.

Frère Jean, in association with the stewards, butlers, bakers, wine-waiters, squires-trenchant, cup-bearers and tasters, brought in four terrific bacon-pasties, so huge that they reminded me of the four bastions of Turin.

God's Truth! How they did drink and enjoy the feast! The dessert was still to come when a west-nor'wester began to swell out their main-, mizzen- and topsails. At which they all sang a variety of canticles in praise of Almighty God in his Heaven.

When the fruit was served, Pantagruel asked, 'Do you think your problems have been fully resolved, my friends?'

'I am no longer yawning, thank God' said Rhizotome.

'I am no longer sleeping like a dog,' said Ponocrates.

'I am no longer dazzled,' replied Gymnaste.

'And I am no longer fasting,' said Eusthenes.

'And therefore, safe from my saliva today will be:

asps,
amphisbaenas,
anerudites,
abedissimons,

---

72. The following reference to Diogenes is also from Erasmus (*Apophthegms*, III, Diogenes, 70).
73. Petosiris was an ancient Egyptian astrologer. The woman satirized in Juvenal (6, 580) would not do anything, not even eat, except when the almanac of Petosiris showed the hours to be propitious.

alhartafz,
ammobates,
apimaos,
alhatrabans,
aractes,
asterions,
alcharates,
arges,
ariadnes,
ascalabes,
ascalabotes,
aemorrhoïdes,
basilisks,
belettes ictides (Greek weazels),
boas,
buprestes,
cantharides,
caterpillars,
crocodiles,
crapaux (toads),
catoblepes,
cerastae,
colotae,
cauquemars (incubi),
canes rabidi, (mad dogs),
colotes,
cycrides,
caphezates,
cauhares,
coulevres (grass-snakes),
cuharsces,
chalhydres,
chroniocolaptes,
chersydri,
conchydri,
cockatrices,
dipsades,
domeses,

dryinades,
dragons,
elopses,
enhydrides,
fanuises,
galeotides,
harmenes,
handons,
icles,
ilicines,
ichneumons,
iarrares,
kesudures,
lepores (the *Aplysia depilans*),
lizards from Chalcis,
myopes,
mantichores,
molures,
myagres,
musirani (shrew-mice),
miliares,
megalauni,
ptyades,
porphyres,
pareades,
phalanges,
penphredones,
pityocampes,
rutules,
rhimories,
rhagions,
rhaganes,
salamanders,
scytalae,
stellions,
scorpaenae,
scorpions,
selsirs,

scalabotins,
solofuidars,
surdi,
sangsues (blood-suckers),
solifugi,
sepae,
stinces,
stufae,
sabtins,
sangles,
sepedones,
scolopenders,
tarantulas,
typholopes,
tetragnates,
teristales,
vipers.'

How Pantagruel, with his household,
raises good weather

CHAPTER 65

*[Rabelais had been accused in print of antifeminism. (By the standard
of his extreme contemporaries he was a moderate but certainly no
platonizing feminist.)*

*Panurge appears pious and tranquil, but merely verbally so and not
for long, as the next chapters convincingly show.*

*The 'Cenomanic Sausage' is the Sausage of Le Mans, but 'Ceno-
manic' suggests being mad about one's* cena, *one's dinner.*

*A joyful banquet raises men's spirits and, by natural sympathy also
raises good weather, for which the companions have sung (in chapter
64) canticles to God.*

*Hercules' awkward attempts to help Atlas hold up the sky come
from Lucian's* Charon, iv. *The Reverend Doctor Rabelais' last words
in print about wine before he died tell how wine brings spiritual
powers to mankind. That was a Classical commonplace, supported*

by Plato, Plutarch and many others. It is summed up in the saying
Vinum acuit ingenium *(Wine sharpens the intellect). The spiritual*
powers of wine are represented mythologically by Bacchus psilax, *the*
'Wingèd Bacchus' of the Amyclaeans (taken from the Description of
Greece *of Pausanias). Thanks to Rabelais The Wingèd Bacchus was*
to become the subject of Renaissance emblems and their learned com-
mentaries. See The Journal of the Warburg and Courtauld Institutes,
43 (1980), pp. 259–62. All the writers insist and assume that the
much-praised wine is drunk in company and in moderation.]

'In which sacred Order of poisonous creatures,' asked Frère
Jean, 'do you place Panurge's wife-to-be?'

'Hey!' Panurge retorted. 'Speaking ill of women, you spruced
up, scabby-arsed monk!'

'By the Cenomanic Sausage!' said Epistemon, 'Euripides
wrote (words said by Andromeda) that, by the inventiveness of
mankind and the instruction of the gods, a useful remedy has
been found against all venomous beasts: but no remedy has so
far been found against a bad woman.'

'That fop of a Euripides always spoke ill of women,' said
Panurge, 'and therefore, by divine vengeance, was eaten by
dogs. Aristophanes casts it in his teeth. Let us get on. If you
have anything to say, say it.'

'I shall urinate now as much as you like,' said Epistemon.

'Now,' said Xenomanes, 'my stomach is economically ballasted: never more will it sag one way more than the other.'

'And I,' said Carpalim, 'need neither wine nor bread:

A truce for wine and a truce for bread.'

'I am no longer bored,' said Panurge. 'Thanks to God and to
you, I'm as gay as a popinjay; as merry as a merlin; as bright
as a butterfly. It is indeed written by that fine Euripides of
yours, and it is recited by Silenus, that memorable toper:

A man is insane: he cannot be right,
Who drinks up his wine without any delight!

'We should, without fail, praise God, our Good Creator, Servator and Conservator, who with this good bread, this good cool wine and these good viands cures us of all such perturbations of both body and soul, not to mention the pleasure and delight which we enjoy when eating and drinking.

'But you are not answering the question of our blessèd and venerable Frère Jean, who asked us, *How to raise good weather.*'

'Since,' said Pantagruel, 'you are happy with the ready solution I have provided to those problems, so am I. We shall have more to say about them if you like at some other time and place. There remains to resolve the problem posed by Frère Jean: *How to raise good weather.* But have we not done so already, just as you wanted? Look at the pennant by the crow's-nest. Look at the wind whistling through the sails. Look at the tautness of the guy-ropes, sheets and stays! While we were raising and emptying our cups, good weather was raised in parallel from an occult sympathy in Nature.

'That, if you believe the wise mythologists, is how Atlas and Hercules raised it, but they raised it half a degree too high: Atlas, because of feasting Hercules, his guest, too convivially; Hercules, because of his preceding thirsts in the deserts of Libya . . .'

'Gosh,' said Frère Jean, interrupting the discourse. 'I have heard from several venerable professors that Tirelupin, your good father's wine-steward, saves over one thousand eight hundred pipes of wine a year by making both visitors and family drink before they feel thirsty.'

'. . . for,' continued Pantagruel, 'just as the camels and dromedaries in the caravan drink for thirsts past, thirsts present and thirsts to come, so did Hercules, and through such excessive *raising of the weather* there was produced a new motion in the heavens, a titubation-cum-trepidation, the subject of much controversy and debate between foolish astrologers.'

'That,' said Panurge, 'is what is stated in a popular saying:

Good weather is raised and the bad weather passes,
Whilst round a big ham we all raise our glasses.'

'And,' said Pantagruel, 'not only have we *raised up good weather* by eating and drinking but we have also greatly lightened our ship: not only lightening it as Aesop's basket was lightened by consuming its contents but also by emancipating ourselves from fasting. For as the body is heavier dead than alive, so too the fasting man is more earthy and heavy than after eating and drinking. And those who, during a long journey, drink and break their fasts in the morning are not wrong to say, "Our horses will go all the better for it."

'Do you not know that the Amyclaeans of old, above all other gods, worshipped and adored noble Father Bacchus, dubbing him *Psilax* in a proper and appropriate act of naming? In the Doric tongue *psila* means *wings*. For, just as birds lightly fly high in the air by the help of their wings, so too, by the help of Bacchus – that is, of good wine, delicious and delightful – the minds of human beings are raised high, their bodies made manifestly merry, and what in them was earthy made supple.'

How, near the isle of the Ganabin, the Muses are saluted at the orders of Pantagruel

CHAPTER 66

[This is an isle of thieves: 'Ganabin, thieves, Hebrew' (Brief Declaration). Gannab appears several times in the Old Testament. Great navigators discovered their own 'Isle of Thieves', Magellan before Rabelais and Drake after him.)

This Isle of Thieves is like Poneropolis, that 'City of the Wicked' in Plutarch (On Curiosity, 520 B–D). These wicked islanders spy out defects in others, preferring the scandalous, the deformed and the ugly to the beautiful and the true. For Erasmus in his adage II, IX, XXII, 'A city of slaves', in Poneropolis were gathered as in a sink, 'flatterers, false-witnesses, and "prevaricatores" – meaning criminal advocates secretly in collusion with their opponents. The end of the Fourth Book recalls the longer end of Pantagruel with its loathing of devilish calumniators, and the Third Book with its warnings about corrupt legal men through whom the devil can appear as an angel of light.

This isle is the antithesis of Parnassus, the mountain of the Muses (and so no doubt associated with plagiarism). Yet it has its own fair stream (Hippocrene?) and there are Muses there too, perhaps the true Muses which the Ganabin steal and plagiarize.

The Conciergerie was a gaol in Paris.

With 'Plus ultra' Panurge recalls the device of the Emperor Charles V mocked in Gargantua.

At the end of this last book the characters of the companions are consolidated. Panurge again talks of the devil and is the embodiment of servile fear. The force of the name of 'Frère Jean des Entommeures' is at last emphasized: he makes entommeures – *mincemeat* – *of his enemies. As for Pantagruel, he is, following Plutarch (On the Daemon of Socrates), a new Socrates.*

In 1548 the inhabitants of the Bordeaux region rebelled against the salt-tax. The bells which called them together to resist were confiscated.]

As the fair wind and that happy converse continued, Pantagruel scanned the distant horizon and descried a mountainous land. He pointed it out to Xenomanes and asked him, 'Can you make out ahead to the larboard a high mountain with twin peaks closely resembling Mount Parnassus in Phocis?'

'Very clearly,' said Xenomanes. 'It is the isle of the Ganabin. Do you wish to go ashore?'

'No,' said Pantagruel.

'You are right,' said Xenomanes. 'There is nothing worth seeing! The inhabitants are all thieves and robbers. However, near that right-hand peak there is the most beautiful spring in the world, and around it stands a very large forest. Your seamen can take on wood and water.'

'Well and learnedly spoken,' said Panurge. 'Ha, da, da! Never let us land on an isle of thieves and robbers. I can tell you that this present isle is like Sark and Herm, the isles I once saw between Brittany and England; such too was the Poneropolis of Philip of Thrace: isles full of criminals, thieves, brigands, murderers and assassins, all descended from their origins in the deep dungeons of the *Conciergerie*. Let's not land there, I beg you. Trust, if not me, the advice of our good and wise

Xenomanes. They are (by the death of the Wooden Ox!) worse
than the cannibals. They'll eat us alive. Go not ashore, I beseech
you. It would be better for you to descend into Avernus. Hark!
By God, either I can hear a horrifying tocsin such as the Gascons
used to ring in the Bordelais to defy the commissioners and
collectors of the salt-levy and the tax-officials, or else I've got a
ringing in my ears.

'Let us sail past. Hau! *Plus ultra*!'

'Go ashore,' said Frère Jean, 'go ashore. Onwards, onwards,
ever onwards! *Never stay: then for lodging never pay!* We'll
massacre the lot of them. Go ashore!'

'The devil may have a part in this,' said Panurge. 'This devil
of a monk here – this mad devil's monk– is afraid of nothing!
He's as rash as all the devils put together and never bothers
about anyone else. He thinks the whole world is a monk like
he is!'

'Go to all the millions of devils, you gangrened old leper,'
replied Frère Jean, 'and may they anatomize your brain and
make *entommeures* of it! This devilish old idiot here is so
cowardly and nasty that he's forever shitting himself out of a
frenzy of funk. Since you're thrown into consternation by such
vain terrors, don't go ashore: stay here with the baggage. Or
else dash through all the millions of devils and hide away under
Proserpine's brave skirts!'

At those words Panurge vanished from the company and hid
below-decks in the pantry, amongst crusts, crumbs and scraps
of bread.

'I can feel in my soul an urge to withdraw,' said Pantagruel,
'as though it were a voice heard from afar telling me that we
must not go ashore. Each and every time that I have felt such
an impulse in my mind I have found myself fortunate when I
rejected and abandoned the course it was withdrawing me away
from, and, on the contrary, similarly fortunate whenever I
followed whither it was urging me. And I have never had cause
to repent of it.'

'That,' said Epistemon, 'is like the daemon of Socrates so
celebrated amongst the Academics.'

'Listen, then,' said Frère Jean. 'While the crews are taking on water, Panurge is lying down below like a wolf in its straw. Would you like to have a good laugh? Then light the powder of the basilisk here, hard by the foc's'le. (It will form a salute on our part to the Muses of this Mount Antiparnassus.) In any case the gunpowder inside it is spoiling.'

'Well said,' Pantagruel replied. 'Summon the Master-gunner.'

The Master-gunner promptly appeared. Pantagruel ordered him to fire the basilisk and then recharge it at once with fresh powder against every contingency. That was instantly done. At that first shot of the basilisk from aboard Pantagruel's ship, the gunners on the other ships, row-barges, galleons and galleasses of the convoy each likewise fired off one of their large, loaded cannons. You may take it that there was a glorious din.

How Panurge messed himself out of sheer funk; and how he mistook the mighty cat Rodilardus for a little devil

CHAPTER 67

[Rabelais returns to scatology – learned scatology – for the last time. In Chapter 52 he had already quoted scatological lines from Catullus. A knowledge of Italian is here simply supposed. Without it, contemporaries would have been lost. (Translations were later supplied by the publisher.) Here the original Italian is given with a translation.

The giants, once coarse and concerned with faeces and grossness, are now ideals: Gargantua, the model king and father; Pantagruel, the model princely son and Socratic sage. It is Panurge now who replaces the young faeces-centred oaf that Gargantua was before being purged of his madness. Scatology provides both jests and a final judgement on Panurge. Panurge also breaks into patois like the Limousin scholar of Pantagruel.

For the first time since Pantagruel, *Pantagruel (the giant) bursts out laughing. He cannot help it. Pantagruel has been an agelast, a non-laugher, throughout the last two books: that too makes him like Socrates, who had a great sense of fun and laughed with his friends, yet was classed as an 'agelast' by Pliny. (Erasmus, Adages, II, V, LXII, 'Unlaughing stone').*

The tale about Villon in England dates from well before the time of Villon, let alone of Thomas Linacre.

The lines attributed to Villon are authentic.

At the battle of Inchkeith (the Isle of Horses) in 1548, some 400 English soldiers were slaughtered by the French.

At the end, Pantagruel talks of God and of cleanliness: Panurge irrepressibly talks of the devil and dung.]

Panurge came tumbling out of the bread-store like a giddy goat: he was in his shirt-sleeves, with his trunk-hose pulled on to only one leg and his beard all besprinkled with breadcrumbs; he was holding on to a large, sleek-haired cat clinging fast to his other stocking. Quivering his jowls like a monkey hunting for fleas in the head, trembling and clacking his teeth, he went over to Frère Jean (who was sitting on the starboard chains) and devoutly begged him to have compassion upon him and to keep him safe with his cutlass, insisting and swearing by his share in Papimania that he had that very hour seen all the devils raging loose from their chains.

'Look-ee 'ere, me friend, me bruvvah, me ghostly Fahver,' said Panurge; 'today all the devils are having a wedding! You never saw such preparations for a diabolical banquet. Can you see that smoke rising from the kitchens of Hell?' – So saying he was pointing at the gun-smoke hanging over all the ships. – 'So many damnèd souls you never have seen! Look-ee 'ere, me friend. Know what? Those souls are such dainty little things, so blond and so tender that you could rightly say they're ambrosia for the Styx. God forgive me, but I took them for the souls of Englishmen, supposing that the Isle of Horses off Scotland had just been sacked this very morn by the Seigneurs de Thermes and d'Essé, and all the English who had surprised it hacked to pieces.'

As he drew near, Frère Jean smelt an odour which was not that of gun-powder. So he tugged out Panurge and saw his shirt all covered with thin excrement and freshly beshitten. The retentive powers of the sinew which restrains the muscle called the sphincter (that is, the arsehole) had been relaxed by the vehemence of the fear which Panurge had felt during his phantasmagorical visions; to which add the thundering of the cannonades, which is more terrifying down below in the cabins than up on deck. For one of the symptoms and by-products of fear is that it usually unlocks the aperture of the pen within which the faeces are temporarily retained.

Messere Pandolfo de la Cassina in Sienna is an example of that: he was travelling by post-horse through Chambéry when, dismounting at the home of that wise burgher Vinet, he grabbed a pitchfork from the stable and said to Vinet:

'*Da Roma in qua io non son andato del corpo. Di gratia piglia in mano.*'

('From Rome up till now I've never been once! Kindly grab hold of this pitchfork and give me a fright.')

Vinet did make several lunges with the pitchfork as if fencing, pretending to want to strike him in earnest. But the Siennese said to him:

'*Se tu non fai altramente, tu non fai nulla. Pero sforzati di adoperarli più guagliardamente.*'

'If you can't do it differently you'll get nowhere. Do try to wield it more vigorously.'

At which Vinet with that pitchfork landed him so great a blow between the neck and the collar-bone that he knocked him to the ground with his feet in the air. Then that Siennese, slobbering and laughing heartily, said to him: 'By Bayard's God's Feast-day! That's what I call

Datum Camberiaci!'

(Given by Our hand, at Chambéry!)

And he lowered his breeches just in time, for he had begun to mute more copiously than nine buffaloes and fourteen arch-priests from Ostia. The Siennese ended by thanking Vinet most graciously:

'*Io ti ringratio, bel messere. Cosi facendo tu m'hai esparmiata la speza d'un servitiale.*'

('I thank you, kind sir. By so doing you have saved me the cost of an enema.')

Another example: Edward the Fifth, King of England.

Maître François Villon, exiled from France, had gone over
to him. The king admitted him to such great intimacy that he
hid none of the little household secrets from him. One day,
when the said king was doing his job on his jakes, he showed
Villon a painting of the arms of France. 'See in what reverence
I hold your French kings! I have their arms nowhere but here
in my privy, hard by my close-stool.'

'Holy God!' said Villon, 'how wise, intelligent and well
informed you are, and careful about your well-being. And how
well you are served by your learned physician Thomas Linacre,
who, noting that you have naturally grown constipated in your
old age so that every day you have to stuff an apothecary up
your bum – I mean a suppository – otherwise you never could
mute, got you, with singular and laudable forethought, to have
the arms of France aptly painted here and nowhere else; for the
mere sight of them gives you such an horrific fear and fright
that you immediately drop pats like eighteen wild oxen from
Paeonia! Were they to be painted elsewhere in your palace – in
your bed-chamber, your hall, your chapel, your galleries or,
Holy God! anywhere else – you would be messing yourself all
over the place the instant you saw them. And if you were to
have a painting of the Great Oriflamme of France here as well,
at the mere sight of it you would be voiding your innards, I
believe, through your fundament. But *hum*, *hum* and again I
say *hum*:

> Aren't I a booby from Paree?
> From Pointoise near Paree, in sum:
> When from a rope I hang, that day
> Neck will know what Bum doth weigh.

'I am a booby, I say: one ill advised, ill informed and slow
on the uptake, for whenever I came here with you it astonished
me that you should already have them unlace your breeches in
your bed-chamber. I really did think your close-stool was there
behind some arras or other, or in the space between your bed
and the wall. Otherwise it seemed to me quite out of place to
unlace yourself in your bed-chamber so far from your family

seat. A truly boobyish thought, wasn't it? The cause arises, by God, from some greater mystery. You do well to act as you do. I mean so well that you could never do better. Have them fully unlace your breeches far off, in plenty of time, for if you were to come in here still unlaced and saw that coat-of-arms, then, Holy God! – note all this well! – the seat of your breeches would do you the office of a lazanon, *pot-de-chambre,* jakes and privy.'

Frère Jean, pinching his nose with his left hand, was, with the index-finger of his right, pointing out to Pantagruel the shirt-tails of Panurge.

Pantagruel, on seeing Panurge so disturbed, transfixed, trembling, incoherent, beshitten and clawed by the talons of the celebrated cat Rodilardus, could not contain his laughter, saying, 'And what are you going to do with that cat?'

'Cat!!!' replied Panurge. 'The devil take me if I didn't think it was that mangy little devilkin I once smartly and quietly nabbed in the great Hutch of Hell, using my stocking as a mitten. To the devil with this devil!

'It's lacerated my skin like the beard of a crayfish!'

So saying, he threw the cat down.

'Go,' said Pantagruel, 'in the name of God go; have a hot bath, cleanse yourself, calm down, put on a white shirt and clothe yourself anew.'

'Are you saying that I'm afraid?' Panurge replied, 'Not a bit. I am, by God's power, more valiant than if I'd swallowed as many flies as have been mixed into dough in Paris from the Feast of Saint John to All-Saints Day. Ha, ha, ha, Houay! What in the devil's name *is* this? Do you call it squitters, pooh, crap, turds, shit, ordure, droppings, faeces, excrement, wolf-muck, scumber, mute, fumets, turds, *scybala* or *spyrathia*[74] It is, I believe, saffron of Hibernia:

74. Rabelais could have taken the word scybala from Philippians 3:8. Erasmus defines σκύβαλον as the dung of dogs. As for spyrathia (σπυραθια) it is a medical term, applied to ball-dung, the round excrement of sheep and goats. The *Brief Declaration* defines them respectively as 'hardened turds' and the 'droppings of goats and sheep.'

Ho, ho, hee,
Safran d'Hibernie.

Selah! Let us drink!'[75]

The end of the fourth book
of the deeds and sayings
of noble Pantagruel.

75. *Selah* is the Hebrew word (a musical notation?) that comes at the end of
some seventy-one of the psalms. Its sense is not clear, but it does suggest
'The End' – not least for a former monk who had chanted the psalms day
after day throughout the year. The *Brief Declaration* defines it as meaning
'certainly'.

THE FIFTH BOOK
OF PANTAGRUEL

Introduction to *The Fifth Book of Pantagruel*

Ever since its publication some eleven years after the death of Rabelais, this book has regularly appeared (originally without warning) in almost all the editions of *Gargantua and Pantagruel*. Until the mid-nineteenth century, it was assumed to be by Rabelais. Currently, though some scholars think parts of the text are based on authentic papers left behind by Rabelais, others (myself included) judge it to be supposititious, but not without interest.

The available texts are:

the Isle Sonante of 1562, published without name or place, consisting of sixteen chapters;

the first edition of the printed version, published in 1564 without name or place, consisting of forty-seven chapters which differ in detail from the Isle Sonante;

a manuscript not in the hand of Rabelais, consisting of part of the Prologue and forty-six chapters (omitting Chapters 24 and 25 of the printed text, but adding one new chapter).

Some think that the Isle Sonante has perhaps the best chance of being based on papers left by Rabelais, but the relationship of the texts is a complex one. Questions of authenticity demand recourse to the evidence of the French texts.

Because of its complicated nature, the text given here is a simplified one: that of the first edition of 1564, with a strict selection of variants from the Isle Sonante of 1562 and from the undated manuscript, which could well date from before 1564. The shorter variants appear in the footnotes; the longer ones can be found in the appendices at the end.

For the most part this translation is based upon the text of

Guy Demerson in *Rabelais: Œuvres completes*; I have found
the work of Guy Demerson particularly useful. As always, there
is a debt, warmly acknowledged, to the Pléiade *Rabelais* of
Mireille Huchon.[1]

---

1.   For publication details, see the Introduction to *Pantagruel*.

The Fifth
and last book
of the Heroic deeds and sayings
of our good Pantagruel

Composed by Maître François Rabelais
Doctor of Medicine

In which is contained the visit to the
Oracle of the Dive Bacbuc and the
Word of the Bottle, for which
the whole of this long voyage
was undertaken.
Newly brought to light.
1564.

Contents

Prologue of Maître François Rabelais
for the Fifth Book of the heroic deeds
and sayings of Pantagruel.
To the kindly readers

[The word 'fat' in the opening paragraph is not the English word for obese but a Provençal word for daft. It is appealing to a theme in the Pantagrueline Prognostication, *Chapter 5.*

The Bagpipes of Prelates *is one of the comic titles from the Library of Saint-Victor in* Pantagruel.

The reader will recognize echoes of the Prologue to the 1548 Fourth Book as well as several other echoes of the four Books. This version of the story of the 'fresh-water physician' taken from the 1548 Prologue is weaker and varies in detail. There are also echoes of Joachim Du Bellay's Defence and Illustration of the French Language *(1549), with its savour of young aspirant Pléiade poets rather than of an author with the secure and outstanding place already earned by Rabelais.*

For Pythagoras cf. Erasmus, within adage I, I, II, and for the obscurity of the numbers of Pythagoras see adage III, VI, XXXII, 'More obscure than Platonic numbers' (which is also important for Pythagoras). Pythagoras' interdiction of beans was an absolute commonplace and much discussed. Horace mentions it in passing, Satires, 2, 7, 63. For other possible echoes of Erasmus, cf. adage I, V, XXV, 'I am holding a wolf by the ears'.

The French queen eulogized is Marguerite de Navarre, to whom Rabelais dedicated the Third Book.

'Rhyparographer' is the surname of Pyreicus in Pliny, Natural History, *35, 10. It means a squalid painter of mean subjects.*

'To grate like a goose among swans' echoes Virgil, Eclogue, *9, 36.]*

'Tireless Drinkers, and you, the most becarbuncled of Syphilitics: while you are at ease and I have nothing more urgent to do, I ask you this, saying, why is it cited nowadays as a common proverb that 'the world is no longer *fat*'?

Now *fat* is a term in Provençalo-Gothic which means

unsalted, saltless, insipid and tasteless; metaphorically *fat* signifies daft, silly, bereft of sense and hare-brained. Would you say (as one may indeed logically infer) that the world was heretofore daft but now become wise? How many and what conditions were required to make it daft? And how many and wise to make it wise? And why was it daft? And why should it now be wise? By what qualities did you recognize its former folly? By what qualities, its present wisdom? Who made it daft? Who made it wise? Who form the greater number: those who liked it daft or those who like it wise? For how long was it daft? How long has it been wise? Whence proceeded its antecedent folly and whence its subsequent wisdom? Why did its antecedent folly end now and not later? Why did its present wisdom begin now and not earlier? What ill did that antecedent folly do to us? And what good, the subsequent wisdom? How could that old folly have been abolished? And how could the present wisdom be restored?

Answer, if you think it right to do so.

I shall not adjure your Reverences any further, fearing to parch your Paternities. Do not be shy: make your confession to Herr der Tyflet, the Enemy of Paradise, the Enemy of the truth. Be of good heart, my lads: for this first part of my sermon have three or five drinks if you're men of mine: if you belong to the Other, then *Get thee behind me, Satan*! For otherwise I swear to you by my great Hurlyburly that if you are not helping me to resolve the aforesaid puzzle, then I for some time now regret having set it before you, even though I am in no less a quandary than if I held a wolf by the ears without hope of succour.

What did you say? I get you: you have not yet decided how to answer. By my beard, no more have I.

I shall merely quote you what a venerable Doctor of Theology – the author of the *Bagpipes of Prelates* – foretold in the spirit of prophecy. What does the scallywag say? Harken, ye old asses' pricks! Hearken:

> That Jubilee when the daft world was shorn
> In figures now exceeds the thirtieth morn
> Supernumerically. Scant respect!
> Daft it appeared, all perseverance wrecked
> Of lengthy bills; no longer avid he;
> For the sweet fruit of grass shall shellèd be,
> Of which the flower in spring feared to be lorn.

You heard that. Did you understand it?

That Doctor is ancient; his words, laconic; his judgement Duns-Scottish and obscure.[1]

He was indeed treating a matter intrinsically deep and difficult, but the best of the exegetes of that good Father expound that *Jubilee* which *exceeds the thirtieth morn* as the years embraced within this current age until one thousand five hundred and fifty. *The flower of it feared to be lorn.* Come spring the world will no more be called daft. The fools – the number of which is infinite as Salomon testifies – will die insane. Then there shall cease all species of madness, which are similarly countless: *The species of mania are infinite*, as Avicenna states. Madness, which was driven back to the centre during the rigours of winter, now appears at the circumference and is, like the trees, in sap. Experience shows us that; you know it; you can see it. And it was long ago investigated by that great and good fellow Hippocrates in his *Aphorisms*, saying, 'For manias, indeed, are . . .' etc.

And so the world, growing wise, will no more fear the flower of beans in spring: that is (as you can piteously believe with a glass in your hand and a tear in your eye) in Lent it will feel no fear from piles of books which could seem to be flowering, florescent and florulent like fair butterflies but are in fact all boring, troubling, endangering, prickling and darkling like the numbers of Pythagoras, who, as Horace testifies, was the Monarch of the Bean.

Such books shall perish and be no more in men's hands, no

---

1. Plays on Duns Scotus' name and *skotinos* (obscure) have already been met in the *Third Book*, Chapter 17. See also for laconic speech Erasmus; *Adages*, II, I, XCII, 'Battologia, Laconismus'.

more be seen nor read. Such was their destiny, and there, their predestined end. In their place succeed *shellèd beans*, that is, those joyful and fruitful books of *pantagruelism* which rumour reports to be selling well nowadays in expectation of the end of the subsequent Jubilee: all the world is given over to studying them, and is therefore called wise. There is the solution and resolution of your problem. On the basis of which establish yourselves as worthy folk. Enjoy a good cough or two and steadily down nine good drinks, since the vines are good and the money-lenders are hanging themselves. If this good weather goes on they will cost me dear in ropes, which, I declare, I shall liberally provide gratis, any and every time they want them, thus saving them the expense of a hangman.

And in order that you may share in our future wisdom, freed from your former folly, erase this instant from your scrolls the credo of that ancient philosopher with the golden thigh who forbade you the use of beans as fodder: take it as true, and admitted as such amongst all good companions, that he forbade them to you with the same motives as the late Dr Amer – that fresh-water physician, the nephew of the Seigneur de Camelotière, the lawyer – who used to order his patients to avoid the wing of a partridge, the rump of a chicken and the neck of a pigeon, saying in Latin: *Wing bad; crupper doubtful; neck good after skin removed*, setting the dainties aside for his own mouth and leaving the sick to gnaw at the bones.[2]

He was succeeded by certain of the becowlèd brethren who forbade us *beans* – that is to say, pantagruelic books – thus imitating Philoxenus and Gnato, those ancient Sicilians who, as architects of their monastic and ventric voluptuousness, used to gob in the dishes during a banquet when the tasty morsels were being served, so that everyone else would thrust them away in disgust.[3]

Thus do those hideous, snot-dripping, mucose and decrepit hypocrites execrate such tasty books in public and private,

---

2.   Cf. a jest in the Prologue to the 1548 *Fourth Book*, one of the sources of this Prologue.
3.   For Philoxenus and Gnatho and their gobbing again see the Prologue to the 1548 *Fourth Book*.

basely gobbing all over them in their impudence. And though we can read in our Gallic tongue nowadays many excellent works in both prose and verse, with only a few relics from the Gothic age and black-beetlery, I have nevertheless chosen (as the proverb goes) to hiss and grate like a goose amongst swans rather than be judged quite dumb amongst so many fine poets and eloquent writers of prose; chosen also to play the role of some village yokel amongst such skilful actors in this noble drama rather than to be ranked with those who but serve as umber and number, merely yawning at the flies, pricking up my ears like an ass in Arcady at the song of the music-makers, and silently showing by signs that they approve of the dramatis personae.

Once I had decided and made my choice I thought that I would be doing no useless or boring task if I trundled my Diogenic barrel about so that you should not say that I live without a model.

I have in mind a great pile of authors like Colinet, Marot, Héroët, Saint-Gelais, Salel, Masuau and a good hundred or so other Gallic poets and writers of prose; and I see that, since they have long shown respect for the School of Apollo and drunk full goblets from the stream of Pegasus amidst the joyful Muses, they bring to the eternal construction of our vulgar tongue nothing less than Parian marble, alabaster, porphyry and fine goldsmiths' solder; they treat nothing less than heroic deeds, great matters, difficult themes both grave and arduous, all spun in crimson-silken rhetoric; by their writings they produce nothing less than heavenly nectar, than precious, laughing, quaffing wine, delicate, delightful and savouring of musk.

And that glory is not the prerogative of the males alone: ladies have shared in it, amongst whom one lady extracted from the blood of France whom you cannot mention without a profection of her notable honours: our whole century is amazed as much by her writings and her transcendent themes as by the elegance of her language and her miracle-working style.

Imitate them, if you know how. In my case I could never pull it off: it is not given to everyone to haunt and inhabit Corinth, no more than everyone was able open-handedly to contribute a golden shekel towards the building of the temple of Solomon. And since it is not within our capacity to achieve such artistic constructions, I am determined to do what Regnault de Montauban did: I will wait upon the masons, boil up the pot for the masons and, since I cannot be their comrade, they will have me as a listener – I mean an indefatigable listener – to their most-excellent writings. You Zoiluses, jealous and envious, will die of fear. Go and hang yourselves and choose a tree for yourself to do it on: you will never lack a rope: meanwhile I declare here, before my Helicon, within the hearing of the heavenly Muses, that if I yet live as long as a dog and three crows in such health and wholeness as did the saintly Jewish captain, as well as Xenophilus the musician and Demonax the philosopher, I shall prove (by not irrelevant arguments and by irrefutable reasons, in the very teeth of who-knows-which compilers of centons, trussers-up of topics treated hundreds and hundreds of times already, pickers-over of old Latin scrap-iron and dealers in second-hand old Latinate words all mouldy and vague) that our vulgar tongue is not so crass, inept, indigent and contemptible as they may reckon it to be. I also beg in all modesty that just as when, long ago, all the treasures were distributed by Phoebus to the great poets, Aesop still found a niche and role as a writer of fables, so too may I. And since I do not aspire to a higher place, may they by special grace not scorn to receive me as a minor rhyparographer, a follower of Pyreicus. They will do so, I am sure, for they are all so good, so human, so gracious and so debonair: none more so.

That is why, ye drinkers, and why, ye sufferers from the gout, those Zoiluses want to have the exclusive enjoyment of such books, for while they read them out loud in their conventicles and build up a cult for the high mysteries contained in them, they appropriate them and their unique reputation to themselves, as Alexander the Great, in similar circumstances, arrogated to himself the books of basic philosophy composed by Aristotle.

Guts to guts: what booze-ups; what scapegraces!

That is why, Drinkers, I counsel you to lay up a good stock of my books while the time is right; as soon as you come across them on the booksellers' stalls you must not only shuck them but devour them like an opiatic cordial and incorporate them within you: it is then that you will discover the good they have in store for all noble bean-shuckers. I offer you now a lovely good basketful of them, harvested in the same garden as the previous ones, most reverently beseeching you to welcome the present volume, whilst hoping for better when the swallows next return.

END OF THE PROLOGUE.

How Pantagruel landed on Ringing Island and of the din which we heard

CHAPTER I

[This chapter comes from the Ringing Island (the Isle Sonante), modified. There are echoes of Rabelaisian words and phrases, especially from the Fourth Book.

For the bees, see Virgil, Georgics, 4:63.

'Fasts of the Four Times' were three fasts a week occurring four times a year.

Cf. three adages of Erasmus: I, I, VII, 'Dordonian bronze', III, VII, XXXIX, 'Corybantiari for to be mad', and I, VIII, LXI, 'Life in a barrel'.

The dock called 'patience' was used in treating leprosy.

The 'times' for verbs are normally called tenses, but 'times' need to be kept here. The aorist is an 'uncertain' tense.

'Esurience' is Hunger.]

Continuing on our way, we sailed for three days without descrying anything. On the fourth we sighted land and were told by our pilot that it was Ringing Island; we heard a din from afar, repetitive and strident. To our ears it sounded like big bells, little bells and middling bells all pealing together as is done on great festival days in Paris, Tours, Jargeau, Nantes and elsewhere. The nearer we drew, the louder it rang in our ears.

We wondered whether it was Dordona with its cauldrons, or the portico in Olympia called Heptaphone, or the never-ending noise emanating from the colossus erected over the tomb of Memnon at Thebes in Egypt; or else the racket that used to be heard around a grave in Lipara, one of the Aeolian Isles: but geography was against it.

'I am wondering,' said Pantagruel, 'whether some bees have attempted to swarm there and whether the neighbourhood has not raised this clanging of pans, cauldrons, basins and corybantic cymbals of Cybele, the great Mother of the Gods, in order to summon them back.

'Hark!'

As we drew nearer still we thought we could hear the indefatigable chanting of the inhabitants of the place amidst the ceaseless pealing of the bells. That is why Pantagruel decided that, before docking at Ringing Island, we should land with our skiff on an eyot hard by a hermitage and a sort of tiny garden.

There we found a nice little hermit called Braguibus, a native of Glenay, who fully instructed us about all that jangling. He regaled us in a very odd fashion: he made us fast for the next four days, asserting that we would not otherwise be admitted on to Ringing Island, since it was then their Fast of the Four Times.

'That is an enigma I don't understand,' said Panurge. 'It would rather be the Season of the Four Winds, since whenever we fast we are stuffed full of flatulence. And anyway, do you have nothing else to do here but fast? It all seems very meagre to me: we could do without so many palatial feasts!'[4]

'In my Donatus,' said Frère Jean, 'I can find but three "times" to verbs: preterite, present and future. That fourth "time" must have been thrown in as a tip for the valet!'

'It is,' said Epistemon, 'an aorist issuing from the very-imperfect preterite of the Greeks and Latins, accepted as a mottled, motley bellicose time. Patience! (as the lepers say).'

'It is a fatal time,' said the hermit, 'as I told you. Whoever would gainsay that is a heretic, good for nothing but the pyre.'

'It is quite certain, Father,' said Panurge, 'that when I'm at sea, I'm more afraid of being wetted than heated, of being drowned than burnt. All right, then! For God's sake let us fast, but I have fasted so long already that the fasts have undermined all my flesh and I fear that the bastions of my body may fall into decay.

'I have another worry too: I might offend you by my fasting, for I know nothing about it and, as many have told me, I make a bad show at it: and I believe them. For my own part, I say, I am not much concerned with fasting: nothing is easier or readier

---

4.   A pun: *palais* means both 'palace' and 'palate'.

to hand. I'm much more concerned not to fast in the future, for then I'll need cloth to full and grist for the mill.

'But let us fast, for God's sake, since we have entered upon the festivities of Esurience: it is a long time since I was last acquainted with them.'

'And if fast we must,' said Pantagruel, 'the only expedient is to get over it quickly as over a bad road.

'I would also like to spend some time with my papers to find out whether studying at sea is as good as studying on land, since Plato, wishing to describe a silly, uncouth and ignorant man, compared him to folk brought up at sea aboard boats, just as we might say *Folk brought up in a barrel*, who peer only through a bung-hole.'

Our fastings were terrifying and very dreadful, for:
– the first was a joust with short staves;
– the second, with drawn foils;
– the third, with whetted blades,
and
– the fourth, with all put to fire and sword.
For such was the decision of the Fatal Sprites.

How Ringing Island had been inhabited by Siticines who had been transfigured into birds

CHAPTER 2

[The opening chapters are a satire of celibate religious Orders.
Strictly 'Siticines' were musicians at Roman funerals, whilst Sicinnistae *danced satyr-dances.]*

'Albian Camat' may be a faulty transcription of Abien Camar, *the Hebrew for a pagan priest.*

Master Aedituus (Temple-keeper) is miscalled Antitus, the name of a cook in the Fourth Book *and of a booby in* Pantagruel.

In French the birds are called Clerigaux, *etc. Here the termination 'goths' seeks to convey the pejorative force of the original -aux.*

The Harpies and the Stimphalides *(foul and befouling birds of prey) were eventually defeated by Hercules.]*

Once our fastings were over, the hermit gave us a letter addressed to a man whom he called Albian Camat, the Master Aedituus of Ringing Island: but Panurge greeted him as Master Antitus. He was a little old man, bald, with an illuminated snout and a ruddy face who offered us a very warm welcome on the recommendation of the hermit, once he learnt that – as was expounded above – we had all fasted.

After we had very well eaten, he explained to us the special features of the island, insisting that it had first been inhabited by Siticines but they (following the natural order, since all things change) had turned into birds.

There I was fully informed of what Atteius Capito, Pollux, Marcellus, Aulus Gellius, Athenaeus, Suidas, Ammonius and others had written on the subject of the Siticines and the Sicinnists; after which it did not seem hard to us to believe in the metamorphoses of Nyctimene, Progne, Itys, Alcyone, Antigone, Tereus and other birds. We had no more doubts either about the children of Matabrune, who were changed into swans, nor about the men of Pallene (in Thrace), who, at the precise moment that they bathed nine times in Lake Triton, were also turned into birds. Thereafter he talked of nothing but birds and cages.

The cages were grand, richly ornate, sumptuous and remarkably constructed. The birds were grand, handsome and becomingly sleek, closely resembling the men of my part of the world. They ate and drank like men, shat like men, broke wind, slept and leapt females like men. In short, on first seeing them, you would have said that they were in fact men, yet according to what Maître Aedituus taught us, they were not men at all, maintaining that they were, on the contrary, neither secular nor of this world.

Their plumage moreover made us wonder: some had plumage which was wholly white; others, entirely black; others, all grey; others half white and half black; others, entirely red; others, half white, half blue. And what a fine sight it was to see them!

The male birds they called Clerigoths, Monkogoths, Priestogoths, Abbégoths, Bishogoths, Cardingoths, plus a Popinjay, who is unique in his species.

He called the female birds Clerickesses, Monkagesses, Priesta-gesses, Abbégesses, Bishogesses, Cardingesses and Popagesses.

He told us, however, that, just as drones haunt bees yet do nothing but eat and spoil everything, so too, for the last three hundred years, on the fifth day after each full moon, a large number of Bigot-tails have somehow flown in amongst those happy birds, shamefully shitting all over their island. So hideous and monstrous are they that everyone has always shunned them, for they all have wry-necks, hairy paws and the claws and bellies of Harpies together with the bums of Stymphalian birds.

It was impossible to exterminate them: for every one of them killed, two dozen fly in. I yearned for a second Hercules, since Frère Jean had sunk into such mind-distracting contemplation that he had lost touch with reality, while there befell Pantagruel what had befallen Messer Priapus when his skin ran out as he contemplated the sacrifices of Ceres.[5]

How there is but one Popinjay on Ringing Island

CHAPTER 3

[Popinjay meant a parrot. Here it also means a pope. There is an allusion to the Great Schism (1378 to 1417) when there were two rival popes.

'Robert Valbringue' may be a confused allusion to Roberval, the explorer who governed Canada.

Cf. two adages of Erasmus: I, V, XXIX, 'More mute than a fish', and 'III, VII, X, 'Africa always brings something new'.]

We then inquired of the Maître Aedituus why, seeing the increase of those venerable birds in their various species, there

5.   Cf. Erasmus, *Adages*, I, VII, XXXV, 'Ficulnus (fig-tree wood)', citing Horace, *Satires*, 1, 7. Priapus, carved from fig-wood, laughed so much at the sacrifices he witnesses that he split his arse (but when laughing at Hecate not Ceres). It must be supposed that Pantagruel too risked splitting the skin of his backside through laughing.

was only one Popinjay. He replied that the cause lay in the original foundation and in ineluctable destiny as determined by the stars, by which Priestogoths and Monkogoths were born of Clerigoths without carnal intercourse (as happens to bees which are brought forth from a young bull prepared according to the art and practice of Aristaeus).

From the Priestogoths are born the Bishogoths, and from them the splendid Cardingoths; any, unless overtaken by death, could well become Popinjay, of which there is usually but one just as there is but one king-bee in a hive and but one sun in this world. When a Popinjay dies, to replace him another is born from the entire tribe of Cardingoths (again, you realize, without carnal intercourse). Accordingly, within that species there is but one individual in an unbroken succession, no more nor less than the Arabian phoenix.

It is true that two Popinjays were delivered into Nature some two thousand seven hundred and sixty moons ago, but that was the greatest disaster ever seen on this island, 'for,' said the Aedituus, 'during that period all the birds despoiled each other and tore the skins off each other, so that the island was put in peril of being robbed of its inhabitants. Part of them adhered to one and supported him: part, to the other, and protected him; part of them stayed as mute as fishes and chanted no more; and some of these bells of ours, as though under an interdict, rang out no more.

'During that period of sedition they summoned to their aid the emperors, kings, dukes, monarchs, counts, barons and corporations who dwelt upon the terra-firma of our continent. But there was no end to that schism and sedition until plurality was brought back to unity when one of them was plucked from this life.'

We then asked what moved those birds to chant thus incessantly. The Aedituus replied it was the bells hanging over their cages. He then said to us:

'Those Monkogoths you can see over there clad in a cape with a hood like a bag for straining hippocras: would you like me to make them chant now like meadow-larks?'

'Kindly do so,' we replied.

Thereupon he rang a bell six times only; whereupon Monko-goths came rushing up and Monkogoths began to sing.

'Now,' said Panurge, 'if I were to ring that bell, would I make those birds sing which have plumage the colour of red herrings?'

'Just the same,' said the Aedituus.

And when Panurge struck it, those smoke-cured birds did come charging up at once, and they all chanted together, but their voices were raucous and nasty. The Aedituus explained that they lived on nothing but fish, as herons and cormorants do in the outside world, and that they were a fifth species of Bigot-tails, newly minted. He further added that he had been warned by Robert Valbringue (who had recently called in on the way back from Africa) that there was a sixth species due to land, which he called Capuchinogoths, glummer, madder and more provoking than any species found on that isle.

'Africa,' said Pantagruel, 'is always bringing forth things new and monstrous.'

How the Birds of Ringing Island were all birds of passage

CHAPTER 4

[Harsh words on monasteries and convents. 'The Ile Bossard' is occu-pied by bossus, hunchbacks, and other misfits. Much the same was said about monks and nuns at the beginning of the Abbaye de Thélème.

There was a French saying, 'Long as a day without bread'.

'Malsueda' is an echo of Virgil, Aeneid, 6, 276, malsueda fames (evil-counselling Hunger).

More of the inmates leave their Ringing Isle these days because of the Reformation.

'A useless burden upon the earth' is applied to monks in the Fourth Book, Chapter 58, where Rabelais attributes this (quite common) saying of Homer, Iliad, 18, 104, to Hesiod.]

'But,' said Pantagruel, 'seeing that you have explained to us how the Popinjay is born from Cardingoths, Cardingoths, from

Bishogoths, Bishogoths, from Priestogoths, and Priestogoths, from Clerigoths, I would dearly like to know whom the Clerigoths are born from.'

'They are all birds of passage. They come to us from the other world, some from a wondrously broad country called *Day-sans-Bread* and some from another land lying towards the setting sun and called *Too-Many-Childer*. Every year those Clerigoths come here in droves from those two lands, leaving behind fathers and mothers and all their friends and neighbours. That is what happens whenever there are so many children, be they male or female, in some noble House in that second land, that if you were to divide up the inheritance between them (as reason requires, Nature ordains and God commands) the family itself would be ruined.

'That is the occasion which leads parents to dump their children on to this Ile Bossard.'

'Ah,' said Panurge, 'The Ile Bouchard, near Chinon!'

'I said this Ile *Bossard*,' replied the Aedituus, 'this Isle of *Hunchbacks*. For here they are usually hunchbacked, one-eyed, lame, one-armed, plagued with the gout, misshapen and deformed, a useless burden upon the earth.'

'That,' said Pantagruel, 'is a custom diametrically opposed to the basic rule observed at the admission of Vestal Virgins: it was, as Labeo Antistius testifies, forbidden to choose any maiden for that honour who had any defect in her soul, any weakness in her senses or any blemish in her body, no matter how trivial or concealed.'

'I am amazed,' continued the Aedituus, 'that mothers in that other world can bear their children nine months in the womb seeing that they cannot bear or abide them nine years in the home – not even seven years in most cases – but, by merely putting a surplice over their clothes and shaving Lord-knows how much hair off their crowns whilst uttering certain evil-averting, expiatory formulas, they clearly and openly turn them before your eyes into such Birds as you see here now by a Pythagorean metempsychosis, without lesion or gash of any kind, just as the priests of Isis were created amongst the Egyptians by tonsuring and the imposition of certain linen stoles.

'But, dear friends, I cannot tell how it can be, nor why it must be, that the females (be they Clerickesses, Monkagesses or Abbégesses) never sing pleasant motets and songs of thankfulness as once were sung to Oromasis by the rule of Zoroaster, but rather songs of cursing and of gloom such as were addressed to the demon Ahriman, songs (sung continually by the young as much as the old) raining imprecations on their kinsfolk and friends who had transformed them into birds.

'An even greater number come to us from *Day-sans-Bread* (which day is excessively long). For when the Asaphis (who inhabit that land) are about to suffer from *malsueda* because they have nothing to eat, and since they neither know what to do nor want to do it – prepared neither to toil at some honest art or craft nor to go loyally into service with some decent family – they all fly here as do those who have been hopelessly crossed in love and likewise those too who have committed a wicked crime and whom men hunt so as to bring them to some shameful death. Here they have their lives assigned: here they who had once been as skinny as magpies quickly grow as plump as dormice; here they find perfect safety, immunity and privilege.'

'But,' asked Pantagruel, 'once they have come here, do those fine birds never return to the world they were hatched in?'

'Some do,' replied the Aedituus, 'formerly, very few, very late in life and very sadly. But since certain eclipses, huge flocks of them have flown back home by virtue of the constellations in the heavens. That in no wise makes us melancholy: those who stay have all the greater pittance!

'Before flying off all of them cast their plumage to the thorns and the nettles.'

We did indeed find a few feathers there; and in our searches we came across an uncovered pot of roses.[6]

---

6. 'To uncover a (or the) pot of roses' meant to uncover a secret or some hidden piece of knavery; more or less, 'To let the cat out of the bag'.

How the Gourmander-Birds on Ringing Island are mute

CHAPTER 5

[The verb gourmander *found here in the original implies both gourmandise and commanding, domineering or acting proudly. There is also a suggestion of avidity. This chapter mentions three Orders of Chivalry: the Order of the Garter, the Order of Saint Michael (who is shown slaying Satan, the Calumniator, the Father of Lies) and the Order of the Golden Fleece. There is a pun between* Gourmanders *and the* Commanders *of such Orders. There are clear allusions to the insignia of the Orders of the Garter, of Saint Michael and of the Golden Fleece.]*

Those words had hardly been uttered before there came flying close by some twenty-five or thirty birds of a hue and plumage which we had not yet seen on that isle. Their plumage kept changing from hour to hour like the skin of a chameleon and like the flower of a tripolion or teucrion. Beneath their left wings all of them had a mark like two diameters each bisecting a circle or like a perpendicular dropping on to a straight horizontal. All were virtually of the same shape but not all of the same colour: in some it was white; in others, green; in others, red; in others, violet, and in others, blue.

'What are these?' asked Pantagruel. 'And how do you call them?'

'They are cross-breeds,' said the Aedituus. 'We call them Gourmanders, and they possess a large number of rich gourmandises in your world.'

'I beg you,' I said, 'to get them to sing a bit so that we may hear their voices.'

'They never sing,' he replied, 'but to make up for it, they put enough food away for two.'

'Where are their females?' I asked.

'They have none,' he replied.

'How is it, then,' argued Panurge, 'that they are all covered with scabs and eaten away by syphilis?'

'Syphilis is a property of this species of bird,' he replied, 'caught from the seas which they haunt at times.'

He then told us of the motive of their coming here:

'For this one here,' he said, 'it was to find out whether there is amongst you a magnificent species of Goth-birds: terrifying birds of prey which however do not answer to the gauntlet nor respond to the lure, but do exist, they say, in your world. Some of them sport a fair and costly jess-strap garter round their legs, to which is attached a varvel-ring on which is inscribed *Honni* to him who *mal y pense*, for all such are condemned to be suddenly shat upon.

'Others it is said wear on the front of their plumage a pectoral badge depicting victory over the Calumniator, or in other cases, the fleece of a ram.'

'That,' said Panurge, 'is true, Master Aedituus, but we do not know any.'

'Now,' said the Aedituus, 'there has been quite enough palavering: now for a drink.'

'And for a feed,' said Panurge.

'Both a feed and a good drink,' said the Aedituus. 'A pair of cards down, then the rest of the suit! Nothing is more dear nor more precious than time: let us spend it on good works.'

He first wanted us to bathe in the thermal springs of the Cardingoths, springs outstandingly beautiful and delightful, and then, on coming out from the baths, have ourselves anointed with precious balm by the Alyptae. But Pantagruel told him that he would drink all too much without any of that.

Whereupon the Aedituus conducted us to a spacious and delightful refectory and said:

'Braguibus the hermit made you fast for four days: here, to balance things up, you shall eat and feed for four days without ceasing.'

'Shall we not get any sleep during all that time?' asked Panurge.

'As you freely wish,' replied the Aedituus, 'for *he who sleeps, drinks*.[7] Good Lord, what good cheer we had. O! what a great man and a good!'

---

7.   The original saying is, 'He who sleeps, eats', that is, being asleep, he can forego a meal even when hungry.

How the birds of Ringing Island are nourished

CHAPTER 6

[There is an echo of two adages of Erasmus: I, I, LXIV, 'To move the Camarina' (that is, to disturb the Camerine marshes and so bring ills on to oneself), and II, VII, XC, 'To thunder in a basin' (as we might say 'To storm in a tea-cup').

These lucky idle birds live in plenty. They are untouchable even by the curses and plagues of Jehovah himself, even if their 'Heaven is as iron' and their 'Earth as brass' as threatened to any Israelite who broke the Covenant. (Leviticus 26:19 and context.)

The famine in Egypt lasted seven years.

For the 'great feast with banners' cf. Chapter 45 of the Fourth Book.

These idle monk-birds have their loving cup as in many English colleges today. The two lines at the end are adapted from an epigram of Victor Brodeau published in the works of Clément Marot.]

Pantagruel showed a glum countenance and seemed displeased about the four-days' stop-over that the Aedituus had prescribed for us. The Aedituus noticed it and said:

'My Lord, you know that for several days before and after the Winter Solstice there never is a storm at sea. That is because of the sympathy the elements have for the halcyons, those birds sacred to Thetis, which are laying their eggs at that time and hatching their young by the shore. Hereabouts the sea atones for that long period of calm: whenever voyagers appear, it never ceases to rage abnormally for four days. We believe the reason to be that Necessity wants to constrain them to remain here for four days, to be well feasted out of the profits from our bell-ringing. Do not therefore consider this time to be lost in idleness. You will be retained here by *force majeure*, unless you prefer to fight against Juno, Neptune, Doris, Aeolus and all the little counter-Joves. Simply make up your mind to have a good time.'

After the first gollops, Frère Jean asked the Aedituus:

'In this isle of yours you have nothing but birds and cages;

the birds neither plough nor cultivate the soil: their sole occupation is to frolic, twitter and sing: so from what lands does this cornucopia come from, this abundance of good and toothsome tidbits?'

'From all over that other world,' replied the Aedituus, 'except for certain lands in the Northern climes who have stirred up the Camerine marshes these last few years, tra-la-la,

> They shall repent of it, ding-dong:
> They shall repent of it, dong-ding.

Now for a drink, my friends. But what land do you come from?'

'From Touraine,' Panurge replied.

'Then you were certainly not hatched by a wretch among magpies,' said the Aedituus, 'since you come from the favoured land of Touraine. So many, many good things reach us annually from Touraine that (as we were told one day by some folk from there who were passing through) the Duc de Touraine has not enough left from all his income to eat his fill of bacon; that is because of the excessive bounty of his forebears, who bestowed upon his sacrosanct birds enough to provide us here with a surfeit of pheasants, partridges, pullets, turkeys and fat Loudun capons, with all sorts of venison and game of all sorts.

'Let us drink, my friends. Just look at this perch-load of birds: see how downy they are and plump from the income arising from our remittances from over yonder. And they sing well for it. You never saw skylarks warbling away in the plain as they do here whenever they espy two gilded banner-staves . . .'

'Ah!' said Frère Jean, 'a feast! With banners!'

'. . . and when I ring those fat bells there which you can see suspended over their cages. Let us drink, my friends. It is certainly a nice day for a drink. But so is every day. Let us drink. I toast you all with a good heart: you are most welcome. And never fear that food and drink might run out, for even if the sky be brass and the Earth be iron, still we would never be short of something to live on, not for seven years, nay for eight; longer than that famine in Egypt. Let us drink together, in harmony and charity.'

'What ease you enjoy in this world, you devils!' Panurge exclaimed. 'And we shall have even more in the next,' replied the Aedituus. 'At the very least we shall not lack the Elysian Fields. Drink up, my friends. And I drink to you person-ally.'

'It was,' I said, 'a most sacred and perfect mind in the original Siticines which found the means for you to enjoy what all humans naturally aspire to but which is vouchsafed to few – nay, strictly speaking, to none: that is, to have Paradise in this life and in the next one too:

> O blessèd folk! O demi-gods!
> Lord! If only it came to me!'

How Panurge related to Maître Aedituus the fable of the war-horse and the ass

CHAPTER 7

[Platonists make ignorance the source of all evil. But these islanders are no Platonists: they are a parody of the Religious, their life is controlled by their regular services and their copious meals.

The chapter includes a delightful fable; perhaps the best-written pages in the entire Fifth Book.

The phrase 'in less time than it takes to cook asparagus' is an expression of the Emperor Augustus (Suetonius, The Lives of the Twelve Caesars, 2, 87).]

Once we had drunk to the full and eaten our fill, the Aedituus brought us into a gilded chamber, well furnished and hung with fine tapestries. He then had us served with myrobalans, a pot of balm and some green preserved-ginger, together with plenty of hippocras and delightful wine. He invited us by means of such antidotes to cast into oblivion and indifference the strains we had undergone at sea, forgetting them all as though with a draft from the waters of Lethe. He also had an abundance of victuals delivered to our ships which were riding in the harbour.

Only then did we settle down for the night, but I could not sleep because of the sempiternal clanging of the bells.

At midnight the Aedituus woke us up for a drink. He was himself the first to have one, and then spoke to us:

'You folk from the other world say that Ignorance is the mother of all evil. And you say truly. Yet you by no means banish her for ever from your minds: you live in her, with her, through her. That is why, day in and day out, so many evils beset you. You are ever complaining, ever lamenting, never satisfied. I can see that even now. For it is Ignorance that keeps you tied to your bed (as the god of War was tied by Vulcan's art): you do not realize that it was your duty to be abstemious with your sleep but never abstemious with the good things of this famous isle. By now you should already have eaten three meals. Believe you me: to eat the foods of this Ringing Island you must get up betimes. Eat them, and they multiply: spare them, and they shrivel. Scythe grass in good season, it comes back all the thicker: never scythe it, in a few years all is carpeted with moss.

'Let us drink, my friends. All of us. The skinniest of our birds are all ringing for us now: if you like we will drink them a toast. Let us drink one, two, three, nine rounds: not with zeal but in charity.'

At the break of day he likewise woke us up again to eat prime-time bread-and-dripping. After that we had only one meal: it lasted all day! I never knew whether it was lunch, dinner, supper or a bite before bedtime. However, we went for strolls over that isle for the next few days to amuse ourselves and listen to the merry song of those favoured birds.

One evening Panurge said to the Aedituus:

'Don't be offended if I tell you, sir, an amusing story of something which happened twenty-three moons ago in the countryside round Châtellerault.

'One morning in the month of April the groom of a certain nobleman was walking his war-horses through the meadows. There he encountered a happy shepherdess keeping watch over her little lambkins 'neath the shade of a little bush. Over an ass and a goat too. He chatted to her, persuading her to get up behind on the crupper to visit his stables and enjoy a nice little country-style bite there. While they were still chattering, the war-horse turned to the ass and said in its ear (the beasts in some places could talk to each other the whole of that year):

'"You poor wretched little donkey. For you I feel pity and compassion. You work hard every day: I can tell that from that rub under your crupper-belt. A good thing too, for God made you for the service of human kind. You are, fellow, a good little donkey. But it does seem a bit tyrannical and unreasonable to me when I see you never sponged down, always poorly curry-combed, poorly caparisoned and poorly fed. Your coat looks like bristles all dirty and shiny. You eat nothing but rushes, thorns and prickly thistles. That is why I summon you, donkey, to pick your way after me and see how we (whom Nature has made for war) are treated and cared for. You will not fail, fellow, to see how I normally live."

'"Indeed, Sir Horse, I will willingly come," the ass replied.

'"In your position you should say, Sir Steed," said the steed.

'"I beg your pardon, Sir Steed," said the ass, "but us village rustics is often wrong and uncouth in our speech.

'"While on the subject, I will willingly obey you, Sir, and follow you – that is, since it pleases you, Sir, to vouchsafe me such an honour, but at a distance for fear of blows: my hide is all quilted with blows."

'The shepherdess mounted and the ass followed after, firmly intending to have a good feed once they had reached the stables. The groom noticed the ass and ordered the stable-lads to greet it with their pitchforks and belabour it with their cudgels. The ass, upon hearing those words, entrusted itself to the god Neptune and began to scamper away with all speed, thinking and arguing to itself:

'"He put it well. My estate is not to follow the courts of great lords: Nature made me merely to help poor folk. Aesop warned me about it in one of his fables. It was presumptuous of me: there's no remedy for me today but to scamper off in less time than it takes to cook asparagus."

'And off trots that ass, breaking wind, bouncing about, kicking its heels and letting off farts.

THE FIFTH BOOK OF PANTAGRUEL

'The shepherdess, on seeing the ass making off, told the
groom it was hers and begged him to treat it well, otherwise
she would leave at once and go on no further. The groom then
commanded that the horses should go without oats for a week
rather than the ass not eat its fill. The hardest thing was to
summon it back, for the stable-lads vainly called and cajoled it:
"Here, donkey; hee-haw donkey."

'"I'm not going to come," said the ass, "I'm too lowly."

'The more kindly they called it, the more wildly it flayed
about, kicking up its heels and farting. They would still be at
it, were it not for the shepherdess who told them that they
should call to it while holding up a sieve full of oats. Which
was done.

'Suddenly the ass faced about saying:

'"For oats I votes; for pitchforks, no. I don't say, *Pass, no
trumps*."

'And so it went over to them, singing harmoniously: it is, as
you know, nice to hear the musical tones of those beasts from
Arcady!

'Once it had come over, they led it next to the war-horse in
the stable. It was rubbed down and sponged, curried and supplied with fresh litter up to its belly and a manger full of oats.
And while the stable-lads were sieving the oats, it lay back its
ears, trying to let them know that it would eat the oats only
too well without any sieving, and that so great an honour did
not become him.

'Once they had both fed, the horse questioned the ass, saying:

'"How are things going for you now, you poor old donkey?
What do you think of such treatment, eh? Yet you didn't want
to come! What have you got to say now?"

'The ass replied:

'"By the fig which one of our forebears ate and so made
Philemon die of laughter, this, Sir Steed, is pure balm. And yet
we are having but half a good time. Do you gentlemen-horses
never, hm, ass about?"

'"What do you mean, donkey, by assing about?" retorted
the horse.

'"Strangullion strike you, donkey! Do you take me for an ass too?"

'"Haw, haw," replied the ass; "I find it hard to learn the courtly language of horses. I mean, do you gentlemen-stallions never, hmm, act the stallion?"

'"Shush, you ass!" said the horse, "If the stable-lads hear you they'll give you such a drubbing with their pitchforks that you'll never again desire to ass about. We in here never dare to get a stiff on for fear of a beating, not even at the tip, not even to urinate. Apart from that, snug as kings."

'"By the pommel of the pack-saddle which I bear," said the ass, "I renounce you, fellow, and say pooh to your litter, pooh to your hay and pooh to your oats. Long live the thistles out in the fields, since there you can stud-it as much as you like. Feed less and cover away: that's my motto. It's hay and fodder to us! O, Sir Steed, my good friend, if only you had seen us at the fairs, my lad, when we're holding our provincial chapter, covering away while our mistresses are selling their chicks and their goslings!"

'At that they parted.

'I have spoken.'

Whereupon Panurge held his peace and uttered not a word more. Pantagruel urged him to end with the moral but the Aedituus retorted:

'One word's enough for the wise. I know well enough what you mean to say and infer by that fable of the ass and the horse. But you are shameless. There's nothing like that for you here, you know. Never mention it again.'

'And yet,' said Panurge, 'I recently met a white-feathered Abbégesse whom I'd rather bestride than lead by the bridle. And if the others are *dain-oiseaux* – young bucks of birds – then she looks to me like a *daine-moiselle* – a doe-bird – I mean an attractive one, a pretty one, well worth a sin or two. God forgive me, but I wasn't thinking any evil: may the evil I was thinking come quick to me now!'

How, with much difficulty, we were shown a Popinjay

CHAPTER 8

[The travellers meet a pope-bird.

Erasmus similarly links Pluto's helmet and Gyges' ring, both of which could render the wearer invisible (Adages, II, X, LXXIX, 'The helmet of Orcus', where Orcus is Pluto).

'Gyges' ring' was widely known from Plato, Cicero and Lucian's Double Indictment (or De Votis).

See also Adages, II, VII, XC, 'Thunder in a basin'. It applied to ineffectual menaces.

Nobody seems to know who Michel de Mâcon was.

One variant reading from the Isle Sonante is preferred: on the mitre (that is mitre, rather than moitié, half or middle).]

The third day, like the first two, were spent on the same feasting and dining. On that third day Pantagruel earnestly pressed to see the Popinjay but the Aedituus replied that it did not allow itself to be seen as easily as all that.

'How then?' asked Pantagruel. 'To make itself invisible does it have Pluto's helmet on its head, Gyges' ring upon its claws, or a chameleon upon its breast?'

'Not so,' replied the Aedituus, 'but it is a little difficult to see by its very nature. Yet, if it can be done, I shall arrange for you to be able to see it.'

Having said that, he left us there chomping away.

Coming back a quarter of an hour later, he told us that the Popinjay was visible at that time and led us discreetly and silently straight to the cage in which it was squatting accompanied by two little Cardingoths and six gross fat Bishogoths. Panurge closely examined its form, gestures and bearing. Then he loudly exclaimed:

'Damn the beast! It looks like a hoopoe-bird!'

'Shush,' said the Aedituus. 'For God's sake. As Michel de Mâcon pointed out wisely: *It has ears.*'

'So does a hoopoe,' said Panurge.

'If ever it hears you blaspheming like that, you're done for, good people. Do you see that basin in its cage? There issues from it thunder, thunderbolts, lightning, devils and tempests, by which you would be swallowed up a hundred feet below ground.'

'It would better,' said Frère Jean, 'to drink and to feast.' Panurge, gazing at the Popinjay and its suite, remained abstracted until he noticed a Madge-owl hidden under its cage. He then exclaimed:

'By God's might! We're being badly lured and allured by a barrelful of lures! By God there is some gulling, lulling and mulling going on in this manor. Just look at that Madge-owl there. This is blue murder!'

'Shush, for God's sake,' said the Aedituus. 'That is no Madge-owl: it is a male, a noble Church-treasury-Owl.'

'Yes,' said Pantagruel, 'but do get the Popinjay to sing us something so that we can hear how harmonious it is.'

'It sings only by its Hours,' replied the Aedituus, 'and it eats only by its Hours too.'

'Well I don't!' said Panurge. 'All hours are good for me. So let's go and drink to each other.'

'At this hour you are talking correctly,' said the Aedituus. 'Talk like that and you'll never be a heretic. Let's go. I share your opinion.'

On our way back to our potations we perceived an ancient green-headed Bishogoth squatting down in the company of some merry Protonotary-Birds which were snoring in an arbour. Near by perched a pretty Abbégesse, which twittered happily away: we took such pleasure in her song that we wished that all our limbs were turned into ears so as to lose nothing of it and to be in no wise distracted by anything else, concentrating on it alone.

Panurge said:

'That beautiful Abbégesse is splitting her temples by the force of her singing while that ugly, fat old Bishogoth goes on snoring. I'll soon get it singing too, in the name of all the devils.'

With that he struck a bell hanging over its cage, but however hard he did so, it never sang but snored all the more.

'By God, you old buzzard,' said Panurge, 'I shall find some other way to make you sing!'

Then, picking up a big stone, he went to strike it on its mitre, but the Aedituus cried out:

'Worthy fellow: beat, batter, kill and slaughter all the kings and princes of the world as you please – by treachery, poison or any other means – or dislodge the angels out of their nests in Heaven: for that, the Popinjay will grant you pardons. But never touch these holy birds if you value the life, well-being and happiness of you, your friends and relations, living or dead: even those born to them hereafter would all suffer for the deed. Consider well that basin.'

'It would be better, then,' said Panurge, 'to drink to each other and have a feast.'

'He puts it well, does Monsieur Antitus,' said Frère Jean. 'When looking at these diabolical birds here we do nothing but blaspheme: when emptying your bottles and wine-jars we do nothing but praise God. So let's drink to one another. O, what a nice saying!'

On the third day the Aedituus (after a drink, of course) granted us our congee. We made him a present of a lovely little penknife from Perche: he was even more delighted with it than Artaxerxes was with the glass of water given him by a peasant. And he thanked us courteously. To our ships he despatched fresh supplies of all sorts of provisions; he wished us a pleasant journey and a safe return at the end of our enterprises, and made us promise *by Jupiter Stone*[8] that our return journey would be via his territories. And in conclusion he said:

'Friends, you should note that, in this world, there are more bollocks than men. Keep that in mind.'

---

8. By Jupiter-stone was a Latin oath. But *pierre* (stone, rock) plays on the name of Peter, whose successor the pope claims to be. At all events the papal Peter thunders like Jove, but since it is from a basin, ineffectually, as in Erasmus's adage, 'To thunder in a basin'.

How we landed upon the Island of Ironmongery

CHAPTER 9

[A chapter partly inspired by the Disciple de Pantagruel. *There is also a debt to Plutarch's* Natural Questions, *1, 1.*

Compare and contrast the plants with hair (roots) in the soil with the fable of Physis *and* Antiphysie *in the Chapter 32 of the* Fourth Book.]*

Our stomachs once properly ballasted, we had the wind astern, and with the mizzen-mainsail hoisted we docked in less than two days at the Isle of Ironmongery: a desert isle, totally uninhabited. There we saw many trees bringing forth mattocks, pickaxes, hoes, scythes, sickles, spades, trowels, hatchets, pruning-hooks, saws, coopers' adzes, pruning-shears, secateurs, pincers, shovels, bradawls, braces and bits.

Other trees bore short daggers, poniards, Venetian stilettos, pen-knives, awls, swords, rapiers, wood-knives, scimitars, tucks, quarrels and carving-knives.

Anyone who wanted any of them needed only to shake the tree and they would come tumbling down like plums. Moreover, as they fell to the ground, they encountered a species of grass called scabbard, into which they sheathed themselves.

But you had to look out to see that they did not drop on your head, feet or other parts of the body when they fell, for they dropped point downwards (so as to run straight into their sheathes) and could do you great harm.

Under some unknown trees I saw certain kinds of plants which grew into pikes, lances, javelins, halberds, boar-spears, partisans, claws, pitchforks and spears: grown tall, they touch against the trees and encounter blades (or sharp-edges), each according to its kind. The trees above them have blades ready for them once they grow tall enough to reach them, just as you have vests ready for little babes when you decide to take them out of their swaddling-clothes.

And so that you do not in future judge the opinions of Plato,

Anaxagoras and Democritus abhorrent – were they minor philosophers? – those trees seemed to us to be earthly animals, not distinct from beasts in having no skin, fat, flesh, veins, arteries, ligaments, sinews, cartilages, adenes, bones, marrow, humours, matrices, brain and recognized articulations, for they do indeed have them, as Theophrastus clearly demonstrates, but in that they have their heads – their trunks, that is – down in the soil with their hair (that is, their roots) while their feet (that is, their branches) are up above, as when a man stands on his head and plays the forked oak.

And just as you Syphilitics can feel well ahead the onset of rain, wind or calm and every change in the weather in your sciatic legs and shoulder-blades, so they too, in their roots, radicles, sap and marrow, have a presentiment of what sort of handles are growing beneath them and prepare the appropriate blades (or sharp-edges) for them. It is true that in every thing save God mistakes sometimes occur: Nature herself is not exempt, as when she brings forth monstrosities and deformed beasts. I noticed some mistakes made by those trees too:

– the bottom half of a pike growing high into the air beneath those ironmongery-trees, encountered, on reaching their branches, not a blade but a besom: still, it would do for sweeping chimneys;

– a partisan encountered shears: but it can be put to good use: it can help rid a garden of caterpillars;

– the staff of a halberd encountered the blade of a scythe and looked like an hermaphrodite: it will serve a turn as a sickle.

A fine thing it is to have faith in God.

As we were returning to our ships, I saw some people or other, behind some sort of bush, doing something or other, somehow sharpening some sort of weapons which they had managed to get hold of somehow, somewhere.

How Pantagruel arrived at an island called Cheating

CHAPTER 10

[The gambling is primarily that of swindlers at dice, a sport condemned by many Renaissance moralists, since lots were the domain of God. The numbers on dice attributed to deities by the ancient Greek sages including the Pythagoreans are known through Plutarch (Isis and Osiris, 354 D–355 A).

The text uses a form 'Sang vréal' for the Holy Grail, presumably a distortion of Rabelais' 'Cratylic' form 'sangréal' met in the Fourth Book *(Chapters 42 and 43), where the* sangréal *of the Chidlings is mustard, and of the Ruachites, wind. Here it is perhaps some sort of scraggy object of veneration appropriate to gamblers, treated with as much respect as the key manuscript of the* Pandects *treasured in Florence, or the Veronica (the cloth said to bear the imprint of the face of Jesus). Compare the antics here with those of Bishop Homenaz unveiling the portrait of the 'Idea' of a pope at the beginning of Chapter 50 of the* Fourth Book.

'Put-a-good-face-on-it' renders Bonne-Mine, *the wife of* Mauvais-Jeu *(Bad-throw).]*

Leaving astern the Isle of Ironmongery, we sailed next day to an island called Cheating, the very Idea of Fontainebleau, for the soil there is so thin that its bones – its rocks that is – poke through its skin; it is sandy, sterile, unhealthy and nasty.

There our pilot pointed out to us two small cubic rocks with eight equal angles. From their appearance they seemed to me to be of alabaster or else covered with snow, but he assured us that they were of knuckle-bone. Within them, he said, was the dark, six-storeyed mansion of the Twenty Devils of Hazard so dreaded in our lands. Amongst which he called the greatest couple of twins, Double-Sixes; the smallest, Double-Ones; the other middling couples, Double-Fives, Double-Fours, Double-Threes and Double-Twos. He called the others Six-Five, Six-Four, Six-Three, Six-Two and Six-One; Five-Four, Five-Three, and so on, consecutively.

I observed at that point that in all the world few ever cast dice without invoking devils, for when they throw two dice on to the table they devoutly cry, 'Darling Double-Six!' – that's the Great Devil – 'Sweet Double-One!' – that's the Tiny Devil – 'Dear little Four-Two', and so on for all the others, invoking them by their personal and family names, indeed not simply invoking them but calling themselves their friends and familiar spirits. When summoned, they admittedly do not come at once, but they have an excuse: they were somewhere else already, having a prior engagement with those who had already invoked them. So you must never say that they have no ears or senses. They do have them: fine ones, I can tell you.

He then informed us that there had been more shipwrecks and disasters around and along those cube-shaped rocks, with greater loss of life and treasure, than around all the Syrtes, Charybdes, Sirens, Scyllas, Strophades and deeps of the sea. I readily believed him, recalling that, formerly amongst the sages of Egypt, Neptune was represented in their hieroglyphics by the prime cube, as was Apollo by the One, Diana by the Deuce, Minerva by the Seven, etc.

He added that there was also a flask of *Sang vréal*, a thing divine, known to but a few. Panurge, by his fine prayers, prevailed upon the local Sindics to show it to us, which was done however with thrice more ceremonial and solemnity than when they display the Pandects of Justinian in Florence or the Veronica in Rome: never had I seen so many pieces of sendal-cloth, so many torches, tapers and jiggery-pokeries. What we were eventually shown was the visage of a roasted rabbit! We saw nothing else worth remembering there except for Put-a-good-face-on-it, the wife of Bad-throw, and for the shells of two eggs laid of yore and hatched by Leda, from which sprung Castor and Pollux, the brothers of fair Helen. The Sindics swapped a small bit of those shells for some bread.

At our departure we purchased a barrel-load of swindlers' caps and bonnets: I doubt that we shall make much profit from their sale, and I believe that those who buy them will make even less when they wear them.

How we sailed by Wicket-Gate, where dwells
Catty-claws, the Archduke of the Furry Scribble-cats

CHAPTER II

[A particularly harsh satire of a whole system of justice, with its grasping legal officials and their corrupt values.

'Catty-claws' renders Grippe-minaud. *'Furry Scribble-cats' renders* Chats-fourrés. *There is play on words:* Chats fourrés *(Furry cats) and* chaffourer *(to scribble, scrabble up paper).*

'Wicket-gate' suggests the prison gate.

The translation follows the text of Demerson. (Several variants, not noted here, between the Isle Sonante and the manuscript have the effect of suppressing any mention of the 'Isle of Procuration' and the 'Chicanous'.

A 'serargeant-at-law' (a portmanteau word) is a grasping serjeant, *a legal official who* serre argent *(clutches money).*

The furs suggests rich ermine robes.

The satire here may be compared with that of Clément Marot in L'Enfer.]

From there we passed Condemnation, which is another completely desert island. Then we sailed to the Isle of Wicket-Gate, where Pantagruel refused go ashore. He did well, for we were arrested – taken prisoner by order of Catty-claws, the Archduke of the Furry Scribble-cats – because one of our band had tried to sell swindlers' hats to a *serargeant-at-law*.

Those Furry Scribble-cats are the most horrifying and terrifying of animals. They eat little children and feed off slabs of marble. Don't you think, Drinkers, that they deserve to have their noses put out? Their fur never grows out from their hides but lies hidden. Each and every one of them sports an open game-bag as his symbol and device, but not all in the same way. Some wear it slung scarf-wise from their necks; others, against their bums, across their guts or at their sides, all for sound professional reasons. They all have claws which are very long, strong and sharp so that nothing escapes them once they get it in their clutches. Some cover their heads with square-caps each with four gutters (or codpieces); others, with caps sporting turned-up brims; others, with square-cornered mortar-boards; others, with mortar-like caparisons. As we went into their lair a beggar from the hospice to whom we had given half-a-testoon, said to us:

'God grant, Good Folk, that you get out of here safely. Consider well the facial expressions of those valiant pillaging-pillars, those flying buttresses of Cattyclavian justice. And take note, that if you live for six Olympiads plus the age of two curs, you will find those Furry Scribble-cats have become lords of all Europe, calm possessors of all the goods and properties contained therein (unless all the goods and income unjustly acquired by them do not, by divine punishment, suddenly perish).

'Take that from a beggar, and take it well.

'Amongst them reigns the Sixth Essence, by means of which they grab everything, devour everything and beshit everything; they burn, batter, behead, slaughter, imprison, ruin and destroy everything before them without any distinction between good and evil. For amongst them vice is called virtue, and wickedness is dubbed goodness; treachery, fealty; and larceny, liberality. Pillaging is their watch-word, and, when done by them, pillaging is adjudged good by every human (except the heretics). And they do all the above by sovereign and unshakable authority.

'As a sign witnessing to my prophecy you will notice that the mangers therein are set *above* the stable-racks. One of these days you may be recalling that. And, should there ever be plagues, famines, wars, floods, cataclysms, conflagrations or disasters in this world, do not attribute them – do not refer them – to the conjunctions of maleficent planets, to the abuses of the Roman curia, to the tyranny of the kings and princes of this world, to the deceits of the black-beetles and false prophets, to the iniquities of usurers, coiners, clippers of testoons, nor to the ignorance, imprudence and impudence of physicians, surgeons and apothecaries, nor yet to the perverted deeds of adulterous, poisoning or infanticidal women: attribute the lot to a destructiveness which surpasses words and to an unbelievable, immeasurable wickedness which is ever being forged and effected in the workshop of those Furry Catty-claws; yet it is no more understood by the world than is the Jewish Cabbala; that is why it is not loathed nor set to rights and punished as by reason it should be. But if it is ever revealed one day to the people and made evident to them, then there has never been an orator so eloquent as by his art to prevent them – nor any law so rigorous and draconian as by fear of retribution to contain them, nor any magistrate so powerful as to restrain them – from grimly burning them alive in their burrows. Their very own children, the Furry Scribble-kittens and their other relatives hold them in revulsion and abomination.

'That explains why, just as Hannibal received from Hamilcar his father the command, sealed by a binding religious oath, to fight the Romans as long as he lived, I too likewise received from my late father an injunction to abide here outside, waiting for Heaven's thunderbolt to fall upon those within and reduce them to ashes (as new sacrilegious Titans fighting against the Divine) since human beings have bodies so inured that they cannot register, feel nor predict the harm that has been done, is being done, and will be done among them; or, if they do feel it, they either cannot or will not destroy them.'

'What's all this!' said Panurge. 'Ah! No! No! By God I'm not going in there. Let's turn back. For God's sake, I say, turn back.

> That noble tramp caused me to fear and wonder,
> Far more than when in autumn heavens thunder.'

On our return we found the gate closed; they told us that it was as easy to get in there as into Avernus: the hard thing was to get out again; we could in no wise do so without a permit and a discharge from those present, for this sole reason: *It's one thing to quit a fair and quite another a market*: and in law we were *pedepulverosi*.[9]

9.   *Pedepulverosi*, the 'Dusty-footed', were in law a class of travellers subject
      to summary jurisdiction. Just above there is an echo of Virgil, *Aeneid*, 6,
      126, 'facilis discensus Averno' (the descent to Avernus – the underworld,
      'Hell' – is easy).

The worst was to come when we passed through the wicket-gate: in order to obtain our permits and discharges we were brought before the most horrid monster ever described. He was called Catty-claws. I could best compare him to a chimera, a sphinx and a Cerberus, or else to that figure of Osiris as the Egyptians portrayed him, having three heads joined together, namely those of a roaring lion, a fawning dog and a yawning wolf, entwined about by a snake biting its own tail, with shimmering rays all round it.[10]

His hands were dripping with blood; his claws were those of a harpy; his snout, like the crow's-bill lancet of a surgeon, his fangs, like a wild boar in its fourth year; his eyes, aflame like the mouth of Hell bedecked with mortars all criss-crossed by pestles. Nothing showed but his claws. The bench on which he sat with the Feral Cats his assessors, consisted of a brand-new fodder-rack, *above* which, just as the beggar had told us, were set, back to front, beautiful and capacious mangers. Above the principal seat hung the portrait of an old crone wearing glasses on her nose and holding the sheath of a sickle in her right hand and a pair of scales in her left. The pans of those scales consisted of two velvet game-bags: one, weighed down, was full of coins; the other, empty, was raised high above the pivot. It was, in my opinion, the symbol of Cattyclavian justice, quite different from the practice of the ancient Thebans, who raised statues to their judges and Dicasts only once they were dead, statues made, according to their merits, of gold, silver and marble, but all without hands.[11]

When we were brought before them some people or other, all bedizened with game-bags and bundles full of big, ragged, old parchments, made us sit down on a low stool.

Panurge said, 'Well now, my friends, you scabby vagabonds. I am much better standing: such stools are too low for a man wearing new breeches and a short doublet.'

'You sit down there!' they replied. 'Let us not have to tell

10.   Cf. Macrobius, *Saturnalia*, I 20 I 3. (The snake biting its tail was an Egyptian hieroglyph for eternity.)
11.   This is a borrowing from Plutarch's *On Isis and Osiris*, 10, 355 A.

you again. If you fail to answer properly, the earth will gape
open this instant and swallow you alive.'

How a riddle was propounded to us by Catty-claws

CHAPTER 12

[In the original much play is made here on the repeated ejaculation
Orça (Now then!) which is taken to be a lawyer's cry actually meaning
not so much 'Now then!' but 'Gold here!' ('gold' in French being or).
In the translation that repeated play on words is rendered by 'For
Gold's sake!' (modelled on 'For God's sake!'). The reply, 'Good Gold!'
has a similar force.

Maidens late abed on Holy Innocents' Day were given a spanking.]

Once we had sat down, Catty-claws, amidst his Furry-cats,
addressed us in an angry raucous voice: 'For Gold's sake! For
Gold's sake! For Gold's sake! . . .'

– 'For drink's sake! For drink's sake!' Panurge muttered
between his teeth –

> 'A tender maiden, blonde and neat,
> An Ethiop son, without a man,
> Did drop: 'twas painless. Quite a feat:
> Bit through her flank as vipers can.
> O'er hill and dale he quickly ran
> (Once pierced impatiently her side.)
> Then confidently far and wide
> He clove the air, he walked the earth.
> A lover of wisdom, terrified,
> Judged him a human being worth.

'Now answer me, for Gold's sake! And, for Gold's sake solve
that riddle at once!'

'Good Gold!' I replied, 'if I had a sphinx at home, Good
Gold! as one of your predecessors, Verres did, then, Good Gold!

I could, Good Gold! resolve that riddle; but I have never even been there and am, Good Gold! quite innocent of the deed.'

'For Gold's sake!' said Catty-claws; 'if that is all you have to say, I shall demonstrate to you (for Gold's sake! by the Styx, since you will say nothing else!) that it would have been better for you to have fallen into the paws of Lucifer and all his devils than into these talons of ours, for Gold's sake! Don't you, for Gold's sake! realize that you wretched man? You plead your innocence, for Gold's sake! as though that merits your escaping from our tortures, for Gold's sake! Our laws are like spiders' webs, for Gold's sake! For silly flies and little butterflies are caught in them, for Gold's sake! whilst the big, evil-doing horse-flies, break them and pass through them, for Gold's sake! We, for Gold's sake! likewise never go in search of important thieves and oppressors. They are too hard on our stomachs, for Gold's sake! and would, for Gold's sake! do us an injury. Now you nice little innocents will get an Innocents-day spanking for Gold's sake! The great Devil himself, for Gold's sake!, will chant you a Mass, for Gold's sake!'

Frère Jean could not abide the discourse of Catty-claws and said, 'Hey! You My-lord-the-devil-in-robes, how do you think he can answer a point he knows nothing about! Aren't you satisfied with the truth?'

'Oh, for Gold's sake!' said Catty-claws. 'Never in all my reign has anyone spoken, for Gold's sake! without being first interrogated by us. Who untied this crazy loon?' –

'You are lying,' muttered Frère Jean without moving his lips.

– 'Do you think you are in the groves of Academe, for Gold's sake! with idle hunters and seekers after Truth! We have better things to do, for Gold's sake! Here, for Gold's sake! you give categorical answers about things you do *not* know. You must, for Gold's sake! confess to having done things which you, for Gold's, sake! have *not* done. You must allege, for Gold's sake! that you know things you have *never* been told of. Here, however angry, you must suffer things quietly, for Gold's sake! Here we pluck the goose, for Gold's sake! without letting it squeal. You, fellow, speak without procuration: I can see that well enough, for Gold's sake! And may that nasty quartan fever of yours, for Gold's sake, *marry* you, for Gold's sake!'

'Marry off monks, would you,' exclaimed Frère Jean, 'by the devils, arch-devils, proto-devils and pan-devils! Ho, hu; ho, hoo. I take you for a heretic.'

How Panurge solved the riddle of Catty-claws

CHAPTER 13

[The bribes which lawyers and judges openly expected were known as spices *(épices). All these legal men love their spices and are avid for gold, not justice.]*

Catty-claws, affecting not to hear that remark, addressed Panurge, saying:

'For Gold's sake, you big-head, for Gold's sake! Have you got nothing to say, for Gold's sake?'

Panurge replied:

'I can clearly see, Good Gold, by the devil! that the plague lurks for us in here, since here, Good Gold by the devil! innocence is not safe and the devil sings Masses. Allow me, I beg you, to pay for the lot, and then let us go, Good Gold by the devil! I can stand no more, Good Gold by the devil!'

'Go?' said Catty-claws. 'Why, for the last three hundred years nobody, for Gold's sake! has ever got away, for Gold's sake! without leaving his hair behind or more often his hide. Why, for Gold's sake! that would be tantamount to saying, for Gold's sake! that the folk brought before us here were unjustly summonsed for Gold's sake! and unjustly treated. You are wretched enough already for Gold's sake! but will be even more so, for Gold's sake! if you fail to solve the riddle propounded to you. What, for Gold's sake! does it mean?'

'It means, replied Panurge, 'Good Gold, by the devil! a black weevil born of a white bean via the hole it pierced by its gnawing, Good Gold by the devil! which weevil (Good Gold, by the devil!) sometimes flies, sometimes crawls along the ground. For which – Good gold, by the devil! – it was deemed by Pythagoras, who was the first lover of wisdom (which is what *philosopher* means in Greek) to have received a human soul by metempsychosis, Good Gold, by the devil! If you fellows were human – Good Gold, by the devil! – your souls after your nasty deaths would, according to his opinion – Good Gold, by the devil! – enter into the bodies of weevils. For in this life you gnaw at everything, eat everything; while in the life to come,

> You will gnaw and eat like vipers
> The very flanks of your mothers.

Good Gold, by the devil there!'

'Bothy of God!' said Frère Jean, 'I could wish with all my heart that the hole in my bum should become such a bean and be nibbled all round by such weevils!'

Those words once said, Panurge tossed into the middle of the courtroom a fat leather purse stuffed with Sun-crowns. At the chinking of that purse all the Furry-cats began to play on their claws as on out-of-tune fiddles. And they all cried out in a loud voice, 'Those are our spices! It was a very good lawsuit, well spiced and succulent. These folk are all right.'

'Gold, that is,' said Panurge. 'Good Sun-crowns.'

'The Court,' said Catty-claws, 'so understands. Good Gold! hmm; Good Gold! hmm; Good Gold! hmm! Off you go, my lads – Good Gold! hmm – and pass Beyond: we are, Good Gold! hmm! more blackish than devilish, Good Gold! hmm, Good Gold! hmm! Good Gold! hmm!'

Leaving by the wicket-gate, we were conducted as far as the port by certain highland Clawyers. There, before we boarded our ships, they warned us that we could not set sail until we had first bestowed lordly presents on Dame Catty-claws and all the female Furry-cats; otherwise they had been commissioned to march us back to the wicket-gate.

'Pooh!' said Frère Jean, 'we shall draw aside and dig into our coffers and make them all happy.'

'But,' said the serving-lads, 'don't forget a tip to buy wine for us poor devils!'

'The wine of poor devils is never forgotten,' replied Frère Jean. 'In all lands and in all seasons it is ever remembered.'

How the Furry-cats live by corruption

CHAPTER 14

[In the still-dominant physics of Aristotle, generation and corruption are twin concepts, succeeding each other. For Rabelais in Pantagruel, *Chapter 8, they will remain until the end of the Age, when Christ returns his Kingdom to God the Father.]*

Those words were not all out of his mouth before Frère Jean perceived sixty-eight galleys and frigates coming into harbour. At which he quickly ran to ask for news and to learn what merchandise the vessels were laden with. He saw they had a cargo of venison, hares, capons, pigeons, pigs, kids, plovers, pullets, ducks, teal, goslings and other kinds of game. Amongst them he also saw several rolls of cloth: velvet, satin and damask. He asked the seafarers where they were bringing such dainty items from, and to whom. They answered that it was for Catty-claws, the Furry-Toms and the Furry-Tabbies.

'What do you call those soothing things,' asked Frère Jean.

'Corruption,' the seafarers replied.

'They live by corruption: they will perish, then, by generation!' said Frère Jean. 'By the might of God, this is how things now stand: their forebears gobbled up the good noblemen (who, as befitted their estate, practised hawking and hunting so as to develop their skills for war and be inured to its hardships; for hunting is a simulacrum of war, and Xenophon was simply telling the truth when he wrote that all good leaders in war came forth from hunting as from the Trojan Horse. I'm no scholar but so I've been told, and I believe it.) After the death of those noblemen their souls, according to the opinion of Catty-claws, enter into wild boars, stags, roebucks, herons, partridges and other such beasts which they had always liked and hunted during their first lives, so these Furry-cats, once they have ruined and swallowed up the noblemen's châteaux, lands, demesnes, possessions, rents and revenues, then go after their blood and souls in that other life.

'What a noble beggar that was who warned us of that fact from the sight of their mangers set *above* the hay-racks.'

'That's all very well,' said Panurge to the travellers, 'but the criers have proclaimed in the name of the Great King that no one, on pain of hanging, should kill stags, does, wild-boars or roebucks.'

'True enough,' replied one of them on behalf of them all, 'but the Great King is courteous and kind, whereas those Furry-cats are madly ravenous for Christian blood, so we have less to fear from offending the Great King and more to hope for from sustaining the Furry-cats through such corruption, especially since Catty-claws himself is marrying off one of his Furred Tabby-kittens to a gross, well-lined Tom. In days gone by we used to call them mere munchers-of-hay; nowadays we call them munchers of hare, partridge, woodcock, pheasant, pullet, roebuck, rabbit and pork. On no other fodder are they fed.'

'Oh pooh! pooh!!' said Frère Jean. 'Next year they shall be termed Turd-munchers, Squitter-munchers, Shit-munchers. Will you trust what I say?'

'Yes, indeed,' the band replied.

'Then let us do two things,' he said. 'First, let's appropriate all that game over there. I'm fed up with salted meats: they overheat my hypochondria. I mean we should pay well for it.

'Secondly: let's go back to the wicket-gate and strip all those devilish Furry-cats!'

'Without fail I shall not go,' said Panurge. 'I am timorous by nature.'

How Frère Jean des Entommeures plans to strip the Furry-cats

CHAPTER 15

[Eurystheus (a grandson of Perseus) was commanded by Juno to impose upon Hercules his twelve labours.

Jupiter appeared to Semele with thunder and lightning (which killed her).

The first mother of Bacchus was Semele; his second mother was Jupiter's thigh, Bacchus having been sewn up in it until he was delivered.

There are echoes of a widely known saying of Horace, listed in the Adages of Erasmus: II, X, XXV, 'A wall of brass'.

Mounts Calpe and Abila are on either side of the straits of Hercules (of Gibraltar).

The name of the 'Subtle Doctor', Duns Scotus, allows of a hidden pun on paying one's scot.]

'By the power of my cloth,' said Frère Jean, 'what sort of voyage are we sailing on here? It's a voyage of men with the runs! All we do is break wind, fart, defecate, fantasize and do nothing. Body of God! it's not in my character. Unless I've done some heroic deed by day I can't sleep at nights. Did you bring me along on this voyage as your companion, merely to sing Mass and to hear confessions! Balm Sunday! The first man who comes to me will find that his penance, the nasty coward, is to cast himself into the depths of the sea, in deduction of the pains of purgatory. And I mean head first. What is it that brought fame and eternal renown to Hercules? Was it not that, in the course of his peregrinations through the world, he freed folk from tyrants, errors, dangers and oppression? He put to death all marauders, monsters, poisonous snakes and evil-doing beasts. Why don't we follow his example and do as he did in all the lands we travel through? He did for the Stymphalides, the Hydra of Lerna, Cacus, Antaeus and the Centaurs. (I'm no scholar but that's what the scholars say.) In imitation of him

let us overthrow these Furry-cats and put them to the sack.
They are but tercels of devils; and we shall deliver this land
from tyranny. If I were as powerful and strong as Hercules was,
why! – I renounce Mahoun! – I shouldn't be asking you for
help or advice! Shall we get going then? We shall easily slay
them, I tell you, and I don't doubt that they will suffer it
patiently, seeing that they have patiently swallowed more
insults from us than ten sows draining their swill!

'Let them have gold coins in their game-bags, I say, and
then they're never troubled by insults or dishonour, even when
drenched in shit. And we doubtless would defeat them, only we
lack the order from Eurystheus. At this time that's all I want,
except that I would like to have Jupiter walking amongst them
for two tiny hours in the guise he once adopted when visiting
Semele, his sweeting, the first of Bacchus' mothers.'

'God,' said Panurge, 'has graciously vouchsafed that you
escape from their claws. As for me, I won't go back. I still feel
troubled and upset from the anguish I suffered there. I was
greatly vexed there for three reasons. First: because I was vexed.
Second: because I was vexed. Third, because I was vexed. Frère
Jean, my old left bollock, hearken to this with your right ear:
each and every time you would go to all the devils before the
judgement-seats of Minos, Aeacus, Rhadamanthus and Dis, I
am ready to maintain an unbreakable comradeship with you,
crossing the Acheron, Styx and Cocytus, drinking bumperfuls
of the waters of Lethe, and paying both our fares for Charon's
barque. But as for that wicket-gate, if you do happen to want
to go back there, press into your company someone else but
me. I will not go back. Let those words be unto you a wall of
brass. Unless I'm dragged there by might and main I shall never
draw nigh there, as long as I love this life, no more than Mount
Calpe will draw nigh to Abila. Did Hercules go back to fetch
the sword he had left in the Cyclops' cavern? That, by Jove, he
did not. I left nothing behind at the wicket-gate: I shall not go
back to it.'

'O, what a frank and great-hearted comrade,' said Frère Jean,
'one with palsied hands! But let us talk about the paying of
your scot, Subtle Doctor. Why did you throw them your purse

crammed with crowns? What moved you to it? Did we have
too many? Wouldn't it have sufficed to toss them a few clipped
testoons?'

'Because with every phrase that they uttered Catty-claws
opened his velvet game-bag and exclaimed, "Good Gold here!
Good Gold here! Good Gold here!" From which I surmised
that we could escape, liberated and free, by tossing them some
good gold there; good gold there; and in God's name, good
gold there, on behalf of all the devils there! Now a velvet
game-bag is not a reliquary for testoons or small coins: it is a
receptacle for Sun-crowns: you know that, Frère Jean, my little
old well-bollocked. When you've roasted as much as I have,
and been roasted as much as I've been, you'll talk a different
jargon. But by their injunction we are obliged to pass through.'

Idle scroungers were still waiting in the harbour hoping for
a few pennies. And seeing that we intended to set sail, they
approached Frère Jean to warn him that there would be no
passing through without our bestowing pourboires to the
Apparitors in line with the rate for the spices.

'By the Holy Hurlyburly,' said Frère Jean. 'Still there, are
you, you every-devil's Griffins! Am I not angry enough already
without you pestering me further. God's Body! I'll give you
your pourboires here and now: I can promise you that for a
certainty.'

Whereupon he drew forth his cutlass and leapt ashore, fully
resolved to slaughter them like felons, but they made off at a
gallop and we saw them no more.

We were not yet free from hassle however, since, while we
were before Catty-claws, some of our sailors, with Pantagruel's
leave, had resorted to a hostelry near the harbour to have a
carousal and a bit of a rest. I do not know whether they had
actually paid their scot, but the old woman who kept the inn
saw Frère Jean on shore and uttered a long lament in the
presence of a serargeant (a son-in-law of one of the Furry-cats)
and two bailiffs as witnesses.

Frère Jean had no patience with their speeches and allegations: he asked, 'My good-for-nothing friends! Do you mean to
say, in short, that our matelots are not decent fellows? Well I

maintain the contrary and will prove that to you by Justice, to whit, by this my Lord Cutlass.'

So saying, he swished about him with his cutlass, but the peasants fled away at a fair pace. Only the old woman was left; she maintained before Frère Jean that those matelots were decent fellows but had paid nothing for the bed they had rested on after dinner. She charged five Touraine shillings for it.

'In truth,' said Frère Jean, 'that was a bargain. They are ungrateful. They won't always get a bed at that price. I will readily pay for the bed but I would like to see it first.'

The old woman brought him to the inn and showed him the bed. Having praised all its qualities, she said that she was not overpricing in asking for five shillings. Frère Jean handed her her five shillings, then, with his cutlass, sliced the quilt and pillows in two and shook the feathers out of the windows to blow with the wind, while the old woman ran downstairs crying, 'Help!' and 'Murder!' and devoted herself to gathering up her feathers.

Frère Jean, quite unconcerned, bore off the quilt, the mattress and the pair of sheets to our ship. Nobody saw him since the air was blanketed with feathers as if by snow. He then said to Pantagruel that beds were much cheaper here than in the Chinonais, despite our having the celebrated Pautille geese, since that old woman had merely asked five dozen pence for a bed which in the Chinonais would fetch a dozen francs at least.[12]

12. This chapter in the Isle Sonante continues and ends as follows: . . . *As soon as Frère Jean and the rest of the company were aboard ship, Pantagruel set sail, but there arose a sirocco so violent that they could not maintain their course and almost strayed into the land of the Furry-cats; but they were swept into a swirling deep, the seas being so high and terrifying. A lad who was above the top-gallant shouted that he could again make out the dread domain of Catty-claws. At which Panurge, mad with fear, yelled: 'Despite the wind and the waves, tug on the bridle! Don't let's go back to that wicked land where I left my purse!' The wind then drove them close to an island at which they dared not land at first but did enter about a mile from there close to some big rocks.*

How we passed Over, and how Panurge
nearly got killed there

CHAPTER 16

*[This Chapter 16 of the printed text of 1564 does not figure in the Isle
Sonante. (In its place is the chapter of the Apedeftes, given at the end
in the Appendix.)*

*This island's name, Oultre (Over, or Beyond) lends itself to plays
on words: passer oultre is 'to go beyond', but also to 'pass over' in the
sense of to die. These fat natives die oultrés, that is, as bloated as
oultres, leathern bottles.*

*Since Panurge does not nearly get killed here, the chapter is taken
to be unfinished.]*

We at once set sail for Over and recounted our adventures to
Pantagruel, who greatly commiserated with us and composed
several elegies about them as a pastime.

Once arrived at Over we rested a while, took on fresh water
and loaded wood for our stores. The natives seemed by their
looks to be good companions and of good cheer. They were all
over-bloated like leathern bottles and gave off greasy farts. We
saw there what we had never seen in any other land: they put
slashes into their skin to make their fat billow out (exactly as
the tarty-farties where I come from have slashes worked into
their breeches and make the taffeta billow out). They maintain
that they do not do it for vainglory or ostentation but because
they could not otherwise be confined to their skins.

By doing so they also grow taller, just as gardeners incise the
bark of their trees to hasten their growth. Near the harbour
there was a tavern with a fine and imposing façade. When we
saw a great number of the Over-bloated rushing in (people of
all sexes, ages and rank) we thought that there must be some
notable feast or banquet, but we were informed that they had
all been invited by their host to a *blowing*. We, not understanding their dialect, thought that they called a blow-out a blowing,
just as we refer to betrothings, weddings, churchings, shearings

and harvestings; we were told that the host had been quite a lad in his time, a good trencherman, a good devourer of Lyonese soups, a notable clock-watcher forever dining like mine Host at Rouillac; and since he had been farting an abundance of grease for the past ten years, he had now reached his *blowings*. In accordance with the customs of his country he was ending his days in a blow-out, since his peritoneum and his flesh had been slashed over so many years that they could no longer hold up his innards and restrain them from dropping as from a stove-in barrel.

'Well now, good folk,' said Panurge, 'could you not ring his guts well round with good, strong bands or great hoops (of sorb-apple wood, or if needs be of iron)? Bound thus, he wouldn't so readily cast out his intestines and so readily burst.'

Those words were not uttered before we heard a sound in the air, loud and rasping as though a great oak had been split in two. His neighbours then said that his bursting was over: that splitting sound had been his dying fart.

Which made me think of that venerable abbot of Castilliers, who deigned to lie with his chamber-maids only when clad in full canonicals. As he was getting old he was badgered by his family and friends to resign his Abbey; he stated and declared that he would never give up before he was laid out, and that the last fart as his Paternity would be the fart of an abbot.

How our ship ran aground; and how we were succoured by voyagers who were vassals of Quintessence

CHAPTER 17

[There is a break in subject here. This and the following chapters show a concern with alchemy.

The philosopher whose wisdom was summed up with the saying 'Bear and forbear' was the Cynic Epictetus. Erasmus (in Adages, II, VII, XIII, *'Sustine et abstine' (that is 'Bear and forebear') explains that we should 'abstain' from illicit things (*ab illicitis temperemus).

The author here thinks temperemus *means we should* temporize *(not, abstain). A real gaffe.*

'*So many valets: so many enemies*' *figures amongst the* Adages *of* Erasmus *(I, III, XXXI) where there is no word of Plautus but much about Seneca, who said it, and Plato.*

'*To avoid Scylla and fall into Charybdis*' *is a commonplace, but also an adage of Erasmus (I, V, IV).*

'*Castor and Pollux above the sails*' *was what the Ancients called Saint Elmo's fire.*

'*Done well, haven't I?*' *is a saying of Pathelin already met in the* Prologue *to the* Fourth Book.

Geber was an eighth-century alchemist.]

Having weighed our anchors and slipped our cables, we set sail, blown by the gentle Zephyr. Some twenty-two miles further on there arose a boisterous whirlwind with a variety of gusts; we skirted it, temporizing by setting our top-gallants and our top-sails, with the sole aim of not being accused of going against the instructions of the pilot, who personally assured us that we had no great good to hope for, and no great harm to fear given the lightness of those breezes, their pleasant skirmishes and the calmness of the air. The philosopher's adage was therefore relevant to us, which tells us to *Bear and forbear*, that is, to temporize.

That whirlwind went on for so long, however, that, at our importuning, the pilot tried forcing a way through it, sticking to our original route. And indeed, after hoisting the mizzen and setting the helm strictly by the needle of the compass, we did force our way through that whirlwind thanks to a stiff gale which was blowing. But we were as discomfited as though we had struck Scylla by avoiding Charybdis: some two miles on our ships were stranded amidst shoals similar to the shallows at Saint-Maixent. All our crew were deeply distressed. A strong wind came whistling through our mizzen; Frère Jean never once gave way to melancholy but consoled this man and heartened that one by gentle words, assuring them that we would soon receive help from Heaven and that he had glimpsed Castor shining atop the lateen-yards.

'Would to God,' said Panurge, 'that I was at this hour upon

land. Nothing more. And that every man-jack of you who loves the briny had two hundred thousand crowns apiece. I would set a calf aside for you and get a hundred bundles of firewood ready against your return. All right then: I agree never to get married: just see that I'm set ashore with a horse to carry me back. I shall manage well enough without a valet. Plautus was telling no lie when he said that the number of our crosses – that is to say of our afflictions, torments and vexations – is in proportion to the number of our valets, yes, even were they to lack the most dangerous and evil part of a valet, his tongue, on account of which alone the torturing, racking and questioning of valets was instituted; there were no other reasons, although in those days and outside this kingdom glossators of the law drew from it an a-logical (i.e., an unreasonable) conclusion.'

Just then there came a ship alongside laden with drums; on it I recognized a few voyagers of good family. Amongst others was Henry Cotiral, an old comrade, who bore a huge ass's prick dangling from his belt in the manner that women carry their rosaries, whilst in his left hand he held a dirty, great, gross, scabby old hat, and in his right hand a big cabbage-stump. He recognized me at sight and cried out with joy and said to me, '*Done well, haven't I!* Look upon this' – displaying his ass's prick – 'it is the true alchemical Amalgam; and this bonnet is our one and only Elixir; and this – here he pointed to his cabbage-stump – is moonwort. When you return we shall make it do its work.'

'But,' said I, 'where do you come from? Where are you going to? What goods are you bringing? Have you smelt the sea-breeze?'

He replied, 'From Quintessence. To Touraine. Alchemy. Arse-deep in it.'

'And who are those people up on deck with you?' I said.

'Songsters,' he replied, 'musicians, poets, astrologers, rhymesters, geomancers, alchymists, horologists. They are all vassals of Quintessence. They all hold beautiful and ample letters of credence from her.'

Those words were hardly out of his mouth when Panurge spoke, annoyed and indignant: 'You lot can do anything; you

can beget fine weather and little children! Why don't you stand
out to sea and tow us straightway out into the main stream?'

'I was about to do so,' said Henry Cotiral. 'At this very
hour, this very moment, immediately now, you will be off the
sea-bottom.'

He then set about staving in one side of his 7532810 big
drums. He placed them with their stove-in sides facing towards
the foc's'le, and then tightly affixed all the cables to their hous-
ings. He then shackled our bow to his stern by their bollards.
To our jubilation he easily tugged us off the sands with the very
first heave; for the sound of the drums combined with the soft
grating of the gravel and the shanties of the crew produced a
harmony for us not less than the harmony of the stars in their
courses, which Plato said he had sometimes heard whilst he
slept at night.[13]

We were loathe to appear ungrateful for that good deed, so
we shared our chidlings with them, piled sausages into their
drums and were hauling sixty-two leathern bottles of wine on
to the deck when two huge physeters impulsively approached
their ship and spouted more water into it than the river Vienne
contains between Chinon and Saumur; those physeters spouted
their drums full of water, soused all their sail-yards, and
swamped their nether-breeches through the top ribbing. On
seeing which, Panurge entered into so excessive a joy and was
so merry that he had a stitch in his side for two hours or more.

'I intended to tip them with wine,' he said, 'but their water
was served most apropos! They never bother with fresh water
except for washing their hands: this lovely salt water will serve
them as borax, nitre and sal ammoniac in Geber's pantry.'

We were not able to have further discussions with them,
principally because the whirlwind had deprived us of free control of the rudder. The pilot begged us to allow the seas to guide
us from now on, not bothering about anything save having a
good time. If we wanted to reach the kingdom of Quintessence
without danger, the right thing was to yield a while to the
current and be borne round this whirlwind.

13.   For the music of the spheres and Plato, see Chapter 4 of the *Third Book*.

How we arrived at the Kingdom of Quintessence, called Entelechy

CHAPTER 18

[A chapter echoing a scholarly quarrel and a learned jest. In Greek entelechy *(coming into actuality) and* endelechy *(duration) are two quite independent words confused even in Antiquity. The confusion is a cause of amusement in Lucian's* Consonants at Law, *10, where the letter D complains to the jury that T 'has robbed her of* entelechy, *wanting it to be called* endelechy *against all the laws'. Guillaume Budé discusses the true meaning of both words in* De Asse *(1515). All the discussion flows from Aristotle (On the Soul, 2, 12); he calls the soul the* entelechia *of the body (that by which it actually is). Cicero made the subject evergreen by his mistake over the word (*Tusculan Epistles, *1, 10).*

Mataeotechny *is a Greek word defined by Quintilian (2, 10, 2–3) as* 'an unprofitable imitation of art which is neither good nor bad but involves a useless expenditure of labour'. *Here that art is alchemy.*

In a jest already met in Rabelais' preliminary epistle to Odet de Châtillon for the Fourth Book, *the portmanteau word* rhubarbative *again links* rebarbative *(crabbed, unattractive) with* rhubarb.*]*

Having skilfully skirted round the whirlwind for half a day, on the next day (the third) it seemed to us that the air was serener than usual; we came ashore safe and sound in the harbour of Mataeotechny, a short distance from the palace of Quintessence.

Once disembarked in that port we found ourselves beard-to-beard with a large number of bowmen and men-at-arms who were guarding the arsenal. They all but frightened us at first since they obliged us all to disarm and then interrogated us roughly, saying, 'What country do you come from, shipmates?'

'Cousins,' said Panurge, 'we hale from Touraine. We are coming now from France, keen to pay our respects to the Dame of Quintessence and to visit this famous kingdom of Entelechy.'

'Do you say Entelechy or Endelechy?' they asked.

Panurge replied, 'Fair Cousins, we are simple, ignorant folk. Please allow for the boorishness of our way of speaking, for our hearts are nevertheless frank and loyal.'

'It is not without cause,' they said, 'that we have questioned you about that variant. A great many of other folk who have passed through here from Touraine appear to be good solid fellows who spoke correctly, but there have come here men from other lands, overweening men, as fierce as Scotsmen, men who, as soon as they arrived, stubbornly wanted to argue the point. They got a good dressing-down despite their putting on rhubarbative faces. Have you such a great superfluity of leisure time in that world of yours that you have no idea how to spend it except by impudently talking, arguing and writing thus about our Sovereign Lady? To meddle in this matter Cicero felt obliged to abandon his *Respublica*; similarly Diogenes Laertius, Theodore Gaza, both Argyropolous and Bessarion, as well as Politian, and Budé and Lascaris and all those wise-foolish devils, the number of whom would not have been large enough without Scaliger, Bigot, Chambrier, François Fleury and Lord knows how many other prinked-out wretches.[14]

'May a nasty quinsy get them by the throat and the epiglottis! We'll . . .'

'What the divel,' said Panurge between his teeth, 'they're flattering the devils.'

'You have not come here to support them in their madness and you have no power of proxy. So we shall say no more about them. Aristotle, the first amongst men and the very model of all philosophy, was godfather to our Sovereign Lady. He very well and appropriately named her Entelechy. That is her true name: Entelechy. Whoever would call her otherwise may go for a shit. Whoever calls her anything else is heavens-wide of the mark. You are most welcome.'

They then embraced us, and we were all very happy.

Panurge said in my ear: 'Were you not, fellow traveller, just a little bit scared by that first clash?'

14. The scholars named are real people who published works touching on the subject, Scaliger doing so after Rabelais was dead. (The presumed misprint Brigot for *Bigot* has been corrected.)

'A little,' I replied.

'I was,' he said, 'more indeed than the soldiers of Ephraim when they were slaughtered and drowned by the Gileadites for saying *Sibboleth* not *Shibboleth*.[15] And (that's enough!) there is not a man in all Beauce who could have stopped up the hole in my bum with a cart-load of hay.'

The Captain, with great ceremonial, subsequently conveyed us in silence to the palace of the queen. Pantagruel wanted to say a word to him, but since the Captain could not reach up to his height, he expressed a desire for a ladder or for very tall stilts. He then said, 'Be that as it may: if our Sovereign Lady so wished we would be as tall as you are. So we shall, when it so pleases her.'

In the first galleries we came across a great multitude of the sick, who were variously segregated according to the variety of their maladies: the lepers were apart; the sufferers from poison here; the sufferers from the plague there; the syphilitics in the front row, and so on.

How Quintessence cured the sick by singing songs

CHAPTER 19

[The first list of Hebrew words would not of course have been under-stood except by at most a handful of readers. The meanings of the second series of Hebrew words could have been partly inferred from their context.

See Lucian's Philosophies for Sale, *and also Erasmus (Adages, IV, III, LXXII, 'More taciturn that Pythagoreans', and III, VII, XCVI, 'To scratch one's head; bite one's nails'.*

For the importance of silence for the Egyptians, see Adages I, VI, LII, 'He made him Harpocrates' (that is, he made him mute like Harpocrates, the Egyptian god of silence portrayed with his finger over his lips). He is mentioned by Catullus, 74. The 'king's touch' is the special power of the kings of England and France to cure scrofula simply by their touch.

15. Judges 12:5–6.

For the 'diphthera', the goat-skin on which Jupiter records all of our deeds, cf. Erasmus, Adages, II, V, XXIV, 'You are speaking of things older than the diphthera' (that is, fabulous nonsense from the distant past), and I, VIII, XXIV, 'A witness from Jove's tables' (citing the indirect evidence of Lucian).

The word 'eginchus' applied to it must be an error for aigiochos (aegis-bearing), the title of Zeus (Jupiter) and also of Athena, the aegis being both the flashing shield of the god and (by a false etymology) the goat-skin of Zeus and of Athena.

The speech of the queen, pompous, obscure, and deliberately obscure, is apparently meant to be taken seriously as saying something deep.]

In the second gallery, by the Captain, we were shown the dame, young (despite being eighteen centuries old) beautiful, refined and gorgeously arrayed, surrounded by her ladies and noblemen.

The Captain said to us, 'Now is not the time to speak to her: simply be attentive spectators of what she does. In your realm you have some kings who, by the power of imagination, merely by the touch of their hands, cure certain maladies such as the king's evil, epilepsy and quartan fevers: our queen cures all maladies without even touching, simply by singing a song appropriate to each illness.'

He then showed us the organ by her playing of which she works her miraculous cures. It was of a strange construction, for its pipes were made of sticks of cassia; its sounding-board, of lignum vitae; its stops, of rhubarb; its pedals, of turpeth; its keyboard, of scammony. While we were contemplating the wonderful and novel way in which that organ was built, there were brought to her (by her abstractors, spodizators, malax-ators, tasters, tabachins, chachanins, neemanins, rabrebans, nereins, rozuins, nedibins, nearins, segamions, perazons, chesi-nins, sarins, sotrins, aboth, enilins, archasdarpenins, mebins, giborins and other of her officers) the lepers. She played them I-know-not-what song and they were all at once perfectly cured. Then there were brought in those who had been poisoned: she sang them a different song: and they were on their feet! Then came the blind, the deaf and the mute who were similarly treated. We were astounded, and rightly so; we fell to the ground, prostrating ourselves as men caught up in ecstasy, as men enraptured in mind-departing contemplation and wonder at the powers which we had seen proceeding from that dame. We found it impossible to utter a word, so we remained thus on the floor until she, touching Pantagruel with a bouquet of species-roses held in her hand, restored us to our senses and set us back on our feet. She then addressed us in words of fine linen such as Parysitis desired to be uttered when addressing Cyrus her son, or at the very least in words of armozean taffeta.

'The candour which scintillates from the circumference of your minds fully convinces me of the virtue hidden within their ventricles; and, having noted the mellifluous suavity of your eloquent courtesies, I am readily persuaded that your heart suffers no vitiation nor any paucity of deep and liberal learning but abounds rather in several peregrine and rare disciplines which nowadays (because of the common practices of the imperite mob) are more easily sought than caught.

'That explains why I, who have in the past overmastered any private emotions, cannot now restrain myself from uttering to you the most trite words in the world, namely: Be ye welcome, most welcome, most utterly welcome.'

Panurge said discreetly to me, 'I am no scholar: you can answer her if you like.' But I made no reply; nor did Pantagruel. We kept mute. Whereupon the queen said:

'From this your silence I realize that not only are you sprung from the School of Pythagoras (in which the antiquity of my progenitors set down roots in successive propagations) but also have, for many a moon, bitten your nails and scratched your head with one finger in Egypt, that celebrated forge of high philosophy. In the School of Pythagoras taciturnity was the symbol of knowledge, and amongst the Egyptians silence was recognized as deifying praise. In Hieropolis the pontiffs sacrificed to their great god in silence, making no noise, uttering no word. My design is not to enter into any privation of gratitude towards you but rather, by living forms (even though their matter strove to abstract itself from me) to eccentricate my thoughts to you.'

Having finished her speech, she addressed her words to her officers and merely said, 'Tabachins: to Panacea!'

At those words the Tabachins told us we must excuse the queen for not having us dine with her, since she never ate anything for dinner but a few categories, jecabots, eminims, dimions, abstractions, harborins, chelimins, second intentions, caradoth, antitheses, metempsychoses and transcendent prolepsies.

We were then taken into a little room, scattered all over with alarms. How we were treated then, Lord only knows. It is said that Jupiter, on the diphthera (the tanned hide of the nanny-goat which suckled him in Candy) which he used as a shield when battling against the Titans (which is why it is surnamed *Eginchus*) writes down everything that happens in the world: well, eighteen goat-skins would not suffice – by my faith, Friends and Drinkers! – to inscribe all the good viands they served up to us, all the side-dishes and the good cheer we were treated to, not even if it were written in such tiny letters as in that *Iliad* of Homer which Cicero claims to have seen: so small that you could cover it with a walnut-shell. On my part, even if I had a hundred tongues, a hundred mouths and a voice of iron, together with the mellifluous linguistic plenitude of Plato I could never, in four volumes, expound to you one-third of the twenty-fourth part of a goldsmith's prime-weight of it. Pantagruel said to me, moreover, that in his opinion the dame, by saying to her Tabachins *To Panacea*, was giving them the watchword which was the symbol amongst them for good cheer, just as Lucullus said *In Apollo* when, though caught unprepared, he wanted to provide a very special feast for his friends. Cicero and Hortensius occasionally did the same.

How the queen passed her time after dinner

CHAPTER 20

[A variation on the theme of the Fountain of Youth.

The 'pox of Rouen' was proverbial.

The 'Tenesian axe' figures in an adage of Erasmus (I, IX, XXIX, 'The two-headed axe'). It represents hurried, harsh or summary justice.

The dances (mainly already found in Athenaeus, Dipnosophists, 147) are not given in the manuscript.

'Art', as often, probably means the Art of Medicine.

The 'malady of Saint Francis' is poverty.]

Once the dinner was quite finished, we were led by a Chachanin into the Hall of that dame and witnessed how after her meal she, together with the ladies and princes of her Court, would sift her time, passing it, sieving it and dredging it through a big and beautiful strainer of blue and white silk. We then realized that they were reviving antiquity, dancing together:

the Cordax,	the Calabrism,
the Emellia,	the Molossian,
the Sicinnis,	the Cenophorum,
the Iambics,	the Mongas,
the Persian,	the Thelmastry,
the Phrygian,	the Floralia,
the Nicatism,	the Pyrrhic,
the Thracian	and hundreds of other dances.

Afterwards we visited the palace at her command and saw things so novel, wonderful and exotic that I am still caught away in the spirit whenever I think of it. Yet nothing amazed us more than the doings of the noblemen of the household – the Abstractors, Parazones, Nebidins, Spodizators and so on – who told us frankly and without any dissimulation how it was that their Lady the queen alone healed the incurables and did the impossible, while they her officers merely did all the rest and

cured the others. There I saw a young Parazon heal syphilitics of
the very finest pox (the pox, you might say, of Rouen) merely
by touching their dentiform vertebra three times with a splinter
from a wooden clog.

I saw another perfectly healing sufferers from various types
of dropsy – tympanies, ascites and hyposarcides – by striking
them nine times on their bellies with a Tenesian axe without
any solution of continuity.

One cured all fevers within the hour merely by hanging a
fox's tail from the sufferers' belts on the left side; one cured
toothache merely by laving the root of the aching tooth with
elderberry vinegar and then letting it dry in the sun for half-an-
hour; another cured all species of gout, both hot and cold, as
well as the natural and sequential, merely by making the sufferers shut their mouths and open their eyes.

Another one I saw curing nine fine noblemen of the malady
of Saint Francis by relieving them of all their debts and sus-
pending a string from their necks: from it there hung a little
box crammed full with six thousand Sun-crowns.

Another cast houses out of windows by some mirific device,
so leaving them cleansed of malaria.

Another cured all three forms of hectic fever (the atrophying,
the consumptive and the wasting) without baths, Stabian milk,
depilatories, pitch-dressings or any other medication, merely
by turning his patients into monks for three months. He assured
me that if they didn't fatten up in the monastic state they never
would, either by nature or by Art. Another I saw accompanied
by a great number of women arranged in two groups: one
group was formed of young maidens, appetizing, tender, blonde
and gracious little things, all well disposed, it seemed, to me; the
other, of old, toothless, bleary-eyed, wrinkled, sun-blackened,
corpse-like old women.

Then Pantagruel was told that he would remould those old
women by his Art, making them youthful again like the young
maidens there present whom he had remoulded that very day,
restoring them to the same beauty, form, elegance, size and
disposition of their limbs as they had had when they had been
fifteen or sixteen, except only for their heels, which remained

much shorter than in their first flush of youth (which explains why they are thenceforth very subject to readily falling backwards whenever they come across a man).

The band of old women were devoutly waiting for the next baking and urgently pressing for it, protesting that it is not tolerable in nature that a well-disposed bum should lack beauty.

That Parazon was in continuous demand for the practice of his Art, and his profits were more than mediocre. Pantagruel asked whether he could recast old men likewise and make them young. The reply was 'No, but the way for men to grow young is to live together with a re-cast woman, for then they catch that fifth kind of syphilis, that hair-drop, called *ophiasis* in Greek, which makes them slough off their hair and skin as snakes do annually: their youth is then renewed in them as it is in the Arabian phoenix.[16]

That is the true fountain of youth. There he who was old and decrepit immediately becomes young, nimble and well disposed in body, as Euripides tells of Iolaus; as happened to the handsome Phaon (so beloved by Sappho through the bounty of Venus); to Tithonus, through Aurora; to Aeson, by Medea's art; and likewise to Jason, who (according to the testimony of Pherecides and Simonides) was given back his youth by her and a fresh colour; as Aeschylus says happened to the nurse-maids of our good Bacchus (and their husbands too).

How the officers of Quintessence worked in a variety of ways, and how the dame appointed us retainers in her retinue with the rank of Abstractors

CHAPTER 21

[Proverbial fun, then playing with alchemy.

The proverbs from the first draw heavily on Erasmus. Some of the French ones are already known to readers of Rabelais. For Erasmus

16. *Ophiasis* in Galen is a bald place on the head, of snake-like or winding form. A relevant adage – not in Erasmus – is 'To live again like the Phoenix'.

see in his Adages: *I, IV, L, 'You are whitening an Ethiopian'; I, III,
L, 'To yoke foxes'; I, IV, LI, 'To plough the shore'; I, IV, XLVIII,
'You are washing a brick (or tile)'; I, IV, LXXV, 'You want water
from a pumice-stone'; I, IV, LXXIX, 'Wool from an ass'; I, IV, LXXX,
'You are shearing an ass'; 'I, III, LI, 'To milk a he-goat (or a buck)';
I, IV, LX, 'To draw water in a sieve'; III, III, XXXIX, 'To wash an
ass's head in nitron'; II, I, LIX, 'To pound water in a mortar'; I, IV,
LXIII, 'You are trying to catch winds in nets'; I, IV, LV, 'To cleave
fire'; I, III, LII, 'About an ass's shadow'; I, III, LIV, 'To dispute about
smoke'; I, III, LIII, 'About goat's wool'.*

*One adage cited in the text is found in the Gospel but is not listed
in Erasmus. It can be found but in the* Adages of Adrian Junius *(Basle,
1558):* 'E spinis uvas colligere' *(To gather grapes from thorns and figs
from thistles).*

*Socrates was praised by Cicero for bringing philosophy down to
earth, but mocked by Aristophanes in* The Clouds *for playing with
fleas.]*

Afterwards I saw a great number of her aforesaid officers, who
were whitening Aethiopians in quite a short time simply by
scratching their bellies with the bottom of a basket.

Others had yoked together three pairs of foxes and were
ploughing up the sandy shore without wasting their seeds.

Others were washing tiles, making them lose colour.

Others were extracting water from that porous lava you call
pumice-stone, giving it a lengthy stir with a pestle in a marble
mortar and so transmuting its substance.

Others sheared asses, finding very good woollen fleeces on
them.

Others gathered grapes from thorns, and figs from thistles.

Others were milking billygoats into sieves, which proved very
economical.

Others scrubbed the heads of their asses yet wasted no soap.

Others hunted winds with nets and caught decuman crayfish
in them. I saw one Spodizator who was ingeniously getting farts
out of a dead donkey and selling some of them at five-pence
per ell.

Others were putrefying sechaboths. A fine dish it made! But

Panurge got violently sick on seeing an Archasdarpanin putrefying a great vatful of human urine by means of horse-dung and a mass of Christian shit. Ugh! Nasty fellow! He, however, retorted that he gave that holy distillation to kings and great princes to drink, by which means he lengthened their lives by a good yard or two.

Others were breaking chidlings across their knees.

Others skinned eels from the tail-end, and they did not scream before they were skinned as do eels from Melun.

Others made great somethings out of nothing, and to that nothing made somethings return.

Others cut fire with a knife and drew up water in a net.

Others made lanterns from bladders, and bronze pots out of clouds.[17] We also saw a dozen others holding a banquet beneath a bower; they drank four sorts of wine, cool and delicious, out of fair and ample bowls, drinking to all with all their might: we were told that they were *improving the weather* in the local way, and that, in days gone by, Hercules too had thus *improved the weather* together with Atlas.

Others were making virtue out of necessity, and it seemed to me very fine and relevant work. They did alchemy on their teeth, producing little to fill their close-stools.[18]

Others were carefully measuring the hopping of fleas along a flat strip of ground; and they assured me that their activity was more than necessary to the governing of kingdoms, the conducting of wars and the administration of states, citing the example of Socrates, who (having been the first to bring philosophy down from the heavens and to make it useful and profitable instead of lazy and inquisitive) employed one half of his time in measuring the hops of fleas, as the quintessential Aristophanes attests.

I saw a pair of Giborins – giants – standing apart as sentinels on a high tower: we were told that they were guarding the

17. The development from here on in this chapter is absent from the manuscript. See Mireille Huchon's Pléiade *Rabelais*, p. 1646. There is a clear echo of the *Fourth Book* (Chapter 65) in what follows.

18. *They did alchemy . . . close-stools*: that is, they picked their teeth fasting and 'extracted' little enough matter to eat and then to excrete.

moon from the wolves. I met four more of them in a corner of a garden, bitterly disputing and ready to tear out each other's hair. On asking what their quarrel arose from, I was told that four days had gone by since they had begun a dispute over three deep, metaphysical propositions. They had promised themselves mountains of gold once they had resolved them. The first concerned the shadow cast by a well-hung ass; the second, the smoke of a lantern; the third, goat's hair: i.e., is it wool?

They went on to tell us how it did not seem odd to them that there could be two contradictory assertions which were both true in mode, form, figure and time. The Sophists of Paris would rather be de-christened than confess it.

We were attentively watching the wondrous acts of those people when their dame appeared with her entourage of nobles (Hesperus was already shining bright.)

Upon her arrival our senses were again troubled and our eyes were dazzled. She at once noticed our awe and said to us:

'What makes human thoughts lose their way within the abysses of wonder is not the supremacy of actions (which they realize to derive from natural causes through the industry of skilled artificers), it is the novelty of the experience entering their senses, since they do not perceive how easy the activity is when serene judgement is allied to scrupulous study. So keep your mind awake and rid yourself of any fear which could seize you when you contemplate what is done before your eyes by my artificers. Of your own free-will see, hear and contemplate everything which my household contains, gradually emancipating yourself from the slavery of ignorance. The matter accords well with my own will, of which I give you knowledge unfeigned (out of consideration for the studious desires of which you seem to me to have provided sufficient proof and a joyful abundance in your minds). I now retain you in the state and office of my Abstractors. As you leave this place, you will be formally enrolled by Geber, my Prime Tabachin.'

Without uttering a word, we humbly thanked her, accepting the offer of the fine position she was conferring on us.

How the queen was served at supper, and
of her manner of eating

CHAPTER 22

[The jest about the 'pâtés in pie-crusts' leaves editors perplexed: perhaps it is partly a veiled account of alchemical sublimation.]

The dame, having finished her discourse, turned round to her noblemen and said:

'The orifice of the stomach (that ambassador for the common victualling of all our limbs, both major and minor) importunes us to restore to limbs, by the distribution of appropriate foods, what has been taken from them through the continuous action of natural heat upon basic humours.[19] It will be your fault alone, O Spodizators, Cesenins, Nemains and Perazons, if our trestle-tables are not promptly set up and abounding in every kind of restoratives. And you my noble Food-Tasters together with my noble Chewer: the proof that I have been given of your industry, interlaced with care and diligence, means that I cannot order you to be attentive to duty and to be ever on your guard. I merely remind you to go on as before.'

Once those words were said, she withdrew for a while with some of her ladies; we were told that it was to have a bath, which was as customary amongst the Ancients as washing our hands before a meal is to us. The trestles were promptly set up and decked with very precious table-cloths. The service was so ordered that the dame ate nothing but ambrosia and drank nothing but heavenly nectar, whilst the lords and ladies of her household were served as we were with all sorts of dishes, as rich and rare and appetizing as any that Apicius ever dreamt up. At dessert there was brought in a ragoût made up of many varied meats, in case hunger had not declared a truce. The serving-platter was of such dimensions and capacity that the

---

19. The manuscript adds: *A penalty is attached by Nature, my Queen, if we do not achieve the resolution of spirits.*

golden plane-tree which Pythius Bithinus gave to King Darius would scarce have covered it. That ragoût was replete with pot-loads of various stews, salads, fricassées, casseroles, goat-meat potages, meats (roasted, boiled and grilled), huge steaks of salted beef, fine old-style hams, deific preserved meats, pastries, pies, a whole world of couscous prepared in the Moorish style, cheeses, junkets, jellies and every kind of fruit. All of which seemed good and appetizing to me, but, being full and replete, I never tasted any. I should warn you, though, that I saw some pâtés in pie-crusts – something quite rare – and those pâtés in pie-crusts were pâtés potted. At the bottom of that ragoût I espied a great many dice, playing-cards, tarot-packs, spillikin-slips, chessmen and draughts, together with a goblet full of Sun-crowns for any who wished to play.

Finally, right at the bottom, I noticed a number of mules wearing fine caparisons with velvet covers; hackneys (for both men and women to ride), dressed in similar trappings, and litters – I don't know how many – similarly lined with velvet and a few Ferrara-style coaches for those who might enjoy themselves out-of-doors.

That did not seem odd to me, but what did seem novel was the dame's way of eating. She masticated nothing: not that she did not have good strong teeth nor that her foods did not require mastication, but such was her manner and custom. Her foods, after the Tasters had assayed them, were taken over by her Chewers and nobly masticated for her, their throats being lined with crimson satin containing streaks of gold and gold-braid, whilst their teeth were of beautiful white ivory: with such help, once they had masticated her food to a turn, they poured it directly into her stomach through a funnel of fine gold.

For the same reason, she never had a stool except by procuration.

How a joyful ball was staged under the form of a tournament in the presence of Quintessence

CHAPTER 23

[Games of chess in the form of a ballet, all influenced by The Dream of Polifilo *of Colonna. The author of the chess chapters tells his tale with a disconcerting mixture of past and present tenses (changing tenses within quite short sentences). He is not followed slavishly here.*

This and the following chapter are not in the manuscript.]

Once that supper was over, a ball was staged in that dame's presence. It took the form of a knightly tournament which was worth not merely watching but being for ever remembered.

To begin with the floor of the Hall was covered with an ample piece of velvet carpet made in the form of a chess-board, that is with squares, half of which were white and the others yellow; each was three spans wide and perfectly squared off on all sides.

Whereupon there entered into that Hall thirty-two young personages, sixteen of which were dressed in cloth-of-gold: namely eight young nymphs, such as were portrayed by the Ancients in the suite of Diana; one king, one queen, two castle-guards, two knights and two archers. The sixteen others were similarly drawn up, all arrayed in cloth-of-silver.

They took up their places on the carpet as follows: the kings stood in the back row on the fourth square, in such a way that the golden king was on a white square and the silver king on a yellow. The queens stood beside their kings, the golden queen on the yellow square, the silver queen on the white, with two archers either side of them, each as guards of their own king and queen. Beside the archers stood two knights, and beside the knights, two castle-guards.

In the row next in front of them stood the eight nymphs. Between the two troops of nymphs, four rows of squares were left empty.

Each troop had musicians on its side, clad in the like livery, one troop in orange damask and the other in white damask; there were eight either side, with various instruments happily contrived, all playing together in a most wonderful concord and harmony but varying in tone, tempi and measure as required by the progress of that ball. I found it all most remarkable, given the many variations of steps, moves, leaps, bounds, returns, flights, ambushes and surprises.

What, it seemed to me, surpassed even more the notions of men was the fact that the personages in that ball should at once understand the tune which was appropriate to each advance or retreat, so that the note of the music had no sooner sounded before they were propelling themselves towards their designated places despite all their motions being so diverse. The nymphs, who are in the front row as ones prepared to join battle, march straight ahead against their foes, stepping from square to square except in their first moves, in which they are free to advance two squares. They alone may never retreat. Should one of them reach as far as the row of their enemy king she is crowned a queen to her own king, from now on taking pieces and making moves with the same privileges of the queen herself; otherwise she may never strike her foes save diagonally – obliquely – and straight ahead. It is, however, never permissible for them or any others to take any of their foes if by so doing they would leave their own king unprotected and exposed to capture.

The kings march and take their enemies from any square on the board, moving only from a white square to an adjacent yellow one and vice-versa, with the exception that at their first move they may (if their row is found to be empty of other officers save either of its castle-guards) set him in their place and withdraw beside him.

The queens manoeuvre and capture more freely than all the others, namely in any way, in any place, in every manner, as far as they like in a straight line (provided that it be not blocked by one of their own side) as well as diagonally, provided that they keep to the colour of their emplacement.

The archers march equally well forwards or backwards, far

and near alike; but they never change from the colour of their original emplacement.

The knights march and take their foes at right-angles, first passing freely over a square even when occupied by one of their men or one of their enemies, and then landing either to the right or to the left, always with a change of colour. Such a leap is greatly detrimental to the adversary and closely to be watched, for they never take anyone openly, face on.

The castle-guards do march and capture face on as well as to the right as to the left and forwards as much as backwards, as do the kings; and they can march as far as they like to any empty space (which the kings may not do).

The rule governing both sides requires the king to be besieged and hemmed in by the enemy at the last stage of the combat, in such a way that he cannot escape on any side whatsoever. When he is so hemmed in that he is unable to flee and incapable of being succoured by his own side, the combat ceases and the besieged king is the loser.

To protect him from such a disaster there are none on his side, male or female, who do not offer their lives nor fail to attack the others everywhere as soon as the music resounds. Whenever anyone took a prisoner from the opposing side, he would bow to him, gently tap him with his right hand, remove him from the enclosure and take his place. Should it transpire that one of the kings was in jeopardy, it was not licit for any opponent to take him: there was a rigorous command to the one who had found him or placed him in jeopardy to make a deep bow and to warn him saying, *God guard thee*, so that he might be succoured and protected by his officers, or might change his position if unfortunately he could not be succoured. At all events he is never taken by an opponent but hailed by him, kneeling upon one knee and saying *Good Day*. With that the tournament ended.

How the thirty-two personages at the ball joined in combat

CHAPTER 24

[The chess ballet continues.
*   The work by Nicolas of Cusa referred to is* De Ludo globi.
*   Enyo is the goddess of war.*
*   The last paragraph forms the end of Chapter 22 in the manuscript*
(where it is numbered 23).]

The two companies thus set out in their places, all the musicians strike up together a martial strain, most frighteningly as for an assault. We then see a tremor run through the warrior-bands as they tense themselves for the fight: the time has come for the clash when they would be called forth from their camp. As the musicians of the band of the silver warriors suddenly stopped playing, only the instruments of the golden warriors resounded. By that they were indicating to us that the golden warrior-band were to attack. Which they soon did, for with a new musical strain we saw the nymph positioned in front of her queen make a full turn to the left towards her king (as though requesting permission to join battle) and also saluting the whole company. Then, with great modesty, she marched two squares forward and curtseyed to the opposing warrior-band, which she then attacked. Thereupon the golden musicians stopped playing and the silver one began.

It should not be passed over in silence at this point that the nymph had turned round to salute the king and his company in order that they should not remain idle. They likewise saluted her back, turning fully round to the left, save for the queen, who turned towards her king on the right. Such salutations were given whenever anyone made a move, and during the whole course of the ball those salutations were returned by each of the two warrior-bands.

At the sound of the silver musicians, the silver nymph who was posted in front of her queen marched forth, gracefully saluting her king and all his company; they saluted her back, just as was related of the golden ones, except that they all now turned to the right and the queen to the left. The nymph positioned herself on the second square forward, curtsied to her opponent, stood facing the first golden nymph, with no distance between them as though ready for the fray, except that they strike sideways only. Their companions followed them, both the golden and the silver, intercalating themselves and showing signs of a skirmish, until the golden nymph who had first entered the field slapped the hand of the silver nymph to her left, removing her from the field and taking her place.

Very soon, with a new strain from the musicians, that nymph was herself struck by a silver archer. A golden nymph drove him elsewhere. The silver knight entered the field: the golden queen positioned herself before her king. Whereupon the silver king, fearing the fury of the golden queen, changed his position, withdrawing to that of his guard to the right; that position seemed well fortified and well defended. Both of the knights who stood on the left – the gold as well as the silver one – made their moves and captured many nymphs from the other side who were unable to withdraw: above all the golden knight who devoted himself to capturing nymphs. But the silver knight was thinking of more important matters while concealing his enterprise; once, when he could have captured a golden nymph, he let her be, went beyond her and so manoeuvred that he took up position near to his adversaries, from which he saluted the enemy king saying, *May God guard thee*. The golden warrior-band, being thus warned to succour their king, a tremor rang though them all, not that they could not easily succour him but because, by saving him, they must irremediably lose their right castle-guard. At which the king withdrew to the left, and the silver knight captured the gold castle-guard, which was a great loss to them. However, the gold warrior-band decided to avenge themselves and surround it on every side so that it could neither flee nor escape from their hands. He made hundreds of attempts to get out; his own side tried hundreds of ruses to protect him, but in the end the gold queen took him.

The gold warrior-band, deprived of one of their officers,

bestir themselves and most imprudently seek means of revenge, laying about them right and left and inflicting great damage among the enemy troops. The silver warrior-band make a ploy, awaiting their time for revenge and offering one of their nymphs to the gold queen, having laid a secret ambush, so that when that nymph is taken the gold knight all but surprises the silver king. The gold knight goes to take the silver king and queen, saying *Good day!* The silver knight salutes them: he is taken by a gold nymph; she is taken by a silver nymph. Bitter is the battle. The castle-guards come out from their positions to help. All is in dangerous confusion. Enyo has yet to declare herself. Once, all the silver warrior-band break right through to the tent of the gold king and are straightway repulsed. Amongst others the gold queen does great deeds of valour: in one venture she takes the archer and then, moving sideways, takes the silver castle-guard.

Seeing which, the silver queen sallies forth and with similar boldness shoots her bolts, takes the last gold castle-guard and likewise one of the nymphs.

The two queens battled long, at times trying to surprise each other, at times trying to save themselves and at others to protect their kings. In the end the gold queen captured the silver, but soon after she was herself taken by a silver knight. At that point there remained to the gold king but three nymphs, one archer and one castle-guard. To the silver king there remained three nymphs and the right-hand knight, which explains why they fought on more cautiously now and slowly.

The two kings looked forlorn over the loss of their beloved queens; all their thoughts and deeds are directed now to elevating their nymphs if they can to that dignity in a new marriage, to loving them with joy and to giving them certain assurances of being welcomed if they break through to the last row of the enemy king. The gold nymphs push ahead and from amongst them a new queen is made: a new crown is set upon her head and new accoutrements are given her. The silver nymphs follow on likewise; they have only a single row to cross before one of them can be made a new queen, but the castle-guard is watching her and so she stays quiet.

When she first appeared the new golden queen wanted to show herself valiant, strong and war-like. She did great feats of arms throughout the field. But while such things were being done, the silver knight took the gold castle-guard who was protecting the skirts of the battle-field. By which means there was made a new silver queen. She too wanted to show herself similarly valiant when she freshly appeared. The battle was joined anew, hotter than before. Hundreds of ruses, hundreds of assaults, hundreds of moves were made by both sides, such that the silver queen clandestinely entered the tent of the gold king saying, *God guard thee!* He could be succoured by his new queen alone. She made no difficulty about endangering herself to save him. Whereupon the silver knight vaulted about in all directions, brought himself near to his queen and threw the golden king into such disarray that he had to lose his queen to save himself. But the golden king took the silver knight. That notwithstanding, the golden archer defended the king with the two nymphs which remained from all their forces, but eventually all of them were taken and removed from the field of battle. The golden king remained, alone. The entire band of silver warriors then bowed low to him and said, *Good day!* since their silver king was left the victor. At those words the two companies of musicians struck up a victory strain together.

And thus did end that first ball in such great joy, with such pleasant gestures, such honourable conduct and such rare gracefulness that we were all laughing in our minds like folk caught away in ecstasy, and we not wrongly felt that we had been transported to the sovereign joys and supreme felicity of the Olympian heavens.

When that first tournament was over, the two warrior-bands returned to their original positions and began to fight a second time as they had previously fought, except that the music was now half a beat more rapid. The moves made were quite different from the first's. There I saw the gold queen, apparently angered by the rout of her army, aroused by the strains of the music: she was amongst the first of the females on to the battle-field accompanied by an archer and a knight; she all but surprised the silver king in his tent, surrounded by his officers. After that, seeing her enterprise discovered, she skirmished amongst the troops and so troubled the silver nymphs and other officers that it was piteous to behold. You would have said that she was some new Penthesilea, an Amazon thundering through the battle-field of the Greeks. But that scuffle did not last long, since the silver warriors, all a-quiver at the loss of their soldiers yet hiding their griefs, secretly set up an ambush for her consisting of one archer in a distant corner and one knight errant, by whom she was taken and removed from the field. Another time she will act more wisely! She will stay close to her king, never venturing far from him and, when go she must, go otherwise supported.

Whereat the silver warriors remained the victors as before.

For the third and final ball the two warrior-bands stood as they had done before, and it seemed to me that they wore happier and more determined expressions than on both former occasions. The music was a fifth more rapid and the strains were Phrygian and bellicose such as Marsyas invented long ago. They then began their tournament and joined battle with such a light touch that they made four moves to a bar, together with the appropriate bows and scrapes as we have described above, so that it was nothing but intertwined leaps, capers and curvets as though by tight-rope dancers. On seeing them twirl round on one foot having made their bow, we likened them to a spinning-top which children play with by whipping it round until its twirls are so rapid that movement seems repose, the top appears still and motionless ('sleeping' as they put it). And if a coloured dot should figure on it, it seems to our gaze to be not a point but a continuous line (as Nicolas of Cusa notes in an inspired work of his).

Then we heard nothing but the clapping of hands and acclamations every time a piece was taken by either side. There is none, even so glum as Cato, be he Crassus the Elder – none such an agelast – not even the misanthropic Timon of Athens, nor even Heraclitus, who loathed the very property of Man which is laughter, who would not have wrinkled his cheeks at the sight of those young warriors, quickly moving to the strains of that rapid music in five hundred diversions, setting forth, jumping, vaulting, cutting capers, curveting and wheeling about together with the queens and the nymphs with such dexterity that never did one obstruct another. The smaller the number that remained on the field the greater our delight at seeing the ploys and ruses they effected to surprise each other as the tone of the music moved them. I shall add that, although this more-than-human spectacle left us dazed, with our minds astonished as we were caught away from ourselves, yet we were even more moved in heart and mind by the strains of the music, and we readily believed that it was by such harmonies that Ismenias stirred up the heart of Alexander the Great (when he was seated at table and quietly dining) to spring to his feet and take up arms.

At the third tournament the gold king was the victor.

During those balls the dame disappeared unseen. We saw her no more. We were indeed taken by the longshoremen of Geber to be enrolled in the estate which she had decreed. We then made our way down to the harbour of Mateotechnia; we went aboard our ships, learning that we had a wind astern, which, if rejected then, could hardly be recovered for three-quarters of the waning moon.

How we landed on the Isle of the Roads, on which the roadways road on their ways

CHAPTER 25

[*In French this is the Isle des Odes, where* ode *has above all its Greek sense of* hodos (ὁδός) *road (as in the English* (h)odometer).

'Nothing is in all parts blessed', *is a saying from Horace* (Odes, *2, 16, 27). That self-movement is the sign of the animal is touched on by Rondibilis in the* Third Book, Chapter *32.*

'Despite Minerva' *is a very well-known adage of Erasmus (I, I, XLII) meaning to do something against intelligence, nature or the heavens.*

'The description of the old road crossing the "Grand-Ours" (The

Great Bear Mountain) probably owes something to Virgil's description of the icy old mountain god (Aeneid, 4, 246ff.).]

After two days' sailing the Isle of the Roads was sighted, on which we noticed something worth remembering: the roadways there are animals (if what Aristotle asserted is true, when he maintained, that is, that self-movement is an irrefutable proof of animality) for there the roadways rode on their ways: some roads are wanderers like planets; others are wending roads, crossing roads and thoroughfares. I noticed that when travellers, servants and the local inhabitants ask, 'Where does this road go to?' and 'Where does this one go?' they receive the reply 'To the parish,' or 'To the town,' or 'To the river,' or 'From Fèverolles to Twelve o'clock.' Then, leaping on to the appropriate road they find themselves taken to their destination without further effort or fatigue, just like those who take a boat on the Rhône to travel from Lyons to Avignon and Arles.

And since, as you know, there is some defect in every thing, and *Nothing is in all parts blessed*, we were told that there was a species of men called highway robbers and pavement thumpers. Those poor old roads fear them and avoid them as we do brigands, for just as we trap wolves with false trails, and woodcocks with nets, those men lie in wait for roads.

I saw one of those villains brought to justice for having, despite Minerva, unlawfully taken the road to school – that's the longest – while another boasted of having in a fair fight taken the shortest; his encounter gave him the advantage of being the first to reach the end of his enterprise. That explains why Carpalim could tell Epistemon that he was no longer surprised to find him always the first at the levees of our good prince Pantagruel, for he had seen him, pisser in hand, pissing against the wall, holding on to the shortest and the less ridden!

I came across the highway to Bourges and saw it stumble along at an abbot's pace; I also saw it give way at the arrival of some carters who threatened to trample over it with their horses' hooves and drive their carts across its belly (as Tullia made her chariot run over the belly of her father, Servius Tullius, the sixth king of the Romans). I similarly recognized the old Picardy-road from Péronne to Saint-Quentin: he looked personally quite presentable. I also recognized between the cliffs that good old road of La Ferrate, which clambers over the Grand-Ours. Looking at him from afar I was reminded of Saint Jerome in a painting, but with a bear not a lion, for he was all hoary with a long, white, ill-combed beard: you could rightly have said they were icicles. He wore a great many rough pine-wood rosaries and was as though propped up on his knees, neither standing nor entirely lying down; and he was beating his bosom with great rugged rocks. We were moved to simultaneous fear and pity.

While we were looking at him, a Bachelor of Arts and giver of courses took us aside, showed us a very smooth road, completely white, which was lightly strewn with straw, and said:

'From this time forth do not despise the opinion of Thales of Miletus, who said that water was the beginning of all things, nor the judgement of Homer affirming that all things have their births in the ocean: the road you see here was born of water and to water it will return. Two months ago boats travelled along here, now wagons do.'

'Truly,' said Pantagruel, 'you make that road appear most pitiable! In our world we see over five hundred of such transfigurations every year.'

Then, contemplating the gaits of those moving roads, he said that, according to his judgement, it was on this isle that Philolaus and Aristarchus had been led to affirm by philosophy – Seleucus reaching the same opinion – that it is the earth not the sky which truly rotates about its poles, despite the contrary appearing to us to be true. Similarly, when we are on the river Loire, it appears to us that the nearby trees are moving, yet they are not: it is we who are moving as the boat sails by.[20]

On our way back to our ship we came across three highwaymen on the shore who were being racked on the wheel; they had been caught laying an ambush. And some great lout was also being roasted over a slow fire: he had so thumped the

20. It was Celio Calcagnini in his posthumous works who widely spread the opinion that the sun remains still whilst the earth moves. It was Lucretius who wrote that the land seems to move when you follow the shore in a boat.

surface of the road that he had fractured one of its ribs. We were told that it was the road leading to the dikes and levees of the Nile in Egypt.[21]

How we visited the Isle of Clogs; and of the Order of the Demisemiquaver Friars

CHAPTER 26

[In French this is the Order of the Frères Fredons. There are Friars Minor and Friars Minim. These Friars are even more minimal.

Fortune, whose forehead is bare, is either grasped by the hair at the back of her head as she sweeps by or grasped not at all.

'Quint' is Quintessence and also a Fifth, which allows of some sporting with musical terms.

The reference to Pontanus echoes Gargantua, Chapter 18.]

We then called at the Isle of Clogs, where they live on nothing but stewed haddock; we were well received, though, by the king of the Isle (Benius, the Third of that Name) and well entertained. After giving us drinks he took us to a new kind of monastery which had been devised, erected and built to his design for the Demisemiquavers – it was thus that he called his Friars, saying that on terra-firma there dwelt the Little Servants and Friends of the Gentle Lady, the boasting and beautiful Friars-Minor (the Semi-breves of papal bulls), the Friars-Minims (those smoky eaters of herrings) and the Minim-crochets. He could find no title even more diminishing than Demisemiquavers.

21. Here the manuscript adds: *There we were told moreover that Panigon had retired to a monastery on that isle in his later years and was living in great holiness in the true Catholic faith, without concupiscence, without emotion and without vice, in innocence, loving his neighbour as himself, and God above all things; wherefore he performed many fine miracles. On our leaving Chothu, I saw a mirific portrait of a valet seeking a master, painted some time ago by Charles Charmoy of Aurleans.* (Cf. the *Fourth Book*, Chapter 10 for Panigon, and Chapter 2 for the Charmoy portrait of the valet.)

By the Statutes and Bull-patent obtained from Dame Quint, who is in every good chord, they were all attired like a mob of incendiaries, except that, just as roof-tilers in Anjou have padded cushions on their knees, they had padded soles over their bellies. (Amongst them padders-up of guts enjoy a high reputation.) The codpieces on their breeches had the form of slippers; each man wore two of them, one sewn on in front and the other behind, asserting that certain terrifying mysteries were duly signified by that cod-piecely duplication.

They wore shoes as round as basins in imitation of those who dwell amidst the Sea of Sand. In addition they wore their beards shaven off, and iron-shod shoes. And to prove that they are never troubled by Fortune he, Benius, had them shaven and shorn like pigs, from their crowns down to their omoplates along the posterior parts of their heads. Their frontal hair, from the parietal bones downwards, was allowed to grow freely. So they were like Anti-Fortunes and like folk who care nothing at all for the things of this world. Each one, even more defiant of many-faceted Fortune, bore a sharp razor – not as she does in her hand but attached to his belt like prayer-beads, – which they whetted twice a day and honed three times a night.

Each wore a round ball on his feet because Fortune is said to have one under hers. The back-flap of their cowls is not secured behind but in front, by which means they kept their faces concealed and could freely mock at Fortune and those whom Fortune favours, neither more nor less than maidens hiding behind their mask-uglies (which you call nose-mufflers and which men of yore call charity, because it covers a great multitude of sins).[22]

They always kept the back of their heads uncovered as we do our faces, which explains why they can travel as they prefer with either belly or bum to the fore. Whenever they went bum-wards you would have reckoned that to be their natural way of walking, as much from their round shoes as from the codpiece which went before them, together with the shaven

---

22. A monastic joke to which Erasmus took exception: charity is like a monastic robe – or as here like a face-mask for ugly ladies – because it covers a multitude of sins. (Cf. I Peter 4:8.)

face, coarsely painted behind, with its two eyes and mouth such as may be seen on Indian coconuts. When they went belly-wards you would have taken them for folk playing at blind-man's-buff. It was a fine sight to behold!

Their way of life is as follows: when bright Lucifer begins to be visible from Earth, they, for charity's sake, boot and spur into each other. Thus booted and spurred, they go to sleep (or at the very least they snore) keeping on their noses their goggles or at very worst their glasses.

We found that way of doing things odd but they satisfied us with their reply: they protested that at the Last Judgement, whenever it came, human beings would be found resting and sleeping; so in order to appear as Fortune's favourites, they keep themselves booted, spurred and ready to mount their steeds whenever the Trumpet shall sound.

At the stroke of noon – and note that all their bells, both in tower and Refectory, were constructed according to the device of Pontanus, namely of fine padded down, whilst their tongues were of foxes' tails – at the stroke, I say, of noon, they awoke, pulled off their boots, pissed (if they wished), defecated (if they wished) and (if they wished) sneezed. But all of them were constrained by statute copiously and amply to yawn.

They had yawns for breakfast. It was for me a pleasant sight to see; for, having put their boots and spurs on the racks, they went down into the cloisters. There they meticulously washed their hands and their mouths and then sat down on a long bench picking their teeth until the Provost gave a signal by whistling through his palm. Whereupon each one opened his jaws as wide as he could and yawned, sometimes for a full half-hour, sometimes less, as the Prior judged proportionate to each day's festival.

After which, they took out a fine procession in which they carried two banners: on one was painted a beautiful portrait of Virtue; on the other, of Fortuna. A leading Demisemiquaver carried Fortuna's banner followed by another carrying Virtue's; he bore in his hand an aspergillum dipped in that fountain of Mercury's which Ovid describes in his *Fasti*, continually lustrating the friar walking before him and carrying Fortuna.

'That order,' said Panurge, 'runs counter to the judgement of Cicero and the Academics, according to which Virtue takes precedence over Fortune.'

But they contended that they were acting rightly, since their intention was to fustigate Fortuna.

During the procession they melodiously demisemiquavered some anthems between their teeth – I could not tell which, as I did not understand their lingo – but by listening attentively I eventually realized that they were singing with their ears. O, what a delightful harmony, so well consonant with the ring of their bells! You will never find them discordant.

Pantagruel made a wonderful and memorable remark about their procession; he said to us:

'Did you see and notice the *finesse* of those Demisemi-quavers? To make their procession they left by one door of the church and came in by another: they were too wily to go back through the one they'd just left by. Upon my honour they are fine folk, as fit to be gilded as a leaden dagger, not finely fined but finely fining, sifted through a fine mesh.'

'Such finesse,' said Frère Jean, 'is distilled from occult philosophy, of which, by the devil, I understand nothing.'

'It is,' said Pantagruel, 'all the more to be feared precisely because nobody understands it. For finesse understood, foreseen and unveiled, loses its name and essence: then we call it boorishness. I tell you on my honour that they know plenty of other tricks.'

Once the procession was over, for a walk and some healthy exercise they resorted to their Refectory, sinking to their knees underneath their tables and each pressing his chest and belly against a lantern. When they had adopted that position, there entered a Great Clog holding a fork in his hand; he so prodded them with his fork that they started off their meal with cheese and ended it with lettuce and mustard (the custom of the Ancients as Martial testifies). Each was finally served with a platterful of mustard: in fact, *served with mustard once the meal is o'er!*

Their regimen was as follows. They eat:

– on Sundays: black-puddings, chidlings, sausages, veal

stewed in lard, hazlets, hogs' hazlets, quails, not including the first course of cheese nor the after-dinner mustard.

– on Mondays: rich peas-with-bacon, with copious footnotes and interlined glosses;

– on Tuesdays a great quantity of holy bread, *fouaces*, cakes, buns and biscuits;

– on Wednesdays: 'rustic fare' (that is, finest sheep's heads, calves' heads and badgers' heads, which all abound in that countryside);

– on Thursdays: seven kinds of soups, always with mustard served between them;

– on Fridays: nothing save sorb-apples, which as far as I could judge from their colour, were not even very ripe.

– on Saturdays: they gnawed at bones (not that they were poor or needy, since each one of them enjoyed the benefice of a very good belly).

For their drink they had some local wine or other which they called 'an Antidote to Fortuna'.

Whenever they wanted to eat or drink they pulled down the flaps of their cowls in front of them to serve as bibs; once dinner was over they thoroughly praised God entirely in demisemiquavers; the rest of the day they spent on works of charity whilst awaiting the Last Judgement;

– on Sundays, they boxed each other's ears;

– on Mondays, they tweaked each other's noses;

– on Tuesdays, they clawed at each other;

– on Wednesdays they wiped snot from each other's conks;

– on Thursdays, they wormed ticks from each other's noses;

– on Fridays, they gave each other a tickle;

– on Saturdays, they lashed each other with whips.

That was their regular regime when residing in their convents. Should they go out by order of the claustral Prior they were rigorously forbidden, under horrifying penalties, ever to touch or eat fish when travelling by river or sea, or meat of any kind when on terra-firma: that was so as to make it evident to all that, whilst being moved by the sight, they were not moved by privilege or concupiscence, remaining as unshakable as the Marpesian Rock.

All this they performed with appropriate and relevant anthems, always chanting with their ears as already said. As the sun sank down into the sea, they booted and spurred one another as before and settled down to sleep with their glasses on their noses. At midnight: enter the Clog.

Everyone got up and whetted and honed his razor. Once the procession was finished, they placed the tables over themselves and began to feed as before.

Frère Jean des Entommeures, on seeing the rejoicing of those Demisemiquaver-Friars and upon learning of the Table of Contents of their Statutes, lost his calm and loudly exclaimed:

'O! what a *rat* in that Table! I'm striking it out, and then, by God, out I go too.[23]

'O! If only Priapus were here as he rightly was for the midnight rites of Canidia, we might see him deeply farting, and demisemiquavering as he counter-farted.[24] Now I know that we are indeed in an antichthonian – an antipodean – land. In Germany they are unfrocking monks and pulling down monasteries: here, on the contrary, they're setting them up, out of kilter and against the grain.

How Panurge, when questioning a Demisemiquaver Friar, received from him no reply save in monosyllables

CHAPTER 27

[Some slight liberties are taken here in the translation to keep the replies monosyllabic, since such humour as there is lies in the monosyllables. Erasmus had made this kind of jest current in his Colloquy Echo, *though here there are no echoes as there were in the* Third Book.]

23. There is a triple pun: *rat* means the rodent, a blunder and shaven (the last suggesting a shaven-pate monk).
24. *Contrepéterie* really means a kind of Spoonerism but can be seen as deriving from *contre* + *pet* (meaning a 'counter-fart' or something similar).

Panurge had done nothing since our arrival except deeply contemplate the sour faces of those royal Demisemiquavers; but
then he tugged one of them by the sleeve – he was as lean as a
soused devil – and asked him:

'Brother Demiseque, Demiseque, Hum-tee-tum Quaver, where
do you keep the girl then?'

The Demisemiquaver Friar replied, 'Down'.

PAN. Got many here? – FR. Few.

PAN. How many are there? – FR. Score.

PAN. How many would you like to have? – FR. More.

PAN. Where do you hide them? – FR. There.

PAN. They're not all of the same age, I suppose, but how do
they hold themselves? – FR. Straight.

PAN. And their complexion? – FR. Fair.

PAN. And their hair? – FR. Blonde.

PAN. And their eyes: how are they? – FR. Black.

PAN. And their titties? – FR. Round.

PAN. Their faces? – FR. Fine.

PAN. Their eyebrows? – FR. Soft.

PAN. Their attractions? – FR. Ripe.

PAN. Their looks? – FR. Frank.

PAN. Their feet, how are they? – FR. Splay.

PAN. Their heels? – FR. Neat.

PAN. The nether parts: what about them? – FR. Nice.

PAN. And their arms? – FR. Long.

PAN. What do they wear on their hands? – FR. Gloves.

PAN. And what of the rings on their fingers? – FR. Gold.

PAN. What do you use for their clothes? – FR. Cloth.

PAN. What cloth do you dress them in? – FR. New.

PAN. What colour is it? – FR. Green.

PAN. Their headgear. What of that? – FR. Blue.

PAN. Their stockings? – FR. Brown.

PAN. All the aforementioned clothes, how do they look? –
FR. Smart.

PAN. What are their shoes made of? – FR. Hide.

PAN. How are they usually? – FR. Foul.

PAN. How do they walk about with them in public? – FR.
Quick.

PAN. Let's get round to the kitchen – I mean the girls' kitchen – let's pick through everything in detail without undue haste. What is there in their kitchen? – FR. Fire.

PAN. What keeps it going? – FR. Wood.

PAN. What's that wood like? – FR. Dry.

PAN. From which trees? – FR. Yew.

PAN. And the kindling and faggots? – FR. Thorn.

PAN. What wood do you burn in your rooms? – FR. Pine.

PAN. And from what other trees? – FR. Limes.

PAN. And those maidens aforesaid – I'll go fifty-fifty with you! – how do you nourish them? – FR. Well.

PAN. What do they eat? – FR. Bread.

PAN. What kind? – FR. Brown.

PAN. And what else? – FR. Meat.

PAN. How cooked? – FR. Roast.

PAN. Do they eat any soups? – FR. None.

PAN. And pastries? – FR. Lots.

PAN. I'll join in! Do they never eat fish? – FR. Yes.

PAN. Hmm. And what else? – FR. Eggs.

PAN. How do they like them? – FR. Boiled.

PAN. But now I ask, how boiled? – FR. Hard.

PAN. Is that their entire meal? – FR. No.

PAN. Well then, what else do they have? – FR. Beef.

PAN. Anything else? – FR. Pork.

PAN. And what else? – FR. Goose.

PAN. And the male gander? – FR. Male.

PAN. Also? – FR. Cock.

PAN. And what do they put in their sauce? – FR. Salt.

PAN. And for the fastidious drinkers amongst them? – FR. Must.

PAN. And to finish up with? – FR. Rice.

PAN. What else? – FR. Milk.

PAN. What else? – FR. Peas.

PAN. What sort of peas do you mean? – FR. Green.

PAN. What do you put with them? – FR. Pork.

PAN. What sorts of fruit? – FR. Ripe.

PAN. Served how? – FR. Raw.

PAN. Then? – FR. Nuts.

PAN. And how do they like their drinks? – FR. Neat.

PAN. What do they drink? – FR. Wine.

PAN. What sort? – FR. White.

PAN. In Winter? – FR. Sound.

PAN. In Spring? – FR. Dry.

PAN. In Summer – FR. Cool.

PAN. In Autumn and at the vendanges? – FR. Sweet.

'By my quim of a frock,' exclaimed Frère Jean, 'how fat those demisemiquavering bitches must be and how well they must trot to it, seeing they're fed such good and such copious fodder.'

'Allow me to finish' (said Panurge).

PAN. When do they go to bed? – FR. Night.

PAN. And when do they get up? – FR. Day.

PAN. Here is the nicest little male Demisemiquaver that I have put through its courses this year. Would to God by the Blessed Saint Demisemiquaver and the venerable Virgin Saint Demisemiquaver that he were the Principal President of the Paris Parlement. Gosh almighty, my friend, how he would expedite his cases! What an abbreviator of lawsuits he would be, what a drainer of quarrels, what a sorter-through of bundles, what a riffler through of papers, what a taker-down of details! Now let us get round to the other viands and talk leisurely and exhaustively of our aforesaid Sisters of Charity. What are their thingummies like? – FR. Big.

PAN. The entrance? – FR. Fresh.

PAN. Deep down it is like a – FR. Pit.

PAN. I mean, what does it feel like inside? – FR. Hot.

PAN. What grows around it? – FR. Hair.

PAN. What sort? – Fr. Red.

PAN. And the older ones? – FR. Grey.

PAN. How are they when it comes to the jump? – FR. Prompt.

PAN. The wriggling of the bottoms? – FR. Quick.

PAN. Do they all do much bumping? – FR. Much.

PAN. Your tools, now: what are they like? – FR. Large.

PAN. And of what shape is the shaft? – FR. Round.

PAN. What colour is the helmet? – FR. Bay.

PAN. When it's over, what are they like? – FR. Limp.

PAN. And the testicles drooping? – FR. So.

PAN. How are they trussed up? – FR. Tight.

PAN. When all is over, how are they? – FR. Drained.

PAN. Now, by the oath you have sworn, when you come to service those girls, how do you lay them? – FR. Back.

PAN. What do they say whilst they jig about? – FR. Nowt.

PAN. They're giving you a good time, but meanwhile they're thinking about their thingummies? – FR. True.

PAN. Have they borne you any children? – FR. None.

PAN. How do you lie together? – FR. Nude.

PAN. By the aforesaid oath you have sworn, how many times, carefully counted, do you normally manage it a day? – FR. Six.

PAN. And a night? – FR. Ten.

'Damme,' (said Frère Jean) 'the lecher can never get beyond *seize*. He must be shy.'[25]

PAN. Could you really do as well, Frère Jean? Good God! He's a bit of a green leper. Can all the others do as well? – FR. All.

PAN. Who is the greatest gallant amongst you? – FR. Me.

PAN. Do you ever serve a fault? – FR. No.

PAN. I'm a bit confused at this point: having emptied and exhausted your spermatic tools the previous day, can there be any more left in them on the morrow? – FR. More.

PAN. Unless I am raving, they use that Indic herb made famous by Theophrastus. But if in the midst of such delights you experience any slackening off in your member from some natural impediment or otherwise, how do you feel? – FR. Bad.

PAN. And what do those maidens do then? – FR. Yell.

PAN. And if you dry up one day? – FR. Worse.

PAN. What do you give them then? – FR. Biffs.

PAN. What do they do then for you? – FR. Shit.

PAN. What do you mean? – FR. Farts.

PAN. Sounding like what? – FR. Quims.

PAN. How do you chastise them? – FR. Hard.

PAN. Until what flows? – FR. Blood.

PAN. What is their complexion like then? – FR. Dyed.

25. The next number after *seize* (sixteen) is the unmonosyllabic *dix-sept*.

970   RABELAIS

PAN. To make it better for you they need . . . ? – FR. Paint.

PAN. So you remain for them an object of . . . ? – FR. Fear.

PAN. And then they think you are . . . ? – FR. Saints.

PAN. By the vine-leaf oaf that you swore, is August the season when you do it most flaccidly? – FR. Hmm.

PAN. And the one in which you do it most vigorously? – FR. March.

PAN. At other times you do it with . . . ? – FR. Glee.

Panurge then said with a smile:

'So that's the poor old worldly Demisemiquaver! Did you hear how definite, peremptory and brief he was in his replies? He answered only in monosyllables. I reckon he would get three bites from one cherry.'

'Golly,' said Frère Jean, 'he never speaks to his maidens like that! He's polysyllabic with them! You were talking about three bites from one cherry: by Saint Grey, I swear that he could reduce a shoulder of mutton to two slices and down a quart of wine at one gulp. See how tired out he is!'

'Such wretched monkish scrap-iron, avid for victuals, can be found all over the world,' said Epistemon. 'And then they tell us that they've nothing in this world but their lives. What the devil more do kings and great princes have?'[26]

---

26. The manuscript adds: 'Moreover I am in faith very bored here,' said Panurge. 'Let us all act each according to his affection. But once I'm married as I wish I shall found a new monkery, I do not mean of monked monks: they are monking monks. I shall nourish _Frère Tens_ or else _Frère Narjorie_. But they won't go as fast as Demisemiquavers – (The end is incomprehensible.)

How the Institution of Lent is displeasing to Epistemon

CHAPTER 28

[Lent is mocked on medical, moral, prudential and theological grounds.

Rabelais was for a while the titular, non-residing curé *of Saint Christophe du Jambet.*

There are some obvious echoes of the four books, including the quotation from Saint Paul (Romans 14:5) 'Let every man be fully persuaded in his own mind', which was so vital for the philosophy and structure of the Third Book *and cited there in Chapter 7.]*

'Did you note how that miserable, wretched Demisemiquaver mentioned March as the month for debauchery?'

'Yes,' replied Pantagruel; 'yet March always falls in Lent, which was instituted for the maceration of the flesh, the disciplining of sensual appetites and the restraining of venereal frenzies.'

'And,' said Epistemon, 'you can judge whether that pope who first instituted it showed any good sense or not: this peasant-like, lecherous Demisemiquaver confesses that he is never more bewrayed in debauchery than during Lent; and for that he gives the convincing reason advanced by all good and learned physicians who assert that there are no foods eaten during the whole course of a year which excite a man more to lubricity than those which are then in season: beans, peas, kidney-beans, chick-peas, onions, walnuts, oysters, herrings, salted fish and garum-sauce, together with salads wholly composed of aphrodisiac herbs such as rocket, garden-cress, tarragon, watercress, water-parsley, rampion, sea-poppy, hops, figs, rice and raisins.'

'You might be surprised to learn,' said Pantagruel, 'that that good pope who instituted the holy time of Lent (noting that that was the season when natural heat, exuded from the central parts of the body to which it had confined itself during the winter chill, is dispersed like the sap in trees to the limbs at the circumference) prescribed the aforementioned foods so as to help the human race to multiply. What made me think so is the fact that the number of children born in October and November inscribed in the baptismal registers at Thouars is greater than those born in the other ten months of the year: those children, if you count backwards, were all forged, conceived and spawned in Lent.'

'I,' said Frère Jean, 'am listening to your words and take no little pleasure in them, but the curé of Jambet attributed that copious impregnation of wives not to Lenten foods but rather to the bent little begging Friars, the little booted preachers and the little bedraggled confessors who, during the time of their imperium, damn all randy husbands three fathoms deep below the talons of Lucifer. Terrified, those husbands no longer dare to swive their chambermaids and so fall back on their wives.

'I have spoken.'

'Interpret the institution of Lent according to your own ideas,' said Epistemon; '*Let every man be fully persuaded in his own mind*. The abolition of Lent seems to me to be imminent; but I know that the physicians are against it: I've heard them say so. For their Art would be held in contempt without Lent, they would earn nothing and nobody would ever fall ill. All maladies are sown in Lent. Lent is the true hot-bed, the natural seed-bed and dispenser of all maladies. And you're still not taking it into account that whilst Lent rots the body it also drives the soul mad. Devils then get busy: black-beetles come out into the open, bigots hold their great assizes as well as their numerous sessions, stations-of-the-Cross, sales of pardons, confessions, flagellations and anathematizings. I do not mean to infer, though, that the Arimaspians are better off than we are in this matter, but I was speaking apropos.'

'Now then,' said Panurge, 'my old bumkin of a demisemi-quavering bollock! What do you think of this one?

'Is he not a heretic?' – FR. Yea.

PAN. Should he be burnt? – FR. Should.

PAN. Soon as possible? – FR. Yes.

PAN. With no parboiling? – FR. None.

PAN. Quick or dead? – FR. Quick.

PAN. Until what follows? – FR. Death.

PAN. Did he make you cross? – FR. Most.

PAN. What did you take him to be? – FR. Daft.

PAN. Do you mean daft or raging mad? – FR. Worse.

PAN. What do you want him to be? – FR. Burnt.

PAN. Have you burnt any others? – FR. Lots.

PAN. Were they heretics too? – FR. Less.

PAN. Will you burn any more? – FR. Heaps.

PAN. Would you redeem any of them? – FR. None.

PAN. They should all be burnt then? – FR. All.

'I cannot tell,' said Epistemon, 'what pleasure you derive from reasoning with this nasty, scruffy old monk; if I didn't know you already, you'd be spawning in my mind a dishonourable impression of yourself.'

'Let's be on our way, for God's sake,' said Panurge. 'I'm so fond of him that, once I'm married, I'd like to bring him before Gargantua, as my wife's fool; he'd be quite a cop –'

'– ulator, yes,' said Epistemon, employing the figure of speech called tmesis.'[27]

'Now comes the time,' said Frère Jean with a laugh, 'when you'll get your deserts, my poor old Panurge. You will never escape being cuckolded right up to your bum!'

How we called at the land of Satin

CHAPTER 29

[A Lucianesque tapestry-land with embroidered flora and fauna.

Charles Marais succeeded Rabelais at the Hôtel-Dieu in Lyons.

In French April fools are April fish.

The remora fish has a name which in Latin means 'delay' or 'hindrance'. It was constantly mentioned for its ability to delay great ships, even stopping them in full sail.]

27. Tmesis in rhetoric is the cutting of a word in two. In the original the tmesis produces *fou* (fool) + *teur* (-tor) making *fouteur*, fucker. The jest is here transposed.

Happy for having seen the new religious order of the Demisemiquaver Friars, we sailed on for two days. On the third our
pilot descried an island. It was of all isles the most beautiful
and delightful. It was called the Isle of Frieze-cloth, for there
the roads are made of such frieze. Upon it lies the land of Satin
– so well known to pages about Court – upon which grow trees
and plants which never lose flower or leaf and which are formed
of damask and velvet with needle-work figures. Beast and bird
were of tapestry-work.

Then we saw several beasts, birds and trees which are like
ours at home in configuration, size, spread and colour, except
that, unlike ours, they do not eat, do not sing and never bite.
There were several others as well which we had not seen before;
including elephants in various attitudes. Amongst them I noted
six bull-elephants and seven cows which had been put on show
by their trainer in the theatre at Rome during the time of
Germanicus, a nephew of the Emperor Claudius. Those were
talented elephants, elephants which were scholars, musicians,
philosophers and dancers (such as could step out a stately
pavane or a galliard). They were seated at table, elegantly
ordered, eating and drinking in silence like caloyers in their
refectory. They have trunks which are two cubits in length
which we call proboscides; with them they suck up water and
they pick up dates, plums and edibles of all sorts. They use
them as fists for attack and defence. In the course of battle they
toss men high into the air and make them split their sides with
laughter as they fall. They have joints and articulations in their
legs: those who have written the contrary have never seen any
save in paintings. Amongst their teeth they have two great horns
(as Juba calls them). Pausanias says that they are indeed horns,
not teeth; Philostratus, that they are teeth, not horns. It's all
the same to me, provided you realize that they are pure ivory,
three or four cubits long and set in the upper jaw-bone not the
lower. Should you believe those who state the contrary – even
Aelian who is a male hawk where lying is concerned – then you
will find yourself in a fix. It was there, in tapestry-work and
nowhere else, that Pliny had seen elephants with jingles dancing
as funambulists on tight-ropes, walking high above the tables

in the midst of a banquet without disturbing the eaters and drinkers.

I also saw a rhinoceros there, exactly like the one that Henry Clerberg showed me some time ago, and hardly differing from a boar which I once saw at Limoges, save that it had a horn on its snout, pointed and a cubit long. It would dare to take on an elephant with it, sticking it into its belly during the fight (the belly being the softest and weakest part of an elephant) and throw it to the ground, dead.

There I also saw thirty-two unicorns. It is a beast of wondrous ferocity, in form exactly like a beautiful steed, except that it has the head of a stag, the feet of an elephant, the tail of a wild boar and, on its forehead, a sharp, black horn, six or seven foot long, which normally droops down like the crest of a turkey-cock, but when it wants to fight or otherwise employ it, it erects it, straight and stiff. I saw one of them, accompanied by various wild animals, purifying a spring with its horn.

Panurge then told me that his own horn was like that, not in overall length but in its powers and capacities, for just as that unicorn cleansed the water in the ponds and springs from filth and poison so that the other species of animals could then safely drink of it, so too you could safely lark about after his horn without risk of canker, pox, clap, stippled pustules or other minor blessings, for if there were to be any infection in a hole of a Memphitic rankness he would clean it out with its sinewy horn.

'Once you're married,' said Frère Jean, 'we'll try that out on your wife; and may God so will it, since you've given us such a lesson in hygiene.'

'Oh, yes,' said Panurge; 'and then you'll quickly get that lovely little pill in your guts by which you graduate to God and which, like Julius Caesar's, is compounded of twenty-two dagger blows.'

'Far better,' said Frère Jean, 'would be a goblet of a good cool wine.'

I also saw there the Golden Fleece which Jason won (and those who maintain that it was not a fleece but a golden apple, since *mêla* in Greek means both apple and sheep, have a poor acquaintance with the land of Satin).

I also saw a chameleon just as Aristotle describes it and like the one I was once shown by Charles Marais, a famous physician in the noble city of Lyons on the Rhone: it lived on air alone.

I also saw three hydras such as I had previously seen elsewhere. They are snakes, each having seven distinct heads.

I also saw fourteen phoenixes there. I have read in various authors that there is never more than one phoenix in the whole world at any one epoch, but according to my humble opinion those who have described it never saw any except in tapestry-land, not even Lactantius Firmianus. I also saw the hide of the ass of Apuleius. And I saw: three hundred and nine pelicans; six thousand and sixteen seleucid birds (proceeding in ranks and gobbling up the grasshoppers in their wheat-fields; some cynamolges, argathiles, caprimulges and tinnunculi – why, even some great-throated pelican jawyers: I mean Vatican lawyers – some stymphalides (harpies), panthers, gazelles, cemades, cynocephali, satyrs, cartazoni, tarands, aurochs, monopes, pephages, cepi, neades, steres, cercopitheci, bisons, musmons, byturi, ophyri, screech-owls and gryphons.

I also saw Mid-Lent (mounted, her stirrups held by Mid-August and Mid-March) as well as werewolves, centaurs, tigers, leopards, hyenas, giraffes and oryxes.

I also saw a *remora* (a tiny 'delay' fish called *echineis* by the Greeks): it was close to a great ship which could not budge even though she was in full sail on the high seas. I can well believe it to be the ship of Periander, the tyrant, which just such a tiny fish brought to a halt despite the wind. It was here, in the land of Satin, that Mutianus saw it, and nowhere else. Frère Jean told us that two sorts of fish used to lord it over the Courts of Parlement, rotting the bodies of all the plaintiffs (noble and commoner, poor and rich, great and small) and driving their souls mad: the first were April fools – fishy false-witnesses – and the venomous delay-fish – an eternity of lawsuits never ending in a judgement.

I also saw sphinxes, raphia, lynxes, cephi (which have front feet like hands and rear legs like a man's) crocutae, eali (which are as big as hippopotamuses, with tails like elephants, jaws like wild-boars and horns which are as mobile as the ears of an ass) and cucrotes (very quick beasts as big as the donkeys in the countryside at Mirebeau): they have necks, tails and chests like those of lions, legs like a stag's and a maw split up to their ears but with only two teeth, one upper and one lower; they speak with a human voice but there they uttered not a word. You tell me that no one has ever seen a saker's eyrie: well I saw eleven of them. Note that well.

I also saw some left-hand halberds, something I had never seen elsewhere.

'I also saw some manticors: very strange beasts, with the body of a lion, a red hide, a face and ears like a man's, and three rows of teeth which intersected each other as when one interlaces the fingers of both hands; they have a sting in their tail with which they prick you as scorpions do; and their voices are most melodious.

I also saw some catoblepes: savage beasts with small bodies but heads disproportionately big: they can scarcely lift them off the ground. Their eyes are so poisonous that anyone who looks into them dies at once, as if he had seen a basilisk.

I also saw some beasts-with-two-backs who seemed to me to be marvellously merry; the motions of their buttocks being more lavish than a wagtail's, with an everlasting stirring of cruppers.

I also saw some mammiferous cray-fish, which I had never seen anywhere else. They marched in excellent order: it did you good to see them.

How in the land of Satin we saw Hear-say, who kept a school for witnesses

CHAPTER 30

[A chapter dealing with false witnesses, including tellers of travellers' tales and marvels.

'Anacampserotes' are fruit said by Pliny to reconcile lovers.

Pierre Gilles (Aegidius) was a friend of Erasmus. In 1533 he published a treatise, On the Latin and French Names of Mediterranean Fishes, *which the Cardinal d'Armagnac persuaded him to dedicate to François I.*

   The people standing behind leaves of mint are liars, 'mint' in French being menthe, *suggesting* mentir, *to tell lies.*

   The famous mill at Bazacle on the Garonne is mentioned in Chapter 14 of Pantagruel.*]*

Penetrating a little deeper into the land of tapestry we saw the Mediterranean Sea, parted and revealed to its uttermost depths just as the Red Sea in the Arabian Gulf parted to make a way for the Israelites to come out from Egypt. There I recognized Triton sounding his mighty horn, Glaucus, Proteus, Mereus and hundreds of other sea-gods and sea-monsters. We also saw an infinity of fish of various kinds: fish dancing, flying, flitting, fighting, eating, breathing, mating, hunting, skirmishing, laying ambushes, arranging truces, trading, swearing oaths and disporting themselves.

   In one corner near by we saw Aristotle standing and holding a lantern like the hermit usually painted close to Saint Christopher; he was contemplating, thinking and writing everything down. Ranged below him like bailiff's witnesses were several other philosophers: Appian, Heliodorus, Athenaeus, Porphyry, Pancrates of Arcadia, Numenius, Posidonius, Ovid, Oppian, Olympius, Seleucus, Leonides, Agathocles, Theophrastus, Demostratus, Mutianus, Nymphodorus, Aelian and five hundred other men of leisure, as were Chrysippus, or Aristarchus of Sola who spent fifty-eight years doing nothing else but study bees.

   Amongst them I espied Peter Gilles, who, sample-bottle in hand, was in deep contemplation, examining the urine of those beautiful fish.

   After having long considered the land of Satin, Pantagruel said, 'I have long here fed my eyes, yet I can in no wise eat my fill: my stomach is barking with a raging hunger.'

   'Let us feed, then,' I said, 'feed and taste those anacampserotes dangling down over there.'

   'Ugh! They are worthless!'

So I plucked some myrobolans which were hanging down near the edge of a tapestry, but I could neither chew them nor swallow them. If you were to try them you would rightly say and swear that they were nothing but twisted silken-thread and had no taste whatsoever. You would have said that Heliogabalus had found in them (as in a transcript from some papal bull) the model of those feasts which he arranged for those whom he had long kept fasting with promises of enjoying eventually a sumptuous, copious, Imperial feast, then feeding them with foods made of wax, marble or clay, and painted in pictures or on table-linen.

So while foraging in that land for something to eat we heard a grating, uncertain noise as of women doing their washing or as of the wooden clappers feeding grain to the mills at Bazacle near Toulouse. Without lingering any further we made our ways towards whence it came; there we saw a little old hunchback, misshapen and grotesque.

His name was Hear-say.

His maw was cloven to the ears; in his mouth were seven tongues; each tongue was slit into seven parts. No matter what the subject, all seven spoke together, saying divers things in divers languages. He also had as many ears scattered over his head and body as Argus of old had eyes. In addition he was blind, with paralysis in his legs.

I saw countless men and women around him, listening and attentive. Some whom I recognized in the troop were cutting fine figures: one of them was holding a map of the world which he was briefly explaining to them in short aphorisms; in no time they became learned scholars, and with a good memory for detail spoke about many marvels, to understand a hundredth part of which a man's lifetime would not suffice: about the Pyramids, the Nile, Babylon, Troglodytes, Himantopodes, Blemmyae, Pygmies and Cannibals; about the Hyperborean Mountains, the Aegipans, and all the devils.

And all from Hear-say.

There I fancy I saw Herodotus, Pliny, Solinus, Berosus, Philostratus, Mela, Strabo and many other Ancients as well as Albertus Magnus the Dominican, Peter Martyr, Pope Pius the

Second, Volaterranus, Paolo Giovio, Jacques Cartier (a brave man), Hayton of Armenia, Marco Polo the Venetian, Ludovico Romano, Pedro Alvarez, and I-know-not-how-many modern historians who write of handsome deeds whilst hiding behind a piece of tapestry.

And all from Hear-say.

Behind a piece of tapestry embroidered with leaves of mint I saw a number of men from Perche and Le Mans standing close to Hear-say; they were good students and quite young. Upon asking in which Faculty they were studying, we heard that, from their youth upwards, they were learning to be witnesses, earning so much money by their profession that, from the time they left their province to the time they came back, they made a decent living from the witnessing-trade, bearing sure witness to anything at all for those who paid most for a day's work.

And all from Hear-say.

Think what you like about them, but they gave us some hunks of their bread and we drank from their barrels. It was good cheer. Then they gave us heartfelt advice: if we wanted to rise in the courts of great noblemen, to be as economical as possible of the truth.

How we descried Lanternland

CHAPTER 31

[Echoes of the four books and of the Disciple de Pantagruel. *The erudition, as so often, is from Pliny.]*

Poorly fed and entertained in the land of Satin, we sailed for three days; on the fourth we happily drew near to Lanternland. As we did so we saw little lights flitting over the sea; I for my part thought they were not Lanterns but fish with flaming tongues gliding out of the water and glowing, or else those glow-worms which you call cicindellas shining out there as they do in my part of the world at eventide when the barley is ripening. But our pilot assured us that they were Lanterns-of-the-Guard who were doing the rounds and reconnoitring the outskirts while escorting a few foreign Lanterns who were like good Franciscans or Jacobins on their way to take their seats at their Provincial Chapter. We still wondered however whether they were signs of a storm, but he stood by what he had said.

How we landed at the port of the Lychnobians and entered Lanternland

CHAPTER 32

[*This chapter shows debts to Lucian's* True History *and to the* Disciple de Pantagruel.

*The Lychnobians are known from an adage of Erasmus, IV, IV, LI, 'Lychnobii (those who live by lamplight)', that is, either by studying or drinking late into the night). The Latins knew that Greek word from Seneca (*Epistle, *122, 16). Here the dominant meaning is of 'something to do with Lantern'. They are apparently male, living off the female Lanterns.*

*'The Lanterns of Aristophanes and of Cleanthes' are proverbial. They constitute an adage of Erasmus (I, VII, LXXII), which also mentions the famous lamp of Epictetus, which Lucian tells us an ignoramus purchased after his death. (*The Ignorant Book-collector, *13.)*

To lantern, lanterner, *is always open to jokes and plays on words, since as well as suggesting lamps it suggests lechery, the female sexual organ and sexual frolics generally.*

'Obeliscolychny', here personified, is a word taken over from the Fourth Book, Chapter 22.]

We at once entered the port of Lanternland. There, on a high lighthouse tower, Pantagruel recognized the Lantern of La Rochelle, who was sending us clear light. We also saw the Lanterns of Pharos, of Nauplion and of the Acropolis of Athens, sacred to Pallas. Hard by the harbour is a small village inhabited by the Lichnobians, who are folk who live off Lanterns just as in our land lay brothers live off nuns. They are studious and decent people. It was there that Demosthenes once lanterned about. From that place we were escorted as far as the palace by three Obeliscolychnies, who formed the military guard of the harbour, wearing tall hats as Albanians do. We expounded to them the reasons for our voyage and our determination to obtain from the Queen of Lanternland a Lantern to enlighten us and guide us throughout the voyage which we were making to the oracle of La Bouteille. They promised to do so right gladly, adding that we had arrived there at a good and opportune moment for making a sound choice of a Lantern, since those ladies were then holding there their Provincial Chapter.

On arriving at the palace, we were presented by two Lanterns, namely the Lanterns of Aristophanes and of Cleanthes, Lanterns-of-Honour to the queen to whom Panurge briefly expounded in Lanternese the objects of our voyage. We received a kind welcome from her and a command to be present at her supper in order to choose more easily the one whom we would like for our guide.

That greatly pleased us and we were not slack, carefully noting and considering every detail in their gestures, dress and deportment as well as in the way table was served.

The queen was dressed in clear crystal and in encrusted damask-work studded with great diamonds. Lanterns of the blood-royal were clad either in translucent stones or paste; the others were clad in horn, paper or oiled cloth. The same applied to the *Falots*, the Fire-baskets, according to their rank and the antiquity of their families. I noticed only one made of earthenware: she, who looked like a pot, ranked amongst the most gorgeous. Astonished by it, I learnt that she was the Lantern of Epictetus; they had once refused to part with her for three thousand drachmas.

I carefully studied the modish accoutrements of Polymix, the Lantern of Martial, and even more Eicosimyx, consecrated of old by Canopa, the daughter of Tisias.[28]

I especially noted Pensila, the lantern formerly taken from

---

28. The name is corrected after the manuscript. It was the daughter of *Critias* who dedicated a twenty-wick lamp to Serapis.

the temple of Apollo Palatine in Thebes and subsequently removed to the city of Cyme in Aeolia by Alexander the Conqueror.

I noted another one which was outstanding because of a beautiful tuft of crimson silk which she wore on her head; I was told that she was Bartolus, the Light of the Law. I noted two others who were outstanding on account of the clyster-bags they wore on their belts. I was told that they were the two Luminaries of the apothecaries, the Great and the Lesser.

When the hour for supper arrived, the queen sat down in the place of honour, and the others in order of rank and dignity. As an entrée, big moulded candles were served, except that the queen was served with a fat, erect, flaming torch of white wax, a little red round the tip. The Lanterns of the blood-royal were also treated differently from the others, as was the Provincial Lantern of Mirebeau for whom a candle of walnut-oil was served, and as was the Provincial Lantern of Bas Poitou whom I saw served with a candle bearing a coat-of-arms. Lord only knows what light they thereafter produced with their wicks.

There is an exception at this point: a number of girl Lanterns chaperoned by a fat one: they did not shine as the others did but emitted what seemed to me to be pale, straw-tumbling colours.[29]

After supper we retired to rest. The following morning the queen made us choose one of the most outstanding Lanterns for our guide. And thus we took our leave.

29. The medieval legal authority Bartolus was surnamed 'the Light of the Law'. Two late medieval books for chemists were *The Luminary of the Apothecaries* and *The Great Luminary of the Apothecaries*.

    MS: . . . fat one. *Then I recalled Matheline, who allowed neither oil nor candle to be put in her body; nor did she shine like the others*, but emitted . . .

How we arrived at the oracle of La Bouteille

CHAPTER 33

*[A Bacchic chapter but one which tramples drunkenness underfoot.
Guillaume Bigot, whose name (probably) appeared corrupted as 'Brigot' in Chapter 18, moved in the circle of the Du Bellays.*

*That Frère Jean calls the last book of the Bible not the Apocalypse
but Revelation is out of character. The title 'Revelation' is usually
either learned or Reformed. The allusion is to Revelation 12:1.]*

With our noble Lantern lighting us and leading us, we arrived
entirely happy at the longed-for isle on which was the oracle of
La Bouteille. Panurge jumped ashore, raised a merry leg in a
jig, and said to Pantagruel:

'Today we have that, at last, which we have sought with so
much moil and toil.'

He then courteously commended himself to our Lantern. She
bade us all be of good hope and never fear no matter what
appeared before us. As we drew near to the temple of the Dive
Bouteille we had to pass through a big vineyard planted with
vines of many wines, such as Falernian, Malmsey, Muscadet,
Tabbia, Beaune, Mirevaux, Orleans, Picardan, Arbois, Coussy,
Anjou, Graves, Corsican, Verron, Nérac and others. That vineyard was planted of old by good old Bacchus, with such a
blessing that it bore leaf, blossom and fruit in all seasons like
the orange-trees at Cyrene. Our splendid Lantern ordered us to
eat three grapes apiece, to put vine-leaves in our shoes and to
hold a green branch in our left hands. At the far end of the
vineyard we passed under an ancient arch on which was delicately carved a memorial to a Drinker, consisting in one place
of a long string of flagons, leathern bottles, glass bottles, flasks,
barrels, demijohns, pots, pint mugs and antique jars hanging
from a shaded trellis.

In another place were great quantities of garlic, onions, shal-
lots, hams, caviar, cheese tarts, smoked ox-tongues, mature

cheeses and similar dainties all interlarded with vine leaves and industriously bound together with vine-stocks.

In another place were hundreds of differently shaped glasses, such as glasses standing on stems, mounted glasses, goblets, tumblers, cups, jars, bowls, beakers and similar Bacchic artillery.

On the façade of the arch, below the frieze, two lines of verse were incised:

> Traveller passing through this site
> Get a Lantern good and bright.

'We have already provided for that,' said Pantagruel, 'for in the whole of Lanternland there is no Lantern better or more divinely favoured than ours.'

That arch led to a beautiful and spacious arbour entirely composed of vine-stocks bedecked with grapes of five hundred different colours and five hundred different shapes, not natural ones but ones fashioned thus by the art of agriculture: they were yellow, blue, tawny, azure, white, black, green, violet, striped and variegated; long, round, triangular, bollockal, regal, bearded, snub-nosed, herbal. The end of the arbour was closed by three venerable ivy-bushes, most verdant and laden with berries. There our most illustrious Lantern bade us each make for himself an Albanian hat out of that ivy and to cover his entire head with it. Which was done without delay.

'The pontiff of Jupiter,' said Pantagruel, 'would never have passed beneath that trellis in ancient times.'

'There was a mystical reason for that,' said our shining Lantern. For in going under it he would have had the wine – the grapes, that is – *above* his head, which would then appear subordinated and dominated by wine: meaning that pontiffs and all great persons who are devoted and dedicated to the contemplation of things divine must maintain their minds in tranquillity, beyond all sensual perturbations, which are more manifested in drunkenness than in any other passion there is. Seeing that you have passed under it, you too would never be

admitted to the oracle of the Dive Bouteille were it not that
Bacbuc, the noble pontiff, saw your shoes full of vine-leaves,
which is an action totally and diametrically opposed to the
above, and a sign that wine is despised by you, trampled upon
and subjugated.'

'I'm sorry,' said Frère Jean, 'but I'm no scholar, yet I find in
my Breviary that, in Revelation, a wondrous sight was seen: a
woman with the moon under her feet. That, as was explained
to me by Bigot, signifies that she was not of the same ilk or
nature as other women who, on the contrary, all have the moon
inside their heads and consequently have brains forever lunatic.
Which leads me readily to believe what you say, my dear lady
Lantern.'

How we went below ground to enter into the
temple of La Bouteille; and how Chinon is
the first town in the world

CHAPTER 34

[*Chinon is the town of Rabelais' pays which he publicly praised in the
episode of Bollux in the Prologue to the Fourth Book. Some thought
its foundation dated from the time of Cain, hence its 'learned' name,
Caynon. (Cain 'builded a city' in Genesis 4:17 and named it after his
son Enoch.)*

The imposing Cave Peinte *at Chinon is now often used for ceremonies connected with Rabelais and wine. Here that 'Painted Cave'
is appropriately associated with Bacchus and Silenus.*

Phlox *in Greek means flame.*]

We then went down below ground through an arbour daubed
with plaster. On its outside surface were crude paintings of
women and satyrs dancing in the company of old Silenus,
laughing astride his donkey. 'There!' I said to Pantagruel: 'That
entrance recalls to mind the *Cave Peinte* of the first town of the
world, for there are similar paintings there of similar freshness.'

'And where and what is that *first town* you speak of?' asked Pantagruel.

'Chinon,' I said, 'otherwise Caynon, in Touraine.'

'I know where Chinon is,' said Pantagruel, 'And the *Cave Peinte* as well: I have drunk many a glass of cool wine in there. And I have no doubt whatsoever that Chinon is an ancient town: its escutcheon witnesses to it, on which it is said:

> Twice or thrice praise Chinon Town;
> Little city: great renown.
> Sited on an ancient Hoe,
> Woods above, the Vienne below.

Yet how could it be the first town in the world? Where can you find that written down? Why such a conjecture?'

'In Holy Writ I find that Cain was the first builder of towns. It is therefore probable that he called the first one after his own name just as, in imitation of him, all other founders and builders of towns have done, imposing their own names upon them: Athene (the Greek Minerva) did so for Athens; Alexander, for Alexandria; Constantine, for Constantinople; Pompey, for Pompeiopolis in Cilicia; Hadrian, for Hadrianopolis; Canaan, for the Canaanites; Sheba, for the Shebans; Assur, for the Assyrians; and similarly for Ptolomais, Caesaria, Tiberium and Herodium in Judaea.'

While we were chatting thus there came forth the Great Flask – our Lantern called him Phlox – the commissioner of the Dive Bouteille; he was accompanied by the temple-guard who were all French Bottlemen. On seeing us bearing (as I said) our Bacchic staffs and crowned with ivy – recognizing also our famous Lantern – he let us safely in and commanded that we be brought at once before Princess Bacbuc, the Lady of Honour of La Bouteille and the Head Priestess of the Mysteries. Which was done.

How we went down the Tetradic Steps; and of the fright which Panurge had

CHAPTER 35

[In mystical systems one rises or penetrates by 'degrees' (that is, by steps). Here those degrees are quite literally steps in a staircase. The Pythagorean number is four, the tetrad, as in the Third Book, *Chapter 29.*

The text uses Plato's term for soul-generation, psychogony. The author has indeed read Plutarch's Commentary on the Psychogony, *which Plato describes in his* Timaeus, *and his number lore from him (1016Aff.)*

Cf. Erasmus, Adages, *III, VI, XXII, 'More obscure than the numbers of Plato', which makes Pythagoras the source of Plato's mathematical obscurity. There are sustained attempts to link this chapter to the four books. One example amongst others: for the bites from dogs' teeth and toothache, cf. the end of* Pantagruel *Chapter 10, variant.*

Also noteworthy is the appearance of the 'favourite number' of Rabelais, seventy-eight.]

We then descended a marble underground step on to a landing. Turning to the left, we went down two more, where there was a similar landing. Then three more, turning on to a similar landing, then, likewise, four more.

Panurge asked, 'Are we there?'

'How many steps have you counted?' said our magnificent Lantern.

'One plus two plus three plus four,' Pantagruel replied.

'How many does that add up to?' she asked.

'Ten,' replied Pantagruel.

'Multiply that resultant,' she said, 'by the Pythagorean tetrad.'

'That makes ten, twenty, thirty, forty,' said Pantagruel.

'And what do those numbers add up to?' she said.

'One hundred,' replied Pantagruel.

'To that, add the Prime Cube, which is eight. At the end of that number of destiny we shall find the door to the Temple. And there wisely note that is the true psychogony of Plato (so famous amongst the Academics, yet so little understood): the half of it is composed of unity, plus the first two simple numbers, plus their squares and their cubes.'[30]

As we went down that number of steps we first needed our legs – for without them we would have simply gone down like barrels rolling into the cellars below – and secondly our bright Lantern, for during our way down no other light appeared to us, any more than if we had been in Saint Patrick's hole in Hibernia or in the cavern of Trophonius in Boeotia.

Once we had gone down seventy-eight stairs, Panurge cried out, addressing his words to our shining Lantern:

'O miracle-working Dame, with a contrite heart I beg you to let us turn back. By the Death of Ox, I am dying of funk. I consent never to get married. You have taken great trouble over me and undergone great toil. God will repay you in his Great Repayment. Nor shall I be ungrateful, once I have issued forth from this Troglodites' cavern. Of your grace, let us go back. I greatly fear lest this be Tenarum, by which men go down to Avernus, and I seem to hear Cerberus barking. Hark! Either my ears are a-tingle or it's him! I'm no devotee of his: no toothache is greater than the ache of dogs' teeth in our legs. If this is the cave of Triphonius, then spectres and hobgoblins will at once gobble us up alive for want of scraps, as they ate one of the halberdiers of Demetrius. Are you there, Frère Jean? Stay close to me, I beg you, old Fat-guts! I'm dying of fright. Have you got your cutlass? I've got no weapons at all, either to defend or attack. Let us go back!'

'I'm here,' said Frère Jean; 'I'm here. Don't be afraid: I've got you by the scruff of the neck. Eighteen devils will never get you out of my arms, even though you have no weapons. No man lacks weapons in his hour of need who combines a stout heart

---

30. The number is as in Plutarch 1017 DF: half of 108. That is: $1 + 2 + 3 + 4 + 9 + 8 + 27$, in other words: the first simple number, 1, plus the next two simple numbers, 2 and 3, plus the squares of 2 and of 3, plus the cubes of 2 and of 3.

with a strong arm. Weapons would rather rain down from Heaven as boulders once did – and they're still there – over the fields of La Crau hard by Les Fosses Mariannes in Provence, in order to help Hercules, who had nothing else to fight with against the two sons of Neptune.

'But what is this? Are we going down to the babies in Limbo – good God they'll shit all over us! – or else to all the devils in Hell? God's Body! Now that I have those vine-leaves in my shoes I'll whack 'em hard! O, how ferociously I shall fight! Where is this? Where are they? It's only their horns that I fear, and the two horns that Panurge the married man will wear shall protect me from them entirely. In the spirit of prophecy I can foresee him there as another horn-bearing, horny Actaeon, with a horn on his bum.'[31]

'When the time comes for marrying off monks, Brother, see you don't wed Quartan Fever. For may I never return safe and sound from these hypogean chambers if I won't ram her for you simply to make you a horn-bearing farter of horns. Apart from that I think that Quartan Fever is very nasty old bag. I remember that Catty-claws wanted to give her to you as a wife, but you called him a heretic.'

Here the conversation was interrupted by our resplendent Lantern who admonished us that here was the place where it behove us solemnly to guard our lips, suppressing speech and stilling our tongues. And she categorically asserted that since we had lined our shoes with vine-leafs we need never fear having to return without the Word of La Bouteille.

'Let us get on, then,' said Frère Jean, 'and charge head-first right through all the devils. You can only die once! I did mean to save my life, though, for some great battle. Charge! Charge! Fight our way through! I've more than enough courage. True, my heart's all of a tremble, but that is not brought on by fear or fever but by the chill and stench of this Underworld.

'Charge! Charge! Let us push, push, pass, press and piss our way through. I am William the Fearless.'[32]

---

31. The manuscript does not give Panurge 'two horns' but an 'Idea of horns'.
32. Cf. the end of Chapter 23 of the *Fourth Book*.

How the doors of the Temple opened by themselves, wonderfully

CHAPTER 36

[The saying ἐν οἴνῳ ἀλήθεια *is better known by its Latin form,* In vino veritas, *which merits a longish commentary by Erasmus (Adages, I, VII, XVII).*

For 'Corinthian brass' see an adage of Adrian Junius (Basle, 1558): 'Corinthian and Ionian words'.

For the herb called 'aetheopis', which opens things, cf. Chapter 62 of the Fourth Book, *where it is one of Rabelais' many debts to Calcagnini.*

The Indian diamond here acts as a lodestone.]

At the bottom of the steps we came to a portal of fine jasper, all laid out and constructed as work in the Doric style, on the tympanum of which was written this saying in Ionic lettering of the finest gold: ἐν οἴνῳ ἀλήθεια, that is to say, 'In wine: Truth'.

The two doors were of a brass similar to that of Corinth, massive and decorated with a motif of exquisitely enamelled vine-leaves, in relief as the sculpture demanded. Both of them came together and shut evenly in their mortises without fastening, closure or lock of any kind. There an Indian diamond as big as an Egyptian bean was simply hanging down; it was set in fine gold raised at two points and hexagonal in shape. On either side of it, cloves of garlic were suspended in a straight line along the wall.

Our noble Lantern then told us that, though she now desisted from conducting us any further, we must accept her excuse as legally binding; we merely had to obey the instructions of the High Priestess Bacbuc, for she herself was not allowed to enter in, for specific reasons which it was better to pass over in silence than reveal to anyone living this mortal life. But she commanded us to be on the alert whatever happened, not to be in any way fearful or afraid, and to put our trust in her for our way back.

She then tugged at the diamond hanging down where the

two doors met, and tossed it to the right into a silver receptacle expressly reserved for it. Then, from the hinges on either side of the gates, she pulled a cord of crimson silk, about a span and a half in length, from which the garlic was suspended; she attached them both to two golden clasps which hung down at the sides precisely for that purpose. She then withdrew.

Suddenly, without being touched by anyone, the two doors swung open. They made no strident squeal when doing so nor any ghastly grating noise such as tough, heavy brass doors usually do, but rather a sweet and pleasant sound which echoed through the vault of the Temple.

Pantagruel understood why as soon as he espied small rollers set beneath the edge of each door and attached to their hinges: as each swung back towards the wall it rubbed against a hard, very even, smoothed-down piece of porphyry, thus producing that sweet, harmonious sound.

I was astounded and wondered how those two doors opened by themselves without being pushed. To understand such a marvel, as soon as we had gone in I cast my eyes on to the gap between the doors and the walls, longing to find out by what power and device they had been thrown back, wondering whether our friendly Lantern had placed against them when they were closed that herb called aetheopis, by means of which one can open all objects which are shut; but I noted that the parts where the two doors were fitted into their inside mortises were made of plates of high-quality steel let into the Corinthian bronze. I also noticed two wide slabs of sky-blue Indian lodestone about half-a-palm thick, very smooth, highly polished and cut flush into the wall of the Temple over their entire thickness at the point where the doors, once wide open, were now arrested by the wall. So it was by the violent appetite of the lodestone that those steel plates had yielded to that motion through an occult and wondrous institution of Nature: as a result, those doors were slowly seized and attracted, but not always: only once that lodestone had been removed was the steel absolved and freed from the subjection it naturally has to a magnet when sited close by; moreover, the two bunches of garlic had been set aside: our merry Lantern had pulled them away and hung them up, because garlic counteracts a lodestone and strips it of its power of attraction.

On one of the tablets I mentioned, on the right, was exquisitely carved in antique Roman script this line of verse in senarian iambics:

Ducunt volentem fata, nolentem trahunt.

(The fates lead the willing: the unwilling they drag.)[33]

On the other tablet I saw on the left, elegantly incised in capital letters this adage:

ALL THINGS MOVE TO THEIR END.[34]

How the floor of the Temple was paved with a wondrous mosaic

CHAPTER 37

[Readers often compare the rich architecture with that of the Dream of Polifilo *of Colonna. The astonishing realism of the painter Xeuxis is mentioned in the* Fourth Book, *Chapter 17. The dominant theme is the vine as the symbol of Bacchus.*

Where the text refers to 'Sositratus' the manuscript rightly reads 'Sosus', as in the source (Pliny, Natural History, 36, 25, 30.]

33. A senarian line of verse consists of six feet, each of which is an iambus or a permitted variant. The line, which is attributed to Cleanthes, is quoted in Latin by Seneca (Epistle 107). It is cited twice by Erasmus (*Adages*, II, III, XLI, 'Against necessity even the gods cannot resist', and V, I, XC, 'There is no fighting against fate'. But most powerful of all is the specific endorsing of this line by Saint Augustine, *City of God*, 5, 8.

34. This line is given in Greek capitals in the manuscript: ΠΡΟΣ ΤΕΛΟΣ ΑΥΤΩΝ ΠΑΝΤΑ ΚΙΝΕΙΤΑΙ. It is presented as adonic verse (of which it is an imperfect example). I do not know its author, but the idea is consonant with that of Gargantua in his letter to his son (*Pantagruel*, Chapter 8) referring to the end of the age 'when all things are brought to their End and period'.

Having read those inscriptions I turned my eyes to contemplating the magnificent temple; I lingered over the incredible art with which the pavement was put together; nothing beneath the canopy of Heaven, now or in the past, can reasonably be compared to it, not even the pavement of the temple of Fortuna in Praeneste in the days of Sylla, nor that of the Greeks called asserotum, which was made in Pergamo by Sositratus; for it was a mosaic formed of little square tablets, each of fine polished stone, each stone in its natural colour: one was of red jasper, delightfully spangled with a variety of colour flecks; another was of snake-stone; another of porphyry; another of wolf's-eye, with a scattering of golden sparks as tiny as atoms; another of agate with a random confusion of tiny flames, milky in colour; another of the choicest chalcedony; another of green jasper with clear red and yellow veins all separated by a diagonal line. The paving above the portico was constructed of a mosaic of little stones fitted together, each with its natural colour, which served to form a figurative design, as though one had strewn a scattering of vine-branches over that pavement without much concern for their order, for in one place they had been thickly strewn, and in another more thinly. That vine-foliage was everywhere remarkable, but particularly so where, in one place, snails were palely inching over the grapes; in another, where little lizards were darting through the branches; and in another, where there were figured grapes, both half and fully ripe. All were made and disposed with such art and decorative skill that they would have easily deceived starlings and other little birds as did the portrait of Zeuxis by Heraclea.

Be that as it may, they deceived us all right, for at the point where the architect had scattered the vine-branches more thickly we – fearing to trip over them – walked with great, high-stepping strides as one does when making one's way through an uneven stony place.

After that I looked attentively at the vault and walls of the temple, which were encrusted all over with a mosaic of marble and porphyry, forming a wonderful mosaic, stretching from one end to the other, beginning on the left of the entrance with an unbelievably elegant representation of the battle which the good god Bacchus won against the Indians.

The description of it is as follows.

How the Battle of Bacchus against the Indians was portrayed on the mosaic-work of the Temple

CHAPTER 38

[After an echo of the Bacchantes *of Euripides, this chapter and Chapters 39 and 42 are exceptionally indebted to Lucian's* Dionysus, *one of the main Bacchic texts of Antiquity. There are also echoes of Plutarch (648 Bff.: Symposiaca, 3, Question 2: 'On ivy and on Bacchus'); indeed all of this Question in Plutarch is concerned with wine. For mint and blood see Aristotle, Problems, 20, 2.]*

It started by depicting various towns, villages, castles, fortresses, fields and forests, all in flames and ablaze. Various demented and dishevelled women were depicted there, frenetically tearing living calves, sheep and ewes to pieces and devouring their flesh. That signified for us how Bacchus, as he went into India, put everything to fire and sword.

Despite which, Bacchus was held in such contempt by the Indians that they did not deign to march out to meet him, having received conclusive news from their spies that there were no fighting-men in his army, only a little old womanish fellow who was always drunk, accompanied by some yokelish lads (stark naked and always dancing and leaping about, with tails and horns like kids) and by a large number of drunken women. They therefore resolved to let them pass through without armed resistance as though a victory over such folk would bring them not honour and glory but shame, dishonour and ignominy.

Bacchus, despised, went on gaining ground, putting everything to the fire (since fire and thunderbolt are the weapons of his father and since even before he was born he had been saluted by Jupiter with the thunderbolts which burnt and destroyed by fire Semele his mother and her house) and likewise to the sword, since Bacchus naturally produces blood in times of peace and draws it off in times of war. Witness the fields of the isle of Samos called panaema (that is, all-blood), where Bacchus overtook the Amazons who were fleeing from the land of the Ephesians and killed them all by phlebotomy, so that that field of battle was drenched and bespattered with blood.

From which you may understand from now on (better than Aristotle ever explained it in his *Problems*) why men of old cited as a current proverb: *In time of war eat not and plant not mint*. The reason is that blows are then regularly struck without discrimination: if any man who has handled or eaten mint is wounded that day, it is impossible (or very hard) to staunch his blood.

Next on that mosaic was portrayed how Bacchus went to war riding in a magnificent chariot drawn by three pairs of young leopards yoked together. His face was as that of a little child (to teach us that no good drinker ever grows old) and as red as a cherubim's, without a hair on his chin. Upon his head he bore sharp horns, topped by a beautiful crown made from vine-branches and grapes, and a mitre of crimson-red. And on his feet he wore gilded buskins.

In his fighting-force there was no man: his whole guard and soldiery consisted of Bassarides, Evantes, Euhyades, Edonides, Trietherides, Ogygiae, Mimallones, Maenads, Thyades and Bacchides, who are raving, raging frenzied women, with belts of live snakes and serpents rather than girdles, with their hair flying in the wind, bands of vine-leaves on their foreheads and clad in the skins of stags and goats; in their hands they wield axes, thyrses, bill-hooks, halberds shaped like pineapples, and special, light little bucklers which clanged and resounded when they were struck ever so lightly, which they used when necessary as tambourines and cymbals. They numbered seventy-nine thousand, two hundred and twenty-seven.

The vanguard was led by Silenus, a man who had in the past gained his complete confidence and whose manly virtue, magnanimity, courage and wisdom he had witnessed on several situations.

He was a shaky, bent little old man, fat, with sagging guts, big straight ears, a pointed aquiline nose and huge shaggy eyebrows; he rode astride a well-hung ass; in his hand he held a stick for support and also to fight with gallantly if ever it were appropriate to dismount; he was dressed in a yellow garment such as women wear.

His unit was composed of young country lads, horned like goats and cruel as lions, quite naked, always singing and dancing lascivious dances: they were called Tityri and Satyrs. They numbered eighty-five thousand, six-score and thirteen.

Pan brought up the rear: a terrifying monster of a man, for with his hairy thighs he was like a goat in his nether limbs; on his head were horns pointing straight up to the heavens. His face was rubicund and flushed, his beard extremely long: he was a bold, courageous, daring male, easily provoked to wrath; in his left hand he held a flute; in his right, a bent stick. His bands were made up of satyrs, hemipans, aegipans, sylvans, fauns, lemures, lares, goblins and hobgoblins, to the number of seventy-eight thousand, one hundred and fourteen.

The watchword, shared by all, was *Euhoe*.

How the assault and attack of our good Bacchus against the Indians were portrayed in the mosaic

CHAPTER 39

[More praise of Bacchus, still closely following the Dionysus *of Plutarch. The last paragraph is indebted to Plutarch's* On Isis and Osiris, *362 C.*

In the third paragraph for 'Words' the manuscript reads 'Echo'.]

Next there were portrayed the violent assault and attack launched by our good Bacchus against the Indians. There I contemplated the leader of the vanguard, Silenus, dripping great drops of sweat and harshly belabouring his ass. And that ass, with its jaws yawning horrifying wide, whisked off the flies, advanced and skirmished about in the most terrifying manner as though it had a horse-fly up its rump.

The satyrs, captains, troop-sergeants, squad-leaders and cor-
porals, all with their trumpets sounding martial strains, madly
dashed around the army, capering like goats with many a
bound, fart, kick and prance, putting heart into their comrades
for a valiant fight. All the figures in the mosaic were crying
Euhoe!

The Maenades were the ones to make the first incursion
against the Indians with hideous yells and a terrifying din from
their cymbals and bucklers. As depicted in that mosaic, the
whole heavens resounded with it: therefore be not so moved to
wonder by the art of Apelles, Aristides of Thebes and others
who have painted peals of thunder, flashes of lightning,
thunderbolts, winds, Words, manners and minds.

In the following, the army of the Indians was portrayed as
aware that Bacchus was laying waste to their land. To the fore
were the elephants, with towers strapped on to them, and
countless fighting men. But that entire army was routed, their
elephants turning back and trampling over them because of the
horrifying tumult of the Bacchides and the panic terror which
had stripped them of their senses.

There you would have seen Silenus fencing with his stave in
the old style of swordsmanship and sharply spurring on that
ass of his, which cavorted along after the elephants with its jaws
agape as though it were braying a martial bray and sounding the
attack, with a bravery equal to that with which it once awoke
Lotis the Nymph at the height of the Bacchanalia, when Priapus,
full of priapism, sought not to apprise her but to priapize her
while she slept

There you would have seen Pan skipping around the
Maenades on his crooked legs, encouraging them to fight valiantly with his rustic pipes. There you would have next seen: a
young Satyr leading in seventeen kings as captives; a Bacchante
hauling along forty-two captains with her snakes; a little faun
bearing twelve standards seized from the enemy; and that good
fellow Bacchus riding securely in his chariot in the midst of the
field, laughing, joking and downing drink for drink with all
comers.

Finally there was portrayed in that mosaic the trophy celebrating the victory and triumph of that good fellow Bacchus. His triumphal car was covered all over with ivy, culled and garnered on Mount Meros for its rarity, which raises the price of everything, particularly of this plant in India. (Later, Alexander the Great, during his Indian triumph, imitated him in that: his car was drawn by elephants yoked together. And subsequently Pompey the Great during his African Triumph in Rome, imitated him.) On his car rode our noble Bacchus, drinking from a two-handed jar (and in that Caius Marius imitated him after his victory over the Cimbri which he won near Aix-en-Provence).

All in Bacchus' army were crowned with ivy: their thyrses, bucklers and drums were covered in it. Why! the very ass of Silenus was caparisoned in it! Flanking the car were the captured Indian princes, bound in chains of gold. The whole company marched with a religious pomp, with joy and happiness beyond utterance, bearing an infinite number of trophies, models of captured towns and spoil from their enemies, all resounding in joyful paeans of victory or little rustic songs and dithyrambs.

At the very end was painted the land of Egypt with the Nile and its crocodiles, long-tailed monkeys, ibises, apes, crested wrens, ichneumons, hippopotamuses and other indigenous creatures. And there was Bacchus, progressing through that land, drawn by two oxen, on one of which was written in letters of gold, Apis, and upon the other, Osiris, because, before the advent of Bacchus, neither bull nor cow had ever been seen in Egypt.

How the Temple was illuminated by
a wondrous lamp

CHAPTER 40

[The lamp shining in the Temple is a real lamp, not a living Lantern. The whole chapter is influenced by the Dream of Polifilo *of Colonna, sometimes closely.]*

Before I embark upon a presentation of La Bouteille I shall
describe for you the wonderful form of a lamp by means of
which light was widely shed over the whole temple so abundantly that even though we were under the ground we could see
there as we can see the sun shining clear and serenely upon the
earth at noon. In the middle of the vault was fixed a ring of
solid gold, as thick as a clenched fist; from it hung three somewhat smaller chains most skilfully forged, forming a triangle,
some two-and-a-half feet up in the air, enclosing a fine golden
disc of such a size that the diameter exceeded two cubits plus
half a span. In it were four buckles or rings, in each of which
was firmly held a hollow ball, scooped out and open at the top
like a little oil-lamp measuring about two spans all round. They
were all of very precious stones: one of amethyst, another
of Libyan ruby, a third of opal, and the fourth of flaming
garnet-stone. Each was full of eau-de-vie, five-times distilled in
a serpentine alembic: it was as inexhaustible as the oil which
Callimachus once placed in Pallas' golden lamp in the Acropolis
at Athens, with a burning wick made partly of asbestos-flax (as
formerly in the temple of Jupiter Ammon where that most
studious of philosophers, Cleombrotus, saw it) and partly of
Carpasian flax (both of which are renewed by fire rather than
consumed by it).

About two-and-a-half feet below that disc, the three chains
were, as originally disposed, buckled on to the three handles
which projected from a great round lamp of purest crystal. It
was about two-and-a-half cubits in diameter. It was open at the
top for about two spans, and into the middle of that aperture
was set a crystalline vessel, similar in shape to a gourd or a
chamber-pot; it reached down to the base of the great lamp and
held just the right amount of the said eau-de-vie for the flame
of the asbestos-flax to be in the very middle of the great lamp.
By which means it seemed that its whole spherical body was
ablaze and radiating flames, because the flame was in its centre,
just at the mid-point.

It was hard to look at it fixedly and constantly (just as you
cannot look at the body of the sun) since the matter was so
astonishingly translucent and the work so finely wrought and

diaphanous that the various colours inherent in the precious stones of the little lamps set above were reflected in the greater lamp set below, so that the light of those four lamps spread flickering and shimmering all over the temple. And when that roving light struck against the polished surface of the marble which lined the inside of the Temple, there appeared all the colours of the rainbow, as when the bright sun strikes the rain-clouds.

It was a wonderful creation, all the more so, it seemed to me, in that all round the substance of the crystal lamp the sculptor had incised an engraving of a spirited and merry battle between little naked putti mounted on little wooden horses, all with whirligigs for lances and shields skilfully composed of bunches of grapes intertwined with vine-branches; their boyish deeds and assaults were portrayed so ingeniously and with such art that Nature could not have done better. They did not seem to have been cut into the crystal but rather to stand out in full relief in the round, or at least as in grotesques, because of the play of that pleasingly variegated inside light shining forth through the carvings.

How we were shown a phantastic fountain by the High-Priestess Bacbuc

CHAPTER 41

[A short chapter in the printed text but not in the manuscript. For the choice and arrangement of the various texts, including the following chapter, see Mireille Huchon in her Pléiade Rabelais, pp. 1673–4.]

While we were in ecstasy, contemplating that wonder-working Temple and that remarkable lamp, the venerable High-Priestess Bacbuc, with a joyful and smiling face, appeared before us with her train. Seeing us attired as we had been instructed, she made no difficulty about bringing us right into the middle of the temple where, below the said lamp, the beautiful, phantastic fountain was to be found.

How the waters of the Fountain tasted of whatever wine the drinkers fancied

CHAPTER 42

[Many items in this chapter derive eventually from Pliny. Over several details the manuscript gives different readings, some perhaps better ones. For example, where the printed editions refer to 'Pluto in limbo', the manuscript speaks of Daedalus, and also adds the Magi (of Classical antiquity) after the Chaldaeans.

For Polycletus see an adage of Cognatus (Cousin), 'The Norm of Polycletus'.

The final paragraph picks up a scriptural quotation, last met in Gargantua, Chapter 5 apropos of true faith: 'For with God nothing is ever impossible' (cited from Luke 1:37 and echoing Genesis 8).

The word 'portri' remains unexplained.

From the last line on p. 1006 the text forms a separate chapter in the manuscript.]

She next commanded us to be offered beakers, chalices and goblets of gold, silver, crystal and porcelain, and we were courteously invited to taste of the spring flowing from that fountain. We were delighted to do so, for, however doleful, it was a phantastic fountain, more costly, rare and miraculous in materials and workmanship than any dreamt up by Pluto in limbo. Its base-work was of the purest, limpidest alabaster, three spans high or a little more, forming on the outside a regular heptagon, complete with stylobates, arulets, wave-shaped mouldings and a surrounding of Doric undulations. At the centre of the space within each angle was sited a fluted pillar in the shape of an ivory or alabaster bobbin such as architects nowadays call *portri*. There were seven in all, one for each angle. From base to architrave they measured a little under seven spans, which is exactly and precisely the length of a diameter passing through the centre from the inner curve of the circumference.

Now those columns were so disposed that when we were looking from behind one of them in order to see the others opposite, we discovered that, regardless of the size of its shaft at that point, the pyramidal cone formed by our line of vision terminated in the said centre where it met the two columns facing it to form an equilateral triangle, two sides of which divided the column (which we wished to measure) into three equal parts, and, touching the outsides of two parallel columns at the division of the third section (which served as their base, their fundamental line, designedly projected towards the over-all centre and, divided equally into two) gave, by just division, the distance of the seven columns opposite in a straight line which originates in the obtuse angle at the top. (You realize that in every figure which contains an uneven number of angles, one of its angles is always equidistant from another two.)

By that it was shown to us, without words, that seven semi-diameters equal – in geometric proportion, amplitude and distance – slightly less than the circumference of the circular figure from which they were abstracted, that is to say rather more than three whole diameters plus a little more than one-and-a-half eighths, or else a little less than one-and-a-half sevenths, according to the Ancient teachings of Euclid, Aristotle, Archimedes and others.[35]

The first column – the one which offered itself to our gaze at the entrance to the temple – was of sky-blue sapphire;

the second, of hyacinth, naturally reproducing (with the letters A and J in various places) the colour of that flower into which was changed the angry blood of Ajax;

the third, of that diamond called *anachite*, as shimmering and dazzling as lightning;

the fourth, of balas ruby, male, and bordering on the amethyst in such a way that its sheen and sparkle eventually seem purple and violet as does the amethyst;

the fifth, of emerald, five hundred times more splendid than ever was that of Serapis within the Egyptian labyrinth, and more gleaming and glowing than those once fixed, to serve as eyes, on to the marble lion hard by the tomb of King Hermias;

35. Cf. what Plutarch writes of Pythagorean mathematical mysticism (*On Isis and Osiris*, 367 E–F).

the sixth, of agate, more gaily twinkling in its distinctive streaks and veins than ever was that agate held so dear by Pyrrhus, the King of Epirus;

the seventh, of moonstone, as transparent and white as beryl and with the splendour of honey from Mount Hymettus; within it there appeared the moon, in form and motion as she is in the heavens, full, silent, waxing, waning.

All those are stones attributed to the seven planets of the heavens by the Chaldaeans of old.

To make it all more understandable to grosser understandings: on the first – of sapphire – there was raised above the capital, in a perpendicular line passing through the centre, a statue of Saturn wielding his scythe; it was made of very costly purified lead, with, at its feet, a crane of gold, skilfully enamelled in the colours naturally appropriate to that bird of Saturn's;

on the second – of hyacinth – there was Jupiter cast in the pewter called *jovetanum*, leftwards looking, with a life-like, enamelled, golden eagle upon his bosom;

on the third, was Phoebus in refined gold, holding a white cockerel in his hand;

on the fourth, was Mars, in Corinthian marble, with a lion at his feet;

on the fifth, was Venus, in copper like that used by Aristonides to make the statue of Athamas, expressing in its blushing whiteness the reproach he felt when gazing at his son Learchus lying dead at his feet from a fall;

on the sixth, Mercury, in quicksilver, malleable and set solid;[36]

on the seventh, Luna, in silver, with a greyhound at her feet.

Now these statues were a little above one third of the height of the columns beneath them; they were presented with such ingenuity following the projections of the mathematicians that the Canon of Polycletus[37] (in the establishing of which

36. The manuscript adds: *at his feet was a stork.*
37. The canon of Polycletus is subject to a long commentary in the *Sylloge* of Gilbert Cognatus. As sculptor and writer Polycletus was held to represent absolute perfection in both his art and in morals. His canon is mentioned by Galen and Saint Jerome amongst many others. Pliny *Natural History*, 34, 8, 19, praises him for having 'created art itself by means of art'.

Polycletus was said to have instructed art by means of art) would scarcely have been admitted there as a yardstick.

The bases of the columns, the capitals, the architraves, the friezes and the cornices were in the Phrygian style, decorated with massive gold, purer and finer than that washed down by the river Lez near Montpellier, the Ganges in India, the Po in Italy, the Hebrus in Thrace, the Tagus in Spain or the Pactolus in Lydia. The small arches spanning the columns were each of the same stone as their columns as far as the next one in order, that is, the sapphire arch leading to hyacinth; the hyacinth, to the diamond, and so on in order.

Above the arches and the capitals of the columns, on the inside, a cupola had been constructed to cover the fountain; it began as a hexagon behind the sites of the planets and gradually developed and ended in a sphere; it was of crystal so refined, so diaphanous and so perfectly and evenly polished all over (without veins, cloudy patches, streaks or stripes) that never did Xenocrates see anything to compare with it.

Within its vaulting there were artistically engraved, in order, with exquisite figures and symbols: the twelve signs of the Zodiac, the twelve months of the year with their attributes; the two solstices, the two equinoxes, the ecliptic together with some of the more noteworthy fixed stars around the Antarctic Pole and elsewhere: all done so artistically that I thought it was the work of King Necepsus or of Petosiris, the ancient mathematician.

At the uppermost point of the cupola, exactly over the middle of the fountain, there were three rare, smooth, pear-shaped pearls, each fashioned into the exact form of a tear-drop. They were joined so as to form a fleur-de-lys which was bigger with its setting than the palm of your hand. From its calyx there emerged a carbuncle as big as an ostrich-egg, cut to form a heptagon, seven being a number much loved by Nature. It was so stupendous and wonderful that we all but lost our sight when we raised our eyes to contemplate it, for neither lightning nor the flaming sun are more coruscating or more brilliant than it then seemed to us. So much so that good judges would readily conclude that there would be more riches and wonders in the fountain and the lamps described than are contained in Asia,

Africa and Europe combined. It would have darkened the *pantarbe*[38] of Iarchas, a magician of India, as easily as the clear sun darkens the stars at noon.

Now let Cleopatra, the Queen of Egypt, boast about the twin pearls dangling from her ears, one of which, valued at ten million sesterces, she dissolved into liquid by the virtue of vinegar in the presence of Anthony the Triumvir.

Let Pompeia Platulina go strutting about in her dress, completely covered in alternate rows of pearls and emeralds, which drew the admiration of all the people in the City of Rome (which was styled the ditch and trading-post of the champion thieves of the entire world).

The outflowing water gushed from that fountain through three pipes and channels made of fine pearls and sited at the apexes of three equilateral angles at the tip of the fountain as described above. Those channels projected in the shape of a double helix.

We had contemplated them and were turning our gaze elsewhere when Bacbuc commanded us to listen to the waters pouring out. Whereupon we heard a sound wondrously harmonious yet deadened and fractured as though coming from underground and from afar; it seemed all the more delectable for that, more than if it had been heard easily and close at hand, so that, just as our minds had been delighted by our contemplating what has been described above through the windows of our eyes, the same delight awaited our ears upon hearing that harmony.

Wherefore Bacbuc said to us:

'Those philosophers of yours deny that motion is produced by the power of forms. Hearken now and behold the contrary: it is entirely via the form of that twin spiral which you can see, together with that five-fold fleuron which vibrates with each internal impulse – as in the case of the vena cava where it enters the right ventricle of the heart – that the waters of this holy fountain filter out, producing a harmony such that it rises to the surface of the sea in your world.'

She then commanded a drink to be served to us.

---

38. The *pantarbe* is a fabulous precious stone of terrifying brilliance, fabled to act as a magnet to gold.

Now to tell you plainly, we are not of the calibre of a bunch of calves which, like sparrows, will only feed if you tap their tails and similarly, never eat nor drink unless you lambast them with a crow-bar. We never decline when anyone courteously invites us to drink.

Bacbuc then questioned us, asking us what we thought of it.

We replied that the waters from the fountain felt good and fresh, more limpid and silvery than those of the Argirodines in Aetolia, of the Peneus in Thessaly, of the Axius in Mygdonia or indeed of the Cydnus in Cilicia: when Alexander of Macedonia saw it to be so fair, so clear and so cool in the heart of summer, he atoned for his pleasure in bathing in it with the evil he foresaw arising from that transient pleasure.

'Ah!' said Bacbuc, 'that is what comes from neither analysing nor understanding the motions made by our muscular tongue when the drink flows over it to descend to the stomach. Travellers! Do you have gullets so daubed, paved and enamelled (as did in ancient days Pithylus, who was surnamed Tenthes) that you did not recognize the savour of the bouquet of this deifying liquor? Bring hither,' she said to her maidens, 'those crud-removers of mine – you know which – so as to scrape, clean and cleanse their palates.'

And so there were brought in lovely, fat, happy hams, lovely, fat, happy smoked ox-tongues, lovely, tasty salted meats, saveloys and botargos, lovely, tasty venison sausages and other such chimney-sweepers of the gullet. At her command we ate until we had to admit that our stomachs had been well and truly scoured clean by a thirst which had quite dreadfully plagued us.

At which she said to us: 'Once a learned and chivalrous Jewish captain was leading through the desert his people, who were extenuated by hunger; from the heavens he obtained manna, the taste of which appeared to their minds as that of viands they had once actually eaten. So too here: when drinking from this miracle-working liquor you will experience the taste of whatever wine you have in mind. Bring your mind to it, and drink!'[39]

39. It is in the Apocrypha (Wisdom 26:20–23) that we are told that the manna provided to the children of Israel under Moses 'tempered itself according to every man's choice'.

Which we did. Panurge then exclaimed, 'This, by God, is wine from Beaune, better than any I have ever yet drunk, or else I shall give myself to ninety devils plus sixteen more. O! If only we could have a gullet three cubits in length so as to prolong the taste, as Philoxenus desired, or one like a crane's, as Melanthius wished!'[40]

'Faith of a lanterning man!' exclaimed Frère Jean. 'This is Grecian wine, bold and with a spring in its step. O! for God's sake, dear Lady, tell me how you get it to be like this!'

'To me,' said Pantagruel, 'they seem like wines from Mirevaux, for I had them in mind before I started to drink. There is only one thing wrong with this one: it is cold: colder than ice, I mean, colder than the waters at Nonacris and Dirce, or the fountain of Conthoporeia in Corinth, which froze the guts and the digestive systems of those who drank of it.'

'Drink once, drink twice, drink thrice,' said Bacbuc, 'having a different wine in mind each time, and you will find the taste, the bouquet and the feel on your tongue of whatever wine you thought of. And from henceforth say that with God nothing is ever impossible.'

'We never said it was,' I replied; 'God, we hold, is Almighty.'[41]

How Bacbuc arrayed Panurge so as to receive the Word of La Bouteille

CHAPTER 43

['Wine of one ear' is the best wine, perhaps so called because it makes the connoisseur bend his head in sign of approval. It appears in Chapter 4 of Gargantua.

40. See two adages of Adrian Junius Basle, 1558: 'Collaria cadavera (Bodies all-neck)' and 'Delicatior Melanthio (More delicate that Melanthius)' as well as, for Philoxenus, an adage of Junius, 'Cubitis adolescere (To grow up by cubits)'.

41. Cf. Pantagruel, (near the end of Chapter 11) and the Third Book (end of Chapter 15).

The description of the temple is partly inspired by Pliny's account of the temple dedicated to Fortuna by Nero.]

Those discussions and wine-bibbings once over, Bacbuc inquired:

'Which of you is it that desires to have the Word of La Dive Bouteille?'

'Me,' said Panurge, 'your most obedient little wine-funnel.'

'Friend,' she said, 'I have only one instruction to give you: that is, when you come to the oracle take care not to listen for the Word, save with one ear.'

'So,' said Frère Jean, 'it's wine of one ear!'

She then vested him in a long smock, placed a beautiful, white, Beguine's bonnet on his head, swaddled him up in a felt filter-cloth for straining hypocras (at the bottom of which she placed three small broaches in place of a tassel), pulled two antique codpieces on to his hands as gloves, girded him with three bagpipes bound together, bathed his face thrice in the above fountain and finally cast a handful of flour in his face, stuck three cock's-feathers on to the right of the hypocras-strainer, made him proceed nine times around the fountain, execute three fine little jumps and bump his bottom seven times on the floor; meanwhile she kept repeating Lord-knows-what spells in the Etruscan tongue and read at times from a manual of ritual which one of her hierophants bore open beside her.

To sum up: I believe that never did Numa Pompilius, the second King of the Romans, nor Caerites of Tuscia, nor the holy Captain of the Jews ever institute as many ceremonies as then I saw, nor did the soothsayers of Memphis institute more for Apis in Egypt, nor the Euboeans for Rhamnusia in the city of Rhamnes; and neither did the Ancients perform so many religious rites for Jupiter Ammon or Feronia as there I looked upon.

She drew him apart, thus arrayed, took him by the right hand and led him by a golden gate out of the temple into a round chapel constructed of transparent crystallized gypsum, through whose solid translucent stone the sunlight came streaming in without window or aperture through a steep fissure in the cliff, filling the main temple so easily and abundantly that the light seemed to spring from within, not to come from outside. The structure was no less wonderful than the sacred temple once in Ravenna or the temple on the Isle of Chemnis in Egypt. And it ought not to be passed over in silence that the round chapel was constructed with such symmetry that the diameter of the ground-plan was equal to the height of the vaulted roof.

In the midst of it, heptagonal in shape, with leaf-work remarkably wrought, stood a fountain of fine alabaster, full of water as clear as any element in its simple state can ever be. In it, entirely encased in pure crystal, stood, half-immersed, La Dive Bouteille, oval in form, except that its mouth was rather more prominent than that shape would allow.

How the High Priestess Bacbuc brought
Panurge before the Bouteille

CHAPTER 44

[As befits this chapter, ithymbies *are Bacchic dances, and an* epilemia *is a song for the wine-harvest. The Word of La Bouteille turns out to be 'Trinch', here spelt phonetically 'Trinck' (an order: 'Drink!' in German, a word normally associated with the excesses of Swiss mercenaries).*

The use of the saying to 'fall between two stools, bum to the ground' raises the first smile for quite some time.

Cf. for this and the following chapter the adage of Cognatus (Gilbert Cousin), 'Drunkenness and love produce secrets', which cites Plato (Alcibiades), 'Truth is the daughter of wine'.

See also the works mentioned in the Introduction to Chapter 65 of the Fourth Book. *They include the later emblems, 'Vinum ingenii fomes' (Wine, the kindling of the intellect); 'Vinum acuit ingenium' (Wine sharpens the intellect) and Mignault's commentaries on two of the* Emblems *of Alciato, 'Vino prudentiam augeri' (By wine wisdom is increased) and 'In Juventam'.]*

Bacbuc, the noble High Priestess, now ordered Panurge to
bow low, kiss the rim of the Fountain, rise, then dance three
ithymbies around it. That done, she bade him fall between two
stools, bum to the ground. She then opened wide her Book of
Ritual, blew down his ear and made him sing an epilemia as
follows:

> Bottle clear!
> From thy lip
> Mysterious
> With one ear
> I seek a nip:
> Quite anxious.
> No delay! Reply, imperious.
> Pronounce Thou me the heart-felt Word.
> Soon, soon be thou by all men clearly heard,
> For this sore old mind of mine now surely knows
> That Truth lies still in thy fine liquor: 'tis not absurd!
> The Truth of Wine thy rounded flanks richly enclose.
> Bacchus of old was victorious in Ind: now even his foes,
> Can find in Wine, of foul deceits, not one single sign.
> Lies are the evil things Bacchus' wines all oppose.
> Old Noah for us once planted Truth with the vine.
> Say thou the Word: thou knowest all my design:
> Set me free of every gripe painfully obnoxious.
> Drops of thy rich, pure Wine here may I sip,
> White Wine or red, both good and mere.
> Bottle clear!
> From thy lip
> Mysterious
> With one ear
> I seek a nip:
> Quite anxious.
> No delay! Reply, imperious

That song once sung, Bacbuc cast I-know-not-what substance
into the Fountain; its waters at once began to seethe and boil
as does the Great Cauldron of Bourgueil when there is a festival

with banners. Panurge, in silence, hearkened with one ear.
Bacbuc, on her knees, remained at his side when there then
came forth from La Dive Bouteille a sound such as is made by
bees when they are born from the flesh of a young ox duly
slaughtered and dressed according to the art discovered by
Aristaeus, or such as is made by a crossbow as the bolt is shot,
or by a sudden, heavy shower.

Whereupon was heard this Word: Trinck.

'Might of God!' exclaimed Panurge. 'She has split or – to tell
no lie – cracked! Thus in our lands speak crystal bottles when
they burst near the fire.'

Bacbuc then rose and gently took Panurge by the arm, saying,

'Friend: render thanks to the heavens. Reason tells you so to
do: you have promptly received the Word of La Dive Bouteille:
I mean the most joyful, holy and the surest Word that I have
ever heard since I began my ministry here at her most-hallowed
Oracle. Arise; let us go and consult that chapter in whose gloss
that Word of beauty is explained.'

'For God's sake let us go there!' said Panurge. 'I'm just as
wise as I was years ago! Where's that Book? Flip through it.
Where's that chapter? Let's see that merry gloss.'

How Bacbuc explains the Word of the Bottle

CHAPTER 45

[*The* Quart, *the* Fourth Book of the Sentences *of Peter Lombard allows
(again) a pun between* fourth *and* quart, *the liquid measure.*

In Ezekiel 3 the Lord gave the prophet a book to eat and digest.

*Hermes Trismegistus was the legendary source of 'hermetic' know-
ledge.*

Panomphaeus is an epithet of Jupiter, the 'author of all the oracles'.

*As elsewhere, 'Aesop's beggar's wallet' is worn over the shoulder
and has a pocket in front and another behind. The theme was
developed at the end of Chapter 15 of the* Third Book.

There are implicit appeals to Chapters 7 and 10 of the Third Book *and to the preliminary poem of* Gargantua *apropos of laughter as the property of man.]*

Bacbuc tossed something or other into the basin of the Fountain and the water at once stopped seething. She led Panurge into the centre of the Greater Temple, in which stood that life-giving Fountain. Then, drawing forth a silver book in the shape of a demijohn (or a *Quart* of the *Sentences*), she immersed it in the fountain and said unto him:

'The philosophers, preachers and divines in your world feed you with fair words through your ears: here we really incorporate our precepts through the mouth. That is why I do not say unto you, "Read this chapter; look upon this gloss." What I say is, "Taste this chapter: ingurgitate this beautiful gloss." In days gone by an ancient prophet of the Jewish people did eat a book and became a clerk up to his teeth. You will now drink a book, and become a clerk up to your liver. Here. Open your mandibles.'

Panurge opened wide his gullet; Bacbuc grasped the silver book, which we took for a real book since its shape was that of a Breviary but this Breviary was a genuine and natural flask, full of Falernian wine, all of which she made Panurge swallow.

'Here,' said Panurge, 'is a noteworthy chapter and a most authentic gloss! Is that all that was meant by the Word of that trismegistical Bottle! A lot of good that is for me!'

'Nothing more,' Bacbuc replied, 'for *Trinck* is a famous pan-omphaeic word, understood by all peoples. Its meaning for us is, Drink! In your world you state that *sack* is a noun common to all languages, rightly and justly accepted by all tongues:[42] that is because all humans, being by nature indigent and all begging from one another, are born with a sack slung over their shoulders as in Aesop's fable.

'No king under the sun, however mighty, can do without other people: no person who is poor, however proud, can do without the rich, not even if he were Hippias the philosopher

---

42. The extraordinary spread of variations of the word *sack* to many languages including Hebrew, Greek, Latin, the Germanic tongues, Welsh, Russian and so on is confirmed by the *Oxford English Dictionary*.

who fended entirely for himself. One can manage without a drink even less than without such a sack. So here we maintain that it is not laughing which is the property of man, but drinking.

'I do not indeed mean drinking purely and simply – the beasts drink like that – I mean drinking wine, good and cool. Note well, my friends, that *Juice of vine makes man divine*: there is no argument clearer than that, no art of divination less fallacious.

'Your Academics strongly support that when tracing the etymology of *vin* (wine) from the Greek *oinos*, which corresponds, they say, to the Latin *vis* (power).[43]

'For wine has the power to flood the mind with all truth, all knowledge and philosophy. If you have noticed what is written in Ionic script over the door of the temple, then you may have understood that Truth lies hidden in wine. La Dive Bouteille sends you thither. Be ye yourselves the interpreters of your enterprise.'

'It is not possible,' said Pantagruel, 'to put it better than this venerable Chief Priestess has done. I said as much to you the very first time you spoke to me about it.[44]

'*Trinck!* therefore: that is what your mind tells you to do when it is enraptured by Bacchic enthusiasm.'

'Then,' said Panurge:

> 'Trinck! and now see in Bacchus' name,
> The backside, Bacchus! of my dame,
> Tamped with my bollocks to the brim
> And fully stuffed, all thanks to him.
> What now? By my humanity
> My heart yearns for paternity.

43. See Plato, *Cratylus*, 406; W. F. Smith, *Rabelais. The Five Books and Minor Writings together with Letters and Documents Illustrating His Life* (London: Alexander Watt, 1896) also cites Calepinus as writing: '*vinum* (wine) derives from *vi* (strength) because it brings strength to the mind, or else from the Greek *oinois*.'

44. See Chapters 9 and 29 of the *Third Book*, where the context is quite different.

My heart tells me, assuredly,
That soon I shall well married be.
Soon married! In my own abode
My wife, ne'er needing other goad,
Will hasten on to Venus' play.
Lord knows what words we then shall say!
I swear that I shall be her plough,
And with my plough-share her endow.
Ploughings galore! For I'm well fed.
I am the perfect ploughman, wed.
Io! *Io*! Of husbands best,
To the wedding with a zest!
Triple-wedded I shall go.
Io. Io. Now Frère Jean know
That true and clear by oath I swear
Infallibility lieth there:
That Oracle is true and fated.'

How Panurge and the others rhyme by poetic frenzy

CHAPTER 46

[Poetic furor is a Classical notion, all the rage with the Pléiade poets in mid- and late sixteenth-century France rather than with the generation of Rabelais. One may compare and contrast what Rabelais wrote of the spirit-raising powers of wine in the Fourth Book *apropos of the wingèd Bacchus, by whom the minds of human beings are raised up high, their bodies made manifestly agile, and what in them was earthy is assuaged. Similarly, compare and contrast what Rabelais wrote on the basis of* The Obsolescence of Oracles *apropos of the death of Pan in the* Fourth Book, Chapters 26 to 28.]*

'Are you mad or under a spell?' said Frère Jean. 'Look! He's foaming at the mouth! Hark at him rhymstering! What the devil has he been eating? He's rolling the eyes in his head like a goat in the throes. Will he be off on his own? Will he go farther off to mute? Will he chew some dog-wort to loosen up his nelly? Or will he, monkish fashion, stick his fist elbow-deep down his throat so as to scour out his abdomen? Will he take a hair of the dog that bit him?'

Pantagruel rebuked Frère Jean, and said to him:

> 'Poets' frenzy true and unabated
> Ecliptic, Bacchus sent and minds are sated
> And then inspired it to intone its song.
>
>> His mind enrapt,
>> By frenzy tapped,
>> The potion lapped,
>> Prophetic mime,
>> From cry to cry,
>> From low to high,
>> Far and near by,
>> Makes mind to climb,
>> Enrapt, to rhyme,
>> King in his time,
>> Of laugh not sigh.
>
> And since he has a mind fantastic
> 'Twould be an action dubbed with foulest slime
> To mock a Drinker rendered so sublime.'

'What?' said Frère Jean, 'are you rhyming too! We're all in for a peppering! Would to God that Gargantua could see us in this state. By God, I don't know what to do: whether or not to rhyme away like you. I don't understand such things anyway, yet we're all deep in rhymstery. By Saint John, I'll do like the others: I shall rhyme away. I can feel it. Wait. And if I fail to spin a rhyme of Crimson cloth, forgive me:

> O Father divine
> Who turned water to wine,[45]
> Make my bum a light
> For my neighbour's sight.'

---

45. A strange error to attribute the first miracle of Jesus, in Cana in Galilee, to the Father, not the Son.

Panurge took over and said:

> 'Ne'er did Pythian Tripod shed
> Truer Oracles from its head;
> Replies more certain or more sure
> Did never from that fountain pour.
> It was transported through the sky
> Hither from places at Delphi.
> If Plutarch of this wine had drunk
> He never would so low have sunk
> To wonder whether he should say
> That oracles have had their day.
> They ceased from making a reply:
> Not hard to know the reason why:
> Delphi's fane has had to flee.
> It now is here. Look up and see
> Who gave reply to those who ask.
> For Athenaeus 'twas a flask,
> A Bottle, indeed, round and clear,
> Full of the good wine 'of one ear'.
> Of wine, I say, of verity.
> There is not more sincerity
> In any art of divination
> Than the bosom-deep insinuation
> Of the good Word drawn from that flasklet
> Now Frère Jean, since I now do ask it,
> While we are here I counsel you
> To seek to yourself a Word so true
> From our Flask trismegistical
> To learn if anything at all
> Can stop you finding now a mate.
> Hold fast. All wobbling abate.
> Play not the fool maid in her bower!
> Just sprinkle here a little flour.'

In poetic rapture Frère Jean replied:

'Well! By Benedick's great Boot
By both his gaiters great to boot
A man who truly knows me well
Would swear an oath that he can tell
That I would fain unfrockèd be
Than trapped within the drudgery
Of single-wife matrimony.
Sela! Despoiled of liberty,
Enslaved to female ne'er I'll be!
Why! not to Alexander's paw
Nor Caesar, nor his son-in-law,
Nor to the grandest knight in all this world.'

Panurge, casting off his over-smock and all his mystical paraphernalia, made reply:

'So beastly fellow, you'll be curled
In coiled damnation like a snake,
Whilst I, on harp, shall music make,
Happy, and saved in Paradise,
From whence I'll piss on you, once, twice,
The worst whoremonger that I know.
You'll be a devil there below
If, as seems likely to us all,
Dame Proserpine has you in thrall,
Pricked on by prick in codpiece hidden,
And ever by your manhood smitten
And by your known Paternity
When you find opportunity
To say sweet nothings; and that said,
To clamber on her in her bed;
And send to fetch you when you dine,
The very best of hellish wine.
Old Lucifer will bring it you.
Then you and she'll know what to do:
She never could refuse a Frère.
And she is nice with lovely hair.'

'Go to the devil, you silly old fool,' said Frère Jean. 'I can rhyme no more: I have rime in the throat. Let us satisfy them hereabouts.'

How, having taken congee of Bacbuc, they quit the Oracle of La Bouteille

CHAPTER 47

[The description of God as the Intellectual Sphere derives from Hermes Trismegistus. It figures in Chapter 13 of the Third Book.

Ceres' daughter is Proserpine, who was ravished by Pluto, the Ruler of the Underworld; Pluto's name was derived by Plato in the Cratylus *from* plutos, *rich. Truth lies hidden: wise men seek it.]*

'You need not worry about that,' replied Bacbuc. 'Everything will be achieved as long as you are satisfied with us. Here, in the environs of these central regions, we firmly place the Supreme Good not in getting and receiving but in giving and distributing: we count ourselves blessèd not if we take or obtain much from others (as the sects of your world erroneously decree) but if we can ever give and dispense much to others. Only one thing I do ask: that you have your names and addresses written here in this book of ritual.'

She then opened a big and beautiful book in which one of her mystagogues traced a number of marks at our dictation; and although she seemed to have been writing, nothing was apparent to us.

Once that was done, she filled three leathern bottles with phantasy-water and personally handed them to us, saying:

'Go now, my friends, under the protection of that Intellectual Sphere, whose centre is everywhere and whose circumference nowhere, whom we call God. And once you have come to your world, bear witness that great treasures and wonders lie under the earth: Ceres (who was already hallowed throughout the whole world because she had revealed and taught the art of agriculture and, through the discovery of corn, had abolished

the brutish eating of acorns from amongst men) not without
cause so greatly lamented the ravishing of her daughter to our
regions below-ground, foreseeing with certainty that she would
find more good things, more excellent things, there than her
mother had ever brought forth above-ground.

'What has become of the art of summoning thunder and fire
down from the heavens? Discovered of old by Prometheus, you
have certainly lost it: it has abandoned your hemisphere and is
practised here below. And you are wrong to be dumbfounded
when, from time to time, you see cities set ablaze by lightning
and burning with fire from the ethereal heights, since you do
not know by whom, through whom and whence comes that
which is for you an awesome prodigy but for us something
everyday and useful. Those philosophers of yours who lament
that everything has already been written by the Ancients and
that nothing is left to discover are plainly wrong. Those
phenomena (as you call them) which appear in the sky, those
things which the earth exhibits to you, as well as everything
that the seas and the rivers too contain, cannot be compared
with what lies hidden below the ground. That is why the Ruler
of the subterranean realms is rightly called in virtually all languages by a term descriptive of riches.

'But when will those philosophers of yours devote their study
and labour to seeking through their entreaties that sovereign
God whom the Egyptians of old called in their own tongue the
Hidden One, the Concealed One, the Veiled One, invoking him
by such a name and beseeching him to reveal and manifest to
them himself and his creation? They were guided also by a good
Lantern, for all the sages and philosophers of old deemed two
things requisite for following surely and pleasantly the way
leading to knowledge of the divine and the quest for wisdom:
the guidance of God and the companionship of Man. Thus
did Zoroaster, amongst the philosophers, take Arimaspes as a
comrade on his wanderings; Aesculapius, Mercury; Orpheus,
Museus; Pythagoras, Aglaophemus. And amongst the princes
and warriors Hercules was accompanied in his most arduous
enterprises by his dearest friend Theseus; Ulysses, by Diomedes;
Aeneas, by Achates. You too have done as much by taking that

shining Lady Lantern for your guide. And now go on your way, in the name of God and under his guidance.'

The end of the *Fifth Book* of the heroic deeds and sayings of noble Pantagruel.

Epigram

['Epigram' is sometimes used with the sense of an inscription (as on a statue). NATVRE QVITE is an anagram of JEAN TVRQVET (that is, of Jean Turquet). The Turquets were a pious French-speaking Piedmontese family, at least one of whose members came to England as a physician, possibly as a refugee after the massacre of Saint Bartholomew's Day.]

Rabelais: is he dead? Another book here take!
No. Look: his better part has claimed back his own mind,
Presenting to us here a work and you will find
Immortal and alive it will him ever make.

NATVRE QVITE

APPENDIX 1: THE ENDING AS FOUND
IN THE MANUSCRIPT

[The manuscript ending is fuller, and is given here for convenience rather than in the smaller print of a footnote.

Gaps in the text are shown thus: [. . .].

See Erasmus, Adages, III, V, XVII, 'Time reveals all things', and II, XL, XXXIV, 'About the lion from its claws'.

There is a quotation from Psalm 42:9: 'Deep calling unto deep'.]

'And so too, amongst the Persians, Zoroaster took Arimaspes as his comrade during the whole of his quest for mystical truth; amongst the Egyptians, Hermes Trismegistus took [. . .]; Aesculapeus took [. . .]; Orpheus in Thrace took Musaeus; there too Aglaophemus took Pythagoras; amongst the Athenians, Plato first took Dion of Syracuse in Sicily, and then, after his death, Xenocrates; and Apollonius took Damis.

'So when your philosophers, guided by God and accompanied by some clear-shining Lantern, devote themselves to careful research and investigations (as is natural to human beings, for which characteristic Herodotus and Homer are called in Greek *alphestai*, that is to say seekers and discoverers), they will find to be true the reply given to Amasis, the king of the Egyptians by the wise Thales: when asked wherein wisdom does most consist, he replied, *In Time, for all things hidden have been and will be uncovered by Time.* That is why the Ancients gave to Saturn the names of Time, and Father of Truth, whilst the daughter of Time was herself called Truth. And they will find without fail that all the knowledge acquired by them and their forebears is hardly the tiniest part of all that is, and what they do not know. From the three leathern wine-skins which now I give you, you will form your judgement, learning, as the adage puts it, *About the lion from its claws.* By the rarefaction of this water of ours which is enclosed therein, and through the intervention of the heat of the heavenly bodies and the fever-heat of the salt sea following the natural transmuting of the elements, there will be engendered therein the healthiest of airs for you, which will serve you as clear, serene and delightful breezes, for the winds are nothing but floating and undulating air. By means of that wind you will (without setting foot on land if you so desire) be wafted straight to the port of Les Sables d'Olonne in Talmondais, by allowing there to blow through your sails (from this little golden mouthpiece which you can see fixed here as on a flute) enough air as you deem necessary for sailing gently, always pleasantly and safely, without hazard or tempest.

'Do not doubt this. Never think that tempests arise and proceed from wind: it is the wind that comes from the tempests as they sally forth from the depths of the Abyss. Never think that rain comes from any weakness in the retentive powers of the heavens and from the weight of the suspended clouds: rain comes when called down by the subterranean regions, just as it had been called from below by the bodies high above. The kingly prophet bears witness to that, when he sang the verse, *Deep calleth unto deep.*

'Two of the three wine-skins are full of the water which I told you of; the third is drawn from the well of the Indian sages which is termed the Cask of the Brahmins. In addition you will find your ships well and duly provided with everything which might prove requisite or useful for the needs of your crew. While you were sojourning here I have had all that very properly seen to.'

Having spoken, she gave us a letter, closed and sealed. After we returned undying thanks, she sent us out by a gate near the chapel, where Bacbuc told us to pose questions twice as tall as Mount Olympus. So, via a land full of all delights, more pleasant and mild than Tempe in Thessaly, more healthy than the part of Egypt facing Libya, more watered and verdant than Themischyra, more fertile than where Mount Taurus faces north or than the Hyperborean Mountains in the Judaic Sea, as fragrant, serene and gracious as Touraine, we found at last our ships in harbour.

APPENDIX 2: CHAPTER 16 *BIS* AS
FOUND IN THE ISLE SONANTE

How Pantagruel arrived at the Isle of the long-fingered and crooked-handed Apedeftes, and of the terrifying adventures and monsters he encountered there

CHAPTER 16 *BIS*

[This chapter is conventionally numbered 16 bis. It is found only in the Isle Sonante, where it forms the conclusion.

The theme is probably a satire of the French Royal Exchequer (the Chambre des Comptes).

The 'Apedeftes' are the Untutored, the Uncouth.

The winepress is a common symbol of torture and oppression.

'Get-a-lot' renders Gaignebeaucoup.]

As soon as the anchors were dropped and the vessel securely moored, the skiff was lowered. As soon as our good Pantagruel had offered up prayers and given thanks to God for having saved him in so great a peril, he boarded the skiff with his men so as to go ashore, which proved very easy since, the sea being calm and the winds having dropped, they had soon reached some cliffs. Once they were ashore, Epistemon, who was gazing with wonder at the site and the strangeness of the rocks, noticed several of the dwellers in that land. The first of them whom he spoke to was clad in a fairly short robe of royal hue and a doublet with worsted panels, satin cuffs and chamois-leather sleeves; he wore a proud Spanish cap and had quite an allure. We later learnt his name was Get-a-lot; he told Epistemon, who asked him what they called those strange cliffs and valleys, that they were a colony called Ledgers, detached from the land of

Procuration, and that beyond those Ledgers, after crossing over a little ford, we would find the land of the Apedeftes.

'By the power of the Extravagantes!' said Frère Jean, 'What do you live on here, good people? May we have a drink from your glass, since I can see no equipment here save parchments, inkhorns and feather-pens?'

'And that,' said Get-a-lot, 'is just what we live on: everyone who has business on this island has to pass through our hands.'

'Why?' said Panurge, 'Are you barbers. Do they have to be shorn?'

'Yes,' said Get-a-lot, 'shorn of the testoons in their purses.'

'By God,' said Panurge, 'you shan't get a penny or a farthing from me. But I pray you, good sir, do take us to those Apedeftes, for we come from the Land of the Learned, where frankly I've never profited much.'

Thus chatting they arrived at the Isle of the Apedeftes, for the water was soon forded. Pantagruel was moved to marvel greatly at the architecture of the home and habitation of the locals, since they dwell in a huge winepress which they reach by climbing up some fifty steps. Before entering the master press – for in this land there are all kinds of presses, little ones, big ones, secret ones and middling ones – you pass through a great peristyle with landscape paintings portraying the ruin of almost everybody: so many gibbets for great robbers, and so many gallows and racks, that it strikes fear into you. Get-a-lot, noting that Pantagruel was lingering over it, said, 'My Lord, let us get on. This is nothing.'

'What!' said Frère Jean. 'Nothing! By the soul of my excited codpiece, Panurge and I are famished and trembling. I would rather have a drink than look upon the ruination of so many.'

'Come along,' said Get-a-lot.

He then brought us to a little winepress which was hidden away to the rear. In their island tongue they called it pithies.[46]

Do not ask if Frère Jean looked after himself there. And Panurge too. For Milanese sausages, turkeys, capons, bustards,

46. Perhaps from the Greek *pithos*, barrel.

malmsey and all good viands were there, ready and beautifully prepared. A squat butler who noticed that Frère Jean was casting amorous glances at a bottle standing near the sideboard apart from the troupe of bottles, said to Pantagruel:

'My Lord, I see that one of your men is ogling that bottle. I beg you not to touch it, since it is for My Lords.'

'How come?' said Panurge, 'Are there lords of the harvest in here? There's a vendange under way, I suppose.'

Whereupon Get-a-lot made us climb a little private staircase and enter a room, from which he showed us My Lords within that master winepress (which no one is permitted to enter without their permission, but whom we could easily see through a little loophole without their seeing us).

Once there, we saw in that winepress some twenty to twenty-five pieces of gallows-fodder around a big hangman's table covered with green beize; they were all watching each other, their hands as long as the legs of a crane and their nails at least two foot in length (for they are forbidden ever to clip them, with the result that they become like the claws of barbed lances or boat-hooks). Just then there was brought in a great bunch of the grapes which grow in the vineyards thereabouts from a stock called *Taxes Extraordinary*, which often weigh down their vine-props. As soon as that bunch arrived they put it into the press: there was not so much as a seed from which they did not extract some juice-of-gold, with the result that the wretched bunch was borne away squeezed as dry and as shrivelled up as anything in this world. Get-a-lot then told us that they seldom have bunches as large as that one, but they always have others in the vine-press.

'But my good companion,' said Panurge, 'do they have plenty of vine-plants coming on?'

'Yes,' said Get-a-lot. 'Plenty. Can you see that little one over there which is being returned to the press? It is of the stock called *Tithes*. The other day they squeezed it out to the ultimate pressing, but the oil stank of priestly coffers and My Lords gleaned little joy from it.'

'Why then,' said Pantagruel, 'are they putting it back into the press?'

'To see,' said Get-a-lot, 'whether they have overlooked any juice or receivables in the dry lump.'

'God's might!' said Frère Jean, 'do you call such folk ignorant? The devil if they don't get oil from a stone.'

'Indeed they do,' said Get-a-lot. 'They put châteaux, domains and woodlands into the press and, from them all, squeeze out potable gold.'

'You mean portable gold,' said Epistemon.

'I said *potable* gold,' said Get-a-lot, 'for they drink many a bottle in here which others may not drink. There are so many vine-plants that nobody knows the number of them. Come up here and look down into that walled garden. You can see hundreds of them, simply waiting for their turn to be squeezed. Look. Some are from the public domain, some from the private: fortifications, loans, gifts, sales of positions, inheritances, petty fees, offices, offertories and posts in the Royal Household.'

'And what is that big one over there, surrounded by all those little ones?'

'That,' said Get-a-lot, 'is the best vine-plant in all the land, the Exchequer. When they put the squeeze on that plant there is not one of My Lords who does not stink of it for six months.'

When those Lords had risen, Pantagruel begged Get-a-lot to bring us to the great winepress, which he readily did. As soon as we were inside, Epistemon, who knew all the languages, started to point out to Pantagruel all the devices on the winepress (which was large and beautiful, made according to Get-a-lot from the wood of the Cross): on each part of it was written its name in the language of the country. The screw of the press was called Receipts; the bowl, Expenditure; the shaft, the State; the levers, Accounts-Rendered-but-not-Received; the beams, Tolerated Postponements; the shafts, Annulments; the twin side-beams, Recuperations; the vats, Accrued Value; the juice-channels, Registers; the pressure-vats, Aquittances; the hods, Validations; the carrying-troughs, Ordinances Enforced; the buckets, Empowerments; and the funnel, Quittances.

'By the Queen of the Chidlings!' said Panurge, 'all the hieroglyphs of Egypt never came near such jargon. The devil! Such jargon follows suit like the droppings of goats. But why, good fellow, are these people called the Ignorants?'

'Because,' said Get-a-lot, 'they are not scholars and must never be so; also because, by their ordinance, there must be no other reason herein but *My Lords have said so*; *My Lords so will it*; and *My Lords so decree.*'

'True God!' said Pantagruel, 'if they make so much out of the bunches, a branch borne in must be worth an oath sworn in.'

'Can you doubt it!' said Get-a-lot. 'Not a month goes by without their having some. And it is not as in your lands, where the branch bears fruit but once a year.'[47]

As we were leaving in order to be escorted through hundreds of other small presses, we espied another person, a little hangman surrounded by five or six of those grubby Ignorants as fractious as a donkey with a squib stuck to its rump. In the language of their country they were called Courractors.[48] They were putting the dry lump of the bunches through again, after having squeezed out the others.

'They are the grimmest rogues I have ever seen,' said Frère Jean. We went from the great press through innumerable little ones crammed with vendangeurs who were raking through the grapes with tools which they called *items of account*. Eventually we came to a low building, where we saw a two-headed hound with the belly of a wolf and the claws of a stage-devil at Lamballe; it was delicately fed on milk from fines. Such was the ordinance of My Lords, for there was not one of them to whom it did not bring in the equivalent of the rent of a good tenant farm.

In the Ignorants' tongue it was called *Double-it*.

Near by was its dam, similar in coat and shape, except that she had four heads, two male, two female. Her name was *Quadruple-it*. It was the fiercest and most dangerous beast in the place, except for the grand-dam we saw shut up in a cage. Her name was *Fees Overdue*.

47. There is a pun in the original, *sarment* meaning both 'vine-branch' and an 'oath'.

48. Another pun: *Courrecteurs* is a portmanteau word combining *courroux* (anger) and *Corrector* (Corrector, Auditor).

Frère Jean, who still had over twenty yards of empty innards yearning for a fricassée of lawyers, was beginning to get cross; he begged Pantagruel to think of dinner, and to bring along Get-a-lot. So, as we left by the back door, we came across an old man bound in chains; half a scholar and half an Ignorant, he was a mongrel devil, decked out with spectacles as a tortoise is with scales. He lived on one kind of food only, called in their tongue *Audit-it*.

At the sight of that protonotoriety Pantagruel asked what brood he belonged to and what he was called. Get-a-lot told us how he had been kept there in chains from ancient times, to the deep displeasure of My Lords, who all but starved him to death, and that his name was Review-the-Books.

'By the Pope's holy bollocks,' said Frère Jean, 'there's a good jigger for you: and I am not at all amazed if My Lords the Ignorants take full account of that bacon-papper! By God, it seems to me, friend Panurge, that, if you look at him closely, he has the look of a Catty-claws. Ignorant as they are, they know as much about him as anyone does. I would send him back where he comes from, after a good walloping with an eel-hide lash.'

'By my spectacles from the Orient,' said Panurge, 'you are right, Frère Jean, my friend. For, judging from the physog of that false villain Audit-it, he is even more ignorant and wicked than these wretched Ignorants here, who do the least harm they can: they gather in the grapes without lengthy lawsuits; in three little words, they strip the vine-close but without all those adjourments and muck-scourings. And that makes the Furry-cats so angry.'

End of the Voyage of the Ringing Isle.

APPENDIX 3: CHAPTER 32 *BIS*

How the Lanternese Ladies were served at supper

CHAPTER 32 *bis*

[The following chapter is to be found in the manuscript of the Fifth
Book. *It is now conventionally referred to as 32 bis. It does not appear
in the printed text.*

There are untranslatable puns in the first paragraph: between sentent
si bon *(smell so good) and* ante-cibum *(Latin, pronounced the French
way, for pills to be taken 'before a meal'); the word used for barley-
water, 'pétassine', is a deformation of* ptisanne, *its first syllable distorted to evoke* pet, *(fart).*

*The note in the manuscript after 'Then were served' is in curious
Latin: 'Servato in 4 libr Panorgum ad nuptias'. It is apparently
intended to mean 'Use in the 4th book, Panurge: at the marriage.'*

The patter at the end of Chapter 38 of the Third Book *'promised'
such a marriage, but such patter is not always a sign of things to come,
as shown by the ends of the other Books and the contents of the Book
which follows them.*

Gaps in the manuscript are shown thus: [. . .].

Unexplained or unknown foods are left as they are.

The list of dances is heavily indebted to the Disciple de Pantagruel,
which was itself indebted to a macaronic book of Antonius de Arena,
Ad suos compagniones studiantes bassas dansas, *of which there were
several editions in the sixteenth century.]*

Rustic reeds together with Breton and Poitevin bagpipes
resounded harmoniously and the food was brought in. To
degrease her stomach the queen swallowed before the first
course a spoonful of fartly-water in lieu of her smell-so-goods.
Then were served:

[*Use in the 4th book, Panurge: at the marriage.*]

four quarters of the sheep which bore Helle and Phryxus over the straits of Propontis;

the two kids of the famous nanny-goat which suckled Jupiter;

the fawns of the doe Egeria who counselled Numa Pompilius;

six goslings hatched by the worthy ilmatic goose which saved the Tarpeian Rock in Rome by her cries;

pigs of the sow [. . .];

the calf of Ino the cow badly guarded of yore by Argus; the lung of the fox which Neptune [. . .] Julius Pollux in *On Dogs*;

the swan into which Jupiter metamorphosed himself out of love for Leda;

the ox Apis of Memphis in Egypt, who refused his fodder from Caesar Germanicus; also the six beeves rustled by Cacus and recovered by Hercules;

the two young roebucks which Corydon recovered for Alexis;

the wild boar of the Erymanthus, Olympian and Caledonian;

the genitals of the bull so beloved by Pasiphaë;

the stag into which Actaeon was transformed;

the liver of Calixto the she-bear;

savoury tidbits;

fools' snares;

horse-chaps;

nightmares vinaigrette;

worrycows;

tasty morsels from Eastangourre;

nonsense pasties;

fine turds, tweak-nose style;

aucbares de mer;

choice-greyhound pie;

pro-dung from the best meat;

ribs of boar;

prime-chews;

brégizollons;
Switzers' *By-Gods!*;
prelinginingues;
snakeweed rolls;
mortified cock-chasers;
high-tree *genabins*;
starabillatz;
corméabotz;
horn-up-arses dressed in turnips;
black gendarmes;
jerangois;
germander hotpot;
burning sighs;
Athenian rump;
brébasenas;
left-overs;
chinfenaux;
boil-biscuits;
volepuginges;
blunderlets;
shitlets;
wonder-bacon bitlets;
crock-pies.

For the second course there were served dishes of:

Swiss hundert-punders;
inter-duchies;
fox-tail-duster delight;
Saint Anthony's nuts;
wanton hares;
bandyélivagues, served rare;
Levantine red mushrooms;
Western threadbare mutterings;
fartaradine;
notrodilles;
collared bullfarts;
squirts-in-breeches;

donkey suet;
hairy scumber;
monkish quims;
bubbles;
spopondriloches
leave-me-in-peaces;
get-thee-out-of-theres;
push-him-out-yourselfs;
clap-your-hands;
Saint Balleran;
épiboches;
tipsy-lime;
March squalls;
trifles;
stiff-stuff;
smubrelotz;
I-swear-by-my-lifes;
Hurtalis;
kneaded-doughlets;
ancrastabotz;
blubber-blabs;
marabires;
gosh's holybloods;
whatnots;
bugbears;
maralipes;
stitched bum-stirrings;
whoops;
marmaladeries in a fine strong-piss;
muvver-of-goshes;
Croquinpédingues;
tintalois;
foot-in-the-doors;
chinfrenaux;
ace of spades pastry-noses;
Balm-Sundays;
whip-lashings;
mistletoe necks

For the last course there were offered dishes of:

> spiced senna-gogs;
> thingumajigs;
> junkets of bum-wipings;
> sandal-sole soup;
> dickory-dockeries;
> mock greedy-girls;
> *hucquemâches*;
> hey nonny nonnies;
> the snows of yesteryear (of which there are an abundance
>   in Lanternland);
> merry grigs;
> dirty-filths;
> *mirelaridaines*;
> *mizenas*;
> *grésamines* (delicious fruits);
> little Maries;
> small chidlings;
> *piedebillories*;
> flybum mix;
> puffs-up-my-bum;
> ugly dials;
> *tritrepolus*;
> *befaibenus*;
> donkey-brains;
> drawfartlets;
> cockerelets;
> *coqilles bétissons*;
> chews;
> din-of-scolds.

For dessert there was brought in a full platter of *Shit drench with blossoming turds*, that is, a full platter of *White honey covered with a wimple of crimson silk*.

    Their drink came in windpipe-ticklers – beautiful antique vessels – and they drank nothing but quantities of oleaginous Greek wine, a pretty unpleasant tipple to my taste, but in

Lanternland it is a deifying cup on which they get drunk just
like human beings, so much so that I saw a toothless old hag
of a Lantern clad in parchment – a corporal over other Lanterns,
young and also female – who cried out to the butlers, 'Our
lamps have gone out'.[49] She was so drunk on that tipple that
her life and her light were doused; Pantagruel was told that such
lanternized female Lanterns often perished that way, especially
when holding chapter-meetings.

Once supper was over and the trestles removed, the minstrels
struck up even more harmoniously than before, and the queen
then headed a double dance in which the male Falots[50] and
female Lanterns danced together. The queen then returned to
her throne while the others, to the heavenly sound of the rustic
pipes, joined in divers dances, including these. You might know
their names:

Hold me tight, Martin,
It's the fair Franciscan nun,
Upon the steps at Arras,
Bastienne,
The Brittany Round-dance,
Alas! And yet she is so fair,
Seven faces,
Revergasse,
The Toads and the Cranes,
The Marchioness,
If I have lost my pretty time,
The thorn,
Most wrong it is,
Frisky,
Too dark am I,
Of my sad grief,
When I recall,
The galliard,

49. 'Our lamps have gone out' – cited in the text from the Latin Vulgate – is
the cry of the foolish virgins in Matthew 25:8.
50. *Falots*, whom we have met already, are male Lanterns; their name allows
a pun on the English word *fellow*, which was known to the French.

The gout,
Vexed by his wife,
The maiden gay,
The ill-wed wife from Provence,
La pamine,
Catherine,
Saint Roc,
Sancerre,
Nevers,
Fair Picardy,
The suffering maid,
Never can I ought without her,
Curé, come and dance,
I stay alone,
I'm a Cabin-boy from Biscay Bay,
Enter the fool,
Come Christmas-tide,
Warm yourselves upon the steps,
The rudder,
Come to the banished maiden,
Foix,
Greenery,
Princess of love,
The heart is mine,
The heart is good,
Enjoyment,
Châteaubriant,
Butter fresh!,
Off she goes!,
The duchy,
Free from care,
Jacqueline,
The great alas,
Such pain have I,
My heart shall be,
La signora,
Fair glance,
Perrichon,

Despite the danger,
The great regrets,
Beneath the little bush's shade,
The pain that wounds me to the heart,
The floral maid,
Brother Pierre,
Be off, regrets,
Each noble city,
Thrust not it all,
The lamb's lament
The Spanish ball,
'Tis simply to give me leave to go,
My cunt a catchpole has become,
Wait not a mickle or a muckle,
The renown of a wandering man,
My sweeting, what has she become?
Waiting for the grace,
In her no longer faith have I,
With plaints and tears I congee take,
Out you come from there, Guillot!,
Love has caused me such displeasure,
The patience of the Moor,
The sighs of the colt,
I know not why,
Let us do it, do it now,
Black and sun-tanned,
The fair French maid,
That is my thought,
O loyal hope!,
My pleasure it is,
Fortune,
The allemande,
My lady's thoughts,
Think ye all of the fear,
Wrongly, fair maiden,
I know not why,
Alas, what has my heart done unto thee?,
O God! What a wife had I,

The hour has come for my complaint,
My heart to love shall be,
What is good, it seems to me,
Born in a happy hour was he,
The squire's lament,
This letter's sadness,
The tall German lad,
For having fulfilled my lover's desire,
Yellow mantles,
The must pressed from the vine,
Entire like is she,
Cremona,
The mercer-maid,
The tripe-maid,
My children,
The false semblance,
La Valentinoise,
Wrongly did Fortune,
Testimony,
Calabria,
L'estrac,
Affaires de cœur,
Hope,
Young Robin,
Sad pleasure,
Rigoron pirouy,
Fledgling,
Biscay,
She who feels pain,
You know what!,
How good it is,
The small alas,
On my return,
No longer do I,
Poor soldier-boys,
The scyther,
'Tis not a game,
O Beauty!,

My queen, I thank thee,
Patience,
Navarre,
Jacques Bourdain,
Rouhaut the Strong,
Noblesse,
Quite to the contrary,
Cabbages,
The ill is mine,
Sweet my Beloved,
The heat,
The châteaux,
The gillyflower,
Go to me,
Swear ye the price,
Night,
Adieu! I'm off,
Good governance,
My sonnet,
Pampeluna,
They have lied,
My Joy!,
Beautiful cousin,
She is returning,
By halves,
All the goods,
As you shall like it,
Since in my love I wretched be,
To the greenwood,
All colours above,
Above 'twas when,
Now is it good to love,
My pleasant fields,
My pretty heart,
Fair foot, fair eye,
Ah! shepherd maiden, my beloved,
The spinstresses,
Pavane,

Alas! And yet you are so fair,
The daisy,
Now good it is,
Wool,
Time past,
The pretty wood,
Comes now the hour,
Most dolorous, he,
Strike now that ancient air,
Hedges.

I also saw them dancing to songs of Poitou sung by a Falot-light from Saint-Maixent or by a mighty yawner from Parthenay-le-Veil. Now you should note, you drinkers, that all was proceeding merrily, and that those courteous Falot-lights were showing off their legs of wood. Towards the end, a nightcap was brought us and the queen showed her generosity by means of draughts of fartly-water. To be our guide she then offered us the choice of any one of her Lanterns we liked. We selected as our choice the Lantern who had been great Maître Pierre Amy's *amie*, whom I had once had the good fortune of knowing. She recognized me too. She seemed to us to be the most alluring, the most learned, the most astute, the most accomplished, the most human, the most debonair and, of all the company, the most suitable one to guide us. We, having humbly thanked that lady the queen, were escorted right up to our ship by seven young dancing Falots, while bright Diana already shed her beams.

As we were leaving the palace I heard the voice of a crooked-legged Falot saying that one single *Good evening* was worth more than all the *Good mornings* there ever were, be they as numerous as all the chestnuts used to stuff geese since the days of Ogyges' great flood, giving us to understand that there is nothing like the night-time for having good fun, when Lanterns are set out accompanied by their noble *Falot-Lights*. On such good fun the Sun can never cast a favouring eye, as is witnessed by Jupiter: when he lay with Alcmene, the mother of Hercules, he caused the Sun to hide herself for two days, having just discovered the furtive affair of Mars and Venus.

THE STORY OF PENGUIN CLASSICS

Before 1946 ...'Classics' are mainly the domain of academics and students, without readable editions for everyone else. This all changes when a little-known classicist, E. V. Rieu, presents Penguin founder Allen Lane with the translation of Homer's *Odyssey* that he has been working on and reading to his wife Nelly in his spare time.

1946 *The Odyssey* becomes the first Penguin Classic published, and promptly sells three million copies. Suddenly, classic books are no longer for the privileged few.

1950s Rieu, now series editor, turns to professional writers for the best modern, readable translations, including Dorothy L. Sayers's *Inferno* and Robert Graves's *The Twelve Caesars*, which revives the salacious original.

1960s The Classics are given the distinctive black jackets that have remained a constant throughout the series's various looks. Rieu retires in 1964, hailing the Penguin Classics list as 'the greatest educative force of the 20th century'.

1970s A new generation of translators arrives to swell the Penguin Classics ranks, and the list grows to encompass more philosophy, religion, science, history and politics.

1980s The Penguin American Library joins the Classics stable, with titles such as *The Last of the Mohicans* safeguarded. Penguin Classics now offers the most comprehensive library of world literature available.

1990s The launch of Penguin Audiobooks brings the classics to a listening audience for the first time, and in 1999 the launch of the Penguin Classics website takes them online to a larger global readership than ever before.

The 21st Century Penguin Classics are rejacketed for the first time in nearly twenty years. This world famous series now consists of more than 1300 titles, making the widest range of the best books ever written available to millions – and constantly redefining the meaning of what makes a 'classic'.

The Odyssey continues ...

The best books ever written

PENGUIN (🐧) CLASSICS

SINCE 1946